THE PORTION
OF LABOR

[See page 67

"'WHAT DID SUCH A GOOD LITTLE GIRL AS YOU BE RUN AWAY FROM FATHER
AND MOTHER FOR?'"

THE PORTION
OF LABOR

by

MARY E. FREEMAN (WILKINS)

AUTHOR OF

"JEROME" "A NEW ENGLAND NUN" ETC.

ILLUSTRATED

THE GREGG PRESS / RIDGEWOOD, N. J.

AMERICANS
IN
FICTION

INTRODUCTION BY PROFESSOR CLARENCE GOHDES
Editor of *American Literature* Magazine

In the domain of literature the play may once have been the chief abstract and chronicle of the times, but during the nineteenth and twentieth centuries the novel has usurped the chief place in holding the mirror up to the homely face of society. On this account, if for no other, the Gregg Press series of reprints of American fiction merits the attention of all students of Americana and of librarians interested in building up adequate collections dealing with the social and literary history of the United States. Most of the three score and ten novels or volumes of short stories included in the series enjoyed considerable fame in their day but have been so long out of print as to be virtually unobtainable in the original editions.

Included in the list are works by writers not presently fashionable in critical circles — but nevertheless well known to literary historians — among them Joel Chandler Harris, Harriet Beecher Stowe, Thomas Bailey Aldrich, and William Gilmore Simms. A substantial element in the list consists of authors who are known especially for their graphic portrayal of a particular American setting, such as Gertrude Atherton (California), Arlo Bates (Boston), Alice Brown (New England), Edward Eggleston (Indiana), Mary Wilkins Freeman (New England), Henry B. Fuller (Chicago), Richard M. Johnston (Georgia), James Lane Allen (Kentucky), Mary N. Murfree (Tennessee), and Thomas Nelson Page (Virginia). There is even a novel by Frederic Remington, one of the most popular painters of the Western cowboy and Indian — and another, an impressive minor classic on the early mining region of Colorado, from the pen of Mary Hallock Foote. The professional student of American literature will rejoice in the opportunity afforded by the collection to extend his reading of fiction belonging to what is called the "local-color movement" — a major current in the development of the national belles-lettres.

Among the titles in the series are also a number of famous historical novels. Silas Weir Mitchell's *Hugh Wynne* is one of the best fictional treatments of the American Revolution. John Esten Cooke is the foremost Southern writer of his day who dealt with the Civil War. The two books by Thomas Dixon are among the most famous novels on the Reconstruction Era, with sensational disclosures of the original Ku Klux Klan in action. They supplied the grist for the first great movie "spectacular" — *"The Birth of a Nation* (1915).

Paul Leicester Ford's *The Honorable Peter Stirling* is justly ranked among the top American novels which portray American politics in action — a subject illuminated by other novelists in the Gregg list — A. H. Lewis, Frances H. Burnett, and Alice Brown, for example. Economic problems are forcefully put before the reader in works by Aldrich, Mrs. Freeman, and John Hay, whose novels illustrate the ominous concern over the early battles between labor and capital. From the sweatshops of Eastern cities in which newly arrived immigrants toiled for pittances, to the Western mining camps where the laborers packed revolvers, the working class of the times enters into various other stories in the Gregg list. The capitalist class, also, comes in for attention, with an account of a struggle for the ownership of a railroad in Samuel Merwin's *The Short-Line War* and with the devastating documentation of the foibles of the newly rich and their wives in the narratives of David Graham Phillips. It was Phillips whose annoying talent for the exposure of abuses led Theodore Roosevelt to put the term "muck-raker" into currency.

While it is apparent that local-color stories, the historical novel, and the economic novel have all been borne in mind in choosing the titles for this important series of reprints, it is evident that careful consideration has also been given to treatments of various minority elements in the American population. The Negro, especially, but also the Indian, the half-breed, Creoles, Cajuns — and even the West Coast Japanese — appear as characters in various of these novels or volumes of short stories and sketches. Joel Chandler Harris's *Free Joe* will open the eyes of readers who know that author solely as the creator of humorous old Uncle Remus. And there is a revelatory volume of dialect tales, written by a Negro author, *The Conjure Woman* by Charles W. Chesnutt.

In literary conventions and the dominating attitudes toward life, the works in the Gregg series range from the adventurous romance illustrated so well by Mayne Reid or the polite urbanity of Owen Wister to the mordant irony of Kate Chopin and the grimmer realism of Joseph Kirkland's own experiences on bloody Civil War battlefields or the depressing display of New York farm life by Harold Frederic. In short, the series admirably illustrates the general qualities of the fiction produced in the United States during the era covered, just as it generously mirrors the geographical regions, the people, and the problems of the times.

ILLUSTRATIONS

THE PORTION OF LABOR

CHAPTER I

On the west side of Ellen's father's house was a file of Norway spruce-trees, standing with a sharp pointing of dark boughs towards the north, which gave them an air of expectancy of progress.

Every morning Ellen, whose bedroom faced that way, looked out with a firm belief that she would see them on the other side of the stone wall, advanced several paces towards their native land. She had no doubt of their ability to do so; their roots, projecting in fibrous sprawls from their trunks, were their feet, and she pictured them advancing with wide trailings, and rustlings as of green draperies, and a loudening of that dreamy cry of theirs which was to her imagination a cry of homesickness reminiscent of their old life in the White North. When Ellen had first heard the name Norway spruce, 'way back in her childhood—so far back, though she was only seven and a half now, that it seemed to her like a memory from another life—she had asked her mother to show her Norway on the map, and her strange convictions concerning the trees had seized her. When her mother said that they had come from that northernmost land of Europe, Ellen, to whose childhood all truth was naked and literal, immediately conceived to herself those veritable trees advancing over the frozen seas around the pole, and down through the vast regions which were painted blue on her map, straight to her father's west yard. There they stood and sang the songs of their own country, with a melancholy sweetness of absence and longing, and were forever thinking to return. Ellen felt always a thrill of happy surprise when she saw them still there of a morning, for she felt that she would miss them sorely when they were gone. She said nothing of all this to her mother; it was one of the secrets of the soul which created her individuality and made her a spiritual birth. She was also silent about her belief concerning the cherry-trees in the east yard. There were three of them, giants of their kind, which filled the east yard every spring as with mountains of white bloom, breathing wide gusts of honey sweetness, and humming with bees. Ellen believed that these trees had once stood in the Garden of Eden, but she never expected to find them missing from the east yard of a morning, for she remembered the angel with the flaming sword, and she knew how one branch of the easternmost tree happened to be blasted as if by fire. And she thought that these trees were happy, and never sighed to the wind as the dark evergreens did, because they had still the same blossoms and the same fruit that they had in Eden, and so did not fairly know that they were not there still. Sometimes Ellen, sitting underneath them on a low rib of rock on a May morning, used to fancy with success that she and the trees were together in that first garden which she had read about in the Bible.

Sometimes, after one of these successful imaginings, when Ellen's mother called her into the house she would stare at her little daughter uneasily, and give her a spoonful of a bitter spring medicine which she had brewed herself. When Ellen's father, Andrew Brewster, came home from the shop, she would speak to him aside as he was washing his hands at the kitchen sink, and tell him that it seemed to her that Ellen looked kind of "pindlin'." Then Andrew, before he sat down at the dinner-table, would take Ellen's face in his two moist hands, look at her with anxiety thinly veiled by facetiousness, rub his rough, dark cheek against her soft, white one until he had reddened it, then laugh, and tell her she looked like a bo'sn. Ellen never quite knew what her father meant by bo'sn, but she understood that it signified something very rosy and hearty indeed.

Ellen's father always picked out for her the choicest and tenderest bits of the humble dishes, and his keen eyes were more watchful of her plate than of his own. Always after Ellen's mother had said to her father that she thought Ellen looked pindling he was late about coming home from the shop, and would turn in at the gate laden with paper parcels. Then Ellen would find an orange or some other delicacy beside her plate at supper. Ellen's aunt Eva, her mother's younger sister, who lived with them, would look askance at the tidbit with open sarcasm. "You jest spoil that young one, Fanny," she would say to her sister.

"You can do jest as you are a mind to with your own young ones when you get them, but you can let mine alone. It's none of your business what her father and me give her to eat; you don't buy it," Ellen's mother would retort. There was the utmost frankness of speech between the two sisters. Neither could have been in the slightest doubt as to what the other thought of her, for it was openly proclaimed to her a dozen times a day, and the conclusion was never complimentary. Ellen learned very early to form her own opinions of character from her own intuition, otherwise she would have held her aunt and mother in somewhat slighting estimation, and she loved them both dearly. They were headstrong, violent-tempered women, but she

3

had an instinct for the staple qualities below that surface turbulence, which was lashed higher by every gust of opposition. These two loud, contending voices, which filled the house before and after shop-hours—for Eva worked in the shop with her brother-in-law—with a duet of discords instead of harmonies, meant no more to Ellen than the wrangle of the robins in the cherry-trees. She supposed that two sisters always conversed in that way. She never knew why her father, after a fiery but ineffectual attempt to quell the feminine tumult, would send her across the east yard to her grandmother Brewster's, and seat himself on the east door-step in summer, or go down to the store in the winter. She would sit at the window in her grandmother's sitting-room, eating peacefully the slice of pound - cake or cooky with which she was always regaled, and listen to the scolding voices across the yard as she might have listened to any outside disturbance. She was never sucked into the whirlpool of wrath which seemed to gyrate perpetually in her home, and wondered at her grandmother Brewster's impatient exclamations concerning the poor child, and her poor boy, and that it was a shame and a disgrace, when now and then a louder explosion of wrath struck her ears.

Ellen's grandmother—Mrs. Zelotes Brewster, as she was called, though her husband Zelotes had been dead for many years—was an aristocrat by virtue of inborn prejudices and convictions, in despite of circumstances. The neighbors said that Mrs. Zelotes Brewster had always been high-feeling, and had held up her head with the best. It would have been nearer the truth to say that she held up her head above the best. No one seeing the erect old woman, in her draperies of the finest black goods to be bought in the city, could estimate in what heights of thin upper air of spiritual con-

4

sequence her head was elevated. She had always a clear sight of the head-tops of any throng in which she found herself, and queens or duchesses would have been no exception. She would never have failed to find some stool of superior possessions or traits upon which to raise herself, and look down upon crown and coronet. When she read in the papers about the marriage of a New York belle to an English duke, she reflected that the duke could be by no means as fine a figure of a man as Zelotes had been, and as her son Andrew was, although both her husband and son had got all their education in the town schools, and had worked in shoe-shops all their lives. She could have looked at a palace or a castle, and have remained true to the splendors of her little one-story-and-a-half house with a best parlor and sitting-room, and a shed kitchen for use in hot weather.

She would not for one instant have been swerved from utmost admiration and faith in her set of white-and-gold wedding china by the contemplation of Copeland and Royal Sèvres. She would have pitted her hair-cloth furniture of the ugliest period of household art against all the Chippendales and First Empire pieces in existence.

As Mrs. Zelotes had never seen any household possessions to equal her own, let alone to surpass them, she was of the same mind with regard to her husband and his family, herself and her family, her son and little granddaughter. She never saw any gowns and shawls which compared with hers in fineness and richness; she never tasted a morsel of cookery which was not as sawdust when she reflected upon her own; and all that humiliated her in the least, or caused her to feel in the least dissatisfied, was her son's wife and her family and antecedents.

Mrs. Zelotes Brewster had considered that her son

5

Andrew was marrying immeasurably beneath him when he married Fanny Loud, of Loudville. Loudville was a humble, an almost disreputably humble, suburb of the little provincial city. The Louds from whom the locality took its name were never held in much repute, being considered of a stratum decidedly below the ordinary social one of the city. When Andrew told his mother that he was to marry a Loud, she declared that she would not go to his wedding, nor receive the girl at her house, and she kept her word. When one day Andrew brought his sweetheart to his home to call, trusting to her pretty face and graceful though rather sharp manner to win his mother's heart, he found her intrenched in the kitchen, and absolutely indifferent to the charms of his Fanny in her stylish, albeit somewhat tawdry, finery, though she had peeped to good purpose from her parlor window, which commanded the road, before she fled kitchenward.

Mrs. Zelotes was beating eggs with as firm an impetus as if she were heaving up earth-works to strengthen her own pride when her son thrust his timid face into the kitchen. "Mother, Fanny's in the parlor," he said, beseechingly.

"Let her set there, then, if she wants to," said his mother, and that was all she would say.

Very soon Fanny went home on her lover's arm, freeing her mind with no uncertain voice on the way, though she was on the public road, and within hearing of sharp ears in open windows. Fanny had a pride as fierce as Mrs. Zelotes Brewster's, though it was not so well sustained, and she would then and there have refused to marry Andrew had she not loved him with all her passionate and ill-regulated heart. But she never forgave her mother-in-law for the slight she had put upon her that day, and the slights which she put upon her later. She would have refused to live next

door to Mrs. Zelotes had not Andrew owned the land
and been in a measure forced to build there. Every
time she had flaunted out of her new house-door in her
wedding finery she had an uncomfortable feeling of
defiance under a fire of hostile eyes in the next house.
She kept her own windows upon that side as clear and
bright as diamonds, and her curtains in the stiffest,
snowy slants, lest her terrible mother-in-law should
have occasion to impeach her housekeeping, she being
a notable housewife. The habits of the Louds of Loudville were considered shiftless in the extreme, and poor
Fanny had heard an insinuation of Mrs. Zelotes to that
effect.

The elder Mrs. Brewster's knowledge of her son's
house and his wife was limited to the view from her
west windows, but there was half-truce when little
Ellen was born. Mrs. Brewster, who considered that
no woman could be obtained with such a fine knowledge
of nursing as she possessed, and who had, moreover, a
regard for her poor boy's pocket-book, appeared for
the first time in his doorway, and opened her heart to
her son's child, if not to his wife, whom she began to
tolerate.

However, the two women had almost a hand-to-hand
encounter over little Ellen's cradle, the elder Mrs. Brewster judging that it was for her good to be rocked to sleep,
the younger not. Little Ellen herself, however, turned
the balance that time in favor of her grandmother, since
she cried every time the gentle, swaying motion was
hushed, and absolutely refused to go to sleep, and her
mother from the first held every course which seemed to
contribute to her pleasure and comfort as a sacred duty.
At last it came to pass that the two women met only
upon that small neutral ground of love, and upon all
other territory were sworn foes. Especially was Mrs.
Zelotes wroth when Eva Loud, after the death of her

7

father, one of the most worthless and shiftless of the Louds of Loudville, came to live with her married sister. She spoke openly to Fanny concerning her opinion of another woman's coming to live on poor Andrew, and paid no heed to the assertions that Eva would work and pay her way.

Mrs. Zelotes, although she acknowledged it no social degradation for a man to work in a shoe-factory, regarded a woman who worked therein as having hopelessly forfeited her caste. Eva Loud had worked in a shop ever since she was fourteen, and had tagged the grimy and leathery procession of Louds, who worked in shoe-factories when they worked at all, in a short skirt with her hair in a strong black pigtail. There was a kind of bold grace and showy beauty about this Eva Loud which added to Mrs. Zelotes's scorn and dislike.

"She walks off to work in the shop as proud as if she was going to a party," she said, and she fairly trembled with anger when she saw the girl set out with her son in the morning. She would have considered it much more according to the eternal fitness of things had her son Andrew been attending a queen whom he would have dropped at her palace on the way. She writhed inwardly whenever little Ellen spoke of her aunt Eva, and would have forbidden her to do so had she dared.

"To think of that child associating with a shopgirl!" she said to Mrs. Pointdexter. Mrs. Pointdexter was her particular friend, whom she regarded with loving tolerance of superiority, though she had been the daughter of a former clergyman of the town, and had wedded another, and might presumably have been accounted herself of a somewhat higher estate. The gentle and dependent clergyman's widow, when she came back to her native city after the death of her husband, found herself all at once in a pleasant little valley of humiliation at the feet of her old friend, and was

8

contented to abide there. "Perhaps your son's sister-in-law will marry and go away," she said, consolingly, to Mrs. Zelotes, who indeed lived in that hope. But Eva remained at her sister's, and, though she had admirers in plenty, did not marry, and the dissension grew.

It was an odd thing that, however the sisters quarrelled, the minute Andrew tried to take sides with his wife and assail Eva in his turn, Fanny turned and defended her. "I am not going to desert all the sister I have got in the world," she said. "If you want me to leave, say so, and I will go, but I shall never turn Eva out of doors. I would rather go with her and work in the shop." Then the next moment the wrangle would recommence, and the harsh trebles of wrath would swell high. Andrew could not appreciate this savageness of race loyalty in the face of anger and dissension, and his brain reeled with the apparent inconsistency of the thing.

"Sometimes I think they are both crazy," he used to tell his mother, who sympathized with him after a covertly triumphant fashion. She never said, "I told you so," but the thought was evident on her face, and her son saw it there.

However, he said not a word against his wife, except by implication. Though she and her sister were making his home unbearable, he still loved her, and, even if he did not, he had something of his mother's pride.

However, at last, when Ellen was almost eight years old, matters came suddenly to a climax one evening in November. The two sisters were having a fiercer dispute than usual. Eva was taking her sister to task for cutting over a dress of hers for Ellen, Fanny claiming that she had given her permission to do so, and Eva denying it. The child sat listening in her little chair with a look of dawning intelligence of wrath and wicked temper in her face, because she was herself in a manner the cause of the dissension. Suddenly Andrew Brewster, with a fiery outburst of inconsequent masculine wrath with the whole situation, essayed to cut the Gordian knot. He grabbed the little dress of bright woollen stuff, which lay partly made upon the table, and crammed it into the stove, and a reek of burning wool filled the room. Then both women turned upon him with a combination of anger to which his wrath was wildfire.

Andrew caught up little Ellen, who was beginning to look scared, wrapped the first thing he could seize around her, and fairly fled across the yard to his mother's. Then he sat down and wept like a boy, and his pride left him at last. "Oh, mother," he sobbed, "if it were not for the child, I would go away, for my home is a hell!"

Mrs. Zelotes stood clasping little Ellen, who clung to her, trembling. "Well, come over here with me," she said, "you and Ellen."

"Live here in the next house!" said Andrew. "Do you suppose Fanny would have the child living under her very eyes in the next house? No, there is no way out of the misery—no way; but if it was not for the child, I would go!"

Andrew burst out in such wild sobs that his mother released Ellen and ran to him; and the child, trembling and crying with a curious softness, as of fear at being heard, ran out of the house and back to her home. "Oh, mother," she cried, breaking in upon the dialogue of anger which was still going on there with her little tremulous flute—"oh, mother, father is crying!"

"I don't care," answered her mother, fiercely, her temper causing her to lose sight of the child's agitation. "I don't care. If it wasn't for you, I would leave him. I wouldn't live as I am doing. I would leave everybody.

10

I am tired of this awful life. Oh, if it wasn't for you, Ellen, I would leave everybody and start fresh!"

"You can leave *me* whenever you want to," said Eva, her handsome face burning red with wrath, and she went out of the room, which was suffocating with the fumes of the burning wool, tossing her black head, all banged and coiled in the latest fashion.

Of late years Fanny had sunk her personal vanity further and further in that for her child. She brushed her own hair back hard from her temples, and candidly revealed all her unyouthful lines, and dwelt fondly upon the arrangement of little Ellen's locks, which were of a fine, pale yellow, as clear as the color of amber.

She never recut her skirts or her sleeves, but she studied anxiously all the slightest changes in children's fashions. After her sister had left the room with a loud bang of the door, she sat for a moment gazing straight ahead, her face working, then she burst into such a passion of hysterical wailing as the child had never heard. Ellen, watching her mother with eyes so frightened and full of horror that there was no room for childish love and pity in them, grew very pale. She had left the door by which she had entered open; she gazed one moment at her mother, then she turned and slipped out of the room, and, opening the outer door softly, though her mother would not have heard nor noticed, went out of the house.

Then she ran as fast as she could down the frozen road, a little, dark figure, passing as rapidly as the shadow of a cloud between the earth and the full moon.

CHAPTER II

THE greatest complexity in the world attends the motive-power of any action. Infinite perspectives of mental mirrors reflect the whys of all doing. An adult with long practice in analytic introspection soon becomes bewildered when he strives to evolve the primary and fundamental reasons for his deeds; a· child so striving would be lost in unexpected depths; but a child never strives. A child obeys unquestioningly and absolutely its own spiritual impellings without a backward glance at them.

Little Ellen Brewster ran down the road that November night, and did not know then, and never knew afterwards, why she ran. Loving renunciation was surging high in her childish heart, giving an indication of tidal possibilities for the future, and there was also a bitter, angry hurt of slighted dependency and affection. Had she not heard them say, her own mother and father say, that they would be better off and happier with her out of the way, and she their dearest loved and most carefully cherished possession in the whole world? It is a cruel fall for an apple of the eye to the ground, for its law of gravitation is of the soul, and its fall shocks the infinite. Little Ellen felt herself sorely hurt by her fall from such fair heights; she was pierced by the sharp thorns of selfish interests which flourish below all the heavenward windows of life.

Afterwards, when her mother and father tried to make her tell them why she ran away, she could not say; the answer was beyond her own power.

There was no snow on the ground, but the earth was frozen in great ribs after a late thaw. Ellen ran painfully between the ridges which a long line of ice-wagons had made with their heavy wheels earlier in the day. When the spaces between the ridges were too narrow for her little feet, she ran along the crests, and that was precarious. She fell once and bruised one of her delicate knees, then she fell again, and struck the knee on the same place. It hurt her, and she caught her breath with a gasp of pain. She pulled up her little frock and touched her hand to her knee, and felt it wet, then she whimpered on the lonely road, and, curiously enough, there was pity for her mother as well as for herself in her solitary grieving. "Mother would feel pretty bad if she knew how I was hurt, enough to make it bleed," she murmured, between her soft sobs. Ellen did not dare cry loudly, from a certain unvoiced fear which she had of shocking the stillness of the night, and also from a delicate sense of personal dignity, and a dislike of violent manifestations of feeling which had strengthened with her growth in the midst of the turbulent atmosphere of her home. Ellen had the softest childish voice, and she never screamed or shouted when excited. Instead of catching the motion of the wind, she still lay before it, like some slender-stemmed flower. If Ellen had made much outcry with the hurt in her heart and the smart of her knee, she might have been heard, for the locality was thickly settled, though not in the business portion of the little city. The houses, set prosperously in the midst of shaven lawns—for this was a thrifty and emulative place, and democracy held up its head confidently—were built closely along the road, though that was lonely and deserted at that hour. It was the hour between half-past six and half-past seven, when people were lingering at their supper-tables, and had not yet started upon their evening pursuits.

13

The lights shone for the most part from the rear windows of the houses, and there was a vague compound odor of tea and bread and beefsteak in the air. Poor Ellen had not had her supper; the wrangle at home had dismissed it from everybody's mind. She felt more pitiful towards her mother and herself when she smelt the food and reflected upon that. To think of her going away without any supper, all alone in the dark night! There was no moon, and the solemn brilliancy of the stars made her think with a shiver of awe of the Old Testament and the possibility of the Day of Judgment. Suppose it should come, and she all alone out in the night, in the midst of all those worlds and the great White Throne, without her mother? Ellen's grandmother, who was of a stanch orthodox breed, and was, moreover, anxious to counteract any possible detriment as to religious training from contact with the degenerate Louds of Loudville, had established a strict course of Bible study for her granddaughter at a very early age. All celestial phenomena were in consequence transposed into a Biblical key for the child, and she regarded the heavens swarming with golden stars as a Hebrew child of a thousand years ago might have done.

She was glad when she came within the radius of a street light from time to time; they were stationed at wide intervals in that neighborhood. Soon, however, she reached the factories. when all mystery and awe, and vague terrors of what beside herself might be near unrevealed beneath the mighty brooding of the night, were over. She was, as it were, in the mid-current of the conditions of her own life and times, and the material force of it swept away all symbolisms and unstable drift, and left only the bare rocks and shores of existence. Always when the child had been taken by one of her elders past the factories, humming like gigantic hives, with their windows alert with eager eyes of toil,

14

glancing out at her over bench and machine, Ellen had seen her secretly cherished imaginings recede into a night of distance like stars, and she had felt her little footing upon the earth with a shock, and had clung more closely to the leading hand of love. "That's where your poor father works," her grandmother would say. "Maybe you'll have to work there some day," her aunt Eva had said once; and her mother, who had been with her also, had cried out sharply as if she had been stung, "I guess that little delicate thing ain't never goin' to work in a shoe-shop, Eva Loud." And her aunt Eva had laughed, and declared with emphasis that she guessed there was no need to worry yet awhile.

"She never shall, while I live," her mother had cried; and then Eva, coming to her sister's aid against her own suggestion, had declared, with a vehemence which frightened Ellen, that she would burn the shop down herself first.

As for Ellen's father, he never at that time dwelt upon the child's future as much as his wife did, having a masculine sense of the instability of houses of air which prevented him from entering them without a shivering of walls and roof into naught but star-mediums by his downrightness of vision. "Oh, let the child be, can't you, Fanny?" he said, when his wife speculated whether Ellen would be or do this or that when she should be a woman. He resented the conception of the woman which would swallow up, like some metaphysical sorceress, his fair little child. So when he now and then led Ellen past the factories it was never with the slightest surmise as to any connection which she might have with them beyond the present one. "There's the shop where father works," he would tell Ellen, with a tender sense of his own importance in his child's eyes, and he was as proud as Punch when Ellen was able to point with her tiny pink finger at the window where father

15

worked. "That's where father works and earns money to buy nice things for little Ellen," Andrew would repeat, beaming at her with divine foolishness, and Ellen looked at the roaring, vibrating building as she might have looked at the wheels of progress. She realized that her father was very great and smart to work in a place like that, and earn money—so much of it. Ellen often heard her mother remark with pride how much money Andrew earned.

To-night, when Ellen passed in her strange flight, the factories were still, though they were yet blazing with light. The gigantic buildings, after a style of architecture as simple as a child's block house, and adapted to as primitive an end, loomed up beside the road like windowed shells enclosing massive concretenesses of golden light. They looked entirely vacant except for light, for the workmen had all gone home, and there were only the keepers in the buildings. There were three of them, representing three different firms, rival firms, grouped curiously close together, but Lloyd's was much the largest. Andrew and Eva worked in Lloyd's.

She was near the last factory when she met a man hastening along with bent shoulders, of intent, middle-aged progress. After he had passed her with a careless glance at the small, swift figure, she smelt coffee. He was carrying home a pound for his breakfast supply. That suddenly made her cry, though she did not know why. That familiar odor of home and the wontedness of life made her isolation on her little atom of the unusual more pitiful. The man turned round sharply when she sobbed. "Hullo! what's the matter, sis?" he called back, in a pleasant, hoarse voice. Ellen did not answer; she fled as if she had wings on her feet. The man had many children of his own, and was accustomed to their turbulence over trifles. He kept on,

16

thinking that there was a sulky child who had been sent on an errand against her will, that it was not late, and she was safe enough on that road. He resumed his calculation as to whether his income would admit of a new coal-stove that winter. He was a workman in a factory, with one accumulative interest in life—coal-stoves. He bought and traded and swapped coal-stoves every winter with keenest enthusiasm. Now he had one in his mind which he had just viewed in a window with the rapture of an artist. It had a little nickel statuette on the top, and that quite crowded Ellen out of his mind, which had but narrow accommodations.

So Ellen kept on unmolested, though her heart was beating loud with fright. When she came into the brilliantly lighted stretch of Main Street, which was the business centre of the city, her childish mind was partly diverted from herself. Ellen had not been down town many times of an evening, and always in hand of her hurrying father or mother. Now she had run away and cut loose from all restrictions of time; there was an eternity for observation before her, with no call in-doors in prospect. She stopped at the first bright shop window, and suddenly the exultation of freedom was over the child. She tasted the sweets of rebellion and disobedience. She had stood before that window once before of an evening, and her aunt Eva had been with her, and one of her young men friends had come up behind, and they had gone on, the child dragging backward at her aunt's hand. Now she could stand as long as she wished, and stare and stare, and drink in everything which her childish imagination craved, and that was much. The imagination of a child is often like a voracious maw, seizing upon all that comes within reach, and producing spiritual indigestions and assimilations almost endless in their effects upon the growth. This window before which Ellen stood was that of a market: a great expanse of plate-glass framing a crude study in the clearest color tones. It takes a child or an artist to see a picture without the intrusion of its second dimension of sordid use and the gross reflection of humanity.

Ellen looked at the great shelf laid upon with flesh and vegetables and fruits with the careless precision of a kaleidoscope, and did not for one instant connect anything thereon with the ends of physical appetite, though she had not had her supper. What had a meal of beefsteak and potatoes and squash served on the little white-laid table at home to do with those great golden globes which made one end of the window like the remove from a mine, those satin-smooth spheres, those cuts as of red and white marble? She had eaten apples, but these were as the apples of the gods, lying in a heap of opulence, with a precious light-spot like a ruby on every outward side. The turnips affected her imagination like ivory carvings: she did not recognize them for turnips at all. She never afterwards believed them to be turnips; and as for cabbages, they were green inflorescences of majestic bloom. There is one position from which all common things can be seen with reflections of preciousness, and Ellen had insensibly taken it. The window and the shop behind were illuminated with the yellow glare of gas, but the glass was filmed here and there with frost, which tempered it as with a veil. In the background rosy-faced men in white frocks were moving to and fro, customers were passing in and out, but they were all glorified to the child. She did not see them as butchers, and as men and women selling and buying dinners.

However, all at once everything was spoiled, for her fairy castle of illusion or a higher reality was demolished, and that not by any blow of practicality, but by pity and sentiment. Ellen was a woman-child, and suddenly

she struck the rock upon which women so often wreck
or effect harbor, whichever it may be. All at once she
looked up from the dazzling mosaic of the window and
saw the dead partridges and grouse hanging in their
rumpled brown mottle of plumage, and the dead rabbits,
long and stark, with their fur pointed with frost, hanging
in a piteous headlong company, and all her delight and
wonder vanished, and she came down to the hard actualities of things. "Oh, the poor birds!" she cried
out in her heart. "Oh, the poor birds, and the poor
bunnies!"

Just at that moment, when the sudden rush of compassion and indignation had swollen her heart to the
size of a woman's, and given it the aches of one, when
her eyes were so dilated with the sight of helpless injury
and death that they reflected the mystery of it and lost
the outlook of childhood, when her pretty baby mouth
was curved like an inverted bow of love with the impulse of tears, Cynthia Lennox came up the street and
stopped short when she reached her.

Suddenly Ellen felt some one pressing close to her,
and, looking up, saw a woman, only middle-aged, but
whom she thought very old, because her hair was white,
standing looking at her very keenly with clear, light-
blue eyes under a high, pale forehead, from which the
gray hair was combed uncompromisingly back. The
woman had been a beauty once, of a delicate, nervous
type, and had a certain beauty now, a something which
had endured like the fineness of texture of a web when
its glow of color has faded. Her black garments draped
her with sober richness, and there was a gleam of dark
fur when the wind caught her cloak. A small tuft of
ostrich plumes nodded from her bonnet. Ellen smelt
flowers vaguely, and looked at the lady's hand, but she
did not carry any.

"Whose little girl are you?" Cynthia Lennox asked,

softly, and Ellen did not answer. "Can't you tell me whose little girl you are?" Cynthia Lennox asked again. Ellen did not speak, but there was the swift flicker of a thought over her face which told her name as plainly as language if the woman had possessed the skill to interpret it.

"Ellen Brewster—Ellen Brewster is my name," Ellen said to herself very hard, and that was how she endured the reproach of her own silence.

The woman looked at her with surprise and admiration that were fairly passionate. Ellen was a beautiful child, with a face like a white flower. People had always turned to look after her, she was so charming, and had caused her mother's heart to swell with pride. "The way everybody we met has stared after that child to-day!" she would whisper her husband when she brought Ellen home from some little expedition; then the two would look at the little one's face with the one holy vanity of the world. Ellen wore to-night the little white shawl which her father had caught up when he carried her over to her grandmother's. She held it tightly together under her chin with one tiny hand, and her face looked out from between the soft folds with the absolute purity of curve and color of a pearl.

"Oh, you darling!" said the woman, suddenly; "you darling!" and Ellen shrank away from her. "Don't be afraid, dear," said Cynthia Lennox. "Don't be afraid, only tell me who you are. What is your name, dear?" But Ellen remained silent; only, as she shrank aloof, her eyes grew wild and bright with startled tears, and her sweet baby mouth quivered piteously. She wanted to run, but the habit of obedience was so strong upon her little mind that she feared to do so. This strange woman seemed to have gotten her in some invisible leash.

"Tell me what your name is, darling," said the

woman, but she might as well have importuned a flower.
Ellen was proof against all commands in that direction.
She suddenly felt the furry sweep of the lady's cloak
against her cheek, and a nervous, tender arm drawing
her close, though she strove feebly to resist. "You
are cold, you have nothing on but this little white shawl,
and perhaps you are hungry. What were you looking
in this window for? Tell me, dear, where is your mother?
She did not send you on an errand, such a little girl
as you are, so late on such a cold night, with no more
on than this?"

A tone of indignation crept into the lady's voice.

"No, mother didn't send me," Ellen said, speaking
for the first time.

"Then did you run away, dear?" Ellen was silent.
"Oh, if you did, darling, you must tell me where you
live, what your father's name is, and I will take you
home. Tell me, dear. If it is far, I will get a carriage,
and you shall ride home. Tell me, dear."

There was an utmost sweetness of maternal persuasion
in Cynthia Lennox's voice; Ellen was swayed by it as a
child might have been swayed by the magic pipe of the
Pied Piper of Hamelin. She half yielded to her leading motion, then she remembered. "No," she cried out,
with a sob of utter desolation. "No, no."

"Why not, dear?"

"They don't want; they don't want. No, no!"

"They don't want you? Your own father and mother
don't want you? Darling, what is the matter?" But
Ellen was dumb again. She stood sobbing, with a
painful restraint, and pulling futilely from the lady's
persuasive hand. But it ended in the mastery of the
child. Suddenly Cynthia Lennox gathered her up
in her arms under her great fur-lined cloak, and carried
her a little farther down the street, then across it to a
dwelling-house, one of the very few which had with-

stood the march of business blocks on this crowded main street of the provincial city. A few people looked curiously at the lady carrying such a heavy, weeping child, but she met no one whom she knew, and the others looked indifferently away after a second backward stare. Cynthia Lennox was one to bear herself with such dignity over all jolts of circumstances that she might almost convince others of her own exemption from them. Her mental bearing disproved the evidence of the senses, and she could have committed a crime with such consummate self-poise and grace as to have held a crowd in abeyance with utter distrust of their own eyes before such unquestioning confidence in the sovereignty of the situation. Cynthia Lennox had always had her own way except in one respect, and that experience had come to her lately.

Though she was such a slender woman, she seemed to have great strength in her arms, and she bore Ellen easily and as if she had been used to such a burden. She wrapped her cloak closely around the child.

"Don't be afraid, darling," she kept whispering. Ellen panted in bewilderment, and a terror which was half assuaged by something like fascination.

She was conscious of a soft smother of camphor, in which the fur-lined cloak had lain through the summer, and of that flower odor, which was violets, though she did not know it. Only the wild American scentless ones had come in little Ellen's way so far.

She felt herself carried up steps, then a door was thrown open, and a warm breath of air came in her face, and the cloak was tossed back, and she was set softly on the floor. The hall in which she stood seemed very bright; she blinked and rubbed her eyes.

The lady stood over her, laughing gently, and when the child looked up at her, seemed much younger than she had at first, very young in spite of her white hair.

22

There was a soft red on her cheek; her lips looked full
and triumphant with smiles; her eyes were like stars.
An emotion of her youth which had never become dulled
by satisfaction had suddenly blossomed out on her
face, and transformed it. An unassuaged longing
may serve to preserve youth as well as an undestroyed
illusion; indeed, the two are one. Cynthia Lennox
looked at the child as if she had been a young mother,
and she her first-born; triumph over the future, and
daring for all odds, and perfect faith in the kingdom of
joy were in her look. Had she nursed one child like
Ellen to womanhood, and tasted the bitter in the cup,
she would not have been capable of that look, and would
have been as old as her years. She threw off her cloak
and took off her bonnet, and the light struck her hair and
made it look like silver. A brooch in the laces at her
throat shone with a thousand hues, and as Ellen gazed
at it she felt curiously dull and dizzy. She did not resist at all when the lady removed her little white shawl,
but stared at her with the look of some small and helpless thing in too large a grasp of destiny to admit of a
struggle. "Oh, you darling!" Cynthia Lennox said,
and stooped and kissed her, and half carried her into a
great, warm, dazzling room, with light reflected in long
lines of gold from picture-frames on the wall, and now
and then startling patches of lurid color blazing forth
unmeaningly from the dark incline of their canvases,
with gleams of crystal and shadows of bronze in set-
tings of fretted ebony, with long swayings of rich
draperies at doors and windows, a red light of fire in
a grate, and two white lights, one of piano keys, the
other of a flying marble figure in a corner, outlined
clearly against dusky red. The light in this room was
very dim. It was all beyond Ellen's imagination. The
White North where the Norway spruces lived would not
have seemed as strange to her as this. Neither would

23

Bluebeard's Castle, nor the House that Jack Built, nor the Palace of King Solomon, nor the tent in which lived little Joseph in his coat of many colors, nor even the Garden of Eden, nor Noah's Ark. Her imagination had not prepared her for a room like this. She had formed her ideas of rooms upon her grandmother's and her mother's and the neighbors' best parlors, with their glories of crushed plush and gilt and onyx and cheap lace and picture - throws and lambrequins. This room was such a heterodoxy against her creed of civilization that it did not look beautiful to her as much as strange and bewildering, and when she was bidden to sit down in a little inlaid precious chair she put down her tiny hand and reflected, with a sense of strengthening of her household faith, that her grandmother had beautiful, smooth, shiny hair-cloth.

Cynthia Lennox pulled the chair close to the fire, and bade her hold out her little feet to the blaze to warm them well. "I am afraid you are chilled, darling," she said, and looked at her sitting there in her dainty little red cashmere frock, with her spread of baby-yellow hair over her shoulders. Then Ellen thought that the lady was younger than her mother; but her mother had borne her and nursed her, and suffered and eaten of the tree of knowledge, and tasted the bitter after the sweet; and this other woman was but as a child in the garden, though she was fairly old. But along with Ellen's conviction of the lady's youth had come a conviction of her power, and she yielded to her unquestioningly. Whenever she came near her she gazed with dilating eyes upon the blazing circle of diamonds at her throat.

When she was bidden, she followed the lady into the dining-room, where the glitter of glass and silver and the soft gleam of precious china made her think for a little while that she must be in a store. She had never

seen anything like this except in a store, when she had
been with her mother to buy a lamp-chimney. So she
decided this to be a store, but she said nothing. She
did not speak at all, but she ate her biscuits, and slice
of breast of chicken, and sponge-cake, and drank her
milk.

She had her milk in a little silver cup which seemed
as if it might have belonged to another child; she also
sat in a small high-chair, which made it seem as if another child had lived or visited in the house. Ellen
became singularly possessed with this sense of the presence of a child, and when the door opened she would
look around for her to enter, but it was always an old
black woman with a face of imperturbable bronze, which
caused her to huddle closer into her chair when she drew
near.

There were not many colored people in the city, and
Ellen had never seen any except at Long Beach, where
she had sometimes gone to have a shore dinner with
her mother and Aunt Eva. Then she always used to
shrink when the black waiter drew near, and her mother
and aunt would be convulsed with furtive mirth. "See
the little gump," her mother would say in the tenderest
tone, and look about to see if others at the other tables
saw how cunning she was—what a charming little
goose to be afraid of a colored waiter.

Ellen saw nobody except the lady and the black
woman, but she was still sure that there was a child in
the house, and after supper, when she was taken up-
stairs to bed, she peeped through every open door with
the expectation of seeing her.

But she was so weary and sleepy that her curiosity
and capacity for any other emotion was blunted. She
had become simply a little, tired, sleepy animal. She
let herself be undressed; she was not even moved to
much self-pity when the lady discovered the cruel

bruise on her delicate knee, and kissed it, and dressed it with a healing salve. She was put into a little night-gown which she knew dreamily belonged to that other child, and was laid in a little bedstead which she noted to be made of gold, with floating lace over the head.

She sleepily noted, too, that there were flowers on the walls, and more floating lace over the bureau. This room did not look so strange to her as the others; she had somehow from the treasures of her fancy provided the family of big bears and little bears with a similar one. Then, too, one of the neighbors, Mrs. George Crocker, had read many articles in women's papers relative to the beautifying of homes, and had furnished a wonderful chamber with old soap-boxes and rolls of Japanese paper which was a sort of a cousin many times removed of this. When she was in bed the lady kissed her, and called her darling, and bade her sleep well, and not be afraid, she was in the next room, and could hear if she spoke. Then she stood looking at her, and Ellen thought that she must be younger than Minnie Swensen, who lived on her street, and wore a yellow pigtail, and went to the high-school. Then she closed her heavy eyes, and forgot to cry about her poor father and mother; still, there was, after all, a hurt about them down in her childish heart, though a great wave of new circumstances had rolled on her shore and submerged for the time her memory and her love, even, she was so feeble and young.

She slept very soundly, and awoke only once, about two o'clock in the morning. Then a passing lantern flashed into the chamber into her eyes, and woke her up, but she only sighed and stretched drowsily, then turned her little body over with a luxurious roll and went to sleep again.

It was poor Andrew Brewster's lantern which flashed

in her eyes, for he was out with a posse of police and sympathizing neighbors and friends searching for his lost little girl. He was frantic, and when he came under the gas-lights from time to time the men that saw him shuddered; they would not have known him, for almost the farthest agony of which he was capable had changed his face.

CHAPTER III

BY the next morning all the city was in a commotion over little Ellen's disappearance. Woods on the outskirts were being searched, ponds were being dragged, posters with a stare of dreadful meaning in large characters of black and white were being pasted all over the fences and available barns, and already three of the local editors had been to the Brewster house to obtain particulars and photographs of the missing child for reproduction in the city papers.

The first train from Boston brought two reporters representing great dailies.

Fanny Brewster, white - cheeked, with the rasped redness of tears around her eyes and mouth, clad in her blue calico wrapper, received them in her best parlor. Eva had made a fire in the best parlor stove early that morning. "Folks will be comin' in all day, I expect," said she, speaking with nervous catches of her breath. Ever since the child had been missed, Eva's anxiety had driven her from point to point of unrest as with a stinging lash. She had pelted bareheaded down the road and up the road; she had invaded all the neighbors' houses, insisting upon looking through their farthest and most unlikely closets; she had even penetrated to the woods, and joined wild-eyed the groups of peering workers on the shore of the nearest pond. That she could not endure long, so she had rushed home to her sister, who was either pacing her sitting-room with inarticulate murmurs and wails of distress in the sympathizing ears of several of the neighboring women,

28

or else was staring with haggard eyes of fearful hope from a window. When she looked from the eastern window she could see her mother-in-law, Mrs. Zelotes Brewster, at an opposite one, sitting immovable, with her Bible in her lap, prayer in her heart, and an eye of grim holding to faith upon the road for the fulfilment of promise. She felt all her muscles stiffen with anger when she saw the wild eyes of the child's mother at the other window. "It is all her fault," she said to herself—"all her fault—hers and that bold trollop of a sister of hers." When she saw Eva run down the road, with her black hair rising like a mane to the morning wind, she was an embodiment of an imprecatory psalm. When, later on, she saw the three editors coming—Mr. Walsey, of *The Spy*, and Mr. Jones, of *The Observer*, and young Joe Bemis, of *The Star*, on his bicycle—she watched jealously to see if they were admitted. When Fanny's head disappeared from the eastern window she knew that Eva had let them in and Fanny was receiving them in the parlor. "She will tell them all about the words they had last night, that made the dear child run away," she thought. "All the town will know what doings there are in our family." Mrs. Zelotes made up her mind to a course of action. Each editor was granted a long audience with Fanny and Eva, who entertained them with hysterical solemnity and displayed Ellen's photographs in the red plush album, from the last, taken in her best white frock, to one when she was three weeks old, and seeming weakly and not likely to live. This had been taken by a photographer summoned to the house at great expense. "Her father has never spared expense for Ellen," said Fanny, with an outburst of grief. "That's so," said Eva. "I'll testify to that. Andrew Brewster never thought anything was too good for that young one." Then she burst out with a sob louder than her sister's. Eva had

29

usually a coarsely well-kempt appearance, her heavy black hair being securely twisted, and her neck ribbons tied with smart jerks of neatness; but to-day her hair was still in the fringy braids of yesterday, and her cotton blouse humped untidily in the back. Her face was red and her lips swollen; she looked like a very bacchante of sorrow, and as if she had been on some mad orgy of grief.

Mr. Walsey, of *The Spy*, who had formerly conducted a paper in a college town and was not accustomed to the feminine possibilities of manufacturing localities, felt almost afraid of her. He had never seen a woman of that sort, and thought vaguely of the French Revolution and fish-wives when she gave vent to her distress over the loss of the child. He fairly jumped when she cut short a question of his with a volley of self-recriminatory truths, accompanied with fierce gesturing. He stood back involuntarily out of reach of those powerful, waving arms. "Do I know of any reason for the child to run away?" shrieked Eva, in a voice shrilly hideous with emotion, now and then breaking into hoarseness with the strain of tears. "I guess I know why, I guess I do, and I wish I had been six foot under ground before I did what I did. It was all my fault, every bit of it. When I got home, and found that Fan had been making that precious young one a dress out of my old blue one, I pitched into her for it, and she gave it back to me, and then we jawed, and kept it up, till Andrew, he grabbed the dress and flung it into the fire, and did just right, too, and took Ellen and run over to old lady Brewster's with her; then Ellen, she see him cryin', and it scared her 'most to death, poor little thing, and she heard him say that if it wasn't for her he'd quit, and then she come runnin' home to her mother and me, and her mother said the same thing, and then that poor young one, she thought she wa'n't wanted nowheres, and she run. She always was as easy to hurt as a baby robin; it didn't take nothing to set her all of a flutter and a twitter; and now she's just flown out of the nest. Oh, my God, I wish my tongue had been torn out by the roots before I'd said a word about her blessed little dress; I wish Fan had cut up every old rag I've got; I'd go dressed in fig-leaves before I'd had it happen. Oh! oh! oh!"

Young Joe Bemis, of *The Star*, was the first to leave, whirling madly and precariously down the street on his wheel, which was dizzily tall in those days. Mrs. Zelotes, hailing him from her open window, might as well have hailed the wind. Her family dissensions were well aired in *The Star* next morning, and she always kept the cutting at the bottom of a little rosewood work-box where she stored away divers small treasures, and never looked at the box without a swift dart of pain as from a hidden sting and the consciousness as of the presence of some noxious insect caged therein.

Mrs. Zelotes was more successful in arresting the progress of the other editors, and (standing at the window, her Bible on the little table at her side) flatly contradicted all that had been told them by her daughter-in-law and her sister. "The Louds always give way, no matter what comes up. You can always tell what kind of a family anybody comes from by the way they take things when anything comes across them. You can't depend on anything she says this morning. My son did not marry just as I wished; everybody knows that; the Louds weren't equal to our family, and everybody knows it, and I have never made any secret as to how I felt, but we have always got along well enough. The Brewsters are not quarrelsome; they never have been. There were no words whatever last night to make my granddaughter run away. Eva and Fanny are all

31

wrong about it. Ellen has been stolen; I know it as well as if I had seen it. A strange-looking woman came to the door yesterday afternoon; she was the tallest woman I ever saw, and she took the widest steps; she measured her dress skirt every step she took, and she spoke gruff. I said then I knew she was a man dressed up. Ellen was playing out in the yard, and she saw the child as she went out, and I see her stoop and look at her real sharp, and my blood run kind of cold then, and I called Ellen away as quick as I could; and the woman, she turned round and gave me a look that I won't ever forget as long as I live. My belief is that that woman was laying in wait when Ellen was going across the yard home from here last night, and she has got her safe somewhere till a reward is offered. Or maybe she wants to keep her, Ellen is such a beautiful child. You needn't put in your papers that my grandchild run away because of quarrelling in our family, because she didn't. Eva and Fanny don't know what they are talking about, they are so wrought up; and, coming from the family they do, they don't know how to control themselves and show any sense. I feel it as much as they do, but I have been sitting here all the morning; I know I can't do anything to help, and I am working a good deal harder, waiting, than they are, rushing from pillar to post and taking on, and I'm doing more good. I shall be the only one fit to do anything when they find the poor child. I've got blankets warming by the fire, and my tea-kettle on, and I'm going to be the one to depend on when she's brought home." Mrs. Zelotes gave a glance of defiant faith from the window down the road as she spoke. Then she settled back in her chair and resumed her Bible, and dismissed the tall and forbidding woman whom she had summoned to save the honor of her family resolutely from her conscience. The

editors of *The Spy* and *The Observer* had a row of
ingratiating photographs of little Ellen from three weeks
to seven years of age; and their opinions as to the cause
of her disappearance, while fully agreeing in all points
of sensationalism with those of young Bemis, of *The
Star*, differed in detail.

Young Bemis read about the mysterious kidnapper,
and wondered, and the demand for *The Star* was chiefly
among the immediate neighbors of the Brewsters. Both
The Observer and *The Spy* doubled their circulation in
one day, and every face on the night cars was hidden
behind poor little Ellen's baby countenances and the
fairy-story of the witch-woman who had lured her away.
Mothers kept their children carefully in-doors that
evening, and pulled down curtains, fearful lest She look
in the windows and be tempted. Mrs. Zelotes also
waylaid both of the Boston reporters, but with results
upon which she had not counted. One presented her
story and Fanny's and Eva's with impartial justice;
the other kept wholly to the latter version, with the
addition of a shrewd theory of his own, deduced from
the circumstances which had a parallel in actual history,
and boldly stated that the child had probably committed
suicide on account of family troubles. Poor Fanny
and Eva both saw that, when night was falling and
Ellen had not been found. Eva rushed out and secured
the paper from the newsboy, and the two sisters gasped
over the startling column together.

"It's a lie! oh, Fanny, it's a lie!" cried Eva. "She
never would; oh, she never would! That little thing,
just because she heard you and me scoldin', and you
said that to her, that if it wasn't for her you'd go away.
She never would."

"Go away?" sobbed Fanny—"go away? I wouldn't
go away from hell if she was there. I would burn; I
would hear the clankin' of chains, and groans, and

screeches, and devils whisperin' in my ears what I had done wrong, for all eternity, before I'd go where they were playin' harps in heaven, if she was there. I'd like it better, I would. And I'd stay here if I had twenty sisters I didn't get along with, and be happier than I would be anywhere else on earth, if she was here. But she couldn't have done it. She didn't know how. It's awful to put such things into papers."

Eva jumped up with a fierce gesture, ran to the stove, and crammed the paper in. "There!" said she; "I wish I could serve all the papers in the country the same way. I do, and I'd like to put all the editors in after 'em. I'd like to put 'em in the stove with their own papers for kindlin's." Suddenly Eva turned with a swish of skirts, and was out of the room and pounding up-stairs, shaking the little house with every step. When she returned she bore over her arm her best dress—a cherished blue silk, ornate with ribbons and cheap lace. "Where's that pattern?" she asked her sister.

"She wouldn't ever do such a thing," moaned Fanny.

"Where's that pattern?"

"What pattern?" Fanny said, faintly.

"That little dress pattern. Her little dress pattern, the one you cut over my dress for her by."

"In the bureau drawer in my room. Oh, she wouldn't."

Eva went into the bedroom, returned with the pattern, got the scissors from Fanny's work-basket, and threw her best silk dress in a rustling heap upon the table.

Fanny stopped moaning and looked at her with wretched wonder. "What be you goin' to do?"

"Do?" cried Eva, fiercely—"do? I'm goin' to cut this dress over for her."

"You ain't."

"Yes, I be. If I drove her away from home, scoldin' because you cut over that other old thing of mine for

34

her, I'm goin' to make up for it now. I'm goin' to
give her my best blue silk, that I paid a dollar and a
half a yard for, and 'ain't worn three times. Yes, I be.
She's goin' to have a dress cut out of it, an' she's comin'
back to wear it, too. You'll see she is comin' home to
wear it."

Eva cut wildly into the silk with mad slashes of her
gleaming shears, while two neighboring women, who
had just come into the room, stared aghast, and even
Fanny was partly diverted from her sorrow.

"She's crazy," whispered one of the women, backing
away as she spoke.

"Oh, Eva, don't; don't do so," pleaded Fanny, tremulously.

"I be," said Eva, and she cut recklessly up the front
breadth.

"You ain't cutting it right," said the other neighbor,
who was skilful in such matters, and never fully moved
from her own household grooves by any excitement.
"If you are a-goin' to cut it at all, you had better cut
it right."

"I don't care how I cut it," returned Eva, thrusting
the woman away. "Oh, I don't care how I cut it; I
want to waste it. I will waste it."

The other neighbor backed entirely out of the room,
then turned and fled across the yard, her calico wrapper
blowing wildly and lashing about her slender legs,
to her own house, the doors of which she locked. Presently the other woman followed her, stepping with the
ponderous leisure which results from vastness of body
and philosophy of mind. The autumn wind, swirling
in impetuous gusts, had little effect upon her broadside
of woollen shawl. She had not come out on that raw
evening with nothing upon her head. She shook the
kitchen door of her friend, and smiled with calm reassurance when it was cautiously set ajar to disclose

a wide-eyed and open-mouthed face of terror. "Who is it?"

"It's me. What have you got your door locked for?"

"I think that Eva Loud is raving crazy. I'm afraid of her."

"Lord! you 'ain't no reason to be 'fraid of her. She ain't crazy. She's only lettin' the birds that fly over your an' my heads settle down to roost. You and me, both of us, if we was situated jest as she is, might think of doin' jest what she's a-doin', but we won't neither of us do it. We'd let our best dresses hang in the closet, safe and sound, while we cut them up in our souls; but Eva, she's different."

"Well, I don't care. I believe she's crazy, and I'm going to keep my doors locked. How do you know she hasn't killed Ellen and put her in the well?"

"Stuff! Now you're lettin' your birds roost, Hattie Monroe."

"I read something that wasn't any worse than that in the paper the other day. I should think they would look in the well. Have Mrs. Jones and Miss Cross gone home?"

"No; they are over there. There's poor Andrew coming now; I wonder if he has heard anything?"

Both women eyed hesitatingly poor Andrew Brewster's dejected figure creeping up the road in the dark.

"You holler and ask him," said the woman in the door.

"I hate to, for I know by his looks he 'ain't heard anything of her. I know he's jest comin' home to rest a minute, so he can start again. I know he 'ain't eat a thing since last night. Well, Maria has got some coffee all made, and a nice little piece of steak ready to cook."

"You holler and ask him."

36

"EVA SPRANG FORWARD AND CLUTCHED HIM BY THE ARM"

"What is the use? Just see the way he walks; I know without askin'."

However, as Andrew neared his house he involuntarily quickened his pace, and his head and shoulders became suddenly alert. It had occurred to him that possibly Fanny and Eva might have had some news of Ellen during his absence. Possibly she might have come home even.

Then he was hailed by the stout woman standing at the door of the next house. "Heard anything yet, Andrew?"

Andrew shook his head, and looked with despairing eyes at the windows where he used to see Ellen's little face. She had not come, then, for these women would have known it. He entered the house, and Fanny greeted him with a tremulous cry. "Have you heard anything; oh, have you heard anything, Andrew?"

Eva sprang forward and clutched him by the arm. "Have you?"

Andrew shook his head, and moved her hand from his arm, and pushed past her roughly.

Fanny stood in his way, and threw her arms around him with a wild, sobbing cry, but he pushed her away also with sternness, and went to the kitchen sink to wash his hands. The four women— his wife, her sister, and the two neighbors—stood staring at him; his face was terrible as he dipped the water from the pail on the sink corner, and the terribleness of it was accentuated by the homely and every-day nature of his action.

They all stared, then Fanny burst out with a loud and desperate wail. "He won't speak to me, he pushes me away, when it is our child that's lost — his as well as mine. He hasn't any feelings for me that bore her. He only thinks of himself. Oh, oh, my own husband pushes me away."

Andrew went on washing his hands and his ghastly

37

face, and made no reply. He had actually at that moment not the slightest sympathy with his wife. All his other outlets of affection were choked by his concern for his lost child; and as for pity, he kept reflecting, with a cold cruelty, that it served her right—it served both her and her sister right. Had not they driven the child away between them?

He would not eat the supper which the neighbors had prepared for him; finally he went across the yard to his mother's. It seemed to him at that time that his mother could enter into his state of mind better than any one else.

When he went out, Fanny called after him, frantically, "Oh, Andrew, you ain't going to leave me?"

When he made no response, she gazed for a second at his retreating back, then her temper came to her aid. She caught her sister's arm, and pulled her away out of the kitchen. "Come with me," she said, hoarsely. "I've got nobody but you. My own husband leaves me when he is in such awful trouble, and goes to that old woman, that has always hated me, for comfort."

The sisters went into Fanny's bedroom, and sat down on the edge of the bed, with their arms round each other. "Oh, Fanny!" sobbed Eva; "poor, poor Fanny! if Andrew turns against you, I will stand by you as long as I live. I will work my fingers to the bone to support you and Ellen. I will never get married. I will stay and work for you and her. And I will never get mad with you again as long as I live, Fanny. Oh, it was all my fault, every bit my fault, but, but—" Eva's voice broke; suddenly she clasped her sister tighter, and then she went down on her knees beside the bed, and hid her tangled head in her lap. "Oh, Fanny," she sobbed out miserably, "there ain't much excuse for me, but there's a little. When Jim Tenny stopped goin' with

38

me last summer, my heart 'most broke. I don't care if you do know it. That's what made me so much worse than I used to be. Oh, my heart 'most broke, Fanny! He's treated me awful, but I can't get over it; and now little Ellen's gone, and I drove her away!"

Fanny bent over her sister, and pressed her head close to her bosom. "Don't you feel so bad, Eva," said she. "You wasn't any more to blame than I was, and we'll stand by each other as long as we live."

"I'll work my fingers to the bone for you and Ellen, and I'll never get married," said Eva again.

CHAPTER IV

ELLEN BREWSTER was two nights and a day at Cynthia Lennox's, and no one discovered it. All day the searching - parties passed the house. Once Ellen was at the window, and one of the men looked up and saw her, and since his solicitude for the lost child filled his heart with responsiveness towards all childhood, he waved his hand and nodded, and bade another man look at that handsome little kid in the window.

"Guess she's about Ellen's size," said the other.

"Shouldn't wonder if she looked something like her," said the first.

"Answers the description well enough," said the other, "same light hair."

Both of the men waved their hands to Ellen as they passed on, but she shrank back afraid. That was about ten o'clock of the morning of the day after Miss Lennox had taken her into her house. She had waked at dawn with a full realization of the situation. She remembered perfectly all that had happened. She was a child for whom there were very few half-lights of life, and no spiritual twilights connected her sleeping and waking hours. She opened her eyes and looked around the room, and remembered how she had run away and how her mother was not there, and she remembered the strange lady with that same odd combination of terror and attraction and docility with which she had regarded her the night before. It was a very cold morning, and there was a delicate film of frost on the windows between the sweeps of the muslin curtains, and the morning sun gave it a rosy glow and a crusting sparkle as of diamonds. The sight of the frost had broken poor Andrew Brewster's heart when he saw it, and reflected how it might have meant death to his little tender child out under the blighting fall of it, like a little house-flower.

Ellen lay winking at it when Cynthia Lennox came into the room and leaned over her. The child cast a timid glance up at the tall, slender figure clad in a dressing-gown of quilted crimson silk which dazzled her eyes, accustomed as she was to morning wrappers of dark-blue cotton at ninety-eight cents apiece; and she was filled with undefined apprehensions of splendor and opulence which might overwhelm her simple grasp of life and cause her to lose all her old standards of value.

She had always thought her mother's wrappers very beautiful, but now look at this! Cynthia's face, too, in the dim, rosy light, looked very fair to the child, who had no discernment for those ravages of time of which adults either acquit themselves or by which they measure their own. She did not see the faded color of the woman's face at all; she did not see the spreading marks around mouth and eyes, or the faint parallels of care on the temples; she saw only that which her unbiased childish vision had ever sought in a human face, love and kindness, and tender admiration of herself; and her conviction of its beauty was complete. But at the same time a bitter and piteous jealousy for her mother and home, and all that she had ever loved and believed in, came over her. What right had this strange woman, dressed in a silk dress like that, to be leaning over her in the morning, and looking at her like that — to be leaning over her in the morning instead of her own mother, and looking at her in that way, when she was

41

not her mother? She shrank away towards the
other side of the bed with that nestling motion which
is the natural one of all young and gentle children
even towards vacancy, but suddenly Cynthia was leaning close over her, and she was conscious again of that
soft smother of violets, and Cynthia's arms were embracing all her delicate little body with tenderest violence,
folding her against the soft red silk over her bosom,
and kissing her little, blushing cheeks with the lightest
and carefulest kisses, as though she were a butterfly
which she feared to harm with her adoring touch.

"Oh, you darling, you precious darling!" whispered
Cynthia. "Don't be afraid, darling; don't be afraid,
precious; you are very safe; don't be afraid. You
shall have such a little, white, new-laid egg for your
breakfast, and some slices of toast, such a beautiful
brown, and some honey. Do you love honey, sweet?
And some chocolate, all in a little pink-and-gold cup
which you shall have for your very own."

"I want my mother!" Ellen cried out suddenly, with
an exceedingly bitter and terrified and indignant cry.

"There, there, darling!" Cynthia whispered; "there
is a beautiful red-and-green parrot down-stairs in a
great cage that shines like gold, and you shall have
him for your own, and he can talk. You shall have
him for your very own, sweetheart. Oh, you darling!
you darling!"

Ellen felt herself overborne and conquered by this
tide of love, which compelled like her mother's, though
this woman was not her mother, and her revolt of loyalty
was subdued for the time. After all, whether we like
it or not, love is somewhat of an impersonal quality to
all children, and perhaps to their elders, and it may
be in such wise that the goddess is evident.

She did not shrink from Cynthia any more then, but
suffered her to lift her out of bed as if she were a baby

and set her on a white fur rug, into which her feet sank, to her astonishment. Her mother had only drawn-in rugs, which Ellen had watched her make. She was a little afraid of the fur rug.

Ellen was very small, and seemed much younger than she was by reason of her baby silence and her little clinging ways. Then, too, she had always been so petted at home, and through never going to school had not been in contact with other children. Often the bloom of childhood is soonest rubbed off by friction with its own kind. Diamond cut diamond holds good in many cases.

Cynthia did not think she was more than six years old, and never dreamed of allowing her to dress herself, and indeed the child had always been largely assisted in so doing. Cynthia washed her and dressed her, and curled her hair, and led her down-stairs into the dining-room of the night before, which Ellen still regarded with wise eyes as the store. Then she sat in the tall chair which must have been vacated by that mysterious other child, and had her breakfast, eating her new-laid egg, which the black woman broke for her, while she leaned delicately away as far as she could with a timid shrug of her little shoulder, and sipping her chocolate out of the beautiful pink-and-gold cup. That, however, Ellen decided within herself was not nearly as pretty as one with "A Gift of Friendship" on it in gilt letters which her grandmother kept on the whatnot in her best parlor. This had been given to her aunt Ellen, who died when she was a young girl, and was to be hers when she grew up. She did not care as much for the egg and toast either as for the griddle-cakes and maple syrup at home. All through breakfast Cynthia talked to her, and in such manner as the child had never heard. That fine voice, full of sweetest modulations and cadences, which used the language

43

with the precision of a musician, was as different from the voices at home with their guttural slurs and maimed terminals as the song of a spring robin from the scream of the parrot which Ellen could hear in some distant room. And what Cynthia said was as different from ordinary conversation to the child as a fairy tale, being interspersed with terms of endearment which her mother and grandmother would have considered high-flown, and have been shamefaced in employing, and full of a whimsical playfulness which had an undertone of pathos in it. Cynthia was not still for a minute, and seemed to feel that much of her power lay in her speech and voice, like some enchantress who cast her spell by means of her silver tongue. Nobody knew how she dreaded that outcry of Ellen's, "I want my mother!" It gave her the sensations of a murderess, even while she persisted in her crime. So she talked, diverting the child's mind from its natural channel by sheer force of eloquence. She told a story about the parrot, which caused Ellen's eyes to widen with thoughtful wonder; she promised her treasures and pleasures which made her mouth twitch into smiles in spite of herself; but with all her efforts, when after breakfast they went into another room, Ellen broke out again, "I want my mother!"

Cynthia turned white and struggled with herself for a moment, then she spoke. That which she was doing of the nature of a crime was in reality more foreign to her nature than virtue, and her instinct was to return to her narrow and straight way in spite of its cramping of love and natural longings. "Who is your mother, darling?" she asked. "And what is your name?"

But Ellen was silent, except for that one cry, "I want my mother!" The persistency of the child, in spite of her youth and her distress, was almost invulner-

44

able. She came of a stiff-necked family on one side at least, and sometimes stiff-neckedness is more pronounced in a child than in an adult, in whom it may be tempered by experience and policy. "I want my mother! I want my mother!" Ellen repeated in her gentle wail as plaintively inconsequent as the note of a bird, and would say no more.

Then Cynthia displayed the parrot, but a parrot was too fine and fierce a bird for Ellen. She would have preferred him as a subject for her imagination, which could not be harmed by his beak and claws, and she liked Cynthia's story about him better than the gorgeous actuality of the bird himself. She shrank back from that shrieking splendor, clinging with strong talons to his cage wires, against which he pressed cruelly his red breast and beat his gold-green wings, and through which he thrust his hooked beak, and glared with his yellow eyes.

Ellen fairly sobbed at last when the parrot thrust out a wicked and deceiving claw towards her, and said something in his unearthly shriek which seemed to have a distinct reference to her, and fired at her a volley of harsh "How do's" and "Good-mornings," and "Good-nights," and "Polly want a cracker's," then finished with a wild shriek of laughter, her note of human grief making a curious chord with the bird's of inhuman mirth. "I want my mother!" she panted out, and wept, and would not be comforted. Then Cynthia took her away from the parrot and produced the doll. Then truly did the sentiment of emulative motherhood in her childish breast console her for the time for her need of her own mother. Such a doll as that she had never seen, not even in the store-windows at Christmas-time. Still, she had very fine dolls for a little girl whose relatives were not wealthy, but this doll was like a princess, and nearly as large as Ellen.

45

Ellen held out her arms for this ravishing creature in a French gown, looked into its countenance of unflinching infantile grace and amiability and innocence, and her fickle heart betrayed her, and she laughed with delight, and the tension of anxiety relaxed in her face.

"Where is her mother?" she asked of Cynthia, having a very firm belief in the little girl-motherhood of dolls. She could not imagine a doll without her little mother, and even in the cases of the store-dolls, she wondered how their mothers could let them be sold, and mothered by other little girls, however poor they might be. But she never doubted that her own dolls were her very own children even if they had been bought in a store. So now she asked Cynthia with an indescribably pitying innocence, "Where is her mother?"

Cynthia laughed and looked adoringly at the child with the doll in her arms. "She has no mother but you," said she. "She is yours, but once she belonged to a dear little boy, who used to live with me."

Ellen stared thoughtfully: she had never seen a little boy with a doll. The lady seemed to read her thought, for she laughed again.

"This little boy had curls, and he wore dresses like a little girl, and he was just as pretty as a little girl, and he loved to play with dolls like a little girl," said she.

"Where is he?" asked Ellen, in a small, gentle voice. "Don't he want her now?"

"No, darling," said Cynthia; "he is not here; he has been gone away two years, and he had left off his baby curls and his dresses, and stopped playing with her for a year before that." Cynthia sighed and drew down her mouth, and Ellen looked at her lovingly and wonderingly.

"Be you his mother?" she asked, piteously; then, before Cynthia could answer, her own lip quivered and

46

she sobbed out again, even while she hugged her doll-child to her bosom, "I want my mother! I want my mother!"

All that day the struggle went on. Cynthia Lennox, leading her little guest, who always bore the doll, traversed the fine old house in search of distraction, for the heart of the child was sore for its mother, and success was always intermittent. The music-box played, the pictures were explained, and even old trunks of laid-away treasures ransacked. Cynthia took her through the hot-houses and gave her all the flowers she liked to pick, to still that longing cry of hers. Cynthia Lennox had fine hot-houses kept by an old colored man, the husband of her black cook. Her establishment was very small; her one other maid she had sent away early that morning to make a visit with a sick sister in another town. The old colored couple had lived in her family since she was born, and would have been silent had she stolen a whole family of children. Ellen caught a glimpse of a bent, dark figure at one end of the pink-house as they entered; he glanced up at her with no appearance of surprise, only a broad, welcoming expansion of his whole face, which caused her to shrink; then he shuffled out in response to an order of his mistress.

Ellen stared at the pinks, swarming as airily as butterflies in motley tints of palest rose to deepest carmine over the blue-green jungle of their stems; she sniffed the warm, moist, perfumed atmosphere; she followed Cynthia down the long perspective of bloom, then she said again that she wanted her mother; and Cynthia led her into the rose-house, then into one where the grapes hung low overhead and the air was as sweet and strong as wine, but even there Ellen wanted her mother.

But it was not until the next morning when she was

47

eating her breakfast that the climax came. Then the door-bell rang, and presently Cynthia was summoned into another room. She kissed Ellen, and bade her go on with her breakfast and she would return shortly; but before she had quite left the room a man stood unexpectedly in the door-way, a man who looked younger than Cynthia. He had a fair mustache, a high forehead scowling over near-sighted blue eyes, and stood with a careless slouch of shoulders in a gray coat.

"Good-morning," he began. Then he stopped short when he saw Ellen in her tall chair staring shyly around at him through her soft golden mist of hair. "What child is that?" he demanded; but Cynthia with a sharp cry sprang to him, and fairly pulled him out of the room, and closed the door.

Then Ellen heard voices rising higher and higher, and Cynthia say, in a voice of shrill passion: "I cannot, Lyman. I cannot give her up. You don't know what I have suffered since George married and took little Robert away. I can't let this child go."

Then came the man's voice, hoarse with excitement: "But, Cynthia, you must; you are mad. Think what this means. Why, if people know what you have done, kept this child, while all this search has been going on, and made no effort to find out who she was—"

"I did ask her, and she would not tell me," Cynthia said, miserably.

"Good Lord! what of that? That is nothing but a subterfuge. You must have seen in the papers—"

"I have not looked at a paper since she came."

"Of course you have not. You were afraid to. Why, good God! Cynthia Lennox, I don't know but you will stand in danger of lynching if people ever find this out, that you have taken in this child and kept her in this way—I don't know what people will do."

Ellen waited for no more; she rose softly, she gathered

48

up her great doll which sat in a little chair near by, she gathered up her pink-and-gold cup which had been given her, and the pinks which had been brought from the hot-house the day before, which Cynthia had arranged in a vase beside her plate, then she stole very softly out of the side door, and out of the house, and ran down the street as fast as her little feet could carry her.

CHAPTER V

THAT morning, after the street in front of Lloyd's factory had been cleared of the flocking employés with their little dinner-boxes, and the great broadside of the front windows had been set with faces of the workers, a distracted figure came past. A young fellow at a window of the cutting-room noticed her first. "Look at that, Jim Tenny," said he, with a shove of an elbow towards his next neighbor.

"Get out, will ye?" growled Jim Tenny, but he looked.

Then three girls from the stitching-room came crowding up behind with furtively tender pressings of round arms against the shoulders of the young men. "We come in here to see if that was Eva Loud," said one, a sharp-faced, alert girl, not pretty, but a favorite among the male employés, to the constant wonder of the other girls.

"Yes, it's her fast enough," rejoined another, a sweet-faced blonde with an exaggeratedly fashionable coiffure and a noticeable smartness in the tie of her neck-ribbon and the set of her cotton waist. "Just look at the poor thing's hair. Only see how frowsly it is, and she has come out without her hat."

"Well, I don't wonder," said the third girl, who was elderly and whose complexion was tanned and weather-beaten almost to the color of the leather upon which she worked. Yet through this seamed and discolored face, with thin grayish hair drawn back tightly from the temples, one could discern, as through a transparent mask, a past prettiness and an exceeding gentleness

50

and faithfulness. "If my sister's little Helen was to be lost I shouldn't know whether my hat was on or not," said she. "I believe I should go raving mad."

"You wouldn't have to slave as you have done supportin' it ever since your sister's husband died," said the pretty girl. "Only look how Eva's waist bags in the back and she 'ain't got any belt on. I wouldn't come out lookin' so."

"I should die if I didn't have something to work for. That's the difference between being a worker and a slave," said the other girl, simply. "Poor Eva!"

"Well, it was a pretty young one," said the first girl.

"Looks to me as if Eva Loud's skirt was comin' off," said the pretty girl. She pressed close to Jim Tenny with a familiar air of proprietorship as she spoke, but the young man did not seem to heed her. He was looking over his bench at the figure on the street below, and his heavy black eyebrows were scowling, and his mouth set.

Jim Tenny was handsome after a swarthy and grimy fashion, for the tint of the leather seemed to have become absorbed into his skin. His black mustache bristled roughly, but his face was freer than usual from his black beard-stubble, because the day before had been Sunday and he had shaved. His black right hand with its squat discolored nails grasped his cutting-knife with a hard clutch, his left held the piece of leather firmly in place, while he stared out with that angry and anxious scowl at Eva, who had paused on the street below, and was staring up at the windows, as if she meditated a wild search in the factory for the lost child. There was a curious likeness between the two faces; people had been accustomed to say that Eva Loud and her gentleman looked more like brother and sister than a courting couple, and there was, moreover, a curious spirit of comradeship between the two. It asserted itself now with the young man, in opposition to the more purely sexual attraction of the pretty girl who was leaning against him, and for whom he had deserted Eva.

After all, friendship and good comradeship are a steadier force than love, if not as overwhelming, and it may be that tortoise of the emotions which outruns the hare.

"Well, for my part, I think a good deal more of Eva Loud than if she had come out all frizzed and ruffled— shows her heart is in the right place," said the man who had spoken first. He spoke with a guttural drawl, and kept on with his work, but there was a meaning in his words for the pretty girl, who had coquetted with him before taking up with Jim Tenny.

"That is so," said another man at Jim Tenny's right. "She is right to come out as she has done when she is so anxious for the child." This man was a fair-haired Swede, and he spoke English with a curious and careful precision, very different from the hurried, slurring intonations of the other men. He had been taught the language by a philanthropic young lady, a college graduate, in whose father's family he had lived when he first came to America, and in consequence he spoke like a gentleman and had some considerable difficulty in understanding his companions.

"Eva Loud has had a damned hard time, take it all together," spoke out another man, looking over his bench at the girl on the street. He was small and thin and wiry, a mass of brown-coated muscles under his loose-hanging gingham shirt. He plied feverishly his cutting-knife with his lean, hairy hands as he spoke. He was accounted one of the best and swiftest cutters in Lloyd's, and he worked unceasingly, for he had an invalid wife and four children to support. Now and then he had to stop to cough, then he worked faster.

"That's so," said the first man.

"Yes, that is so," said the Swede, with a nod of his fair head.

"And now to lose this young one that she set her life by," said the first girl, with an evident point of malice in her tone, and a covert look at the pretty girl at Jim Tenny's side. Jim Tenny paled under his grime; the hand which held the knife clinched.

"What do you s'pose has become of the young one?" said the first girl. "There's a good many out from the shop huntin' this mornin', ain't there?"

"Fifty," said the first man, laconically.

"You three were out all day yesterday, wa'n't you?"

"Yes, Jim and Carl and me were out till after midnight."

"Well, I wonder whether the poor little young one is alive? Don't seem as if she could be—but—"

"Look there! look there!" screamed the elderly girl suddenly. "Look at *there !*" She began to dance, she laughed, she sobbed, she waved her lean hands frantically out of the window, leaning far over the bench. "Look at there!" she kept crying. Then she turned and ran out of the room, with the other girls and half the cutting-room after her.

"Damn it, she's got the child!" said the thin man. He kept on working, his dark, sinewy hands flying over the sheets of leather, but the tears ran down his cheeks. Lloyd's emptied itself into the street, and surrounded Eva Loud and Ellen, who, running aimlessly, had come straight to her aunt. Jim Tenny was first.

Eva stood clasping the child, who was too frightened to cry, and was breathing in hushed gasps, her face hidden on her aunt's broad bosom. Eva had caught her up at the first sight of her, and now she stood clasping her fiercely, and looking at them all as if she thought they wanted to rob her of the child. Even when a great cheer went up from the crowd, and was echoed by

53

another from the factory, with an accompaniment of waving bare, leather-stained arms and hands, that expression of desperate defiance instead of the joy of recovery did not leave her face, not until she saw Jim Tenny's face working with repressed emotion and met his eyes full of the memory of old comradeship. Then her bold heart and her pride all melted and she burst out in a great wail before them all.

"Oh, Jim!" she cried out. "Oh, Jim, I lost you, and then I thought I'd lost her! Oh, Jim!"

Then there was a chorus of feminine sobs, for Eva's wild weeping had precipitated the ready sympathy of half the girls present. The men started a cheer to cover a certain chivalrous shamefacedness which was upon them at the sight of the girl's grief, and another cheer from the factory echoed it. Then came another sound, the great steam-whistle of Lloyd's; then the whistles of the other neighboring factories responded, and people began to swarm out of them, and the windows to fill with eager faces. Jim Tenny grasped Eva's arm with a grasp like a vise. "Come this way," said he, sharply. "Come this way, Eva."

"Oh, Jim! oh, Jim!" Eva sobbed again; but she followed him, little Ellen's golden fleece tossing over her shoulder.

"She's got her; she's got her!" shouted the people.

Then the leather-stained hands gyrated, the cheers went up, and again the whistles blew.

Jim Tenny, with his hand on Eva's arm, pushed his way through the crowd.

"Where you goin', Jim?" asked the pretty girl at his elbow, but he pushed past her roughly, and did not seem to hear. Eva's face was all inflamed and convulsed with sobs, but she did not dream of covering it— she was full of the holy shamelessness of grief and joy. "Let me see her! let me see her! Oh, the dear little

54

thing, only look at her ! Where have you been, precious?
Are you hungry? Oh, Nellie, she is hungry, I know!
She looks thin. Run over to the bakery and buy her
some cookies, quick! Are you cold? Give her this
sacque. Only look at her! Kate, only look at her!
Are you hurt, darling? Has anybody hurt you? If
anybody has, he shall be hung! Oh, you darling!
Only see her, 'Liza."

But Jim Tenny, his mouth set, his black brows scowling, his hard grasp on Eva's arm, pushed straight
through the gathering crowd until they came to Clarkson's stables at the rear of Lloyd's, where he kept his
horse and buggy—for he lived at a distance from his
work, and drove over every morning. He pointed to a
chair which a hostler had occupied, tilted against the
wall, for a morning smoke, after the horses were fed
and watered, and which he had vacated to join the
jubilant crowd. "Sit down there," he said to Eva.
Then he hailed a staring man coming out of the office.
"Here, help me in with my horse, quick!" said he.

The man stared still, with slowly rising indignation.
He was portly and middle-aged, the senior partner of
the firm, who seldom touched his own horses of late
years, and had a son at Harvard. "What's to pay?
What do you mean? Anybody sick?" he asked.

"Help me into the buggy with my horse!" shouted
Jim Tenny. "I tell you the child is found, and I've
got to take it home to its folks."

"Don't they know yet? Is that it?"

"Yes, I tell you." Jim was backing out his horse
as he spoke.

Mr. Clarkson seized a harness and threw the collar
over the horse's head, while Jim ran out the buggy.
When Mr. Clarkson lifted Eva and Ellen into the buggy
he gave the child's head a pat. "God bless it!" he said,
and his voice broke.

The horse was restive. Jim took a leap into the buggy at Eva's side, and they were out with a dash and a swift rattle. The crowd parted before them, and cheer after cheer went up. The whistles sounded again. Then all the city bells rang out. They were signalling the other searchers that the child was found. Jim and Eva and Ellen made a progress of triumph down the street. The crowd pursued them with cheers of rejoicing; doors and windows flew open; the house-yards were full of people. Jim drove as fast as he could, scowling hard to hide his tenderness and pity. Eva sat by his side, weeping in her terrible candor of grief and joy, and Ellen's golden locks tossed on her shoulder.

CHAPTER VI

As Jim Tenny, with Eva Loud and the child, drove down the road towards the Brewster house, his horse and buggy became the nucleus of a gathering procession, shouting and exclaiming, with voices all tuned to one key of passionate sympathy. There were even many women of the poorer class who had no sense of indecency in following the utmost lead of their tender emotions. Some of them bore children of their own in their arms, and were telling them with passionate croonings to look at the other little girl in the carriage who had been lost, and gone away a whole day and two nights from her mother. They often called out fondly to Ellen and Eva, and ordered Jim to wait a moment that they might look at the poor darling. But Jim drove on as fast as he was able, though he had sometimes to rein his horse sharply to avoid riding down some lean racing boys, who would now and then shoot ahead of him with loud whoops of triumph. Once as he drove he laid one hand caressingly over Eva's. "Poor girl!" he said, hoarsely and shamefacedly, and Eva sobbed loudly. When Jim reached Mrs. Zelotes Brewster's house there was a swift displacement of lights and shadows in a window, a door flew open, and the gaunt old woman was at the wheel.

"Stop!" she cried. "Stop! Bring her in here to me! Let me have her! Give her to me; I have got everything ready! Come, Ellen — come to grandmother!"

Then there was a mad rush from the opposite direction, and the child's mother was there, reaching into the buggy with fierce arms of love and longing. "Give her to me!" she shrieked out. "Give me my baby, Eva Loud! Oh, Ellen, where have you been?"

Fanny Brewster dragged her child from her sister's arms so forcibly that she seemed fairly to fly over the wheel. Then she strained her to her hungry bosom, covering her with kisses, wetting her soft face and yellow hair with tears.

"My baby, mother's darling, mother's baby!" she gasped out with great pants of satisfied love; but another pair of lean, wiry old arms stole around the child's slender body.

"Give her to me!" demanded Mrs. Zelotes Brewster. "She is my son's child, and I have a right to her! You will kill her, goin' on so over her. Give her to me! I have everything all ready in my house to take care of her. Give her to me, Fanny Loud!"

"Keep your hands off her!" cried Fanny. "She's my own baby, and nobody's goin' to take her away from me, I guess."

"Give her to me this minute!" said Mrs. Zelotes Brewster. "You'll kill her, goin' on so. You're frightenin' her to death. Give her to me this minute!"

Ellen, meanwhile, that little tender blossom tossed helplessly by contending waves of love, was weeping and trembling with joy at the feel of her mother's arms and with awe and terror at this tempest of passion which she had evoked.

"Give her to me!" demanded Mrs. Zelotes Brewster.

The crowd who had followed stood gaping with working faces. The mothers wept over their own children. Eva stood at her sister's elbow, with a hand on one of the child's, which was laid over Fanny's shoulder. Jim Tenny had his face hidden on his horse's neck.

" ' SHE'S GOT HER ! ' SHOUTED THE PEOPLE "

"Give her to me!" said Mrs. Zelotes again. "Give her to me, I say! I am her own grandmother!"

"And I am her own mother!" called out Fanny, with a great master-note of love and triumph and defiance. "I'm her own mother, and I've got her, and nobody but God shall take her from me again." The tears streamed down her cheeks; she kissed the child with pale, parted lips. She was at once pathetic and terrible. She was human love and selfishness incarnate.

Mrs. Zelotes Brewster stared at her, and her face changed suddenly and softened. She turned and went back into her own house. Her gray head appeared a second beside her window, then sank out of sight. She was kneeling there with her Bible at her side, a sudden sweet humility of thankfulness rising from her whole spirit like a perfume, when Fanny, with Eva following, still clinging to the child's little hand over her sister's shoulder, went across the yard to her own house to tell her husband. The others followed, and stood about outside, listening with curiosity sanctified by intensest sympathy. One nervous-faced boy leaped on the slant of the bulkhead to peer in a window of the sitting-room, and when his mother pulled him back forcibly, rubbed his grimy little knuckles across his eyes, and a dark smooch appeared on his nose and cheeks. He was a young boy, very small and thin for his age. He whispered to his mother and she nodded, and he darted off in the direction of his own home.

Andrew Brewster had just come home after an all-night's search, and he was in his bedroom in the bitter sleep of utter exhaustion and despair. Suddenly his heart had failed him and his brain had reeled. He had begun to feel dazed, to forget for a minute what he was looking for. He had made incoherent replies to the men with him, and finally one, after a whispered consultation with the others, had said: "Look at here, Andrew, old fellow; you'd better go home and rest a bit. We'll look all the harder while you're gone, and maybe she'll be found when you wake up."

"Who will be found?" Andrew asked, with a dazed look. He reeled as if he were drunk.

"Ain't had anything, has he?" one of the men whispered.

"Not a drop to my knowledge."

Andrew's lips trembled perceptibly; his forehead was knitted with vacuous perplexity; his eyes reflected blanks of unreason; his whole body had an effect of weak settling and subsidence. The man who worked next to him in the cutting-room at Lloyd's, and had searched at his side indefatigably from the first, stole a tender hand under his shoulder. "Come along with me, old man," he said, and Andrew obeyed.

When Fanny and Eva came in with the child, he lay prostrate on the bed, and scarcely seemed to breathe. A great qualm of fear shot over Fanny for a second. His father had died of heart-disease.

"Is he—dead?" she gasped to Eva.

"No, of course he ain't," said Eva. "He's asleep; he's wore out. Andrew, Andrew, Andrew, wake up! She's found, Andrew; Ellen's found." But Andrew did not stir.

"He is!" gasped Fanny, again.

"No, he ain't. Andrew, Andrew Brewster, wake up, wake up! Ellen's here! She's found!"

Fanny put Ellen down, and bent over Andrew and listened. "No, I can hear him breathe," she cried. Then she kissed him, and leaned her mouth close to his ear. "Andrew!" she said, in a voice which Eva and Ellen had never heard before. "Andrew, poor old man, wake up; she's found! Our child is found!"

When Andrew still did not wake, but only stirred,

60

and moaned faintly, Fanny lifted Ellen onto the bed. "Kiss poor father, and wake him," she told her.

Ellen, whose blue eyes were big with fright and wonder, whose lips were quivering, and whose little body was vibrating with the strain of her nerves, laid her soft cheek against her father's rough, pale one, and stole a little arm under his neck. "Father, wake up!" she called out in her little, trembling, sweet voice, and that reached Andrew Brewster in the depths of his own physical inertness. He opened his eyes and looked at the child, and the light came into them, and then the sound of his sobbing filled the house and reached the people out in the yard, and an echo arose from them. Gradually the crowd dispersed. Jim Tenny, before he drove away, went to the door and spoke to Eva.

"Anything I can do?" he asked, with a curious, tender roughness. He did not look at her as he spoke.

"No; thank you, Jim," replied Eva.

Suddenly the young man reached out a hand and stroked her rough hair. "Well, take care of yourself, old girl," he said.

Eva went to her sister as Jim went out of the yard. Ellen was in the sitting-room with her father, and Fanny had gone to the kitchen to heat some milk for the child, whom she firmly believed to have had nothing to eat during her absence.

"Fanny," said Eva.

"Well?" said Fanny. "I can't stop; I must get some milk for her; she must be 'most starved."

Fanny turned and looked at Eva, who cast down her eyes before her in a very shamefacedness of happiness and contrition.

"Why, what is it?" repeated Fanny, staring at her.

"I've got Jim back, I guess, as well as Ellen," said Eva, "and I'm going to be a good woman."

After all the crowd of people outside had gone, the

61

little nervous boy raced into the Brewster yard with a tin cup of chestnuts in his hand. He knocked at the side door, and when Fanny opened it he thrust them upon her. "They're for her!" he blurted out, and was gone, racing like a deer.

"Don't you want the cup back?" Fanny shouted after him.

"No, ma'am," he called back, and that, although his mother had charged him to bring back the cup or he would get a scolding.

CHAPTER VII

ELLEN had clung fast all the time to her doll, her bunch of pinks, and her cup and saucer; or, rather, she had guarded them jealously. "Where did you get all these things?" her aunt Eva had asked her, amazedly, when she first caught sight of her, and then had not waited for an answer in her wild excitement of joy at the recovery of the child. The great, smiling wax doll had ridden between Jim and Eva in the buggy, Eva had held the pink cup and saucer with a kind of mechanical carefulness, and Ellen herself clutched the pinks in one little hand, though she crushed them against her aunt's bosom as she sat in her lap. Ellen's grandmother and aunt had glanced at these treasures with momentary astonishment, and so had her mother, but curiosity was in abeyance for both of them for the time; rapture at the sight of the beloved child at whose loss they had suffered such agonies was the one emotion of their souls. But later investigation was to follow.

When Ellen did not seem to care for her hot milk liberally sweetened in her own mug, and griddle-cakes with plenty of syrup, her mother looked at her, and her eyes of love sharpened with inquiry. "Ain't you hungry?" she said. Ellen shook her head. She was sitting at the table in the dining-room, and her father, mother, and aunt were all hovering about her, watching her. Some of the neighbor women were also in the room, staring with a sort of deprecating tenderness of curiosity.

"Do you feel sick?" Ellen's father inquired, anxiously.

63

"You don't feel sick, do you?" repeated her mother. Ellen shook her head.

Just then Mrs. Zelotes Brewster came in with her black - and - white - checked shawl pinned around her gaunt old face, which had in it a strange softness and sweetness, which made Fanny look at her again, after the first glance, and not know why.

"We've got our blessing back again, mother," said her son Andrew, in a broken voice.

"But she won't eat her breakfast, now mother has gone and cooked it for her, so nice, too," said Fanny, in a tone of confidence which she had never before used towards Mrs. Zelotes.

"You don't feel sick, do you, Ellen?" asked her grandmother.

Ellen shook her head. "No, ma'am," said she.

"She says she don't feel sick, and she ain't hungry," Andrew said, anxiously.

"I wonder if she would eat one of my new dough-nuts. I've got some real nice ones," said a neighbor— the stout woman from the next house, whose breadth of body seemed to symbolize a corresponding spiritual breadth of motherliness, as she stood there looking at the child who had been lost and was found.

"Don't you want one of Aunty Wetherhed's nice doughnuts?" asked Fanny.

"No; I thank you," replied Ellen. Eva started suddenly with an air of mysterious purpose, opened a door, ran down cellar, and returned with a tumbler of jelly, but Ellen shook her head even at that.

"Have you had your breakfast?" said Fanny.

Then Ellen was utterly quiet. She did not speak, she made no sign or motion. She sat still, looking straight before her.

"Don't you hear, Ellen?" said Andrew. "Have you had your breakfast this morning?"

64

"Tell Auntie Eva if you have had your breakfast," Eva said.

Mrs. Zelotes Brewster spoke with more authority, and she went further.

"Tell grandmother if you have had your breakfast, and where you had it," said she.

But Ellen was dumb and motionless. They all looked at one another. "Tell Aunty Wetherhed: that's a good girl," said the stout woman.

"Where are those things she had when I first saw her?" asked Mrs. Zelotes, suddenly. Eva went into the sitting-room, and fetched them out—the bunch of pinks, the cup and saucer, and the doll. Ellen's eyes gave a quick look of love and delight at the doll.

"She had these, luggin' along in her little arms, when I first caught sight of her comin'," said Eva.

"Where did you get them, Ellen?" asked Fanny. "Who gave them to you?"

Ellen was silent, with all their inquiring eyes fixed upon her face like a compelling battery. "Where have you been, Ellen, all the time you have been gone?" asked Mrs. Zelotes. "Now you have got back safe, you must tell us where you have been."

Andrew stooped his head down to the child's, and rubbed his rough cheek against her soft one, with his old facetious caress. "Tell father where you've been," he whispered. Ellen gave him a little piteous glance, and her lip quivered, but she did not speak.

"Where do you s'pose she got them?" whispered one neighbor to another.

"I can't imagine; that's a beautiful doll."

"Ain't it? It must have cost a lot. I know, because my Hattie had one her aunt gave her last Christmas; that one cost a dollar and ninety-eight cents, and it didn't begin to compare with this. That's a handsome cup and saucer, too."

"Yes, but you can get real handsome cups and saucers to Crosby's for twenty-five cents. I don't think so much of that."

"Them pinks must have come from a greenhouse."

"Yes, they must."

"Well, there's lots of greenhouses in the city besides the florists. That don't help much." Then the first woman inclined her lips closely to the other woman's ear and whispered, causing the other to start back. "No, I can't believe she would," said she.

"She came from those Louds on her mother's side," whispered the first woman, guardedly, with dark emphasis.

"Ellen," said Fanny, suddenly, and almost sharply, "you didn't take those things in any way you hadn't ought to, did you? Tell mother."

"Fanny!" cried Andrew.

"If she did, it's the first time a Brewster ever stole," said Mrs. Zelotes. Her face was no longer strange with unwonted sweetness as she looked at Fanny.

Andrew put his face down to Ellen's again. "Father knows she didn't steal the things; never mind," he whispered.

Suddenly the stout woman made a soft, ponderous rush out of the room and the house. She passed the window with oscillating swiftness.

"Where's Miss Wetherhed gone?" said one woman to another.

"She's thought of somethin'."

"Maybe she left her bread in the oven."

"No, she's thought of somethin'."

A very old lady, who had been sitting in a rocking-chair on the other side of the room, rose trembling and came to Ellen and leaned over her, looking at her with small, black, bright eyes through gold-rimmed spectacles. The old woman was deaf, and her voice was

66

shrill and high-pitched to reach her own consciousness.
"What did such a good little girl as you be run away
from father and mother for?" she piped, going back
to first principles and the root of the whole matter,
since she had heard nothing of the discussion which
had been going on about her, and had supposed it to
deal with them.

Ellen gasped. Suddenly all her first woe returned
upon her recollection. She turned innocent, accusing
eyes upon her father's loving face, then her mother's
and aunt's. "You said—you said—you—" she stammered out, but then her father and mother were both
down upon their knees before her in her chair embracing her, and Eva, too, seized her little hands. "You
mustn't ever think of what you heard father and
mother say, Ellen," Andrew said, solemnly. "You
must forget all about it. Father and mother were both
very wrong and wicked—"

"And Aunt Eva, too," sobbed Eva.

"And they didn't mean what they said," continued
Andrew. "You are the greatest blessing in this whole
world to father and mother; you're all they have got.
You don't know what father and mother have been
through, thinking you were lost and they might never
see their little girl again. Now you mustn't ever think
of what they said again."

"And you won't ever hear them say it again, Ellen,"
Fanny Brewster said, with a noble humbling of herself
before her child.

"No, you won't," said Eva.

"Mother is goin' to try to do better, and have more
patience, and not let you hear such talk any more,"
said Fanny, kissing Ellen passionately, and rising
with Andrew's arm around her.

"I'm going to try, too, Ellen," said Eva.

The stout woman came padding softly and heavily

into the room, and there was a bright-blue silken gleam in her hand. She waved a whole yard of silk of the most brilliant blue before Ellen's dazzled eyes. "There!" said she, triumphantly, "if you will tell Aunty Wetherhed where you've been, and all about it, she'll give you all this beautiful silk to make a new dress for your new dolly."

Ellen looked in the woman's face, she looked at the blue silk, and she looked at the doll, but she was silent.

"Only think what a beautiful dress it will make!" said a woman.

"And see how pretty it goes with the dolly's light hair," said Fanny.

"Ellen," whispered Andrew, "you tell father, and he'll buy you a whole pound of candy down to the store."

"I shouldn't wonder if I could find something to make your dolly a cloak," said a woman.

"And I'll make her a beautiful little bonnet, if you'll tell," said another.

"Only think, a whole pound of candy!" said Andrew.

"I'll buy you a gold ring," Eva cried out—"a gold ring with a little blue stone in it."

"And you shall go to ride with mother on the cars to-morrow," said Fanny.

"Father will get you some oranges, too," said Andrew.

But Ellen sat silent and unmoved by all that sweet bribery, a little martyr to something within herself; a sense of honor, love for the lady who had concealed her, and upon whom her confession might bring some dire penalty; or perhaps she was strengthened in her silence by something less worthy—possibly that stiff-neckedness which had descended to her from a long line of Puritans upon her father's side. At all events she was silent, and opposed successfully her one little new will to the onslaught of all those older and more experienced ones before her, though nobody knew
68

at what cost of agony to herself. She had always been a singularly docile and obedient child; this was the first persistent disobedience of her whole life, and it reacted upon herself with a cruel spiritual hurt. She sat clasping the great doll, the pinks, and the pink cup and saucer before her on the table—a lone little weak child, opposing her single individuality against so many, and to her own hurt and horror and self-condemnation, and she did not weaken; but all at once her head drooped on one side, and her father caught her.

"There! you can all stop tormentin' this blessed child!" he cried. "Ellen, Ellen, look at father! Oh, mother, look here; she's fainted dead away!"

"Fanny!"

When Ellen came to herself she was on the bed in her mother's room, and her aunt Eva was putting some of her beautiful cologne on her head, and her mother was trying to make her drink water, and her grandmother had a glass of her currant wine, and they were calling to her with voices of far-off love, as if from another world.

And after that she was questioned no more about her mysterious journey.

"Wherever she has been, she has got no harm," said Mrs. Zelotes Brewster, "and there's no use in trying to drive a child, when it comes of our family. She's got some notion in her head, and you've got to leave her alone to get over it. She's got back safe and sound, and that's the main thing."

"I wish I knew where she got those things," Fanny said. Looseness of principle as to property rights was not as strange to her imagination as to that of her mother-in-law.

For a long time afterwards she passed consciously and uneasily by cups and saucers in stores, and would not look their way lest she should see the counterpart of

Ellen's, which was Sèvres, and worth more than the whole counterful, had she only known it, and she hurried past the florists who displayed pinks in their windows. The doll was evidently not new, and she had not the same anxiety with regard to that.

No one was allowed to ask Ellen further questions that day, not even the reporters, who went away quite baffled by this infantile pertinacity in silence, and were forced to draw upon their imaginations, with results varying from realistic horrors to Alice in Wonderland. Ellen was kissed and cuddled by some women and young girls, but not many were allowed to see her. The doctor had been called in after her fainting-fit, and pronounced it as his opinion that she was a very nervous child, and had been under a severe strain, and he would not answer for the result if she were to be further excited.

"Let her have her own way: if she wants to talk, let her, and if she wants to be silent, let her alone. She is as delicate as that cup," said the doctor, looking at the shell-like thing which Ellen had brought home, with some curiosity.

70

CHAPTER VIII

THAT evening Lyman Risley came to see Cynthia. He looked at her anxiously and scrutinizingly when he entered the room, and did not respond to her salutation.

"Well, I have seen the child," he said, in a hushed voice, with a look towards the door as he seated himself before the fire and spread out his hands towards the blaze. He looked nervous and chilly.

"How did she look?" asked Cynthia.

"Why in the name of common-sense, Cynthia," he said, abruptly, without noticing her query, "if you had to give that child china for a souvenir, didn't you give her something besides Royal Sèvres?" Lyman Risley undoubtedly looked younger than Cynthia, but his manner even more than his looks gave him the appearance of comparative youth. There was in it a vehemence and impetuosity almost like that of a boy. Cynthia, with her strained nervous intensity, seemed very much older.

"Why not?" said she.

"Why not? Well, it is fortunate for you that those people have a knowledge for the most part of the fundamental properties of the drama of life, such as bread-and-butter, and a table from which to eat it, and a knife with which to cut it, and a bed in which to sleep, and a stove and coal, and so on, and so on, and that the artistic accessories, such as Royal Sèvres, which is no better than common crockery for the honest purpose of holding the tea for the solace of the thirsty mouth of labor, is beneath their attention."

"How does the child look, Lyman?" asked Cynthia
Lennox. She was leaning back in a great crimson-
covered chair before the fire, a long, slender, graceful shape, in a clinging white silk gown which
was a favorite of hers for house wear. The light
in the room was subdued, coming mostly through
crimson shades, and the faint, worn lines on Cynthia's
face did not show; it looked, with her soft crown of gray
hair, like a cameo against the crimson background
of the chair. The man beside her looked at her with
that impatience of his masculine estate and his superior
youth, and yet with the adoration which nothing could
conquer. He had passed two-thirds of his life, metaphorically, at this woman's feet, and had formed a habit
of admiration and lovership which no facts nor developments could ever alter. He was frowning, he replied
with a certain sharpness, and yet he leaned towards
her as he spoke, and his eyes followed her long, graceful
lines and noted the clear delicacy of her features against
the crimson background. "How the child looked—
how the child looked; Cynthia, you do not realize what
you did. You have not the faintest realization of what
it means for a woman to keep a lost child hidden away
as you did, when its parents and half the city were
hunting for it. I tell you I did not know what the
consequences might be to you if it were found out.
There is wild blood in a city like this, and even the staid
old New England stream is capable of erratic currents.
I tell you I have had a day of dreadful anxiety, and
it was worse because I had to be guarded. I dared
scarcely speak to any one about the matter. I have
listened on street corners; I have made errands to newspaper offices. I meant to get you away if— Well,
never mind—I tell you, you do not realize what you
did, Cynthia."

Cynthia glanced at him without moving her head,

72

then she looked away, her face quivering slightly, more as if from a reflection of his agitation than from her own. "You say you saw her," she said.

"This afternoon," the man went on, "I got fairly desperate. I resolved to go to the fountain-head for information, and take my chances. So down I went to Maple Street, where the Brewsters live, and I rang the front-door bell, and the child's aunt, a handsome, breathless kind of creature, came and ushered me into the best parlor, and went into the next room— the sitting-room—to call the others. I caught sight of enough women for a woman's club in the sitting-room. Then Andrew Brewster came in, and I offered my legal services out of friendly interest in the case, and in that way I found out what I wanted to. Cynthia, that child has not told."

Cynthia raised herself and sat straight, and her face flashed like a white flame. "Were they harsh to her?" she demanded. "Were they cruel? Did they question her, and were they harsh and cruel because she would not tell? Why did you not tell them yourself? Why did you not, Lyman Risley? Why did you not tell the whole story rather than have that child blamed? Well, I will go myself. I will go this minute. They shall not blame that darling. What do you think I care for myself? Let them lynch me if they want to. I will go this minute!" Cynthia sprang to her feet, but Risley, with a hoarse shout under his breath, caught hold of her and forced her back.

"For God's sake, sit down, Cynthia!" he said. "Didn't you hear the door-bell? Somebody is coming."

The door-bell had in fact rung, and Cynthia had not noticed it. She lay back in her chair as the door opened, and Mrs. Norman Lloyd entered. "Good-evening, Cynthia," she said, beamingly. "I thought I would stop a few minutes on my way to meeting. I'm rather

73

early. No, don't get up," as Cynthia rose. "Don't get up; I can only stay a minute. Never mind about giving me a chair, Mr. Risley—thank you. Yes, this is a real comfortable chair." Mrs. Lloyd, seated where the firelight played over her wide sweep of rich skirts, and her velvet fur-trimmed cloak and plumed bonnet, beamed upon them with an expansive benevolence and kindliness. She was a large, handsome, florid woman. Her grayish-brown hair was carefully crimped, and looped back from her fat, pink cheeks, a fine shell-and-gold comb surmounted her smooth French twist, and held her bonnet in place. She unfastened her cloak, and a diamond brooch at her throat caught the light and blazed red like a ruby. She was the wife of Norman Lloyd, the largest shoe-manufacturer in the place. There was between her and Cynthia a sort of relationship by marriage. Norman Lloyd's brother George had married Cynthia's sister, who had died ten years before, and of whose little son, Robert, Cynthia had had the charge. Now George, who was a lawyer in St. Louis, had married again. Mrs. Norman had sympathized openly with Cynthia when the child was taken from Cynthia at his father's second marriage. "I call it a shame," she had said, "giving that child to a perfect stranger to bring up, and I don't see any need of George's marrying again, anyway. I don't know what I should do if I thought Norman would marry again if I died. I think one husband and one wife is enough for any man or woman if they believe in the resurrection. It has always seemed to me that the answer to that awful question in the New Testament, as to whose wife that woman who had so many husbands would be in the other world, meant that people who had done so much marrying on earth would have to be old maids and old bachelors in heaven. George ought to be ashamed of himself, and Cynthia ought to keep that child."

Ever since she had been very solicitously friendly towards Cynthia, who had always imperceptibly held herself aloof from her, owing to a difference in degree. Cynthia had no prejudices of mind, but many of nerves, and this woman was distinctly not of her sort, though she had a certain liking for her. Every time she was brought in contact with her she had a painful sense of a grating adjustment as of points of meeting which did not dovetail as they should. Norman Lloyd represented one of the old families of the city, distinguished by large possessions and college training, and he was the first of his race to engage in trade. His wife came from a vastly different stock, being the daughter of a shoe-manufacturer herself, and the granddaughter of a cobbler who had tapped his neighbor's shoes in his little shop in the L of his humble cottage house. Mrs. Norman Lloyd was innocently unconscious of any reason for concealing the fact, and was fond, when driving out to take the air in her fine carriage, of pointing out to any stranger who happened to be with her the house where her grandfather cobbled shoes and laid the foundation of the family fortune. "That all came from that little shop of my grandfather," she would say, pointing proudly at Lloyd's great factory, which was not far from the old cottage. "Mr. Lloyd didn't have much of anything when I married him, but I had considerable, and Mr. Lloyd went into the factory, and he has been blessed, and the property has increased until it has come to this." Mrs. Lloyd's chief pride was in the very facts which others deprecated. When she considered the many-windowed pile of Lloyd's, and that her husband was the recognized head and authority over all those throngs of grimy men, walking with the stoop of daily labor, carrying their little dinner-boxes

75

with mechanical clutches of leather-tanned fingers, she used to send up a prayer for humility, lest evil and downfall of pride come to her. She was a pious woman, a member of the First Baptist Church, and active in charitable work. Mrs. Norman Lloyd adored her husband, and her estimate of him was almost ludicrously different from that of the grimy men who flocked to his factory, she seeing a most kindly spirited and amiable man, devoting himself to the best interests of his employés, and striving ever for their benefit rather than his own, and the others seeing an aristocrat by birth and training, who was in trade because of shrewd business instincts and a longing for wealth and power, but who despised, and felt himself wholly superior to, the means by which it was acquired.

"We ain't anything but the rounds of the ladder for Norman Lloyd to climb by, and he only sees and feels us with the soles of his patent-leathers," one of the turbulent spirits in his factory said. Mrs. Norman Lloyd would not have believed her ears had she heard him.

Mrs. Lloyd had not sat long before Cynthia's fire that evening before she opened on the subject of the lost child. "Oh, Cynthia, have you heard—" she began, but Risley cut her short.

"About that little girl who ran away?" he said. "Yes, we have; we were just talking about her."

"Did you ever hear anything like it?" said Mrs. Lloyd. "They say they can't find out where she's been. She won't tell. Don't you believe somebody has threatened her if she does?"

Cynthia raised herself and began to speak, but a slight, almost imperceptible gesture from the man beside her stopped her.

"What did you say, Cynthia?"

"There is no accounting for children's freaks,"

said Risley, shortly and harshly. Mrs. Lloyd was not thin-skinned; such a current of exuberant cordiality emanated from her own nature that she was not very susceptible to any counter-force. Now, however, she felt vaguely and wonderingly, as a child might have done, that for some reason Lyman Risley was rude to her, and she had a sense of bewildered injury. Mrs. Lloyd was always, moreover, somewhat anxious as to the relations between Cynthia and Lyman Risley. She heard a deal of talk about it first and last; and while she had no word of unkind comment herself, yet she felt at times uneasy. " Folks do talk about Cynthia and Lyman Risley keeping company so long," she told her husband; " it's as much as twenty years. It does seem as if they ought to get married, don't you think so, Norman? Do you suppose it is because the property was left that way—for you know Lyman hasn't got anything besides what he earns—or do you suppose it is because Cynthia doesn't want to marry him? I guess it is that. Cynthia never seemed to me as if she would ever care enough about any man to marry him. I guess that's it; but I do think she ought to stop his coming there quite so much, especially when people know that about her property."

Cynthia's property was hers on condition that her husband took her name if she married, otherwise it was forfeited to her sister's child. " Catch a Risley ever taking his wife's name!" said Mrs. Lloyd. " Of course Cynthia would be willing to give up the money if she loved him, but I don't believe she does. It seems as if Lyman Risley ought to see it would be better for him not to go there so much if they weren't going to be married."

So it happened when Risley caught up her question to Cynthia in that peremptory fashion, Mrs. Lloyd felt in addition to the present cause some which had gone

before for her grievance. She addressed herself thereafter entirely and pointedly to Cynthia. "Did you
ever see that little girl, Cynthia?" said she.

"Yes," replied Cynthia, in a voice so strange that
the other woman stared wonderingly at her.

"Ain't you feeling well, Cynthia?" she asked.

"Very well, thank you," said Cynthia.

"When did you see her?" asked Mrs. Lloyd. Cynthia
opened her mouth as if to speak, then she glanced at
Risley, whose eyes held her, and laughed instead—a
strange, nervous laugh. Happily, Mrs. Lloyd did not
wait for her answer. She had her own important information to impart. She had in reality stopped for
that purpose. "Well, I have seen her," she said.
"I met her in front of Crosby's one day last summer.
And she was so sweet-looking I stopped and spoke
to her—I couldn't help it. She had beautiful eyes,
and the softest light curls, and she was dressed so
pretty, and the flowers on her hat were nice. The
embroidery on her dress was very fine, too. Usually,
you know, those people don't care about the fineness,
as long as it is wide, and showy, and bright-colored.
I asked her what her name was, and she answered
just as pretty, and her mother told me how old she was.
Her mother was a handsome woman, though she had
an up-and-coming kind of way with her. But she seemed real pleased to have me notice the child. Where do
you suppose she was all that time, Cynthia?"

"She was in some safe place, undoubtedly," said
Risley, and again Mrs. Lloyd felt that she was snubbed,
though not seeing how nor why, and again she rebelled
with that soft and gentle persistency in her own course
which was the only rebellion of which she was capable.

"Where do you suppose she was, Cynthia?" said she.

"I think some woman must have seen her, and coaxed
her in and kept her, she was such a pretty child," said

78

Cynthia, defiantly and desperately. But the other woman looked at her in wonder.

"Oh, Cynthia, I can't believe that," said she. "It don't seem as if any woman could be so bad as that when the child's mother was in such agony over her." And then she added, "I can't believe it, because it seems to me that if any woman was bad enough to do that, she couldn't have given her up at all, she was such a beautiful child." Mrs. Norman Lloyd had no children of her own, and was given to gazing with eyes of gentle envy at pretty, rosy little girls, frilled with white embroidery like white pinks, dancing along in leading hands of maternal love. "It don't seem to me I could ever have given her up, if I had once been bad enough to steal her," she said. "What put such an idea into your head, Cynthia?"

When the church-bell clanged out just then Lyman Risley had never been so thankful in his life. Mrs. Lloyd rose promptly, for she had to lead the meeting, that being the custom among the sisters in her church. "Well," said she, "I am thankful she is found, anyway; I couldn't have slept a wink that night if I had known she was lost, the dear little thing. Good-night, Cynthia; don't come to the door. Good-night, Mr. Risley. Come and see me, Cynthia—do, dear."

When Mrs. Norman Lloyd was gone, Risley looked at Cynthia with a long breath of relief, but she turned to him with seemingly no appreciation of it, and repeated her declaration which Mrs. Lloyd's coming had interrupted: "Lyman, I am going there to-night—this minute. Will you go with me? No, you must not go with me. I am going!" She sprang to her feet.

"Sit down, Cynthia," said Risley. "I tell you they were not harsh to her. You don't seem to consider that they love the child—possibly better than you can—and would not in the nature of things be harsh to

79

her under such circumstances. Sit down and hear the rest of it."

"But they will be harsh by-and-by, after the first joy of finding her is over," said Cynthia. "I will go and tell them the first thing in the morning, Lyman."

"You will do nothing so foolish. They are not only not insisting upon her telling her secret, but announced to me their determination not to do so in the future. I wish you could have seen that man's face when he told me what a delicate, nervous little thing his child was, and the doctor said she must not be fretted if she had taken a notion not to tell; and I wish you could have seen the mother and the aunt, and the grandmother, Mrs. Zelotes Brewster. They would all give each other and themselves up to be torn of wild beasts first. It is easy to see where the child got her extraordinary strength of will. They took me out in the sitting-room, and there was a wild flurry of feminine skirts before me. I had previously overheard myself announced as Lawyer Risley by the aunt, and the response from various voices that they were 'goin'' if he was comin' out in the sittin'-room.' It always made them nervous to see lawyers. Well, I followed the parents and the grandmother and the aunt out. I dared not refuse when they suggested it, and I hoped desperately that the child would not remember me from that one scared glance she gave at me this morning. But there she sat in her little chair, holding the doll you gave her, and she looked up at me when I entered, and I have never in the whole course of my existence seen such an expression upon the face of a child. Remember me? Indeed she did, and she promised me with the faithfulest, stanchest eyes of a woman set in a child's head that she would not tell; that I need not fear for one minute; that the lady who had given her the doll was quite safe. She knew, and she must have heard what I said to you this morning. She is the most wonderful child I have ever seen."

Cynthia had sank back in her chair. Lyman Risley put his cigar back between his lips; Cynthia was quite still, her delicate profile towards him.

"I assure you there is not the slightest danger of their troubling the child because of her silence, and you would do an exceedingly foolish thing, and its consequences would react not upon yourself only, but—upon others, were you to confess the truth to them," he said after a little. "You must think of others—of your friends, and of your sister's boy, whose loss led you into this. This would—well, it would get into the papers, Cynthia."

"Do you think that the doll continued to please her?" asked Cynthia.

"Cynthia, I want you to promise," said her friend, persistently.

"Very well, I will promise, if you will promise to let me know the minute you hear that they are treating her harshly because of her silence."

Suddenly Cynthia turned her face upon him. "Lyman," said she, "do you think that I could do anything for her—"

"Do anything for her?" he repeated, vaguely.

"Yes; they cannot have money. They must be poor: the father works in the factory. Would they allow me—"

The lawyer laughed. "Cynthia," he said, "you do not realize that pride finds its native element in all strata of society, and riches are comparative. Let me inform you that these Brewsters, of whom this child sprung, claim as high places in the synagogue as any of your Lennoxes and Risleys, and, what is more, they believe themselves there. They have seen the tops of their neighbors' heads as often as you or I. The mere fact of familiarity with shoe-knives and leather, and hand-skill instead of brain-skill, makes no difference with such inherent confidence of importance as theirs. The Louds, on the other side—the handsome aunt is a Loud—are rather below caste, but they make up for it with defiance. And as for riches, I would have you know that the Brewsters are as rich in their own estimation as you in yours; that they have possessions which entirely meet their needs and their æsthetic longings; that not only does Andrew Brewster earn exceedingly good wages in the shop, and is able to provide plenty of nourishing food and good clothes, but even by-and-by, if he prospers and is prudent, something rather extra in the way of education—perhaps a piano. I would have you know that there is a Rogers group on a little marble-topped table in the front window, and a table in the side window with a worked spread, on which reposes a red plush photograph album; that there is also a set of fine parlor furniture, with various devices in the way of silken and lace scarfs over the corners and backs of the chairs and sofa, and that there is a tapestry carpet; that in the sitting-room is a fine crushed-plush couch, and a multiplicity of rocking-chairs; that there is a complete dining-set in the next room, the door of which stood open, and even a side-board with red napkins, and a fine display of glass, every whit as elegant in their estimation as your cut glass in yours. The child's father owns his house and land free of encumbrance. He told me so in the course of his artless boasting as to what he might some day be able to do for the precious little creature of his own flesh and blood; and the grandmother owns her comfortable place next door, and she herself was dressed in black silk, and I will swear the lace on her cap was real, and she wore a great brooch containing hair of the departed, and it was set in pearl. What are you going to do in the face of opulence like this, Cynthia?"

Cynthia did not speak; her face looked as still as if it were carved in ivory.

"Cynthia," said the man, in a harsh voice, "I did not dream you were so broken up over losing that little boy of your sister's, poor girl."

Cynthia still said nothing, but a tear rolled down her cheek. Lyman Risley saw it, then he looked straight ahead, scowling over his cigar. He seemed suddenly to realize in this woman whom he loved something anomalous, yet lovely—a beauty, as it were, of deformity, an over-development in one direction, though a direction of utter grace and sweetness, like the lip of an orchid.

Why should she break her heart over a child whom she had never seen before, and have no love and pity for the man who had laid his best at her feet so long?

He saw at a flash the sweet yet monstrous imperfection of her, and he loved her better for it.

83

CHAPTER IX

AFTER Ellen's experience in running away, she dreamed her dreams with a difference. The breath of human passion had stained the pure crystal of her childish imagination; she peopled all her air-castles, and sounds of wailing farewells floated from the White North of her fancy after the procession of the evergreen trees in the west yard, and the cherry-trees on the east had found out that they were not in the Garden of Eden. In those days Ellen grew taller and thinner, and the cherubic roundness of her face lengthened into a sweet wistfulness of wonder and pleading, as of one who would look farther, since she heard sounds and saw signs in her sky which indicated more beyond. Andrew and Fanny watched her more anxiously than ever, and decided not to send her to school before spring, though all the neighbors exclaimed at their tardiness in so doing. "She'll be two years back of my Hattie gettin' into the high-school," said one woman, bluntly, to Fanny, who retorted, angrily,

"I don't care if she's ten years behind, if she don't lose her health."

"You wait and see if she's two years behind!" exclaimed Eva, who had just returned from the shop, and had entered the room bringing a fresh breath of December air, her cheeks glowing, her black eyes shining.

Eva was so handsome in those days that she fairly forced admiration, even from those of her own sex whose delicacy of taste she offended. She had a parcel in

84

her hand, which she had bought at a store on her way home, for she was getting ready to be married to Jim Tenny. "I tell you there don't nobody know what that young one can do," continued Eva, with a radiant nod of triumph. "There ain't many grown-up folks round here that can read like her, and she's studied geography, and she knows her multiplication - table, and she can spell better than some that's been through the high-school. You jest wait till Ellen gets started on her schoolin'—she won't stay in the grammar-school long, I can tell you that. She'll go ahead of some that's got a start now and think they're 'most there." Eva pulled off her hat, and the coarse ·black curls on her forehead sprang up like released wire. She nodded emphatically with a good-humored combativeness at the visiting woman and at her sister.

"I hope your cheeks are red enough," said Fanny, looking at her with grateful admiration.

The visiting woman sniffed covertly, and a retort which seemed to her exceedingly witty was loud in her own consciousness. "Them that likes beets and pinies is welcome to them," she thought, but she did not speak. "Well," said she, "folks must do as they think best about their own children. I have always thought a good deal of an education myself. I was brought up that way." She looked with eyes that were fairly cruel at Eva Loud and Fanny, who had been a Loud, who had both stopped going to school at a very early age.

Then the rich red flamed over Eva's forehead and neck as well as her cheeks. There was nothing covert about her, she would drag an ambushed enemy forth into the open field even at the risk of damaging disclosures regarding herself.

"Why don't you say jest what you mean, right out, Jennie Stebbins?" she demanded. "You are hintin' that Fanny and me never had no education, and twittin' us with it.''

"It wa'n't our fault," said Fanny, no less angrily.

"No, it wa'n't our fault," assented Eva. "We had to quit school. Folks can live with empty heads, but they can't with empty stomachs. It had to be one or the other. If you want to twit us with bein' poor, you can, Jennie Stebbins."

"I haven't said anything," said Mrs. Stebbins, with a scared and injured air. "I'd like to know what you're making all this fuss about? I don't know. What did I say?"

"If I'd said anything mean, I wouldn't turn tail an' run, I'd stick to it about one minute and a half, if it killed me," said Eva, scornfully.

"You know what you was hintin' at, jest as well as we do," said Fanny; "but it ain't so true as you and some other folks may think, I can tell you that. If Eva and me didn't go to school as long as some, we have always read every chance we could get."

"That's so," said Eva, emphatically. "I guess we've read enough sight more than some folks that has had a good deal more chance to read. Fanny and me have taken books out of the library full as much as any of the neighbors, I rather guess."

"We've read every single thing that Mrs. Southworth has ever written," said Fanny, "and that's sayin' considerable."

"And all Pansy's and Rider Haggard's," declared Eva, with triumph.

"And every one of The Duchess and Marie Corelli, and Sir Walter Scott, and George Macdonald, and Laura Jean Libbey, and Charles Reade, and more, besides, than I can think of."

"Fanny has read 'most all Tennyson," said Eva, with loyal admiration; "she likes poetry, but I don't

very well. She has read most all Tennyson and Long-
fellow, and we've both read *Queechee*, and *St. Elmo*,
and *Jane Eyre.*"

"And we've read the Bible through," said Fanny,
"because we read in a paper once that that was a complete education. We made up our minds we'd read it
through, and we did, though it took us quite a while."

"And we take *Zion's Herald*, and *The Rowe Gazette*,
and *The Youth's Companion*," said Eva.

"And we've both of us learned Ellen geography and
spellin' and 'rithmetic, till we know most as much as
she does," said Fanny.

"That's so," said Fanny. "I snum, I believe I
could get into the high-school myself, if I wasn't goin'
to git married," said Eva, with a gay laugh. She was
so happy in those days that her power of continued
resentment was small. The tide of her own bliss returned upon her full consciousness and overflowed, and
crested, as with glory, all petty annoyances.

The visiting woman took up her work, and rose to
go with a slightly abashed air, though her small brown
eyes were still blanks of impregnable defence. "Well,
I dunno what I've said to stir you both so," she remarked again. "If I've said anythin' that riled you,
I'm sorry, I'm sure. As I said before, folks must do
as they are a mind to with their own children. If they
see fit to keep 'em home from school until they're women
grown, and if they think it's best not to punish 'em
when they run away, why they must. I 'ain't got no
right to say anythin', and I 'ain't."

"You—" began Fanny, and then she stopped short,
and Eva began arranging her hair before the glass.
"The wind blew so comin' home," she said, "that my
hair is all out." The visiting woman stared with a
motion of adjustive bewilderment, as one might before a
sudden change of wind, then she looked, as a shadowy

87

motion disturbed the even light of the room and little Ellen passed the window. She knew at once, for she had heard the gossip, that the ready tongues of recrimination were hushed because of the child, and then Ellen entered.

The winter afternoon was waning and the light was low; the child's face, with its clear fairness, seemed to gleam out in the room like a lamp with a pale luminosity of its own.

The three women, the mother, and aunt, and the visiting neighbor, all looked at her, and Ellen smiled up at them as innocently sweet as a flower. There was that in Ellen's smile and regard at that time which no woman could resist. Suddenly the visiting neighbor laid a finger softly under her chin and tilted up her little face towards the light. Then she said with that unconscious poetry of bereavement which sees a likeness in all fair things of earth to the face of the lost treasure, "I do believe she looks like my first little girl that died."

After the visiting woman had gone, Fanny and Eva calling after her to come again, they looked at each other, then at Ellen. "That little girl that died favored the Stebbinses, and was dark as an Injun," said Fanny, "no more like Ellen—"

"That's so," acquiesced Eva; "I remember that young one. Lookin' like Ellen—I'd like to see the child that did look like her; there ain't none round these parts. I wish you could have seen folks stare at her when I took her down street yesterday. One woman said, 'Ain't she pretty as a picture,' so loud I heard it, but Ellen didn't seem to."

"Sometimes I wonder if we'll make her proud," Fanny said, in a hushed voice, with a look of admiration that savored of worship at Ellen.

"She don't ever seem to notice," said Eva, with a

88

hushed response. Indeed, Ellen had seemed to pay no attention whatever to their remarks, whether from an innate humility and lack of self-consciousness, or because she was so accustomed to adulation that it had become as the breath of her nostrils, to be taken no more account of. She had seated herself in her favorite place in a rocking-chair at a west window, with her chin resting on the sill, and her eyes staring into the great out-of-doors, full of winds and skies and trees and her own imaginings.

She would sit so, motionless, for hours at a time, and sometimes her mother would rouse her almost roughly. "What be you thinkin' about, settin' there so still?" she would ask, with eyes of vague anxiety fixed upon her, but Ellen could never answer.

Though it was getting late, it did not seem dark as early as usual, since there was a full moon and there was snow on the ground which gave forth a pale light in a wide surface of reflection. However, the moon was behind clouds, for it was beginning to snow again quite heavily, and the white flakes drove in whirlwinds past the street-lamp on the corner of the street. Now and then a tramping and muffled figure came into the radius of light, then passed into the white gloom beyond.

Fanny was preparing supper, and the light from the dining-room shone in where Ellen sat, but the sitting-room was not lighted. Ellen began to smell the fragrance of tea and toast, and there was a reflection of the dining-room table and lamp outside pictured vividly against the white sheet of storm.

Ellen knew better, but it amused her to think that her home was out-of-doors as well as under her father's and mother's roof. Eva passed her with her hands full of kindlings. She was going to make a fire in the parlor-stove, for Jim Tenny was coming that evening. She laid a tender hand on Ellen's head as she passed, and smoothed her hair. Ellen had a sort of acquiescent wonder over her aunt Eva in those days. She heard people say Eva was getting ready to be married, and speculated. "What is getting ready to be married?" she asked Eva.

"Why, getting your clothes made, you little ninny," Eva answered.

The next day Ellen had watched her mother at work upon a new little frock for herself for some time before she spoke.

"Mother," she said.

"Yes, child."

"Mother, you are making that new dress for me, ain't you?"

"Of course I am; why?"

"And you made me a new coat last week?"

"Why, you know I did, Ellen; what do you mean?"

"And you are going to make me a petticoat and put that pretty lace on it?"

"You know I am, Ellen Brewster, what be you drivin' at?"

"Be I a-gettin' ready to be married, mother?" asked Ellen, with the strangest look of wonder and awe and anticipation.

Fanny had told this saying of the child's to everybody, and that evening when Jim Tenny came he caught up Ellen and gave her a toss to the ceiling, a trick of his which filled Ellen with a sort of fearful delight, the delight of helplessness in the hands of strength, and the titillation of evanescent risk.

"So you are gettin' ready to be married, are you?" Jim Tenny said, with a great laugh, looking at her soberly, with big black eyes. Jim Tenny was a handsome fellow, and much larger and stronger than her father. Ellen liked him; he often brought candies in his pocket for her, and they were great friends, but she could never understand why he stayed in the parlor all alone with her aunt Eva, instead of in the sitting-room with the others.

Ellen had looked back at him as soberly. "Mother says I 'ain't," she replied, "but—"

"But what?"

"I am getting most as many new clothes as Aunt Eva, and she is."

"And you think maybe you are gettin' ready to be married, after all, hey?"

"I think maybe mother wants to surprise me," Ellen said.

Jim Tenny had all of a sudden shaken convulsively as if with mirth, but his face remained perfectly sober.

That evening after the parlor door was closed upon Jim and Eva, Ellen wondered what they were laughing at.

To-night when she saw Eva enter the room, a lighted lamp illuminating her face fairly reckless with happiness, to light the fire in the courting-stove as her sister facetiously called it, she thought to herself that Jim Tenny was coming, that they would be shut up in there all alone as usual, and then she looked out at the storm and the night again, and the little home picture thrown against it. Then she saw her father coming into the yard with his arms full of parcels, and she was out of her chair and at the kitchen door to meet him.

Andrew had brought as usual some dainties for his darling. He watched Ellen unwrap the various parcels, not smiling as usual, but with a curious knitting of his forehead and pitiful compression of mouth. When she had finished and ran into the other room to show a great orange to her aunt, he drew a heavy sigh that was almost a groan. His wife coming in from the kitchen with a dish heard him, and looked at him with quick anxiety, though she spoke in a merry, rallying way.

"For the land sake, Andrew Brewster, what be you groanin' that way for?" she cried out.

Andrew's tense face did not relax; he strove to push past her without a word, but Fanny stood before him. "Now, look at here, Andrew," said she, "you 'ain't goin' to walk off with a face like that, unless I know what the matter is. Are you sick?"

"No, I ain't sick, Fanny," Andrew said; then in a low voice, "Let me go, I will tell you by-and-by."

"No, Andrew, you have got to tell me now. I'm goin' to know whatever has happened."

"Wait till after supper, Fanny."

"No, I can't wait. Look here, Andrew, you are my husband, and there ain't no trouble that can come to you in this world that I can't bear, except not knowin'. You've got to tell me what the matter is."

"Well, keep quiet till after supper, then," said Andrew. Then suddenly he leaned his face close to her and whispered with a hiss of tragedy, "Lloyd's shut down."

Fanny recoiled and looked at him.

"When?"

"The foreman gave notice to-night."

"For how long? Did he say?"

"Oh, till business got better—same old story. Unless I'm mistaken, Lloyd's will be shut down all winter."

"Well, it ain't so bad for us as for some," said Fanny. Both pride and a wish to cheer her husband induced her to say that. She did not like to think that, after the fine marriage she had made, she needed to be as distressed at a temporary loss of employment as others. Then, too, that look of overhanging melancholy in Andrew's face alarmed her; she felt that she must drive it away at any cost.

"Seems to me it's bad enough for anybody," said Andrew, morosely.

"Now, Andrew, you know it ain't. Here we own the house clear, and we've got that money in the savings-bank, and all that's your mother's is yours in the end. Of course we ain't always thinkin' of that, and I'm sure I hope she'll outlive me, but it's so. You know we sha'n't starve if you don't have work."

"We shall starve in the end, and you know I've been—" Andrew stopped suddenly as he heard Ellen and his sister-in-law coming. He shook his head at his wife with a warning motion that she should keep silence.

"Don't Eva know?" she whispered.

"No, she came out early. Do for Heaven's sake keep quiet till after supper."

Eva was sharp-eyed, and all through supper she watched Andrew, and the lines of melancholy on his face, which did not disappear even when he forced conversation.

"What in creation ails you, Andrew?" she burst out, finally. "You look like a walking funeral."

Andrew made no reply, and Fanny volunteered an answer. "He's all tired out," she said; "he's got a little cold. Eat some more of the stew, Andrew; it'll do you good, it's nice and hot."

"You can't cheat me," said Eva. "There's something to pay." She took a mouthful, then she stared at Andrew, with a sudden pallor. "It ain't anythin' about Jim, is it?" she gasped out. "Because if it is, there's no use in your waitin' to tell me, you might as well have it over at once. You won't make it any easier for me, I can tell you that."

"No, it ain't anything about Jim, in the way you mean, Eva," her sister said, soothingly. "Eat your supper and don't worry."

"What do you mean by that? Jim ain't sick?"

"No, I tell you; don't be a goose, Eva."

"He ain't been anywhere with—"

"Do keep still, Eva!" Fanny cried, impatiently. "If I didn't have any more faith than that in a man, I'd give him up. I don't think you're fair to Jim. Of course he ain't been with that girl, when he's goin' to marry you next month."

"I'm just as fair to Jim as he deserves," Eva said, simply. "I think just as much of him, but what a man's done once he may do again, and I can't help it if I think of it, and he shouldn't be surprised. He's brought it on himself. I've got as much faith in him as anybody can have, seein' as he's a man. Well, if it ain't that, Andrew Brewster, what is it?"

"Now, you let him alone till after supper, Eva," Fanny said. "Do let him have a little peace."

"Well, I'll get it out of him afterwards," Eva said.

As soon as she got up from the table she pushed him into the sitting-room. "Now, out with it," said she. Ellen, who had followed them, stood looking at them both, her lips parted, her eyes full of half-alarmed curiosity.

"Lloyd's has shut down, if you want to know," Andrew said, shortly.

"Oh my God!" cried Eva. Andrew shrank from her impatiently. She made that ejaculation because she was a Loud, and had an off-streak in her blood. Not one of Andrew's pure New England stock would have so expressed herself. He sat down beside the lamp and took up the evening paper. Eva stood looking at him a minute. She was quite pale, she was weighing consequences. Then she went out to her sister. "Well, you know what's happened, Fan, I s'pose," she said.

"Yes, I'm awful sorry, but I tell Andrew it ain't so bad for us as for some; we sha'n't starve."

"I don't know as I care much whether I starve or not," said Eva. "It's goin' to make me put off my weddin'; and if I do put it off, Jim and me will never get married at all; I feel it in my bones."

"Why, what should you have to put it off for?" asked Fanny.

"Why? I should think you'd know why without askin'. Ain't I spent every dollar I have saved up on my weddin' fixin's, and Jim, he's got his mother on his hands, and she's been sick, and he ain't saved up anything. If you s'pose I'm goin' to marry him and make him any worse off than he is now you're mistaken."

"Well, mebbe Jim can work somewhere else, and mebbe Lloyd's won't be shut up long," Fanny said, consolingly. "I wouldn't give up so, if I was you."

"I might jest as well," Eva returned. "It's no use, Jim and me will never get married." Eva's face was curiously set; she was not in the least loud nor violent as was usually the case when she was in trouble, her voice was quite low, and she spoke slowly.

Fanny looked anxiously at her. "It ain't as though you hadn't a roof to cover you," she said, "for you've got mine and Andrew's as long as we have one ourselves."

"Do you think I'd live on Andrew long?" demanded Eva.

"You won't have to. Jim will get work in a week or two, and you'll get married. Don't act so. I declare, I'm ashamed of you, Eva Loud. I thought you had more sense, to give up discouraged at no more than this. I don't see why you jump way ahead into trouble before you get to it."

"I've got to it, and I can feel the steam of it in my face," Eva said, with unconscious imagery. Then she lit a lamp, and went up-stairs to change her dress before Jim Tenny arrived.

It was snowing hard. Ellen sat in her place by the window and watched the flakes drive past the radiance of the street-lamp on the corner, and past the reflection of the warm, bright room. Now she could see, since the light was in the room where she sat, her father beside the table reading his paper, and shadowy images of all the familiar things projecting themselves like a mirage of home into the night and storm. Ellen could see, even without turning round, that her father looked very sober, and did not seem to be much interested in his paper, and a vague sense of calamity oppressed her. She did not know just what might be involved in Lloyd's shutting down, but she saw that her father and aunt were disturbed, and her imaginings were half eclipsed by a shadow of material things. Ellen dearly loved this early evening hour when she could stare out into the mystery of the night, herself sheltered under the wing of home, and the fancies which her childish brain wove were as a garment of spirit for the future; but to-night she did not dream so much as she wondered and reflected. Pretty soon Ellen saw a man's figure plodding through the fast-gathering snow, and heard her aunt Eva make a soft, heavy rush down the front stairs, and she knew the man was Jim Tenny, and her aunt had been watching for him. Ellen wondered why she had watched up in her cold room, why she had not sat down-stairs where it was warm, and let Jim ring the door-bell. Ellen liked Jim Tenny, but there was often that in her aunt's eyes regarding him which made Ellen look past him and above him to see if there was another man there. Ellen heard the fire crackling in the parlor-stove, and saw the light shining under the parlor threshold, and heard the soft hum of voices. Her mother, having finished washing up the supper dishes, came in presently and seated herself beside the lamp with her needle-work.

96

"You don't feel any wind comin' in the window?" she said, anxiously, to Ellen.

"No, ma'am," replied Ellen.

Andrew looked up quickly. "You're sure you don't?" he said.

"No, sir."

Ellen watched her mother sewing out in the snowy yard, then a dark shadow came between the reflection and the window, then another. Two men treading in the snow in even file, one in the other's foot-tracks, came into the yard.

"Somebody's comin'," said Ellen, as a knock, came on the side door.

"Did you see who 'twas?" Fanny asked, starting up.

"Two men."

"It's somebody to see you, Andrew," Fanny said, and Andrew tossed his paper on the table and went to the door.

When the door was opened Ellen heard a man cough.

"I should think anybody was crazy to come out such a night as this, coughin' that way," murmured Fanny. "I do believe it's Joe Atkins; sounds like his cough." Then Andrew entered with the two men stamping and shaking themselves.

"Here's Joseph Atkins and Nahum Beals," Andrew said, in his melancholy voice, all unstirred by the usual warmth of greeting. The two men bowed stiffly.

"Good-evenin'," Fanny said, and rose and pushed forward the rocking-chair in which she had been seated to Joseph Atkins, who was a consumptive man with an invalid wife, and worked next Andrew in Lloyd's.

"Keep your settin', keep your settin'," he returned in his quick, nervous way, as if his very words were money for dire need, and sat himself down in a straight chair far from the fire. The other man, Nahum Beals, was very young. He seated himself next to Joseph,

G 97

and the two side by side looked with gloomy significance at Andrew and Fanny. Then Joseph Atkins
burst out suddenly in a rattling volley of coughs.

"You hadn't ought to come out such a night as this,
I'm afraid, Mr. Atkins," said Fanny.

"He's been out jest as bad weather as this all winter,"
said the young man, Nahum Beals, in an unexpectedly
deep voice. "The workers of this world can't afford
to take no account of weather. It's for the rich folks
to look out betwixt their lace curtains and see if it looks
lowery, so they sha'n't git their gold harnesses and their
shiny carriages, an' their silks an' velvets an' ostrich
feathers wet. The poor folks that it's life and death to
have to go out whether or no, no matter if they've got
an extra suit of clothes or not. They've got to go out
through the drenchin' rain and the snow-drifts, to
earn money so that the rich folks can have them gold-
plated harnesses and them silks and velvets. Joe's
been out all winter in weather as bad as this, after he's
been standin' all day in a shop as hot as hell, drenched
with sweat. One more time won't make much difference."

"It would be 'nough sight better for me if it did,"
said Joseph Atkins, chokingly, and still with that same
seeming of hurry.

Fanny had gone out to the dining-room, and now she
returned stirring some whiskey and molasses in a cup.

"Here," said she, "you take this, Mr. Atkins; it's
real good for a cough. Andrew cured a cold with it
last month."

"Mine ain't a cold, and it can't be cured in this world,
but it's better for me, I guess," said Joe Atkins, chokingly, but he took the cup.

"Now, you hadn't ought to talk so," Fanny said.
"You had ought to think of your wife and children."

"My life is insured," said Joseph Atkins.

"We ain't got no money and no jewelry, and no silver to leave them we love—all we've got to leave 'em is the price of our own lives," said Nahum Beals.

"I wish I had got my life insured," Andrew said.

"Don't talk so, Andrew," Fanny cried, with a shudder.

"My life is insured for two thousand dollars," Joe Atkins said, with an odd sort of pride. "I had it done three years ago. My lungs was sound as anybody's then, but that very next summer I worked up under that tin roof, and came out as wet as if I'd been dipped in the river, into an east wind, and got a chill. It was the only time I ever struck luck—to get insured before that happened. Nobody'd look at me now, and I dunno what they'd do. I 'ain't laid up a cent, I've had so much sickness in my family."

"If you hadn't worked that summer in the annex under that tin roof, you'd be as well as you ever was now," said Nahum Beals.

"I worked there 'longside of you that summer," said Andrew to Joe, with bitter reminiscence. "We used to strip like a gang of convicts, and we stood in pools of sweat. It was that awful hot summer, and the room had only that one row of windows facing the east, and the wind never that way."

"Not till I came out of the shop that night I took the chill," said Joe.

Suddenly the young man, Nahum Beals, hit his knees a sounding slap, which made Ellen, furtively and timidly attentive at her window, jump. "It seems sometimes as if the Almighty himself was in league with 'em," he shouted out, "but I tell you it won't last, it won't last."

"I don't see much sign of any change for the better," Andrew said, gloomily.

"I tell you, sir, it won't last," repeated Nahum Beals. "I tell you, the Lord only raises 'em up higher and higher that He may dash 'em lower when the time comes. The same earth is beneath the high places of this life, and the lowly ones, and the law that governs 'em is the same, and—the higher the place the longer the fall, and the longer the fall the sorer the hurt." Nahum Beals sprang to his feet with a strange abandon of self-consciousness and a fiery impetus for one of his New England blood. He had a delicate, nervous face, like a woman's, his blue eyes gleamed like blue flames under his overhang of white forehead, he shook his head as if it were maned like a lion, and, though he wore his thin, fair hair short, one could seem to see it flung back in glistening lines. He spread his hands as if he were addressing an audience, and as he did so the parlor door opened and Jim Tenny and Eva stood there, listening.

"I tell you, sir," shouted Nahum Beals, "the time will come when you will all thank God that you belong to the poor and down-trodden of this earth, and not to the rich and great—the time will come. There's knives to sharpen to-day, and wood for scaffolds as plenty as in the days of the French Revolution, and the hand that marks the time of day on the clock of men's patience with wrong and oppression has near gone round to the same hour and minute."

Andrew Brewster looked at him, with a curious expression half of disgust, half of sympathy. His sense of dignity in the face of adversity inherited from his New England race was shocked; he was not one to be blindly swayed by another's fervor even when his own wrongs were in question. He would not have made a good follower in a revolution, nor a leader. He would simply have found his own place of fixed principle and abided there. Then, too, he had a judicial mind which could combine the elements of counsels for and against his own cause.

"Now, look at here," he said, slowly, "I ain't goin'
to say I don't think we ain't in a hard place, and that
there's somethin' wrong that's to blame for it, but I
dunno but you go most too far, Nahum; or, rather, I
dunno as you go far enough. I dunno but we've got
to dig down past the poor and the rich, farther into the
everlastin' foundations of things to get at what's the
trouble."

Jim Tenny, standing in the parlor doorway, with an
arm around Eva's waist, broke in suddenly with a
defiant laugh. "I don't care nothin' about the everlastin' foundations of things, and I don't care a darn
about the rich and the poor," he proclaimed. "I'm
willin' to leave that to lecturers and dynamiters, and let
'em settle it if they can. I don't grudge the rich nothin',
and I ain't goin' to call the Almighty to account for
givin' somebody else the biggest piece of pie; mebbe it
would give me the stomach-ache. All I'm concerned
about is Lloyd's shut-down."

"That's so," said Eva.

"I tell you, sir, it ain't the facts of the case, but the
reason for the facts, which we must think of," maintained Nahum Beals.

"I don't care a darn for the facts nor the reasons,"
said Jim Tenny; "all I care about is I'm out of work
maybe till spring, with my mother dependent on me,
and not a cent laid up, I've been so darned careless,
and here's Eva says she won't marry me till I get work."

"I won't," said Eva, who was very pale, except for
burning spots on her cheeks.

"She's afraid she won't get frostin' on her cake,
and silk dresses, I expect," Jim Tenny said, and laughed, but his laugh was very bitter.

"Jim Tenny, you know better than that," Eva cried,
sharply. "I won't stand that."

Jim Tenny, with a quick motion, unwound his arm

from Eva's waist and stripped up his sleeve. "There, look at that, will you," he cried out, shaking his lean, muscular arm at them; "look at that muscle, and me tellin' her that I could earn a livin' for her, and she afraid. I can dig if I can't make shoes. I guess there's work in this world for them that's willin', and don't pick and choose."

"There ain't," declared Nahum, shortly.

"You can't dig when the ground's froze hard," Eva said, with literal meaning.

"Then I'll take a pickaxe," cried Jim.

"You can dig, but who's goin' to pay you for the diggin'?" demanded Nahum Beals.

"The idea of a girl's bein' afraid I wa'n't enough of a man to support a wife with an arm like that," said Jim Tenny, "as if I couldn't dig for her, or fight for her."

"The fightin' has got to come first in order to get the diggin', and the pay for it," said Nahum.

"Now, look at here," Andrew Brewster broke in, "you know I'm in as bad a box as you, and I come home to-night feelin' as if I didn't care whether I lived or died; but if it's true what McGrath said to-night, we've got to use common-sense in lookin' at things even if it goes against us. If what McGrath said was true, that Lloyd's losing money keeping on, I dunno how we can expect him or any other man to do that."

"Why not he lose money as well as we?" demanded Nahum, fiercely.

"'Cause we 'ain't got none to lose," cried Jim Tenny, with a hard laugh, and Eva and Fanny echoed him hysterically.

Nahum took no notice of the interruption. Tragedy, to his comprehension, never verged on comedy. One could imagine his face of intense melancholy and de- nunciation relaxed with laughter no more than that of the stern prophet of righteous retribution whose name he bore.

"Why shouldn't Norman Lloyd lose money?" he demanded again. "Why shouldn't he lose his fine house as well as I my poor little home? Why shouldn't he lose his purple and fine linen as well as Jim his chances of happiness? Why shouldn't he lose his diamond shirt-studs, and his carriage and horses, as well as Joe his life?"

"Well, he earned his money, I suppose," Andrew said, slowly, "and I suppose it's for him to say what he'll do with it."

"Earned his money? He didn't earn his money," cried Nahum Beals. "We earned it, every dollar of it, by the sweat of our brows, and it's for us, not him, to say what shall be done with it. Well, the time will come, I tell ye, the time will come."

"We sha'n't see it," said Joe Atkins.

"It may come sooner than you think," said Nahum. Then Nahum Beals, with a sudden access of bitterness, broke in. "Look at Norman Lloyd," he cried, "havin' that great house, and horses and carriages, and dressin' like a dude, and his wife rustlin' in silks so you can hear her comin' a mile off, and shinin' like a jeweller's window—look at 'em all—all the factory bosses—livin' like princes on the money we've earned for 'em; and look at their relations, and look at the rich folks that ain't never earned a cent, that's had money left 'em. Go right up and down the Main Street, here in this city. See the Lloyds and the Maguires and the Marshalls and the Risleys and the Lennoxes—"

"There ain't none of the Lennoxes left except that one woman," said Andrew.

"Well, look at her. There she is without chick or child, rollin' in riches, and Norman Lloyd's her own brother-in-law. Why don't she give him a little money to run the factory this winter, so you and me won't have to lose everythin'?"

"I suppose she's got a right to do as she pleases with her own," said Andrew.

"I tell you she ain't," shouted Nahum. "She ain't the one to say, 'It's the Lord, and He's said it.' Cynthia Lennox and all the women like her are the oppressors of the poor. They are accursed in the sight of the Lord, as were those women we read about in the Old Testament, with their mantles and crisping-pins. Their low voices and their silk sweeps and their shrinkin' from touchin' shoulders with their fellow-beings in a crowd don't alter matters a mite."

"Now, Nahum," cried Jim Tenny, with one of his sudden turns of base when his sense of humor was touched, "you don't mean to say that you want Cynthia Lennox to give you her money?"

"I'd die, and see her dead, before I'd touch a dollar of her money!" cried Nahum—"before I'd touch a dollar of her money or anything that was bought with her money, her money or any other rich person's. I want what I earn. I don't want a gift with a curse on it. Let her keep her fine things. She and her kind are responsible for all the misery of the poor on the face of the earth."

"Seems to me you're reasonin' in a circle, Nahum," Andrew said, good-humoredly.

"Look here, Andrew, if you're on the side of the rich, why don't you say so?" cried Eva.

"He ain't," returned Fanny — "you know better, Eva Loud."

"No, I ain't," declared Andrew. "You all of you know I'm with the class I belong to; I ain't a toady to no rich folks; I don't think no more of 'em than you do, and I don't want any favors of 'em—all I want is pay for my honest work, and that's an even swap, and

I ain't beholden, but I want to look at things fair and square. I don't want to be carried away because I'm out of work, though, God knows, it's hard enough."

"I don't know what's goin' to become of us," said Joseph Atkins—then he coughed.

"I don't," Jim Tenny said, bitterly.

"And God knows I don't," cried Eva, and she sat down in the nearest chair, flung up her hands before her face, and wept.

Then Fanny spoke to Ellen, who had been sitting very still and attentive, her eyes growing larger, her cheeks redder with excitement. Fanny had often glanced uneasily at her, and wished to send her to bed, but she was in the habit of warming Ellen's little chamber at the head of the stairs by leaving open the sitting-room door for a while before she went to it, and she was afraid of cooling the room too much for Joseph Atkins, and had not ventured to interrupt the conversation. Now, seeing the child's fevered face, she made up her mind. "Come, Ellen, it's your bed-time," she said, and Ellen rose reluctantly, and, kissing her father, she went to her aunt Eva, who caught at her convulsively and kissed her, and sobbed against her cheek. "Oh, oh!" she wailed, "you precious little thing, you precious little thing, I don't know what's goin' to become of us all."

"Don't, Eva," said Fanny, sharply; can't you see she's all wrought up? She hadn't ought to have heard all this talk."

Andrew looked anxiously at his wife, rose, and caught up Ellen in his arms with a hug of fervent and protective love. "Don't you worry, father's darlin'," he whispered. "Don't you worry about anythin' you have heard. Father will always have enough to take care of you with."

Jim Tenny, when Andrew set the child down, caught

her up again with a sounding kiss. "Don't you let your big ears ache, you little pitcher," said he, with a gay laugh. "Little doll-babies like you haven't anythin' to worry about if Lloyd's shut down every day in the year."

"They're the very ones whom it concerns," said Nahum Beals, when Ellen and her mother had gone up-stairs.

"Well, I wouldn't have had that little nervous thing hear all this, if I'd thought," Andrew said, anxiously.

Joseph Atkins, whom Fanny had stationed in a sheltered corner near the stove when she opened the door, peered around at Andrew.

"Seems as if she was too young to get much sense of it," he remarked. "My Maria, that's her age, wouldn't."

"Ellen hears everything and makes her own sense of it," said Andrew, "and the Lord only knows what she's made of this. I hope she won't fret over it."

"I wish my tongue had been cut off before I said anything before her," cried Eva. "I know just what that child is. She'll find out what a hard world she's in soon enough, anyway, and I don't want to be the one to open her eyes ahead of time."

Ellen went to bed quietly, and her mother did not think she had paid much attention to what had been going on, and said so when she went down-stairs after Ellen had been kissed and tucked in bed and the lamp put out. "I guess she didn't mind much about it, after all," she said to Andrew. "I guess the room was pretty warm, and that was what made her cheeks so red."

But Ellen, after her mother left her, turned her little head towards the wall and wept softly, lest some one hear her, but none the less bitterly that she had no right conception of the cause of her grief. There was over her childish soul the awful shadow of the labor and poverty of the world. She knew naught of the sub-

106

stance behind the shadow, but the darkness terrified her all the more, and she cried and cried as if her heart would break. Then she, with a sudden resolution, born she could not have told of what strange understanding and misunderstanding of what she had heard that evening, slipped out of bed, groped about until she found her cherished doll, sitting in her little chair in the corner. She was accustomed to take the doll to bed with her, and had undressed her for that purpose early in the evening, but she had climbed into bed and left her sitting in the corner.

"Don't you want your dolly?" her mother had asked.

"No, ma'am; I guess I don't want her to-night," Ellen had replied, with a little break in her voice. Now, when she reached the doll, she gathered her up in her little arms, and groped her way with her into the closet. She hugged the doll, and kissed her wildly, then she shook her. "You have been naughty," she whispered —"yes, you have, dreadful naughty. No, don't you talk to me; you have been naughty. What right had you to be livin' with rich folks, and wearin' such fine things, when other children don't have anything. What right had that little boy that was your mother before I was, and that rich lady that gave you to me? They had ought to be put in the closet, too. God had ought to put them all in the closet, the way I'm goin' to put you. Don't you say a word; you needn't cry; you've been dreadful naughty."

Ellen set the doll, face to the wall, in the corner of the closet, and left her there. Then she crept back into bed, and lay there crying over her precious baby shivering in her thin night-gown all alone in the dark closet. But she was firm in keeping her there, since, with that strange, involuntary grasp of symbolism which has always been maintained by the baby-fingers of humanity for the satisfying of needs beyond resources and the solving of problems outside knowledge, she had a conviction that she was, in such fashion, righting wrong and punishing evil. But she wept over the poor doll until she fell asleep.

108

CHAPTER X

WHEN Ellen woke the next morning she had a curious
feeling, as if she were blinded by the glare of many
hitherto unsuspected windows opening into the greatness outside the little world, just large enough to contain
them, in which she had dwelt all her life with her parents,
her aunt, her grandmother, and her doll. She tried to
adjust herself to her old point of view with her simple
childish recognition of the most primitive facts as a
basis for dreams, but she remembered what Mr. Atkins,
who coughed so dreadfully, had said the night before;
she remembered what the young man with the bulg-
ing forehead, who frightened her terribly, had said;
she remembered the gloomy look in her father's face,
the misery in her aunt Eva's; and she remembered
her doll in the closet—and either everything was different or had a different light upon it. In reality
Ellen's evening in the sound and sight of that current
of rebellion against the odds of life which has taken
the poor off their foothold of understanding since the
beginning of the world had aged her. She had lost
something out of her childhood. She dreaded to go
down - stairs; she had a feeling of shamefacedness
struggling within her; she was afraid that her father
and mother would look at her sharply, then look again,
and ask her what the matter was, and she would not
know what to say. When she went down, and backed
about for her mother to fasten her little frock as was her
wont, she was careful to keep her face turned away;
but Fanny caught her up and kissed her in her usual

way, and then her aunt Eva sung out to know if she wanted to go on a sleigh-ride, and had she seen the snow; and then her father came in and that look of last night had gone from his face, and Ellen was her old self again until she was alone by herself and remembered.

Fanny and Andrew and Eva had agreed to say nothing before the child about the shutting-up of Lloyd's, and their troubles in consequence. "She heard too much last night," Andrew said; "there's no use in her botherin' her little head with it. I guess that baby won't suffer."

"She's jest the child to fret herself most to pieces thinkin' we were awful poor, and she would starve or somethin'," Fanny said.

"Well, she sha'n't be worried if I can help it, no matter what happens to me," Eva said.

After breakfast that morning Eva went to work on a little dress of Ellen's. When Fanny told her not to spend her time over that, when she had so much sewing of her own to do, Eva replied with a gay, hard laugh, that she guessed she'd wait and finish her weddin'-fix when she was goin' to be married.

"Eva Loud, you ain't goin' to be so silly as to put off your weddin'," Fanny cried out.

"I dunno as I've put it off; I dunno as I want to get married, anyhow," Eva said, still laughing. "I dunno, but I'd rather be old maid aunt to Ellen."

"Eva Loud," cried her sister; "do you know what you are doin'?"

"Pretty well, I reckon," said Eva.

"Do you know that if you put off Jim Tenny, and he not likin' it, ten chances to one Aggie Bemis will get hold of him again?"

"Well," said Eva, "let her. I won't have been the one to drag him into misery, anyhow."

"Well, if you can feel that way," Fanny returned, looking at her sister with a sort of mixed admiration and pity.

"I can. I tell you what 'tis, Fanny. When I look at Jim, handsome and head up in the air, and think how he'd look all bowed down, hair turnin' gray, and not carin' whether he's shaved and has on a clean shirt or not, 'cause he's got loaded down with debt, and the grocery-man and the butcher after him, and no work, and me and the children draggin' him down, I can bear anything. If another girl wants to do it, she must, though I'd like to kill her when I think of it. I can't do it, because—I think too much of him."

"He might lose his work after he was married, you know."

"Well, I suppose we'd have to run the risk of that; but I'm goin' to start fair or not at all."

"Well, maybe he'll get work," Fanny said.

"He won't," said Eva. She began to sing "Nancy Lee" over Ellen's dress.

After breakfast Ellen begged a piece of old brown calico of her mother. "Why, of course you can have it, child," said her mother; "but what on earth do you want it for? I was goin' to put it in the rag-bag."

"I want to make my dolly a dress."

"Why, that ain't fit for your dolly's dress. Only think how queer that beautiful doll would look in a dress made of that. Why, you 'ain't thought anything but silk and satin was good enough for her."

"I'll give you a piece of my new blue silk to make your doll a dress," said Eva.

But Ellen persisted. When the doll came out of her closet of vicarious penance she was arrayed like a very scullion among dolls, in the remnant of the dress in which Fanny Brewster had done her house-work all summer.

"There," Ellen told the doll, when her mother did not

hear "you look more like the way you ought to, and you ought to be happy, and not ever think you wish you had your silk dress on. Think of all the poor children who never have any silk dresses, or any dresses at all—nothing except their cloth bodies in the coldest weather. You ought to be thankful to have this." For all which good advice and philosophy the little mother of the doll would often look at the discarded beauty of the wardrobe, with tears in her eyes and fondest pity in her heart; but she never flinched. When the young man Nahum Beals came in, as he often did of an evening, and raised his voice in fierce denunciation against the luxury and extravagance of the rich, Ellen would listen and consider that he would undoubtedly approve of what she had done, did he know, and would allow that she had made her small effort towards righting things.

"Only think what Mr. Beals would say if he saw you in your silk dress; why, I don't know but he would throw you out of the window," she told her doll once.

Ellen did not feel any difference in her way of living after her father was out of work. "She ain't goin' to be stented in one single thing; remember that," Andrew told Fanny, with angry emphasis. "That little, delicate thing is goin' to have everything she needs, if I spend every cent I've saved and mortgage the place."

"Oh, you'll get work before it comes to that," Fanny said, consolingly.

"Whether I do or not, it sha'n't make any difference," declared Andrew. "I'm goin' to hire a horse and sleigh and take her sleigh-ridin' this afternoon. It 'll be good, and she's been talkin' about a sleigh-ride ever since snow flew."

"She could do without that," Fanny said, doubtfully.

"Well, she ain't goin' to."

So it happened that the very day after Lloyd's had

shut down, when every man out of employment felt poorer than he did later when he had grown accustomed to the sensation of no money coming in, Andrew Brewster hired a horse and double sleigh, and took Ellen, her mother, grandmother, and aunt out sleigh-riding. Ellen sat on the back seat of the sleigh, full of that radiant happiness felt by a child whose pleasures have not been repeated often enough for satiety. The sleigh slid over the blue levels of snow followed by long creaks like wakes of sound, when the livery-stable horse shook his head proudly and set his bells in a flurry. Ellen drew a long breath of rapture. These unaccustomed sounds held harmonies of happiness which would echo through her future, for no one can estimate the immortality of some little delight of a child. In all her life, Ellen never forgot that sleigh-ride. It was a very cold day, and the virgin snow did not melt at all; the wind blew a soft, steady pressure from the west, and its wings were evident from the glistening crystals which were lifted and borne along. The trees held their shining boughs against the blue of the sky, and burned and blazed here and there as with lamps of diamonds. The child looked at them, and they lit her soul. Her little face, between the swan's-down puffs of her hood, deepened in color like a rose; her blue eyes shone; she laughed and dimpled silently; she was in too much bliss to speak. The others kept looking at her, then at one another. Fanny nudged her mother-in-law, behind the child's back, and the two women exchanged glances of confidential pride. Andrew and Eva kept glancing around at her, and asking if she were having a good time. Eva was smartly dressed in her best hat, gay with bows and red wings bristling as sharply as the head-dress of an Indian chief in the old pictures. She had a red coat, and a long fur boa wound around her throat; the clear crimson of her cheeks, her great black eyes, and her heavy black braids were so striking that people whom they met looked long at her. Eva talked fast to Andrew, and laughed often and loudly.

Whenever that strident laugh of hers rang out, Mrs. Zelotes Brewster, on the seat behind, moved her be-shawled shoulders with a shivering hunch of disgust. "Can't you tell that girl not to laugh so loud when we're out ridin'," she said to her son that evening; "I saw folks lookin'."

"Oh, never mind, mother," Andrew said; "the poor girl's got a good deal on her mind."

"I suppose you mean that Tinny feller," said Mrs. Zelotes, alluding to something which had happened that afternoon in the course of the sleigh-ride.

The sleighing that day was excellent, for there had been an ice coating on the road before, and the last not very heavy snowfall had been just enough. The Brewsters passed and met many others: young men out with their sweethearts, whole families drawn by the sober old horse as old as the grown-up children; rakish young men driving stable teams, leaning forward with long circles of whip over the horses' backs, leaving the scent of cigars behind them; and often, too, two young ladies in dainty turnouts; and sometimes two girls or four girls from Lloyd's, who had clubbed together and hired a sleigh, taking reckless advantage of their en-forced vacation.

"There's Daisy and Hat Sears, and—and there's Nell White and Eaat Ryoce in the team behind," Eva said.

"I should think they better be savin' their money if Lloyd's has shut up," said Mrs. Zelotes, severely.

"We ain't savin' ours, or Andrew ain't," Eva retorted, with a laugh.

"It's different with us," said Mrs. Zelotes, proudly, "though I shouldn't think it was right for Andrew to hire a team every day."

"Sometimes I think folks might just as well have a little as they're goin' along, for half the time they never seem to get there," Eva said, with another hard laugh at her own wit; and just then she saw something which made her turn deathly white, and catch her breath with a gasp in spite of herself, though that was all. She held up her head like a queen and turned her handsome white face full towards Jim Tenny and the girl for whom he had jilted her before, as they drove past, and bowed and smiled in a fashion which made the red flame up over the young man's swarthy cheek, and the pretty girl at his side shrink a little and avert her tousled fair head with a nervous giggle.

Mrs. Zelotes Brewster twisted herself about and looked after them. "There's John Tibbets and his wife in that sleigh; he's thrown out of work as well as you, Andrew," said Fanny, hastily. "See that feather in her bonnet blow; it's standin' up straight." But Fanny's manœuvre to turn the attention of her mother-in-law was of no avail, for nothing short of sudden death could interpose an effectual barrier between Mrs. Zelotes Brewster's tongue and mind set with the purpose of speech. "Was that the Tinny fellow?" she demanded.

"Yes; I guess so. I didn't notice in particular," Fanny replied, in a low voice. Then she added, pointing to an advancing sleigh. "Good land, there's that Smith girl. They said she wasn't able to ride out. Seems to me she's taken a queer day for it."

"Was that that Tinny fellow?" Mrs. Zelotes asked again. She leaned forward and gave Eva a hard nudge on her red-coated elbow.

"Yes, it was," Eva answered, calmly.

"Who was that girl with him?"

"It was Aggie Bemis."

Mrs. Zelotes gave a sniff, then she settled back, studying Eva's back with a sort of reflective curiosity. Presently she fumbled under the sleigh cushion for an extra shawl which she had brought, and handed it up to Eva. "Don't you want this extra shawl?" she asked, while Fanny stared at her wonderingly. Mrs. Zelotes's civilities towards her sister had been few and far between.

"No, thank you," Eva replied, with a start.

"Hadn't you better? It must be pretty cold sitting up there. You must take all the wind. You can wrap this shawl all round your face and ears, and I don't want it."

"No, thank you; I'm plenty warm," Eva replied. She swallowed hard, and set her mouth hard. There was something about this kindness of her old disapprover which touched her deeply, and moved her to weakness more than had the sight of her recreant lover with another girl. Fanny saw the little quiver pass over her sister's face, and leaned over and whispered.

"I shouldn't be a mite surprised if that girl asked Jim to take her. It would be just like her."

"It don't make any odds whether she did or not," returned Eva, with no affectation of secrecy. "I don't care which way 'twas." She sat up straighter than ever, and some men in a passing sleigh turned to look after her.

"I 'spose she don't think my shawl looks genteel enough to wear," Mrs. Zelotes said to Fanny; "but she's dreadful silly."

They drove through the main street of the city and passed Cynthia Lennox's house. Ellen looked at it with the guilt of secrecy. She thought she saw the lady's head at a front window, and the front door opened and Cynthia came down the walk with a rich sweep of black draperies, and the soft sable toss of plumes.

"There's Cynthia Lennox," said Fanny. "She's a handsome-lookin' woman, ain't she?"

"She's most as old as Andrew, but you'd never suspect it," said Mrs. Zelotes. She had used to have a fancy that Andrew and Cynthia might make a match. She had seen no reason to the contrary, and she always looked at Cynthia with a curious sense of injury and resentment when she thought of what might have been.

As Cynthia Lennox swept down the walk to-day, the old lady said, sharply:

"I don't see why she should walk any prouder than anybody else. I don't know why she should, if she's right-minded. The Lennoxes wasn't any grander than the Brewsters way back, if they have got a little more money of late years. Cynthia's grandfather, old Squire Lennox, used to keep the store, and live in one side of it, and her mother's father, Calvin Goodenough, kept the tavern. I dunno as she has so much to be proud of, though she's handsome enough, and shows her bringin' up, as folks can't that ain't had it." Fanny winced a little; her bringing up was a sore subject with her.

"Well, folks can't help their bringin' up," she retorted, sharply.

"There's Lloyd's team," Andrew said, quickly, partly to avert the impending tongue-clash between his wife and mother.

He reined his horse to one side at a respectful distance, and Norman H. Lloyd, with his wife at his side, swept by in his fine sleigh, streaming on the wind with black fur tails, his pair of bays stepping high to the music of their arches of bells. The Brewsters eyed Norman Lloyd's Russian coat with the wide sable collar turned up around his proud, clear-cut face, the fur-gauntleted hands which held the lines and the whip, for Mr. Lloyd preferred to drive his own blooded pair, both from a love of horseflesh and a greater confidence in his own guidance than in that of other people. Mr. Lloyd was no coward, but he would have confided to no man his sensations had he sat behind those furnaces of fiery motion with other hands than his own upon the lines.

"I should think Mis' Lloyd would be afraid to ride with such horses," said Mrs. Zelotes, as they leaped aside in passing; then she bowed and smiled with eager pleasure, and yet with perfect self-respect. She felt herself every whit as good as Mrs. Norman Lloyd, and her handsome Paisley shawl and velvet bonnet as genteel as the other woman's sealskins and floating plumes. Mrs. Lloyd loomed up like a vast figure of richness enveloped in her bulky winter wraps; her face was superb with health and enjoyment and good-humor. Her cheeks were a deep crimson in the cold wind; she smiled radiantly all the time as if at life itself. She had no thought of fear behind those prancing bays which seemed so frightful to Mrs. Zelotes, used to the steadiest stable team a few times during the year, and driven with a wary eye to railroad crossings and a sense of one's mortality in the midst of life strong upon her. Mrs. Norman Lloyd had never any doubt when her husband held the lines. She would have smiled behind ostriches and zebras. To her mind Norman Lloyd was, as it were, impregnable to all combinations of alien strength or circumstances. When she bowed on passing the Brewsters, she did not move her fixed smile until she caught sight of Ellen. Then emotion broke through the even radiance of her face. She moved her head with a flurry of nods; she waved her hand; she even kissed it to her.

"Bow to Mis' Lloyd, Ellen," said her grandmother; and Ellen ducked her head solemnly. She remembered what she had heard the night before, and the sleigh swept by, Mrs. Lloyd's rosy face smiling back over the black fringe of dancing tails. Eva had shot a swift glance of utmost rancor at the Lloyds, then sat stiff and upright until they passed.

"I wouldn't ask Ellen to bow to that woman," said she, fiercely, between her teeth. "I hate the whole tribe."

No one heard her except Andrew, and he shook the lines over the steady stable horse, and said, "G'lang!" hoarsely.

Mrs. Norman Lloyd, in the other sleigh, had turned to her husband with somewhat timid and deprecating enthusiasm. "Ain't she a sweet little girl?" said she.

"What little girl?" Lloyd asked, abstractedly. He had not looked at the Brewsters at all.

"That little Ellen Brewster who ran away and was gone most three days a little while ago. She was in that sleigh we just passed. She is just the sweetest child I ever laid eyes on," and Norman Lloyd smiled vaguely and coldly, and cast a glance over his sable-clad shoulders to see how far behind the team whose approaching bells he heard might be.

"I suppose her father and aunt are out of work on account of the closing of the factory," remarked Mrs. Lloyd, and a shadow of reflection came over her radiant face.

"Yes, I believe they worked there," Lloyd replied, shaking loose the reins and speeding the horses, that he might not be overtaken. In a few minutes they reached the factory neighborhood. There were three factories: two of them on opposite sides of the road, humming with labor, and puffing with jets of steam at different points; Lloyd's, beyond, was as large as both those standing hushed with windows blank in the afternoon sunshine.

"I suppose the poor men feel pretty badly at being thrown out of work," Mrs. Lloyd said, looking up at the windows as she slipped past in her nest of furs.

"They feel so badly that I have seen a round dozen since we started out taking advantage of their liberty to have a sleigh-ride with livery teams at a good round price," Lloyd replied, with languid emphasis. He never spoke with any force of argument to his wife, nor indeed to any one else, in justification of his actions. His reasons for action were in most cases self-evolved and entirely self-regulated. He had said not a word to any one, not even to his foreman, of his purpose to close the factory until it was quite fixed; he had asked no advice, explained to no one the course of reasoning which led to his doing so. Rowe was a city of strikes, but there had never been a strike at Lloyd's because he had abandoned the situation in every case before the clouds of rebellion were near enough for the storm to break. When Briggs and McGuire, the rival manu-facturers at his right and left, had resorted to cut prices when business was dull, as a refuge from closing up, Lloyd closed with no attempt at compromise.

"I suppose they need a little recreation," Mrs. Lloyd observed, thinking of the little girl's face peeping out between her mother and grandmother in the sleigh they had just passed.

"Their little recreation is on about the same scale for them as my hiring a special railroad train every day in the week to go to Boston would be for me," returned Lloyd, setting his handsome face ahead at the track.

"It does seem dreadful foolish," said his wife, "when they are out of work, and maybe won't earn any more money to support their families all winter—" Mrs. Lloyd hesitated a minute. "I wonder," said she, "if they feel sort of desperate, and think they won't have enough for their families, anyway—that is, enough to feed them, and they might as well get a little good time out of it to remember by-and-by when there ain't enough bread-and-butter. I dunno but we might do something like that, if we were in their places — don't you, Norman?''

" No, I do not," replied Lloyd; " and that is the reason why you and I are not in their places."

Mrs. Lloyd put her sealskin muff before her face as they turned a windy corner, and reflected that her husband was much wiser than she, and that the world couldn't be regulated by women's hearts, pleasant as it would be for the world and the women, since the final outcome would doubtless be destruction.

Mrs. Norman Lloyd was an eminent survival of the purest and oldest-fashioned femininity, a very woman of St. Paul, except that she did not keep silence in the sanctuary.

Just after they had turned the corner they passed an outlying grocery store much frequented as a lounging-place by idle men. There was a row of them on the wooden platform (backed against the wall), cold as it was, watching the sleighs pass, and two or three knots gathered together for the purposes of confabulation. Nearly all of them were employés of Lloyd's, and they had met at that unseasonable hour on that bitter day, drifting together unconsciously as towards a common nucleus of trouble, to talk over the situation.

When these men, huddled up in their shabby great-coats, with caps pulled over shaggy brows and sullenly flashing eyes, saw the Lloyds approaching, the rumble of conversation suddenly ceased. They all stood staring when their employer passed. Only one man, Nahum Beals, looked fairly at Lloyd's face with a denouncing flash of eyes.

To this man Lloyd, recognizing him and some of the others as his employés, bowed. Nahum Beals stood glaring at him in accusing silence, and his head was as immovable as if carved in stone. The other men, with their averted eyes, made a curious, motionless tableau of futile and dumb resistance to power which might have been carved with truth on the face of the rock from the beginning of the earth.

122

CHAPTER XI

THE closing of Lloyd's marked, in some inscrutable way, the close of the first period of Ellen Brewster's childhood. Looking back in later years, she always felt her retrospective thought strike a barrier there, beyond which her images of the past were confused. Yet it was difficult to tell why it was so, for after the first the child could, it seemed, have realized no difference in her life. Now and then she heard some of that conversation characterized at once by the confidence of wrong and injustice, and the logical doubt of it, by solid reasoning which, if followed far enough, refuted itself, by keen and unanswerable argument, and the wildest and most futile enthusiasm. But she had gained nothing except the conviction of the great wrongs of the poor of this earth and the awful tyranny of the rich, of the everlasting moaning of Lazarus at the gates and the cry for water later on from the depths of the rich man's hell. Somehow that last never comforted Ellen; she had no conception of the joy of the injured party over righteous retribution. She pitied the rich man and Lazarus impartially, yet all the time a spirit of fierce partisanship with these poor men was strengthening with her growth, their eloquence over their wrongs stirred her soul, and set her feet outside her childhood. Still, as before said, there was no tangible difference in her daily life. The little petted treasure of the Brewsters had all her small luxuries, sweets, and cushions of life, as well after as before the closing of Lloyd's. And the preparations for her aunt's wedding went on also. The sight of her lover sleigh-riding with her rival that afternoon had been too much for the resolution of Eva Loud's undisciplined nature. She had herself gone to Jim Tenny's house that evening, and called him to account, to learn that he had seriously taken her resolution not to marry at present to proceed from a fear that he would not provide properly for her, and that he had in this state of indignation been easily led by the sight of Aggie Bemis's pretty face in her front door, as he drove by, to stop. She had told Jim that she would marry him as she had agreed if he looked at matters in that way, and had passed Aggie Bemis's window leaning on Jim's arm with a side stare of triumph.

"Be you goin' to get married next month after what you said this mornin'?" her sister asked, half joyfully, half anxiously.

"Yes, I be," was all Eva replied, and Fanny stared at her; she was so purely normal in her inconsistency as to seem almost the other thing.

The preparations for the wedding went on, but Eva never seemed as happy as she had done before the closing of Lloyd's. Jim Tenny could get no more work, and neither could Andrew.

Fanny lamented that the shop had closed at that time of year, for she had planned a Christmas tree of unprecedented splendor for Ellen, but Mrs. Zelotes was to be depended upon as usual, and Andrew told his wife to make no difference. "That little thing ain't goin' to be cheated nohow," he said one night after Ellen had gone to bed and his visiting companions of the cutting-room had happened in.

"I know my children won't get much," Joseph Atkins said, coughing as he spoke; "they wouldn't if Lloyd's hadn't shut down. I never see the time when I could afford to make any account of Christmas, much as ever I could manage a turkey Thanksgiving day."

"The poor that the Lord died for can't afford to keep his birthday; it is the rich that he's going to cast into outer darkness, that keep it for their own ends, and it's a blasphemy and a mockery," proclaimed Nahum Beals. He was very excited that night, and would often spring to his feet and stride across the room. There was another man there that night, a cousin of Joseph Atkins, John Sargent by name. He had recently moved to Rowe, since he had obtained work at McGuire's, "had accepted a position in the finishing-room of Mr. H. S. McGuire's factory in the city of Rowe," as the item in the local paper put it. He was a young man, younger than his cousin, but he looked older. He had a handsome face, under the most complete control as to its muscles. When he laughed he gave the impression of the fixedness of merriment of a mask. He looked keenly at Nahum Beals with that immovable laugh on his face, and spoke with perfectly good-natured sarcasm. "All very well for the string-pieces of the bridge from oppression to freedom," he said, "but you need some common-sense for the ties, or you'll slump."

"What do you mean?"

"We ain't in the Old Testament, but the nineteenth century, and those old prophets, if they were alive to-day, would have to step down out of their flaming chariots and hang their mantles on the bushes, and instead of standing on mountain-tops and tellin' their enemies what rats they were, and how they would get what they deserved later on, they would have to tell their enemies what they wanted them to do to better matters, and make them do it."

"Instead of standing by your own strike in Greenboro, you quit and come here to work in McGuire's the minute you got a chance," said Nahum Beals, sullenly, and

Sargent responded, with his unrelaxing laugh, "I left enough strikers for the situation in Greenboro; don't you worry about me."

"I think he done quite right to quit the strike if he got a chance to work," Joseph Atkins interposed. "Folks have got to look out for themselves, labor reform or no labor reform."

"That's the corner-stone of labor reform, seems to me," said Andrew.

"Seems to me sometimes you talk like a damned scab," cried Nahum Beals, fiercely, red spots flickering in his thin cheeks. Andrew looked at him, and spoke with slow wrath. "Look here, Nahum Beals," he said, "you're in my house, but I ain't goin' to stand no such talk as that, I can tell you."

John Sargent laid a pacifically detaining hand on Nahum Beals's arm as he strode past him. "Oh, Lord, stop rampagin' up and down like a wildcat," he said. "What good do you think you're doin' tearin' and shoutin' and insultin' people? He ain't talkin' like a scab, he's only talkin' a tie to your string-piece."

"That's so," said Joseph Atkins. Sargent boarded with him, and the board money was a godsend to him, now he was out of work. John Sargent had fixed his own price, and it was an unheard-of one for such simple fare as he had. His weekly dollars kept the whole poor family in food. But John Sargent was a bachelor, and earning remarkably good wages, and Joseph Atkins's ailing wife, whom illness and privation had made unnaturally grasping and ungrateful, told her cronies that it wasn't as if he couldn't afford it.

Up-stairs little Ellen lay in her bed, her doll in her arms, listening to the low rumble of masculine voices in the room below. Her mother had gone out, and there were only the men there. They were smoking, and the odor of their pipes floated up into Ellen's cham-

ber through the door-cracks. She thought how her
grandmother Brewster would sniff when she came in
next day. She could hear her saying, "Well, for my
part, if those men couldn't smoke their old pipes somewhere else besides in my sittin'-room, I wouldn't have
'em in the house." But that reflection did not trouble
Ellen very long, and she had never been disturbed
herself by the odor of the pipes. She thought of them
insensibly as the usual atmosphere when men were
gathered together in any place except the church. She
knew that they were talking about that old trouble, and
Nahum Beals's voice of high wrath made her shrink;
but, after all, she was removed from it all that night
into a little prospective paradise of her own, which, as
is the case in childhood, seemed to overgild her own
future and all the troubles of the world. Christmas was
only a week distant, she was to have a tree, and the
very next evening her mother had promised to take
her down-town and show her the beautiful, lighted
Christmas shops. She wondered, listening to that
rumble of discontent below, why grown-up men and
women ever fretted when they were at liberty to go down-
town every evening when they chose and look at the
lighted shops, for she could still picture pure delight for
others without envy or bitterness.

The next day the child was radiant; she danced rather
than walked; she could not speak without a smile; she
could eat nothing, for her happiness was so purely
spiritual that desires of the flesh were in abeyance.
Her heart beat fast; the constantly recurring memory of
what was about to happen fairly overwhelmed her as
with waves of delight.

"If you don't eat your supper you can't go, and
that's all there is about it," her mother told her when
they were seated at the table, and Ellen sat dreaming
before her toast and peach preserve.

"You must eat your supper, Ellen," Andrew said, anxiously. Andrew had on his other coat, and he had shaved, and was going too, as was Mrs. Zelotes Brewster.

"She 'ain't eat a thing all day, she's so excited about goin'," Fanny said. "Now, Ellen, you must eat your supper, or you can't go—you'll be sick."

And Ellen ate her supper, though exceeding joy as well as exceeding woe can make food lose its savor, and toast and preserves were as ashes on her tongue when the very fragrance of coming happiness was in her soul.

When, finally, in hand of her mother, while Andrew walked behind with her grandmother, she went towards the lights of the town, she had a feeling as of wings on her feet. However, she walked soberly enough with wide eyes of amazement and delight at everything—the long, silver track of the snowy road under the light of the full moon, the slants of the house roofs sparkling with crusts of crystals, the lighted windows set with house plants, for the dwellers in the outskirts of Rowe loved house plants, and their front windows bloomed with the emulative splendor of geraniums from fall to spring. She saw behind them glimpses of lives and some doings as real as her own, but mysterious under the locks of other personalities, and therefore as full of possibilities of preciousness as the sheet of morning dew over a neighbor's yard; she had often believed she saw diamonds sparkle in that, though never in her own. She had proved it otherwise too often. So Ellen, seeing through a window a little girl of her own age in a red frock, straightway believed it to be satin of the richest quality, and, seeing through another window a tea-table spread, had no doubt that the tin teapot was silver. A girl with a crown of yellow braids pulled down a curtain, and she thought her as beautiful as an angel; but of all this she said nothing at all, only walked soberly on, holding fast to her mother's hand.

When they were half-way to the shops, a door of a white house close to the road flew open and shut again with a bang, there was a scúrry and grating slide on the front walk, then the gate was thrown back, and a boy dashed through with a wild whoop, just escaping contact with Mrs. Zelotes Brewster. "You'd better be careful," said she, sharply. "It ain't the thing for boys to come tearin' out of yards in the evenin' without seein' where they are goin'."

The boy cast an abashed glance at her. The street-lamp shone full on his face, which was round and reddened by the frosty winds, with an aimlessly grinning mouth of uncertain youth, and black eyes with a bold and cheerful outlook on the unknown. He was only ten, but he was large for his age. Ellen, when he looked from her grandmother back at her, thought him almost a man, and then she saw that he was the boy who had brought the chestnuts to her the night when she had returned from her runaway excursion. The boy recognized her at the same moment, and his mouth seemed to gape wider, and a moist red overspread his face down to his swathing woollen scarf. Then he gave another whoop significant of the extreme of nervous abashedness and the incipient defiance of his masculine estate, there was a flourish of heels, followed by a swift glimmering slide of steel, and he was off trailing his sled.

"That's that Joy boy that brought Ellen the chestnuts that time," Fanny said. "Do you remember him, Ellen?"

"Yes, ma'am," replied Ellen. The look of the boy in her face had bewildered and confused her, without her knowing the why of it. It was as if she had spelled a word in her reading-book whose meaning she could not grasp.

"I don't care who he is," said Mrs. Zelotes, "he 'ain't no business racin' out of gates that way, and his folks hadn't ought to let a boy no older than that out alone of nights."

They kept on, and the boy apparently left them far behind in his career of youthful exuberance, until they came to the factories. Andrew looked up at the windows of Lloyd's, dark except for a faint glimmer in a basement window from the lamp of the solitary watchman, and drew a heavy sigh.

"It ain't as bad for you as it is for some," his mother said, sharply, and then she jumped aside, catching her son's arm as the boy sprang out of a covering shadow under the wall of Lloyd's and dashed before them with another wild whoop and another glance of defiant bashfulness at Ellen.

"My land! it's that boy again," cried Mrs. Zelotes. "Here, you boy !—boy ! What's your name?"

"His name is Granville Joy," Ellen replied, unexpectedly.

"Why, how did you know, child?" her grandmother asked. "Seems to me he's got a highfalutin' name enough. Here you, Granville—if that's your name—don't you know any better than to—" But the boy was gone, his sled creaking on the hard snow at his heels, and a faint whoop sounded from the distance.

"I guess if I had the bringin' up of that boy there wouldn't be such doin's," said Mrs. Zelotes, severely. "His mother's a pretty woman, but I don't believe she's got much force. She wouldn't have given him such a name if she had."

"She named him after the town she came from," said Fanny. "She told me once. She's a real smart woman, and she makes that boy stand around."

"She must; it looks as if he was standin' round pretty lively jest now," said Mrs. Zelotes. "Namin' of a boy after a town! They'd better wait and name a town after the boy if he amounts to anything."

"His mother told me he was goin' into the first grammar-school next year," said Fanny.

"I pity his teacher," said Mrs. Zelotes, and then she recoiled, for the boy made another dart from behind a lamp-post, crossed their path, and was off again.

"My land!" gasped Mrs. Zelotes, "you speak to him, Andrew." But Andrew laughed. "Might as well speak to a whirlwind," said he. "He ain't doin' any harm, mother; it's only his boyish antics. For Heaven's sake, let him enjoy himself while he can, it won't be long before the grind-mill in there will get hold of him, and then he'll be sober enough to suit anybody," and Andrew pointed at Lloyd's as he spoke.

"Boys can be boys," said Mrs. Zelotes, severely, "and they can have a good time, but they can behave themselves."

None of them looking after that flying and whooping figure ahead had the slightest idea of the true situation. They did not know that the boy was confused by the fires, none the less ardent that they were so innocent, of a first love for Ellen; that, ever since he had seen her little, fair face on her aunt's shoulder the day when she was found, it had been even closer to his heart than his sled and his jackstones and his ball, and his hope of pudding for dinner. They did not know that he had toiled at the wood-pile of a Saturday, and run errands after school, to earn money to buy Christmas presents for his mother and Ellen; that he had at that very minute in his purse in the bottom of his pocket the sum of eighty-nine cents, mostly in coppers, since his wage was generally payable in that coin, and his pocket sagged arduously therefrom. They did not know that he was even then bound upon on errand to the grocery store for a bag of flour to be brought home on his sled, and would thereby swell his exchequer by another cent. They did not know what dawning chords of love, and knowledge of love, that wild whoop expressed; and the boy dodged and darted and hid, and appeared before them all the way to the busy main street of Rowe; and, after they had entered the great store where the finest Christmas display was held, he stood before the window staring at Ellen vanishing in a brilliant vista, and whooped now and then, regardless of public opinion.

Ellen, when once she was inside the store, forgot everything else. She clung more tightly to her mother's hand, as one will cling to any wonted stay of love in the midst of strangeness, even of joy, and she saw everything with eyes which photographed it upon her very soul. At first she had an impression of a dazzling incoherence of splendor, of a blare as of thousands of musical instruments all sounding different notes of delight, of a weaving pattern of colors, too intricate to master, of a mingled odor of paint and varnish, and pine and hemlock boughs, and then she spelled out the letters of the details. She looked at those counters set with the miniature paraphernalia of household life which give the first sweet taste of domesticity and housekeeping joys to a little girl.

There were the sets of dolls' furniture, and the dolls, dishes, and there was a counter with dolls' cooking-stoves and ranges bristling with the most delightful realism of pots and pans, at which she gazed so fixedly and breathlessly that she looked almost stupid. Her elders watched half in delight, half with pain, that they could not purchase everything at which she looked. Mrs. Zelotes bought some things surreptitiously, hiding the parcels under her shawl. Andrew, whispering to a salesman, asked the price of a great cooking-stove at which Ellen looked long. When he heard the amount he sighed. Fanny touched his arm comfortingly.

" There would be no sense in your buying that, if you had all the money in creation," she said, in a hushed voice. " There's a twenty-five-cent one that's good enough. I'm going to buy that for her to-morrow. She'll never know the difference." But Andrew Brewster, nevertheless, went through the great, dazzling shop with his heart full of bitterness. It seemed to him monstrous and incredible that he had a child as beautiful and altogether wonderful as that, and could not buy the whole stock for her if she wanted it. He had never in his whole life wanted anything for himself that he could not have, enough to give him pain, but he wanted for his child with a longing that was a passion. Her little desires seemed to him the most important and sacred needs in the whole world. He watched her with pity and admiration, and shame at his own impotence of love to give her all.

But Ellen knew nothing of it. She was radiant. She never thought of wanting all those treasures further than she already had them. She gazed at the wonders in that department where the toy animals were kept, and which resembled a miniature menagerie, the silence broken by the mooing of cows, the braying of donkeys, the whistle of canaries, and the roars of mock-lions when their powers were invoked by the attendants, and her ears drank in that discordant babel of tiny mimicry like music. There was no spirit of criticism in her. She was utterly pleased with everything.

When her grandmother held up a toy-horse and said the fore-legs were too long, Ellen wondered what she meant. To her mind it was more like a horse than any real one she had ever seen.

As she gazed at the decorations, the wreaths, the gauze, the tinsel, and paper angels, suspended by invisible wires over the counters, and all glittering and shining and twinkling with light, a strong whiff of evergreen fragrance came to her, and the aroma of fir-balsam, and it was to her the very breath of all the mysterious joy and hitherto untasted festivity of this earth into which she had come. She felt deep in her childish soul the sense of a promise of happiness in the future, of which this was a foretaste. When she went into the department where the dolls dwelt, she fairly turned pale. They swung, and sat, and lay, and stood, as in angelic ranks, all smiling between shining fluffs of hair. It was a chorus of smiles, and made the child's heart fairly leap. She felt as if all the dolls were smiling at her. She clung fast to her mother's hand, and hid her face against her skirt.

"Why, what is the matter, Ellen?" Fanny asked. Ellen looked up, and smiled timidly and confusedly, then at that dazzle of waxen faces and golden locks above skirts of delicate pink and blue and white, like flower petals.

"You never saw so many dolls together before, did you, Ellen?" said Andrew; then he added, wistfully, "There ain't one of 'em any bigger and prettier than your own doll, be they, Ellen?" And that, although he had never recovered from his uneasiness about that mysterious doll.

Ellen had not seen Cynthia Lennox since that morning several weeks ago when she had run away from her, except one glimpse when she was sleigh-riding. Now all at once, when they had stopped to look at some wonderful doll-houses, she saw her face to face. Ellen had been gazing with rapture at a great doll-house completely furnished, and Andrew had made one of his miserable side inquiries as to its price, and Fanny had said, quite loud, "Lord, Andrew, you might just as well ask the price of the store! You know such a thing as that is out of the question for any child unless her father is rich as Norman Lloyd," and Ellen, who had not noticed what they were saying, looked up, when a faint breath of violets smote her sense with a quick memory, and there was the strange lady who had taken her into her house and kept her and given her the doll, the strange lady whom the gentleman said might be punished for keeping her if people were to know.

Cynthia Lennox went pale when, without knowing what was going to happen, she looked down and saw suddenly the child's innocent face looking into hers. She stood wavering in her trailing, fur-lined, and softly whispering draperies, so marked and set aside by her grace and elegance and countenance of superiority and proud calm that people turned to look after her more than after many a young beauty, and did not, for a second, know what to say or do. She had no mind to shrink from a recognition of the child; she had no fear of the result, but there was a distinct shrinking at a scene with that flashing-eyed and heavy-browed mother of the child in such a place as that. She would undoubtedly speak very loud. She expected the volley of recrimination in a high treble which would follow the announcement in that sweet little flute which she remembered so well.

"Mamma, that is the lady who kept me, and would not let me go home."

But Ellen, after a second's innocent and startled regard, turned away with no more recognition than if she had been a stranger. She turned her little back to her, and looked at the doll-house. A great flush flamed over Cynthia Lennox's face, and a qualm of mortal shame. She took an impetuous glide forward, and was just about to speak and tell the truth, whatever the consequences, and not be outdone in magnanimity by that child, when a young girl with a sickly but impudent and pretty face jostled her rudely. The utter pertness of her ignorant youth knew no respect

135

for even the rich Miss Cynthia Lennox. "Here's your parcel, lady," she said, in her rough young voice, its shrillness modified by hoarseness from too much shouting for cash boys during this busy season, and she thrust, with her absent eyes upon a gentleman coming towards her, a parcel into Cynthia's hands. Somehow the touch of that parcel seemed to bring Cynthia to her senses. It was a kodak which she had been purchasing for the little boy who had lived with her, and whom it had almost broken her heart to lose. She remembered what her friend Lyman Risley had said, that it might make trouble for others besides herself. She took her parcel with that involuntary meekness which the proudest learn before the matchless audacity of youthful ignorance when it fairly asserts itself, and passed out of the store to her waiting carriage. Ellen saw her.

"That was Cynthia Lennox, wasn't it?" Fanny said, with something like awe. "Wasn't that an elegant cloak she had on? I guess it was Russian sable."

"I don't care if it was, it ain't a mite handsomer than my cape lined with squirrel," said Mrs. Zelotes.

Ellen looked intently at a game on the counter. It was ten o'clock when Ellen went home. She had been into all the principal stores which were decorated for Christmas. Her brain resembled a kaleidoscope as she hurried along at her mother's hand. Every thought seemed to whirl the disk, and new and more dazzling combinations appeared, but the principle which underlay the whole was that of the mystery of festivity and joy upon the face of the earth, of which this Christmas wealth was the key.

The Brewsters had scarcely reached the factory neighborhood when there was a swift bound ahead of them and the familiar whoop.

"There's that boy again," said Mrs. Zelotes.

She made various remonstrances, and even Andrew, when the boy had passed his own home in his persistent dogging of them, called out to him, as did Fanny, but he was too far ahead to hear. The boy followed them quite to their gate, proceeding with wild spurts and dashes from shadow to shadow, and at last reappeared from behind one of the evergreen trees in the west yard, springing out of its long shadow with strange effect. He darted close to Ellen as she passed in the gate, crammed something into her hand, and was gone. Andrew could not catch him, though he ran after him. "He ran like a rabbit," he said, coming breathlessly into the house, where they were looking at the treasure the boy had thrust upon Ellen. It was a marvel of a patent top, which the boy had long desired to own. He had spent all his money on it, and his mother was cheated of her Christmas present, but he had given, and Ellen had received, her first token of love.

CHAPTER XII

THE next spring Ellen went to school. When a
child who has reigned in undisputed sovereignty at
home is thrust among other children at school, one of
two things happens: either she is scorned and rebelled
against, and her little crown of superiority rolled in
the dust of the common playground, or she extends
the territories of her empire. Ellen extended hers,
though involuntarily, for there was no conscious
thirst for power in her.

On her first morning at school, she seated herself
at her desk and looked forth from the golden cloud
of her curls, her eyes full of innocent contemplation,
her mouth corners gravely drooping. She knew one
little girl who sat not far from her. The little girl's
name was Floretta Vining. Floretta was built on the
scale of a fairy, with tiny, fine, waxen features, a little
tossing mane of flaxen hair, eyes a most lovely and
perfect blue, with no more depth in them than in the
blue of china, and an expression of the sweetest and
most innocent inanity and irresponsibility. Nobody
ever expected anything of this little Floretta Vining.
She was always a negative success. She smiled
around from the foot of her curving class, and never
had her lessons, but she never disobeyed the rules,
except that of punctuality.

Floretta was late at school. She came daintily up
the aisle, two cheap bangles on one wrist slipping over
a slim hand, and tinkling. Floretta's mother had a
taste for the cheaply decorative. There was an abun-

dance of coarse lace on Floretta's frock, and she wore a superfluous sash which was not too fresh. Floretta toed out excessively, her slender little feet pointing out sharply, almost at right angles with each other, and Ellen admired her for that. She watched her coming, planting each foot as carefully and precisely as a bird, her lace frills flouncing up and down, her bangles jingling, and thought how very pretty she was.

Ellen felt herself very loving towards the teacher and Floretta Vining. Floretta leaned forward as soon as she was seated and gazed at her with astonishment, and that deepening of amiability and general sweetness which one can imagine in the face of a doll after persistent scrutiny. Ellen smiled decorously, for she was not sure how much smiling was permissible in school. When she smiled guardedly at Floretta, she was conscious of another face regarding her, twisted slightly over a shabby little shoulder covered with an ignominious blue stuff, spotted and faded. This little girl's wisp of brown braid was tied with a shoe-string, and she looked poorer than any other child in the school, but she had an honest light in her eyes, and Ellen considered her to be rather more beautiful than Floretta.

She was Maria Atkins, Joseph Atkins's second child. Ellen sat with her book before her, and the strange, new atmosphere of the school-room stole over her senses. It was not altogether pleasant, although it was considered that the ventilation was after the most approved modern system. She perceived a strong odor of peppermints, and Floretta Vining was waving ostentatiously a coarse little pocket-handkerchief scented with New-mown Hay. There was also a strong effusion of stale dinners and storm-beaten woollen garments, but there was, after all, that savor of festivity which Ellen was apt to discover in the new. She looked over her book

139

with utter content. In a line with her, on the boys'
side, there appeared a covertly peeping face under a
thatch of light hair, and Ellen, influenced insensibly
by the boy's shyly worshipful eyes, looked and saw
Granville Joy. She remembered the Christmas top,
and blushed very pink without knowing why, and
flirted all her curls towards the boys' side.

Ellen, from having so little acquaintance with boys,
had had no very well-defined sentiments towards them,
but now, on being set apart with her feminine element,
and separated so definitely by the middle aisle of the
school-room, she began to experience sensations both
of shyness and exclusiveness. She did not think the
boys, in their coarse clothes, with their cropped heads,
half as pretty as the girls.

The teacher coming down the aisle laid a caressing
hand on Ellen's curls, and the child looked up at her
with that confidence which is exquisite flattery.

After she had passed, Ellen heard a subtle whisper
somewhere at her back; it was half audible, but its
meaning was entirely plain. It signified utmost scorn
and satirical contempt. It was fine-pointed and far-
reaching. A number looked around. It was as expressive as a whole sentence, and, being as concentrated, was fairly explosive with meaning.

"H'm, ain't you pretty? Ain't you dreadful pretty,
little dolly-pinky-rosy. H'm, teacher's partial. Ain't
you pretty? Ain't you stuck up? H'm."

Ellen, not being used to the school vernacular, did
not fairly apprehend all this, and least of all that it
was directed towards herself. She cast a startled look
around, then turned to her book. She leaned back in
her seat and held her book before her face with both
hands, and began to read, spelling out the words noiselessly. All at once, she felt a fine prick on her head,
and threw back one hand and turned quickly. The

little girl behind was engrossed in study, and all Ellen could see was the parting in her thick black hair, for her head was supported by her two hands, her elbows were resting on her desk, and she was whispering the boundaries of the State of Massachusetts.

Ellen turned back to her reading-book, and recommenced studying with the painful faithfulness of the new student; then came again that small, fine, exasperating prick, and she thrust her face around quickly to see that same faithfully intent little girl.

Ellen rubbed her head doubtfully, and tried to fix her attention again upon her book, but presently it came again; a prick so small and fine that it strained consciousness; an infinitesimal point of torture, and this time Ellen, turning with a swift flirt of her head, caught the culprit. It was that faithful little girl, who held a black-headed belt-pin in her hand; she had been carefully separating one hair at a time from Ellen's golden curls, and tweaking it out.

Ellen looked at her with a singular expression compounded of bewilderment, of injury, of resentment, of alarm, and of a readiness to accept it all as a somewhat peculiar advance towards good-fellowship and a merry understanding. But the expression on that dark, somewhat grimy little face, looking out at her from a jungle of coarse, black locks, was fairly impish, almost malicious. There was not merriment in it so much as jibing; instead of that soft regard and worshipful admiration which Ellen was accustomed to find in new eyes, there was resentful envy.

Then Ellen shrank, and bristled with defiance at the same time, for she had the spirit of both the Brewsters and the Louds in her, in spite of her delicacy of organization. She was a fine instrument, capable of chords of tragedy as well as angelic strains. She saw that the little girl who was treating her so was

141

dressed very poorly, that her dress was not only shabby, but actually dirty; that she, as well as the other girl whom she noticed, had her braid tied with an old shoe-string, and that a curious smell of leather pervaded her. Ellen continued to regard the little girl, then suddenly she felt a hand on her shoulder, and the teacher, Miss Rebecca Mitchell, was looking down at her. "What is the trouble?" asked Miss Mitchell. That look of half-wondering admiration to which Ellen was accustomed was in the teacher's eyes, and Ellen again thought her beautiful.

One of the first, though a scarcely acknowledged principle of beauty, is that of reflection of the fairness of the observer. Ellen being as innocently self-seeking for love and admiration as any young thing for its natural sustenance, was quick to recognize it, though she did not understand that what she saw was herself in the teacher's eyes, and not the teacher. She gazed up in that roseate face with the wide mouth set in an inverted bow of smile, curtained, as it were, with smoothly crinkled auburn hair clearly outlined against the cheeks, at the palpitating curve of shiny black-silk bosom, adorned with a festoon of heavy gold watch-chain, and thought that here was love, and beauty, and richness, and elegance, and great wisdom, calling for reverence but no fear. She answered not one word to the teacher's question, but continued to gaze at her with that look of wide-eyed and contemplative regard. "What is the trouble, Ellen?" repeated Miss Mitchell. "Why were you looking around so?" Ellen said nothing. The little girl behind had her head bent over her book so low that the sulky curves of her mouth did not show. The teacher turned to her—"Abby Atkins," said she, "what were you doing?"

Abby Atkins did not raise her studious head. She did not seem to hear.

"Abby Atkins," said the teacher, sharply, "answer me. What were you doing?" Then the little girl answered, with a sulky note, half growl, half whimper, like some helpless but indomitable little trapped animal, "Nothin'."

"Ellen," said the teacher, and her voice changed indescribably. "What was she doing?" Ellen did not answer. She looked up in the teacher's face, then cast down her eyes and sat there, her little hands folded in tightly clinched fists in her lap, her mouth a pink line of resistance. "Ellen," repeated the teacher, and she tried to make her voice sharp, but in spite of herself it was caressing. Her heart had gone out to the child the moment she had seen her enter the school-room. She was as helpless before her as before a lover. She was wild to catch her up and caress her instead of pestering her with questions. "Ellen, you must answer me," she said, but Ellen sat still.

Half the scholars were on their feet, reaching and craning their necks. The teacher turned on them, and there was no lack of sharpness in her tone. "Sit down this moment, every one of you," she called. "Abby Atkins, if there is any more disturbance, I shall know what is at the root of the matter. If I see you turning around again, Ellen, I shall insist upon knowing why." Then the teacher placed a caressing hand upon Ellen's yellow head, and passed down the aisle to her desk.

Ellen had no more trouble during the session. Abby Atkins was commendably quiet and studious, and when called out to recitation made the best one in her class. She was really brilliant in a defiant, reluctant fashion. However, though she did not again disturb Ellen's curls, she glowered at her with furtive but un-relaxed hostility over her book. Especially a blue ribbon which confined Ellen's curls in a beautiful bow fired her eyes of animosity. She looked hard at it, then she pulled her black braid over her shoulder and felt of the hard shoe-string knot, and frowned with an ugly frown of envy and bitterest injury, and asked herself the world-wide and world-old question as to the why of inequality, and, though it was based on such trivialities as blue ribbons and shoe-strings, it was none the less vital to her mind. She would have loved, have gloried, to pull off that blue ribbon, put it on her own black braid, and tie up those yellow curls with her own shoe-string with a vicious yank of security. But all the time it was not so much because she wanted the ribbon as because she did not wish to be slighted in the distribution of things. Abby Atkins cared no more for personal ornament than a wild cat, but she wanted her just allotment of the booty of the world. So at recess she watched her chance. Ellen was surrounded by an admiring circle of big girls, gushing with affection. "Oh, you dear little thing," they said. "Only look at her beautiful curls. Give me a kiss, won't you, darling?" Little reverent fingers twined Ellen's golden curls, red apples were thrust forward for her to take bites, sticky morsels of candy were forced secretly into her hands. Abby Atkins stood aloof. "You mean little thing," one of the big girls said suddenly, catching hold of her thin shoulder and shaking her—"you mean little thing, I saw you."

"So did I," said another big girl, "and I was a good mind to tell on you."

"Yes, you had better look out, and not plague that dear little thing," said the other.

"You ought to be ashamed of yourself," chimed in still another big girl. "Only look how pretty she is, the little darling—the idea of your tormenting her. You deserve a good, hard whipping, Abby Atkins."

This big girl was herself a beauty and wore a fine

and precise blue-ribbon bow, and Abby Atkins looked at her with a scowl of hatred.

"She's an ugly little thing," said the big girls among themselves as they went edging gently and imperceptibly away towards a knot of big boys, and then Abby Atkins's chance had come. She advanced with a spring upon Ellen Brewster, and she pulled that blue ribbon off her head so cruelly and fiercely that she pulled out some of the golden hairs with it and threw it on the ground, and stamped on it. Then she seized Ellen by the shoulders and proceeded to shake her for wearing a blue ribbon when she herself wore a shoe-string, but she reckoned without Ellen. One would as soon have expected to meet fight in a little child angel as in this Ellen Brewster, but she did not come of her ancestors for nothing.

Although she was so daintily built that she looked smaller, she was in reality larger than the other girl, and as she straightened herself in her wrath she seemed a head taller and proportionately broad. She tossed her yellow head, and her face took on an expression of noble courage and indignation, but she never said a word. She simply took Abby Atkins by the arms and lifted her off her feet and seated her on the ground. Then she picked up her blue ribbon, and walked off, and Abby scrambled to her feet and looked after her with a vanquished but untamed air. Nobody had seen what happened except Abby's younger sister Maria and Granville Joy. Granville pressed stealthily close to Ellen as she marched away and whispered, his face blazing, his voice full of confidence and congratulation, "Say, if she'd been a boy, I'd licked her for you, and you wouldn't hev had to tech her yourself;" and Maria walked up and eyed her prostrate but defiantly glaring sister—"I ain't sorry one mite, Abby Atkins," she declared—"so there."

"You go 'long," returned Abby, struggling to her feet, and shaking her small skirts energetically.

"Your dress is jest as wet as if you'd set down in a puddle, and you'll catch it when you get home," Maria said, pitilessly.

"I ain't afraid."

"What made you touch her, anyhow; she hadn't done nothin'?"

"If you want to wear shoe-strings when other folks wear ribbons, you can," said Abby Atkins. She walked away, switching, with unabated dignity in the midst of defeat, the draggled tail of her poor little dress. She had gone down like a cat; she was not in the least hurt except in her sense of justice; that was jarred to a still greater lack of equilibrium. She felt as if she had been floored by Providence in conjunction with a blue bow, and her very soul rose in futile rebellion. But, curiously enough, her personal ire against Ellen vanished.

At the afternoon recess she gave Ellen the sound half of an old red Baldwin apple which she had brought for luncheon, and watched her bite into it, which Ellen did readily, for she was not a child to cherish enmity, with an odd triumph. "The other half ain't fit to eat, it's all wormy," said Abby Atkins, flinging it away as she spoke.

"Then you ought to have kept this," Ellen cried out, holding towards her the half, minus one little bite. But Abby Atkins shook her head forcibly. "That was why I gave it to you," said she. "Say, didn't you never have to tie up your hair with a shoe-string?" Ellen shook her head, looking at her wonderingly. Then with a sudden impulse she tore off the blue ribbon from her curls. "Say, you take it," she said, "my mother won't care. I'd jest as lief wear the shoe-string, honest."

"I don't want your blue ribbon," Abby returned,

stoutly; "a shoe-string is a good deal better to tie the hair with. I don't want your blue ribbon; I don't want no blue ribbon unless it's mine."

"It would be yours if I give it to you," Ellen declared, with blue eyes of astonishment and consternation upon this very strange little girl.

"No, it wouldn't," maintained Abby Atkins.

But it ended in the two girls, with that wonderful and inexplicable adjustment of childhood into one groove after harsh grating on different levels, walking off together with arms around each other's waist, and after school began Ellen often felt a soft, cat-like pat on her head, and turned round with a loving glance at Abby Atkins.

Ellen talked more about Abby Atkins than any other of the children when she got home, and while her mother looked at it all easily, her grandmother was doubtful. "There's others that I should rather have Ellen thick with," said she. "I 'ain't nothin' against the Atkinses, but they can't have been as well brought up as some, they have had so little to do with, and their mother's been ailin' so long."

"Ellen may as well begin as she can hold out, and be intimate with them that will be intimate with her," Eva said, rather bitterly. Eva was married by this time, and living with Jim and his mother. She wore in those days an expression of bitterly defiant triumph and happiness, as of one who has wrested his sweet from fate under the ban of the law, and is determined to get the flavor of it though the skies fall. "I suppose I did wrong marrying Jim," she often told her sister, "but I can't help it."

"Maybe Jim will get work before long," her sister would say, consolingly.

"I have about given up," Eva would reply. "I guess Jim will have to roost on a flour-barrel at Mun-

sey's store the rest of his days; but as long as he belongs to me, it don't make so much difference."

Eva had taken up an agency for a cosmetic which
was manufactured by a woman in Rowe. She had one
window of the north parlor in the Tenny cottage, which
had been given up to her when she married Jim, filled
with the little pink boxes containing the "Fairy Cream,"
and a great sign, but the trade languished. Both Eva
and Jim had tried in vain to obtain employment in factories in other towns.

Lloyd's had not reopened, although it was April,
and Andrew was drawing on his savings. Fanny
had surreptitiously answered an advertisement pur-
porting to give instructions to women as to the earning
of large sums of money at home, and was engaged with
a stock of glass and paints which she hurriedly swept
out of sight when any one's shadow passed the window,
and later she found herself to be the victim of a small
swindling conspiracy, and lost the dollar which she had
invested. But Ellen knew nothing of all this. She
lacked none of her accustomed necessaries nor luxuries,
and with her school a new life full of keen, new savors
or relish began for her. There were also new affections
in it.

Ellen was as yet too young, and too confident in love,
to have new affections plunge her into anything but a
delightful sort of anti-blossom tumult. There was no
suspense, no doubt, no jealousy, only utter acquiescence
of single - heartedness, admiration, and trust. She
thought Abby Atkins and Floretta Vining lovely and
dependable: she parted from them at night without a
pang, and looked forward blissfully to the meeting next
morning. She also had sentiments equally peaceful
and pronounced, though instinctively more secret,
towards Granville Joy. She used to glance over towards the boys' side and meet his side-long eyes without

so much a quickening of her pulses as a quickening of her imagination.

"I know who your beau is," Floretta Vining, who was in advance of her years, said to her once, and Ellen looked at her with half-stupid wonder.

"His first name begins with a G and his last with a J," Floretta tittered, and Ellen continued to look at her with the faintest suspicion of a blush, because she had a feminine instinct that a blush was in order, not because she knew of any reason for it.

"He is," said Floretta, with another exceedingly foolish giggle. "My, you are as red as a beet."

"I ain't old enough to have a beau," Ellen said, her soft cheeks becoming redder, and her baby face all in a tremor.

"Yes, you be," Floretta said, with authority, "because you are so pretty, and have got such pretty curls. Ben Simonds said the other day you were the prettiest girl in school."

"Then do you think he is my beau, too?" asked Ellen, innocently. But Floretta frowned, and tittered, and hesitated.

"He said except one," she faltered out, finally.

"Well, who was that?" asked Ellen.

"How do I know?" pouted Floretta. "Mebbe it was me, though I don't think I'm so very pretty."

"Then Ben Simonds is your beau," said Ellen, reflectively.

"Yes, I guess he is," admitted Floretta.

That night, amid much wonder and tender ridicule, Ellen told her mother and Aunt Eva, and her father, that Ben Simonds was Floretta's beau, and Granville Joy was hers. But Andrew laughed doubtfully.

"I don't want that little thing to get such ideas into her head yet a while," he told Fanny afterwards, but she only laughed at him, seeing nothing but the childish play of the thing; but he, being a man, saw deeper.

However, Ellen's fondest new love was not for any of her little mates, but for her school-teacher. To her the child's heart went out in worship. All through the spring she offered her violets—violets gathered laboriously after school in the meadow back of her grandmother's house. She used to skip from hillock to hillock of marsh grass with wary steps, lest she might slip and wet her feet in the meadow ooze and incur her mother's displeasure, for Fanny, in spite of her worship of the child, could speak with no uncertain voice. She pulled up handfuls of the flowers, gleaming blue in the dark-green hollows. Later she carried roses from the choice bush in the yard, and, later, pears from her grandmother's tree. She used to watch for Miss Mitchell at her gate and run to meet her, and seize her hand and walk at her side, blushing with delight. Miss Mitchell lived not far from Ellen, in a tidy white house with a handsome smoke-tree on one side of the front walk and a willow with upside-down branches on the other. Miss Mitchell had been born and brought up in this house, but she had been teaching school in a distant town ever since Ellen's day, so they had never been acquainted before she went to school. Miss Mitchell lived alone with her mother, who was an old friend of Mrs. Zelotes. Ellen privately thought her rather better - looking than her own grandmother, though her admiration was based upon wholly sentimental reasons. Old Mrs. Mitchell might have earned more money in a museum of freaks than her daughter in a district school. She was a mountain of rotundity, a conjunction of palpitating spheres, but the soul that dwelt in this painfully ponderous body was as mellow with affection and kindliness as a ripe pear, and the voice that proceeded from her ever-smiling lips was a

hoarse and dove-like coo of love. Ellen at first started a
little aghast at this gigantic fleshliness, this general
slough and slump of outline, this insistency of re-
pellent curves, and then the old woman spoke and
thrust out a great, soft hand, and the heart of the child
overleaped her artistic sense and her reason, and she
thought old Mrs. Mitchell beautiful. Mrs. Mitchell never failed to regale her with a superior sort of cooky,
and often with a covert peppermint, and that although
the Mitchells were not well off. The old place was
mortgaged, and Miss Mitchell had hard work to pay
the interest. Ellen had the vaguest ideas about the
mortgage, and was half inclined to think it might be a
disfiguring patch in the plastering of the sitting-room,
which hung down in an unsightly fashion with a disclosure of hairy edges, and threatened danger to the
heads underneath.

Often of a Saturday afternoon Ellen went to visit
Miss Mitchell and her mother, and really preferred
them to friends of her own age. Miss Mitchell had a
store of superannuated paper dolls which dated from
her own childhood. Their quaint costumes, and old-
fashioned coiffures, and simpers were of overwhelming interest to Ellen. Even at that early age she had a
perception of the advantages of an atmosphere to art,
and even to the affections. Without understanding it,
she loved those obsolete paper-dolls and those women
of former generations better because they gave her
breathing-scope for her imagination. She could love
Abby Atkins and Floretta Vining at one bite, as it
were, and that was the end of it, but she could sit and
ponder and dream over Miss Mitchell and her mother,
and see whole vistas of them in receding mirrors of
affection.

As for the teacher and her mother, they simply adored
the child—as indeed everybody did. She continued at

her first school for a year, which was one of the hardest
financially ever experienced in Rowe. Norman Lloyd
during all that time did not reopen his factory, and in
the autumn two others shut down. The streets were
full of the discontented ranks of impotent labor, and
all the public buildings were props for the weary shoulders of the unemployed. On pleasant days the sunny
sides of the vacant factories, especially, furnished set-
tings for lines of scowling faces of misery.

This atmosphere affected Ellen more than any one
realized, since the personal bearing of it was kept from
her. She did not know that her father was drawing
upon his precious savings for daily needs, she did
not know how her aunt Eva and her uncle Jim were
getting into greater difficulties every day, but she was
too sensitive not to be aware of disturbances which
were not in direct contact with herself. She never
forgot what she had overheard that night Lloyd's
had shut down; it was always like a blot upon the face
of her happy consciousness of life. She often overheard, as then, those loud, dissenting voices of her father
and his friends in the sitting-room, after she had gone
to bed; and then, too, Abby Atkins, who was not spared
any knowledge of hardship, told her a good deal. "It's
awful the way them rich folks treat us," said Abby
Atkins. "They own the shops and everything, and
take all the money, and let our folks do all the
work. It's awful. But then," continued Abby Atkins,
comfortingly, "your father has got money saved in
the bank, and he owns his house, so you can get along
if he don't have work. My father 'ain't got any, and
he's got the old-fashioned consumption, and he coughs,
and it takes money for his medicine. Then mother's
sick a good deal too, and has to have medicine. We
have to have more medicine than most anything else,
and we hardly ever have any pie or cake, and it's all the

152

fault of them rich folks." Abby Atkins wound up
with a tragic climax and a fierce roll of her black eyes.

That evening Ellen went in to see her grandmother,
and was presented with some cookies, which she did
not eat.

"Why don't you eat them?" Mrs. Zelotes asked.

"Can I have them to do just what I want to with?"
asked Ellen.

"What on earth do you want to do with a cooky
except eat it?" Ellen blushed; she had a shamed-
faced feeling before a contemplated generosity.

"What do you want to do with them except eat them?"
her grandmother asked, severely.

"Abby Atkins don't have any cookies 'cause her
father's out of work," said Ellen, abashedly.

"Did that Atkins girl ask you to bring her cookies?"

"No, ma'am."

"You can do jest what you are a mind to with 'em,"
Mrs. Zelotes said, abruptly.

Ellen never knew why her grandmother insisted
upon her drinking a little glass of very nice and very
spicy cordial before she went home, but the truth was,
that Mrs. Zelotes thought the child so angelic in this
disposition to give up the cookies which she loved to
her little friend that she was straightway alarmed and
thought her too good to live.

The next day she told Fanny, and said to her, with
her old face stern with anxiety, that the child was lookin'
real pindlin', and Ellen had to take bitters for a month
afterwards because she gave the cookies to Abby Atkins.

CHAPTER XIII

IN all growth there is emulation and striving for precedence between the spiritual and the physical, and this very emulation may determine the rate of progression of the whole. Sometimes the one, sometimes the other, may be in advance, but all the time the tendency is towards the distant goal. Sometimes the two keep abreast, and then there is the greatest harmony in speed. In Ellen Brewster at twelve and fifteen the spiritual outstripped the physical, as is often the case. Her eyes grew intense and hollow with reflection under knitting brows, her thin shoulders stooped like those of a sage bent with study and contemplation. She was slender to emaciation; her clothes hung loosely over her form, which seemed as sexless as a lily-stem; indeed, her body seemed only made for the head, which was flower-like and charming, but almost painful in its delicacy, and with such weight of innocent pondering upon the unknown conditions of things in which she found herself. At times, of course, there were ebullitions of youthful spirit, and the child was as inconsequent as a kitten. At those times she was neither child nor woman; she was an anomalous thing made up not so much of actualities as of instincts. She romped with her mates as unseen and uncomprehended of herself as any young animal, but the flame of her striving spirit made everything full of unread meaning.

Ellen was accounted a most remarkable scholar. She had left Miss Mitchell's school, and was in one

154

of a higher grade. At fifteen she entered the high-school and had a master.

Andrew was growing old fast in those days, though not so old as to years. Though he was far from old, his hair was gray, his back bent. He moved with a weary shuffle. The men in the shop began to eye him furtively. "Andrew Brewster will get fired next," they said. "The boss 'ain't no use for men with the first snap gone." Indeed, Andrew was constantly given jobs of lower grades, which did not pay so well. Whenever the force was reduced on account of dulness in trade, Andrew was one of the first to be laid aside on waiting orders in the regular army of toil. On one of these occasions, in the spring after Ellen was fifteen, his first fit of recklessness seized him. One night, after loafing a week, he came home with fever spots in his cheeks and a curiously bright, strained look in his eyes. Fanny gazed sharply at him across the supper-table. Finally she laid down her knife and fork, rested her elbows on the table, and fixed her eyes commandingly upon him. "Andrew Brewster, what is the matter?" said she. Ellen turned her flower-like face towards her father, who took a swallow of tea without saying a word, though he shuffled his feet uneasily. "Andrew, you answer me," repeated Fanny.

"There ain't anything the matter," answered Andrew, with a strange sullenness for him.

"There is, too. Now, Andrew Brewster, I ain't goin' to be put off. I know you're on the shelf on account of hard times, so it ain't that. It's something new. Now I want to know what it is."

"It ain't anything."

"Yes, it is. Andrew, you ought to tell me. You know I ain't afraid to bear anything that you have to bear, and Ellen is getting old enough now, so she can understand, and she can't always be spared. She'd

better get a little knowledge of hardships while she has
us to help her bear 'em.''

"This ain't a hardship, and there ain't anything to
spare, Ellen,'' said Andrew; and he laughed with a
hilarity totally unlike him.

That was all Fanny could get out of him, but she
was half reassured. She told Eva that she didn't
believe but he had been buying some Christmas present
that he knew was extravagant for Ellen, and was afraid
to tell her because he knew she would scold. But
Andrew had not been buying Christmas presents, but
speculating in mining· stocks. He had resisted the
temptation long. Year in and year out he had heard
the talk right and left in the shop, on the street, and at
the store of an evening. "I'll give you a point,'' he
had heard one say to another during a discussion as to
prices and dividends. He had heard it all described
as a short cross-cut over the fields of hard labor to wealth
and comfort, and he had kept his face straight ahead
in his narrow track of caution and hereditary instincts
until then. "The savings bank is good enough for
me,'' he used to say; "that's where my father kept his
money. I don't know anything about your stocks.
I'd rather have a little and have it safe.'' The men
could not reason him out of his position, not even when
Billy Monroe made fifteen hundred dollars on a Colorado mine which had cost him fifteen cents per share,
and left the shop, and drove a fast horse in a Goddard
buggy.

It was even reported that fifteen hundred was fifteen thousand, but Andrew was proof against this
brilliant loadstar of success, though many of his mates
followed it afar, just before the shares dropped below
par.

Jim Tenny went with the rest. "Tell you what
'tis, Andrew, old man,'' he said, clapping Andrew

on the shoulder as they were going out of the shop one
night, "you'd better go in too."

"The savings-bank is good enough for me," said
Andrew, with his gentle doggedness.

"You can buy a trotter," urged Jim.

"I never was much on trotters," replied Andrew.

"I ain't going to walk home many times more, you
bet," Jim said to Eva when he got home, and then he
bent back her tensely set face and kissed it. Eva was
crocheting hoods for fifteen cents apiece for a neighboring woman who was a padrone on a small scale, having taken a large order from a dealer for which she
realized twenty cents apiece, and employed all the
women in the neighborhood to do the work.

"Why not?" said she.

"Oh," said Jim, gayly, "I've bought some of that
'Golden Hope' mining stock. Billy Monroe has just
made fifteen thousand on it, and I'll make as much in
a week or two."

"Oh, Jim, you 'ain't taken all the money out of the
bank?"

"Don't you worry, old girl," replied Jim. "I guess
you'll find I can take care of you yet."

But the stock went down, and Jim's little venture
with it.

"Guess you were about right, old man," he said to
Andrew.

Andrew was rather looked up to for his superior
caution and sagacity. He was continually congrat-
ulated upon it. "Savings-banks are good enough
for me," he kept repeating. But that was four years
ago, and now his turn had come; the contagion of
speculation had struck him at last. That was the way
with Lloyd's failing employés.

Andrew kept his stock certificate in a little, tin, trunk-
shaped box which had belonged to his father. It had

a key and a tiny padlock, and he had always stored in it the deed of his house, his savings-bank book, and his insurance policy. He carried the key in his pocket. Fanny never opened the box, or had any curiosity about it, believing that she was acquainted with its contents; but now when, on coming unexpectedly into the bedroom — the box was always kept at the head of the bed—she heard a rattle of papers, and caught Andrew locking the box with a confused air, she began to suspect something. She began to look hard at the box, to take it up and shake it when her husband was away. Fanny was crocheting hoods as well as Eva. Ellen wished to learn, but her mother would not allow that. "You've got enough to do to study your lessons," she said. Andrew watched his wife crochet with ill-concealed impatience.

"I ain't goin' to have you do that long," he said— "workin' at that rate for no more money. That Mrs. William Pendergrass that lets out these hoods is as bad as any factory boss in the country."

"Well, she got the chance," said Fanny, "and they won't let out the work except that way; they can get it done so much cheaper."

"Well, you sha'n't have it, anyhow," said Andrew, smiling mysteriously.

"Why, you ain't goin' to work again, be you, Andrew?"

"You wait."

"Well, don't you talk the way poor Jim did. Eva wasn't going to crochet any more hoods, and now Jim's out of work again. Eva told me yesterday that she didn't know where the money was comin' from. Jim's mother owns the place, and it ain't worth much, anyhow, and they can't take it from her in her lifetime, even if she was willing to let it go. Eva said she was goin' to try again for work herself in the shop.

She thought maybe there might be some kind of a job she could get. Don't you talk like Jim did about his good-for-nothin' mining stock. I've been glad enough that you had sense enough to keep what little we had where 'twas safe."

"Ain't it most time for Ellen to be comin' home?" asked Andrew, to turn the conversation, as he felt somewhat guilty and uncomfortable, though his eyes were jubilant. He had very little doubt about the success of his venture. As it is with a man who yields to love for the first time in his life, it was with Andrew in his tardy subjection to the hazards of fortune. He was a much more devoted slave than those who had long wooed her. He had always taken nothing but the principal newspaper published in Rowe, but now he subscribed to a Boston paper, the one which had the fullest financial column, though Fanny exclaimed at his extravagance.

Along in midsummer, in the midst of Ellen's vacation, the mining stock dropped fast a point or more a day. Andrew's heart began to sink, though he was far from losing hope. He used to talk it over with the men who advised him to buy, and come home fortified.

All he had to do was to be patient; the fall meant nothing wrong with the mine, only the wrangle of speculators. "It's like a football, first on one side, and then on the other," said the man, "but the football's there all the same, and if it's that you want, you're all right."

One night when Nahum Beals and Atkins and John Sargent were in, Andrew repeated this wisdom, concealing the fact of its personal application. He was anxious to have some confirmation.

"I suppose it's about so," he said.

Then John Sargent spoke up. "No, it is not so,"

he said—"that is, not in many cases. There isn't any football—that's the trouble. There's nothing but the money; a lot of fools have paid for it when it never existed out of their imagination."

"About so," said Nahum Beals. Andrew and Atkins exchanged glances. Atkins was at once sympathizing and triumphant.

"Lots of those things appear to be doing well, and to be all right," said Andrew, uneasily. "The directors keep saying that they are in a prosperous condition, even if the stock drops." He almost betrayed himself.

John Sargent laughed that curious, inflexible laugh of his. "Lord, I know all about that," said he. "I had some once. First one thing and then another came up to hinder the working of the mine and the payments of dividends. First there wasn't any water, an unprecedented dry season in those parts, oldest inhabitants for evidence. Then there was too much water, no way to mine except they employed professional divers, everything under water. Then the transportation was to pay; then, when that was remedied, the ore didn't come out in shape to transport in the rough and had to be worked up on the premises, and new mills had to be built and new machinery put in, and a few little Irish dividends were collected for that. Then when they got the mills up and the machinery in, they struck another kind of ore that ought to be transported; then there came a landslide and carried half the road into a cañon. So it went on, one thing and another. If ever that darned mine had got into working order, right kind of ore, water enough and not too much, roads and machinery all right, and everything swimming, the Day of Judgment would have come."

"Did you ever get anything out of it?" inquired Andrew.

"Anything out of it?" repeated the other. "Yes.

I got enough worldly wisdom never to buy any more mining stock, after I had paid assessments on it for two years and the whole thing went to pieces."

"It may come up yet," said Andrew.

"There's nothing to come up," said John Sargent. He had been away from Rowe a year, but had just returned, and was again boarding with Atkins, and all the family lived on his board money. Andrew and Nahum Beals were smoking pipes. Andrew gently, like a philosopher, who smokes that he may dream; Nahum with furious jets and frequent removals of his pipe for scowling speeches. John Sargent did not smoke at all. He had left off cigars first, then even his pipe. He gave the money which he saved thereby to Mrs. Atkins as a bonus on his board money.

The lamp burned dimly in the blue fog of tobacco smoke, and the windows where the curtains were not drawn were blanks of silvery moonlight. Ellen sat on the doorstep outside and heard the talk. She did not understand it, nor take much interest in it. Their minds were fixed upon the way of living, and hers upon life itself. She could bring her simplicity to bear upon the world-old question of riches and poverty and labor, but this temporal adjunct of stocks and markets was as yet beyond her. Her mother had gone to her aunt Eva's and she sat alone out in the wide mystery of the summer night, watching the lovely shift of radiance and shadows, as she might have watched the play of a kaleidoscope, seeing the beauty of the new combinations, and seeing without comprehending the unit which governed them all. The night was full of cries of insistent life and growth, of birds and insects, of calls of children, and now and then the far-away roar of railroad trains. It was nearly midsummer. The year was almost at its height, but had not passed it. Growth and bloom was still in the ascendant, and had not yet attained that maturity of perfection beyond which is the slope of death.

Everywhere about her were the revolutions of those unseen wheels of nature whose immortal trend is towards the completion of time, and whose momentum can overlap the grave; and the child was within them and swept onward with the perfecting flowers, and the ripening fruit, and the insects which were feeling their wings; and all unconsciously, in a moment as it were, she unfolded a little farther towards her own heyday of bloom. Suddenly from those heights of the primitive and the eternal upon which a child starts and where she still lingered she saw her future before her, shining with new lights, and a wonderful conviction of bliss to come was over her. It was that conviction which comes at times to all unconquered souls, and which has the very essence of truth in it, since it overleaps the darkness of life that lies between them and that bliss. Suddenly Ellen felt that she was born to great happiness, and all that was to come was towards that end. Her heart beat loud in her ears. There was a whippoorwill calling in some trees to the left; the moon was dim under a golden dapple of clouds. She could not feel her hands or her feet; she seemed to feel nothing except her soul.

Then she heard, loud and sweet and clear, a boy's whistle, one of the popular tunes of the day. It came nearer and nearer, and it was in the same key with the child's thoughts and dreams. Then she saw a slender figure dark against the moonlight stop at a fence, and she jumped up and ran towards it with no hesitation through the dewy grass; and it was the boy, Granville Joy. He stood looking at her. He had a handsome, eager face, and Ellen looked at him, her lips parted, her face like a lily in the white light.

"Hulloo," said the boy.

"Hulloo," Ellen responded, faintly.

Granville extended one rough, brown, boyish hand over the fence, and Ellen laid her little, soft hand in it. He pulled her gently close, then Ellen lifted her face, and the boy bent his, and the two kissed each other over the fence. Then the boy went on down the street, but he did not whistle, and Ellen went back to the doorstep, and, looking about to be sure that none of the men in the sitting-room saw, pulled off one little shoe and drew forth a sprig of southernwood, or boy's-love, which was crushed under her foot.

That day Floretta Vining had told her that if she would put a sprig of boy's-love in her shoe, the very first boy she met would be the one she was going to marry; and Ellen, who was passing from one grade of school to another, had tried it.

CHAPTER XIV

THE high-school master was a distant relative of the Lloyd's, through whom he had obtained the position. One evening when he was taking tea with them at Cynthia Lennox's, he spoke of Ellen. "I have one really remarkable scholar," he said, with a curious air of self-gratulation, as if he were principally responsible for it; "her name is Brewster—Ellen Brewster."

"Good land! That must be the child that ran away five or six years ago, and all the town up in arms over it," said Mrs. Norman Lloyd. "Don't you remember, Cynthia?"

"Yes," replied Cynthia, and continued pouring tea. Cynthia was very little changed. In some faces time seems to engrave lines delicately, once for all, and then lay by. She was rather more charming now than when one had looked at her with any expectancy of youth, since there was now no sense of disappointment.

"I remember that," said Norman Lloyd. "The child would never tell where she had been. A curious case."

"Well," said the school-master, "leaving that childish episode out of the question, she has a really remarkable mind. If she were a boy, I should advise a thorough education and a profession. I should as it is, if her family were able to bear the expense. She has that intuitive order of mind which is wonderful enough, though not, after all, so rare in a girl; but in addition she has the logical, which, according to my experience,

164

is almost unknown in a woman. She ought to have an education."

"But," said Risley, "what is the use of educating that unfortunate child?"

"What do you mean?"

"What I say. What is the use? There she is in her sphere of life, the daughter of a factory operative, in all probability in after-years to be the wife of one and the mother of others. Nothing but a rich marriage can save her, and that she is not likely to make. Milkmaids are more likely to make rich marriages than factory girls; there is a certain savor of romance about milk, and the dewy meadows, and the breath of kine, but a shoe factory is brutally realistic and illusionary. Now, why do you want to increase the poor child's horizon farther than her little feet can carry her? Fit her to be a good female soldier in the ranks of labor, to be a good wife and mother to the makers of shoes, to wash and iron their uniforms of toil, to cook well the food which affords them the requisite nourishment to make shoes, to appreciate book-lore, which is a pleasure and a profit to the makers of shoes; possibly in the non-event of marriage she will make shoes herself. The system of education in our schools is all wrong. It is both senseless and futile. Look at the children filing past to school, and look at their fathers, and their mothers too, filing past to the factory. Look at their present, and look at their future. And look at the trash taught them in their text-books—trash from its utter dissociation with their lives. You might as well teach a Zulu lace-work, instead of the use of the assagai."

"Now look here, Mr. Risley," said the school-master, his face flushing, "is not—I beg your pardon, of course— this view of yours a little narrow and ultra-conservative? You do not want to establish a permanent factory-operative class in this country, do you? That is what your theory would ultimately tend towards. Ought not these children be given their chance to rise in the ranks; ought they to be condemned to tread in the same path as their fathers?"

"I would have those little paths which intersect every unoccupied field in this locality worn by the feet of these men and their children after them unto the third and fourth generation," said Risley. "If not, where is our skilled labor?"

"Oh, Mr. Risley," said Mrs. Lloyd, anxiously, "you wouldn't want all those dear little children to work as hard as their fathers, and not do any better, would you?"

"If they don't, who is going to make our shoes, dear Mrs. Lloyd?" asked Risley.

Mrs. Lloyd and the school-master stared at him, and Lloyd laughed his low, almost mirthless laugh.

"Don't you know, Edward," he said, "that Mr. Risley is not in earnest, and speaks with the deadly intent of an anarchist with a bomb in his bag? He is the most out-and-out radical in the country. If there were a strike, and I did not yield to the demands of the oppressed, and imported foreign labor, I don't know that my life would be safe from him."

"Then you do approve of a higher education?" asked the school-master, while Mrs. Lloyd stared from one to the other in bewilderment.

"Yes, if we and our posterity have to go barefoot," said Risley, laughing out with a sudden undertone of seriousness.

"I suppose everybody could get accustomed to going barefoot after a while," said Mrs. Lloyd. "Do you suppose that dear little thing was barefooted when she ran away, Cynthia?"

Risley answered as if he had been addressed. "I

can vouch for the fact that she was not, Mrs. Lloyd," he said. "They would sooner have walked on red-hot ploughshares themselves than let her."

"Her father is getting quite an old man," Norman Lloyd said, with no apparent relevancy, as if he were talking to himself.

All the time Cynthia Lennox had been quietly sitting at the head of the table. When the rest of the company had gone, and she and Risley were alone, seated in the drawing-room before the parlor fire, for it was a chilly day, she turned her fair, worn face towards him on the crimson velvet of her chair. "Do you know why I did not speak and tell them where the child was that time?" she asked.

"Because of your own good sense?"

"No; because of you."

He looked at her adoringly. She was older than he, her beauty rather recorded than still evident on her face; she had been to him from the first like a fair, forbidden flower behind a wall of prohibition, but nothing could alter his habit of loving her.

"Yes," said she. "It was more on your account than on my own; confession would be good for the soul. The secret has always rankled in my pride. I would much rather defy opinion than fly before it. But I know that you would mind. However, there was another reason."

"What?"

She hesitated a little and colored, even laughed a little, embarrassed laugh which was foreign to her. "Well, Lyman," said she, finally, "one reason why I did not speak was that I see my way clear to making up to that child and her parents for any wrong which I may have done them by causing them a few hours' anxiety. When she has finished the high-school I mean to send her to college."

CHAPTER XV

WHEN Ellen was about sixteen, in her second year at the high-school, her own family never looked at her without a slight shock of wonder, as before the unexpected. Her mates, being themselves in the transition state, received her unquestioningly as a fellow-traveller, and colored like themselves with the new lights of the journey. But Ellen's father and mother and grandmother never ceased regarding her with astonishment and admiration and something like alarm. While they regarded Ellen with the utmost pride, they still privately regretted this perfection of bloom which was the forerunner of independence of the parent stalk —at least, Andrew did. Andrew had grown older and more careworn; his mine had not yet paid any dividends, but he had scattering jobs of work, and with his wife's assistance had managed to rub along, and his secret was still safe.

One day in February there was a half - holiday. Lloyd's was shut for the rest of the day, for his brother in St. Louis was dead, and had been brought to Rowe to be buried, and his funeral was at two o'clock.

"Goin' to the funeral, old man?" one of Andrew's fellow-workmen had asked, jostling him as he went out of the shop at noon. Before Andrew could answer, another voice broke in fiercely. It belonged to Joseph Atkins, who was ghastly that day.

"I ain't goin' to no funerals," he said; "guess they won't shut up shop for mine." Then he coughed. His daughter Abby, who had been working in the factory for some time then, pressed close behind her father, and the expression in her face was an echo of his.

"When I strike, that's what I'm going to strike for—to have the shop shut up the day of my funeral," said she; and the remark had a ghastly flippancy, contradicted by her intense manner. A laugh went around, and a young fellow with a handsome, unshaven face caught her by the arm.

"You'd better strike to have the shop shut up the day you're married," said he; but Abby flung away from him.

"I'll thank you to let me alone, Tom Hardy," she said, with a snap; and the men laughed harder.

Abby was attractive to men in spite of her smallness and leanness and incisiveness of manner. She was called mighty smart and dry, which was the shop synonym for witty, and her favors, possibly because she never granted them, were accounted valuable. Abby Atkins had more admirers than many a girl who was prettier and presumably more winning in every way, and could have married twice to their once. But Abby had no wish for a lover. "I've got all I can do to earn my own living and the living of them that belong to me," said she.

That afternoon Andrew Brewster stayed at home. After dinner Eva Tenny and her little girl came in, and Ellen went down street on an errand.

Mrs. Zelotes Brewster was crossing her yard to her son's house when she saw Ellen passing, and paused to gaze at her with that superb pride which pertains to self and is yet superior to it. It was the idealized pride of her own youth. When she proceeded again against the February gusts, it was with an unconscious aping of her granddaughter's freedom of gait. Mrs. Zelotes wore an old red cashmere scarf crossed over her bosom;

she held up her black skirts in front, and they trailed pointedly in the rear; she also stood well back on her heels, and when she paused in the wind-swept yard presented a curious likeness to an old robin pausing for reconnoitre. Fanny and Eva Tenny in the next house saw her coming.

"Look at her holding up her dress in front and letting it drag in the back," said Eva. "It always seemed to me there was somethin' wrong about any woman that held up her dress in front and let it drag behind."

Eva retained all the coarse beauty of her youth, but lines of unalterable hardness were fixed on her forehead and at her mouth corners, and the fierce flush in her cheeks was as set as paint. Her beauty had endured the siege; no guns of mishaps could affect it, but that charm of evanescence which awakens tenderness was gone. Jim Tenny's affection seemed to be waning, and Eva looked at herself in the glass even when bedecked with tawdry finery, and owned that she did not wonder. She strained up her hair into the latest perkiness of twist, and crimped it, and curled her feathers, and tied her ribbons not as much in hope as in a stern determination to do her part towards the furbishing of her faded star of attraction. "Jim don't act as if he thought so much of me, an' I dun'no' as I wonder," she told her sister.

Fanny looked at her critically. "You mean you ain't so good-lookin' as you used to be?" said she.

Eva nodded.

"Well, if that is all men care for us," said Fanny.

"It ain't," said Eva, "only it's the key to it. It's like losin' the key and not bein' able to get in the door in consequence."

"It wa'n't my husband's key," said Fanny, with a glance at her own face, faded as to feature and bloom, but intensified as to love and daily duty, like that of a dog sharpened to one faithfulness of existence.

"Andrew ain't Jim," said Eva, shortly.

"I know he ain't," Fanny assented, with emphasis.

"But I wouldn't swap off my husband for a dozen of yours," said Eva.

"Well, I wouldn't swap off mine for a thousand of yours," returned Fanny, sharply; and there might have been one of the old-time tussles between the sisters had not Eva's violent, half-bitter sense of humor averted it. She broke into a hard laugh.

"Good Lord," she said, "I dun'no' as I should want a thousand like Jim. Seems to me it would be considerable care."

Fanny began to speak, but checked herself. She had heard rumors regarding Jim Tenny of late and had flown fiercely with denial at the woman who told her, and had not repeated them to her sister.

She was thinking how she had heard that Jim had been seen driving in Wenham with Aggie Morse several times lately. Aggie Morse had been Aggie Bemis, Jim's old sweetheart. She had married a well-to-do merchant in Wenham, who died six months before and left her with considerable property. It was her own smart little turn-out in which she had been seen with Jim.

Eva was working in the shop, and Jim had been out of employment for nearly a year, and living on his wife. There was a demand for girls and not for men just then, so Jim loafed. His old mother cared for the house as well as she was able, and Eva did the rest nights and mornings. At first Jim had tried to help about the house-work, but Eva had interfered.

"It ain't a man's work," said she. "Your mother can leave the hard part of it till I get home." Eva used to put the money she earned surreptitiously into

171

her husband's pockets that he might not feel his manly pride injured, but she defeated her own ends by her very solicitude. Jim Tenny began to reason that his wife saw his shame and ignominious helplessness, else she would not have been so anxious to cover it. The stoop of discouragement which Eva used to fear for his shoulders did not come, but, instead, something worse—the defiant set-back of recklessness. He took his wife's earnings and despised himself. Whenever he paid a bill, he was sure the men in the store said, the minute his back was turned, "It's his wife's money that paid for that." He took to loafing on sunny corners, and eying the passers-by with the blank impudence of regard of those outside the current of life. When his wife passed by on her way from the shop he nodded to her as if she were a stranger, and presently followed her home at a distance. He would not be seen on the street with her if he could avoid it. If by any chance when he was standing on his corner of idleness his little girl came past, he melted away imperceptibly. He could not bear it that the child should see him standing there in that company of futility and openly avowed inadequacy. The child was a keen-eyed, slender little girl, resembling neither father nor mother, but looking rather like her paternal grandmother, who was a fair, attenuated woman, with an intelligence which had sharpened on herself for want of anything more legitimate, and worn her out by the unnatural friction. The little Amabel, for Eva had been romantic in the naming of her child, was an old-fashioned-looking child in spite of Eva's careful decoration of the little figure in the best childish finery which she could muster.

Little Amabel was reading a child's book at another window. When Mrs. Zelotes entered she eyed her with the sharpness and inscrutable conclusions therefrom of a kitten, then turned a leaf in her book.

When Mrs. Zelotes had greeted her daughter-in-law and Eva, she looked with disapproval at Amabel.

"When I was a little girl I should have been punished if I hadn't got up and curtsied and said good-afternoon when company came in," she remarked, severely.

Amabel was not a favorite outside of her own family. People used to stare aghast at her unexpected questions and demands delivered in a shrill clarion as from some summit of childish wisdom, and they said she was a queer child. She yielded always to command from utter helplessness, but the why of obedience was strongly alert within her. The child might have been in some subtle and uncanny fashion the offspring of her age and generation instead of her natural parents, she was so unlike either of them, and so much a product of the times, with her meekness and slavishness of weakness and futility, and her unquenchable and unconquerable vitality of dissent.

Ellen adored the little Amabel. Presently, when she returned from her errand down-town, she cried out with delight when she saw her; and the child ran to meet her, and clung to her, with her flaxen head snuggled close to her cheek. Ellen caught the child up, seated herself, and sat cuddling her as she used to cuddle her doll.

"You dear little thing!" she murmured, "you dear little thing! You did come to see Ellen, didn't you?" And the child gazed up in the young girl's face with a rapt expression. Nothing can express the admiration, which is almost as unquestionable as worship, of a very little girl for a big one. Amabel loved her mother with a rather unusual intensity for a child, but Ellen was what she herself would be when she

173

was grown up. Through Ellen her love of self and her ambition budded into blossom. Ellen could do nothing wrong because she did what she herself would do when she was grown. She never questioned Ellen for her reasons.

Mrs. Zelotes kept looking at the two, with pride in Ellen and disapproval of her caresses of the child. "Seems to me you might speak to your own folks as well as to have no eyes for anybody but that child," she said, finally.

"Why, grandma, I spoke to you just a little while ago," returned Ellen. "You know I saw you just a few minutes before I went down-town." Ellen straightened the child on her knees, and began to try to twist her soft, straight flaxen locks into curls. Andrew lounged in from the kitchen and sat down and regarded Ellen fondly. The girl's cheeks were a splendid color from her walk in the cold wind, her hair around her temples caught the light from the window, and seemed to wreathe her head with a yellow flame. She tossed the child about with lithe young arms, whose every motion suggested reserves of tender strength. Ellen was more beautiful than she had ever been before, and yet something was gone from her face, though only temporarily, since the lines for the vanished meaning was still there. All the introspection and dreaminess and poetry of her face were gone, for the girl was, for the time, overbalanced on the physical side of her life. The joy of existence for itself alone was intoxicating her. The innocent frivolities of her sex had seized her too, and the instincts which had not yet reached her brain nor gone farther than her bounding pulses of youth. "Ellen is getting real fond of dress," Fanny often said to Andrew. He only laughed at that. "Well, pretty birds like pretty feathers, and no wonder," said he. But he did not laugh when Fanny

174

added that Ellen seemed to think more about the
boys than she used to. There was scarcely a boy
in the high - school who was not Ellen's admirer.
It was a curious happening in those days when
Ellen was herself in much less degree the stuff of
which dreams are made than she had been and
would be thereafter, that she was the object of so
many. Every morning when she entered the school-
room she was reflected in a glorious multiple of ideals
in no one could tell how many boyish hearts. Floretta Vining began to imitate her, and kept close to
Ellen with supremest diplomacy, that she might thereby catch some of the crumbs of attention which fell
from Ellen's full table. Often when some happy boy
had secured a short monopoly of Ellen, his rival took
up with Floretta, and she was content, being one of
those purely feminine things who have no pride when
the sweets of life are concerned. Floretta dressed her
hair like Ellen's, and tied her neck-ribbons the same
way; she held her head like her, she talked like her,
except when the two girls were absolutely alone; then
she sometimes relapsed suddenly, to Ellen's bewilderment, into her own ways, and her blue eyes took on an
expression as near animosity as her ingratiating politic
nature could admit.

Ellen did not affiliate as much with Floretta as with
Maria Atkins. Abby had gone to work in the shop,
and so Ellen did not see so much of her. Maria was not
as much a favorite with the boys as she had been since
they had passed and not yet returned to that stage
when feminine comradeship satisfies; so Ellen used
to confide in her with a surety of sympathy and no con-
tention. Once, when the girls were sleeping together,
Ellen made a stupendous revelation to Maria, having
first bound her to inviolable secrecy. "I love a boy,"
said she, holding Maria's little arm tightly.

"I know who," said Maria, with a hushed voice.

"He kissed me once, and then I knew it," said Ellen.

"Well, I guess he loves you," said Maria. Ellen shivered and drew a fluttering sigh of assent. Then the two girls lay in each other's arms, looking at the moonlight which streamed in through the window. God knew in what realms of pure 'romance, and of passion so sublimated by innocence that no tinge of earthliness remained, the two wandered in their dreams.

At last, that afternoon in February. Ellen put down little Amabel and got out her needle-work. She was making a lace neck-tie for her own adornment. She showed it to her grandmother at her mother's command. "It's real pretty," said Mrs. Zelotes. "Ellen takes after the Brewsters; they were always handy with their needles."

"Can uncle sew?" asked little Amabel, suddenly, from her corner, in a tone big with wonder.

Eva and the others chuckled, but Mrs. Zelotes eyed the child severely. "Little girls shouldn't ask silly questions," said she.

Andrew passed his hand with a rough caress over the small flaxen head. "Uncle Andrew can't sew anything but shoes," said he.

Little Amabel's question had aroused in Mrs. Zelotes a carping spirit even against Ellen. Presently she turned to her. "I heard something about you," said she. "I want to know if it is true. I heard that you were walking home from school with that Joy boy one day last week." Ellen looked at her grandmother without flinching, though the pink was over her face and neck.

"Yes'm, I did," said she.

"Well, I think it's about time it was put a stop to," said Mrs. Zelotes. "That Joy boy!"

Then Fanny lost her temper. "I can manage my

own daughter, Grandma Brewster," said she, "and I'll thank you to attend to your own affairs."

"You don't seem to know enough to manage her," retorted Mrs. Zelotes, "if you let her go traipsin' round with that Joy boy."

The warfare waged high for a time. Andrew withdrew to the kitchen. Ellen took little Amabel up in her own chamber and showed her her beautiful doll, which looked not a day older, so carefully had she been cherished, than when she first had her. Ellen felt both resentment and shame, and also a fierce dawning of partisanship towards Granville Joy. "Why should my grandmother speak of him so scornfully?" she asked herself. "He is a real good boy."

That night was very cold, a night full of fierce white glitter of frost and moonlight, and raging with a turbulence of winds. Ellen lay awake listening to them. Presently between the whistle of the wind she heard another, a familiar pipe from a boyish throat. She sprang out of bed and peeped from her window, and there was a dark, slight figure out in the yard, and he was looking up at her window, whistling. Shame, and mirth, and also exultation, which overpowered them both, stirred within the child's breast. She had read of things like this. Here was her boy lover coming out this bitter night just for the sake of looking up at her window. She adored him for it. Then she heard a window raised with a violent rasp across the yard, and saw her grandmother's night-capped head thrust forth. She heard her shrill, imperious voice call out quite distinctly, "Boy, who be you?"

The lovelorn whistler ceased his pipe, and evidently, had he consulted his own discretion, would have shown a pair of flying heels, but he walked bravely up to the window and the night-capped head and replied. Ellen could not hear what he said, but she distinguished

M   177

plainly enough her grandmother's concluding remarks.

"Go home," cried Mrs. Zelotes; "go home just as fast as you can and go to bed. Go home!" Mrs. Zelotes made a violent shooting motion with her hands and her white head as if he were a cat, and Granville Joy obeyed. However, Ellen heard his brave, retreating whistle far down the road. She went back to bed, and lay awake with a fervor of young love roused into a flame by opposition swelling high in her heart. But the next afternoon, after school, Ellen, to Granville Joy's great bliss and astonishment, insinuated herself, through the crowd of out-going scholars, close to him, and presently, had he not been so incredulous, for he was a modest boy, he would have said it was by no volition of his own that he found himself walking down the street with her. And when they reached his house, which was only half-way to her own, she looked at him with such a wistful surprise as he motioned to leave her that he could not mistake it, and he walked on at her side quite to her own house. Granville Joy was a gentle boy, young for his age, which was a year more than Ellen's. He had a face as gentle as a girl's, and really beautiful. Women all loved him, and the school-girls raised an admiring treble chorus in his praise whenever his name was spoken. He was saved from effeminacy by nervous impulses which passed for sustained manly daring. "He once licked a boy a third bigger than he was, and you needn't call him sissy," one girl said once to a decrying friend. To-day, as the boy and girl neared Mrs. Zelotes's house, Granville was conscious of an inward shrinking before the remembrance of the terrible old lady. He expected every minute to hear the grating upward slide of the window and that old voice, which had in it a terrible intimidation of feminine will. Gran-

"HE FOUND HIMSELF WALKING HOME FROM SCHOOL
WITH HER"

ville had a mother as gentle as himself, and a woman with the strength of her own conviction upon her filled him with awe as of something anomalous. He wondered uneasily what he should do if the old lady were to hail him and call him to an account again, whether it would be a more manly course to face her, or obey, since she was Ellen's grandmother. He kept an uneasy eye upon the house, and presently, when he saw the stern old face at the window, he quailed a little. But Ellen for the first time in her life took his arm, and the two marched past under the fire of Mrs. Zelotes's gaze. Ellen had retaliated, not nobly, but as naturally under the conditions of her life at that time as the branch of a tree blows east before the west wind.

CHAPTER XVI

ELLEN, when she graduated, was openly pronounced the flower of her class. Not a girl equalled her, not a boy surpassed her. When Ellen came home one night about two months before her graduation, and announced that she was to have the valedictory, such a light of pure joy flashed over her mother's face that she looked ten years younger.

"Well, I guess your father will be pleased enough," she said. She was hard at work, finishing women's wrappers of cheap cotton. The hood industry had failed some time before, since the hoods had gone out of fashion. The same woman had taken a contract to supply a large firm with wrappers, and employed many in the neighborhood, paying them the smallest possible prices. This woman was a usurer on a scale so pitiful and petty that it almost condoned usury. Sometimes a man on discovering the miserable pittance for which his wife toiled during every minute which she could snatch from her household duties and the care of her children, would inveigh against it. "That woman is cheating you," he would say, to be met with the argument that she herself was only making ten cents on a wrapper. Looked at in that light, the wretched profit of the workers did not seem so out of proportion. It was usury in a nutshell, so infinitesimal as almost to escape detection. Fanny worked every minute which she could secure on these wrappers — the ungainly, slatternly home-gear of other poor women. There was an air of dejected femininity and

180

slipshod drudgery about every fold of one of them when it was hung up finished. Fanny used to keep them on a row of hooks in her bedroom until a dozen were completed, when she carried them to her employer, and Ellen used to look at them with a sense of depression. She imagined worn, patient faces of the sisters of poverty above the limp collars, and poor, veinous hands dangling from the clumsy sleeves.

Fanny would never allow Ellen to assist her in this work, though she begged hard to do so. "Wait till you get out of school," said she. "You've got enough to do while you are in school."

When Ellen told her about the valedictory, Fanny was so overjoyed that she lost sight of her work, and sewed in the sleeves wrong. "There, only see what you have made me do!" she cried, laughing with delight at her own folly. "Only see, you have made me sew in both these sleeves wrong. You are a great child. Another time you had better keep away with your valedictories till I get my wrapper finished." Ellen looked up from the book which she had taken.

"Let me rip them out for you, mother," she said.

"No, you keep on with your study—it won't take me but a minute. I don't know what your father will say. It is a great honor to be chosen to write the valedictory out of that big class. I guess your father will be pleased."

"I hope I can write a good one," said Ellen.

"Well, if you can't, I'd give up my beat," said the mother, looking at her with enthusiasm, and speaking with scornful chiding. "Why don't you go over and tell your grandmother Brewster? She'll be tickled 'most to death."

Ellen had not been gone long when Andrew came home, coming into the yard, bent as if beneath some invisible burden of toil. Just then he had work, but not in Lloyd's. He had grown too old for Lloyd's, and had been discharged long ago.

He had so far been able to conceal from Fanny the fact that he had withdrawn all his little savings to invest in that mining stock. The stock had not yet come up, as he had expected. He very seldom had a circular reporting progress nowadays. When he did have one in the post-office his heart used to stand still until he had torn open the envelope and read it. It was uniformly not so hopeful as formerly, while speciously apologetic. Andrew still had faith, although his heart was sick with its long deferring. He could not actually believe that all his savings were gone, sunken out of sight forever in this awful shaft of miscalculation and misfortune. What he dreaded most was that Fanny should find out, as she would have to were he long out of employment.

Andrew, when he entered the house on his return from work, had come to open a door into the room where his wife was, with a deprecating and apologetic air. He gained confidence when, after a few minutes, the sore subject had not been broached.

To-night, as usual, when he came into the sitting-room where Fanny was sewing it was with a sidelong glance of uneasy deprecation towards her, and an attempt to speak easily, as if he had nothing on his mind. "Pretty warm day," he began, but his wife cut him short. She faced around towards him beaming, her work—a pink wrapper—slid from her lap to the floor. "What do you think, Andrew?" she said. "What do you s'pose has happened? Guess." Andrew laughed gratefully, and with the greatest alacrity. Surely this was nothing about mining-stocks, unless, indeed, she had heard, and the stocks had gone up, but that seemed too much like the millennium. He dismissed that from his mind before it entered. He stood before her in his worn clothes. He always wore a collar and a black tie, and his haggard face was carefully shaven. Andrew was punctiliously neat, on Ellen's account. He was always thinking, suppose he should meet Ellen coming home from school, with some young ladies whose fathers were rich and did not have to work in the shop, how mortified she might feel if he looked shabby and unkempt.

"Guess, Andrew," she said.

"What is it?" said Andrew.

"Oh, you guess."

"I don't see what it can be, Fanny."

"Well, Ellen has got the valedictory. What's the matter with you? Be you deaf? Ellen has got the valedictory out of all them girls and boys."

"She has, has she?" said Andrew. He dropped into a chair and looked at his wife. There was something about the intense interchange of confidence of delight between these two faces of father and mother which had almost the unrestraint of lunacy. Andrew's jaw fairly dropped with his smile, which was a silent laugh rather than a smile; his eyes were wild with delight. "She has, has she?" he kept repeating.

"Yes, she has," said Fanny. She tossed her head with an incomparable pride; she coughed a little, affected cough. "I s'pose you know what a compliment it is?" said she. "It means that she's smarter than all them boys and girls—the smartest one in her whole class."

"Yes, I s'pose it does," said Andrew. "So she has got it! Well!"

"There she comes now," said Fanny, "and Grandma Brewster."

Andrew borrowed money to buy a gold watch and chain for a graduating gift for his daughter. He would scarcely have essayed anything quite so magnificent, but Fanny innocently tempted him. The two had been sitting in the door in the cool of the evening, one day in June, about two weeks before the graduation, and had just watched Ellen's light muslin skirts flutter out of sight. She had gone down-town to purchase some ribbon for her graduating dress—she and Floretta Vining, who had come over to accompany her. "I feel kind of anxious to have her have something pretty when she graduates," Fanny said, speaking as if she were feeling her way into a mind of opposition. Neither she nor Andrew had ever owned a watch, and the scheme seemed to her breathless with magnificence.

"Yes, she ought to have something pretty," agreed Andrew.

"I don't want her to feel ashamed when she sees the other girls' presents," said Fanny.

"That's so," assented Andrew.

"Well," said Fanny, "I've been thinkin'—"

"What?"

"Well, I've been thinkin' that—of course your mother is goin' to give her the dress, and that's all, of course, and it's a real handsome present. I ain't sayin' a word against that; but there ain't anybody else to give her much except us. Poor Eva 'd like to, but she can't; it takes all she earns, since Jim's out of work, and I don't know what she's goin' to do. So that leaves nobody but us, and I've been thinkin'—I dun'no' what you'll say, Andrew, but I've been thinkin'— s'pose you took a little money out of the bank, and —got Ellen—a watch." Fanny spoke the last word in a faint whisper. She actually turned pale in the darkness.

"A watch?" repeated Andrew.

"Yes, a watch. I've always wanted Ellen to have a gold watch and chain. I've always thought she

184

could, and so she could if you hadn't been out of work so much."

"Yes, she could," said Andrew—"a watch and mebbe a piano. I thought I'd be back in Lloyd's before now. Well, mebbe I shall before long. They say there's better times comin' by fall."

"Well, Ellen will be graduated by that time," said Fanny, "and she ought to have the watch now if she's ever goin' to. She'll never think so much of it. Floretta Vining is goin' to have a watch, too. Mrs. Cross says her mother told her so; said Mr. Vining had it all bought — a real handsome one. I don't believe Sam Vining can afford to buy a gold watch. I don't believe it is all gold, for my part. They 'ain't got as much as we have, if Sam has had work steadier. I don't believe it's gold. I don't want Ellen to have a watch at all unless it's a real good one. It seems to me you'd better take a little money out and buy her one, Andrew."

"Well, I'll see," said Andrew. He had a terrible sense of guilt before Fanny. Suppose she knew that there was no money at all in the bank to take out?

"Well, I'll buy her one if you say so," said he, in a curious, slow, stern voice. In his heart was a fierce rising of rebellion, that he, hard-working and frugal and self-denying all his life, should be denied the privilege of buying a present for his darling without resorting to deception, and even almost robbery. He did not at that minute blame himself in the least for his misadventure with his mining stock. Had not the same relentless Providence driven him to that also? His weary spirit took for the first time a poise of utter self-righteousness in opposition to this Providence, and he blasphemed in his inner closet of self, before the face of the Lord, as he comprehended it.

"Well, I have a sort of set my heart on it," said Fanny.

"She shall have the watch," repeated Andrew, and his voice was fairly defiant.

After Fanny had gone into the house and lighted her lamp, and resumed work on her wrapper, Andrew still sat on the step in the cool evening. There was a full moon, and great masses of shadows seemed to float and hover and alight on the earth with a gigantic brooding as of birds. The trees seemed redoubled in size from the soft indetermination of the moonlight which confused shadow and light, and deceived the eye as with soft loomings out of false distances. There was a tall pine, grown from a sapling since Ellen's childhood, and that looked more like a column of mist than a tree, but the Norway spruces clove the air sharply like silhouettes in ink, and outlined their dark profiles clearly against the silver radiance.

To Andrew, looking at it all, came the feeling of a traveller who passes all scenes whether of joy or woe, being himself in his passing the one thing which remains, and somehow he got from it an enormous comfort.

"We're all travellin' along," he said aloud, in a strained, solemn voice.

"What did you say, Andrew?" Fanny called from the open window.

"Nothin'," replied Andrew.

186

CHAPTER XVII

ELLEN had always had objective points, as it were,
in her life, and she always would have, no matter how
long she lived. She came to places where she stopped
mentally, for retrospection and forethought, wherefrom
she could seem to obtain a view of that which lay behind, and of the path which was set for her feet in
advance. She saw the tracked and the trackless.
Once, going with Abby Atkins and Floretta in search
of early spring flowers, Ellen had lingered and let
them go out of sight, and had sat down on a springing
mat of wintergreen leaves under the windy outstretch
of a great pine, and had remained there quite deaf
to shrill halloos. She had sat there with eyes of inward
scrutiny like an Eastern sage's, motionless as on a
rock of thought, while her daily life eddied around
her. Ellen, sitting there, had said to herself: "This
I will always remember. No matter how long I live,
where I am, and what happens to me, I will always
remember how I was a child, and sat here this morning
in spring under the pine-tree, looking backward and
forward. I will never forget."

When, finally, Abby and Floretta had run back, and
spied her there, they had stared half frightened. "You
ain't sick, are you, Ellen?" asked Abby, anxiously.

"What are you sitting there for?" asked Floretta.

Ellen had replied that she was not sick, and had risen
and run on, looking for flowers, but the flowers for her
bloomed always against a background of the past,
and nodded with forward flings of fragrance into the

future; for the other children, who were wholly of their own day and generation, they bloomed in the simple light of their own desire of possession. They picked only flowers, but Ellen picked thoughts, and they kept casting bewildered side-glances at her, for the look which had come into her eyes as she sat beneath the pine-tree lingered.

It was as if a rose had a second of self-consciousness between the bud and the blossom; a bird between its mother's brooding and the song. She had caught sight of the innermost processes of things, of her wheels of life.

Ellen waked up on that June morning, and the old sensation of a pause before advance was upon her, and the strange solemnity which was almost a terror, from the feeble clutching of her mind at the comprehension of infinity. She looked at the morning sunlight coming between the white slants of her curtains, an airy flutter of her new dress from the closet, her valedictory, tied with a white satin ribbon, on the stand, and she saw quite plainly all which had led up to this, and to her, Ellen Brewster; and she saw also the inevitableness of its passing, the precious valedictory being laid away and buried beneath a pile of future ones; she saw the crowd of future valedictorians advancing like a flock of white doves in their white gowns, when hers was worn out, and its beauty gone, pressing forward, dimming her to her own vision. She saw how she would come to look calmly and coldly upon all that filled her with such joy and excitement to-day; how the savor of the moment would pass from her tongue, and she said to herself that she would always remember this moment.

Then suddenly—since she had in herself an impetus of motion which nothing, not even reflection, could long check—she saw quite plainly a light beyond, after all this should have passed, and the leaping power of her spirit to gain it. And then, since she was healthy, and given only at wide intervals to these Eastern lapses of consciousness from the present, she was back in her day, and alive to all its importance as a part of time.

She felt the bounding elation of tossing on the crest of her wave of success, and the full rainbow glory of it dazzled her eyes. She was first in her class, she was valedictorian, she had a beautiful dress, she was young, she was first. It is a poor spirit, and one incapable of courage in defeat, who feels not triumph in victory. Ellen was triumphant and confident. She had faith in herself and the love and approbation of everybody.

When she was seated with her class on the stage in the city hall, where the graduating exercises were held, she saw herself just as she looked, and it was with a satisfaction which had nothing weakly in its vein, and smiled radiantly and innocently at herself as seen in this mirror of love and appreciation of all who knew her.

When the band stopped playing, and Ellen, who as valedictorian came last as the crown and capsheaf of it all, stepped forward from the semicircle of white-clad girls and seriously abashed boys, there was a subdued murmur and then a hush all over the hall. Andrew and Fanny and the grandmother, seated directly in front of the stage—for they had come early to secure good seats—heard whispers of admiration on every side. It was admiration with no dissent—such jealous ears as theirs could not be deceived. Fanny's face was blazing with the sweet shame of pride in her child; Andrew was pale; the grandmother sat as if petrified, with a proud toss of her head. They looked straight ahead; they dared not encounter each other's eyes, for they were more self-conscious than Ellen. They felt the attention of the whole assembly upon them. Andrew was conscious of feeling ill and faint. His own joy seemed to overwhelm him. He forgot his stocks, he forgot his borrowed money, he forgot Lloyd's; he was perfectly happy at the sight of that beautiful young creature of his own heart, who was preferred before all others in the sight of the whole city. In truth, there was about Ellen a majesty and nobility of youth and innocence and beauty which overawed. The other girls of the class were as young and as pretty, but none of them had that indescribable quality which seemed to raise her above them all. Ellen still kept her blond fairness, but there was nothing of the doll-like which often characterizes the blond type. Although she was small, Ellen's color had the firmness and unwavering of tinted marble; she carried her crown of yellow braids as if it had been gold; she moved and looked and spoke with decision. The violent and intense temperament which she had inherited from two sides of her family had crystallized in her to something more forcible, but also more impressive. However, she was, after all, only a young girl, scarcely more than a child, whatever her principle of underlying character might be, and when she stood there before them all—all her townspeople who represented her world, the human shore upon which her own little individuality beat—when she saw those attentive faces, row upon row, all fixed upon her, she felt her heart pound against her side; she had no sensation of the roll of paper in her hand; an awful terror as of suddenly discovered depths came over her, as the wild clapping of hands to which her appearance had given rise died away. Ellen stood still, holding the valedictory as if it had been a stick. A little wondering murmur began to be heard. Andrew felt as if he were dying. Fanny gripped his arm hard. Mrs. Zelotes had the look of one about to spring. Ellen had the terrible sensation which has in it a nightmare of inability to move, allied with the intensest consciousness. She knew that she was to read her valedictory, she knew that she must raise that white-ribboned roll and read, or else be disgraced forever, and yet she was powerless. But suddenly some compelling glance seemed to arouse her from this lock of nerve and muscle; she raised her eyes, and Cynthia Lennox, on the farther side of the hall, was gazing full at her with an indescribable gaze of passion and help and command. Her own mother's look could not have influenced her. Ellen raised her valedictory, bowed, and began to read. Andrew looked so pale that people nudged one another to look at him. Mrs. Zelotes settled back, relaxing stiffly from her fierce attitude. Fanny wiped her forehead with a cheap lace-bordered handkerchief. There was a stifled sob farther back, that came from Eva Tenny, who sat back on account of a break across the shoulders in the back of her silk dress. Amabel, anæmic and eager in a little, tawdry, cheap muslin frock, sat beside her, with worshipful eyes on Ellen. "What ailed her?" she whispered, hitting her mother with a sharp little elbow. "Hush up!" whispered Eva, angrily, surreptitiously wiping her eyes. In front, directly in her line of vision, sat the woman of whom she was jealous—the young widow, who had been Aggie Bemis, arrayed in a handsome India silk and a flower-laden hat. Eva's hat was trimmed with a draggled feather and a bunch of roses which she had tried to color with aniline dye. When she got home that night she tore the feather out of the hat and flung it across the room. She wished to do it that afternoon every time she looked at the other woman's roses against the smooth knot of her brown hair, and that repressed impulse, with her alarm at Ellen's silence, had made her almost hysterical. When Ellen's clear young voice rose and filled the hall she calmed herself. Ellen had not folded back her first page with a flutter of the white satin ribbons before people began to sit straight and stare at each other incredulously. The subject of the valedictory, as well as those of the other essays, had been allotted, and Ellen's had been "Equality," and she had written a most revolutionary valedictory. Ellen had written with a sort of poetic fire, and, crude as it all was, she might have had the inspiration of a Shelley or a Chatterton as she stood there, raising her fearless young front over the marshalling of her sentiments on the smooth sheets of foolscap. Her voice, once started, rang out clear and full. She had hesitated at nothing, she flung all castes into a common heap of equality with her strong young arms, and she set them all on one level of the synagogue. She forced the employer and his employé to one bench of service in the grand system of things; she gave the laborer, and the laborer only, the reward of labor. As Ellen went on reading calmly, with the steadfastness of one promulgating principles, not the excitement of one carried away by enthusiasm, she began to be interrupted by applause, but she read on, never wavering, her clear voice overcoming everything. She was quite innocently throwing her wordy bomb to the agitation of public sentiment. She had no thought of such an effect. She was stating what she believed to be facts with her youthful dogmatism. She had no fear lest the facts strike too hard. The school-master's face grew long with dismay; he sat pulling his mustache in a fashion he had when disturbed. He glanced uneasily now and then at Mr. Lloyd, and at another leading manufacturer who was present. The other manufacturer sat quite stolid and unsmiling beside a fidgeting wife, who presently arose and swept out with a loud rustle of silks. She looked back once and beckoned angrily to her husband, but he did not stir. He was on the school-board. The schoolmaster trembled when he saw that imperturbable face

THE VALEDICTORY

of storing recollection before him. Mr. Lloyd leaned towards Lyman Risley, who sat beside him and whispered and laughed. It was quite evident that he did not consider the flight of this little fledgling in the face of things seriously. But even he, as Ellen's clearly delivered sentiments grew more and more defined—almost anarchistic—became a little grave in spite of the absurd incongruity between them and the girlish lips. Once he looked in some wonder at the school-teacher as much as to say, "Why did you permit this?" and the young man pulled his mustache harder.

When Ellen finished and made her bow, such a storm of applause arose as had never before been heard at a high-school exhibition. The audience was for the most part composed of factory employés and their families, as most of the graduates were of that class of the community. Many of them were of foreign blood, people who had come to the country expecting the state of things advocated in Ellen's valedictory, and had remained more or less sullen and dissenting at the non-fulfilment of their expectation. One tall Swede, with a lurid flashing of blue eyes under a thick, blond thatch, led the renewed charges of applause. Red spots came on his cheeks, gaunt with high cheekbones; his cold Northern blood was up. He stood upreared against a background of the crowd under the balcony; he stamped when the applause died low; then it swelled again and again like great waves. The Swede brandished his long arms, he shouted, others echoed him. Even the women hallooed in a frenzy of applause, they clapped their hands, they stood up in their seats. Only a few sat silent and contemptuous through all the enthusiasm. Thomas Briggs, the manufacturer, was one of them. He sat like a rock, his great, red, imperturbable face of dissent fixed straight ahead. Mrs. Lloyd clapped wildly, on account of the girl who had read the valedictory. She had slept through the greater part of it, for it was very warm, and the heat always made her drowsy. She kept leaning towards Cynthia as she clapped, and asking in a loud whisper if she wasn't sweet. Cynthia did not applaud, but her delicate face was pale with emotion. Lyman Risley, beside her, was clapping energetically. "She may have a bomb somewhere concealed among those ribbons and frills," he said to Lloyd when the applause was waxing loudest, and Lloyd laughed.

As for Ellen, when the storm of applause burst at her feet, she stood still for a moment bewildered. Then she bowed again and turned to go, then the compelling uproar brought her back. She stood there quite piteous in her confusion. This was too much triumph, and, moreover, she had not the least idea of the true significance of it all. She was like a chemist who had brought together, quite ignorantly and unwittingly, the two elements of an explosive. She thought that her valedictory must have been well done, that they liked it, and that was all. She had no sooner finished reading than the ushers began in the midst of the storm of applause to approach the stage with her graduating presents. They were laden with great bouquets and baskets of flowers, with cards conspicuously attached to most of them. Cynthia Lennox had sent a basket of roses. Ellen took it on her arm, and wondered when she saw the name attached to the pink satin bow on the handle. She did not look again towards Cynthia since the old impulse of concealment on her account came over her. Ellen had great boxes of candy from her boy admirers, that being a favorite token of young affection upon such occasions. She had a gift-book from her former school-teacher, and a ninety-eight-cent gilded vase from Eva and Amabel, who had been saving money to buy it. She heard a murmur of admiration

194

when she had finally reached her seat, after the storm of applause had at last subsided, and she unrolled the packages with trembling fingers.

"My, ain't that handsome!" said Floretta, pressing her muslin-clad shoulder against Ellen's. "My, didn't they clap you, Ellen! What's that in that package?"

The package contained Ellen's new watch and chain. Floretta had already received hers, and it lay in its case on her lap. Ellen looked at the package, not hearing in the least the Baptist minister who had taken his place on the stage, and was delivering an address. She had felt her aunt Eva's and Amabel's eager eyes on her when she unrolled the gaudy vase; now she felt her father's and mother's. The small, daintily tied package was inscribed "Ellen Brewster, from Father and Mother."

"Why don't you open it?" came in her ear from Floretta. Maria was leaning forward also, over her lapful of carnations which John Sargent had presented to her.

"Why don't she open it?" she whispered to Floretta. They were all quite oblivious of the speaker, who moved nervously back and forth in front of them, so screening them somewhat from the observation of the audience. Still Ellen hesitated, looking at the little package and feeling her father's and mother's eyes on her face.

Finally she untied the cord and took out the jeweller's case from the wrapping-paper. "My, you've got one too, I bet!" whispered Floretta. Ellen opened the box, and gazed at her watch and chain; then she glanced at her father and mother down in the audience, and the three loving souls seemed to meet in an ineffable solitude in the midst of the crowd. All three faces were pale—Ellen's began to quiver. She felt Floretta's shoulder warm through her thin sleeve against hers.

"My! you've got one—I said so," she whispered. "It isn't chased as much as mine, but it's real handsome. My, Ellen Brewster, you ain't going to cry before all these people!"

Ellen smiled against a sob, and she gave her head a defiant toss. Down in the audience Fanny had her handkerchief to her eyes, and Andrew sat looking sternly at the speaker. Ellen said to herself that she would not cry—she would not, but she sat gazing down at her flower-laden lap and the presents. The golden disk under her fixed eyes waxed larger and larger, until it seemed to fill her whole comprehension as with a golden light of a suffering, self-denying love which was her best reward of life and labor on the earth.

CHAPTER XVIII

AFTER the exhibition there was a dance. The Brewsters, even Mrs. Zelotes, remained to see the last of Ellen's triumph. Mrs. Zelotes was firmly convinced that Ellen's appearance excelled any one's in the hall. Not a girl swung past them in the dance but she eyed her white dress scornfully, then her rosy face, and sniffed with high nostrils like an old war-horse. " Jest look at that Vining girl's dress, coarse enough to strain through," she said to Fanny, leaning across Andrew, who was sitting rapt, his very soul dancing with his daughter, his eyes never leaving her one second, following her fair head and white flutter of muslin ruffles and ribbons around the hall.

"Yes, that's so," assented Fanny, but not with her usual sharpness. A wistful softness and sweetness was on her coarsely handsome face. Once she reached her hand over Andrew's and pressed it, and blushed crimson as she did so. Andrew turned and smiled at her. All that annoyed Andrew was that Ellen danced with Granville Joy often, and also with other boys. It disturbed him a little, even while it delighted him, that she should dance at all, that she should have learned to dance. Andrew had been brought up to look upon dancing as an amusement for Louds rather than for Brewsters. It had not been in vogue among the aristocracy of this little New England city when he was young.

Mrs. Zelotes watched Ellen dance with inward delight and outward disapproval. "I don't approve of dancing, never did," she said to Andrew, but she was furious once when Ellen sat through a dance. Towards the end of the evening she saw with sudden alertness Ellen dancing with a new partner, a handsome young man, who carried himself with more assurance than the school-boys. Mrs. Zelotes hit Andrew with her sharp elbow.

"Who's that dancing with her now?" she said.

"That's young Lloyd," answered Andrew. He flushed a little, and looked pleased.

"Norman Lloyd's nephew?" asked his mother, sharply.

"Yes, he's on here from St. Louis. He's goin' into business with his uncle," replied Andrew. "Sargent was telling me about it yesterday. Young Lloyd came into the post-office while we were there." Fanny had been listening. Immediately she married Ellen to young Lloyd, and the next moment she went to live in a grand new house built in a twinkling in a vacant lot next to Norman Lloyd's residence, which was the wonder of the city. She reared this castle in Spain with inconceivable swiftness, even while she was turning her head towards Eva on the other side, and prodding her with an admonishing elbow as Mrs. Zelotes had prodded Andrew. "That's Norman Lloyd's nephew dancing with her now," she said. Eva looked at her, smiling. Directly the idea of Ellen's marriage with the young man with whom she was dancing established full connections and ran through the line of Ellen's relatives as though an electric wire.

As for Ellen, dancing with this stranger, who had been introduced to her by the school-master, she certainly had no thought of a possible marriage with him, but she had looked into his face with a curious, ready leap of sympathy and understanding of this other soul which she met for the first time. It seemed to her that

198

she must have known him before, but she knew that she had not. She began to reflect as they were whirling about the hall, she gazed at that secret memory of hers, which she had treasured since her childhood, and discovered that what had seemed familiar to her about the young man was the face of a familiar thought. Ever since Miss Cynthia Lennox had told her about her nephew, the little boy who had owned and loved the doll, Ellen had unconsciously held the thought of him in her mind. "You are Miss Cynthia Lennox's nephew," she said to young Lloyd.

"Yes," he replied. He nodded towards Cynthia, who was sitting on the opposite side from the Brewsters, with the Norman Lloyds and Lyman Risley. "She used to be like a mother to me," he said. "You know I lost my mother when I was a baby."

Ellen nodded at him with a look of pity of that marvellous scope which only a woman in whom the maternal slumbers ready to awake can compass. Ellen, looking at the handsome face of the young man, saw quite distinctly in it the face of the little motherless child, and all the tender pity which she would have felt for that child was in her eyes.

"What a beautiful girl she is," thought the young man. He smiled at her admiringly, loving her look at him, while not in the least understanding it. He had asked to be presented to Ellen from curiosity. He had not been at the exhibition, and had heard the school-master and Risley talking about the valedictory. "I didn't know that you taught anarchy in school, Mr. Harris," Risley had said. He laughed as he said it, but Harris had colored with an uneasy look at Norman Lloyd, whose face wore an expression of amusement. "Perhaps I should have," he began, but Lloyd interrupted him. "My dear fellow," he said, "you don't imagine that any man in his senses could take seriously enough to be annoyed by it that child's effusion on her nice little roll of foolscap tied with her pretty white satin rribbon?"

"She is just as sweet as she can be," said Mrs. Norman, "and I thought her composition was real pretty. Didn't you, Cynthia?"

"Very," replied Cynthia.

"What you are worrying about it for, Edward, I don't see," said Mrs. Norman to the school-master.

"Well, I am glad if it struck you that way," said he, "but when I heard the applause from all those factory people"—he lowered his voice, since a number were sitting near—"I didn't know, but—" He hesitated.

"That the spark that would fire the mine might be in that pretty little beribboned roll of foolscap," said Risley, laughing. "Well, it was a very creditable production, and it was written with the energy of conviction. The Czar and that little school-girl would not live long in one country, if she goes on as she has begun."

It was then that young Lloyd, who had just come in, and was standing beside the school-master, turned eagerly to him, and asked who the girl was, and begged him to present him.

"Perhaps he'll fall in love with her," said Mrs. Norman, directly, when the two men had gone across the hall in quest of Ellen. Her husband laughed.

"You have not seen your aunt for a long time," Ellen said to young Lloyd, when they were sitting out a dance after their waltz together.

"Not since—I—I came on—with my father when he died," he replied. Again Ellen looked at him with that wonderful pity in her face, and again the young man thought he had never seen such a girl.

"I think your aunt is beautiful," Ellen said, presently, gazing across at Cynthia.

"Yes, she must have been a beauty when she was young."

"I think she is now," said Ellen, quite fervently, for she was able to disabuse her mind of associations and rely upon pure observation, and it was quite true that leaving out of the question Cynthia's age and the memory of her face in stronger lights at closer view, she was as beautiful from where they sat as some graceful statue. Only clear outlines showed at that distance, and her soft hair, which was quite white, lay in heavy masses around the intense repose of her face.

"Yes—s," admitted Robert, somewhat hesitatingly. "She used to think everything of me when I was a little shaver," he said.

"Doesn't she now?"

"Oh yes, I suppose she does, but it is different now. I am grown up. A man doesn't need so much done for him when he is grown up."

Then again he looked at Ellen with eyes of pleading which would have made of the older woman what he remembered her to have been in his childhood, and hers answered again.

Robert did not say anything to her about the valedictory until just before the close of the evening, when their last dance together was over.

"I am sorry I did not have a chance to hear your valedictory," he said. "I could not come early."

Ellen blushed and smiled, and made the conventional school-girl response. "Oh, you didn't miss anything," said she.

"I am sure I did," said the young man, earnestly. Then he looked at her and hesitated a little. "I wonder if you would be willing to lend it to me?" he said, then. "I would be very careful of it, and would return it immediately as soon as I had read it. I should be so interested in reading it."

"Certainly, if you wish," said Ellen, "but I am afraid you won't think it is good."

"Of course I shall. I have been hearing about it, how good it was, and how you broke up the whole house."

Ellen blushed. "Oh, that was only because it was the valedictory. They always clap a good deal for the valedictory."

"It was because it was you, you dear beauty," thought the young man, gazing at her, and the impulse to take her in his arms and kiss that blush seized upon him. "I know they applauded your valedictory because it was worthy of it," said he, and Ellen's eyes fell before his, and the blush crept down over her throat, and up to the soft toss of hair on her temples. The two were standing, and the man gazed at Ellen's pink arms and neck through the lace of her dress, those incomparable curves of youthful bloom shared by a young girl and a rose; he gazed at that noble, fair head bent not so much before him as before the mystery of life, of which a perception had come to her through his eyes, and he said to himself that there never was such a girl, and he also wondered if he saw aright, he being one who seldom entirely lost the grasp of his own leash. Having the fancy and the heart of a young man, he was given like others of his kind to looking at every new girl who attracted him in the light of a problem, the unknown quantity being her possible interest for him, but he always worked it out calmly. He kept himself out of his own shadow, when it came to the question of emotions, in something the same fashion that his uncle Norman did. Now, looking at Ellen Brewster with the whole of his heart setting towards her in obedience to that law which had brought him into being, he yet was saying quite coolly and loudly in his own inner consciousness, "Wait, wait, wait! Wait until to-

202

morrow, see how you feel then. You have felt in much this way before. Wait! Perhaps you don't see it as it is. Wait!"

He realized his own wisdom all the more clearly when Ellen led him to the settee where her relatives sat guarding her graduation presents and her precious valedictory. She presented him gracefully enough. Ellen knew nothing of society etiquette, she had never introduced such a young gentleman as this to any one in her life, but her inborn dignity of character kept her self-poise perfect. Still, when young Lloyd saw the mother coarsely perspiring and fairly aggressive in her delight over her daughter, when poor Andrew hoped he saw him well, and Mrs. Zelotes eyed him with sharp approbation, and Eva, conscious of her shabbiness, bowed with a stiff toss of her head and sat back sullenly, and little Amabel surveyed him with uncanny wisdom divided between himself and Ellen, he became conscious of a slight disappearance of his glamour. He thanked Ellen most heartily for the privilege which she granted him, when she took the valedictory from the heap of flowers, and took his leave with a bow which made Fanny nudge Andrew, almost before the young man's back was turned.

Then she looked at Ellen, but she said nothing. A sudden impulse of delicacy prevented her. There was something about this beloved daughter of hers which all at once seemed strange to her. She began to associate her with the sacred mystery of life as she had never done. Then, too, there was the more superficial association with one of another class which she held in outward despite but inward awe.

Ellen gathered up her presents into her lap, and sat there a few minutes through the last dance, which she had refused to Granville Joy, who went away with nervous alertness for another girl, and nobody spoke to her.

When young Lloyd and Cynthia Lennox and the others left, as they did directly, Fanny murmured, "They've gone," and they all knew what she meant. She was thinking—and so were they all, except Ellen— that that was the reason, because he had to go, that he had not asked Ellen for the last dance.

As for Ellen, she sat looking at her gold watch and chain, which she had taken out of the case. Her face grew intensely sober, and she did not notice when young Lloyd left. All at once she had reflected how her father had never owned a watch in his whole life, though he was a man, but he had given one to her. She reflected how he had so little work, how shabby his clothes were, how he must have gone without himself to buy this for her. and the girl had such a heart of gold that it rose triumphantly loyal to its first loves and tendernesses, and her father's old, worn face came between her and that of the young man who might become her lover.

CHAPTER XIX

THE day after Ellen's graduation there might have been seen a touching little spectacle passing along the main street of Rowe about ten o'clock in the forenoon. It was touching because it gave evidence of that human vanity common to all, which strives to perpetuate the few small, good things that come into the hard lives of poor souls, and strives with such utter futility. Ellen held up her fluffy skirts daintily, the wind caught her white ribbons and the loose locks of her yellow hair under her white hat. She carried Cynthia Lennox's basket of roses on her arm, and each of the others was laden with bouquets. Little Amabel clasped both slender arms around a great sheaf of roses; the thorns pricked through her thin sleeves, but she did not mind that, so upborne with the elation of the occasion was she. Her small, pale face gazed over the mass of bloom with challenging of admiration from every one whom she met. She was jealous lest any one should not look with full appreciation of Ellen.

Ellen was the one in the little procession who had not unmixed delight in it. She had a certain shamefacedness about going through the streets in such a fashion. She avoided looking at the people whom she met, and kept her head slightly bent and averted, instead of carrying it with the proud directness which was her habit. She felt vaguely that this was the element of purely personal vanity which degrades a triumph, and the weakness of delight and gloating in the faces of her relatives irritated her. It was a sort of unveiling of love, and the girl was sensitive enough to understand it. "Oh, mother, I don't want to have us all go through the street with all these flowers, and me in my white dress," she had said. She had looked at her mother with a shrinking in her eyes which was incomprehensible to the other coarser-natured woman.

"Nonsense," she had said. "Sometimes you have real silly notions, Ellen." Fanny said it adoringly, for even silliness in this girl was in a way worshipful to her. Ellen, with her heart still softened almost to grief by the love shown her on the day before, had yielded, but she was glad when they arrived at the photograph studio. She had particularly dreaded passing Lloyd's, for the thought came to her that possibly young Mr. Lloyd might see her. She supposed that he was likely to be in the office. When they passed the office-windows she looked the other way, but before she was well past, her aunt Eva hit her violently and laughed loudly. Ellen shrank, coloring a deep crimson. Then her mother also laughed, and even Amabel, shrilly, with precocious recognition of the situation. Only Mrs. Zelotes stalked along in silent dignity.

"Don't laugh so loud, he'll hear you," said she, severely.

"It was that young man who was at the hall last night, and he was looking at you awful sharp," said little Amabel to Ellen, squeezing her warm arm, and sending out that shrill peal of laughter again.

"Don't, dear," said Ellen. She felt humiliated, and the more so because she was ashamed of being humiliated by her own mother and aunt. "Why should I be so sensitive to things in which they see no harm?" she asked herself, reprovingly.

As for young Lloyd, he had, ever since he parted with the girl the night before, that sensation of actual contact which survives separation, and had felt the light

206

pressure of her hand in his all night, and along with it that ineffable pain of longing which would draw the substance of a dream to actuality and cannot. He saw her with her coarsely exultant relatives, the inevitable blur of her environments, and felt himself not so much disillusioned as confirmed. He had been constantly saying to himself, when the girl's face haunted his eyes, and her hand in his own, that he was a fool, that he had felt so before, that he must have, that there was no sense in it, that he was Robert Lloyd, and she a good girl, a beautiful girl, but a common sort of girl, born of common people to a common lot. "Now," he said to himself, with a kind of bitter exultation, "there, I told you so." The inconceivable folly of that glance of the mother at him, then at Ellen, and the meaning laughter, repelled him to the point of disgust. He turned his back to the window and resumed his work, but, in spite of himself, the pathos of the picture which he had seen began to force itself upon him, and he thought almost tenderly and forgivingly that she, the girl, had not once looked his way. He even wondered, pityingly, if she had been mortified and annoyed by her mother's behavior. A great anger on Ellen's behalf with her mother seized upon him. How pretty she did look moving along in that little flower-laden procession, he thought, how very pretty. All at once a desire for the photograph which would be taken seized him, for he divined the photograph. However, he said to himself that he would send back the valedictory which he had not yet read by post, with a polite note, and that would be the end.

But it was only the next evening that Robert Lloyd with the valedictory in hand got off the trolley-car in front of the Brewster house. He had proved to himself that it was an act of actual rudeness to return anything so precious and of so much importance to the owner by the post, that he ought to call and deliver it in person. When he regained his equilibrium from the quick sidewise leap from the car, and stood hesitating a little, as one will do before a strange house, for he was not quite sure as to his bearings, he saw a white blur as of feminine apparel in the front doorway. He advanced tentatively up the little path between two rows of flowering bushes, and Ellen rose.

"Good-evening, Mr. Lloyd," she said, in a slightly tremulous voice.

"Oh, good-evening, Miss Brewster," he cried, quickly. "So I am right! I was not sure as to the house."

"People generally tell by the cherry-trees in the yard," replied Ellen, taking refuge from her timidity in the security of commonplace observation, as she had done the night before, giving thereby both a sense of disappointment and elusiveness.

"Won't you walk in?" she added, with the prim politeness of a child who accosts a guest according to rule and precept. Ellen had never, in fact, had a young man make a formal call upon her before. She reflected now, both with relief and trepidation, that her mother was away, having gone to her aunt Eva's. She had an instinct which she resented, that her mother and this young man were on two parallels which could never meet. Her father was at home, seated in the south door with John Sargent and Nahum Beals and Joe Atkins, but she never thought of such a thing as her father's receiving a young man caller, though she would not have doubted so much his assimilating with Robert Lloyd. She understood that the young man might look at her mother with dissent, while she resented it, but with her father it was different.

The group of men at the south door were talking in loud, fervent voices which seemed to rise and fall like waves. Nahum Beals's strained, nervous tones were paramount. "Mr. Beals is talking about the labor question, and he gets quite excited," Ellen remarked, somewhat apologetically, as she ushered young Lloyd into the parlor.

Lloyd laughed. "It sounds as if he were leading an army," he said.

"He is very much in earnest," said the girl.

She placed painstakingly for her guest the best chair, which was a spring rocker upholstered with crush-plush. The little parlor was close and stuffy, and the kerosene-lamp, with the light dimmed by a globe decorated with roses, heated the room still further. This lamp was Fanny's pride. It had, in her eyes, the double glory of high art and cheapness. She was fond of pointing at it, and inquiring, "How much do you think that cost?" and explaining with the air of one who expects her truth to be questioned that it only cost forty-nine cents. This lamp was hideous, the shape was aggressive, a discordant blare of brass, and the roses on the globe were blasphemous. Somehow this lamp was the first thing which struck Lloyd on entering the room. He could not take his eyes from it. As for Ellen, long acquaintance had dulled her eyes. She sat in the full glare of this hideous lamp, and Lloyd considered that she was not so pretty as he had thought last night. Still, she was undeniably very pretty. There was something in the curves of her shoulders, in her pink-and-white cotton waist, that made one's fingers tingle, and heart yearn, and there was an appealing look in her face which made him smile indulgently at her as he might have done at a child. After all, it was probably not her fault about the lamp, and lamps were a minor consideration, and he was finical, but suppose she liked it? Lloyd, sitting there, began to speculate if it were possible for one's spiritual nature to be definitely damaged by hideous lamps. Then he caught sight of a plate decorated with postage-stamps, with a perforated edge through which ribbons were run, and he wondered if she possibly made that.

"They are undoubtedly perfectly moral people," he told his aunt Cynthia afterwards, "but I wonder that they keep such an immoral plate.'' However, that was before he fell in love with Ellen, while he was struggling with himself in his desire to do so, and making all manner of sport of himself by way of hindrance.

Ellen at that age could have had no possible conception of the sentiment with which the young man viewed her environment. She was sensitive to spiritual discords which might arise from meeting with another widely different nature, but when it came to material things, she was at a loss. Then, too, she was pugnaciously loyal to the glories of the best parlor. She was innocently glad that she had such a nice room into which to usher him. She felt that the marble-top table, the plush lambrequin on the mantle-shelf, the gilded vases, the brass clock, the Nottingham lace curtains, the olive-and-crimson furniture, the pictures in cheap gilt frames, the heavily gilded wall-paper, and the throws of thin silk over the picture corners must prove to him the standing of her family. She felt an ignoble satisfaction in it, for a certain measure of commonness clung to the girl like a cobweb. She was as yet too young to bloom free of her environment, her head was not yet over the barrier of her daily lot; her heart never would be, and that was her glory. Young Lloyd handed her the roll of valedictory as soon as he entered.

"I am very much obliged to you for allowing me to read it," he said.

Ellen took it, blushing. Her heart sank a little. She thought to herself that he probably did not like it. She looked at him proudly and timidly, like a child half holding, half withdrawing its hand for a sweet.

It suddenly came to her that she would rather this young man would praise her valedictory than any one else, that if he had been present when she read it in the hall, and she had seen him standing applauding, she could not have contained her triumph and pride. She was not yet in love with him, but she began to feel that in his approbation lay the best coin of her realm.

"It is very well written, Miss Brewster," said Robert, and she flushed with delight.

"Thank you," she said.

But the young man was looking at her as if he had something besides praise in mind, and she gazed at him, shrinking a little as before a blow whose motion she felt in the air. However, he laughed pleasantly when he spoke.

"Do you really believe that?" he asked.

"What?" she inquired, vaguely.

"Oh, all that you say in your essay. Do you really believe that all the property in the world ought to be divided, that kings and peasants ought to share and share alike?"

She looked at him with round eyes. "Why, of course I do!" she said. "Don't you?"

Robert laughed. He had no mind to enter into an argument with this beautiful girl, nor even to express himself forcibly on the opposite side.

"Well, there are a number of things to be considered," he said. "And do you really believe that employer and employés should share alike?"

"Why not?" said she.

Her blue eyes flashed, she tossed her head. Robert smiled at her.

"Why not?" she repeated. "Don't the men earn the money?"

"Well, no, not exactly," said Robert. "There is the capital."

"The profit comes from the labor, not from the capital," said Ellen, quickly. "Doesn't it?" she continued, with fervor, and yet there was a charming timidity, as before some authority.

"Possibly," replied Robert, guardedly; "but the question is how far we should go back before we stop in searching for causes."

"How far back ought we to go?" asked Ellen, earnestly.

"I confess I don't know," said Robert, laughingly. "I have thought very little about it all."

"But you will have to, if you are to be the head of Lloyd's," Ellen said, with a severe accent, with grave, blue eyes full on his face.

"Oh, I am not the head of Lloyd's yet," he answered, easily. "My uncle is far from his dotage. Then, too, you know that I was never intended for a business man, but a lawyer, like my father, if there had not been so little for my father's second wife and the children—" He stopped himself abruptly on the verge of a confidence. "I think I saw you on your way to the photographer to-day," he said, and Ellen blushed, remembering her aunt Eva's violent nudge, and wondering if he had noticed. She gave him a piteous glance.

"Yes," she said. "All the girls have their pictures taken in their graduating dresses with their flowers."

"You looked to me as if the picture would be a great success," said Robert. He longed to ask for one and yet did not, for a reason unexplained to himself. He knew that this innocent, unsophisticated creature would see no reason on earth why he should not ask, and no reason why she should not grant, and on that account he felt prohibited. That night, after he had gone, Ellen wondered why he had not asked for one of her pictures, and felt anxious lest he should have seen the nudge.

212

"Well," she said to herself, "if he finds any fault with anything that my mother has done, I don't want him to have one."

Robert stayed a long time. He kept thinking that he ought to go, and also that he was bored, and yet he felt a singular unwillingness to leave, possibly because of his sense that the visit was in a measure forbidden by prudence. The longer he remained, the 'prettier Ellen looked to him. New beauties of line and color seemed to grow apparent in the soft glow from the hideous lamp. There was a wonderful starry radiance in her eyes now and then, and when she turned her head her eyeballs gleamed crimson and her hair seemed to toss into flame. When she spoke, he was conscious of unknown depths of sweetness in her voice, and it was so with her smile and her every motion. There was about the girl a mystery, not of darkness but of light, which seemed to draw him on and on and on without volition. And yet she said nothing especially remarkable, for Ellen was only a young girl, reared in a little provincial city in common environments. She would have been a great genius had she more than begun to glimpse the breadth and freedom of the outer world through her paling of life. She was too young and too unquestioning of what she had learned from her early loves.

"Have you always lived here in Rowe?" asked Lloyd.

"Yes," said she. "I was born here, and I have lived here ever since."

"And you have never been away?"

"Only once. Once I went to Dragon Beach and stayed a fortnight with mother." She said this with a visible sense of its importance. Dragon Beach was some ten miles from Rowe, a cheap seashore place, built up with flimsy summer cottages of factory hands. Andrew had hired one for a fortnight once when Ellen was ailing, and it had been the event of a lifetime to the family. They hereafter dated from the year "we went to Dragon Beach."

Lloyd looked with a quick impulse of compassionate tenderness at this child who had been away from Rowe once to Dragon Beach. He had his own impressions of Dragon Beach and also of Rowe.

"I suppose you enjoyed that?" said he.

"Very much. The sea is beautiful."

So, after all, it was the sea which she had cared for at Dragon Beach, and not the clam-bakes and merry-go-rounds and women in wrappers in the surf. Robert felt rebuked for thinking of anything but the sea in his memory of Dragon Beach; there was a wonderful water-view there.

All the time they sat there in the parlor, the murmur of conversation at the south door continued, and now and again over it swelled the fervid exhortations of Nahum Beals. Not a word could be distinguished, but the meaning was beyond doubt. That voice was full of denunciation, of frenzied appeal, of warning.

"Who is it?" asked Lloyd, after an unusually loud burst.

"Mr. Beals," replied Ellen, uneasily. She wished that he would not talk so loud.

"He sounds as if he were preaching fire and brimstone," said Robert.

"No, he is talking about the labor question," replied Ellen.

Then she looked confused, for she remembered that this young man's uncle was the head of Lloyd's, that he himself would be the head of Lloyd's some day. All at once, along with another feeling which seemed about to conquer her, came a resentment against this young man with his fine clothes and his gentle manners. Two men passed the windows and one of them looked in, and when the electric-light flashed on his face she saw Granville Joy, and the man with him was in his shirt-sleeves. She saw those white shirt-sleeves swing into the darkness, and felt at once antagonized against herself and against Robert, and yet she knew that she had never seen a man like him.

"I suppose he has settled it," said Robert.

"I don't know," replied Ellen.

"He sounds dangerous."

"Oh, no. He is a good man. He wouldn't hurt anybody. He has always talked that way. He used to come here and talk when I was a child. It used to frighten me at first, but it doesn't now. It is only the way that poor people are treated that frightens me."

Again Robert had a sensation of moving unobtrusively aside from a direct encounter. He looked across the room and started at something which he espied for the first time.

"Pardon me," he said, rising, "but I am interested in dolls. I see you still keep your doll, Miss Brewster."

Ellen sat stupefied. All at once it dawned upon her what might happen. In the corner of the parlor sat her beloved doll, still beloved, though the mother and not the doll had outgrown her first condition of love. The doll, in the identical dress in which she had come from Cynthia's so many years ago, sat staring forth with the fixed radiance of her kind, seated stiffly in a tiny rocking-chair, also one of the treasures of Ellen's childhood. It was a curious feature for the best parlor, but Ellen had insisted upon it. "She isn't going to be put away up garret because I have outgrown her," said she. "She's going to sit in the parlor as long as she lives. Suppose I outgrew you, and put you up in the garret; you wouldn't like it, would you, mother?"

"You are a queer child," Fanny had said, laughing, but she had yielded.

When young Lloyd went close to examine the doll, Ellen's heart stood still. Suppose he should recognize it? She tried to tell herself that it was impossible. Could any young man recognize a doll after all those years? How much did a boy ever care for a doll, anyway? Not enough to think of it twice after he had given it up. It was different with a girl. Her doll meant—God only knew what her doll meant to her; perhaps it had a meaning of all humanity. But the boy, what had he cared for the doll? He had gone away out West and left it.

But Lloyd remembered. He stared down at the doll a moment. Then he took her up gingerly in her fluffy pink robes of an obsolete fashion. He held her at arm's length, and stared and stared. Suddenly he parted the flaxen wig and examined a place on the head. Then he looked at Ellen.

"Why, it is my old doll," he cried, with a great laugh of wonder and incredulity. "Yes, it is my old doll! How in the world did you come by my doll, Miss Brewster? Account for yourself. Are you a child kidnapper?"

Ellen, who had risen and come forward, stood before him, absolutely still, and very pale.

"Yes, it is my doll," said Lloyd, with another laugh. "I will tell you how I know. Of course I can tell her face. Dolls look a good deal alike, I suppose, but I tell you I loved this doll, and I remember her face, and that little cast in her left eye, and that beautiful, serene smile; but there's something besides. Once I burned her head with the red-hot end of the poker to see if she would wake up. I always had a notion when I was a child that it was only a question of violence to make her wake up and demonstrate some existence besides that

216

eternal grin. So I burned her, but it made no difference; but here is the mark now—see."

Ellen saw. She had often kissed it, but she made no reply. She was occupied with considerations of the consequences.

"How did you come by her, if you don't mind telling?" said the young man again. "It is the most curious thing for me to find my old doll sitting here. Of course Aunt Cynthia gave her to you, but I didn't know that she was acquainted with you. I suppose she saw a pretty little girl getting around without a doll after I had gone, and sent her, but—"

Suddenly between the young man's face and the girl's flashed a look of intelligence. Suddenly Robert remembered all that he had heard of Ellen's childish escapade. He *knew*. He looked from her to the doll, and back again. "Good Lord!" he said. Then he set the doll down in her little chair all of a heap, and caught Ellen's hand, and shook it.

"You are a trump, that is what you are," he said; "a trump. So she—" He shook his head, and looked at Ellen, dazedly. She did not say a word, but looked at him with her lips closed tightly.

"It is better for you not to tell me anything," he said; "I don't want to know. I don't understand, and I never want to, how it all happened, but I do understand that you are a trump. How old were you?" Robert's voice took on a tone of tenderness.

"Eight," replied Ellen, faintly.

"Only a baby," said the young man, "and you never told! I would like to know where there is another baby who would do such a thing." He caught her hand and shook it again. "She was like a mother to me," he said, in a husky voice. "I think a good deal of her. I thank you."

Suddenly to the young man looking at the girl a

217

conviction as of some subtle spiritual perfume came; he
had seen her beauty before, he had realized her charm,
but this was something different. A boundless approbation and approval which was infinitely more precious
than admiration seized him. Her character began to
reveal itself, to come in contact with his own; he felt
the warmth of it through the veil of flesh. He felt a
sense of reliance as upon an inexhaustibility of goodness in another soul. He felt something which was
more than love, being purely unselfish, with as yet no
desire of possession. "Here is a good, true woman,"
he said to himself. "Here is a good, true woman, who
has blossomed from a good, true child." He saw a
wonderful faithfulness shining in her blue eyes, he
saw truth itself on her lips, and could have gone down
at the feet of the little girl in the pink cotton frock.
Going home he tried to laugh at himself, but could not
succeed. It is easy to shake off the clasp of a hand of
flesh, but not the clasp of another soul.

Ellen on her part was at once overwhelmed with
delight and confusion. She felt the fervor of admiration in the young man's attitude towards her, but
she was painfully conscious of her undeservingness.
She had always felt guilty about her silence and disobedience towards her parents, and as for any self-ap-
probation for it, that had been the farthest from her
thoughts. She murmured something deprecatingly,
but Lloyd cut her short.

"It's no use crying off," said he; "you are one girl
in a thousand, and I thank you, I thank you from the
bottom of my heart. It might have made awful trouble.
My aunt Lizzie told me what a commotion there was
over it."

"I ran away," said Ellen, anxiously. Suddenly it
occurred to her he might think Cynthia worse than
she had been.

"Never mind," said Lloyd—"never mind. I know what you did. You held your blessed little tongue to save somebody else, and let yourself be blamed."

The door which led into the sitting-room opened, and Andrew looked in.

He made a shy motion when he saw Lloyd; still, he came forward. His own callers had gone, and he had heard voices in the parlor, and had feared Granville Joy was calling upon Ellen.

As he came forward, Ellen introduced him shyly. "This is Mr. Lloyd, father," she said. "Mr. Lloyd, this is my father." Then she added, "He came to bring back my valedictory." She was very awkward, but it was the charming awkwardness of a beautiful child. She looked exceedingly childish standing beside her father, looking into his worn, embarrassed face.

Lloyd shook hands with Andrew, and said something about the valedictory, which he had enjoyed reading.

"She wrote it all herself without a bit of help from the teacher," said Andrew, with wistful pride.

"It is remarkably well written," said Robert.

"You didn't hear it read at the hall?" said Andrew.

"No, I had not that good fortune."

"You ought to have heard them clap," said Andrew.

"Oh, father," murmured Ellen, but she looked innocently at her father as if she delighted in his pride and pleasure without a personal consideration.

The front door opened. "That's your mother," said Andrew.

Fanny looked into the lighted parlor, and dodged back with a little giggle.

Ellen colored painfully. "It is Mr. Lloyd, mother," she said.

Then Fanny came forward and shook hands with Robert. Her face was flaming—she cast involuntary glances at Andrew for confirmation of her opinion. She was openly and shamelessly triumphant, and yet all at once Robert ceased to be repelled by it. Through his insight into the girl's character, he had seemed to gain suddenly a clearer vision for the depths of human love and pity which are beneath the coarse and the common. When Fanny stood beside her daughter and looked at her, then at Robert, with the reflection of the beautiful young face in her eyes of love, she became at once pathetic and sacred.

"It is all natural," he said to himself as he was going home.

CHAPTER XX

ROBERT LLOYD when he came to Rowe was confronted with one of the hardest tasks in the world, that of adjustment to circumstances which had hitherto been out of his imagination. He had not dreamed of a business life in connection with himself. Though he had always had a certain admiration for his successful uncle, Norman Lloyd, yet he had always had along with the admiration a recollection of the old tale of the birthright and the mess of pottage. He had expected to follow the law, like his father, but when he had finished college, about two years after his father's death, he had to face the unexpected. The stocks in which the greater part of the elder Lloyd's money had been invested had depreciated; some of them were for the time being quite worthless as far as income was concerned. There were two little children—girls—by his father's second marriage, and there was not enough to support them and their mother and allow Robert to continue his reading for the law. So he pursued, without the slightest hesitation, but with bitter regret, the only course which he saw open before him. He wrote to his uncle Norman, and was welcomed to a position in his factory with more warmth than he had ever seen displayed by him. In fact, Norman Lloyd, who had no son of his own, saw with a quickening of his pulses the handsome young fellow of his own race who had in a measure thrown himself upon his protection. He had never shared his wife's longing for children as children, and had never cared for Robert when a child; but now, when he was a man grown and bore his name, he appealed to him.

Norman Lloyd was supposed to be heaping up riches, and wild stories of his wealth were told in Rowe. He gave large sums to public benefactions, and never stinted his wife in her giving within certain limits. It would have puzzled any one when faced with facts to understand why he had the name of a hard man, but he had it, whether justly or not. "He's as hard as nails," people said. His employés hated him—that is, the more turbulent and undisciplined spirits hated him, and the others regarded him as slaves might a stern master. When Robert started his work in his uncle's office he started handicapped by this sentiment towards his uncle. He looked like his uncle, he talked like him, he had his same gentle stiffness, he was never unduly familiar. He was at once placed in the same category by the workmen.

Robert Lloyd did not concern himself in the least as to what the employés in his uncle's factory thought of him. Nothing was more completely out of his mind. He was conscious of standing on a firm base of philanthropic principle, and if ever these men came directly under his control, he was resolved to do his duty by them so far as in him lay.

Ellen, since her graduation, had been like an animal which circles about in its endeavors to find its best and natural place of settlement.

"What shall I do next?" she had said to her mother. "Shall I go to work, or shall I try to find a school somewhere in the fall, or shall I stay here, and help you with some work I can do at home? I know father cannot afford to support me always at home."

"I guess he can afford to support his only daughter at home a little while after she has just got out of

222

school," Fanny had returned indignantly, with a keen pain at her heart.

Fanny mentioned this conversation to Andrew that night after Ellen had gone to bed.

"What do you think—Ellen was asking me this afternoon what she had better do!" said she.

"What she had better do?" repeated Andrew, vaguely. He looked shrinkingly at Fanny, who seemed to him to have an accusing air, as if in some way he were to blame for something. And, indeed, there were times when Fanny in those days did blame Andrew, but there was some excuse for her. She blamed him when her own back was filling her very soul with the weariness of its ache as she bent over the seams of those grinding wrappers, and when her heart was sore over doubt of Ellen's future. At those times she acknowledged to herself that it seemed to her that Andrew somehow might have gotten on better. She did not know how, but somehow. He had not had an expensive family. "Why had he not succeeded?" she asked herself. So there was in her tone an unconscious recrimination when she answered his question about Ellen.

"Yes—what she had better go to work at," said Fanny, dryly, her black eyes cold on her husband's face.

Andrew turned so white that he frightened her. "Go to work!" said he. Then all at once he gave an exceedingly loud and bitter groan. It betrayed all his pride in and ambition for his daughter and his disgust and disappointment over himself. "Oh! my God, has it come to this," he groaned, "that I cannot support my one child!"

Fanny laid down her work and looked at him. "Now, Andrew," said she, "there's no use in your taking it after such a fashion as this. I told Ellen that it was all nonsense—that she could stay at home and rest this summer."

"I guess, if she can't—" said Andrew. He dropped his gray head into his hands, and began to sob dryly. Fanny, after staring at him a moment, tossed her work onto the floor, went over to him, and drew his head to her shoulder.

"There, old man," said she, "ain't you ashamed of yourself? I told her there was no need for her to worry at present. Don't do so, Andrew; you've done the best you could, and I know it, if I stop to think, though I do seem sort of impatient sometimes. You've always worked hard and done your best. It ain't your fault."

"I don't know whether it is or not," said Andrew, in a high, querulous voice like a woman's. "It seems as if it must be somebody's fault. If it ain't my fault, whose is it? You can't blame the Almighty."

"Maybe it ain't anybody's fault."

"It must be. All that goes wrong is somebody's fault. It can't be that it just happens—that would be worse than the other. It is better to have a God that is cruel than one that don't care, and it is better to be to blame yourself, and have it your fault, than His. Somehow, I have been to blame, Fanny. I must have. It would have been enough sight better for you, Fanny, if you'd married another man."

"I didn't want another man," replied Fanny, half angrily, half tenderly. "You make me all out of patience, Andrew Brewster. What's the need of Ellen going to work right away? Maybe by-and-by she can get an easy school. Then, we've got that money in the bank."

Andrew looked away from her with his face set. Fanny did not know yet about his withdrawal of the money for the purpose of investing in mining-stocks.

He never looked at her but the guilty secret seemed to force itself between them like a wedge of ice.

"Then Grandma Brewster has got a little something," said Fanny.

"Only just enough for herself," said Andrew. Then he added, fiercely, "Mother can't be stinted of her little comforts even for Ellen."

"I 'ain't never wanted to stint your mother of her comforts," Fanny retorted, angrily.

"She 'ain't got but a precious little, unless she spends her principal," said Andrew. "She 'ain't got more'n a hundred and fifty or so a year clear after her taxes and insurance are paid."

"I ain't saying anything," said Fanny. "But I do say you're dreadful foolish to take on so when you've got so much to fall back on, and that money in the bank. Here you haven't had to touch the interest for quite a while and it has been accumulating."

It was agreed between the two that Ellen must say nothing to her grandmother Brewster about going to work.

"I believe the old lady would have a fit if she thought Ellen was going to work," said Fanny. "She 'ain't never thought she ought to lift her finger."

So Ellen was charged on no account to say anything to her grandmother about the possible necessity of her going to work.

"Your grandmother's awful proud," said Fanny, "and she's always thought you were too good to work."

"I don't think anybody is too good to work," replied Ellen, but she uttered the platitude with a sort of mental reservation. In spite of herself, the attitude of worship in which she had always seen all who belonged to her had spoiled her a little. She did look at herself with a sort of compunction when she realized the fact that she might have to go to work in the shop some time. School-teaching was different, but could she earn enough school-teaching? There was a sturdy vein in the girl. All the time she pitied herself she blamed herself.

"You come of working-people, Ellen Brewster. Why are you any better than they? Why are your hands any better than their hands, your brain than theirs? Why are you any better than the other girls who have gone to work in the shops? Do you think you are any better than Abby Atkins?"

And still Ellen used to look at herself with a pitying conviction that she would be out of place at a bench in the shoe-factory, that she would suffer a certain indignity by such a course. The realization of a better birthright was strong upon her, although she chided herself for it. And everybody abetted her in it. When she said once to Abby Atkins, whom she encountered one day going home from the shop, that she wondered if she could get a job in her room in the fall, Abby turned upon her fiercely.

"Good Lord, Ellen Brewster, you ain't going to work in a shoe-shop?" she said.

"I don't see why not as well as you," returned Ellen.

"Why not?" repeated the other girl. "Look at yourself, and look at us!"

As she spoke, Ellen saw projected upon her mental vision herself passing down the street with the throng of factory operatives which her bodily eyes actually witnessed. She had come opposite Lloyd's as the six o'clock whistle was blowing. She saw herself in her clean, light summer frock, slight and dainty, with little hands like white flowers in the blue folds of her skirt, with her fine, sensitive outlook of fair face, and her dainty carriage; and she saw others—those girls and women in dingy skirts and bagging blouses, with coarse hair strained into hard knots of exigency from

226

patient, or sullen faces, according to their methods of bearing their lots; all of them rank with the smell of leather, their coarse hands stained with it, swinging their poor little worn bags which had held their dinners. There were not many foreigners among them, except the Irish, most of whom had been born in this country, and a sprinkling of fair-haired, ruddy Swedes and keen Polanders, who bore themselves better than the Americans, being not so apparently at odds with the situation.

The factory employés in Rowe were a superior lot, men and women. Many of the men had put on their worn coats when they emerged from the factory, and their little bags were supposed to disguise the fact of their being dinner satchels. And yet there was a difference between Ellen Brewster and the people among whom she walked, and she felt it with a sort of pride and indignation with herself that it was so.

"I don't see why I should be any better than the rest," said she, defiantly, to Abby Atkins. "My father works in a shop, and you are my best friend, and you do. Why shouldn't I work in a shop?"

"Look at yourself," repeated the other girl, mercilessly. "You are different. You ain't to blame for it any more than a flower is to blame for being a rose and not a common burdock. If you've got to do anything, you had better teach school."

"I would rather teach school," said Ellen, "but I couldn't earn so much unless I got more education and got a higher position than a district school, and that is out of the question."

"I thought maybe your grandmother could send you," said Abby.

"Oh no, grandma can't afford to. Sometimes I think I could work my own way through college, if it wasn't for being a burden in the mean time, but I don't know."

Suddenly Abby Atkins planted herself on the sidewalk in front of Ellen, and looked at her sharply, while an angry flush overspread her face.

"I want to know one thing," said she.

"What?"

"It ain't true what I heard the other day, is it?"

"I don't know what you heard."

"Well, I heard you were going to be married."

Ellen turned quite pale, and looked at the other girl with a steady regard of grave, indignant blue eyes.

"No, I am not," said she.

"Well, don't be mad, Ellen. I heard real straight that you were going to marry Granville Joy in the fall."

"Well, I am not," repeated Ellen.

"I didn't suppose you were, but I knew he had always wanted you."

"Always wanted me!" said Ellen. "Why, he's only just out of school!"

"Oh, I know that, and he's only just gone to work, and he can't be earning much, but I heard it."

The stream of factory operatives had thinned; many had taken the trolley-cars, and others had gone to the opposite side of the street, which was shady. The two girls were alone, standing before a vacant lot grown to weeds, rank bristles of burdock, and slender spikes of evanescent succory. Abby burst out in a passionate appeal, clutching Ellen's arm hard.

"Ellen, promise me you never will," she cried.

"Promise you what, Abby?"

"Oh, promise me you never will marry anybody like him. I know it's none of my business—I know that is something that is none of anybody's business, no matter how much they think of anybody; but I think more of you than any man ever will, I don't care who he is. I know I do, Ellen Brewster. And don't you ever marry a man like Granville Joy, just an ordinary man who works in the shop, and will never do anything but work in the shop. I know he's good, real good and steady, and it ain't against him that he ain't rich and has to work for his living, but I tell you, Ellen Brewster, you ain't the right sort to marry a man like that, and have a lot of children to work in shops. No man, if he thinks anything of you, ought to ask you to; but all a man thinks of is himself. Granville Joy, or any other man who wanted you, would take you and spoil you, and think he'd done a smart thing." Abby spoke with such intensity that it redeemed her from coarseness. Ellen continued to look at her, and two red spots had come on her cheeks.

"I don't believe I'll ever get married at all," she said.

"If you've got to get married, you ought to marry somebody like young Mr. Lloyd," said Abby.

Then Ellen blushed, and pushed past her indignantly.

"Young Mr. Lloyd!" said she. "I don't want him, and he doesn't want me. I wish you wouldn't talk so, Abby."

"He would want you if you were a rich girl, and your father was boss instead of a workman," said Abby.

Then she caught hold of Ellen's arm and pressed her own thin one in its dark-blue cotton sleeve lovingly against it.

"You ain't mad with me, are you, Ellen?" she said, with that indescribable gentleness tempering her fierceness of nature which gave her caresses the fascination of some little, untamed animal. Ellen pressed her round young arm tenderly against the other.

"I think more of you than any man I know," said she, fervently. "I think more of you than anybody except father and mother, Abby."

The two girls walked on with locked arms, and each was possessed with that wholly artless and ignorant

passion often seen between two young girls. Abby felt
Ellen's warm round arm against hers with a throbbing
of rapture, and glanced at her fair face with adoration.
She held her in a sort of worship, she loved her so
that she was fairly afraid of her. As for Ellen, Abby's
little, leather-stained, leather-scented figure, strung
with passion like a bundle of electric wire, pressing
against her, seemed to inform her farthest thoughts.

"If I live longer than my father and mother, we'll
live together, Abby," said she.

"And I'll work for you, Ellen," said Abby, rapt-
urously.

"I guess you won't do all the work," said Ellen.
She gazed tenderly into Abby's little, dark, thin face.
"You're all worn out with work now," said she, "and
there you bought that beautiful pin for me with your
hard earnings."

"I wish it had been a great deal better," said Abby,
fervently.

She had given Ellen a gold brooch for a graduating-
gift, and had paid a week's wages for it, and gone
without her new dress, and stayed away from the graduation, but that last Ellen never knew; Abby had told
her that she was sick.

That evening Robert Lloyd and his aunt Cynthia
Lennox called on the Brewsters. Ellen was under the
trees in the west yard when she heard a carriage stop
in front of the house and saw the sitting-room lamp
travel through the front entry to the front door. She
wondered indifferently who it was. Carriages were not
given to stopping at their house of an evening; then
she reflected that it might be some one to get her
mother to do some sewing, and remained still.

It was a bright moonlight night; the whole yard
was a lovely dapple of lights and shadows. Ellen

230

had a vivid perception of the beauty of it all, and also that unrest and yearning which comes often to a young girl in moonlight. This beauty and strangeness of familiar scenes under the silver glamour of the moon gave her, as it were, an assurance of other delights and beauties of life besides those which she already knew, and along with the assurance came that wild yearning. Ellen seemed to scent her honey of life, and at the same time the hunger for it leaped to her consciousness. She had begun by thinking of what Abby had said to her that afternoon, and then the train of thought led her on and on. She quite ignored all about the sordid ways and means of existence, about toil and privation and children born to it. All at once the conviction was strong upon her that love, and love alone, was the chief end and purpose of life, at once its source and its result, the completion of its golden ring of glory. Her thought, started in whatever direction, seemed to slide always into that one all-comprehending circle—she could not get her imagination away from it. She began to realize that the mind of mortal man could not get away from the law which produced it. She began to understand dimly, as one begins to understand any great truth, that everything around her obeyed that unwritten fundamental law of love, expressed it, sounded it, down to the leaves of the trees casting their flickering shadows on the silver field of moonlight, and the long-drawn chorus of the insects of the summer night. She thought of Abby and how much she loved her; then that love seemed the step which gave her an impetus to another love. She began to remember Granville Joy, how he had kissed her that night over the fence and twice since, how he had walked home with her from entertainments, how he had looked at her. She saw the boy's face and his look as plain as if he stood before her, and her heart leaped with a shock of pain which was joy.

Then she thought of Robert Lloyd, and his face came before her. Ellen had not thought as much of Robert as he of her. For some two weeks after his call she had watched for him to come again; she had put on a pretty dress and been particular about her hair, and had stayed at home expecting him; then when he had not come, she had put him out of mind resolutely. When her mother and aunt had joked her about him she had been sensitive and half angry. "You know it is nothing, mother," she said; "he only came to bring back my valedictory. You know he wouldn't think of me. He'll marry somebody like Maud Hemingway." Maud Hemingway was the daughter of the leading physician in Rowe, and regarded with a mixture of spite and admiration by daughters of the factory operatives. Maud Hemingway was attending college, and rode a saddle-horse when home on her vacations. She had been to Europe.

But that evening in the moonlight Ellen began thinking again of Robert Lloyd. His face came before her as plainly as Granville Joy's. She had arrived at that stage when life began to be as a picture-gallery of love. Through this and that face the goddess might look, and the look was what she sought; as yet, the man was a minor quantity.

All at once it seemed to Ellen, looking at her mental picture of young Lloyd, that she could see love in his face yet more plainly, more according to her conception of it, than in the other. She began to build an air-castle which had no reference whatever to Robert's position, and to his being the nephew of the richest factory-owner in Rowe, and so far as that went he had not a whit the advantage of Granville Joy in her eyes. But Robert's face wore to her more of the guise of that for which the night and the moonlight, and her youth, had made her long. So she began innocently to imag-

ine a meeting with him at a picnic which would be held
some time at Liberty Park. She imagined their walking side by side, through a lovely dapple of moonlight
like this, and saying things to each other. Then all
at once the man of her dreams touched her hand in a
dream, and a faintness swept over her. Then suddenly, gathering shape out of the indetermination of
the shadows and the moonlight, came a man into the
yard, and Ellen thought with awe and delight that it
was he; but instead Granville Joy stood before her,
lifting his hat above his soft shock of hair.

"Hullo!" he said.

"Good-evening," responded Ellen, and Granville
Joy felt abashed. He lay awake half the night reflecting that he should have greeted her with a "Good-
evening" instead of "Hullo," as he had been used to
do in their school-days; that she was now a young
lady, and that Mr. Lloyd had accosted her differently.
Ellen rose with a feeling of disappointment that Granville was himself, which is the hardest greeting possible
for a guest, involving the most subtle reproach in the
world—the reproach for a man's own individuality.

"Oh, don't get up, Ellen," the young man said,
awkwardly. "Here—I'll sit down here on the rock."
Then he flung himself down on the ledge of rock which
cropped out like a bare rib of the earth between the
trees, and Ellen seated herself again in her chair.

"Beautiful night, ain't it?" said Granville.

Ellen noticed that Granville said "ain't" instead of
"isn't," according to the fashion of his own family,
although he was recently graduated from the high-
school. Ellen had separated herself, although with
no disparaging reflections, from the language of her
family. She also noticed that Granville presently said
"wa'n't" instead of "wasn't." "Hot yesterday, wa'n't
it?" said he.

233

"Yes, it was very warm," replied Ellen. That "wa'n't" seemed to insert a tiny wedge between them. She would have flown at any one who had found fault with her father and mother for saying "wa'n't," but with this young man in her own rank and day it was different. It argued something in him, or a lack of something. An indignation all out of proportion to the offence seized her. It seemed to her that he had in this simple fashion outraged that which was infinitely higher than he himself. He had not lived up to her thought of him, and fallen short by a little slip in English which argued a slip in character. She wanted to reproach him sharply—to ask him if he had ever been to school.

He noticed her manner was cool, and was as far as the antipodes from suspecting the cause. He never knew that he said "ain't" and "wa'n't," and would die not knowing. All that he looked at was the substance of thought behind the speech. And just then he was farther than ever from thinking of it, for he was single-hearted with Ellen.

The boy crept nearer her on the rock with a shy, nestling motion; the moonlight shone full on his handsome young face, giving it a stern quality. "Ellen, look at here," he said.

Then he stopped. Ellen waited, not dreaming what was to follow. She had never had a proposal; then, too, he had just been chased out of her mental perspective by the other man.

"Look at here, Ellen," said Granville. He stopped again; then when he spoke his voice had an indescribably solemn, beseeching quality. "Oh, Ellen," he said, reaching up and catching her hand. He dragged himself nearer, leaned his cheek against her hand, which it seemed to burn; then he began kissing it with soft, pouting lips.

Ellen tried to pull her hand away. "Let my hand go this minute, Granville Joy," she said, angrily.

The boy let her hand go immediately, and stood up, leaning over her.

"Don't be angry; I didn't mean any harm, Ellen," he whispered.

"I shall be angry if you do such a thing again," said Ellen. "We aren't children; you have no right to do such a thing, and you know it."

"But I thought maybe you wouldn't mind, Ellen," said Granville. Then he added, with his voice all husky with emotion and a kind of fear: "Ellen, you know how I feel about you. You know how I have always felt."

Ellen made no reply. It seemed inconceivable that she for the minute should not know his meaning, but she was bewildered.

"You know I've always counted on havin' you for my wife some day when we were both old enough," said the boy, "and I've gone to work now, and I hope to get bigger pay before long, and—"

Ellen rose with sudden realization. "Granville Joy," cried she, with something like panic in her voice, "you must not! Oh, if I had known! I would not have let you finish. I would not, Granville." She caught his arm, and clung to it, and looked up at him pitifully. "You know I wouldn't have let you finish," she said. "Don't be hurt, Granville."

The boy looked at her as if she had struck him.

"Oh, Ellen," he groaned. "Oh, Ellen, I always thought you would!"

"I am not going to marry anybody," said Ellen. Her voice wavered in spite of herself; the young man's look and voice were shaking her through weakness of her own nature which she did not understand, but which might be mightier than her strength. Something crept into her tone which emboldened the young man to seize her hand again. "You do, in spite of all you say—" he began; but just then a long shadow fell athwart the moonlight, and Ellen snatched her hand away imperceptibly, and young Lloyd stood before them.

CHAPTER XXI

GRANVILLE JOY was employed in Lloyd's, and Robert had seen him that very day and spoken to him, but he did not recognize him, not until Ellen spoke. "This is Mr. Joy, Mr. Lloyd," she said; "perhaps you know him. He works in your uncle's shop." She said it quite simply, as if it was a matter of course that Robert was on speaking terms with all the employés in his uncle's factory.

Granville colored. "I saw Mr. Lloyd this afternoon in the cutting-room," he said, "and we had some talk together; but maybe he don't remember, there are so many of us." Granville said "so many of us" with an indescribably bitter emphasis. Suddenly his gentleness seemed changed to gall. It was the terrible protest of one of the herd who goes along with the rest, yet realizes it, and looks ever out from his common mass with fierce eyes of individual dissent at the immutable conditions of things. Immediately, when Granville saw the other young man, this gentleman in his light summer clothes, who bore about him no stain nor odor of toil, he felt that here was Ellen's mate; that he was left behind. He looked at him, not missing a detail of his superiority, and he saw himself young and not ill-looking, but hopelessly common, clad in awkward clothes; he smelled the smell of leather that steamed up in his face from his raiment and his body; and he looked at Ellen, fair and white in her dainty muslin, and saw himself thrust aside, as it were, by his own judgment as to the fitness of things, but with no less bitterness. When he said "there are so many of us," he felt the impulse of revolution in his heart; that he would have liked to lead the "many of us" against this young aristocrat. But Robert smiled, though somewhat stiffly, and bowed. "I beg your pardon, Mr. Joy," he said; "I do remember, but for a minute I did not."

"I don't wonder," said Granville, and again he repeated, "There are so many of us," in that sullen, bitter tone.

"What is the matter with the fellow?" thought Robert; but he said, civilly enough: "Oh, not at all, Mr. Joy. I will admit there are a good many of you, as you say, but that would not prevent my remembering a man to whom I was speaking only a few hours ago. It was only the half-light, and I did not expect to see you here."

"Mr. Joy is a very old friend of mine," Ellen said, quickly, with a painful impulse of loyalty. The moment she saw her old school-boy lover intimidated, and manifestly at a disadvantage before this elegant young gentleman, she felt a fierce instinct of partisanship. She stood a little nearer to him. Granville's face lightened, he looked at her gratefully, and Robert stared from one to the other doubtfully. He began to wonder if he had interrupted a love-scene, and was at once pained with a curious, new pain, and indignant. Then, too, he scarcely knew what to do. He had been sent to ask Ellen to come into the parlor.

"My aunt is in the house," he said.

"Your aunt?"

"Yes, my aunt, Miss Lennox."

Ellen gave a great start, and stared at him. "Does she want to see me?" she asked, abruptly.

Robert glanced at Granville. He was afraid of being rude towards this possible lover, but the young man was quick to perceive the situation.

"I guess I must be going," he said to Ellen.

"Must you hurry?" she returned, in the common, polite rejoinder of her class in Rowe.

"Yes, I guess I must," said Granville. He held out his hand towards Ellen, then drew it away, but she extended hers resolutely, and so forced his back again. "Good-night," she said, kindly, almost tenderly, and again Robert thought with that sinking at his heart that here was quite possibly the girl's lover, and all his dreams were thrown away.

As for Granville, he glowed with a sudden triumph over the other. Again he became almost sure that Ellen loved him after all, that it was only her maiden shyness which had led her to refuse him. He pressed her hand hard, and held it as long as he dared; then he turned to Robert. "I'll bid you good-evening, sir," he said, with awkward dignity, and was gone.

"I will go in and see your aunt," Ellen said to Robert, regarding him as she spoke with a startled expression. It had flashed through her mind that Miss Lennox had possibly come to confess the secret of so many years ago, and she shrank with terror as before the lowering of some storm of spirit. She knew how little was required to lash her mother's violent nature into fury. "She was not—?" she began to say to Robert, then she stopped; but he understood. "Don't be afraid, Miss Brewster," he said, kindly. "It is not a matter of by-gones, but the future. My aunt has a plan for you which I think you will like."

Ellen looked at him wonderingly, but she went with him across the moonlit yard into the house.

She found Miss Cynthia Lennox, fair and elegant in a filmy black gown, and a broad black hat draped with lace and violets shading her delicate, clear-cut face, and her father and mother. Fanny's eyes were red. She looked as if she had been running—in fact, one could easily hear her breathe across the room. "Ellen, here is Miss Lennox," she said. Ellen approached the lady, who rose, and the two shook hands. "Good-evening, Miss Brewster," said Cynthia, in the same tone which she might have used towards a society acquaintance. Ellen would never have known that she had heard the voice before. As she remembered it, it was full of intensest vibrations of maternal love and tenderness and protection beyond anything which she had ever heard in her own mother's voice. Now it was all gone, and also the old look from her eyes. Cynthia Lennox was, in fact, quite another woman to the young girl from what she had been to the child. In truth, she cared not one whit for Ellen, but she was possessed with a stern desire of atonement, and far stronger than her love was the appreciation of what that mother opposite must have suffered during that day and night when she had forcibly kept her treasure. The agony of that she could present to her consciousness very vividly, but she could not awaken the old love which had been the baby's for this young girl. Cynthia felt much more affection for Fanny than for Ellen. When she had unfolded her plan for sending Ellen to college, and Fanny had almost gone hysterical with delight, she found it almost impossible to keep her tears back. She knew so acutely how this other woman felt that she almost seemed to lose her own individuality. She began to be filled with a vicarious adoration of Ellen, which was, however, dissipated the moment she actually saw her. She realized that this grown-up girl, who could no longer be cuddled and cradled, was nothing to her, but her sympathy with the mother remained.

Ellen remained standing after she had greeted Cynthia. Robert went over to the mantle-piece and stood leaning against it. He was completely puzzled and disturbed by the whole affair. Ellen looked at Cynthia, then at her parents. "Ellen, come here, child," said her father, suddenly, and Ellen went over to him, sitting on the plush sofa beside her mother.

Andrew reached up and took hold of Ellen's hands, and drew her down on his knee as if she had been a child. "Ellen, look here," he said, in an intense, almost solemn voice, "father has got something to tell you."

Fanny began to weep almost aloud. Cynthia looked straight ahead, keeping her features still with an effort. Robert studied the carpet pattern.

"Look here, Ellen," said Andrew; "you know that father has always wanted to do everything for you, but he ain't able to do all he would like to. God hasn't prospered him, and it seems likely that he won't be able to do any more than he has done, if so much, in the years to come. You know father has always wanted to send you to college, and give you an extra education so you could teach in a school where you would make a good living, and now here Miss Lennox says she heard your composition, and she has heard a good deal about you from Mr. Harris, how well you stood in the high-school, and she says she is willing to send you to Vassar College."

Ellen turned pale. She looked long at her father, whose pathetic, worn, half-triumphant, half-pitiful face was so near her own; then she looked at Cynthia, then back again. "To Vassar College?" she said.

"Yes, Ellen, to Vassar College, and she offers to clothe you while you are there, but we thank her, and tell her that ain't necessary. We can furnish your clothes."

"Yes, we can," said Fanny, in a sobbing voice, but with a flash of pride.

"Well, what do you say to it, Ellen?" asked Andrew,

and he asked it with the expression of a martyr. At that moment indescribable pain was the uppermost sensation in his heart, over all his triumph and gladness for Ellen. First came the anticipated agony of parting with her for the greater part of four years, then the pain of letting another do for his daughter what he wished to do himself. No man would ever look in Ellen's eyes with greater love and greater shrinking from the pain which might come of love than Andrew at that moment.

"But—" said Ellen; then she stopped.

"What, Ellen?"

"Can you spare me for so long? Ought I not to be earning money before that, if you don't have much work?"

"I guess we can spare you as far as all that goes," cried Andrew. "I guess we can. I guess we don't want you to support us."

"I rather guess we don't," cried Fanny.

Ellen looked at her father a moment longer with an adorable look, which Robert saw with a sidewise glance of his downcast eyes, then at her mother. Then she slid from her father's knee and crossed the room and stood before Cynthia. "I don't know how to thank you enough," she said, "but I thank you very much, and not only for myself but for them"; she made a slight, graceful, backward motion of her shoulder towards her parents. "I will study hard and try to do you credit," said she. There was something about Ellen's direct, childlike way of looking at her, and her clear speech, which brought back to Cynthia the little girl of so many years ago. A warm flush came over her delicate cheeks; her eyes grew bright with tenderness.

"I have no doubt as to your doing your best, my dear," she said, "and it gives me great pleasure to do this for you."

"'I'LL STUDY HARD AND TRY TO DO YOU CREDIT'"

With that, said with a graceful softness which was charming, she made as if to rise, but Ellen still stood before her. She had something more to say. "If ever I am able," she said—"and I shall be able some day if I have my health—I will repay you." Ellen spoke with the greatest sweetness, yet with an inflexibility of pride evident in her face. Cynthia smiled. "Very well," she said, "if you feel better to leave it in that way. If ever you are able you shall repay me; in the mean time I consider that I am amply paid in the pleasure it gives me to do it." Cynthia held out her slender hand to Ellen, who took it gratefully, yet a little constrainedly.

In the opposite corner the doll sat staring at them with eyes of blank blue and her vacuous smile. A vague sense of injury was over Ellen, in spite of her delight and her gratitude — a sense of injury which she could not fathom, and for which she chided herself. However, Andrew felt it also.

After this surprising benefactress and Robert had gone, after repeated courtesies and assurances of obligation on both sides, Andrew turned to Fanny. "What does she do it for?" he asked.

"Hush; she'll hear you."

"I can't help it. What does she do it for? Ellen isn't anything to her."

Fanny looked at him with a meaning smile and nod which made her tear-stained face fairly grotesque.

"What do you mean lookin' that way?" demanded Andrew.

"Oh, you wait and see," said Fanny, with meaning, and would say no more. She was firm in her conclusion that Cynthia was educating their girl to marry her favorite nephew, but that never occurred to Andrew. He continued to feel, while supremely grateful and overwhelmed with delight at this good fortune for Ellen,

243

the distrust and resentment of a proud soul under obligation for which he sees no adequate reason, and especially when it is directed towards a beloved one to whom he would fain give of his own strength and treasure.

As for Ellen, she was in a tumult of wonder and delight, but when she looked at the doll in her corner there came again that vague sense of injury, and she felt again as if in some way she were being robbed instead of being made the object of benefit.

After Ellen had gone to bed that night she wondered if she ought to go to college, and maybe gain thereby a career which was beyond anything her own loved ones had known, and if it were not better for her to go to work in the shop after all.

CHAPTER XXII

WHEN Mrs. Zelotes was made acquainted with the plan for sending Ellen to Vassar she astonished Fanny. Fanny ran over the next morning, after Andrew had gone to work, to tell her mother-in-law. She sat a few minutes in the sitting-room, where the old lady was knitting, before she unfolded the burden of her errand.

"Cynthia Lennox came to our house last night with Robert Lloyd," she said, finally.

"Did they?" remarked Mrs. Zelotes, who had known perfectly well that they had come, having recognized the Lennox carriage in the moonlight, and having been ever since devoured with curiosity, which she would have died rather than betray.

"Yes, they did," said Fanny. Then she added, after a pause which gave wonderful impressiveness to the news, "Cynthia Lennox wants to send Ellen to college —to Vassar College."

Then she jumped, for the old woman seemed to spring at her like released wire.

"Send her to college!" said she. "What does she want to send her to college for? What right has Cynthia Lennox got to send Ellen Brewster anywhere?"

Fanny stared at her dazedly.

"What right has she got interfering?" demanded Mrs. Zelotes again.

"Why," replied Fanny, stammering, "she thought Ellen was so smart. She heard her valedictory, and the school-teacher had talked about her, what a good scholar she was, and she thought it would be nice for

245

her to go to college, and she should be very much obliged herself, and feel that we were granting her a great pleasure and privilege if we allowed her to send Ellen to Vassar."

All unconsciously Fanny imitated to the life Cynthia's soft elegance of speech and language.

"Pshaw!" said Mrs. Zelotes; but still she said it not so much angrily as doubtfully. "It's the first time I ever heard of Cynthia Lennox doing such a thing as that," said she. "I never knew she was given to sending girls to college. I never heard of her giving anything to anybody."

Fanny looked mysteriously at her mother-in-law with sudden confidence. "Look here," she said.

"What?"

The two women looked at each other, and neither said a word, but the meaning of one flashed to the other like telegraphy.

"Do you s'pose that's it?" said Mrs. Zelotes, her old face relaxing into half-shamed, half-pleased smiles.

"Yes, I do," said Fanny, emphatically.

"You do?"

"Yes, I 'ain't a doubt of it."

"He did act as if he couldn't take his eyes off her at the exhibition," agreed Mrs. Zelotes, reflectively; "mebbe you're right."

"I know I'm right just as well as if I'd seen it."

"Well, mebbe you are. What does Andrew say?"

"Oh, he wishes he was the one to do it."

"Of course he does—he's a Brewster," said his mother.

"But he's got sense enough to be pleased that Ellen has got the chance."

"He ain't any more pleased than I be at anything that's a good chance for Ellen," said the grandmother; but all the same, after Fanny had gone, her joy had a sharp sting for her. She was not one who could take a gift to her heart without feeling its sharp edge.

Had Ellen's sentiment been analyzed, she felt in something the same way that her grandmother did. However, she had begun to dream definitely about Robert, and the reflection had come, too, that this might make her more his equal, as nearly his equal as Maud Hemingway.

Maud Hemingway went to college, and so would she. Of the minor accessories of wealth she thought not so much. She looked at her hands, which were very small and as delicately white as flowers, and reflected with a sense of comfort, of which she was ashamed, that she would not need ever to stain them with leather now. She looked at the homeward stream of dingy girls from the shops, and thought with a sense of escape that she would never have to join them; but she was conscious of loving Abby better, and Maria, who had also entered Lloyd's. Abby, when she heard the news about Vassar, had looked at her with a sort of fierce exultation.

"Thank the Lord, you're out of it, anyhow!" she cried, fervently, as a soul might in the midst of flames.

Maria had smiled at her with the greatest sweetness and a certain wistfulness. Maria was growing delicate, and seemed to inherit her father's consumptive tendencies.

"I am so glad, Ellen," she said. Then she added, "I suppose we sha'n't see so much of you."

"Of course we sha'n't, Maria Atkins," interposed Abby, "and it won't be fitting we should. It won't be best for Ellen to associate with shop-girls when she's going to Vassar College."

But Ellen had cast an impetuous arm around a neck of each.

"If ever I do such a thing as that!" said she. "If

247

ever I turn a cold shoulder to either of you for such a reason as that! What's Vassar College to hearts? That's at the bottom of everything in this world, anyhow. I guess you'll see it won't make any difference unless you keep on thinking such things. If you do— if you think I can do anything like that—I won't love you so much."

Ellen faced them both with gathering indignation. Suddenly this ignoble conception of herself in the minds of her friends stung her to resentment. But Abby seized her in two wiry little arms.

"I never did, I never did!" she cried. "Don't I know what you are made of, Ellen Brewster? Don't you think I know? But after all, it might be better for you if you were worse. That was all I meant."

Ellen, one afternoon, set out in her pretty challis, a white ground with long sprays of blue flowers running over it, and a blue ribbon at her neck and waist, and her leghorn hat with white ribbons, and a knot of forget-me-nots under the brim. She wore her one pair of nice gloves, too, but those she did not put on until she reached the corner of the street where Cynthia lived. Then she rubbed them on carefully, holding up her challis skirts under one arm.

Cynthia was at home, seated on the back veranda, in a rattan chair, with a book which she was not reading. Ellen stood before her, in her cheap attire, which she wore with an air which seemed to make it precious, such faith she had in it. Ellen regarded her coarse blue-flowered challis with an innocent admiration which seemed almost able to glorify it into silk. Cynthia took in at a glance the exceeding commonness of it all; she saw the hat, the like of which could be seen in the milliners' windows at fabulously low prices; the foam of spurious lace and the spray of wretched blue flowers made her shudder. "The poor child, she must have

248

something better than that," she thought, and insensibly she also thought that the girl must lose her evident faith in the splendor of such attire; must change her standard of taste. She rose and greeted Ellen sweetly, though somewhat reservedly. When the two were seated opposite each other, Cynthia tried to talk pleasantly, but all the time with a sub-consciousness as one will have of some deformity which must be ignored. The girl looked so common to her in this array that she began to have a hopeless feeling of disgust about it all. Was it not manifestly unwise to try to elevate a girl who took such evident satisfaction in a gown like that, in a hat like that? Ellen wore her watch and chain ostentatiously. The watch was too large for a chatelaine, but she had looped the heavy chain across her bosom, and pinned it with the brooch which Abby Atkins had given her, so it hung suspended. Cynthia riveted her eyes helplessly upon that as she talked.

"I hope you are having a pleasant vacation," said she, as she looked at the watch, and all at once Ellen knew.

Ellen replied that she was having a very pleasant vacation, then she plunged at once into the subject of her call, though with inward trembling.

"Miss Lennox," said she—and she followed the lines of a little speech which she had been rehearsing to herself all the way there—"I am very grateful to you for what you propose doing for me. It will make a difference to me during my whole life. I cannot begin to tell you how grateful I am."

"I am very grateful to be allowed to do it," replied Cynthia, with her unfailing refrain of gentle politeness, but a kindly glance was in her eyes. Something in the girl's tone touched her. It was exceedingly earnest, with the simple earnestness of childhood. Moreover,

Ellen was regarding her with great, steadfast, serious eyes, like a baby's who shrinks and yet will have her will of information.

"I wanted to say," Ellen continued—and her voice became insensibly hushed, and she cast a glance around at the house and the leafy grounds, as if to be sure that no one was within hearing—"that I should never under any circumstances have said anything regarding what happened so long ago. That I never have and never should have, that I never thought of doing such a thing."

Then the elder woman's face flushed a burning red, and she knew at once what the girl had suspected. "You might proclaim it on the house-tops if it would please you," she cried out, vehemently. "If you think—if you think—"

"Oh, I do not!" cried Ellen, in an agony of pleading. "Indeed, I do not. It was only that—I—feared lest you might think I would be mean enough to tell."

"I would have told, myself, long ago if there had been only myself to consider," said Cynthia, still red with anger, and her voice strained. All at once she seemed to Ellen more like the woman of her childhood. "Yes, I would," said she, hotly—"I will now."

"Oh, I beg you not!" cried Ellen.

"I will go with you this minute and tell your mother," Cynthia said, rising.

Ellen sprang up and moved towards her as if to push her back in her chair. "Oh, please don't!" she cried. "Please don't. You don't know mother; and it would do no good. It was only because I wondered if you could have thought I would tell, if I would be so mean."

"And you thought, perhaps, I was bribing you not to tell, with Vassar College," Cynthia said, suddenly.

250

"Well, you have suspected me of something which was undeserved."

"I am very sorry," Ellen said. "I did not suspect, really, but I do not know why you do this for me." She said the last with her steady eyes of interrogation on Cynthia's face.

"You know the reasons I have given."

"I do not think they were the only ones," Ellen replied, stoutly. "I do not think my valedictory was so good as to warrant so much, and I do not think I am so smart as to warrant so much, either."

Cynthia laughed. She sat down again. "Well," she said, "you are not one to swallow praise greedily." Then her tone changed. "I owe it to you to tell you why I wish to do this," she said, "and I will. You are an honest girl, with yourself as well as with other people —too honest, perhaps, and you deserve that I should be honest with you. I am not doing this for you in the least, my dear."

Ellen stared at her.

"No, I am not," repeated Cynthia. "You are a very clever, smart girl, I am sure, and it will be a nice thing for you to have a better education, and be able to take a higher place in the world, but I am not doing it for you. When you were a little child I would have done everything, given my life almost, for you, but I never care so much for children when they grow up. I am not doing this for you, but for your mother."

"My mother?" said Ellen.

"Yes, your mother. I know what agony your mother must have been in, that time when I kept you, and I want to atone in some way. I think this is a good way. I don't think you need to hesitate about letting me do it. You also owe a little atonement to your mother. It was not right for you to run away, in the first place."

"Yes, I was very naughty to run away," Ellen said,

starting. She rose, and held out her hand. "I hope you will forgive me," she said. "I am very grateful, and it will make my father and mother happier than anything else could, but indeed I don't think—it is so long ago—that there was any need—"

"I do, for the sake of my own distress over it," Cynthia said, shortly. "Suppose, now, we drop the subject, my dear. There is a taint in the New England blood, and you have it, and you must fight it. It is a suspicion of the motives of a good deed which will often poison all the good effect from it. I don't know where the taint came from. Perhaps the Pilgrim Fathers', being necessarily always on the watch for the savage behind his gifts, have affected their descendants. Anyway, it is there. I suppose I have it."

"I am very sorry," said Ellen.

"I also am sorry," said Cynthia. "I did you a wrong, and your mother a wrong, years ago. I wonder at myself now, but you don't know the temptation. You will never know how you looked to me that night."

Cynthia's voice took on a tone of ineffable tenderness and yearning. Ellen saw again the old expression in her face; suddenly she looked as before, young and beautiful, and full of a boundless attraction. The girl's heart fairly leaped towards her with an impulse of affection. She could in that minute have fallen at her feet, have followed her to the end of the world. A great love and admiration which had gotten its full growth in a second under the magic of a look and a tone shook her from head to foot. She went close to Cynthia, and leaned over her, putting her round, young face down to the elder woman's. "Oh, I love you, I love you," whispered Ellen, with a fervor which was strange to her.

But Cynthia only kissed her lightly on her cheek,

and pushed her away softly. "Thank you, my dear," she said. "I am glad you came and spoke to me frankly, and I am glad we have come to an understanding."

Ellen, after she had taken her leave, was more in love than she had ever been in her life, and with another woman. She thought of Cynthia with adoration; she dreamed about her; the feeling of receiving a benefit from her hand became immeasurably sweet.

CHAPTER XXIII

ELLEN, under the influence of that old fascination which Cynthia had exerted over her temporarily in her childhood, and which had now assumed a new lease of life, would have loved to see her every day, but along with the fascination came a great timidity and fear of presuming. She felt instinctively that the fascination was an involuntary thing on Cynthia's part. She kept repeating to herself what she had said, that she was not sending her to Vassar because she loved her. Strangely enough, this did not make Ellen unhappy in the least, she was quite content to do all the loving and adoring herself. She made a sort of divinity of the older woman, and who expects a divinity to step down from her marble heights, and love and caress? Ellen began to remember all Cynthia's ways and looks, as a scholar remembers with a view to imitation. She became her disciple. She began to move like Cynthia, and to speak like her, though she did not know it. Her imitation was totally unconscious; indeed, it was hardly to be called imitation: it was rather the following out of the leading of that image of Cynthia which was always present before her mind. Ellen saw Cynthia very seldom. Once or twice she arrayed herself in her best and made a formal call of gratitude, and once Fanny went with her. Ellen saw the incongruity of her mother in Cynthia's drawing-room with a torture which she never forgot. Going home she clung hard to her mother's arm all the way. She was fairly fierce with love and loyalty. She was so indignant with herself

254

that she had seen the incongruity. "I think our parlor is enough sight prettier than hers," she said, defiantly, when they reached home and the hideous lamp was lighted. Ellen looked around the ornate room, and then at her mother, as with a challenge in behalf of loyalty, and of that which underlies externals.

"I rather guess it is," agreed Fanny, happily, "and I don't s'pose it cost half so much. I dare say that mat on her hearth cost as much as all our plush furniture and the carpet, and it is a dreadful dull, homely thing."

"Yes, it is," said Ellen.

"I wish I'd been able to keep my hands as white as Miss Lennox's, an' I wish I'd had time to speak so soft and slow," said Fanny, wistfully. Then Ellen had her by both shoulders, and was actually shaking her with a passion to which she very seldom gave rein.

' Mother," she cried—"mother, you know better, you know there is nobody in the whole world to me like my own mother, and never will be. It isn't being beautiful, nor speaking in a soft voice, nor dressing well, it's the being you—*you*. You know I love you best, mother, you know, and I love my own home best, and everything that is my own best, and I always will." Ellen was almost weeping.

"You silly child," said Fanny, tenderly. "Mother knows you love her best, but she wishes for your sake, and especially since you are going to have advantages that she never had, that she was a little different."

"I don't, I don't," said Ellen, fiercely. "I want you just as you are, just exactly as you are, mother."

Fanny laughed tearfully, and rubbed her coarse black head against Ellen's lovingly with a curious, cat-like motion, then bade her run away or she would not get her dress done. A dressmaker was coming for

255

a whole week to the Brewster house to make Ellen's outfit. Mrs. Zelotes had furnished most of the materials, and Andrew was to pay the dressmaker. "You can take a little more of that money out of the bank," Fanny said. "I want Ellen to go looking so she won't be ashamed before the other girls, and I don't want Cynthia Lennox thinking she ain't well enough dressed, and we ought to have let her do it. As for being beholden to her for Ellen's clothes, I won't."

"I rather guess not," said Andrew, but he was sick at heart. Only that afternoon the man from whom he had borrowed the money to buy Ellen's watch and chain had asked him for it. He had not a cent in advance for his weekly pay; he could not see where the money for Ellen's clothes was coming from. It was long since the "Golden Hope" had been quoted in the stock-list, but the next morning Andrew purchased a morning paper. He had stopped taking one regularly. He put on his spectacles, and spread out the paper in his shaking hands, and scrutinized the stock-list eagerly, but he could not find what he wanted. The "Golden Hope" had long since dropped to a still level below all record of fluctuations. A young man passing to his place at the bench looked over his shoulder. "Counting up your dividends, Brewster?" he asked, with a grin.

Andrew folded up the paper gloomily and made no reply.

"Irish dividends, maybe," said the man, with a chuckle at his own wit, and a backward roll of a facetious eye.

"Oh, shut up, you're too smart to live," said the man who stood next at the bench. He was a young fellow who had been a school-mate of Ellen in the grammar-school. He had left to go to work when she had entered the high-school. His name was Dixon. He was wiry and alert, with a restless sparkle of bright eyes

in a grimy face, and he cut the leather with lightning-
like rapidity. Dixon had always thought Ellen the
most beautiful girl in Rowe. He looked after Andrew
with a sharp pain of sympathy when he went away
with the roll of newspaper sticking out of his pocket.

"Poor old chap," he said to the facetious man, thrusting his face angrily towards him. "He has had a devil
of a time since he begun to grow old. You ought to
be ashamed of yourself. Wait till you begin to drop
behind. It's what's bound to come to the whole boiling
of us."

"Mind your jaw," said the first man, with a scowl.

"You'd better mind yours," said Dixon, slashing
furiously at the leather.

That noon Dixon offered Andrew, shamefacedly, taking him aside lest the other men see, a piece of pie
of a superior sort which his mother had put into his
dinner bag, but Andrew thanked him kindly and refused it. He could eat nothing whatever that noon.
He kept thinking about the dressmaker, and how Fanny
would ask him again to take some of that money out
of the bank to pay her, and how the money was already
taken out.

That evening, when he sat down to the tea-table
furnished with the best china and frosted cake in honor
of the dressmaker, and heard the radiant talk about
Ellen's new frills and tucks, he had a cold feeling at
his heart. He was ashamed to look at the dressmaker.

"You won't know your daughter when we get her
fixed up for Vassar," she told Andrew, with a smirk
which covered her face with a network of wrinkles
under her blond fluff of hair.

"Do have some more cake, Miss Higgins," said
Fanny. She was radiant. The image of her daughter
in her new gowns had gone far to recompense her for all
her disappointments in life, and they had not been few.

"What, after all, did it matter?" she asked herself, "if a woman was growing old, if she had to work hard, if she did not know where the next dollar was coming from, if all the direct personal savor was fast passing out of existence, when one had a daughter who looked like that?" Ellen, in a new blue dress, was ravishing. The mother looked at her when she was trying it on, with the possession of love, and the dressmaker as if she herself had created her.

After supper Ellen had to try on the dress again for her father, and turn about slowly that he might see all its fine points.

"There, what do you think of that, Andrew?" asked Fanny, triumphantly.

"Ain't she a lady?" asked the dressmaker.

"It is very pretty," said Andrew, smiling with gloomy eyes. Then he heaved a great sigh, and went out of the south door to the steps. "Your father is tired to-night," Fanny said to Ellen with a meaning of excuse for the dressmaker.

The dressmaker reflected shrewdly on Andrew's sigh when she was on her way home. "Men don't sigh that way unless there's money to pay," she thought. "I don't believe but he has been speculating." Then she wondered if there was any doubt about her getting her pay, and concluded that she would ask for it from day to day to make sure.

So the next night after tea she asked, with one of her smirks of amiability, if it would be convenient for Mrs. Brewster to pay her that night. "I wouldn't ask for it until the end of the week," said she, "but I have a bill to pay." She said "bill" with a murmur which carried conviction of its deception. Fanny flushed angrily. "Of course," said she, "Mr. Brewster can pay you just as well every night if you need it." Fanny emphasized the "need" maliciously. Then she turned to Andrew. "Andrew," said she, "Miss Higgins needs the money, if you can pay her for yesterday and to-day."

Andrew turned pale. "Yes, of course," he stammered. "How much?"

"Six dollars," said Fanny, and in her tone was unmistakable meaning of the dearness of the price. The dressmaker was flushed, but her thin mouth was set hard. It was as much as to say, "Well, I don't care so long as I get my money." She was unmarried, and her lonely condition had worked up her spirit into a strong attitude of defiance against all masculine odds. She had once considered men from a matrimonial point of view. She had wondered if this one and that one wanted to marry her. Now she was past that, and considered with equal sharpness if this one or that one wanted to cheat her. She had missed men's love through some failing either of theirs or hers. She did not know which, but she was determined that she would not lose money. So she bore Fanny's insulting emphasis with rigidity, and waited for her pay.

Andrew pulled out his old pocket-book, and counted the bills. Miss Higgins saw that he took every bill in it, unless there were some in another compartment, and of that she could not be quite sure. But Andrew knew. He would not have another penny until the next week when he received his pay. In the meantime there was a bill due at the grocery store, and one at the market, and there was the debt for Ellen's watch. However, he felt as if he would rather owe every man in Rowe than this one small, sharp woman. He felt the scorn lurking within her like a sting. She seemed to him like some venomous insect. He went out to the door-step again, and wondered if she would want her pay the next night when she went home.

CHAPTER XXIV

ELLEN had a flower-garden behind the house, and a row of sweet-peas which was her pride. It had occurred to her that she might venture, although Cynthia Lennox had her great garden and conservatories, to carry her a bunch of these sweet-peas. She had asked her mother what she thought about it. "Why, of course, carry her some if you want to," said Fanny. "I don't see why you shouldn't. I dare say she's got sweet-peas, but yours are uncommon handsome, and, anyway, it ought to please her to have some given her. It ain't altogether what's given, it's the giving."

So Ellen had cut a great bouquet of the delicate flowers, selecting the shades carefully, and set forth. She was as guiltily conscious as a lover that she was making an excuse to see Miss Lennox. She hurried along in delight and trepidation, her great bouquet shedding a penetrating fragrance around her, her face gleaming white out of the dusk. She had to pass Granville Joy's house on her way, and saw with some dismay, as she drew near, a figure leaning over the gate.

He pushed open the gate when she drew near, and stood waiting.

"Good - evening, Ellen," he said. He was mindful not to say "Hullo" again. He bowed with a piteous imitation of Robert Lloyd, but Ellen did not notice it.

"Good-evening," she returned, rather stiffly, then she added, in a very gentle voice, to make amends, that it was a beautiful night.

260

The young man cast an appreciative glance at the crescent moon in the jewel-like blue overhead, and at the soft shadows of the trees.

"Yes, beautiful," he replied, with a sort of gratitude, as if the girl had praised him instead of the night.

"May I walk along with you?" he asked, falling into step with her.

"I am going to take these sweet-peas to Miss Lennox," said Ellen, without replying directly.

She was in terror lest Granville should renew his appeal of a few weeks before, and she was in terror of her own pity for him, and also of that mysterious impulse and longing which sometimes seized her to her own wonder and discomfiture. Sometimes, in thinking of Granville Joy, and his avowal of love, and the touch of his hand on hers, and his lips on hers, she felt, although she knew she did not love him, a softening of her heart and a quickening of her pulse which made her wonder as to her next movement, if it might be something which she had not planned. And always, after thinking of Granville, she thought of Robert Lloyd; some mysterious sequence seemed to be established between the two in the girl's mind, though she was not in love with either.

Ellen was just at that period almost helpless before the demands of her own nature. No great stress in her life had occurred to awaken her to a stanchness either of resistance or yielding. She was in the full current of her own emotions, which, added to a goodly flood inherited from the repressed passion of New England ancestors, had a strong pull upon her feet. Sooner or later she would be given that hard shake of life which precipitates and organizes in all strong natures, but just now she was in a ferment. She walked along under the crescent moon, with the young man at her side whose every thought and imagination was dwelling upon her with love. She was conscious of a tendency of her own imagination in his direction, or rather in the direction of the love and passion which he represented, and all the time her heart was filled with the ideal image of another woman. She was prostrated with that hero-worship which belongs to young and virgin souls, and yet she felt the drawing of that other admiration which is more earthly and more fascinating, as it shows the jewel tints in one's own soul as well as in the other.

As for Granville Joy, who had scrubbed his hands and face well with scented soap to take away the odor of the leather, and put on a clean shirt and collar, being always prepared for the possibility of meeting this dainty young girl whom he loved, he walked along by her side, casting, from time to time, glances which were pure admiration at the face over the great bunch of sweet-peas.

"Don't you want me to carry them for you?" he asked.

"No, thank you," replied Ellen. "They are nothing to carry."

"They're real pretty flowers," said Granville, timidly.

"Yes, I think they are."

"Mother planted some, but hers didn't come up. Mother has got some beautiful nasturtiums. Perhaps you would like some," he said, eagerly.

"No, thank you, I have some myself," Ellen said, rather coldly. "I'm just as much obliged to you."

Granville quivered a little and shrank as a dog might under a blow. He saw this dainty girl-shape floating along at his side in a flutter of wonderful draperies, one hand holding up her skirts with maddening revelations of whiteness. If a lily could hold up her petals out of the dust she might do it in the same fashion as

262

Ellen held her skirts, with no coarse clutching nor crumpling, not immodestly, but rather with disclosures of modesty itself. Ellen's wonderful daintiness was one of her chief charms. There was an immaculateness about her attire and her every motion which seemed to extend to her very soul, and hedged her about with the lure of unapproachableness. It was more that than her beauty which roused the imagination and quickened the pulses of a young man regarding her.

Granville Joy did not feel the earth beneath his feet as he walked with Ellen. The scent of the sweet-peas came in his face, he heard the soft rustle of Ellen's skirts and his own heart-beats. She was very silent, since she did not wish him to go with her, though she was all the time reproaching herself for it. Granville kept casting about for something to say which should ingratiate him with her. He was resolved to say nothing of love to her.

"It is a beautiful night," he said.

"Yes, it is," agreed Ellen, and she looked at the moon. She felt the boy's burning, timid, worshipful eyes on her face. She trembled, and yet she was angry and annoyed. She felt in an undefined fashion that she herself was the summer night and the flowers and the crescent moon, and all that was fair and beautiful in the whole world to this other soul, and shame seized her instead of pride. He seemed to force her to a sight of her own pettiness, as is always the case when love is not fully returned. She made an impatient motion with the shoulder next Granville, and walked faster.

"You said you were going to Miss Lennox's," he remarked, anxiously, feeling that in some way he had displeased her.

"Yes, to carry her some sweet-peas."

"She must have been real good-looking when she was young," Granville said, injudiciously.

"When she was young," retorted Ellen, angrily. "She is beautiful now. There is not another woman in Rowe as beautiful as she is."

"Well, she is good-looking enough," agreed Granville, with unreasoning jealousy. He had not heard of Ellen's good fortune. His mother had not told him. She was a tenderly sentimental woman, and had always had her fancies with regard to her son and Ellen Brewster. When she heard the news she reflected that it would perhaps remove the girl from her boy immeasurably, that he would be pained, so she said nothing. Every night when he came home she had watched his face to see if he had heard.

Now Ellen told him. "You know what Miss Cynthia Lennox is going to do for me," she said, abruptly, almost boastfully, she was so eager in her partisanship of Cynthia.

Granville looked at her blankly. They were coming into the crowded, brilliantly lighted main street of the city, and their two faces were quite plain to each other's eyes.

"No, I don't," said he. "What is it, Ellen?"

"She is going to send me to Vassar College."

Granville's face whitened perceptibly. There was a queer sound in his throat.

"To Vassar College!" he repeated.

"Yes, to Vassar College. Then I shall be able to get a good school, and teach, and help father and mother."

Granville continued to look at her, and suddenly an intense pity sprang into life in the girl's heart. She felt as if she were looking at some poor little child, instead of a stalwart young man.

"Don't look so, Granville," she said, softly.

"Of course I am glad at any good fortune which can come to you, Ellen," Granville said then, huskily. His lips quivered a little, but his eyes on her face were

264

brave and faithful. Suddenly Ellen seemed to see in this young man a counterpart of her own father. Granville had a fine, high forehead and contemplative outlook. He had been a good scholar. Many said that it was a pity he had to leave school and go to work. It had been the same with her father. Andrew had always looked immeasurably above his labor. She seemed to see Granville Joy in the future just such a man, a finer animal harnessed to the task of a lower, and harnessed in part by his own loving faithfulness towards others. Ellen had often reflected that, if it hadn't been for her and her mother, her father would not have been obliged to work so hard. Now in Granville she saw another man whom love would hold to the ploughshare. A great impulse of loyalty as towards her own came over her.

"It won't make any difference between me and my old friends if I do go to Vassar College," she said, without reflecting on the dangerous encouragement of it.

"You can't get into another track of life without its making a difference," returned Granville, soberly. "But I am glad. God knows I'm glad, Ellen. I dare say it is better for you than if—" He stopped then and seemed all at once to see projected on his mirror of the future this dainty, exquisite girl, with her fine intellect, dragging about a poor house, with wailing children in arm and at heel, and suddenly a great courage of renunciation came over him.

"It *is* better, Ellen," he said, in a loud voice, like a hero's, as if he were cheering his own better impulses on to victory over his own passions. "It is better for a girl like you, than to—"

Ellen knew that he meant to say, "to marry a fellow like me." Ellen looked at him, the sturdy backward fling of his head and shoulders, and the honest regard of his pained yet unflinching eyes, and a great weakness of natural longing for that which she was even now deprecating nearly overswept her. She was nearer loving him that moment than ever before. She realized something in him which could command love—the renunciation of love for love's sake.

"I shall never forget my old friends, whatever happens," she said, in a trembling voice, and it might have all been different had they not then arrived at Cynthia Lennox's.

"Shall I wait and go home with you, Ellen?" Granville asked, timidly.

"No, thank you. I don't know how long I shall stay," Ellen replied. "You are real kind, but I am not a bit afraid."

"It is sort of lonesome going past the shops."

"I can take a car," Ellen said. She extended her hand to Granville, and he grasped it firmly.

"Good-night, Ellen; I am always glad of any good fortune that may come to you," he said.

But Granville Joy, going alone down the brilliant street, past the blaze of the shop-windows and the knots of loungers on the corners, reflected that he had seen the fiery tip of a cigar on the Lennox veranda, that it might be possible that young Lloyd was there, since Miss Lennox was his aunt, and that possibly the aunt's sending Ellen to Vassar might bring about something in that quarter which would not otherwise have happened, and he writhed at the fancy of that sort of good fortune for Ellen, but held his mind to it resolutely as to some terrible but necessary grindstone for the refinement of spirit. "It would be a heap better for her," he said to himself, quite loud, and two men whom he was passing looked at him curiously. "Drunk," said one to the other.

When he was on his homeward way he overtook a slender girl struggling along with a kerosene-can in one hand and a package of sugar in the other, and, seeing that it was Abby Atkins, he possessed himself of both. She only laughed and did not start. Abby Atkins was not of the jumping or screaming kind, her nerves were so finely balanced that they recovered their equilibrium, after surprises, before she had time for manifestations. There was a curious healthfulness about the slender, wiry little creature who was overworked and under-fed, a healthfulness which seemed to result from the action of the mind upon a meagre body.

"Hullo, Granville Joy!" she said, in her good-comrade fashion, and the two went on together. Presently Abby looked up in his face.

"Know about Ellen?" said she. Granville nodded.

"Well, I'm glad of it, aren't you?" Abby said, in a challenging tone.

"Yes, I am," replied Granville, meeting her look firmly.

Suddenly he felt Abby's little, meagre, bony hand close over the back of his, holding the kerosene-can. "You're a good fellow, Granville Joy," said she.

Granville marched on and made no response. He felt his throat fill with sobs, and swallowed convulsively. Along with this womanly compassion came a compassion for himself, so hurt on his little field of battle. He saw his own wounds as one might see a stranger's.

"Think of Ellen dogging around to a shoe-shop like me and the other girls," said Abby, "and think of her draggin' around with half a dozen children and no money. Thank the Lord she's lifted out of it. It ain't you nor me that ought to grudge her fortune to her, nor wish her where she might have been otherwise."

"That's so," said the young man.

Abby's hand tightened over the one on the kerosene-can. "You are a good fellow, Granville Joy," she said again.

CHAPTER XXV

ROBERT LLOYD was sitting on the veranda behind the green trail of vines when Ellen came up the walk. He never forgot the girl's face looking over her bunch of sweet-peas. There was in it something indescribably youthful and innocent, almost angelic. The light from the window made her hair toss into gold; her blue eyes sought Cynthia with the singleness of blue stars. It was evident whom she had come to see. She held out her flowers towards her with a gesture at once humble and worshipful, like that of some devotee at a shrine.

She said "Good-evening" with a shy comprehensiveness, then, to Cynthia, like a child, "I thought maybe you would like some of my sweet-peas."

Both gentlemen rose, and Risley looked curiously from the young girl to Cynthia, then placed his chair for her, smiling kindly.

"The sweet-peas are lovely," Cynthia said. "Thank you, my dear. They are much prettier than any I have had in my garden this year. Please sit down," for Ellen was doubtful about availing herself of the proffered chair. She had so hoped that she might find Cynthia alone. She had dreamed, as a lover might have done, of a tête-à-tête with her, what she would say, what Cynthia would say. She had thought, and trembled at the thought, that possibly Cynthia might kiss her when she came or went. She had felt, with a thrill of spirit, the touch of Cynthia's soft lips on hers, she had smelt the violets about her clothes. Now it was all spoiled. She remembered

268

things which she had heard about Mr. Risley's friendship with Cynthia, how he had danced attendance upon
her for half a lifetime, and thought that she did not
like him. She looked at his smiling, grizzled, blond
face with distrust. She felt intuitively that he saw
straight through her little subterfuge of the flowers,
that he divined her girlish worship at the shrine of Cynthia, and was making fun of her.

"Do you object to a cigar, Miss Brewster?" asked
Robert, and Risley looked inquiringly at her.

"Oh, no," replied Ellen, with the eager readiness
of a child to fit into new conditions. She thought of
the sitting-room at home, blue with the rank pipe-smoke
of Nahum Beals and his kind. She pictured them to
herself sitting about on these warm evenings in their
shirt-sleeves, and she saw the two gentlemen in their
light summer clothes with their fragrant cigars at
their lips, and all of a sudden she realized that between
these men and the others there was a great gulf, and
that she was trying to cross it. She did not realize, as
later, that the gulf was one of externals, and of width
rather than depth, but it seemed to her then that from
one shore she could only see dimly the opposite. A
great fear and jealousy came over her as to her own
future accessibility to those of the other kind among
whom she had been brought up, like her father and
Granville.

Ellen felt all this as she sat beside Cynthia, who
was casting about in her mind, in rather an annoyed
fashion, for something to say to this young beneficiary
of hers which should not have anything to do with the
benefit.

Finally she inquired if she were having a pleasant
vacation, and Ellen replied that she was. Risley looked
at her beautiful face with the double radiance of the
electric-light and the lamp-light from the window on

it, giving it a curious effect. It suddenly occurred to him to wonder why everybody seemed to have such an opinion as to the talents of this girl. Why did Cynthia consider that her native ability warranted this forcible elevation of her from her own sphere and setting her on a height of education above her kind? She looked and spoke like an ordinary young girl. She had a beautiful face, it is true, and her shyness seemed due to the questioning attitude of a child rather than to self-consciousness, but, after all, why did she give people that impression? Her valedictory had been clever, no doubt, and there was in it a certain fire of conviction, which, though crude, was moving; but, after all, almost any bright girl might have written it. She had been a fine scholar, no doubt, but any girl with a ready intelligence might have done as well. Whence came this inclination of all to rear the child upon a pedestal? Risley wondered, looking at her, narrowing his keen, light eyes under reflective brows, puffing at his cigar; then he admitted to himself that he was one with the crowd of Ellen's admirers. There was somehow about the girl that which gave the impression of an enormous reserve out of all proportion to any external evidence. "The child says nothing remarkable," he told Cynthia, after she had gone that evening, "but somehow she gives me an impression of power to say something extraordinary, and do something extraordinary. There is electricity and steel behind that soft, rosy flesh of hers. But all she does which is evident to the eye of man is to worship you, Cynthia."

"Worship me?" repeated Cynthia, vaguely.

"Yes, she has one of those aberrations common to her youth and her sex. She is repeating a madness of old Greece, and following you as a nymph might a goddess."

"It is only because she is grateful," returned Cynthia, looking rather annoyed.

"Gratitude may be a factor in it, but it is very far from being the whole of the matter. It is one of the spring madnesses of life; but don't be alarmed, it will be temporary in the case of a girl like that. She will easily be led into her natural track of love. Do you know, Cynthia, that she is one of the most normal, typical young girls I ever saw, and that makes me wonder more at this impression of unusual ability which she undoubtedly gives. She has all the weaknesses of her age and sex, she is much younger than some girls of her age, and yet there is the impression which I cannot shake off."

"I have it, too," said Cynthia, rather impatiently.

"Cynthia Lennox, I don't believe you care in the least for this young devotee of yours, for all you are heaping benefits upon her," Risley said, looking at her quizzically.

"I am not sure that I do," replied Cynthia, calmly.

"Then why on earth—?"

Suddenly Cynthia began speaking rapidly and passionately, straightening herself in her chair. "Oh, Lyman, do you think I could do a thing like that, and not repent it and suffer remorse for it all these years?" she cried.

"A thing like that?"

"Like stealing that child," Cynthia replied, in a whisper.

"Stealing the child? You did not steal the child."

"Yes, I did."

"Why, it was only a few hours that you kept her."

"What difference does it make whether you steal anything for a few hours or a lifetime? I kept her, and she was crying for her mother, and her mother was suffering tortures all that time. Then I kept it secret

271

all these years. You didn't know what I have suffered, Lyman."

Cynthia regarded him with a wan look.

Risley half laughed, then checked himself. "My poor girl, you have the New England conscience in its worst form," he said.

"You yourself told me it was a serious thing I was doing," Cynthia said, half resentfully. "One does not wish one's sin treated lightly when one has hugged its pricks to one's bosom for so long—it detracts from the dignity of suffering."

"So I did, but all those years ago!"

"If you don't leave me my remorse, how can I atone for the deed?"

"Cynthia, you are horribly morbid."

"Maybe you are right, maybe it is worse than morbid. Sometimes I think I am unnatural, out of drawing, but I did not make myself, and how can I help it?" Cynthia spoke with a pathetic little laugh.

She leaned her head back in her chair, and looked at a star through a gap in the vines. The shadows of the leaves played over her long, white figure. Again to Risley, gazing at her, came the conviction as of subtle spiritual deformity in the woman; she was unnatural in something the same fashion that an orchid is unnatural, and it was worse, because presumably the orchid does not know it is an orchid and regret not being another, more evenly developed, flower, and Cynthia had a full realization and a mental mirror clear enough to see the twist in her own character.

Risley had never kissed her in his life, but that night, when they parted, he laid a hand on her soft, gray hair, and smoothed it back with a masculine motion of tenderness, leaving her white forehead, which had a candid, childish fulness about the temples, bare. Then he put his lips to it.

"You are a silly girl, Cynthia," he said.

"I wish I were different, Lyman," she responded. and, he felt, with a double meaning.

"I don't," he said, and stroked her hair with a great tenderness, which seemed for the time to quite fill and satisfy his heart. He was a man of measureless patience, born to a firm conviction of the journey's end.

"There are worse things than loving a good woman your whole life and never having her," he said to himself as he went home, but he said it without its full meaning. Risley's "nerves" were always lighted by the lamp of his own hope, which threw a gleam over unknown seas.

8

CHAPTER XXVI

ROBERT LLOYD accompanied Ellen home, though she had said timidly that she was not in the least afraid, that she would not trouble any one, that she could take a car. Cynthia herself had insisted that Robert should escort her.

"It's too late for you to be out alone," she said, and the girl seemed to perceive dimly a hedge of conventionality which she had not hitherto known. She had often taken a car when she was alone of an evening, without a thought of anything questionable. Some of the conductors lived near Ellen, and she felt as if she were under personal friendly escort. "I know the conductor on that car, and it would take me right home, and I am not in the least afraid," she said to Robert, as the car came rocking down the street when they emerged from Cynthia's grounds.

"It's a lovely night," Robert said, speaking quickly as they paused on the sidewalk. "I am not going to let you go alone, anyway. We will take the car if you say so, but what do you say to walking? It's a lovely night."

It actually flashed through Ellen's mind—to such small issues of finance had she been accustomed—that the young man might insist upon paying her car-fare if he went with her on the car.

"I would like to walk, but I am sorry to put you to so much trouble," she said, a little awkwardly.

"Oh, I like to walk," returned Robert. "I don't walk half enough," and they went together down the

274

lighted street. Suddenly to Ellen there came a vivid remembrance, so vivid that it seemed almost like actual repetition of the time when she, a little child, maddened by the sudden awakening of the depths of her nature, had come down this same street. She saw that same brilliant market-window where she had stopped and stared, to the momentary forgetfulness of her troubles in the spectacular display of that which was entirely outside them. Curiously enough, Robert drew her to a full stop that night before the same window. It was one of those strange cases of apparent telepathy which one sometimes notices. When Ellen looked at the market-window, with a flash of reminiscence, Robert immediately drew her to a stop before it. "That is quite a study in color," he said. "I fancy there are a good many unrecognized artists among market-men."

"Yes, it is really beautiful," agreed Ellen, looking at it with eyes which had changed very little from their childish outlook. Again she saw more than she saw. The window differed materially from that before which she had stood fascinated so many years ago, for that was in a different season. Instead of frozen game and winter vegetables, were the products of summer gardens, and fruits, and berries. The color scheme was dazzling with great heaps of tomatoes, and long, emerald ears of corn, and baskets of apples, and gold crooks of summer squashes, and speckled pods of beans.

"Suppose," said Robert, as they walked on, "that all the market-men who had artistic tastes had art educations and set up studios and painted pictures, who would keep the markets?"

He spoke gayly. His manner that night was younger and merrier than Ellen had ever seen it. She was naturally rather grave herself. What she had seen of life had rather disposed her to a hush of respect than to hilarity, but somehow his mood began to infect her.

275

"I don't know," she answered, laughing, "I suppose somebody would keep the markets."

"Yes, but they would not be as good markets. That is, they would not do as artistic markets, and they would not serve the higher purpose of catering to the artistic taste of man, as well as to his bodily needs."

"Perhaps a picture like that is just as well and better than it would be painted and hung on a wall," Ellen admitted, reflectively.

"Just so—why is it not?" Robert said, in a pleased voice.

"Yes, I think it is," said Ellen. "I do think it is better, because everybody can see it there. Ever so many people will see it there who would not go to picture-galleries to see it, and then—"

"And then it may go far to dignify their daily needs," said Robert. "For instance, a poor man about to buy his to-morrow's dinner may feel his soul take a little fly above the prices of turnips and cabbages."

"Maybe," said Ellen, but doubtfully.

"Don't you think so?"

"The prices of turnips and cabbages may crowd other things out," Ellen replied, and her tone was sad, almost tragic. "You see I am right in it, Mr. Lloyd," she said, earnestly.

"You mean right in the midst of the kind of people whom necessity forces to neglect the æsthetic for the purely useful?"

"Yes," said Ellen. Then she added, in an indescribably pathetic voice, "People have to live first before they can see, and they can't think until they are fed, and one needs always to have had enough turnips and cabbages to eat without troubling about the getting them, in order to see in them anything except food."

Lloyd looked at her curiously. "Decidedly this

276

child can think," he reflected. He shrugged his arm, on which Ellen's hand lay, a little closer to his side.

Just then they were passing the great factories—Lloyd's, and Briggs's, and Maguire's. Many of the windows in Briggs's and Maguire's reflected light from the moon and the electric-lamps on the street. Lloyd's was all dark except for one brilliant spark of light, which seemed to be threading the building like a will-. o'-the-wisp. "That is the night-watchman," said Robert. "He must have a dull time of it."

"I should think he might be afraid," said Ellen.

"Afraid of what?"

"Of ghosts."

"Ghosts in a shoe-shop?" asked Robert, laughing.

"I don't believe there has been another building in the whole city which has held so many heart-aches, and I always wondered if they didn't make ghosts instead of dead people," Ellen said.

"Do you think they have such a hard time?"

"I know they do," said Ellen. "I think I ate the knowledge along with my first daily bread."

Robert Lloyd looked down at the light, girlish figure on his arm, and again the resolution that he would not talk on such topics with a young girl like this came over him. He felt a reluctance to do so which was quite apart from his masculine scorn of a girl's opinion on such matters. Somehow he did not wish to place Ellen Brewster on the same level of argument on which another man might have stood. He felt a jealousy of doing so. She seemed more within his reach, and infinitely more for his pleasure, where she was. He looked admiringly down at her fair face fixed on his with a serious, intent expression. He was quite ready to admit that he might fall in love with her. He was quite ready to ask now why he should not. She was a beautiful girl, an uncommon girl. She was going to be

277

thoroughly educated. It would probably be quite possible to divorce her entirely from her surroundings. He shuddered when he thought of her mother and aunt, but, after all, a man, if he were firm, need not marry the mother or aunt. And all this was in spite of a resolution which he had formed on due consideration after his last call upon Ellen. He had said to himself that it would not in any case be wise, that he had better not see more of her than he could help. Instead of going to see her, he had gone riding with Maud Hemingway, who lived near his uncle's, in an old Colonial house which had belonged to her great-grandfather. The girl was a good comrade, so good a comrade that she shunted, as it were, love with flings of ready speech and friendly greeting, and tennis-rackets and riding-whips and foils. Robert had been teaching Maud to fence, and she had fenced too well. Still, Robert had said to himself that he might some day fall in love with her and marry her. He charged his memory with the fact that this was a much more rational course than visiting a girl like Ellen Brewster, so he stayed away in spite of involuntary turnings of his thoughts in that direction. However, now when the opportunity had seemed to be fairly forced upon him, what was he to do? He felt that he was stirred as he had never been before. The girl's very soul seemed to meet his when she looked up at him with those serious blue eyes of hers. He knew that there had never been any like her for him, but he felt as if in another minute, if they did not drop topics which he might as well have discussed with another man, this butterfly of femininity which so delighted him would be beyond his hand. He wanted to keep her to her rose.

"But the knowledge must not imbitter your life," he said. "It is not for a little, delicate girl to worry herself over the problems which are too much for men."

In spite of himself a tenderness had come into his voice. Ellen looked down and away from him. She trembled.

"It seems to me that the problems of life, like those in the algebra we studied at school, are for everybody who can read them, whether men or women," said she, but her voice was unsteady.

"Some of them are for men to read and struggle with for the sake of the women," said Robert. His voice had a tender inflection. They were passing a garden full of old-fashioned flowers, bordered with box. The scent of the box seemed fairly to clamor over the garden fence, drowning out the smaller fragrances of the flowers, like the clamor of a mob. Even the sweetness of the mignonette was faintly perceived.

"How strong the box is," said Ellen, imperceptibly shrinking a little from Robert.

When they reached the Brewster house Robert said, as kindly as Granville Joy might have done, "Cannot we get better acquainted, Miss Brewster? May I call upon you sometimes?"

"I shall be happy to see you," Ellen said, repeating the formula of welcome like a child, but she knew when she repeated it that it was very true. After she had parted from young Lloyd, she went into the sitting-room where were her mother and father, her mother sewing on a wrapper, her father reading the paper. Both of them looked up as the girl entered, and both stared at her in a bewildered way without rightly knowing why. Ellen's cheeks were a wonderful color, her eyes fairly blazed with blue light, her mouth was smiling in that ineffable smile of a simple overflow of happiness.

"Did you ride home on the car?" asked Fanny. "I didn't hear it stop."

"No, mother."

"Did you come home alone?" asked Andrew, abruptly.

"No," said Ellen, blinking before the glare of the lamp. Fanny looked at Andrew. "Who did come home with you?" she asked, in a foolish, fond voice.

"Mr. Robert Lloyd. He was sitting on the piazza when I got there. I told Miss Lennox I had just as soon come on the cars alone, but she wouldn't let me, and then he said it would be pleasant to walk, and—"

"Oh, you needn't make so many excuses," said Fanny, laughing.

Ellen colored until her face was a blaze of roses, she blinked harder, and turned her head away impatiently.

"I am not making excuses," said she, as if her modesty were offended. "I wish you wouldn't talk so, mother. I couldn't help it."

"Of course you couldn't," her mother called out jocularly, as Ellen went into the other room to get her lamp to go to bed.

Fanny was radiant with delight. After Ellen had gone up-stairs, she kept looking at Andrew, and longing to confide in him her anticipation with regard to Ellen and young Lloyd, but she refrained, being doubtful as to how he would take it. Andrew looked very sober. The girl's beautiful, metamorphosed face was ever before his eyes, and it was with him as if he were looking after the flight of a beloved bird into a farther blue which was sacred, even from the following of his love.

CHAPTER XXVII

ELLEN'S first impulse, when she really began to love Robert Lloyd, was not yielding, but flight; her first sensation, not happiness, but shame. When he left her that night she realized, to her unspeakable dismay and anger, that he had not left her, that he would never in her whole life, or at least it seemed so, leave her again. Everywhere she looked she saw his face projected by her memory before her with all the reality of life. His face came between her and her mother's and father's, it came between her and her thoughts of other faces. When she was alone in her chamber, there was the face. She blew out the lamp in a panic of resentment and undressed in the dark, but that made no difference. When she lay in bed, although she closed her eyes resolutely, she could still see it.

"I won't have it; I won't have it," she said, quite aloud in her shame and rebellion. "I won't have it. What does this mean?"

In spite of herself the sound of his voice was in her ears, and she resented that; she fought against the feeling of utter rapture which came stealing over her because of it. She felt as if she wanted to spring out of bed and run, run far away into the freedom of the night, if only by so doing she could outspeed herself. Ellen began to realize the tyranny of her own nature, and her whole soul arose in revolt.

But the girl could no more escape than a nymph of old the pursuit of the god, and there was no friendly deity to transform her into a flower to elude him. When

281

she slept at last she was overtaken in the innocent passion of dreams, and when she awoke it was, to her
angry sensitiveness, not alone.

When she went down-stairs all her rosy radiance of
the night before was eclipsed. She looked pale and
nervous. She recoiled whenever her mother began to
speak. It seemed to her that if she said anything,
and especially anything congratulatory about Robert
Lloyd, she would fly at her like a wild thing. Fanny
kept looking at her with loving facetiousness, and Ellen
winced indescribably; still, she did not say anything
until after breakfast, when Andrew had gone to work.
Andrew was unusually sober and preoccupied that
morning. When he went out he passed close to Ellen,
as she sat at the table, and tilted up her face and
kissed her. "Father's blessin'," he whispered, hoarsely, in her ear. Ellen nestled against him. This natural
affection, before which she need not fly nor be ashamed,
which she had always known, seemed to come before
her like a shield against all untried passion. She felt
sheltered and comforted. But Andrew passed Eva
Tenny coming to the house on his way out of the yard,
and when she entered Fanny began at once:

"Who do you s'pose came home with Ellen last
night?" said she. She looked at Eva, then at Ellen,
with a glance which seemed to uncover a raw surface
of delicacy. Ellen flushed angrily.

"Mother, I do wish—" she began; but Fanny cut
her short.

"She's pretendin' she don't like it," she said, almost
hilariously, her face glowing with triumph, "but she
does. You ought to have seen her when she came in
last night."

"I guess I know who it was," said Eva, but she echoed
her sister's manner half-heartedly. She was looking
very badly that morning, her face was stained, and

her eye hard with a look as if tears had frozen in them. She had come in a soiled waist, too, without any collar.

"For Heaven's sake, Eva Tenny, what ails you?" Fanny cried.

Eva flung herself for answer on the floor, and fairly writhed. Words were not enough expression for her violent temperament. She had to resort to physical manifestations or lose her reason. As she writhed, she groaned as one might do who was dying in extremity of pain.

Ellen, when she heard her aunt's groans, stopped, and stood in the entry viewing it all. She thought at first that her aunt was ill, and was just about to call out to know if she should go for the doctor, all her grievances being forgotten in this evidently worse stress, when her mother fairly screamed again, stooping over her sister, and trying to raise her.

"Eva Tenny, you tell me this minute what the matter is."

Then Eva raised herself on one elbow, and disclosed a face distorted with wrath and woe, like a mask of tragedy.

"He's gone! he's gone!" she shrieked out, in an awful, shrill voice, which was like the note of an angry bird. "He's gone!"

"For God's sake, not—Jim?"

"Yes, he's gone! he's gone! Oh, my God! my God! he's gone!"

All at once the little Amabel appeared, slipping past Ellen silently. She stood watching her mother. She was vibrating from head to foot as if strung on wires. She was not crying, but she kept catching her breath audibly; her little hands were twitching in the folds of her frock; she winked rapidly, her lids obscuring and revealing her eyes until they seemed a series of blue sparks. She was no paler than usual—that was scarcely possible—but her skin looked transparent, pulses were evident all over her face and her little neck.

"You don't mean he's gone with—?" gasped Fanny.

Suddenly Eva raised herself with a convulsive jerk from the floor to her feet. She stood quite still. "Yes, he has gone," she said, and all the passion was gone from her voice, which was much more terrible in its calm.

"You don't mean with—?"

"Yes; he has gone with Aggie." Eva spoke in a voice like a deaf-mute's, quite free from inflections. There was something dreadful about her rigid attitude. Little Amabel looked at her mother's eyes, then cowered down and began to cry aloud. Ellen came in and took her in her arms, whispering to her to soothe her. She tried to coax her away, but the child resisted violently, though she was usually so docile with Ellen.

Eva did not seem to notice Amabel's crying. She stood in that horrible inflexibility, with eyes like black stones fixed on something unseeable.

Fanny clutched her violently by the arm and shook her.

"Eva Tenny," said she, "you behave yourself. What if he has run away? You ain't the first woman whose husband has run away. I'd have more pride. I wouldn't please him nor her enough. If he's as bad as that, you're better off rid of him."

Eva turned on her sister, and her calm broke up like ice under her fire of passion.

"Don't you say one word against him, not one word!" she shrieked, throwing off Fanny's hand. "I won't hear one word against my husband."

Then little Amabel joined in. "Don't you say one word against my papa!" she cried, in her shrill, childish treble. Then she sobbed convulsively, and pushed Ellen away. "Go away!" she said, viciously, to her. She was half mad with terror and bewilderment.

"Don't you say one word against Jim," said Eva again. "If ever I hear anybody say one word against him I'll—"

"You don't mean you're goin' to stan' up for him, Eva Tenny?"

"As long as I draw the breath of life, and after, if I know anything," declared Eva. Then she straightened herself to her full height, threw back her shoulders, and burst into a furious denunciation like some prophetess of wrath. The veins on her forehead grew turgid, her lips seemed to swell, her hair seemed to move as she talked. The others shrank back and looked at her; even little Amabel hushed her sobs and stared, fascinated. "Curses on the grinding tyranny that's brought it all about, and not on the poor, weak man that fell under it!" she cried. "Jim ain't to blame. He's had bigger burdens put on his shoulders than the Lord gave him strength to bear. He had to drop 'em. Jim has tried faithful ever since we were married. He worked hard, and it wa'n't never his fault that he lost his place, but he kept losin' it. They kept shuttin' down, or dischargin' him for no reason at all, without a minute's warnin'. An' it wa'n't because he drank. Jim never drank when he had a job. He was just taken up and put down by them over him as if he was a piece on a checker-board. He lost his good opinion of himself when he saw others didn't set any more by him than to shove him off or on the board as it suited their play. He began to think maybe he wa'n't a man, and then he began to act as if he wasn't a man. And he was ashamed of his life because he couldn't support me and Amabel, ashamed of his life because he had to live on my little earnin's. He was ashamed to look me in the face, and ashamed to look his own child in the face. It was only night before last he was talkin' to me, and I didn't know what he meant then, but I know

now. I thought then he meant something else, but now I know what he meant. He sat a long time leanin' his head on his hands, whilst I was sewin' on wrappers, after Amabel had gone to bed, and finally he looks up and says, 'Eva, you was right and I was wrong.'

"'What do you mean, Jim?' says I.

"'I mean you was right when you thought we'd better not get married, and I was wrong,' says he; and he spoke terrible bitter and sad. I never heard him speak like it. He sounded like another man. I jest flung down my sewin' and went over to him, and leaned his poor head against my shoulder. 'Jim,' says I, 'I 'ain't never regretted it.' And God knows I spoke the truth, and I speak the truth when I say it now. I 'ain't never regretted it, and I don't regret it now." Eva said the last with a look as if she were hurling defiance, then she went on in the same high, monotonous key above the ordinary key of life. "When I says that, he jest gives a great sigh and sort of pushes me away and gets up. 'Well, I have,' says he; 'I have, and sometimes I think the best thing I can do is to take myself out of the way, instead of sittin' here day after day and seein' you wearin' your fingers to the bone to support me, and seein' my child, an' bein' ashamed to look her in the face. Sometimes I think you an' Amabel would be a damned sight better off without me than with me, and I'm done for anyway, and it don't make much difference what I do next.'

"'Jim Tenny, you jest quit talkin' in such a way as this,' says I, for I thought he meant to make away with himself, but that wa'n't what he meant. Aggie Bemis had been windin' her net round him, and he wa'n't nothin' but a man, and all discouraged, and he gave in. Any man would in his place. He ain't to blame. It's the tyrants that's over us all that's to blame." Eva's voice shrilled higher. "Curse them!" she shrieked. "Curse them all!—every rich man in this gold-ridden country!"

"Eva Tenny, you're beside yourself," said Fanny, who was herself white to her lips, yet she viewed her sister indignantly, as one violent nature will view another when it is overborne and carried away by a kindred passion.

"Wonder if you'd be real calm in my place?" said Eva; and as she spoke the dreadful impassibility of desperation returned upon her. It was as if she suffered some chemical change before their eyes. She became silent and seemed as if she would never speak again.

"You hadn't ought to talk so," said Fanny, weakly, she was so terrified. "You ought to think of poor little Amabel," she added.

With that, Eva's dreadful, expressionless eyes turned towards Amabel, and she held out her hand to her, but the child fairly screamed with terror and clung to Ellen. "Oh, Aunt Eva, don't look at her so, you frighten her," Ellen said, trembling, and leaning her cheek against Amabel's little, cold, pale one. "Don't cry, darling," she whispered. "It is just because poor mother feels so badly."

"I am afraid of my mamma, and I want papa!" screamed Amabel, quivering, and stiffening her slender back.

Eva continued to keep her eyes fixed upon her, and to hold out that commanding hand.

Fanny went close to her, seized her by both shoulders, and shook her violently. "Eva Tenny, you behave yourself!" said she. "There ain't no need of your acting this way if your man has run away with another woman, and as for that child goin' with you, she sha'n't go one step with any woman that looks and acts as you do. Actin' this way over a good-for-nothin' fellow like Jim Tenny!"

287

Again that scourge of the spirit aroused Eva to her normal state. She became a living, breathing, wrathful, loving woman once more. "Don't you dare say a word against Jim!" she cried out; "not one word, Fanny Brewster; I won't hear it. Don't you dare say a word!"

"Don't you say a word against my papa!" shrilled Amabel. Then she left Ellen and ran to her mother, and clung to her. And Eva caught her up, and hugged the little, fragile thing against her breast, and pounced upon her with kisses, with a fury as of rage instead of love.

"She always looked like Jim," she sobbed out; "she always did. Aggie Bemis shall never get her. I've got her in spite of all the awful wrong of life; it's the good that had to come out of it whether or no, and God couldn't help Himself. I've got this much. She always looked like Jim."

Eva set Amabel down and began leading her out of the room.

"You ain't goin'?" said Fanny, who had herself begun to weep. "Eva, you ain't goin'? Oh, you poor girl!"

"Don't!—you said that like Jim," Eva cried, with a great groan of pain.

"Eva, you ain't goin'? Wait a little while, and let me do somethin' for you."

"You can't do anything. Come, Amabel."

Eva and Amabel went away, the child rolling eyes of terror and interrogation at them, Eva impervious to all her sister's pleading.

When Andrew heard what had happened, and Fanny repeated what Eva had said, his blame for Jim Tenny was unqualified. "I've had a hard time enough, knocked about from pillar to post, and I know what she means when she talks about a checker-board. God

288

knows I feel myself sometimes as if I wasn't anything but a checker - piece instead of a man," he said, "but it's all nonsense blamin' the shoe manufacturers for his runnin' away with that woman. A man has got to use what little freedom he's got right. It ain't any excuse for Jim Tenny that he's been out of work and got discouraged. He's a good-for-nothing cur, an' I'd like to tell him so."

"It won't do for you to talk to Eva that way," said Fanny. They were all at the supper-table. Ellen was listening silently.

"She does right to stand up for her husband, I suppose," said Andrew, "but anybody's got to use a little sense. It don't make it any better for Jim, tryin' to shove blame off his shoulders that belongs there. The manufacturers didn't make him run off with another woman and leave his child. That was a move he made himself."

"But he wouldn't have made that move if the manufacturers hadn't made theirs," Ellen said, unexpectedly.

"That's so," said Fanny.

Andrew looked uneasily at Ellen, in whose cheeks two red spots were burning, and whose eyes upon his face seemed narrowed to two points of brightness. "There's nothing for you to worry about, child," he said.

All this was before the dressmaker, who listened with no particular interest. Affairs which did not directly concern her did not awaken her to much sharpness of regard. She had been forced by circumstances into a very narrow groove of life, a little foot-path as it were, fenced in from destruction by three dollars a day. She could not, view it as keenly as she might, see that Jim Tenny's elopement had anything whatever to do with her three dollars per day. She, therefore, ate her supper. At first Andrew had looked warningly at Fanny

T 289

when she began to discuss the subject before the dress-maker, but Fanny had replied, "Oh, land, Andrew, she knows all about it now. It's all over town."

"Yes, I heard it this morning before I came," said the dressmaker. "I think a puff on the sleeves of the silk waist will be very pretty, don't you, Mrs. Brewster?"

Ellen looked at the dressmaker with wonder; it seemed to her that the woman was going on a little especial side track of her own outside the interests of her kind. She looked at her pretty new things and tried them on, and felt guilty that she had them. What business had she having new clothes and going to Vassar College in the face of that misery? What was an education? What was anything compared with the sympathy which love demanded of love in the midst of sorrow? Should she not turn her back upon any purely personal advantage as she would upon a moral plague?

When Ellen's father said that to her at the supper-table she looked at him with unchildlike eyes. "I think it is something for me to worry about, father," she said. "How can I help worrying if I love Aunt Eva and Amabel?"

"It's a dreadful thing for Eva," said Fanny. "I don't see what she is going to do. Andrew, pass the biscuits to Miss Higgins."

"It seems to me that the one that is the farthest behind anything that happens on this earth is the one to blame," said Ellen, reverting to her line of argument.

"I don't know but you've got to go back to God, then," said Andrew, soberly, passing the biscuits. Miss Higgins took one.

"No, you haven't," said Ellen—"you haven't, because men are free. You've got to stop before you get to God. When a man goes wrong, you have got to look and see if he is to blame, if he started himself, or other men have been pushing him into it. It seems to me that other men have been pushing Uncle Jim into it. I don't think factory-owners have any right to discharge a man without a good reason, any more than he has a right to run the shop."

"I don't think so, either," said Fanny. "I think Ellen is right."

"I don't know. It is all a puzzle," said Andrew. "Something's wrong somewhere. I don't know whether it's because we are pushed or because we pull. There's no use in your worrying about it, Ellen. You've got to study your books." Andrew said this with a look of pride at Ellen and sidelong triumph at the dress-maker to see if she rightly understood the magnitude of it all, of the whole situation of making dresses for this wonderful young creature who was going to Vassar College.

"I don't know but this is more important than books," said Ellen.

"Oh, maybe you'll find out something in your books that will settle the whole matter," said Andrew. Ellen was not eating much supper, and that troubled him. Andrew always knew just how much Ellen ate.

"I don't know what Aunt Eva and poor little Amabel will do," said she. Ellen's lip quivered.

"Pass the cake to Miss Higgins," said Fanny, sharply, to Andrew. She gave him a significant wink as she did so, not to talk more about it.

"Try some of that chocolate cake, Miss Higgins."

"Thank you," said Miss Higgins, unexcitedly.

Andrew had his own cause of worry, and finally reverted to it, eating his food with no more conception of the savor than if it were in another man's mouth. He was sorry enough for his wife's sister, and recognized it as an added weight to his own burden, but just at present all he could think of was the question if Miss

Higgins would ask for her pay again that night. He had not a dollar in his pocket. He had been dunned that afternoon by the man who had lent the money to buy Ellen's watch, there were two new dunning letters in his pocket, and now if that keen little dressmaker, who fairly looked to him like a venomous insect, as she sat eating rather voraciously of the chocolate cake, should ask him again for the three dollars due her that night! He would not have cared so much, if it were not for the fact that she would ask him before his wife and Ellen, and the question about the money in the savings-bank, which was a species of nightmare to him, would be sure to come to the front.

Suddenly it struck Andrew that he might run away, that he might slip out after supper, and either go into his mother's house or down the street. He finally decided on the former, since he reasoned, with a pitiful cunning, that if he went down the street he would have to take off his slippers and put on his shoes, and that would at once betray him and lead to the possible arrest of his flight.

So after supper, while Miss Higgins was trying a waist on Ellen, and Fanny was clearing the table, Andrew, bareheaded and in his slippers, prepared to carry his plan into execution. He got out without being seen, and hurried around the rear of the house, out of view from the sitting-room windows, resolving on the way that in order to avert the danger of a possible following him to the sanctuary of his mother's house, he had perhaps better slip down into the orchard behind it and see if the porter apples were ripe. But when, stooping as if beneath some invisible shield, and moving with a low glide of secrecy, he had gained the yard between the two houses, the yard where the three cherry-trees stood, he heard Fanny's high, insistent voice calling him, and knew that it was all over.

Fanny had her head thrust out of her bedroom window. "Andrew! Andrew!" she called.

Andrew stopped. "What is it?" he asked, in a gruff voice. He felt at that moment savage with her and with fate. He felt like some badgered animal beneath the claws and teeth of petty enemies which were yet sufficient to do him to death. He felt that retreat and defence were alike impossible and inglorious. He was aware of a monstrous impatience with it all, which was fairly blasphemy. "What is it?" he said, and Fanny realized that something was wrong.

"Come here, Andrew Brewster," she said, from the bedroom window, and Andrew pressed close to the window through a growth of sweetbrier which rasped his hands and sent up a sweet fragrance in his face. Andrew tore away the clinging vines angrily.

"Well, what is it?" he said again.

"Don't spoil that bush, Ellen sets a lot by it," said Fanny. "What makes you act so, Andrew Brewster?" Then she lowered her voice. "She wants to know if she can have her pay to-night," she whispered.

"I 'ain't got a cent," replied Andrew, in a dogged, breathless voice.

"You 'ain't been to the bank to-day, then?"

"No, I 'ain't."

Fanny still suspected nothing. She was, in fact, angry with the dressmaker for insisting upon her pay in such a fashion. "I never heard of such a thing as her wantin' to be paid every night," she whispered, angrily, "and I'd tell her so, if I wasn't afraid she'd think we couldn't pay her. I'd never have had her; I'd had Miss Patch, if I'd known she'd do such a mean thing, but, as it is, I don't know what to do. I 'ain't got but a dollar and seventy-three cents by me. You 'ain't got enough to make it up?"

"No, I 'ain't."

" Well, all is, I've got to tell her that it ain't convenient
for me to pay her to-night, and she shall have it all
together to-morrow night, and to-morrow you'll have
to go to the bank and take out the money, Andrew.
Don't forget it."

"Well," said Andrew.

Fanny retreated, and he heard her high voice explaining to Miss Higgins. He tore his way through
the clinging sweetbrier bushes and ran with an unsteady, desperate gait down to the orchard behind his
mother's home, and flung himself at full length in
the dewy grass under the trees with all the abandon,
under stress of fate, of a child.

CHAPTER XXVIII

ANDREW BREWSTER, lying in the dewy grass under the apple-trees, giving way for almost the first time since his childhood to impulses which had hitherto, from his New England heredity, stiffened instead of relaxed his muscles of expression, felt as if he were being stung to death by ants. He was naturally a man of broad views, who felt the indignity of coping with such petty odds. "For God's sake, if I had to be done to death, why couldn't it have been for something?" he groaned, speaking with his lips close to the earth as if it were a listening ear. "Why need it all have been over so little? It's just the little fight for enough to eat and wear that's getting the better of me that was a man, and able to do a man's work in the world. Now it has come to this! Here I am runnin' away from a woman because she wants me to pay her three dollars, and I am afraid of another woman because—I've been and fooled away a few hundred dollars I had in the savings-bank. I'm afraid —yes, it has come to this. I am afraid, afraid, and I'd run away out of life if I knew where it would fetch me to. I'm afraid of things that ain't worth being afraid of, and it's all over things that's beneath me." There came over Andrew, with his mouth to the moist earth, feeling the breath and the fragrance of it in his nostrils, a realization of the great motherhood of nature, and a contempt for himself which was scorching and scathing before it. He felt that he came from that mighty breast which should produce only sons of might, and was

295

spending his whole life in an ignominy of fruitless climbing up mole-hills. "Why couldn't I have been more?" he asked himself. "Oh, my God, is it my fault?" He said to himself that if he had not yielded to the universal law and longing of his kind for a home and a family, it might have been better. He asked himself that question which will never be answered with a surety of correctness, whether the advancement of the individual to his furthest compass is more to the glory of life than the blind following out of the laws of existence and the bringing others into the everlasting problem of advance. Then he thought of Ellen, and a great warmth of conviction came over the loving heart of the man; all his self-contempt vanished. He had her, this child who was above pearls and rubies, he had her, and in her the furthest reach of himself and progression of himself to greater distances than he could ever have accomplished in any other way, and it was a double progress, since it was not only for him, but also for the woman he had married. A great wave of love for Fanny came over him. He seemed to see that, after all, it was a shining road by which he had come, and he saw himself upon it like a figure of light. He saw that he lived and could never die. Then, as with a remorseless hurl of a high spirit upon needle-pricks of petty cares, he thought again of the dressmaker, of the money for Ellen's watch, of the butcher's bill, and the grocer's bills, and the money which he had taken from the bank, and again he cowered beneath and loathed his ignoble burden. He dug his hot head into the grass. "Oh, my God! oh, my God!" he groaned. He fairly sobbed. Then he felt a soft wind of feminine skirts caused by the sudden stoop of some one beside him, and Ellen's voice, shrill with alarm, rang in his ears. "Father, what is the matter? Father!"

Such was the man's love for the girl that his first

thought was for her alarm, and he pushed all his own troubles into the background with a lightning-like motion. He raised himself hastily, and smiled at her with his pitiful, stiff face. "It's nothing at all, Ellen, don't you worry," he said.

But that was not enough to satisfy her. She caught hold of his arm and clung to it. "Father," she said, in a tone which had in it, to his wonder, a firm woman-liness — his own daughter seemed to speak to him as if she were his mother — "you are not telling me the truth. Something is the matter, or you wouldn't do like this."

"No, there's nothin', nothin' at all, dear child," said Andrew. He tried to loosen her little, clinging hand from his arm. "Come, let's go back to the house," he said. "Don't you mind anything about it. Some-times father gets discouraged over nothin'."

"It isn't over nothing," said Ellen. "What is it about, father?"

Andrew tried to laugh. "Well, if it isn't over nothin', it's over nothin' in particular," said he; "it's over jest what's happened right along. Sometimes father feels as if he hadn't made as much as he'd ought to out of his life, and he's gettin' older, and he's feelin' kind of discouraged, that's all."

"Over money matters?" said Ellen, looking at him steadily.

"Over nothin'," said her father. "See here, child, father's ashamed that he gave way so, and you found him. Now don't you worry one mite about it—it's nothing at all. Come, let's go back to the house," he said.

Ellen said no more, but she walked up from the field holding tightly to her father's poor, worn hand, and her heart was in a tumult. To behold any convulsion of nature is no light experience, and when it is a storm of the spirit in one beloved the beholder is swept along with it in greater or less measure. Ellen trembled as she walked. Her father kept looking at her anxiously and remorsefully. Once he reached around his other hand and chucked her playfully under the chin. "Scared most to death, was she?" he asked, with a shamefaced blush.

"I know something is the matter, and I think it would be better for you to tell me, father," replied Ellen, soberly.

"There's nothing to tell, child," said Andrew. "Don't you worry your little head about it." Between his anxiety lest the girl should be troubled, and his intense humiliation that she should have discovered him in such an abandon of grief which was almost like a disclosure of the nakedness of his spirit, he was completely unnerved. Ellen felt him tremble, and heard his voice quiver when he spoke. She felt towards her father something she had never felt before—an impulse of protection. She felt the older and stronger of the two. Her grasp on his hand tightened, she seemed in a measure to be leading him along.

When they reached the yard between the houses Andrew cast an apprehensive glance at the windows. "Has she gone?" he asked.

"Who, the dressmaker?"

"Yes."

"She hadn't when I came out. I saw you come past the house, and I thought you walked as if you didn't feel well, so I thought I would run out and see."

"I was all right," replied Andrew. "Have you got to try on anything more to-night?"

"No."

"Well, then, let's run into grandma's a minute."

"All right," said Ellen.

Mrs. Zelotes was sitting at her front window in the dusk, looking out on the street, as was her favorite custom. The old woman seldom lit a lamp in the summer evening, but sat there staring out at the lighted street and the people passing and repassing, with her mind as absolutely passive as regarded herself as if she were travelling and observing only that which passed without. At those times she became in a fashion sensible of the motion of the world, and lost her sense of individuality in the midst of it. When her son and granddaughter entered she looked away from the window with the expression of one returning from afar, and seemed dazed for a moment.

"Hullo, mother!" said Andrew.

The room was dusky, and they moved across between the chairs and tables like two shadows.

"Oh, is it you, Andrew?" said his mother. "Who is that with you—Ellen?"

"Yes," said Ellen. "How do you do, grandma?"

Mrs. Zelotes became suddenly fully awake to the situation; she collected her scattered faculties; her keen old eyes gleamed in a shaft of electric-light from the street without, which fell full upon her face.

"Set down," said she. "Has the dressmaker gone?"

"No, she hadn't when I came out," replied Ellen, "but she's most through for to-night."

"How do your things look?"

"Real pretty, I guess."

"Sometimes I think you'd better have had Miss Patch. I hope she 'ain't got your sleeves too tight at the elbows."

"They seem to fit very nicely, grandma."

"Sleeves are very particular things; a sleeve wrong can spoil a whole dress."

Suddenly the old woman turned on Ellen with a look of extremest facetiousness and intelligence, and

the girl winced, for she knew what was coming. "I
see you goin' past with a young man last night, didn't
I?" said she.

Ellen flushed. "Yes," she said, almost indignantly,
for she had a feeling as if the veil of some inner sacred-
ness of her nature were continually being torn aside.
"I went over to Miss Lennox, to carry some sweet-
peas, and Mr. Robert Lloyd was there, and he came
home with me."

"Oh!" replied her grandmother.

Ellen's patience left her at the sound of that "Oh,"
which seemed to rasp her very soul. "You have none
of you any right to talk and act as you do," said she.
"You make me ashamed of you, you and mother;
father has more sense. Just because a young man
makes me a call to return something, and then walks
home with me, because he happened to be at the house
where I call in the evening! I think it's a shame.
You make me feel as if I couldn't look him in the
face."

"Never mind, grandma didn't mean any harm,"
Andrew said, soothingly.

"You needn't try to excuse me, Andrew Brewster,"
cried his mother, angrily. "I guess it's a pretty to-do,
if I can't say a word in joke to my own granddaughter.
If it had been a poor, good-for-nothing young feller
workin' in a shoe-factory, I s'pose she'd been tickled to
death to be joked about him, but now when it begins to
look as if somebody that was worth while had come
along—"

"Grandma, if you say another word about it, I will
never speak to Robert Lloyd again as long as I live,"
declared Ellen.

"Never mind, child," whispered Andrew.

"I do mind, and I mean what I say," Ellen cried.
"I won't have it. Robert Lloyd is nothing to me, and

I am nothing to him. He is no better than Granville Joy. There is nothing between us, and you make me too ashamed to think of him."

Then the old woman cried out, in a tone of triumph, "Well, there he is, turnin' in at your gate now."

CHAPTER XXIX

ELLEN rose without a word, and fled out of the room and out of the house. It seemed to her, after what had happened, after what her mother and grandmother had said and insinuated, after what she herself had thought and felt, that she must. She longed to see Robert Lloyd, to hear him speak, as she had never longed for anything in the world, and yet she ran away as if she were driven to obey some law which was coeval with the first woman and beyond all volition of her individual self.

When she reached the head of the little cross street on which the Atkinses lived, she turned into it with relief. The Atkins house was a tiny cottage, with a little kitchen ell, and a sagging piazza across the front. On this piazza were shadowy figures, and the dull, red gleam of pipes, and one fiery tip of a cigar. Joe Atkins, and Sargent, and two other men were sitting out there in the cool of the evening. Ellen hurried around the curve of the foot-path to the kitchen door. Abby was in there, working with the swift precision of a machine. She washed and wiped dishes as if in a sort of fury, her thin elbows jerking, her mouth compressed.

When Ellen entered, Abby stared, then her whole face lighted up, as if from some internal lamp. "Why, Ellen, is that you?" she said, in a surprisingly sweet voice. Sometimes Abby's sharp American voice rang with the sweetness of a soft bell.

"I thought I'd run over a minute," said Ellen.

302

The other girl looked sharply at her. "Why, what's the matter?" she said.

"Nothing is the matter. Why?"

"Why, I thought you looked sort of queer. Maybe it's the light. Sit down; I'll have the dishes done in a minute, then we'll go into the sitting-room."

"I'd rather stay out here with you," said Ellen.

Abby looked at her again. "There is something the matter, Ellen Brewster," said she; "you can't cheat me. You would never have run over here this way in the world. What has happened?"

"Let's go up to your room after the dishes are done, and then I'll tell you," whispered Ellen. The men's voices on the piazza could be heard quite distinctly, and it seemed possible that their own conversation might be overheard in return.

"All right," said Abby. "Of course I have heard about your aunt," she added, in a low voice.

"Yes," said Ellen, and she felt shamed and remorseful that her own affairs had been uppermost in her mind, and that Abby had supposed that she might be disturbed over this great trouble of her poor aunt's.

"I think it is dreadful," said Abby. "I wish I could get hold of that woman." By "that woman" she meant the woman with whom poor Jim Tenny had eloped.

"I do," said Ellen, bitterly.

"But it's something besides that made you run over here," said Abby.

"I'll tell you when we go up to your room," replied Ellen.

When the dishes were finished, and the two girls in Abby's little chamber, seated side by side on the bed, Ellen still hesitated.

"Now, Ellen Brewster, what is the matter? You said you would tell, and you've got to," said Abby.

Ellen looked away from her, blushing. The electric-light from the street shone full in the room, which was wavering with grotesque shadows.

"Well," said she, "I ran away."

"You ran away! What for?"

"Oh, because."

"Because what?"

"Because I saw somebody coming."

"Saw who coming?"

Ellen was silent.

"Not Granville Joy?"

Ellen shook her head.

"Not—?"

Ellen looked straight ahead.

"Not young Mr. Lloyd?"

Ellen was silent with the silence of assent.

"Did he go into your house?"

Ellen nodded.

"Where were you?"

"In grandma's."

"And you ran away, over here?"

Ellen nodded.

"Why, Ellen Brewster, didn't you want to see him?"

Ellen turned from Abby with an impatient gesture, buried her face in the bed, and began to weep.

Abby leaned over her caressingly. "Ellen dear," she whispered, "what is the matter; what are you crying for? What made you run away?"

Ellen sobbed harder.

Abby looked at Ellen's prostrate figure sadly. "Ellen," she began; then she stopped, for her own voice quivered. Then she went on, quite steadily. "Ellen," she said, "you like him."

"No, I don't," declared Ellen. "I won't. I never will. Nothing shall make me."

But Abby continued to look at her sadly and jealously.

"There's a power over us which is too strong for girls," said she, "and you've come under it, Ellen, and you can't help it." Then she added, with a great, noble burst of utter unselfishness: "And I'm glad, I'm glad, Ellen. That man can lift you out of the grind."

But Ellen sat up straight and faced her, with burning cheeks, and eyes shining through tears. "I will never be lifted out of the grind as long as those I love are in it," said she.

"Do you suppose it would make it any better for your folks to see you in it all your life along with them?" said Abby. "Suppose you married a fellow like Granville Joy?"

U

CHAPTER XXX

ELLEN looked at the other girl in a kind of rage of maidenly shame. "Why have I got to get married, anyway?" she demanded. "Isn't there anything in this world besides getting married? Why do you all talk so about me? You don't seem so bent on getting married yourself. If you think so much of marriage, why don't you get married yourself, and let me alone?"

"Nobody wants to marry me that I know of," replied Abby, quite simply. Then she, too, blazed out. "Get married!" she cried. "Do you really think I would get married to the kind of man who would marry me? Do you think I could if I loved him?" A great wave of red surged over the girl's thin face, her voice trembled with tenderness. Ellen knew at once, with a throb of sympathy and shame, that Abby did love some one.

"Do you think I would marry him if I loved him?" demanded Abby, stiffening herself into a soldier-like straightness. "Do you think? I tell you what it is," she said, "I was lookin' only to-day at David Mendon at the cutting-bench, cutting away with his poor little knife. I'd like to know how many handles he's worn out since he began. There he was, putting the pattern on the leather, and cuttin' around it, standin' at his window, that's a hot place in summer and a cold one in winter, and there's where he's stood for I don't know how many years since before I was born. He's one of the few that Lloyd's has hung on to when he's got older, and I thought to myself, good Lord, how that

306

poor man must have loved his wife, and how he must love his children, to be willin' to turn himself into a machine like that for them. He never takes a holiday unless he's forced into it; there he stands and cuts and cuts. If I were his wife, I would die of shame and pity that I ever led him into it. Do you think I would ever let a man turn himself into a machine for me, if I loved him? I guess I wouldn't! And that's why, when I see a man of another sort that you won't have to break your own heart over, whether you marry him or not, payin' attention to you, I am glad. It's a different thing, marriage with a man like Robert Lloyd, and a man like that would never think of me. I'm right in the ranks, and you ain't."

"I am," said Ellen, stoutly.

"No, you ain't; you don't belong there, and when I see a chance for you to get out where you belong—"

"I don't intend to make marriage a stepping-stone," said Ellen. "Sometimes—" She hesitated.

"What?" asked the other girl.

"Sometimes I think I would rather not go to college, after all."

"Ellen Brewster, are you crazy? Of course, you will go to college unless you marry Robert Lloyd. Perhaps he won't want to wait." Then Abby, dauntless as she was, shrank a little before Ellen's wrathful retort.

"Abby Atkins, you ought to be ashamed of yourself!" she cried. "There he's been to see me just twice, the first time on an errand, and the next with his aunt, and he's walked home with me once because he couldn't help it; his aunt told him to!"

"But here he is again to-night," said Abby, apologetically.

"What of that? I suppose he has come on another errand."

"Then what made you run away?"

"Because you have all made me ashamed of my life to look at him," said Ellen, hotly.

Then down went her head on the bed again, and Abby was leaning over her, caressing her, whispering fond things to her like a lover.

"There, there, Ellen," she whispered. "Don't be mad, don't feel bad. I didn't mean any harm. You are such a beauty—there's nobody like you in the world—that everybody thinks that any man who sees you must want you."

"Robert Lloyd doesn't, and if he did I wouldn't have him," sobbed Ellen.

"You sha'n't if you don't want him," said Abby, consolingly.

After a while the two girls bathed their eyes with cold water, and went down-stairs into the sitting-room. Maria was making herself a blue muslin dress, and her mother was hemming the ruffles. There was a cheap blue shade on the lamp, and Maria herself was clad in a blue gingham. All the blue color and the shade on the lamp gave a curious pallor and unreality to the homely room and the two women. Mrs. Atkins's hair was strained back from her hollow temples, which had noble outlines.

"I'm going to walk a little way with Ellen, she's going home," said Abby.

"Very well," said her mother. Maria looked wistfully at them as they went out. She went on sewing on her blue muslin, rather sadly. She coughed a little.

"Why don't you put up your sewing for to-night and go to bed, child?" said her mother.

"I might as well sit here and sew as go to bed and lie there. I shouldn't sleep," replied Maria, with the gentlest sadness conceivable. There was in it no shadow of complaining. Of late years all the fire of resistance had seemed to die out in the girl. She was

unfailingly sweet, but nerveless. Often when she
raised a hand it seemed as if she could not even let it
fall, as if it must remain poised by some curious inertia.
Still, she went to the shop every day and did her work
faithfully. She pasted linings in shoes, and her slender
little fingers used to fly as if they were driven by some
more subtle machine than any in the factory. Often
Maria felt vaguely as if she were in the grasp of some
mighty machine worked by a mighty operator; she
felt, as she pasted the linings, as if she herself were also
a part of some monstrous scheme of work under greater
hands than hers, and there was never any getting back
of it. And always with it all there was that ceaseless,
helpless, bewildered longing for something, she was
afraid to think what, which often saps the strength
and life of a young girl. Maria had never had a lover
in her life; she had not even good comrades among
young men, as her sister had. No man at that time
would have ever looked twice at her, unless he had
fallen in love with her, and had been disposed to pick
her up and carry her along on the hard road upon which
they fared together. Maria was half fed in every sense;
she had not enough nourishing food for her body, nor
love for her heart, nor exercise for her brain. She had
no time to read, as she was forced to sew when out of
the shop if she would have anything to wear. When
at last she went up-stairs to bed, before Abby returned,
she sat down by her window, and leaned her little, peaked
chin on the sill and looked out. The stars were unusually bright for a summer night; the whole sky
seemed filled with a constantly augmenting host of
them. The scent of tobacco came to her from below.
To the lonely girl the stars and the scent of the tobacco
served as stimulants; she formed a forcible wish. "I
wish," she muttered to herself, "that I was either an
angel or a man." Then the next minute she chided

herself for her wickedness. A great wave of love for God, and remorse for impatience and melancholy in her earthly lot, swept over her. She knelt down beside her bed and prayed. An exultation half - physical, half-spiritual, filled her. When she rose, her little, thin face was radiant. She seemed to measure the shortness of the work and woe of the world as between her thumb and finger. The joy of the divine filled all her longing. When Abby came home, who shared her chamber, she felt no jealousy. She only inquired whether she had gone quite home with Ellen. "Yes, I did," replied Abby. "I don't think it is safe for her to go past that lonely place below the Smiths'."

"I'm glad you did," said Maria, with an angelic inflection in her voice.

"Robert Lloyd came to see Ellen, and she ran away over here, and wouldn't see him, because they had all been plaguing her about him," said Abby. "I wish she wouldn't do so. It would be a splendid thing for her to marry him, and I know he likes her, and his aunt is going to send her to college."

"That won't make any difference to Ellen, and everything will be all right anyway, if only she loved God," said Maria, still with that rapt, angelic voice.

"Shucks!" said Abby. Then she leaned over her sister, caught her by her little, thin shoulders and shook her tenderly. "There, I didn't mean to speak so," said she. "You're awful good, Maria. I'm glad you've got religion if it's so much comfort to you. I don't mean to make light of it, but I'm afraid you ain't well. I'm goin' to get you some more of that tonic to-morrow."

CHAPTER XXXI

WHEN Ellen reached home that night she found no one there except her father, who was sitting on the door-step in the north yard. Her mother had gone to see her aunt Eva as soon as the dressmaker had left. "Who was that with you?" Andrew asked, as she drew near.

"Abby," replied Ellen.

"So you went over there?"

Ellen sat down on a lower step in front of her father. "Yes," said she. She half laughed up in his face, like a child who knows she has been naughty, yet knows she will not be blamed since she can count so surely on the indulgent love of the would-be blamer.

"Ellen, your mother didn't like it."

"They had said so many things to me about him that I didn't feel as if I could see him, father," she said.

Andrew put a hand on her head. "I know what you mean," he replied, "but they didn't mean any harm; they're only looking out for your best good, Ellen. You can't always have us; it ain't in the course of nature, you know, Ellen."

There was a tone of inexorable sadness, the sadness of fate itself in Andrew's voice. He had, as he spoke, the full realization of that stage of progress which is simply for the next, which passes to make room for it. He felt his own nothingness. It was the throe of the present before the future: it was the pang of anticipatory annihilation.

"Don't talk that way, father," said Ellen. "Neither you nor mother are old people."

"Oh, well, it's all right, don't you worry," said Andrew.

"How long did he stay?" asked Ellen. She did not look at her father as she spoke.

"Oh, he didn't stay at all, after they found out you had gone."

Ellen sighed. After a second Andrew sighed also. "It's gettin' late," said he, heavily; "mebbe we'd better go in before your mother comes, Ellen. Mebbe you'll get cold out here."

"Oh no, I shall not," said Ellen, "and I want to hear about poor Aunt Eva. I don't see what she is going to do."

"It's a dreadful thing makin' a mistake in marriage," said Andrew.

"Uncle Jim was a good man if he hadn't had such a hard time."

Andrew looked at her, then he spoke impressively. "Look here, Ellen," he said, "you are a good scholar, and you are smarter in a good many ways than father has ever been, but there's one thing you want to remember; you want to be sure before you blame the Lord or other men for a man's goin' wrong, if it ain't his own fault at the bottom of things."

"There's mother," cried Ellen; "there's mother and Amabel. Where's Aunt Eva? Oh, father, what do you suppose has happened? Why do you suppose mother is bringing Amabel home?"

"I don't know," replied Andrew, in a troubled voice.

He and Ellen rose and hastened forward to meet Fanny and Amabel. The child hung at her aunt's hand in a curious, limp, disjointed fashion; her little face, even in the half light, showed ghastly. When she saw Ellen she let go of Fanny's hand and ran to her and threw both her little arms around her in a fierce clutch as of terror, then she began to sob wildly, "Mamma, mamma, mamma!"

Fanny leaned her drawn face forward, and whispered to Andrew and Ellen over Amabel's head, under cover of her sobs, "Hush, don't say anything. She's gone mad, and, and—she tried to—kill Amabel."

CHAPTER XXXII

AMABEL was a very nervous child, and she was in such terror from her really terrific experience that she threatened to go into convulsions. Andrew went over for his mother, whom he had always regarded as an incontestable authority about children. She, after one sharp splutter of wrath at the whole situation, went to work with the resolution of an old soldier.

"Heat some water, quick," said she to Andrew, "and get me a wash-tub."

Then she told Fanny to brew a mess of sage tea, and began stripping off Amabel's clothes.

"Let me alone! Mamma, mamma, mamma!" shrieked the child. She fought and clawed like a little, wild animal, but the old woman, in whose arms great strength could still arise for emergencies, and in whose spirit great strength had never died, got the better of her.

When Amabel's clothing was stripped off, and her little, spare body, which was brown rather than rosy, although she was a blonde, was revealed, she was as pitiful to see as a wound. Every nerve and pulse in that tiny frame, about which there was not an ounce of superfluous flesh, seemed visible. The terrible sensitiveness of the child appeared on the surface. She shrank, and wailed in a low, monotonous tone like a spent animal overtaken by pursuers. But Mrs. Zelotes put her in the tub of warm water, and held her down, though Amabel's face, emerging from it, had the expression of a wild thing.

"There, you keep still!" said she, and her voice was tender enough, though the decision of it could have moved an army.

When Amabel had had her hot bath, and had drunk her sage tea by compulsory gulps, and been tucked into Ellen's bed, her childhood reasserted itself. Gradually her body and her bodily needs gained the ascendancy over the unnatural strain of her mind. She fell asleep, and lay like one dead. Then Ellen crept downstairs, though it was almost midnight, where her father and mother and grandmother were still talking over the matter. Fanny seemed almost as bad as her sister. It was evident that there was in the undisciplined Loud family a dangerous strain if too far pressed. She was lying down on the lounge, with Andrew holding her hand.

"Oh, my God! Oh, my God! Poor Eva!" she kept repeating.

Then she threw off Andrew's hand, sprang to her feet, and began to walk the room.

"She'll be as bad as her sister if she keeps on," said Mrs. Zelotes, quite audibly, but Fanny paid no attention to that.

"What is goin' to be done? Oh, my God, what is goin' to be done?" she wailed. "There she is locked up with two men watchin' her lest she do herself a harm, and it's got to cost eighteen dollars a week, unless she's put in with the State poor, and then nobody knows how she'll be treated. Oh, poor Eva, poor Eva! Albert Riggs told me there were awful things done with the State poor in the asylums. He's been an attendant in one. He says we've got to pay eighteen dollars a week if we want to have her cared for decently, and where's the money comin' from?" Fanny raised her voice higher still.

"Where's the money comin' from?" she demanded,

315

with an impious inflection. It was as if she questioned
that which is outside of, and the source of, life. Everything with this woman, whose whole existence had been
bound and tainted by the need of money, resolved itself
into that fundamental question. All her woes hinged
upon it; even her misery was deteriorated by mammon.

"Where's the money comin' from?" she demanded
again. "There's Jim gone, and all his mother's got
is that little, mortgaged place, and she feeble, and there
ain't a cent anywhere, unless—" She turned fiercely
to Andrew, clutching him hard by the arm.

"You must take every cent of that money out of the
savings-bank," she cried, "every cent of it. I'm your
wife, and I've been a good wife to you, you can't say I
haven't."

"Yes, of course you have, poor girl! Don't, don't!"
said Andrew, soothingly. He was very pale, and shook
from head to foot as he tried to calm Fanny.

"Yes, I've been a good, faithful wife," Fanny went
on, in her high, hysterical voice. "Even your mother
can't say that I haven't; and Eva is my own sister, and
you ought to help her. Every cent of that money will
have to come out of the savings-bank, and the house
here will have to be mortgaged; it's only my due. I
would do as much for you if it was your sister. Eva
ain't goin' to suffer."

"I guess if you mortgage this house that you had from
your father, to keep a woman whose husband has gone
off and left her," said Mrs. Zelotes, "I guess if you don't
go and get him back, and get the law to tackle him!"

Then Fanny turned on her. "Don't you say a word,"
said she. "My sister ain't goin' to suffer, I don't care
where the money comes from. It's mine as much as
Andrew's. I've half supported the family myself sewin'
on wrappers, and I've got a right to have my say. My
sister ain't goin' to suffer! Oh, my God, what's goin'

316

to become of her? Poor Eva, poor Eva! Eighteen dollars a week; that's as much as Andrew ever earned. Oh, it was awful, it was awful! There, when I got in there, she had a—knife, the—carving knife, and she had Amabel's hair all gathered up in one hand, and her head tipped back, and poor old mother Tenny was holding her arms, and screamin', and it was all I could do to get the knife away," and Fanny stripped up her sleeves, and showed a glancing cut on her arm.

"She did that before I got it away from her," she said. "Think of it, my own sister! My own sister, who always thought so much of me, and would have had her own fingers cut to the bone before she would have let any one touch me or Ellen! Oh, poor Eva, poor Eva! What is goin' to become of her, what is goin' to become of her?"

Mrs. Zelotes went out of the house with a jerk of angry decision, and presently returned with a bottle half full of whiskey.

"Here," said she to Ellen, "you pour out a quarter of a tumbler of this, and fill it up with hot water. I ain't goin' to have the whole family in an asylum because Jim Tenny has run off with another woman, if I can help it!"

The old woman's steady force of will asserted itself over the hysterical nature of her daughter-in-law. Fanny drank the whiskey and water and went to bed, half stupefied, and Mrs. Zelotes went home.

"You ring the bell in the night if she's taken worse, and I'll come over," said she to her son.

When Ellen and her father were left alone they looked at each other, each with pity for the other. Andrew laid a tender, trembling hand on the girl's shoulder. "Somehow it will all come out right," he whispered. "You go to bed and go to sleep, and if Amabel wakes up and makes any trouble you speak to father."

317

"Don't worry about me, father," returned Ellen. "It's you who have the most to worry over." Then she added—for the canker of need of money was eating her soul, too—"Father, what is going to be done? You can't pay all that for poor Aunt Eva. How much money have you got in the bank?"

"Not much, not much, Ellen," replied Andrew, with a groan.

"It wouldn't last very long at eighteen dollars a week?"

"No, no."

"It doesn't seem as if you ought to mortgage the house when you and mother are getting older. Father—"

"What, Ellen?"

"Nothing," said Ellen, after a little pause. It had been on her lips to tell him that she must go to work, then she refrained. There was something in her father's face which forbade her doing so.

"Go to bed, Ellen, and get rested," said Andrew. Then he rubbed his head against hers with his curious, dog-like method of caress, and kissed her forehead.

"You go to sleep and get rested yourself, father," said Ellen.

"I guess I won't undress to-night, but I'll lay on the lounge," said Andrew.

"Well, you speak to me if mother wakes up and takes on again. Maybe I can do something."

"All right, dear child," said Andrew, lovingly and wearily. He had a look as if some mighty wind had passed over him and he were beaten down under it, except for that one single uprearing of love which no tempest could fairly down.

Ellen went up-stairs, and lay down beside poor little Amabel without undressing herself. The child stirred, but not to awake, when she settled down beside her, and reached over her poor little claw of a hand to the girl, who clasped it fervently, and slipped a protecting arm under the tiny shoulders. Then the little thing nestled close to Ellen, with a movement of desperate seeking for protection. "There, there, darling, Ellen will take care of you," whispered Ellen. But Amabel did not hear.

CHAPTER XXXIII

THE next afternoon poor Eva Tenny was carried away, and Andrew accompanied the doctor who had her in charge, as being the only available male relative. As he dressed himself in his Sunday suit, he was aware —to such pitiful passes had financial straits brought him—of a certain self-congratulation, that he would not be at home when the dressmaker asked for money that night, and that no one would expect him to go to the bank under such circumstances. But Andrew, in his petty consideration as to personal benefit from such dire calamity, reckoned without another narrow traveller. Miss Higgins stopped him as he was going out of the door, looking as if bound to a funeral in his shabby Sunday black, with his solemn, sad face under his well-brushed hat.

"I hate to say anything when you're in such trouble, Mr. Brewster," said she, "but I do need the money to pay a bill, and I was wondering if you could leave what was due me yesterday, and what will be due me to-day."

But Fanny came with a rush to Andrew's relief. She was in that state of nervous tension that she was fairly dangerous if irritated. "Look here, Miss Higgins," said she. "We hesitated a good deal about havin' you come here to-day, anyway. Ellen wanted to send you word not to. We are in such awful trouble, that she said it didn't seem right for her to be thinkin' about new clothes, but I told her she'd got to have the things if she was going to college, and so we decided to have you come, but we 'ain't had any time nor any heart

320

to think of money. We've got plenty to pay you in the bank, but my husband 'ain't had any time to go there this mornin', what with seein' the doctor, and gettin' the certificate for my poor sister, and all I've got to say is: if you're so dreadful afraid as all this comes to, that you have to lose all sense of decency, and dun folks so hard, in such trouble as we be, you can put on your things and go jest as quick as you have a mind to, and I'll get Miss Patch to finish the work. I've been more than half a mind to have her, anyway. I was very strongly advised to. Lots of folks have talked to me against your fittin', but I've always had you, and I thought I'd give you the chance. Now if you don't want it, you jest pack up and go, and the quicker the better. You shall have your pay as soon as Mr. Brewster can get round after he has carried my poor sister to the asylum. You needn't worry." Fanny said the last with a sarcasm which seemed to reach out with a lash of bitterness like a whip. The other woman winced, her eyes were hard, but her voice was appeasing.

"Now, I didn't think you'd take it so, Mrs. Brewster, or I wouldn't have said anything," she almost wheedled. "You know I ain't afraid of not gettin' my pay, I—"

"You'd better not be," said Fanny.

"Of course I ain't. I know Mr. Brewster has steady work, and I know your folks have got money."

"We've got money enough not to be beholden to anybody," said Fanny. "Andrew, you'd better be goin' along or you'll be late."

Andrew went out of the yard with his head bent miserably. He had felt ashamed of his fear, he felt still more ashamed of his relief. He wondered, going down the street, if it might not be a happier lot to lose one's wits like poor Eva, rather than have them to the full responsibility of steering one's self through such straits of misery.

"I hope you won't think I meant any harm," the dressmaker said to Fanny, quite humbly.

There was that about the sister of another woman who was being carried off to an insane asylum which was fairly intimidating.

Miss Higgins sewed meekly during the remainder of the day, having all the time a wary eye upon Fanny. She went home before supper, urging a headache as an excuse. She was in reality afraid of Fanny.

Andrew was inexpressibly relieved when he reached home to find that the dressmaker was gone, and Fanny, having sent Amabel to bed, was chiefly anxious to know how her sister had reached the asylum. It was not until the latter part of the evening that she brought up the subject of the bank. "Do look out to-morrow, Andrew Brewster, and be sure to take that money out of the bank to pay Miss Higgins," she said. "As for being dunned again by that woman, I won't! It's the last time I'll ever have her, anyway. As far as that is concerned, all the money will have to come out of the bank if poor Eva is to be kept where she is. How much money was there that she had?"

"Just fifty-two dollars and seventy cents," replied Andrew. "Jim had left a little that he'd scraped together somehow, with the letter he wrote to her, and he told her if he had work he'd send her more."

"I'd die before I'd touch it," said Fanny, fiercely. Then she looked at Andrew with sudden pity. "Poor old man," she said; "it's mighty hard on you when you're gettin' older, and you never say a word to complain. But I don't see any other way than to take that money, do you?"

"No," said Andrew.

"And you don't think I'm hard to ask it, Andrew?"

"No."

"God knows if it was your sister and my money,

322

I would take every dollar. You know I would, Andrew."

"Yes, I know," replied Andrew, hoarsely.

"Mebbe she'll get better before it's quite gone," said Fanny. "You say the doctor gave some hope?"

"Yes, he did, if she was taken proper care of."

"Well, she shall be. I'll go out and steal before she sha'n't have proper care. Poor Eva!" Fanny burst into the hysterical wailing which had shaken her from head to foot at intervals during the last twenty-four hours. Andrew shuddered, thinking that he detected in her cries a resemblance to her sister's ravings. "Don't, don't, Fanny," he pleaded. "Don't, poor girl." He put his arm around her, and she wept on his shoulder, but with less abandon. "After all, we've got each other, and we've got Ellen, haven't we, Andrew?" she sobbed.

"Yes, thank God," said Andrew. "Don't, Fanny."

"That—that's more than money, more than all the wages for all the labor in the world, and that we've got, haven't we, Andrew? We've got what comes to us direct from God, haven't we? Don't think I'm silly, Andrew—haven't we?"

"Yes, yes, we have—you are right, Fanny," replied Andrew.

"I guess I am, too," she assented, looking up in Andrew's poor, worn face with eyes of sudden bravery. "We'll get along somehow—don't you worry, old man. I guess we'll come out all right, somehow. We'll use that money in the bank as far as it goes, and then I guess some way will be opened."

Then there came over Andrew's exaltation, to which Fanny's words had spurred his flagging spirit, a damper of utter mortification and guilt. He felt that he could bear this no longer. He opened his mouth to tell her what he had done with the money in the bank, when

323

there came a knock on the door, and Fanny fled into the bedroom. She had unfastened her dress, and her face was stained with tears. She shut the bedroom door tightly as Andrew opened the outer one.

The man who had loaned him the money to buy Ellen's watch stood there. His name was William Evarts, and he worked in the stitching - room of McGuire's factory, in which Andrew was employed. He was reported well-to-do, and to have amassed considerable money from judicious expenditures of his savings, and to be strictly honest, but hard in his dealings. He was regarded with a covert disfavor by his fellow-workmen, as if he were one of themselves who had somehow elevated himself to a superior height by virtue of their backs. If William Evarts had acquired prosperity through gambling in mines, they would have had none of that feeling; they would have recognized the legitimacy of luck in the conduct of affairs. He was in a way a reproach to them. "Why can't you get along and save as well as William Evarts?" many a man's monitor asked of him. "He doesn't earn any more than you do, and has had as many expenses in his family." The man not being able to answer the question to his own credit, disliked William Evarts who had instigated it.

Andrew, who had in his character a vein of sterling justice, yet felt that he almost hated William Evarts as he stood there before him, small and spare, snapping as it were with energy like electric wires, the strong lines in his clean-shaven face evident in the glare of the street-lamp.

"Good-evening," Andrew said, and he spoke like a criminal before a judge, and at that moment he felt like one.

"Good-evening," responded the other man. Then he added, in a hushed voice at first, for he had fineness to appreciate a sort of indecency in dunning, in asking a man for even his rightful due, and he had a regard for possible listening ears of femininity, "I was passing by, and I thought I'd call and see if it was convenient for you to pay me that money."

"I'm sorry," Andrew responded, with utter subjection. He looked and felt ignoble. "I haven't got it, Evarts."

"When are you going to have it?" asked the other, in a slightly raised, ominous voice.

"Just as soon as I can possibly get it," replied Andrew, softly and piteously. Ellen's chamber was directly overhead. He thought of the possibility of her overhearing.

"Look at here, Andrew Brewster," said the other man, and this time with brutal, pitiless force. When it came to the prospect of losing money he became as merciless as a machine. Something diabolical in remorselessness seemed to come to the surface, and reveal wheels of grinding for his fellow-men. "Look at here," he said, "I want to know right out, and no dodging. Have you got the money to pay me—yes or no?"

"No," said Andrew then, with a manliness born of desperation. He had the feeling of one who will die fighting. He wished that Evarts would speak lower on account of Ellen, but he was prepared to face even that. The man's speech came with the gliddering rush of an electric car; it was a concentration of words into one intensity of meaning; he elided everything possible, he ran all his words together. He spoke something in this wise: "GoddamnyouAndrewBrewster, for comin'to borrow money to buy your girl a watch when you had nothin' to pay for't with, what business had yourgirlwithawatchanyhow,I'dliket'know? Mygirl'ain't got no watch. I'veputmymoneyinthebank. It'srobbery. I'llhavethelawonye. I'llsueyou. I'll—"

At that moment something happened. The man, William Evarts, who was talking with a vociferousness which seemed cutting and lacerating to the ear, who was brandishing an arm for emphasis in a circle of frenzy, fairly jumped to one side. The girl, Ellen Brewster, in a light wrapper, which she had thrown over her night-gown, came with such a speed down the stairs which led to the entry directly before the door, that she seemed to be flying. White ruffles eddied around her little feet, her golden hair was floating out like a flag. She came close to William Evarts. "Will you please not speak so loud," said she, in a voice which her father had never heard from her lips before. It was a voice of pure command, and of command which carried with it the consciousness of power to enforce. She stood before William Evarts, and her fine smallness seemed intensified by her spirit to magnificence. The man shrank back a little, he had the impression as of some one overtowering him, and yet the girl came scarcely to his shoulder. "Please do not speak so loud, you will wake Amabel," she said, and Evarts muttered, like a dog under a whip, that he didn't want to wake her up.

"You must not," said Ellen. "Now here is the watch and chain. I suppose that will do as well as your money if you cannot afford to wait for my father to pay you. My father will pay you in time. He has never borrowed anything of any man which he has not meant to pay back, and will not pay back. If you cannot afford to wait, take the watch and chain."

The man looked at her stupefied.

"Here," said Ellen; "take it."

"I don't want your watch an' chain," muttered Evarts.

"You have either got to take them or wait for your money," said Ellen.

326

"I'll wait," said Evarts. He was looking at the girl's face with mingled sentiments of pity, admiration, and terror.

"Very well, then," said Ellen. "I will promise you, and my father will, that you shall have your money in time, but how long do you want to wait?"

"I'll wait any time. I ain't in any straits for the money, if I get it in the end," said Evarts.

"You will get it in the end," said Ellen. Evarts turned to Andrew.

"Look here, give me your note for six months," said he, "and we'll call it all right."

"All right," said Andrew, again.

"If you are not satisfied with that," said Ellen, with a tone as if she were conferring inestimable benefits, so proud it was, "you can take the watch and chain. It is not hurt in the least. Here." She was fairly insolent. Evarts regarded her with a mixture of admiration and terror. He told somebody the next day that Andrew Brewster had a stepper of a daughter, but he did not give his reasons for the statement. He had a sense of honor, and he had been in love with a girl as young before he married his wife, who had been a widow older than he, worth ten thousand dollars from her first husband. He could no more have taken the girl's watch and chain than he could have killed her.

"I'm quite satisfied," he replied to her, making a repellant motion towards the watch and dangling chain glittering in the electric-light.

"Very well, then," said Ellen, and she threw the chain over her neck.

"You just bring that I O U to the shop to-mor-mor," said Evarts to Andrew; then, with a "Good-evening," he was off. They heard him hail an electric-car passing, and that, although he never took a car, but walked to save the fare. He had been often heard

to say that he for one did not support the street railroad.

After he had gone, Ellen turned to her father, and
flung a silent white arm slipping from her sleeve loose
around his neck, and pulled his head to her shoulder.
"Now look here, father," she said, "you've been through
lots to-day, and you'd better go to bed and go to sleep.
I don't think mother was waked up—if she had been,
she would have been out here."

"Look here, Ellen, I want to tell you," Andrew began, pitifully. He was catching his breath like a child
with sobs.

"I don't want to hear anything," replied Ellen, firmly. "Whatever you did was right, father."

"I ought to tell you, Ellen!"

"You ought to tell me nothing," said Ellen. "You
are all tired out, father. You can't do anything that
isn't right for me. Now go to bed and go to sleep."

Ellen stroked her father's thin gray hair with exactly the same tender touch with which he had so often
stroked her golden locks. It was an inheritance of
love reverting to its original source. She kissed him
on his lined forehead with her flower-like lips, then she
pushed him gently away. "Go softly, and don't wake
mother," whispered she; "and, father, there's no need
to trouble her with this. Good-night."

CHAPTER XXXIV

ELLEN'S deepest emotion was pity for her father, so intense that it was actual physical pain.

"Poor father! Poor father! He had to borrow the money to buy me my watch and chain," she kept repeating to herself. "Poor father!"

To her New England mind, borrowing seemed almost like robbing. She actually felt as if her father had committed a crime for love of her, but all she looked at was the love, not the guilt. Suddenly a conviction which fairly benumbed her came over her—the money in the savings-bank; that little hoard, which had been to the imagination of herself and her mother a sheet-anchor against poverty, must be gone. "Father must have used it for something unbeknown to mother," she said to herself—"he must, else he would not have told Mr. Evarts that he could not pay him." It was a hot night, but the girl shivered as she realized for the first time the meaning of the wolf at the door. "All we've got left is this house—this house and—and—our hands," thought Ellen. She saw before her her father's poor, worn hands, her mother's thin, tired hands, jerking the thread in and out of those shameful wrappers; then she looked at her own, as yet untouched by toil, as white and small and fair as flowers. She thought of the four years before her at college, four years before she could earn anything—and in the mean time? She looked at the pile of her school-books on the table. She had been studying hard all summer. The thirst for knowledge was as intense in her as the thirst for stimulants in a drunkard.

"I ought to give up going to college, and go to work in the shop," Ellen said to herself, and she said it as one might drive a probing-knife into a sore. "I ought to," she repeated. And yet she was far from resolving to give up college. She began to argue with herself the expediency, supposing that the money in the bank was gone, of putting a mortgage on the house. If her father continued to have work, they might get along and pay for her aunt, who might, as the doctor had said, not be obliged to remain long in the asylum if properly cared for. Would it not, after all, be better, since by a course at college she would be fitted to command a larger salary than she could in any other way. "I can support them all," reflected Ellen. At that time the thought of Robert Lloyd, and that awakening of heart which he had brought to pass, were in abeyance. Old powers had asserted themselves. This love for her own blood and their need came between her and this new love, half of the senses, half of the spirit.

Amabel waked up in the early sultry dawn of the summer day with the bewilderment of one in a new world. She stared at the walls of the room, at the shaft of sunlight streaming in the window, then at Ellen.

"Where am I?" she inquired, in a loud, querulous plaint. Then she remembered, but she did not cry; instead, her little face took on a painfully old look.

"You are here with cousin Ellen, darling, don't you know?" Ellen replied, leaning over her, and kissing her.

Amabel wriggled impatiently away, and faced to the wall. "Yes, I know," said she.

That morning Amabel would not eat any breakfast, and Fanny suggested that Ellen take her for a ride on the street-cars. "We can get along without you for an

330

hour," she whispered, "and I am afraid that child will be sick."

So Ellen and Amabel set out, leaving Fanny and the dressmaker at work, and when they were returning past the factories the noon whistles were blowing and the operatives were streaming forth.

Ellen was surprised to see her father among them as the car swept past. He walked down the street towards home, his dinner-bag dangling at his side, his back more bent than ever.

She wondered uneasily if her father was ill, for he never went home to dinner. She looked back at him as the car swept past, but he did not seem to see her. He walked with an air of seeing nothing, covering the ground like an old dog with some patient, dumb end in view, heeding nothing by the way. It puzzled her also that her father had come out of Lloyd's instead of McGuire's, where he had been employed all summer. Ellen, after she reached home, watched anxiously for her father to come into the yard, but she did not see him. She assisted about the dinner, which was a little extra on account of the dressmaker, and all the time she glanced with covert anxiety at the window, but her father did not pass it. Finally, when she went out to the pump for a pitcher of water, she set the pitcher down, and sped to the orchard like a wild thing. A suspicion had seized her that her father was there.

Sure enough, there he was, but instead of lying face down on the grass, as he had done before, he was sitting back against a tree. He had the air of having settled into such a long lease of despair that he had sought the most comfortable position for it. His face was ghastly. He looked at Ellen as she drew near, and opened his mouth as if to speak, but instead he only caught his breath. He stared hard at her, then he closed his eyes as if not to see her, and motioned her away with one hand with an inarticulate noise in his throat.

But Ellen sat down beside him. She caught his two hands and looked at him. "Father, look at me," said she, and Andrew opened his eyes. The expression in them was dreadful, compounded of shame and despair and dread, but the girl's met them with a sort of glad triumph and strength of love. "Now look here, father," she said, "you tell me all about it. I didn't want to know last night. Now I want to know. What is the matter?"

Andrew continued to look at her, then all at once he spoke with a kind of hoarse shout. "I'm discharged! I'm discharged," he said, "from McGuire's; they've got a boy who can move faster in my place—a boy for less pay, who can move faster. I hurried over to Lloyd's to see if they would take me on again; I've always thought I should get back into Lloyd's, and I saw the foreman, and he told me to my face that I was too old, that they wanted younger men. And I went into the office to see Lloyd, pushed past the foreman, with him damning me, and I saw Lloyd."

"Was young Mr. Lloyd there?" asked Ellen, with white lips.

"No; I guess he had gone to dinner. And Lloyd looked at me, and I believe he counted every gray hair in my head, and he saw my back, and he saw my hands, and he said—he said I was too old."

Andrew snatched his hands from Ellen's grasp, pressed them to his face, and broke into weeping. "Oh, my God, I'm too old, I'm too old!" he sobbed; "I'm out of it! I'm too old!"

Ellen regarded him, and her face had developed lines of strength hitherto unrevealed. There was no pity in it, hardly love; she looked angry and powerful. "Father, stop doing so, and look at me," she said. She dragged her father's hands from his face, and he stared at her with his inflamed eyes, half terrified, half sustained. At that moment he realized a strength of support as from his own lost youth, a strength as of eternal progress which was more to be relied upon than other human strength. For the first time he leaned on his child, and realized with wonder the surety of the stay.

"Now, father, you stop doing so," said Ellen. "You can get work somewhere; you are not old. Call yourself old! It is nonsense. Are you going to give in and be old because two men tell you that you are? What if your hair is gray! Ever so many young men have gray hair. You are not old, and you can get work somewhere. McGuire's and Lloyd's are not the only factories in the country."

"That ain't all," said Andrew, with eyes like a beseeching dog's on her face.

"I know that isn't all," said Ellen. "You needn't be afraid to tell me, father. You have taken the money out of the savings-bank for something."

Again Andrew would have snatched his hands from the girl's and hidden his face, but she held them fast. "Yes, I have," he admitted, in a croaking voice.

"Well, what if you have?" asked Ellen. "You had a right to take it out, didn't you? You put it in. I don't know of anybody who had a better right to take it out than you, if you wanted to."

Andrew stared at her, as if he did not hear rightly. "You don't know what I did with it, Ellen," he stammered.

"It is nobody's business," replied Ellen. She had an unexplained sensation as if she were holding fast to her father's slipping self-respect which was dragging hard at her restraining love.

"I put it in a worthless gold-mine out in Colorado—

333

the same one your uncle Jim lost his money in," groaned Andrew.

"Well, it was your money, and you had a perfect right to," said Ellen. "Of course you thought the mine was all right or you wouldn't have put the money into it."

"God knows I did."

"Well, the best business men in the world make mistakes. It is nobody's business whether you took the money out or not, or what you used it for, father."

"I don't see how the bills are going to be paid, and there's your poor aunt," said Andrew. He was leaning more and more heavily upon this new tower of strength, this tender little girl whom he had hitherto shielded and supported. The beautiful law of reverse of nature had come into force.

Ellen set her mouth firmly. "Don't you worry, father," said she. "We will think of some way out of it. There's a little money to pay for Aunt Eva, and maybe she won't be sick long. Does mother know, father?"

"She don't know about anything, Ellen," replied Andrew, wretchedly.

"I know she doesn't know about your getting thrown out of work—but about the bank?"

"No, Ellen."

Ellen rose. "You stay here, where it is cool, till I ring the dinner-bell, father," she said.

"I don't want any dinner, child."

"Yes, you do, father. If you don't eat your dinner you will be sick. You come when the bell rings."

Andrew knew that he should obey, as he saw the girl's light dress disappear among the trees.

Ellen went back to the pump, and carried her pitcher of water into the house. Her mother met her at the door. "Where have you been all this time, Ellen Brew-

ster?" she asked, in a high voice. "Everything is
getting as cold as a stone."

Ellen caught her mother's arm and drew her into
the kitchen, and closed the door. Fanny turned pale
as death and looked at her. "Well, what has happened
now?" she said. "Is your father killed?"

"No," said Ellen, "but he is out of work, and he
can't get a job at Lloyd's, and he took all that money
out of the savings-bank a long time ago, and put it
into that gold-mine that Uncle Jim lost in."

Fanny clutched the girl's arm in a grasp so hard that
it left a blue mark on the tender flesh. She looked at
her, but did not speak one word.

"Now, mother," said Ellen, "you must not say one
word to father to scold him. He's got enough to bear
as it is."

Fanny pushed her away with sudden fierceness.
"I guess I don't need to have my own daughter teach
me my duty to my husband," said she. "Where is
he?"

"Down in the orchard."

"Well, ring the bell for dinner loud, so he can hear
it."

When Andrew came shuffling wearily up from the
orchard, Fanny met him at the corner of the house, out
of sight from the windows. She was flushed and perspiring, clad in a coarse cotton wrapper, revealing all
her unkempt curves. She went close to him, and thrust
one large arm through his. "Look here, Andrew,"
said she, in the tenderest voice he had ever heard from
her, a voice so tender that it was furious, "you needn't
say one word. What's done's done. We shall get
along somehow. I ain't afraid. Come in and eat your
dinner!"

The dressmaking work went on as usual after dinner. Andrew had disappeared, going down the road

towards the shop. He tried for a job at Briggs's, with no success, then drifted to the corner grocery.

Ellen sat until nearly three o'clock sewing. Then she went up-stairs and got her hat, and went secretly out of the back door, through the west yard, that her mother should not see her. However, her grandmother called after her, and wanted to know where she was going.

"Down street, on an errand," answered Ellen.

"Well, keep on the shady side," called her grandmother, thinking the girl was bound to the stores for some dressmaking supplies.

That night Miss Higgins did not ask for her pay; she had made up her mind to wait until her week was finished. She went away after supper, and Ellen followed her to the door. "We won't want you to-morrow, Miss Higgins," said she, "and here is your pay." With that she handed a roll of bills to the woman, who stared at her in amazement and growing resentment.

"If my work ain't satisfactory," said she—

"Your work is satisfactory," said Ellen, "but I don't want any more work done. I am not going to college."

There was something conclusive and intimidating about Ellen's look and tone. The dressmaker, who had been accustomed to regard her as a child, stared at her with awe, as before a sudden revelation of force. Then she took her money, and went down the walk.

When Ellen re-entered the sitting-room her father and mother, who had overheard every word, confronted her.

"Ellen Brewster, what does this mean?"

Andrew looked as if he would presently fall to the floor.

"It means," said Ellen—and she looked at her parents with the brave enthusiasm of a soldier on her beautiful face—she even laughed—"it means that I am going to work—I have got a job in Lloyd's."

336

When Ellen made that announcement, her mother did a strange thing. She ran swiftly to a corner of the room, and stood there, staring at the girl, with back hugged close to the intersection of the walls, as if she would withdraw as far as possible from some threatening ill. At that moment she looked alarmingly like her sister; there was something about Fanny in her corner, calculated, when all circumstances were taken into consideration, to make one's blood chill, but Andrew did not look at her. He was intent upon Ellen, and the facing of the worst agony of his life, and Ellen was intent upon him. She loved her mother, but the fear as to her father's suffering moved her more than her mother's. She was more like her father, and could better estimate his pain under stress. Andrew rose to his feet and stood looking at Ellen, and she at him. She tried to meet the drawn misery and incredulousness of his face with a laugh of reassurance.

"Yes, I've got a job in Lloyd's," said she. "What's the matter, father?"

Then Andrew made an almost inarticulate response; it sounded like a croak in an unknown tongue.

Ellen continued to look at him, and to laugh.

"Now look here, father," said she. "There is no need for you and mother to feel bad over this. I have thought it all over, and I have made up my mind. I have got a good high-school education now, and the four years I should have to spend at Vassar I could do nothing at all. There is awful need of money here, and not only for us, but for Aunt Eva and Amabel."

"You sha'n't do it!" Andrew burst out then, in a great shout of rage. "I'll mortgage the house—that'll last awhile. You sha'n't, I say! You are my child, and you've got to listen. You sha'n't, I say!"

"Now, father," responded Ellen's voice, which seemed to have in it a wonderful tone of firmness against which his agonized vociferousness broke as against a rock, "this is nonsense. You must not mortgage the house. The house is all you have got for your and mother's old age. Do you think I could go to college, and let you give up the house in order to keep me there? And as for grandma Brewster, you know what's hers is hers as long as she lives—we don't want to think of that. I have got this job now, which is only three dollars a week, but in a year the foreman said I might earn fifteen or eighteen, if I was quick and smart, and I will be quick and smart. It is the best thing for us all, father."

"You sha'n't!" shouted Andrew. "I say you sha'n't!"

Suddenly Andrew sank into a chair, his head lopped, he kept moving a hand before his eyes, as if he were brushing away cobwebs. Then Fanny came out of her corner.

"Get the camphor, quick!" she said to Ellen. "I dun'no' but you've killed your father."

Fanny held her husband's head against her shoulder, and rubbed his hands frantically. The awful strained look had gone from her face. Ellen came with the camphor, and then went for water. Fanny rubbed Andrew's forehead with the camphor, and held the bottle to his nose. "Smell it, Andrew," she said, in a voice of ineffable tenderness and pity. Ellen returned with a glass of water, and Andrew swallowed a little obediently. Finally he made out to stagger into the bedroom with Fanny's and Ellen's assistance. He sat down weakly on the bed, and Fanny lifted his legs up. Then he sank and closed his eyes as if he were spent. In fact, he was. At that moment of Ellen's announcement some vital energy in him suddenly relaxed like overstrained rubber. His face, sunken in the pillow, was both ghastly and meek. It was the face of a man who could fight no more. Ellen knelt down beside him, sobbing.

"Oh, father!" she sobbed, "I think it is for the best. Dear father, you won't feel bad."

"No," said Andrew, faintly. There was a slight twitching in his hand, as if he wished to put it on her head, then it lay thin and inert on the coverlid. He tried to smile, but his face settled into that look of utter acquiescence of fate.

"I s'pose it's the best you can do," he muttered.

"Have you told Miss Lennox?" gasped Fanny.

"Yes."

"What did she say?"

"She was sorry, but she made no objection," replied Ellen, evasively.

Fanny came forward abruptly, caught up the camphor-bottle, and began bathing Andrew's forehead again.

"We won't say any more about it," said she, in a harsh voice. "You'd better go over to your grandma Brewster's and see if she has got any whiskey. I think your father needs to take something."

"I don't want anything," said Andrew, feebly.

"Yes, you do, too, you are as white as a sheet. Go over and ask her, Ellen."

Ellen ran across the yard to her grandmother's, and the old woman met her at the door. She seemed to have an instinctive knowledge of trouble.

"What's the matter?" she asked.

"Father's a little faint, and mother wants me to borrow the whiskey," said Ellen. She had not at that time the courage to tell her grandmother what she had done.

Mrs. Zelotes ran into the house, and came out with the bottle.

"I'm comin' over," she announced. "I'm kind of worried about your father; he 'ain't looked well for some

339

time. I wonder what made him faint. Maybe he ate something which hurt him."

Ellen said nothing. She fled up-stairs to her chamber, as her grandmother entered the bedroom. She felt cowardly, but she thought that she would let her mother tell the news.

She sat down and waited. She knew that presently she would hear the old woman's voice at the foot of the stairs. She was resolved upon her course, and knew that she could not be shaken in it, yet she dreaded unspeakably the outburst of grief and anger which she knew would come from her grandmother. She felt as if she had faced two fires, and now before the third she quailed a little.

It was not long before the expected summons came.

"Ellen—Ellen Brewster, come down here!"

Ellen went down. Her grandmother met her at the foot of the stairs. She was trembling from head to foot; her mouth twisted and wavered as if she had the palsy.

"Look here, Ellen Brewster, this ain't true?" she stammered.

"Yes, grandma," answered Ellen. "I have thought it all over, and it is the only thing for me to do."

Her grandmother clutched her arm, and the girl felt as if she were in the grasp of another will, which was more conclusive than steel.

"You sha'n't!" she said, whispering, lest Andrew should hear, but with intense force.

"I've got to, grandma. We've got to have the money."

"The money," said the old woman, with an inflection of voice and a twist of her features indicative of the most superb scorn—"the money! I guess you ain't goin' to lose such a chance as that for money. I guess I've got two hundred and ten dollars a year income,

340

and I'll give up a half of that, and Andrew can put a mortgage on the house, if that Tenny woman has got to be supported because her husband has run off and left her and her young one. You sha'n't go to work in a shop."

"I've got to, grandma," said Ellen.

The old woman looked at her. It was like a duel between two strong wills of an old race. "You sha'n't," she said.

"Yes, I shall, grandma."

Then the old woman turned upon her in a fury of rage. "You're a Loud all over, Ellen Brewster," said she. "You 'ain't got a mite of Brewster about you. You 'ain't got any pride! You'd just as soon settle down and work in a shop as do anything else."

Fanny pushed before her. "Look here, Mother Brewster," said she, "you can just stop! Ellen is my daughter, and you 'ain't any right to talk to her this way. I won't have it. If anybody is goin' to blame her, it's me."

"Who be you?" said Mrs. Zelotes, sniffing.

Then she looked at them both, at Ellen and at her mother.

"If you go an' do what you've planned," said she to Ellen, "an' if you uphold her in it," to Fanny, "I've done with you."

"Good riddance," said Fanny, coarsely.

"I ain't goin' to forget that you said that," cried Mrs. Zelotes. She held up her dress high in front and went out of the door. "I ain't comin' over here again, an' I'll thank you to stay at home," said she. Then she went away.

Soon after Fanny heard Ellen in the dining-room setting the table for supper, and went out.

"Where did you get that money you paid the dressmaker with?" she asked, abruptly.

"I borrowed it of Abby," replied Ellen.

"Then she knows?"

"Yes."

Fanny continued to look at Ellen with the look of one who is settling down with resignation under some knife of agony.

"Well," said she, "there's no need to talk any more about it before your father. Now I guess you had better toast him some bread for his supper."

"Yes, I will," replied Ellen. She looked at her mother pitifully, and yet with that firmness which had seemed to suddenly develop in her. "You know it is the best thing for me to do, mother?" she said, and although she put it in the form of a question, the statement was commanding in its assertiveness.

"When are you—goin' to work?" asked Fanny.

"Next Monday," replied Ellen.

CHAPTER XXXV

WHEN Ellen had gone to the factory to apply for work neither of the Lloyds were in the office, only a girl at the desk, whom she knew slightly. Ellen had hesitated a little as she approached the girl, who looked around with a friendly smile.

"I want to see—" Ellen began, then she stopped, for she did not exactly know for whom she should ask. The girl, who was blond and trim, clad coquettishly in a blue shirt-waist and a duck skirt, with a large, cheap rhinestone pin confining the loop of her yellow braids, looked at her in some bewilderment. She had heard of Ellen's good-fortune, and knew she was to be sent to Vassar by Cynthia Lennox. She did not dream that she had come to ask for employment.

"You want to see Mr. Lloyd?" she asked.

"Oh no!" replied Ellen.

"Mr. Robert Lloyd?" The girl, whose name was Nellie Stone, laughed a little meaningly as she said that.

Ellen blushed. "No," she said. "I think I want to see the foreman."

"Which foreman?"

"I don't know," replied Ellen. "I want to get work if I can. I don't know which foreman I ought to see."

"To get work?" repeated the girl, with a subtle change in her manner.

"Yes," said Ellen. She could hear her heart beat, but she looked at the other girl's pretty, common face with the most perfect calmness.

343

"Mr. Flynn is the one you want to see, then," said the girl. "You know Ed Flynn, don't you?"

"A little," replied Ellen. He had been a big boy when she entered the high-school, and had left the next spring.

"Well, he's the one you want," said Nellie Stone. Then she raised her voice to a shrill peal as a boy passed the office door.

"Here, you, Jack," said she, "ask Mr. Flynn to come here a minute, will you?"

"He don't want to see you," replied the boy, who was small and spare, laden heavily with a great roll of wrapping paper borne bayonet fashion over his shoulder. His round, impish face grinned back at the girl at the desk.

"Quit your impudence," she returned, half laughing herself. "I don't want to see him; it is this young lady here; hurry up."

The boy gave a comprehensive glance at Ellen. "Guess he'll come," he called back.

Flynn appeared soon. He was handsome, well shaven and shorn, and he held himself smartly. He also dressed well in a business suit which would not have disgraced the Lloyds. His face lit up with astonishment and pleasure when he saw Ellen. He bowed and greeted her in a rich voice. He was of Irish descent but American born. Both his motions and his speech were adorned with flourishes of grace which betrayed his race. He placed a chair for Ellen with a sweep which would have been a credit to the stage. All his actions had a slight exaggeration as of fresco painting, which seemed to fit them for a stage rather than a room, and for an audience rather than chance spectators.

"No, thank you," replied Ellen. Then she went straight to the matter in hand. "I have called to see

344

if I could get a job here?" she said. She had been formulating her speech all the way thither. Her first impulse was to ask for employment, but she was sure as to the manner in which a girl would ordinarily couch such a request. So she asked for a job.

Flynn stared at her. "A job?" he repeated.

"Yes, I want very much to get one," replied Ellen. "I thought there might be a vacancy."

"Why, I thought—" said the young man. He was very much astonished, but his natural polish could rise above astonishment. Instead of blurting out what was in his mind as to her change of prospects, he reasoned with incredible swiftness that the change must be a hard thing to this girl, and that she was to be handled the more tenderly and delicately because she was such a pretty girl. He became twice as polite as before. He moved the chair nearer to her.

"Please sit down," he said. He handed to her the wooden arm-chair as if it had been a throne. Nellie Stone bent frowning over her day-book.

"Now let me see," said the young man, seriously, with perfect deference of manner, only belied by the rollicking admiration in his eyes. "You have never held a position in a factory before, I think?"

"No," replied Ellen.

"There is at present only one vacancy that I can think of," said Flynn, "and that does not pay very much, but there is always a chance to rise for a smart hand. I am sure you will be that," he added, smiling at her.

Ellen did not return the smile. "I shall be contented to begin for a little, if there is a chance to rise," she said.

"There's a chance to rise to eighteen dollars a week," said Flynn. He smiled again, but it was like smiling at seriousness itself. Ellen's downright, searching eyes upon his face seemed almost to forbid the fact of her own girlish identity.

"What is the job you have for me?" said she.

"Tying strings in shoes," answered Flynn. "Easy enough, only child's play, but you won't earn more than three dollars a week to begin with."

"I shall be quite satisfied with that," said Ellen. "When shall I come?"

"Why, to-morrow morning; no, to-morrow is Friday. Better come next Monday and begin the week. That will give you one day more off, and the hot wave a chance to get past." Flynn spoke facetiously. It was a very hot day, and the air in the office like a furnace. He wiped his forehead, to which the dark rings of hair clung. The girl at the desk glanced around adoringly at him.

"I would rather not stop for that if you want me to begin at once," said Ellen.

Flynn looked abashed. "Oh, we'd rather have you begin on the even week—it makes less bother over the account," he said. "Monday morning at seven sharp, then."

"Yes," said Ellen.

Flynn walked off with an abrupt duck of his head. He somehow felt that he had been rebuffed, and Ellen rose.

"I told you you'd get one," said the girl at the desk. "Catch Ed Flynn not giving a pretty girl a job." She said it with an accent of pain as well as malice. Ellen looked at her with large, indignant eyes. She had not the least idea what she meant, at least she realized only the surface meaning, and that angered her.

"I suppose he gave me the job because there was a vacancy," she returned, with dignity.

The other girl laughed. "Mebbe," said she.

Ellen continued to look at her, and there was something in her look not only indignant, but appealing. Nellie Stone's expression changed again. She laughed uneasily. "Land, I didn't mean anything," said she. "I'm glad for you that you got the job. Of course you wouldn't have got it if there hadn't been a chance. One of the girls got married last week, Maud Millet. I guess it's her place you've got. I'm real glad you've got it."

"Thank you," said Ellen.

"Good-bye," said the girl.

"Good-bye," replied Ellen.

On Monday morning the heat had broken, and an east wind with the breath of the sea in it was blowing. Ellen started for her work at half-past six. She held her father's little, worn leather-bag, in which he had carried his dinner for so many years. The walk was so long that it would scarcely give her time to come home at noon, and as for taking a car, that was not to be thought of for a moment on account of the fare.

Ellen walked along briskly, the east wind blew in her face, she smelled the salt sea, and somehow it at once soothed and stimulated her. Without seeing the mighty waste of waters, she seemed to realize its presence; she gazed at the sky hanging low with a scud of gray clouds, which did not look unlike the ocean, and the sense of irresponsibility in the midst of infinity comforted her.

"I am not Ellen Brewster after all," she thought. "I am not anything separate enough to be worried about what comes to me. I am only a part of greatness which cannot fail of reaching its end." She thought this all vaguely. She had no language for it, for she was very young; it was formless as music, but as true to her.

When she reached the cross-street where the Atkinses lived Abby and Maria came running out.

347

"My land, Ellen Brewster," said Abby, half angrily, "if you don't look real happy! I believe you are glad to go to work in a shoe-shop!"

Ellen laughed. Maria said nothing, but she pressed close to her as she walked along. She was coughing a little in the east wind. There had been a drop of twenty degrees in the night, and these drops of temperature in New England mean steps to the tomb.

"You make me mad," said Abby. Her voice broke a little. She dashed her hand across her eyes angrily. "Here's Granville Joy," said she; "you'll be in the same room with him, Ellen." She said it maliciously. Distress over her friend made her fairly malicious.

Ellen colored. "You are hard to talk to," said she, in a low voice, for Granville was coming nearer, gaining on them from behind.

"She don't mean it," whispered Maria.

When Granville caught up with them, Ellen pressed so close to Maria that he was forced to walk with Abby or pass on. She returned his "Good-morning," then did not look at him again. Presently Willy Jones appeared, coming so imperceptibly that he seemed almost impossible.

"Where did he come from?" whispered Ellen to Maria.

"Hush," replied Maria; "it's this way 'most every morning. All at once he comes, and he generally walks with me, because he's afraid Abby won't want him, but it's Abby."

This morning, Willy Jones, aroused, perhaps, to self-assertion by the presence of another man, walked three abreast with Abby and Granville, but on the other side of Granville. Now and then he peered around the other man at the girl, with soft, wistful blue eyes, but Abby never seemed to see him. She talked fast, in a harsh, rather loud voice. She uttered bitter witticisms which made her companions laugh.

348

"Abby is so bright," whispered Maria to Ellen, "but I wish she wouldn't talk so. Abby doesn't feel the way I wish she did. She rebels. She would be happier if she gave up rebelling and believed." Maria coughed as she spoke.

"You had better keep your mouth shut in this east wind, Maria," her sister called out sharply to her.

"I'm not talking much, Abby," replied Maria.

Presently Maria looked at Ellen lovingly. "Do you feel very badly about going to work?" she asked, in a low voice.

"No, not now. I have made up my mind," replied Ellen. The east wind was bringing a splendid color to her cheeks. She held up her head as she marched along, like one leading a charge of battle. Her eyes gleamed as with blue fire, her yellow hair sprung and curled around her temples.

They were now in the midst of a great, hurrying procession bound for the factories. Some of the men walked silently, with a dogged stoop of shoulders and shambling hitch of hips; some of the women moved droopingly, with an indescribable effect of hanging back from the leading of some imperious hand of fate. Many of them, both men and women, walked alertly and chattered like a flock of sparrows. Ellen moved with this rank and file of the army of labor, and all at once a sense of comradeship seized her. She began to feel humanity as she had never felt it before. The sense of her own littleness aroused her to a power of comprehension of the grandeur of the mass of which she was a part. She began to lose herself and sense humanity.

When the people reached the factories, two on one side of the road, one, Lloyd's, on the other, they began streaming up the outside stairs and disappearing like swarms of bees in hives. Two flights of stairs, one on each side, led to a platform in front of the entrance of Lloyd's.

When Ellen set her foot on one of these stairs the seven-o'clock steam-whistle blew, and a mighty thrill shot through the vast building. Ellen caught her breath. Abby came close to her.

"Don't get scared," said she, with ungracious tenderness; "there's nothing to be scared at."

Ellen laughed. "I'm not scared," said she. Then they entered the factory, humming with machinery, and a sensation which she had not anticipated was over her. Scared she was not; she was fairly exultant. All at once she entered a vast room in which eager men were already at the machines with frantic zeal, as if they were driving labor herself. When she felt the vibration of the floor under her feet, when she saw people spring to their stations of toil, as if springing to guns in a battle, she realized the might and grandeur of it all. Suddenly it seemed to her that the greatest thing in the whole world was work and that this was one of the greatest forms of work—to cover the feet of progress of the travellers of the earth from the cradle to the grave. She saw that these great factories, and the strength of this army of the sons and daughters of toil, made possible the advance of civilization itself, which cannot go barefoot. She realized all at once and forever the dignity of labor, this girl of the people, with a brain which enabled her to overlook the heads of the rank and file of which she herself formed a part. She never again, whatever her regret might have been for another life for which she was better fitted, which her taste preferred, had any sense of ignominy in this. She never again felt that she was too good for her labor, for labor had revealed itself to her like a goddess behind a sordid veil. Abby and Maria looked at her wonderingly. No other girl had ever entered Lloyd's with such a look on her face.

"Are you sick?" whispered Abby, catching her arm.

"No," said Ellen. "No, don't worry me, Abby. I think I shall like it."

"I declare you make me mad," said Abby, but she looked at her adoringly. "Here's Ed Flynn," she added. "He'll look out for you. Good-bye, I'll see you at noon." Abby went away to her machine. She was stitching vamps by the piece, and earning a considerable amount. The Atkinses were not so distressed as they had been, and Abby was paying off a mortgage.

When the foreman came towards Ellen she experienced a shock. His gay, admiring eyes on her face seemed to dispel all her exaltation. She felt as if her feet touched earth, and yet the young man was entirely respectful, and even thoughtful. He bade her "Good-morning," and conducted her to the scene of her labor. One other girl was already there at work. She gave a sidewise glance at Ellen, and went on, making her fingers fly. Mr. Flynn showed Ellen what to do. She had to tie the shoes together with bits of twine, laced through eyelet holes. Ellen took a piece of twine and tied it in as Flynn watched her. He laughed pleasantly.

"You'll do," he said, approvingly. "I've been in here five years, and you are the first girl I ever saw who tied a square knot at the first trial. Here's Mamie Brady here, she worked a solid month before she got the hang of the square knot."

"You go along," admonished the girl spoken of as "Mamie Brady." Her words were flippant, even impudent, but her tone was both dejected and childish. She continued to work without a glance at either of them. Her fingers flew, tying the knots with swift jerks.

"Well, you help Miss Brewster, if she needs any help," said Flynn, as he went away.

"We don't have any misses in this shop," said the girl to Ellen, with sarcastic emphasis.

"I don't care anything about being called miss," replied Ellen, picking up another piece of string.

"What's your first name?"

"Ellen."

"Oh, land! I know who you be. You read that essay at the high-school graduation. I was there. Well, I shouldn't think you would want to be called miss if you feel the way you said you did in that."

"I don't want to," said Ellen.

The girl gave a swift, comprehensive glance at her as her fingers manipulated the knots.

"You won't earn twenty cents a week at the rate you're workin'," she said; "look at me."

"I don't believe you worked any faster than I do when you hadn't been here any longer," retorted Ellen.

"I did, too; you can't depend on a thing Ed Flynn says. You're awful slow. He praises you because you are good-lookin'."

Ellen turned and faced her. "Look here," said she.

The other girl looked at her with unspeakable impudence, and yet under it was that shadow of dejection and that irresponsible childishness.

"Well, I am lookin'," said she, "what is it?"

"You need not speak to me again in that way," said Ellen, "and I want you to understand it. I will not have it."

"My, ain't you awful smart," said the other girl, sneeringly, but she went on with her work without another word. Presently she said to Ellen, kindly

352

enough: "If you lay the shoes the way I do, so, you
can get them faster. You'll find it pays. Every little
saving of time counts when you are workin' by the
piece."

"Thank you," said Ellen, and did as she was instructed. She began to work with exceeding swiftness
for a beginner. Her fingers were supple, her nervous
energy great. Flynn came and stood beside her,
watching her.

"If you work at that rate, you'll make it pretty
profitable," he said.

"Thank you," said Ellen.

"And a square knot every time," he added, with
almost a caressing inflection. Mamie Brady tied in
the twine with compressed lips. Granville Joy passed
them, pushing a rack full of shoes to another department, and he glanced at them jealously. Still he was
not seriously alarmed as to Flynn, who, although
he was good-looking, was a Catholic. Mrs. Zelotes
seemed an effectual barrier to that.

"Ed Flynn talks that way to everybody," Mamie
Brady said to Ellen, after the foreman had passed
on. She said it this time quite inoffensively. Ellen
laughed.

"If I *do* tie the knots square, that is the main thing,"
she said.

"Then you don't like him?"

"I never spoke two words to him before the day I
applied for work," Ellen replied, haughtily. She
was beginning to feel that perhaps the worst feature of her going to work in a factory would be this
girl.

"I've known girls who would be willing to go down
on their knees and tie his shoes when they hadn't seen
more of him than that," said the girl. "Ed Flynn
is an awful masher."

z

353

Ellen went on with her work. The girl, after a side glance at her, went on with hers.

Gradually Ellen's work began to seem mechanical. At first she had felt as if she were tying all her problems of life in square knots. She had to use all her brain upon it; after a while her brain had so informed her fingers that they had learned their lesson well enough to leave her free to think, if only the girl at her side would let her alone. The girl had a certain harsh beauty, coarsely curling red hair, a great mass of it, gathered in an untidy knot, and a brilliant complexion. Her hands were large and red. Ellen's contrasted with them looked like a baby's.

"You 'ain't got hands for workin' in a shoe-shop," said Mamie Brady, presently, and it was impossible to tell from her tone whether she envied or admired Ellen's hands, or was proud of the superior strength of her own.

"Well, they've got to work in a shoe-shop," said Ellen, with a short laugh.

"You won't find it so easy to work with such little mites of hands when it comes to some things," said the girl.

It began to be clear that she exulted in her large, coarse hands as being fitted for her work.

"Maybe mine will grow larger," said Ellen.

"No, they won't. They'll grow all bony and knotty, but they won't grow any bigger."

"Well, I shall have to get along with them the best way I can," replied Ellen, rather impatiently. This girl was irritating to a degree, and yet there was all the time that vague dejection about her, and withal a certain childishness, which seemed to insist upon patience. The girl was really older than Ellen, but she was curiously unformed. Some of the other girls said openly that she was "lacking."

354

"You act stuck up. Are you stuck up?" asked Mamie Brady, suddenly, after another pause.

Ellen laughed in spite of herself. "No," said she, "I am not. I know of no reason that I have for being stuck up."

"Well, I don't know of any either," said the other girl, "but I didn't know. You sort of acted as if you felt stuck up."

"Well, I don't."

"You talk stuck up. Why don't you talk the way the rest of us do? Why do you say 'am not,' and 'ar'n't'; why don't you say 'ain't'?"

The girl mimicked Ellen's voice impishly.

Ellen colored. "I am going to talk the way I think best, the way I have been taught is right, and if that makes you think I am stuck up, I can't help it."

"My, don't get mad. I didn't mean anything," said the other girl.

All the time while Ellen was working, and even while the exultation and enthusiasm of her first charge in the battle of labor was upon her, she had had, since her feminine instincts were, after all, strong with her, a sense that Robert Lloyd was under the same great factory roof, in the same human hive, that he might at any moment pass through the room. That, however, she did not think very likely. She fancied the Lloyds seldom went through the departments, which were in charge of foremen. Mr. Norman Lloyd was at the mountains with his wife, she knew. They left Robert in charge, and he would have enough to do in the office. She looked at the grimy men working around her, and she thought of the elegant young fellow, and the utter incongruity of her being among them seemed so great as to preclude the possibility of it. She had said to herself when she thought of obtaining work in Lloyd's that she need not hesitate about it on account of Robert. She had heard her father say that the elder Lloyd almost never came in contact with the men, that everything was done through the foremen. She reasoned that it would be the same with the younger Lloyd. But all at once the girl at her side gave her a violent nudge, which did not interrupt for a second her own flying fingers.

"Say," she said, "ain't he handsome?"

Ellen glanced over her shoulder and saw Robert Lloyd coming down between the lines of workmen. Then she turned to her work, and her fingers slipped and bungled, her ears rang. He passed without speaking.

Mamie Brady openly stared after him. "He's awful handsome, and an awful swell, but he's awful stuck up, just like the old boss," said she. "He never notices any of us, and acts as if he was afraid we'd poison him. My, what's the matter with you?"

"Nothing," said Ellen.

"You look white as a sheet; ain't you well?"

Ellen turned upon her with sudden fury. She had something of the blood of the violent Louds and of her hot-tempered grandmother. She had stood everything from this petty, insistent tormentor.

"Yes, I am well," she replied, "and I will thank you to let me alone, and let me do my work, and do your own."

The other girl stared at her a minute with curiously expressive, uplifted eyebrows.

"Whew!" she said, in a half whistle then, and went on with her work, and did not speak again.

Ellen was thankful that Robert Lloyd had not spoken to her in the factory, and yet she was cut to the quick by it. It fulfilled her anticipations to the letter. "I was right," she said to herself; "he can never think of me again. He is showing it." Somehow, after

356

he had passed, her enthusiasm, born of a strong imagination, and her breadth of nature failed her somewhat. The individual began to press too closely upon the aggregate. Suddenly Ellen Brewster and her own heartache and longing came to the front. She had put herself out of his life as completely as if she had gone to another planet. Still, feeling this, she realized no degradation of herself as a cause of it. She realized that from his point of view she had gone into a valley, but from hers she was rather on an opposite height. She on the height of labor, of skilled handiwork, which is the manifestation in action of brain-work, he on the height of pure brain-work unpressed by physical action.

At noon, when she was eating her dinner with Abby and Maria, Abby turned to her and inquired if young Mr. Lloyd had spoken to her when he came through the room.

"No, he didn't," replied Ellen.

Abby said nothing, but she compressed her lips and gave her head a hard jerk. A girl who ran a machine next to Abby's came up, munching a large piece of pie, taking clean semicircular bites with her large, white teeth.

"Say," she said, "did you see the young boss's new suit? Got up fine, wasn't he?"

"I'd like to see him working where I be for an hour," said a young fellow, strolling up, dipping into his dinner-bag. He was black and greasy as to face and hands and clothing. "Guess his light pants and vest would look rather different," said he, and everybody laughed except the Atkins girls and Ellen.

"I guess he washed his hands, anyway, before he ate his dinner," said Abby, sharply, looking at the young man's hands with meaning.

The young fellow colored, though he laughed. "There ain't a knife in this shop so sharp as some

357

women's tongues," said he. "I pity the man that gets you."

"There won't any man get me," retorted Abby. "I've seen all I want to see of men, working with 'em every day."

"Mebbe they have of you," called back the young fellow, going away.

"The saucy thing!" said the girl who stitched next to Abby.

"There isn't any excuse for a man's eating his dinner with hands like that," said Abby. "It's worse to poison yourself with your own dirt than with other folks'. It hurts your own self more."

"He ain't worth minding," said the girl.

"Do you suppose I do mind him?" returned Abby. Maria looked at her meaningly. The young man, whose name was Edison Bartlett, had once tried to court Abby, but neither she nor Maria had ever told of it.

"His clothes were a pearl gray," said the girl at the stitching-machine, reverting to the original subject.

"Good gracious, who cares what color they were?" cried Abby, impatiently.

"He looked awful handsome in 'em," said the girl. "He's awful handsome."

"You'd better look at handsome fellows in your own set, Sadie Peel," said Abby, roughly.

The girl, who was extremely pretty, carried herself well, and dressed with cheap fastidiousness, colored.

"I don't see what we have to think about sets for," said she. "I guess way back the Peels were as good as the Lloyds. We're in a free country, where one is as good as another, ain't we?"

"No one is as good as another, except in the sight of the Lord, in any country on the face of this earth," said Abby.

"If you are as good in your own sight, I don't see

that it makes much difference about the sight of other human beings," said Ellen. "I guess that's what makes a republic, anyway."

Sadie Peel gave a long, bewildered look at her, then she turned to Abby.

"Do you know where I can get somebody to do accordion-plaiting for me?" she asked.

"No," said Abby. "I never expect to get to the height of accordion-plaiting."

"I know where you can," said another girl, coming up. She had light hair, falling in a harsh, uncurled bristle over her forehead; her black gown was smeared with paste, and even her face and hands were sticky with it.

"There's a great splash of paste on your nose, Hattie Wright," said Abby.

The girl took out a crumpled handkerchief and began rubbing her nose absently while she went on talking about the accordion-plaiting.

"There's a woman on Joy Street does it," said she. "She lives just opposite the school-house, and she does it awful cheap, only three cents a yard." She thrust the handkerchief into her pocket.

"You haven't got it half off," said Abby.

"Let it stay there, then," said the girl, indifferently. "If you work pasting linings in a shoe-shop you've got to get pasted yourself."

Ellen looked at the girl with a curious reflection that she spoke the truth, that she really was pasted herself, that the soil and the grind of her labor were wearing on her soul. She had seen this girl out of the shop— in fact, only the day before—and no one would have known her for the same person. When her light hair was curled, and she was prettily dressed, she was quite a beauty. In the shop she was a slattern, and seemed to go down under the wheels of her toil.

"On Joy Street, you said?" said Sadie Peel.

"Yes. Right opposite the school-house. Her name is Brackett."

Then the one-o'clock whistle blew, and everybody, Ellen with the rest, went back to their stations. Robert Lloyd did not come into the room again that afternoon. Ellen worked on steadily, and gained swiftness. Every now and then the foreman came and spoke encouragingly to her.

"Look out, Mamie," he said to the girl at her side, "or she'll get ahead of you."

"I don't want to get ahead of her," said Ellen, unexpectedly.

Flynn laughed. "If you don't, you ain't much like the other girls in this shop," said he, passing on with his urbane, slightly important swing of shoulders.

"Did you mean that?" asked Mamie Brady.

"Yes, I did. It seems to me you work fast enough for any girl. A girl isn't a machine."

"You're a queer thing," said Mamie Brady. "If I were you, I would just as soon get ahead as not, especially if Ed Flynn was goin' to come and praise me for it."

Ellen shrugged her shoulders and tied another knot.

"You're a queer thing," said Mamie Brady, while her fingers flew like live wires.

CHAPTER XXXVI

THAT night, when Ellen went down the street towards home with the stream of factory operatives, she computed that she must have earned about fifty cents, perhaps not quite that. She was horribly tired. Although the work in itself was not laborious, she had been all day under a severe nervous tension.

"You look tired to death, Ellen Brewster," Abby said, in a half-resentful, half-compassionate tone. "You can never stand this in the world."

"I am no more tired than any one would be the first day," Ellen returned, stoutly, "and I'm going to stand it."

"You act to me as if you liked it," said Abby, with an angry switch like a cat.

"I do," Ellen returned, almost as angrily. Then she turned to Abby. "Look here, Abby Atkins, why can't you treat me half-way decent?" said she. "You know I've got to do it, and I'm making the best of it. If anybody else treated me the way you are doing, I don't know what you would do."

"I would kill them," said Abby, fiercely; "but it's different with me. I'm mad to have you go to work in the shop, and act as if you liked it, because I think so much of you." Abby and Ellen were walking side by side, and Maria followed with Sadie Peel.

"Well, I can't help it if you are mad at me," said Ellen. "I've had everything to contend against, my

361

father and mother, and my grandmother won't even speak to me, and now if you—" Ellen's voice broke.

Abby caught her arm in a hard grip.

"I ain't," said she; "you can depend on me. You know you can, in spite of everything. You know why I talk so. If you've set your heart on doing it, I won't say another word. I'll do all I can to help you, and I'd like to hear anybody say a word against you for going to work in the shop, that's all."

Ellen and Abby almost never kissed each other; Abby was not given to endearments of that kind. Maria was more profuse with her caresses. That night when they reached the corner of the cross street where the Atkinses lived, Maria went close to Ellen and put up her face.

"Good-night," said she. Then she withdrew her lips suddenly, before Ellen could touch them.

"I forgot," said she. "You mustn't kiss me. I forgot my cough. They say it's catching."

Ellen caught hold of her little, thin shoulders, held her firmly, and kissed her full on her lips.

"Good-night," said she.

"Good-night, Ellen," called Abby, and her sharp voice rang as sweet as a bird's.

When Ellen came in sight of her grandmother's house, she saw a window-shade go down with a jerk, and knew that Mrs. Zelotes had been watching for her, and was determined not to let her know it. Mrs. Pointdexter came out of her grand house as Ellen passed, and took up her station on the corner to wait for a car. She bowed to Ellen with an evasive, little, sidewise bow. Her natural amiability prompted her to shake hands with her, call her "my dear," and inquire how she had got on during her first day in the factory, but she was afraid of her friend, whose eye she felt upon her around the edge of the drawn curtain.

It was unusually dark that night for early fall, and the rain came down in a steady drizzle, as it had come all day, and the wind blew from the ocean on the east. The lamp was lighted in the kitchen when Ellen turned into her own door-yard, and home had never looked so pleasant and desirable to her. For the first time in her life she knew what it was to come home for rest and shelter after a day of toil, and she seemed to sense the full meaning of home as a refuge for weary labor.

When she opened the door, she smelled at once a particular kind of stew of which she was very fond, and knew that her mother had been making it for her supper. There was a rush of warm air from the kitchen which felt grateful after the damp chill outside.

Ellen went into the kitchen, and her mother stood there over the stove, stirring the stew. She looked up at the girl with an expression of intense motherliness which was beyond a smile.

"Well, so you've got home?" she said.

"Yes."

"How did you get along?"

"All right. It isn't hard work. Not a bit hard, mother."

"Ain't you tired?"

"Oh, a little. But no more than anybody would be at first. I don't look very tired, do I?" Ellen laughed.

"No, you don't," said Fanny, looking at her cheeks, reddened with the damp wind. The mother's look was admiring and piteous and brave. No one knew how the woman had suffered that day, but she had kept her head and heart above it. The stew for Ellen's supper was a proof of that.

"Where's father?" asked Ellen, taking off her hat and cape, and going to the sink to wash her face and hands. Fanny saw her do that with a qualm. Ellen had always used a dainty little set in her own room.

Now she was doing exactly as her father had always done on his return from the shop—washing off the stains of leather at the kitchen sink. She felt instinctively that Ellen did it purposely, that she was striving to bring herself into accord with her new life in all the details.

Little Amabel came running out of the dining-room, and threw her arms around Ellen's knees as she was bending over the sink. "I've set the table!" she cried.

"Look out or you'll get all splashed," laughed Ellen.

"And I dusted," said Amabel.

"She's been as good as a kitten all day, and a sight of help," said Fanny.

"She's a good girl," said Ellen. "Cousin Ellen will kiss her as soon as she gets her face washed."

She caught hold of a fold of the roller towel, and turned her beautiful, dripping face to her mother as she did so.

"That stew does smell so good," said she. "Where did you say father was?"

"I thought we'd just have some bread and milk for dinner, and somethin' hearty to-night, when you came home," said Fanny. "I thought maybe a stew would taste good."

"I guess it will," said Ellen, stooping down to kiss Amabel. "Where did you say father was?"

"Uncle Andrew has been lyin' down all day most," whispered Amabel.

"Isn't he well?" Ellen asked her mother, in quick alarm.

"Oh yes, he's well enough." Fanny moved close to the girl with a motion of secrecy. "If I were you I wouldn't say one word about the shop, nor what you did, before father to-night; let him kind of get used to it. Amabel mustn't talk about it, either."

"I won't," said Amabel, with a wise air.

364

"You know father had set his heart on somethin' pretty different for you," said Fanny.

Fanny hushed her voice as Andrew came out of the dining-room, staggering a little as if the light blinded him. His nervous strength of the morning had passed and left him exhausted. He moved and stood with a downward lope of every muscle, expressing unutterable patience, which had passed beyond rebellion and questioning.

He stood before Ellen like some old, spent horse. He was expecting to hear something about the shop—expecting, as it were, a touch on a sore, and he waited for it meekly.

Ellen turned her lovely, glowing face towards him.

"Father," she said, as if nothing out of the common had happened, "are you going down-town to-night?"

Andrew brightened a little. "I can if you want anything, Ellen," he said.

"Well, I don't want you to go on purpose, but I do want a book from the library."

"I'd just as soon go as not, Ellen," said Andrew.

"It'll do him good," whispered Fanny, as she passed Ellen, carrying the dish of stew to the dining-room.

"Well, then, I'll give you my card after supper," said Ellen. "Supper is ready now, isn't it, mother? I'm as hungry as a bear."

Andrew, when he was seated at the table and was ladling out the stew, had still that air of hopeless and defenceless apology towards life, but he held his head higher, and his frown of patient gloom had relaxed.

Then Ellen said something else. "Maybe I can write a book some time," said she.

A sudden flash illumined Andrew's face. It was like the visible awakening of hope and ambition.

"I don't see why you can't," he said, eagerly.

"Maybe she can," said Fanny. "Give her some more of the potatoes, Andrew."

"I'll have plenty of time after—evenings," said Ellen.

"I guess lots of folks write books that sell, and sell well, that don't have any more talent than you," said Andrew. "Only think how they praised your valedictory."

"Well, it can't do any harm to try," said Ellen, "and you could copy it for me, couldn't you, father? Your writing is so fine, it would be as good as a typewriter."

"Of course I can," said Andrew.

When Andrew went down to the library, passing along the drenched streets, seeing the lamps through shifting veils of heavy mist, he was as full of enthusiasm over Ellen's book as he had been over the goldmine. The heart of a man is always ready to admit a ray of sunshine, and it takes only a small one to dispel the shadows when love dwells therein.

366

CHAPTER XXXVII

ELLEN actually went to work, with sheets of fools-cap and a new bottle of ink, on a novel, which was not worth the writing; but no one could estimate the comfort and encouragement it was to Andrew. Ellen worked an hour or two every evening on the novel, and next day Andrew copied it in a hand like copperplate—large, with ornate flourishes. Andrew's handwriting had always been greatly admired, and, strangely enough, it was not in the least indicative of his character, being wholly acquired. He had probably some ability for drawing, but this had been his only outlet.

At the head of every chapter of Ellen's novel were birds and flowers done in colored inks, and every chapter had a tail-piece of elegant quirls and flourishes. Fanny admired it intensely. She was not quite so sure of Ellen's work as she was of her husband's. She felt herself a judge of one, but not of the other.

" If Ellen could only write as well as you copy, it will do," she often said to Andrew.

"What she is writing is beautiful," said Andrew, fervently. He was quite sure in his own mind that such a book had never been written, and his pride in his decorations was a minor one.

Ellen, although she was not versed in the ways of books, yet had enough of a sense of the fitness of things, and of the ridiculous, to know that the manuscript, with its impossible pen-and-ink birds and flowers heading and finishing every chapter, was grotesque in the extreme. She felt divided between a desire to laugh

367

and a desire to cry whenever she looked at it. About her own work she felt more than doubtful; still, she was somewhat hopeful, since her taste and judgment, as well as her style, were alike crude. She told Abby and Maria what she was doing, under promise of strict secrecy, and after a while read them a few chapters.

"It's beautiful," said Maria—"perfectly beautiful. I had a Sunday-school book this week which I know wasn't half as good."

Ellen looked at Abby, who was silent. The three girls were up in Ellen's room. It was midwinter, some months after she had gone to work in the shop, and she had a fire in her little, air-tight stove.

"Well, what do you think of it, Abby?" asked Ellen. Ellen's cheeks were flushed as if with fever. She looked eagerly at the other girl.

"Do you want me to tell you the truth?" asked Abby, bluntly.

"Yes, of course I do."

"Well, then, I don't know a thing about books, and I'd knock anybody else down that said it, but it seems to me it's trash."

"Oh, Abby," murmured Maria.

"Never mind," said Ellen, though she quivered a little, "I want to know just how it looks to her."

"It looks to me just like that," said Abby—"like trash. It sounds as if, when you began to write it, you had mounted upon stilts, and didn't see things and people the way they really were. It ain't natural."

"Do you think I had better give it up, then?" asked Ellen.

"No, I don't, on account of your father."

"I believe it would about break father's heart," said Ellen.

"I don't know but it's worth as much to write a book for your father, to please him, and keep his

368

spirits up, as it is to write one for the whole world," said Abby.

"Only, of course, she can't get any money for it," said Maria. "But I don't believe Abby is right, and don't you get discouraged, Ellen. It sounds beautiful to me."

"Well, I suppose it is worth keeping on with for father's sake," said Ellen; but she had a discouraged air. She never again wrote with any hope or heart; she had faith in Abby's opinion, for she knew that she was always predisposed to admiration in her case.

Ellen at that time was earning more, for she had advanced, and had long ago left her station beside Mamie Brady; and now in a month or two she would have a machine. The girls, many of them, said openly that her rapid promotion was due to favoritism, and that Ed Flynn wouldn't do as much for anybody but Ellen Brewster. Flynn hung about her in the shop a good deal, but he had made no efforts to pay her decided attention. His religion was the prime factor for his hesitation. He could not see his way clear towards open addresses with a view to marriage. Still, he had a sharp eye for other admirers, and Ellen had not been in the factory two months before Granville Joy was sent into another room. Robert Lloyd, to whom the foreman appealed for confirmation of the plan, coincided with readiness.

"That fellow ain't strong enough to run that machine he's doing now," said Flynn.

"Then put him on another," Robert said, coloring. It was not quite like setting his rival in the front of the battle; still, he felt ashamed of himself. Quicker than lightning it had flashed through his mind that young Joy could thus be sent into a separate room from Ellen Brewster.

"I think he had better take one of the heel-shaving

machines below," said Flynn, "and let that big Swede, that's as strong as an ox, and never jumped at anything in his life, take his place here."

"All right," said Lloyd, assuming a nonchalant air. "Make the change if you think it advisable, Flynn."

While such benevolence towards a possible rival had its suspicious points, yet there was, after all, some reason for it. Granville Joy, who was delicately organized as to his nerves, was running a machine for cutting linings, and this came down with sharp thuds which shook the factory, and it was fairly torture to him. Every time the knife fell he cringed as if at a cannon report. He had never grown accustomed to it. His face had acquired a fixed expression of being screwed to meet a shock of sound. He was manifestly unfit for his job, but he received the order to leave with dismay.

"Hasn't my work been satisfactory?" he asked Flynn.

"Satisfactory enough," replied the foreman, genially, "but it's too hard for you, man."

"I 'ain't complained," said Joy, with a flash of his eyes. He thought he knew why this solicitude was shown him.

"I know you 'ain't," said Flynn, "but you 'ain't got the muscle and nerve for it. That's plain enough to see."

"I 'ain't complained, and I'd rather stay where I be," said Joy, angrily.

"You'll go where you are sent in this factory, or be damned," cried Flynn, walking off.

Joy looked after him with an expression which transformed his face. But the next morning the stolid Swede, who would not have started at a bomb, was at his place, and he was below, where he could not see Ellen.

Robert never spoke to Ellen in the factory, and had never called upon her since she entered. Now and then he met her on the street and raised his hat, that was all. Still, he began to wonder more and more if his aunt had not been mistaken in her view of the girl's motive for giving up college and going to work. Then, later on, he learned from Lyman Risley that a small mortgage had been put on the Brewster house some time before. In fact, Andrew, not knowing to whom to go, and remembering his kindness when Ellen was a child, had applied to him for advice concerning it. "He had to do it to keep his wife's sister in the asylum," he told Robert; "and that poor girl went to work because she was forced into it, not because she preferred it, you may be sure of that."

The two men were walking down the street one wind-swept day in December, when the pavement showed ridges of dust as from a mighty broom, and travellers walked bending before it with backward-flying garments.

"You may be right," said Robert; "still, as Aunt Cynthia says, so many girls have that idea of earning money instead of going to school."

"I know the pitiful need of money has tainted many poor girls with a monstrous and morbid overvalue of it," said Risley, "and for that I cannot see they are to blame; but in this case I am sure it was not so. That poor child gave up Vassar College and went to work because she was fairly forced into it by circumstances. The aunt's husband ran away with another woman, and left her destitute, so that the support of her and her child came upon the Brewsters; and Brewster has been out of work a long time now, I know. He told me so. That mortgage had to be raised, and the girl had to go to work; there was no other way out of it."

"Why didn't she tell Aunt Cynthia so?" asked Robert.

"Because she is Ellen Brewster, the outgrowth of the child who would not—" Risley checked himself abruptly.

"I know," said Robert, shortly.

The other man started. "How long have you known —she did not tell?"

Robert laughed a little. "Oh no," he replied. "Nobody told. I went there to call, and saw my own old doll sitting in a little chair in a corner of the parlor. She did not tell, but she knew that I knew. That child was a trump."

"Well, what can you expect of a girl who was a child like that?" said Risley. "Mind you, in a way I don't like it. This power for secretiveness and this rigidity of pride in a girl of that age strike me rather unpleasantly. Of course she was too proud to tell Cynthia the true reason, and very likely thought they would blame her father, or Cynthia might feel that she was in a measure hinting to her to do more."

"It would have looked like that," said Robert, reflecting.

"Without any doubt that was what she thought; still, I don't like this strength in so young a girl. She will make a more harmonious woman than girl, for she has not yet grown up to her own character. But depend upon it, that girl never went to work of her own free choice."

"You say the father is out of work?" Robert said.

"Yes, he has not had work for six months. He said, with the most dejected dignity and appeal that I ever saw in my life, that they begin to think him too old, that the younger men are preferred."

"I wonder," Robert began, then he stopped confusedly. It had been on his tongue to say that he wondered if he could not get some employment for him

372

at Lloyd's; then he remembered his uncle, and stopped. Robert had begun to understand the older man's methods, and also to understand that they were not to be cavilled at or disputed, even by a nephew for whom he had undoubtedly considerable affection.

"It is nonsense, of course," said Risley. "The man is not by any means old or past his usefulness, although I must admit he has that look. He cannot be any older than your uncle. Speaking of your uncle, how is Mrs. Lloyd?"

"I fear Aunt Lizzie is very far from well," replied Robert, "but she tries to keep it from Uncle Norman."

"I don't see how she can. She looked ghastly when I met her the other day."

"That was when Uncle Norman was in New York," said Robert. "It is different when he is at home." As he spoke, an expression of intensest pity came over the young man's face. "I wonder what a woman who loves her husband will not do to shield him from any annoyance or suffering," he said.

"I believe some women are born fixed to a sort of spiritual rack for the sake of love, and remain there through life," said Risley. "But I have always liked Mrs. Lloyd. She ought to have good advice. What is it, has she told you?"

"Yes," said Robert.

"It will be quite safe with me."

Robert whispered one word in his ear.

"My God!" said Risley, "that? And do you mean to say that she has had no advice except Dr. Story?"

"Yes, I took her to New York to a specialist some time ago. Uncle Norman never knew it."

"And nothing can be done?"

"She could have an operation, but the success would be very doubtful."

"And that she will not consent to?"

373

"She has not yet."

"How long?"

"Oh, she may live for years, but she suffers horribly, and she will suffer more."

"And you say he does not know?"

"No."

"Why, look here, Robert, dare you assume the responsibility? What will he say when he finds out that you have kept it from him?"

"I don't care," said Robert. "I will not break an oath exacted by a woman in such straits as that, and I don't see what good it could do to tell him."

"He might persuade her to have the operation."

"His mere existence is persuasion enough, if she is to be persuaded. And I hope she may consent before long. She has seemed a little more comfortable lately, too."

"I suppose sometimes those hideous things go away as mysteriously as they come," said Risley.

"Yes," replied Robert. "Going back to our first subject—"

Risley laughed. "Here she is coming," he said.

In fact, at that moment they came abreast the street that led to the factories, and the six-o'clock whistle was just dying away in a long reverberation, and the workmen pouring out of the doors and down the stairs. Ellen had moved quickly, for she had an errand at the grocery-store before she went home. She was going to get some oysters for a hot stew for supper, of which her father was very fond. She had a little oyster-can in her hand when she met the two gentlemen. She had grown undeniably thinner since summer, but she was charming. Her short black skirt and her coarse gray jacket fitted her as well as if they had been tailor-made. There was nothing tawdry or slatternly about her. She looked every inch a lady, even with the drawback of an oyster-can, and mittens instead of gloves.

Both Risley and Robert raised their hats, and Ellen bowed. She did not smile, but her face contracted curiously, and her color obviously paled. Risley looked at Robert after they had passed.

"I have called on her twice." said Robert, as if answering a question. His relations with the older man had become very close, almost like those of father and son, though Risley was hardly old enough for that relation.

"And you haven't been since she went to work?"

"No."

"But you would have, had she gone to college instead of going to work in a shoe-factory?" Risley's voice had a tone of the gentlest conceivable sarcasm.

Robert colored. "Yes, I suppose so," he said. Then he turned to Risley with a burst of utter frankness. "Hang it! old fellow," he said, "you know how I have been brought up; you know how she—you know all about it. What is a fellow to do?"

"Do what he pleases. If it would please me to call on that splendid young thing, I should call if I were the Czar of all the Russias."

"Well, I will call," said Robert.

CHAPTER XXXVIII

THE very next evening Robert Lloyd went to call on Ellen. As he started out he was conscious of a strange sensation of shock, as if his feet had suddenly touched firm ground. All these months since Ellen had been working in the factory he had been vacillating. He was undoubtedly in love with her; he did not for a moment cheat himself as to that. When he caught a glimpse of her fair head among the other girls, he realized how unspeakably dear she was to him. Ellen never entered nor left the factory that he did not know it. Without actually seeing her, he was conscious of her presence always. He acknowledged to himself that there was no one like her for him, and never would be. He tried to interest himself in other young women, but always there was Ellen, like the constant refrain of a song. All other women meant to him not themselves, but Ellen. Womanhood itself was Ellen for his manhood. He knew it, and yet that strain of utterly impassionate judgment and worldly wisdom which was born in him kept him from making any advances to her. Now, however, the radicalism of Risley had acted like a spur to his own inclination. His judgment was in abeyance. He said to himself that he would give it up; he would go to see the girl—that he would win her if he could. He said to himself that she had been wronged, that Risley was right about her, that she was good and noble.

As the car drew near the Brewsters, his tenderness seemed to outspeed the electricity. The girl's fair

376

face was plain before his eyes, as if she were actually there, and it was idealized and haloed as with the light of gold and precious stones. All at once, since he had given himself loose rein, he overtook, as it were, the true meaning of her. "The dear child," he thought, with a rush of tenderness like pain—"the dear child. There she gave up everything and went to work, and let us blame her, rather than have her father blamed. The dear, proud child. She did that rather than seem to beg for more help."

When Robert got off the car he was ready to fall at her feet, to push between her and the roughness of life, between her and the whole world.

He went up the little walk between the dry shrubs and rang the bell. There was no light in the front windows nor in the hall. Presently he heard footsteps, and saw a glimmer of light advancing towards him through the length of the hall. There were muslin-curtained side-lights to the door. Then the door opened, and little Amabel Tenny stood there holding a small kerosene lamp carefully in both hands. She held it in such a manner that the light streamed up in Robert's face and nearly blinded him. He was dimly conscious of a little face full of a certain chary innocence and pathos regarding him.

"Is Miss Ellen Brewster at home?" asked Robert, smiling down at the little thing.

"Yes, sir," replied Amabel.

Then she remained perfectly still, holding the lamp, as if she had been some little sculptured light-bearer. She did not return his smile, and she did not ask him in. She simply regarded him with her sharp, innocent, illuminated face. Robert felt ridiculously nonplussed.

"Did you say she was in, my dear?" he asked.

"Yes, sir," replied Amabel, then relapsed into silence.

"Can I see her?" asked Robert, desperately.

"I don't know," replied Amabel. Then she stood still, as before, holding the lamp.

Robert began to wonder what he was to do, when he heard a woman's voice calling from the sitting-room at the end of the hall, the door of which had been left ajar :

"Amabel Tenny, what are you doin'? You are coldin' the house all off! Who is it?"

"It's a man, Aunt Fanny," called Amabel.

"Who is the man?" asked the voice. Then, much to Robert's relief, Fanny herself appeared.

She colored a flaming red when she saw him. She looked at Amabel as if she had an impulse to shake her.

"Why, Mr. Lloyd, is it you?" she cried.

"Good-evening, Mrs. Brewster; is—is your daughter at home?" asked Robert. He felt inclined to roar with laughter, and yet a curious dismay was beginning to take possession of him.

"Yes, Ellen is at home," replied Fanny, with alacrity. "Walk in, Mr. Lloyd." She was blushing and smiling as if she had been her own daughter. It was foolish, yet pathetic. Although Fanny asked the young man to walk in, and snatched the lamp peremptorily from Amabel's hand, she still hesitated. Robert began to wonder if he should ever be admitted. He did not dream of the true reason for the hesitation. There was no fire in the parlor, and in the sitting-room were Andrew, John Sargent, and Mrs. Wetherhed. It seemed to her highly important that Ellen should see her caller by herself, but how to take him into that cold parlor?

Finally, however, she made up her mind to do so. She opened the parlor door.

"Please walk in this way, Mr. Lloyd," said she, and Robert followed her in.

It was a bitter night outside, and the temperature in the unused room was freezing. The windows behind the cheap curtains were thickly furred with frost.

"Please be seated," said Fanny.

She indicated the large easy-chair, and Robert seated himself without removing his outer coat, yet the icy cold of the cushions struck through him.

Fanny ignited a match to light the best lamp with its painted globe. Her fingers trembled. She had to use three matches before she was successful.

"Can't I assist you?" asked Robert.

"No, thank you," replied Fanny; "I guess the matches are damp. I've got it now." Her voice shook. She turned to Robert when the lamp was lighted, still holding the small one, which she had set for the moment on the table. The strong double light revealed her face of abashed delight, although the young man did not understand it. It was the solicitude of the mother for the child which dignified all coarseness and folly.

"I guess you had better keep on your overcoat a little while till I get the fire built," said she. "This room ain't very warm."

Robert tried to say something polite about not feeling cold, but the lie was too obvious. Instead, he remarked that his coat was very warm, as it was, indeed, being lined with fur.

"I'll have the fire kindled in a minute," Fanny said.

"Now don't trouble yourself, Mrs. Brewster," said Robert. "I am quite warm in this coat, unless," he added, lamely, "I could go out where you were sitting."

"There's company out there," said Fanny, with embarrassed significance. She blushed as she spoke, and Robert blushed also, without knowing why.

"It's no trouble at all to start a fire," said Fanny; "this chimney draws fine. I'll speak to Ellen."

Robert, left alone in the freezing room, felt his dis-

379

may deepen. Barriers of tragedy are nothing to those of comedy. He began to wonder if he were not, after all, doing a foolish thing. The hall door had been left ajar, and he presently became aware of Amabel's little face and luminous eyes set therein.

Robert smiled, and to his intense astonishment the child made a little run to him and snuggled close to his side. He lifted her up on his knee, and wrapped his fur coat around her. Amabel thrust out one tiny hand and began to stroke the sable collar.

"It's fur," said she, with a bright, wise look into Robert's face.

"Yes, it's fur," said he. "Do you know what kind?"

She shook her head, with bright eyes still on his.

"It is sable," said Robert, "and it is the coat of a little animal that lives very far north, where it is as cold and colder than this all the time, and the ice and snow never melts."

Suddenly Amabel slipped off his knee, pushing aside his caressing arm with a violent motion. Then she stood aloof, eying him with unmistakable reproof and hostility. Robert laughed.

"What is the matter?" he said.

"What does he do without his coat if it is as cold as that where he lives?" asked Amabel, severely. There was almost an accent of horror in her childish voice.

"Why, my dear child," said Robert, "the little animal is dead. He isn't running around without his coat. He was shot for his fur."

"To make you a coat?" Amabel's voice was full of judicial severity.

"Well, in one way," replied Robert, laughing. "It was shot to get the fur to make somebody a coat, and I bought it. Come back here and have it wrapped round you; you'll freeze if you don't."

Amabel came back and sat on his knee, and let him

wrap the fur-lined garment around her. A strange sensation of tenderness and protection came over the young man as he felt the little, slender body of the child nestle against his own. He had begun to surmise who she was. However, Amabel herself told him in a moment.

"My mamma's sick, and they took her to an asylum. And my papa has gone away," she said.

"You poor little soul," said Robert, tenderly. Amabel continued to look at him with eyes of keenest intelligence, while one little cheek was flattened against his breast.

"I live with Uncle Andrew and Aunt Fanny now," said she, "and I sleep with Ellen."

"But you like living here, don't you, you dear?" asked Robert.

"Yes," said Amabel, "and I like to stay with Ellen, but—but—I want to see my mamma and papa," she wailed, suddenly, in the lowest and most pitiful wail imaginable.

"Poor little darling," said Robert, stroking her flaxen hair. Amabel looked up at him with her little face all distorted with grief.

"If you had been my papa, would you have gone away and left Amabel?" she asked, quiveringly. Robert gathered her to him in a strong clasp of protection.

"No, you little darling, I never should," he cried, fervently.

At that moment he wished devoutly that he had the handling of the man who had deserted this child.

"I like you most as well as my own papa," said Amabel. "You ain't so big as my papa." She said that in a tone of evident disparagement.

Then the sitting-room door opened, and Fanny and Ellen and Andrew appeared, the last with a great basket of wood and kindlings.

Robert set down Amabel, and sprang to his feet to greet Andrew and Ellen. Andrew, after depositing his basket beside the stove, shook hands with a sort of sad awkwardness. Robert saw that the man had aged immeasurably since he had last seen him.

"It is a cold night, Mr. Brewster," he said, and knew the moment he said it that it was not a happy remark.

"It is pretty cold," agreed Andrew, "and it's cold here in this room."

"Oh, it'll be warm in a minute; this stove heats up quick," cried Fanny, with agitated briskness. She began pulling the kindlings out of the basket.

"Here, you let me do that," said Andrew, and was down on his knees beside her. The two were cramming the fuel into the little, air-tight stove, while Robert was greeting Ellen. The awkwardness of the situation was evidently overcoming her. She was quite pale, and her voice trembled as she returned his good-evening. Amabel left the young man, and clung tightly to Ellen's hand, drawing her skirt around her until only her little face was visible above the folds.

The fumes from a match filled the room, and the fire began to roar.

"It'll be warm in a minute," said Fanny, rising. "You leave the register open till it's real good and hot, Ellen, and there's plenty more wood in the basket. Here, Amabel, you come out in the other room with Aunt Fanny."

But Amabel, instead of obeying, made a dart towards Robert, who caught her up, laughing, and smuggled her into the depths of his fur-lined coat.

"Come right along, Amabel," said Fanny.

But Amabel clung fast to Robert, with a mischievous roll of an eye at her aunt.

"Amabel," said Fanny, authoritatively.

"Come, Amabel," said Andrew.

"THE AWKWARDNESS OF THE SITUATION WAS EVIDENTLY
OVERCOMING HER"

"Oh, let her stay," Robert said, laughing. "I'll keep her in my coat until it is warm."

"I'm afraid she'll bother you," said Fanny.

"Not a bit," replied Robert.

"You are a naughty girl, Amabel," said Fanny; but she went out of the room, with Andrew at her heels. She did not know what else to do, since the young man had expressed a desire to keep the child. She had thought he would have preferred a *tête-à-tête* with Ellen. Ellen sat down on the sofa covered with olive-green plush, beyond the table, and the light of the hideous lamp fell full upon her face. She was thin, and much of her lovely bloom was missing between her agitation and the cold; but Robert, looking at her, realized how dear she was to him. There was something about that small figure, and that fair head held with such firmness of pride, and that soul outlooking from steady blue eyes, which filled all his need of life. His love for the pearl quite ignored its setting of the common and the ridiculous. He looked at her and smiled. Ellen smiled back tremulously, then she cast down her eyes. The fire was roaring, but the room was freezing. The sitting-room door was opened a crack, and remained so for a second, then it was widened, and Andrew peeped in. Then he entered, tiptoeing gingerly, as if he were afraid of disturbing a meeting. He brought a blue knitted shawl, which he put over Ellen's shoulders.

"Mother thinks you had better keep this on till the room gets warm," he whispered. Then he withdrew, shutting the door softly.

Robert, left alone with Ellen in this solemnly important fashion, felt utterly at a loss. He had never considered himself especially shy, but an embarrassment which was almost ridiculous was over him. Ellen sat with her eyes cast down. He felt that the child on his knee was regarding them both curiously.

"If you have come to see Ellen, why don't you speak to her?" demanded Amabel, suddenly. Then both Robert and Ellen laughed.

"This is your aunt's little girl, isn't she?" asked Robert.

Amabel answered before Ellen was able. "My mamma is sick, and they carried her away to the asylum," she told Robert. "She—she tried to hurt Amabel; she tried to"—Amabel made that hideous gesture with her tiny forefinger across her throat. "Mamma was sick or she wouldn't," she added, challengingly, to Robert.

"Of course she wouldn't, you poor little soul," said Robert.

Suddenly Amabel burst into tears, and began to wriggle herself free from his arms. "Let me go," she demanded; "let me go. I want Ellen."

When Robert loosened his grasp she fled to Ellen, and was in her lap with a bound.

"I want my mamma—I want my mamma," she moaned.

Ellen leaned her cheek against the poor little flaxen head. "There, there, darling," she whispered, "don't. Mamma will come home as soon as she gets better."

"How long will that be, Ellen?"

"Pretty soon, I hope, darling. Don't."

Poor Eva Tenny had been in the asylum some four months, and the reports as to her condition were no more favorable. Ellen's voice, in spite of herself, had a hopeless tone, which the child was quick to detect.

"I want my mamma," she repeated. "I want her, Ellen. It has been to-morrow, and to-morrow, and to-morrow after that, and the to-morrows are yesterdays, and she hasn't come."

"She will come some time, darling."

Robert sat eying the two with intensest pity. "Do you like chocolates, Amabel?" he asked.

The child repeated that she wanted her mother still, as with a sort of mechanical regularity of grief, but she fastened her eyes on him.

"Because I am going to send you a big box of them to-morrow," said Robert.

Amabel turned to Ellen. "Does he mean it?" she asked.

"I guess so," replied Ellen, laughing.

Amabel, looking from one to the other, also began to laugh unwillingly.

Then the sitting-room door opened, and Fanny called sharply and imperatively, "Amabel, Amabel; come!"

Amabel clung more tightly to Ellen, who began to gently loosen her arms.

"Amabel Tenny, come this minute. It is your bed-time," said Fanny.

"I guess you had better go, darling," whispered Ellen.

"I don't want to go to bed till you do, Ellen," whispered the child.

Ellen gently but firmly unclasped the clinging arms. "Run along, dear," she whispered.

"I will send those chocolates to-morrow," suggested Robert.

Amabel seemed to do everything by sudden and violent impulses. All at once she ceased resisting. She slid down from Ellen's lap as quickly as she had gotten into it. She clutched her neck with two little, wiry arms, kissed her hard on the mouth, darted across the room to Robert, threw her arms around his neck and kissed him, then flew out of the room.

"She is an interesting child," said Robert, who felt, like most people, the delicate flattery of a child's unsolicited caresses.

2 B   385

"I am very fond of her," replied Ellen.

Then the two were silent. Robert suddenly realized that there was little to say unless he ventured on debatable ground. It would be too absurd of him to commence making love at once, and as for asking Ellen about her work, that seemed a subject better let alone.

Ellen herself opened the conversation by inquiring for his aunt.

"Aunt Cynthia is very well," replied Robert. "I was in there last evening. You have not been to see her lately, Miss Brewster."

Robert realized as soon as he had said that that he had made a mistake.

"No," replied Ellen. She obviously paled a little, and looked at him wistfully. The young man could not stand it any longer, so straight into the heart of the matter he lunged.

"Look here, Miss Brewster," he said, "why on earth didn't you tell Aunt Cynthia?"

"Tell her?" repeated Ellen, vaguely.

"Yes; make a clean breast of it to her. Tell her just why you went to work, and gave up college?"

Ellen colored, and looked at him half defiantly, half piteously. "I told her all I ought to," she said.

"But you did not; pardon me," said Robert, " you did not tell her half enough. You let her think that you actually of your own free choice went to work in the factory rather than go to college."

"So I did," replied Ellen, looking at him proudly.

"Of course you did, in one sense, but in another you did not. You deliberately chose to make a sacrifice; but it was a sacrifice. You cannot deny that it was a sacrifice."

Ellen was silent.

"But you gave Aunt Cynthia the impression that it was not a sacrifice," said Robert, almost severely.

Ellen's face quivered a little. "I saw no other way to do," she said, faintly. The authoritative tone which this young man was taking with her stirred her as nothing had ever stirred her in her life before. She felt like a child before him.

"You have no right to give such a false impression of your own character," said Robert.

"It was either that or a false impression of another," returned Ellen, tremulously.

"You mean that she might have blamed your parents, and thought that they were forcing you into this?"

Ellen nodded.

"And I suppose you thought, too, that maybe Aunt Cynthia would suspect, if you told her all the difficulties, that you were hinting for more assistance."

Ellen nodded, and her lip was quivering. Suddenly all her force of character seemed to have deserted her, and she looked more like a child than Amabel. She actually put both her little fists to her eyes. After all, the girl was very young, a child forced by the stress of circumstances to premature development, but she could relapse before the insistence of another nature.

Robert looked at her, his own face working, then he could bear it no longer. He was over on the sofa beside Ellen and had her in his arms. "You poor little thing," he whispered. "Don't. I have loved you ever since the first time I saw you. I ought to have told you so before. Don't you love me a little, Ellen?"

But Ellen released herself with a motion of firm elusiveness and looked at him. The tears still stood in her eyes, but her face was steady. "I have been putting you out of my mind," said she.

"But could you?" whispered Robert, leaning over her.

Ellen did not reply, but looked down and trembled.

"Could you?" repeated Robert, and there was in his

voice that masculine insistence which is a true note of nature, and means the subjugation of the feminine into harmony.

Ellen did not speak, but every line in her body betrayed helpless yielding.

"You know you could not," said Robert with triumph, and took her in his arms again.

But he reckoned without the girl, who was, after all, stronger than her natural instincts, and able to rise above and subjugate them. She freed herself from him resolutely, rose, and stood before him, looking at him quite unfalteringly and accusingly.

"Why do you come now?" she asked. "You say you have loved me from the first. You came to see me, you walked home with me, and said things to me that made me think—" She stopped.

"Made you think what, dear?" asked Robert. He was pale and indescribably anxious and appealing. It was suddenly revealed to him that this plum was so firmly attached to its bough of individuality that possibly love itself could not loosen it.

"You made me think that perhaps you did care a little," said Ellen, in a low but unfaltering voice.

"You thought quite right, only not a little, but a great deal," said Robert, firmly.

"Then," said Ellen, "the moment I gave up going to college and went to work you never came to see me again; you never even spoke to me in the shop; you went right past me without a look."

"Good God! child," Robert interposed, "don't you know why I did that?"

Ellen looked at him bewildered, then a burning red overspread her face. "Yes," she replied. "I didn't. But I do now. They would have talked."

"I thought you would understand that," said Robert. "I had only the best motives for that. I cannot speak to you in the factory any more than I have done. I cannot expose you to remark; but as for my not calling, I believed what you said to my aunt and to me. I thought that you had deliberately preferred a lower life to a higher one—that you preferred earning money to something better. I thought—"

Robert fairly started as Ellen began talking with a fire which seemed to make her scintillate before his eyes.

"You talk about a lower and a higher life," said she. "Is it true? Is Vassar College any higher than a shoe-factory? Is any labor which is honest, and done with the best strength of man, for the best motives, to support the lives of those he loves, or to supply the needs of his race, any higher than another? Where would even books be without this very labor which you despise — the books which I should have learned at college? Instead of being benefited by the results of labor, I have become part of labor. Why is that lower?"

Robert stared at her.

"I have come to feel all this since I went to work," said Ellen, speaking in a high, rapid voice. "When I went to work, it was, as you thought, for my folks, to help them, for my father was out of work, and there was no other way. But since I have been at work I have realized what work really is. There is a glory over it, as there is over anything which is done faithfully on this earth for good motives, and I have seen the glory, and I am not ashamed of it; and while it was a sacrifice at first, now, while I should like the other better, I do not think it is. I am proud of my work."

The girl spoke with a sort of rapt enthusiasm. The young man stared, bewildered.

Robert caught Ellen's little hands, which hung, tightly clinched, in the folds of her dress, and drew her down to his side again. "See here, dear," he said, "maybe you are right. I never looked at it in this way before, but you do not understand. I love you; I want to marry you. I want to make you my wife, and lift you out of this forever."

Then again Ellen freed herself, and straightened her head and faced him. "There is nothing for me to be lifted out of," said she. "You speak as if I were in a pit. I am on a height."

"My God! child, how many others feel as you, do you think, out of the whole lot?" cried Robert.

"I don't know," replied Ellen, "but it is true. What I feel is true."

Robert caught up her little hand and kissed it. Then he looked at its delicate outlines. "Well, it may be true," he said, "but look at yourself. Can't you see that you are not fashioned for manual labor? Look at this little hand."

"That little hand can do the work," Ellen replied, proudly.

"But, dear," said Robert, "admitting all this, admitting that you are not in a position to be lifted—admitting everything—let us come back to our original starting-point. Dear, I love you, and I want you for my wife. Will you marry me?"

"No, I never can," replied Ellen, with a long, sobbing breath of renunciation.

"Why not? Don't you love me?"

"Yes. I think it must be true that I do. I said I wouldn't; I have tried not to, but I think it must be true that I do."

"Then why not marry me?"

"Because it will be impossible for my father and mother to get along and support Amabel and Aunt Eva without my help," said Ellen, directly.

"But I—" began Robert.

"Do you think I will burden you with the support of a whole family?" said Ellen.

"Ellen, you don't know what I would be willing to do if I could have you," cried the young man, fervently. And he was quite in earnest. At that moment it seemed to him that he could even come and live there in that house, with the hideous lamp, and the crushed-plush furniture, and the eager mother; that he could go without anything and everything to support them if only he could have this girl who was fairly storming his heart.

"I wouldn't be willing to have you," said Ellen, firmly. "As things are now I cannot marry you, Mr. Lloyd. Then, too," she added, "you asked me just now how many people looked at all this labor as I do, and I dare say not very many. I know not many of your kind of people. I know how your uncle looks at it. It would hurt you socially to marry a girl from a shoe-shop. Whether it is just or not, it would hurt you. It cannot be, as matters are now, Mr. Lloyd."

"But you love me?"

Ellen suddenly, as if pushed by some mighty force outside herself, leaned towards him, and he caught her in his arms. He tipped back her face and kissed her, and looked down at her masterfully.

"We will wait a little," he said. "I will never give you up as long as I live if you love me, Ellen."

CHAPTER XXXIX

WHEN Ellen went out into the sitting-room that evening, after Robert Lloyd had taken leave, her father and mother were still there, although the callers had gone. Both of them looked furtively at her as she went through the room to the kitchen to get a lamp, then they looked at each other. Fanny was glowing with half shame-faced triumph; Andrew was pale. Ellen did not re-enter the room, but simply paused at the door, before going up-stairs, and they had a vision of a face in a tumult of emotions, with eyes and hair illuminated to excess of brilliancy by the lamp which she held.

"Good-night," she called, and her voice did not sound like her own.

"Something has happened," Fanny whispered to Andrew, when Ellen's chamber door had closed.

"Do you suppose she's goin' to?" whispered Andrew, in a sort of breathless fashion. His eyes on his wife's face were sad and wistful.

"Hush! How do I know?" asked Fanny. "I always told you he liked her."

However, Fanny looked disturbed. Presently she went out in the kitchen to mix up some bread, and she wept a little, standing in a corner, with her face hidden in the folds of an old shawl which hung there on a peg. Dictatorial towards circumstances as she was when her beloved daughter came in question, and proud as she was at the prospect of an advantageous marriage for her, she remembered her sister in the asylum, she remembered how Andrew was out of work, and she

392

could not understand how it was to be managed. And all this was aside from the grief which she would have felt in any case at losing Ellen.

As for Andrew, the next morning he put on his best clothes and went by trolley-cars to the next manufacturing town, not a city like Rowe, but a busy little place with two large factories, and tried in vain to get a job there. As he came home on the crowded car, his face was so despairing that the people looked curiously at him. Andrew had always been mild and peaceable, but at that moment anarchistic principles began to ferment in him. When a portly man, swelling ostentatiously with broadcloth and fine linen, wearing a silk hat, and carrying a gold-headed cane like a wand of office, got into the car, Andrew looked at him with a sidelong glance which was almost murderous. The spiritual bomb, which is in all our souls for our fellow-men, began to swell towards explosion. This man was the proprietor of one of the great factories in Leavitt, the town where Andrew had vainly sought a job. He had been in the office when Andrew entered, and the latter had heard his low voice of instruction to the foreman that that man was too old. The manufacturer, who weighed heavily, and described a vast curve of opulence from silk hat to his patent-leathers, sat opposite, his gold-headed cane planted in the aisle, his countenance a blank of complacent power. Andrew felt that he hated him.

The man's face was not intellectual, not as intellectual as Andrew's. He gave the impression of the force of matter oncoming and irresistible, some inertia which had started Heaven knew how. This man had inherited great wealth, as Andrew knew. He had capital with which to begin, and he had strength to roll the accumulating ball. Andrew felt more and more how he hated this man. He had told his foreman that Andrew was too old, and Andrew knew that he was no older, if as old, as the man himself.

"If I had been born under the Czar, and done with it, I should have felt differently," he told himself. "But who is this man? What right has he to say that his fellow-men shall or shall not? Does even his own property give him the right of dictation over others? What is property? Is it anything but a temporary lease while he draws the breath of life? What of it in the tomb, to which he shall surely come? Shall a temporary possession give a man the right to wield eternal power? For the power of giving or withholding the means of life may produce eternal results."

When the man rose and moved down the car, oscillating heavily, steadying himself with his gold-headed cane, and got out in front of a portentous mansion, Andrew would scarcely have recognized the look in his own eyes had he seen himself in a mirror.

"That chap is pretty well fixed," said a man next him, to one on the other side.

"A cool half-million," replied the other.

"More than that," said the first speaker. "His father left him half a million to start with, besides the business, and he's been piling up ever since."

"Do you work there?"

"Did, but I had what was mighty nigh a sunstroke last summer; had to quit. It was damned hot up there under the roof. It's the same old factory his father had."

"Goin' to work again?"

"Next week, if I'm able, but I dun'no' whether I can stay there longer than till spring. It's damned hot up there under the roof."

The man who spoke had a leaden hue of face, something ghastly, as if the deadly heat had begun a work of decomposition. Andrew looked at him, and his hatred against the rich man who had built himself a stately mansion, and kept his fellow-creatures at work for him in an unhealthy factory in tropical heat, and had condemned him for being too old, was redoubled.

"Andrew Brewster, where have you been?" Fanny asked, when he got home.

"I've been to Leavitt," answered Andrew, shortly.

"To see if you could get a job there?"

"Yes."

Fanny did not ask if he had been successful. She sighed, and took another stitch in the wrapper which she was making. That sigh almost drove Andrew mad.

"I don't see what has got you into such a habit of sighing," he said, brutally.

Fanny looked at him with reproachful anger. "Andrew Brewster, you ain't like yourself," said she.

"I can't help it."

"There's no need for you to pitch into me because you can't get work; I ain't to blame. I'm doing all I can. I won't stand it, and you might as well know it first as last."

Fanny glared angrily at her husband, then the tears sprang to her eyes.

Andrew hesitated a moment, then he leaned over her and put his thin cheek against her rough black hair. "The Lord knows I don't mean to be harsh to you, you poor girl," said he, "but I wish I was dead."

Fanny seemed to spring into resistance like a wire. "Then you are a coward, Andrew Brewster," said she, hotly. "Talk about wishin' you was dead. I 'ain't got time to die. You'd 'nough sight better go out into the yard and split up some of that wood."

"I didn't mean to speak so, Fanny," said Andrew, "but sometimes I get desperate, and I've been thinking of Ellen."

"Don't you suppose I have?" asked Fanny, angrily.

"Well, there's one thing about it; we won't stand in her way," said Andrew.

"No, we won't," replied Fanny. "I'll go out washing first."

"She hasn't said anything?"

"No."

As time went on Ellen still said nothing. She had made a curious compact for a young girl with her lover. She had stipulated that no engagement was to exist, that she should be perfectly free—when she said that she thought of Maud Hemingway, but she said it without a tremor—and if years hence both were free and of the same mind they might talk of it again.

Robert had rebelled strenuously. "You know this will shut me off from seeing much of you," he said. "You know I told you how it will be about my even talking much to you in the factory."

"Yes, I understand that now," replied Ellen, blushing; "and I understand, too, that you cannot come to see me very often under such circumstances without making talk."

"How often?" Robert asked, impetuously.

Ellen hesitated, her lip quivered a little, but her voice was firm. "Not oftener than two or three times a year, I am afraid," said she.

"Great Scott!" cried Robert. Then he caught her in his arms again. "Do you suppose I can stand that?" he whispered. "Ellen, I cannot consent to this!"

"It is the only way," said she. She freed herself from him enough to look into his eyes with a brave, fearless gaze of comradeship, which somehow seemed to make her dearer than anything else.

"But to see you to speak to only two or three times a year!" groaned Robert. "You are cruel, Ellen. You don't know how I love you."

"There isn't any other way," said Ellen. Then

396

she looked up into his face with a brave innocence of confession like a child. "It hurts me, too," said she.

Robert had her in his arms, and was covering her face with kisses. "You darling," he whispered. "It shall not be long. Something will happen. We cannot live so. We will let it go so a little while, but something will turn up. I shall have a more responsible place and a larger salary, then—"

"Do you think I will let you?" asked Ellen, with a great blush.

"I will, whether you will let me or not," cried Robert; and at that moment he felt inclined to marry the entire Brewster family rather than give up this girl.

However, as he went home, walking that he might think the better, he had to confess to himself that the girl was right; that, as matters were, anything definite was out of the question. He had to admit that it might be a matter of years.

CHAPTER XL

WHEN Ellen had been at work in the factory a year, she was running a machine and working by the piece, and earning on an average eighteen dollars a week. Of course that was an unusual advance for a girl, but Ellen was herself unusual. She came to work in those days with such swiftness and unswerving accuracy that she seemed fairly a part of the great system of labor itself. While she was at her machine, her very individuality seemed lost; she became an integral part of a system.

"She's one of the best hands we ever had," Flynn told Norman Lloyd one day.

"I am glad to hear that," Lloyd responded, smiling with that peculiar smile of his which was like a cold flash of steel.

"Curse him, he thinks no more of anybody in this shop than he does of the machine they work," Flynn thought as he watched the proprietor walking with his stately descent down the stairs. The noon whistle was blowing, and the younger Lloyd went leaping down the stairs and joined his uncle, then the two walked down the street, away from the factory. The factory at that time of year began to present, in spite of its crude architecture, quite a charming appearance, from the luxuriant vines which covered it and were beginning to get autumnal tints of red and russet. All the front of Lloyd's was covered with vines, which had grown with amazing swiftness. Mrs. Lloyd often used to look at them and reflect upon them with complacency.

"I should think it would make it pleasanter for the

men to work in the factory, when it looks so pretty and
green," she told her husband one of the hottest days
of the preceding summer. As she spoke she compressed
her lips in a way which was becoming habitual to her.
It meant the endurance of a sharp stab of vital pain.
There was a terrible pathos in the poor woman's appearance at that time. She still kept about. Her malady did not seem to be on the increase, but it endured.
Her form had changed indescribably. She had not
lost flesh, but she had a curious, distorted look, and one
on seeing her had a bewildered feeling, and looked again
to be sure that he had seen aright. Her ghastly pallor
she concealed in a manner which she thought distinctly
sinful. She painted and powdered. She did not dare
purchase openly the concoctions which were used for
improving her complexion, but she went to a manicure
and invested in a colored salve for her finger-nails.
This, with rather surprising skill for such a conscience-
pricked tyro, she applied to the pale curves of her cheeks
and her blue lips. She took more pains than ever before with her dress, and it was all to deceive her husband, that he should not be annoyed. She felt a desperate shame because of her illness; she felt it to be a
direct personal injury to this masculine power which
had been set over her gentle femininity. It was not
so much because she was afraid of losing his affection
that she concealed her affliction from him, as because
she felt that the affliction itself was somehow an act
of disloyalty. Her terrible malady had in a way affected her reasoning powers, so that they had become
distorted by a monstrous growth of suffering, like her
body. She would not give up going about as usual,
and was never absent from church. She drove about
with her husband in his smart trap. Twice she had
gone with Robert to consult the New York specialist,
taking times when Norman was away on business.

She still would not consent to an operation, and lately the specialist had been lukewarm in advising it. He had indeed been doubtful from the first.

Mrs. Lloyd treated Robert with a soft affection which was almost like that of a mother. One night, when he returned late from a call on Ellen, she sat up waiting for him. He had not called on Ellen before for several months, and it was nearly midnight when he returned.

"Why, Aunt Lizzie, are you up?" he cried, as he entered the library door and saw his aunt's figure, clad in shining black satin, gleaming with jet, in the depths of an easy-chair.

Mrs. Lloyd looked up at him with an expression of patient suffering. "I couldn't go to sleep if I went to bed, Robert," she replied, in a hushed voice. She found it a comfort sometimes to confess her pain to him. Robert went over to her, and drew her large, crinkled, blond head to his shoulder as if she had been a child.

"Poor thing," he whispered, stroking her face pitifully. "Is it very terrible?" he asked, with his lips close to her ear.

"Terrible," she whispered back. "Oh, Robert, you do not know; pray God you may never know."

"I wish to God I could bear it for you, Aunt Lizzie," Robert said, fervently.

"Oh, hush! If you or Norman had to bear anything like this, I should curse God and die," she answered, and she shut her mouth hard, and her whole face was indicative of a repressed shriek.

"Aunt Lizzie, don't you think you ought to go to New York, that you ought—" Robert began, but she stopped him with an almost fierce peremptoriness. "Robert Lloyd, I have trusted you," she said. "For God's sake, don't forsake me. Don't say a word to me about that; when I can I will. It means my death, anyhow. Dr. Evarts thought so; you can't deny it."

"I think he thought there was a chance, Aunt Lizzie," Robert returned, but he said it faintly.

"You can't cheat me," replied Mrs. Lloyd. "I know." She had a lapse from pain, and her features began to assume their natural expression. She looked at him almost smiling, and as if she turned her back upon her own misery. "Where have you been, Robert?" she asked.

Robert colored a little, but he answered directly enough. "I have been to make a call on Miss Brewster," he said.

"You don't go there very often," said Mrs. Lloyd.

"No, not very often."

"She's a beautiful girl, as beautiful a girl as I ever laid eyes on, if she does work in the shop," said Mrs. Lloyd, "and she's a good girl, too; I know she is. She was the sweetest little thing when she was a child, and she 'ain't altered a mite!" Then Mrs. Lloyd looked with a sort of wistful curiosity at Robert.

"I think it is all true, what you say, Aunt Lizzie," replied Robert.

Mrs. Lloyd continued to look at him with that wistful scrutiny.

"Robert," she began, then she hesitated.

"What, Aunt Lizzie?"

"If—ever you wanted to marry that girl, I don't see any reason why you shouldn't, for my part."

Robert pulled a chair close to his aunt, and sat down beside her, still holding her hand.

"I've a good mind to tell you the whole story, Aunt Lizzie," he said.

"I wish you would, Robert. You know I think as much of you as if you were my own son, and I won't tell anybody, not even your uncle, if you don't want me to."

"Well, then, it is all in a nutshell," said Robert.
"I like her, you know, and I think I have ever since
I saw her in her little white gown at the high-school
exhibition."

"Wasn't she sweet?" said his aunt.

"And she likes me, too, I think."

"Of course she does."

"But you know what my salary is, and her whole
family is in a measure dependent upon her."

"Hasn't her father got work?"

"No."

"I'll speak to Norman," cried Mrs. Lloyd, quickly.
"I know he would do it for me."

"But even then, Aunt Lizzie, there is the aunt in the
asylum, and the child, and—"

"Your uncle will pay you more."

"It isn't altogether that; in fact, it isn't that at all
which is at the bottom of the difficulty. The difficulty
is with Ellen herself. She will never consent to my
marrying her, and having to support her family, while
matters are as now. You don't know how proud she
is, Aunt Lizzie."

"She is a splendid girl."

"As far as I am concerned I would marry the whole
lot on a little more than I have now, but she would not
let me do it. There's nothing to do but to wait."

"Perhaps the aunt will get well and her husband
will come back; and I will see, anyway, if Norman
won't give her father work," said Mrs. Lloyd.

"I think you had better not, Aunt Lizzie."

"Why not, Robert?"

"There are reasons why I think you had better not."
Robert would not tell her that Ellen had begged him not
to use any influence of his to get her father work.

"After the way father has been turned off, I can't
stand it," she had said, with a sort of angry dignity

which was unusual to her. In fact, her father himself had begged her not to make use of Robert in any way for his own advancement.

"If they don't want me for my work, I don't want to crawl in because the nephew of the boss likes my daughter," he had said. This speech was fairly rough for him, but Ellen had understood.

"I know what you mean, father," she said.

"I'd rather work in the road," said Andrew. That autumn he was getting jobs of clearing up yards of fallen leaves, and gathering feed-corn and pumpkins, and earning a pittance. Fanny continued to work on her wrappers. "It's a mercy wrappers don't go out of fashion," she often said.

"I suppose things that folks can get for nothing ain't so apt to go out of fashion," Andrew retorted, bitterly. He hated the wrappers with a deadly hatred. He hated the sight of the limp row of them on his bed-room wall. Nobody knew how the family pinched and screwed in those days.

They were using the small fund which they secured from the house mortgage, Ellen's earnings, and Fanny's and Andrew's, and every cent had to be counted, but there was something splendid in their loyalty to poor Eva in the asylum. The thought of deserting her in her extremity never occurred to them.

Mrs. Lloyd spoke of her that night, when she and Robert were talking together in the library.

"They are good folks, to keep on doing for that poor woman in the asylum," she said.

"They would never desert a dog that belonged to them," Robert answered, fervently. "I tell you that trait is worth a good many others, Aunt Lizzie."

"I guess it is," said his aunt. Then another paroxysm of pain seized her. She looked at Robert with a convulsed, speechless face. He held her hands more

403

tightly, his own face contracting in sympathy, and watched his aunt with a sort of angry helplessness. But he felt as if he wanted to fight something for the sake of this poor, oppressed, innocent creature; indeed, he felt fairly blasphemous. But this time the pain passed quickly, and Mrs. Lloyd looked at her nephew with an expression of relief and gentleness which was almost angelic. When the pain was over she thought again of the Brewsters, and how they would not have forsaken her in her misery, had she belonged to them, any more than they had forsaken the insane aunt.

"They are good folks," said she, "and that is the main thing. That is the main thing to consider when you are marrying into a family, Robert. It is more than riches and position. The power they've got of loving and standing by each other is worth more than anything else."

"You are right, Aunt Lizzie, I guess there's no doubt of that," said Robert.

"And that girl's beautiful," said Mrs. Lloyd. She gazed at the young man with a delicate understanding and sympathy which was almost beyond that of a sweetheart. Robert felt as if a soft hand of tenderness and blessing were laid on his inmost heart. He looked at her like a grateful child.

"There isn't anybody like her, is there, Aunt Lizzie?" he asked.

"No, I don't think there is, dear boy," said Mrs. Lloyd. "I do think she is the sweetest little thing I ever saw in my life."

Robert brought his aunt's hand to his lips and kissed it. It seemed to him for a minute as if the love and sympathy of this martyr were almost more precious than the love of Ellen herself.

He realized when he was in his own room, and the house was quiet, how much he loved his aunt, and how hard her pain and probably inevitable doom were for him to bear. Then something came to him which he had never felt before—a great, burning anxiety and tenderness and terror over Ellen, because she was of the weaker half of creation, which is born to the larger share of pain in the world. He felt that he would almost have given her up, yielded up forever all his delight in her, to spare her; for the pain of knighthood, which is in every true lover, awoke in his heart.

CHAPTER XLI

NAHUM BEALS was a laster in Lloyd's. Late in the autumn, when Ellen had been in the factory a little over a year, there began to be a subtle condition of discontent and insubordination. Men gathered in muttering groups, of which Nahum Beals seemed always to be the nucleus. His high, rampant voice, restrained by no fear of consequences, always served as the keynote to the chorus of rebellion. Ellen paid little attention to it. She was earning good wages, and personally she had nothing of which to complain. She had come to regard Beals as something of a chronic fanatic, but as she knew that the lasters were fairly paid, she had not supposed it meant anything. However, one night, going home from the factory, her eyes were opened. Abby and Maria Atkins and Mamie Brady were with her, and shortly after they had left the shop Abby stopped Granville Joy, Frank Dixon, and Willy Jones, who with another young man were swinging past without noticing the girls, strange to say. Abby caught Joy by the arm.

"Hold on a minute, Granville Joy," said she. "I want to know what's up with the lasters."

Granville laughed, with an uneasy, sidelong, deprecating glance at Ellen. "Oh, nothing much," said he.

Willy Jones stood still, coloring, gazing at Abby with a half-terrified expression. Dixon walked on, and the other young man, Amos Lee, who was dark and slight and sinewy, stared from one to the other with quick flashes of black eyes. He looked almost

406

as if he had gypsy blood in him, and he came of a family which was further on the outskirts of society than the Louds had been.

When Granville replied "nothing much" to Abby's question, Amos Lee frowned with a swift contraction of dissent, but did not speak until Abby had retorted. "You needn't talk that way to me, Granville Joy," said she. "You can't cheat me. I know something's up."

"It ain't nothin', Abby," said Granville, but it was quite evident that he was lying.

Then Lee spoke up, in a sudden fury of enthusiasm. "There is somethin' up," said he, "and I don't care if you do know it. There's—" he stopped as Granville clutched his arm violently and whispered something.

"Well, maybe you're right," said Lee to Joy. "Look here," he continued to Abby, "you and Ellen come along here a little ways, and I'll tell you."

After Maria and Mamie had passed on, Joy and Jones and Lee, standing close to the two girls, began to talk, Lee leading.

"Well, look here," he said, in a hushed voice. "We've found out—no matter how, but we've found out—that the boss is goin' to dock the lasters' pay."

"How much?" asked Abby.

"Fifteen per cent."

"Good Lord!" said Abby.

"We ain't going to stand it," said Lee.

"I don't see how we can stand it," said Willy Jones, with a slightly interrogative tone directed towards Abby. Granville looked at Ellen.

"Are you sure?" she asked.

"Perfectly sure," replied Granville. "What do you think about it, Ellen?"

"What are you going to do?" asked Ellen, thoughtfully.

"Strike for fifteen per cent. more before he has a chance to dock us," cried Lee, with a hushed vehemence, looking about warily to make sure that no one overheard.

"The worst of it is, I know it all comes from Nahum Beals, and he's half cracked," said Abby, bluntly.

"He's got the right of it, anyhow," said Lee.

The two girls walked on, while the men lingered behind to talk.

"Do you suppose it is true, Abby?" asked Ellen.

"I don't know. I should, if it wasn't for that Lee fellow. I can't bear him. And that Nahum Beals, I believe he's half mad."

"I feel the same way about him," said Ellen; "but think what it would mean, fifteen per cent. less on their wages."

"It doesn't mean so much for those young fellows, except Willy Jones; he's got enough on his shoulders."

"No, but ever so many of the lasters have large families."

"I hope they don't drag Willy Jones into it," said Abby. She looked back as she spoke. Willy, in the little knot of men, was looking after her, and their eyes met. Abby colored.

"It's a shame to dock his wages," she said.

"Whose—Willy Jones's?"

"Yes. I hope he won't get into any trouble. I can't bear that Lee."

"Still, to dock their wages fifteen per cent.," said Ellen, thoughtfully.

"What right has Mr. Lloyd?"

"I suppose he'd say he has the right because he has the capital."

"I don't see why that gives him the right."

"You'd better go and talk to him," said Abby. "As for me, I made up my mind when I went to work in

408

the shop that I'd got to be a bond-slave, all but my soul. That can kick free, thank the Lord."

"I didn't make up my mind to it," said Ellen. "I am not going to be a slave in any way, and I am not going to approve of others being slaves."

"You think they ought to strike?"

"Yes, if it is true that Mr. Lloyd is going to dock their wages, but I don't feel sure that it is true. Mr. Beals is a queer man. Sometimes I have thought he was dangerous."

CHAPTER XLII

TUESDAY evening was one of those marvellously clear atmospheres of autumn which seem to be clearer from the contrast to the mists of the recent summer. The stars swarmed out in unnumbered hosts.

"Seems to me I never saw so many stars," one would say to another. The air had the sharp cleave of the frost in it. Everything was glittering with a white rime—the house roofs, and the levels of fields on the outskirts of the little city.

Ellen had an errand down-town that evening, and she wrapped herself up warmly, putting on a fur collar which she had not worn since the winter before. She felt strangely nervous and disturbed as she set out.

"Don't you want your father to go with you?" asked Fanny, for in some occult fashion the girl's perturbation seemed to be communicated to her. She followed her to the door.

"Seems kind of lonesome for you to go alone," she said, anxiously.

"As if I minded! Why, it is as bright as day with the electric-lights, and there are houses almost all the way," laughed Ellen.

"Your father could go with you, or he could go for you."

"No, he couldn't go for me. I want to get one of the new catalogues at the library and pick out a book, and there is no sense in dragging father out. He has a cold, too. Why, there is nothing in the world to be afraid of, mother."

410

"Well, don't be any longer than you can help," said Fanny.

Ellen, as she passed her grandmother's house, saw a curtain drawn with a quick motion. That happened nearly every time she passed. She knew that the old woman was always on the lookout for her, and always bent on concealing it. Mrs. Zelotes never went into her son's house, and never spoke to Ellen in those days. She had aged rapidly during the past year, and even her erect carriage had failed her. She stooped rigidly when she walked. She was fairly racked with love and hatred of Ellen. She adored her, she could have kissed the ground she walked on, and yet she was so full of wrath against her for thwarting her hopes for her own advancement that she was conscious of cruel impulses in her direction.

Ellen walked along rapidly under the vast canopy of stars, about which she presently began to have a singular impression. She felt as if they were being augmented, swelled as if by constantly oncoming legions of light from the space beyond space, and as if her little space of individuality, her tiny foothold of creation, was being constantly narrowed by them.

"I never saw so many stars," she said to herself. She looked with wonder at the Milky Way, which was like a zone of diamond dust. Suddenly a mighty conviction of God, which was like the blazing forth of a new star, was in her soul. Ellen was not in a sense religious, and had never united with the Congregational Church, which she had always attended with her parents; she had never been responsive to efforts made towards her so-called conversion, but all at once, under the stars that night, she told herself with an absolute certainty of the truth of it. "There is something beyond everything, beyond the stars, and beyond all poor men, and beyond me, which is enough for all needs. We shall have our portion in the end."

She had been feeling discouraged lately, although she would not own it even to herself. She saw Robert but seldom, and her aunt was no better. She often wondered if there could be anything before her but that one track of drudgery for daily bread upon which she had set out. She wondered if she ought not to say positively to Robert that there must be no thought of anything between them in the future. She wondered if she were not wronging him. Once or twice she had seen him riding with Miss Hemingway, and thought that, after all, that was a girl better suited to him, and perhaps if he had no hope whatever of her he might turn to the other to his own advantage. But to-night, with the clear stimulus of the frost in her lungs, and her eyes and soul dazzled with the multiplicity of stars, she began to have a great impetus of courage, like a soldier on the morning of battle. She felt as if she could fight for her joy and the joy of others, and victory would in the end be certain; that the chances of victory ran to infinity, and could not be measured.

However, all the while, in spite of her stimulation of spirits, there was that vague sense of excitement, as over some impending crisis. That she could not throw off. Suddenly she found herself searching the road ahead of her, and often turning at the fancied sound of a footstep. She began to wish that her father had come with her; then she told herself how foolish she was, for he had a cold, and this keen air would have been sure to give him more. The electric-car passed her, and she had a grateful sense of companionship. She looked after its diminishing light in the distance, and almost wished that she had stopped it, but car-fares had to be counted carefully.

She began to dread unspeakably passing the factories.

She told herself that there was no sense in it, that it was not late, that the electric-light made it like high noon, that there was a watchman in each building, that there was nothing whatever to fear; but it was in vain. It was only by a great effort of her will that she did not turn and go back home when she reached Lloyd's.

Lloyd's came first; then, a few rods farther, on the other side of the street, McGuire's, and then Briggs's.

Ellen had a library book under her arm, and she clutched her dress-skirt firmly. A terror as to the supernatural was stealing over her. She felt as she had when waking in the night from some dreadful dream, though all the time she was dinning in her ears how foolish she was. She saw the lantern of the night-watchman in Lloyd's moving down a stair which crossed a window.

She came opposite Lloyd's, and, just as she did so, saw a dark figure descending the right-hand flight of stairs from the entrance platform. She thought, from something in the carriage, that it was Mr. Lloyd, and hung back a little, reflecting that she would keep behind him all the way to town.

The man reached the ground at the foot of the stairs, then there was a flash of fire from the shadow underneath, and a shot rang out. Ellen did what she could never have counted upon herself for doing. She ran straight towards the man, who had fallen prostrate like a log, and was down on the ground beside him, with his head on her lap, shouting for the night-watchman, whose name was McLaughlin.

"McLaughlin!" she shouted. But there was no need of it, for he had heard the shot. The cry had not left Ellen's lips before she was surrounded by men, one of whom was Granville Joy, one was Dixon, and one was John Sargent.

Joy and Sargent had met down-town, and were walk-

413

ing home together, when the shot rang out, and they had rushed forward. Then there was McLaughlin, the watchman of Lloyd's, and the two watchmen from Briggs's and McGuire's came pelting down their stairs, swinging their lanterns.

They all stood around the wounded man and Ellen, and stared for a second. They were half stupefied.

"My God! this is a bad job," said Dixon.

"Go for a doctor," cried Ellen, hoarsely.

"We're a pack of fools," ejaculated Sargent, suddenly. Then he gave Granville Joy a push on the back. "Run for your life for the first doctor," he cried, and was down on his knees beside the wounded man. Lloyd seemed to be quite insensible. There was a dark spot which was constantly widening in a hideous circle of death on his shirt-front when Sargent opened his coat and vest tenderly.

"Is he—" whispered Ellen. She held one of Lloyd's hands in a firm clutch as if she would in such wise hold him to life.

"No, not yet," whispered Sargent. Dixon knelt down on the other side, and. took Lloyd's other hand and felt his pulse. McLaughlin was rushing aimlessly up and down, talking as he went.

"I never heard a thing till that shot came," he kept repeating. "He'd jest been in to get his pocketbook he'd left in the office. I never heard a thing till I heard that shot."

Sargent was opening Lloyd's shirt. "McLaughlin, for God's sake stop talking and run for another doctor, in case Joy does not get one at once," he cried; "then go to his house, and tell young Lloyd, but don't say anything to his wife."

"Poor Mrs. Lloyd," whispered Ellen.

The sick man sighed audibly. It seemed as if he had heard. The other watchmen stood looking on helplessly.

"Why in thunder don't you two scatter, and see if you can't catch him," cried Dixon to them. "He can't be far off."

But the words had no sooner left his mouth than up came a great Swede who was one of the workmen in Lloyd's, and he had Nahum Beals in a grasp as imperturbable as fate. The assassin, even with the strength of his fury of fanaticism, was as a reed in the grasp of this Northern giant. The Swede held him easily, walking him before him in a forced march. He had a hand of Nahum's in each of his, and he compelled Nahum's right hand to retain the hold of the discharged pistol. There was something terrible about the Swede as he drew near, a captor as unyielding and pitiless as justice itself. He was even smiling with a smile which showed his gums from ear to ear, but there was no joy in his smile, and no triumph. His blue eyes surveyed them all with the placid content of achievement.

"I have him," he said. "I heard him shoot, and I heard him run, and I stood still until he ran into my arms. I have him."

Nahum, in the grasp of this fate, was quivering from head to foot, but not from fear.

"Is he dead?" he shouted, eagerly.

"Hush up, you murderer," cried Dixon. "We didn't want any such work as this, damn you. Keep fast hold of him, Olfsen."

"I will keep him fast," replied the Swede, smiling.

Then there was a swift clatter of wheels, and two doctors drove up, and men came running. The space in front of Lloyd's was black with men. Robert Lloyd was among them. Granville Joy had met him on the street.

"You'd better go down to the factory, quick," he had said, hoarsely. "There's trouble there; your uncle—"

Robert pushed through the crowd, which made way

respectfully for him. He knelt down beside the wounded man. "Is he—" he whispered to Sargent.

"Not yet," whispered Sargent, "but I'm afraid it's pretty bad."

"You here?" Robert said to Ellen.

"Yes," she answered, "I was passing when I heard the shot."

"See here," said Robert, "I don't know but I am asking a good deal, but will you get into Dr. James's buggy, and let his man drive you to my aunt's, and you break it to her? She likes you. I must stay with him. I don't want her to know it first when he is brought home."

"Yes, that will be the best way," said the other physician, who was the one regularly employed by the Lloyds. "Some one must tell her first, and if she knows this young lady—"

"I will go," said Ellen.

Dr. Story whispered something to Ellen as she was getting into the buggy. Then Dr. James's man drove her away down the street.

There was a little black mare harnessed to the buggy, and she went with nervous leaps of speed. When Ellen reached the Lloyd house she saw that it was blazing with light. Norman Lloyd was fond of brilliant light, and would have every room in his house illuminated from garret to cellar.

As Ellen went up the stone steps she saw a woman's figure in the room at the right, which moved to an attitude of attention when she rang the bell.

Before Ellen could inquire for Mrs. Lloyd of the maid who answered her ring there was a shrill cry from the room on the right.

"Who is it? Who is it?" demanded the voice.

Then, before Ellen could speak, Mrs. Lloyd came running out.

416

"What is it?" she said. "Tell me quick. I know
something has happened. Tell me quick. You came
in Dr. James's buggy, and the man was driving fast.
Tell me."

"Oh, Mrs. Lloyd," said Ellen. Then she could say
no more, but the other woman knew.

"Is he dead?" she asked, hoarsely.

"Oh, no, no, not dead."

"Hurt?"

Ellen nodded, trembling.

"How?"

"He was shot."

"Who shot him?"

"One of the workmen. They have him. Carl Olfsen found him."

"One of the workmen, when he has always been so
good!"

Suddenly Mrs. Lloyd seemed to gather herself together into the strength of action.

"Are they bringing him home?" she asked Ellen, in
a sharp, decisive voice.

"I think they must be by this time."

"Then I've got to get ready for him. Come, quick."

There was by that time a man and two women ser-
vants standing near them, aghast. Mrs. Lloyd turned
to the man.

"Go down to the drug-store and get some brandy,
there isn't any in the house," said she; "then come back
as quick as you can. Maggie, you see that there is
plenty of hot water. Martha, you and Ellen come up-
stairs with me, quick."

Ellen followed Mrs. Lloyd and the maid up-stairs,
and, before she knew what she was doing, was assisting
to put the room in perfect readiness for the wounded
man. The maid was weeping all the time she worked,
although she had never liked Mr. Lloyd. There was

something about her mistress which was fairly abnormal. She kept looking at her. This gentle, soft-natured woman had risen above her own pain and grief to a sublime strength of misery.

"Get the camphor, quick, Martha," she said to the maid, who flew out, with the tears streaming. Ellen stood on one side of the bed, and Mrs. Lloyd on the other. Mrs. Lloyd had stripped off the blankets, and was pinning the sheet tightly over the mattress. She seemed to know instinctively what to do.

"I wish you would bring that basin over here, and put it on the stand," said Mrs. Lloyd. "Martha, you fetch more towels, and, Maggie, you run up garret and bring down some of those old sheets from the trunk under the window, quick."

This maid, who was as large and as ample as her mistress, fled out of the room with heavy, noiseless pads of flat feet.

All the time Mrs. Lloyd worked she was evidently listening. She paid no attention to Ellen except to direct her. All at once she gave a great leap and stood still.

"They're coming," said she, though Ellen had heard nothing. Ellen went close to her, and took her two fat, cold hands. She could say nothing. Then she heard the roll of carriage-wheels in the street below.

Mrs. Lloyd pulled her hands away from Ellen's and went to the head of the stairs.

"Bring him right up here," she ordered, in a loud voice.

Ellen stood back, and the struggling procession with the prostrate man in the midst labored up the broad stairs.

"Bring him in here," said Mrs. Lloyd, "and lay him on the bed."

When Lloyd was stretched on the bed, the crowd drew back a little, and she bent over him.

Then she turned with a sort of fierceness to the doctors.

"Why don't you do something?" she demanded. She raised a hand with a repellant gesture towards the other men.

"You had better go now," said she. "I thank you very much. If there is anything you can do, I will let you know."

When Mrs. Lloyd was left with the two doctors and a young assistant, Robert, and Ellen, she said, cutting her words short as if she released every one from a mental grip:

"I have got everything ready. Shall I go out now?"

"I think you had better, Mrs. Lloyd," said the family physician, pityingly. He went close to Ellen.

"Can't you stay with her a little while?" he whispered. Ellen nodded.

Then the physician spoke quite loudly and cheerfully to Mrs. Lloyd.

"We are going to probe for the ball," he said. "We must all hope for the best, Mrs. Lloyd."

Mrs. Lloyd made no reply. She bent again over her husband with a rigid face, and kissed him on his white lips, then she went out, with Ellen following.

Norman Lloyd lived only two hours after he was shot. The efforts to remove the ball had to be abandoned. He was conscious only a few minutes. He suddenly began to look about him with comprehension.

"Robert," he said, in a far-away voice.

Robert stooped closely over his uncle. The dying man looked up at him with an expression which he had never worn in life.

"That man was insane," whispered he, faintly. Then he added, "Look out for her, if she has to go through the operation. Take care of her. Make it as easy for her as you can."

"Then you know, Uncle Norman," gasped Robert. "All the time, but it—pleased her to think I—did not. Don't let her know I knew. Take care—"

Then Norman Lloyd relapsed into unconsciousness, and the whole room and the whole house became clamorous with his stertorous breathing. Mrs. Lloyd and Ellen came and stood in the doorway. The doctor whispered to them. Then the breathing ceased, although at first it was inconceivable that the silence did not continue to ring with it, and Mrs. Lloyd came into the room.

CHAPTER XLIII

WHEN Mrs. Lloyd entered the room, the attention of every one was taken from the dead man on the bed and concentrated upon the woman. Dr. Story, a nervous, intense, elderly man with a settled frown of perplexity over keen eyes, which he had gotten from a struggle of forty years with unanswerable problems of life and death, stepped towards her hastily. Robert pressed close to her side. Ellen came behind her, holding in a curious, instinctive fashion to a fold of the older woman's gown, as if she had been a mother holding back a child from a sudden topple to its hurt. Everybody expected her to make some heart-breaking manifestation. She did nothing. At that moment the sublime unselfishness of the woman, which was her one strength of character, seemed actually to spread itself, as with wings, before them all. She moved steadily, close to her husband on the bed. She gazed at that profile of rigid calmness and enforced peace, which, although the head lay low, seemed to have an effect of upward motion, as if it were cleaving the mystery of space. Mrs. Lloyd laid her hand upon her husband's forehead; she felt a slight incredulousness of death, because it was still warm. She took his hands, drew them softly together, and folded them upon his breast. Then she turned and faced them all with an angelic expression.

"He did not realize it to suffer much?" she said

"No, Mrs. Lloyd," replied Dr. Story, quickly. "No, I assure you that he suffered very little."

"He seemed very happy when he died, Aunt Lizzie," said Robert, huskily.

Mrs. Lloyd looked away from them all around the room. It was a magnificent apartment. Norman Lloyd had had an artistic taste as well as wealth. The furnishings had always been rather beyond Mrs. Lloyd's appreciation, but she admired them kindly. She took in every detail; the foam of rich curtains at the great windows, the cut-glass and silver on the dressing-table, the pale softness of a polar-bear skin beside the bed, the lifelike insistence of the costly pictures on the walls.

"He's gone where it is a great deal more beautiful," she said to them, like a child. "He's gone where there's better treasures than these which he had here."

They all looked at her in amazement. It actually seemed as if, for the moment, the woman's sole grief was over the loss to her husband of those things which he had on earth—the treasures of his mortal state.

Robert took hold of his aunt's arm and led her, quite unresisting, from the room, and as she went she felt for Ellen's hand. "It is time she was home," she said to Robert. "Her folks will be worried about her. She's been a real comfort to me."

It was the first time that Ellen had ever seen death, that she had ever seen the living confronted with it. She felt as if a wave were breaking over her own head as she clung fast to Mrs. Lloyd's hand.

"Sha'n't I stay?" she whispered, pitifully, to her. "If I can send word to my mother—"

"No, you dear child," replied Mrs. Lloyd, "you've done enough, and you will have to be up early in the morning." Then she checked herself. "I forgot," said she to Robert; "the factory will be closed till after the funeral, won't it?"

"Of course it will, Aunt Lizzie."

"And the workmen will be paid just the same, of course," said Mrs. Lloyd. "Now, can't you take her home, Robert?"

"Oh, don't mind about me," cried Ellen.

"You can have a horse put into the buggy," said Mrs. Lloyd.

"Oh, you mustn't leave her now," Ellen whispered to Robert. "Let somebody else take me—Dr. James—"

"I would rather you took her," said Mrs. Lloyd. "And you needn't worry about his leaving me, dear child; the doctor will stay until he comes back."

As Robert was finally going out his aunt caught his arm and looked at him with a radiant expression. "He will never know about *me* now," said she, "and it won't be long before I— Oh, I feel as if I had gotten rid of my own death."

She was filled with inexpressible thankfulness that she had herself to bear what she had dreaded for her husband. "Only think how hard it would have been for Norman," she said to Cynthia, the next day.

Cynthia looked at her wonderingly. She could have understood this feeling over a dearly beloved child. "You are a good woman, Lizzie," she said, in a tone of pitiful respect.

"Not half as good a woman as he was a man," returned Mrs. Lloyd, jealously. "Norman wasn't a professor, I know, but he was a believer. You don't think it is necessary to be a professor in order to be saved, do you, Cynthia?"

"I certainly do not," Cynthia replied. "I wish you would go and lie down, Lizzie."

"Oh, I can't. I wouldn't let anybody do these things but me, for the whole world." Mrs. Lloyd was arranging flowers, tuberoses and white carnations, in vases, and the whole house was scented with them. She looked ghastly, yet still unconquerably happy. She

423

had now no reason to conceal the ravages of disease, and her color was something frightful. Still, she did not suffer as much, for her mind had overborne her body to such an extent that she had the mastery for the time, to a certain extent, of those excruciating stabs of pain. People looked at her incredulously. They could not believe that she felt as she talked, that she was as happy and resigned as she looked, but it was all true. It was either an abnormal state into which her husband's death had thrown her, or one too normal to be credited. She looked at it all with a supreme childishness and simplicity. She simply believed that her husband was in heaven, where she should join him; that he was beyond all suffering which might have come to him through her, and all that troubled her was the one consideration of his having been forced to leave his treasures of earth. She looked at various things which had been prized by the dead man, and found her chief comfort in saying to the minister or Cynthia or Robert that Norman had loved these, but he would have that which was infinitely more precious. She even gazed out of the window, that Tuesday night, and saw her nephew driving away with Ellen, and reflected, with pain, that her husband had been fond and proud of that bay. She was a little at a loss to conceive what could make up to her husband for that in another world, but she succeeded, and evolved from her own loving fancy, and her recollection of the Old Testament, a conception of some wonderful creature, shod with thunder and maned with a whirlwind. Her disease, and a drug she had been taking of late, stimulated her imagination to results of grotesque pathos, but she was comforted.

That night when they were alone, Robert turned to the girl at his side with a sudden motion. It was no time for love-making, for that was in the mind of neither

424

of them, but the bereavement of this other woman, and the tragedy of her state, filled him with a sort of protective pain towards the girl who might some time have to suffer through him the same loss.

"Are you all tired out, dear?" he said, and passed his free arm around her waist.

"No," replied Ellen. Then, since she was only a girl, and overwrought, having been through a severe strain, she broke down, and began to cry.

Robert drew her closer, and she hid her face on his shoulder. "Poor little girl, it has been very hard for you," he whispered.

"Oh, don't think of me," sobbed Ellen. "But I can't bear it, the way she acts and looks. It is sadder than grief."

"She is not going to live long herself, dear," said Robert, in a stifled voice.

"And he—did not know?"

"Hush! yes; but you must never tell any one. She tried to keep it from him. That is her comfort."

"Oh," said Ellen. She looked up at the white face of the young man bending over her, and suddenly the realization of a love that was mightier than all the creatures who came of it and all who followed it was over her.

CHAPTER XLIV

WHEN Ellen did not return, there was some alarm in the Brewster household. Mrs. Zelotes came over, finally, in a quiver of anxiety.

"Maybe I had better start out and see if I can find her," said Andrew.

"I think you had better," returned his mother. "She went before eight o'clock, and it's most midnight, and I've set at my window watchin' ever since. I don't see what you've been thinkin' about, waitin' all this time. I guess if I was a man I shouldn't have waited."

"I think she may have gone in to see Abby Atkins— it's on the way—and not realized how late it was," said Fanny, obstinately, but with a very white face. She drew her thread through with a jerk. It knotted, and she broke it off viciously.

"Fiddlesticks!" said her mother-in-law.

"There's no use imaginin' things," said Fanny, angrily; "but I think myself you'd better go now, Andrew, and see if you can see anything of her."

"I'm goin' with him," announced Mrs. Zelotes.

"Now, mother, you'd better stay where you be," said Andrew, putting on his hat. Then the door flew open, and Amos Lee, who had seen the light in the windows, and was burning to impart the news of the tragedy, rushed in.

"Heard what's happened?" he cried out.

They all thought of Ellen. "What?" demanded Andrew, in a terrible voice. Fanny dropped her work and stared at him, with her chin falling as if she were dying. Mrs. Zelotes made a queer gurgling noise in her throat. Lee stared at them a second, bewildered by the effect of his own words, although they had for him such a tragic import. Andrew caught hold of him in a grasp like the clamp of a machine. "What?" he demanded again.

"The boss has been shot," cried Lee, getting his breath.

Andrew dropped his arm, and they all stared at him. Lee went on fluently, as if he were a fakir at a fair.

"Nahum Beals did it. The boss went back to the office to get his pocketbook; McLaughlin saw him; then he went down the stairs; Nahum, he—he fired; he had been hidin' underneath the stairs. Carl Olfsen caught him, and he's in jail. Your daughter she was there when the shot came, and run up and held his head. The young boss he sent her in Dr. James's buggy to Mrs. Lloyd to break the news. She 'ain't got home?"

"No," gasped Andrew.

"The boss has been shot; he's dead by this time," repeated Lee. "Beals did it; they've got him." There was the most singular evenness and impartiality in his tone, although he was evidently strained to a high pitch of excitement. It was impossible to tell whether he exulted in or was aghast at the tragedy.

"Oh, that poor woman!" cried Fanny.

"I'd like to know what they'll do next," cried Mrs. Zelotes. "I should call it pretty work."

"Nahum Beals has acted to me as if he was half crazy for some time," said Fanny.

"No doubt about it," said Lee; "but I shouldn't wonder if he had to swing."

"It's dreadful," said Fanny. "I wonder when she's comin' home."

"Seems as if they might have got somebody besides that girl to have gone there," said Mrs. Zelotes.

"She happened to be right on the spot," said Lee, importantly.

Andrew seemed speechless; he leaned against the mantel-shelf, gazing from one to the other, breathing hard. He had had bitter feelings against the murdered man, and a curious sense of guilt was over him. He felt almost as if he were the murderer.

" Andrew, I dun'no' but you'd better go up there and see if she's comin' home," said Fanny; and he answered heavily that maybe he had better, when they heard wheels, which stopped before the house.

"They're bringin' her home," said Lee.

Andrew ran and threw open the front door. He had a glimpse of Robert's pale face, nodding to him from the buggy as he drove away, and Ellen came hastening up the walk.

"Well, Ellen, this is pretty dreadful news," said her father, tremulously.

"So you have heard?"

"Amos Lee has just come in. It's a terrible thing, Ellen."

" Yes, it's terrible," returned Ellen, in a quick, strained voice. She entered the sitting-room, and when she met her mother's anxious, tender eyes, she stood back against the wall, with her hands to her face, sobbing. Fanny ran to her, but her grandmother was quicker. She had her arms around the girl before the mother had a chance.

" If they couldn't get somebody besides you," she said, in a voice of intensest love and anger, "I should call it pretty work. Now you go straight to bed, Ellen Brewster, and I'm goin' to make a bowl of sage tea, and bring it up, and see if it won't quiet your nerves. I call it pretty work."

"Yes, you'd better go to bed, Ellen," said Andrew, gulping as if he were swallowing a sob.

Mrs. Zelotes fairly forced Ellen towards the door, Fanny following.

"Don't talk and wake Amabel," whispered Ellen, forcing back her sobs.

"Was he dead when you got there, Ellen?" called out Lee.

Mrs. Zelotes turned back and looked at him. "It's after midnight, and time for you to be goin' home," she said. Then the three disappeared. Lee grinned sheepishly at Andrew.

"Your mother is a stepper of an old woman," said he.

"It's awful news," said Andrew, soberly. "Whatever anybody may have felt, nobody expected—"

"Of course they didn't," retorted Lee, quickly. "Nahum went a step too far." He started for the door as he spoke.

"Well, he was crazy, without any doubt!" said Andrew.

"He'll have to swing for it all the same," said Lee, going out.

"It don't seem right, if he wasn't himself when he did it."

"Lord, we're all crazy when it comes to things like that," returned Lee. Before closing the door he flashed his black eyes and white teeth at Andrew, who felt repelled.

He sat down beside the table and leaned his head upon it. To his fancy all creation seemed to circle about that one dead man. Mr. Lloyd had been for years the arbiter of his destiny, almost of his life. Andrew had regarded him with almost feudal loyalty and admiration, and lately with bitter revolt and hatred, and now he was dead. He felt no sorrow, but rather a terrible remorse because he felt no sorrow. All the bitter thoughts which he had ever had against Lloyd seemed to marshal themselves before him like an ac-

cusing legion of ghosts. And with it all there was a
sense of desolation, as if some force which had been
necessary to his full living had gone out of creation.

"It's over thirty years since I went to work under
him," Andrew thought, and he gave a dry sob. At
that moment a wonderful pity and sorrow for the dead
man seemed to spring up in his soul like a light. He
felt as if he loved him.

Norman Lloyd's funeral was held in the First Baptist
Church of Rowe. It was crowded. Mr. Lloyd had
been the most prominent manufacturer and the wealth-
iest man in the city. His employés filled up a great
space in the body of the church.

Andrew went with his mother and wife. They arrived quite early. When Andrew saw the employés
of Lloyd's marching in, he drew a great sigh. He
looked at the solemn black thing raised on trestles before
the pulpit with an emotion which he could not himself
understand. "That man 'ain't treated me well enough
for me to care anything about him," he kept urging
upon himself. "He never paid any more attention to
me than a gravel-stone under his feet; there ain't any
reason why I should have cared about him, and I don't;
it can't be that I do." Yet arguing with himself in
this way, he continued to eye the casket which held
his dead employer with an unyielding grief.

Mrs. Zelotes sat like a black, draped statue at the
head of the pew, but her eyes behind her black veil
were sharply observant. She missed not one detail.
She saw everything; she counted the wreaths and
bouquets on the casket, and stored in her mind, as
vividly as she might have done some old mourning-
piece, the picture of the near relatives advancing up
the aisle.

Mrs. Lloyd came leaning on her nephew's arm, and

there were Cynthia Lennox and a distant cousin, an elderly widow who had been summoned to the house of death.

Ellen sat in the body of the church, with the employés of Lloyd's, between Abby Atkins and Maria. She glanced up when the little company of mourners entered, then cast her eyes down again and compressed her lips. Maria began to weep softly, pressing her handkerchief to her eyes. Ellen's mother had begged her not to sit with the employés, but with her and her father and grandmother in their own pew, but the girl had refused.

"I must sit where I belong," said she.

"Maybe she thinks it would look as if she was putting on airs on account of—" Fanny said to Andrew when Ellen had gone out.

"I guess she's right," returned Andrew.

The employés had contributed money for a great floral piece composed of laurel and white roses, in the shape of a pillow. Mannie Brady, who sat behind Ellen, leaned over, and in a whisper whistled into her ear.

"Ain't it handsome?" said she. "Can you see them flowers from the hands?"

Ellen nodded impatiently. The great green and white decoration was in plain view from her seat, and as she looked at it she wondered if it were a sarcasm or poetic truth beyond the scope of the givers, the pillow of laurel and roses, emblematic of eternal peace, presented by the hard hands of labor to dead capital.

Of course the tragic circumstances of Norman Lloyd's death increased the curiosity of the public. Gradually the church became crowded by a slow and solemn pressure. The aisles were filled. The air was heavy with the funeral flowers. The minister spoke at length, descanting upon the character of the deceased, his

431

uprightness and strict integrity in business, avoiding pitfalls of admissions of weaknesses with the expertness of a juggler. He was always regarded as very apt at funerals, never saying too much and never too little. The church was very still, the whole audience wrapped in a solemn hush, until the minister began to pray; then there was a general bending of heads and devout screening of faces with hands. Then all at once a sob from a woman sounded from the rear of the church. It was hysterical, and had burst from the restraint of the weeper. People turned about furtively.

"Who was that?" whispered Mamie Brady, after a prolonged stare over her shoulders from under her red frizzle of hair. "It ain't any of the mourners."

Ellen shook her head.

"Do keep still, Mamie Brady," whispered Abby Atkins.

The sob came again, and this time it was echoed from the pew where sat the members of the dead man's family. Mrs. Lloyd began weeping convulsively. Her state of mind had raised her above natural emotion, and yet her nerves weakly yielded to it when given such an impetus. She wept like a child, and now and then a low murmur of heart-broken complaint came from her lips, and was heard distinctly over the church. Other women began to weep. The minister prayed, and his words of comfort seemed like the air in a discordant medley of sorrow.

Andrew Brewster's face twitched; he held his hands clutched tightly. Fanny was weeping, but the old woman at the head of the pew sat immovable.

When the services were over, and the great concourse of people had passed around the casket and viewed the face of the dead, with keen, sidewise observation of the funeral flowers, Mrs. Zelotes pressed out as fast as she was able without seeming to crowd, and caught up with Mrs. Pointdexter, who had sat in the rear of the church.

She came alongside as they left the church, and the two old women moved slowly down the sidewalk, with lingering glances at the funeral procession drawn up in front of the church.

"Who was that cryin' so in back; did you see?" asked Mrs. Zelotes of Mrs. Pointdexter, whose eyes were red, and whose face bore an expression of meek endurance of a renewal of her own experience of sorrow.

"It was Joe Martin's wife," said she. "I sat just behind her."

"What made her?"

Then both started, for the woman who had sobbed came up behind them, her brother, an elderly man, trying to hold her back.

"You stop, John," she cried. "I heard what she said, and I'm goin' to tell her. I'm goin' to tell everybody. Nobody shall stop me. There the minister spoke and spoke and spoke, and he never said a word as to any good he'd done. I'm goin' to tell. I wanted to stan' right up in the church an' tell everybody. He told me not to say a word about it, an' I never did whilst he was livin', but now I'm goin' to stan' up for the dead." The woman pulled herself loose from her brother, who stood behind her, frightened, and continually thrusting out a black-gloved hand of remonstrance. People began to gather. The woman, who was quite old, had a face graven with hard lines of habitual restraint, which was now, from its utter abandon, at once pathetic and terrible. She made a motion as if she were thrusting her own self into the background.

"I'm goin' to speak," she said, in a high voice. "I held my tongue for the livin', but I'm goin' to speak for the dead. My poor husband died twenty years ago, got his hand cut in a machine in Lloyd's, and had lockjaw, and I was left with my daughter that had spinal disease, and my little boy that died, and my own health none too good, and—and he—he—came to my house, one night after the funeral, and—and told me he was goin' to look out for me, and he has, he has. That blessed man gave me five dollars every week of my life, and he buried poor Annie when she died, and my little boy, and he made me promise never to say a word about it. Five dollars every week of my life— five dollars."

The woman's voice ended in a long-drawn, hysterical wail. The other women who had been listening began to weep. Mrs. Pointdexter, when she and Mrs. Zelotes moved on, was sobbing softly, but Mrs. Zelotes's face, though moved, wore an expression of stern conjecture.

"I'd like to know how many things like that Norman Lloyd did," said she. "I never supposed he was that kind of a man."

She had a bewildered feeling, as if she had to reconstruct her own idea of the dead man as a monument to his memory, and reconstruction was never an easy task for the old woman.

434

CHAPTER XLV

A SHORT time after Norman Lloyd's death, Ellen, when she had reached the factory one morning, met a stream of returning workmen. They swung along, and on their faces were expressions of mingled solemnity and exultation, as of children let out to play because of sorrow in the house, which will not brook the jarring inconsequence of youth.

Mamie Brady, walking beside a young man as red-haired as herself, called out, with ill-repressed glee, "Turn round, Ellen Brewster; there ain't no shop to-day."

The young man at her side, nervously meagre, looked at Ellen with a humorous contortion of his thin face, then he caught Mamie Brady by the arm, and swung her into a hopity-skip down the sidewalk. Just behind them came Granville Joy, with another man. Ellen stopped. "What is it?" she said to him. "Why is the shop closed?"

Granville stopped, and let the stream of workmen pass him and Ellen. They stood in the midst of it, separating it, as rock will separate a current. "Mrs. Lloyd is dead," Granville replied, soberly.

"I heard she was very low last night," Ellen returned, in a hushed voice.

Then she passed Granville, who stood a second gazing wistfully after her, before he resumed his homeward way. He told himself quite accurately that she had purposely refrained from turning, in order to avoid walking with himself. A certain resentment seized him. It seemed to him that something besides his love had been slighted. "She needn't have thought I was going to make love to her going home in broad daylight with all these folks," he reflected, and he threw up his head impatiently.

The man with whom he had been walking when Ellen appeared lingered for him to rejoin him. "Wonder how many shops they'd shut up for you and me," said the man, with a sort of humorous bitterness. He had a broad face, seemingly fixed in an eternal mask of laughter, and yet there were hard lines in it, and a forehead of relentless judgment overhung his wide bow of mouth and his squat and wrinkled nose.

"Guess not many," replied Granville, echoing the man in a way unusual to him.

"And yet if it wa'n't for us they couldn't keep the shop running at all," said the man, whose name was Tom Peel.

"That's so," said Granville, with a slight glance over his shoulder.

Ellen had met the Atkins girls, and had turned, and was coming back with them. It was as he had thought.

"If the new boss cuts down fifteen per cent., as the talk is, what be you goin' to do?" asked Tom Peel.

"I ain't goin' to stand it," replied Granville, fiercely.

"Ain't goin' to be swept clean by the new broom, hey?" said the man, with a widened grin.

"No!" thundered Granville—"not by him, nor any one like him. Damn him!"

Tom Peel's grin widened still further into an intense but silent laugh.

Meantime Ellen was walking with Abby and Maria.

"I wonder how we're going to get along with young Lloyd," said Abby.

Ellen looked at her keenly. "Why?" she said.

"Oh, I heard the men talking the other night after

436

I'd gone to bed. Maybe it isn't true that he's thinking of cutting down the wages."

"It can't be," said Ellen.

"I say so, too," said Maria.

"Well, I hope not," said Abby. "You can't tell. Some chimneys always have the wind whistling in them, and I suppose it's about so with a boot and shoe shop. It don't follow that there's going to be a hurricane."

They had come to the entrance of the street where the Atkins sisters lived, and Ellen parted from them.

She kept on her way quite alone. They had walked slowly, and the other operatives had either boarded cars or had gone out of sight.

Ellen, when she turned, faced the northwest, out of which a stiff wind was blowing. She thrust a hand up each jacket-sleeve, folding her arms, but she let the fierce wind smite her full in the face without blenching. She had a sort of delight in facing a wind like that, and her quick young blood kept her from being chilled. The sidewalk was frozen. There was no snow, and the day before there had been a thaw. One could see on this walk, hardened into temporary stability, the footprints of hundreds of the sons and daughters of labor. Read rightly, that sidewalk in the little manufacturing city was a hieroglyphic of toil, and perhaps of toil as tending to the advance of the whole world. Ellen did not think of that, for she was occupied with more personal considerations, thinking of the dead woman in the great Lloyd house. She pictured her lying dead on that same bed whereon she had seen her husband lie dead. All the ghastly concomitants of death came to her mind. "They will turn off all that summer heat, and leave her alone in this freezing cold," she thought. She remembered the sound of that other woman's kind voice in her ears, and she saw her face when she told her the dreadful news of her husband's death. She felt a sob rising in her throat, but forced it back. What Abby had told concerning Mrs. Lloyd's happiness in the face of death seemed to her heartbreaking, though she knew not why. That enormous, almost transcendent trust in that which was absolutely unknown seemed to engulf her.

When she reached home, her mother looked at her in astonishment. She was sewing on the interminable wrappers. Andrew was paring apples for pies. "What be you home for—be you sick?" asked Fanny. Andrew gazed at her in alarm.

"No, I am not sick," replied Ellen, shortly. "Mrs. Lloyd is dead, and the factory's closed."

"I heard she was very low—Mrs. Jones told me so yesterday," said Fanny, in a hushed voice. Andrew began paring another apple. He was quite pale.

"When is the funeral to be, did you hear?" asked Fanny. Ellen was hanging up her hat and coat in the entry.

"Day after to-morrow."

"Have you heard anything about the hands sending flowers?"

"No."

"I suppose they will," said Fanny, "as long as they sent one to him. Well, she was a good woman, and it's a mark of respect, and I 'ain't anything to say against it, but I can't help feeling as if it was a tax."

CHAPTER XLVI

IT was some time after Mrs. Lloyd's death. Ellen had not seen Robert except as she had caught from time to time a passing glimpse of him in the factory. One night she overheard her father and mother talking about him after she had gone to bed, the sitting-room door having been left ajar.

"I thought he'd come and call after his aunt died," she heard Fanny say. "I've always thought he liked Ellen, an' here he is now, with all that big factory, an' plenty of money."

"Mebbe he will," replied Andrew, with a voice in which were conflicting emotions, pride and sadness, and a struggle for self-renunciation.

"It would be a splendid thing for her," said Fanny.

"It would be a splendid thing for *him*," returned Andrew, with a flash.

"Land, of course it would! You needn't be so smart, Andrew Brewster. I guess I know what Ellen is, as well as you. Any man might be proud to get her—I don't care who—whether he's Robert Lloyd, or who, but that don't alter what I say. It would be a splendid chance for Ellen. Only think of that great Lloyd house, and it must be full of beautiful things—table linen, and silver, and what-not. I say it would be a splendid thing for her, and she'd be above want all her life—that's something to be considered when we 'ain't got any more than we have to leave her, and she workin' the way she is."

"Yes, that's so," assented Andrew, with a heavy

439

sigh, as of one who looks upon life from under the mortification of an incubus of fate.

"We'd ought to think of her best good," said Fanny, judiciously. "I've been thinkin' every evening lately that he'd be comin'. I've had the fire in the parlor stove all ready to touch off, an' I've kept dusted in there. I know he liked her, but mebbe he's like all the rest of the big-bugs."

"What do you mean?" asked Andrew, with an inward qualm of repulsion. He always hated unspeakably to hear his wife say "big-bugs" in that tone. Although he was far from being without humility, he was republican to the core in his estimate of his own status in his own free country. In his heart, as long as he kept the law of God and man, he recognized no "big-bugs." It was one of the taints of his wife's ancestry which grated upon him from time to time.

"Oh, well, mebbe he don't want to be seen callin' on a shop-girl."

"Then he'd better keep away, that's all!" cried Andrew, furiously.

"Oh, well, mebbe it ain't so," said Fanny. "He's always seemed to me like a sensible feller, and I know he's liked Ellen, an' lots of girls that work in shops marry rich. Look at Annie Graves, married that factory boss over to Pemberton, an' has everythin'. She'd worked in his factory years. Mebbe it ain't that."

"Ellen don't act as if she minded anything about his not comin'," said Andrew, anxiously.

"Land, no; she ain't that kind. She's too much like her grandmother, but there 'ain't been a night lately that she 'ain't done her hair over when she got home from the shop and changed her dress."

"She always changes her dress, don't she?" said Andrew.

"Oh yes, she always has done that. I guess she

likes to get rid of the leather smell for a while; but she has put on that pretty, new, red silk waist, and I've seen her watchin', though she's never said anything."

"You don't suppose she—" began Andrew, in a voice of intensest anxiety and indignant tenderness.

"Land, no; Ellen Brewster ain't a girl to fret herself much over any man unless she's sure he wants her; trust her. Don't you worry about that. All I mean is, I know she's had a kind of an idea that he might come."

Ellen, up-stairs, lay listening against her will, and felt herself burning with mortified pride and shame. She said to herself that she would never put on that red silk waist again of an evening; she would not even do her hair over. It was quite true that she had thought that Robert might come, that he might renew his offer, now that he was so differently situated, and the obstacles, on his side, at least, removed. She told herself all the time that the obstacles on her own were still far from removed. She asked herself how could she, even if this man loved her and wished to marry her, allow him to support all her family, although he might be able to do so. She often told herself that she ought perhaps to have pride enough to refuse, and yet she watched for him to come. She had reflected at first that it was, of course, impossible for him to seem to take advantage of the deaths which had left him with this independence, that he must stay away for a while from motives of delicacy; but now the months were going, and she began to wonder if he never would come. Every night, when she took off the pretty, red silk waist, donned in vain, and let down her fair lengths of hair, it was with a sinking of her heart, and a sense of incredulous unhappiness. Ellen had always had a sort of sanguinity of happiness and of the petting of Providence as well as of her friends. However, the girl had, in spite of her childlike trust in the beauty of her life, plenty of strength to meet its refutal, and a pride equal to her grandmother's. In case Robert Lloyd should never approach her again, she would try to keep one face of her soul always veiled to her inmost consciousness.

The next evening she was careful not to put on her red silk waist, but changed her shop dress for her old blue woollen, and only smoothed her hair. She even went to bed early in order to prove to her mother that she expected nobody.

"You ain't goin' to bed as early as this, Ellen?" her mother said, as she lighted her lamp.

"Yes, I'm going to bed and read."

"Seems as if somebody might be in," said Fanny, awkwardly.

"I don't know who," Ellen returned, with a gentle haughtiness.

Andrew colored. He was at his usual task of paring apples. Andrew, in lieu of regular work outside, assisted in these household tasks, that his wife might have more time to sew. He looked unusually worn and old that night.

"If anybody does come, Ellen will have to get up, that's all," said Fanny, when the girl had gone upstairs. Then she pricked up her ears, for the electric-car had stopped before the house. Then it went on, with a sharp clang of the bell and a gathering rush of motion.

"That car stopped," Fanny said, breathlessly, her work falling from her fingers. Andrew and she both listened intently, then footsteps were heard plainly coming around the path at the side of the house.

Fanny's face fell. "It's only some of the men," said she, in a low voice. Then there came a knock on the side door, and Andrew ushered in John Sargent, Joe Atkins, and Amos Lee. Nahum Beals did not come

442

in those days, for he was in prison awaiting trial for the murder of Norman Lloyd. However, Amos Lee's note was as impressive as his. He called often with Sargent and Atkins. They could not shake him off. He lay in wait for them at street corners, and joined them. He never saw Ellen alone, and did not openly proclaim his calls as meant for her. She prevented him from doing that in a manner which he could not withstand, full of hot and reckless daring as he was. When he entered that night he looked around with keen furtiveness, and was evidently listening and watching for her, though presently his voice rose high in discussion with the others. After a while the man who lived next door dropped in, and his wife with him. She and Fanny withdrew to the dining-room with their sewing—for the woman also worked on wrappers —and left the sitting-room to the men.

"It beats all how they like to talk," said the woman, with a large-minded leniency, "and they never get anywhere," she added. "They work themselves all up, and never get anywhere; but men are all like that."

"Yes, they be," assented Fanny.

"Jest hear that Lee feller," said the woman.

Amos Lee's voice was audible over the little house, and could have been heard in the yard, for it had an enormous carrying quality. It was the voice of a public ranter. Ellen, up in her chamber, lying in her bed, with a lamp at her side, reading, closely covered from the cold—for the room was unheated—heard him with a shiver of disgust and repulsion, and yet with a fierce sympathy and loyalty. She could not distinguish every word he said, but she knew well what he was talking about.

Mrs. Lloyd's death had made a certain hush in the ferment of revolt at Lloyd's, but now it was again on the move. There was a strong feeling of dislike to

443

young Lloyd among the workmen. His uncle had heaped up ill-feeling as well as wealth as a heritage for him. The older Lloyd had never been popular, and Robert had succeeded to all his unpopularity, and was fast gathering his own. He was undoubtedly disposed to follow largely his uncle's business methods. He had admired them, they had proved successful, and he had honestly seen nothing culpable in them as business methods go; so it was not strange that he tried to copy them when he came into charge of Lloyd's. He was inclined to meet opposition with the same cool inflexibility of persistency in his own views, and was disposed to consult his own interests and carry out his own plans with no more brooking of interference than the skipper of a man-o'-war. Therefore, when it happened, shortly after his aunt's death, that he conceived a dissatisfaction with some prominent spirits among union men, he discharged them without the slightest reference to the fact that they were old and skilful workmen, and employed non-union men from another town in their places. He had, indeed, the object of making in time his factory entirely non-union. He said to himself that he would be dictated to by no labor organization under the sun, and that went a step beyond his uncle, inasmuch as the elder Lloyd had always made his own opinion subservient to good business policy; but Robert was younger and his blood hotter. It happened, also, a month later, when he began to see that business had fallen off considerably (indeed, it was the beginning of a period of extreme business depression), and that he could no longer continue on the same scale with the same profits, that instead of assembling the men in different departments, communicating the situation to them, and submitting them a reduced price-list for consideration, as was the custom with the more

444

pacific of the manufacturers in the vicinity, he posted it up in the different rooms with no ado whatever. That had been his uncle's method, but never in the face of such brewing discontent as was prevalent in Lloyd's at that time. It was an occasion when the older man would have shut down, but Robert had, along with his arbitrary impetuosity, a real dislike to shut down on account of the men, for which they would have been the last to give him credit. "Poor devils," he told himself, standing in the office window one night, and seeing them pour out and disappear into the early darkness beyond the radius of the electric-lights, "I can't turn them adrift without a dollar in midwinter. I'll try to run the factory a while longer on a reduced scale, if I only meet expenses."

He saw Ellen going out, descending the steps with the Atkins girls, and as she passed the light, her fair head shone out for a second like an aureole. A great wave of tenderness came over him. He reflected that it would make no difference to her, that it was only a question of time before he lifted her forever out of the ranks of toil. The impulse was strong upon him to go to see her that night, but he had set himself to wait three months after his aunt's death, and the time was not yet up. He had a feeling that he might seem to be, and possibly would be, taking advantage of his bereavement if he went sooner, and that Ellen herself might think so.

It was that very night that Ellen had gone to bed early, to prove not only to her mother but to herself that she did not expect him, and the men came to see Andrew. Once she heard Amos Lee's voice raised to a higher pitch than ever, and distinguished every word.

"I tell you he's goin' to cut the wages to-morrow," said he.

There was a low rumble of response, which Ellen

could not understand, but Lee's answer made it evident.

"How do I know?" he thundered. "It is in the air. He don't tell any more than his uncle did; but you wait and see, that's all."

"I don't believe it," the girl up-stairs said to herself, indignantly and loyally. "He can't cut the wages of all those poor men, he with all his uncle's money."

But the next morning the reduced price-list was posted on the walls of the different rooms in Lloyd's.

CHAPTER XLVII

THERE was a driving snow-storm the next day. When Ellen started for the factory the white twilight of early morning still lingered. Everywhere were the sons and daughters of toil plodding laboriously and noiselessly through the snow, each keeping in the track of the one who went before. There was no wind blowing, and the snow was in a blue-white level; the trees bent stiffly and quietly beneath a heavy shag of white, and now and then came a clamor of birds, which served to accentuate the silence and peace. Ellen could always be forced by an extreme phase of nature to forgetfulness of her own stresses. For the time being she forgot everything; her vain watching for Robert, the talk of trouble in the factory, the disappointment in her home—all were forgotten in the contemplation, or rather in the absorbing, of this new-old wonder of snow.

There was a survival of the old Greek spirit in the girl, and had she come to earth without her background of orthodox traditions, she might have easily found her own deities in nature. The peace of the snow enveloped her soul as well as the earth, and she became a beneficiary of the white storm; the graceful droop of the pine boughs extended to her thoughts, and the clamor of the birds aroused in her a winged freedom, so that she felt at once peace and a sort of ecstasy. She walked in the track of a stolidly plodding man before her, as different a person as if she were an inhabitant of another planet. He was digesting the soggy.

447

sweet griddle-cakes which he had eaten for breakfast, and revolving in his mind two errands for his wife—one, a pail of lard; the other, three yards of black dress braid; he was considering the surface scum of existence, that which pertained solely to his own petty share of it; the girl, the clear residue of life which was, and had been, and would be. Each was on the way to humble labor for daily bread, but with a difference of eternity between them.

But when Ellen reached the end of the cross street where the Atkins girls lived, she heard a sound which dispelled her rapt state. Her far vision became a near one; she saw, as it were, the clouded window-glass between her mortal eyes and the beyond, and the sound of a cough brought it about. Abby and Maria were coming towards her through the snow. Maria was coughing violently, and Abby was scolding her.

"I don't care anything about it, Maria Atkins," Abby was saying, "you ought to be ashamed of yourself coming out such a morning as this. There isn't any sense in it. You know you'll catch cold, and then there'll be two of you to take care of. You don't help a mite doing so, you needn't think you do."

When Abby caught sight of Ellen she hastened forward, while Maria, still coughing, trailed behind, lifting her little, heavy, snow-bound feet wearily.

"Ellen, I wish you'd tell Maria to turn around and go home," she said. "Just hear her cough, and out in all this snow, and getting her skirts draggled. She hasn't got common-sense, you tell her so."

Ellen stopped, nodding assentingly. "I think she's right, Maria," she said. "You ought not to be out such a morning as this. You had better go home."

Maria came up smiling, though her lips were quite white, and she controlled her cough to convulsive motions of her chest.

"I am no worse than usual," said she. "I feel better than I generally do in the morning. I haven't coughed any more, if I have as much, and I am holding my dress up high, and you know how warm the factory is. It will be enough sight warmer than it is at home. It is cold at home."

"Lloyd don't have to save coal," said Abby, bitterly, "but that don't alter the fact of your getting your skirts draggled."

Maria pulled up her skirts so high that she exposed her slender ankles, then seeing that she had done so, she let them fall with a quick glance at two men behind them.

"The snow will shake right off; it's light, Abby," she said.

"It ain't light. I should think you might listen to Ellen, if you won't to me."

Ellen pressed close to Maria, and pulled her thin arm through her own. "Look here," she said, "don't you think—"

Then Maria burst out with a pitiful emphasis. "I've got to go," she said. "Father had a bad spell last night; he can't get out. He'll lose his place this time, we are afraid, and there's a note coming due that father says he's paid, but the man didn't give it up, and he's got to pay it over again; the lawyer says there is no other way, and we can't let John Sargent do everything. He's got a sister out West he's about supporting since her husband died last fall. I've got to go to work; we've got to have the money, Ellen, and as for my cough, I have always coughed. It hasn't killed me yet, and I guess it won't yet for a while." Maria said the last with a reckless gayety which was unusual to her.

Abby trudged on ahead with indignant emphasis. "I'd like to know what good it is going to do to work and earn and pay up money if everybody is going

2 F   449

to be killed by it?" she said, without turning her head.

Ellen pulled up Maria's coat-collar around her neck and put an extra fold of her dress-skirt into her hand.

"There, you can hold it up as high as that, it looks all right," said she.

"I wish Robert Lloyd had to get up at six o'clock and trudge a mile in this snow to his work," said Abby, with sudden viciousness. "He'll be driven down in his Russian sleigh by a man looking like a drum-major, and cut our poor little wages, and that's all he cares. Who's earning the money, he or us, I'd like to know? I hate the rich!"

"If it's true, what you say," said Maria, "it seems to me it's like hating those you have given things to, and that's worse than hating your enemies."

"Don't say given, say been forced to hand over," retorted Abby, fiercely; "and don't preach, Maria Atkins, I hate preaching; and do have sense enough not to talk when you are out in this awful storm. You can keep your mouth shut, if you can't do anything else!"

Ellen had turned quite white at Abby's words.

"You don't think that he means to cut the wages?" she said, eagerly.

"I know he does. I had it straight. Wait till you get to the shop."

"I don't believe it."

"You wait. Norman Lloyd was as hard as nails, and the young one is just like him." Abby looked relentlessly at Ellen.

"Maybe it isn't so," whispered Maria to Ellen.

"I don't believe it is," responded Ellen, but Abby heard them, and turned with a vicious jerk.

"Well, you wait!" said she.

The moment Ellen reached the factory she realized that something unwonted had happened. There were groups of men, talking, oblivious even of the blinding storm, which was coming in the last few minutes with renewed fury, falling in heavy sheets like dank shrouds.

Ellen saw one man in a muttering group throw out an arm, whitened like a branch of a tree, and shake a rasped, red fist at the splendid Russian sleigh of the Lloyd's, which was just gliding out of sight with a flurry of bells and a swing of fur tails, the whole surmounted by the great fur hat of the coachman. Abby turned and looked fiercely at Ellen.

"What did I tell you?" she cried.

Even then Ellen would not believe. She caught a glimpse of Robert's fair head at the office window, and a great impulse of love and loyalty came over her.

"I don't believe it," she said aloud to Maria. Maria held her arm tightly.

"Maybe it isn't so," she said.

But when they entered the room where they worked, there was a sullen group before a placard tacked on the wall. Ellen pressed closely, and saw what it was— a reduced wage-list. Then she went to her machine.

CHAPTER XLVIII

ELLEN had a judicial turn of mind, as her school-master had once said of her. She was able to look at matters from more than one stand-point, but she reasoned with a New Testament clearness of impartiality. She was capable of uncompromising severity, since she brought such a clear light of youth and childhood to bear upon even those things which needed shadows for their true revelation. Everything was for her either black or white. She had not lived long enough, perhaps she never would, for a comprehension of half-tones. The situation to her mind was perfectly simple, and she viewed it with a candor which was at once terrible and cruel, for it involved cruelty not only to Robert but to herself. She said to herself, here was this rich man, this man with accumulation of wealth, not one dollar of which he had earned himself, either by his hands or his brains, but which had been heaped up for his uncle by the heart and back breaking toil of all these poor men and women; and now he was going to abuse his power of capital, his power to take the bread out of their mouths entirely, by taking it out in part. He was going to reduce their wages, he was deliberately going to cause privation, and even suffering where there were large families. She felt the most unqualified dissent and indignation, and all the love which she had for the man only intensified it. Love, with a girl like this, tended to clearness of vision instead of blindness. She judged him as she would have judged herself. As she stood working at her machine, stitching linings

452

to vamps, she kept a sharply listening ear for what went on about her, but there was very little to hear after work had fairly commenced and the great place was in full hum. The demand of labor was so imperative that the laborers themselves were merged in it; they ceased to be for the time, and, instead of living, they became parts of the struggle for life. A man hustling as if the world were at stake to get his part of a shoe finished as soon as another man, so as not to clog and balk the whole system, had no time for rebellion. He was in the whirlpool which was mightier than himself and his revolt. After all, a man is a small and helpless factor before his own needs. For a time those whirring machines, which had been evolved in the first place from the brains of men, and partook in a manner of both the spirit and the grosser elements of existence, its higher qualities and its sordid mechanism, like man himself, had the best of it. The swart arms of the workmen flew at their appointed tasks, they fed those unsatisfied maws, the factory vibrated with the heavy thud of the cutting-machines like a pulse, the racks with shoes in different stages of completion trundled from one department to another, propelled by men with tense arms and doggedly bent heads.

Ellen worked with the rest, but she was one of the few whose brain could travel faster than her hands. She thought as she worked, for her muscles did not retard her mind. She was composed of two motions, one within the other, and the central motion was so swift that it seemed still.

Ed Flynn came down the room and bent over her.

"Good-morning," he said. He was too gayly confident to be entirely respectful, but he had always a timidity of bearing which sat oddly upon him before Ellen. He looked half boldly, half wistfully at her fair face, and challenged her with gay eyes, which had in their depths a covert seriousness.

Ellen stood between Abby Atkins and Sadie Peel at her work. Sadie Peel turned on the foreman coquettishly and said, "You'd better go an' talk to Mamie Brady, she's got on a new blue bow on her red hair. Why don't you give her some better work than tying those old shoes? Here she's been workin' in this shop two years. You needn't come shinin' round Ellen an' me! We don't want you."

Flynn colored angrily and shot a vicious glance at the girl.

"It's a pretty hard storm," he said to Ellen, as if the other girl had not spoken.

"You needn't pretend you don't hear me, Ed Flynn," called out the girl. Her cheap finery was in full force that morning, not a lock of her brown hair was unstudied in its arrangement, and she was as conscious of her pose before her machine as if she had been on the stage. She knew just how her slender waist and the graceful slope of her shoulders appeared to the foreman, and her voice, in spite of its gay rallying and audacity, was wheedling.

Flynn caught hold of her shoulders, round and graceful under her flannel blouse, and shook her, half in anger, half in weakness.

"You shut up, you witch," said he. Then he turned to Ellen again, and his whole manner and expression changed.

"I'm sorry about that new list," he said, very low, in her ear. Ellen never looked at him, and did not make a motion as if she heard.

"It's a hard storm," the foreman said again, almost appealingly.

"Yes, it is very hard," replied Ellen, slipping another shoe under the needles.

"What on earth ails you this morning, Ellen Brewster?" Sadie Peel said to her, when the foreman had gone. "You look queer and act queer."

"Ellen ain't in the habit of joking with Ed Flynn," said Abby Atkins, on the other side, with sarcastic emphasis.

"My, don't you feel big!" sneered Sadie Peel. There was always a jarring inconsequence about this girl, she was so delicately pretty and refined in appearance, her ribbons weit so profuse and cheap, and her manners were so recklessly coarse.

Ellen said nothing, but worked steadily.

"Mame Brady's just gone on Ed Flynn, and he goes with her just enough to keep her hangin', and I don't believe he means to marry her, and I think it's mean," said Sadie Peel.

"She ought to have more sense than to take any stock in him," said Abby.

"She ain't the only one," said Sadie. "Nellie Stone in the office has been daft over him since she's been there, and he don't look at her. I don't see what there is about Ed Flynn, for my part."

"I don't," said Abby, dryly.

"Well, I don't know. He's pretty good-looking," said Sadie Peel, "and he's got a sort of a way with him." All the time the girl was talking her heart was aching. The foreman had paid her some little attention, which she had taken seriously, but nobody except her father had known it, or known when he had fallen off. Sometimes Flynn, meeting the father's gaze as he passed him at his work at the cutting-bench, used to waver involuntarily, though he asked himself with perfect good faith what was it all about, for he had done the girl no harm. He felt more guilty concerning Mamie Brady.

Ellen worked on, with her fingers flying and her forehead tense with thought. The chatter of the girls

455

ceased. They were too busy to keep it up. The hum of work continued. Once Ellen knew, although she did not see him, by some subtle disturbance of the atmosphere, a little commotion which was perfectly silent, that Robert Lloyd had entered the room. She knew when he passed her, and she worked more swiftly than ever. After he had gone out there was a curiously inarticulate sound like a low growl of purely animal dissent over the room; a word of blasphemy sounded above the din of the machines. Then all went on as before until the noon whistle blew.

Even then there was not so much discussion as might have been expected. Robert, since the storm was so heavy, remained in the office, and sent a boy out for a light luncheon, and the foremen were much in evidence. There was always an uncertainty about their sentiments, occupying as they did a position half - way between employer and employés; and then, too, they were not affected by the cut in wages. The sentiments of the unaffected are always a matter of suspicion to those who suffer themselves. There were grumblings carried on in a low key behind Flynn's back, but the atmosphere for the most part was one of depression. Ellen ate her luncheon with Maria and Abby. Willy Jones came up timidly when they were nearly finished, feeling his way with a remark about the storm, which was increasing.

"All the cars are tied up," he said, "and the noon train isn't in."

He leaned, with a curious effort at concealment from them all and himself, upon the corner of the bench near Abby. Then a young man passed them, with such an air of tragedy and such a dead-white face that they all stared after him.

"What in the world ails you, Ben Simmons?" called out Sadie Peel. But he did not act as if he heard. He crossed vehemently to the other side of the room, and

456

stood at a window, looking out at the fierce white slant of the storm.

"What in creation ails him?" cried Sadie Peel.

"I guess I know," Willy Jones volunteered, timidly.

"What?"

"He was going to get married, and this cut in his wages is going to put a stop to it. I heard him say so this morning."

"Married! Who to?" asked Sadie Peel.

"Floretta Vining."

"My land!" cried Sadie Peel. "So she did take up with him after the school-teacher went away. I always said she would. I always knew Edward Harris wouldn't marry her, and I always said Ben Simmons would get her if he hung on long enough. Floretta was bound to marry somebody; she wasn't going to wind up an old maid; and if she couldn't get one, she'd take another. I suppose Ben has got that sick sister of his to do for since her father died, and thinks he can't get married with any less pay. Floretta won't make a very cheap wife. She's bound to have things whether or no, and Ben 'ain't never earned so much as some. He's awful steady, but he's slow as cold molasses, and he won't let his sister suffer for no Floretta."

"That's so; I don't believe he would," said Abby. "What any man in his senses wants a doll like that for enough to look as if he was dead when he's got to put off marrying her!"

"That's because you ain't a man, Abby Atkins," said Sadie Peel. "All the men think of is looks, and little fine airs and graces."

"It seems as if they might get along," ventured Willy Jones, "as if they might do with less for a while."

Then Ellen turned to him unexpectedly. "There's no use in talking about doing with less when every single cent has to count," said she, sternly. "Ben

457

Simmons has his taxes and insurance, and a steady
doctor's bill for his sister, and medicines to buy. He
can't have laid up a cent, for he's slow, though he's
a good workman. You can't do with less when you
haven't any more than enough."

"That's so," said Abby. Then she turned a tender,
conciliating, indulgent gaze on the young man at her
side. "If I were Floretta Vining," said she, "and if
Ellen were, we would go without things, and never
know it. We'd go to work; but Floretta, she's different.
We went to school with Floretta Vining."

"Floretta Vining is dreadful fond of men, but she
wouldn't go without a yard of ribbon for one if he was
dying," said Sadie Peel, conclusively. "It's awful
hard on Ben Simmons, and no mistake."

"What?" said Amos Lee, coming up.

"Oh, what's hard on all of us? What's the use of
asking?" said the girl, with a bitter coquetry. "I
shouldn't think any man with horse-sense would ask
what's hard on us when he's seen the ornaments tacked
up all over the shop this morning."

"That's so," said Lee, with a glance over his shoulder.
Flynn was at the other end of the room. Granville Joy,
Dixon, and one or two other men were sauntering up.
For a second the little group looked at one another.

"What are you going to do?" asked Ellen, in a low
voice, which had an intonation that caused the others
to start.

"I know what I'll do, if I can get enough to back me,"
cried Lee, in a loud voice.

"Hush up!" said Sadie Peel. Then her father came
along smiling his imperturbable smile on his wide face,
which had a Slavonic cast, although he was New England born and bred. He looked from one to the other
without saying a word.

"We're deciding whether to strike or not, father,"

said Sadie, in a flippant manner. She raised a hand and adjusted a stray lock of hair as she spoke, then she straightened her ribbon stock. Her father said nothing, but his face assumed a stolidity of expression.

"I know what I'll do," proclaimed Amos Lee again.

"Hush up!" cried Sadie Peel again, with a giggle. "Here's Ed Flynn." And the foreman came sauntering up as the one-o'clock whistle blew, and the workers sprang to their posts of work.

CHAPTER XLIX

THE snow increased all day. When the six-o'clock whistle blew, and the workmen streamed out of the factories, it was a wild waste of winter and storm. The wind had come up, and the light snow arose in the distance like white dancers of death, spinning furiously over the level, then settling into long, gravelike ridges. Ellen glanced into the office as she passed the door, and saw Robert Lloyd talking busily with Flynn and another foreman by the name of Dennison. As she passed, Robert turned with a look as if he had been watching for her, and came forward hastily.

"Miss Brewster!" he called.

Mamie Brady, following close behind, gave Ellen an admonishing nudge. "Boss wants to see you," she whispered, loudly. Ellen stopped, and Robert came up.

"Please step in here a moment, Miss Brewster," he said, and colored a little.

Granville Joy, who was following Ellen, looked keenly at him, some one sniggered aloud, and a girl said quite audibly, "My land!"

Ellen followed Robert into the office, and he bent over her, speaking rapidly, in a low voice.

"You must not walk home in this snow," he said, "and the cars are not running. You must let me take you. My sleigh is at the door."

Ellen turned white. Somehow this protecting care for herself, in the face of all which she had been considering that day, gave her a tremendous shock. She

460

felt at once touched and more indignant than she had ever been in her whole life. She had been half believing that Robert was neglecting her, that he had forgotten her; all day she had been judging his action of cutting the wages of the workmen from her unswerving, child-like, unshadowed point of view, and now this little evidence of humanity towards her, in the face of what she considered wholesale inhumanity towards others, made her at once severe to him and to herself, and she forced back sternly the leap of pleasure and happiness which this thought of her awakened. "No, thank you," she said, shortly; "I am much obliged, but I would rather walk."

"But you cannot, in this storm," pleaded Robert, in a low voice.

"Yes, I can; it is no worse for me than for others. There is Maria Atkins, she has been coughing all day."

"I will take her too. Ellen, you cannot walk. You must let me take you."

"I am much obliged, but I would rather not," replied Ellen, in an icy tone. She looked quite hard in his face.

Robert looked at her perplexed. "But it is drifting," he said.

"It is no worse for me than for the others." Ellen turned to go. Her attitude of rebuff was unmistakable.

Robert colored. "Very well; I will not urge you," he said, coldly. Then he returned to his desk, and Ellen went out. She caught up with Maria Atkins, who was struggling painfully through the drifts, leaning on Abby's arm, and slipped a hand under her thin shoulder.

"I expect nothing but she'll get her death out in this storm," grumbled Abby. "What did he want, Ellen?"

"Nothing in particular," replied Ellen. Uppermost in her mind at that moment was the charge of cruelty against Robert for not taking her hint as to Maria.

"He can ask me to ride because he has amused himself with me, but as for taking this poor girl, whom he does not love, when it may mean life or death to her, he did not think seriously of doing that for a moment," she thought.

Maria was coughing, although she strove hard to smother the coughs. Granville Joy, who was plodding ahead, turned and waited until they came up.

"You had better let me carry you, Maria," he said, jocularly, but his honest eyes were full of concern.

"He is enough sight kinder than Robert Lloyd," thought Ellen; "he has a better heart." And then the splendid Lloyd sleigh came up behind them and stopped, tilting to a drift. Robert, in his fur-lined coat, sprang out and went up to Maria.

"Please let me take you home," he said, kindly. "You have a cold, and this storm is too severe for you to be out. Please let me take you home."

Maria looked at him, fairly gasping with astonishment. She tried to speak, but a cough choked her.

"You had better go if Mr. Lloyd will take you," Abby said, decisively. "Thank you, Mr. Lloyd; she isn't fit to be out." She urged her sister towards the sleigh, and Robert assisted her into the fur-lined nest.

"I can sit with the driver," said Robert to Abby, "if you will come with your sister."

"No, thank you," replied Abby. "I am able to walk, but I will be much obliged if you will take Maria home."

Robert sprang in beside Maria, and the sleigh slid out of sight.

"I never!" said Abby. Ellen said nothing, but plodded on, her eyes fixed on the snowy track.

"I am glad she had a chance to ride," said Granville Joy, in a tentative voice. He looked uneasily at Ellen.

"It beats the Dutch," said Abby. She also regarded

Ellen with sympathy and perplexity. When they reached the street where she lived, up which the sleigh had disappeared, she let Granville go on ahead, and she spoke to Ellen in a low tone. "Why didn't he ask you?" she said.

"He did," replied Ellen.

"In the office?"

"Yes."

"And you wouldn't?"

"No."

"Why not?"

"I don't care to accept favors from a man who oppresses all my friends!"

"He was good to take in Maria," said Abby, in a perplexed voice. "His uncle would never have thought of it."

Ellen made no reply. She stood still in the drifting snow, with her mouth shut hard.

"You feel as if this cutting wages was a pretty hard thing?" said Abby.

"Yes, I do."

"Well, so do I. I wonder what they will do about it. I don't know how the men feel. Somehow, folks can't seem to think or plan much in a storm like this. There's the sleigh coming back."

"Good-night," Ellen said, hurriedly, and trudged on as fast as she was able in order not to have the Lloyd sleigh pass her; it had to turn after reaching the end of the street. Ellen caught up with Granville Joy. Robert, glancing over the waving fringe of fur tails, saw disappearing in the pale gleam of the electric-light the two dim figures veiled by the drifting snow. He thought to himself, with a sharp pain, that perhaps, after all, Granville Joy was the reason for her rebuff. It never occurred to him that his action in cutting the wages could have anything to do with it.

463

Ellen went along with Granville, who was anxious to offer her his arm, but did not quite dare. He kept thrusting out an elbow in her direction, and an inarticulate invitation died in his throat. Finally, when they reached an unusually high drift of snow, he plucked up sufficient courage.

"Take my arm, won't you?" he said, with a pitiful attempt at ease, then stared as if he had been shot, at Ellen's reply.

"No, thank you," she said. "I think it is easier to walk alone in snow like this."

"Maybe it is," assented Granville, dejectedly. He walked on, scuffling as hard as he could to make a path for Ellen with the patient faithfulness of a dog.

"What are you going to do about the cut in wages?" Ellen asked, presently.

Granville started. The sudden transition from personalities to generalities confused him.

"What?" he said.

Ellen repeated her question.

"I don't know," said Granville. "I don't think the boys have made up their minds. I don't know what they will do. They have been weeding out union men. I suppose the union would have something to say about it otherwise. I don't know what we will do."

"I shouldn't think there would be very much doubt as to what to do," said Ellen.

Granville stared at her over his shoulder in a perplexed, admiring fashion. "You mean—?" he asked.

"I shouldn't think there would be any doubt."

"Well, I don't know. It is a pretty serious thing to get out of work in midwinter for a good many of us, and as long as the union isn't in control, other men can come in. I don't know."

"I know," said Ellen.

"You mean—?"

"I mean that I do not think it right, that it is unjust, and I believe in resisting injustice."

"Men have resisted injustice ever since the Creation," said Granville, in a bitter voice.

"Well, resistance can continue as long as life lasts," returned Ellen. Just then came a fiercer blast than ever, laden with a stinging volley of snow, and seemed to sweep the words from the girl's mouth. She bent before it involuntarily, and the conviction forced itself upon her that, after all, resistance to injustice might be as futile as resistance to storm, that injustice might be one of the primal forces of the world, and one of the conditions of its endurance, and yet with the conviction came the renewed resolution to resist.

"What can poor men do against capital unless they are backed up by some labor organization?" asked Granville. "And I don't believe there are a dozen in the factory who belong to the union. There has been an understanding, without his ever saying so that I know of, that the old boss didn't approve of it. So lots of us kept out of it, we wanted work so bad. What can we do against such odds?"

"When right is on your side, you have all the odds," said Ellen, looking back over her snow - powdered shoulder.

"Then you would strike?"

"I wouldn't submit."

"Well, I don't know how the boys feel," said Granville. "I suppose we'll have to talk it over."

"I shouldn't need to talk it over," said Ellen. "You've gone past your house, Granville."

"I ain't going to let you go home alone in such a storm as this," said Granville, in a tender voice, which he tried to make facetious. "I wouldn't let any girl go home alone in such a storm."

Ellen stopped short. "I don't want you to go home with me, thank you, Granville," she said. "Your mother will have supper ready, and I can go just as well alone."

"Ellen, I won't let you go alone," said the young man, as a wilder gust came. "Suppose you should fall down?"

"Fall down!" repeated Ellen, with a laugh, but her regard of the young man, in spite of her rebuff, was tender. He touched her with his unfailing devotion; the heavy trudging by her side of this poor man meant, she told herself, much more than the invitation of the rich one to ride behind his bays in his luxurious sleigh. This meant the very bone and sinew of love. She held out her little, mittened hand to him.

"Good-night, Granville," she said.

Granville caught it eagerly. "Oh, Ellen," he murmured.

But she withdrew her hand quickly. "We have always been good friends, and we always will be," said she, and her tone was unmistakable. The young man shrank back.

"Yes, we always will, Ellen," he said, in a faithful voice, with a note of pain in it.

"Good-night," said Ellen again.

"Good-night," responded Granville, and turned his plodding back on the girl and retraced his laborious steps towards his own home, which he had just passed. There come times for all souls when the broad light of the path of humanity seems to pale to insignificance before the intensity of the one little search-light of personality. Granville Joy felt as if the eternal problem of the rich and poor, of labor and capital, of justice and equality, was as nothing before the desire of his heart for that one girl who was disappearing from his sight behind the veil of virgin snow.

CHAPTER L

WHEN Ellen came in sight of her house that night she saw her father's bent figure moving down the path with sidewise motions of a broom. He had been out at short intervals all the afternoon, that she should not have to wade through drifts to the door. The electric-light shone full on this narrow, cleared track and the toiling figure.

"Hullo, father!" Ellen called out. Andrew turned, and his face lit with love and welcome and solicitude.

"Be you dreadful snowy?" he asked.

"Oh no, father, not very."

"It's an awful storm."

"Pretty bad, but I got along all right. The snow-plough has been out."

"Wait a minute till I get this swept," said Andrew, sweeping violently before her.

"You needn't have bothered, father," said Ellen.

"I 'ain't anything else to do," replied Andrew, in a sad voice.

"There's mother watching," said Ellen.

"Yes, she's been diggin' at them wrappers all day."

"I suppose she has," Ellen returned, in a bitter tone. Her father stared at her. Ellen never spoke like that. For the first time she echoed him and her mother. Something like terror came over him at the sound of that familiar note of his own life from this younger one. He seemed to realize dimly that a taint of his nature had descended upon his child.

When Ellen entered the house, the warm air was full

467

of savory odors of toast and tea and cooking meat and
vegetables.

"You'd better go right up-stairs and put on a dry
dress, Ellen," said Fanny. "I put your blue one out
on your bed, and your shoes are warming by the sitting-room stove. I've been worrying as to how you
were going to get home all day." Then she stopped
short as she caught sight of Ellen's face. "What on
earth is the matter, Ellen Brewster?" she said.

"Nothing," said Ellen. "Why?"

"You look queer. Has anything happened?"

"Yes, something has happened."

"What?"

Andrew turned pale. He stood in the entry with his
snowy broom in hand, staring from one to the other.

"Nothing that you need worry about," said Ellen.
"I'll tell you when I get my dress changed."

Ellen pulled off her rubbers, and went up-stairs to her
chamber. Fanny and Andrew stood looking at each
other.

"You don't suppose—" whispered Andrew.

"Suppose what?" responded Fanny, sharply.

They continued to look at each other. Fanny answered Andrew as if he had spoken, with that jealous
pride for her girl's self-respect which possessed her even
before the girl's father.

"Land, it ain't that," said she. "You wouldn't
catch Ellen lookin' as if anything had come across her
for such a thing as that."

"No, I suppose she wouldn't," said Andrew; and he
actually blushed before his wife's eyes.

That afternoon Mrs. Wetherhed had been in, and
told Fanny that she had heard that Robert Lloyd was
to be married to Maud Hemingway; and both Andrew
and Fanny had thought of that as the cause of Ellen's
changed face.

"You'd better take that broom out into the shed, and get the snow off yourself, and come in and shut the door," Fanny said, shortly. "You're colding the house all off, and Amabel has got a cold, and she's sitting right in the draught."

"All right," replied Andrew, meekly, though Fanny had herself been holding the sitting-room door open. In those days Andrew felt below his moral stature as head of the house. Actually, looking at Fanny, who was earning her small share towards the daily bread, she seemed to him much taller than he, though she was a head shorter. He thought so little of himself, he seemed to see himself as through the wrong end of a telescope. Fanny went into the sitting-room and shut the door with a bang. Amabel did not look up from her book. She was reading a library book much beyond her years, and sniffing pathetically with her cold. Amabel had begun to discover an omnivorous taste for books, which stuck at nothing. She understood not more than half of what she read, but seemed to relish it like indigestible food.

When Ellen came down-stairs, and sat beside the coal stove to change her shoes, she looked at the book which Amabel was reading. "You ought not to read that book, dear," she said. "Let Ellen get you a better one for a little girl to-morrow."

But Amabel, without paying the slightest heed to Ellen's words, looked up at her with amazement, as Andrew and Fanny had done. "What's the matter, Ellen?" she asked, in her little, hoarse voice.

Fanny and Andrew, who had just entered, stood waiting. Ellen bent over her shoe, drawing in the strings firmly and evenly.

"Mr. Lloyd has reduced the wage-list," she said.

"How much?" asked Andrew, in a hoarse voice.

"Ten per cent."

There was a dead silence. Andrew and Fanny looked at Ellen like people who are uncertain of their next move; Amabel stared from one to the other with her weak, watery eyes. Ellen continued to lace her shoes.

"What do you think about it, Ellen?" asked Andrew, almost timidly.

"I know of only one thing to think," replied Ellen, in a dogged voice.

As she spoke she pulled the tag off a shoe-string because it would not go through the eyelet.

"What is that?" asked Fanny, in a hard voice.

"I think it is cruelty and tyranny," said Ellen, pulling the rough end of the string through the eyelet.

"I suppose the times are pretty hard," ventured Andrew; but Ellen cut him short.

"Robert Lloyd has half a million, which has been accumulated by the labor of poor men in prosperous times," said she, with her childlike severity and pitilessness. "There is no question about the matter."

Then Fanny flung all self-interest to the wind and was at her daughter's side like a whirlwind. The fact that the two were of one blood was never so strongly evident. Red spots glowed in the elder woman's cheeks and her black eyes blazed.

"Ellen's right," said she; "she's right. For a man worth half a million to cut down the wages of poor, hard-working folks in midwinter is cruelty. I don't care who does it."

"Yes, it is," said Ellen.

Fanny opened her mouth to tell Ellen of the rumor concerning Robert's engagement to Maud Hemingway, then she refrained, for some reason which she could not analyze. In her heart she did not believe the report to be true, and considered the telling of it a slight to Ellen, but it influenced her in her indignation against Robert for the wage-cutting.

"What are they going to do?" asked Andrew.

"I don't know," replied Ellen.

"Did he—young Lloyd—talk to the men?"

"No; notices were tacked up all over the shop."

"That was the way his uncle would have done," said Andrew, in a curious voice of bitterness and respect.

"So you don't know what they are going to do?" said Fanny.

"No."

"Well, I know what I would do," said Fanny. "I never would give in, if I starved—never!"

CHAPTER LI

WHEN Ellen started for the factory the next morning the storm had not ceased; the roads were very heavy, although the snow-plough had been out at intervals all night, and there was a struggling line of shovelling men along the car-track, but the cars were still unable to penetrate the drifts. When Ellen passed her grandmother's house the old woman tapped sharply on the window and motioned her back frantically with one bony hand. The window was frozen to the sill with the snow, and she could not raise it. Ellen shook her head, smiling. Her grandmother continued to wave her back, the lines of forbidding anxiety in her old face as strongly marked as an etching in the window frame. This love, which had at once coerced and fondled the girl since her birth, was very precious to her. This protection, which she was forced to repel, smote her like a pain.

"Poor old grandmother!" she thought; "there she will worry about me all day because I have gone out in the storm." She turned back and waved her hand and nodded laughingly; but the old woman continued that anxiously imperative backward motion until Ellen was out of sight.

Ellen walked in the car-track, as did everybody else, that being better cleared than the rest of the road. She was astonished that she heard nothing of the cut in wages from the men. There seemed to be no excitement at all. They merely trudged heavily along, their whitening bodies bent before the storm. There was

472

an unusual doggedness about this march to the factory this morning, but that was all. Ellen returned the muttered greeting of several, and walked along in silence with the rest. Even when Abby Atkins joined her there was little said. Ellen asked for Maria, and Abby replied that she had taken more cold yesterday, and could not speak aloud; then relapsed into silence, making her way through the snow with a sort of taciturn endurance. Ellen looked at the struggling procession of which she was a part, all slanting with the slant of the storm, and a fancy seized her that rebellion and resistance were hopeless, that those parallel lines of yielding to the onslaughts of fate were as inevitable as life itself, one of its conditions. Men could not help walking that way when the bitter storm-wind was blowing; they could not help living that way when fate was in array against their progress. Then, thinking so, a mightier spirit of revolt than she had ever known awoke within her. She, as she walked, straightened herself. She leaned not one whit before the drive of the storm. She advanced with no yielding in her, her brave face looking ahead through the white blur of snow with a confidence which was almost exultation.

"What do you think the men will do?" she said to Abby when they came in sight of Lloyd's, shaggy with fringes and wreaths and overhanging shelvings of snow, roaring with machinery, with the steady stream of labor pouring in the door.

"Do?" repeated Abby, almost listlessly. "Do about what?"

"About the cut in wages?"

Abby turned on her with sudden fire. "Oh, my God, what can they do, Ellen Brewster?" she demanded. "Haven't they got to live? Hasn't Lloyd got it all his own way? How are men to live in weather like this without work? Bread without butter is better

473

than none at all, and life at any cost is better than
death for them you love. What can they do?"

"It seems to me there is only one thing to do,"
replied Ellen.

Abby stared at her wonderingly. "You don'i
mean—" she said, as they climbed up the stairs.

"I mean I would do anything, at whatever cost to
myself, to defeat injustice," said Ellen, in a loud, clear
voice.

Several men turned and looked back at her and
laughed bitterly.

"It's easy talking," said one to another.

"That's so," returned the other.

The people all settled to their work as usual. One
of the foremen (Dennison), who was anxious to curry
favor with his employer, reported to him in an undertone in the office that everything was quiet. Robert
nodded easily. He had not anticipated anything else.
In the course of the morning he looked into the room
where Ellen was employed, and saw with relief and concern her fair head before her machine. It seemed to
him that he could not bear it one instant longer to have
her working in this fashion, that he must lift her out
of it. He still tingled with his rebuff of the night before, but he had never loved her so well, for the idea
that the cut in wages affected her relation to him never
occurred to him. As he walked through the room
none of the workers seemed to notice him, but worked
with renewed energy. He might have been invisible
for all the attention he seemed to excite. He looked
with covert tenderness at the back of Ellen's head,
and passed on. He reflected that he had adopted
the measure of wage-cutting with no difficulty whatever.

"All it needs is a little firmness," he thought, with
a boyish complacency in his own methods. "Now I

can keep on with the factory, and no turning the poor people adrift in midwinter."

At noon Robert put on his fur-lined coat and left the factory, springing into the sleigh, which had drawn up before the door with a flurry of bells. He had an errand in the next town that afternoon, and was not going to return. When the sleigh had slid swiftly out of sight through the storm, which was lightening a little, the people in the office turned to one another with a curious expression of liberty, but even then little was said. Nellie Stone was at the desk eating her luncheon; Ed Flynn and Dennison and one of the lasters, who had looked in and then stepped in when he saw Lloyd was gone, were there. The laster, who was young and coarsely handsome, had an admiration for the pretty girl at the desk. Presently she addressed him, with her mouth full of apple-pie.

"Say, George, what are you fellows going to do?" she asked.

Dennison glanced keenly from one to the other; Flynn shrugged his shoulders and looked out of the window.

"Looks as if it was clearing up," he remarked.

"What are you going to do?" asked Nellie Stone again, with a coquettish flirt of her blond fluff of hair.

"Grin and bear it, I s'pose," replied the young laster, with an adoring look at her.

"My land! grin and bear a cut of ten per cent.? Well, I don't think you've got much spunk, I must say. Why don't you strike?"

"Who's going to feed us?" replied the laster, in a tender voice.

"Feed you? Oh, you don't want much to eat. Join the union. It's ridiculous so few of the men in Lloyd's belong to it, anyway; and then the union will feed you, won't it?"

"The union did not do what it promised in the Scarboro strike," interposed Dennison, curtly.

"Oh, we all know where you are, Frank Dennison," said the girl, with a soft roll of her blue eyes. "Besides, it's easy to talk when you aren't hit. Your wages aren't cut. But here is George May here, he's in a different box."

"He's got nobody dependent on him, anyway," said Flynn.

"If I wasn't going to get married I'd strike," cried the young man, with a fervent glance at the girl. She colored, half pleased, half angry, and the other men chuckled. She took another bite of pie to conceal her confusion. She preferred Flynn to the laster, and while she was not averse to proving to the former the triumph of her charms over another man, did not like too much concessions.

"You'd better go and eat your dinner, George May," she said, in her sweet, shrill voice. "First thing you know the whistle will blow. Here's yours, Ed." With that she pulled out a leather bag from under the desk, where she had volunteered to place it for warmth and safety against the coil of steam-pipes.

"I don't believe your coffee is very cold, Ed," said she.

The laster glared from one to the other jealously. Dennison went towards a shelf where he had stored away his luncheon, when he stopped suddenly and listened, as did the others. There came a great uproar of applause from the next room beyond. Then it subsided, and a girl's clear, loud voice was heard.

"What is going on?" cried Nellie Stone. She jumped up and ran to the door, still eating her pie, and the men followed her.

At the end of one of the work-rooms, backed against a snowy window, clung about with shreds of the driv-

476

ing storm, stood Ellen Brewster, with some other girls around her, and a few men on the outskirts, and a steady, curious movement of all the other workmen towards her, as of iron filings towards a magnet, and she was talking.

Her voice was quite audible all over the great room. It was low-pitched, but had a wonderful carrying quality, and there was something marvellous in its absolute confidence.

"If you men will do nothing, and say nothing, it is time for a girl to say and act," she proclaimed. "I did not dream for a minute that you would yield to this cut in wages. Why should you have your wages cut?"

"The times are pretty hard," said a doubtful voice among her auditors.

"What if the times are hard? What is that to you? Have you made them hard? It is the great capitalists who have made them hard by shifting the wealth too much to one side. They are the ones who should suffer, not you. What have you done, except come here morning after morning in cold or heat, rain or shine, and work with all your strength? They who have precipitated the hard times are the ones who should bear the brunt of them. Your work is the same now as it was then, the strain on your flesh and blood and muscles is the same, your pay should be the same."

"That's so," said Abby Atkins, in a reluctant, surly fashion.

"That's so," said another girl, and another. Then there was a fusilade of hand-claps started by the girls, and somewhat feebly echoed by the men.

One or two men looked rather uneasily back towards Dennison and Flynn and two more foremen who had come forward.

"It ain't as though we had something to fall back on," said a man's grumbling voice. "It's easy to talk

when you 'ain't got a wife and five children dependent
on you."

"That's so," said another man, doggedly.

"That has nothing to do with it," said Ellen, firmly. "We can all club together, and keep the wolf from
the door for those who are hardest pressed for a while;
and as for me, if I were a man—"

She paused a minute. When she spoke again her
voice was full of childlike enthusiasm; it seemed to
ring like a song.

"If I were a man," said she, "I would go out in the
street and dig—I would beg, I would steal—before I
would yield—I, a free man in a free country—to
tyranny like this!"

There was a great round of applause at that. Dennison scowled and said something in a low voice to
another foreman at his side. Flynn laughed, with a
perplexed, admiring look at Ellen.

"The question is," said Tom Peel, slouching on the
outskirts of the throng, and speaking in an imperturbable, compelling, drawling voice, "whether the free
men in the free country are going to kick themselves
free, or into tighter places, by kicking."

"If you have got to stop to count the cost of bravery
and standing up for your rights, there would be no
bravery in the world," returned Ellen, with disdain.

"Oh, I am ready to kick," said Peel, with his mask-
like smile.

"So am I," said Granville Joy, in a loud voice. Amos
Lee came rushing through the crowd to Ellen's side.
He had been eating his dinner in another room, and
had just heard what was going on. He opened his
mouth with a motion as of letting loose a flood of ranting, but somebody interposed. John Sargent, bulky
and irresistible in his steady resolution, put him aside
and stood before him.

478

"Look here," he said to them all. "There may be truth in what Miss Brewster says, but we must not act hastily; there is too much at stake. Let us appoint a committee and go to see Mr. Lloyd this evening, and remonstrate on the cutting of the wages." He turned to Ellen in a kindly, half-paternal fashion. "Don't you see it would be better?" he said.

She looked at him doubtfully, her cheeks glowing, her eyes like stars. She was freedom and youth incarnate, and rebellious against all which she conceived as wrong and tyrannical. She could hardly admit, in her fire of enthusiasm, of pure indignation, of any compromise or arbitration. All the griefs of her short life, she had told herself, were directly traceable to the wrongs of the system of labor and capital, and were awakening within her as freshly as if they had just happened.

She remembered her father, exiled in his prime from his place in the working world by this system of arbitrary employment; she remembered her aunt in the asylum; poor little Amabel; her own mother toiling beyond her strength on underpaid work; Maria coughing her life away. She remembered her own life twisted into another track from the one which she should have followed, and there was for the time very little reason or justice in her. That injustice which will arise to meet its kind in equal combat had arisen in her heart. Still, she yielded. "Perhaps you are right," she said to Sargent. She had always liked John Sargent, and she respected him.

"I am sure it is the best course," he said to her, still in that low, confidential voice.

It ended in a committee of four—John Sargent, Amos Lee, Tom Peel, and one of the older lasters, a very respectable man, a deacon in the Baptist Church—being appointed to wait on Robert Lloyd that evening.

When the one-o'clock whistle blew, Ellen went back

to her machine. She was very pale, but she was conscious of a curious steadiness of all her nerves. Abby leaned towards her, and spoke low in the roar of wheels. "I'll back you up, if I die for it," she said.

But Sadie Peel, on the other side, spoke quite openly, with a laugh and shrug of her shoulders. "Land," she said, "father'll be with you. He's bound to strike. He struck when he was in McGuire's. Catch father givin' up anything. But as for me, I wish you'd all slow up an' stick to work, if you do get a little less. If we quit work I can't have a nearseal cape, and I've set my heart on a nearseal cape this winter."

CHAPTER LII

ELLEN resolved that she would say as little as possible about the trouble at home that night. She did not wish her parents to worry over it until it was settled in one way or another.

When her mother asked what they had done about the wage-cutting, she replied that a committee had been appointed to wait on Mr. Lloyd that evening, and talk it over with him; then she said nothing more.

"He won't give in if he's like his uncle," said Fanny.

Ellen went on eating her supper in silence. Her father glanced at her with sharp solicitude.

"Maybe he will," said he.

"No, he won't," returned Fanny.

Ellen was very pale and her eyes were bright. After supper she went to the window and pressed her face against the glass, shielding her eyes from the in-door light, and saw that the storm had quite ceased. The stars were shining and the white boughs of the trees lashing about in the northwest wind. She went into the entry, where she had hung her hat and coat, and began putting them on.

"Where are you going, Ellen?" asked her mother.

"Just down to Abby's a minute."

"You don't mean to say you are goin' out again in this snow, Ellen Brewster? I should think you were crazy." When Fanny said crazy, she suddenly started and shuddered as if she had struck herself. She thought of Eva. Always the possibility of a like doom was in her own mind.

"It has stopped snowing, mother," Ellen said.

"Stopped snowing! What if it has? The roads ain't cleared. You can't get down to Abby Atkins's without gettin' wet up to your knees. I should think if you got into the house after such a storm you'd have sense enough to stay in. I've worried just about enough."

Ellen took off her coat and hat and hung them up again. "Well, I won't go if you feel so, mother," she said, patiently.

"It seems as if you might get along without seein' Abby Atkins till to-morrow mornin', when you'd seen her only an hour ago," Fanny went on, in the high, nagging tone which she often adopted with those whom she loved the dearest.

"Yes, I can," said Ellen. It seemed to her that she must see somebody with whom she could talk about the trouble in the factory, but she yielded. There was always with the girl a perfect surface docility, as that she seemed to have no resistance, but a little way down was a rock-bed of firmness. She lighted her lamp, and took her library book and went up-stairs to bed to read. But she could not read, and she could not sleep when she had put aside her book and extinguished her lamp. She could think of nothing except Robert, and what he would say to the committee. She lay awake all night thinking of it. Ellen was a girl who was capable of the most devoted love, and the most intense dissent and indignation towards the same person. She could love in spite of faults, and she could see faults in spite of love. She thought of Robert Lloyd as of the one human soul whom she loved best out of the whole world, whom she put before everybody else, even her own self, and she also thought of him with a wrath which was pitiless and uncompromising, and which seemed to tear her own heart to pieces, for one

cannot be wroth with love without a set-back of torture.
"If he does not give in and raise the wages, I shall hate
him," thought Ellen; and her heart stung her as if at
the touch of a hot iron, and then she could have struck
herself for the supposition that he would not give in.
"He must," she told herself, with a great fervor of
love. "He must."

But when she went down to breakfast the next morning her mother stared at her sharply.

"Ellen Brewster, what is the matter with you?"
she cried.

"Nothing. Why?"

"Nothing! You look like a ghost."

"I feel perfectly well," said Ellen. She made an effort
to eat as much breakfast as usual in order that her
mother should not suspect that she was troubled. When
at last she set out for the factory, in the early morning
dusk, she was chilled and trembling with excitement.

The storm had quite ceased, and there was a pale
rose-and-violet dawn-light in the east, and presently
came effects like golden-feathered shafts shooting over
the sky. The road was alive with shovelling men,
construction-cars of the railroad company were labor-
ing back and forth to clear the tracks, householders
were making their way from their doors to their gates,
clearing their paths, lifting up the snow in great, glittering, blue-white blocks on their clumsy shovels. Everywhere were the factory employés hastening to their
labor; the snow was dropping from the overladen tree
branches in great blobs; there was an incessant, shrill
chatter of people, and occasional shouts. It was the
rally of mankind after a defeat by a primitive force of
nature. It was the eternal reassertion of human life
and a higher organization over the elemental. Men
who had walked doggedly the morning before now
moved with a spring of alacrity, although the road was

483

very heavy. There was a new light in their eyes; their cheeks glowed. Ellen had no doubt whatever that if Robert Lloyd had not yielded the attitude of the employés of Lloyd's would be one of resistance. She herself seemed to breathe in resistance to tyranny, and strength for the right in every breath of the clear, crisp morning air. She felt as if she could trample on herself and her own weakness, for the sake of justice and the inalienable good of her kind, with as little hesitation as she trampled on the creaking snow. Yet she trembled with that deadly chill before a sense of impending fate. When she returned the salutations of her friends on the road she felt that her lips were stiff.

"You look dreadful queer, Ellen," Abby Atkins said, anxiously, when she joined her. Maria also was out that morning.

"Have you heard what they are going to do?" Ellen asked, in a sort of breathless fashion.

"You mean about the wage-cutting? Don't look so, Ellen."

Maria pressed close to Ellen, and slid her thin arm through hers.

"Yes," said Ellen. "What did John Sargent say when he got home last night?"

Abby hesitated a second, looking doubtfully at Ellen. "I don't see that there is any need for you to take all this so much to heart," she said.

"What did he say?"

"Well," Abby replied, reluctantly, "I believe Mr. Lloyd wouldn't give in. Ellen Brewster, for Heaven's sake, don't look so!"

Ellen walked on, her head high, her face as white as death. Maria clung closely to her, her own lips quivering.

"What are the men going to do, do you think?" asked Ellen, presently, in a low voice.

484

"I don't know," replied Abby. "John Sargent seems to think they'll give in. He says he doesn't know what else they can do. The times are hard. I believe Amos Lee and Tom Peel are for striking, but he says he doesn't believe the men will support them. The amount of it all is, a man with money has got it all his own way. It's like fighting with bare hands to oppose him, and getting yourself cut, and not hurting him at all. He's got all the weapons. We simply can't go without work all winter. It is better to do with less than with nothing at all. What can a man like Willy Jones do if he hasn't any work? He and his mother would actually suffer. What could we do?"

"I don't think we ought to think so much about that," said Ellen.

"What do you think we ought to think about, for goodness' sake?"

"Whether we are doing right or not, whether we are furthering the cause of justice and humanity, or hindering it. Whether it is for good in the long run or not. There have always been martyrs; I don't see why it is any harder for us to be martyrs than for those we read about."

Sadie Peel came pressing up behind eagerly, her cheeks glowing, holding up her dress, and displaying a cheap red petticoat. "Ellen Brewster," she exclaimed, "if you dare say anything more to-day I'm goin' to talk. Father is tearing, though he goes around looking as if he wouldn't jump at a cannon-ball. Do, for Heaven's sake, keep still; and if you can't get what you want, take what you can get. I ain't goin' to be cheated out of my nearseal cape, nohow."

"Sadie Peel, you make me tired," cried Abby Atkins. "I don't say that I'm striking, but I'd strike for all a nearseal cape. I'm ashamed of you."

"I don't care if you be," said the girl, tossing her

485

head. "A nearseal cape means as much to me as some other things to you. I want Ellen Brewster to hold her tongue."

"Ellen Brewster will hold her tongue or not, just as she has a mind to," responded Abby, with a snap. She did not like Sadie Peel.

"Oh, stick up for her if you want to, and get us all into trouble."

"I shall stick up for her, you can be mighty sure of that," declared Abby.

Ellen walked on as if she heard nothing of it at all, with little Maria clinging closely to her. Robert Lloyd got out of his sleigh and went up-stairs just before they reached the factory, and she heard a very low, subdued mutter of execration.

"They don't mean to strike," she told herself. "They mean to submit."

All went to their tasks as usual. In a minute after the whistle blew the great pile was in the full hum of labor. Ellen stood for a few moments at her machine, then she left it deliberately, and made her way down the long room to where John Sargent stood at his bench cutting shoes, with a swift faithfulness born of long practice. She pressed close to him, while the men around stared.

"What is going to be done?" she asked, in a low voice.

Sargent turned and looked at her in a troubled fashion, and spoke in a pacific, soothing tone, as her father might have done. He was much older than Ellen.

"Now look here, child," he said, "I don't dare take the responsibility of urging all these men into starvation this kind of weather. The times are hard. Lloyd has some reason—"

Ellen walked away from him swiftly and went to the row of lasting-machines where Amos Lee and Tom

486

Peel stood. She walked up to them and spoke in a loud, clear voice.

"You are not going to give in?" said she. "You don't mean to give in?"

Lee turned and gave her one stare, and left his machine.

"Not another stitch of work will I do under this new wage-list, so help me, God!" he proclaimed.

Tom Peel stood for a second like an automaton, staring at them both. Then he turned his back to his post.

"I'm with ye," he said.

The lasters, for some occult reason, were always the most turbulent element in Lloyd's. In less than three minutes the enthusiasm of revolt had spread, and every laster had left his machine. In a half-hour more there was an exodus of workmen from Lloyd's. There were very few left in the factory. Among them were John Sargent, the laster who was a deacon and had formed one of the consulting committee, Sadie Peel, who wanted her nearseal cape, and Mamie Brady, who would do nothing which she thought would displease the foreman, Flynn.

"If father's mind to be such a fool, it's no reason why I should," said Sadie Peel, stitching determinedly away. Mamie Brady looked at Flynn, when he came up to her, with a gentle, wheedling smile. There was no one near, and she fancied that he might steal a kiss. But instead he looked at her, frowning.

"No use you tying away any longer, Mamie," he said. "The strike's on."

CHAPTER LIII

THAT was one of the strangest days which Ellen had ever passed. The enforced idleness gave her an indefinite sense of guilt. She tried to assist her mother about the household tasks, then she tried to sew on the wrappers, but she was awkward about it, from long disuse.

"Do take your book and sit down and read and rest a little, now you've got a chance," said Fanny, with sharp solicitude.

She said never one word concerning it to Ellen, but all the time she thought how Ellen had probably lost her lover. It was really doubtful which suffered the more that day, the mother or the daughter. Fanny, entirely faithful to her own husband, had yet that strange vicarious affection for her daughter's lover, and a realization of her state of mind, of which a mother alone is capable. It is like a cord of birth which is never severed. Not one shadow of sad reflection passed over the bright enthusiastic face of the girl but was passed on, as if driven by some wind of spirit, over the face of the older woman. She reflected Ellen entirely.

As for Andrew, his anxiety was as tender, and less subtle. He did not understand so clearly, but he suffered more. He was clumsy with this mystery of womanhood, but he was unremitting in his efforts to do something for the girl. Once he tiptoed up to Fanny and whispered, when Ellen was in the next room, that he hoped she hadn't made any mistake, that it seemed to him she looked pretty pale.

488

"Mistake?" cried Fanny, tossing her head, and staring at him proudly. "Haven't you got any spirit, and you a man, Andrew Brewster?"

"I ain't thinking about myself," said Andrew.

And he was quite right. Andrew, left to himself and his purely selfish interests, could have struck with the foremost. He would never have considered himself when it came to a question of a conscientious struggle against injustice, though he was so prone to look upon both sides of an argument that his decision would have been necessarily slow; but here was Ellen to consider, and she was more than himself. While he had been, in the depths of his heart, fiercely jealous of Robert Lloyd, yet the suspicion that his girl might suffer because of her renunciation of him hurt him to the quick. Ellen had told him all she had done in the interests of the strike, and he had no doubt that her action would effectually put an end to all possible relations between the two. He tried to imagine how a girl would feel, and being a man, and measuring all passion by the strength of his own, he exaggerated her suffering. He could eat nothing, and looked haggard. He remained out-of-doors the greater part of the day. After he had cleared his own paths, he secured a job clearing some for a more prosperous neighbor. Andrew in those days grasped eagerly at any little job which could bring him in a few pennies. He worked until dark, and when he went home he saw with a great throb of excitement the Lloyd sleigh waiting before his door.

Robert had heard from Dennison of Ellen's attitude about the strike. He had been incredulous at first, as indeed he had been incredulous about the strike. He had looked out of the office window with the gaze of one who does not believe what he sees when he had heard that retreating tramp of the workmen on the stairs.

489

"What does all this mean?" he said to Dennison, who entered, pale to his lips.

"It means a strike," replied Dennison. Nellie Stone rolled her pretty eyes around at the two men from under her fluff of blond hair. Flynn came in and stood in a curious, non-committal attitude.

"A strike!" repeated Robert, vaguely. "What for?" It seemed incredible that he should ask, but he did. The calm masterfulness of his uncle, which could not even imagine opposition, had apparently descended upon him.

Both foremen stared at him. Nellie Stone smiled a little covertly.

"Why, you know you had a committee wait upon you last night, Mr. Lloyd," replied Dennison.

Flynn looked out of the window at the retreating throngs of workmen, and gave a whistle under his breath.

"Have they struck because of the wage-cutting?" asked Robert, in a curious, boyish, incredulous, aggrieved tone. Then all at once he colored violently. "Let them strike, then!" he cried. He threw himself into a chair and took up the morning paper, with its glaring headlines about the unprecedented storm, as if nothing had happened. Nellie Stone, after a sly wink at Flynn, which he did not return, began writing again. Flynn went out, and Dennison remained standing in a rather helpless attitude. A strike in Lloyd's was unprecedented, but this manner of receiving the news was more unprecedented still. The proprietor was apparently reading the morning paper with much interest, when two more foremen, heads of other departments, came hurrying in.

"I have heard already," said Robert, in response to their gasped information. Then he turned another page of the paper.

"What's to be done, sir?" said one of the new-comers, after a prolonged stare at his companion and Dennison. He was a spare man, with a fierce glimmer of blue eyes under bent brows.

"Let them strike if they want to," replied Robert.

It was in his mind to explain at length to these men his reasons for cutting the wages—for his own attitude as he knew it himself was entirely reasonable—but the pride of a proud family was up in him.

"The strike would never have been on, for the men went to work quietly enough, if it hadn't been for that Brewster girl," Dennison said, presently, but rather doubtfully. He was not quite sure how the information would be received.

Robert dropped his paper, and stared at him with angry incredulity.

"What are you talking about?" he said. "What had Miss Brewster to do with it?"

He said "Miss Brewster" with a meaning emphasis of respect, and Dennison was quick to adopt the hint.

"Oh, nothing," he replied, uneasily, "only she talked with them."

"You mean that Miss Brewster talked to the men?"

"Yes; she said a good deal yesterday, and to-day the men would not have struck if it had not been for her. It only needs a spark to set them off sometimes."

Robert was very pale. "Well," he said, coolly, "there is no need for you to remain longer, since the factory is shut down. You may as well go."

"The engineer is seeing to the fires, Mr. Lloyd," said Dennison.

"Very well." Robert turned to the girl at the desk. "The factory is closed, Miss Stone," he said; "there is no need for you to remain longer to-day. Come to-morrow at ten o'clock, and I will have something for you

491

to do with regard to settling up accounts. There is nothing in shape now."

That afternoon Robert went to see Ellen. He could not wait until evening.

Fanny greeted him at the door, and there was the inevitable flurry about lighting the parlor stove, and presently Ellen entered.

She had changed the gown which she had worn at her factory-work for her last winter's best one. Her young face was pale, almost severe, and she met him in a way which made her seem a stranger.

Robert realized suddenly that she had, as it were, closed the door upon all their old relations. She seemed years older, and at the same time indefinably younger, since she was letting the childish impulses, which are at the heart of all of us untouched by time and experience, rise rampant and unchecked. She was following the lead of her own convictions with the terrible unswerving of a child, even in the face of her own hurt. She was, metaphorically, bumping her own head against the floor in her vain struggles for mastery over the mighty conditions of her life.

She bowed to Robert, and did not seem to see his proffered hand.

"Won't you shake hands with me?" he asked, almost humbly, although his own wrath was beginning to rise.

"No, I would rather not," she replied, with a straight look at him. Her blue eyes did not falter in the least.

"May I sit down?" he said. "I have something I would like to say to you."

"Certainly, if you wish," she replied. Then she seated herself on the sofa, with Robert opposite in the crushed-plush easy-chair.

The room was still very cold, and the breath could be seen at the lips of each in white clouds. Robert had on his coat, but Ellen had nothing over her blue gown. It was on Robert's tongue to ask if she were not cold, then he refrained. The issues at stake seemed to make the question frivolous to offensiveness. He felt that any approach to tenderness when Ellen was in her present mood would invoke an indignation for which he could scarcely blame her, that he must try to meet her on equal fighting-ground.

Ellen sat before him, her little, cold hands tightly folded in her lap, her mouth set hard, her steady fire of blue eyes on his face, waiting for him to speak.

Robert felt a decided awkwardness about beginning to talk. Suddenly it occurred to him to wonder what there was to say. It amounted to this: they were in their two different positions, their two points of view— would either leave for any argument of the other? Then he wondered if he could, in the face of a girl who wore an expression like that, stoop to make an argument, for the utter blindness and deafness of her very soul to any explanation of his position was too evident in her face.

"I called to tell you, if you will permit me, how much I regret the unfortunate state of affairs at the factory," Robert said, and the girl's eyes met his as with a flash of flame.

"Why did you not prevent it, then?" asked she. Ellen had all the fire of her family, but a steadiness of manner which never deserted her. She was never violent.

"I could not prevent it," replied Robert, in a low voice. Ellen said nothing.

"You mistake my position," said Robert. It was in his mind then to lay the matter fully before her, as he had disdained to do before the committee, but her next words deterred him.

"I understand your position very fully," said she.

493

Robert bowed.

"There is only one way of looking at it," said Ellen, in her inexpressibly sweet, almost fanatical voice. She tossed her head, and the fluff of fair hair over her temples caught a beam of afternoon sunlight.

"She is only a child," thought Robert, looking at her. He rose and crossed over to the sofa, and sat down beside her with a masterful impatience. "Look here, Ellen," he said, leaving all general issues for their own personal ones. "you are not going to let this come between us?"

Ellen sat stiff and straight, and made no reply.

"All this can make very little difference to you," Robert urged. "You know how I feel. That is, it can make very little difference to you if you still feel as you did. You must know that I have only been waiting—that I am eager and impatient to lift you out of it all."

Ellen faced him. "Do you think I would be lifted out of it now?" she said.

"Why, but, Ellen, you cannot—"

"Yes, I can. You do not know me."

"Ellen, you are under a total misapprehension of my position."

"No, I am not. I apprehend it perfectly."

"Ellen, you cannot let this separate us."

Ellen looked straight ahead in silence.

"You at least owe it to me to tell me if, irrespective of this, your feelings have changed," Robert said, in a low voice.

Ellen said nothing.

"You may have come to prefer some one else," said Robert.

"I prefer no one before my own, before all these poor people who are a part of my life," Ellen cried out, suddenly, her face flaming.

"Then why do you refuse to let me act for their final good? You must know what it means to have them thrown out of work in midwinter. You know the factory will remain closed for the present on account of the strike."

"I did not doubt it," said Ellen, in a hard voice. All the bitter thoughts to which she would not give utterance were in her voice.

"I cannot continue to run the factory at the present rate and meet expenses," said Robert; "in fact, I have been steadily losing for the last month." He had, after all, descended to explanation. "It amounts to my either reducing the wage-list or closing the factory altogether," he continued. "For my own good I ought to close the factory altogether, but I thought I would give the men a chance."

Robert thought by saying that he must have finally settled matters. It did not enter his head that she would really think it advisable for him to continue losing money. The pure childishness of her attitude was something really beyond the comprehension of a man of business who had come into hard business theories along with his uncle's dollars.

"What if you do lose money?" said Ellen.

Robert stared at her. "I beg your pardon?" said he.

"What if you do lose money?"

"A man cannot conduct business on such principles," replied Robert. "There would soon be no business to conduct. You don't understand."

"Yes, I do understand fully," replied Ellen.

Robert looked at her, at the clear, rosy curve of her young cheek, the toss of yellow hair above a forehead as candid as a baby's, at her little, delicate figure, and all at once such a rage of masculine insistence over all this obstinacy of reasoning was upon him that it was all he could do to keep himself from seizing her in his arms and forcing her to a view of his own horizon. He felt himself drawn up in opposition to an opponent at once too delicate, too unreasoning, and too beloved to encounter. It seemed as if the absurdity of it would drive him mad, and yet he was held to it. He tried to give a desperate wrench aside from the main point of the situation. He leaned over Ellen, so closely that his lips touched her hair.

"Ellen, let us leave all this," he pleaded; "let me talk to you. I had to wait a little while. I knew you would understand that, but let me talk to you now."

Ellen sat as rigid as marble. "I wish to talk of nothing besides the matter at hand, Mr. Lloyd," said she. "That is too close to my heart for any personal consideration to come between."

496

CHAPTER LIV

WHEN Robert went home in the winter twilight he was more miserable than he had ever been in his life. He felt as if he had been assaulting a beautiful alabaster wall of unreason. He felt as if that which he could shatter at a blow had yet held him in defiance. The idea of this girl, of whom he had thought as his future wife, deliberately setting herself against him, galled him inexpressibly, and in spite of himself he could not quite free his mind of jealousy. On his way home he stopped at Lyman Risley's office, and found, to his great satisfaction, that he was alone, writing at his desk. Even his stenographer had gone home. He turned around when Robert entered, and looked at him with his quizzical, yet kindly, smile.

"Well, how are you, boy?" he said.

Robert dropped into the first chair, and sat therein, haunched up as in a lapse of despair and weariness.

"What is the matter?" asked Risley.

"You have heard about the trouble in the factory?"

For answer Risley held up a night's paper with glaring head-lines.

"Yes, of course it is in the papers," assented Robert, wearily.

Risley stared at him in a lazily puzzled fashion. "Well," he said, "what is it all about? Why are you so broken up about it?" Risley laid considerable emphasis on the *you*.

"Yes," cried Robert, in a sudden stress of indignation. "You look at it like all the rest. Why are all the laborers to be petted and coddled, and the capitalists held up to execration? Good Lord, isn't there any pity for the rich man without his drop of water, in the Bible or out? Are all creation born with blinders on, and can they only see before their noses?"

"What are you talking about, Robert?" said Risley, laughing a little.

"I say why should all the sympathy go to the workmen who are acting like the pig-headed idiots they are, and none for the head of the factory, who has the sharp-edged, red-hot brunt of it all to bear?"

"You wouldn't look at it that way if you were one of the poor men just out on strike such weather as this," said Risley, dryly. He glanced as he spoke at the window, which was beginning to be thickly furred with frost in spite of the heat of the office. Robert followed his gaze, and noted the spreading fairy jungle of crystalline trees and flowers on the broad field of glass.

"Do you think that is the worst thing in the world to bear?" he demanded, angrily.

"What? Cold and hunger not only for yourself, but for those you love?"

"Yes."

"Well, I think it is pretty bad," replied Risley.

"Well, suppose you had to bear that, at least for those you loved, and—and—" said the young man, lamely.

Risley remained silent, waiting.

"If I had been my uncle instead of myself I should simply have shut down with no ado," said Robert, presently, in an angry, argumentative voice.

"I suppose you would; and as it was?"

"As it was, I thought I would give them a chance. Good God, Risley, I have been running the factory at a loss for a month as it is. With this new wage-list I should no more than make expenses, if I did that. What was it to me? I did it to keep them in some sort

of work. As for myself, I would much rather have
shut down and done with it, but I tried to keep it running on their account, poor devils, and now I am exe-
crated for it, and they have deliberately refused what
little I could offer."

"Did you explain all this to the committee?" asked
Risley.

"Explain? No! I told them my course was founded
upon strict business principles, and was as much for
their good as for mine. They understood. They
know how hard the times are. Why, it was only
last week that Weeks & McLaughlin failed, and that
meant a heavy loss. I didn't explain." Then Robert
hesitated and colored. "I have just explained to her,"
he said, with a curious hang of his head, like a boy,
"and if my explanation was met in the same fashion
by the others in the factory I might as well have addressed the north wind. They are all alike; they are a
different race. We cannot help them, and they cannot
help themselves, because they are themselves."

"You mean by her, Ellen Brewster?" Risley said.

Robert nodded gloomily.

"That is all in the paper," said Risley—"what she
said to the men."

Robert made an impatient move.

"If ever there was a purely normal outgrowth, a perfect flower of her birth and environments and training, that girl is one," said Risley, with an accent of
admiration.

"She is infected with the ranting idiocy of those
with whom she has been brought in daily contact,"
said Robert; but even as he spoke he seemed to see the
girl's dear young face, and his voice faltered.

"Even as you may be infected with the conservatism
of those with whom you are brought in contact," said
Risley, dryly.

"What a democrat you are, Risley!" said Robert, impatiently. "I believe you would make a good walking delegate."

Risley laughed. "I think I would myself," he said. "Wouldn't she listen to you, Robert?"

"She listened with such utter dissent that she might as well have been dumb. It is all over between us, Risley."

"How precipitate you are, you young folks!" said the other, good-humoredly.

"How precipitate? Do you mean to say—?"

"I mean that you are forever thinking you are on the brink of nothingness, when the true horizon-line is too far for you ever to reach in your mortal life."

"Not in this case," said Robert.

"You know nothing about it. But if you will excuse me, it seems to me that the matter of all these people being reduced to starvation in a howling winter is of more importance than the coming together of two people in the bonds of wedlock. It is the aggregate against the individual."

"I don't deny that," said Robert, doggedly, "but I am not responsible for the starvation, and the aggregate have brought it on themselves."

"You have shut down finally?"

"Yes, I have. I would rather shut down than not, as far as I am concerned. It is distinctly for my interest. The only one objection is losing experienced workmen, but in a community like this, and in times like this, that objection is reduced to a minimum. I can hire all I want in the spring if I wish to open again. I should run a risk of losing on every order I should have to fill in the next three months, even with the reduced list. I would rather shut down than not; I only reduced the wages for them."

Robert rose as he spoke. He felt in his heart that

he had gotten scant sympathy and comfort. The older man looked with pity at the young fellow's handsome, gloomy face.

"There's one thing to remember," he said.

"What?"

"All the troubles of this world are born with wings." Risley laughed, as he spoke, in his half-cynical fashion.

As Robert walked home—for there was no car due—he felt completely desolate. It seemed to him that everybody was in league against him. When he reached his uncle's splendid house and entered, he felt such an isolation from his kind in the midst of his wealth that something like an actual terror of solitude came over him.

The impecunious cousin of his aunt's who had come to her during her last illness acted as his housekeeper. There was something inexpressibly irritating about this woman, who had suffered so much, and was now nestling, with a sense of triumph over the passing of her griefs, in a luxurious home.

She asked Robert if it were true that the factory was closed, and he felt that she noted his gloomy face, and realized a greater extent of comfort from her own exemption from such questions.

"Business must be a great care," said she, and a look of utter peaceful reflection upon her own lot overspread her face.

After supper Robert went down to his aunt Cynthia's. He had not been there for a long time. The minute he entered she started up with an eagerness which had been completely foreign to her of late years.

"What is the matter, Robert?" she asked, softly. She took both his hands as she spoke, and her look in his face was full of delicate caressing.

Robert succumbed at once to this feminine solicitude,

of which he had had lately so little. He felt as if he had relapsed into childhood. A sense of injury which was exquisite, as it brought along with it a sense of his demand upon love and sympathy, seized him.

"I am worried beyond endurance, Aunt Cynthia," said he.

"About the strike? I have read the night papers."

"Yes; I tried to do what was right, even at a sacrifice to myself, and—"

Cynthia had read about Ellen, but she was a woman, and she said nothing as to that.

"I tried to do what was right," Robert said, fairly broken down again.

Cynthia had seated herself, and Robert had taken a low foot-stool at her side. It came over him as he did so that it had been a favorite seat of his when a child. As for Cynthia, influenced by the appealing to the vulnerable place of her nature, she put her slim hands on her nephew's head, and actually seemed to feel his baby curls.

"Poor boy," she whispered.

Robert put both his arms around her and hid his face on her shoulder, for love is a comforter, in whatever guise.

CHAPTER LV

ON the day after the strike Ellen went to McGuire's
and to Briggs's, the two other factories in Rowe, to see
if she could obtain a position; but she was not successful. McGuire had discharged some of his employés,
reducing his force to its smallest possible limits, since
he had fewer orders, and was trying in that way to avert
the necessity of a cut in wages, and a strike or shut-
down. McGuire's was essentially a union factory, as
was Briggs's. Ellen would have found in either case
difficulty about obtaining employment, because she did
not belong to the union, if for no other reason. At
Briggs's she encountered the proprietor himself in the
office, and he dismissed her with a bluff, almost brutal,
peremptoriness which hurt her cruelly, although she
held up her head high as she left. Briggs turned to a
foreman who was standing by before she was well out
of hearing.

"I like that!" he said. "Mrs. Briggs read about
that girl in the paper last night, and the strike wouldn't
have been on at Lloyd's if it hadn't been for her. I would
as soon take a lighted match into a powder-magazine."

The foreman grinned. "She's a pretty, mild-looking
thing," he said; "doesn't look as if she could say boo
to a goose."

"That's all you can tell," returned Briggs. "Deliver me from a light-complexioned woman. They're
all the very devil. Mrs. Briggs says it's the same girl
that read that composition that made such a stir at the
high-school exhibition. She'd make more trouble

503

in a factory than a dozen ordinary girls, and just now, when everything is darned ticklish-looking."

"That's so," assented the foreman, "and all the more because she's good-looking."

"I don't know what you call good-looking," returned Briggs.

He had two daughters, built upon the same heavy lines as himself and wife, and he adored them. Insensibly he regarded all more delicate feminine beauty as a disparagement of theirs. As Briggs spoke, the foreman seemed to see in the air before his eyes the faces of the two Briggs girls, large and massive, and dull of hue, the feminine counterpart of their father's.

"Well, maybe you're right," said he, evasively. "I suppose some might call her good-looking."

As he spoke he glanced out of the window at Ellen's retreating figure, moving away over the snow-path with an almost dancing motion of youth and courage, though she was sorely hurt. The girl had scarcely ever had a hard word said to her in her whole life, for she had been in her humble place a petted darling. She had plenty of courage to bear the hard words now, but they cut deeply into her unseasoned heart.

Ellen went on past the factories to the main street of Rowe. She had no idea of giving up her efforts to obtain employment. She said to herself that she must have work. She thought of the stores, that possibly she might obtain a chance to serve as a sales-girl in one of them. She actually began at the end of the long street, and worked her way through it, with her useless inquiries, facing proprietors and superintendents, but with no success. There was not a vacancy in more than one or two, and there they wished only experienced hands. She found out that her factory record told against her. The moment she admitted that she had worked in a factory the cold shoulder was turned. The position of a

shop-girl was so far below that of a sales-lady that the
effect upon the superintendent was almost as if he had
met an unworthy aspirant to a throne. He would smile
insultingly and incredulously, even as he regarded her.

"You would find that our goods are too fine to handle
after leather. Have you tried all the shops?"

At last Ellen gave that up, and started homeward.
She paused once as she came opposite an intelligence
office. There was one course yet open to her, but from
that she shrank, not on her own account, but she dared
not—knowing what would be the sufferings of her relatives should she do so—apply for a position as a servant.

As for herself, strained as she was to her height of
youthful enthusiasm for a great cause, as she judged
it to be, clamping her feet to the topmost round of her
ladder of difficulty, she would have essayed any honest
labor with no hesitation whatever. But she thought
of her father and mother and grandmother, and went
on past the intelligence office.

When she came to her old school-teacher's—Miss
Mitchell's—house, she paused and hesitated a moment,
then she went up the little path between the snow-banks
to the front door, and rang the bell. The door was opened
before the echoes had died away. Miss Mitchell had
seen her coming, and hastened to open it. Miss Mitchell
had not been teaching school for some years, having
retired on a small competency of her savings. Her
mortgage was paid, and there was enough for herself
and her mother to live upon, with infinite care as to details of expenditure. Every postage-stamp and car-
fare had its important part in the school-teacher's system of economy; but she was quite happy, and her large
face wore an expression of perfect peace and placidity.

She was a woman who was not tortured by any strong,
ungratified desires. Her allotment of the gifts of the
gods quite satisfied her.

When Ellen entered the rather stuffy sitting-room
—for Miss Mitchell and her mother were jealous of any
breath of cold air after the scanty fire was kindled—
it was like entering into a stratum of peace. It seemed
quite removed from the turmoil of her own life. The
school-teacher's old mother sat in her rocker close to
the stove, stouter than ever, filling up her chair with
those wandering curves and vague outlines which
only the over-fleshy human form can assume. She
looked as indefinite as a quivering jelly until one reached
her face. That wore a fixedness of amiability which
accentuated the whole like a high light. She had not
seen Ellen for a long time, and she greeted her with
delight.

"Bless your heart!" said she, in her sweet, throaty,
husky voice. "Go and get her some of them cookies,
Fanny, do." The old woman's faculties were not in
the least impaired, although she was very old, neither
had her hands lost their cunning, for she still retained
her skill in cookery, and prepared the simple meals
for herself and daughter, seated in a high chair at the
kitchen table to roll out pastry or the famous little cookies which Ellen remembered along with her childhood.

There was something about these cookies which
Miss Mitchell presently brought to her in a pretty
china plate, with a little, fine-fringed napkin, which
was like a morsel of solace to the girl. With the first
sweet crumble of the cake on her plate, she wished to
cry. Sometimes the rush of old, kindly, tender associations will overcome one who is quite equal to the
strain of present emergency. But she did not cry; she
ate her cookies, and confided to Miss Mitchell and her
mother her desire to obtain a position elsewhere, since
her factory-work had failed her. It had occurred to
her that possibly Miss Mitchell, who was on the school-
board, might know of a vacancy in a primary school

for the coming spring term, and that she might obtain it.

"I think I know enough to teach a primary school," Ellen said.

"Of course you do, bless your heart," said old Mrs. Mitchell. "She knows enough to teach any kind of a school, don't she, Fanny? You get her a school, dear, right away."

But Miss Mitchell knew of no probable vacancy, since one young woman who had expected to be married had postponed her marriage on account of the strike in Lloyd's, and the consequent throwing out of employment of her sweetheart. Then, also, Miss Mitchell owned with hesitation, in response to Ellen's insistent question, that she supposed that the fact that she had worked in a shop might in any case interfere with her obtaining a position in a school.

"There is no sense in it, dear child; I know," she said, "but it might be so."

"Yes, I supposed so," replied Ellen, bitterly. "They would all say that a shop-girl had no right to try to teach school. Well, I'm much obliged to you, Miss Mitchell."

"What are you going to do?" Miss Mitchell asked, anxiously, following her to the door.

"I'm going to Mrs. Doty, to get some of the wrappers that mother works on, until something else turns up," replied Ellen.

"It seems a pity."

Ellen smiled bravely. "Beggars mustn't be choosers," she said. "If we can only keep along, somehow, I don't care."

There came a vehement pound of a stick on the floor, for that was the way the old woman in the sitting-room commanded attention. Miss Mitchell opened the door on a crack, that she might not let in the cold air.

"What is it, mother?" she said.

"You get Ellen a school right away, Fanny."

"All right, mother; I'll do my best."

"Get her the grammar-school you used to have."

"All right, mother."

There was something about the imperative solicitude of the old woman which comforted Ellen in spite of its futility as she went on her way. The good-will of another human soul, even when it cannot be resolved into active benefits, has undoubtedly a mighty force of its own. Ellen, with the sweet of the cookies still lingering on her tongue, and the sweet of the old woman's kindness in her soul, felt refreshed as if by some subtle spiritual cake and wine. She even went to the door of Mrs. Doty's house. Mrs. Doty was the woman who let out wrappers to her impecunious neighbors with an undaunted heart. She had no difficulty there. The demand for cheap wrappers was not on the wane, even in the hard times. When Ellen reached her grandmother's house, with a great parcel under her arm, Mrs. Zelotes opened her side door.

"What have you got there, Ellen Brewster?" she called out sharply.

"Some wrappers," replied Ellen, cheerfully.

"Are you going to work on wrappers?"

"Yes, grandma."

The door was shut with a loud report.

When Ellen entered the house and the sitting-room, her mother looked up from a pink wrapper which she was finishing.

"What have you got there?" she demanded.

"Some wrappers."

"Why, I haven't finished the last lot."

"These are for me to make, mother."

Andrew got up and went out of the room. Fanny shut her mouth hard, and drew her thread through with a jerk.

"Well," she said, in a second, "take off your things, and let me show you how to start on them. There's a little knack about it."

509

CHAPTER LVI

THAT was a hard winter for Rowe. Aside from
the financial stress, the elements seemed to conspire
against the people who were so ill-prepared to meet
their fury. It was the coldest winter which had been
known for years; coal was higher, and the poor people
had less coal to burn. Storm succeeded storm; then,
when there came a warm spell, there was an epidemic
of the grippe, and doctors' bills to pay and quinine to
buy—and quinine was very dear.

The Brewsters managed to keep up the interest on
the house mortgage, but their living expenses were reduced to the smallest possible amount. In those days
there was no wood laid ready for kindling in the parlor
stove, since there was neither any wood to spare nor
expectation of Robert's calling. Ellen and her mother
sat in the dining - room, for even the sitting-room fire
had been abolished, and they heated the dining-room
whenever the weather admitted it from the kitchen
stove, and worked on the wrappers for their miserable
pittance.

The repeated storms were in a way a boon to Andrew,
since he got many jobs clearing paths, and thus secured
a trifle towards the daily expenses.

In those days Mrs. Zelotes watched the butcher-
cart anxiously when it stopped before her son's
house, and she knew just what a tiny bit of meat
was purchased, and how seldom. On the days
when the cart moved on without any consultation at the tail thereof, the old woman would buy

an extra portion, cook it, and carry some over to her son's.

Times grew harder and harder. Few of the operatives who had struck in Lloyd's succeeded in obtaining employment elsewhere, and most of them joined the union to enable them to do so. There was actual privation. One evening, when the strike was some six weeks old, Abby Atkins came over in a pouring rain to see Ellen. There were a number of men in the dining-room that night. Amos Lee and Frank Dixon were among them. It was a singular thing that Andrew, taking, as he had done, no active part in any rebellion against authority, should have come to see his house the headquarters for the rallies of dissension. Men seemed to come to Andrew Brewster's for the sake of bolstering themselves up in their hard position of defiance against tremendous odds, though he sat by and seldom said a word. As for Ellen, she and her mother on these occasions sat out in the kitchen, sewing on the endless seams of the endless wrappers. Sometimes it seemed to the girl as if wrappers enough were being made to clothe not only the present, but future generations of poor women. She seemed to see whole armies of hopeless, overburdened women, all arrayed in these slouching garments, crowding the foreground of the world.

That evening little Amabel, who had developed a painful desire to make herself useful, having divined the altered state of the family finances, was pulling out basting-threads, with a puckered little face bent over her work. She was a very thin child, but there was an incisive vitality in her, and somehow Fanny and Ellen contrived to keep her prettily and comfortably clothed.

"I've got to do my duty by poor Eva's child, if I starve," Fanny often said.

When the side door opened, Ellen and her mother thought it was another man come to swell the company in the dining-room.

"It beats all how men like to come and sit round and talk over matters; for my part, I 'ain't got any time to talk; I've got to work," remarked Fanny.

"That's so," rejoined Ellen. She looked curiously like her mother that night, and spoke like her. In her heart she echoed the sarcasm to the full. She despised those men for sitting hour after hour in a store, or in the house of some congenial spirit, or standing on a street corner, and talking—talking, she was sure, to no purpose. As for herself, she had done what she thought right; she had, as it were, cut short the thread of her happiness of life for the sake of something undefined and rather vague, and yet as mighty in its demands for her allegiance as God. And it was done, and there was no use in talking about it. She had her wrappers to make. However, she told herself, extenuatingly, "Men can't sew, so they can't work evenings. They are better off talking here than they would be in the billiard-saloon." Ellen, at that time of her life, had a slight, unacknowledged feeling of superiority over men of her own class. She regarded them very much as she regarded children, with a sort of tolerant good-will and contempt. Now, suddenly, she raised her head and listened. "That isn't another man, it's a woman—it's Abby," she said to her mother.

"She wouldn't come out in all this rain," replied Fanny. As she spoke, a great, wind-driven wash of it came over the windows.

"Yes, it is," said Ellen, and she jumped up and opened the dining-room door.

Abby had entered, as was her custom, without knocking. She had left her dripping umbrella in the entry, and her old hat was flattened on to her head with wet, and several damp locks of her hair straggled from under it and clung to her thin cheeks. She still held up her wet skirts around her, as she had held them out-of-doors, but she was gesticulating violently with her other hand. She was repeating what she had said before. Ellen had heard her indistinctly through the door.

"Yes, I mean just what I say," she cried. "Get up and go to work, if you are men! Stop hanging around stores and corners, and talking about the tyranny of the rich, and go to work, and make them pay you something for it, anyhow. This has been kept up long enough. Get up and go to work, if you don't want those belonging to you to starve."

Abby caught sight of Ellen, pale and breathless, in the door, with her mother looking over her shoulder, and she addressed her with renewed violence. "Come here, Ellen," she said, "and put yourself on my side. We've got to give in."

"You go away," cried little Amabel, in a shrill voice, looking around Ellen's arm; but nobody paid any attention to her.

"I never will," returned Ellen, with a great flash, but her voice trembled.

"You've got to," said Abby. "I tell you there's no other way."

"I'll die before I give up," cried Lee, in a loud, threatening voice.

"I'm with ye," said Tom Peel.

Dixon and the young laster who sat beside him looked at each other, but said nothing. Dixon wrinkled his forehead over his pipe.

"Then you'd better go to work quick, before some that I know of, who are enough sight better worth saving than you are, starve," replied Abby, unshrinkingly. "If I could I would go to Lloyd's and open it on my own account to-morrow. I believe in bravery, but nothing except fools and swine jump over precipices."

Abby passed through the room, sprinkling raindrops from her drenched skirts, and went into the kitchen with Ellen. Fanny cast an angry glance at her, then a solicitous one at her dripping garments.

"Abby Atkins, you haven't got any rubbers on," said she.

"Rubbers!" repeated Abby.

"You just slip off those wet skirts, and Amabel will fetch you down Ellen's old black petticoat and brown dress. Amabel—"

But Abby seated herself peremptorily before the kitchen stove and extended one soaked little foot in its shabby boot. "I'm past thinking or caring about wet skirts," said she. "Good Lord, what do wet skirts matter? We can't make wrappers any longer. We had to sell the sewing-machine yesterday to pay the rent or be turned out, and we haven't got a thing to eat in the house except potatoes and a little flour. We haven't had any meat for a week. Nice fare for a man like poor father and a girl like Maria! We have come down to the kitchen fire like you, but we can't keep it burning as late as this. The rest went to bed an hour ago to keep warm. Maria has got more cold. She did seem better one spell, but now she's worse again. Our chamber is freezing cold, and we haven't had a fire in it since the strike. John Sargent has ransacked every town within twenty miles for work, but he can't get any, and his sick sister keeps sending to him for money. He looks as if he was just about done, too. He went off somewhere after supper. A great supper! He don't smoke a pipe nowadays. Father don't get the medicine he ought to have, and that cold spell he just about perished for a little whiskey. The bedroom was like ice with no fire in the sitting-room, and he didn't sleep warm. It's one awful thing after another happening. Did you know Mamie Brady took laudanum last night?"

"Good land!" said Fanny.

"Yes, she did. Ed Flynn has been playing fast and loose with her for a long time, and she's none too well balanced, and when it came to her not having enough to eat, and to keep her warm, and her mother nagging at her all the time—you know what an awful hard woman her mother is—she got desperate. She gulped it down when the last car went past and Ed Flynn hadn't come; she had been watchin' out for him; then she told her mother, and her mother shook her, then run for Dr. Fox, and he called in Dr. Lord, and they worked with a stomach-pump till morning, and she isn't out of danger yet. Then that isn't all. Willy Jones's mother is failing. He was over to our house last evening, telling us about it, and he fairly cried, poor boy. He said he actually could not get her what she needed to make her comfortable this awful winter. It was all he could do with odd jobs to keep the roof over their heads, that she hadn't actually enough to eat and keep her warm. It seemed as if he would die when he told about it. And that isn't all. Those little Blake children next door are fairly starving. They are going around to the neighbors' swill-buckets—it's a fact— just like little hungry dogs, and it's precious little they find in them. Mrs. Wetherhed has let her sewing-machine go, and Edward Morse is going to be sold out for taxes. And that isn't all." Abby lowered her voice a little. She cast an apprehensive glance at the door of the other room, and at Amabel. "Mamie Bemis has gone to the bad. I had it straight. She's in Boston. She didn't have enough to pay for her board, and got desperate. I know her sister did wrong, but that was no reason why she should have, and I don't believe she would if it hadn't been for the strike. It's all on account of the strike. There's no use talking: before the sparrow flies in the eyes of the tiger, he'd better count the cost."

Fanny, quite white, stood staring from Abby to Ellen, and back again.

Amabel was holding fast to a fold of Ellen's skirt. Ellen looked rigid.

"I knew it all before," she said, in a low voice.

Suddenly Abby jumped up and caught the other girl in a fierce embrace. "Ellen," she sobbed—"Ellen, isn't there any way out of it? I can't see—"

Ellen freed herself from Abby with a curious imperative yet gentle motion, then she opened the door into the other room again. The loud clash of voices hushed, and every man faced towards her standing on the threshold, with her mother and Abby and little Amabel in the background. "I want to say to you all," said Ellen, in a clear voice, "that I think I did wrong. I have been wondering if I had not for some time, and growing more and more certain. I did not count the cost. All I thought of was the principle, but the cost is a part of the principle in this world, and it has to be counted in with it. I see now. I don't think the strike ought ever to have been. It has brought about too much suffering upon those who were not responsible for it, who did not choose it of their own free will. There are children starving, and people dying and breaking their hearts. We have brought too much upon ourselves and others. I am sorry I said what I did in the shop that day, if I influenced any one. Now I am not going to strike any longer. Let us all accept Mr. Lloyd's terms, and go back to work."

But Ellen's voice was drowned out in a great shout of wrath and dissent from Lee. He directly leaped to the conclusion that the girl took this attitude on account

of Lloyd, and his jealousy, which was always smouldering, flamed.

"Well, I guess not!" he shouted. "I rather guess
not! I've struck, and I'm going to stay struck! I ain't
goin' to back out because a girl likes the boss, damn
him!"

Andrew and the young laster rose and moved quietly
before Ellen. Tom Peel said nothing, but he grinned
imperturbably.

"I 'ain't had a bit of tobacco, and the less said about
what I've had to eat the better," Lee went on, in a loud,
threatening voice, "but I ain't going to give up. No,
miss; you've het up the fightin' blood in me, and it
ain't so easy coolin' of it down."

The door opened, and Granville Joy entered. He
had knocked several times, but nobody had heard him.
He looked inquiringly from one to another, then moved
beside Andrew and the laster.

Dixon got up. "It looks to me as if it was too soon
to be giving up now," he said.

"It's easy for a man who's got nobody dependent upon
him to talk," cried Abby.

"I won't give up!" cried Dixon, looking straight at
Ellen, and ignoring Abby.

"That's so," said Lee. "We don't give up our rights
for bosses, or bosses' misses."

As he said that there was a concerted movement of
Andrew, the laster, and Granville. Granville was
much slighter than Lee, but suddenly his right arm
shot out, and the other man went down like a log. Andrew followed him up with a kick.

"Get out of my house," he shouted, "and never set
foot in it again! Out with ye!"

Lee was easily cowed. He did not attempt to make
any resistance, but gathered himself up, muttering,
and moved before the three into the entry, where he

517

had left his coat and hat. Dixon and Peel followed him. When the door was shut, Ellen turned to the others, with a quieting hand on Amabel's head, who was clinging to her, trembling.

"I think it will be best to talk to John Sargent," said she. "I think a committee had better be appointed to wait upon Mr. Lloyd again, and ask him to open the factory. I'm not going to strike any longer."

"I'm sure I'm not," said Abby.

"Abby and I are not going to strike any longer," said Ellen, in an indescribably childlike way, which yet carried enormous weight with it.

CHAPTER LVII

ELLEN had not arrived at her decision with regard to the strike as suddenly as it may have seemed. All winter, ever since the strike, Ellen had been wondering, not whether the principle of the matter was correct or not, that she never doubted; she never swerved in her belief concerning the cruel tyranny of the rich and the helpless suffering of the poor, and their good reason for making a stand, but she doubted more and more the wisdom of it. She used to sit for hours up in her chamber after her father and mother had gone to bed, wrapped up in an old shawl against the cold, resting her elbows on the window-sill and her chin on her two hands, staring out into the night, and reflecting. Her youthful enthusiasm carried her like a leaping-pole to conclusions beyond her years. "I wonder," she said to herself, "if, after all, this inequality of possessions is not a part of the system of creation, if the righting of them is not beyond the flaming sword of the Garden of Eden? I wonder if the one who tries to right them forcibly is not meddling, and usurping the part of the Creator, and bringing down wrath and confusion not only upon his own head, but upon the heads of others? I wonder if it is wise, in order to establish a principle, to make those who have no voice in the matter suffer for it—the helpless women and children?" She even thought with a sort of scornful sympathy of Sadie Peel, who could not have her nearseal cape, and had not wished to strike. She reflected, as she had done so many times before, that the world was very old—thousands of years old—

and inequality was as old as the world. Might it not even be a condition of its existence, the shifting of weights which kept it to its path in the scheme of the universe? And yet always she went back to her firm belief that the strikers were right, and always, although she loved Robert Lloyd, she denounced him. Even when it came to her abandoning her position with regard to the strike, she had not the slightest thought of effecting thereby a reconciliation with Robert.

For the first time, that night when she had gone to bed, after announcing her determination to go back to work, she questioned her affection for Robert. Before she had always admitted it to herself with a sort of shamed and angry dignity. "Other women feel so about men, and why should I not?" she had said; "and I shall never fail to keep the feeling behind more important things." She had accepted the fact of it with childlike straightforwardness as she accepted all other facts of life, and now she wondered if she really did care for him so much. She thought over and over everything Abby had said, and saw plainly before her mental vision those poor women parting with their cherished possessions, the little starving children snatching at the refuse-buckets at the neighbors' back doors. She saw with incredulous shame, and something between pity and scorn, Mamie Bemis, who had gone wrong, and Mamie Brady, who had taken her foolish, ill-balanced life in her own hands. She remembered every word which she had said to the men on the morning of the strike, and how they had started up and left their machines. "I did it all," she told herself. "I am responsible for it all—all this suffering, for those hungry little children, for that possible death, for the ruin of another girl." Then she told herself, with a stern sense of justice, that back of her responsibility

came Robert Lloyd's. If he had not cut the wages
it would never have been. It seemed to her that she
almost hated him, and that she could not wait to strive
to undo the harm which she had done. She could not
wait for morning to come.

She lay awake all night in a fever of impatience.
When she went down-stairs her eyes were brilliant,
there were red spots on her cheeks, her lips were tense,
her whole face looked as if she were strained for some
leap of action. She took hold of everything she touched
with a hard grip. Her father and mother kept watching her anxiously. Directly after breakfast Ellen put
on her hat and coat.

"What are you going to do?" asked Fanny.

"I am going over to see John Sargent, and ask him
to get some other men and go to see Mr. Lloyd, and tell
him we are willing to go to work again," replied Ellen.

Ellen discovered, when she reached the Atkins house,
that John Sargent had already resolved upon his course
of action.

"The first thing he said when he came in last night
was that he couldn't stand it any longer, and he was
going to see the others, and go to Lloyd, and ask him
to open the shop on his own terms," said Abby. "I told
him how we felt about it."

"Yes, I am ready to go back whenever the factory is
opened," said Ellen. "I am glad he has gone."

Ellen did not remain long. She was anxious to return and finish some wrappers she had on hand. Abby
promised to go over and let her know the result of the
interview with Lloyd.

It was not until evening that Abby came over, and
John Sargent with her. Lloyd had not been at home
in the morning, and they had been forced to wait until
late afternoon. The two entered the dining-room, where
Ellen and her mother sat at work.

Abby spoke at once, and to the point. "Well," said she, "the shop's going to be opened to-morrow."

"On what terms?" asked Ellen.

"On the boss's, of course," replied Abby, in a hard voice.

"It's the only thing to do," said Sargent, with a sort of stolid assertion. "If we are willing to be crushed under the Juggernaut of principle, we haven't any right to force others under, and that's what we are doing."

"Bread without butter is better than no bread at all," said Abby. "We've got to live in the sphere in which Providence has placed us." The girl said "Providence" with a sarcastic emphasis.

Andrew was looking at Sargent. "Do you think there will be any trouble?" he asked.

Sargent hesitated, with a glance at Fanny. "I don't know; I hope not," said he. "Lee and Dixon are opposed to giving in, and they are talking hard to-night in the store. Then some of the men have joined the union since the strike, and of course they swear by it, because it has been helping them, and they won't approve of giving up. But I doubt if there will be much trouble. I guess the majority want to go to work, even the union men. The amount of it is, it has been such a tough winter it has taken the spirit out of the poor souls." Sargent, evidently, in yielding was resisting himself.

"You don't think there will be any danger?" Fanny said, anxiously, looking at Ellen.

"Oh no, there's no danger for the girls, anyhow. I guess there's enough men to look out for them. There's no need for you to worry, Mrs. Brewster."

"Mr. Lloyd did not offer to do anything better about the wages?" asked Ellen.

Sargent shook his head.

"Catch him!" said Abby, bitterly.

Ellen had a feeling as if she were smiting in the

face that image of Robert which always dwelt in her heart.

"Well," said Abby, with a mirthless laugh, "there's one thing: according to the Scriptures, it is as hard for the rich man to get into heaven as it is for the poor men to get into their factories."

"You don't suppose there will be any danger?" Fanny said again, anxiously.

"Danger—no; who's afraid of Amos Lee and a few like him?" cried Abby, contemptuously; "and Nahum Beals is safe. He's going to be tried next month, they say, but they'll make it imprisonment for life, because they think he wasn't in his right mind. If he was here we might be afraid, but there's nobody now that will do anything but talk. I ain't afraid. I'm going to march up to the shop to-morrow morning and go to work, and I'd like to see anybody stop me."

However, before they left, John Sargent spoke aside with Andrew, and told him of a plan for the returning workmen to meet at the corner of a certain street, and go in a body to the factory, and suggested that there might be pickets posted by the union men, and Andrew resolved to go with Ellen.

The next morning the rain had quite ceased, and there was a faint something, rather a reminiscence than a suggestion, of early spring in the air. People caught themselves looking hard at the elm branches to see if they were acquiring the virile fringe of spring or if their eyes deceived them, and wondered, with respect to the tips of maple and horse-chestnut branches, whether or not they were swollen red and glossy. Sometimes they sniffed incredulously when a soft gust of south wind seemed laden with fresh blossom fragrance.

"I declare, if I didn't know better, I should think I smelled apple blossoms," said Maria.

"Stuff!" returned Abby. She was marching along

523

with an alert, springy motion of her lean little body. She was keenly alive to the situation, and scented something besides apple blossoms. She had tried to induce Maria to remain at home. "I don't know but there'll be trouble, and if there is, you'll be just in the way," she told her before they left the house, but not in their parents' hearing.

"Oh, I don't believe there'll be any. Folks will be too glad to get back to work," replied Maria. She had a vein of obstinacy, gentle as she was; then, too, she had a reason which no one suspected for wishing to be present. She would not yield when John Sargent begged her privately not to go. It was just because she was afraid there might be trouble, and he was going to be in it, that she could not bear to stay at home herself.

Andrew had insisted upon accompanying Ellen in spite of her remonstrances. "I've got an errand down to the store," he said, evasively; but Ellen understood.

"I don't think there is any danger, and there wouldn't be any danger for me—not for the girls, sure," she said; but he persisted.

"Don't you say a word to your mother to scare her," he whispered. But they had not been gone long before Fanny followed them, Mrs. Zelotes watching her furtively from a window as she went by.

All the returning employés met, as agreed upon, at the corner of a certain street, and marched in a solid body towards Lloyd's. The men insisted upon placing the girls in the centre of this body, although some of them rebelled, notably Sadie Peel. She was on hand, laughing and defiant.

"I guess I ain't afraid," she proclaimed. "Father's keepin' on strikin', but I guess he won't see his own daughter hurt; and now I'm goin' to have my nearseal cape, if it is late in the season. They're cheaper now, that's one good thing. On some accounts the strike has

524

been a lucky thing for me." She marched along, swing
ing her arms jauntily. Ellen and Maria and Abby were
close together. Andrew was on the right of Ellen,
Granville Joy behind; the young laster, who had called
so frequently evenings, was with him. John Sargent
and Willy Jones were on the left. They all walked in
the middle of the street like an army. It was covertly
understood that there might be trouble. Some of the
younger men from time to time put hands on their
pockets, and a number carried stout sticks.

The first intimation of disturbance came when they
met an electric-car, and all moved to one side to let
it pass. The car was quite full of people going to
another town, some thirty miles distant, to work in a
large factory there. Nearly every man and woman
on the car belonged to the union.

As this car slid past a great yell went up from the
occupants; men on the platforms swung their arms in
execration and derision. "Sc-ab, sc-ab!" they called.
A young fellow leaped from the rear platform, caught
up a stone and flung it at the returning Lloyd men, but
it went wide of its mark. Then he was back on the
platform with a running jump, and one of the Lloyd
men threw a stone, which missed him. The yell of
"Scab, scab!" went up with renewed vigor, until it
died out of hearing along with the rumble of the car.

"Sometimes I wish I had joined the union and stuck
it out," said one of the Lloyd men, gloomily.

"For the Lord's sake, don't show the white feather
now!" cried a young fellow beside him, who was striding
on with an eager, even joyous outlook. He had fighting blood, and it was up, and he took a keen delight
in the situation.

"It's easy to talk," grumbled the other man. "I
don't know but all our help lies in the union, and we've
been a pack of fools not to go in with them, because we

hoped Lloyd would weaken and take us back. He hasn't weakened; we've had to. Good God, them that's rich have it their own way!"

"I'd have joined the union in a minute, and got a job, and got my nearseal cape, if it hadn't been for father," said Sadie Peel, with a loud laugh. "But, my land! if father'd caught me joinin' the union I dun'no' as there would have been anything left of me to wear the cape."

They all marched along with no disturbance until they reached the corner of the street into which they had to turn in order to approach Lloyd's. There they were confronted by a line of pickets, stationed there by the union, and the real trouble began. Yells of "Scab, scab!" filled the air.

"Good land, I ain't no more of a scab than you be!" shrieked Sadie Peel, in a loud, angry voice. "Scab yourself! Touch me if you dasse!"

Many young men among the returning force had stout sticks in their hands. Granville Joy was one of them. Andrew, who was quite unarmed, pressed in before Ellen. Granville caught him by the arm and tried to draw him back.

"Look here, Mr. Brewster," he said, "you keep in the background a little. I am young and strong, and here are Sargent and Mendon. You'd better keep back."

But Ellen, with a spring which was effectual because so utterly uncalculated, was before Granville and her father, and them all. She reasoned it out in a second that she was responsible for the strike, and that she would be in the front of whatever danger there was in consequence. Her slight little figure passed them all before they knew what she was doing. She was in the very front of the little returning army. She saw the threatening faces of the pickets; she half turned, and waved an arm of encouragement, like a general in a

"'IF YOU WANT TO KILL A GIRL FOR GOING BACK TO WORK TO SAVE HERSELF
FROM STARVATION, DO IT!'"

battle. "Strike if you want to," she cried out, in her sweet young voice. "If you want to kill a girl for going back to work to save herself and her friends from starvation, do it. I am not afraid! But kill me, if you must kill anybody, because I am the one that started the strike. Strike if you want to."

The opposing force moved aside with an almost imperceptible motion. Ellen looked like a beautiful child, her light hair tossed around her rosy face, her eyes full of the daring of perfect confidence. She in reality did not feel one throb of fear. She passed the picket-line, and turned instinctively and marched backward with her blue eyes upon them all. Abby Atkins sprang forward to Ellen's side, with Sargent and Joy and Willy Jones and Andrew. Andrew kept calling to Ellen to come back, but she did not heed him.

The little army was several rods from the pickets before a shot rang out, but that was fired into the air. However, it was followed by a fierce clamor of "Scab" and a shower of stones, which did little harm. The Lloyds marched on without a word, except from Sadie Peel. She turned round with a derisive shout.

"Scab yourselves!" she shrieked. "You dassen't fire at me. You're scabs yourselves, you be!"

"Scabs, scabs!" shouted the men, moving forward.

"Scab yourself!" shouted Sadie Peel.

Abby Atkins caught hold of her arm and shook her violently. "Shut up, can't you, Sadie Peel," she said.

"I'll shut up when I get ready, Abby Atkins! I ain't afraid of them if you be. They dassen't hit me. Scab, scab!" the girl yelled back, with a hysteric laugh.

"Don't that girl know anything?" growled a man behind her.

"Shut up, Sadie Peel," said Abby Atkins.

"I ain't afraid if you be, and I won't shut up till I get

527

ready, for you or anybody else. I'm goin' to have my nearseal cape! Hi!"

"I ain't afraid," said Abby, contemptuously, "but I've got sense."

Maria pressed close to Sadie Peel. "Please do keep still, Sadie," she pleaded. "Let us get into the factory as quietly as we can. Think, if anybody was hurt."

"I ain't afraid," shrieked the girl, with a toss of her red fringe, and she laughed like a parrot. Abby Atkins gripped her arm so fiercely that she made her cry out with pain. "If you don't keep still!" she said, threateningly.

Willy Jones was walking as near as he could, and he carried his right arm half extended, as if to guard her. Now and then Abby turned and gave him a push backward.

"They won't trouble us girls, and you might as well let us and the men that have sticks go first," she said in a whisper.

"If you think—" began the young fellow, coloring.

"Oh, I know you ain't afraid," said Abby, "but you've got your mother to think of, and there's no use in running into danger."

The pickets were gradually left behind; they were, in truth, half-hearted. Many of them had worked in Lloyd's, and had small mind to injure their old comrades. They were not averse to a great show of indignation and bluster, but when it came to more they hesitated.

Presently the company came into the open space before Lloyd's. Robert and Lyman Risley and several foremen were standing at the foot of the stairs. The windows of the factory were filled with faces, and derisive cries came from them. Lloyd's tall shaft of chimney was plumed with smoke. The employés advanced towards the stairs, when suddenly Amos Lee, Dixon, and a dozen others appeared, coming with a rush from around a corner of the building, and again the air was filled with the cry of "Scab!" Ellen and Abby linked arms and sprang forward before the men with an impetuous rush, with Joy and Willy Jones and Andrew following. Ellen, as she rushed on towards the factory stairs, was conscious of no fear at all, but rather of a sort of exaltation of courage. It did not really occur to her that she could be hurt, that it could be in the heart of Lee or Dixon, or any of them, actually to harm her. She was throbbing and intense with indignation and resolution. Into that factory to her work she was bound to go. All that intimidated her in the least was the fear for her father. She rushed as fast as she could that her father might not get before her and be hurt in some way.

"Scab! scab!" shouted Lee and the others.

"Scab yourself!" shrieked Sadie Peel. Her father was one of the opposing party, and that gave her perfect audacity. "Look out you don't hit me, dad," she cried to him. "I'm goin' to get my nearseal cape. Don't you hit your daughter, Tom Peel!" She raced on with a sort of hoppity-skip. She caught a young man near her by the arm and forced him into the same dancing motion.

They were at the foot of the stairs, when Robert, watching, saw Lee with a pistol in his hand aim straight at Ellen. He sprang before her, but Risley was nearer, and the shot struck him. When Risley fell, a great cry, it would have been difficult to tell whether of triumph or horror, went up from the open windows of the other factories, and men came swarming out. Lee and his companions vanished.

A great crowd gathered around Risley until the doctors came and ordered them away, and carried him

2 L   529

in the ambulance to the hospital. He was not dead, but evidently very seriously injured.

When the ambulance had rolled out of sight, the Lloyd employés entered the factory, and the hum of machinery began.

Fanny and Andrew stood together before the factory after Ellen had entered. Andrew had started when he had seen his wife.

"You here?" he said.

"I rather guess I'm here," returned Fanny. "Do you s'pose I was goin' to stay at home, and not know whether you and her were shot dead or not?"

"I guess it's all safe now," said Andrew. He was very pale. He looked at the blood-stained place where Lyman Risley had lain. "It's awful work," he said.

"Who did it?" asked Fanny, sharply. "I heard the shot just before I got here."

"I don't know for sure, and guess it's better I don't," replied Andrew, sternly.

Then all at once as they stood there a woman came up with a swift, gliding motion and a long trail of black skirts straight to Fanny, who was the only woman there. There were still a great many men and boys standing about. The woman, Cynthia Lennox, caught Fanny's arm with a nervous grip. Her finely cut face was very white under the nodding plumes of her black bonnet.

"Is he in there?" she asked, in a strained voice, pointing to the shop.

Fanny stared at her. She was half dazed. She did not know whether she was referring to the wounded man or Robert.

Andrew was quicker in his perceptions.

"They carried him off to the hospital in the ambulance," he told her. Then he added, as gently as if he had been addressing Ellen: "I guess he wasn't hurt so very bad. He came to before they took him away."

"You don't know anything about it," Fanny said, sharply. "I heard them say something about his eyes."

"His eyes!" gasped Cynthia. She held tightly to Fanny, who looked at her with a sudden passion of sympathy breaking through her curiosity.

"Oh, I guess he wasn't hurt so very bad; he *did* come to. I heard him speak," she said, soothingly. She laid her hard hand over Cynthia's slim one.

"They took him to the hospital?"

"Yes, in the ambulance."

"Is—my nephew in there?"

"No; he went with him."

Cynthia looked at the other woman with an expression of utter anguish and pleading.

"Look here," said Fanny; "the hospital ain't very far from here. Suppose we go up there and ask how he is? We could call out your nephew."

"Will you go with me?" asked Cynthia, with a heart-breaking gasp.

If Ellen could have seen her at that moment, she would have recognized her as the woman whom she had known in her childhood. She was an utter surprise to Fanny, but her sympathy leaped to meet her need like the steel to the magnet.

"Of course I will," she said, heartily.

"I would," said Andrew—"I would go with her, Fanny."

"Of course I will," said Fanny; "and you had better go home, I guess, Andrew, and see how I left the kitchen fire. I don't know but the dampers are all wide open."

Fanny and Cynthia hastened in one direction towards the hospital, and Andrew towards home;

but he paused for a minute, and looked thoughtfully up at the humming pile of Lloyd's. The battle was over and the strike was ended. He drew a great sigh, and went home to see to the kitchen fire.

CHAPTER LVIII

LYMAN RISLEY was very seriously injured. There was, as the men had reported, danger for his eyes. When Robert was called into the reception-room of the hospital to see his aunt, he scarcely recognized her. Her soft, white hair was tossed about her temples, her cheeks were burning. She ran up to him like an eager child and clutched his arm.

"How is he?" she demanded. "Tell me quick!"

"They are doing everything they can for him. Why, don't, poor Aunt Cynthia!"

"His eyes, they said—"

"I hope he will come out all right. Don't, dear Aunt Cynthia." The young man put his arm around his aunt and spoke soothingly, blushing like a girl before this sudden revelation of an under-stratum of delicacy in a woman's heart.

Cynthia lost control of herself completely; or, rather, the true self of her rose uppermost, shattering the surface ice of her reserve. "Oh," she said—"oh, if he— if he is—blind, if he is—I—I—will lead him everywhere all the rest of his life; I will, Robert."

"Of course you will, dear Aunt Cynthia," replied Robert, soothingly.

Suddenly Cynthia's face took on a new expression. She looked at Robert, deadly pale, and her jaw dropped. "He will not—die," she said, with stiff lips. "It is not as bad as that?"

"Oh no, no; I am sure he will not," Robert cried, wonderingly and pityingly. "Don't, Aunt Cynthia."

533

"If he dies," she said—"if he dies—and he has loved me all this time, and I have never done anything for him—I cannot bear it; I will not bear it; I will not, Robert!"

"Oh, he isn't going to die, Aunt Cynthia."

"I want to go to him," she said. "I *will* go to him."

Robert looked helplessly from her to Fanny. "I am afraid you can't just now, Aunt Cynthia," he replied.

Fanny came resolutely to his assistance. "Of course you can't, Miss Lennox," she said. "The doctors won't let you see him now. You would do him more harm than good. You don't want to do him harm!"

"No, I don't want to do him harm," returned Cynthia, in a wailing, hysterical voice. She threw herself down upon a sofa and began sobbing like a child, with her face hidden.

A young doctor entered and stood looking at her.

Robert turned to him. "It is my aunt, and she is agitated over Mr. Risley's accident," he said, coloring a little.

Instantly the young physician's face lost its expression of astonishment and assumed the soothing gloss of his profession. "Oh, my dear Miss Lennox," he said, "there is no cause for agitation, I assure you. Everything is being done for Mr. Risley."

"Will he be blind?" gasped Cynthia, with a great vehemence of woe, which seemed to gainsay the fact of her years. It seemed as if such an outburst of emotion could come only from a child all unacquainted with grief and unable to control it.

The young doctor laughed blandly. "Blind? No, indeed," he replied. "He might have been blind had this happened twenty-five years ago, but with the resources of the present day it is a different matter. Pray don't alarm yourself, dear Miss Lennox."

"Can you call a carriage for my aunt?" asked Robert. He went close to Cynthia and laid a hand on her slender shoulder. "I am going to have a carriage come for you, and perhaps Mrs. Brewster will be willing to go home with you in it."

"Of course I will," replied Fanny.

"You hear what Dr. Payson says, that there is nothing to be alarmed about," Robert said, in a low voice, with his lips close to his aunt's ear.

Cynthia made no resistance, but when the carriage arrived, and she was being driven off, with Fanny by her side, she called out of the window with a fierce shamelessness of anxiety, "Robert, you must come and tell me how he is this afternoon, or I shall come back here and see him myself."

"Yes, I will, Aunt Cynthia," he replied, soothingly. He met the doctor's curious eyes when he turned. The young man had a gossiping mind, but he forbore to say what he thought, which was to the effect that—why under the heavens, if that woman cared as much as that for that man, she had not married him, instead of letting him dangle after her so many years? But he merely said:

"There is no use in saying anything to excite a woman further when she is in such a state of mind, but—" Then he paused significantly.

"You think the chances of his keeping his eyesight are poor?" said Robert.

"Mighty poor," replied the doctor.

Robert stood still, with his pale, shocked face bent upon the carpet. He could not seem to comprehend at once the enormity of it all; his mind was grasping at and trying to assimilate the horrible fact with an infinite pain.

"Have they got the man that did it?" asked the doctor.

"I don't know. I had to see to poor Risley," replied

Robert. "I hope to God they have." Then all at once
he thought, with keen anxiety, of Ellen. Who knew
what new tragedy had happened? "I must go back
to the factory," he said, hurriedly. "I will be back
here in an hour or so, and see how he is getting on.
For Heaven's sake, do all you can!"

Robert was desperately impatient to be back at the
factory. He was full of vague anxiety about Ellen.
He could not forget that the shot which had hit poor
Risley had been meant for her, and he remembered the
look on the man's face as he aimed. He found a carriage at the street corner, and jumped in, and bade the
man drive fast.

When Robert entered the great building, and felt the
old vibration of machinery, he had a curious sensation,
one which he had never before had and which he had
not expected. For the first time in his life he knew
what it was to have a complete triumph of his own will
over his fellow-men. He had gotten his own way. All
this army of workmen, all this machinery of labor, was
set in motion at his desire, in opposition to their own.
He realized himself a leader and a conqueror. He went
into the office, and Flynn and Dennison came forward,
smiling, to greet him.

"Well," said Dennison, "we're off again." He spoke
as if the factory were a ship which had been launched
from a shoal.

"Yes," replied Robert, gravely.

Nellie Stone, at the desk, was glancing around, with
a half-shy, half-coquettish look.

"How is Mr. Risley?" asked Flynn.

"He is badly hurt," replied Robert. "Have they
found the man? Do you know what has been done
about it?"

"They've got all the police force of the city out,"
replied Flynn, "but it's no use. They'll never catch

Amos Lee. His mother was a gypsy, I've always heard. He knows about a thousand ways out of traps, and there's plenty to help him. They've got Dixon under arrest, and Tom Peel; but they didn't have any fire-arms on 'em, and they can't prove anything. Peel says he's ready to go back to work." Flynn had a somewhat seedy and downcast appearance, although he fought hard for his old jaunty manner. His impulsive good-nature had gotten the better of his judgment and his own wishes, and he had gone to Mamie Brady and offered to marry her out of hand if she recovered from her attempted suicide. The night before he had watched, turn and turn about, with her mother. He gave a curious effect of shamefaced and melancholy virtue. He followed Robert to one side when he was hanging up his hat and coat. "I'm going to tell you, Mr. Lloyd," he said, rather awkwardly; "maybe you won't be interested in the midst of all this, but it all came from the strike. She's better this morning, and I'm going to marry her, poor girl."

Robert looked at him in a dazed fashion. For a moment he had not the slightest idea what he was talking about.

"I'm going to marry Mamie Brady," explained Flynn. "She took laudanum. It all happened on account of the strike. I'll own I'd been flirting some with her, but she'd never done it if she hadn't been out of work, too. She said so. Her mother made her life a hell. I'm going to marry her, and take her out of it."

"It's mighty good of you," Robert said, rather stupidly.

"There ain't no other way for me to do," replied Flynn. "She thinks the world of me, and I suppose I'm to blame."

"I hope she'll make you a good wife and you'll be happy," said Robert.

"She thinks all creation of me," replied Flynn, with the simplest vanity and acquiescence in the responsibility laid upon him in the world. "That shot wasn't meant for Mr. Risley," said Flynn, as Robert approached the office door. His eyes flashed. He himself would gladly have been shot for the sake of Ellen Brewster. He was going to marry, and try to fulfil his simple code of honor, but all his life he would be married to one woman, with another ideal in his heart; that was inevitable.

"I know it wasn't," Robert replied, grimly.

"Everything is quiet now," said Dennison, with his smooth smile. Robert made no reply, but entered the great work-room. "He's mighty stand-offish, now he's got his own way," Dennison remarked in a whisper to Nellie Stone. He leaned closely over her. Flynn had followed Robert. The girl glanced up at the foreman, who was unmarried, although years older than she, and her face quivered a little, but it seemed due to a surface sensitiveness.

"I want to know if you've heard that Ed is going to marry Mamie Brady, after all," she whispered.

Dennison nodded.

She knitted her forehead over a column of figures. Dennison leaned his face so close that his blond-bearded cheek touched hers. She made a little impatient motion.

"Oh, go long, Jim Dennison," she said, but her tone was half-hearted.

Dennison persisted, bending her head gently backward until he kissed her. She pushed him away, but she smiled weakly.

"You didn't want Ed Flynn. Why, he's a Roman Catholic, and you're Baptist, Nell," he said.

"Who said I did?" she retorted, angrily. "Why, I wouldn't marry Ed Flynn if he was the last man in the world."

"You'd 'nough sight better marry me," said Dennison.

"Go along; you're fooling."

"No, I ain't. I mean it, honest."

"I don't want to marry anybody yet awhile," said Nellie Stone; but when Dennison kissed her again she did not repulse him, and even nestled her head with a little caressing motion into the hollow of his shoulder.

Then they both started violently apart as Flynn entered.

"Say!" he proclaimed, "what do you think? The boss has just told the hands that he'll split the difference and reduce the wages five instead of ten per cent."

539

CHAPTER LIX

WHEN Robert Lloyd entered the factory that morning he experienced one of those revulsions which come to man in common with all creation. As the wind can swerve from south to east, and its swerving be a part of the universal scheme of things, so the inconsistency of a human soul can be an integral part of its consistency. Robert, entering Lloyd's, flushed with triumph over his workmen, filled also with rage whenever he thought of poor Risley, became suddenly, to all appearances, another man. However, he was the same man, only he had come under some hidden law of growth. All at once, as he stood there amidst those whirring and clamping machines, and surveyed those bowed and patient backs and swaying arms of labor, standing aside to allow a man bending before a heavy rack of boots to push it to another department, he realized that his triumph was gone.

Not a man or woman in the factory looked at him. All continued working with a sort of patient fierceness, as if storming a citadel—as, indeed, they were in one sense—and waging incessant and in the end hopeless warfare against the destructive forces of life. Robert stood in the midst of them, these fellow-beings who had bowed to his will, and saw, as if by some divine revelation, in his foes his brothers and sisters. He saw Ellen's fair head before her machine, and she seemed the key-note of a heart-breaking yet ineffable harmony of creation which he heard for the first time. He was a man whom triumph did not exalt as much as it humil-

540

iated. Who was he to make these men and women do his bidding? They were working as hard as they had worked for full pay. Without doubt he would not gain as much comparatively, but he was going to lose nothing actually, and he would not work as these men worked. He saw himself as he never could have seen himself had the strike continued; and yet, after all, he was not a woman, to be carried away by a sudden wave of generous sentiment and enthusiasm, for his business instincts were too strong, inherited and developed by the force of example. He could not forget that this had been his uncle's factory.

He shut his mouth hard, and stood looking at the scene of toil, then he resolved what to do.

He spoke to Flynn, who could not believe his ears, and asked him over.

"I beg your pardon, sir," he said.

"Go and speak to the engineer, and tell him to shut down," said Robert.

"You ain't going to turn them out, after all?" gasped Flynn. He was deadly white.

"No, I am not. I only want to speak to them," replied Robert, shortly.

When the roar of machinery had ceased, Robert stood before the employés, whose faces had taken on an expression of murder and menace. They anticipated the worst by this order.

"I want to say to you all," said Robert, in a loud, clear voice, "that I realize it will be hard for you to make both ends meet with the cut of ten per cent. I will make it five instead of ten per cent., although I shall actually lose by so doing unless business improves. I will, however, try it as long as possible. If the hard times continue, and it becomes a sheer impossibility for me to employ you on these terms without abandoning the plant altogether, I will approach you again, and

541

trust that you will support me in any measures I am forced to take. And, on the contrary, should business improve, I promise that your wages shall be raised to the former standard at once."

The speech was so straightforward that it sounded almost boyish. Robert, indeed, looked very young as he stood there, for a generous and pitying impulse does tend to make a child of a man. The workmen stared at him a minute, then there was a queer little broken chorus of "Thank ye's," with two or three shrill crows of cheers.

Robert went from room to room, repeating his short speech, then work recommenced.

"He's the right sort, after all," said Granville Joy to John Sargent, and his tone had a quality of heroism in it. He was very thin and pale. He had suffered privations, and now came additional worry of mind. He could not help thinking that this might bring about an understanding between Robert and Ellen, and yet he paid his spiritual dues at any cost.

"It's no more than he ought to do," growled a man at Granville's right. "S'pose he does lose a little money?"

"It ain't many out of the New Testament that are going to lose a little for the sake of their fellow-men, I can tell you that," said John Sargent. He was cutting away deftly and swiftly, and thinking with satisfaction of the money which he would be able to send his sister, and also how the Atkins family would be no longer so pinched. He was a man who would never come under the grindstone of the pessimism of life for his own necessities, but lately the necessities of others had almost forced him there. Now and then he glanced across the room at Maria, whose narrow shoulders he could see bent painfully over her work. He was in love with Maria. but no one suspected it, least of all Maria herself.

"Lord! don't talk about the New Testament. Them days is past," growled the man on the other side of Joy.

"They ain't past for me," said John Sargent, stoutly. A dark flush rose to his cheek as if he were making a confession of love.

"Lord! don't preach," said the other man, with a sneer.

Ellen had stopped work .with the rest when Robert addressed them. Then she recommenced her stitching without a word. Her thoughts were in confusion. She had so long held one attitude towards him that she could not readily adjust herself to another. She was cramped with the extreme narrowness of the enthusiasm of youth. At noontime she heard all the talk which went on about him. She heard some praise him, and some speak of him as simply doing his manifest duty, and some say openly that he should have put the wages back upon the former footing, and she did not know which was right. He did not come near her, and she was very glad of that. She felt that she could not bear it to have him speak to her before them all.

When she went home at night the news had preceded her. Fanny and Andrew looked up eagerly when she entered. "I hear he has compromised," said Andrew, with doubtful eyes on the girl's face.

"Yes; he has cut the wages five instead of ten per cent.," replied Ellen, and it was impossible to judge of her feelings by her voice. She took off her hat and smoothed her hair.

"Well, I am glad he has done that much," said Fanny, "but I won't say a word as long as you ain't hurt."

With that she went into the kitchen, and Ellen and Andrew heard the dishes rattle. "Your mother's been dreadful nervous," whispered Andrew. He looked at Ellen meaningly. Both of them thought of poor Eva Tenny. Lately the reports with regard to her had been more encouraging, but she was still in the asylum.

Suddenly, as they stood there, a swift shadow passed the window, and they heard a shrill scream from upstairs. It sounded like "Mamma, mamma!" "It's Amabel!" cried Ellen. She clutched her father by the arm. "Oh, what is it—who is it?" she whispered, fearfully.

Andrew was suddenly white and horror-stricken. He took hold of Ellen, and pushed her forcibly before him into the parlor. "You stay in there till I call you," he said, in a commanding voice, the like of which the girl had never heard from him before; then he shut the door, and she heard the key turn in the lock.

"Father, I can't stay in here," cried Ellen. She ran towards the other door into the front hall, but before she could reach it she heard the key turn in that also. Andrew was convinced that Eva had escaped from the asylum, and thus made sure of Ellen's safety in case she was violent. Then he rushed out into the kitchen, and there was Amabel clinging to her mother like a little wild thing, and Fanny weeping aloud.

When Andrew entered Fanny flew to him. "O Andrew—O Andrew!" she cried. "Eva's come out! She's well! she's cured! She's as well as anybody! She is! She says so, and I know she is! Only look at her!"

"Mamma, mamma!" gasped Amabel, in a strange, little, pent voice, which did not sound like a child's. There was something fairly inhuman about it. "Mamma," as she said it, did not sound like a word in any known language. It was like a cry of universal childhood for its parent. Amabel clung to her mother, not only with her slender little arms, but with her legs and breast and neck; all her slim body became as a vine with tendrils of love and growth around her mother.

As for Eva, she could not have enough of her. She

544

was intoxicated with the possession of this little creature of her own flesh and blood.

"She's grown; she's grown so tall," she said, in a high, panting voice. It was all she could seem to realize —the fact that the child had grown so tall—and it filled her at once with ineffable pain and delight. She held the little thing so close to her that the two seemed fairly one. "Mamma, mamma!" said Amabel again.

"She has—grown so tall," panted Eva.

Fanny went up to her and tried gently to loosen her grasp of the little girl. In her heart she was not yet quite sure of her. This fierceness of delight began to alarm her. "Of course she has grown tall, Eva Tenny," she said. "It's quite a while since you were— taken sick."

"I ain't sick now," said Eva, in a steady voice. "I'm cured now. The doctors say so. You needn't be afraid, Fanny Brewster."

"Mamma, mamma!" said Amabel. Eva bent down and kissed the little, delicate face; then she looked at her sister and at Andrew, and her own countenance seemed fairly illuminated. "I 'ain't *told* you all," said she. Then she stopped and hesitated.

"What is it, Eva?" asked Fanny, looking at her with increasing courage. The tears were streaming openly down her cheeks. "Oh, you poor girl, what have you been through?" she said. "What is it?"

"I 'ain't got to go through anything more," said Eva, still with that rapt look over Amabel's little, fair head. "He's—come back."

"Eva Tenny!"

"Yes, he has," Eva went on, with such an air of inexpressible triumph that it had almost a religious quality in it. "He has. He left her a long time ago. He—he wanted to come back to me and Amabel, but he was ashamed, but finally he came to the asylum,

2 M   545

and then it all rolled off, all the trouble. The doctors said I had been getting better, but they didn't know. It was—Jim's comin' back. He's took me home, and I've come for Amabel, and—he's got a job in Lloyd's, and he's bought me this new hat and cape." Eva flirted her free arm, and a sweep of jetted silk gleamed, then she tossed her head consciously to display a hat with a knot of pink roses. Then she kissed Amabel again. "Mamma's come back," she whispered.

"Mamma, mamma!" cried Amabel.

Andrew and Fanny looked at each other.

"Where is he?" asked Andrew, in a slow, halting voice.

Eva glanced from one to the other defiantly. "He's outside, waitin' in the road," said she; "but he ain't comin' in unless you treat him just the same as ever. I've set my veto on that." Eva's voice and manner as she said that were so unmistakably her own that all Fanny's doubt of her sanity vanished. She sobbed aloud.

"O God, I'm so thankful! She's come home, and she's all right! O God, I'm so thankful!"

"What about Jim?" asked Eva, with her old, proud, defiant look.

"Of course he's comin' in," sobbed Fanny. "Andrew, you go—"

But Andrew had already gone, unlocking the parlor door on his way. "It's your aunt Eva, Ellen," he said as he passed. "She's come home cured, and your uncle Jim is out in the yard, and I'm goin' to call him in. I guess you'd better go out and see her."

CHAPTER LX

LLOYD'S had been running for two months, and spring had fairly begun. It was a very forward season. The elms were leafed out, the cherry and peach blossoms had fallen, and the apple-trees were in full flower. There were many orchards around Rowe. The little city was surrounded with bowing garlands of tenderest white and rose, the well-kept lawns in the city limits were like velvet, and golden-spiked bushes and pink trails of flowering almond were beside the gates. Lilacs also, flushed with rose, purpled the walls of old houses. One morning Ellen, on her way to the factory, had for the first time that year a realization of the full presence of the spring. All at once she knew the goddess to be there in her whole glory.

"Spring has really come," she said to Abby. As she spoke she jostled a great bush of white flowers, growing in a yard close to the sidewalk, and an over-powering fragrance, like a very retaliation of sweet-ness, came in her face.

"Yes," said Abby; "it seems more like spring than it did last night, somehow!" Abby had gained flesh, and there was a soft color on her cheeks, so that she was almost pretty, as she glanced abroad with a sort of bright gladness and a face ready with smiles. Maria also looked in better health than she had done in the winter. She walked with her arm through Ellen's.

Suddenly a carriage, driven rapidly, passed them, and Cynthia Lennox's graceful profile showed like a drooping white flower in a window.

547

Sadie Peel came up to them with a swift run. "Say!" she said, "know who that was?"

"We've got eyes," replied Abby Atkins, shortly.

"Who said you hadn't? You needn't be so up an' comin', Abby Atkins; I didn't know as you knew they were married, that's all. I just heard it from Lottie Snell, whose sister works at the dressmaker's that made the wedding fix. Weddin' fix! My land! Think of a weddin' without a white dress and a veil! All she had was a gray silk and a black velvet, and a black lace, and a travellin'-dress!"

Abby Atkins eyed the other girl sharply, her curiosity getting the better of her dislike. "Who did she marry?" said she, shortly. "I suppose she didn't marry the black velvet, or the lace, or the travelling-dress. That's all you seem to think about."

"I *thought* you didn't know," replied Sadie Peel, in a tone of triumph. "They've kept it mighty still, and he's been goin' there so long, ever since anybody can remember, that they didn't think it was anything more now than it had been right along. Lyman Risley and Cynthia Lennox have just got married, and they've gone down to Old Point Comfort. My land, it's nice to have money, if you be half blind!"

Ellen looked after the retreating carriage, and made no comment.

She was pale and thin, and moved with a certain languor, although she held up her head proudly, and when people asked if she were not well, answered quickly that she had never been better. Robert had not been to see her yet. She had furtively watched for him a long time, then she had given it up. She would not acknowledge to herself or any one else that she was not well or was troubled in spirit. Her courage was quite equal to the demand upon it, yet always she was aware of a peculiar sensitiveness to all happenings, whether directly concerned with herself or not, which made life an agony to her, and she knew that her physical strength was not what it had been. Only that morning she had looked at her face in the glass, and had seen how it was altered. The lovely color was gone from her cheeks, there were little, faint, downward lines about her mouth, and, more than that, out of her blue eyes looked the eternal, unanswerable question of humanity, "Where is my happiness?"

It seemed to her when she first set out that she could not walk to the factory. That sense of the full presence of the spring seemed to overpower her. All the revelation of beauty and sweetness seemed a refinement of torture worse to bear than the sight of death and misery would have been. Every blooming apple-bough seemed to strike her full on the heart.

"Only look at that bush of red flowers in that yard," Maria said once, and Ellen looked and was stung by the sight as by the contact of a red flaming torch of spring. "What ails you, dear; don't you like those flowers?" Maria said, anxiously.

"Yes, of course I do; I think they are lovely," replied Ellen, looking.

She looked after the carriage which contained the bridal party; she thought how the bridegroom had almost lost his eyesight to save her, and her old adoration of Cynthia seemed to rise to a flood-tide. Then came the thought of Robert, how he must have ceased to love her—how some day he would be starting off on a bridal trip of his own. Maud Hemingway, with whom she had often coupled him in her thoughts, seemed to start up before her, all dressed in bridal white. It seemed to her that she could not bear it all. She continued walking, but she did not feel the ground beneath her feet, nor even Maria's little, clinging fingers of tenderness on her arm. She became to her own understanding like an instrument which is played upon with such results of harmonies and discords that all sense of the mechanism is lost.

"Well, Ellen Brewster," said Sadie Peel, in her loud, strident voice, "I guess you wouldn't have been walkin' along here·quite so fine this mornin' if it hadn't been for Mr. Risley. You'd ought to send him a weddin'-present—a spoon, or something."

"Shut up," said Abby Atkins; "Ellen has worried herself sick over him as it is." She eyed Ellen anxiously as she spoke. Maria clung more closely to her.

"Shut up yourself, Abby Atkins," returned Sadie Peel. "He's got a wife to lead him around, and I don't see much to worry about. A great weddin'! My goodness, if I don't get married when I'm young enough to wear a white dress and veil, catch me gettin' married at all!"

Sadie Peel sped on with her news to a group of girls ahead, and the wheels of the carriage flashed out of sight in the spring sunlight. It was quite true that Risley and Cynthia had been married that morning. He had not entirely lost his vision, although it would always be· poor, and he would live happily, although in a measure disappointedly, feeling that his partial helplessness was his chief claim upon his wife's affection. He had gotten what he had longed for for so many years, but by means which tended to his humiliation instead of his pride. But Cynthia was radiant. In caring for her half-blind husband she attained the spiritual mountain height of her life. She possessed love in the one guise in which he appealed to her, and she held him fast to the illumination of her very soul.

After the carriage had passed out of sight Abby came close on the other side of Ellen and slid her arm through hers. "Say!" she began.

"What is it?" asked Ellen.

Abby blushed. "Oh, nothing much," she replied, in a tone unusual for her. She took her arm away from Ellen's, and laughed a little foolishly.

Ellen stared at her with grave wonder. She had not the least idea what she meant.

Abby changed the subject. "Going to the park opening to-night, Ellen?" she asked.

"No, I guess not."

"You'd better. Do go, Ellen."

"Yes, do go, Ellen; it will do you good," said Maria. She looked into Ellen's face with the inexpressibly pure love of one innocent girl for another.

The park was a large grove of oaks and birch-trees which had recently been purchased by the street railway company of Rowe, and it was to be used for the free entertainment of the people, with an undercurrent of consideration for the financial profit of the company.

"I'm afraid I can't go," said Ellen.

"Yes, you can; it will do you good; you look like a ghost this morning," said Abby.

"Do go, Ellen," pleaded Maria.

However, Ellen would not have gone had it not been for a whisper of Abby's as they came out of the factory that night.

"Look here, Ellen, you'd better go," said she, "just to show folks. That Sadie Peel asked me this noon if it was true that you had something on your mind, and was worrying about—well, you know what—that made you look so."

Ellen flushed an angry red. "I'll stop for you and Maria to-night," she answered, quickly.

"All right," Abby replied, heartily; "we'll go on the eight-o'clock car."

Ellen hurried home, and changed her dress after supper, putting on her new green silk waist and her spring hat, which was trimmed with roses. When she went down-stairs, and told her mother where she was going, she started up.

"I declare, I'd go too if your father had come home," she said. "I don't know when I've been anywhere; and Eva was in this afternoon and said that she and Jim were going."

"I wonder where father is?" said Ellen, uneasily. "I don't know as I ought to go till he comes home."

"Oh, stuff!" replied Fanny. "He's stopped to talk at the store. Oh, here he is now. Andrew Brewster, where in the world have you been?" she began as he entered; but his mother was following him, and something in their faces stopped her. Fanny Brewster had lived for years with this man, but never before had she seen his face with just that expression of utter, unreserved joy; although joy was scarcely the word for it, for it was more than that. It was the look of a man who has advanced to his true measure of growth, and regained self-respect which he had lost. All the abject bend of his aging back, all the apologetic patience of his outlook, was gone. She stared at him, hardly believing her eyes. She was as frightened as if he had looked despairing instead of joyful. "Andrew Brewster, what is it?" she asked. She tried to smile, to echo the foolish width of grimace on his face, but her lips were too stiff.

Ellen looked at him, trembling, and very white under her knot of roses. Andrew held out a paper and tried to speak, but he could not.

"For God's sake, what is it?" gasped Fanny.

Then Mrs. Zelotes spoke. "That old mining-stock has come up," said she, in a harsh voice. "He'd never ought to have bought it. I should have told him better if he had asked me, but it's come up, and it's worth considerable more than he paid for it. I've just been down to Mrs. Pointdexter's, and Lawyer Samson was

552

in there seeing her about a bond she's got that's run
out, and he says the mine's going to pay dividends, and
for Andrew to hold on to part of it, anyhow. I bought
this paper, and it's in it. He never ought to have bought
it, but it's come up. I hope it will learn him a lesson.
He's had enough trouble over it."

Nothing could exceed the mixture of recrimination
and exultation with which the old woman spoke. She
eyed Fanny accusingly; she looked at Andrew with
grudging triumph. "Lawyer Samson says it will
make him rich, he guesses; at any rate, he'll come out
whole," said she. "I hope it will learn you a lesson."

Andrew dropped into a chair. His face was distended
with a foolish smile like a baby's. He seemed to smile
at all creation. He looked at his wife and Ellen; then
his face again took on its expression of joyful vacuity.

Fanny went close to him and laid a firm hand on
his shoulder. "You 'ain't had a mite of supper, Andrew Brewster," said she; "come right out and have
something to eat."

Andrew shook his head, still smiling. His wife and
daughter looked at him alarmedly, then at each other.
Then his mother went behind him, laid a hard, old hand
on each shoulder, and shook him.

"If you *have* got a streak of luck, there's no need
of your actin' like a fool about it, Andrew Brewster,"
said she. "Go out and eat your supper, and behave
yourself, and let it be a lesson to you. There you had
worked and saved that little money you had in the bank,
and you bought an old mine with it, and it might have
turned out there wasn't a thing in it, no mine at all, and
there was. Just let it be a lesson to you, that's all;
and go out and eat your supper, and don't be too set up
over it."

Andrew looked at his wife and mother and daughter,
still with that expression of joy, so unreserved that it

553

was almost idiotic. They had all stood by him loyally; he had their fullest sympathy; but had one of them fully understood? Not one of them could certainly understand what was then passing in his mind, which had been straitened by grief and self-reproach, and was now expanding to hold its full measure of joy. That poor little sum in the bank, that accumulation of his hard earnings, which he had lost through his own bad judgment, had meant much more than itself to him, both in its loss and its recovery. It was more than money; it was the value of money in the current coin of his own self-respect.

His mother shook him again, but rather gently. "Get up this minute, and go out and eat your supper," said she; "and then I don't see why you can't go with Fanny and me to the park opening. They say lots of folks are goin', and there's goin' to be fireworks. It'll distract your mind. It ain't safe for anybody to dwell too much on good luck any more than on misfortune. Go right out and eat your supper; it's most time for the car."

Andrew obeyed.

CHAPTER LXI

THE new park, which had been named, in honor of the president of the street railway company, Clemens Park, was composed of a light growth of oak and birch trees. With the light of the full moon, like a broadside of silvery arrows, and the frequent electric-lights filtering through the young, delicate foliage, it was much more effective than a grove of pine or hemlock would have been.

When the people streamed into it from the crowded electric-cars, there were exclamations of rapture. Women and girls fairly shrieked with delight. The ground, which had been entirely cleared of undergrowth, was like an etching in clearest black and white, of the tender dancing foliage of the oaks and birches. The birches stood together in leaning, white-limbed groups like maidens, and the rustling spread of the oaks shed broad flashes of silver from the moon. In the midst of the grove the Hungarian orchestra played in a pavilion, and dancing was going on there. Many of the people outside moved with dancing steps. Children in swings flew through the airs with squeals of delight. There was a stand for the sale of ice-cream and soda, and pretty girls blossomed like flowers behind the counters. There were various rustic adornments, such as seats and grottos, and at one end of the grove was a small collection of wild animals in cages, and a little artificial pond with swans. Now and then, above the chatter of the people and the music of the orchestra, sounded the growl of a bear or the shrill screech of a paroquet, and the people all stopped and listened and laughed. This little titillation of the unusual in the midst of their sober walk of life affected them like champagne. Most of them were of the poorer and middle classes, the employés of the factories of Rowe. They moved back and forth with dancing steps of exultation.

"My, ain't it beautiful!" Fanny said, squeezing Andrew's arm. He had his wife on one arm, his mother on the other. For him the whole scene appeared more than it really was, since it reflected the joy of his own soul. There was for him a light greater than that of the moon or electricity upon it — that extreme light of the world — the happiness of a human being who blesses in a moment of prosperity the hour he was born. He knew for the first time in his life that happiness is as true as misery, and no mere creation of a fairy tale. No trees of the Garden of Eden could have outshone for him those oaks and birches. No gold or precious stones of any mines on earth can equal the light of the little star of happiness in one human soul.

Fanny, as they walked along, kept looking at her husband, and her own face was transfigured. Mrs. Zelotes, also, seemed to radiate with a sort of harsh and prickly delight. She descanted upon the hard-earned savings which Andrew had risked, but she held her old head very high with reluctant joy, and her bonnet had a rakish cant.

Ellen, with Abby and Maria, walked behind them.

Presently Andrew met another man who had also purchased stock in the mine, and stopped to exchange congratulations. The man's face was flushed, as if he had been drinking, but he had not. On his arm hung his wife, a young woman with a showy red waist and some pink ribbon bows on her hat. She was teetering a little in time to the music, while a little girl clung to her skirts and teetered also.

556

"Well, old man," said the new-comer, with a hoarse sound in his throat, "they needn't talk to us any more, need they?"

"That's so," replied Andrew, but his joy in prosperity was not like the other man's. It placed him heights above him, although from the same cause. Prosperity means one thing to one man, and another to his brother. Presently they met Jim Tenny and Eva and Amabel. They were walking three abreast, Amabel in the middle. Jim Tenny looked hesitatingly at them, although his face was widened with irrepressible smiles. Eva gazed at them with defiant radiance. "Well," said she, "so luck has turned?"

Amabel laughed out, and her laugh trilled high with a note of silver, above the chatter of the crowd and the blare and rhythmic trill of the orchestra. "I've had an ice-cream, and I'm going to have a new doll and a doll-carriage," said she. "Oh, Ellen!" She left her father and mother for a second and clung to Ellen, kissing her; then she was back.

"Well, Andrew?" said Jim. He had a shamed face, yet there was something brave in it struggling for expression.

"Well, Jim?" said Andrew.

The two shook hands solemnly. Then they walked on together, and the sisters behind, with Amabel clinging to her mother's hand. "Jim's goin' to work if he *has* had a little windfall," said Eva, proudly. "Oh, Fanny, only think what it means!"

"I hope it will be a lesson to both of them," said Mrs. Zelotes, stalking along after, but she smiled harshly.

"Oh, land, don't croak, if you've got a chance to laugh! There's few enough chances in this world," cried Eva, with boisterous good humor. "As for me, I've come out of deep waters, and I'm goin' to take what comfort I can in the feel of the solid ground under my feet." She began to force Amabel into a dance in time with the music, and the child shrieked with laughter.

"S'pose she's all right?" whispered Mrs. Zelotes to Fanny.

"Land, yes," replied Fanny; "it's just like her, just the way she used to do. It makes me surer than anything else that she's cured."

The girls behind were loitering. Abby turned to Ellen and pointed to a rustic seat under a clump of birches.

"Let's sit down there a minute, Ellen," said she.

"All right," replied Ellen. When she and Abby seated themselves, Maria withdrew, standing aloof under an oak, looking up at the illumined spread of branches with the rapt, innocent expression of a saint.

"Why don't you come and sit down with us, Maria?" Ellen called.

"In a minute," replied Maria, in her weak, sweet voice. Then John Sargent came up and joined her.

"She'll come in a minute," Abby said to Ellen. "She —she—knows I want to tell you something."

Abby hesitated. Ellen regarded her with wonder.

"Look here, Ellen," said Abby; "I don't know what you're going to think of me after all I've said, but—I'm going to get married to Willy Jones. His mother has had a little money left her, and she owns the house clear now, and I'm going to keep right on working; and—I never thought I would, Ellen, you know; but I've come to think lately that all you can get out of labor in this world is the happiness it brings you, and—the love. That's more than the money, and—he wants me pretty bad. I suppose you think I'm awful, Ellen Brewster." Abby spoke with triumph, yet with shame. She dug her little toe into the shadow-mottled ground.

"Oh, Abby, I hope you'll be real happy," said Ellen. Then she choked a little.

"I've made up my mind not to work for nothing,"

said Abby; "I've made up my mind to get whatever work is worth in this world if I can, and—to get it for him too."

"I hope you will be very happy," said Ellen again.

"There he is now," whispered Abby. She rose as Willy Jones approached, laughing confusedly. "I've been telling Ellen Brewster," said Abby, with her perfunctory air.

Ellen held out her hand, and Willy Jones grasped it, then let it drop and muttered something. He looked with helpless adoration at Abby, who put her hand through his arm reassuringly.

"Let's go and see the animals," said she; "I haven't seen the animals."

"I guess I'll go and see if I can find my father and mother," returned Ellen. "I want to see my mother about something."

"Oh, come with us." Abby grasped Ellen firmly around the waist and kissed her. "I don't love him a mite better than I do you," she whispered; "so there! You needn't think you're left out, Ellen Brewster."

"I don't," replied Ellen. She tried to laugh, but she felt her lips stiff. An unconquerable feeling of desolation was coming over her, and in spite of herself her tone was somewhat like that of a child who sees another with all the cake.

"I suppose you know Floretta got married last night," said Abby, moving off with Willy Jones. John Sargent and Maria had long since disappeared from under the oak.

Ellen, left alone, looked for a minute after Abby and Willy, and noted the tender lean of the girl's head towards the young man's shoulder; then she started off to find her father and mother. She could not rid herself of the sense of desolation. She felt blindly that if she could not get under the shelter of her own loves of life she could not bear it any longer. She had borne up bravely

559

under Robert's neglect, but now all at once, with the sight of the happiness of these others before her eyes, it seemed to crush her. All the spirit in her seemed to flag and faint. She was only a young girl, who would fall to the ground and be slain by the awful law of gravitation of the spirit without love. "Anyway, I've got father and mother," she said to herself.

She rushed on alone through the merry crowd. The orchestra was playing a medley. The violins seemed to fairly pierce thought. A Roman-candle burst forth on the right with a great spluttering, and the people, shrieking with delight, rushed in that direction. Then a rocket shot high in the air with a splendid curve, and there was a sea of faces watching with speechless admiration the dropping stars of violet and gold and rose.

Ellen kept on, moving as nearly as she could in the direction in which her party had gone. Then suddenly she came face to face with Robert Lloyd.

She would have passed him without a word, but he stood before her.

"Won't you speak to me?" he asked.

"Good-evening, Mr. Lloyd," returned Ellen.

Then she tried to move on again, but Robert still stood before her.

"I want to say something to you," he said, in a low voice. "I was coming to your house to-night, but I saw you on the car. Please come to that seat over there. There is nobody in that direction. They will all go towards the fireworks now."

Ellen looked at him hesitatingly. At that moment she seemed to throw out protecting antennæ of maiden-liness; and, besides, there was always the memory of the cut in wages, for which she still judged him; and then there was the long neglect.

"Please come," said Robert. He looked at her at

once like a conqueror and a pleading child. Ellen placed her hand on his arm, and they went to the seat under the clump of birches. They were quite alone, for the whole great company was streaming towards the fireworks. A fiery wheel was revolving in the distance, and rockets shot up, dropping showers of stars. Ellen gazed at them without seeing them at all.

Robert, seated beside her, looked at her earnestly. "I am going to put back the wages on the old basis to-morrow," he said.

Ellen made no reply.

"Business has so improved that I feel justified in doing so," said Robert. His tone was almost apologetic. Never as long as he lived would he be able to look at such matters from quite the same standpoint as that of the girl beside him. She knew that, and yet she loved him. She never would get his point of view, and yet he loved her. "I have waited until I was able to do that before speaking to you again," said Robert. "I knew how you felt about the wage-cutting. I thought when matters were back on the old basis that you might feel differently towards me. God knows I have been sorry enough for it all, and I am glad enough to be able to pay them full wages again. And now, dear?"

"It has been a long time," said Ellen, looking at her little hands, clasped in her lap.

"I have loved you all the time, and I have only waited for that," said Robert.

Later on Robert and Ellen joined Fanny and the others. It was scarcely the place to make an announcement. After a few words of greeting the young couple walked off together, and left the Brewsters and Tennys and Mrs. Zelotes standing on the outskirts of the crowd watching the fireworks. Granville Joy stood near them. He had looked at Robert and Ellen with a white

face, then he turned again towards the fireworks with a
gentle, heroic expression. He caught up Amabel that
she might see the set piece which was just being put up.
"Now you can see, Sissy," he said.

Eva looked away from the fireworks after the retreating pair, then meaningly at Fanny and Andrew.
"That's settled," said she.

Andrew's face quivered a little, and took on something of the same look which Granville Joy's wore.
All love is at the expense of love, and calls for
heroes.

"It 'll be a great thing for her," said Fanny, in his
ear; "it 'll be a splendid thing for her, you know that,
Andrew."

Andrew gazed after the nodding roses on Ellen's hat
vanishing towards the right. Another rocket shot up,
and the people cried out, and watched the shower of stars
with breathless enjoyment. Andrew saw their up-
turned faces, in which for the while toil and trial were
blotted out by that delight in beauty and innocent pleasure of the passing moment which is, for human souls,
akin to the refreshing showers for flowers of spring;
and to him, since his own vision was made clear by
his happiness, came a mighty realization of it all, which
was beyond it all. Another rocket described a wonderful golden curve of grace, then a red light lit all the
watching people. Andrew looked for Ellen and Robert,
and saw the girl's beautiful face turning backward
over her lover's shoulder. All his life Andrew had
been a reader of the Bible, as had his father and mother
before him. To-day, ever since he had heard of his
good fortune, his mind had dwelt upon certain verses
of Ecclesiastes. Now he quoted from them. "Live
joyfully with the wife whom thou lovest all the days
of the life of thy vanity, which He hath given thee under
the sun, all the days of thy vanity, for that is thy por-

tion in this life and in thy labor which thou takest under the sun."

Ellen saw her father, and smiled and nodded, then she and her lover passed out of sight. Another rocket trailed its golden parabola along the sky, and dropped with stars; there was an ineffably sweet strain from the orchestra; the illuminated oaks tossed silver and golden boughs in a gust of fragrant wind. Andrew quoted again from the old King of Wisdom—"I withheld not my heart from any joy, for my heart rejoiced in all my labor, and that was my portion of labor." Then Andrew thought of the hard winter which had passed, as all hard things must pass, of the toilsome lives of those beside him, of all the work which they had done with their poor, knotted hands, of the tracks which they had worn on the earth towards their graves, with their weary feet, and suddenly he seemed to grasp a new and further meaning for that verse of Ecclesiastes.

He seemed to see that labor is not alone for itself, not for what it accomplishes of the tasks of the world, not for its equivalent in silver and gold, not even for the end of human happiness and love, but for the growth in character of the laborer.

"That is the portion of labor," he said. He spoke in a strained, solemn voice, as he had done before. Nobody heard him except his wife and mother. His mother gave a sidewise glance at him, then she folded her cape tightly around her and stared at the fireworks, but Fanny put her hand through his arm and leaned her cheek against his shoulder.

THE END

THE GOOD SOLDIER ŠVEJK

JAROSLAV HAŠEK

THE GOOD SOLDIER ŠVEJK

AND HIS FORTUNES IN THE WORLD WAR

IN A NEW AND UNABRIDGED TRANSLATION
BY CECIL PARROTT
WITH THE ORIGINAL ILLUSTRATIONS
BY JOSEF LADA

THOMAS Y. CROWELL COMPANY
NEW YORK   ESTABLISHED 1834

Manufactured in the United States of America

Library of Congress Cataloging in Publication Data

Hašek, Jaroslav, 1883-1923.
The good soldier Švejk and his fortunes in the
World War.

Translation of Osudy dobrého vojaka Švejka za
světové války.
I. Lada, Josef, 1887-1957, illus. II. Title.
PZ3.H2693Go20   [PG5038.H28]   891.8'6'35
ISBN 0-690-00466-4 (pbk)   73-13703
ISBN 0-690-00123-1

3   4   5   6   7   8   9   10

Contents

THE GOOD SOLDIER ŠVEJK

Part I · Behind the Lines

Part II · At the Front

Introduction

JAROSLAV HAŠEK, the author of *The Good Soldier Švejk*, was a true bohemian within the meaning of the term 'La Bohème' but a very untypical Czech. The son of an impoverished schoolmaster who drank himself to death, he was left at the age of thirteen without adequate parental control and quickly acquired the tastes and habits of a hobo or beatnik.

This born truant first saw the light of day in Prague on 30 April 1883 in a house in a street called appropriately enough Školská, or 'School Street'. At school he was idle and in the family's straitened circumstances after his father's death he was offered employment in a chemist's shop belonging to a Mr Kokoška. This brief episode in his life is reflected not only in *The Good Soldier Švejk* but also in his stories *From an Old Chemist's Shop*. Thus already in his teens Hašek was beginning to store up material for later literary use.

In 1899 at the age of sixteen he was admitted to the recently founded Czechoslavonic Commercial Academy, where for the first time he appears to have done a little study and to have acquitted himself creditably. But he also began to develop a taste for what were to be the main occupations of his life – writing and vagrancy. A Prague newspaper, *Národní listy*, published anonymously his first story at a time when the young author was making vacation trips in Moravia, Slovakia, Hungary and Galicia. He set off without a penny in his pocket and supported himself by begging, consorting with gipsies, tramps and vagabonds and acquiring many bad habits from them.

His good record at the Commercial Academy won Hašek a place in the Slavia Bank in 1902 but he threw it up and went off to Slovakia instead. A few weeks later he returned and was indulgently taken back, but when a month later he absconded on another jaunt he was justifiably given notice. From then on he resolved to try to live by his writing, but in the course of the eight years from 1900 to 1908 he was only able to get published 185 short feuilletons – a quite insufficient number to enable him to support himself in a regular existence.

Not only was Hašek a true bohemian: he was a born mischief-maker and hoaxer as well. As a schoolboy he had taken part in the anti-German riots in Prague in 1897, tearing down proclamations of martial law, damaging emblems of the Austro-Hungarian monarchy, breaking windows of government offices and joyfully helping to set fire to the yard of a Prague German. In 1906 he systematized these perverse proclivities by joining the anarchist movement, which naturally led to further conflicts with the police and short periods of arrest and imprisonment. But in the same year he encountered a new and unexpected influence. He met Jarmila Mayerová, the daughter of a Prague stucco decorator, and fell deeply in love with her. But there was trouble in store for him because his vagabond life and radical convictions were unlikely to find favour with her respectable bourgeois parents.

In 1907 his anarchist activities increased. He became editor of the anarchist journal *Komuna* and gave lectures to miners and textile workers in the provinces. Austrian police informers reported that he was particularly dangerous and his movements were closely watched. During an anarchist demonstration he was arrested for assaulting a police constable and sentenced to a month's imprisonment. From gaol he sent out love poems to Jarmila, as a result of which her father tried to prevent her from seeing any more of him and instructed her to warn him that any further anarchist involvement on his part would make it impossible for them to see each other again, let alone think of marriage. Hašek promised to give up anarchism, but continued to go about in such ragged clothes that his future father-in-law insisted that if he was to be a serious contender for Jarmila's hand he must at least dress himself decently and find some permanent employment. Again Hašek promised to obey. His conflicts with the police became fewer. The following year he was only summonsed twice, once because he tried to tear down a flag on the Wenceslas Square and another time for breach of public order. But this was more than Jarmila's parents could tolerate and they took their daughter away from Prague. Her undesirable but importunate suitor followed her all the way into the country and when he had no money for his railway ticket back to Prague he tramped the whole sixty miles on foot.

In 1909 he seemed to be making a genuine effort to prove to Jarmila's parents that he was capable of maintaining himself and her. In this year he wrote sixty-four stories, most of which were published in the paper *Karikatury*, which was edited by the artist Josef Lada, the illustrator of the present edition of *The Good Soldier Švejk*. Later he succeeded a journalist friend of his as editor of a journal called *The Animal World*, but was soon dismissed for writing articles about non-existent animals which he had invented – in fact exactly what Marek claimed to have done in the present book.

Preparations for the wedding were now under way and Jarmila's parents insisted that it must be celebrated in a church. For this purpose Hašek had to agree to return to the Catholic fold, which he had deserted some three years earlier. The wedding finally took place on 13 May 1910. Hašek now had his Jarmila, but his marriage with her inevitably brought him into circles where he was unlikely to feel at his ease. Nevertheless 1910 was a bumper year for his literary output and he wrote and published seventy-five stories.

In 1911 he published in *Karikatury* the first of his stories about 'The Good Soldier Švejk'. They consisted of a number of tales about a soldier who had not quite yet developed into the famous character of the present book but bore a strong resemblance to him. The next year they were included in a book of short stories under the title of *The Good Soldier Švejk and Other Strange Stories*, although the Švejk stories only took up twenty-nine pages. Meanwhile Hašek had shown himself utterly incapable of living a regular life or of keeping up to the standards which Jarmila and her parents demanded of him. He had already perpetrated little hoaxes on the readers of *The Animal World*. He now carried this art a stage farther by pretending one day to commit suicide by jumping off the Charles Bridge at the spot where the legendary St John of Nepomuk was thrown into the water. The police were called and took him off to a mental home. Here he was able to gather material for the passages in the present book which describe Švejk's adventures among the lunatics. After that Hašek took it into his head to form his own 'cynological institute' (his own pretentious name for a dog-fancier's shop). He was helped in the business by Jarmila and again his experiences in this pursuit are to be found in the pages not only of this book but of others of his works too. A year or two later he was to publish an article, 'Cynological Institute', in the fashionable Prague illustrated, *Světozor*. He explained how he had found the word 'cynological' in an encyclopedia, and had hit on the name 'institute' after walking past the Agricultural Institute. 'I am now at last the owner of an Institute,' he wrote.

His next escapade was to found a new political party called '*The Party of Moderate and Peaceful Progress Within the Limits of the Law*'. It was the time of the elections to the Austro-Hungarian parliament and he stood as a candidate for it, publicly debunking the monarchy, its institutions and its social and political system. Of course it was only another hoax, designed partly to satisfy Hašek's innate thirst for exhibitionism and partly to bolster the finances of the pub where the election meetings were held.

In 1912 Jarmila bore him a son, Richard, but the marriage had not proved a happy one and was soon to break up. Hašek lost a promising job with a leading Prague paper after publicly attacking the leaders of the political party controlling it. Jarmila left him and went to live with her parents, while Hašek reverted to his former bohemian existence. He continued to write prolifically and could now draw on his experiences of married life. His breach with Jarmila led to his almost total alienation from society and from now on he lived in the 'underground'. He was not registered anywhere and the police searched for him in vain.

The outbreak of the First World War found him living spasmodically with the cartoonist Lada, who afterwards related that Hašek wrote many stories and cooked many wonderful meals during his stay with him. Indeed, he had the reputation of being as talented a cook as he was a writer, and the culinary details in *The Good Soldier Švejk* merit serious study.

It was at this time that Hašek perpetrated what was probably his most daring hoax. He has collected around him as many legends as the saints, and one version of what happened is as follows. He decided to fool the authorities by taking a room at U Valšů, which was notorious for being half-hotel and half-brothel, and registering himself there as a Russian. The name he wrote in the visitor's book sounded Russian enough, but when read backwards in Czech it became 'Kiss my arse.' When required to state what he was doing in Prague he wrote that he was looking into the activities of the Austrian general staff. At the time war fever was at its height and the police were at once alerted and the hotel surrounded. They thought they had caught an important spy and were disappointed and embarrassed when they found that it was none other than the by now notorious hooligan Hašek. Asked why he had done it Hašek replied in all innocence that he had wanted to assure himself that the Austrian police were operating effectively. He got off lightly with only five days' imprisonment.

In 1915 he was called up and drafted to the 91st Infantry Regiment in České Budějovice – the very same regiment to which Švejk himself belonged. Like Marek in *The Good Soldier Švejk* he was admitted as a one-year volunteer and the privileges of his rank were later withdrawn from him. In his case it was because it had been subsequently discovered that he was entered on the police records as a dangerous anarchist. From Southern Bohemia the 91st soon moved to Királyhida in Hungary and from there to the front.

During his brief spell in the regiment Hašek carefully observed the officers, N.C.O.s and men he came into contact with – especially his battalion commander, Captain Ságner, his company commander, Lieutenant Lukas, the lieutenant in the reserve, Mechálek, and finally Lieutenant Lukas's batman, a private called Strašlipka. The names of all these men, who were to appear later under the same or different names in *The Good Soldier Švejk*, could afterwards be found in the records of the 91st regiment. Hašek was particularly attached to Lieutenant Lukas. He was not in fact Lukas's batman but served under him, admired him greatly and wrote a number of poems to him. The lieutenant, who lived in retirement in the Czechoslovak Republic after the war, kept the poems long after Hašek's death, but after his own death they unaccountably disappeared.

Hašek also saw a lot of the quartermaster sergeant-major, Vaněk, whom he assisted with the accounts and whose office he shared. Lieutenant Mechálek was the model for the notorious Lieutenant Dub. There is mention too of a Cadet Biegler and a Major Wenzel in the records, but no trace of any Josef Švejk or of a one-year volunteer Marek. It appears that Hašek took the name of Josef Švejk from a respectable parliamentary deputy of that name. It is to be presumed that for the characters of Švejk and Marek he drew on his own personal experiences, except that Strašlipka, the real batman, seems to have been part model for Švejk. Photographs are preserved of these various members of the regiment and they have little in common with the illustrations which Lada drew and are included in this volume. The photograph of Strašlipka is much closer to the image the reader forms of Švejk than Lada's brilliant but farcical caricatures. Hašek himself never saw any of the illustrations contained in the present volume but they have now become inseparable from the book.

Hašek's long trek by train and on foot from Királyhida to the front in Galicia provided him with the material for the journey he describes in the book. But he did not stay long at the front. He was taken prisoner on 23 September 1915 after having been cut off in a dug-out as the result of a sudden Russian breakthrough. Although Lieutenant Lukas personally tried to persuade him to retreat with the others he would not follow them and gave himself up to the Russians.

Conditions in the Russian prisoner-of-war camps at that time were terrible, not least for the Czechs. The Russians regarded their fellow Slavs as the least privileged category among the prisoners and considered them devoted enough to Mother Russia to be proud to undergo the worst suffering and take upon themselves the most arduous labours. Hašek was sent first to a camp near Kiev and later to another one at Totskoye near the southernmost point of the Urals. Here he was fortunate to be able to escape the worst rigours of the camp by working in the very comfortable office of one of the camp commanders. Like most of the other prisoners he caught spotted typhus but the attack was not a serious one.

One day the news reached him that a military volunteer unit was about to be formed drawn from the Czechs and Slovaks in Russia. It was to be the nucleus of the future Czech Legion and he at once applied to serve in it. He was accepted and immediately employed on recruiting service by the Union of Czech Associations in Russia. His literary gifts predisposed him for journalistic and propaganda work and it was natural that he should be employed in this capacity. In his spare time he worked on a journal, *Čechoslován*, which was published by the Czech colony in Kiev, and it was here that he began to write a second series of stories about Švejk which bore the title *The Good Soldier Švejk In Captivity*. It was published in Kiev in book form in 1917.

It was hardly to be expected that Hašek would be a very reliable employee of the Union and he often caused them embarrassment by his freelance writings. He lampooned the leadership in an article in the *Čechoslován* called 'The Pickwick Club' and was disciplined for it. He was not only strongly pro-Czech and anti-Austrian but very Russophil as well. He greeted the news of the coronation of the new Austrian emperor in 1916 with the words: 'We started our revolution to overthrow the Hapsburg dynasty and call to the Czech throne a member of the great family of the Romanovs.' Even after the Russian February Revolution Hašek continued to express pro-monarchical views and attack the Bolsheviks. But after the October Revolution his views became more radical. He was strongly opposed to plans to send the Legion away from Russia to fight on the Western Front, believing that it should remain on Russian soil and fight the Germans there. When the Legion left Kiev to move into the interior of Russia in preparation for its later transhipment to the West, Hašek did not go with it. At the end of February 1918 he left for Moscow to join the Red Army. A month later he had become a member of the Bolshevik Party. Hašek could no longer agitate for the Legion to fight the Germans in Russia, as the Bolsheviks had signed a peace treaty with the Central Powers on 3 March. The Legion proclaimed him a traitor and issued an order for his arrest. Later Hašek was sent to the town of Samara to work for the Bolsheviks, but after it fell into the hands of the Legion he had hastily to disappear into the Central Asian provinces of Russia disguised as a German colonist. When the Red Army established control in Russia and the Legion was gradually withdrawn Hašek started to make a career for himself in the Russian Bolshevik Party organization – to become in fact an *apparatchik*. In December 1918 he was appointed Deputy Commandant of the town of Bugulma. The Czech Red Army man became the Soviet Commissar Gashek (the Russians, having no 'h' in their alphabet, spell and pronounce his name in this way). The little town has since been immortalized in the amusing stories about Soviet life which the author published on his return to Prague. In 1919 he was appointed Secretary of the Committee of Foreign Communists in the Russian town of Ufa, in the same year Secretary of the Party Cell of the printing office of *The Red Arrow*, and a year later Head of the International Section of the Political Department of the 5th Army. He is also said to have completed a course at the Soviet Communist Party School. More significant was the surprising fact that he gave up drinking and led an orderly and sober life for thirty months.

It seems improbable that Hašek – bohemian and anarchist as he was – would have been able to adapt himself to the rigidities of the Soviet system for any length of time but fortunately he had other options open to him. And when a visiting Czechoslovak Social Democratic delegation invited him to come back and help the party in his own country, he readily agreed. On 19 December 1920 he suddenly turned up in Czechoslovakia and began to write articles in *Rudé Právo*, the organ of the Left Wing of the Social Democratic Party. He could not return to Jarmila, because he had brought another wife with him from Russia. Some say that she was an aristocrat, a relative of Prince Lvov, but it is possible that this was another of Hašek's yarns. None the less he was anxious to re-establish contact with Jarmila and enlist her help in finding permanent employment. But this was no simple task. In the new Republic Hašek was not highly thought of nationally, politically or socially. He was branded as a traitor, a Bolshevik and finally a bigamist. Unable to secure a steady job he drifted back into his drunken vagabond existence of the pre-war years. However, he had to maintain himself and his new Russian wife and this spurred him to try his hand at a complete novel for the first time. Early in 1921 he started writing *The Good Soldier Švejk* and in the summer of the same year moved to Lipnice on the Sázava which lies some hundred miles to the east of Prague and where in its beautiful surroundings he hoped to be able to concentrate on his writing with least disturbance. The novel was to extend to four volumes and no publisher was anxious to handle it. Consequently Hašek was forced to publish the first volume privately and distribute it himself together with his friend, Franta Sauer. But after the success of the initial volume a publisher was found who was ready to take over the remaining parts. Although Hašek did not make much money out of the first volume he earned enough to buy a cottage at Lipnice, where he could begin to dictate the subsequent volumes.

But his renewed irregular life coming on top of his hard existence in Russia had taken a severe toll of his health. After the abstemiousness of thirty months his system could ill support a return to the orgies and excesses of his youth. He fell seriously ill and died on 3 January 1923. The only mourners at his funeral were his eleven-year-old son, Richard, and a few friends. The fourth volume of his book remained unfinished. A friend of his, Karel Vaněk, completed it but the ending, although illustrated by Lada, has been omitted from recent versions because it is not only spurious but generally considered to be of inferior quality. It is not included in the present volume.

Although *The Good Soldier Švejk* was a popular success from the beginning it was not taken seriously by the literary critics for many years. Indeed, books on the First World War did not begin to attract serious notice until some ten years after it had ended. In the immediate post-war years people were still under the spell of the emotions it had unleashed. It had been grand and heroic, from whichever side you

looked at it. Only after a distance of years were people able to free
themselves from this obsession and to view it critically and dispassion-
ately. And for the Czechs it was particularly difficult to do so. Even if
they had been forced to fight on the wrong side many of them had
'done their bit' and were not unproud of it. Some on the other hand
had later deserted to the Russians and helped to form the Czech Legion
there. For a short time the Legion had become the most formidable
force in Russia and had even inflicted defeats on the Red Army. When
the legionaries eventually returned home after the war they became
part of the national legend. And there were many Czechs who thought
then and still do now that Švejk himself is not a good advertisement
for the Czech character. When the new Republic was trying to establish
its identity and reputation abroad patriots did not wish to be associated in the minds of foreign readers with the qualities which seemed
to characterize Švejk. But these fears were unjustified. Although
'Schweikism' is a word often used to characterize the passive resistance of the Czechs, anyone who reads the book carefully and knows
the Czechs will perceive that Švejk is not necessarily a Czech figure.
He might be any Central European and is in fact a 'Mr Everyman',
in the sense that he resembles any 'little man' who gets caught up in
the wheels of a big bureaucratic machine.

A true appreciation of the book requires a full understanding of
Švejk's character. It is a complex one. Although he was discharged
from military service for patent idiocy, as he proudly tells everyone,
he is far from being a fool. He is quite capable of making himself
appear a fool to save a situation, and it was probably to this resource-
fulness that he owed his discharge from the army. Švejk speaks most
of the time in double-talk. He pretends to be in agreement with anyone
he is dealing with, particularly if he happens to be a superior officer.
But the irony underlying his remarks is always perceptible. Not only
are his observations and explanations ironical, but so too are many of
his actions. One example of this is his *apparent* efforts to get to the
front by protesting his patriotism and devotion to the monarchy, when
it is clear that his actions only impede the achievement of his proclaimed objective.

Švejk is no ignoramus. He is the brother of a schoolmaster and is
clearly an educated man. Although he expresses himself in the Prague
vernacular he has a rich literary vocabulary combined with an almost
encyclopedic knowledge, no doubt derived from considerable reading

of newspapers and journals. He is a close observer of human nature and some of his deductions are penetrating. In dealing with his superiors he masks his real views and, indeed, even when talking to people of his own class he rarely reveals his true thinking. At the end of Part I, in conversation with a soldier he says exactly what he thinks of Austria-Hungary: 'A monarchy as idiotic as this ought not to exist at all.' None the less he accepts with resigned and even cheerful equanimity all the struggles and privations of army life in wartime. Although he evidently has no high opinion of most of his superiors he is capable of personal devotion at least to the officer whose batman he originally was, Lieutenant Lukáš. In situations where he has the upper hand he can be decisive to the point of ruthlessness. The way he punishes Baloun for cheating his master contrasts strikingly with the picture some people may have formed of him as a slippery and refractory orderly. Švejk grows in stature as he proves his superiority to those around him. He is a complete match for any of the soldiers or N.C.O.s who are unlucky enough to be his escorts. He is capable of reducing Lieutenant Dub to a state of speechlessness. At the same time he has a disarming way of attracting the admiration and approval of some stupid general or colonel. He has 'a way with him'. Few people, not even stern judge advocates, can resist his good-natured but unflinching blue eyes.

Moreover, unlike his creator, Švejk is no anarchist. He believes in law and order and means what he says when he asserts that discipline must be preserved. At the same time he is full of human feeling and compassion. 'Mistakes must occur,' he says, and he is always ready to excuse or defend, when others attack or complain. These can be the characteristics of Czechs but are not necessarily such. Some of the characteristics are common to many who are placed in the position in which Švejk finds himself. But the combination of all these traits makes Švejk unique.

One writer who recognized the greatness of Hašek's novel soon after it was written was Max Brod, the man who had diagnosed the genius of Kafka and Janáček. 'Hašek was a humorist of the highest calibre,' he wrote. 'A later age will perhaps put him on a level with Cervantes and Rabelais.' Max Brod saw that there was something of the Sancho Panza in Švejk. There is some truth in this. Lieutenant Lukáš might well have said to his batman, and in fact did say in so many words, what Don Quixote said to Sancho Panza: 'If you tell your story that way, Sancho, and repeat everything you have to say twice over, you will not be done in two days. Tell it consequentially like an intelligent man, or else be quiet.' And Švejk might well have replied like Sancho, although he did not: 'The way I am telling it is the way all stories are told in my country, and I don't know any other way of telling it.' But while Sancho is the foil to Don Quixote, Švejk is the main character of the Czech novel. And Sancho has neither the education nor the courage of Švejk. 'I've never read any histories at all, because I can't read or write,' says Sancho, who also admits to his master that he is very peaceable by nature and 'all against shoving himself into brawls and quarrels'. But Švejk is certainly not the man to pull his punches, as can be seen by the way he joins Vodička in the brawl with the Hungarians or eggs Kunert on to complain against Lieutenant Dub.

The parallel with Rabelais is more valid. In this book Hašek comes near to scraping the barrel in coarseness and nastiness. Here of course he is showing his true colours as the anarchist who wants to shake the bourgeoisie out of its comfortable complacency and hypocritical respectability, and he does not scruple to rake about in the dirt just for the sake of the stench. There were times in Prague when to invent a new anecdote all one had to do was to mention the name of the wife of a prominent political leader and add to it as much filth as possible. This is exactly Hašek's method of treating the Catholic Church. Some of the episodes dealing with the army chaplain can hardly be said to embellish the work. Hašek was consumed with such a bitter hatred of the Church and religion that in this book and many of his other stories he shot wide of the mark and the reader soon becomes surfeited, if not nauseated. One should note that he was more tolerant towards the Orthodox Church.

Nor should one blind oneself to Hašek's shortcomings as a writer. He is certainly a master of character-drawing and dialogue. Indeed, it is his dialogue which often provides the material for the characterization. And he displays considerable ingenuity, inventiveness and imagination too in devising the innumerable stories which Švejk and the characters tell in the course of the book. But his own comments and descriptions are less successful. He was good at recording what he had heard in life, especially over a drink at the pub – the stories, the conversations, the adventures. But he can be surprisingly lame in his descriptions and unconvincing in his narrative style. His greatest achievement is to maintain the momentum of the book and the raciness of the narrative in spite of introducing so many stories which hold back the action. He wrote carelessly and quickly. Sometimes it is apparent that he must have been drunk when he was writing, so confused do his thoughts and sentences become. But with all its imperfections *The Good Soldier Švejk* is a classic and I know of no novel which conveys so poignantly not only the ugliness of war but the utter futility of anything connected with it.

This rendering of *The Good Soldier Švejk* into English for the first time in an unabridged and unbowdlerized version will give English-speaking readers the chance of reviewing their opinions of the author and his leading character. But it is of course impossible to convey to a reader who does not know Czech or German finer points which must inevitably be lost in translation. Josef Švejk is inseparable from the manner in which he expresses himself. The language of Švejk *is* Švejk himself. Unfortunately it is impossible to reproduce this in English without running the risk of distorting his image, his period and his milieu.

THE ILLUSTRATIONS

Although Josef Lada (1887–1957) had been Hašek's friend since 1907 and had published in 1911 some of his stories in the humorous journal *Karikatury*, which he was then editing, it was not until 1921 that Hašek asked him to design a cover for the weekly parts in which *The Good Soldier Švejk* was then making its first appearance. Lada accepted the commission and did the drawing. He relates that it was approved by Hašek and his friend Sauer, who were the joint private publishers, but not only was the promised payment for it never made but Lada had to foot the bill for the meal over which the transaction was concluded.

This sketch was the first illustration which Lada made of Švejk. It bore little resemblance to the later illustrations with which we are now so familiar, but it was the only Lada illustration which Hašek personally approved.

It was not until 1924 – a year after Hašek's death – that Lada was commissioned to draw 540 pictures of Švejk for the Sunday supplement of the Czech daily *České Slovo*. These appeared each week in serial form, and each illustration was accompanied by a much shortened text adapted from the book by the artist himself. In these pictures Lada changed the figure of Švejk and created other characters after his own fancy. He also invented a brief ending for the unfinished book and illustrated it accordingly. This 'strip' version of Švejk was very popular and soon led to the appearance of a new edition of the book with about a quarter of Lada's original illustrations. But there were some changes in the drawings. Švejk was now shown with his head shaven from the very beginning. In fact he became less and less like Strašlipka, on whom he was probably modelled, and more a figure of Lada's own. The present translation reproduces 156 of these drawings.

If none of them were seen or approved by Hašek, and if many of the figures depicted bear little resemblance to the living persons who inspired Hašek's characters, they are now as inseparable from his *Švejk* as Tenniel's drawings are from *Alice in Wonderland*. For all their deviations, they reproduce very faithfully in caricature the picture which many Czechs had of Austro-Hungarian officialdom. But if Lada seems to have had no mercy on Austrian officials he is hardly more indulgent when he depicts his own countrymen – high or low. In this he was at one with Hašek, for the biggest *blbec* in the book ('idiot' – to use Hašek's favourite word), Lieutenant Dub, is a Czech and is caricatured without mercy.

Although Lada was a serious artist who achieved fame in his water-colours, *paysages*, animal pictures and book illustrations, he is known today mainly as the illustrator of the characters in Hašek's tales. He is said to have made 1,339 sketches to accompany Hašek's various works and 909 for *The Good Soldier Švejk* alone. His clear-cut drawings in bold strokes, which immortalize the humorous gestures of the people of that period and region, effectively combine the primitive and the popular. They are as much a revolt against the glorification of Czech history and legend, as shown by Mánes and Aleš in their innumerable heroic visions of Libuše, Žižka or Jiří of Poděbrady, as Hašek's writings are against national romanticism in Czech literature from Jirásek to Medek.

NOTE ON THE TRANSLATION

The translator of *The Good Soldier Švejk* is faced with a number of problems at the very outset. First there is no authorized text of the work. Only the first and second editions were seen by the author during his lifetime, but there is no certainty that even these texts represent what he actually wrote or approved. Only a part of the manuscript has been preserved. The author, it appears, cared little about what he had written once he had sent it off to the printer.

Broadly speaking there are two groups of texts – the texts published before the war, which were assumed to be what the author himself had written, and the texts published from the 1950s onwards which were revised in orthography, grammar and syntax. In making this translation I have drawn on both groups and have chosen whichever version seemed clearer and more consistent. Discrepancies between the texts, except in spelling and syntax, are not substantial, the only major difference being the omission in the post-war editions of a 'message' from Hašek to President Masaryk which was to be found in the pre-war editions, and which is included in this translation. (See footnote on p. 680.)

I have already referred to the language in which Švejk expresses himself and the impossibility of reproducing this in English. Švejk and many of the other characters in the book use what is called 'obecná čeština' or *common* Czech, which is not quite the same as *literary* or *book* Czech. The use of common Czech in Bohemia and Moravia is by no means confined to the uneducated. The Czechs are a democratic people and when they get together and let their hair down, whether they are educated or not, they speak a more or less common vernacular. This cannot be adequately rendered in English, since the only thinkable equivalent would be dialect or bad English. Either would be false and out of place in this context. We also have to remember that the action is taking place during the First World War in the Austro-Hungarian Empire among Czechs and it will create a wrong atmosphere if the language used in the English translation is associated with people and conditions of a very different kind. Much of the charm of Švejk's narration lies in his use of common Czech.

Another problem is that although in the Austro-Hungarian army the nationalities spoke their own languages among themselves, the language of command was German. Thus in the book there are a large number of German words and phrases, some of which are distorted by Czech mispronunciation, and this adds a peculiar colour and humour to the language. It also has some significance whether the characters speak German or Czech and what kind of German or Czech they speak. This too cannot be adequately conveyed in translation.

A further complication is the richness of Czech 'bad language' as compared with our own. In common with other Slavic languages and with German, Czech can boast a wide range of words of abuse in all shades of intensity. We cannot match these in Britain, where – no doubt under the influence of puritanism – the bulk of our terms of abuse are too mild and our strong expressions are limited to one or two hackneyed obscenities. Czech words of abuse generally involve domestic animals, excrement or the parts of the body connected with it. The English relate mainly to sexual functions or perversions, although there is in this respect a narrow area of common ground between the two languages. If the reader finds a certain monotony in the words chosen by the translator I hope he will realize that the bandsman has to operate within the limits of his instrument.

It is characteristic of Švejk's way of telling a story that he does not bother about syntax. This of course is an indication of his mentality and a part of his character, but it is also a reflection of the author's disregard of grammatical rules. In translating Švejk's lengthy anecdotes it has been found necessary to break up some of his sentences so that the reader can understand their drift and get the point of the story. In doing this the translator risks incurring the charge of having tried to 'edit' Hašek. In fact any translator of Hašek has to exercise very considerable self-restraint, since it is often tempting completely to re-write him. But if this were carried too far the book would not be Hašek's any more. It follows from what has been written above that there are passages in the original of *The Good Soldier Švejk* which may be not too intelligible. In these cases the translator has had to try to make them so. Fortunately these cases are very few and not of vital importance.

This is the first unabridged and unbowdlerized version of *The Good Soldier Švejk* in English. The only previous translator reduced the book to less than two-thirds of this volume. There is no doubt that Hašek was writing to make money and that he spun out the book to increase his earnings. No one would deny that it needs pruning. But it is a different matter when censorship is applied to it. Hašek regaled his readers with words which had never appeared in Czech literature before. In his postscript to the first volume he explains why he did this and how important it was to him. As far as the translation goes the omission of anecdotes because they are 'dirty' or of references to monarchs or the deity because they might be treasonable or blasphemous could hardly be justified in 1930 and would certainly be indefensible in 1973. Today 'The Good Soldier Švejk' must stand as he is, without any fig-leaf.

I owe a great debt to Dr Dana Kňourková for the invaluable assistance she gave me in reading my manuscript and helping to solve the many problems connected with the translation.

CECIL PARROTT

Guide to the Pronunciation of Czech Names

The first syllable always bears the stress. However, the unstressed syllables are not swallowed as in English. Each syllable is pronounced clearly, whether stressed or not.

Baloun = Bah-lohn
České Budějovice = Che-skeh Boo-dye-yo-vi-tseh
Dub = Doop
Konopiště = Kon-o-pish-tyeh
Lukáš = Loo-kaahsh
Matušič = Mah-too-shich
Na Bojišti = Nah Bo-yish-tyee
Palivec = Pah-li-vets

Piešťany = Pee-ye-shty-ah-nee
Písek = Pee-sek
Putim = Poo-tyim
Ságner = Saah-gnehr
Švejk = Shvayk
Vaněk = Vah-nyek
Vodička = Vo-dyich-kah
Vršovice = Vrr-sho-vi-tseh

Czech vowels are short or long. The diacritic marks which look like acute accents and the small circle occurring on 'u' (ů) indicate that the vowel is long.

The use of a hook (or an apostrophe) on a consonant letter has the effect of softening it:

ť (or t') sounds like 't' in 'tune' in contrast with hard 't' in 'top'
ď (or d') sounds like 'd' in 'duke' in contrast with hard 'd' in 'done'
ň sounds like the French 'gn' in 'Champagne'

The same effect, i.e. softening of the previous consonant, is produced by 'i' or 'í' or 'ě' when following 'd', 't', or 'n'.

Otherwise Czech 'č' sounds like 'ch' in 'chop';
    'š' sounds like 'sh' in 'short';
    'ž' resembles the sound denoted by 's' in 'pleasure'.

The most difficult Czech sound is probably 'ř', which sounds somewhat like 'rzh' (compare 'Dvořák' – Dvo-rzhaahk).

Czech 'r' is pronounced exactly like the Scottish 'r', and Czech 'ch' like 'ch' in 'loch'.

CISLEITHANIA.
OR AUSTRIA
'THE AUSTRIAN
LANDS'

TRANSLEITHANIA
OR HUNGARY
'THE LANDS OF THE
HUNGARIAN CROWN'

ANNEXED BY
AUSTRIA-HUNGARY
IN 1908

G

Prague

BOHEMIA

SEE MAP B

České
Budějovice

MORAV

SWITZERLAND

GERMANY

Vienna

Bra

Bruck an der Leitha

Királyh

River Leitha

AUSTRIA

Venice

CROATIA

S

BOSN

HERZE

ITALY

Adriatic Sea

DALMATIA

SVEJK'S JOURNEY WITH HIS REGIMENT TO THE FRONT

NY

RUSSIAN POLAND

Cracow

SEE MAP C

Przemyśl

Lwów

Żółtańce

Sanok

Stara Sól

Lupka Pass

GALICIA

Medzilaborce

Humenné

Sátoraljaújhely

Miskolc

A

BUKOVINA

RUSSIAN UKRAINE

Füzesabony

Budapest

River Danube

G A R Y

TRANSYLVANIA

RUMANIA

SERBIA

A.

THE
AUSTRO-
HUNGARIAN
MONARCHY

(1) Five minutes before the train reached Tábor Švejk and a railwayman had their hands on the handle of the alarm signal and it is really a mystery how it happened that the train came to a halt. When he finally reached Tábor Švejk sat drinking, missed all the trains to České Budějovice and was told by the lieutenant on duty to walk there.

(2) Here Švejk was helped by a motherly old woman.

(3) Here Švejk met Farmer Melichárek who took him for a deserter.

(4) Here at Putim Švejk slept in the haystack in gay company.

(5) Here Švejk met a resourceful and garrulous tramp.

(6) Here Švejk and the tramp were feasted by an even more garrulous shepherd in the Schwarzenberg sheep-fold.

(7) Here Švejk found himself back again at Putim. He was arrested by the gendarmerie and taken for a Russian spy.

(8) Švejk was escorted to Písek by the corporal (or rather Švejk escorted him!) and was then sent to České Budějovice by train.

Milevsko

Tábor

B. ŠVEJK'S ANABASIS

THIS IS WHERE ŠVEJK SHOULD HAVE GONE

České Budějovice

BATTLE FRONT

Żółtańce

Lwów

River Bug

ŠVEJK'S REGIMENT

C.   ŠVEJK'S JOURNEY
WITH HIS REGIMENT

Austro-Hungarian Currency

1 guilder = 2 crowns
1 guilder = 100 kreutzers
1 crown = 100 hellers
1 kreutzer = 2 hellers

Part I

BEHIND THE LINES

Preface

GREAT times call for great men. There are unknown heroes who are modest, with none of the historical glamour of a Napoleon. If you analysed their character you would find that it eclipsed even the glory of Alexander the Great. Today you can meet in the streets of Prague a shabbily dressed man who is not even himself aware of his significance in the history of the great new era. He goes modestly on his way, without bothering anyone. Nor is he bothered by journalists asking for an interview. If you asked him his name he would answer you simply and unassumingly: 'I am Švejk . . .'

And this quiet, unassuming, shabbily dressed man is indeed that heroic and valiant good old soldier Švejk. In Austrian times his name was once on the lips of all the citizens of the Kingdom of Bohemia, and in the Republic his glory will not fade either.

I am very fond of the good soldier Švejk and in relating his adventures during the world war I am convinced that this modest, anonymous hero will win the sympathy of all of you. Unlike that stupid fellow Herostrates he did not set fire to the temple of the Goddess in Ephesus just to get himself into the newspapers and school books.

And that is enough.

THE AUTHOR

I

The Good Soldier Švejk Intervenes in the Great War

'AND so they've killed our Ferdinand,'[1] said the charwoman to Mr Švejk, who had left military service years before, after having been finally certified by an army medical board as an imbecile, and now lived by selling dogs – ugly, mongrel monstrosities whose pedigrees he forged.

Apart from this occupation he suffered from rheumatism and was at this very moment rubbing his knees with Elliman's embrocation.

'Which Ferdinand, Mrs Müller?' he asked, going on with the

1. The Archduke Franz Ferdinand, nephew of the Austrian Emperor, Franz Joseph, was assassinated with his wife at Sarajevo by the Serbian nationalist, Gavrilo Princip, in 1914.

massaging. 'I know two Ferdinands. One is a messenger at Průša's, the chemist's, and once by mistake he drank a bottle of hair oil there. And the other is Ferdinand Kokoška who collects dog manure. Neither of them is any loss.'

'Oh no, sir, it's His Imperial Highness, the Archduke Ferdinand, from Konopiště, the fat churchy one.'

'Jesus Maria!' exclaimed Švejk. 'What a grand job! And where did it happen to His Imperial Highness?'

'They bumped him off at Sarajevo, sir, with a revolver, you know. He drove there in a car with his Archduchess.'

'Well, there you have it, Mrs Müller, in a car. Yes, of course, a gentleman like him can afford it, but he never imagines that a drive like that might finish up badly. And at Sarajevo into the bargain! That's in Bosnia, Mrs Müller. I expect the Turks did it. You know, we never ought to have taken Bosnia and Herzegovina from them.[1] And so you see, Mrs Müller. His Imperial Highness now rests with the angels. Did he suffer long?'

'His Imperial Highness was done for at once, sir. You know, a revolver isn't just a toy. Not long ago there was a gentleman in Nusle, where I come from, who fooled about with a revolver too. And what happened? He shot his whole family and the porter too who came up to see who was doing the shooting there on the third floor.'

'There are some revolvers, Mrs Müller, that won't go off even if you bust yourself. There are lots of that type. But for His Imperial Highness I'm sure they must have bought something better. And I wouldn't mind betting, Mrs Müller, that the chap who did it put on smart togs for the occasion. Potting at an Imperial Highness is no easy job, you know. It's not like a poacher potting at a gamekeeper. The question is how you get at him. You can't come near a fine gentleman like that if you're dressed in rags. You've got to wear a topper, so the cops don't nab you beforehand.'

'They say there were a lot of them, sir.'

'Well, of course, Mrs Müller,' said Švejk, finishing massaging his knees. 'If you wanted to kill His Imperial Highness or for that matter even His Imperial Majesty the Emperor, you'd certainly need advice. Several heads are wiser than one. One chap advises you this, another

1. After the Russo-Turkish war of 1877–8 Austria-Hungary occupied Bosnia and Herzegovina. They remained under Turkish suzerainty until 1908 when Austria-Hungary annexed them.

that, and then "the deed is crowned with success", as our national anthem says. The main thing is to watch out for the moment when a gentleman like that rides past. Just like old Luccheni, if you remember, who stabbed our late lamented Elizabeth[1] with a file. He just went for a stroll with her. Who's going to trust anybody now? After that there'll be no more strolls for empresses! And a lot of other persons'll have it coming to them too, you know. You mark my words, Mrs Müller, it'll be the turn of the Tsar and the Tsarina next and maybe, though God forbid, even of His Imperial Majesty the Emperor, now they've started with his uncle.[2] He's got a lot of enemies, the old gentleman has. Even more than Ferdinand. Not long ago a gentleman was telling us in the pub that a time would come when all these emperors would get done in one after the other, and all the king's horses and all the king's men wouldn't save them. After that he hadn't any money to pay his bill and the landlord had to have him arrested. And he hit the landlord across the jaw once and the policeman twice. So after that they took him away in a drunks' cart to sober him up again. Well, Mrs Müller, what a world we live in, to be sure! What a loss for Austria again! When I was in the army an infantryman once shot a captain. He loaded his rifle and went into his office. They told him he had no business there, but he went on insisting he must speak to the captain. The captain came out and at once gave him "confined to barracks!" But he took up his rifle and bang it went, plum through the captain's heart. The bullet flew out of his back and damaged the office into the bargain. It smashed a bottle of ink which messed up the official documents.'

'Oh, goodness, and what happened to that soldier?' asked Mrs Müller later, while Švejk was dressing.

'He hanged himself on his braces,' said Švejk, cleaning his bowler. 'And what's more they weren't even his. He'd borrowed them from the warder on the excuse that his trousers were falling down. Do you think he should have waited until they shot him? You know, Mrs Müller, in a situation like that anyone would be in a flap. They reduced the warder to the ranks because of it and gave him six months. But he didn't sit them out. He ran away to Switzerland and today he's a preacher of some church or other. Today there are very few honest

1. The Empress Elizabeth of Austria was stabbed by an anarchist in 1898 in Switzerland.
2. In fact Franz Ferdinand was the Emperor's nephew.

people about, Mrs Müller. I can imagine that His Imperial Highness, the Archduke Ferdinand, made a mistake in Sarajevo about that chap who shot him. He saw a gentleman and thought, "He must be a decent fellow who's giving me a cheer." And instead of that he gave him bang! bang! Did he give him one bang or several, Mrs Müller?'

'The newspaper says, sir, that His Imperial Highness was riddled like a sieve. He emptied all his cartridges into him.'

'Well, it goes jolly quickly, Mrs Müller, terribly quickly. I'd buy a Browning for a job like that. It looks like a toy, but in a couple of minutes you can shoot twenty archdukes with it, never mind whether they're thin or fat. Although, between you and me, Mrs Müller, a fat archduke's a better mark than a thin one. You may remember the time they shot that king of theirs in Portugal? He was a fat chap too. After all, you wouldn't expect a king to be thin, would you? Well, now I'm going to the pub, The Chalice, and if anyone comes here for that miniature pinscher, which I took an advance on, tell them I've got him in my kennels in the country, that I've only just cropped his ears, and he mustn't be moved until they heal up, otherwise they'll catch cold. Would you please give the key to the house-porter.'

There was only one guest sitting at The Chalice. It was the plain-clothes police officer, Bretschneider, who worked for the State Security. The landlord, Palivec, was washing up the glasses and Bretschneider was vainly endeavouring to engage him in serious conversation.

Palivec was notorious for his foul mouth. Every second word of his was 'arse' or 'shit'. But at the same time he was well read and told everyone to read what Victor Hugo wrote on this subject when he described the last answer Napoleon's Old Guard gave to the British at the Battle of Waterloo.[1]

'Well, it's a glorious summer!' said Bretschneider, embarking on his serious conversation.

'Shit on everything!' answered Palivec, putting the glasses away into a cupboard.

'It's a fine thing they've done to us at Sarajevo,' said Bretschneider with a faint hope.

'Which Sarajevo?' asked Palivec. 'Do you mean the wine cellar at

1. When the British Commander called upon Marshal Cambronne to surrender he is reputed to have said: '*Merde*! The guard dies but does not yield.'

Nusle? They're always fighting there, you know. Of course it's Nusle.'

'At Sarajevo in Bosnia, Mr Palivec. They've just shot His Imperial Highness, the Archduke Ferdinand, there. What do you say to that?'

'I don't poke my nose into things like that. They can kiss my arse

if I do!' Palivec replied politely, lighting his pipe. 'Nowadays, if anyone got mixed up in a business like that, he'd risk breaking his neck. I'm a tradesman and when anyone comes in here and orders a beer I fill up his glass. But Sarajevo, politics or the late lamented Archduke are nothing for people like us. They lead straight to Pankrác.'[1]

Bretschneider lapsed into silence and looked disappointedly round the empty pub.

'Hallo, there used to be a picture of His Imperial Majesty hanging here once,' he started up again after a while. 'Just where the mirror hangs now.'

1. The Prague prison.

'Yes, you're right,' Palivec replied. 'It did hang there, but the flies used to shit on it, so I put it away in the attic. You know, somebody might be so free as to pass a remark about it and then there could be unpleasantness. I don't want that, do I?'

'In Sarajevo it must have been a pretty ugly business, Mr Palivec.'

This crafty direct question evoked an extremely cautious answer from Palivec: 'At this time of the year it's scorching hot in Bosnia and Herzegovina. When I served there, they had to put ice on our lieutenant's head.'

'Which regiment did you serve in, Mr Palivec?'

'I can't possibly remember anything so unimportant. Bloody nonsense of that sort never interested me and I've never bothered my head about it,' answered Palivec. 'Curiosity killed a cat.'

Bretschneider finally relapsed into silence. His gloomy face only lit up on the arrival of Švejk who came into the pub, ordered a dark black beer and remarked: 'Today they'll be in mourning in Vienna too.'

Bretschneider's eyes gleamed with hope, and he said laconically: 'On Konopiště there are ten black flags.'

'There should be twelve,' said Švejk, after he had taken a swig.

'What makes you think twelve?' asked Bretschneider.

'To make it a round number. A dozen adds up better, and dozens always come cheaper,' answered Švejk.

There was a silence, which Švejk himself broke with a sigh: 'And so he's already lying with God and the angels. Glory be! He didn't even live to be Emperor. When I was serving in the army a general once fell off his horse and killed himself without any fuss. They wanted to help him back onto his horse, to lift him up, but to their surprise he was completely dead. And he was going to be promoted Field Marshal. It happened at a review. These reviews never come to any good. In Sarajevo there was a review too. I remember once at a parade like that I had twenty buttons missing from my uniform and they sent me into solitary confinement for a fortnight, where I lay for two days trussed up like Lazarus. But in the army you must have discipline, otherwise why would anyone bother at all? Our Lieutenant Makovec always used to say: "There's got to be discipline, you bloody fools, otherwise you'd be climbing about on the trees like monkeys, but the army's going to make human beings of you, you god-forsaken idiots." And isn't that true? Just imagine a park, let's say at Charles Square, and on every tree an undisciplined soldier! It's enough to give you a nightmare!'

'At Sarajevo,' Bretschneider resumed, 'it was the Serbs who did it.'

'You're wrong there,' replied Švejk. 'It was the Turks, because of Bosnia and Herzegovina.' And Švejk expounded his views on Austrian foreign policy in the Balkans. In 1912 the Turks lost the war with Serbia, Bulgaria and Greece. They had wanted Austria to help them, and when this didn't happen, they shot Ferdinand.

'Do you like the Turks?' said Švejk, turning to Palivec. 'Do you like those heathen dogs? You don't, do you?'

'One customer is as good as another,' said Palivec, 'never mind a Turk. For tradesmen like us politics doesn't enter into it. Pay for your beer, sit down in my pub and jabber what you like. That's my principle. It's all the same to me whether our Ferdinand was done in by a Serb or Turk, Catholic or Moslem, anarchist or Young Czech.'[1]

'All right now, Mr Palivec,' resumed Bretschneider, who was again beginning to despair of catching either of them out, 'but all the same you'll admit that it's a great loss for Austria.'

Švejk replied for the landlord: 'Yes, it's a loss indeed, there's no denying it. A shocking loss. You can't replace Ferdinand by any twopenny-halfpenny idiot. Only he ought to have been still fatter.'

'What do you mean?' Bretschneider livened up.

'What do I mean?' Švejk answered happily. 'Just this. If he'd been fatter then of course he'd certainly have had a stroke long ago, when he was chasing those old women at Konopiště when they were collecting firewood and picking mushrooms on his estate, and he wouldn't have had to die such a shameful death. Just imagine, an uncle of His Imperial Majesty and shot! Why, it's a scandal! The newspapers are full of it. Years ago in our Budějovice a cattle-dealer called Břetislav Ludvík was stabbed in the market place in a petty squabble. He had a son called Bohuslav, and wherever that lad came to sell his pigs, no one wanted to buy anything from him and everyone said: "That's the son of that chap who was stabbed. He's probably a first-class bastard too!" There was nothing for him to do but to jump into the Vltava from that bridge at Krumlov, and they had to drag him out, resurrect

1. A member of the Czech National Liberal Party led by Dr Kramář, later to be the first Premier of the Czechoslovak Republic.

him, pump water out of him, and of course he had to die in the arms of the doctor just when he was giving him an injection.'

'You do make strange comparisons, I must say,' said Bretschneider significantly. 'First you talk about Ferdinand and then about a cattle-dealer.'

'Oh, no, I don't,' Švejk defended himself. 'God forbid my wanting to compare anyone to anybody else. Mr Palivec knows me very well. I've never compared anyone to anybody else, have I? But I wouldn't for the life of me want to be in the skin of that Archduke's widow. What's she going to do now? The children are orphans and the family estate at Konopiště has no master. Marry a new Archduke? What would she get out of that? She'd only go with him to Sarajevo again and be widowed a second time. You know years ago there was a game-keeper in Zliv near Hluboká.[1] He had a very ugly name – Pind'our.[2] Some poachers shot him, and he left a widow and two little babes. Within a year she married another gamekeeper, Pepík Šavel from Mydlovary. And they shot him too. And then she married a third time, again a gamekeeper, and said: "Third time lucky. If it doesn't succeed this time, then I don't know what I shall do." Well, of course, they shot him too, and with all these gamekeepers she had six children altogether. She even went to the office of His Highness the Prince at Hluboká and complained that she'd had trouble with those game-keepers. And so they recommended her a fellow called Jareš[3] who was a water bailiff in the watch tower at Ražice. And, can you imagine it? He was drowned when they were fishing the lake out. And she had two children by him. And then she took a pig-gelder from Vodňany and one night he hit her over the head with his axe and went and gave himself up voluntarily. And when they hanged him afterwards at the district court at Písek he bit the priest's nose and said he didn't regret anything. And he also said something extremely nasty about His Imperial Majesty.'

'And you don't happen to know what he said?' Bretschneider asked hopefully.

'I can't tell you, because no one dared repeat it. But I'm told that it was something so dreadful and horrible that one of the magistrates went mad, and they keep him to this very day in solitary confinement,

---

1. Famous estate of Prince Schwarzenberg in Southern Bohemia.
2. 'Little cock'.
3. Hašek's grandfather was called Jareš and was a water bailiff.

so that it shan't get out. It wasn't the usual sort of insulting remark which people make about His Imperial Majesty when they're tight.'

'And what sort of insulting remark do people make about His Imperial Majesty when they're tight?' asked Bretschneider.

'Now come, gentlemen, please change the subject,' said Palivec. 'You know, I don't like it. Somebody might talk out of turn and we'd be sorry for it.'

'What sort of insulting remarks do people make about His Imperial Majesty when they're tight?' Švejk repeated. 'All kinds. Get drunk, have the Austrian national anthem played and you'll see what you start saying! You'll think up such a lot about His Imperial Majesty, that if only half of it were true it would be enough to disgrace him all his life. But the old gentleman really doesn't deserve it. Just think! His son Rudolf[1] – lost in tender years, in full flower of his manhood. His wife Elizabeth – stabbed with a file. And then Jan Orth – also lost. His brother, the Emperor of Mexico[2] – put up against a wall and shot in a fortress somewhere. And now again in his old age they've shot his uncle. A chap needs iron nerves for that. And then some drunken bastard starts to swear at him. If the balloon went up today I'd go as a volunteer and serve His Imperial Majesty to my last drop of blood.'

Švejk took a deep draught of beer and continued:

'Do you really think His Imperial Majesty is going to put up with this sort of thing? If so, you don't know him at all. There'll have to be a war with the Turks. "You killed my uncle and so I'll bash your jaw." War is certain. Serbia and Russia will help us in it. There won't half be a blood bath.'

Švejk looked beautiful in this prophetic moment. His simple face, smiling like a full moon, beamed with enthusiasm. Everything was so clear to him.

'It may be,' he said, continuing his account of Austria's future, 'that if we have war with the Turks the Germans'll attack us, because the Germans and the Turks stick together. You can't find bigger bastards anywhere. But we can ally ourselves with France which has had a down

1. Rudolf, the son of the Emperor Franz Joseph and heir to the throne, died mysteriously at his hunting lodge of Mayerling.

2. Archduke Johann gave up his Hapsburg title and called himself Johann Orth. Ferdinand Maximilian, the brother of the Emperor, was crowned Emperor of Mexico. He was taken prisoner and executed in 1867.

on Germany ever since 1871. And then the balloon'll go up. There'll be war. I won't say any more.'

Bretschneider stood up and said solemnly:

'You don't need to. Just come along with me into the passage. I've got something to say to you there.'

Švejk followed the plain-clothes police officer into the passage where a little surprise awaited him. His drinking companion showed him his eaglet[1] and announced that he was arresting him and would take him at once to police headquarters. Švejk tried to explain that the gentleman must be mistaken, that he was completely innocent and that he had not uttered a single word capable of offending anyone.

However, Bretschneider told him that he had in fact committed several criminal offences, including the crime of high treason.

Then they returned to the pub and Švejk said to Palivec:

'I've had five beers, a couple of frankfurters and a roll. Now give me one more slivovice and I must go, because I'm under arrest.'

1. The two-headed eagle was the warrant of the Austrian State Security.

Bretschneider showed Palivec his eaglet, stared at him for a moment and then asked:

'Are you married?'

'I am.'

'And can Madam carry on the business for you during your absence?'

'She can.'

'Then it's all right, Mr Palivec,' said Bretschneider gaily. 'Call your wife here, give the business over to her, and in the evening we'll come for you.'

'Take it easy,' Švejk consoled him. 'I'm only going there for high treason.'

'But what am I going for?' moaned Palivec. 'After all, I've been so careful.'

Bretschneider smiled and said triumphantly:

'Because you said the flies shitted on His Imperial Majesty. They'll certainly knock His Imperial Majesty out of your head there.'

And so Švejk left The Chalice under the escort of the plain-clothes police officer. When they went out into the street his face lit up with its good-natured smile and he asked:

'Should I step down from the pavement?'

'What do you mean?'

'I thought as I'm under arrest I've no right to walk on the pavement.'

When they passed through the door of police headquarters Švejk said:

'Well, the time passed very pleasantly for us there. Do you often go to The Chalice?'

And while they were escorting Švejk to the reception office Palivec at The Chalice handed over the running of the pub to his weeping wife, consoling her in his own inimitable way:

'Don't cry, don't howl. What can they do to me because of some shit on a picture of His Imperial Majesty?'

And thus it was that the good soldier Švejk intervened in the great war in his own sweet, charming way. It will interest historians that he saw far into the future. If the situation subsequently developed otherwise than he had expounded it at The Chalice we must bear in mind that he had never had any preparatory training in diplomacy.

2

The Good Soldier Švejk at
Police Headquarters

THE Sarajevo assassination had filled police headquarters with numerous victims. They were brought in one after another, and the old inspector at the reception office said in his kindly tone:

'That Ferdinand is going to cost you dear.'

When they had locked Švejk up in one of the numerous cells on the first floor, he found six persons already assembled there. Five of them were sitting round the table, and in a corner a middle-aged man was sitting on a bunk, as though trying to avoid the company of the others.

Švejk started asking them in turn why they had been arrested.

From the five sitting at the table he received almost exactly the same answer:

'Because of Sarajevo.' 'Because of Ferdinand.' 'Because of the murder of His Imperial Highness.' 'For Ferdinand.' 'Because they did away with His Imperial Highness at Sarajevo.'

The sixth, who was avoiding the company of the other five, said he did not want to have anything to do with them, in case any suspicion should fall on him. He was only detained here for attempted robbery with murder on a farmer Giles from Holice.

Švejk sat down at the table with the conspirators, who were recounting for at least the tenth time how they had got there.

All, except one, had been taken in a pub, a wine cellar or a café. The exception was an unusually fat gentleman with glasses and tear-stained eyes, who had been arrested in his apartment, because two days before the murder at Sarajevo he had stood drinks to two Serbian students of engineering at the pub U Brejšky and had been seen by detective Brixi drunk in their company in Montmartre in Řetězová Street where, as he had already confirmed by his signature on the police report, he had stood them drinks too.

In reply to all questions during the preliminary investigation at police headquarters he repeated the stereotyped moan:

'I keep a stationer's shop.'

Whereupon he received the equally stereotyped reply:

'That's no excuse.'

The short gentleman, who had been taken in the wine cellar, was a professor of history and was expounding to the landlord the history of various assassinations. He was arrested at the very moment when he had completed a psychological analysis of every assassination and was saying:

'The idea of an assassination is as simple as Columbus's egg.'

'Yes, just as simple as you're for Pankrác,' said the police inspector during the interrogation, capping his remark.

The third conspirator was the president of the charity organization Dobromil at Hodkovičky. On the day the assassination took place Dobromil had organized a garden party with a concert. The sergeant of the gendarmerie came to ask the public to go home, as Austria was in mourning, whereupon the president of Dobromil said good-naturedly:

'Just wait a moment until we have finished playing "Hej Slované".'[1]

Now he was sitting there with bowed head and lamenting:

1. Famous patriotic song in Bohemia calling for the wider use of the Czech language.

'In August we have new elections for the presidency. If I'm not home by then I may not be elected. It's the tenth time I'm president. I'll never survive the shame.'

The late lamented Ferdinand played an odd trick on the fourth detainee, a man of sterling character and blameless reputation. For two whole days he had avoided any talk about Ferdinand until in the evening in the café, while playing mariáš[1] and trumping the king of spades with the seven of clubs, he said:

'Seven pips like at Sarajevo.'

The fifth man, who as he said himself was detained there 'because of that murder of His Imperial Highness at Sarajevo', was so scared that his hair and beard were still standing on end and his head reminded one of a stable pinscher.

This man had not uttered a single word in the restaurant where he had been arrested. He had not even read the newspapers about the murder of Ferdinand and was sitting alone at the table, when a gentleman came up to him, sat down opposite him and said to him quickly:

'Have you read it?'

'No.'

'Do you know about it?'

'No.'

'And do you know what it's about?'

'No, I'm not interested.'

'But you ought to be interested.'

'I don't know what I ought to be interested in. I just smoke my cigar, drink my few glasses, have my supper and don't read the newspapers. The newspapers tell lies. Why should I get excited?'

'And so you're not even interested in the murder at Sarajevo then?'

'I'm not interested in any murder at all, whether it's at Prague, Vienna, Sarajevo or London. For that there are authorities, courts and police. If at any time anywhere they kill anybody it only serves him right. Why is he such a bloody careless fool to let himself get killed?'

Those were his last words in this conversation. From that moment he went on repeating aloud at intervals of five minutes:

'I'm innocent. I'm innocent.'

He screamed out these words at the gate of police headquarters; he is going to repeat them when he is transferred to the criminal court in Prague; and with these words he will enter his prison cell.

1. A popular Czech card game.

When Švejk had heard all these dreadful conspiratorial tales he thought it right to explain to the others the utter hopelessness of their position.

'We're all of us in a nasty jam,' he began his words of comfort. 'You're not right when you say that nothing can happen to you or any of us. What have we got the police for except to punish us for talking out of turn? If the times are so dangerous that archdukes get shot, no one should be surprised if he's carried off to police headquarters. They're doing all this to make a splash, so that Ferdinand can have some publicity before his funeral. The more of us there are here, the better it'll be for us, because it'll be all the jollier. When I was in the army half a company of us were sometimes locked up together. And how many innocent people used to be condemned! And not only in the army but in the civil courts too. I remember once a woman was sentenced for strangling her newly-born twins. Although she swore on oath that she couldn't have strangled twins, when she'd given birth to only one little girl, which she had succeeded in strangling quite painlessly, she was sentenced for double murder all the same. Or that innocent gipsy in Záběhlice, who broke into a greengrocer's shop on Christmas Day in the night. He swore that he'd gone there to get warm, but it didn't help. Once it gets into the hands of the courts it's bad. But that bad has to be. Perhaps all people aren't such scoundrels as you'd think them to be. But how can you tell the good chap from the rotter, especially nowadays at such a serious time as this when they've bumped off Ferdinand? When I served in the army in Budějovice the captain's dog got shot in a forest behind the parade ground. When he learnt about it he summoned us all, made us fall in and ordered every tenth man to step forward. Of course it goes without saying that I was one of the tenth men. And so we stood at attention without batting an eyelid. The captain went along our ranks and said: "You bastards, you, you swine, you, you brutes, you spotted hyenas, you, because of that dog I'd like to send every bloody one of you into solitary confinement, make macaroni out of you, shoot you up and make kedgeree out of you. And to show you I'm not going to be soft with you I'm giving all of you fourteen days c.b." And so there you see. Then it was all because of a mangy cur and now it's all because of no less a person than His Imperial Highness. You have to have some horror, to make the mourning worth while.'

'I'm innocent, I'm innocent,' repeated the man with his hair on end.

'Jesus Christ was innocent too,' said Švejk, 'and all the same they crucified him. No one anywhere has ever worried about a man being innocent. *Maul halten und weiter dienen*![1] – as they used to tell us in the army. That's the best and finest thing of all.'

Švejk lay down on the bunk and fell asleep contentedly.

Meanwhile they brought in two new detainees. One of them was a Bosnian. He walked up and down the cell grinding his teeth and every time he opened his mouth said: '*Jebe ti dušu.*'[2] He was tortured by the thought that his pedlar's basket would get lost at police headquarters.

The other new guest was the landlord Palivec. When he saw his friend Švejk, he woke him up and called out in the most tragic tones:

'Now I'm here too!'

Švejk shook his hand cordially and said:

'I'm glad about that, really I am. I knew that gentleman would keep his word when he said that they'd come for you. Punctiliousness like that is a good thing.'

But Palivec remarked that punctiliousness of that sort was not worth a shit and lowering his voice asked Švejk whether the other gentlemen under arrest were thieves, because it might harm his business.

Švejk explained to him that all of them belonged to the same party arrested because of the Archduke, except the man who had been arrested for attempted robbery with murder on a farmer Giles from Holice.

Palivec took umbrage at this and said that he was not here for any pip-squeak of an Archduke but because of His Imperial Majesty. And because the others began to show interest he told them how his flies had defiled His Imperial Majesty.

'They fouled him up for me, the vermin,' he said, ending the description of his adventure, 'and finally they got me locked up. I'll never forgive those flies for that,' he added menacingly.

Švejk went back to bed, but he did not sleep long because they came to take him away for questioning.

And so, mounting the staircase to the 3rd Department for questioning, Švejk carried his cross up on to the hill of Golgotha, sublimely unconscious of his martyrdom.

Observing the notice that spitting in the corridors was prohibited,

1. Famous phrase of Švejk: 'Grin and bear it and get on with the job.'
2. A common obscene oath in Serbian: 'Fuck your soul!'

he asked the policeman to allow him to spit in the spittoon, and, beaming with his natural simplicity, said as he came into the office:

'A very good evening to you all, gentlemen.'

Instead of a reply, someone pummelled him under the ribs and stood him in front of a table, behind which there sat a gentleman with a cold official face and features of such bestial cruelty that he might have just fallen out of Lombroso's book, *Criminal Types*.

He gave Švejk a bloodthirsty look and said:

'Take that idiotic expression off your face.'

'I can't help it,' replied Švejk solemnly. 'I was discharged from the army for idiocy and officially certified by a special commission as an idiot. I'm an official idiot.'

The gentleman of the criminal type ground his teeth:

'What you're accused of and you've committed proves you've got all your wits about you.'

And now he proceeded to enumerate to Švejk a whole series of different crimes, beginning with high treason and ending with abuse of His Majesty and members of the Imperial Family. The central gem of this collection was Švejk's approval of the murder of the Archduke Ferdinand, from which there branched out a string of fresh crimes, among which the shining light was the crime of incitement, as it had all happened in a public place.

'What do you say to that?' the gentleman with features of bestial cruelty asked triumphantly.

'There's a lot of it,' Švejk replied innocently. 'You can have too much of a good thing.'

'So there you are, then, you admit it's true?'

'I admit everything. You've got to be strict. Without strictness no one would ever get anywhere. When I was in the army . . .'

'Shut your mug!' shouted the police commissioner, 'and speak only when you're questioned! Do you understand?'

'Of course I understand,' said Švejk. 'Humbly report, I understand and am able to orientate myself in everything you are pleased to say, sir.'

'Whom are you in contact with?'

'My charwoman, your honour.'

'And you don't have any friends in political circles here?'

'Yes, I do, your honour. I subscribe to the afternoon edition of *Národní Politika* – "The Bitch".'[1]

1. A famous Prague conservative daily which ceased to appear in 1945.

'Get out!' the gentleman with the bestial appearance roared at Švejk. As they were leading him out of the office, Švejk said:

'Good night, your honour.'

Back in his cell Švejk told all the detainees that this kind of interrogation was fun. 'They shout at you a bit and finally they kick you out.

'In the old days,' continued Švejk, 'it used to be worse. I once read in a book how the accused had to walk on red-hot iron and drink molten lead, to prove whether they were innocent or not. Or else they put their legs into Spanish boots or strung them up on the ladder if they wouldn't confess. Or they burnt their hips with a fireman's torch like they did to St John of Nepomuk.[1] They say that when they did it to him he screamed like blue murder and didn't stop until they had thrown him from Eliška's bridge in a watertight sack. There were many cases like that and even after that they went and quartered the chap or stuck him on a stake somewhere near the Museum. And if a chap like that was only thrown into a dungeon he felt as if he were reborn.

'Nowadays it's fun being locked up,' Švejk continued with relish. 'There's no quartering, no Spanish boots. We've got bunks, a table, a bench. We're not all squashed together like sardines: we get soup; they give us bread and bring us a jug of water. We've got our latrines right under our snouts. You can see progress in everything. It's true that it's a bit far to the interrogation room. You've got to go along more than three corridors and up one staircase, but on the other hand it's clean and lively in the corridors. They bring one person here, another there – young, old, male and female. You can be glad that at least you're not alone here. Everyone goes his own sweet way and no one need be afraid that in the office they'll tell him: "Well, we've considered your case and tomorrow you'll be quartered or burnt. The choice is up to you." That certainly wasn't an easy choice to make, and I think, gentlemen, that many of us at a time like that would be completely flummoxed by it. Yes, nowadays things have improved for our good.'

He had just finished his defence of the modern way of imprisoning citizens, when a warder opened the door and shouted:

'Švejk, get dressed and come for interrogation.'

1. A Czech prelate who was tortured and thrown into the Vltava by order of Wenceslas IV in 1398. He was later canonized and became the symbol of the Counter-Reformation.

'I shall indeed,' answered Švejk. 'I've got no objection, but I'm afraid that there may be some mistake here. I've already been thrown out from interrogation once. And I'm afraid that these other gentlemen who are here with me will be cross with me if I go twice for interrogation when they haven't been there even once the whole evening. They might be jealous of me.'

'Get out and stop talking drivel,' was the reply to Švejk's gentlemanly utterance.

Švejk again found himself face to face with the gentleman of criminal type, who without beating about the bush asked him harshly and irrevocably:

'Do you confess to everything?'

Švejk fixed his good blue eyes on the ruthless man and said softly:

'If you want me to confess, your worship, I shall. It can't do me any harm. But if you say: "Švejk, don't confess to anything", I'll wriggle and wriggle out of it until there isn't a breath left in my body.'

The severe gentleman wrote something on the documents and handing Švejk a pen invited him to sign it.

And Švejk signed Bretschneider's deposition with the following addition:

All the above-named accusations against me are founded on fact.

Josef Švejk

When he had signed, he turned to the severe gentleman:

'Have I got to sign anything else? Or am I to come back in the morning?'

'In the morning you'll be taken off to the criminal court' was the answer.

'At what time, your worship? So that I don't oversleep, for Christ's sake.'

'Get out!' For the second time that day there was a roar from the other side of the table in front of which Švejk was standing.

Returning to his new home behind bars Švejk told the policeman who was escorting him:

'Everything here goes like a house on fire.'

As soon as the door closed behind him, his fellow prisoners deluged him with questions of all kinds, to which he replied clearly:

'I've just admitted that I might have murdered the Archduke Ferdinand.'

Six men crouched in horror under the lice-ridden blankets. Only the Bosnian said:

'*Dobro došli.*'[1]

As he lay down on the bunk Švejk said:

'It's stupid that we haven't got an alarm clock here.'

But in the morning he was woken up without an alarm clock, and at six o'clock sharp he was carried away to the criminal court in the Green Antony.[2]

'The early bird catches the worm,' said Švejk to his fellow travellers when the Green Antony drove out of the gates of police headquarters.

1. 'Welcome.'
2. Black Maria.

3

Švejk before the Medical Experts

THE clean, cosy cubicles of the regional criminal court made the most favourable impression on Švejk – the white-washed walls, the black-painted bars and the fat Mr Demartini, the chief warder for the prisoners on remand, with his purple facings and purple braid on his government-supplied cap. Purple is the colour prescribed not only here, but also at religious services on Ash Wednesday and Good Friday.

The glorious times of Roman rule over Jerusalem were coming back. The prisoners were led out and brought before the Pontius Pilates of 1914 down on the ground floor. And the examining magistrates, the Pilates of modern times, instead of honourably washing their hands, sent to Teissig's for goulash and Pilsen beer and passed more and more indictments to the Director of Prosecutions.

Here all logic mostly disappeared and the § triumphed. The § strangled, went mad, fumed, laughed, threatened, murdered and gave no quarter. The magistrates were jugglers with the law, high priests of its letter, devourers of the accused, tigers of the Austrian jungle, who measured their spring on the accused by the number of clauses.

The exception were a few gentlemen (as at police headquarters) who did not take the law quite so seriously, for everywhere wheat can be found among the tares.

It was to one of these gentlemen that they conducted Švejk for questioning. He was an elderly gentleman of affable appearance who, when he was once interrogating the notorious murderer, Valeš, never failed to tell him: 'Be so good as to sit down, Mr Valeš. There is an empty chair just here.'

When they led Švejk before him, with his natural amiability he asked him to sit down and said:

'So you are this Mr Švejk, then?'

'I think I must be,' answered Švejk, 'because my papa was Mr Švejk and my mamma was Mrs Švejk. I can't disgrace them by denying my own name.'

A kindly smile flitted across the face of the examining magistrate: 'Well, you've been up to a fine lot of things. You've certainly got a great deal on your conscience.'

'I've always got a great deal on my conscience,' said Švejk, smiling even more affably than the magistrate. 'I've probably got more on my conscience than Your Worship is pleased to have.'

'Well, that's clear from the statement you've signed,' said the magistrate in a no less affable tone. 'They didn't bring any pressure on you at the police station, did they?'

'Why, of course not, Your Worship. I asked them myself if I had to sign it, and when they told me to do so I obeyed. After all, I wouldn't want to quarrel with them just because of my signature, would I? It certainly wouldn't be in my interest to do that. There must be law and order.'

'Do you feel completely well, Mr Švejk?'

'Not completely well, no, I wouldn't say that, Your Worship. I've got rheumatism and I rub myself with Elliman's embrocation.'

The old gentleman again gave a kindly smile. 'What would you say if we were to have you examined by our medical experts?'

'I don't think that I can be so bad that these gentlemen need unnecessarily waste their time on me. I was examined by one doctor already at police headquarters to see if I'd got V.D.'

'You know, all the same, Mr Švejk, we'll try with these medical experts. We'll set up a nice commission and keep you in remand under investigation. In the meantime you'll have a nice rest. Now just one more question: is it true, as it is stated in the report, that you declared and widely disseminated the view that war would soon break out?'

'Oh, yes, Your Worship, and it will break out very soon indeed.'

'And you don't occasionally feel run down by any chance?'

'Oh, no, sir, I was only once nearly run down by a car on Charles Square but that was many years ago.'

That concluded the interrogation. Švejk shook hands with the magistrate and after having returned to his cell said to his neighbours:

'Now all because of that murder of His Imperial Highness, the Archduke Ferdinand, they're going to have me examined by the medical experts.'

'I've been examined by those medical experts too,' said a young man. 'That was when I had to come before a jury about some carpets. They certified me as feeble-minded. Now I've embezzled a steam threshing machine and they can't do anything to me. My lawyer told me yesterday that once I've been certified feeble-minded, I'll have the benefit of it for the rest of my life.'

'I don't trust those medical experts at all,' observed the man with the intelligent appearance. 'Once when I forged some bills of exchange I prepared myself for all eventualities and went to lectures by the psychiatrist Dr Heveroch, and when they caught me, I pretended to be a paralytic, exactly as Dr Heveroch had described one. I bit one of the medical experts on the commission in the leg, drank ink out of the ink pot and relieved myself, if you'll pardon the expression, gentlemen, in the corner in the view of the whole commission. But because I bit one of them through the calf they certified me as completely fit and so I was done for.'

'I'm not a bit afraid of these gentlemen's examinations,' said Švejk.

'When I was in the army a vet examined me and it didn't turn out at all badly.'

'Medical experts are swine,' the short man with a stoop broke in. 'Not long ago quite by chance they dug up a skeleton in my meadow, and the medical experts said that it was murdered forty years ago by some blunt object on the head. I'm thirty-eight and I've been gaoled, although I have my birth certificate, an extract from the parish register and my identity card.'

'I think that we should be fair about everything,' said Švejk. 'After all, anybody can and must make a mistake, the more he thinks about a thing. Medical experts are human beings and human beings have their faults. Once in Nusle, just by the bridge across the Botič, a gentleman came up to me in the night, when I was coming back from U Banzetů, and hit me over the head with a knout. And when I was lying on the ground he flashed his torch on me and said: "It's a mistake. It's not him." And he got so angry because he'd made a mistake that he hit me on the back again. It's only human nature that a chap should go on making mistakes until he dies. It's just like that gentleman who one night found a mad, half-frozen dog, took it home with him and put it in his wife's bed. As soon as it had got warmed up it bit the whole family and tore to pieces and devoured the baby in the cradle. Or I can give you an example of a mistake a turner who lives in our house once made. He opened the chapel at Podolí with his key, because he thought it was his kitchen, and lay down on the altar because he thought that he was home in bed. And then he pulled over himself some cloths with holy inscriptions and put the New Testament and other sacred books under his head to make it higher. In the morning he was found by the sexton and when he came to himself he told him quite good-humouredly that it was only a little mistake. "A nice little mistake," said the sexton, "when all because of it we shall have to have the church re-consecrated." After that the turner came before the medical experts and they proved to him that he had been completely sensible and sober, because if he had been tight, they said, he wouldn't have been able to fit the key into the lock of the chapel door. Afterwards that turner died in Pankrác. I can also give you another example of how a police dog at Kladno made a mistake. It was an Alsatian which belonged to the famous cavalry captain, Rotter. Captain Rotter bred these dogs and experimented with them on tramps, until all the tramps began to avoid the district of Kladno. And so he gave orders that the gendarmes must bring in some suspicious individual without fail. Well, once they brought him a quite respectably dressed man, whom they'd found in the Forest of Lány sitting on a tree stump. The captain at once had a piece of his coat-tails cut off and given to his police dogs to sniff. And then they took the man away to a brick works behind the town and set their trained dogs on to his tracks. The dogs found him and brought him back again. Then the man had to climb up a ladder to a loft, leap over a wall and jump into a lake with the dogs after him. In the end it turned out that he was a deputy of the Czech Radical Party who had gone for an outing in the woods of Lány after having got bored with parliament. And that's why I say that people are erring creatures by nature, they make errors, never mind whether they're learned people or stupid uneducated idiots. Even ministers make mistakes.'

The commission of medical experts, which had to decide whether Švejk's mental horizon did or did not correspond to all the crimes with which he was charged, consisted of three unusually solemn gentlemen whose views were such that the view of each differed gloriously from any of the views of the other two.

Three different scientific schools and psychiatric views were represented there.

If in the case of Švejk complete agreement had been reached between these opposing scientific camps, it can be explained purely and simply by the stunning impression he produced upon them when he entered the room where his mental state was to be examined and, observing a picture of the Austrian monarch hanging on the wall, cried out:

'Long live our Emperor, Franz Joseph I, gentlemen.'

The case was clear as daylight. Švejk's spontaneous declaration disposed of a whole range of questions, and there only remained a few very important questions which were needed so that from Švejk's answers the initial opinion of him could be confirmed according to the system of the psychiatrist Dr Kallerson, Dr Heveroch and the Englishman, Weiking.

'Is radium heavier than lead?'

'Please, sir, I haven't weighed it,' answered Švejk with his sweet smile.

'Do you believe in the end of the world?'

'I'd have to see that end first,' Švejk answered nonchalantly. 'But certainly I shan't see it tomorrow.'

'Would you know how to calculate the diameter of the globe?'

'No, I'm afraid I wouldn't,' answered Švejk, 'but I'd like to ask you a riddle myself, gentlemen. Take a three-storied house, with eight windows on each floor. On the roof there are two dormer windows

and two chimneys. On every floor there are two tenants. And now, tell me, gentlemen, in which year the house-porter's grandmother died?'

The medical experts exchanged knowing looks, but nevertheless one of them asked this further question:

'You don't know the maximum depth of the Pacific Ocean?'

'No, please sir, I don't,' was the answer, 'but I think that it must be definitely deeper than the Vltava below the rock of Vyšehrad.'

The chairman of the commission asked briefly: 'Is that enough?', but nonetheless another member requested the following question:

'How much is 12,897 times 13,863?'

'729,' answered Švejk, without batting an eyelid.

'I think that that will do,' said the chairman of the commission. 'You can take the accused back where he came from.'

'Thank you, gentlemen,' replied Švejk deferentially. 'For me it will do too.'

After his departure the three agreed that Švejk was a patent imbecile and idiot according to all the natural laws invented by the luminaries of psychiatry.

The report which was passed to the examining magistrate contained *inter alia* the following:

The undersigned medical experts certify the complete mental feebleness and congenital idiocy of Josef Švejk, who appeared before the aforesaid commission and expressed himself in terms such as: 'Long live our Emperor Franz Joseph I', which utterance is sufficient to illuminate the state of mind of Josef Švejk as that of a patent imbecile.

The undersigned commission accordingly recommends:

1. That the investigation of Josef Švejk be quashed.
2. That Josef Švejk be sent to a psychiatrical clinic for observation to establish how far his mental state is a danger to his surroundings.

While this report was being compiled Švejk was telling his fellow prisoners: 'They didn't care a hoot about Ferdinand, but talked to me about even stupider nonsense. Finally we agreed that what we talked about was quite enough for us and we parted.'

'I don't believe anyone,' observed the short man with a stoop on whose meadow a skeleton happened to have been dug up. 'They're all of them a gang of crooks.'

'There have to be crooks in this world too,' said Švejk, lying down on his straw mattress. 'If everyone were honest with each other, they'd soon start punching each other's noses.'

4

Švejk Thrown out of the Lunatic Asylum

WHEN Švejk subsequently described life in the lunatic asylum, he did
so in exceptionally eulogistic terms: 'I really don't know why those
loonies get so angry when they're kept there. You can crawl naked on
the floor, howl like a jackal, rage and bite. If anyone did this anywhere
on the promenade people would be astonished, but there it's the most
common or garden thing to do. There's a freedom there which not
even Socialists have ever dreamed of. A chap can pass himself off as
God Almighty, the Virgin Mary, the Pope, the King of England,
His Imperial Majesty or St Wenceslas, although the chap who said he
was St Wenceslas was tied up naked all day long and lay in solitary
confinement. There was also a chap who shouted out that he was the
Archbishop, but all he did was to eat, and, if you'll pardon the expression, do something else which rhymes with it – excrete – but no
one's ashamed of doing that there. One chap even pretended to be St
Cyril and St Methodius just to get a double portion. And there was
one gentleman there who was pregnant and invited everyone to the
christening. There were many people shut up there who were chess
players, politicians, fishermen and scouts, stamp collectors and amateur
photographers. One person was there because of some old pots which
he called funerary urns. One was in a straitjacket all the time so that he
shouldn't be able to calculate when the world would come to an end.
And I also met a certain number of professors there. One of them
used to follow me about all the time and expatiate on how the cradle
of the gipsy race was in the Krkonoše, and the other explained to me
that inside the globe there was another globe much bigger than the
outer one.

'Everyone there could say exactly what he pleased and what was
on the tip of his tongue, just as if he was in parliament. Sometimes they used to tell each other fairy stories and started fighting when
something very bad happened to a princess. The wildest of them all
was a gentleman who pretended to be the sixteenth volume of *Otto's
Encyclopedia* and asked everybody to open him and to find the entry:

"Cardboard box stapling machine", otherwise he would be done for. He only quietened down when they put him in a straitjacket. Then he was happy, because he thought he had got into a bookbinder's press and begged to be given a modern trim. It was really like living in paradise there. You could kick up a row, fight, sing, cry, bleat, yell, jump, say your prayers, turn somersaults, crawl on all fours, hop, run about, dance, skip, squat all day on your haunches and climb up the walls. No one would come to you and tell you: "You mustn't do that, sir. It's not decent. You should be ashamed of yourself. Aren't you properly brought up?" It's true however that there are loonies there who are quite quiet. There was one well brought-up inventor, for instance, who continually picked his nose and said only once a day: "I've just discovered electricity." As I say it was very pleasant there and those few days which I spent in the lunatic asylum are among the loveliest hours of my life.'

And indeed the very welcome which awaited Švejk in the asylum, when they had taken him away from the criminal court and brought him there for observation, surpassed his expectations. First they stripped him naked, then they gave him a hospital gown and led him off to have a bath, holding him familiarly under his arms, while one of the male nurses entertained him by telling him some jokes about Jews. In the bathroom they immersed him in a tub of warm water, and then pulled him out and put him under a cold douche. They repeated this three times and then asked him how he liked it. Švejk said that it was better than in the baths near the Charles Bridge, and that he liked bathing very much. 'If you'll only cut my nails and my hair too, I'll have everything I need to make me completely happy,' he added with a pleasant smile.

And this request of his was granted too, and after they had thoroughly rubbed him down with a sponge as well, they wrapped him in a sheet, carried him off to the first ward, put him on to a bed, covered him with a quilt and asked him to go to sleep.

And even today Švejk talks about it with affection: 'Just imagine, they carried me, really carried me off. I was in a state of utter bliss at that moment.'

And indeed he fell blissfully asleep on the bed. Then they woke him to offer him a mug of milk and a roll. The roll was already cut up into little pieces and while one of the warders held both his arms, the other dipped the pieces of roll into the milk and fed him like a goose is

fed on dumplings. When they had finished feeding him, they took him under the arms and led him off to the W.C., where they asked him to perform his large and small bodily needs.

And Švejk talks with affection about this lovely moment too and I certainly do not need to reproduce his words describing what they did with him after that. I will only mention that he said:

'One of them held me in his arms while I was doing it.'

When they brought him back, they put him to bed again and asked him once more to go to sleep. But just as he had dozed off they woke him up and took him to the examination room, where, standing stark naked before two doctors, he was reminded of the glorious time when he was called up. The German word '*tauglich*' or 'fit for service' fell spontaneously from his lips.

'What are you saying?' asked one of the doctors. 'Take five paces forward and five to the rear.'

Švejk took ten.

'But I told you to take five,' said the doctor.

'A few paces more or less are all the same to me,' said Švejk.

After that the doctors asked him to sit down on a chair and one of them tapped him on the knee. Then he said to the other doctor that the reflexes were perfectly correct, whereupon the other shook his head and began to tap Švejk's knee himself, while the first doctor opened wide Švejk's eyelids and examined his pupils. After that they went away to a table and let fall one or two expressions in Latin.

'Listen, can you sing?' one of them asked Švejk. 'Would you please sing us a song?'

'With pleasure, gentlemen,' Švejk answered. 'I haven't any voice or musical ear, you know, but I'll have a shot. I'll do it to please you, if you want to be amused.'

And Švejk struck up:

> 'The little monk sat in the chair
> And scalding tears ran down his cheeks.
> Feverishly he tore his hair . . .

'I'm afraid I don't know any more,' continued Švejk. 'If you like I can also sing you:

> 'Oh, 'tis heavy on my heart,
> My bosom heaves with leaden pain,
> As I sit here and gaze afar,
> To where I'm bound by love's sweet chain . . .

'And I can't remember any more of that either,' sighed Švejk. 'I also know the first verse of "Where is my home?"¹ and "General Windischgrätz as the cock did crow". And a few folk songs too, like "God save our Emperor and land", "When we marched to Jaroměř" and "Hail to Thee, Holy Virgin, hail a thousand times" ...'

The learned doctors exchanged glances, and one of them put the following question to Švejk:

'Have you ever had your mental condition examined?'

'In the army,' Švejk replied solemnly and proudly, 'I was officially certified by military doctors as a patent idiot.'

'I believe you're a malingerer!' the other doctor shouted at Švejk.

'What, me, gentlemen?' said Švejk, defending himself. 'No, I assure you I'm no malingerer. I'm a genuine idiot. You only have to ask at České Budějovice or at the reserve command at Karlín.'

1. Afterwards the Czech national anthem.

The elder of the two doctors waved his hand in a gesture of despair and pointing to Švejk said to the nurses: 'Give this man back his clothes and send him to the third class in the first corridor. Then one of you come back and take all his papers to the office. And tell them there to settle the case quickly, so that we don't have him round our necks for long.'

The doctors cast another devastating look at Švejk who backed deferentially to the door, bowing politely. When one of the nurses asked him what nonsense he was up to now, he answered: 'As I'm not dressed, I'm naked and I wouldn't like to show these gentlemen anything, in case they should think me rude or vulgar.' From the moment the nurses received orders to return Švejk's clothes to him, they no longer showed the slightest concern for him. They told him to get dressed, and one of them took him to the third class where, during the few days it took the office to complete his discharge formalities, he had an opportunity of carrying on his agreeable observations. The disappointed doctors gave him a certificate that he was a 'malingerer whose mind was affected', but as they discharged him before he was given any lunch it led to a minor scene.

Švejk declared that if they threw anyone out of a lunatic asylum they had no right to do so without giving him lunch.

This breach of the public peace was stopped by a police officer who had been summoned by the asylum porter and who took Švejk off to the police station in Salmova Street.

5

Švejk at the Police Station in Salmova Street

AFTER Švejk's beautiful, sunny days in the asylum came hours full of persecution. Police Inspector Braun set the scene for his meeting with Švejk with all the cruelty of Roman lictors in the time of the charming Emperor Nero. With the same ruthlessness as they said: 'Throw this scoundrel of a Christian to the lions', Inspector Braun said: 'Put him behind bars.'

Not a word more or less, except that Inspector Braun's eyes shone with a peculiarly perverted lust.

Švejk bowed and said proudly: 'I'm ready, gentlemen. I believe behind bars means the same as a prison cell, and that's not too bad.'

'Don't make yourself too much at home here,' answered the police officer, whereupon Švejk piped up: 'I'm quite modest and grateful for anything you do for me.'

In the cell a man was sitting on a plank-bed deep in thought. He sat listlessly, and it was clear from his expression that when the key grated in the lock of the cell he did not believe that the door would open to set him free.

'My compliments, Your Honour,' said Švejk, sitting down beside him on the plank-bed. 'What time might it be?'

'Time is not my master,' the thoughtful man answered.

'It's not too bad here,' Švejk continued: 'They've at least planed the wood on this plank-bed.'

The solemn man made no reply. He stood up and began to rush about in the tiny space between the door and the bed, as if he were hurrying to save something.

In the meantime Švejk observed with interest the writings scrawled upon the walls. There was one inscription in which an unknown prisoner solemnly pledged to heaven a fight to the death with the police. It read: 'You won't half catch it.' Another prisoner had written: 'Buzz off, you cops.' Another merely recorded the plain fact: 'I was locked up here on 5 June 1913 and wasn't too badly treated. Josef Mareček, tradesman from Vršovice.' And there was another inscription which was earth-shaking in its profundity: 'Have mercy, Almighty God . . .' And underneath: 'Kiss my a—.' The letter 'a' had been crossed out however and instead was written in capitals: 'COAT TAILS'. Beside it some poetical soul had written the lines: 'I sit in

sorrow by the stream. The sun is hid behind the fells. I watch the radiant mountain tops, Where my best beloved dwells.'

The man who was rushing between the door and the plank-bed as though he was trying to win a marathon race stopped and breathlessly resumed his seat. He plunged his head in his hands and suddenly screamed: 'Let me out!'

'No, they won't let me out,' he said to himself. 'They won't. They won't. I've been here since six o'clock this morning.'

He then had a fit of expansiveness, stood up erect and asked Švejk:

'You don't by any chance have a strap on you, so that I can end it all?'

'That's something I can very gladly help you with,' answered Švejk, undoing his belt. 'I've never yet seen anyone hang himself on a strap in a prison cell.

'Only it's a nuisance that there's no hook here,' he went on, looking around him. 'The window latch won't bear your weight, unless you hang yourself kneeling by the plank-bed, like the monk did in the Emmaus monastery, when he hanged himself on a crucifix because of a young Jewess. I'm very fond of suicides, so just carry on. Well begun is half done.'

The gloomy man, into whose hands Švejk had pushed the strap, gave it one look, threw it into the corner and burst out crying, smearing his tears with his black hands and shrieking out: 'I've got little children! I'm here for drunkenness and immoral practices. My God, my poor wife, what will they say to me in the office? I've got little children! I'm here for drunkenness and immoral practices' etc. etc. *ad infinitum*.

At last, however, he calmed down a little, went to the door and began to kick it and pound it with his fists. From behind the door could be heard steps and a voice: 'What do you want?'

'Let me out,' he said in a voice which sounded as if he had nothing left to live for. 'Where to?' came the answer from the other side.

'To my office,' answered the unfortunate father, official, drunkard and libertine.

Laughter could be heard in the quiet of the passage, horrible laughter, and the steps went away again.

'It seems to me that that gentleman must hate you if he laughs at you like that,' said Švejk, when the despairing man sat down beside him again. 'A policeman like that might do a lot of harm when he gets angry, and when he gets angrier still he might do anything. Just sit down quietly, if you don't want to hang yourself, and wait and see how things develop. If you're an official, you're married and you have little babes, it's frightful, I must admit. If I'm not mistaken you're probably convinced that they'll sack you from the office.'

'I can't say,' he sighed, 'because I don't remember myself what I was up to. I only know that I got thrown out from somewhere and that I wanted to get back there to light a cigar. But it started splendidly. Our departmental chief was celebrating his name day and invited us to a wine restaurant. Then we went to a second, a third, a fourth, a fifth, a sixth, a seventh, an eighth, a ninth . . .'

'Wouldn't you like me to help you count?' asked Švejk. 'I'm a bit of an expert. One night I was in twenty-eight pubs. But, God's truth, I never had at the most more than three glasses of beer in any one of them.'

'In short,' continued the unfortunate subordinate of the departmental chief who had celebrated his name day in such magnificent style, 'when we'd been in about a dozen different night dens we discovered we'd lost our chief, although we'd tied him with string and led him with us like a little dog. And so we went to look for him everywhere and finally we all lost each other until in the end I found myself in one of those night cafés in Vinohrady, a very decent place, where I drank a liqueur straight out of the bottle. What I did afterwards I can't remember. I only know that when they brought me to the police station here two policemen reported that I was drunk, had been behaving immorally, had hit a lady, taken down somebody else's hat from the peg and cut it in shreds with my penknife, chased away the ladies' orchestra, accused the head waiter in front of everyone of stealing twenty crowns, smashed the marble slab at the table where I was sitting and intentionally spat into the black coffee of a stranger at the next table. I didn't do anything else. At least I can't remember having done so. And, believe me, I'm a decent, intelligent man who hasn't a thought for anything except his family. What do you say to that? I'm certainly not a hooligan!'

Švejk made no reply but asked with interest: 'Did you have much trouble smashing that marble slab or did you do it at one go?'

'At one go,' answered the intelligent gentleman.

'Then you're for it,' said Švejk pensively. 'They'll prove to you that you coached yourself for it with intensive training. And that stranger's coffee which you spat into, was it with rum or not?'

And without waiting for an answer he explained:

'If it was with rum, then it'll be worse for you, because it's more expensive. In the court they reckon up every item and add them together so that it amounts at least to a crime.'

'In the court ...' the conscientious paterfamilias whispered dejectedly and, hanging his head, lapsed into that unpleasant state in which a man is devoured by the reproaches of his conscience.[1]

---

1. Some writers use the expression: 'gnawed by the reproaches of his conscience'. I do not regard this expression as altogether appropriate. After all, a tiger devours a man and does not gnaw him. (Author's note.)

'And do they know at home that you're in gaol,' Švejk asked, 'or will they wait till it's in the paper?'

'Do you think it will be in the paper?' was the naïve question of the victim of the name day party of his departmental chief.

'Why, it's a dead certainty,' was the frank answer, for Švejk was never one to conceal anything from others. 'All the newspaper readers will get a great kick out of what you did. I also like to read that column about drunks and their escapades. Not long ago at the pub The Chalice one of the guests didn't do anything more than break his own head with a glass. He threw the glass up into the air and then stood underneath it. But they carried him off and the very next morning we read it in the papers. Or in Bendlovka I once slapped an undertaker's mute and he slapped me back. To restore peace between us they had to arrest us both, and at once it was in the afternoon paper. Or when that Councillor smashed two cups in the café The Corpse, do you imagine they spared him? It was immediately in the newspapers the day after. All you can do is to send a correction to the papers from gaol saying that the information published about you has nothing to do with you, and that you're no relative of the person of that name and have no connection with him. And you must write home and tell them to cut your correction out of the paper and keep it, so that you can read it when you've served out your sentence.

'Aren't you cold?' asked Švejk, who was full of compassion when he saw that the intelligent gentleman was shivering. 'This year the summer has turned very cold.'

'I am done for,' sobbed Švejk's companion. 'I've lost my promotion now.'

'You certainly have,' Švejk agreed readily. 'And if they don't take you back in to the office after you've served out your sentence I don't know whether you'll find another job so quickly, because anyone at all you wanted to work for, even if it was a skinner, would require from you a certificate of good conduct. No, a moment of debauchery like what you've indulged in costs you dear. And will your wife and children have anything to live on while you're sitting in gaol? Or will she have to go and beg and teach the babes all sorts of vices?'

A sob could be heard:

'My poor little babes! My poor wife!'

The conscienceless penitent stood up and started talking about his babes: he had five. The eldest was twelve and was one of those scouts.

He only drank water and ought to have been an example to his father, who had misbehaved like this for the first time in his life.

'A scout?' exclaimed Švejk. 'I like hearing about those scouts. Once in Mydlovary near Zliv, district Hluboká, police district České Budějovice, just when we of the 91st were doing our training, the peasants from the neighbourhood started a hunt for scouts who were swarming in the parish wood. They caught three of them. When they tied up the smallest of them, he moaned, squealed and wailed so much that we hardened soldiers could not bear the sight of it and thought it better to clear off. While these three scouts were being tied up they bit eight peasants. Afterwards under the torture of the birch they confessed before the mayor that there wasn't a single meadow in the region they hadn't flattened out while they lay sunbathing. And then again they said that it was only by pure accident that the field of standing corn near Ražice burnt down. It was just before the harvest and they only happened to be roasting a deer on a spit in the middle of it – one they'd stalked and killed with their knives in the parish wood. In their hide-out in the wood were found more than half a hundred-weight of gnawed bones of poultry and game, an enormous quantity of cherry stones, heaps of cores of unripe apples and other good things.'

The scout's poor father was not to be comforted, however.

'What have I done?' he wailed. 'My reputation is ruined.'

'It certainly is,' said Švejk with his characteristic frankness. 'After all you've done your reputation will certainly be ruined for life. When your friends have read all about it in the newspapers they'll certainly add something to it of their own. They always do that, but don't be worried about it. There are ten times more people in the world with blemished reputations than there are with unblemished ones! That's just a very unimportant trifle.'

In the passage energetic steps could be heard, the key grated in the lock, the door opened and a policeman called Švejk's name.

'Excuse me,' said Švejk chivalrously, 'I've only been here since twelve noon, but this gentleman has been here since six o'clock this morning. I'm not in any hurry anyway.'

Instead of getting an answer Švejk was dragged into the passage by the powerful arm of a policeman and silently led up the stairs to the first floor. In the second room a police inspector was sitting at a table. He was a fat gentleman of amiable countenance and said to Švejk:

'So you're this Švejk, then? And how did you get here?'

'The most common or garden way in the world,' answered Švejk. 'I came here under the escort of a police officer, because I wasn't going to put up with them throwing me out of the lunatic asylum without any lunch. It was as though they took me for a kicked-out whore.'

'All right, Švejk,' said the inspector affably, 'why should we have to be bothered with you here at Salmova Street? Wouldn't it be better to send you to police headquarters?'

'You're master of the situation, as the saying goes,' said Švejk with composure. 'A walk to police headquarters now in the evening would be quite a pleasant little stroll.'

'I am glad that we agree about that,' said the inspector cheerfully. 'It's much better when we agree, isn't it, Švejk?'

'And I'm always awfully glad to take advice from anyone too,' replied Švejk. 'I'll never forget your kindness to me, inspector. Believe me I won't.'

Bowing deferentially he went down to the guardroom accompanied by the police officer, and a quarter of an hour later could be seen at the corner of Ječná Street and Charles Square under the escort of another police officer who was carrying under his arm a voluminous book of prisoners' records with the German title *Arrestantenbuch*.

At the corner of Spálená Street Švejk and his escort met a crowd of people who were surging round a placard that had been hung up.

'That's His Imperial Majesty's proclamation on the declaration of war,' said the police officer to Švejk.

'I prophesied it,' said Švejk, 'but in the lunatic asylum they still don't know about it, although they should have got it from the horse's mouth.'

'What do you mean?' the police officer asked Švejk.

'Because they've got a lot of officer gentlemen locked up there,' Švejk explained, and when they reached another crowd of people surging in front of the proclamation, Švejk shouted out:

'God save our Emperor Franz Joseph! We shall win this war!'

Someone in the enthusiastic crowd banged his hat over his ears, and so the good soldier Švejk, surrounded by a crowd of people, stepped once more through the gates of police headquarters.

'Quite definitely we'll win this war. I repeat it once more, gentlemen!'

And with these words Švejk took leave of the crowd which accompanied him.

And somewhere from the dim ages of history the truth dawned upon Europe that the morrow would obliterate the plans of today.

Švejk Home Again after having Broken
through the Vicious Circle

THE spirit of alien authority pervaded the building of the police headquarters – an authority which was ascertaining how enthusiastic the population were for the war. With the exception of a few people who were ready to admit that they were sons of a nation which had to bleed for interests completely alien to it, police headquarters presented the finest collection of bureaucratical beasts of prey, to whom gaols and gallows were the only means of defending the existence of the twisted clauses of the law.

They treated their victims with malicious affability, weighing every word carefully in advance.

'I am very sorry that you've fallen into our hands again,' said one of these black and yellow striped vultures, when they brought Švejk before him. 'We thought that you'd reform, but we've been disappointed.'

Švejk mutely nodded his head and assumed so innocent an expression that the black and yellow vulture looked at him inquiringly and said emphatically:

'Take that imbecile expression off your face.'

But he immediately went over to an amiable tone and continued:

'Of course it's very disagreeable for us to keep you in custody, and I can assure you that in my opinion your guilt can't be so enormous. With your absence of intelligence you must obviously have been led astray. Tell me, Mr Švejk, who was it really who led you to commit such stupidities?'

Švejk coughed and replied:

'Begging your pardon, sir, I know nothing of any stupidities.'

'But wasn't it stupidity, Mr Švejk,' he said in an artificially paternal tone, 'when, according to the deposition of the police officer who brought you here, you caused a crowd of people to collect in front of the war proclamation which was posted up at the corner, and you

incited people with shouts of: "God Save Our Emperor Franz Joseph!
This war is already won!"?'

'I couldn't hang back,' declared Švejk, fixing his honest eyes on the
eyes of the inquisitor. 'I was so angry when I saw how they were all
reading this proclamation and none of them were expressing any joy.
There were no shouts of "God Save Our Emperor", no hurrahs, nothing at all, inspector. It was just as if they didn't care. An old soldier
of the 91st regiment like me couldn't go on looking at it and so I
shouted out those words. And I believe that had you been in my place
you'd have done exactly the same as I did. If there's a war it must be
won and people must call out "God Save Our Emperor." No one will
talk me out of that!'

Crushed and overcome the black and yellow wolf could not withstand
the gaze of the pure and innocent lamb, Švejk. He lowered his gaze on
to the official documents and said:

'I give you full marks for your enthusiasm, but if only it had been
displayed in different circumstances! After all you know very well that
you were under police escort and that a patriotic pronouncement like
that could and must have been regarded by the public as ironic rather
than serious.'

'When a chap is being led under police escort,' answered Švejk,
'it's a very hard moment in his life. And if a man, even in such a
difficult moment as that, doesn't forget what he ought to do when
there's a war on, I think he's not so bad after all.'

The black and yellow wolf growled and looked Švejk in the eyes once
more.

Švejk parried with the innocent, gentle, modest and tender warmth
of his gaze.

For a moment they both went on staring fixedly at each other.

'Go to hell, Švejk,' said the official at last, 'and if you ever come here
again, I shan't ask you any questions but march you straight off to the
military court at Hradčany. Do you understand?'

But before he could say Jack Robinson, Švejk had stepped towards
him, kissed his hand and said:

'May the good Lord reward you for everything! If at any time you
should need a thoroughbred little dog, just ask me. I deal in dogs.'

And so Švejk found himself at liberty again and on his way home.

He could not make up his mind whether he should stop first at The
Chalice. Finally he decided he would and opened the door through

which he had gone out some time ago under the escort of detective Bretschneider.

A deathly silence reigned in the bar. A few guests sat there, including the sexton from St Apollinaire. They looked very gloomy. Behind the serving counter sat Mrs Palivec and stared dully at the beer taps.

'Well, here I am back again,' said Švejk gaily. 'May I have a glass of beer, please? What's happened to Mr Palivec? Is he home again too?'

Instead of replying Mrs Palivec burst into tears and concentrating all her misery on to a special stress on every word groaned out:

'A week ago he – got – ten – years.'

'There you are, then,' said Švejk, 'so he's already served seven days of it.'

'He was always so careful,' sobbed Mrs Palivec. 'He always said that about himself.'

The customers in the bar maintained a stubborn silence, as though the spirit of Palivec was haunting the room and urging them to even greater caution.

'Caution is the mother of wisdom,' said Švejk, sitting down at a table to a glass of beer. In the foam there were little holes made by Mrs Palivec's tears as they fell into it when she brought the glass to the table for Švejk. 'We're living in such times that we are forced to be cautious.'

'Yesterday we had two funerals,' said the sexton of St Apollinaire, changing the subject.

'That means somebody must have died,' said another customer, whereupon a third added:

'Were they funerals with a catafalque?'

'I'd like to know,' said Švejk, 'what military funerals are going to be like now there's a war on.'

The customers rose, paid and went out noiselessly. Švejk was left alone with Mrs Palivec.

'I never imagined that they'd sentence an innocent man to ten years,' he said. 'Sentencing an innocent man to five years, that's something I've heard of, but ten, that's a bit too much.'

'Well, you see, he confessed everything, my old man,' sobbed Mrs Palivec. 'What he was saying here about those flies and that picture he repeated at police headquarters and before the court. I was a witness at the trial, but what evidence could I give when they told me that as I was in a state of relations with my husband I could forgo giving evidence? I was so scared of that "state of relations", in case it might lead to something else, that I got out of giving evidence and he, poor dear, gave me such a look! I shall never forget that look to my dying day. And after the sentence had been passed and they were leading him off he shouted to them in the passage, as though he'd gone off his head: "Long live Free Thinking!"'

'And Mr Bretschneider doesn't come here any more?' asked Švejk.

'He's been here several times,' answered Mrs Palivec. 'He drank a beer or two, asked me who comes here and listened to the customers talking about football. As soon as they catch sight of him they start talking about nothing else but football. And he had the jerks as though any moment he'd go mad and have a fit. And all that time he only succeeded in catching an upholsterer from Příčná Street.'

'It's all a matter of training,' observed Švejk. 'Was that upholsterer a stupid fellow?'

'Rather like my husband,' she replied, weeping. 'Mr Bretschneider asked him if he would fire against the Serbs. And he said he couldn't shoot, that he was once at the shooting range and shot through a whole crown. Then we all heard how Mr Bretschneider took out his notebook and said: "Aha, and here's another nice case of treason!", and he went away with that upholsterer from Příčná Street, who never came back.'

'Lots of them never come back,' said Švejk. 'Can I have a rum, please?'

Švejk was just having a second glass of rum, when Bretschneider came into the bar. Throwing a quick glance at the bar and the empty rooms he sat down next to Švejk and ordering a beer waited to see what he would say.

Švejk took down a newspaper from the hanger and looking at the last page of advertisements said:

'Well, I never! Look at that! A Mr Čimpera of Straškov no. 5, near Račiněves, is selling a farm with nine acres of land convenient for school and railway station.'

Bretschneider drummed his fingers nervously and turning to Švejk said:

'I'm surprised that you're interested in farming, Mr Švejk.'

'Oh, it's you, is it?' said Švejk, shaking his hand. 'I couldn't recognize you at first. I have a very bad memory. The last time we parted, if I remember aright, was in the reception office at police headquarters. What have you been doing since then? Do you come here often?'

'I've come here today because of you,' said Bretschneider. 'I was told at police headquarters that you sell dogs. I need a nice miniature pinscher or a pom or something of that kind.'

'I can get any for you,' replied Švejk. 'Do you want a thoroughbred animal or a common cur?'

'I think I'll plump for a thoroughbred,' replied Bretschneider.

'And why don't you have a police dog?' asked Švejk. 'Wouldn't you like one that picks up the scent at once and leads you to the scene of the crime? There's a butcher in Vršovice who has one and he uses it for drawing his cart. You might very well say that that dog has missed its vocation.'

'I should like a pom,' said Bretschneider with quiet obstinacy, 'a pom that doesn't bite.'

'Do you want a pom without teeth then?' asked Švejk. 'I know of one. It belongs to a pub keeper in Dejvice.'

'Then I'd rather have a miniature pinscher,' replied Bretschneider, whose cynological capacities were very elementary and who would never have learnt anything about dogs at all, if he had not got those orders from police headquarters.

But the instructions were precise, clear and firm – to get on to familiar terms with Švejk on the basis of his dog-dealing; for which purpose he had the right to choose assistants and dispose of funds for the purchase of dogs.

'There are bigger and smaller miniature pinschers,' said Švejk. 'I know of two small ones and three big ones. You can nurse all five of them on your lap. I can recommend them to you very warmly.'

'That's what I'd like,' said Bretschneider. 'And how much would it be if I only took one?'

'It goes by sizes,' answered Švejk. 'It depends on the size, you see. A miniature pinscher's not a calf. With miniature pinschers it's just the opposite, the smaller they are the dearer they come.'

'I'm considering getting larger ones which would be good watch-dogs,' answered Bretschneider, who was beginning to fear that he might overburden the secret funds of the State Police.

'All right, then,' said Švejk. 'I can sell you the bigger ones for fifty crowns and bigger ones still for forty-five crowns. But we've forgotten one thing. Are they to be puppies or grown dogs, dogs or bitches?'

'It's all the same to me,' answered Bretschneider, who was here on unfamiliar ground. 'Get them for me and I'll come and fetch them tomorrow at seven o'clock in the evening. Is that all right?'

'Come along and it'll be all right,' answered Švejk drily, 'but in this case I must ask you for a deposit of thirty crowns.'

'By all means,' said Bretschneider, paying out the money, 'and now let's have a quarter-litre of wine on me.'

When they had drunk it up Švejk stood Bretschneider another quarter and then Bretschneider invited Švejk not to be afraid of him, saying that today he was not on duty and that it was all right to speak to him about politics.

Švejk declared that he never spoke about politics in a pub, that politics in general were only for babies.

Bretschneider's views were, on the contrary, more revolutionary. He

said that every weak state was doomed to extinction and asked Švejk
what were his views on this subject.

Švejk said that he had nothing to do with the state, but that he had
once had to look after a St Bernard puppy in a weak state. He had fed
it on army biscuits but it had pegged out all the same.

When each of them had had a fifth quarter-litre Bretschneider
declared that he was an anarchist and asked Švejk what organization he
would recommend him to join.

Švejk said that an anarchist once purchased from him a Leonberger
dog for a hundred crowns and never paid him the last instalment.

During the sixth quarter-litre Bretschneider talked about revolution
and against mobilization, whereupon Švejk leaned towards him and
whispered in his ear:

'A customer's just come in. Be careful he doesn't hear you otherwise
you might be in trouble. You see the landlord's wife's already in tears.'

Mrs Palivec was indeed crying on her chair behind the service
counter.

'What are you crying for, Mrs Palivec?' asked Bretschneider. 'In
three months' time we'll have won the war, there'll be an amnesty, your
husband'll return and then we'll have a fine celebration.

'Or don't you think that we shall win?' he asked, turning to Švejk.

'Why keep on always playing that gramophone record?' said Švejk.
'We've got to win and that's that. And now I must go home.'

Švejk paid his bill and returned to his old charwoman, Mrs Müller,
who was scared when she realized that the man who was opening the
door of the flat with his latch key was Švejk.

'O Lord, sir, I thought you wouldn't be returning here for many
years,' she said with her usual frankness. 'And so in the meanwhile out
of charity I took a porter from a night club as a lodger, because we've
had a police search here three times, and when they couldn't find anything they said it was all up with you because you were so cunning.'

Švejk was at once able to convince himself that the unknown lodger
had made himself very much at home. He was sleeping in his bed and
was indeed so noble as to be content with only half of it, having
placed in the other half a long-haired creature, who gratefully slept
embracing him round the neck, while articles of male and female
attire were scattered higgledy-piggledy round the bed. From this
chaos it was evident that the night-club porter had returned with his
lady in a jocund mood.

'Sir,' said Švejk, shaking the intruder. 'Make sure that you're not late for lunch. I should hate it if you had to say that I had thrown you out after you'd lost your chance of getting any lunch.'

The porter from the night club was very sleepy and it took a long

time before he understood that the owner of the bed had returned home and was making a claim to it.

Like all night-club porters this gentleman declared that he would smash anyone who woke him up, and tried to go on sleeping.

In the meantime Švejk collected parts of his clothing, brought them to his bed and, shaking him energetically, said:

'If you don't dress, I'll try to fling you out just as you are on to the street. It'll be a great advantage for you if you're properly dressed when you fly out.'

'I wanted to sleep until eight o'clock in the evening,' said the porter in a startled voice as he put on his pants. 'I am paying the mistress two crowns a day for the bed and I'm allowed to bring here young ladies from the club. Mařena, get up!'

As he was putting on his collar and tying his tie he recovered sufficiently to be able to assure Švejk that the night club Mimosa was really one of the most respectable night clubs and that ladies were only admitted there who had a clean police book and he cordially invited Švejk to come and visit it.

On the other hand his female companion was not at all pleased with Švejk and used some very choice expressions, of which the choicest of all was:

'You son of an archbishop, you!'

After the departure of the intruders Švejk went to settle accounts with Mrs Müller but found no trace of her except for a scrap of paper, upon which with unusual ease in her scrawly handwriting she had recorded her thoughts about the unfortunate episode of the loan of Švejk's bed to the porter from the night club.

'Excuse me, sir, if I don't see you any more, because I am going to jump out of the window.'

'She's lying,' said Švejk and waited.

Half an hour later the unfortunate Mrs Müller crept into the kitchen and it was clear from her distraught expression that she was expecting words of consolation from Švejk.

'If you want to jump out of the window,' said Švejk, 'go into the sitting-room. I've opened the window for you. I wouldn't advise you to jump out of the kitchen window, because you'd fall on to the rose bed in the garden, damage the bushes and have to pay for them. From the window of the sitting-room you'll fall beautifully on to the pavement and if you're lucky you'll break your neck. If not you'll only break all your ribs, arms and legs, and you'll have to pay for hospital charges.'

Mrs Müller burst into tears, went quietly into the sitting-room and shut the window. Then, coming back, she said: 'It's terribly draughty there and it wouldn't be good for your rheumatism, sir.'

Then she went to make the bed, put it all in order with unusual care and, returning to Švejk in the kitchen, remarked with tears in her eyes: 'Those two puppies, sir, which we had in the court-yard have pegged out. And that St Bernard, it ran away when the police made their search.'

'Oh, my God,' shouted Švejk, 'he'll get himself into a fine mess. The police will be after him soon.'

'He bit one police inspector when they pulled him out from underneath the bed during the search,' continued Mrs Müller. 'Before
that, one of those gentlemen said that there was somebody under
the bed, and so they called that St Bernard to come out in the name of
the law and, when he wouldn't, they dragged him out. And he was
going to gobble them up, but then he bolted out of the door and never
returned. They also cross-questioned me about who comes to see us,
whether we get any money from abroad, and then they started insinu-
ating that I was a fool, when I told them that we only get money from
abroad very rarely, the last being from the headmaster in Brno, that
advance of sixty crowns for an angora cat which you advertised in
Národní Politika and instead of which you sent him that blind fox-
terrier puppy in a date box. After that they talked to me very affably
and recommended me that porter from the night club, so that I
shouldn't be afraid of being alone in the flat, that very man you've just
thrown out . . . .'

'I've always had bad luck with those authorities, Mrs Müller. Now
you'll see how many of them are going to come here to buy dogs,'
sighed Švejk.

I don't know whether those gentlemen who examined the police
archives after the overthrow of the Austro-Hungarian monarchy
succeeded in deciphering the items of the secret funds of the State
Police, where it was written: B . . . forty crowns, F . . . fifty crowns,
L . . . eighty crowns etc., but they certainly were deceived if they
thought that B, F, L were the initials of any gentlemen who for forty,
fifty, eighty etc. crowns sold the Czech nation to the black and yellow
eagle.

'B' stands for St Bernard, 'F' for fox-terrier and 'L' for Leonberger.
All these dogs Bretschneider took from Švejk to police headquarters.
They were ghastly mongrels, which had no connection whatsoever
with any thoroughbred race which Švejk pretended them to be, when
he sold them to Bretscheider.

The St Bernard was a mixture of mongrel poodle and a common
street cur; the fox-terrier had the ears of a dachshund and was the size
of a butcher's dog, with bandy legs as though it had suffered from
rickets. The head of the Leonberger recalled the hairy muzzle of a
stable pinscher. It had a stubbed tail, was the height of a dachshund
and had bare hindquarters like the famous naked American dogs.

Later detective Kalous came to buy a dog and returned with a wildly·staring monster which was reminiscent of a spotted hyena with the mane of a collie, and in the accounts of the secret fund came a new item: M . . . ninety crowns.

That monster was passing itself off as a mastiff . . .

But not even Kalous succeeded in getting any information out of Švejk. He fared the same as Bretschneider. Švejk diverted the deftest political conversations to the curing of distemper in puppies and the most cunningly prepared traps always ended in Bretschneider bringing back from Švejk another unbelievable mongrel monster.

And that was the end of the famous detective Bretschneider. When he had seven monsters of this kind in his flat, he shut himself up with them in the back room and starved them so long that they finally gobbled him up.

He was so honourable that he saved the state the expense of a funeral.

In his personal file at police headquarters there were recorded under the column 'Advancement in service' the following poignant words: 'Devoured by his own dogs.'

When Švejk learnt later about this tragic event he said:

'It gives me a headache to think how they are going to put all his pieces together when the day of the last judgement comes.'

7

Švejk Goes to the War

AT the time when the forests on the river Raab in Galicia saw the Austrian armies fleeing across the river and when down in Serbia one after the other of the Austrian divisions were taken with their pants down and got the walloping they had long deserved, the Austrian Ministry of War suddenly remembered Švejk. Why, even he might help to get the Monarchy out of the mess.

When they brought Švejk the order to report within a week for a medical examination on Střelecký Ostrov, he happened to be lying in bed, stricken once more by rheumatism.

Mrs Müller was making coffee for him in the kitchen.

'Mrs Müller,' Švejk called softly from his room, 'Mrs Müller, come here for a moment.'

When the charwoman stood by his bed, Švejk repeated in the same soft voice: 'Sit down, Mrs Müller.'

There was something mysterious and solemn in his voice.

When she had sat down, Švejk drew himself up in bed and announced: 'I'm going to the war!'

'Holy Mother!' shrieked Mrs Müller. 'What ever are you going to do there?'

'Fight,' answered Švejk in sepulchral tones. 'Things are going very badly for Austria. Up above they're already creeping on us at Cracow and down below on Hungary. They're crushing us like a steam-roller on all sides and that's why they're calling me up. I read you yesterday from the newspaper, didn't I, that dark clouds were enveloping our dear fatherland.'

'But you can't move.'

'That doesn't matter, Mrs Müller, I shall go to the war in a bath-chair. You know that confectioner round the corner? Well, he has just the right kind of bathchair. Years ago he used to push his lame and wicked old grandfather about in it in the fresh air. Mrs Müller, you're going to push me to the war in that bathchair.'

Mrs Müller burst into tears: 'Oh dear, sir, shouldn't I run for the doctor?'

'You'll not run anywhere, Mrs Müller. Except for my legs I'm completely sound cannon-fodder, and at a time when things are going badly for Austria every cripple must be at his post. Just go on making the coffee.'

And while Mrs Müller, tear-stained and distraught, poured the coffee through the strainer, the good soldier Švejk started singing in bed:

> 'General Windischgrätz as the cock did crow
> Unfurled his banner and charged the foe.
> Rataplan, rataplan, rataplan.
>
> Charged the foe and brandished his sword
> Calling to Mary, Mother of the Lord.
> Rataplan, rataplan, rataplan.'

The panic-stricken Mrs Müller under the impact of this awe-inspiring war-song forgot about the coffee and trembling in every limb listened in horror as the good soldier Švejk continued to sing in bed:

> 'With Mary Mother and bridges four,
> Piedmont, strengthen your posts for war.
> Rataplan, rataplan, rataplan.
>
> At Solferino there was battle and slaughter,
> Piles of corpses and blood like water.
> Rataplan, rataplan, rataplan.
>
> Arms and legs flying in the air,
> For the brave 18th were fighting there.
> Rataplan, rataplan, rataplan.
>
> Boys of the 18th, don't lose heart!
> There's money behind in the baggage cart.
> Rataplan, rataplan, rataplan.'

'For God's sake, sir, please!' came the piteous voice from the kitchen, but Švejk was already ending his war-song:

> 'Money in the cart and wenches in the van!
> What a life for a military man!
> Rataplan, rataplan, rataplan.'

Mrs Müller burst out of the door and rushed for the doctor. She returned in an hour's time, while Švejk had slumbered off.

And so he was woken up by a corpulent gentleman who laid his hand on his forehead for a moment and said:

'Don't be afraid. I am Dr Pávek from Vinohrady – let me feel your pulse – put this thermometer under your armpit. Good – now show me your tongue – a bit more – keep it out – what did your father and mother die of?'

And so at a time when it was Vienna's earnest desire that all the peoples of Austria-Hungary should offer the finest examples of loyalty and devotion, Dr Pávek prescribed Švejk bromide against his patriotic enthusiasm and recommended the brave and good soldier not to think about the war:

'Lie straight and keep quiet. I'll come again tomorrow.'

When he came the next day, he asked Mrs Müller in the kitchen how the patient was.

'He's worse, doctor,' she answered with genuine grief. 'In the night he was singing, if you'll pardon the expression, the Austrian national anthem, when the rheumatism suddenly took him.'

Dr Pávek felt obliged to react to this new manifestation of loyalty on the part of his patient by prescribing a larger dose of bromide.

The third day Mrs Müller informed him that Švejk had got even worse.

'In the afternoon he sent for a map of the battlefield, doctor, and in the night he was seized by a mad hallucination that Austria was going to win.'

'And he takes his powders strictly according to the prescription?'

'Oh, no, doctor, he hasn't even sent for them yet.' Dr Pávek went away after having called down a storm of reproaches on Švejk's head and assured him that he would never again come to cure anybody who refused his professional help and bromide.

Only two days remained before Švejk would have to appear before the call-up board.

During this time Švejk made the necessary preparations. First he sent Mrs Müller to buy an army cap and next he sent her to borrow the bathchair from the confectioner round the corner – that same one in which the confectioner once used to wheel about in the fresh air his lame and wicked old grandfather. Then he remembered he needed crutches. Fortunately the confectioner still kept the crutches too as a family relic of his old grandfather.

Now he only needed the recruit's bunch of flowers for his button-hole. Mrs Müller got these for him too. During these last two days she got noticeably thinner and wept from morning to night.

And so on that memorable day there appeared on the Prague streets a moving example of loyalty. An old woman pushing before her a bathchair, in which there sat a man in an army cap with a finely polished Imperial badge and waving his crutches. And in his button-hole there shone the gay flowers of a recruit.

And this man, waving his crutches again and again, shouted out to the streets of Prague: 'To Belgrade, to Belgrade!'

He was followed by a crowd of people which steadily grew from the small group that had gathered in front of the house from which he had gone out to war.

Švejk could see that the policemen standing at some of the crossroads saluted him.

At Wenceslas Square the crowd around Švejk's bathchair had grown by several hundreds and at the corner of Krakovská Street they beat up a student in a German cap who had shouted out to Švejk:

'*Heil! Nieder mit den Serben!*'[1]

At the corner of Vodičkova Street mounted police rode in and dispersed the crowd.

When Švejk showed the district police inspector that he had it in black and white that he must that day appear before the call-up board, the latter was a trifle disappointed; and in order to reduce disturbances to a minimum he had Švejk and his bathchair escorted by two mounted police all the way to the Střelecký Ostrov.

The following article about this episode appeared in the *Prague Official News*:

A CRIPPLE'S PATRIOTISM

Yesterday afternoon the passers-by in the main streets of Prague were witnesses of a scene which was an eloquent testimony to the fact that in these great and solemn hours the sons of our nation can furnish the finest examples of loyalty and devotion to the throne of the aged monarch. We might well have been back in the times of the ancient Greeks and Romans, when Mucius Scaevola had himself led off to battle, regardless of his burnt arm. The most sacred feelings and sympathies were nobly demonstrated yesterday by a cripple on crutches who was pushed in an invalid chair by his aged mother. This son of the Czech people, spontaneously and regardless of his infirmity, had himself driven off to war to sacrifice his life and possessions for his emperor. And if his call: 'To Belgrade!' found such a lively echo on the streets of Prague, it only goes to prove what model examples of love for the fatherland and the Imperial House are proffered by the people of Prague.

The *Prager Tagblatt* wrote in the same strain, ending its article by saying that the cripple volunteer was escorted by a crowd of Germans who protected him with their bodies from lynching by the Czech agents of the Entente.

Bohemie published the same report and urged that the patriotic cripple should be fittingly rewarded. It announced that at its offices it was ready to receive gifts from German citizens for the unknown hero.

If in the eyes of these three journals the Czech lands could not have produced a nobler citizen, this was not the opinion of the gentlemen at the call-up board – certainly not of the chief army doctor Bautze, an utterly ruthless man who saw in everything a criminal attempt to evade military service, the front, bullets, and shrapnel.

1. 'Down with the Serbs.'

This German's stock remark was widely famous: 'The whole Czech people are nothing but a pack of malingerers.'

During the ten weeks of his activities, of 11,000 civilians he cleaned out 10,999 malingerers, and he would certainly have got the eleven thousandth by the throat, if it had not happened that just when he shouted 'About turn!' the unfortunate man was carried off by a stroke.

'Take away that malingerer!' said Bautze, when he had ascertained that the man was dead.

And on that memorable day it was Švejk who stood before him. Like the others he was stark naked and chastely hid his nudity behind the crutches on which he supported himself.

'That's really a remarkable fig-leaf,' said Bautze in German. 'There were no fig-leaves like that in paradise.'

'Certified as totally unfit for service on grounds of idiocy,' observed the sergeant-major, looking at the official documents.

'And what else is wrong with you?' asked Bautze.

'Humbly report, sir, I'm a rheumatic, but I will serve His Imperial Majesty to my last drop of blood,' said Švejk modestly. 'I have swollen knees.'

Bautze gave the good soldier Švejk a blood-curdling look and roared out in German: 'You're a malingerer!' Turning to the sergeant-major he said with icy calm: 'Clap the bastard into gaol at once!'

Two soldiers with bayonets took Švejk off to the garrison gaol.

Švejk walked on his crutches and observed with horror that his rheumatism was beginning to disappear.

Mrs Müller was still waiting for Švejk with the bathchair above on the bridge but when she saw him under bayoneted escort she burst into tears and ran away from the bathchair, never to return to it again.

And the good soldier Švejk walked along unassumingly under the escort of the armed protectors of the state.

Their bayonets shone in the light of the sun and at Malá Strana before the monument of Radetzky Švejk turned to the crowd which had followed them and called out:

'To Belgrade! To Belgrade!'

And Marshal Radetzky looked dreamily down from his monument at the good soldier Švejk, as, limping on his old crutches, he slowly disappeared into the distance with his recruit's flowers in his button-hole. Meanwhile a solemn-looking gentleman informed the crowd around that it was a 'dissenter' they were leading off.

8

Švejk the Malingerer

IN these great times the army doctors took unusual pains to drive the devil of sabotage out of the malingerers and restore them to the bosom of the army.

Various degrees of torture had been introduced for malingerers and suspected malingerers, such as consumptives, rheumatics, people with hernia, kidney disease, typhus, diabetes, pneumonia and other illnesses.

The tortures to which the malingerers were subjected were systematized and the grades were as follows:

1. Strict diet, a cup of tea each morning and evening for three days, during which, irrespective, of course, of their complaints, aspirin to be given to induce sweating.

2. To ensure they did not think that war was all beer and skittles, quinine in powder to be served in generous portions, or so-called 'quinine licking'.

3. The stomach to be pumped out twice a day with a litre of warm water.

4. Enemas with soapy water and glycerine to be applied.

5. Wrapping up in a sheet soaked in cold water.

There were stalwart men who endured all five degrees of torture and let themselves be carried off to the military cemetery in a simple coffin. But there were also pusillanimous souls who, when they reached the stage of the enema, declared that they were now well and desired nothing better than to march off to the trenches with the next march battalion.

In the garrison prison Švejk was put into the sanatorium hut among pusillanimous malingerers of this very type.

'I can't stand it any longer,' said his neighbour in the next bed, who was brought in from the consulting room after having had his stomach pumped for the second time.

This man was shamming short-sightedness.

'Tomorrow I'll join the regiment,' decided his other neighbour on the left, who had just had an enema and who had been shamming deafness.

In the bed by the door a consumptive who was wrapped up in a cold wet sheet was slowly dying.

'That's the third this week,' observed his neighbour on the right. 'And what's your trouble?'

'I've got rheumatism,' answered Švejk, upon which there was a hearty guffaw all round. Even the dying consumptive, who was shamming tuberculosis, joined in the laughter.

'Don't try and climb in here with rheumatism,' a fat man warned Švejk solemnly. 'Rheumatism here doesn't mean more than a chilblain. I'm anaemic, I've lost half my stomach and five of my ribs, but no one believes me. We even had a fellow here who was deaf and dumb. For a fortnight they wrapped him up every half-hour in a cold wet sheet and every day they gave him an enema and pumped his stomach. All the nurses thought he'd won through and would go home, when the doctor prescribed him an emetic. It could have torn him in half and so he lost courage. "I can't go on being deaf and dumb," he said. "My speech and hearing have returned." All the patients urged him not to ruin himself but he insisted that he could hear and speak just like other people. And he reported to this effect at the doctor's visit next morning.'

'He kept it up for quite a long time,' remarked a man, who was pretending to have one leg four inches shorter than the other. 'Not like that chap who shammed a stroke. All they had to do was to give him three doses of quinine, one enema and a day's fasting. He confessed and by the time they started pumping out his stomach there wasn't a trace left of his stroke. The chap who held out longest of all was the one who had been bitten by a mad dog. He bit, he howled – it's true he could do it splendidly – but he just couldn't manage to foam at the mouth. We did our best to help him. Several times we tickled him for a whole hour before the doctor's visit until he had convulsions and got blue all over, but the foam wouldn't come and didn't in fact come at all. It was really terrifying. When he gave in one morning at the doctor's visit we were quite sorry for him. He stood by his bed erect as a candle, saluted and said: "Humbly report, sir, the dog I was bitten by may not have been mad after all." The doctor gave him such a queer look that he began to tremble all over and went on: "Humbly report, sir, I wasn't bitten by a dog at all. It was I who bit myself in the arm." After that confession they put him under investigation for self-mutilation on the charge that he had tried to bite off his arm to get out of going to the front.'

'All those kinds of illnesses where you have to foam at the mouth are difficult to sham,' said the fat malingerer. 'Take for instance epilepsy. We had an epileptic here who always used to tell us that one fit wasn't enough and so he put on some ten a day. He writhed in convulsions, clenched his fists, rolled his eyes wildly, flung himself about on the floor, stuck out his tongue, in short, I can tell you, it was a magnificent first-class epilepsy, the genuine thing. But suddenly he got boils, two on the neck and two on the back, and it was all over with his writhing and flinging himself about on the floor, when he couldn't move his head and wasn't able either to sit or lie down. He got fever and in delirium he let out everything at the doctor's visit. He gave us a lot of trouble over his boils, because he had to lie here with them another three days and got another diet – coffee and rolls in the morning, soup, dumplings and gravy for lunch, and porridge or soup in the evening. And with our hungry, pumped-out stomachs and strict diet we had to watch this fellow bolting the food, smacking his lips, panting and belching with repletion. In this way he broke down another three who confessed as well. They had been suffering from heart disease.'

'The best thing to sham,' said one of the malingerers, 'is insanity. There are two of our teachers lying in the ward next door and one of them shrieks out incessantly day and night: "Giordano Bruno's stake is still smouldering. Reopen the trial of Galileo." And the other one barks, first three times slowly: bow—wow—wow, then five times quickly in succession: bowwowwowwowwow, and then once more slowly, and so it goes on without a break. They've managed to keep it up for over three weeks now. Originally I wanted to be insane too, have religious mania and preach about papal infallibility, but in the end I fixed myself up with cancer of the stomach from a barber in Malá Strana for fifteen crowns.'

'I know a chimney-sweep in Břevnov,' remarked another patient. 'For ten crowns he'll give you such a fever that you'll jump out of the window.'

'That's nothing,' said another. 'In Vršovice there's a midwife who for twenty crowns will dislocate your leg so well that you'll be a cripple until your death.'

'I had my leg dislocated for ten crowns,' came a voice from the row of beds by the window, 'for ten crowns and three glasses of beer.'

'My illness has cost me more than two hundred already,' announced his neighbour, a dried-up stick. 'You tell me any poison I haven't taken. You won't find it. I'm a living repository of poisons of all kinds. I've taken mercury chloride, I've breathed in mercury fumes, I've chewed arsenic, I've smoked opium, I've drunk tincture of opium, I've sprinkled morphine on bread, I've swallowed strychnine, I've drunk a solution of phosphorus in carbon sulphide as well as picric acid. I've destroyed my liver, my lungs, my kidneys, my gall-bladder, my brain, my heart and my intestines. No one knows what kind of illness I have.'

'The best thing to do,' explained somebody from the door, 'is to inject paraffin under the skin of your arm. My cousin was so fortunate as to have his arm cut off under the elbow and today he has no trouble for the rest of the war.'

'So you see,' said Švejk, 'everyone has to go through all that for His Imperial Majesty – even stomach-pumping and enemas. When I served years ago in my regiment it was even worse. In those days they used to truss the patient and throw him into a hole to recuperate him. There weren't any bunks like there are here or spittoons either. Just a bare plank-bed and the patients lay on it. Once one had a genuine typhus and the other next to him had smallpox. Both were trussed, and the regimental doctor kicked them in the belly for being malingerers. And when both these soldiers died it came up in parliament and was in the newspapers. They immediately forbade us to read those newspapers and searched our boxes in case we had them. And as I always have bad luck, I was the only one in the whole regiment they found them on. So I was taken off on regimental report and our colonel, who was a bloody half-wit, God help him, started to roar at me to stand straight and to tell him who it was who wrote that in the newspapers or he'd break my jaw wide open and have me locked up till I was black in the face. Then came the regimental doctor, brandishing his fist under my nose and shouting in German: "You dirty hound, you lousy scab, you miserable turd, you Socialist sod!" I looked them all squarely in the eyes without blinking and kept quiet, my right hand at the peak of my cap and my left on the seam of my trousers. They ran around me like dogs and yapped at me, but I did nothing. I kept mum, saluted, left hand on the seam of my trousers. When they had been raging like this for about half an hour, the colonel rushed at me and roared: "Are you a half-wit or aren't you?" – "Humbly report, sir, I'm a half-wit." – "Very well then. Twenty-one days strict confinement for imbecility, two days a week fasting, a month confined to barracks, forty-eight hours in handcuffs, immediate arrest, don't let him eat, truss him, show him that the monarchy doesn't need half-wits. We'll flog those newspapers out of your head, you bastard," the colonel decided after flying around for a long time. But while I was sitting in jug miracles were happening in the barracks. Our colonel forbade our soldiers to read anything at all, even the *Prague Official News*. In the canteen they weren't even allowed to use the newspapers for wrapping up frankfurters or bits of cheese. From that time all the soldiers started to read, and our regiment became the best educated. We read all the newspapers and in every company they made up rhymes and songs against the colonel. And when anything happened in the regiment you'd always find some public benefactor who sent it to the newspapers under the title: "Maltreatment of the troops". And they didn't stop at that. They wrote to the parliamentary deputies in Vienna, asking them to take up their case, and the deputies began to make interpellations one after the other, saying that our colonel was a monster and suchlike. A minister sent a commission to us to investigate the case and a Franta Henčl from Hluboká got two years for being the chap who got on to the deputies in Vienna, because of the knock across the jaw he got from the colonel on the drill-ground. Later when the commission went away our colonel made us all fall in, the whole regiment, and told us that a soldier is a soldier, that he must shut his mug and do his job, and if he doesn't like anything then it's a breach of discipline. "So you, you bloody bastards, thought that that commission would help you?" said the colonel. "A shit they helped you! And now every company will march past me and repeat aloud what I've said." And so we marched to where the colonel stood, one company after the other, eyes right, and our hands on our rifle slings and shouted at him: "And so we, we bloody bastards, thought that that commission would help us. A shit they helped us!" The colonel doubled up with laughter until the eleventh company marched up. They marched, they stamped, but when they reached the colonel – nothing at all, not the faintest sound! The colonel got red as a turkey-cock, marched the eleventh company back and made them repeat the operation once more. They marched past in silence and each rank after the other stared the colonel insolently in the eyes. "Stand at ease!" said the colonel and paced up and down the yard, lashing his boots with his riding crop and spitting about the place. Then he suddenly stopped and roared out "Dismiss!", mounted his old crock and away he was out of the gate. We waited to see what would happen to the eleventh company, but still there was nothing. We waited one day, then another and then a whole week, but still nothing happened. The colonel never appeared in the barracks at all, which gave great joy to the men, the N.C.O.s and the officers. After that we got a new colonel and it was rumoured that the old one was in a sanatorium because he had written a letter in his own hand to His Imperial Majesty telling him that the eleventh company had mutinied.'

The time for the doctor's afternoon round approached. Dr Grünstein went from bed to bed, followed by the medical orderly officer with his notebook.

'Macuna?'

'Present!'

'Enema and aspirin! Pokorný?'

'Present!'

'Stomach pump and quinine! Kovařík?'

'Present!'

'Enema and aspirin! Kot'átko?'

'Present!'

'Stomach pump and quinine!'

And so it went on, one after the other, mercilessly, mechanically, briskly.

'Švejk?'

'Present!'

Dr Grünstein looked at the new acquisition.

'What's the matter with you?'

'Humbly report, I've got rheumatism!'

In the course of his practice Dr Grünstein had grown accustomed to be gently ironical, which was much more effective than shouting.

'Aha, rheumatism,' he said to Švejk. 'Then you've got a jolly serious illness. It's really a coincidence getting rheumatism just at a time when there is a world war on and you've got to go to the front. I think you must be awfully sorry.'

'Humbly report, sir, I am awfully sorry.'

'Well, there you are, you see, he's awfully sorry. It's really awfully nice of you that with your rheumatism you've not forgotten us just at this particular moment. In peacetime a poor chap like him runs about like a young goat, but as soon as war breaks out he immediately gets rheumatism and suddenly his knees don't work. Your knees hurt, I suppose?'

'Humbly report, they do, sir.'

'And you can't sleep a wink the whole night, can you? Rheumatism's a very dangerous, painful and grave illness. We've already had good experience with rheumatics here. Strict diet and other treatment of ours have proved very effective. Here you'll be fit quicker than in Piešt'any[1] and you'll march to the front like greased lightning.'

Turning to the hospital orderly he said:

'Write this down: Švejk, strict diet, stomach pump twice a day, enema once a day, and we'll see how it goes after that. For the time being take him to the consulting room, pump his stomach and when he comes to, give him an enema, but a real good one, until he screams blue murder and his rheumatism gets frightened and runs away.'

Then turning to all the beds the doctor made a speech full of noble and rational moral maxims: 'Don't imagine that I'm just a bloody half-wit who swallows all your bull. Your tricks don't rattle me in the least. I know you're all malingerers and you want to desert from the war. And I'll treat you as such. I've survived hundreds and hundreds of soldiers like you. Masses of people have lain on these beds here who had nothing wrong with them at all except that they hadn't got a soldier's guts. While their comrades were fighting on the battlefield they thought they'd lounge about in bed, get hospital rations and wait until the war flew by. But they all found they'd made a bloody mistake, and all of you'll find you've made a bloody mistake too. In twenty years time you'll be still screaming in your sleep, when you dream of how you tried it on with me.'

'Humbly report, sir,' came a gentle voice from the bed at the window, 'I'm well again. I noticed in the night that my asthma's gone.'

'Your name?'

'Kovařík. Humbly report, I have to have an enema.'

'Good, you'll still get an enema for the road,' Dr Grünstein decided, 'so that you don't complain that we didn't give you treatment here. Now, all the patients whose names I've read out, fall in and follow the orderly, so that each can get what's due to him.'

1. A famous spa in Slovakia for the treatment of rheumatism.

And each one got a handsome dose of what had been prescribed. And if any of them tried to work on those who were executing the orders by means of prayers or threats that they might too once join the medical corps and the executioners might fall into their hands, Švejk at least bore himself with steadfastness.

'Don't spare me,' he invited the myrmidon who was giving him the enema. 'Remember your oath. Even if it was your father or your own brother who was lying here, give him an enema without batting an eyelid. Try hard to think that Austria rests on these enemas and victory is ours.'

The next day on his round Dr Grünstein asked Švejk how he was enjoying being in the military hospital.

Švejk answered that it was a fair and high-minded institution. In reward he received the same as the day before plus aspirin and three quinine powders which they dissolved into water so that he should drink them at once.

And not even Socrates drank his hemlock bowl with such composure as did Švejk his quinine, when Dr Grünstein was trying out on him all his various degrees of torture.

When they wrapped Švejk up in a wet sheet in the presence of the doctor his answer to the question how he liked it now was: 'Humbly report, sir, it's like being in a swimming pool or at the seaside.'

'Have you still got rheumatism?'

'Humbly report, sir, it doesn't seem to want to get better.'

Švejk was subjected to new tortures.

At that time the widow of the infantry general, Baroness von Botzenheim, took great pains to find that soldier about whom *Bohemie* had recently published a report that, cripple as he was, he had had himself pushed in a bathchair shouting: 'To Belgrade!'; which patriotic pronouncement induced the editorial staff of *Bohemie* to invite their readers to organize collections in aid of the loyal and heroic cripple.

Finally, after inquiries at police headquarters it was ascertained that the man in question was Švejk and after that it was easy to make a search for him. Baroness von Botzenheim went to the Hradčany taking with her her lady companion and her footman with a hamper.

The poor baroness had no idea what it meant for someone to be lying in the hospital of the garrison gaol. Her visiting card opened the prison door for her, in the office they were awfully nice to her, and in five minutes she learnt that 'the good soldier Švejk', whom she was looking for, lay in the third hut, bed number seventeen. She was accompanied by Dr Grünstein himself, who was quite flabbergasted by it.

Švejk was just sitting up in bed after the usual daily procedure prescribed by Dr Grünstein, surrounded by a group of emaciated and starved malingerers, who had not yet given up and were stubbornly struggling with Dr Grünstein on the battlefield of strict diet.

Anyone who had listened to them would have had the impression that he was in the company of epicures, in a school of *cordon bleu* cuisine or a course for gourmets.

'You can even eat ordinary suet cracklings if they are warm,' a patient with 'inveterate stomach catarrh' was just telling the others at this moment. 'As the suet boils, you squeeze the cracklings dry, add salt and pepper, and I can tell you that goose cracklings are not in the same class.'

'You leave goose cracklings alone,' said a man with 'cancer of the stomach'. 'There's nothing to touch them. What are pork cracklings in comparison? Of course you must fry them until they're golden brown, like the Jews do. They take a fat goose, draw the fat off with the skin and fry it.'

'You know, you're quite wrong as far as pork cracklings are concerned,' Švejk's neighbour put in. 'Of course I'm talking about cracklings of home-made fat, what they call home-made cracklings. They're not brown and they're not yellow. They must be something between the two shades. These kinds of cracklings mustn't be either too soft or too hard. And they mustn't be crunchy or they're over-cooked. They must melt on the tongue and you mustn't feel the fat dripping on your chin.'

'Which of you have eaten horse cracklings?' chimed in a new voice, but there was no answer because at that moment the medical orderly ran in:

'Everybody in bed! An archduchess is coming here. Don't anyone dare show his dirty legs outside the bed.'

And not even an archduchess could have entered the ward with such dignity as did Baroness von Botzenheim. After her the whole suite poured in, including even the quartermaster sergeant-major of the hospital who saw in all this the mysterious hand of Accounts Control, which was going to tear him away from his fat feeding trough at the base and deliver him to the tender mercies of the shrapnel some-where under the barbed wire posts.

He was pale, but Dr Grünstein was even paler. Before his eyes there danced the old baroness's small visiting card with her title, 'Widow of a general', and everything which could be associated with it like connections, protection, complaints, transfer to the front and other frightful things.

'Here you have Švejk,' he said, endeavouring to preserve an arti-ficial composure and leading the Baroness von Botzenheim to Švejk's bed. 'He behaves with great patience.'

Baroness von Botzenheim sat down on the chair prepared for her at Švejk's bed and said: 'Tshech zoldier, goot zoldier, krippl – zoldier iss brafe zoldier. I lof fery moch Tshech Austrian.'

At that she stroked Švejk on his unshaven cheeks and went on:

'I reat eferyzink in ze newspapers, I brink you yum yum, zomzink to bite, to shmoke, to zuck, Tshech zoldier, goot zoldier. Johann, come here!'

Her footman, whose bristly side-whiskers recalled the notorious killer Babinský, dragged a voluminous hamper to the bed, while the old baroness's companion, a tall lady with a tearful face, sat down on Švejk's bed and smoothed out his straw pillow under his back with the fixed idea that this was what ought to be done for sick heroes.

In the meantime the baroness drew presents out of the hamper: a dozen roast chickens wrapped up in pink silk paper and tied with a yellow and black silk ribbon, two bottles of a war liqueur with the label: '*Gott strafe England.*'[1] On the back of the label was a picture of Franz Joseph and Wilhelm clasping hands as though they were going to play the nursery game: 'Bunny sat alone in his hole. Poor little bunny, what's wrong with you that you can't hop!'[2]

Then she took out of the hamper three bottles of wine for the con-valescent and two boxes of cigarettes. She set out everything elegantly on the empty bed next to Švejk's, where she also put a beautifully bound book, *Stories from the Life of our Monarch*, which had been written by the present meritorious chief editor of our official *Czechoslovak Republic* who doted on old Franz. Packets of chocolate with the same inscription, '*Gott strafe England*', and again with pictures of the Austrian and German emperors, found their way to

1. 'God punish England.'
2. Czech children's game.

the bed. On the chocolate they were no longer clasping hands; each was acting on his own and turning his back to the other. There was a beautiful toothbrush with two rows of bristles and the inscription '*Viribus unitis*',[1] so that anyone who cleaned his teeth should remember Austria. An elegant and extremely useful little gift for the front and the trenches was a manicure set. On the case was a picture showing shrapnel bursting and a man in a steel helmet rushing forward with fixed bayonet. And underneath it was written in German: 'For God, Emperor and Fatherland!' There was a tin of biscuits without a picture on it but with a verse in German instead, together with a Czech translation on the back:

> Austria, thou noble house,
> Thy banners wide unfurl!
> Thy flags shall flutter proud on high.
> Austria shall never die!

The last gift was a white hyacinth in a flower-pot.

When all of this lay unpacked on the bed the Baroness von Botzenheim could not restrain her tears for emotion. Several famished malingerers felt their mouths water. The baroness's companion propped up the seated Švejk and wept too. There was a silence of the grave which was suddenly broken by Švejk who said with his hands clasped in prayer:

'Our Father, which art in heaven, hallowed be Thy name. Thy kingdom come. . . . Pardon me, your ladyship, it's not right. I mean to say: O God our Father in heaven, bless for us these gifts that we may enjoy them thanks to Thy goodness. Amen.'

After these words he took a chicken from the bed and started to devour it under the horrified gaze of Dr Grünstein.

'Ach, how he enjoys it, poor soldier,' the old baroness whispered enthusiastically to Dr Grünstein. 'He's certainly well again and can go to the battlefield. I'm really very glad that my gifts stand him in such good stead.'

Then she walked from bed to bed, distributing cigarettes and chocolate creams. When she came back again to Švejk after her promenade, she stroked his hair, said in German: 'God protect you all!' and went out of the door with her whole escort.

Before Dr Grünstein could return from below, where he had gone

---

1. 'With united forces'. The device of the Emperor Franz Joseph.

to see the baroness out, Švejk had distributed the chickens. They were bolted by the patients so quickly that Dr Grünstein found only a heap of bones gnawed cleanly, as though the chickens had fallen alive into a nest of vultures and the sun had been beating down on their gnawed bones for several months.

The war liqueur and the three bottles of wine had also disappeared. The packets of chocolate and the box of biscuits were likewise lost in the patients' stomachs. Someone had even drunk up the bottle of nail-polish which was in the manicure set and eaten the toothpaste which had been enclosed with the toothbrush.

When Dr Grünstein returned he resumed his belligerent pose and delivered a long speech. A stone fell from his heart now that the visitors had gone. The pile of gnawed bones confirmed his belief that they were all incorrigible.

'Men,' he burst out, 'if you'd had a little sense, you'd have left it all untouched and said to yourselves: "If we eat it all up, then the

doctor won't believe that we're very ill." Now you've yourselves
provided me with proof that you don't appreciate my kindness. I
pump your stomachs, I give you enemas, I try to keep you on strict
diet and you go and stuff up your stomachs again. Do you want to
get stomach catarrh? You're making a great mistake. Before your
stomach tries to digest all this I'll clean it out for you so thoroughly
that you'll remember it to your dying day and tell your children how
you once gobbled up chickens, and gorged yourself on various other
delicacies, and how they didn't stay in your stomach fifteen minutes,
because they pumped it out while it was still warm. And now fall in all
of you, one after the other, so that you don't forget that I'm not a
bloody fool like you are, but a little bit cleverer than the whole lot of
you together. In addition I want to inform you that tomorrow I'm
going to send a commission to you, because you've been lazing around
here far too long and there's nothing wrong with any of you if in those
five minutes you could pig it and stuff your stomachs up so chock-full
as you did just now. One, two, three, march!'

When it was Švejk's turn Dr Grünstein looked at him and a memory
of the mysterious visit of the day prompted him to ask: 'You know
Her Excellency?'

'She's my stepmother,' Švejk answered calmly. 'In tender years she
abandoned me and now she's found me again. . . .'

And Dr Grünstein said tersely: 'Afterwards give Švejk an extra
enema.'

In the evening melancholy reigned among the bunks. A few hours
earlier all of them had had in their stomachs various good and tasty
things and now they only had weak tea and a slice of bread.

From the window could be heard the voice of no. 21: 'Do you
know, chaps, that I prefer fried chicken to roast?'

Somebody growled: 'Give him the blanket treatment', but they
were all so weak after the unsuccessful banquet that no one stirred.

Dr Grünstein was as good as his word. In the morning there came
several military doctors from the famous commission.

They went solemnly past the rows of beds and said nothing else
but 'Put out your tongue!'

Švejk put his tongue out so far that his face made an idiotic grimace
and his eyes screwed up:

'Humbly report, sir, I don't have a longer tongue than that.'

And an interesting discussion arose between Švejk and the com-

mission. Švejk asserted that he had made this observation in case they might think he was trying to hide his tongue from them.

The members of the commission, however, were remarkably divided in their conclusions about Švejk.

Half of them insisted that Švejk was 'a half-wit', while the other half insisted he was a scoundrel who was trying to make fun of the war.

'It'll be a bloody miracle,' roared the chairman of the commission at Švejk, 'if we don't get the better of you.'

Švejk looked at the whole commission with the godlike composure of an innocent child.

The senior staff doctor came up close to Švejk:

'I'd like to know, you swine, what you're thinking about now?'

'Humbly report, sir, I don't think at all.'

'Himmeldonnerwetter,' bawled one of the members of the commission, rattling his sabre. 'So he doesn't think at all. Why in God's name don't you think, you Siamese elephant?'

'Humbly report, I don't think because that's forbidden to soldiers on duty. When I was in the 91st regiment some years ago our captain always used to say "A soldier mustn't think for himself. His superiors do it for him. As soon as a soldier begins to think he's no longer a soldier but a dirty, lousy civilian. Thinking doesn't get you anywhere..."'

'Shut your mug!' the chairman of the commission interrupted Švejk in fury. 'We know all about you already. The swine thinks he'll be taken for a genuine idiot. You're not an idiot at all, Švejk. You're cunning, you're foxy, you're a scoundrel, you're a hooligan, you're a lousy bastard, do you understand...?'

'Humbly report, sir, I understand.'

'I've already told you to shut your mug. Did you hear?'

'Humbly report, sir, I heard that I must shut my mug.'

'Himmelherrgott, then shut it! When I've given you orders, you know very well that you must stop talking rot!'

'Humbly report, sir, I know well I must stop talking rot.'

The military gentlemen exchanged glances and called the sergeant-major:

'Take this man to the office,' said the senior staff doctor pointing to Švejk, 'and wait for our announcement and report. At the garrison they'll knock all this drivel out of his head. The fellow's as fit as a fiddle. He's only shamming and into the bargain he talks rot and tries to make fun of his superiors. He thinks they're only here for his amusement and that the whole war's a joke, a laughing matter. At the garrison, Švejk, they'll soon show you that war's no picnic.'

Švejk went off with the sergeant-major to the office and on the way through the courtyard hummed to himself:

> 'I always thought
> That war was fun.
> A week or two
> And home I'd run . . .

And while in the office the duty officer was bellowing at Švejk that bastards like him ought to be shot, in the wards upstairs the commission was making short shrift with the malingerers. Of seventy patients only two got through. One had had a leg torn off by a shell and the other suffered from genuine bone decay.

These two were the only ones who did not hear the word '*Tauglich*'. All the others, including even the three dying of consumption, were certified fit for service at the front, whereupon the senior staff doctor did not deny himself the opportunity of making a speech.

His speech was interlarded with the most variegated oaths and was brief in content. They were all swine and dung and only if they were to fight valiantly for His Imperial Majesty would they be fit to return to human society and after the war be forgiven for having tried to get out of military service and been malingerers. He himself however didn't believe that this would happen and thought the gallows were in store for them all.

A youngish army doctor whose soul was still pure and uncorrupted asked the senior staff doctor if he might say a few words too. His speech distinguished itself from that of his superior by its optimism and naïvety. He spoke in German.

He dwelt long on the fact that each of them who was leaving the hospital to join their regiments at the front must be conqueror and knight. He was convinced they would be skilful in handling their weapons on the battlefield and honourable in all their dealings in war and in private life. They would be unconquerable warriors, mindful of the glory of Radetzky and Prince Eugène of Savoy. With their blood they would fertilize the vast fields of glory of the monarchy and victoriously accomplish the task to which history had predestined them. With fearless courage, despising their lives, they would charge forward under the bullet-ridden ensigns of their regiments towards new glories and new victories.

Later in the corridor the senior staff doctor said to this naïve man: 'My dear colleague, I can assure you it's all a complete waste of time. Why, not even Radetzky or your Prince Eugène of Savoy could make soldiers out of bastards like them. Whether you speak to them like an angel or a devil, it all comes to the same thing. They're a gang of crooks.'

Švejk in the Garrison Gaol

FOR people who did not want to go to the front the last refuge was the garrison gaol. I once knew a probationary teacher who was a mathematician and did not want to serve in the artillery and shoot people. So he stole a lieutenant's watch to get himself into the garrison gaol. He did this deliberately. War neither impressed nor enchanted him. Shooting at the enemy and killing with shrapnel and shells equally unhappy probationary teachers of mathematics serving on the other side seemed to him sheer idiocy.

'I don't want to be hated for my brutality,' he said to himself, and calmly stole the watch. First they examined his mental condition but, when he said he wanted to get rich quick, they sent him off to the garrison gaol. There were a lot more people like that sitting there for theft or fraud – idealists and non-idealists. There were people who saw the war as a way of increasing their income, those various quarter-master sergeants at the base or at the front who were up to all possible kinds of fiddles with messing and pay, and also petty thieves who were a thousand times more honest than the blackguards who sent them there. And soldiers sat there who had committed various other offences of a purely military kind such as insubordination, attempted mutiny or desertion. Then came the political prisoners who were in a special class; eighty per cent of them were utterly innocent and of these ninety-nine per cent were sentenced.

The whole establishment of the office of the judge advocate was magnificent. Every state on the brink of total political, economic and moral collapse has an establishment like this. The aura of past power and glory clings to its courts, police, gendarmerie and venal pack of informers.

In every military unit Austria had her snoopers who spied on their comrades, sleeping on the same bunks with them and sharing their bread on the march.

In addition the garrison gaol was supplied with material by the

State Security, Messrs Klíma, Slavíček and Co. The military censorship consigned here the writers of letters exchanged between the men at the front and the despairing ones they had left behind at home. The gendarmes even brought here poor old peasant pensioners who had written letters to the front, and the court-martial jugged them for twelve years as a punishment for their words of consolation and their descriptions of the misery at home.

From the Hradčany garrison the road led through Břevnov to the drill-ground at Motol. Along it a procession would pass, headed by a man under military escort with his hands manacled and followed by a cart with a coffin on it. On the drill-ground was heard the curt order: 'Fire!' And then in all the regiments and battalions they read out the regimental order that one more man had been shot for mutiny during call-up, when his wife, not bearing to be parted from him, had been slashed by the captain's sabre.

And in the garrison gaol the triumvirate – Staff Warder Slavík, Captain Linhart and Sergeant-Major Řepa, alias 'the hangman', were getting on with the job! How many did they flog in solitary confinement? Perhaps in the Republic today Captain Linhart is still a captain. I hope for his sake his years of service in the garrison gaol will count towards his pension. They do in the case of Slavíček and Klíma from the State Security. Řepa has returned to civilian life and carries on his profession as a master builder. Perhaps he is a member of one of the patriotic societies in the Republic.

Under the Republic Staff Warder Slavík became a thief and is today in gaol. The poor man could not set himself up so comfortably in the Republic as the other military gentlemen did.

It was quite natural that when he took charge of Švejk Staff Warder Slavík gave him a look of mute reproach, as much as to say:

'So you've got a tarnished reputation too, if you've got yourself here? Well, love, we'll sweeten your stay here, as we do for anyone who's fallen into our hands, and you know that our hands aren't exactly the ladies' kind.'

And to add weight to his look he thrust his muscular fat fist under Švejk's nose and said:

'Sniff that, you bastard!'

Švejk sniffed it and observed:

'I wouldn't like to get that in the nose. It smells of the graveyard.'

This calm, considered remark appealed to the staff warder.

'Hey,' he said, prodding Švejk in the stomach with his fist, 'stand straight! What's that you've got in your pockets? If it's cigarettes, you can leave them here. And hand over your money too so that they don't

steal it off you. Haven't you got anything else? Honest to God? Don't tell lies, now. You'll be punished for lying.'

'Where shall we put him?' asked Sergeant-Major Řepa.

'In no. 16,' the staff warder decided, 'among the pants. Don't you see that Captain Linhart has marked his papers: "Guard and watch closely!"'

'Oh, yes, indeed,' he declared solemnly to Švejk, 'vermin are treated like vermin. If anyone gets awkward we drag him off to the solitary. There we break all his ribs and leave him until he's a goner. That's our right. Like we did with that butcher, eh, Řepa?'

'Yes, he gave us a lot of trouble, sir,' replied Sergeant-Major Řepa dreamily. 'What a body! I stamped on him for more than five minutes, until his ribs began to crack and blood poured out of his mouth. And he lived for another ten days. A really tough customer.'

'So you see, you bastard, what happens here when anyone starts getting awkward or trying to escape,' said Staff Warder Slavík, concluding his pedagogical discourse. 'It's sheer suicide, and by the way suicide's punished too. And God help you, you miserable shit, if when there's an inspection you take it into your head to complain about anything. When there's an inspection and you're asked: "Have you any complaints?" you have to stand at attention, you stinking vermin, salute and answer: "Humbly report, none. I'm completely satisfied." Now what are you going to say, you lousy oaf? Repeat what I said!'

'Humbly report, none. I'm completely satisfied,' Švejk repeated with such a sweet expression on his face that the staff warder was misled and took it for honest zeal and decency.

'Now strip down to your pants and go to no. 16,' he said affably, without adding either 'shit', 'stinking vermin' or 'lousy oaf' as he usually did.

In no. 16 Švejk encountered twenty men in their pants. They were all men whose papers had been marked 'Guard and watch closely!' and who were now being watched very carefully so that they should not escape.

If those pants had been clean and there had been no bars on the windows, you might at first glance have supposed that you were in the dressing-room of some bathing establishment.

Sergeant-Major Řepa handed Švejk over to the 'cell commander', a hairy fellow in an unbuttoned shirt. He wrote Švejk's name down on a piece of paper which was hanging on the wall and said to him:

'Tomorrow we're going to have a show. They'll take us to the chapel to hear a sermon. We shall all of us be standing in our pants right under the pulpit. There'll be some fun.'

As in all prisons and penitentiaries the local chapel was very popular in the garrison gaol too. Not that enforced attendance at it brought the congregation nearer to God or that the prisoners learned more about morality. There could be no question of any nonsense of that kind.

The service and sermons were a marvellous thrill in the boredom of the garrison gaol. It was not a question of getting nearer to God, but of the hope of finding on the way in the corridor or in the courtyard a fag-end or a cigar-end. A little fag-end, lying about hopelessly in a spittoon or somewhere in the dust on the floor, stole the show and God was nowhere. That little stinking object triumphed over God and the salvation of the soul.

Then on top of that came the sermon, which was a rare picnic, for the chaplain, Otto Katz, was really a lovely man. His sermons were unusually exciting and amusing and they refreshed the boredom of the garrison gaol. He could drivel so beautifully about the infinite grace of God, and give uplift to the abandoned prisoners and disgraced men. He could let off such resounding oaths from the pulpit and the altar. He could roar out his ' Ite, missa est' so gorgeously at the altar, conduct the whole service in such an original way and turn the whole order of the Holy Mass upside down. When he was thoroughly drunk he could invent entirely new prayers and a new Holy Mass, even a liturgy of his own, something which was quite unheard of here.

And then, what a scream when he sometimes slipped and fell over with the chalice, the holy sacrament or the missal, loudly accusing the server from the prison unit of having purposely tripped him up and dealing him out solitary confinement or irons before the Holy Communion itself.

And the recipient was happy because it was an inseparable part of the whole pantomime in the prison chapel. He played a leading part in the piece and acquitted himself honourably in it.

The chaplain, Otto Katz, the most perfect of army chaplains, was a Jew. By the way, there's nothing odd about that. Archbishop Kohn was a Jew too and a friend of Machar[1] into the bargain.

Chaplain Otto Katz had an even more colourful past than the famous Archbishop Kohn.

He studied at the Commercial Academy and served in the forces as a one-year volunteer. He mastered so thoroughly bills of exchange and the laws about them that within a year he brought the firm of Katz and Co. Ltd to such a glorious and successful bankruptcy that old Mr Katz went off to North America, pulling off a kind of settlement unbeknown to his creditors or his partner, who went off to the Argentine.

And so after having disinterestedly bestowed the firm of Katz and

1. At the turn of the century the Czech poet J. S. Machar (1864–1942) defended Dr Theodor Kohn, Archbishop of Olomouc, against attacks on his Jewish origin.

Co. upon North and South America, young Otto Katz found himself in the position of a man who had no hopes of inheriting anything, had nowhere to lay his head and must therefore join the army.

Before this, however, Otto Katz had hit upon an awfully fine idea. He had himself baptized. He turned to Christ to help him make a career. He applied to him in absolute confidence that this was a business transaction between him and the Son of God.

He was solemnly baptized in the Emmaus monastery in Prague. Father Alban himself[1] dipped him in the font. It was a magnificent spectacle; it was attended by a pious major from the regiment where Otto Katz served, an old maid from the Institute of Gentlewomen on the Hradčany and a large-jowled representative of the consistory, who acted as his godfather.

The officers' examination went off well, and the newly-fledged Christian Otto Katz stayed in the army. At first he thought he was going to do well and even wanted to study on staff courses.

But one day he got drunk and went into a monastery, gave up the sword and donned the cassock. He was received by the archbishop on the Hradčany and managed to get himself into the seminary. Before his ordination he got drunk as a fish in a very respectable house served by ladies in the alley behind U Vejvodů, and straight from a whirl of voluptuous pleasures and delights went to have himself ordained. After his ordination he went to his regiment to try and get them to help him get a job. After he was appointed chaplain, he bought a horse, rode through the streets of Prague and took a merry part in all the drinking bouts with the officers of his regiment.

In the corridor of the house where he lived the curses of dissatisfied creditors could very often be heard. He also brought home tarts from off the streets or sent his orderly to fetch them. He loved playing färbl,[2] and there were certain conjectures and presumptions that he cheated, but nobody caught him out with an ace hidden in the wide sleeves of his chaplain's cassock. In officer circles they called him 'Holy Father'.

He never prepared his sermons beforehand and in this he differed from his predecessor who also used to visit the garrison gaol. The latter was possessed by the fixed idea that the men in the garrison gaol

1. Alban Schachleitner, a Benedictine monk, said later to have emigrated to Germany and become a Nazi.

2. An illegal Austrian card game.

could be reformed from the pulpit. This venerable chaplain piously rolled his eyes, explaining to the prisoners that prostitutes should be reformed and care for unmarried mothers improved, and held forth about the bringing up of illegitimate children. His sermons were of an abstract character with no connection whatsoever with life today. They were very boring.

Chaplain Otto Katz, on the contrary, delivered sermons which everybody looked forward to.

It was a festive moment when they led the 'number sixteens' to the chapel in their pants, because to allow them to be dressed entailed the risk that one of them might escape. They put these twenty angels in white pants right under the pulpit. Some of them, upon whom fortune had smiled, were chewing fag-ends which they had found on the way, because as was only natural they had no pockets and there was nowhere to put them.

Around them stood the rest of the garrison prisoners and gazed with relish at the twenty men in pants beneath the pulpit. The chaplain climbed up in to it, clinking his spurs.

'Attention!' he shouted. 'Let us pray, forward after me, repeating what I say! And you at the back there, you bastard, don't snot into your hands! You're in the temple of the Lord, and I'll have you locked up for it. I wonder if you haven't forgotten the Lord's Prayer, you oafs? All right, let's try it – well, I knew it wouldn't go. What the hell does the Lord's Prayer mean to you? All you care about is two helpings of meat and bean salad, stuffing yourself up, lying on your backsides on your bunk and picking your nose without a thought for the Lord. Isn't that right?'

He stared down from the pulpit at the twenty white angels in pants, who were thoroughly enjoying themselves like all the rest. At the back they were playing 'flesh'.[1]

'This is first-class,' Švejk whispered to his neighbour, who was suspected of having taken an axe and chopped off all his mate's fingers to get him out of military service – at the price of three crowns.

'You wait,' was the answer. 'Today he's properly oiled again. He'll tell us once more about the thorny path of sin.'

True enough the chaplain was in an excellent mood that day. He did

1. A game among soldiers where one soldier bares his buttocks and the others hit him from behind. If he can guess which of the others has hit him, that soldier has to change places with him.

not know himself why he was doing it, but he continually leaned out
of the pulpit and nearly overbalanced.

'Sing something, boys,' he shouted down to them, 'or do you want
me to teach you a new song? Now sing with me:

> 'Of all people in the world,
> I love my love the best.
> I'm not her only visitor;
> I queue up with the rest.
> Her lovers are innumerable.
> Now, tell me, pray, her name?
> It is the Virgin Mary —

'You'll never learn it, you bastards,' continued the chaplain. 'I'd
like to have you all shot, do you understand? I state this from this
holy place of God, you scoundrels, because God's a thing that's not
afraid of you and'll give you hell, and all because you hesitate to turn
to Christ and you'd rather go along the thorny path of sin.'

'Now it's coming. He's properly oiled,' whispered Švejk's neighbour
delightedly.

'The thorny path of sin, you bloody half-wits, is the path of the
battle against vice. You are the prodigal sons who prefer to loll about
in quod rather than return to the bosom of Our Father. But lift up
your eyes to heaven on high, and you will be victorious and peace will
abide in your souls, you gutter-snipes. I'd be glad if the person at the
back would stop snorting. He's not a horse and he's not in a stable.
He's in the Temple of the Lord. Let me tell you that, ducks. Now then,
where was I? Yes,' he continued in German, 'about peace in your
souls. Very good. Bear in mind, you cattle, that you're human beings
and that you must look through the dark clouds into the wide spaces
and know that everything here lasts only for a moment, while God is
for eternity. Very good, wasn't it, gentlemen?' (He lapsed into German
again.) 'I ought to pray for you day and night, that merciful God, you
bloody imbeciles, may infuse your cold hearts with His spirit and wash
away your sins with His holy mercy, that you may be His for evermore
and that He may love you for ever, you blackguards. But that's just
where you're wrong. I'm not going to lead you into paradise.' The
chaplain hiccoughed. 'No, I won't,' he repeated obstinately. 'I won't
do anything for you. I wouldn't dream of it, because you are incorrigible
scum. On your ways you will not be guided by the grace of the

Lord, the breath of God's love will not be wafted on to you, because the Lord would not dream of having anything to do with such twisters as you. Do you hear that, you down there below in those pants?'

Twenty pairs of pants looked up and said as with one voice: 'Humbly report, sir, we hear.'

'It's not enough just to hear,' the chaplain continued. 'Dark is the cloud of life and God's smile will not take away your woe, you bloody apes, for God's goodness has its bounds too. And don't choke yourself, you bounder at the back there, or I'll have you locked up until you're black in the face! And you down there, don't think that you're in the tap room! God is supremely merciful, but only to decent people and not to the scum of human society who won't be guided by His laws or by service regulations. That's what I wanted to tell you. You don't know how to pray, and you think that going to chapel is some kind of entertainment like being at a theatre or cinema. But I'll knock that out of your heads so that you don't think that I'm here to amuse you and bring pleasure to your lives. I'll send each one of you into solitary confinement, that's what I'll do, you sods. I'm wasting my time on you and I see it's all quite useless. If the field marshal himself or the archbishop had been here you wouldn't reform, you wouldn't incline to the Lord. But all the same one of these days you'll remember how I was trying to do you some good.'

Among the twenty pants a sob could be heard. It was Švejk, who had burst into tears.

The chaplain looked down. There stood Švejk rubbing his eyes with his fist. Round him were signs of gleeful appreciation.

Pointing to Švejk the chaplain continued:

'Let every one of you take an example from this man. What is he doing? He's crying. Don't cry, I tell you, don't cry! Do you want to reform? That's not so easy for you, my lad. You're crying now, but when you go back to your cell you'll be just as big a bastard as you were before. You'll have to think a lot about the unending grace and mercy of God. You'll have to work hard to see that your sinful soul finds the right path to tread in this world. Just now we saw a man who wants to be reformed bursting into tears. And what do the rest of you do? Nothing at all. Over there someone's chewing something, as though his parents had been ruminants, and over there they're searching for lice in their shirts in the Temple of the Lord. Can't you do your scratching at home? Must you reserve it just for the divine service?

And, Staff Warder, you never notice anything either. After all, you're all soldiers and not a lot of half-witted civilians. You've got to behave as befits soldiers even if you're in a church. For Christ's sake, get on with searching for God, and do your searching for lice at home. That's all I've got to say, you gutter-snipes, and I request you to behave yourselves at Mass, so that it doesn't happen as it did last time, when people in the back rows were bartering government linen for bread and then gorging it during the elevation of the Host.'

The chaplain came down from the pulpit and went off to the vestry, followed by the staff warder. After a while the staff warder came out, went straight up to Švejk, pulled him out of the group of twenty pants and led him away to the vestry.

The chaplain was sitting very comfortably on a table and rolling a cigarette.

When Švejk came in, the chaplain said:

'Oh, here you are! I've been thinking it all over and I believe I've seen through you. D'you understand, you bastard? It's the first case I've had of anyone blubbing in the church here.'

He jumped down from the table and, standing beneath a huge gloomy painting of St Francis of Sales, jerked at Švejk's shoulder and shouted:

'Confess that you only blubbed for fun, you sod.'

And St Francis of Sales gazed inquiringly down from his portrait at Švejk. From another painting on the other side, a martyr gazed open-mouthed at him, while Roman mercenaries were sawing through his buttocks. During this operation no suffering could be detected on the martyr's face, nor the joy nor the glory of martyrdom either. He only stared, open-mouthed, as though he wanted to say: 'How on earth did this happen to me? What on earth are you doing to me, gentlemen?'

'Humbly report, sir,' said Švejk deliberately, staking everything on a single card, 'I confess to God Almighty and to you, venerable Father, who are God's deputy, that I was really only blubbing for fun. I saw that for your preaching you needed a reformed sinner, and that you were looking for him in vain in your sermon. And so I really wanted to give you a pleasure, so that you shouldn't think that there weren't any just men left, and at the same time I wanted to have a little fun on my own to get some relief.'

The chaplain looked searchingly at Švejk's artless countenance. A sunbeam played on the melancholy face of St Francis of Sales and warmed the staring eyes of the martyr on the opposite wall.

'I'm beginning to take a fancy to you,' said the chaplain, sitting on the table again. 'Which regiment do you belong to?' He began to hiccough.

'Humbly report, sir, I belong and don't belong to the 91st regiment and I haven't the faintest idea how I really stand.'

'And what are you in gaol here for?' inquired the chaplain, continuing to hiccough.

From the chapel were wafted in this direction the sounds of a harmonium which was a substitute for an organ. The musician, a teacher who had been gaoled for desertion, wailed out on the harmonium the most mournful hymn tunes. With the hiccoughing of the chaplain these sounds blended to form a new Doric scale.

'Humbly report, sir, I really don't know why I am in gaol here, but I don't complain. It's just my bad luck. My intentions are always the best, and in the end I always get the worst of it, just like that martyr there in the picture.'

The chaplain looked at the picture, smiled and said:

'Yes, I've really taken to you. I must ask the judge advocate about you and I won't stay talking to you any longer. I must get that Holy Mass off my chest! About turn! Dismiss!'

When Švejk returned to his family group of pants beneath the pulpit, he replied very drily and laconically to their questions about what the chaplain had wanted of him in the vestry:

'He's sozzled.'

The chaplain's new performance, the Holy Mass, was followed by all with close attention and unconcealed enjoyment. One man under the pulpit even bet that the monstrance would fall out of the chaplain's hands. He wagered his whole portion of bread against two across the jaw and won his bet.

What inspired the souls of everyone in the chapel at the sight of the chaplain's ministration was not the mysticism of the faithful or the piety of true Catholics; it was the feeling we have in the theatre when we do not know what the play is about, when the plot develops and we breathlessly wait to see how it is going to end. They were absorbed in the scene which the chaplain with great devotion presented to them before the altar.

They surrendered completely to the aesthetic enjoyment of the vestments which the chaplain had put on inside out and watched all the happenings at the altar with ardent sympathy and enthusiasm.

The red-haired server, a deserter from the ranks of the sextons, a specialist in petty larcenies in the 28th regiment, was doing his level best to conjure up in his memory the whole ritual, technique and text of the Holy Mass. He was both server and prompter to the chaplain, who quite frivolously turned whole sentences upside down and instead of getting to the ordinary Mass found himself at that point of the prayer book where the Advent Mass came. He then began to sing this to the general satisfaction of the congregation.

He had neither voice nor musical ear, and under the vaulting of the chapel there resounded such a squealing and caterwauling as could only be heard in a pig-sty.

'He's really well sozzled today,' those sitting in front of the altar said with great joy and relish. 'He isn't half oiled. He's been at it again! He must have got tight with some tarts somewhere.'

And now for about the third time the strains of '*Ite, missa est!*' rang out from the altar like a Red Indian war-whoop until the windows rattled.

Then the chaplain looked once more into the chalice, in case there should still be a drop of wine left in it, made a gesture of annoyance and addressed his listeners:

'Well, now you can go home, you bastards. It's all over. I observed that you don't show that true piety you ought to have when you are in church in the presence of the Holy of Holies, you cads. When you're face to face with God Almighty you're not ashamed to laugh aloud, cough and snigger, shuffle your feet, even in my presence, who represent here the Virgin Mary, Jesus Christ and God the Father, you bloody imbeciles. If you do this again next time you'll get the hell you deserve and you'll learn that there's not only that hell which I preached to you about in my last sermon but one, but a hell on earth as well. And if you should by any chance save yourself from the first one, I'll see you don't escape from the second. Dismiss!'

The chaplain, who had just given such a wonderful practical demonstration of that damnable old custom – prison visiting – went into the vestry, changed his clothes, poured out some sacramental wine from the cask into a flagon, drank it up and with the help of the red-haired server mounted his horse which was tied up in the courtyard. Then he remembered Švejk, dismounted again and went to the office of Judge Advocate Bernis.

Judge Advocate Bernis was a man who liked society. He was an elegant dancer and a rake who was frightfully bored here and spent his time writing German verses for girls' autograph albums so as to have a supply always at hand. He was the most important element in the whole apparatus of military justice, and because he had such a tremendous pile of unfinished cases and muddled documents he was held in respect by the whole military court on Hradčany. He kept losing the documents for the indictment and was compelled to invent new ones. He mixed up names, lost the threads of the indictments and spun new ones just as they happened to come into his head. He tried deserters for theft and thieves for desertion. He brought in political cases which he had fabricated himself. He invented all kinds of hocus-pocus to convict men of crimes they had never even dreamt of. He invented insults to the monarch and always attributed fabricated incriminating statements to anyone, if the indictment and informers' reports had got lost in the unending chaos of documents and official correspondence.

'Hallo,' said the chaplain, shaking his hand. 'How are you?'

'Not very well,' answered Bernis. 'They've mucked up my papers and I can't make bloody head or tail of them. Yesterday I put up the material I'd processed on a fellow had up for mutiny, and they sent it back saying that in this case it wasn't a question of mutiny but of stealing a tin. And I'd taken the trouble to give it a completely different number, and it beats me how they managed to discover it.'

The judge advocate spat.

'Are you still playing cards?' asked the chaplain.

'I've lost everything I had at cards. The last time it happened I was playing makao with that bald-headed colonel and I had to throw everything I'd got down his bloody maw. But I know of a nice young bird. And what are you doing, Holy Father?'

'I need a batman,' said the chaplain. 'Last time I had an old book-keeper without academic education but a prize bastard. He kept on snivelling and praying that God would save him, and so in the end I drafted him off to the front with a march battalion. They say it was cut to pieces. Then they sent me a little chap, who did nothing but sit in the pub and drink at my expense. He was quite a tolerable cove, but had sweaty feet. So I drafted him off too. Today when I was preaching I found a bastard who started blubbing just for fun. That's the kind of cove I need. He's called Švejk and sits in no. 16. I'd like to know why they've put him there and whether it wouldn't be possible somehow to arrange for me to get him out.'

The judge advocate started looking in the drawers for the files on Švejk, but as usual he couldn't find anything.

'Captain Linhart'll have them,' he said after a long search. 'God knows where all these files of mine get to. I must have sent them to Linhart. I'll telephone to him at once – Hallo! It's Lieutenant Bernis speaking, sir. Please, have you by any chance some files about a man called Švejk. . . . They must be with me? I'm surprised. . . . I took them over from you? Well, I'm very surprised. . . . He's at present in no. 16 . . . I know, sir, that I've got the no. 16 file with me. But I thought that Švejk's papers must be lying around somewhere in your tray. . . . You'd be glad if I didn't speak to you in that tone? Papers don't lie around in your tray? . . . Hallo, hallo . . .'

Bernis sat down at the table and angrily condemned the disorderly way the investigations were being carried out. There was a long-standing feud between him and Captain Linhart in which they were both very consistent. If Bernis got hold of papers belonging to Linhart, he arranged them in a way that no one could make head or tail of them. Linhart did exactly the same with papers belonging to Bernis. And of course they lost each other's enclosures.[1]

(The papers on Švejk were not found until after the war. They were in the archives of the Army Legal Department and were minuted: 'Planned to throw off his hypocritical mask and come out publicly against our ruler and our state.' The papers had been stuck into files dealing with a certain Josef Koudela. On the file cover was a cross and underneath it 'Action completed' with the date.)

'So I've lost Švejk,' said Bernis. 'I'll have him sent for, and if he doesn't confess to anything, I'll let him go and have him drafted to you and you can settle it with his regiment.'

After the chaplain had gone Bernis had Švejk brought before him but left him standing at the door, because he had just received a telephone message from police headquarters that the material which was required for prosecution document no. 7267 about infantryman

1. Thirty per cent of the people who sat in the garrison gaol went on sitting there throughout the whole war without once being brought up for interrogation. (Author's note.)

Maixner, had arrived in office no. 1 and been signed for by Captain Linhart.

Meanwhile Švejk inspected the judge advocate's office.

One could not say that it made a very favourable impression, especially the photographs on the walls. They were photographs of various executions carried out by the army in Galicia and Serbia. They were artistic photographs of charred cottages and trees with branches sagging under the weight of bodies strung up on them. Particularly fine was a photograph from Serbia of a whole family strung up – a small boy and his father and mother. Two soldiers with bayonets were guarding the tree, and an officer stood victoriously in the foreground smoking a cigarette. On the other side in the background a field kitchen could be seen in full operation.

'Well, what's the trouble with you, Švejk?' asked Bernis, when he had filed away the telephone message. 'What have you been up to? Are you going to confess or wait until a charge is brought against you? It can't go on like this. Don't imagine that you're before a court where you'll be tried by lunatic civilians. Ours are courts-martial – the Imperial and Royal Military Court. The only way you can save yourself from a severe and just punishment is to confess.'

Bernis had a special method when he had lost the material against the accused. As you can see, there was nothing special about it and so we need not be surprised if the results of such an examination and cross-questioning always amounted to nix.

And Bernis felt he was always so clairvoyant that, without having any material against the accused and without knowing what he was accused of or why he was imprisoned in the garrison gaol but simply by observing the behaviour and physiognomy of the man who had been brought before him for interrogation, he could deduce why they had imprisoned him.

His clairvoyance and knowledge of human nature was so great that a gipsy who was sent by his regiment to the garrison gaol for stealing a few dozen shirts (he was helping the storekeeper in a store) was accused by him of political crimes; allegedly he had spoken in a pub somewhere with some soldiers about the setting up of an independent national state made up of the lands of the Bohemian crown and Slovakia and ruled by a Slav king.

'We have material evidence,' he said to the unfortunate gipsy. 'There's nothing left for you but to confess in which pub you said it, which regiment those soldiers came from, who listened to you and when it took place.'

The unfortunate gipsy invented not only the date but the pub and the regiment which his alleged listeners came from, and when he left the interrogation he ran away from the garrison altogether.

'So you won't confess to anything,' said Bernis, when Švejk remained deathly silent. 'You won't say why you're here and why they've put you in gaol? You could at least have told me, before I tell you it myself. I warn you once more that you'd better confess. It will be easier for you because it helps the investigation and alleviates the punishment. In that respect it's just the same here as in a civil court.'

'Humbly report, sir,' Švejk piped up good-naturedly, 'I am here in garrison gaol because I'm a foundling.'

'What do you mean by that?'

'Humbly report, sir, I can explain it quite simply. In our street there's a coal merchant and he had an entirely innocent two-year-old little boy. This laddie once walked all the way from Vinohrady to Libeň, where a policeman found him sitting on the pavement. So he took him to the police station and locked him up there – a two-year-old child. The little boy was, as you see, quite innocent and yet he was locked up. And if he'd been able to speak and anyone had asked him why he was locked up there, he wouldn't have known either. And it's rather like that with me. I'm a foundling too.'

The keen gaze of the judge advocate passed swiftly over Švejk's figure and face and foundered on them. Such unconcern and innocence radiated from the whole of the being which stood before him that Bernis began to pace nervously up and down his office and, if he had not given his word to the chaplain, God knows what might have happened to Švejk.

Finally he came to a standstill again by his table.

'Listen,' he said to Švejk, who was gazing unconcernedly in front of him. 'If ever I meet you again, you'll never forget it. Take him away!'

When they took Švejk back to no. 16 Bernis had Staff Warder Slavík called before him.

'Until further orders,' he said laconically, 'Švejk is sent to Chaplain Katz for his disposal. Prepare his discharge papers and have him escorted to the chaplain by two men!'

'Is he to be put in handcuffs for the journey, sir?'

The judge advocate banged his fist on the table.

'You're an oaf. I told you quite distinctly to make his discharge papers out.'

And all the bile which had accumulated in the judge advocate's soul in the course of that day because of Captain Linhart and Švejk poured out like a wild torrent on the head of the staff warder. At the end of it Bernis said:

'And now do you understand that you are a prize royal oaf?'

This is something which should only be said to kings and emperors, but even this simple staff warder, who was no royal personage, was not very pleased about it. On his way back from the judge advocate's office he gave a cruel kicking to a prisoner on fatigue duty who was cleaning the corridor.

As for Švejk, the staff warder made up his mind that he must spend at least one night more in the garrison gaol so as to derive a little more benefit from it.

The night spent in the garrison gaol will always rank among Švejk's most affectionate memories.

Next to no. 16 was the 'black hole', a murky pit for solitary confinement, from which could be heard during that night the howls of a soldier whose ribs were being broken by Sergeant-Major Řepa at the orders of Staff Warder Slavík because of a disciplinary offence.

When the howling stopped there could be heard in no. 16 the smashing of lice which got in between the fingers of the prisoners during their search.

Above the doors in an aperture in the wall a paraffin lamp, fitted with a protective grille, emitted a feeble light and smoked. The smell of paraffin mingled with the natural exhalations of unwashed human bodies and the stench of the bucket, which every time it was used had its surface stirred up and added a new wave of stink to no. 16.

The bad food made the digestive process difficult for everyone, and the majority suffered from wind, which they released into the stillness of the night, answering each other with these signals to the accompaniment of various witticisms.

In the corridors could be heard the measured tread of the sentries. From time to time the aperture in the door opened and a warder peered through the peephole.

From the middle bunk could be heard a voice quietly saying:

'Before I tried to escape and before they brought me here among you I was in no. 12. There they keep the light cases. Once they brought in a chap from somewhere in the country. The good fellow had got fourteen days because he allowed soldiers to stay overnight with him. At first they thought that it was a plot but then it turned out that he did it for money. He should have been locked up among the lightest cases but because it was full there he came to us. And you can't imagine all the things he brought with him from home and what they sent him, because he somehow got permission to order his own food and make things cosy for himself. And he got permission to smoke. He had two hams, giant loaves of bread, eggs, butter, cigarettes – well, in short he had in his two knapsacks everything you could dream of. And the bastard thought that he must guzzle it all up himself. We started begging him to share it with us, when he didn't hit on the idea himself, like others did when they got something. But he was a mean bastard and said no: he'd be locked up for fourteen days and the cabbage and rotten potatoes, which they gave us for mess rations, would ruin his stomach. He said he'd give us all his mess rations and army bread: it wasn't worth having and we could share it among ourselves or have it in turns. I tell you that he was such a gent that he didn't even want to sit on the bucket and waited until the next day for the exercise hour so that he could do it in the latrine in the courtyard. He was so spoiled that he even brought his own toilet paper. We told him that we didn't care a damn about his rations and we braved it out one, two, three days. The bastard guzzled ham, spread butter on his bread, shelled his eggs – in short he lived like a pig in clover. He smoked cigarettes and wouldn't give anyone even a puff. He said that we weren't allowed to smoke and if the warder were to see him giving us a puff they'd lock him up. As I said we stood it for three days. But on the fourth day in the night we did it. The bastard woke up early, and I forgot to tell you that in the early morning, at noon and in the evening, before he began to stuff himself, he always prayed and prayed for a very long time. And so this time he prayed and then looked for his knapsacks under his bunk. Yes, the knapsacks were there, but they were dried up and shrunk like dried prunes. He began to shriek that he had been robbed and that we'd only left him his toilet paper. And then for about five minutes he thought that we were only joking and that we had hidden it somewhere. He said still quite merrily: "I know you're only teasing. I know you'll give it back to me, but it was neatly done." There was a chap among us from Libeň and he said, "Look, cover yourself with your blanket and count up till ten. And then look in your knapsacks." And he covered himself and counted one, two, three, like an obedient little boy . . . and then the chap from Libeň said again: "You mustn't do it so quickly, you must do it very slowly." And there he was under the blanket counting slowly at intervals: one – two – three – . . . and when he got to ten he climbed out of his bunk and looked into his knapsacks. "Jesus Mary, chaps," he began hollering, "they're just as empty as they were before." And all the time his face was so bloody silly that we could all have split our sides with laughter. And then that chap from Libeň went on: "Try once more." And believe me he was so crazy after all this that he tried again, and when he saw that there was still nothing there except toilet paper he began to bang on the door and to shout out: "They've robbed me, they've robbed me, help, open, for Christ's sake, open." And then they all came rushing in and called the staff warder and Sergeant-Major Řepa. We all said with one voice that he had gone mad, that the day before he gorged far into the night and guzzled everything up. But he just wept and kept on saying: "Surely there must be some crumbs left somewhere." And then they started looking for the crumbs and couldn't find any because we were quite clever too. What we had not been able to guzzle ourselves we sent by rope-post up to the second storey. They couldn't prove anything on us, although that stupid fool kept on with his: "But surely there must be some crumbs left." The whole day he ate nothing and looked carefully to see whether anyone ate or smoked anything. And at lunch the next day again he didn't touch his rations, but in the evening the rotten potatoes and cabbage seemed to appeal to him, only he didn't pray as much as he did when he used to tuck into his ham and eggs. Then one of us somehow got some fags from outside, and then he began talking to us for the first time, asking us to give him a puff. But we didn't give him anything.'

'I was afraid you'd give him a puff,' remarked Švejk. 'That would've spoiled the whole story. You only find noble actions like that in novels, but in the garrison gaol in such circumstances it would be sheer lunacy.'

'And you didn't give him the blanket treatment?' someone asked.

'We didn't think of it.' Then a discussion began in hushed tones as to whether he should have had the blanket treatment or not. The majority were for it.

The conversation gradually died out. They were falling asleep, scratching themselves under their armpits, on their chests and on their bellies – at those points in their underclothes where the lice congregated most. They went to sleep, drawing the lice-ridden blankets over their heads, so that the light of the paraffin lamp shouldn't disturb them . . .

At eight o'clock in the morning they called Švejk to go to the office.

'On the left-hand side of the door leading into the office there's a spittoon and they throw fag-ends into it,' one man informed Švejk. 'And on the first floor you'll pass another one. They don't sweep the passages till nine o'clock, so something may still be there.'

But Švejk disappointed their hopes. He never came back to no. 16. The nineteen pairs of pants made various deductions and conjectures about him.

A freckled soldier belonging to the Landwehr who had a very lurid imagination spread the news that Švejk had shot his captain and would be led away the same day to the drill-ground at Motol for execution.

Švejk Batman to the Chaplain

I

ŠVEJK'S odyssey began anew under the honourable escort of two soldiers with fixed bayonets who had to conduct him to the chaplain.

His escort were men who complemented each other. If one was lanky, the other was small and tubby. The lanky one limped with his right foot and the small tubby one with his left. Both served behind the lines because sometime before the war they had been totally exempted from military service.

They walked solemnly alongside the pavement and from time to time looked sideways at Švejk, who strode in the middle and saluted everyone he saw. His mufti and the military cap he got when he joined up had got lost in the garrison stores. Before they discharged him they had given him an old military uniform which had belonged to some pot-bellied fellow who was taller than him by a head.

As for the trousers three more Švejks could have got into them. An endless succession of baggy folds from his feet up to where his trousers reached over his chest involuntarily evoked the admiration of the spectators. A vast tunic with patches on the elbows, covered with grease and dirt, dangled around Švejk like a coat on a scarecrow. His trousers hung on him like a circus clown's costume. The military cap, which they had also changed in the garrison gaol, came down over his ears.

Švejk answered the smiles of the spectators with a sweet smile of his own and the warm tender look of his good-natured eyes.

And so they marched to the chaplain's apartment at Karlín.

The first of the two to speak to Švejk was the small tubby one. They were just at that moment in Malá Strana down under the arcades.

'Where do you come from?' asked the small tubby one.

'From Prague.'

'And you're not going to run away?'

Now the lanky one joined the conversation. It is a very remarkable phenomenon that people who are small and fat are generally good-humoured optimists, whereas people who are lanky and spindly are on the contrary sceptics.

And so the lanky one said: 'He'd run away if he could.'

'But why should he?' replied the small tubby one. 'Now he's out of the garrison gaol he's practically free. I'm carrying it in the bundle here.'

'What's in that bundle for the chaplain?' asked the lanky one.

'I don't know.'

'There, you see. You don't know and yet you talk about it.'

They crossed the Charles Bridge in complete silence. In Charles Street the small tubby one spoke to Švejk again:

'Do you know why we're taking you to the chaplain?'

'For confession,' said Švejk nonchalantly. 'Tomorrow they're going to hang me. This is what they always do on these occasions and they call it spiritual consolation.'

'And why are they going to...?' the lanky one asked cautiously, while the tubby one looked pityingly at Švejk.

Each was a small tradesman from the country, a paterfamilias.

'I don't know,' replied Švejk, with his good-natured smile. 'I haven't the faintest idea. It must be fate.'

'Perhaps you were born under an unlucky star,' remarked the little fellow with a knowing air and in sympathy. 'At home in Jasenná near Josefov during the war with Prussia they hanged someone just like that. They came to fetch him, didn't say anything to him, and hanged him in Josefov.'

'If you ask me,' said the lanky one sceptically, 'they don't hang a person for nothing at all. There must always be some reason for it, so they can justify it.'

'When there isn't a war on,' remarked Švejk, 'they justify it, but when there is, they don't worry about you. You could just as well fall at the front or be hanged at home – six of one or half a dozen of the other.'

'I say, you're not a "political", are you?' asked the lanky one. The tone of his question indicated that he was beginning to take to Švejk.

'Yes, I'm much too political,' replied Švejk with a smile.

'You aren't a National Socialist?'[1] Now it was the turn of the small

1. A Czech political party dating from Austrian times. Later Eduard Beneš became one of its leaders.

tubby one to start being cautious. Breaking in on the conversation he said: 'What's that got to do with us anyway? There are lots of people around everywhere and they're watching us. If we could only take off our bayonets in a passage somewhere without attracting attention. You won't run away from us, will you? We'd have trouble if you did. Aren't I right, Toník?' he said to the lanky one, who answered quietly: 'We could take off our bayonets. After all, he's one of us.'

He ceased being a sceptic and his heart filled with compassion for Švejk. They looked for a suitable passage where they could take off their bayonets and the tubby one allowed Švejk to walk alongside him.

'You'd like a smoke, wouldn't you?' he said. 'I wonder whether . . .' He wanted to say: 'I wonder whether they allow you to have a smoke before they hang you', but he did not complete the sentence, realizing that it might be tactless.

They all had a smoke and Švejk's escort began to tell him about their families in the country near Hradec Králové, their wives and children, their plot of land and their cow.

'I'm thirsty,' said Švejk.

The lanky one and the small tubby one exchanged glances.

'We might drop in somewhere for a quick one,' said the little fellow, feeling he could count on the lanky one's consent, 'but somewhere where it won't attract attention.'

'Let's go to Kuklík,' Švejk suggested. 'You can put your rifles in the kitchen there. The landlord, Serabona, is a Sokol[1] and you don't need to be afraid of him.

'They play the violin and the accordion there,' continued Švejk, 'and tarts come in and various other members of good society who aren't allowed in at the Represent'ák.'[2]

The lanky one and the small one exchanged glances once more and then the lanky one said: 'Very well, then, let's go. It's still a long way to Karlín.'

On the way Švejk told them various stories, and they arrived at Kuklík in a good mood and did exactly as Švejk had advised. They put

1. Czech patriotic sports club whose members wore falcon feathers on their hats. (Sokol = falcon.)

2. The Representational Hall – a complex in the centre of Prague containing a café, a restaurant, several reception rooms and the Smetana Hall, the largest concert hall.

their rifles in the kitchen and went into the bar, where the violin and accordion filled the room with the strains of the popular song:

> At Pankrác there's a hill
> And on that hill there stands
> A lovely row of trees . . .

A young lady who was sitting on the knees of a jaded youth with smoothly parted hair was singing in a hoarse voice: 'I had a girl lined up and now another's pinched her.'

At one table a drunken sardine-hawker was asleep. He woke up from time to time, struck the table with his fist, stuttered out: 'It's no good', and fell asleep again. Under a mirror behind the billiard table sat three other young ladies who shouted at a railway guard: 'Young man, stand us a glass of vermouth.' Near the orchestra two people were quarrelling about whether Mařka had been caught the previous night by the patrol or not. One of them saw it with his own eyes and the other maintained that she had gone to bed with a soldier at the hotel U Valšů.[1]

By the door a soldier was sitting with a number of civilians and telling them how he had been wounded in Serbia. He had a bandaged arm and his pockets were full of cigarettes they had given him. He said that he couldn't drink any more, but one of the company, a bald-headed old man, kept on offering him something: 'Have another, soldier. Who knows if we'll ever meet again. Shall I get them to play something for you? Do you like "The Orphan Child"?'

This was the bald-headed old man's favourite song, and sure enough presently the violin and accordion started to wail it out, while tears came into his eyes and he started to sing in a tremulous voice: 'When it grew to wiser years, it asked about its mamma, it asked about its mamma . . .'

From the other table somebody said: 'Stop it, can't you? Go and stuff it up! String yourself up on a hook! Get to bloody hell with your orphan child!'

And as a final trump the rival table began to sing: 'To part, to part, It breaks my heart, my heart . . .'

'Franta,' they called to the wounded soldier when they had out-sung and drowned the 'Orphan Child', 'leave them and come and sit

1. A louche house in Prague where rooms could be rented by the hour.

with us. They can go to hell. You come and bring the cigarettes here.
You won't amuse those mugs.'

Švejk conjured up memories of the time when he often used to sit
here before the war. The police inspector, Drašner, used to raid the
place and the prostitutes were scared of him and made up songs about
him full of *double-entendres*. He remembered how once they sang in a
chorus:

> When Drašner made his raid
> Mařena wasn't afraid.
> In all the hullaballoo
> She'd knocked back quite a few.

Just at that moment who should have come in but the terrible and
ruthless Drašner himself, accompanied by his men. It was like shooting
into a flock of partridges. The plain-clothes police herded all the
people together in a bunch. And Švejk found himself in it too, because with his usual bad luck he had said to Inspector Drašner when
he was asked to show his papers: 'Have you got permission for this
from police headquarters?' Švejk also remembered a poet who used
to sit there under the mirror, and in the general uproar of Kuklík
amidst the strains and sounds of the accordion used to write poems and
recite them to the prostitutes.

On the other hand Švejk's escort had no such reminiscences. For
them it was a quite new experience and they began to like it. The
first who found complete satisfaction here was the small tubby one,
because people of his type tend to be not only optimists but epicures.
The lanky one struggled with himself for a short time. And just as he
had already lost his scepticism, so he now began gradually to lose his
self-control and the rest of his good sense also.

'I'm going to have a dance,' he said after his fifth beer, when he
saw how couples were dancing the 'Šlapák'.

The little one abandoned himself completely to dissipation. A
young lady sat next to him and told him dirty stories. His eyes sparkled.

Švejk drank. The lanky one finished his dance and returned with
his partner to the table. Then they sang, danced, drank without
interruption and spanked their lady companions. And in the atmosphere of venal love, nicotine and alcohol there was ever present, if
barely perceptible, the old slogan: *'Après nous le déluge!'*

In the afternoon a soldier came up to them and offered them a boil
with blood poisoning for five guilders. He had with him a hypodermic

syringe and could inject paraffin into their legs or arms.[1] With this they would be in bed for at least two months and if they fed the wound with saliva they could perhaps spin it out to half a year and be completely discharged from the army.

The lanky one, who had completely lost his mental balance, had himself injected intravenously in the leg with paraffin. The soldier did it for him in the W.C.

As it was already getting towards evening Švejk proposed that they resume their journey to the chaplain. The small tubby one, who was already beginning to wander, tried to persuade Švejk to stay a little longer. The lanky one was also of the opinion that the chaplain could wait. But Švejk was not enjoying it any more at Kuklík and threatened to go on alone.

And so they left, but he had to promise them that they would all stop somewhere again.

They stopped at a small café at Florence, where the tubby one pawned his silver watch so that they could go on having fun.

When they left, Švejk was already leading them by the arm. It gave him an awful lot of trouble. Their feet kept on slipping, and they were all the time wanting to go somewhere. The small tubby one almost lost the bundle for the chaplain, and so Švejk was forced to carry it himself.

Švejk had continually to alert them when an officer or an N.C.O. came by. After superhuman efforts and struggles he managed to bring them to the house in Královská Avenue where the chaplain lived.

He fixed the bayonets on their rifles himself and by poking them in the ribs forced them to lead him instead of his leading them.

On the first floor, where there was a visiting card on the door: 'Otto Katz, Chaplain', a soldier came to open. From the drawing-room could be heard voices and the clinking of bottles and glasses.

'Hum – bly – report – sir,' said the lanky one with an effort in broken German and saluting the soldier: 'One – bundle – and one man delivered.'

'Come in,' said the soldier. 'However did you manage to get into that state? The chaplain's the same way . . .' The soldier spat.

---

1. This is a fairly well proved method of getting into hospital. But the smell of the paraffin, which remains in the boil, gives it away. Petrol is better, because it evaporates quicker. Subsequently a mixture of ether and petrol used to be injected and later other improvements were introduced. (Author's note.)

The soldier went off with the bundle. They waited in the hall for a long time until the door opened and through it there flew rather than walked the chaplain himself. He was in his waistcoat and held a cigar in his hand. 'So you're here already,' he said to Švejk, 'and these people brought you. Hey, have you got any matches?'

'Humbly report, sir, I haven't.'

'Hey, and why haven't you got any? Every soldier should have matches so that he can light up. A soldier who hasn't got any matches is . . . what is he?'

'Humbly report, sir, he's without matches,' answered Švejk.

'Very good. He's without matches and can't give anyone a light. Well, that's one essential point and now here's another. Do your feet stink, Švejk?'

'Humbly report, sir, they don't.'

'Well, that was the second point. And now for the third. Do you drink spirits?'

'Humbly report, sir, I don't drink spirits, only rum.'

'Good. Just have a look at this soldier here. I borrowed him for the day from Lieutenant Feldhuber. He's his batman. And he doesn't drink anything. He is a t- t- total abstainer, and that's why he is going to be drafted to the front. Be- because a man like him is no use to me. He's not a batman, he's a cow. A cow also drinks only water and lows like an ox.

'You're a teetotaller,' he said, addressing the soldier. 'You ought to be ashamed of yourself, you nincompoop. You deserve a few across the jaw.'

The chaplain addressed himself to those who had escorted Švejk and who in their endeavour to stand straight were wobbling about, vainly trying to prop themselves up on their rifles.

'You are dr- drunk,' said the chaplain. 'You got drunk while on duty, and I'm going to have you l- locked up for that. Švejk, remove their rifles and take them into the kitchen. You're to guard them until the patrol comes to fetch them. I shall teleph- teleph- telephone to the barracks.'

And so on this occasion too the truth of Napoleon's saying, 'In war the situation changes every moment', was entirely borne out.

In the morning these two had led Švejk under bayonet escort and had been afraid he might run away. Then he led them and now finally had to guard them.

They were not at first fully aware of this rapid change of fortune and it only dawned on them when they were sitting in the kitchen and saw Švejk standing at the door with rifle and bayonet.

'I could do with a drink,' sighed the little optimist, while the lanky one again had a fit of scepticism and said that the whole thing was a

piece of lousy treason. He started loudly accusing Švejk of having landed them in this mess and reproached him that he had promised them that he would be hanged the next day. And now they could see that it was all a trick with his confession and his hanging.

Švejk was silent and walked up and down by the door.

'We've been bloody asses!' shouted the lanky one.

In the end, having listened to all the accusations, Švejk declared:

'Now at any rate you can see that the army's no picnic. I'm only doing my duty. I got into this just the same way as you did, but as the saying is: Fortune smiled on me.'

'I could do with a drink,' repeated the optimist in desperate tones.

The lanky one got up and reeled towards the door. 'Let's go home,' he said to Švejk. 'Chum, don't be a bloody fool.'

'Get back,' answered Švejk. 'I've got to guard you. Now we don't know each other any longer.'

The chaplain appeared in the door: 'I – I – can't get through on the phone to the barracks, so you go home and remem-mem-member that when you're on duty you can't go and get yourselves sozzled. Quick march!'

To the honour of the chaplain may it be said that he did not get through to the barracks because he had no telephone at home and in fact was talking to a lamp-stand.

II

Švejk had been the chaplain's batman for three days, but during all this time he had seen him only once. On the third day Lieutenant Helmich's batman arrived to tell Švejk to come and fetch his chaplain.

On the way he told Švejk that the chaplain had had a quarrel with the lieutenant, had smashed the piano, was dead drunk and refused to go home.

Lieutenant Helmich was also drunk and had thrown the chaplain out into the corridor, where he was sitting on the floor by the door-way and dozing.

When Švejk reached the spot he shook the chaplain, and when the latter began to growl and opened his eyes, Švejk saluted and said:

'Humbly report, sir, I'm here.'

'And what do you want – here?'

'Humbly report, sir, I have to come and fetch you.'

'So you have to come and fetch me, have you? And where are we going?'

'To your apartment, sir.'

'Why do I have to go to my apartment – aren't I in my apartment?'

'Humbly report, sir, you're in the corridor of somebody else's house.'

'And how – did – I – get here?'

'Humbly report, sir, you were here on a visit.'

'N- n- not on a v- visit. You're m- m- making a mistake.'

Švejk lifted the chaplain and propped him up against the wall. The

chaplain lurched from side to side and rolled over on him saying:
'I'm falling on you!

'Falling on you,' he repeated with an idiotic grin. Finally Švejk
managed to press the chaplain to the wall, where in this new position
he started to doze again.

Švejk woke him up. 'What can I do for you?' said the chaplain
making a vain attempt to drag himself along by the wall and sit on the
floor. 'Who are you, anyhow?'

'Humbly report, sir,' replied Švejk, pushing the chaplain back
against the wall once more, 'I'm your batman, Your Reverence, sir.'

'I haven't got any batman,' said the chaplain with an effort, making
another attempt to fall on to Švejk. 'And I'm not a Reverence.

'I'm a pig,' he added with the sincerity of a drunkard. 'Let me go,
sir, I don't know you.'

The little tussle ended in a complete victory for Švejk. He took
advantage of it to drag the chaplain down the stairs into the carriage
entrance, where the chaplain tried to stop him from dragging him
into the street. 'I don't know you, sir,' he kept on saying to Švejk
during the struggle. 'Do you know Otto Katz? That's me.

'I've been with the archbishop,' he shouted, clinging to the gate in
the carriage entrance. 'The Vatican's interested in me, do you understand?'

Švejk dropped the 'humbly report, sir' and spoke to the chaplain in
very familiar tones.

'Drop it, I tell you,' he said, 'or I'll bash your flipper. We're going
home and no more nonsense. Just shut up.'

The chaplain let go of the door and rolled over on to Švejk: 'Well,
let's go somewhere, but I won't go to U Šuhů. [1] I've got debts there.'

Švejk pushed him and carried him out of the carriage entrance and
dragged him along the pavement in the direction of his home.

'Who is that gentleman?' asked one of the spectators in the street.

'He's my brother,' answered Švejk. 'He got leave and came to visit
me. He was so happy that he got drunk. You see he thought I was dead.'

The chaplain, who caught the last words, hummed a tune from an
operetta which no one would have recognized, rose up and addressed the
spectators: 'Whoever of you is dead must report to Army Corps
headquarters within three days so that his corpse can be sprinkled with
holy water.'

1. A notorious brothel.

And he lapsed into silence, endeavouring to fall nose-first on the pavement, while Švejk held him under the arm and dragged him home.

With his head thrust forward and his legs trailing behind and dangling like those of a cat with a broken backbone, the chaplain was

humming to himself: '*Dominus vobiscum – et cum spiritu tuo. Dominus vobiscum.*'

When they reached the droshky rank Švejk propped the chaplain against the wall and went to haggle with a droshky driver about his transport.

One of the drivers said he knew the gentleman very well, had had him as a passenger once and wouldn't ever take him again.

'He spewed over everything,' he stated bluntly, 'and didn't even pay for the ride. I drove him for more than two hours before he found where he lived. Only after a week, when I had been to see him at least three times, did he give me anything and then it was only five crowns for all that.'

After long haggling one of the drivers agreed to take them.

Švejk returned to the chaplain, who was sleeping. Someone had removed and carried off his bowler (for he generally went about in mufti).

Švejk woke him up and with the help of the driver got him to the droshky. Once inside the chaplain fell into a state of complete torpor. Mistaking Švejk for Colonel Just of the 75th infantry regiment he repeated several times: 'Don't be angry, old chap, if I call you by your Christian name. I'm a pig.'

At one moment it seemed that the jolting of the droshky on the cobbles was bringing him to his senses. He sat up straight and began to sing a snatch of an unknown song. Perhaps it was only his fancy:

> 'I recall that lovely time
> When he rocked me on his knee.
> We were living in those days
> At Merklín near Domažlice-e-e.'

After a while he fell again into complete torpor. Then turning to Švejk he winked an eye and asked: 'How are you today, madam? . . .

'Are you going somewhere for the summer?' he said after a short pause, and seeing everything double he asked: 'So you already have a grown-up son, have you?' Saying this he pointed to Švejk.

'Sit down!' shouted Švejk, when the chaplain tried to climb on to the seat. 'Otherwise I'll teach you how to behave!'

The chaplain became quiet and stared out of the droshky with his little piggy eyes. He had not the faintest idea what was actually happening to him.

He no longer had a clue and turning to Švejk said dejectedly: 'Madam, give me first class.' Then he tried to take his trousers down.

'Button yourself up at once, you swine!' Švejk shouted at him. 'All the droshky drivers know you only too well already. You spewed all over yourself once, and now this! Don't imagine you'll get away with it without paying like last time!'

The chaplain with a melancholy expression propped his head on his hands and began to sing: 'No one loves me any more . . .' but he broke off his song suddenly and remarked in German: 'Excuse me, old man. You're a bloody idiot. I can sing what I like.'

He appeared to want to whistle some tune, but instead he emitted from his mouth such a powerful 'Whoa' that the droshky came to a standstill.

When afterwards at Švejk's order they continued their journey further, the chaplain began to try to light his cigarette holder.

'It doesn't burn,' he said despondently, when he had used up a whole box of matches. 'You're blowing at it.'

But at that moment he lost the thread again and started to laugh: 'This is a lark. We're alone in the tram, aren't we, my dear colleague?' He began to rummage in his pockets.

'I've lost my ticket,' he shouted. 'Stop, I must find my ticket!'

He waved his hand resignedly: 'All right, let's go on . . .'

He then began to wander: 'In the vast majority of cases. . . . Yes, all right. . . . In all cases. . . . You're quite wrong. . . . Second floor? . . . That's just an excuse. . . . It's not my concern, but yours, my dear madam. . . . Bill, please. . . . I had a black coffee!'

In a half dream he began to squabble with an imaginary enemy who was disputing his rights to sit by the window in a restaurant. Then he began to mistake the droshky for a train and, leaning out of the window, shrieked at the street in Czech and German: 'Nymburk, all change!'

Švejk pulled him back and the chaplain forgot about the train and began to give various animal imitations. He spent longest over the cock and his cock-a-doodle-do resounded triumphantly from the droshky.

For some time he was very active and restless and tried to fall out of the droshky, swearing at the passers-by and calling them gutter-snipes. Then he threw his handkerchief out of the droshky and shouted that they must stop because he had lost his luggage. Then he began to tell a story: 'In Budějovice there was once a drummer. He got married. A year later he died.' He burst out laughing: 'Isn't that a good story?'

All this time Švejk treated the chaplain with ruthless severity.

On the various occasions when the chaplain tried some tricks on him such as falling out of the droshky, or breaking the seat, Švejk gave him one or two punches under the ribs, which the chaplain accepted with unusual apathy.

Only once did he make an attempt to mutiny and jump out of the droshky, saying that he wouldn't go any further and that he knew that they were going to Podmokly instead of Budějovice. In the course of one minute Švejk had liquidated his mutiny completely and forced him to return to his previous position on the seat, taking care that he did not fall asleep. The mildest thing he said during all this was: 'Don't fall asleep, you death's-head!'

Suddenly the chaplain had an attack of melancholy and began to sob, asking Švejk whether he had a mother.

'Folks, I'm all alone in this world,' he shouted from the droshky. 'Take care of me!'

'Don't make a scandal,' Švejk rebuked him. 'Stop or else everyone will say you're tight.'

'I haven't touched a drop, old man,' answered the chaplain, 'I'm completely sober.'

But suddenly he stood up, saluted, and said in German: 'Humbly report, sir, I'm sozzled.

'I'm a filthy hog,' he repeated ten times in succession in hopeless and sincere despair.

And turning to Švejk he persistently begged and entreated: 'Throw me out of the car. Why are you taking me with you?'

He sat down again and muttered: 'Rings are forming round the moon. Captain, do you believe in the immortality of the soul? Can a horse get to heaven?'

He started to laugh aloud, but in a moment again grew sad and looked apathetically at Švejk, saying: 'Excuse me, sir, I've seen you somewhere before. Were you ever in Vienna? I remember you from the seminary.'

He amused himself for a while by reciting Latin verses: '*Aurea prima sata est aetas, quae vindice nullo* . . .

'I can't go on,' he said. 'Throw me out. Why won't you throw me out? I won't do anything to myself.

'I want to fall on my nose,' he announced in a resolute tone.

'Sir,' he continued again imploringly, 'dear old man, give me one across the jaw.'

'One or several?' asked Švejk. 'Two? Here you are . . .'

The chaplain counted the blows aloud as they came, beaming blissfully all the time.

'That does one a lot of good,' he said. 'It helps the stomach and promotes the digestion. Give me another one.'

'Thank you very much,' he called, when Švejk immediately obliged him. 'I'm completely satisfied. Tear open my waistcoat please.'

He expressed the most varied wishes. He wanted Švejk to dislocate his leg, to throttle him for a bit, to cut his nails and to pull out his front teeth.

He exhibited yearnings for martyrdom, asking him to cut off his head and throw him in a sack into the Vltava.

'Some stars round my head would suit me very well,' he said with enthusiasm. 'I should need ten.'[1]

Then he began to speak about the races and quickly went over to the ballet, which however did not detain him for long either.

'Do you dance the czardas?' he asked Švejk. 'Do you know the bear dance? Like this . . .'

He tried to jump in the air but fell on Švejk, who began to box him and then laid him out on the seat.

'I want something,' shouted the chaplain, 'but I don't know what. Don't you know what I want?' He hung his head in complete resignation.

'What business of mine is it what I want?' he said solemnly. 'And it's no business of yours either, is it, sir? I don't know you. How dare you rebuke me? Do you know how to fence?'

For a moment he became more aggressive and tried to push Švejk off the seat.

Then when Švejk had calmed him down and had not scrupled to give him a taste of his physical superiority, the chaplain asked: 'Is it Monday or Friday today?'

He was anxious to know too whether it was December or June and exhibited a great aptitude for asking the most diverse questions such as: 'Are you married? Do you like gorgonzola? Did you have bugs at home? Are you all right? Has your dog had distemper?'

He became communicative. He told how he owed money for riding breeches, a whip and a saddle, that he'd had V.D. some years ago and had cured it with permanganate.

'There was no idea of trying anything else, no time for it,' he said with a belch. 'It may seem to you pretty drastic, but tell me, hic, hic, what am I to do, hic, hic? You must forgive me.

'Thermos flask,' he continued, forgetting what he had been talking about a moment ago, 'is the name for receptacles which keep drinks and food in their original warmth. Which do you think, my dear colleague, is the fairer game, färbl or vingt-et-un?

1. Another reference to St John of Nepomuk. The statue of the saint has stars over the halo, which symbolize the miracles which took place at his martyrdom.

'Really, I've seen you somewhere before,' he called out, trying to embrace Švejk and kiss him with salivary lips. 'We were at school together. You're a good chap,' he said, tenderly stroking his own leg. 'How you've grown from the time when I saw you last. The pleasure of seeing you makes up for all my sufferings.'

A poetic mood came over him and he began to speak of going back to the sunshine of happy faces and warm hearts.

Then he knelt down and began to pray 'Ave Maria', laughing to split his sides.

When they stopped before his apartment, it was very difficult to get him out of the droshky.

'We aren't there yet,' he shrieked. 'Help! They're kidnapping me! I want to go on.' He was literally torn out of the droshky like a boiled snail from its shell. At one moment it seemed as if he would be pulled apart, because his legs got stuck behind the seat.

He laughed loudly when this was happening, saying he had diddled them: 'You are tearing me apart, gentlemen.'

Then he was dragged through the carriage entrance up the steps to his apartment and, once inside, thrown like a sack on to the sofa. He declared that he wouldn't pay for the car which he hadn't ordered, and it took more than a quarter of an hour for them to explain to him that it was a droshky.

And even then he did not agree, objecting that he only drove in a fiacre.

'You're trying to diddle me,' he declared, winking knowingly at Švejk and at the droshky driver. 'We walked here.'

And suddenly in an outburst of generosity he threw his purse to the driver: 'Take it all. I can pay. A kreutzer more or less doesn't make any difference to me.'

He should really have said 'thirty-six kreutzers' because that was all the purse contained. Fortunately the driver subjected him to an exhaustive search, talking of swipes over the jaw as he did so.

'All right, then, give me one,' the chaplain answered. 'D'you think I couldn't take it? I could manage five from you.'

In the chaplain's waistcoat pocket the driver found ten crowns. He went away cursing his fate and the chaplain for wasting his time and ruining his business.

The chaplain took some time to fall asleep because he kept on

making new plans. He wanted to do all sorts of things, play the piano, take dancing lessons and fry fish.

Then he promised Švejk his sister, although he did not have one. And he also asked to be taken off to bed, and finally he fell asleep, asserting that he wished to be regarded as a human being, which was just as valuable an entity as a pig.

III

When Švejk entered the chaplain's room in the morning, he found him lying on the sofa and puzzling hard how it could happen that someone had wetted him in such a peculiar way that he had got stuck to the leather couch with his trousers.

'Humbly report, sir,' said Švejk, 'that in the night you ...'

In a few words he explained to the chaplain that he was terribly mistaken if he thought that he had been wetted. The chaplain, who had an unusually heavy hangover, was in a depressed mood.

'I can't remember,' he said, 'how I got from the bed on to the sofa.'

'You never were in the bed, sir. As soon as we got here we laid you on the sofa. That's as far as we could manage.'

'And what have I been up to? Was I up to anything at all? Wasn't I perhaps drunk?'

'Not half!' answered Švejk, 'to-hotally you were, sir. A little delirium came over you. I hope it'll help you if you change your clothes and wash.'

'I feel as if someone had given me a drubbing,' complained the chaplain. 'And I'm thirsty too. Did I have a brawl yesterday?'

'It wasn't too bad, sir. The thirst is the result of the thirst you had yesterday. A chap doesn't get over it so quickly. I knew a cabinet-maker who got drunk for the first time on New Year's Eve in 1910 and on the morning of the first of January he had such a thirst and felt so bad that he bought a salted herring and started drinking again. And he has gone on doing that every day for four years and no one can help him because he always buys his salted herrings on Saturday for the whole week. It's a proper merry-go-round, as our old sergeant-major in the 91st regiment always used to say.'

The chaplain was suffering from a hundred-per-cent hangover and was in a state of utter depression. Anyone who had been listening to him at that moment would have been convinced that he regularly attended the lectures of Dr Alexander Batěk ('We must declare war to the death on the demon of alcohol, who slaughters our best men') and had been reading his 'Hundred ethical sparks'.

He modified it slightly, it's true. 'If,' he said, 'you drank noble drinks like arak, maraschino, cognac – all right! But yesterday I drank some frightful borovička.[1] I'm surprised I could swill that stuff like I did. It had a disgusting taste. If it had only been griotte. People think up different kinds of filth and drink them like water. A borovička like that doesn't even taste good, it doesn't have any colour and burns your throat. If it had only been the genuine article, distilled from juniper, like what I once drank in Moravia. But it was made out of some kind of wood alcohol and scented oils. Look how I am belching.

'Alcohol's poison,' he decided. 'It must be original and genuine and not manufactured synthetically in a factory as the Jews do it. It's the same with rum. Good rum's a rarity.

'If we only had here genuine ořechovka,'[2] he sighed. 'That would put my stomach right. The sort of ořechovka which Captain Šnábl in Bruska has.'

He began rummaging in his pockets and examining his purse.

'I've only got thirty-six kreutzers. What about selling the sofa?' he reflected. 'What do you think? Would anyone buy it? I'll tell the landlord that I've lent it to somebody or that somebody's stolen it. But no, I'll keep the sofa. I'll send you to Captain Šnábl to ask him to lend me a hundred crowns. The day before yesterday he had a win at cards. If you don't get anything from him, then go to the barracks at Vršovice to Lieutenant Mahler. If you don't succeed with him, you can go to the Hradčany to Captain Fišer. You can tell him that I've got to pay for my horse's fodder and I've spent the money on drink. And if you don't have any luck with him we'll pawn the piano and damn what happens. I'll write you a few general lines. Don't let yourself get fobbed off. Say that I need it and that I'm quite broke. Think up whatever you like, but don't return empty-handed, otherwise I'll march you off to the front. Ask Captain Šnábl where he buys his ořechovka and buy two bottles of it.'

Švejk discharged his mission brilliantly. His sincerity and honest

1. Schnaps made out of juniper.
2. The same, made out of walnut.

countenance won him complete confidence and no one doubted the truth of what he was saying.

He considered it appropriate, in the presence of Captain Šnábl, Captain Fišer and Lieutenant Mahler, not to say that the chaplain had to pay for his horse's fodder, but to support his request for a loan

by saying that the chaplain had to pay paternity alimony. He was given money at all three places.

Having acquitted himself honourably on his expedition and brandishing on return the three hundred crowns, the chaplain, who had by this time taken a bath and put on clean clothes, was very surprised.

'I took the whole lot at one go,' said Švejk, 'so that we shouldn't have to worry our heads about money again tomorrow or the day after tomorrow. It went pretty smoothly, but I had to go on my knees to

Captain Šnábl. He's a real swine. But when I told him that we have to pay alimony . . .'

'Alimony?' the chaplain repeated in horror.

'Yes, alimony, sir, compensation for the women, you know. You told me that I should think up something and I couldn't hit on anything else. Where I come from, a cobbler paid alimony to five different girls. He was quite desperate about it and had to go and borrow money too. But everybody was ready to believe that he was in a frightful situation. They asked me what the girl was like and I said she was very pretty and not yet fifteen. And so they wanted her address.'

'You certainly made a nice mess of it, Švejk,' sighed the chaplain and began to walk up and down his room.

'That's another nice scandal,' he said, clutching his head. 'I've got a terrible headache.'

'I gave them the address of an old, deaf lady in the street where I live,' explained Švejk. 'I wanted to do the thing properly, because an order is an order. I wouldn't let myself be fobbed off, and I had to think up something. And now they're waiting in the hall for the piano. I brought them here, so that they could take it away to the pawnshop, sir. It won't be a bad thing when that piano's gone. There will be more room here and we shall have more money altogether. And we shall have peace for a day or two. And if the landlord asks what we're going to do with the piano, I'll say that there are strings broken in it and that we've sent it to the factory for repair. I've already told the concierge so that she won't think it strange when they take away the piano and load it on the van. And I also have a purchaser for the sofa. He's a friend of mine, a dealer in second-hand furniture, and he's coming here this afternoon. A leather sofa fetches a good price today.'

'Is that all you've done, Švejk?' asked the chaplain, continuing to clutch his head and looking desperate.

'Humbly report, sir, instead of two bottles of ořechovka which Captain Šnábl buys, I've brought five so that we can have something in reserve to drink. Can they come and take the piano before they shut the pawnshop?'

The chaplain waved his hand hopelessly and a few minutes later they were already loading the piano on to the van.

When Švejk returned from the pawnshop, he found the chaplain sitting in front of an open bottle of ořechovka and swearing, because the cutlet he had got for lunch had been underdone.

He was again half-seas over. He declared to Švejk that from to-morrow he would lead a new life. Drinking alcohol was vulgar materialism and one must live a spiritual life.

He spoke philosophically for about half an hour. When he opened the third bottle, the furniture-dealer arrived, and the chaplain sold him the sofa for a song. He invited him to talk to him and was very discontented when the furniture-dealer excused himself on the grounds that he had still to go and buy a bedside table.

'It's a pity that I haven't got one,' said the chaplain reproachfully. 'A man can't think of everything.'

After the furniture-dealer had gone the chaplain started up a friendly conversation with Švejk, with whom he drank another bottle. Part of his talk was taken up with his personal attitude to women and cards.

They were sitting for a long time. And evening found them deep in friendly conversation.

In the night however their relationship changed. The chaplain returned to his condition of the day before, mixed Švejk up with someone else and said to him: 'Oh no, please don't leave now! Do you remember that red-haired cadet from the baggage train?'

This idyll continued until Švejk said to the chaplain: 'Look, I'm fed up. Now you'll climb into bed and snooze, do you understand?'

'I'm climbing in, my dear boy, I'm climbing in – why shouldn't I climb in?' babbled the chaplain. 'D'you remember how we were in the fifth form together and I used to do your Greek exercises for you? You've got a villa at Zbraslav. And you can go by steamer on the Vltava. Do you know what the Vltava is?'

Švejk forced him to take off his boots and undress. The chaplain obeyed with a protest directed to some unknown persons.

'You see, gentlemen,' he said to the cupboard and to the ficus, 'how my relations treat me.

'I don't know my relations,' he suddenly decided, getting into bed. 'Even if heaven and earth were to conspire against me, I don't know them . . .'

And the room resounded with his snoring.

IV

It was during these days too that Švejk went to visit his old char-woman, Mrs Müller. In his apartment Švejk found her cousin, who told him in tears that Mrs Müller had been arrested the same evening that she pushed Švejk off to the war in a bathchair. They had court-martialled the old lady and, finding no evidence against her, had taken her off to a concentration camp at Steinhof. A card had already come from her.

Švejk took this precious household relic and read:

Dear Aninka,
We are enjoying ourselves very much here. We are all well. The woman in the next bed to me has spotted ——— and also there are here people with small ———. Otherwise everything is in order.

We have plenty to eat and collect potato ——— for soup. I have heard that Mr Švejk is already ——— so find out somehow, where he is laid, so that after the war we can decorate his grave. I forgot to tell you that in the right-hand corner in the attic there is a little dog in a box, a miniature pinscher puppy. But he hasn't had anything to eat for several weeks, ever since they came to fetch me because of———. So I suppose that it's already too late and the little dog is also resting with ———.

And across the whole letter there was a pink stamp in German: 'Censored, Imperial and Royal Concentration Camp, Steinhof.'

'And the little dog was really dead,' sobbed Mrs Müller's cousin, 'and you'd never recognize your apartment either. I've got some dress-makers lodging there. And they've turned it into a real lady's fashion parlour. Everywhere there are fashion pictures on the walls and flowers in the windows.'

Mrs Müller's cousin was not to be comforted.

Amid continuous sobbing and lamentations she finally expressed the fear that Švejk had deserted from the army and wanted to ruin her too and bring her into misery. Finally she spoke to him as though he were an infamous adventurer.

'That's really priceless,' said Švejk. 'I really love that. And let me tell you, Mrs Kejř, that you are absolutely right about my getting out. I had to kill fifteen sergeants and sergeant-majors. But don't tell anybody . . .'

And Švejk left his home, which was so unwelcoming to him, saying: 'Mrs Kejř, I've got some collars and shirt-fronts at the laundry. Please fetch them for me so that when I come back from the war I'll have some mufti to put on. And please see too that the moths don't get at my suits in the wardrobe. And give my love to those young ladies who are sleeping in my bed.'

And then Švejk went to pay a visit to The Chalice. When Mrs Palivec saw him she declared that she wouldn't serve him, as he had probably deserted.

'My husband,' she started the same old gramophone record, 'was

so careful and he's there; he's locked up, poor dear, all for nothing. And people like you are free to roam about and desert from the army. They were looking for you here again only last week.

'We are more cautious than you,' she concluded, 'and all the same we're in the soup. Not everyone has your luck.'

This conversation was overheard by an elderly man, a locksmith from Smíchov, who came up to Švejk and said: 'Excuse me, sir, do you mind waiting for me outside? I've got something to talk to you about.'

In the street he talked confidentially to Švejk, believing him to be a deserter on the basis of Mrs Palivec's opinion.

He told him that he had a son, who had deserted too and was with his grandmother at Jasenná near Josefov.

Disregarding Švejk's assurances that he was not a deserter, he pressed a twenty-crown piece into his hand.

'That's a bit of first aid,' he said, dragging him into a wine restaurant at the corner. 'I understand you. You don't need to be afraid of me.'

Švejk returned late at night to the chaplain who had not yet come home.

He did not come till next morning, when he woke up Švejk and said: 'Tomorrow we're going to celebrate a drumhead mass. Make some black coffee and put some rum in it. Or, still better, make some grog.'

in Bremen from a debauched sailor, who used to
so strong that if anyone fell into the sea he could s
English Channel. After a weak grog he'd drown lik

'After a grog like this, Švejk, we'll be able to celeb
drumhead mass,' reflected the chaplain. 'I think I ou
farewell words first. A drumhead mass is not such fun as
garrison gaol or preaching to those rascals. You have to
wits about you. We have a field altar. It's a folding
tion.

'Jesus Mary, Švejk,' he cried, holdin
bloody idiots. Do you know where
altar? In the sofa which we sold.'

'Oh dear, that's really a misfor
fact I know that furniture-deale
his wife. He's in jug because
Vršovice has got our sofa. It'
field altar. The best thing
look for it, because I th
brate a mass.'

'A field altar's real
in a melancholy voi
carpenters have a
being lent to us
my own, but whe

He reflected: 'Supp
from Lieutenant Wittinge
races and won it for "Sport-
He did the forty-kilometre stretch
48 minutes, as he always boasted abou
already yesterday. I'm a bloody fool leaving
moment. Why didn't I look inside that sofa? Blo

Under the influence of the grog, prepared after th
debauched sailor, he began torpidly to swear at himself and
in the most diverse maxims where he really belonged.

'Well, we'd better go and have a look for that field altar,' suggeste
Švejk. 'It's already daybreak.'

'I still have to put on my uniform and drink another grog.'

At last they went out. On their way to the wife of the furniture-dealer
the chaplain told Švejk that the day before he had won a lot of money

---

11

Švejk Goes with the Chaplain to Celebrate a Drumhead Mass

1

PREPARATIONS for the slaughter of mankind have always been made
in the name of God or some supposed higher being which men have
devised and created in their own imagination.

Before the ancient Phoenicians cut a prisoner's throat they also
performed religious ceremonies just as solemnly as did new generations
some thousand years later before marching to war and destroying their
enemies with fire and sword.

The cannibals of the Guinea Islands and Polynesia sacrifice to their
gods and perform the most diverse religious rites before ceremoniously devouring their captives or unnecessary people like missionaries, travellers, agents of various business firms or persons who
are just inquisitive. As the culture of vestments has not yet reached
them they decorate the outsides of their thighs with bunches of gaudy
feathers of forest birds.

Before the Holy Inquisition burnt its victims, it performed the most
solemn religious service – a High Mass with singing.

When criminals are executed, priests always officiate, molesting the
delinquents with their presence.

In Prussia the unfortunate victim was led to the block by a pastor,
in Austria to the gallows by a Catholic priest, in France to the guillo-
tine, in America to the electric chair by a clergyman and in Spain
to a chair where he was strangled by an ingenious appliance. In
Russia the revolutionary was taken off by a bearded Orthodox priest
etc.

Everywhere on these occasions they used to march about with a
crucified Christ figure, as if to say: 'They're only cutting your head off,
they're only hanging you, strangling you, putting fifteen thousand volts
into you, but think what that chap there had to go through.'

The great shambles of the world war did not take place without the

Slavs...

Through... driven there no... and generals, but a... and made them perjure t... on land, in the air, on the se... Drumhead masses were genera... tachment left for the front and once u... some bloody massacre and carnage. I re... drumhead mass was being celebrated. There was n... bomb on us and hit the field altar. There was no... chaplain except some bloodstained rags. ... prepared the same kind of fun out of this, and on the other s... Afterwards they wrote about him as a martyr, while our a... We had a great deal of glory for the chaplains on the other s... at the spot where they buried the remains of the chaplain, there ap- peared overnight this epitaph:

What may hit us has now hit you.
You always said we'd join the saints.
Well, now you've caught it at Holy Mass.
And where you stood are only stains.

II

Švejk brewed a splendid grog which eclipsed the grogs of old sea-dogs. Pirates of the eighteenth century might have drunk a grog like that and been satisfied with it.

The chaplain was delighted. 'Where did you learn to make such a marvellous thing?' he asked.

'Years ago as a wandering apprentice,' answered Švejk, 'I learned it

1. St Adalbert – a Czech patron saint.

...mbling at 'God's blessing' and that if all went well he'd buy the piano back from the pawnbroker.

It was rather like when heathens promise to bury an offering. From the sleepy wife of the furniture-dealer they learnt the address of the teacher in Vršovice, the new owner of the sofa. The chaplain displayed unusual generosity. He pinched her cheek and tickled her under the chin.

They went to Vršovice on foot, as the chaplain avowed that he must have a turn in the fresh air to distract his thoughts.

An unpleasant surprise awaited them in the apartment of the teacher at Vršovice who was a pious old gentleman. Finding the field altar in the sofa the old gentleman had thought that this must be some divine dispensation and had given it to the vestry of the local church in Vršovice, stipulating that on the other side of the folding altar there should be the inscription: 'Presented for the honour and praise of God by Mr Kolařík, retired teacher, in the year of our Lord 1914'. He displayed great embarrassment because they came on him in his underclothes.

From their conversation with him it was clear that he attributed to the discovery the significance of a miracle and a divine direction. He said that when he bought the sofa an inner voice said to him: 'Look at what's in the drawer of the sofa.' He claimed he had also had a vision of an angel who gave him the direct command: 'Open the drawer of the sofa.' He obeyed.

And when he saw the miniature folding altar in three sections with a recess for a tabernacle he had knelt down in front of the sofa and prayed long and fervently and praised God. Regarding it as a direction from heaven he adorned the church in Vršovice with it.

'We don't think this at all funny,' said the chaplain. 'An object of this kind which didn't belong to you, you should at once have taken to the police and not to any blasted vestry.'

'Because of that miracle,' added Švejk, 'you may face a lot of trouble. You bought a sofa and not the altar, which belongs to the army authori-ties. A divine dispensation like that can cost you dear. You ought not to have paid any attention to the angels. There was a man in Zhoř who dug up a chalice in a field. It had been stolen from a church and kept there for better times until it was forgotten. He also took it as a divine dispensation and instead of melting it down went to the vicar with it and said he wanted to present it to the church. And the vicar thought that he had been moved by pangs of conscience and sent for the mayor. The mayor sent for the gendarmerie and, although he was innocent, he was sentenced for stealing church property, just because he kept on babbling about some miracle. He wanted to defend himself and also

talked about an angel, but he mixed the Virgin Mary into it and got ten years. You'd do best to come with us to the local vicar here and get him to return us the army property. A field altar isn't a cat or a sock that you can give away to anyone you like.'

The old gentleman trembled all over and his teeth chattered as he put on his clothes: 'I really meant no harm. I thought that with a divine dispensation like that I could use it for the adornment of our poor Church of our Lord in Vršovice.'

'At the expense of the army authorities, no doubt,' Švejk said sternly and harshly. 'Thank God for a divine dispensation like that! A fellow called Pivoňka of Chotěboř also thought it was a divine dispensation when a halter with somebody else's cow in it got into his hand by accident.'

The poor old gentleman was quite confused by these remarks and made no further attempts to defend himself, trying to dress as quickly as possible and settle the whole business.

The vicar at Vršovice was still asleep and when he was awoken by the noise started to swear, because in his drowsiness he thought that he had to go and administer the last rites to somebody.

'They shouldn't bother people with this extreme unction,' he growled, dressing himself unwillingly. 'People take it into their heads to die when a chap's having a really good sleep. And afterwards you have to haggle with them about the fee.'

And so they met in the hall. One, the representative of the Lord for the Catholic civilians of Vršovice, the other, the representative of God on earth for the military authorities.

Altogether, however, it was nothing more than a dispute between a civilian and a soldier.

When the vicar asserted that the field altar did not belong to the sofa, the chaplain declared that in that case it belonged all the less to the vestry of a church which was attended only by civilians.

Švejk made various remarks to the effect that it was an easy job to fit up a poor church at the expense of the army authorities. He pronounced the word 'poor' in inverted commas.

Finally they went to the vestry of the church and the vicar handed over the field altar in return for the following receipt:

Received a field altar which accidentally found its way into the church at Vršovice.   *Chaplain Otto Katz*

The famous field altar came from the Jewish firm of Moritz Mahler in Vienna, which manufactured all kinds of accessories for mass as well as religious objects like rosaries and images of saints.

The altar was made up of three parts, liberally provided with sham gilt like the whole glory of the Holy Church.

It was not possible without considerable ingenuity to detect what the pictures painted on these three parts actually represented. What was certain was that it was an altar which could have been used equally well by heathens in Zambesi or by the Shamans of the Buriats and Mongols.

Painted in screaming colours it appeared from a distance like a coloured chart intended for testing colour-blind railway workers. One figure stood out prominently – a naked man with a halo and a body which was turning green, like the parson's nose of a goose which has begun to rot and is already stinking. No one was doing anything to this saint. On the contrary, he had on both sides of him two winged creatures which were supposed to represent angels. But anyone looking at them had the impression that this holy naked man was shrieking with horror at the company around him, for the angels looked like fairy-tale monsters and were a cross between a winged wild cat and the beast of the apocalypse.

Opposite this was a picture which was meant to represent the Holy Trinity. By and large the painter had been unable to ruin the dove. He had painted a kind of bird which could equally well have been a pigeon or a White Wyandotte. God the Father looked like a bandit from the Wild West served up to the public in an American film thriller.

The Son of God on the other hand was a gay young man with a handsome stomach draped in something that looked like bathing drawers. Altogether he looked a sporting type. The cross which he had in his hand he held as elegantly as if it had been a tennis racquet.

Seen from afar however all these details ran into each other and gave the impression of a train going into a station.

What the third picture represented was quite impossible to make out. The soldiers always argued about it and tried to solve the enigma. One even thought that it was a landscape from the Sázava valley. But underneath it was the inscription in German: 'Holy Mary, Mother of God, have mercy on us.'

Švejk deposited the field altar safely in the droshky and seated himself next to the driver on the box. The chaplain made himself comfortable inside the droshky with his feet on the Holy Trinity.

Švejk chatted with the driver about the war. The driver was a rebel. He made various remarks about the victory of the Austrian forces such as: 'They made it hot for you in Serbia', etc. When they crossed the customs point the official asked them what they were taking with them. Švejk answered:

'The Holy Trinity and the Virgin Mary together with the chaplain.'

Meanwhile on the parade ground the march detachments were waiting impatiently. And they had waited a long time. For they had had to fetch the sports cup from Lieutenant Wittinger and then the monstrance, the pyx and other accessories of the mass, including a bottle of sacramental wine, from the Břevnov monastery. From this one may conclude that it is no simple matter to celebrate a drumhead mass.

'We muddle along as we can,' said Švejk to the driver.

And he was right. For when they reached the drill-ground and were at the platform with the wooden framework and table, on which the field altar was to be placed, it turned out that the chaplain had forgotten the server.

Before it had always been an infantryman who served, but he had preferred to get himself transferred to telephones and had gone to the front.

'Never mind, sir,' said Švejk, 'I can manage that too.'

'But you can't serve?'

'I've never done it,' answered Švejk, 'but there's no harm in having a shot. Today there's a war on and in wartime people do things which they never dreamed of doing before. I'll manage to cope with that stupid "*et cum spiritu tuo*" to your "*dominus vobiscum*". And I think it's not very difficult to walk around you like a cat round hot porridge, and wash your hands and pour wine out of the flask . . .'

'All right,' said the chaplain, 'but don't go and pour me out any water. Better put wine in the other flask too. As to the rest I'll always tell you whether you have to go to the right or to the left. If I whistle once very softly that means go to the right. Twice means to the left. And you don't need to drag the missal about much. It's great fun really. Got stage fright?'

'I'm not frightened of anything, sir, not even of serving.'

The chaplain was right when he said: 'It's great fun really.'

Everything went like a house on fire.

The chaplain's address was very brief.

'Soldiers! We have met here, so that before we go to the battlefield we may incline our hearts to God, that he may grant us victory and keep us safe and sound. I won't detain you long and wish you all the best.'

'Stand at ease!' shouted an old colonel on the left flank.

A drumhead mass is called a 'drumhead' mass because it comes under the same rules as military tactics in the field. During the long manoeuvres of the armies in the Thirty Years' War drumhead masses were apt to be extremely lengthy too.

In modern tactics, where the movements of armies are rapid and brisk, drumhead masses must be equally rapid and brisk.

And so this one lasted exactly ten minutes and those who were close by wondered very much why the chaplain whistled during it.

Švejk quickly mastered the signals. Now he walked to the right of the altar and now he was on the left; and he said nothing else but: '*Et cum spiritu tuo.*'

It looked like a Red Indian dance round a sacrificial stone, but it made a good impression, for it banished the boredom of the dusty melancholy drill-ground with its avenue of plum trees behind and its latrines, the odour of which replaced the mystical scent of incense in Gothic churches.

Everyone enjoyed themselves immensely. The officers standing round the colonel were cracking jokes with each other and so everything was as it should be. Here and there among the rank and file could be heard the words: 'Give me a puff.'

And from the companies blue clouds of tobacco smoke rose to heaven as from a burnt offering. All the N.C.O.s started smoking when they saw that the colonel himself had lit a cigarette.

At last the words 'Let us pray' were heard. There was a whirl of dust and a grey rectangle of uniforms bowed their knees before Lieutenant Wittinger's sports cup, which he won for 'Sport-Favorit' in the Vienna–Mödling race.

The cup was filled full and the general opinion in the ranks of the chaplain's manipulations was: 'He's swilled it all right!'

This performance was repeated twice. After that once more: 'Let us pray', whereupon the band did its best with the Austrian national anthem. Then came 'attention' and 'quick march'.

'Collect all this stuff,' said the chaplain to Švejk, pointing to the field altar, 'so that we can take it all back where it belongs!'

So they drove off with their droshky, returned everything like good boys, except for the bottle of sacramental wine.

And when they were home again and had told the unfortunate droshky driver to apply to the regimental command for payment for the long drive Švejk said to the chaplain: 'Humbly report, sir, must a server be of the same confession as the man he's assisting?'

'Of course,' answered the chaplain, 'otherwise the mass wouldn't be valid.'

'Then, sir, a great mistake has been made,' said Švejk. 'I'm a man without confession. It's always me that has the bad luck.'

The chaplain looked at Švejk, was silent for a moment, then patted him on the shoulder and said: 'You can drink up what's left in the bottle of sacramental wine and imagine that you've been taken back into the bosom of the Church.'

A Religious Debate

IT happened that for whole days at a time Švejk never saw the man who had the cure of army souls. The chaplain divided his time between duties and debauchery and came home very rarely; when he did he was filthy and unwashed like a mewing tom-cat when it makes its amorous expeditions on the tiles.

When he came back, if he was able to express himself at all, he talked to Švejk for a bit before falling asleep. He spoke of lofty aims, inspiration and the pleasure of meditation.

Sometimes too he tried to speak in verse and quoted Heine.

Švejk and the chaplain celebrated one more drumhead mass for the sappers, to which another chaplain had been invited by mistake, a former catechist. He was an extraordinarily pious man, who stared at his colleague in amazement when he offered him a sip of cognac out of the field-flask which Švejk always carried with him for religious functions of this kind.

'It's a good brand,' said Chaplain Katz. 'Have a drink and go home. I'll do the job myself, because I need to be in the open air. I've got a bit of a headache.'

The pious chaplain went away shaking his head, and as usual Katz acquitted himself nobly of his task.

This time it was wine and soda water which was transubstantiated into the blood of our Lord, and the sermon was longer, every third word being 'and so forth and of course'.

'Today, my men, you are going to the front and so forth. Incline your hearts now to God and so forth and of course. You don't know what's going to happen to you and so forth and of course.'

And from the altar there continued to thunder: 'And so forth and of course', alternating with God and all the saints.

In his enthusiasm and rhetorical flights the chaplain presented Prince Eugène of Savoy as a saint who would protect them when they built bridges over the rivers.

Nonetheless the drumhead mass ended without any untoward incident. It was pleasant and amusing. The sappers enjoyed themselves very much.

On the way back the chaplain and Švejk were not allowed into the tram with their folding field altar.

'I'll break this saint on your head,' Švejk said to the conductor.

When they finally got home they found that somewhere on the way they had lost the tabernacle.

'It doesn't matter,' said Švejk. 'The early Christians served Holy Mass without a tabernacle. If we advertised for it somewhere, the honest man who found it could ask us for a reward. If it had been money, then I don't suppose any honest finder would have been found, although such people do exist. In our regiment at Budějovice there was a soldier, a dear old fathead, who once found six hundred crowns in the street and gave it up to the police. In the newspapers they wrote about him as an honest finder, but it only brought discredit on him. No one would talk to him; everyone said: "You half-wit, what's this bloody nonsense you've done? Why, you must be quite disgusted with yourself, if you've still any sense of honour left." He had a girl and she wouldn't speak to him any more. When he came home on leave his friends threw him out of the pub during a dance-party because of it. He got ill and took it all so much to heart that he finally threw himself under a train. And then again in our street there was a tailor who found a golden ring. People warned him not to give it up to the police, but he wouldn't listen. He got an unusually kind reception there and was told that the loss of a golden ring with a diamond had already been notified to them. But then they looked at the stone and said to him: "My good man, you know very well that it's glass and not diamond. How much did they give you for that diamond? We know very well *your* kind of honest finder." In the end it came out that another man had lost a gold ring with a false diamond, a kind of family heirloom, but the tailor sat three days in prison all the same, because he got het up and insulted a policeman. He was given the legal reward of ten per cent, which was one crown twenty hellers because that trash was worth twelve crowns, but he threw it in the gentleman's face. The gentleman then sued him for insulting his honour, so he got another ten crowns fine. Afterwards he used to say everywhere that every honest finder deserves twenty-five strokes, let them flog him black and blue, flog him publicly so that people should remember and take a lesson from it. I don't think that anyone'll bring our tabernacle back, even though it has the regimental crest on the back, because no one wants to have anything to do with army property. They'd rather throw it in the water somewhere, so as not to have further complications with it. Yesterday at the pub, The Golden Wreath, I spoke to a man from the country. He was fifty-six and was going to the office of the district hejtman[1] in Nová Paka to ask why they had requisitioned his carriage. On the way back, when they had thrown him out of the hejtman's office, he had a look at the baggage train which had just come in and was standing on the square. A young man asked him to wait a moment by the horses, which were to fetch tinned goods for the army, and then he never came back. When the baggage train moved off this chap had to go with them and found himself in Hungary, where he in his turn asked someone to wait by the baggage train in his place. It was only in this way that he saved himself, otherwise they'd have dragged him off to Serbia. When he arrived he looked absolutely terrified and would never have anything to do with army property any more.'

In the evening they received a visit from the pious chaplain who had wanted to serve the drumhead mass for the sappers that morning. He was a fanatic who wanted to bring everyone close to God. When he had been a catechist he had developed religious feelings in children by slapping their faces and there had appeared from time to time in various journals articles about 'the sadistic catechist', 'the slapping catechist'. He was convinced that a child learns the catechism best with the help of the birch.

He limped a little on one foot, which had been caused by a visit made to him by the father of one of his pupils, whose face he had slapped for having expressed certain doubts about the Holy Trinity. He got three slaps on the face himself. One for God the Father, a second for God the Son and a third for the Holy Ghost.

Today he had come to lead his colleague Katz on to the right path and to have a heart-to-heart talk with him. He began it with the remark: 'I'm surprised that you've got no crucifix hanging here. Where do you say your breviary prayers? And there's not a single portrait of the saints on the walls of your room. What's that hanging over your bed?'

Katz smiled: 'That's Susanna and the Elders, and that naked woman underneath is an old friend of mine. On the right there's something Japanese, depicting the sexual act betweeen a geisha and an old Japan-

1. Representative of the central government in a district.

ese Samurai. Very original, isn't it? The breviary's in the kitchen.
Švejk, bring it here and open it on the third page.'

Švejk went away, and from the kitchen could be heard the sound of
corks being drawn from three bottles of wine.

The pious chaplain was aghast when the three bottles made their
appearance on the table.

'It's a light sacramental wine, brother,' said Katz, 'of very good
quality, a Riesling. It tastes like Moselle.'

'I'm not going to drink,' said the pious chaplain stubbornly. 'I've
come to have a heart-to-heart talk with you.'

'That'll dry up your throat, my dear colleague,' said Katz. 'Have a
drink and I'll listen. I'm a very tolerant fellow and can listen to other
views.'

The pious chaplain drank a little and rolled his eyes.

'It's a devilish good wine, my dear colleague, isn't it?'

The fanatic said sternly: 'It has not escaped me that you are swearing.'

'That's habit,' answered Katz. 'Sometimes I even catch myself blaspheming. Pour the chaplain out some more, Švejk. I can assure you that I also say: "Himmelherrgott, krucifix and sakra." I think that when you've served in the army as long as I have you'll find yourself doing it too. It isn't at all difficult or complicated and it's very familiar to us clergy – heaven, God, the cross and the holy sacrament. Doesn't that sound marvellously professional? Drink a bit more, my dear colleague.'

The former catechist sipped mechanically. It was obvious that he wanted to say something, but could not. He was collecting his thoughts.

'My dear colleague,' continued Katz, 'cheer up! Don't sit there so miserably, as though they were going to hang you in five minutes' time. I've heard about you, how once on a Friday by mistake you ate a pork cutlet in a restaurant, because you thought that it was Thursday, and how you stuck your finger down your throat in the W.C. to get rid of it, because you thought God would obliterate you. I'm not afraid of eating meat in Lent and I'm not afraid of hell-fire either. Excuse me, please go on drinking. Are you better now? Or do you have progressive views about hell and keep up with the spirit of the times and the reformists? I mean, instead of ordinary cauldrons with sulphur for poor sinners, there are Papin's pots[1] and high-pressure boilers. The sinners are fried in margarine, there are grills driven by electricity, steam rollers roll over the sinners for millions of years, the gnashing of the teeth is produced with the help of dentists with special equipment, the howling is recorded on gramophones, and the records are sent upstairs to paradise for the entertainment of the just. In paradise sprays with eau de cologne operate and the Philharmonic Orchestra plays Brahms so long that you prefer hell and purgatory. The cherubs have aeroplane propellers in their behinds so as not to have to work so hard with their wings. Drink, my dear colleague! Švejk, pour him out some cognac. I don't think he's feeling well.'

When the pious chaplain came round he started to whisper: 'Religion is a matter of rational reasoning. Whoever does not believe in the existence of the Holy Trinity . . .'

'Švejk,' Katz interrupted him, 'pour out one more cognac for the chaplain, so as to bring him round! Tell him something, Švejk!'

'Humbly report, sir,' said Švejk, 'near Vlašim there was a dean who

1. Quick-boiling kettles invented by the French physicist Papin in 1781.

had a charwoman, when his old housekeeper ran away from him with the boy and the money. And this dean in his declining years started studying St Augustine, who is said to be one of the Holy Fathers, and he read there that whoever believes in the Antipodes will be damned. And so he called his charwoman and said to her: "Listen, you once told me that your son was a fitter and that he went to Australia. That would be in the Antipodes and according to St Augustine's instructions everyone who believes in the Antipodes is damned." "Reverend sir," the woman answered, "after all my son sends me letters and money from Australia." "That's a snare of the devil," replied the dean. "According to St Augustine Australia doesn't exist at all and you are just being seduced by the Anti-Christ." On Sunday he anathematized her publicly and shouted out that Australia didn't exist. So they took him straight out of the church into the lunatic asylum. More people like him ought to be put there. In the Convent of the Sisters of St Ursula they have a bottle of the Holy Virgin's milk with which she suckled the baby Jesus, and in the orphanage at Benešov, after they'd brought them water from Lourdes, the orphans got diarrhoea the like of which the world has never seen.'

Black spots were dancing in front of the pious chaplain's eyes and he only came to himself after another cognac, which went to his head.

Blinking his eyes he asked Katz: 'Don't you believe in the Immaculate Conception of the Virgin Mary? Don't you believe that the thumb of St John the Baptist, which is preserved in the Piarists' monastery, is genuine? Do you believe in the Lord at all? And if you don't, why are you a chaplain?'

'My dear colleague,' answered Katz, patting him familiarly on the back, 'until the state recognizes that soldiers who are going to their death at the front don't need the blessing of God for it, the chaplaincy remains a decently paid profession, where a chap isn't overworked. It was better for me than running about on the drill-ground and going on manoeuvres. Then I used to get orders from my superiors but now I do what I like. I represent someone who doesn't exist and myself play the part of God. If I don't want to absolve anybody's sins then I don't, even if they beg me on their bended knees. But you'd find bloody few people nowadays who'd go that far.'

'I love God,' declared the pious chaplain, beginning to hiccough. 'I love him very much. Give me a little wine. I respect God,' he continued.

'I respect and honour him very much. I respect no one as much as I respect him.'

He struck the table with his fist until the bottles jumped. 'God is an exalted being, something unearthly. He's honourable in his dealings. He's a radiant revelation, and no one's going to convince me of the contrary. I respect St Joseph too, I respect all the saints, except St Serapion. He's got such an ugly name.'

'He ought to apply to have it changed,' observed Švejk.

'I love St Ludmila and St Bernard,' continued the former catechist. 'He saved many pilgrims in St Gothard. He carries a bottle of cognac around his neck and looks for people caught in snow drifts.'

The conversation took a new turn. The pious chaplain started getting completely muddled. 'I honour the Innocents. They have their Saints' day on the twenty-eighth of December. I hate Herod. When the hens sleep, you can't get any new-laid eggs.'

He gave a guffaw and began to sing 'Holy, Holy, Holy, Lord God of Sabaoth.'

He broke off at once, and turning to Katz and getting up asked him sharply: 'You don't believe that the fifteenth of August is the day of the Assumption of the Virgin Mary?'

The fun was in full swing. More bottles appeared, and from time to time Katz could be heard saying: 'Say that you don't believe in God, otherwise I won't let you have a drop!'

It was as though the times of the persecution of the early Christians had returned. The former catechist sang a song of the martyrs of the Roman arena and yelled out: 'I believe in God. I won't forswear him. You can keep your wine. I can send for some myself.'

Finally they put him to bed. Before he fell asleep he proclaimed, raising his right hand in a solemn oath: 'I believe in God the Father, Son and Holy Ghost. Bring me the breviary.'

Švejk put into his hand a book which was lying on the night table. The pious chaplain then fell asleep with Boccaccio's *Decameron* in his hand.

Švejk Administers Extreme Unction

CHAPLAIN OTTO KATZ sat glumly over a circular which he had just brought from the barracks. It contained secret instructions from the War Ministry.

For the duration of the war the War Ministry suspends all operative regulations concerning the administering of extreme unction to soldiers of the army and lays down the following regulations for army chaplains:

§*1*. At the front extreme unction is cancelled.

§*2*. Those who are seriously ill and wounded are forbidden to go back to the base for extreme unction. Army chaplains are required at once to hand over such cases to the appropriate military authorities for further action.

§*3*. In army hospitals at the base extreme unction can be administered *en masse* on the basis of a certificate from the army doctors, provided it does not entail difficulties for the appropriate military institutions.

§*4*. In exceptional cases the Military Hospitals Command at the base may allow individuals to receive extreme unction.

§*5*. Army chaplains are obliged, if called on by the Military Hospitals Command, to administer extreme unction to those designated by the Command.

After that the chaplain read once more the order informing him that the next day he must go to the army hospital at Charles Square to administer extreme unction to the seriously wounded.

'Listen, Švejk,' the chaplain called out, 'isn't this a bloody nuisance? Just as if I was the only chaplain in the whole of Prague! Why don't they send that pious priest who slept here the other day? We've got to go and administer it at Charles Square. I've already forgotten how to do it.'

'Then we'll buy a catechism, sir. It'll be there,' said Švejk. 'It's a kind of Baedeker for spiritual pastors. In the Emmaus monastery a gardener's assistant, who worked there once, wanted to join the ranks of the lay brothers and get a cowl so as not to tear his clothes. He had to buy a catechism and learn how to make the sign of the cross, who alone is preserved from original sin, what it means to have a clean conscience, and other trifles like that. And after that he secretly flogged half the cucumbers from the monastery garden and left the monastery in disgrace. When I met him he said: "I could have flogged those cucumbers just as well without the catechism." '

When Švejk brought the catechism, which he had purchased, the chaplain turned the pages in it and said: 'Look, extreme unction can only be administered by a priest and then only with oil which has been consecrated by a bishop. So you see, Švejk, you yourself can't administer extreme unction. Read out to me how one does it.'

Švejk read out: 'It's done like this: the priest anoints the sick man on all his senses, at the same time praying as follows: "By this Holy Unction and by His Holy Mercy may God forgive thee for all the sins thou hast committed through thine eyes, thine ears, thy smell, thy taste, thy words, thy touch and thy gait." '

'I'd like to know, Švejk,' said the chaplain, 'how a man can sin with his touch. Can you tell me?'

'In lots of ways, sir. You can put your hands into someone else's pocket, or on the dance floor – well, you know what goes on there!'

'And by his gait, Švejk?'

'When he begins to limp so as to arouse people's pity.'

'And by his smell?'

'When he doesn't like stink or stinkers.'

'And his taste, Švejk?'

'When he has a taste for somebody.'

'And his words?'

'That goes together with ears. When someone chatters a lot and someone else listens to him.'

After these philosophical reflections the chaplain was silent and said: 'And so we need oil consecrated by a bishop. Here's ten crowns. Go and buy a bottle. Obviously they won't have this kind of oil at the military stores.'

Švejk set out on his journey in search of oil which had been consecrated by a bishop. This errand was more difficult than looking for the water of life in Božena Němcová's fairy tales.[1]

He went into various chemists and as soon as he said: 'Please, I want a bottle of oil consecrated by a bishop', they either burst out

---

1. Božena Němcová, one of the greatest Czech writers and a collector of Czech and Slovak fairy tales.

laughing or hid in a panic under the counter. All this time Švejk's countenance was unusually solemn.

And so he decided to try his luck at surgeries. In the first they had him thrown out by a dispenser. In the second they wanted to telephone for an ambulance. And in the third the head of the surgery said that Poláks Ltd in Dlouhá Avenue, a firm dealing in oil and lacquers, would certainly have in stock the oil he wanted.

Poláks Ltd in Dlouhá Avenue was a very efficient firm. They never let a customer go without satisfying his requirements. If he wanted copaiba balsam they poured out turpentine for him and that did just as well.

When Švejk came in and asked for ten crowns' worth of oil consecrated by a bishop, the manager said to the assistant: 'Pour him out a gill of hempseed oil number three, Mr Tauchen.'

And the assistant, wrapping the bottle up in paper, said to Švejk in a completely business-like way: 'It's of the finest quality. If you would like a paint-brush, lacquer or varnish, don't hesitate to apply to us. We shall serve you reliably.'

In the meantime the chaplain was learning up again in the catechism what he had forgotten from his time at the seminary. He enjoyed very much some unusually witty sentences which made him laugh heartily: 'The name "extreme" or "last unction" derives from the fact that this unction is usually the last of all the unctions which the church administers to anyone.'

Or: 'Extreme unction may be received by every Catholic Christian who is seriously ill and has at last come to his senses.'

'The patient is to receive extreme unction, if possible, while his memory still holds.'

Then an orderly came with a packet, in which the chaplain was informed that the next day extreme unction would be attended by the Association of Gentlewomen for the Religious Education of the Troops.

This association consisted of hysterical old women who distributed to the soldiers in the hospitals icons of saints and stories about a Catholic warrior dying for His Imperial Majesty. These stories had a coloured illustration of a battlefield. There were lying about everywhere human corpses and horse carcasses, overturned munition trains and gun carriages. On the horizon villages were burning and shrapnel bursting. In the foreground lay a dying soldier with his leg torn off. An angel was bending over him and bringing him a wreath with the inscription on the ribbon: 'This very day you will be with me in paradise.' And the dying man was smiling blissfully, as though they were bringing him an ice cream.

When Otto Katz had read the contents of the packet he spat and reflected: 'Tomorrow is going to be some day.'

He knew the harpies, as he called them, from the church of St Ignatius, where years ago he used to preach to the troops. At that time he used to put a lot of feeling into his sermons, and the 'Association' used to sit behind the colonel. Two tall and skinny women in black dresses with rosaries once came up to him after the sermon and talked to him for two hours about the religious education of the troops, until he got angry and said to them: 'Excuse me, my good ladies, the captain's expecting me for a game of färbl.'

'And so here's the oil,' said Švejk solemnly, when he returned from Poláks Ltd. 'Hempseed oil number three, finest quality. We can anoint a whole battalion with it. The firm is a reliable one. It sells varnish, lacquer and brushes as well. Now we only need a bell.'

'Why a bell, Švejk?'

'We have to ring it on the way, so that people take their hats off to us when we transport the Lord, sir, with this hempseed oil number three. It's always done, and very many people, to whom it meant nothing, have been put in gaol because they didn't take their hats off. On a similar occasion in Žižkov a vicar once beat a blind man because he didn't take his hat off and he was put in gaol too, because they proved to him before the courts that he was not deaf and dumb, but only blind, and that he had heard the ringing of the bell and caused a scandal, although it was at night time. That's just like at Corpus Christi. At another time people would never look at us, but now they'll take their hats off to us. If you don't mind, sir, I'll fetch it at once.'

Having obtained permission Švejk produced a bell in half an hour.

'It's from the door of the roadside inn U Křížků,' he said. 'It cost me just five minutes' panic, and I had to wait a long time, because people never stopped going by.'

'I'm going to the café, Švejk. If anybody should come, tell him to wait.'

About an hour later there arrived an elderly grey-haired gentleman of erect carriage and stern countenance.

His whole appearance exhaled cold anger and rage. He looked as if he had been sent by fate to destroy our miserable planet and to obliterate all traces of it in the universe.

His words were harsh, dry and severe: 'Not at home? So he's gone to a café, has he? So I've got to wait, have I? Very well, I'll wait till the morning. He's got money for a café, but not to pay his debts. Calls himself a priest! Lousy rat!'

He spat in the kitchen.

'Sir, don't spit here!' said Švejk, looking at the stranger with interest.

'I shall spit once more, as you see, like this,' said the severe gentleman obstinately, spitting on the floor a second time. 'He should be ashamed. An army chaplain. What a disgrace!'

'If you've had any education,' Švejk reminded him, 'then you should have cured yourself of spitting in someone else's house. Or do you think that when there's a world war on, you can do what you please? You've got to behave decently and not like a hooligan. You've got to act politely, talk decently and not carry on like a damned scoundrel, you bloody fool of a civilian, you!'

The stern gentleman got up from his chair, began to shake with fury and shouted: 'You dare tell me I'm not a decent man? Then what am I, tell me . . .'

'You're a dirty pig,' answered Švejk, looking him straight in the eye. 'You spit on the floor as though you were in a tram, a train or a public place. I've always wondered why there are notices hanging everywhere that spitting is prohibited, and now I see it's all because of you. They must know you very well everywhere.'

The stern man began to change colour and tried to answer with a torrent of oaths directed at Švejk and the chaplain.

'Have you finished your speechifying?' Švejk asked composedly (when the gentleman had delivered himself of his last: 'You're both scoundrels. Like master like dog'), 'or would you like to say something more before you fly down the stairs?'

As the stern gentleman had exhausted himself to such an extent that no valuable and effective oath came to his mind, he fell silent, and Švejk took it as a sign that there was no point in waiting for anything further.

And so he opened the door, placed the stern gentleman at it with his face towards the corridor and gave him a kick worthy of the shoot of the best player in an international football championship team.

And behind the stern gentleman Švejk's voice carried all the way down the steps:

'Next time when you visit decent people, see you behave decently.'

The stern gentleman walked for a long time up and down underneath the windows and waited for the chaplain.

Švejk opened the window and watched him.

At last the chaplain came back. He took the stern gentleman into his room and sat him down on a chair opposite him.

Švejk silently brought in a spittoon and placed it in front of the guest.

'What are you doing, Švejk?'

'Humbly report, sir, there's already been some unpleasantness here with this gentleman concerning spitting on the floor.'

'Leave us alone together, Švejk. We have business to transact.'

Švejk saluted.

'Humbly report, sir, I'm leaving you.'

He went into the kitchen and in the next room a very interesting conversation took place.

'You've come for the money for that bill of exchange, if I am not mistaken?' the chaplain asked his guest.

'Yes, and I hope . . .'

The chaplain sighed.

'A man is often brought into a situation where hope is the only thing left. How beautiful is that little word "hope", from that three-leafed clover, which exalts man above the chaos of life: faith, hope, charity.'

'I hope, chaplain, that the sum . . .'

'Of course, worthy sir,' the chaplain interrupted him. 'Allow me to repeat once more, that the word "hope" is a great strength to man in his struggle with life. And you don't lose hope. How wonderful it is to have a definite ideal, to be an innocent, clean being, who lends money on bills of exchange and has the hope that he will be paid back at the right time. To hope, to hope unremittingly that I shall pay you twelve hundred crowns, when I haven't even a hundred in my pocket!'

'And so you . . .' stammered the guest.

'Yes, and so I,' answered the chaplain.

The guest's face again assumed an obstinate and wrathful expression.

'Sir, this is fraud!' he said, getting up.

'Calm yourself, worthy sir.'

'It's fraud,' the visitor shouted obstinately. 'You have disgracefully abused my confidence.'

'Sir,' said the chaplain, 'a change of air will certainly do you good. It is too sultry here.

'Švejk!' he called to the kitchen. 'This gentleman wants to go out in the fresh air.'

'Humbly report, sir,' came the answer from the kitchen, 'I've already thrown that gentleman out once.'

'Repeat the operation!' came the order, which was executed quickly, briskly and ruthlessly.

'It's good, sir, that we got rid of him before he caused a scandal,' said Švejk, when he returned from the entrance hall, 'In Malešice there was once a pub-keeper, a literary fellow, who always had a quotation from the Holy Bible for all occasions, and when he flogged anybody with a knout he always used to say: "He that spareth his rod hateth his son, but he that loveth him chasteneth him betimes. I'll teach you to fight in my pub."'

'You see, Švejk, what happens to a fellow who doesn't honour priests,' smiled the chaplain. 'St John Chrysostom said: "Whoever honours a priest honours Christ. Who humiliates a priest humiliates Christ the Lord, whose representative the priest is!" We must make thorough preparations for tomorrow. Make some fried eggs and ham. Brew a claret punch, and then we'll devote ourselves to meditation, for, as it is said in the evening prayer, "By God's mercy all the snares of the enemy have been turned aside from this dwelling."'

There are people in the world who are very obstinate and to their number belonged the man who had twice been thrown out of the chaplain's apartment. Just as supper was ready someone rang the bell. Švejk went to open the door and returned after a moment to report: 'He's here again, sir. I've shut him up for the moment in the bathroom, so we can eat our supper in peace.'

'That's not right, Švejk,' said the chaplain. ' "A guest in the house is God in the house." At banquets in old times they used to entertain themselves with monsters. Bring him here so that he can amuse us.'

Švejk returned in a moment with the obstinate man who stared sullenly in front of him.

'Sit down,' the chaplain invited him politely. 'We're just finishing our supper. We've had lobster, salmon and now fried eggs and ham as well. We have marvellous blow-outs when people lend us money.'

'I hope that I am not here just for your amusement,' said the sullen man. 'This is the third time I've come. I hope now that everything will be explained.'

'Humbly report, sir,' observed Švejk, 'he's a real leech, like that fellow Boušek from Libeň. Eighteen times in one evening they threw him out of Exners and he always came back saying he'd forgotten his pipe. He crept in through the window, through the door, from the kitchen, over the wall into the saloon, through the cellar to the bar, and he would have come down the chimney if the firemen hadn't pulled him down off the roof. He was so persistent that he would have made a good minister or parliamentary deputy. They did for him what they could.'

The obstinate man, as though taking no notice of what was being said, repeated stubbornly: 'I want to have this matter cleared up and I demand a hearing.'

'That's granted to you,' said the chaplain. 'Speak, worthy sir. Speak as long as you like and we shall meanwhile continue our feast. I hope it won't disturb your story. Švejk, bring in the food.'

'As you well know,' said the obstinate man, 'a war is raging. I lent you the sum before the war and if there had not been a war I should not have insisted on the repayment. But I have had unfortunate experiences.'

He took a notebook from his pocket and continued: 'I have it all recorded here. Lieutenant Janata owed me seven hundred crowns and had the cheek to fall at the battle of the Drina. Lieutenant Prášek was captured on the Russian front and owes me two thousand crowns. Captain Wichterle, owing me the same amount, got himself killed by his own soldiers at Ruska Rava.[1] Lieutenant Machek, taken prisoner in Serbia, owes me fifteen hundred crowns. There are more people like that here. One falls in the Carpathians with an unpaid bill of exchange of mine; another gets taken prisoner; another gets drowned in Serbia; and a fourth dies in a hospital in Hungary. Now you can understand my fears that this war will ruin me if I'm not energetic and ruthless. You could say that you are in no direct danger. But look.'

He thrust his notebook under the nose of the chaplain. 'You see, Chaplain Matyáš at Brno died in an isolation hospital a week ago. I could have torn my hair out. He owed me eighteen hundred crowns and went into a cholera ward to administer extreme unction to a man who meant nothing to him.'

'That was his duty, my dear sir,' said the chaplain; 'I'm going to administer extreme unction tomorrow too.'

'And in a cholera ward too,' observed Švejk. 'You can go with us so that you can see what it means to sacrifice oneself.'

'Chaplain,' said the obstinate man, 'believe me, I am in a desperate situation. Is this war being waged to put out of the way all who owe me money?'

'When they call you up and you go to the front,' observed Švejk again, 'the chaplain and I will celebrate Holy Mass, so that it may please God in heaven that the first shell should tear you to pieces.'

'Sir, this is a serious matter,' the leech said to the chaplain. 'I request that your servant should not intervene in our business, so that we can settle it at once.'

'Just as you wish, sir,' replied Švejk. 'Be so good as to order me specifically not to interfere in your affairs, otherwise I shall continue to defend your interests as it befits a decent soldier. This gentleman

1. A railway junction in Galicia where there was heavy fighting between the Russian and Austrian troops in 1914–15.

is quite right. He wants to go away from here alone. I don't like scenes either. I'm a social man.'

'Švejk, I'm getting bored with this,' said the chaplain, as though he did not notice the presence of his guest. 'I thought this chap would amuse us, tell us some stories, and instead he asks me to order you not to interfere, although you've had to deal with him twice already. On an evening like this when I have in front of me such an important religious rite, when I have to turn all my thoughts to God, he bothers me with a stupid story about a wretched twelve hundred crowns, distracts me from searching my conscience and from God and wants me to tell him once more that I'm not going to give him anything at the moment. I don't want to speak to him any longer, so that this holy evening is not ruined. You say to him, Švejk: "The chaplain is not going to give you anything!"'

Švejk discharged the order, bawling it into the guest's ear.

The obstinate guest continued to sit there, however.

'Švejk,' suggested the chaplain, 'ask him how long he intends to sit gaping here?'

'I won't move from here until I get my money!' the leech retorted obstinately.

The chaplain got up, went to the window and said: 'In that case I give him over to you, Švejk. Do with him what you like.'

'Come here, sir,' said Švejk, seizing the unwelcome guest by the shoulder. 'Third time lucky.'

And he repeated his performance quickly and elegantly, while the chaplain drummed a funeral march on the window.

The evening, which was devoted to meditation, passed through several phases. The chaplain drew close to God with such piety and ardour that at midnight the following strains could be heard from his apartment:

> 'When we marched away,
> The girls all cried their eyes out . . .

And the good soldier Švejk sang with him.

In the military hospital two men were longing for extreme unction – an old major and a bank manager who was an officer in the reserve. Both had got bullets in the stomach in the Carpathians and lay in adjoining beds. The officer in the reserve considered it his duty to have

extreme unction administered to him, because his superior officer was longing for it too. He regarded it as a breach of discipline not to have it. The pious major did it out of calculation, imagining that a prayer could cure an invalid. However, the night before the extreme unction both of them died, and when in the morning the chaplain arrived with Švejk, both the officers lay underneath a sheet with black faces, like all those who die of asphyxiation.

'We were making such a splash, sir, and now they've gone and spoilt things,' Švejk grumbled, when they told them in the office that these two no longer needed anything.

And it was true that they had made a great splash. They had driven there in a droshky. Švejk had rung the bell, and the chaplain had held in his hands the bottle with the oil, which was wrapped up in a table napkin. He solemnly blessed all the passers-by with it and they took off their hats.

There were not many of them, it is true, although Švejk tried to make a tremendous row with the bell.

One or two innocent street urchins ran behind the droshky, and one of them seated himself behind, whereupon his comrades broke out in unison: 'After the carriage, after the carriage!'

And Švejk rang the bell, the droshky driver hit backwards with his whip, in Vodičkova Street a woman concierge who was a member of the congregation of the Virgin Mary trotted after the droshky and caught up with it. She received a blessing on the way, made the sign of the cross, spat and shouted: 'They're driving like Jehu with the Lord! It's enough to give you T.B.!' after which she returned breathlessly to her old place.

It was the droshky driver's mare which was most worried by the sound of the bell. It must have reminded her of something that had happened in the past, because she continually looked behind and from time to time tried to dance on the cobbles.

And so this was the great splash which Švejk talked about. In the meantime the chaplain went into the office to settle the financial side of the extreme unction and calculated to the quartermaster sergeant-major that the army authorities owed him one hundred and fifty crowns for the consecrated oil and the journey.

Then followed a quarrel between the commandant of the hospital and the chaplain, in the course of which the chaplain hit the table several times with his fist and said: 'Don't imagine, captain, that extreme unction is *gratis*. When an officer of the Dragoons is ordered to go to the stud farm for horses, they pay him subsistence too. I am really sorry that these two did not live to get their extreme unction. It would have been fifty crowns more.'

In the meantime Švejk waited down in the guardhouse with the bottle of holy oil which aroused genuine interest among the soldiers.

One expressed the view that this oil could be used very successfully for cleaning rifles and bayonets.

A young soldier from the Bohemian-Moravian Highlands, who still believed in God, asked them not to talk about these things and not to bring into discussion the mysteries of the sacrament. We must, he said, live in hope, like Christians.

An old reservist looked at the raw recruit and said: 'Nice hope that a shrapnel tears off your head! They've pulled the wool over our eyes. Once a deputy from the Clerical Party came to our village and spoke to us about God's peace, which spans the earth, and how the Lord did not want war and wanted us all to live in peace and get on together like brothers. And look at him now, the bloody fool! Now that war has broken out they pray in all the churches for the success of our arms, and they talk about God like a chief of the general staff who guides and directs the war. From this military hospital I've seen many funerals go out and cartfuls of hacked-off arms and legs carried away.'

'And the soldiers are buried naked,' said another soldier, 'and into the uniform they put another live man. And so it goes on for ever and ever.'

'Until we've won,' observed Švejk.

'And that bloody half-wit wants to win something,' a corporal chimed in from the corner. 'To the front with you, to the trenches! You should be driven for all you're worth on to bayonets over barbed wire, mines and mortars. Anyone can lie about behind the lines, but no one wants to fall in action.'

'I think that it's splendid to get oneself run through with a bayonet,' said Švejk, 'and also that it's not bad to get a bullet in the stomach. It's even grander when you're torn to pieces by a shell and you see that your legs and belly are somehow remote from you. It's very funny and you die before anyone can explain it to you.'

The young soldier gave a heartfelt sigh. He was sorry for his young life. Why was he born in such a stupid century to be butchered like an ox in a slaughterhouse? Why was all that necessary?

A soldier, who was a teacher by profession and seemed to read his thoughts, observed: 'Some scientists explain war by the appearance of sun spots. As soon as a sun spot like that appears, something frightful always happens. The conquest of Carthage . . .'

'To hell with your learning,' the corporal interrupted him. 'Go and sweep the room instead. Today it's your turn. What the hell do we care about any bloody sun spots? Even if there were twenty of them I wouldn't buy them.'

'Those sun spots are really very important,' put in Švejk. 'Once there was a sun spot like that and the very same day I was beaten up at U Banzetů at Nusle. From that time whenever I went anywhere I always looked in the newspapers to see if a sun spot hadn't appeared. And as soon as one did, then count me out, I said. I didn't go anywhere and that was the only way I managed to survive. At the time when the volcano Mont-Pellé destroyed the whole island of Martinique, a professor wrote in *Národní Politika* that he had long ago told readers about a big sun spot. But *Národní Politika* didn't get to the island in time, and so the people on it caught it proper.'

Meanwhile upstairs in the office the chaplain met a lady from the Association of Gentlewomen for the Religious Education of the Troops, an old repulsive siren, who went round the hospital from the early morning and distributed everywhere icons of saints, which the wounded and the sick soldiers threw into the spittoons.

And when she went round she infuriated everybody with her stupid chatter about their having honestly to repent their sins and really reform so that after death God could give them everlasting salvation.

She was pale when she talked with the chaplain. She said that the war instead of ennobling soldiers made beasts of them. Downstairs the patients had stuck their tongues out at her and told her she was a scarecrow and a frightful skinny old frump. 'Oh, how dreadful, chaplain,' she said in German. 'The people have been corrupted.'

And she described how she saw the religious education of a soldier. Only when he believes in God and has religious feelings can a soldier fight bravely for His Imperial Majesty and not fear death, because then he knows that paradise awaits him.

She babbled on and said a few more stupid things like this, and it was clear that she was resolved not to let the chaplain go. But he excused himself in a rather ungallant way.

'We're going home, Švejk!' he called to the guardhouse. On the way back they made no splash.

'Next time anyone who likes can administer extreme unction,' said the chaplain. 'Fancy having to haggle about money for every soul you want to save. Their accounts are the only thing they think about.'

Seeing a bottle of 'consecrated' oil in Švejk's hand, he frowned: 'It would be better, Švejk, if you polished my boots and your own with this.'

'I'll see if I can't oil the lock with it,' added Švejk. 'It squeaks frightfully when you come home at night.'

Thus ended the extreme unction which never was.

Švejk Batman to Lieutenant Lukáš

I

ŠVEJK'S good fortune did not last long. Unrelenting fate severed the friendly relations between him and the chaplain. If until this event the chaplain had been a likeable person, what he now did was calculated to strip from him his likeable image.

The chaplain sold Švejk to Lieutenant Lukáš, or, to be more correct, gambled him away at cards, just as they used to sell serfs in Russia in the old days. It happened quite unexpectedly. Lieutenant Lukáš gave a splendid party and they played vingt-et-un.

The chaplain lost everything and said in the end: 'How much will you advance me on my batman? He's a screaming half-wit and an interesting personality, a kind of *non plus ultra*. You never had a batman like him before.'

'I'll advance you a hundred crowns,' Lieutenant Lukáš offered. 'If I don't get them back the day after tomorrow, you can send me this rare specimen. My own batman is a disgusting fellow. He's always groaning, writes letters home and at the same time steals what he can lay his hands on. I've already beaten him, but it doesn't do any good. I box his ears whenever I meet him, but that doesn't help either. I've knocked out some of his front teeth, but even that hasn't improved the bastard.'

'Agreed, then,' said the chaplain light-heartedly. 'Either a hundred crowns the day after tomorrow or Švejk.'

And he gambled away those hundred crowns too and went home sadly. He knew for certain and had never doubted that in two days he could not possibly rustle up those hundred crowns and that he had actually bartered Švejk away basely and despicably.

'I might just as well have said two hundred,' he said to himself angrily, but when he changed on to the tram which would soon take him home he had an attack of conscience and sentimentality.

'It wasn't gentlemanly of me to do it,' he thought, as he rang at the door of his apartment. 'How can I look into his stupid, kind eyes?'

'My dear Švejk,' he said, when he was home. 'Today something unusual happened. I had awfully bad luck in cards. I went "banco"[1] and had the ace in my hand, and then a ten came. But the banker had the knave in his hand and made twenty-one too. I drew an ace or a

ten several times but the banker always had the same. I went through all my money.'

He paused: 'And finally I gambled you away. I borrowed a hundred crowns on you and if I don't return it by the day after tomorrow you won't belong to me any longer but to Lieutenant Lukáš. I'm really very sorry . . .'

'If it's only a hundred crowns,' said Švejk, 'I can lend it to you.'

'Give it to me,' said the chaplain, brightening up. 'I'll take it at once to Lukáš. I should really hate to have to part with you.'

1. i.e. staked the whole contents of the bank.

Lukáš was very surprised when he saw the chaplain again.

'I'm coming to repay my debt,' said the chaplain, looking around triumphantly. 'Let me join the game.'

'Banco,' shouted the chaplain when it was his turn. 'I'm only one pip over,' he announced.

'All right, then. Banco again,' he said, when the second round came. 'And blind.'

'Paying twenty,' announced the banker.

'I've got nineteen altogether,' said the chaplain quietly and paid the bank the last forty crowns of the hundred which Švejk had lent him to ransom himself from his new serfdom.

On his way home the chaplain came to the conclusion that it was all finished, that nothing could save Švejk, and that it was predestined that he should be Lieutenant Lukáš's batman.

And when Švejk opened the door he told him: 'It's all up, Švejk. No one can escape his fate. I have lost you and your hundred crowns too. I did my utmost, but fate was stronger than me. I've thrown you into the clutches of Lieutenant Lukáš and the time is coming when we must part.'

'And was there a lot in the bank?' asked Švejk calmly. 'Didn't you get a chance of being Forehand very often? If the right card doesn't come it's very bad, but sometimes it's awful when the cards are too good. At Zderaz there was once a tinsmith called Vejvoda and he always used to play mariáš in a pub behind the Century Café. Once the devil whispered into his ear: "How about a game of vingt-et-un at ten-heller stakes?" And so they played vingt-et-un at ten hellers and he held the bank. They all joined the game and then the bank grew to ten crowns. Old Vejvoda wanted to help the others and so he kept on saying: "Low and bad is safe." But you can't imagine what bad luck he had. However low his card was it was never worse than what the others had. The bank grew and grew and there was already a hundred crowns in it. None of the players had enough to go "banco" and Vejvoda sat there sweating. You couldn't hear anything except his "Low and bad is safe." One after another people joined in with ten-crown stakes and all of them burst. A master chimney-sweep got furious and went home for more money. He went "banco" when there was already more than a hundred and fifty in the bank. Vejvoda wanted to get himself out of the game and, as he confessed afterwards, he tried to push the bidding up to as much as thirty just so as not to

win. But instead he got two aces. He pretended he had nothing and said on purpose: "Paying sixteens." And that chimney-sweep had only fifteen. Wasn't that bad luck? Old Vejvoda was quite pale and miserable. All around they were swearing and muttering that he was cheating and that he'd already been flogged for card-sharping, although he was really a very honest player. And so they all of them paid him crown after crown and there was already five hundred crowns there. The landlord couldn't stand it any longer. He had money ready to pay to the brewery and so he took it, sat down, pushed forward two hundred and then two hundred again. After that he shut his eyes, spun the chair round for luck and said he'd go "banco". "And we'll play 'Ouvert',"[1] he declared. I don't know what old Vejvoda wouldn't have given to have lost. Everybody was amazed when he drew a card from the pack and it was a seven and he took it. The landlord was smiling up his sleeve, because he had twenty-one. Old Vejvoda drew a second seven and still he took it. "Now an ace or ten will come," said the landlord maliciously. "I bet my last shirt, Mr Vejvoda, that you'll burst." There was a deathly silence. Vejvoda drew again and a third seven appeared. The landlord turned white as a sheet, because it was his last sou. He went into the kitchen and a short time afterwards his apprentice boy ran in and called us to come and cut the landlord down, because he was hanging on a window-handle. And so we cut him down, revived him and the game went on. No one had any money left at all. Everything was in the bank, in front of Vejvoda, who only went on saying: "Low and bad is safe." And he would have given everything in the world to burst but because he had to expose his hand on the table he couldn't cheat and intentionally overbid. They were all furious over his good luck and arranged that when they had no more money left they would give him I.O.U.s. It went on for several hours and thousands and thousands heaped up in front of old Vejvoda. The chimney-sweep was already more than one and a half million in debt to the bank, a coalman from Zderaz about a million, a porter from the Century Café eight times a hundred thousand and a medico over two million. In the pool alone there was more than three hundred thousand on little bits of paper. Old Vejvoda tried all different tricks. He went continually to the W.C. and always asked someone else to draw for him and when he returned they told him that he had drawn and got twenty-one. They

1. The player has to expose his hand before the opening lead and permit his opponents to see all his cards.

sent for new cards, but still that didn't help. When Vejvoda stopped at fifteen, the other had only fourteen. They all looked furiously at old Vejvoda and the man who swore at him most was a paver who had only put in eight crowns in cash. He stated openly that a man like Vejvoda shouldn't be allowed to go about free but deserved to be beaten up, thrown out and drowned like a puppy. You can't imagine old Vejvoda's despair. Finally he had an idea. "I'm going to the W.C.," he said to the chimney-sweep. "Draw for me, will you?" And then he went out just as he was without a hat on to the street and straight to Myslíkova Street for the police. He found a patrol and told them that in such and such a pub they were playing gambling games. The police ordered him to go ahead and they would follow immediately after. He came back and was told that in the meanwhile the medico had lost over two million and the porter over three. In the pool there were I.O.U.s for five times a hundred thousand crowns. After a while the policemen burst in; the paver screamed out, "Everyone for himself!" but it was no good. They confiscated the bank and took all the players off to the police station. The coalman from Zderaz resisted and so they brought him along in the drunks' cart. In the bank there were I.O.U.s for over half a milliard and fifteen hundred crowns in cash. "I've never copped as much as that before," said the police inspector, when he saw such dizzy sums. "It's worse than in Monte Carlo." All of them except old Vejvoda had to stay there till morning. He was released for turning king's evidence and was promised that he would get as his lawful reward a third of the money confiscated in the bank, about one hundred and sixty million or more. But before the morning he was already off his head and was going about Prague ordering burglar-proof safes by the dozen. That's what they call success at cards.'

And then Švejk went off to brew some grog. And it happened that when with some difficulty he succeeded in getting the chaplain into bed that night the latter burst into tears and cried: 'I've bartered you, my friend, I've shamefully bartered you. Curse me, beat me, I'll take it. I let you down. I can't look you in the eyes. Tear me, bite me, destroy me. I don't deserve anything better. Do you know what I am?'

And the chaplain pressing his tear-stained face into the pillow said gently in a soft tender voice: 'I'm a bastard without any character at all,' and fell asleep like a log.

The next day, shunning Švejk's gaze, the chaplain went out early and returned late at night with a fat infantryman.

'Show him, Švejk, where everything is so that he can get his bearings,' he said, again avoiding his gaze. 'And show him how to make
grog. Tomorrow you are to report to Lieutenant Lukáš.'

Švejk spent the night agreeably with the new man making grog. By
the morning the fat infantryman could hardly stand on his legs and
was humming a strange pot-pourri of various national songs, which he
mixed up together: 'Around Chodov there runs a stream, My love
serves red beer there, Mountain, mountain, thou art high, Maidens
went along the path, On the White Mountain a peasant is ploughing.'

'I'm not worried about you,' said Švejk. 'With a talent like that you'll
keep your job with the chaplain.'

And so it happened that in the morning Lieutenant Lukáš saw for
the first time the decent and honest countenance of the good soldier
Švejk, who announced to him: 'Humbly report, sir, I am Švejk whom
the chaplain gambled away at cards.'

II

The institution of officers' orderlies is of very ancient origin. It seems
that even Alexander the Great had his batman. What is certain,
however, is that in the period of feudalism the knights' hirelings performed this role. What else was Don Quixote's Sancho Panza? I am
surprised that no one has yet written up the history of army orderlies.
If anyone had, we should read in it how at the siege of Toledo the Duke
of Almavira was so hungry that he ate his orderly without salt, which
the duke himself mentions in his memoirs, relating that his orderly had
fine, tender, succulent meat tasting like something between chicken
and donkey.

In an old German book about the art of war we find directions for
orderlies. The batman of the old days had to be pious, virtuous, truthful, modest, brave, courageous, honest and industrious. In short he
had to be a model man. Modern times have changed this type considerably. The modern batman is usually not pious or virtuous or truthful. He tells lies, cheats his master and very often turns his superior's life
into sheer hell. He is a cunning slave, who thinks out the most varied
forms of treacherous ploys to embitter his master's life. In this new
generation of batmen you will not find such self-sacrificing creatures
as would let themselves be eaten by their masters without salt, like the
noble Fernando, batman of the Duke of Almavira. On the other

hand we find that commanders who wage a life and death struggle with their orderlies of modern times adopt the most varied methods to preserve their authority. It is a certain kind of terror. In 1912 there was a trial in Graz in which the leading figure was a captain who had kicked his batman to death. He was acquitted then because it was only the second time he had done it. In the eyes of gentlemen like this the life of a batman has no value at all. He is only an object, often an Aunt Sally, a slave, a maid of all work. It is not surprising that such a position requires of the slave that he should be crafty and cunning. His position on this planet can be compared only with the sufferings of the pot-boys of old days, who were trained to be conscientious by means of blows and torture.

There are however cases where a batman rises to the position of a favourite, and then he becomes the terror of the company or the battalion. All the N.C.O.s try to bribe him. He decides questions of leave and can use his influence and see that it goes well with those who are sent on report. These favourites were usually rewarded in wartime with the large and small silver medals for bravery and valour.

In the 91st regiment I knew several of them. One batman received the large silver medal because he was an adept in roasting the geese he had stolen. Another got the small silver medal because he used to get from his home wonderful food hampers so that in the time of the most acute famine his master stuffed himself up so much that he could hardly walk.

And his master formulated the citation for his decoration as follows:

'For displaying unusual bravery and courage in battle, despising death and not abandoning his superior officer for a moment under the powerful fire of the advancing enemy.'

But in fact he was plundering hen coops somewhere in the base.

The war changed the relationship between the batman and his master and made him the creature who was most hated by the rank and file. The batman always got a whole tin of meat, where otherwise it would be divided among five. His field-flask was always full of rum or cognac. The whole day this type of creature munched chocolate and devoured sweet biscuits reserved for officers, smoked his master's cigarettes, cooked for hours on end and wore an extra tunic.

The batman was on the closest terms with the company orderly and gave him fat pickings from his table and from all those privileges which he enjoyed. He allowed into the triumvirate the quartermaster sergeant-major. This trio lived in direct contact with the officer and knew all the operations and war plans.

The unit whose corporal was friendly with the batman was always best informed about when things would start.

When he said: 'At 2.35 we shall start hopping it,' then at 2.35 exactly the Austrian soldiers began to disengage from the enemy.

The batman was on the most intimate terms with the field-kitchen and always liked to hang around the cauldron and give orders as though he were in a restaurant and had the menu before him.

'I'd like a rib,' he would say to the cook. 'Yesterday you gave me the tail. And add a piece of liver to my soup. You know I don't eat milt.'

But the batman was always in best form when starting a panic. When the trenches were being bombed his heart ran down into his pants. In such times he was always in the most secure cover together with his luggage and that of his master. He covered his head with a rug, in case a shell should find him, and he had no other wish than that his master should be wounded and that he could go with him to the base as far as possible behind the front line.

He cultivated panic systematically by the use of a certain measure of secrecy. 'I've got a hunch that they're packing the telephone up,' he would say confidentially to the units. And he was happy when he was able to say: 'Now they've packed it up.'

No one loved a retreat as much as he did. In such moments he forgot that shell and shrapnel were flying over his head and pushed on indefatigably with the luggage to staff headquarters, where the baggage train was standing. He loved the Austrian baggage train and was very happy when he could travel on it. In emergencies he would use the ambulance two-wheelers. When he had to go on foot he gave the impression of being a completely broken man. In that case he abandoned his master's luggage in the trenches and took only his own property with him.

Should it happen that the officer escaped capture by running away and the batman was caught, he never forgot under any circumstances to take his master's luggage with him into captivity. It then passed into his ownership and he clung to it with might and main.

I once saw a captured batman who had gone on foot with others from Dubno to Darnica beyond Kiev. Besides his own haversack he had with him the haversack of his superior officer who had escaped capture, five handcases of different shape and size, two blankets and a pillow, apart from another piece of luggage which he carried on his head. He complained that the Cossacks had stolen two of his cases.

I shall never forget that man who dragged himself in this way across the whole of the Ukraine. He was a walking removal van, and I can

never understand how he was able to carry off this luggage and drag it for so many hundreds of kilometres and then go with it as far as Tashkent, look after it and die of spotted typhus on it in a prison camp.

Today batmen are scattered over the whole of our republic and they tell of their heroic deeds. It was they who stormed Sokal, Dubno, Niš and the Piave. Every one of them is a Napoleon: 'I told our colonel to ring staff headquarters and say it can start.'

Most of them were reactionaries and the rank and file hated them. Some of them were informers and it was their special delight to watch someone being seized and bound.

They developed into a special caste. Their selfishness knew no bounds.

III

Lieutenant Lukáš was a typical regular officer of the ramshackle Austrian monarchy. The cadet school had turned him into a kind of amphibian. He spoke German in society, wrote German, read Czech books, and when he taught in the course for one-year volunteers, all of whom were Czechs, he told them in confidence: 'Let's be Czechs, but no one need know about it. I'm a Czech too.'

He equated being a Czech with membership of some sort of secret organization, to which it was wiser to give a wide berth.

Otherwise he was a decent man, who was not afraid of his superiors and looked after his company at manoeuvres, as was seemly and proper. He always found them comfortable quarters in barns and often let the soldiers roll out a barrel of beer at the expense of his own modest salary.

He liked it when his men sang songs on the march. They had to sing even when they went to and from drill. And walking by the side of his company he sang with them:

> 'And when it was midnight black
> The oats jumped out of the sack,
> Tantantara! Zing! Bum!'

He enjoyed the affection of his men because he was unusually just and was not in the habit of bullying anyone.

The N.C.O.s trembled before him and in a month he could reduce the most brutal sergeant-major to a perfect lamb.

He could shout, it is true, but he never swore. He used choice expressions and sentences. 'You see,' he said, 'I really don't like punishing you, my boy, but I can't help it, because the efficiency and courage of an army depends on discipline, and without discipline an army is a reed swaying in the wind. If you don't have your uniform in order and your buttons properly sewn on or if they're missing it is obvious that you are neglecting the responsibilities you owe to the army. Perhaps it may seem incomprehensible to you that you are being put in detention just because yesterday at an inspection there was one button missing on your tunic, in other words, a tiny unimportant matter which in civil life would be completely overlooked. But, you see, in the army neglect of your personal appearance like that must result in your punishment. And why? It's not a question here of a missing button but of your having to get used to order. Today you forget to sew on a button and start getting slack. Tomorrow you'll already find it a bore to dismantle your rifle and clean it. The day after you'll forget your bayonet in a pub somewhere, and finally you'll fall asleep at your post, because with that unfortunate button you already started on the downward career of a scrimshanker. So that's it, my boy, and I am punishing you to save you from an even worse punishment for things you might do if you slowly but surely began to forget your duties. I am sending you to detention for five days, and over your bread and water I want you to reflect that punishment is not revenge but just a means of education. Its object is to reform and improve the soldier who is being punished.'

He should have been a captain long since but his cautiousness in the nationality question had not helped him, because he always behaved towards his superiors with complete frankness and any kind of bootlicking in official relations was beneath him.

This is what he had retained of the character of a peasant from South Bohemia, where he was born in a village among dark forests and lakes.

Although he was just to the soldiers and did not bully them he had one special trait in his character. He hated his batmen, because he always had the bad luck to get the most disgusting and mean ones imaginable. He hit them across the jaw, boxed their ears and tried to train them by precept and deed, not looking upon them as soldiers. He struggled with them hopelessly for a number of years, changed them continually and finally sighed: 'Now I've got another filthy bastard.' He regarded his batmen as the lowest form of animal life.

He was very fond of animals. He had a Harz canary, an Angora cat and a stable pinscher. All the batmen in turn treated these animals no worse than Lieutenant Lukáš treated them when they too did something mean.

They starved the canary. One batman knocked one of the Angora cat's eyes out. They beat the stable pinscher every time they saw it, and finally one of Švejk's predecessors took the wretched animal off to Pankrác to the skinner, where he had him put away, paying ten crowns for it from his own pocket without any regrets. Then he simply told the lieutenant that the dog had run away from him on a walk. The very next day that batman was marching with the company to the drill-ground.

When Švejk came to report to Lukáš that he was starting his duties the latter took him into the sitting-room and said: 'The chaplain recommended you and I hope you won't disgrace his recommendation. I've already had a dozen batmen and not one of them has ever settled down with me. I must warn you that I'm strict and that I punish terribly any meanness or lying. I require you always to tell me the truth and to carry out all my orders without grumbling. If I say to you: "Jump into the fire", then you must jump into the fire, even though you don't want to. What are you looking at?'

Švejk was looking with interest sideways at the wall where a cage hung with a canary in it, and fixing his kindly eyes on the lieutenant he answered in a gentle, good-natured tone: 'Humbly report, sir, there's a Harz canary there.'

And after having interrupted in this way the flow of the lieutenant's words Švejk adopted a military stance and looked him straight in the eyes without blinking.

The lieutenant wanted to say something sharp, but observing the innocent expression on Švejk's face said nothing more than 'The chaplain recommended you as a frightful idiot and I think he was not wrong.'

'Humbly report, sir, he certainly was not wrong. When I was serving as a regular I got a complete discharge for idiocy and for patent idiocy into the bargain. In our regiment only two of us were discharged in this way, me and a Captain von Kaunitz. And whenever that captain went out in the street, if you'll pardon me, sir, he always at the same time picked his left nostril with his left hand, and his right nostril with his right hand, and when he went with us to the parade ground he always made us adopt a formation as though it was going to be a march past and said: "Men, ahem, remember, ahem, that today is Wednesday, because tomorrow will be Thursday, ahem." '

Lieutenant Lukáš shrugged his shoulders, like a man who did not know how to express a certain thought and could not immediately find words to do so.

He went from the door to the window on the other side of the room past Švejk and back again. All this time Švejk did 'eyes right' or 'eyes left' wherever the lieutenant was and did it with such a marked expression of innocence on his face that the lieutenant lowered his gaze to the carpet and said something which had no connection at all with Švejk's observation about the stupid captain: 'Yes. With me there's got to be order, cleanliness and no lying. I like honesty. I hate lies and I punish them mercilessly. Do you understand?'

'Humbly report, sir, I understand. There's nothing worse than when someone tells a lie. As soon as he starts getting tied up he's done for. In a village behind Pelhřimov there was once a teacher called Marek who used to keep company with the daughter of the gamekeeper

Špera. The gamekeeper gave him to understand that if ever he had a rendezvous with the girl in the forest and he found him there, he'd shoot a brush full of salt into his backside. The teacher sent him a message that it was not true, but once when he was going to meet the girl the gamekeeper caught him, and was just about to carry out the operation on him when the teacher excused himself by saying that he was only picking flowers. And then after that he said he had gone to catch some beetles and got more and more tied up until finally he got into a panic and swore that he had gone out to set traps for hares. And so the good gamekeeper seized him and took him away to the gendarmerie station, and from there the case went to the courts and the

teacher might easily have been sent to prison for it. If he'd said just
the bare truth he'd only have got the brushes with the salt. I'm of the
opinion that it's always best to confess, to be open and, if I've done
something, to come and say: ' 'Humbly report, I've done this and
that." And as for honesty that's always a jolly good thing because it's
always the best policy. It's just like in those walking races. As soon
as a chap begins to cheat and run he's already disqualified. That
happened to my cousin. An honest man's respected everywhere, he's
honoured, satisfied with himself and feels new-born when he can go
to bed and say: "Today I've played the game again!" '

While he was speaking Lieutenant Lukáš sat for a long time on his
chair, looking at Švejk's boots and thinking: 'My God! I often talk
drivel like this too and the only difference is the form I serve it up in.'

Nonetheless, not wishing to lose his authority, he said when Švejk
had ended:

'With me you must clean your boots, have your uniform in order,
your buttons properly sewn on and give an impression of being a soldier and not a miserable civvy. It's extraordinary how none of you seem
to be able to carry yourselves like soldiers. Only one of all my batmen
looked like a real warrior and in the end he went and stole my full-
dress uniform and sold it in the Jewish quarter.'

He was silent and then continued, explaining to Švejk all his duties,
in the course of which he did not forget to lay the main emphasis on
the fact that he must be loyal and never talk about what was happening
at his home.

'Ladies pay me visits,' he added. 'Sometimes one of them stays overnight, if I'm not on duty the next day. If that happens you'll bring us
our coffee in bed, when I ring. Do you understand?'

'Humbly report, I understand, sir. If I should come to the bed without warning it might perhaps be disagreeable for a lady. I once brought
a young lady home and my charwoman brought us coffee in bed just
when we were enjoying ourselves immensely. She got frightened and
poured the coffee all over my back and said into the bargain: "A very
good morning to you." I know what is seemly and proper, when there's
a lady sleeping somewhere.'

'Good, Švejk, we must always show exceptional tact to the ladies,'
said the lieutenant, who was getting into a better temper, because the
conversation was touching a subject which filled his leisure hours between the barracks, the parade ground and card-playing.

Women were the life and soul of his apartment. It was they who made his home for him. There were several dozen of them and many tried during their stay to adorn his flat with various bric-à-brac.

One lady, the wife of a café proprietor, who lived with him for a whole fortnight until her husband came for her and took her home, embroidered for him a delightful table runner, put monograms on all his underclothing and might indeed perhaps have completed the embroidery of the wall hangings, if her husband had not destroyed the idyll.

Another lady, whom her parents fetched after three weeks, wanted to turn his bedroom into a lady's boudoir and placed everywhere various fancy things and little vases and hung a picture of the guardian angel over his bed.

In all corners of his bedroom and dining room the traces of a feminine hand could be felt. And this extended to the kitchen, where could be seen the most varied kitchen implements and utensils, which had been the magnificent gift of the lovesick wife of a factory-owner. Together with her passion she brought with her a gadget for cutting all kinds of greens and cabbages, a machine for making breadcrumbs and scraping liver, various casseroles, roasters, frying pans, basting ladles and God knows what else.

But she went away after a week, because she could not reconcile herself to the thought that the lieutenant had besides her some twenty other loves, which left certain traces on the performance of the noble male in uniform.

Lieutenant Lukáš also carried on a voluminous correspondence. He had an album of his lady loves and a collection of various relics, because for the last two years he had evinced a tendency to fetishism. Thus he had a number of different ladies' garters, four delightful pairs of ladies' knickers with embroidery and three transparent fine thin chemises, cambric kerchiefs and even a corset and a number of stockings.

'Today I'm on duty,' he said. 'I shan't come back till night. Have everything ready and put the apartment in order. My last batman went off today to the front in the march column because of his skulduggery!'

After giving further orders concerning the canary and the Angora cat he went away without forgetting to make a few remarks about honesty and order while still in the doorway.

After his departure Švejk put everything into the finest order, so that when Lieutenant Lukáš returned to his home at night he could report to him:

'Humbly report, sir, everything is in order. Only the cat has got into mischief and eaten up your canary.'

'What?' thundered the lieutenant.

'Humbly report, sir, it was like this: I knew that cats hate canaries and like to insult them. And so I thought I'd introduce them to each other, and if the brute tried anything on I'd flay her so that she'd remember to her dying day how to behave towards canaries, because I'm very fond of animals. In the house where I live there's a hat-maker and he trained his cat so well that after eating up three of his canaries she didn't eat any more – a canary could sit on her if it liked. And I wanted to try that out too and so I took the canary out of its cage and let her smell it, and she, the little monkey, bit its head off before I realized it. I really never expected such caddishness from her. If it had been a sparrow, sir, I wouldn't have said anything, but a lovely canary like that from the Harz. And how greedily she gobbled it up, feathers and all, and at the same time purred out of sheer joy. They say cats have no musical education and can't stand it when a canary sings, because the brutes don't understand it. I swore at the cat, but I swear to God that I didn't do anything to her and waited for you to come to decide what's to be done with her, the scabby beast.'

While saying this Švejk looked into the lieutenant's eyes with such sincerity that although the latter approached him at first with certain cruel intentions he moved away from him again, sat down on a chair and asked:

'Listen, Švejk, are you really God's prize oaf?'

'Humbly report, sir,' Švejk answered solemnly, 'I am! Ever since I was little I have had bad luck like that. I always want to put something right, to do good, but nothing ever comes out of it except trouble for me and all around. I really wanted these two to get to know each other so that they would understand each other, and I can't help it if she ate it up and it was the end of the acquaintance. In a house called U Štupartů some years ago a cat even ate up a parrot, because it laughed and mimicked her miaowing. But cats cling pretty obstinately to their lives. If you want me to do her in, sir, then I'll have to crush her in the door. Otherwise she'll never be finished.'

And Švejk with the most innocent of countenances and his gentle good-humoured smile gave the lieutenant an account of how cats are executed, the content of which would certainly send any society for the prevention of cruelty to animals into a lunatic asylum.

In telling this he revealed such expert knowledge that Lieutenant Lukáš forgot his anger and asked:

'So you know how to look after animals? Have you got some feeling for them? Do you love them?'

'I like dogs best of all, sir,' said Švejk, 'because they offer a profitable business for anyone who knows how to sell them. I wasn't able to do it, because I've always been honest. But all the same people used to be after me and say I'd sold them a lame duck instead of a healthy thoroughbred, as though all dogs must be thoroughbred and healthy. And everyone at once asked for a pedigree, so that I had to have pedigrees printed and turn some mongrel from Košíře, which had been born in a brickworks, into the most thoroughbred aristocrat from the Bavarian kennels of Armin von Barheim. And really people were only too happy if it turned out so well that they had a thoroughbred at home. I could perhaps have offered them a Vršovice pom as a dachshund, and they would only have been rather surprised that such a rare dog, coming all the way from Germany, was shaggy and didn't have bow legs. They do that in all kennels. You should see, sir, the fiddles which go on with these pedigrees in the big kennels. There are really very few dogs existing which could say of themselves: "I'm a thoroughbred." Either its mamma forgot herself with some frightful monstrosity, or its granny did, or else it's had several papas and inherited a bit from each. From one its ears, from another its tail, from another again the tufts on its snout, from a third its muzzle, from a fourth its hobbling legs and from a fifth its size. And if it had had twelve such papas, you can imagine, sir, what such a dog looks like. I once bought a dog like that called Balabán. After all his papas he was so ugly that all dogs avoided him and I only bought him out of pity because he was so abandoned. And he always used to sit at home in a corner and was so unhappy, till I had to sell him as a stable pinscher. What gave me the most trouble was dyeing him, so that he had a pepper and salt colour. In this condition he went with his master to Moravia and from that time on I've never set eyes on him any more.'

The lieutenant began to be extremely interested by this cynological lecture and Švejk was able to continue without interruption.

'Dogs can't dye their hair like ladies do. This always has to be done by the person who wants to sell them. If a dog is so old that it's completely grey and you want to sell it as a year-old puppy or pretend that the old dodderer is only nine months old, then you must buy some silver nitrate, dissolve it and paint the dog black so that it looks quite new. And you must feed it like a horse with arsenic, so that it gains strength, and you must clean its teeth with sand paper like they use for cleaning rusty knives. And before you lead it out to be sold to a customer, you must pour some slivovice down its throat, so that it gets a bit tipsy. Then it'll immediately get lively, gay, bark joyfully and make friends with anyone, like a drunken town councillor. But the main thing is this: you must talk to people, sir, and go on talking to them until the customer gets completely crazy. If anyone wants to buy a miniature pinscher off you and you have nothing else at home but a pointer, you must be able to talk him into taking away with him a pointer and not a miniature pinscher, and if by chance you only have a miniature pinscher at home and someone comes to buy a fierce German mastiff for a watch dog, you must fool him so that he takes away in his pocket the tiny little miniature pinscher instead of the mastiff. When I used to be in the dog business, a lady came in to tell me that her parrot had flown out into her garden, so she said, and that some little boys who were playing Indians in front of her villa had just seized it, torn all the feathers from its tail and decked themselves up in them like police. And this parrot, out of the shame of being tailless, fell ill, and the vet finished it off with some powders. And so she wanted to buy a new parrot, a respectable one, not a vulgar one which would do nothing but swear. What could I do when I hadn't a parrot at home and didn't know of one? I only had at home a savage bulldog, which was completely blind. And so, sir, I had to spend from four o'clock in the afternoon to seven o'clock in the evening talking that lady into buying that blind bulldog instead of a parrot. It was worse than any diplomatic situation, and when she was going out I said: "Now let the boys try to pull *his* tail out", and I never spoke to this lady any more, as she had to leave Prague on account of that bulldog, because it bit everyone in the house. Believe me, sir, it's very difficult to get hold of a decent animal.'

'I'm very fond of dogs,' said the lieutenant. 'Some of my friends at the front have their dogs with them there and have written to me that the war passes very pleasantly when you have as a companion such a faithful and devoted animal. And so I see you know all breeds of dogs very well, and I hope that if I ever should have a dog you'd look after it properly. Which breed do you think is the best? I mean as a companion, you know? I once had a stable pinscher, but I don't know . . .'

'In my opinion, sir, a stable pinscher is a very nice dog. Not everyone likes them, it is true, because they have wire hair and very stiff whiskers on their muzzle, so that they look like a released convict. They are so ugly that they're beautiful and at the same time they're very clever. What's an idiotic Great St Bernard in comparison? They're even cleverer than fox-terriers. I knew one . . .'

Lieutenant Lukáš looked at his watch and interrupted Švejk's conversation:

'It's getting late. I must have a good sleep. Tomorrow I'm on duty again and you can spend the whole day finding a stable pinscher for me.'

He went to bed, and Švejk lay down on a sofa in the kitchen and read the newspaper which the lieutenant had brought with him from the barracks.

'Well, here you are then,' said Švejk to himself, following with interest the summary of the day's news. 'The sultan has decorated Kaiser Wilhelm with the War Medal, and I haven't even got the small silver medal yet.'

He thought for a moment and then jumped up: 'I nearly forgot . . .'

He went into the bedroom of the lieutenant who was already fast asleep and woke him:

'Humbly report, sir, I've no orders about that cat.'

And the sleepy lieutenant, half-awake, turned over on the other side, and growled: 'Three days confined to barracks!' and went on sleeping.

Švejk went softly out of the room, dragged the wretched cat from underneath the sofa and said to her: 'You've got three days confined to barracks. Dismiss!'

And the Angora cat crawled back under the sofa again.

IV

Švejk was just starting to go and look for a stable pinscher when a young lady rang the bell and asked to speak to Lieutenant Lukáš. Beside her stood two heavy suitcases, and Švejk caught a glimpse of a porter's cap disappearing down the stairs.

'He's not at home,' said Švejk firmly, but the young lady was already in the hall and gave the categorical order to Švejk: 'Carry the suitcases in!'

'Not without the lieutenant's permission, madam,' said Švejk. 'The lieutenant gave express orders that I must never do anything without his permission.'

'You're dotty,' the young lady cried. 'I've come to stay with him.'

'I have no information at all about that,' answered Švejk. 'The lieutenant is on duty today. He won't be back before night and I've had orders to go and find him a stable pinscher. I know nothing about any suitcases or any lady. Now I'm going to lock up the apartment and I'd be glad if you would kindly go away. I've not been informed and so I can't leave in the apartment any strange person whom I don't know. Once they left someone in the house of the pastry cook Bělčický in our street and he opened their wardrobe and ran away.

'I've nothing against you,' continued Švejk, when he noticed that the young lady was getting desperate and beginning to cry, 'but you definitely can't stay here, you must admit that, because the apartment has been put in my charge and I'm responsible for every little thing in it. And so I must ask you again if you would very kindly spare yourself the effort. Until I receive orders from the lieutenant I don't even know my own brother. I'm sincerely sorry that I have to talk to you in this way, but in the army there's got to be order.'

In the meantime the young lady had pulled herself together a little. She took out of her bag a visiting card, wrote a few lines on it in pencil, put it into a charming little envelope and said dejectedly: 'Take this to the lieutenant. Meanwhile I shall wait here for an answer. Here's five crowns for your trouble.'

'That's not going to help,' answered Švejk, offended by the obstinacy of the unexpected guest. 'Keep those five crowns. They are here on the chair, and, if you like, come with me to the barracks and wait for me there. I'll deliver your letter and bring you the answer. But I'm afraid that it's not possible for you to wait here.'

With these words he dragged the suitcases into the hall and rattling the keys like the turnkey of a castle said significantly at the door: 'We're locking up!'

The young lady went out dejectedly into the corridor. Švejk shut the door and went ahead. The visitor trotted behind him like a little dog and caught up with him when he went to buy some cigarettes at a tobacconist.

Now she walked beside him and tried to start a conversation with him.

'You'll really deliver it?'

'Of course I'll deliver it, if I said so.'

'And you're sure you'll find the lieutenant?'

'That I don't know.'

They walked side by side again in silence until after quite a long time his companion began to speak again:

'Do you think, then, that you won't find the lieutenant?'

'No, I don't think that.'

'And where do you think he might be?'

'I don't know.'

Then the conversation was interrupted for a long time until it was resumed once more by a question from the young lady:

'You haven't lost that letter?'

'I haven't lost it yet.'

'And so you'll be sure to give it to the lieutenant?'

'Yes.'

'And you'll find him?'

'I've already said I don't know,' answered Švejk. 'It amazes me how people can be so inquisitive and continually ask the same question. It's just as though I stopped every second person on the street and asked them what was the date today.'

In this way her attempts to make a deal with Švejk came to a definite end and the rest of the journey to the barracks passed in complete silence. It was only when they stopped at the barracks that Švejk invited the young lady to wait and started to chat with the soldiers at the gate about the war, which must have made the young lady awfully happy, because she walked up and down the pavement nervously and appeared extremely miserable when she saw that Švejk was persisting in his talk, with just as stupid an expression on his face as could be seen on the photograph published at that time in the *World War Chronicle* under the headline: 'The Heir to the Austrian throne in conversation with the two pilots who shot down a Russian aeroplane'.

Švejk sat down on a bench at the gate and explained that on the Carpathian battle front the army's attack had failed, but on the other hand the commander of Przemyśl, General Kusmanek, had reached Kiev and that behind us in Serbia there remained eleven bases and that the Serbs would soon be too tired to go on running after our troops.

And then he started criticizing certain famous battles and made the truly Archimedean discovery that a detachment has to give itself up when it is encircled on all sides.

When he had been talking long enough, he thought it right to go out and tell the desperate lady that he would be back again at once, and that she shouldn't go anywhere. Then he went upstairs to the office, where he found Lieutenant Lukáš, who was just at that moment solving for a subaltern a trenches exercise and was reproaching him for not being able to draw and for having no idea at all about geometry.

'Look, this is how you have to draw it. If on a given straight line we have to draw a perpendicular line, we must draw it so that it makes a right angle with it. Do you understand? If you do it this way, you will have your trenches running in the right direction and not in the direction of the enemy. You will be six hundred metres away from him. But the way you've drawn it you'd be pushing our positions into the enemy's line and you'd be standing with your trenches perpendicular over the enemy, whereas you need an obtuse angle. It's really quite simple after all, isn't it?'

And the lieutenant in reserve, who in civil life was a bank cashier, stood in complete despair over these plans. He could not understand anything and heaved a sigh of relief when Švejk advanced towards the lieutenant:

'Humbly report, sir, a lady sends you this letter and is waiting for an answer.' And as he said this he gave a knowing and familiar wink.

What the lieutenant read did not make a favourable impression on him. It was written in German.

Dear Heinrich,
My husband is persecuting me. I absolutely must stay a few days with you. Your batman is a proper swine. I am unhappy.

> Your Katy

Lieutenant Lukáš sighed, took Švejk into an empty office next door, shut the door and began to walk up and down between the tables. When he finally stopped by Švejk he said: 'The lady writes that you're a swine. What on earth have you done to her?'

'I haven't done anything to her, humbly report, sir. I've behaved very respectably, but she wanted to install herself in the apartment at once. And because I had not had any orders from you I didn't leave her alone there. Into the bargain she brought two suitcases with her, as if she was coming home.'

The lieutenant gave another loud sigh and Švejk did the same.

'What did you say?' shouted the lieutenant menacingly.

'Humbly report, sir, it's a difficult case. Two years ago a young lady came into an upholsterer's in Vojtěšská Street and he couldn't get her out of the apartment and had to gas both her and himself, and that was the end of the fun. It's difficult with women. I can see right through them.'

'A difficult case,' repeated the lieutenant after Švejk, and he had never uttered a more truthful word. Dear Heinrich was definitely in an ugly situation. A wife, persecuted by her husband, comes to him on a visit of several days, just when he's expecting to have Mrs Micková from Třeboň. She is coming to him for three days to repeat what she regularly offers him every quarter, when she comes to Prague to do her shopping. And then the day after, a young lady is going to come.

She had definitely promised him that she would let herself be seduced after having thought it over for a whole week, as she was going to be married to an engineer a month later.

The lieutenant now sat on the table with his head in his hands. He pondered in silence, but for the time being he could think of nothing else except at last to sit down at the table, take official paper and envelope and write as follows:

Dear Katy,

On duty until nine p.m. Back at ten. Please make yourself at home with me. As for my batman, Švejk, I've already given him orders to oblige you in everything.

Your Heinrich

'Take this letter to the lady,' said the lieutenant. 'Your orders are to behave to her politely and tactfully and to fulfil all her wishes, which you must regard as a command. You must behave gallantly and serve her decently. Here's a hundred crowns, for which you must account to me, in case she may want to send you for something and you can order her lunch, dinner and so on. Then buy three bottles of wine and a packet of cigarettes. All right, then. Nothing more for the present. You can go, and once more let me impress upon you that you must obey her slightest whim.'

The young lady had already lost all hope of seeing Švejk and was therefore very surprised when she saw him coming out of the barracks in her direction with a letter.

After saluting her he handed her the letter and reported: 'By orders of the lieutenant, madam, I am to behave to you politely and tactfully, serve you decently and obey your slightest whim. I am to feed you and buy for you whatever you wish. I have received from the lieutenant a hundred crowns, but out of it I have to buy three bottles of wine and a packet of cigarettes.'

When she had read the letter her resolution returned, which was manifested by her ordering Švejk to call a fiacre, and when this was done, she bade him sit on the box-seat with the driver.

They drove home. When they were in the apartment the lady was excellent in playing the role of mistress of the house. Švejk had to carry her suitcases into the bedroom and beat the carpets in the court-yard, and a tiny little spider's web behind a mirror brought her to a state of fury.

Everything seemed to confirm that she intended to dig herself in for a long time in the position she had won.

Švejk sweated. After he had beaten the carpets, she took it into her head that the curtains had to be taken down and beaten too. Then he got orders to clean the windows in the sitting-room and in the kitchen. After that she began to move the furniture about, doing

so very nervily, and when Švejk moved it all from corner to corner she was not pleased and made new plans and thought out new arrangements.

She turned everything in the apartment upside down but gradually her energy in building the nest began to peter out and she stopped harrying him.

She took clean bed linen out of the linen cupboard and put the covers on the pillows and eiderdown. It was clear that she did this with

affection for the bed, which object induced in her a sensual trembling of the nostrils.

Then she sent Švejk to get lunch and wine. And before he came back she changed into a transparent gown, which made her exceptionally alluring and attractive.

At lunch she consumed a bottle of wine, smoked many cigarettes and got into bed, while Švejk in the kitchen was enjoying his army bread, which he soaked in a glass of some sweet spirit.

'Švejk!' could be heard from the bedroom, 'Švejk!'

Švejk opened the door and saw the young lady in an alluring position on the pillows.

'Come in!'

Švejk walked towards the bed. With a peculiar smile she measured up his stocky figure and powerful thighs.

Pulling aside the delicate material which veiled and concealed everything, she said severely: 'Take off your boots and trousers! Come on! . . .'

And so it happened that the good soldier Švejk could report to the lieutenant when he returned from the barracks: 'Humbly report, sir, I've fulfilled all the lady's wishes and served her decently according to your orders.'

'Thank you, Švejk,' replied the lieutenant. 'And did she have lots of wishes?'

'About six,' answered Švejk. 'And now she is sleeping as though quite exhausted by the ride. I *did* obey her slightest whim, sir.'

V

While masses of armies, pinned to the forests by the Dunajec and the Raab, stood under a rain of shells, and artillery of heavy calibre was tearing to pieces whole companies and burying them in the Carpathians, and while the horizons on all the battlefields blazed with burning villages and towns, Lieutenant Lukáš and Švejk went through an unpleasant idyll with the lady who had run away from her husband and had now made herself mistress of the house.

When she went out for a walk Lieutenant Lukáš held a council of war with Švejk on how to get rid of her.

'It would be best, sir,' said Švejk, 'if her husband, who she's run away from and who's looking for her, as you said was stated in the letter which I brought you, got to know where she was and came to fetch her away. We could send him a telegram that she's with you and that he could come and fetch her. There was a similar case last year in a villa in Všenory. But then the telegram was sent to the husband by the wife herself, and he came for her and boxed them both across the ears. Then they happened to be both civilians but in this present case the husband wouldn't dare to assault an officer. Besides, you're not guilty at all, because you never invited anybody, and when she ran away from home she did it at her own risk. You'll see that a telegram like that'll do a power of good. Even if there are a few swipes across the jaw . . .'

'He's very intelligent,' Lieutenant Lukáš interrupted him. 'I know him. He's a wholesaler in hops. I must definitely speak to him. I'll send a telegram.'

The telegram he sent was very laconic and commercial: 'The present address of your wife is . . .' Then followed the address of Lieutenant Lukáš's apartment.

And so it happened that Mrs Katy had a very unpleasant surprise when the hop-merchant burst in through the door. He looked very circumspect and careful when Mrs Katy, who did not lose her composure at this moment, introduced both gentlemen to each other: 'My husband – Lieutenant Lukáš.' She couldn't think of anything else.

'Please sit down, Mr Wendler,' Lieutenant Lukáš said in a welcoming tone and took a cigarette case from his pocket. 'May I offer you one?'

The intelligent hop-merchant took a cigarette with great propriety and puffing smoke from his mouth said in measured tones: 'Will you soon be going to the front, lieutenant?'

'I've applied to be transferred to the 91st regiment at Budějovice, where I shall probably be sent as soon as I have finished the one-year volunteers' training school. We need a lot of officers and it is an unhappy feature of the situation today that young people who are qualified to be accepted as one-year volunteers don't apply for it. They prefer to remain ordinary infantrymen rather than try to become cadets.'

'The war has inflicted considerable damage on the hop trade, but I don't think it can last long,' remarked the hop-merchant, looking now at his wife and now at the lieutenant.

'Our situation is very good,' said Lieutenant Lukáš. 'Today no one doubts any longer that the war will end in a victory of the Central Powers. France, England and Russia are too weak against the Austro-

Turco-German granite. It's true that we have suffered some small reverses on some fronts. But as soon as we break through the Russian front between the Carpathian ridge and the middle Dunajec, there's no doubt at all that it will mean the end of the war. And the French too will very soon be threatened with the loss of the whole of Eastern France and the penetration of the German army into Paris. That's now quite certain. Apart from that our manoeuvres in Serbia continue very successfully, and the departure of our troops, which is in fact only a redeployment, has been misinterpreted by many people in a way which is in complete conflict with what cool reason demands in time of war. We shall very soon see that our well-calculated manoeuvres on the southern front are bearing fruit. Please look here.'

Lieutenant Lukáš took the hop-merchant gently by the arm, led him to a map of the battlefields which was hanging on the wall and showed him certain points, explaining: 'The Eastern Beskyds are an excellent base for us. As you can see here we have great support in the Carpathian sector. If we make a powerful strike on this line we shan't stop until we're in Moscow. The war will end before we think.'

'And what about Turkey?' asked the hop-merchant, thinking all the time how he could come to the point which he had come for.

'The Turks are holding well,' replied the lieutenant, leading him to the table again. 'The President of the Turkish parliament, Hali Bej, and Ali Bej have come to Vienna. Marshal Liman von Sanders has been appointed commander of the Turkish Dardanelles army. Goltz Pasha has just come from Constantinople to Berlin, and Enver Pasha, Vice Admiral Usedom Pasha and General Dzevad Pasha have been decorated by our Emperor. This is a fairly considerable number of decorations in such a short time.'

They all sat in silence opposite each other, until the lieutenant considered it appropriate to interrupt the embarrassing situation with the words: 'When did you arrive, Mr Wendler?'

'This morning.'

'I'm very glad that you found me at home, because in the afternoon I always go to the barracks and I have night duty. Because my flat is actually empty the whole day I have been able to offer madame hospitality. She is not troubled by anyone during her stay in Prague. Being an old acquaintance . . .'

The hop-merchant gave a cough: 'Katy is certainly a strange

woman, lieutenant. Please accept my warmest thanks for everything which you've done for her. She took it into her head to go to Prague out of the blue, because, so she said, she had to take a cure for her nerves. I was away, I came home and found the house empty. Katy had gone.'

Trying to put on as agreeable an expression as possible he shook his finger at her and asked her with a forced smile: 'And so you thought, did you, that when I was travelling you could travel too? Of course you didn't realize ...'

Lieutenant Lukáš, seeing that the conversation was taking an awkward turn, led the intelligent hop-merchant back to the map of the battlefields again and showed him places which had been underlined, saying: 'I forgot to point out to you one very interesting circumstance – this great bend which is facing south-west, where this group of mountains forms a major bridgehead. It is just against this spot that the Allies' offensive is directed. By closing this railway line, which links the bridgehead with the enemy's main defence line, communication between the right flank and the Northern Army on the Vistula must be broken. Is that quite clear to you now?'

The hop-merchant answered that everything was quite clear to him and fearing with his natural tact that what he said might be taken up as a hint he mentioned on returning to his place: 'During the war our hops have lost their markets abroad. France, England, Russia and the Balkans are now lost for hops. We're still sending hops to Italy but I'm afraid that Italy will get drawn into it soon. But when we've won it'll be we who will dictate the prices for our goods.'

'Italy is keeping strictly neutral,' the lieutenant said to him to cheer him up. 'She's ...'

'Then why doesn't she admit that she's bound by the Triple Alliance with Austria-Hungary and Germany?' the hop-merchant suddenly burst out in anger. His head became suddenly full of everything – hops, his wife, the war. 'I expected that Italy would march against France and Serbia. The war would then have been over. The hops in my stores are rotting, in the home market trade is poor, export amounts to nothing, and Italy is keeping strictly neutral. Why did Italy renew her Triple Alliance with us in 1912? Where is the Italian Minister of Foreign Affairs, the Marquis of San Giuliano? What's that gentleman doing? Is he asleep or what? Do you know what annual turnover I had before the war and what I have now?'

'You mustn't think that I don't follow events,' he continued. He looked furiously at the lieutenant, who was calmly blowing from his mouth rings of cigarette smoke which caught and broke each other up while Mrs Katy followed the operation with close interest. 'Why did the Germans go back to the frontier, when they'd already been near

Paris? Why is such heavy gunfire going on again between the Maas and Moselle? Do you know that at Combres and Woewre near the Marche three breweries have been burnt down, where we used to send every year more than five hundred sacks of hops? And in the Vosges the Hartmansweiler brewery has burnt down and the enormous brewery in Niederaspach near Mülhausen has been razed to the ground. That means the loss of twelve hundred sacks of hops for my firm every year. Six times the Germans have fought the Belgians for the Klosterhoek brewery. There you have a loss of 350 sacks of hops a year.'

He was so furious that he couldn't go on speaking, but only stood up, advanced towards his wife and said: 'Katy, you come home with me at once. Put on your things.

'All these happenings irritate me very much,' he said a moment later in an apologetic tone. 'Before, I used to be completely calm.'

And when she went away to put on her things he said in a low voice to the lieutenant: 'This is not the first time she's behaved like this. Last year she went away with a probationary teacher and I found them as far away as Zagreb. I used the opportunity to make a contract with the city brewery in Zagreb for 600 sacks of hops.

'Yes, the south used to be a gold mine. Our hops went as far as Constantinople. Today we are half-ruined. If the government limits production of beer at home it will deal us the final blow.'

And lighting the cigarette which had been offered to him he said in despair: 'Warsaw alone used to buy 2,370 sacks of hops. The largest brewery there is the Augustinian. Its representative used to visit me regularly each year. It is enough to make one desperate. It's a good thing I've got no children.'

This logical deduction from the yearly visit of the representative from the Augustinian brewery in Warsaw caused the lieutenant to give a gentle smile which the hop-merchant noticed and so he went on in his explanation: 'The Hungarian breweries in Sopron and in Gross-Kanisza bought from my firm for their export beer, which they exported as far as Alexandria, an average of a thousand sacks of hops a year. Now they refuse to order anything on account of the blockade. I offer them hops thirty per cent cheaper but they don't order a single sack. Stagnation, decay, misery and on top of that domestic troubles.'

The hop-merchant was silent for a moment, but his silence was interrupted by Mrs Katy, who was ready for the journey: 'What are we to do with my suitcases?'

'They'll come and fetch them, Katy,' said the hop-merchant with relief. He was glad in the end that everything had gone off without a row and a scandalous scene. 'If you want to do any more shopping, it's high time that we went. The train goes at 2.20.'

Both took friendly leave of the lieutenant and the hop-merchant was so glad that it was all over that on his way to the hall he said to the lieutenant: 'If you should be wounded at the front, and God forbid that you should, come and convalesce with us. We'll look after you with every care.'

Returning to the bedroom where Mrs Katy had dressed for the

journey, the lieutenant found on the wash-basin four hundred crowns and the following letter:

Lieutenant, you didn't stand up for me before that gorilla of a husband of mine, that prize blockhead. You allowed him to drag me away with him like some chattel he had forgotten in your apartment. And in doing so you took the liberty to observe that you had offered me hospitality. I hope that I have not caused you more expense than the enclosed four hundred crowns, which please share with your servant.

Lieutenant Lukáš stood for a moment with the letter in his hand and then slowly tore it in pieces. With a smile he looked at the money lying on the wash-basin and, seeing that when she was doing her hair before the mirror in her agitation she had forgotten her comb on the table, he placed it among his fetish relics.

Švejk returned in the afternoon. He had gone to look for a stable pinscher for the lieutenant.

'Švejk,' said the lieutenant, 'you're in luck. That lady who stayed with me has gone. Her husband took her away. And for all the services which you performed for her she left four hundred crowns on the wash-basin. You must thank her nicely or rather her husband, because it's his money which she took with her on the journey. I shall dictate to you a letter.'

He dictated:

'Honoured Sir,
Please convey my most cordial thanks for the four hundred crowns which madam, your wife, gave me for the services which I performed for her during her visit to Prague. Everything which I did for her I did with pleasure and therefore I cannot accept this sum but send it . . .

'Now then, just go on writing, Švejk. What are you fidgeting about? Where did I stop?'

'But send it . . .' said Švejk with a trembling voice full of tragic emotion.

'Good, then:

'. . . but send it back with the assurance of my deepest respect. Respectful greetings and a hand-kiss to madam. Josef Švejk, officer's orderly to Lieutenant Lukáš.

'Finished?'
'Humbly report, sir, the date is missing.'

'20 December 1914. Now write the envelope, take these four hundred crowns, carry them to the post office and send them to that address.'

And Lieutenant Lukáš began happily to whistle an aria from the operetta *The Divorced Lady*.

'One thing more, Švejk,' he called out when Švejk was going to the post office. 'What about that dog which you went to look for?'

'I've got my hands on one, sir, a jolly pretty animal, but it'll be difficult to get it. Tomorrow I hope that I'll be able to bring it after all. It bites.'

VI

Lieutenant Lukáš had not heard the last word, though it was so important. 'The beast bit for all it's worth,' Švejk had wanted to repeat, but in the end he thought: 'What business is it of the lieutenant's? He wants a dog, and he'll get one!'

It's of course an easy thing to say: 'Get me a dog!' Dog-owners are very careful about their dogs even if they are not thoroughbreds. And a mongrel whose only function in life is to warm the feet of an old woman is adored by its owner and no one is allowed to hurt a hair of its head.

But the dog, especially if it is a thoroughbred, must feel instinctively that one fine day it will be purloined from its master. It lives in continual fear that it will and must be stolen. For instance, when a dog is out for a walk it goes away from its master for a moment. At first it's happy and skittish. It plays with other dogs and climbs on their backs for immoral purposes and they climb on his. It smells the kerbstones, lifts its leg at every corner and even over the greengrocer woman's basket of potatoes: in short it has such *joie de vivre* and the world seems just as wonderful to it as it does to a young man when he has passed his school-leaving examination.

But suddenly you notice that its gaiety vanishes and it feels that it's got lost. And now it is assailed for the first time by real despair. It runs in a panic about the streets, sniffs, whines and drags its tail between its legs in utter hopelessness. It puts its ears back and rushes along in the middle of the street no one knows where.

If it could speak it would cry: 'Jesus Mary, someone's going to steal me!'

Have you ever been in a kennel and seen dogs which are panicky? They've all been stolen. The large city has evolved a special class of thief who lives exclusively on the theft of dogs. There exist tiny breeds of drawing-room dogs, tiny miniature pinschers which fit like a very small glove into the pocket of an overcoat or a lady's muff. And they even get pulled out from there, poor things. The savage German spotted mastiff gets kidnapped at night while it is ferociously guarding a villa in the suburbs. The police dog is whisked off under the detective's nose. You take a dog out on a lead, someone cuts the lead in two, the dog's gone and you are left looking idiotically at an empty strap. Fifty per cent of the dogs which you meet in the streets have changed their masters several times, and very often after years you may buy back your own dog which someone had stolen from you as a puppy once when you took it for a walk. The danger of being stolen is worst when dogs are led out to perform their small and large bodily needs. It is just when they are engaged in doing the latter that most of them get lost. That is why every dog, when it is so occupied, looks cautiously around itself.

There are various modes of operation resorted to by dog-thieves. They steal dogs either directly in pickpocket fashion or by cunningly enticing the unfortunate creature. It is only in a school reader or natural history primer that a dog is a faithful animal. Once allow even the most faithful of dogs to smell a fried horsemeat sausage and it's lost. It forgets its master by whose side it is walking, turns round and follows you with its mouth watering, and in anticipation of the great joy over the sausage it wags its tail in a very friendly way and distends its nostrils like the wildest stallion when it is being led off to the mare.

In Malá Strana near the Castle Steps there is a small pub. Two men were sitting there one day in the back in the dusk. One was a soldier and the other a civilian. Leaning forward to each other they whispered mysteriously. They looked like conspirators from the days of the Venetian Republic.

'Every day at eight o'clock,' the civilian whispered, 'the maid takes it out to the corner of Havlíček Square on the way to the park. But it's a real brute and bites for all it's worth. You can't stroke it.'

And leaning closer to the soldier he whispered in his ear: 'It doesn't even touch sausage.'

'Not even fried?' asked the soldier.

'Not even fried.'

Both spat.

'Well, what does the brute eat?'

'God knows. These dogs are as spoiled and pampered as an arch-bishop.'

The soldier and the civilian clinked glasses and the latter whispered again: 'Once a black pom which I needed for some kennels over the Klamovka wouldn't look at sausage either. I followed it for three days, until I couldn't hold out any longer and asked the lady who was leading it straight out what it actually was fed on, because it was so beautiful. The lady was flattered and said that it liked cutlets best. And so I bought it a schnitzel. I thought a schnitzel was better. And do you know the brute wouldn't even look at it, because the schnitzel was veal and it was used to pork. So after all I had to buy it a pork cutlet. I let the dog smell it first, and then I ran away with the dog following me. The lady shouted: "Puntík, Puntík!", but where was her dear Puntík? It ran after the pork cutlet as far as the corner and beyond. Then I put a lead round its neck and the next day it was already in the kennels over the Klamovka. It had a patch of white tufts under its neck and they blacked it over and nobody recognized it. But the other dogs, and there were a lot of them, all went for fried horsemeat sausage. It would be best if you asked the maid what the dog likes to eat most; you're a soldier, you've a fine figure and she's more likely to tell you. I've already asked her, but she looked at me as though she wanted to stab me and said: "What business is it of yours?" She isn't very pretty, she's like a monkey but with a soldier like you she'll certainly talk.'

'Is it really a stable pinscher? My lieutenant doesn't want anything else.'

'It's a very natty stable pinscher. Pepper and salt, real thoroughbred just as you're Švejk and I'm Blahník. What I want to know is what it eats and I'll give it that and bring it to you.'

Both friends clinked their glasses again. When before the war Švejk was still making his living on the sale of dogs Blahník used to supply him with them. He was an experienced man and it was said of him that he bought suspicious dogs illegally from the skinner's yard and resold them. He even once had rabies and was quite at home in the Pasteur Institute in Vienna. Now he considered it his duty to give his disinterested help to the soldier Švejk. He knew all the dogs in the whole of Prague and its surroundings and spoke quietly because he had to be careful not to betray himself to the landlord. Six months ago he had carried away from him a dachshund puppy concealed under his coat, and given it a baby's bottle to suck, so that the stupid puppy obviously regarded him as its mummy and never made a sound.

On principle he only stole thoroughbreds and might have been a legal expert on them. He supplied all kennels and private persons as opportunity offered, and when he walked along the street all the dogs which he had once stolen growled at him. It sometimes happened that when he stood somewhere near a shop window a dog, anxious to pay him back, would lift its leg over him and besprinkle his trousers.

At eight o'clock the next morning the good soldier Švejk could be seen walking at the corner of Havlíček Square by the park. He was waiting for the maid with the stable pinscher. Finally she came and a whiskered, bristly dog with a rough coat and wise black eyes ran past him. It was skittish like all dogs are when they have performed their needs and ran after sparrows which were breakfasting on horse dung in the street.

Then the woman who was looking after the dog came past Švejk. She was an elderly spinster and her hair was neatly plaited into a crown. She whistled to the dog and brandished a chain and an elegant whip.

Švejk spoke to her:

'Excuse me, miss, would you please tell me which is the way to Žižkov?'

She stopped and looked at him, to see whether the question was honestly meant and the good-natured face of Švejk told her that actually this soldier perhaps really wanted to go to Žižkov. The expression of her face softened and she gladly explained how to get there.

'I've only recently been transferred to Prague,' said Švejk. 'I don't come from here. I'm from the country. You aren't from Prague either, are you?'

'I'm from Vodňany.'

'Then we're not far away from each other,' answered Švejk. 'I'm from Protivín.'

This knowledge of the topography of South Bohemia, which Švejk had acquired once during manoeuvres there, filled the good lady's heart with a local patriotic glow.

'Then you certainly know the butcher Pejchar in the square at Protivín?'

'Why, of course I do! He's my brother. At home they all like him very much,' said Švejk. 'He's very good and helpful. He has good meat and gives good weight.'

'You aren't by chance one of Jareš's sons?' asked the maid, beginning to feel drawn to the unknown soldier.

'I am.'

'And which Jareš, the one from Krč near Protivín or from Ražice?'

'From Ražice.'

'Does he still deliver beer?'

'Yes, he does still.'

'But he must be a long way past sixty already?'

'He was sixty-eight last spring,' answered Švejk composedly. 'Now he has got a dog and it goes around with him. It sits on his cart. It's just the same kind of dog as that one there running after the sparrows. A lovely little dog, very lovely.'

'That's ours,' Švejk's new friend explained to him. 'I work for the colonel here. Don't you know our colonel?'

'I do. He's bally intelligent,' said Švejk. 'In Budějovice we had a colonel like that.'

'Our master is very strict, and when people were recently saying that we'd been beaten in Serbia, he came home in a frightful rage, threw all the plates around in the kitchen and wanted to give me notice.'

'So that's your doggie?' Švejk interrupted her. 'It's a pity that my lieutenant can't stand dogs, because I'm very fond of them myself.' He was quiet for a moment and suddenly blurted out: 'But not every dog will eat anything.'

'Our Fox is very faddy. At one time he wouldn't eat any meat at all, but now he does again.'

'And what does he like to eat best?'

'Liver, boiled liver.'

'Veal or pork?'

'It's all the same to him.' Švejk's 'fellow countrywoman' smiled, since she took his last question for an unsuccessful attempt to be funny.

They walked together for a little and then they were joined by the stable pinscher which was put on to the chain. It was very friendly to Švejk and tried to tear his trousers with its muzzle. It jumped up at him, but suddenly stopped as though it sensed what Švejk was planning for it, and walked sadly and despondently, looking sideways at Švejk as though it wanted to say: 'And so now it's coming to me too?'

Then she told him as well that she came here with the dog every evening at six o'clock and that she didn't trust any of the men in Prague; she had once put an advertisement in the newspaper, to which she received an answer from a locksmith offering to marry her. But he had wheedled eight hundred crowns out of her for some invention of his and disappeared. In the country people were definitely more honest. If she were to marry she would only take a man from the country, and only after the end of the war. She regarded war marriages as stupid, because a war bride was generally left a widow.

Švejk gave her good reason to hope that he would come at six o'clock and went away to tell his friend, Blahník, that the dog ate liver of any kind.

'I'll treat him to ox liver,' Blahník decided. 'That was how I got the St Bernard belonging to the company director, Vydra, which was a jolly faithful animal. Tomorrow I'll bring you the dog safe and sound.'

Blahník was as good as his word. When Švejk had finished cleaning the apartment in the morning he heard a barking at the door and Blahník dragged in the protesting stable pinscher, which was even more bristly than nature had bristled it. It rolled its eyes wildly and looked so surly that it recalled a hungry tiger in a cage in a zoological garden when it sees a well-fed visitor standing before it. It ground its teeth and growled, as though it wanted to say: 'I'll tear you to pieces. I'll gobble you up.'

They tied the dog to the kitchen table and Blahník described how he had purloined it.

'I went purposefully past it and held the boiled liver wrapped up in paper. It began to sniff and to jump up on me. I didn't give it anything, but just walked on, the dog following me. By the park I turned into Bredovská Street and there I gave it its first piece. It ate it while it was going along so as not to lose sight of me. I turned into Jindřišská Street, where I gave it another portion. And when it'd eaten that up, I put it on a chain and dragged it through Wenceslas Square to Vinohrady and then on to Vršovice. On the way it played me some fantastic tricks. When I crossed the tram lines it lay down and wouldn't move. Perhaps it wanted to be run over. I've brought with me a blank pedigree, which I bought at Fuchs the stationers. Do you know how to forge the pedigree, Švejk?'

'It must be written in your hand. Write that the dog comes from the kennels of von Bülow at Leipzig. Its father was Arnheim von Kahls-berg, its mother Emma von Trautensdorf, descended on the father's side from Siegfried von Busenthal. Its father won the first prize at the Berlin Exhibition of stable pinschers in 1912. The mother was decorated with the gold medal of the Nuremberg society for the breeding of thoroughbred dogs. How old do you think it is?'

'Two years by its teeth.'

'Write down that it's one and a half.'

'It's badly cropped, Švejk. Look at its ears.'

'We can put that right. We can if necessary clip them when it gets used to us. Now it could only make it more angry.'

The stolen animal growled furiously, panted, rushed around and then lay down. With tongue hanging out it waited, tired and exhausted, to see what was going to happen to it next.

Gradually it grew calmer and only occasionally whined piteously.

Švejk offered it the remains of the liver, which Blahník had given him. But it took no notice of it, gave it a defiant look and gazed at it as though it meant to say: 'I burnt my fingers once. You can eat it your-selves.'

It lay down in resignation and pretended to doze. Suddenly it got something into its head, jumped up and began to stand on its hind legs and beg with its front paws. It had capitulated.

But this moving scene had no effect on Švejk.

'Lie down,' he shouted at the wretched animal, which lay down again and whined piteously.

'What name shall I put on its pedigree?' asked Blahník. 'It was called Fox, so we must find something like it, which it will understand at once.'

'Why not perhaps "Max"? Look, Blahník, how it pricks up its ears. Get up, Max!'

The unfortunate stable pinscher, which had been robbed of its home and name, stood up and waited for further orders.

'I think we ought to untie it,' Švejk decided. 'We shall see what it'll do then.'

When it was untied, it made its way to the door, where it barked three times at the handle, obviously relying on the generosity of these evil men. Seeing however that they had no understanding for its yearning to get out, it made a little pool by the door, convinced that they would throw it out as people used to do to it when it was young and the colonel was teaching it in a strict military fashion to be house-trained.

Instead Švejk observed: 'It's a cunning one, to be sure, a bit of a Jesuit.' He gave it a blow with his belt and dipped its muzzle in the puddle, so that it had a hard time licking itself clean.

It whined at this humiliation and began to run round the kitchen, desperately sniffing at its own tracks. Then out of the blue it went to the table, ate up the rest of the liver which was lying on the floor, lay down near the stove and fell asleep after all this adventure.

'How much do I owe you?' Švejk asked Blahník, when the latter took his leave of him.

'Don't mention it, Švejk,' said Blahník gently. 'For an old friend I'd do anything, especially when he's serving in the army. Goodbye, my boy, and don't ever lead it across Havlíček Square, in case any misfortune should happen. If you should ever need another dog, you know where I live.'

Švejk let Max sleep very long and in the meantime bought half a pound of liver at the butcher's, boiled it and waited until Max woke up, letting it smell a piece of warm liver.

Max began to lick its lips in its sleep, then it stretched, sniffed the liver and ate it up. After that it went to the door and repeated its experiments with the door handle.

'Max!' Švejk called to it. 'Come here!'

It came distrustfully. Švejk took it on his lap, stroked it, and Max for the first time wagged the remains of its clipped tail in a friendly way, snapped gently at Švejk's hand, held it in its jaws and looked very wisely at Švejk, as though it was going to say: 'There's nothing to be done. I know I've lost.'

Švejk went on stroking it and began to talk to it in a tender tone:

'There was once a doggie who was called Fox and it lived with a colonel. The maid took it for a walk and a gentleman came and stole it. Fox came to the army to a lieutenant and they gave it the name of Max. Max, give me your paw! Now you see, you bastard, that we shall be good friends if you'll be obedient and good. Otherwise you'll have a hell of a war.'

Max jumped down from Švejk's lap and began happily to jump up on him. By the evening when the lieutenant returned from the barracks Švejk and Max were the very best of friends.

Looking at Max Švejk thought philosophically: 'After all, by and large every soldier's stolen from his home too.'

Lieutenant Lukáš was very agreeably surprised when he saw the dog, which also manifested great pleasure when it again saw a man with a sabre.

In reply to the question where it came from and how much it cost, Švejk said with perfect composure that the dog had been given him by a friend, who had just been called up.

'Good, Švejk,' said the lieutenant, playing with Max. 'On the first of the month you'll get fifty crowns from me for the dog.'

'I can't accept that, sir.'

'Švejk,' said the lieutenant sternly, 'when you began your service with me I explained to you that you must obey all my orders. When I tell you that you'll get fifty crowns, you must take them and spend them on drink. What will you do, Švejk, with these fifty crowns?'

'Humbly report, sir, I shall spend them on drink according to your orders.'

'And in case I should forget this, Švejk, I order you to report to me that I have to give you fifty crowns for the dog. Do you understand? Are you sure the dog hasn't got fleas? You'd better give it a bath and comb it. Tomorrow I'm on duty, but the day after I'll take it for a walk.'

While Švejk was giving Max a bath, its former owner, the colonel, was thundering at home and threatening that he would bring the thief before a court-martial and have him shot, hung, gaoled for twenty years and quartered.

'Bugger that blasted bloody swine,' could be heard in German all over the colonel's apartment so that the windows rattled. 'I'll be even with that murderous assassin.'

Over the heads of Švejk and Lieutenant Lukáš a catastrophic storm was brewing.

15

Catastrophe

COLONEL FRIEDRICH KRAUS, who bore the additional title of von Zillergut after a village in the district of Salzburg which his ancestors had already completely fleeced in the eighteenth century, was a most venerable idiot. Whenever he was relating something, he could only speak in platitudes, asking whether everybody could understand the most primitive expressions: 'And so a window, gentlemen, yes. Well, do you know what a window is?'

Or: 'A track which has a ditch on each side of it is called a road. Yes, gentlemen. Now, do you know what a ditch is? A ditch is an excavation on which several people work. It is a hollow. Yes. They work with picks. Now, do you know what a pick is?'

He suffered from a mania for explanations, which he gave with the enthusiasm of an inventor expounding his work.

'A book, gentlemen, is a number of squares of paper cut in different ways and of varying format which are printed on and put together, bound and gummed. Yes. Well, do you know, gentlemen, what gum is? Gum is adhesive material.'

He was so colossally stupid that the officers avoided him from afar so as not to have to hear from him that the pavement divided the street from the carriage-way and that it was a raised paved strip along the façade of the house. And the façade of the house was that part of it which we see from the street or from the pavement. We cannot see the rear part of the house from the pavement, a fact we can immediately prove to ourselves by stepping into the carriage-way.

He was ready to demonstrate this interesting fact at once. Fortunately however he was run over. From that time he became even more raving mad. He stopped officers on the street and engaged them in unendingly long conversations about omelettes, the sun, thermometers, doughnuts, windows and postage stamps.

It was really remarkable how this fat-head managed to be promoted so quickly and to have behind him such very influential people as a

general of the Supreme Command who backed him up in spite of his
utter military incompetence.

At manoeuvres he performed miracles with his regiment. He never
arrived at any position in time, led his regiment in column formation
against machine-guns, and once many years ago at the Imperial manoeuvres in South Bohemia he and his regiment got completely lost and
finally reached Moravia, where they wandered about with him for
several days after the manoeuvres were over and the troops were back
in the barracks. But he got away with it.

His friendly relations with the general and other no less fat-headed
military dignitaries of old Austria brought him various decorations and
orders, by which he felt extraordinarily honoured and considered himself to be the best soldier under the sun and the best theoretician in
strategy and all military sciences.

At regimental reviews he used to start talking with the men and
always asked them the same question:

'Why are the rifles which have been introduced into the army called
"manlichers"?'[1]

In the regiment he was nicknamed 'the manlicher lunatic'. He was
extraordinarily vindictive, ruined his subordinate officers if he did not
like them, and when they wanted to get married sent up very bad
reports attached to their applications.

He had lost half his left ear, which had been cut off in his youth by
a rival in a duel fought merely to establish the truth of the fact that
Friedrich Kraus von Zillergut was an utter imbecile.

If we analyse his mental capacities, we reach the conclusion that they
were not one wit better than those which had made the big-lipped
Franz Joseph Hapsburg celebrated as a patent idiot.

In each you found the same torrent of words, the same store of
colossal naïvety. At a banquet in the officers' club Colonel Kraus von
Zillergut said quite out of the blue, when there had been mention of
Schiller: 'Now, gentlemen, I saw a steam plough yesterday. It was
driven by a locomotive, but mark my words, gentlemen, not just by
one locomotive, but by two. I see the smoke, I come nearer and there
is one locomotive and on the other side another. Tell me, gentlemen,
isn't that funny? Two locomotives, as though one were not enough.'

He was silent for a moment and then remarked: 'When the petrol in
the car is used up it has to stop. I saw that yesterday too. And then

1. The old-fashioned repeater rifle called after the name of its inventor.

they talk nonsense about perpetual motion, gentlemen! It doesn't go, it stands still, it doesn't move, it hasn't got petrol. Isn't that funny?'

With all his stupidity he was immensely pious. In his apartment he had a house altar. He often went to the church of St Ignatius for confession and communion and after the outbreak of the war prayed for the success of the Austrian and German arms. He mixed Christianity with dreams of German hegemony. God had to help them seize the wealth and lands of the conquered.

He flew into a passion when he read in the newspaper that prisoners had been taken again.

He said: 'What's the point of taking prisoners? They all ought to be shot. No mercy. Dance among the corpses. All the civilians in Serbia should be burnt to a man and the children finished off with the bayonet.'

He was no worse than the German poet Vierordt, who published during the war verses demanding that Germany should have a soul of iron and hate and kill millions of French devils.

> Let the piles of human bones and burning flesh
> Rise to the clouds over the mountains . . .

Having finished his teaching at the course for one-year volunteers Lieutenant Lukáš took Max out for a walk.

'I take the liberty of warning you, sir,' said Švejk solicitously, 'that you must be very careful with that dog in case it runs away. It may perhaps be homesick for its old home and take to its heels if you let it off the lead. And also I wouldn't advise you to take it along Havlíček Square. That's the beat of a savage butcher's dog from The Image of the Virgin, which bites frightfully. As soon as it sees a strange dog in its area it's at once jealous of it for fear it should eat up something. It's like the beggar of St Haštal.'[1]

Max jumped about merrily and got under the lieutenant's feet, wound its lead round his sabre and expressed unusual joy at going for a walk.

They went out on to the street, and Lieutenant Lukáš went with the dog in the direction of Příkopy. He was to meet a lady at the corner of

1. A church in Prague where a beggar, who had made its porch his permanent beat, was arrested by the police for driving away other beggars.

Panská Street. He was deep in thoughts about his work. What should he lecture on to the volunteers in the school tomorrow? How do we determine the height of a given hill? Why do we reckon the height from sea level? How can we establish from its height above sea level the height of a mountain from its foot? Damn it! Why does the Ministry of War put such things into the school programme? Clearly it's a matter for the artillery. And there are after all general staff maps. When the enemy is on elevation 312 it's no use thinking why the height of the hill should be reckoned from sea level or calculating how high the hill is. We look at the map and we have it there.

He was jerked out of these thoughts by a severe 'Halt!', just when he came near Panská Street.

Simultaneously with the 'Halt!' the dog tried to wriggle out of its lead and threw itself with a joyful bark on the man who had just said severely 'Halt!'

In front of the lieutenant stood Colonel Kraus von Zillergut. Lieutenant Lukáš saluted the colonel and stood before him, apologizing that he had not seen him.

Colonel Kraus was known among the officers for his passion for halting people.

He regarded saluting as something on which the success of the war depended and on which the whole power of the army was built.

'A soldier must put his soul into his salute,' he used to say. It was the finest kind of corporal's mysticism.

He saw to it that those who saluted did so according to the smallest niceties of the instructions, accurately and with dignity.

He lay in wait for all who passed him, from infantryman up to lieutenant-colonel. If any infantryman saluted casually as though when he touched his cap he were saying 'God bless' the colonel took him straight off to the barracks for punishment.

For him it was no excuse to say: 'I did not see you, sir.'

'A soldier,' he used to say, 'must pick out his superior officer in a crowd and think of nothing else but carrying out the duties which are prescribed in service orders. When he falls on the battlefield he must salute before he dies. Anyone who doesn't know how to salute, pretends he doesn't see me, or salutes casually I regard as vermin.'

'Lieutenant,' said Colonel Kraus in an awesome voice, 'the lower ranks must always pay respect to the higher. This order has not been rescinded. And next: since when do officers promenade about with stolen dogs? Yes, with stolen dogs. A dog which belongs to someone else is a stolen dog.'

'This dog, sir . . .' Lieutenant Lukáš objected.

'Belongs to me, lieutenant,' the colonel interrupted him harshly. 'It's my Fox.'

And Fox or Max remembered its old master and drove the new one entirely out of its heart. It tore itself loose, jumped up on the colonel and showed such joy as only a love-sick sixth former is capable of when he finds understanding on the part of his beloved.

'Promenading with stolen dogs, lieutenant, is not compatible with the honour of an officer. Didn't you know that? An officer may not buy a dog unless he has assured himself beforehand that he can do so without consequences!' Colonel Kraus thundered on, stroking Fox-Max, who began to growl meanly at the lieutenant and to bare its teeth, as though the colonel had pointed to the lieutenant and said: 'Seize him!'

'Lieutenant,' continued the colonel, 'would you consider it right to ride about on a stolen horse? Did you not read the advertisement in *Bohemie* and in the *Tagblatt* about the loss of my stable pinscher? You didn't read the advertisement which your superior officer put into the newspaper?'

The colonel clapped his hands.

'Really, these young officers! Where has discipline gone? The colonel puts in advertisements and the lieutenant doesn't read them.'

'If only I could give you a few across the jaw, you bloody old dotard,' Lieutenant Lukáš thought to himself, looking at the colonel's side whiskers which were reminiscent of an orang-outang.

'Come with me for a moment,' said the colonel. And so they walked along and had a very pleasant conversation:

'At the front, lieutenant, a thing like this cannot happen to you again. Promenading with stolen dogs behind the lines is certainly very agreeable. Yes, walking about with your superior officer's dog at a time when every day we are losing a hundred officers on the battlefield. And advertisements are not read! For a hundred years I could insert notices that my dog is lost. Two hundred years! Three hundred years!'

The colonel blew his nose noisily, which with him was always a sign of great fury, and said: 'You can go on with your walk.' Then he turned round and went away, angrily striking with his riding whip across the ends of his officer's greatcoat.

Lieutenant Lukáš crossed to the opposite pavement and heard once more: 'Halt!' The colonel had just stopped an unfortunate infantry-man in the reserve, who was thinking about his mother at home and had not noticed him.

The colonel took him in person to the barracks for punishment and swore at him for being a swine and bastard.

'What shall I do with Švejk,' thought the lieutenant. 'I'll smash his jaw, but that's not enough. Even tearing his skin from his body in little strips would be too good treatment for that blackguard.' Disregarding the fact that he was due to meet a lady, he set off home in a fury.

'I'll kill him, the dirty hound,' he said to himself as he got into the tram.

Meanwhile the good soldier Švejk was deep in conversation with an orderly from the barracks. The soldier had brought the lieutenant some documents to sign and was now waiting.

Švejk treated him to coffee and they discussed together how Austria would be smashed.

They carried on this conversation as though it could be taken for granted. There was an endless series of utterances which would certainly have been defined in the court as treasonable and for which both of them would have been hanged.

'His Imperial Majesty must be completely off his rocker by this time,' declared Švejk. 'He was never bright, but this war'll certainly finish him.'

'Of course he's off his rocker,' the soldier from the barracks asserted with conviction. 'He's so gaga he probably doesn't know there's a war on. Perhaps they're ashamed of telling him. If his signature's on the manifesto to his peoples, then it's a fraud. They must have had it printed without his knowledge, because he's not capable of thinking about anything at all.'

'He's finished,' added Švejk knowingly. 'He wets himself and they have to feed him like a little baby. Recently a chap at the pub told us that His Imperial Majesty has two wet nurses and is breast-fed three times a day.'

'If only it was all over,' sighed the soldier from the barracks, 'and they knocked us out, so that Austria at last had peace!'

And both continued the conversation until finally Švejk condemned Austria for ever with the words: 'A monarchy as idiotic as this ought not to exist at all', whereupon the other, to complete his utterance by adding something of a practical kind, said: 'When I get to the front I'll hop it pretty quick.'

And when both continued to interpret the views of the average Czech about the war, the soldier from the barracks repeated what he had heard that day in Prague, that guns could be heard at Náchod and that the Tsar of Russia would soon be in Cracow.

Then they related how our corn was being carted away to Germany and how German soldiers were getting cigarettes and chocolate.

Then they remembered the times of the old wars, and Švejk solemnly argued that when in the olden days they threw stink-pots into a beleaguered castle it was no picnic to have to fight in such a stink. He had read that they had besieged a castle somewhere for three years and the enemy did nothing else except amuse themselves every day in this way with the beleaguered inside.

He would certainly have added something else interesting and informative if their conversation had not been interrupted by the return of Lieutenant Lukáš.

Casting at Švejk a fearful, crushing glance, he signed the documents and after dismissing the soldier motioned Švejk to follow him into his sitting-room.

Frightful lightning shafts darted from the lieutenant's eyes. Sitting on the chair he looked at Švejk and pondered how he should start the massacre.

'First I'll give him a few across the jaw,' he thought. 'Then I'll break his nose and tear off his ears. And after that we'll see.'

But he was confronted by the honest and kindly gaze of the good and innocent eyes of Švejk who dared to interrupt the calm before the storm with the words: 'Humbly report, sir, you've lost your cat. She ate up the boot polish and permitted herself to pass out. I threw her into the cellar – but next door. You won't find again such a good and beautiful Angora cat.'

'What shall I do with him?' flashed through the lieutenant's mind. 'For Christ's sake, what an idiotic expression he has.'

And the kindly innocent eyes of Švejk continued to glow with gentleness and tenderness, combined with an expression of complete composure; everything was in order and nothing had happened, and if something had happened, it was again quite in order that anything at all was happening.

Lieutenant Lukáš jumped up, but did not hit Švejk as he had originally intended to do. He brandished his fist under his nose and roared out: 'Švejk, you *stole* the dog!'

'Humbly report, sir, I know of no such case recently and I would like to observe, sir, that you yourself took Max this afternoon out for a walk and so I couldn't have stolen it. I saw at once when you came back without the dog that something must have happened. That's called a situation. In Spálená Street there is a bag-maker named Kuneš and he couldn't take a dog out for a walk without losing it. Usually he left it somewhere at a pub or someone stole it from him or borrowed it and never returned it . . .'

'Švejk, you bastard, you, Himmellaudon, hold your tongue! Either you're a cunning blackguard or else you're a camel and a fat-headed idiot. You're a real object lesson, but I tell you you'd better not try anything on me! Where did you get that dog from? How did you get hold of it? Do you know that it belongs to our colonel, who took it off with him when we happened to meet? Do you realize that this is a colossal world scandal? So speak the truth now! Did you steal it or not?'

'Humbly report, sir, I didn't steal it.'

'Did you know that it was a stolen dog?'

'Humbly report, sir, I knew it was stolen.'

'Švejk, Jesus Mary, Himmelherrgott, I'll have you shot, you bastard, you cattle, you oaf, you pig. Are you really such a half-wit?'

'Humbly report, sir, I am.'

'Why did you bring me a stolen dog? Why did you put that beast into my apartment?'

'To give you a little pleasure, sir.'

And Švejk's eyes looked kindly and tenderly into the face of the lieutenant, who sat down and sighed: 'Why did God punish me with this bastard?'

The lieutenant sat on the chair in quiet resignation and felt he had not the strength even to roll a cigarette, let alone give Švejk one or two across the jaw, and he had no idea why he sent Švejk to get *Bohemie* and *Tagblatt* so that Švejk could read the colonel's advertisement about the stolen dog.

With the newspaper open on the advertisement pages Švejk returned.

He beamed and proclaimed joyfully: 'It's there, sir. The colonel describes that stolen stable pinscher so beautifully that it's a pure joy, and into the bargain he offers the finder of it a hundred crowns. That's quite a handsome reward. Generally they only give fifty. A chap called Božetěch from Košíře made a business just out of this. He always stole dogs, then looked in the advertisements to see whether one had run away and at once went there. On one occasion he stole a beautiful black pom, and because the owner didn't advertise it in the newspapers, he tried to put an advertisement in himself. He spent ten crowns on advertisements until finally a gentleman announced that it was his dog, that he had lost it and that he had thought that it would be useless to try and look for it, as he didn't believe any longer in people's honesty. But now he saw that all the same there were honest people to be found, and this gave him tremendous pleasure. He said he was opposed on principle to rewarding honesty, but as a souvenir he would give him his book on indoor and outdoor plant cultivation. The good Božetěch took that black pom by its back legs and hit the gentleman over the head with it and from that time he swore he wouldn't put in any more advertisements. He'd rather sell a dog to a kennel, if no one wanted to advertise for it.'

'Go to bed, Švejk,' the lieutenant ordered. 'You are capable of drivelling on like this till tomorrow morning.' And he went to bed too. In the night he dreamt of Švejk, how Švejk had also stolen the horse of the Heir to the Throne and brought it to him, and how the Heir to the Throne had recognized the horse at a review, when the unfortunate Lieutenant Lukáš rode on it at the head of his company.

In the morning the lieutenant felt as if he had gone through a night of debauch during which he had been knocked many times over the head. An unusually oppressive nightmare clung to him. Exhausted by the frightful dream he fell asleep towards the morning, only to be woken by a knocking on the door. The kindly face of Švejk appeared and asked when he should wake the lieutenant.

The lieutenant groaned in bed: 'Get out, you monster, this is sheer hell!'

But when he was already up and Švejk brought him his breakfast, the lieutenant was surprised by a new question from Švejk: 'Humbly report, sir, would you wish me to look for another nice doggie for you?'

'You know, Švejk, that I feel like having you court-martialled,' said the lieutenant with a sigh, 'but they'd only acquit you, because they'd never have seen anything so colossally idiotic in all their lives. Do look at yourself in the mirror. Doesn't it make you sick to see your own drivelling expression? You're the most idiotic freak of nature that I've ever seen. Now, tell me the truth, Švejk, do you really like yourself?'

'Humbly report, sir, I don't. In this mirror I am somehow lopsided or something. But the glass is not properly cut. At the Chinaman, Staněk's, they once had a convex mirror and when anybody looked at himself in it he wanted to spew. A mug like this, a head like a slop-pail, a belly like a sozzled canon, in short a complete scare-crow. Then the Governor of Bohemia passed by and saw himself in it and the mirror had to be removed at once.'

The lieutenant turned away, sighed and thought it right to pay attention to his coffee rather than to Švejk.

Švejk was already pottering about in the kitchen, and Lieutenant Lukáš heard him singing:

> 'Grenevil is marching through the Powder Gate.
> Swords are flashing, pretty girls are weeping . . . '

And then there came from the kitchen another song:

> 'We're the boys who make the noise,
> Win the hearts of all the tarts,
> Draw our pay and then make hay.'

'You certainly make hay, you bastard,' the lieutenant thought to himself and spat.

Švejk's head appeared in the doorway: 'Humbly report, sir, they've come here for you from the barracks. You're to go at once to the colonel. His orderly officer is here.'

And he added confidentially: 'Perhaps it's because of that dog.'

'I've already heard,' said the lieutenant, when the orderly officer wanted to report to him in the hall.

He said this dejectedly and went out casting an annihilating glance at Švejk.

This was not regimental report. It was something worse. When the lieutenant stepped into his office the colonel sat in his chair frowning frightfully.

'Two years ago, lieutenant,' said the colonel, 'you asked to be transferred to the 91st regiment in Budějovice. Do you know where Budějovice is? It's on the Vltava, yes, on the Vltava, where the Ohře or something like that flows into it. The town is big, so to speak, and friendly, and if I'm not mistaken it has an embankment. Do you know what an embankment is? It is a wall built over the water. Yes. However, this is not relevant here. We had manoeuvres there.'

The colonel was silent, and looking at the ink pot passed quickly to another subject: 'My dog's ruined after having been with you. He won't eat anything. Look, there's a fly in the ink pot. It's very strange that flies should fall into the ink pot in winter. That's disorderly.'

'Well, say your say, you bloody old dodderer,' thought the lieutenant to himself.

The colonel got up and walked once or twice up and down the office.

'I've thought for a long time, lieutenant, what I ought to do with you to prevent this *recurring*, and I remembered that you wanted to be transferred to the 91st regiment. The high command recently informed us that there is a great shortage of officers in the 91st regiment because they have all been *killed by the Serbs*. I give you my word of honour that within three days you will be in the 91st regiment in Budějovice, where they are forming *march battalions for the front*. You don't need to thank me. The army requires officers who . . .'

And not knowing what else to say he looked at his watch and pronounced: 'It's half past ten and high time to go to regimental report.'

And with this the agreeable conversation came to an end, and the lieutenant felt very relieved when he left the office and went to the volunteers' school, where he announced that very soon he would be going to the front and was therefore organizing a farewell evening party in Nekázanka.

Returning home he said significantly to Švejk: 'Do you know, Švejk, what a march battalion is?'

'Humbly report, sir, a march battalion is a *maršbaťák* and a march company is a *marškumpačka*. We always use abbreviations.'

'Very well then, Švejk,' said the lieutenant in a solemn voice. 'I wish to tell you that you are going with me on the *maršbaťák*, if you like such abbreviations. But don't think that at the front you'll be able to drop such bloody awful clangers as you've done here. Are you happy?'

'Humbly report, sir, I'm awfully happy,' replied the good soldier Švejk. 'It'll be really marvellous when we both fall dead together for His Imperial Majesty and the Royal Family . . .'

Epilogue to Part I, 'Behind the Lines'

As I finish the first part of the book *The Good Soldier Švejk and his Fortunes in the World War* ('Behind the Lines') I should like to announce that two further volumes will be published in quick succession: 'At the Front' and 'In Captivity'. And in these two further volumes the soldiers and civilian population will go on talking and acting as they do in real life.

Life is no finishing school for young ladies. Everyone speaks the way he is made. The protocol chief, Dr Guth, speaks differently from Palivec, the landlord of The Chalice, and this novel is neither a handbook of drawing-room refinement nor a teaching manual of expressions to be used in polite society. It is a historical picture of a certain period of time.

Where it is necessary to use a strong expression which was actually said, I am not ashamed of reproducing it exactly as it was. I regard the use of polite circumlocutions or asterisks as the stupidest form of sham. The same words are used in parliament too.

It was once said, and very rightly, that a man who is well brought-up may read anything. The only people who boggle at what is perfectly natural are those who are the worst swine and the finest experts in filth. In their utterly contemptible pseudo-morality they ignore the contents and madly attack individual words.

Years ago I read a criticism of a novelette, in which the critic was furious because the author had written: 'He blew his nose and wiped it.' He said that it went against everything beautiful and exalted which literature should give the nation.

This is only a small illustration of what bloody fools are born under the sun.

Those who boggle at strong language are cowards, because it is real life which is shocking them, and weaklings like that are the very people who cause most harm to culture and character. They would like to see the nation grow up into a group of over-sensitive little people – masturbators of false culture of the type of St Aloysius, of whom it is said in the book of the monk Eustachius that when he heard a man breaking wind with deafening noise he immediately burst into tears and could only be consoled by prayers.

People like that proclaim their indignation in public but take unusual pleasure in going to public lavatories to read obscene inscriptions on the walls.

In using a few strong expressions in my book I have done nothing more than affirm *en passant* how people actually talk.

We cannot expect the inn-keeper Palivec to speak with the same refinement as Mrs Laudová, Doctor Guth, Mrs Olga Fastrová[1] and a whole series of others who would like to turn the whole Czechoslovak Republic into a big salon with parquet flooring, where people go about in tail-coats, white ties and gloves, speak in choice phrases and cultivate the refined behaviour of the drawing-room. But beneath this camouflage these drawing-room lions indulge in the worst vices and excesses.

I use this opportunity to draw your attention to the fact that Palivec is still alive. He survived the war, which he spent in gaol, and has remained just as he was when he had that spot of trouble with the portrait of the Emperor Franz Joseph.

He came to see me when he read that he was in the book, and he bought more than twenty copies of the first instalment and distributed them to his friends, thus contributing to its dissemination.

It gave him sincere pleasure that I wrote about him and described him as being renowned for his foul mouth.

'No one's likely to change me,' he said. 'I've always spoken all my whole life just as bawdily as I think, and I shall go on doing so. I'm not going to put a table napkin over my mug just for the sake of some cow or other. Today I'm famous.'

His self-confidence has indeed grown considerably. His fame rests on a number of strong expressions. This is enough to make him happy and if in reproducing his speech faithfully and accurately it had perhaps been my intention to warn him that he shouldn't talk like that (which of course it was not) I should certainly have insulted this good man.

In unrefined language he unconsciously expressed in a simple and honest way the detestation the ordinary Czech feels for Byzantine

1. People of Hašek's time who wrote on morals and behaviour.

methods. It was in his blood – this lack of respect for the Emperor and for polite phrases.

Otto Katz is also still alive. He is the real personification of the chaplain. When the monarchy collapsed he threw everything over, left the Church and today is manager in a bronze and dye factory in North Bohemia. He wrote me a long letter, in which he threatened to pay me out for what I'd done. A certain German newspaper published a translation of that chapter where he is described as he actually looked. And so I went to see him and it all went off very well. At two o'clock in the morning he could no longer stand on his legs but preached and said: 'I am Otto Katz, chaplain, you plaster-cast blockheads.'

Lots of people of the type of the late Bretschneider, who under old Austria was a member of the secret police, are still knocking about today in the Republic. They are extremely interested in what people are talking about.

I do not know whether I shall succeed in achieving my purpose with this book. The fact that I have already heard one man swear at another and say 'You're about as big an idiot as Švejk' does not prove that I have. But if the word 'Švejk' becomes a new choice specimen in the already florid garland of abuse I must be content with this enrichment of the Czech language.

                                                              JAROSLAV HAŠEK

Part II

AT THE FRONT

I

Švejk's Misadventures in the Train

IN a second-class compartment of the Prague-České Budějovice express there were three people: Lieutenant Lukáš, an elderly gentleman opposite with a completely bald pate, and Švejk, who stood modestly at the door to the corridor and was just braving himself to receive a new volley of oaths from Lieutenant Lukáš, who, disregarding the presence of the bald civilian, kept thundering at Švejk throughout the journey that he was the Almighty's choicest quadruped and so on.

It all concerned a mere trifle – the number of pieces of luggage which Švejk was supposed to be looking after.

'So they've stolen one of our cases, have they?' the lieutenant reproached Švejk. 'Anyone can say that, you bastard!'

'Humbly report, sir,' Švejk put in gently, 'they really did steal it. On the station there are always a lot of crooks like that knocking about and I imagine that one of them *undoubtedly* took a liking to your case. This chap *undoubtedly* took advantage of the moment when I slipped away from our luggage to tell you that everything was all right with it. He probably stole our case just at that favourable opportunity. They're always waiting for such an opportunity, you know. Two years ago at the North West station they robbed a young lady of a pram and a little girl in swaddling clothes and were so decent as to hand the little girl in at the police station in our street, saying that they had found her abandoned in the carriage entrance. Then the press tried to make out that the poor young lady was an unnatural mother.'

And Švejk underlined: 'At stations there always have been thefts and always will be. It can't be otherwise.'

'I'm convinced, Švejk,' the lieutenant put in, 'that one day you'll come to a really sticky end. I still don't know whether you're just pretending to be a mule or whether you were born one. What was in the suitcase?'

'Nothing in particular, sir, really,' answered Švejk, keeping his eyes fixed on the bald cranium of the civilian opposite, who appeared to take no interest whatsoever in the whole business and went on reading his *Neue Freie Presse*. 'In the whole suitcase there was only the mirror from the sitting-room and the iron clothes-rack from the hall, so we've really not suffered any loss at all, because the mirror and the clothes-rack both belonged to the landlord.'

Seeing the lieutenant's threatening gesture, Švejk continued in an amiable tone: 'Humbly report, sir, I really didn't know beforehand that the suitcase would be stolen, and as for the mirror and the clothes-rack I told the landlord that we would return them to him when we came home after the war. In enemy countries there are lots of mirrors and clothes-racks, so that even in this case neither the landlord nor us'll suffer any loss. As soon as we conquer a city . . .'

'Hold your tongue, Švejk!' the lieutenant interjected in an awe-inspiring voice: 'Some time I'm going to have you court-martialled. Think carefully whether you aren't the bloodiest fool and bastard in the whole world. In a thousand years no one else could make such a prize idiot of himself as you have done in these few weeks. I hope you've noticed that too?'

'Humbly report, I have, sir. I've got, as they say, a well-developed talent for observation when it's already too late and some unpleasant-ness has happened. I have the same sort of luck as a chap called Nechleba from Nekázanka, who went into the pub there called The Bitches' Grove. He always wanted to do good and start to lead a new life from Saturday onwards, but he always said the next day: "And in the small hours, chaps, I observed that I was lying on a plank-bed." And it always happened to him when he intended to go home respect-ably that in the end it turned out that he broke a fence somewhere, unharnessed some droshky driver's horse or wanted to clean his pipe with a cock's feather from the hat of a police patrol. He was quite desperate about it, and what worried him most of all was that this bad luck had been handed down from generation to generation. His grand-father once went out on his apprentice travels . . .'

'Oh, for God's sake, Švejk, don't pester me with your stories.'

'Humbly report, sir, everything I tell you is holy truth. His grand-father went out on his apprentice travels . . .'

'Švejk!' the lieutenant burst out in fury. 'Once more I order you not to tell me any more stories. I don't want to hear them. I'll deal with you when we get to Budějovice. Do you know, Švejk, that I'm going to have you gaoled?'

'Humbly report, sir, I don't know,' said Švejk gently. 'You haven't mentioned it yet.'

The lieutenant involuntarily ground his teeth, gave a deep sigh, took out from his coat a copy of *Bohemie* and read reports of the great victories and the activities in the Mediterranean of the German submarine 'E'. But when he got to the news of a new German invention for blowing up towns by special bombs dropped from aeroplanes which exploded three times in succession, he was roused by the voice of Švejk addressing himself to the bald-headed gentleman:

'Excuse me, your honour, don't you happen to be Mr Purkrábek, the representative of the Slavia Insurance Company?'

When the bald-headed gentleman did not reply, Švejk said to the lieutenant:

'Humbly report, sir, I once read in the newspapers that a normal man ought to have on his head an average of sixty to seventy thousand hairs and that dark-haired people have less, as can be seen from many examples.'

And he continued inexorably on: 'Once a medico in the café U Špírků said that loss of hair was caused by emotional excitement in childbed.'

And now something frightful happened. The bald-headed gentleman jumped up, roared at Švejk in German: 'Outside with you, you swine, you', kicked him out into the corridor and returned to the compartment, preparing a nice little surprise for the lieutenant by introducing himself to him.

There had been a little mistake. The bald-headed individual was not Mr Purkrábek of the Slavia Insurance Company, but only Major-General von Schwarzburg. The major-general, dressed in mufti, was just making a journey of inspection of the garrisons and was on his way to give Budějovice a surprise.

He was the most frightful inspecting general ever born, and if he found anything that was not in order he spoke with the garrison commander like this:

'Have you got a revolver?' 'Yes, I have.' 'Good! In your place I should certainly know what to do with it, because what I see here is not a garrison but a bloody piggery.'

And indeed after his inspections someone always shot himself somewhere or other, which induced Major-General von Schwarzburg to conclude with satisfaction: 'That's how it should be! That's a soldier for you!'

It seemed that he was not at all happy if anyone remained alive after his inspection. He had a mania for drafting an officer to the most unpleasant places. On the slightest provocation an officer would have to take leave of his garrison and make a pilgrimage to the Montenegrin frontier or to some drunken desperate garrison in a filthy corner of Galicia.

'Lieutenant,' he said, 'where were you at cadet school?'

'In Prague.'

'And so you've been to a cadet school and don't even know that an officer is responsible for his subordinate. That's a fine state of affairs. Next you talk with your servant as though he were your intimate friend. You allow him to speak without first being spoken to. That's still finer. Thirdly you allow him to insult your superiors. That's finest of all. As a result of all this I shall take the consequential measures. What's your name, lieutenant?'

'Lukáš.'

'And what regiment do you serve in?'

'I was ...'

'Thank you. We're not talking about where you were. I want to know where you are now.'

'In the 91st infantry regiment, sir. They transferred me ...'

'Transferred you? That was very sensible of them. It won't do you any harm to go as soon as possible with the 91st regiment and have a look at the front somewhere.'

'That's already been decided, sir.'

The major-general now gave a lecture on how he had observed in recent years that officers were in the habit of talking with their subordinates in a familiar tone, in which he saw the danger of a spread of democratic principles. A soldier must be kept in a state of terror; he must tremble in front of his superior; he must be in mortal dread of him. Officers must keep the men ten paces from their person and not allow them to think independently or even think at all. That had been the tragic mistake of recent years. In the old days the men feared their officers like fire and brimstone, but nowadays ...

The major-general waved his hand in a hopeless gesture: 'Nowadays most officers spoil their soldiers. That's what I wished to convey.'

The major-general took up his newspaper again and immersed himself in it once more. Lieutenant Lukáš turned deadly pale and went out into the corridor to settle accounts with Švejk.

He found him standing by the window with such a blissful and contented expression as could only grace a month-old baby which had drunk and sucked its fill and was now enjoying its bye-byes.

The lieutenant stopped, nodded to Švejk and showed him an empty compartment. He followed Švejk into it and closed the door.

'Švejk,' he said solemnly, 'the moment has finally come when you are going to get the most colossal swipe across the jaw the world has ever seen. Why on earth did you attack that bald-headed gentleman? Do you realize he is Major-General von Schwarzburg?'

'Humbly report, sir,' replied Švejk, assuming the expression of a martyr, 'I never in my life had the slightest intention of insulting anybody and I never had any idea or even dreamed of any major-general. He really is the spit and image of Mr Purkrábek, the representative of the Slavia Insurance Company. He used to come to our local pub and once when he fell asleep at the table some charitable person wrote in an indelible pencil on his bald head: "Allow us to propose to you our scheme for safeguarding your children's dowries and trousseaux by means of an insurance policy as per schedule 3c enclosed." Of course everybody went away, leaving me alone with him and, because I always have bad luck, when he woke up and looked at himself in the mirror he got furious and thought that it was me who had done it. He wanted to give me one across the jaw too.'

The little word 'too' dropped so touchingly, so gently and so reproachfully from Švejk's lips that the lieutenant's poised hand fell back into its place.

But Švejk continued: 'That gentleman ought not to have got so angry over a tiny little mistake like that. He really should have sixty to seventy thousand hairs, as it was stated in that article on what every normal man should have. It had never in my life occurred to me that there could exist a bald major-general. It's a tragic mistake, as they say, and it can happen to anybody when he makes a remark and the other party at once catches on to it. Years ago a tailor called Hývl told us how he travelled from the place where he was working in Steiermark to Prague via Leoben and had with him a ham which he had bought in Maribor. While he was travelling in the train he thought he was the only Czech among all the passengers, and when somewhere near St Moritz he started to slice up the ham, the gentleman sitting opposite him began to cast loving eyes on it and his mouth started to water. When the tailor noticed this he said aloud to himself: "You'd like to have a bite, wouldn't you, you old bastard?" And the gentleman replied in Czech: "Of course I would if you'd only let me." And so both of them together wolfed up the ham completely before they reached Budějovice. That gentleman's name was Vojtěch Rous.'

Lieutenant Lukáš gave Švejk a look and went out of the compartment. When he was sitting in his place again after a little time the honest face of Švejk appeared in the door.

'Humbly report, sir, we shall be in Tábor in five minutes' time. The train stops there for five minutes. Have you any orders for food? In the old days they used to have here some very good . . .'

The lieutenant jumped up in fury and said to Švejk in the corridor: 'Once more I must warn you that the less I see of you the more pleased I shall be. I'd be happiest of all if I never set eyes on you again, and you can be sure I'll see to that. Keep out of my sight altogether. Don't let me catch even a glimpse of you, you mule, you oaf, you half-wit.'

'Just as you order, sir.'

Švejk saluted, turned round and marched in military step to the end of the corridor, where he sat down in the corner in the guard's seat and started a conversation with a railwayman: 'May I ask you something, please?'

The railwayman, who obviously manifested no desire for conversation, gave a faint and uninterested nod.

'I used to see a lot of a good man called Hofmann,' Švejk went on expansively, 'and he always maintained that these alarm signals never work. In other words they don't function properly when you pull that handle. To tell you the truth I've never taken any interest in such things, but when I saw this alarm signal here I felt I'd like to know what the position is if by any chance I needed to use it at any time.'

Svejk stood up and walked with the railwayman towards the alarm brake: 'For use in emergency'.

The railwayman considered it his duty to explain to Švejk the working of the whole mechanism of the alarm signal: 'He was right when he told you that you have to pull it by this handle, but he was lying when he said that it doesn't work. It always brings the train to a halt, because it is connected with the engine through all the carriages. The alarm brake must function.'

Both of them had their hands on the handle at this moment and it is really a mystery how it happened that they pulled it and the train came to a halt.

They could neither of them agree on who had actually done it and given the alarm signal.

Švejk asserted that it couldn't be him, because he wasn't a hooligan. 'I'm very surprised myself that the train suddenly stopped,' he said

good-humouredly to the guard. 'It was going and then suddenly it stopped. It really annoys me more than it does you.'

A solemn gentleman came to the defence of the railwayman and asserted that he had heard that it was the soldier who first began the conversation about alarm signals.

As against that Švejk spoke continually of his honesty and how he had no interest in making the train late, because he was going to the front.

'The station master will explain that to you,' the guard decided. 'It will cost you twenty crowns.'

Meanwhile one could see passengers getting out of the carriages, the chief guard blowing his whistle and a lady running madly with her case across the line into the fields.

'It's really worth twenty crowns,' said Švejk with equanimity and perfect calm. 'And that's really very cheap. Once when His Imperial Majesty was on a visit to Žižkov, a chap called Franta Šnor stopped his carriage by kneeling before His Imperial Majesty in the middle of the road. Then the police commissioner of that district told Mr Šnor with tears in his eyes that he ought not to have done that to him in his district. He ought to have done it in a street lower down, which was in the district of Chief Commissioner Kraus. It was there that he should have made his obeisance. After that they put Mr Šnor in gaol.'

Švejk looked around just when the circle of listeners was swelled by the arrival of the chief guard.

'Well, let's go on now,' said Švejk. 'It's not at all nice when a train is late. If it were in peacetime, who the hell would care, but when there's a war on, everyone has to know that in every train there are military personalities – major-generals, lieutenants and batmen. Every single delay of this kind can be touch and go. Napoleon was five minutes late at Waterloo and after that he and all his glory went down the drain . . .'

At that moment Lieutenant Lukáš pushed through the group of listeners. He was ghastly pale and could utter nothing but: 'Švejk!'

Švejk saluted and said: 'Humbly report, sir, they're shoving the blame on to me for having stopped the train. The State Railways have very peculiar seals on their emergency brakes. A chap shouldn't really come anywhere near them, otherwise he might have an accident, and they might demand twenty crowns from him as they're now doing from me!'

The chief guard was already outside. He gave the signal and the train went off again.

The audience went back to their places in the compartments. Lieutenant Lukáš did not utter another word and went to sit down too.

There remained only the guard, Švejk and the railwayman. The guard took out a notebook and made a report of the whole incident. The railwayman looked spitefully at Švejk, who asked calmly: 'Have you been long with the railway?'

Because the railwayman did not answer, Švejk declared that he knew a certain Mlíčko František from Uhříněves near Prague. He too once pulled the alarm brake and was so frightened that for a whole fortnight he lost his power of speech and regained it only when he came to see a certain Vaněk, a gardener, at Hostivař. There he got into a brawl and they broke a knout across him. 'That happened in May 1912,' Švejk added.

The railwayman opened the door of the W.C. and locked himself inside.

The guard remained with Švejk and tried to get a twenty crowns' fine out of him, stressing that if he didn't pay it he'd have to take him to the station master at Tábor.

'All right,' said Švejk. 'I'm always glad to talk to educated people and it will be a great pleasure for me when I see that station master at Tábor.'

Švejk took a pipe out of his tunic, lit it and, emitting the pungent smoke of army tobacco, continued: 'Years ago the station master at Svitava was a Mr Wagner. He was a devil to his subordinates and gave them hell whenever he could, but the chap he was most down on was the points-man Jungwirt. Finally in despair the wretched man went and drowned himself in the river. But before doing so, he wrote a letter to the station master saying that he'd come and haunt him in the night. And to tell you the honest truth, that was exactly what he did. In the night the good station master was sitting at his telegraph receiver when the bell rang and he received the following telegram: "How are you, you old bastard? Jungwirt." This lasted a whole week and the station master began to send official telegrams across all the lines to answer the ghost: "Forgive me, Jungwirt." And in the night the receiver knocked out the following reply: "Go and hang yourself on the signals at the bridge. Jungwirt." And the station master obeyed. Afterwards they gaoled the telegraphist from the station before Svitava. You see, there are more things in heaven and earth than are dreamt of in our philosophy.'

The train went in to the station at Tábor and Švejk, before leaving the train in the company of the guard, reported to Lieutenant Lukáš as was proper: 'Humbly report, sir, they're taking me to the station master.'

Lieutenant Lukáš did not answer. He was overcome by general apathy to everything. It dawned on him that the best thing to do was not to give a damn for the whole business, either for Švejk or for the bald-headed major-general opposite. It would be better to sit still, get out of the train at Budějovice, report to the barracks and go to the front with a march company. At the front he could get himself killed if necessary and be quit of this miserable world, in which a hideous brute like Švejk was rampaging about.

When the train moved off Lieutenant Lukáš looked out of the window and saw Švejk standing on the platform, absorbed in a serious conversation with the station master. He was surrounded by a crowd of people in which could be seen several railway uniforms.

Lieutenant Lukáš sighed. It was not a sigh of compassion. It was a relief to him that Švejk had remained on the platform. Why, even that bald-headed major-general no longer seemed to him such a loathsome monster.

The train had long ago wheezed its way in the direction of České Budějovice but on the platform the number of people around Švejk did not grow any less.

Švejk spoke of his innocence and was so successful in convincing the crowd of it that a lady exclaimed: 'Another case of a poor soldier being harried.'

The crowd accepted this verdict and one gentleman announced to the station master that he would pay Švejk's twenty crowns' fine. He was convinced that the soldier had not done it.

'Just look at him,' he said, drawing his deduction from the very innocent expression on the face of Švejk, who, turning to the crowd, declared: 'Folks, I'm innocent.'

Then the gendarmerie sergeant appeared, took a citizen out of the crowd, arrested him and led him off with the words: 'You'll answer for this; I'll teach you to incite people! If you handle soldiers like this no one can expect of them that Austria'll win the war.'

The unfortunate citizen could do nothing else but aver frankly that he was a master butcher from the Old Gate and had no such intentions.

Meanwhile the good man who believed in Švejk's innocence paid the fine for him in the office and took him off to the third-class restaurant where he treated him to a glass of beer. Discovering that all his papers and his railway warrant were with Lieutenant Lukáš, he generously gave Švejk ten crowns for his ticket and further expenses.

When he went away he said to Švejk in confidence: 'All right, my good soldier, if, as I said, you're taken prisoner in Russia, give my regards to the brewer Zeman at Zdolbunov. You've got my name written down, haven't you? Only keep your wits about you and see you don't stay long at the front.'

'You needn't worry about that,' said Švejk. 'It's always interesting to see foreign parts free.'

Švejk remained sitting at the table and, while he quietly drank away the ten crowns given to him by the generous benefactor, people on the platform who had not been present at Švejk's interview with the station master and only saw the crowd from a distance were telling each other that a spy had just been caught there and had been photographing the station. But this was contradicted by a lady who declared that it wasn't a spy, but that she had heard how a dragoon had beaten up an officer by the ladies' lavatory, because he'd pursued there the dragoon's girlfriend who had come to see him off.

However, these adventurous speculations, which were characteristic of the wartime nerviness, were nipped in the bud by the gendarmerie who cleared the platform. And Švejk went on drinking quietly, thinking tenderly of his lieutenant. What would he do when he came to České Budějovice and could not find his batman anywhere in the train?

Before the arrival of the passenger train the third-class restaurant filled up with soldiers and civilians. They were predominantly soldiers of various regiments and formations and the most diverse nationalities whom the whirlwinds of war had swept into the Tábor hospitals. They were now going back to the front to get new wounds, mutilations and pains and to earn the reward of a simple wooden cross over their graves. Years after on the mournful plains of East Galicia a faded Austrian soldier's cap with a rusty Imperial badge would flutter over it in wind and rain. From time to time a miserable old carrion crow would perch on it, recalling fat feasts of bygone days when there used to be spread for him an unending table of human corpses and horse carcasses, when just under the cap on which he perched there lay the daintiest morsels of all – human eyes.

One of these candidates for suffering who had been released from a military hospital after an operation came and sat next to Švejk in a dirty uniform covered with traces of blood and mud. He was somehow shrivelled, skinny and miserable. He put on the table a small package, took out a shabby purse and counted his money. Then he looked at Švejk and asked him: '*Magyarúl?*'[1]

'I'm a Czech, old chap,' answered Švejk. 'Would you like a drink?'
'*Nem tudom, barátom.*'[2]

---

1. 'Do you speak Hungarian?'
2. 'I don't understand, my friend.'

'That doesn't matter, old boy,' Švejk said invitingly, putting his own full glass in front of the unhappy soldier. 'Just have a good drink.'

He understood, drank and thanked Švejk: '*Köszönöm szivesen.*'[1] Then he went on to examine the contents of his purse and finally gave a sigh. Švejk understood that the Hungarian would like to order a beer

but did not have enough money and so he ordered a glass for him, whereupon the Hungarian thanked him again and tried to explain something to him with the help of gestures. He pointed to his shot arm and said in international language: 'Pif, paf, poof!'

Švejk shook his head in sympathy and the crippled convalescent explained further to Švejk, by holding his left hand half a metre above the ground and then raising three fingers, that he had three little children.

'*Nincs ham, nincs ham,*' he continued, wishing to tell him that they had nothing to eat at home, and he wiped the tears from his eyes with the dirty sleeve of his military greatcoat, where there was a hole from a

1. 'Thank you very much.'

bullet which had penetrated his body – all for the sake of the King of Hungary.[1]

It was not surprising that in a conversation like that Švejk gradually parted with every one of those ten crowns and was slowly but surely cutting himself off from České Budějovice, losing the possibility of buying a railway ticket with every glass of beer which he stood himself and the Hungarian convalescent.

Another train to Budějovice passed through the station but Švejk went on sitting at the table and listening to the Hungarian repeating his: 'Pif, paf, poof! *Három gyermek nincs ham, éljen!*'[2]

He said the last words when Švejk clinked glasses with him.

'Just go on drinking, you Hungarian bastard,' replied Švejk. 'Soak yourself! You wouldn't treat us like this ...'

From the next table a soldier said that when they came to Szeged with the 28th regiment the Hungarians had pointed at them and put their hands up.[3]

This was the honest truth, but this soldier had obviously been insulted by it, although it was a common occurrence among all Czech soldiers and in the end the Hungarians did the same themselves, when they had got tired of brawling for the sake of the King of Hungary.

Then this soldier sat down next to Švejk and told how they had given the Hungarians a rough time in Szeged and beaten them out of several pubs. Saying this he gave full credit to the Hungarians for their ability to brawl and said that he had got a knife wound in the back, so that he had to be sent to the base to be cured.

But now when he returned the captain of his battalion would obviously put him in gaol, because he had not had time to pay the Hungarian back for the knife wound as was only fit and proper. The fellow should have got his due and the honour of the whole regiment have been preserved.

But Švejk was suddenly set upon by the commander of the army control, a sergeant-major, accompanied by four soldiers with bayonets, who began: '*Ihre Dokumenten*, your tokuments? I zees, you zits, not goes, zits, trinks, keep on trinks, zoldier!'

'Haven't got any documents, *miláčku*,'[4] answered Švejk. 'Lieu-

---

1. The Emperor Franz Joseph was also King of Hungary.
2. 'Three children, nothing to eat, here's how!'
3. A dig at the Czech troops for surrendering and deserting to the enemy.
4. Czech for 'sweetheart'.

tenant Lukáš, regiment number 91, took them with him and I stayed here on the station.'

'What does the word *milatschku* mean?' the sergeant-major said in German to one of his soldiers, an old Landwehr man, who seemed to do everything to spite him because he replied calmly in the same language:

'*Miláčku*? That's the same as "Mr Sergeant-Major".'

The sergeant-major went on talking to Švejk: 'Efrey soldat most haf tokuments. Vizout tokuments I lock him op at Bahnhofs-Militärkommando,[1] like a mad dog, ze lousy brute.'

They took Švejk to the station army headquarters where in the guardroom the men sat looking exactly like the old Landwehr man who had been able to find such an excellent translation in German for the word '*miláčku*' for the benefit of his born enemy, His Lordship, the sergeantmajor.

The guard-room was decorated with lithographs, which the Ministry

1. Army headquarters at the station.

of War had had distributed at that time to all offices which were visited by the troops as well as to schools and barracks.

The good soldier Švejk was welcomed by a picture which, according to the title, showed how Sergeant František Hammel and Corporals Paulhart and Bachmayer of the Imperial and Royal 21st Artillery Regiment encouraged the men to endurance. On the other side there hung a picture with the inscription: 'Sergeant Jan Danko of the 5th regiment of the Honvéd Hussars reconnoitring the position of an enemy battery.'

On the right side lower down hung the placard: '*Rare examples of valour.*'

With the aid of placards like this, in which the examples and texts were invented and written up by various conscripted German journalists, idiotic old Austria tried to inspire troops who never read them; and when these examples of valour were sent to them at the front bound in books, they rolled cigarettes out of them from pipe tobacco or disposed of them still more appropriately, so that their use could correspond to the value and spirit of the rare examples of valour which had been so glowingly written up.

While the sergeant-major went off to find an officer, Švejk read on a placard:

BRAVE DRIVER JOSEF BONG

The men of the Ambulance Corps transported the seriously wounded to carts prepared in a sheltered ravine. As soon as a cart was full they drove away with it to the first-aid post. When the Russians discovered these carts they began to shell them. The horse of driver Josef Bong of the Imperial and Royal 3rd Army Service Squadron was killed by shrapnel. Bong moaned: 'My poor Dobbin, it's all over with you!' At that very moment he was hit himself by a piece of shrapnel. In spite of this he unharnessed his horse and dragged the three-span cart back to safe shelter. After that he returned for the harness of his slaughtered horse. The Russians went on shooting. 'Just go on shooting, you blasted devils! I'm not going to leave the harness here!', and he went on unfastening the harness from the horse muttering these words. At last he finished and dragged himself back to the cart with the harness. Here he had to listen to a thundering rebuke from the ambulance men for his long absence. The brave soldier excused himself: 'I did not want to abandon the harness. It's practically new. It would have been a pity, I thought. We don't have too many of these things.' He then went to the first-aid post and only then reported himself wounded. His captain later decorated his breast with the silver medal for bravery.

When Švejk had finished reading this and the sergeant-major had not yet returned he said to the Landwehr men in the guard-room: 'That's a very fine example of valour. If we go on doing that we shall have nothing but new harness in the army. But when I was in Prague I read in the *Prague Official Gazette* of an even finer example – a one-year volunteer, Dr Josef Vojna. He was in Galicia in the 7th battalion of the Field Rifles, and when it came to a bayonet charge he got a bullet in his head. When they took him away to the first-aid post he shouted at them that he didn't need to be bandaged for a slash like that. And he wanted to advance again immediately with his company, but a shell cut off his ankle. Again they were going to carry him away, but he began to hobble towards the battle line with a stick and defended himself with it against the enemy. But a new shell came flying at him and tore off the arm in which he held the stick. And so he transferred the stick to his other arm and shouted out that he'd never forgive them that. God knows what might have happened to him if, after a short time, a piece of shrapnel hadn't finally murdered him. Perhaps if they hadn't finished him off he too might have got the silver medal for bravery. When his head had been blown off and it was rolling down it still went on shouting: "Never mind if death is near! Do your job and never fear!"'

'That's what they write in the newspapers,' said one of the men, 'but if the writer saw all this he'd be off his chump in an hour.'

The Landwehr man spat: 'In Čáslav, where I live, there was an editor from Vienna, a German. He was serving as an ensign. He refused to speak Czech with us, but when he was drafted to the march company, where there were nothing but Czechs, he was suddenly able to speak it.'

The sergeant-major appeared in the door, gave a furious look and fired off:

'If man go avay tree minute, zen of course he hear nozing but "Tschech, Tschechs".'

Going outside, obviously to the restaurant, he pointed at Švejk and told the corporal of the Landwehr to bring the lousy bastard at once before the lieutenant when he arrived.

'The lieutenant's fooling around again with the telegraph girl at the station,' said the corporal, after he had gone. 'He's been running after her for a fortnight and he's always frightfully furious when he comes from the telegraph office and he says about her: "She's a whore. She won't sleep with me!"'

And now he was obviously in just such a furious temper, because when shortly afterwards he came in he could be heard banging some books about on the table.

'Can't be helped, old man. You've got to go to him,' the corporal said to Švejk in sympathy. 'Lots of people have passed through his hands, old and young soldiers.'

And he led Švejk into the office, where behind a table on which there was a mess of papers a young lieutenant sat looking extremely furious.

When he saw Švejk and the corporal he said very promisingly: 'Ha!' Then followed the report of the corporal: 'Humbly report, sir, this man was found on the station without any documents.'

The lieutenant nodded, as though wishing to indicate that he had calculated years ago that on this very day and at this very hour Švejk would be found on the station without any documents, since anyone who looked at Švejk at this moment could not escape the impression that a man with such a face and figure as his could not possibly have any documents on him. At that moment Švejk looked as if he had fallen down from the sky from some other planet and he was now looking with naïve wonder at a new world where people were demanding from him idiotic nonsense which he had never heard of before, like documents.

The lieutenant looked at Švejk and reflected for a moment on what he should say to him and what questions he should put to him.

In the end he asked: 'And what were you doing at the station?'

'Humbly report, sir, I was waiting for the train to České Budějovice, so that I could rejoin my 91st regiment, where I am serving as batman to Lieutenant Lukáš. I had to leave him behind, when I was brought before the station master for a fine. I was under suspicion of having used the safety and emergency brake and stopped the express in which we were travelling.'

'You're driving me up the wall,' shouted the lieutenant. 'Speak connectedly and to the point and cut out all this drivel.'

'Humbly report, sir, we had bad luck from the very first moment that Lieutenant Lukáš and I got into that express, which was to take us away and convey us as quickly as possible to our 91st Imperial and Royal Infantry Regiment. First we lost a suitcase and then again, so as to get it quite straight, a major-general, who was completely bald . . .'

'Himmelherrgott,' sighed the lieutenant.

'Humbly report, sir, it's got to be shaken out of me like out of a hairy rug in order to get a proper view of all the events, if I'm permitted to quote the favourite words of the late lamented cobbler Petrlík, when he ordered his apprentice to take down his trousers before he started flogging him with a strap.'

And while the lieutenant snorted Švejk continued:

'Well, somehow or other I didn't find favour in the eyes of that bald-headed major-general and so I was sent out into the corridor by Lieutenant Lukáš, whose batman I am. And then in the corridor I was accused of doing what I've just told you. Before that matter could be settled I had to stay behind alone on the platform. The train had gone, the lieutenant and the suitcases and all my documents had gone too, and I was standing there gaping like an orphan without any documents.'

Švejk looked at the lieutenant with an expression of such moving tenderness that the latter was at once clear in his mind that it was the complete truth he was hearing from this bastard, who gave the impression of being a congenital idiot.

The lieutenant now recited to Švejk all the trains that had left for Budějovice after the express and asked him why he had missed all of them.

'Humbly report, sir,' answered Švejk, smiling affably, 'while I was waiting for the next train I suffered the misfortune that I sat down at a table and started drinking one glass of beer after another.'

'I've never seen such a bloody coot as this before,' the lieutenant thought to himself. 'He admits everything. When I think of all the people who I have had before me and who have all denied the charges, and this one calmly says: "I missed all the trains, because I drank one glass of beer after another." '

He put all these thoughts together in one sentence, and pronounced them to Švejk: 'You're degenerate, you bastard. Do you know what it means when you call somebody degenerate?'

'Humbly report, sir, at the corner of Na Bojišti and Kateřinská Street, where I live, there was once a degenerate. His father was a Polish count and his mother a midwife. He used to sweep the streets but in the bars he never allowed anyone to call him anything else than "My Lord".'

The lieutenant thought it proper to find a way of liquidating the case and so he said with emphasis: 'Let me tell you, you blasted fool, you bloody oaf, that you're going to the booking office and you'll buy a ticket and go to Budějovice. If ever I find you here again I'll deal with you as a deserter. Dismiss!'

Because Švejk failed to move but continued to stand with his hand at the peak of his cap the lieutenant shouted out in German: 'Clear

out! Don't you hear? Dismiss! Corporal Palánek, take this bloody half-wit to the booking office and buy him a ticket to České Budějovice!'

Corporal Palánek appeared a moment later in the office again. In the half-open door the good-natured face of Švejk peeped in behind Palánek.

'Well, what's the matter now?'

'Humbly report, sir,' Corporal Palánek whispered mysteriously, 'he hasn't any money for the ticket and I haven't either. They wouldn't take him free, because he hasn't got any military documents to show he's going to his regiment.'

The lieutenant did not hesitate to solve this difficult question with the judgement of Solomon.

'Then let him walk,' he decided. 'Let them gaol him at his regiment for coming late. Who on earth wants to be plagued with him here?'

'There's nothing to be done, old chap,' said Corporal Palánek to Švejk when they left the office. 'You must go to Budějovice on foot, old man. In the guard-room we've got an army loaf, and we'll give it you for the journey.'

And half an hour later, when they had treated Švejk to black coffee and given him a packet of army tobacco and an army loaf for his journey to the regiment, Švejk walked out of Tábor in the darkness of the night through which his singing resounded.

He was singing an old army song:

> 'When we marched to Jaroměř,
>   Believe it, if you like, or not . . .'

And God knows how it happened, but the good soldier Švejk instead of going south to Budějovice went on marching straight to the west.

He trudged through the snow along the road in the frost wrapped up in his military greatcoat, like the last of Napoleon's old guard returning from the Moscow campaign, with the only difference that he sang merrily to himself:

> 'I went out for a little stroll
> Into the green, green grove.'

And in the snowed-in forests in the stillness of the night the echo resounded until the dogs started to bark in all the villages.

When he got tired of singing, he sat down on a heap of gravel, lit his pipe and after a rest trudged on towards the new adventures of his Budějovice anabasis.

2

Švejk's Budějovice Anabasis

XENOPHON, that warrior of ancient times, travelled through the whole of Asia Minor and got to God knows where without any maps at all. And the Goths of old too made their expeditions without any knowledge of topography. Marching forward all the time is what is called an anabasis: penetrating into unknown regions: being cut off by enemies who are waiting for the first convenient opportunity to wring your neck. If anyone has a good brain, like Xenophon or all those thieving tribes who came to Europe from God knows where in the Caspian or Sea of Azov, he can work real wonders on a march.

Caesar's Roman legions penetrated somewhere to the north by the Gallic Sea and they had no maps either. Once they said they would march back to Rome again by another route so that they could get more out of it. And they got there too. And it is obviously from that time that people say that all roads lead to Rome.

And all roads lead to České Budějovice too. The good soldier Švejk was fully convinced of this when instead of the Budějovice region he saw villages in the Milevsko region.

All the same he went steadily forward, for no good soldier can allow a Milevsko to stop him from getting to České Budějovice.

And so Švejk turned up west of Milevsko at Květov, after having rung all the changes in the repertoire of army songs which he knew from his various marches, and so just before Květov he was compelled to start again with the song:

> 'When we marched away,
> All the girls began to cry . . .'

An old woman who was returning from church on the way from Květov to Vráž, which was still in a westerly direction, hailed Švejk with the Christian greeting: 'Good morning, soldier, where are you bound for?'

'I'm going to my regiment at Budějovice, mother,' answered Švejk, 'to the war.'

'Then you're going wrong, soldier,' said the old woman in a scared voice. 'You'll never get there this way through Vráž. If you go straight on you'll get to Klatovy.'

'I believe that a man can get to Budějovice even from Klatovy,' said Švejk resignedly. 'It's certainly a tidy walk, if a chap's hurrying to get to his regiment to avoid any trouble through not being punctual at his destination for all his goodwill.'

'We've already had a chap like you here. He had to go to Pilsen to the Landwehr. He was called Toníček Mašků,' the old woman said with a sigh. 'He was a relation of my niece and he went away. And a week later the gendarmerie were looking for him, because he hadn't reported to his regiment. After another week he turned up here in mufti saying he had been allowed home on leave. But the mayor went to the gendarmerie and they pulled him out of that "leave". Now he's written from the front that he's wounded and that he's lost a leg.'

The old woman looked pityingly at Švejk: 'You can wait in that spinney there, soldier. I'll bring you some of our potatoes. They'll warm you up a bit. You can see our cottage from here. It's just to the right behind the spinney. You mustn't go through our village of Vráž. The gendarmes there are like hawks. You can go afterwards from the spinney towards Malčín. But after that, soldier, avoid Čížová. The gendarmerie there would flay you and they always catch dissenters. Go straight through the wood to Sedlec by Horažd'ovice. There's a very good gendarme there who lets everybody through the village. Have you got any papers on you?'

'I haven't, mother!'

'Then don't go there. It's better you go to Radomyšl, but see that you get there by evening. Then all the gendarmes are in the pub. And there in the Lower Street behind St Florian you'll find a house painted blue below and you can ask for Farmer Melichárek. That's my brother. You can give him my love and he'll show you how to get to Budějovice from there.'

For over half an hour Švejk waited in the spinney for the old woman. When he had warmed himself with the potato soup which she had brought him in a pot covered with a pillow so as not to get cold, she took out of her kerchief a hunk of bread and a piece of bacon, stuck all of it into Švejk's pocket, made the sign of the cross on him and said that she had two grandsons in the army.

Then she repeated to him in detail through which villages he had to go and which he had to avoid. Finally she took a crown out of the pocket of her coat so that in Malčín he could buy some spirit for his journey, because Radomyšl was very far away.

Following the instructions of the old woman Švejk walked from Čížová towards Radomyšl to the east and thought to himself that he could not help getting to Budějovice from any point of the compass.

From Malčín he was accompanied by an old accordion player, whom he had found in a pub when he bought the spirit for that long journey to Radomyšl.

The accordion player took Švejk for a deserter and advised him to go with him to Horažd'ovice, where he had a married daughter whose husband was a deserter too. The accordion player had obviously had a drop too much in Malčín.

'She has been keeping her husband hidden in a stable for two months already,' he confided to Švejk, 'so she can hide you too and you'll be able to stay there until the end of the war. And if there are two of you it'll be jollier.'

When Švejk politely declined this invitation the accordion player suddenly got very angry and went off to the left over the fields, threatening Švejk that he would denounce him to the gendarmerie in Čížová.

Towards evening in Radomyšl in the Lower Street behind St Florian Švejk found Farmer Melichárek. When he conveyed greetings from his sister in Vráž it did not have any effect on the farmer.

He insisted repeatedly on seeing Švejk's papers. He was rather a prejudiced person, talking all the time about robbers, vagabonds and thieves, masses of whom were infesting the whole district of Písek.

'They run away from the army, they don't want to serve in it and then they roam about the whole district and steal,' he said with emphasis to Švejk, looking him straight in the eyes. 'And they all look as innocent as lambs.

'Yes, of course, people always get worked up when it's a question of telling the truth,' he added, when Švejk got up from the bench. 'If a chap has a clean conscience, he sits still and lets his papers be examined. But if he hasn't got any . . .'

'Well, goodbye to you, grandfather.'

'And goodbye to you too, and next time try and catch someone who isn't quite as sharp as me.'

When Švejk went off into the darkness, the old man still went on grumbling for quite a time: 'He says he's going to Budějovice to join his regiment. From Tábor. And the rascal goes first to Horažďovice and only then to Písek. Why, he's making a trip round the world.'

Švejk went on walking almost the whole night until somewhere near Putim he found a haystack in a field. As he was scratching the straw apart he heard a voice quite near him saying: 'What's your regiment? Where are you off to?'

'The 91st. I'm going to Budějovice.'

'Why should you be going there?'

'I've got my lieutenant there.'

He could hear close to him not just one person laughing but three. When the laughter died down Švejk asked what regiment they belonged to. He discovered that two of them were from the 35th and one from the artillery, also from Budějovice.

A month ago the 35th had deserted just before they should have marched to the front, and the artilleryman had been on the tramp from the day he was called up. He was from here at Putim and the haystack belonged to him. At night he always slept in the haystack. The day before he had found the other two in the wood and had taken them with him to his rick.

All cherished the hope that the war must be over in a month or two. They imagined that the Russians were already beyond Budapest and in Moravia. This was what people were saying everywhere in Putim. In the morning before dawn the dragoon's wife would bring them breakfast. After that the men of the 35th would go on to Strakonice, because one of them had an aunt there, and she again had a friend in the mountains beyond Sušice. He had a saw mill and they would find good shelter there.

'And you of the 91st can go with us too, if you like,' they offered
Švejk. 'Shit on your lieutenant!'

'That won't be so easy,' answered Švejk and he squeezed and crawled
deeper into the haystack.

When he woke up next morning they were all of them gone and one
of them, obviously the dragoon, had placed at his feet a slice of bread
for the journey.

Švejk walked through the forests and near Štěkno he met a tramp,
an old gaffer, who welcomed him like an old friend with a nip of
brandy.

'Don't walk about in that,' he told Švejk. 'That army uniform of
yours could cost you hell. Now it's full of gendarmes everywhere and
there's no chance of doing any begging in those clothes. Today, of
course, it's not us the gendarmes chase like they did before. Now it's
only you they're after.

'It's only you they're after,' he repeated in a tone of such conviction
that Švejk thought it wiser not to tell him anything about the 91st
regiment. Let him take him for what he thought him to be. Why
destroy the good old fellow's illusions?

'And where are you bound for?' the tramp asked after a while, when
they had both lit their pipes and were slowly walking round the
village.

'To Budějovice.'

'For the love of Christ!' the tramp said in horror. 'They'll round
you up there in a jiffy, before you can say Jack Robinson. You must
wear mufti and be in rags. You must hobble about like a cripple.

'But don't be afraid. Now we'll go to Strakonice, Volyň, and Dub,
and it'll be hellishly bad luck if we don't scrounge some mufti there. In
Strakonice the people are still so idiotically honest that they often leave
their doors open for you at night and in the daytime they don't lock
them at all. In winter when they go off and have a chat with a neighbour you can pick up some mufti straight away. What do you need?
You have boots, so all you want is something to put over you. Is your
army greatcoat old?'

'Yes, it is.'

'Well, keep it. People go about in that in the country. You need
trousers and a jacket. When we get that mufti we'll sell your army
trousers and tunic to the Jew Herrman at Vodňany. He buys everything that's army and sells it again in the villages.

'Today we'll go to Strakonice,' he unfolded his plan further. 'Four hours from here is the old Schwarzenberg sheep-fold. The shepherd there is a friend of mine. He's an old gaffer too. And so we'll stay the night there and in the morning we'll move on to Strakonice to see if we can't scrounge some mufti somewhere in the neighbourhood.'

In the sheep-fold Švejk found the nice old gaffer, who remembered how his grandfather used to tell him stories about the French wars. He was about twenty years older than the old tramp and called him 'lad' just as he did Švejk.

'Well, you see, lads,' he explained, when they sat round the stove, on which potatoes were boiling in their jackets, 'at that time my grandfather dissented too just like your soldier here is doing. But they caught him in Vodňany and flogged his arse so much that strips flew off it. But he had luck after all. Jareš's son, the grandfather of old Jareš, the water bailiff from Ražice near Protivín, got some powder and lead in him at Písek for desertion. And before they shot him on the ramparts at Písek he ran the gauntlet of the soldiers in the street and got six hundred blows with sticks, so that when death came it was a relief and redemption for him. But when did you run away?' he turned to Švejk with tearful eyes.

'After call-up, when they took us away to the barracks,' answered Švejk, realizing that a soldier must not shatter the illusions of the old shepherd.

'Did you climb over the wall?' the shepherd asked curiously, obviously recalling how his grandfather used to tell of how he too climbed over the barrack wall.

'There was no other way, granddad.'

'And the guard was strong and they shot at you?'

'Yes, they did, granddad.'

'And where are you off to now?'

'He's off his head,' the tramp answered in place of Švejk. 'He insists on going to Budějovice. You know, he's a foolish young puppy and goes to his ruin. I must give him a few lessons. We'll try and scrounge some mufti for him and then everything'll be all right. We'll manage somehow until the spring and after that we'll go and take work with a farmer. This year there'll be a great shortage of labour, there'll be famine and they say all tramps will be rounded up and put on to farm work. And so I think it's better to go of your own accord. There won't be many farm workers. They'll all be wiped out.'

'You think that it won't be over this year?' asked the shepherd. 'Well, of course you're right, lad! There have been long wars in the past. There was the Napoleonic war and then the Swedish wars and the Seven Years' War, as they used to tell us. And people deserved these wars. The good Lord couldn't stand it any longer; people were getting so uppish, you see. They didn't even want to have mutton under their whiskers, they wouldn't even swallow that, lads. In the old days they used to come queuing up here in the hope I'd sell them some mutton under the counter, but in recent years they've guzzled nothing but pork and poultry, all soaked in butter or lard. And so the good Lord got angry with them because of their pride, but they won't come to their senses again until they're cooking goosefoot like they did in the Napoleonic wars. Our lords and masters too didn't know what to do, they were so debauched. The old Prince Schwarzenberg drove about in an ordinary carriage but the young prince, that greenhorn, does nothing but stink around in a motor-car. The good Lord will rub his nose in petrol one of these fine days.'

The water in which the potatoes were cooking on the stove began to bubble and after a short silence the old shepherd said in prophetic tones: 'And His Imperial Majesty won't win this war. There's no enthusiasm for it at all, because, as our schoolmaster in Strakonice says, he wouldn't have himself crowned. Now he can talk as much soft soap as he likes. When you promised you'd be crowned you should have kept your word, you old bastard!'

'Perhaps he'll manage to do it now,' said the tramp.

'Nobody cares a hell any more about it now, lad,' the shepherd said irritably. 'You ought to be there when the neighbours get together down in Skočice. Everyone has a friend at the front and you should hear how they talk. After this war they say there'll be freedom and there won't be any noblemen's palaces or emperors, and the princes'll have their estates all taken away. The gendarmes already took off a chap called Kořínek because of talk like that. They said it was seditious. Yes, today it's gendarmerie law.'

'But so it was before,' replied the tramp. 'I remember how in Kladno there used to be a captain of the gendarmerie called Rotter. One fine day he began to breed those, what do you call them, police dogs, which are like wolves and follow everything when they're trained. And that captain at Kladno had his arse full with all those trainee dogs. He had a special little house for them, where they lived like lords. And one day he had the idea of experimenting with them on us poor tramps. So he gave orders that the gendarmerie in the whole Kladno district should round up the tramps, every man jack of them, and hand them all over to him. And once I was tramping from Lány and kept deep in the woods so that only a glimmer of me could be seen, but it was no good. I didn't get to the gamekeeper's lodge I was making for before they caught me and took me to the captain. And, chaps, you couldn't think or imagine what I had to go through with that captain and his dogs. First of all he made them all smell me, and then I had to climb up a ladder. And when I was on the top he set one of his monsters after me and the bloody brute pulled me down from the ladder on to the ground and kneeled on me, growling and snarling in my face. Then they took the brute away and told me to hide somewhere – anywhere I liked. I went into the woods towards the valley of Kačák, down into a ravine, and half an hour later two of those wolfhounds caught up with me, knocked me over and, while one of them held me by the throat, the other ran off to Kladno. An hour later Captain Rotter himself came with his gendarmes, shouted at the dogs, gave me five crowns and permission to beg in the Kladno region for two whole days. But did I do it? You bet! I rushed off like a madman towards the Beroun district and didn't show myself any more near Kladno. All the tramps avoided it because that captain made his experiments on all of them. He was frightfully fond of those dogs. At the gendarmerie stations they used to say that when he came on an inspection and saw a wolfhound anywhere he didn't make any inspection at all but spent the whole day happily drinking with the sergeant.'

And while the shepherd sieved the potatoes and poured into the dish sour sheep's milk the tramp continued to impart his memories of gendarmerie justice: 'In Lipnice there was a gendarmerie sergeant down underneath the castle. He lived in the gendarmerie station itself and I, being a simple old chap, was always under the impression that a gendarmerie station must be in some prominent place like in the square or somewhere like that and certainly not somewhere in a side street. And so I kept to the side streets of that little country town and didn't look at the street signs. I took one house after the other until I got to the first floor of an ordinary cottage, opened the door and announced, "Have pity on a poor tramp." Good Lord, chaps, I could have dropped through the floor. It was the gendarmerie station. There were rifles along the wall, a crucifix on the table, a register on the chest and His

Imperial Majesty looked down at me directly over the table. And before I could stammer anything, the sergeant jumped at me and gave me such a blow on the jaw at the door that I flew out down those wooden stairs to the very bottom and only stopped when I got to Kejžlice. That's gendarmerie law.'

They started to eat and soon went to sleep stretched out on the benches in the warm sitting-room.

In the night Švejk quietly dressed and went out. The moon was just rising in the east and in its waking light Švejk marched to the east, repeating: 'It's not possible for me not to get to Budějovice.'

And because when Švejk came out of the woods he saw on the right a town, he took a more northerly course and then turned to the south, where again there could be seen a town of some kind. (It was Vodňany.) And so he moved away in the opposite direction over the meadows and the early sun welcomed him on the snow-covered slopes above Protivín.

'Forward the brave!' said the good soldier Švejk to himself. 'Duty calls. I must get to Budějovice.'

But by an unfortunate chance instead of going from Protivín south to Budějovice Švejk directed his steps to the north towards Písek.

About noon Švejk saw a village in front of him. Coming down from a small hill he thought: 'It's no good going on like this. I'll ask how I can get to Budějovice.'

And going into the village he was very surprised when he saw its name marked on a post by the first house: 'Putim'.

'Jesus Christ,' sighed Švejk. 'Here I am back in Putim where I slept in the haystack.'

And so he was not the slightest bit surprised when he saw behind the little lake a white-washed house on which a 'chicken' was hanging (the name given in some places to the Austrian 'eaglet') and a gendarme walking out of it like a spider guarding its web.

The gendarme went straight up to Švejk and said nothing except, 'Where are you off to?'

'To my regiment at Budějovice.'

The gendarme smiled sarcastically: 'But you're going away from Budějovice. Your Budějovice is far behind you,' and he took Švejk into the gendarmerie station.

The sergeant of the Putim gendarmerie was renowned throughout the whole district for his very tactful and shrewd way of conducting business. He never swore at those he detained or arrested, but subjected them to such a searching cross-examination that even an innocent man could do nothing but confess.

Two gendarmes at the station assisted him and the cross-examination

was always accompanied by the grins of the whole staff of the gendarmerie.

'The secret of criminal investigation lies in shrewdness and good manners,' the sergeant always said to his subordinates. 'Bellowing at anybody doesn't help. You must always be gentle with delinquents and suspects, but at the same time ensure that they are drowned in a flood of questions.'

'Welcome here, soldier,' said the sergeant. 'Sit down and make yourself at home. Anyway, you must be tired after your journey. Tell us where you're going.'

Švejk repeated that he was going to České Budějovice to join his regiment.

'Then of course you've taken the wrong turning,' said the sergeant with a smile, 'because you're now going away from České Budějovice, as I can easily convince you. Over your head there's a map of Bohemia. Have a look at it, soldier. To the south of us is Protivín. South of Protivín is Hluboká and south of that is České Budějovice. And so you see you're not going *to* Budějovice but *away from* it.'

The sergeant looked affably at Švejk, who said with composure and dignity: 'But I'm going to Budějovice all the same.' This was more effective even than Galileo's famous statement, 'But it goes round all the same!', because Galileo must certainly have been furious when he said it.

'You know, soldier,' the sergeant said to Švejk with the same affability, 'I shall disabuse you of that idea, and you yourself will come to share my opinion that every denial only makes a confession more difficult!'

'You're absolutely right,' said Švejk. 'Every denial makes a confession more difficult and vice versa.'

'And so you see, soldier, that you're coming to that conclusion of your own accord. Answer me frankly where you were coming from when you set out for this Budějovice of yours. I say intentionally "of yours", because there must obviously be another Budějovice which lies somewhere to the north of Putim and hasn't yet been recorded on any map!'

'I came from Tábor.'

'And what were you doing in Tábor?'

'I was waiting for a train to Budějovice.'

'And why didn't you take that train to Budějovice?'

'Because I didn't have a ticket.'

'But you were a soldier. Why didn't they give you as a soldier a free railway warrant.'

'Because I didn't have any documents on me.'

'Ah, there we have it,' said the sergeant triumphantly to one of his men. 'He's not nearly as stupid as he pretends to be. He's beginning to shoot a good line.'

The sergeant began again, as though he had not heard the last reply about the documents:

'And so you left Tábor. Where did you go then?'

'To České Budějovice.'

The sergeant's face assumed an expression of some severity and his gaze fell on the map.

'Can you show us on the map by what route you went to Budějovice?'

'I can't remember all the places. All I can remember is that I've already been in Putim once.'

All the staff of the gendarmerie station looked at each other inquiringly and the sergeant continued: 'And so in Tábor you were on the railway station. Have you got anything on you? Take it out.'

When they had made a thorough search of Švejk's person and found nothing except a pipe and some matches, the sergeant asked Švejk: 'Tell me, why do you have absolutely nothing on you?'

'Because I don't need anything.'

'Oh, my God,' sighed the sergeant, 'you really are a martyrdom. You said that you've already been in Putim once. What did you do here then?'

'I walked past Putim to Budějovice.'

'Now see how tied up you're getting. You yourself said that you were going to Budějovice and now we've convinced you that you were coming away from it.'

'I suppose I must have gone round in a circle.'

The sergeant again exchanged a knowing glance with the whole personnel of the station. 'A fine circle, that circle of yours! I think that you must be just loafing about the district. Did you stay long on the station at Tábor?'

'I stayed until the last train left for Budějovice.'

'And what did you do there?'

'I talked to the soldiers.'

Another very knowing look from the sergeant to the staff.

'And what did you talk about, for instance, and what did you ask them about?'

'I asked them their regiment and where they were going.'

'Excellent. And you didn't happen to ask them for example how many men there would be in a regiment and how they were distributed?'

'No, I didn't ask that because I knew it by heart ages ago.'

'And so you're perfectly informed about the composition of our army?'

'Of course, sergeant.'

And the sergeant now played his last trump, looking around triumphantly at his gendarmes:

'Do you speak Russian?'

'No, I don't.'

The sergeant nodded to the lance-corporal and when both of them had gone out into the next room he rubbed his hands with the enthusiasm of complete victory and certainty and said: 'Did you hear that? He doesn't speak Russian! He's a cunning one! He's confessed everything except the most important thing. Tomorrow we shall send him to the district officer in Písek. Criminology depends on shrewdness and good manners. You saw how I drowned him in a flood of questions. Who would have thought that of him? He looks so stupid and idiotic, but it's just with people of his kind that you need to have all your wits about you. Now lock him up somewhere and I'll go and write a report about it.'

And that very afternoon towards evening the gendarmerie sergeant, smiling sweetly, drew up a report in every sentence of which occurred in German: 'Under suspicion of espionage.'

When Sergeant Flanderka had spent a little time writing his odd official German the situation became gradually clearer to him, and when he ended with the words: 'And so I beg humble leave to report that the enemy officer will today be sent to Gendarmerie District Command in Písek,' he smiled over his work and called to the lance-corporal: 'Have you given the enemy officer anything to eat?'

'By your orders, sergeant, we serve food only to those who are brought in and interrogated before twelve o'clock.'

'This is a great exception,' said the sergeant solemnly. 'This is a high-ranking officer, someone from their general staff. You know, the Russians would never send here a mere corporal as a spy. Send to The Old Tom Cat for some lunch for him. If they haven't got anything left they'd better cook something specially. After that let them make tea with rum and send everything here. Don't say who it's for. Don't mention to anybody at all who we've got here. It's a military secret. What is he doing now?'

'He asked for a little tobacco. He's sitting in the guard-room and behaving as contentedly as if he were at home. "It's very cosy and warm in here," he said, "and your stove doesn't smoke. I like being here with you very much. But if the stove should smoke, have the chimney swept. But only in the afternoon and never when the sun's right over it."'

'That's very cunning of him,' said the sergeant, his voice full of enthusiasm. 'He acts as though it didn't concern him. And yet he knows that he'll be shot. We must respect a man like that, even if he is our enemy. A man like that goes to certain death. I don't know whether we would be capable of it in his place. We might perhaps waver or give in, but he sits there calmly and says: "It's very cosy and warm in here and your stove doesn't smoke." That's character, lance-corporal. For that you need iron nerves, self-denial, firmness and enthusiasm. . . . If there were enthusiasm like that in Austria . . . but don't let's talk about that. After all, even we have our enthusiasts. Did you read in *Národní Politika* of that Lieutenant Berger of the artillery who climbed up on a high fir tree and set up an observation post on its branches? When our men retreated he couldn't climb down any more, otherwise he would have been taken prisoner. And so he waited there until our troops drove the enemy out again and it took fourteen days. He was fourteen whole days on top of that tree and so as not to die of hunger he gnawed away the whole crown of the tree and fed himself on little shoots and needles. And when our men arrived he had grown so weak that he couldn't keep himself up on the top any longer and fell down and killed himself. He was posthumously decorated with the Golden Cross of Merit for valour.'

And the sergeant added solemnly: 'That was a sacrifice, lance-corporal, that was heroism! Now see how we've got lost in talking again. Run and order that lunch and meanwhile send the man to me.'

The lance-corporal brought in Švejk and the sergeant motioned him in a friendly way to sit down. Then he started to ask him first of all whether he had any parents.

'No. I haven't.'

It occurred to the sergeant immediately that it was better so, because at least there would be nobody to mourn the unfortunate man. He looked at the good-natured face of Švejk and in a fit of good humour suddenly patted him on the back, leant towards him and asked him in a fatherly tone:

'Well, and how do you like being in Bohemia?'

'I like it everywhere in Bohemia,' answered Švejk. 'On my journey I found very good people everywhere.'

The sergeant nodded his head in agreement: 'Our people are very good and well behaved. A theft or a brawl here or there doesn't affect the overall picture. I've been here already fifteen years and if I reckon up I can say that every year there's only about three quarters of a murder.'

'You mean an uncompleted murder?' asked Švejk.

'No, I don't mean that. In the course of fifteen years we've investigated only eleven murders. Of those five were murders with robbery and the remaining six were just the ordinary kind which are of no importance.'

The sergeant was silent and returned to his interrogation method: 'What did you want to do in Budějovice?'

'Take up my duty in the 91st regiment.'

The sergeant ordered Švejk back to the guard-room and then quickly, so that he should not forget, he added the following entry to his report to the district gendarmerie commander in Písek: 'Having a complete mastery of Czech, he planned to enrol in the 91st infantry regiment in České Budějovice.'

The sergeant rubbed his hands joyfully, delighting in the wealth of collected material and the accurate results of his method of investigation. He recalled his predecessor, Sergeant Bürger, who never spoke with a detainee at all, never asked him anything, but sent him at once to the district court with a short report: 'According to the information of the lance-corporal this man has been detained as a vagabond and beggar.' Was that an investigation?

And the sergeant, looking at the pages of his report, smiled with satisfaction and took out of his writing desk a secret instruction of the gendarmerie headquarters in Prague stamped as usual: '*Strictly confidential!*' and read it over to himself again:

All gendarmerie stations are strictly enjoined to keep exceptionally careful watch on all persons passing through their district. As a result of the movement of our troops in Eastern Galicia some Russian units have crossed the Carpathians and taken up positions within the confines of our Empire, as a consequence of which the front has been pushed deeper to the west of the Monarchy. Thanks to this new situation and to the fluidity of the front, Russian spies have been able to penetrate deeper into the territory of our Monarchy, above all in Silesia and Moravia, from where, according to confidential information, a large number of Russian intelligence agents have found their way into Bohemia. It has been ascertained that among them are many Russian Czechs educated in the higher military staff schools of Russia. They speak perfect Czech and appear to be especially dangerous intelligence agents, because they can and do disseminate treasonable propaganda among the Czech population. The regional High Command therefore orders that all suspicious elements should be detained and that vigilance must be increased particularly in those places which have in their vicinity garrisons, military centres and stations through which army trains pass. Those detained must be subject to an immediate examination and passed on to a higher authority.

Sergeant Flanderka again smiled with a satisfied smile and put the secret instruction away with other documents into the file with the inscription: '*Secret Orders*'.

There were many of them, which the Ministry of the Interior drew up with the collaboration of the Ministry of Regional Defence, to which the gendarmerie was subordinated.

The regional headquarters of the gendarmerie in Prague could not cope with their duplication and distribution.

There were:

Orders for the control of the attitude of the local population.

Directives on how to converse with the local inhabitants and elicit from them what influence the news from the front had on their attitude.

A questionnaire on how the local population reacted to the war loans which had been issued and the collections which had been instituted.

A questionnaire on the morale of those called up and those who were to be called up.

A questionnaire on the morale of the members of the local government and the intelligentsia.

An order for the immediate supply of information about the political party affiliations of the local population and the strength of the various political parties.

An order for the control of the activity of the leaders of the local political parties and information on the degree of loyalty of certain political parties represented in the local population.

A questionnaire on what newspapers, journals and brochures came to the district of the gendarmerie station.

Instructions on how to obtain information on the contacts of people suspected of disloyalty and what their disloyalty consisted in.

Instructions on how to recruit paid denouncers and informers among the local population.

Instructions for paid informers from the local population who were officially registered at the gendarmerie station.

Every day brought new instructions, directives, questionnaires and orders.

Swamped with this flood of inventions emanating from the Austrian Ministry of the Interior, Sergeant Flanderka had amassed an enormous backlog of unprocessed papers and answered the questionnaires in a stereotyped way: everything was in perfect order here and the loyalty of the local population could be graded I.a.

The Austrian Ministry of the Interior invented the following grades for unshakeable loyalty to the monarchy: I.a, I.b, I.c; II.a, II.b, II.c; III.a, III.b, III.c; IV.a, IV.b, IV.c. The last fours in Roman figures meant, in conjunction with 'a', treason and the gallows, with 'b', internment, with 'c', 'keep under observation and behind bars'.

In the sergeant's desk were all sorts of printed papers and lists. The government wanted to know what every citizen thought about it.

Sergeant Flanderka would often wring his hands in desperation over these printed circulars which grew inexorably with every post. As soon as he saw the familiar envelopes with the stamps, 'Official – Postage free', his heart always began to thump and at night, pondering over it all, he came to the conviction that he would not live to see the end of the war; the regional command of the gendarmerie would deprive him of his last remnant of reason and he would not be able to enjoy

the victory of the Austrian arms, since by then he would certainly be completely off his nut. And the district command bombarded him daily with questions as to why questionnaire no. $\frac{72345}{721\,af}$ d had not been answered, what action had been taken on instruction no. $\frac{88\,992}{822gfeh}$ z, and what were the practical results of directive no. $\frac{123456}{1922bir}$ V etc.

He had the greatest trouble over the instructions on how to recruit paid denouncers and informers from the local population. Finally, as he considered it impossible to find anyone in the region of Blata, where the people had very thick skulls, he hit on the idea of taking into his service the village herdsman. He was a village idiot who always jumped in the air when people called out to him: 'Pepek, ups-a-daisy!' He was one of those unfortunate figures whom nature and humanity have neglected, a cripple, who for a few guilders yearly and a little food pastured the village cattle.

And so the sergeant had him fetched and said to him: 'Do you know, Pepek, who old Procházka is?'

'Meaeaea,' Pepek bleated.

'Don't bleat but remember that this is how they call His Imperial Majesty. You know who His Imperial Majesty is?'

'That's Sperial Madesty.'

'Well done, Pepek! Now remember that when you go begging for food from house to house, if you should hear anybody say that His Imperial Majesty is an ox or something like that, then come and inform me at once. You'll get six kreutzers. And if you hear anyone say that we shan't win the war, then you must come to me, you understand, and tell me who said it. Then I'll give you another six kreutzers. But if I hear you're concealing something from me, then it'll be all up with you. I'll have you arrested and sent off to Písek. And, now, ups-a-daisy!' When Pepek had jumped, he gave him twelve kreutzers and happily wrote a report to the district gendarmerie command saying that he had recruited an informer.

The next day the vicar came to him and told him in secret that that very morning outside the village he had met the village herdsman, Pepek Vyskoč, who had told him: 'Your reverence, the sergeant told me yesterday that His Sperial Madesty is an ox and that we shan't win the war. Meaeaea. Ups-a-daisy!'

After further explanation and discussion with the priest Sergeant Flanderka had the village herdsman arrested. Afterwards Pepek was condemned at the Hradčany to twelve years' imprisonment for treasonable subversion, incitement, lese-majesty and several other crimes and offences.

He conducted himself in court as he did on the pastures or among his neighbours. In reply to all questions he bleated like a goat and after the sentence had been pronounced he uttered the sounds: 'Meaeaea. Ups-a-daisy!' and jumped. For this he was given the disciplinary punishment of a hard bunk, solitary confinement and three days' fast.

From that time onwards the gendarmerie sergeant had no informer and had to content himself with inventing one, giving him a fictitious name and raising his own salary by fifty crowns a month, which he spent on drink in The Old Tom Cat. When he had drunk his tenth glass he had a fit of conscience, the beer grew bitter in his mouth and he always heard from his neighbours the same remark: 'Today our sergeant is rather sad, as though he wasn't in a good mood.' Then he went home and after he had left somebody always said: 'Our men must have been caught with their pants down in Serbia somewhere. That's why the sergeant hasn't got anything to say.'

But at home the sergeant could at least fill in one more questionnaire: 'The mood of the population: I.a.'

There were often long sleepless nights for the sergeant. He was always expecting an inspection or an investigation. At night he dreamed of the hangman's rope, how they were taking him to the gallows and how finally at the end the Minister of Regional Defence himself asked him right under the gallows: 'Sergeant, where is your answer to circular no. $\frac{1789678}{23792}$ X.Y.Z.?'

And now! It was as if the old German hunting greeting: 'Weidmannsheil!' resounded from all the corners of the gendarmerie station. And Sergeant Flanderka had no doubt that the district commander would pat him on the back and say: 'Sergeant, I congratulate you.'

The sergeant painted in his mind other alluring pictures which had taken shape in some corner of his official brain: decoration, accelerated promotion to the highest rank, appreciation of his criminological capabilities opening the way to a brilliant career.

He called the lance-corporal and asked him: 'Did you get the lunch?'

'They brought him smoked ham with cabbages and dumplings. The soup was already off. He's drunk his tea and wants another cup.'

'Let him have it!' the sergeant agreed magnanimously. 'When he's drunk it, bring him to me.'

'Well then now. Did you enjoy it?' the sergeant asked, when half an hour later the lance-corporal brought in Švejk, who was replete and happy as always.

'It wasn't so bad, sergeant. I could have done with a little more of that cabbage. But never mind! I know you were not prepared for it. The smoked ham was well smoked. It must have been home-smoked from a pig which had been home-reared. The tea with the rum did me good too.'

The sergeant looked at Švejk and began: 'Is it true that in Russia they drink a lot of tea? Have they got rum there also?'

'You can find rum all over the world, sergeant.'

'Don't quibble,' thought the sergeant to himself. 'You ought to have paid more attention before to what you were saying!' And, leaning towards Švejk, he asked him in a confidential tone: 'Are there pretty girls in Russia?'

'You can find pretty girls all over the world, sergeant.'

'Oh, you bastard!' thought the sergeant to himself once more. 'You'd give anything to get out of this now.' And the sergeant came out with his forty-two pounder.

'What did you want to do in the 91st regiment?'

'I wanted to go with them to the front.'

The sergeant looked at Švejk with satisfaction and observed: 'That's right. That's the best way of getting to Russia.'

'Indeed, very well thought out.' The sergeant glowed with satisfaction, observing what effect his words had on Švejk.

But he could not read from the expression of Švejk's eyes anything except the most complete calm.

'This fellow doesn't bat an eyelid,' the sergeant thought to himself in alarm. 'That's their military training. If I were in his situation and someone were saying this to me my knees would begin to shake...'

'Tomorrow we'll take you off to Písek,' he mentioned casually. 'Have you ever been to Písek?'

'In 1910 at the Imperial manoeuvres.'

After this answer the sergeant's smile was still more friendly and triumphant. He felt in his heart that he had excelled himself with his system of questioning.

'Did you go through all the manoeuvres?'

'Of course I did, sergeant, as an infantryman.' And then again just as calmly as before Švejk looked at the sergeant, who squirmed with pleasure and could hardly stop himself from immediately making a report of it. He called the lance-corporal to take Švejk away and completed his report: 'His plan was as follows: to insinuate himself into the ranks of the 91st infantry regiment, to volunteer at once for the front and at the first opportunity get to Russia, because he realized that any other way back would be impossible owing to the vigilance of our security organs. That he would have been able to get on very well in the 91st infantry regiment is quite understandable, because by his own admission he confessed after a further cross-examination that in 1910 he took part in all the Imperial manoeuvres in the region of Písek, as an infantryman. From this it is clear that he is very able in his profession. I should like to add that the indictments which I have collected are the result of my own system of cross-examination.'

The lance-corporal appeared in the door: 'Sergeant, he wants to go to the rears.'

'Fix bayonets!' the sergeant decided. 'But wait a moment! No, bring him here.'

'You want to go to the rears?' said the sergeant in a friendly tone. 'Isn't there something else behind this?' and he focused his gaze on Švejk's face.

'Honestly, it's only a question of number two, sergeant,' answered Švejk.

'To make sure there's nothing else behind it,' the sergeant repeated significantly, girding himself with his official revolver, 'I shall accompany you there myself!'

'This is a very good revolver,' he said to Švejk on the way. 'Seven shots and it shoots very accurately.'

But before they went out into the courtyard he called the lance-corporal and said to him mysteriously: 'You must fix bayonets and when he's inside station yourself at the back of the rear, so that he doesn't dig himself a tunnel out through the dung pit.'

The latrine was the usual small wooden shack, standing despondently in the middle of the yard over a pit full of dung water, which oozed out of the heap of manure near by.

It was already an old veteran, into which whole generations had discharged their bodily needs. Now Švejk sat inside it, holding with one hand the door by the cord, while behind him through the window the lance-corporal watched his hind quarters in case he should dig himself out.

And on the door were fixed the hawk-like eyes of the gendarmerie sergeant who was considering into which leg he should shoot if Švejk attempted to escape.

But the door calmly opened and there emerged a satisfied Švejk who remarked to the sergeant:

'I hope I wasn't too long inside? I hope I haven't kept you waiting?'

'Oh, not at all, not at all,' answered the sergeant, thinking in his mind: 'What polite, decent people they are. He knows what's in store for him, but all honour to him. Up to the last he's a gentleman. Would one of our own people be the same in his place?'

In the gendarmerie station the sergeant went on sitting next to Švejk on the empty bunk of the gendarme Rampa, who was on duty until the next morning. He had to go the rounds of the villages and at that very moment was sitting peacefully in The Black Horse in Protivín

playing mariáš with the master cobblers and explaining in the intervals that Austria was bound to win.

The sergeant lit his pipe and offered Švejk to fill his, the lance-corporal put a log in the stove, and the gendarmerie station changed into the most agreeable spot on the globe, into a quiet corner, a warm nest in the approaching winter twilight when it was time for friendly chat.

Nevertheless no one spoke. The sergeant was pursuing a certain line of thought and at last expressed it, turning to the lance-corporal: 'In my view it's not right to hang spies. A man who sacrifices himself for his duty, for his, let us say, fatherland, ought to be dispatched in an honourable fashion, with powder and lead. What do you think, lance-corporal?'

'Certainly he should only be shot and not hanged,' the lance-corporal agreed. 'Let's say that they sent us and told us: "You must find out how many machine-guns the Russians have in their machine-gun detachment." And then we had to disguise ourselves and go. Why should they have to hang me like some robber and murderer?'

The lance-corporal got so excited that he stood up and called out: 'I insist on being shot and buried with full military honours.'

'But the snag is,' said Švejk, 'that if a chap's clever nobody can ever prove anything against him.'

'Oh yes they can!' said the sergeant emphatically, 'if they are clever too and have *their method*. You'll see for yourself.

'You'll see,' he repeated in a placid tone and gave a friendly smile. 'No one succeeds in wriggling out of it with us, do they, lance-corporal?'

The lance-corporal nodded in agreement and mentioned that in the case of some people the game was already up in advance and even a mask of complete calm would not help, because the calmer anyone seemed to be the more it was proof against him.

'You are of my school,' the sergeant affirmed proudly. 'Calm, that's a soap bubble. And artificial calm is a *corpus delicti*.' And breaking off the exposition of his theory he turned to the lance-corporal and asked: 'What are we going to have for dinner tonight?'

'Aren't you going to the pub tonight, sergeant?'

With this question there arose for the sergeant a new and difficult problem which had to be solved at once.

What if the man were to take advantage of his absence during the night and run away? The lance-corporal was of course a reliable man and careful, but two tramps already had escaped from him. In fact it had happened because he had not wanted to trudge with them in winter through the snow all the way to Písek, and so he set them free in the fields near Ražice and fired a shot into the air *pro forma*.

'We'll send our old woman to fetch us dinner and she can also bring us beer in a jug,' said the sergeant, solving the difficult problem. 'Let the old woman run about a bit.'

And old Pejzlerka, who served them as a charwoman, certainly did run about.

After dinner the path between the gendarmerie station and The Old

Tom Cat was busy the whole time. The unusually frequent footmarks of the heavy big boots of old Pejzlerka on this connecting line indicated that the sergeant was compensating himself fully for his absence from The Old Tom Cat.

And when old Pejzlerka finally appeared at the bar with the message

that the sergeant sent his compliments and would like a bottle of kontušovka[1] sent up to him the landlord could not control his curiosity.

'Who have they got there?' old Pejzlerka answered. 'Why – some suspicious individual. Just before I went away they both had their arms round his neck and the sergeant was stroking him on the head and saying to him: "My lovely Slav bastard, my little spy!"'

And when it was already long past midnight the lance-corporal fell asleep, stretched out on his bunk in full uniform and snoring deeply.

Opposite him sat the sergeant with the rest of the kontušovka at the bottom of the bottle. He had his arm round Švejk's neck, tears ran

1. A kind of Polish vodka.

down his tanned cheeks and his whiskers were stuck together with
kontušovka. He jabbered: 'Say that in Russia they haven't got such
good kontušovka as this! Say it, so I can go to bed in peace! Confess it
like a man!'

'They haven't.'

The sergeant rolled over on to Švejk.

'You've made me happy. You've confessed. That's how it should be
at a cross-examination. If I'm guilty, why should I deny it?'

He got up and staggering into his room with the empty bottle
babbled: 'If he hadn't taken the wrong t-t-turning everything might
have been di-different.'

Before he threw himself on to his bed in his uniform he took out of
his writing-desk his report and tried to supplement it with the following material:

'I must add in addition that Russian kontušovka on the basis of
paragraph fifty-six . . .' He made a blot and licked it. Smiling idiotically, he threw himself on the bed and fell asleep like a log.

In the morning the lance-corporal, lying on his bed by the opposite
wall, started such a snoring, accompanied by a whistling in the nose,
that it woke Švejk up. He got up, shook the lance-corporal and went
back to bed. But already the cocks had begun to crow, and when afterwards the sun came up, old Pejzlerka, who had also overslept as a result
of her nocturnal running about, came to light the stoves, she found the
door open and everything plunged in deep slumber. The paraffin lamp
in the guard-room was still smoking. Old Pejzlerka raised the alarm,
pulled the lance-corporal and Švejk out of bed and said to the lance-
corporal: 'Aren't you ashamed of going to bed fully dressed like one of
the Lord's cattle?' and she reminded Švejk that he might at least do up
his fly buttons when he saw a woman.

Finally she energetically urged the sleepy lance-corporal to go and
wake the sergeant, since it was not decent for people to sleep so long.

'You've certainly fallen into fine hands,' the old woman grumbled to
Švejk, when the lance-corporal went to wake the sergeant. 'One's as
big a boozer as the other. They'd booze away their nose between their
eyes. They owe me my wages for three years and when I remind them
of it the sergeant always says: "Be quiet, old woman, or I'll have you
put in gaol: we know your son's a poacher and steals wood from the
estate." And so I have been martyring myself with them for four years
now.' The old woman gave a deep sigh and went on grumbling. 'Be

sure to be on your guard with that sergeant. He's as oily as you make them and a first-class bastard into the bargain. Whenever he can he'll do anyone down and have them put in gaol.'

The sergeant was very difficult to wake up. The lance-corporal had hard work convincing him that it was already morning.

Finally he surfaced, rubbed his eyes and began to have a vague memory of what had happened the night before. Suddenly there came to him a frightful thought, to which he gave expression, looking uncertainly at the lance-corporal: 'Has he run away?'

'Why, of course not. He's an honest fellow.'

The lance-corporal began to walk up and down the room, looked out of the window, came back again, tore a piece of paper from the newspapers on the table and rolled a paper pellet out of it between his fingers. It was obvious that he wanted to say something.

The sergeant looked at him in some uncertainty and at last, to confirm for certain what he only suspected, he said: 'I'll help you, lance-corporal. Yesterday I suppose I made an exhibition of myself again, didn't I?'

The lance-corporal looked reproachfully at his superior: 'If you knew, sergeant, all you said yesterday and the sort of conversation you had with him.'

Bending close to the sergeant's ear, he whispered: 'You said that all of us, Czechs and Russians, are of the same Slav blood; that Nikolai Nikolaevich[1] will be in Přerov next week; that Austria can't hold out, and that, when he is interrogated again, he must deny everything and talk nonsense so as to be able to hold out till the Cossacks come and free him; that it must come to breaking point very soon; that it will be just like it was during the Hussite wars; the peasants will come with their flails to Vienna; that His Imperial Majesty is a feeble old dotard and will kick the bucket very soon; that Kaiser Wilhelm is a reptile, and that you'll send him money in gaol to improve his conditions and many other things like that . . .'

The lance-corporal moved away from the sergeant: 'I can remember all that very well, because to begin with I was only a little tipsy. After that I got completely sozzled too and I don't know any more.'

The sergeant looked at the lance-corporal.

'But what I can remember,' he declared, 'is that you said that we're

1. The Grand Duke Nicholas who was commander-in-chief of the Russian armed forces.

pigmies compared with the Russians and that you shouted out in front of our old woman: "Long live Russia!" '

The lance-corporal began to walk nervously up and down the room.

'You bellowed like a bull,' said the sergeant, 'and then you threw yourself on to the bed and began to snore.'

The lance-corporal stopped by the window and drumming with his fingers on it declared: 'Sergeant, you didn't exactly keep your mouth shut in front of our old woman either and I remember how you said to her: "Remember, old woman, that every emperor and king thinks only of his own pocket, and that's why they wage war, even if it's only an old dotard like old Procházka,[1] whom they can't let out of the rears in case he should shit up the whole of Schönbrunn." '

'You mean to say I said that?'

'Yes, sergeant, you said that, before you went out into the courtyard to vomit, and into the bargain you shouted: "Old woman, stick your finger down my throat!" '

'You said some fine things too,' the sergeant interrupted him, 'when you hit on the stupid idea that Nikolai Nikolaevich would be King of Bohemia.'

'I don't remember that,' the lance-corporal said timidly.

'Of course you wouldn't remember it. You were absolutely pickled. You had pig's eyes and when you wanted to go outside, you climbed up the stove instead of going through the door.'

Neither of them spoke until the sergeant broke the long silence: 'I've always told you that alcohol is death. You can't take much and yet you drink. What would have happened if he had run away? How could we have explained it? O God, my head's splitting.

'I tell you, lance-corporal,' the sergeant went on, 'that just because he didn't run away it's quite clear what a dangerous and cunning fellow he is. When they come to cross-examine him he'll say that the door was open the whole night, that we were drunk and that he could have run away a thousand times if he had felt guilty. It's a piece of luck that they won't believe a fellow like him and when we say under official oath that it's all a fabrication and an impudent lie on his part, not even the Lord God himself will help him and he'll have another article of the law round his neck. In his case of course it doesn't make much difference. If only my head didn't ache so much!'

1. Czech nickname for Emperor Franz Joseph.

There was a silence. After a moment the sergeant said: 'Get hold of our old woman.'

'Listen, old woman,' said the sergeant to Pejzlerka, looking her sternly in the eye, 'go and collect a crucifix on a stand from somewhere and bring it here.'

Pejzlerka's questioning look produced an explosion on the part of the sergeant: 'You'd better make sharp!'

The sergeant took out of the table drawer two candles on which there were traces of the sealing wax which he used to seal official documents, and when in fear and trembling Pejzlerka finally came in with the crucifix the sergeant put the cross between both candles on the edge of the table, lit the candles and said in a solemn voice: 'Sit down, old woman.'

The terror-stricken Pejzlerka sank down on the sofa and looked wild-eyed at the sergeant, the candles and the crucifix. Panic seized her and as she had her hands on her apron you could see that they were trembling with her knees.

The sergeant walked gravely round her and stopping a second time in front of her announced in a solemn voice: 'Yesterday evening you witnessed a great event, old woman. It may well be that your feeble mind cannot grasp it. That soldier is an intelligence officer, a spy, old woman.'

'Jesus Mary,' shrieked Pejzlerka. 'Dear Holy Virgin from Skočice!'

'Quiet, old woman! In order to get something out of him we had to say various things to him. You heard what strange things we said, didn't you?'

'Yes, sir, I did,' Pejzlerka whispered with a quaking voice.

'But everything we said, old woman, was only designed to make him confess, to make him trust us. And we succeeded. We got everything out of him we wanted. We trapped him.'

The sergeant interrupted his address for a moment to adjust the wick on the candles and then he continued gravely, looking severely at Pejzlerka: 'You were present and you are initiated into the whole secret. This secret is an official one. And you must not say a single word about it to anyone. Not even on your deathbed, otherwise they wouldn't be allowed to bury you in the churchyard.'

'Jesus, Mary, Joseph,' whined Pejzlerka, 'why was I so unfortunate ever to set foot here!'

'Don't howl, old woman. Get up. Approach the crucifix. Put up the two fingers of your right hand. You will take an oath. Speak after me!'

Pejzlerka staggered to the table incessantly moaning: 'Virgin Mary of Skočice, why did I ever set foot here.'

And the careworn face of Christ looked down on her from the cross, the candles smoked and everything appeared dreadful and unearthly to Pejzlerka. She was completely lost, her knees knocked and her hands trembled.

She raised the two fingers of her hand and the sergeant solemnly and emphatically recited for her to repeat: 'I swear before God Almighty and you, sergeant, that I shall never to the day of my death mention a word of what I have heard and seen here, even if I were asked by anybody about it. So help me God.

'And now kiss the crucifix too, old woman,' the sergeant ordered, when Pejzlerka had taken the oath to the accompaniment of terrible sobbing and had crossed herself devoutly.

'And now you can take the crucifix back to where you borrowed it from and tell them I needed it for a cross-examination!'

The shattered Pejzlerka went out from the room on tip-toe with the crucifix and from the window she could be seen continually looking back at the gendarmerie station, as though she wanted to convince herself that this was not merely a dream, but that just a moment ago she had really lived through the most ghastly experience in her whole life.

The sergeant meanwhile re-wrote his report, which he had supplemented the night before with the blots he had tried to lick away together with the handwriting, just as if there had been jam on the paper.

Now he re-wrote it completely and remembered that he had not asked one question. He summoned Švejk and asked him: 'Do you know how to take photographs?'

'Yes, I do.'

'Then why don't you have a camera with you?'

'Because I don't have one,' came the honest and clear answer.

'And if you had had one would you have taken photographs?' the sergeant asked.

'If ifs and ans were pots and pans,' Švejk answered simply, and calmly endured the puzzled expression on the face of the sergeant, whose head had just then begun to ache again so that he could not think out any other question except: 'Is it difficult to photograph a station?'

'Easier than anything else,' answered Švejk, 'because it doesn't move but always stands in the same place and you don't have to tell it to smile.'

The sergeant was then able to supplement his report as follows: 'To report no. 2172, I have the honour to add ...'

And the sergeant went on writing: 'Among other things during my cross-examination he confessed that he knew how to take photographs and that he liked best photographing stations. It is true that no camera was found on him, but one can presume that he has it hidden somewhere and therefore doesn't carry it on him, so as to divert attention away from himself, which is supported by the evidence of his own confession that he would photograph if he had a camera on him.'

The sergeant, having a terrible head after the night before, got more and more mixed up in his report about the photographing and went on writing: 'It is clear that by his own confession only the fact that he didn't have a camera on him prevented him from photographing the station buildings and places of strategic importance in general, and it is indisputable that he would have done so, if he had had that relevant photographic instrument on him which he had hidden somewhere. It is only thanks to the fact that he did not have a camera handy that no photographs were found on him.'

'That's enough,' said the sergeant and signed it.

He was completely satisfied with his work and read it to the lance-corporal with great pride.

'That's a success,' he said to the lance-corporal. 'There you are, that's the way to write reports! Everything must be put in. A cross-examination, my friend, is not a simple matter, and the main thing is that everything is put neatly into the report so that the people at the top are so foxed by it that their eyes boggle. Bring our man in so that we can finish with him.

'And so now the lance-corporal will take you away to the district gendarmerie command at Písek,' he said gravely to Švejk. 'According to the regulations you ought really to be put in handcuffs. But because I think you're a decent fellow we shan't do that. I'm sure you won't try to escape on the way.'

Obviously touched by the sight of Švejk's good-natured face the sergeant added: 'And I hope you won't think badly of me. Take him away, lance-corporal. Here you have the report.'

'Then goodbye and God speed,' added Švejk gently. 'Thank you, sergeant, for everything you've done for me. When I have the chance I'll write to you and if I should ever come round here again I'll drop in on you.'

Švejk went out with the lance-corporal on to the road and anyone who had met them, engaged as they were in friendly conversation, might have taken them for old friends who by chance were going the same way to the town, perhaps to the church.

'I never imagined,' Švejk was saying, 'that the way to Budějovice would involve such difficulties. It reminds me of the case of the butcher Chaura from Kobylisy. Once in the night he came to Palacký's monument at Moráň and went round and round it until morning, because he thought that the wall didn't have any end. He was quite out of his mind about it and by morning he couldn't go on any more and began to shout: "Help, police!" When the cops came he asked them the way to Kobylisy saying that he'd already been walking around a wall for five hours and there was no end to it yet. And so they took him with them and he smashed everything in solitary confinement in his cell.'

The lance-corporal did not say a word but thought to himself: 'What yarns you're spinning! You're starting with your fairy tales about Budějovice again.'

They walked past a lake and Švejk asked the lance-corporal with some interest whether there were many poachers of fish in the region.

'Here everyone's a poacher,' answered the lance-corporal. 'They wanted to throw the last sergeant into the water. The water bailiff on the dam keeps on shooting bristles into their backsides, but it doesn't help. They carry metal plates in their trousers, you see.'

The lance-corporal started to talk about progress, how quickly people get on to everything, and how people cheat each other. He developed a new theory that the war was a great blessing for humanity, because in the battles not only good people were shot but lots of rogues and bastards too.

'In any case there are too many people in the world,' he said reflectively. 'Each one's breathing down the other's neck and it's awful how humanity breeds.'

They approached a roadside pub.

'It's blowing bloody awful,' said the lance-corporal. 'I think that a wee dram won't do us any harm. Don't tell anybody I'm taking you to Písek. It's a state secret.'

Before the eyes of the lance-corporal there danced the instructions of the central authorities about suspicious and conspicuous people and of the duties of every gendarmerie station: 'Keep them away from all contact with the local population and take strict care that on their way to a higher authority there are no unnecessary conversations in the region.'

'It mustn't be let out who you are,' the lance-corporal said again. 'What you've done is nobody's business. We mustn't allow panic to spread. Panic's a very bad thing in these times of war,' he continued. 'You say something and it spreads like an avalanche over the whole region. Do you understand?'

'Well, I shan't spread any panic,' said Švejk, and he was as good as his word, because when the landlord talked to him, he said emphatically: 'My brother here says we'll be in Písek at one o'clock.'

'And so your brother's got leave?' the inquisitive pub-keeper asked the lance-corporal, who without batting an eyelid had the cheek to answer brazenly: 'Today's his last day!'

'We bamboozled him all right,' he said, smiling to Švejk, when the pub-keeper ran out somewhere. 'Only no panic of any kind. It's wartime.'

When the lance-corporal before going into the roadside pub declared that a wee dram would do no harm, he was an optimist, because he forgot about the quantity, and when he had drunk twelve he stated quite firmly that until three o'clock the commander of the district gendarmerie station would be at lunch and that it was useless to come there earlier and in addition a blizzard was starting. If they reached Písek by four o'clock in the afternoon it would be loads of time. Even six would be time enough. It would be dark anyhow as you could see by the weather that day. It was all the same whether they went now or later. Písek couldn't run away.

'Let's be glad that we sit in a warm place,' was his decisive word. 'Out there in the trenches in stinking weather like this those chaps go through a lot more than we do sitting by the stove.'

The big old stove glowed with heat and the lance-corporal found that one could very well top up the outer warmth with an inner warmth attained through the help of various sweet and potent spirits, as they say in Galicia.

In this isolated spot the landlord had eight kinds of spirit; he was bored to death and drank to the sound of the wailing wind which whistled behind every corner of the building.

The lance-corporal went on inviting the landlord to keep in step with him, accusing him of drinking too little, which was obviously an injustice, because he could hardly stand on his legs and wanted all the time to play färbl. He maintained that in the night he had heard gunfire from the east, upon which the lance-corporal hiccupped: 'Only no panic, for God's sake! About that there are in- in- instructions.'

And he went on to explain that instructions were a collection of immediate orders. In doing so he betrayed some secret directives. But the landlord no longer understood anything. He was only capable of stating that the war could not be won by instructions.

It was already dark when the lance-corporal decided that he and Švejk would now set off on the road to Písek. In the blizzard they could not see more than a step or two in front of them and the lance-corporal kept on saying: 'Go on following your nose until Písek.'

When he had said this for the third time his voice no longer sounded from the road but from somewhere below, where he had slipped down the slope on the snow. With the help of his rifle he scrambled laboriously up on to the road again. Švejk heard him giggling to himself: 'Skating rink.' After a time he could not be heard any more on the road, because he had again slipped down the slope and was bawling so loud that he drowned the wind: 'I'm falling. Panic!'

The lance-corporal was transformed into a busy ant, which whenever it falls down anywhere stubbornly tries to climb up again.

Five times the lance-corporal repeated his excursion down the slope and when he was again at Švejk's side he said helplessly and desperately: 'I could easily lose you.'

'Don't be afraid, lance-corporal,' said Švejk. 'We'll get on best if we fasten ourselves together. Then neither of us can lose the other: Have you got handcuffs with you?'

'Every gendarme must always carry handcuffs on him,' said the lance-corporal firmly, stumbling around Švejk. 'That's our daily bread.'

'Then let's link up,' Švejk suggested. 'Why not try?'

With a masterly flick of his hand the lance-corporal fastened the handcuffs to Švejk and the other end of them to the wrist of his right hand; now they were linked together like twins. Stumbling on the road, they could not separate. The lance-corporal dragged Švejk over piles of stones and when he fell down he pulled Švejk down with him. When this happened the handcuffs cut their hands until finally the lance-corporal said that they couldn't go on like this and that he must unfasten them again. After long and vain attempts to free himself and Švejk from the handcuffs he sighed, 'We're linked until kingdom come.'

'Amen,' added Švejk, and they continued their laborious journey.

The lance-corporal was seized with a fit of deep depression and

when late in the evening after terrible trials they got to the gendarmerie headquarters at Písek, he was completely broken and said on the steps: 'Now it'll be frightful. We can't get away from each other.'

And truly it was frightful, when the sergeant sent for the commander of the station, Captain König.

The captain's first words were: 'Breathe on me!

'Now I understand,' said the captain, taking in the situation with his keen experienced nose. 'Rum, kontušovka, čert, jeřabinka, ořechovka, višňovka, vanilková.'[1]

1. Various kinds of schnaps made out of rowan berries, walnuts, cherries, vanilla, etc.

'Sergeant,' he said turning to his subordinate, 'here you see what a gendarme should *not* look like. Conduct like this is an offence on which a court-martial will have to give its verdict. Handcuffing himself to a delinquent! Coming here sozzled, dead drunk. Crawling here like an animal! Take the handcuffs off him!

'Well, what is it?' he said, turning to the lance-corporal who with his free arm was saluting upside down.

'Humbly report, sir, I bring a report.'

'A report on you is going to the court,' said the captain tersely: 'Sergeant, gaol both the men, bring them tomorrow for interrogation, study the report from Putim carefully and send it to me to my house.'

The captain of the gendarmerie at Písek was a very officious man, very thorough in prosecuting his subordinates and outstanding in bureaucratic matters.

In the gendarmerie stations in his district no one could ever say that the storm had passed. It came back with every communication signed by the captain, who spent the whole day issuing reprimands, admonitions and warnings to the whole district.

Ever since the outbreak of war heavy black clouds had loured over the gendarmerie stations in the Písek district.

It was a truly ghostly atmosphere. The thunderbolts of bureaucracy rumbled and struck the gendarmerie sergeants, lance-corporals, men and employees. For every twopenny halfpenny thing there was a disciplinary investigation.

'If we want to win the war,' he said on his inspections of the gendarmerie stations, 'then "a" must be "a", "b" "b"; and everywhere there must be a dot on the "i".'

He felt himself encircled by treason on all sides and was absolutely convinced not only that every gendarme in his district had sins on his conscience as a result of the war, but that everybody at this important time was guilty of some dereliction of duty.

And from above he was bombarded with official communications in which the Ministry of Regional Defence pointed out that according to the information of the Ministry of War soldiers from the Písek district were deserting to the enemy.

And they drove him into testing the loyalty of his district. It looked ghastly. The women from the neighbourhood went to see their husbands off to the war and he knew for certain that their husbands promised them not to let themselves be killed for His Imperial Majesty.

The yellow and black horizon was beginning to become overcast with the clouds of revolution. In Serbia and in the Carpathians battalions went over to the enemy: the 28th and the 11th regiments. In the latter were soldiers from the Písek district and region. In the sultry calm before the storm of the approaching revolution recruits from Vodňany arrived with carnations of black organdie. Soldiers on their way from Prague passed through Písek station and threw back the cigarettes and chocolate which Písek society ladies had given them in their pig trucks.

Then a battalion on its way to the front went past and some Písek Jews bawled out in German: 'God save the Emperor! Down with the Serbs!' They got such a beating up that they could not show themselves in the streets for a week.

And while these episodes took place, showing clearly that when 'God save our Emperor' was played on the organ in the churches it was only a pitiful veneer and universal sham, there came from the gendarmerie stations the familiar answers to the questionnaire à la Putim saying that everything was in the best order, that there was no anti-war agitation anywhere and the attitude of the population was I.a, enthusiasm I.a–b.

'You're not gendarmes but village cops,' the gendarmerie captain used to say on his inspections. 'Instead of sharpening your vigilance a thousand per cent you're slowly turning into cattle.'

Having made this zoological discovery, he added: 'You lounge about at home and think: "They can kiss our arses with that war of theirs."'

This was always followed by a list of all the duties of the unfortunate gendarmes, a lecture on the general situation and how to keep everything firmly in hand, so that it should really be as it ought to be. After this description of the glowing image of gendarmerie perfection, aimed at the strengthening of the Austrian monarchy, there followed threats, disciplinary investigations, transfers and oaths.

The captain was firmly convinced that he stood here on guard, that he was preserving something and that all these gendarmes from the gendarmerie stations who were under his orders were a bunch of do-nothing egoists, bastards, crooks for whom nothing else but brandy, beer and wine had any meaning. Because they had low wages they accepted bribes to be able to booze and they were slowly but surely breaking Austria up. The only man he trusted was his own sergeant in the district command, but that sergeant always said at the pub: 'Today that silly old crackpot of ours has been a scream again . . .'

The captain studied the report of the gendarmerie sergeant from Putim about Švejk. Before him stood his gendarmerie sergeant Matějka and thought to himself that as far as he was concerned the captain could go to hell with all his reports because down at the Otava they were waiting for him to take part in a game of 'Schnapsen'.[1]

'I told you last time, Matějka,' the captain said, 'that the biggest bloody fool I've ever known is the gendarmerie sergeant in Protivín, but judging by this report here the sergeant from Putim has gone one better. That soldier, whom that spirit-sodden scoundrel of a lance-corporal brought here, and whom he was linked with like two dogs, is certainly not a spy. He's undoubtedly a common or garden deserter. Here the idiot writes such stupid rubbish that every little child could see at a first glance that he was as tight as a papal prelate.

'Bring that soldier here at once,' he ordered, after he had studied the report from Putim for a while. 'I've never in my life seen such a tissue of bunkum and on top of all this he sends as escort for this suspicious bastard a sod like his own lance-corporal. These people still don't know me. I can be a devil. Until I've made them shit with fright three times a day they seem to think that they can put anything across me.'

The captain began to expatiate on how the gendarmerie nowadays had a negative attitude to all orders and how it was obvious that every sergeant when he wrote his report had a lark with it just to make a bigger mess of things.

When the warning came from above that the possibility could not be excluded of intelligence agents roaming about the countryside, the gendarmerie sergeants began to manufacture them wholesale and if the war lasted any longer it would be a giant madhouse. In the office they must send a telegram to Putim summoning the sergeant to Písek the next day. He'd knock out of his head that 'very important event', which he wrote about at the beginning of his report.

'Which regiment have you deserted from?' were the captain's welcoming words to Švejk.

'I haven't deserted from any regiment.'

The captain looked at Švejk and saw such composure in his calm face that he asked: 'How did you get hold of that uniform?'

1. A card game, also known as 'sixty-six'.

'Every soldier gets a uniform when he's called up,' answered Švejk with a placid smile. 'I serve in the 91st regiment and not only did I not desert from my regiment, but quite the *contrary*.'

He pronounced the word 'contrary' with such emphasis that the captain assumed a piteous expression and asked: 'How do you mean – the *contrary*?'

'It's a terribly simple matter,' Švejk confided. 'I'm going to my regiment, I'm looking for it and not deserting from it. I want nothing better than to get to my regiment as soon as possible. I'm already quite nervy when I think how I'm obviously getting farther and farther away from České Budějovice, and the whole regiment is waiting for me there. The sergeant in Putim showed me on the map that Budějovice is to the south, but instead of sending me there he directed me to the north.'

The captain waved his hand as though meaning to say: 'He perpetrates much worse things than directing people to the north.'

'And so you can't find your regiment?' he said. 'Have you gone to look for it?'

Švejk explained to him the whole situation. He named Tábor and all the places he'd passed through on the way to Budějovice: Milevsko – Květov – Vráž – Malčín – Čížová – Sedlec – Horažd'ovice – Radomyšl – Putim – Štěkno – Strakonice – Volyň – Dub – Vodňany – Protivín and finally Putim again.

With enormous enthusiasm Švejk described his struggle with fate, how he had tried with might and main to get to his 91st regiment at Budějovice disregarding all obstacles and how all his efforts had been in vain.

He spoke passionately and the captain mechanically drew with his pencil on a piece of paper the vicious circle which the good soldier Švejk could not get out of when he set out to join his regiment.

'That was a labour of Hercules,' he said at last, when he had listened with enjoyment to Švejk's description of how irritated he was that it was taking him so long to get to his regiment. 'It must have been a wonderful sight to see you wandering round and round Putim.'

'It could have been decided already then,' Švejk remarked, 'if it hadn't been for that sergeant in that miserable hole. He never asked my name or my regiment and somehow or other everything was frightfully mysterious to him. He should have had me taken away to Budějovice and in the barracks they would have told him whether I was that Švejk who was looking for his regiment or some suspicious individual.

By now I might have already been a whole day with my regiment and be carrying out my military duties.'

'Why didn't you point out in Putim that it was a mistake?'

'Because I saw that it was useless to talk to him. That was what the old pub-keeper Rampa at Vinohrady said when someone wanted to get something from him on tick: there are times when a man is as deaf as a post to everything.'

The captain did not pause long for reflection. He merely concluded that such a round-about journey by a man who wanted to get to his regiment was a sign of the deepest human degeneration and he had the following knocked out on the typewriter in the office, observing all the rules and embellishments of officialese:

To the Illustrious Command of the Imperial and Royal Infantry Regiment no. 91 at České Budějovice.

Enclosed please find Josef Švejk, who according to the statement of the same should be an infantryman of the same regiment, detained on the basis of his statements in Putim, Písek district, by the gendarmerie station under suspicion of desertion. The same asserts that he is making for his above-mentioned regiment. The enclosed has a small stocky figure, a symmetrical face and nose and blue eyes without special characteristics. In annex b.1. is transmitted the account for the messing of the enclosed for kind remittal to the accounts of the Ministry of Regional Defence with the request for confirmation of the receipt of the enclosed. In annex c.1. is sent for confirmation a list of army property which the detained had on him on the day of his arrest.

Švejk's journey from Písek to Budějovice in the train passed off briskly and swiftly. His companion was a young gendarme, a novice whose eyes never left Švejk's face and who was scared to death that Švejk might run away from him. During the whole journey he was trying to solve a difficult problem: 'If I had now to go and do number one or number two, what would I do?'

He solved it by accepting that Švejk must act as his chaperone.

Throughout the whole journey with Švejk, from the station to the Mariánské barracks in Budějovice, he had his eyes fixed convulsively on Švejk, and whenever they came to a corner or to a cross-roads he told Švejk, as though quite casually, how many loaded cartridges they were given for each escort, upon which Švejk answered that he was convinced that no gendarme would shoot anyone on the street, in case he should cause an accident.

The gendarme wrangled with him and in this way they reached the barracks.

On duty in the barracks for the second day was Lieutenant Lukáš. All unsuspecting he sat at his desk in the office, when they suddenly brought Švejk to him with the papers.

'Humbly report, sir, I'm here again,' Švejk said, saluting and putting on a solemn expression.

This whole scene was witnessed by Company Sergeant-Major Kot'átko, who later related that when Švejk announced himself Lieutenant Lukáš jumped up, put his hands to his head and fell backwards on top of Kot'átko, and that when they revived him Švejk, who had been saluting all this time, repeated: 'Humbly report, sir, I'm here again!' Then Lieutenant Lukáš, white as a sheet, took with trembling hands the papers which concerned Švejk, signed them, asked everybody to go out, told the gendarme that everything was all right and locked himself into the office together with Švejk.

And so ended Švejk's Budějovice anabasis. It is certain that if Švejk had been granted liberty of movement he would have got to Budějovice on his own. However much the authorities may boast that it was they who brought Švejk to his place of duty, this is nothing but a mistake. With Švejk's energy and irresistible desire to fight, the authorities' action was like throwing a spanner into the works.

Švejk and Lieutenant Lukáš looked one another straight in the eye.

The lieutenant's eyes had a dreadful, menacing and desperate gleam in them, while Švejk looked at the lieutenant tenderly and kindly, as though he were looking at his dearest one whom he had lost and found again.

In the office it was as still as the grave. Nearby from the corridor someone could be heard walking about. It was some conscientious one-year volunteer, who had had to stay at home because of a cold, as could be told from his voice, since he was giving a very nasal performance of what he had learnt by heart in German: how members of the Imperial Household must be received at fortresses. One could hear clearly: 'As soon as the exalted personages approach the fortress, a salute is to be fired on all bastions and fortifications. The commandant will receive them on horseback with dirk in hand. He will then ride forward.'

'Shut up there,' the lieutenant roared into the corridor. 'Get to hell out of it! If you've got fever, stay at home in bed!'

The eager volunteer could be heard going away and from the end of the corridor was audible the faint echo of his nasal entoning: 'At the moment when the commandant salutes, the firing is to be repeated. It will be repeated a third time when the exalted personages alight.'

And again the lieutenant and Švejk went on staring at each other in silence, until finally Lieutenant Lukáš said with harsh irony: 'Hearty welcome, Švejk, to České Budějovice. He that is born to be hanged will never be drowned. There's already an arrest order out for you and tomorrow you will be at regimental report. I'm not going to be bothered with you any more. I've suffered more than enough from you, and my patience is shattered to smithereens. When I think that I managed to live so long with such a bloody half-wit as you . . .'

He began to walk up and down the office: 'No, it's frightful. Now I'm amazed that I didn't shoot you. What would have happened to me if I had? Absolutely nothing. I'd have been acquitted. Do you realize that?'

'Humbly report, sir, I realize it fully.'

'Don't start again, Švejk, with that bullshit of yours, or something really will happen. In the end we'll put a stop to your tricks once and for all. You have raised your idiocy to the degree of infinity until everything has burst catastrophically.'

REGIMENTS
ARREST.

Lieutenant Lukáš rubbed his hands: 'It's all up with you, Švejk.' He returned to his table and wrote a few lines on a piece of paper, called the guard in front of the office and ordered him to lead Švejk off to the prison warder and to give him the note.

They led Švejk off across the courtyard and the lieutenant with unconcealed delight watched the prison warder unlock the door with the black and yellow label, 'Regimental arrest'. He saw how Švejk disappeared behind that door and how a moment later the warder emerged from it alone.

'Now, thank the Lord!' the lieutenant thought aloud. 'At last he's there.'

In the dark spaces of the dungeon of the Mariánské barracks Švejk was welcomed cordially by a fat one-year volunteer who was sprawling about on a straw mattress. He was the only prisoner and was bored to death for the second day. To Švejk's question why he was in gaol he answered that it was for nothing. He had boxed the ears of an artillery lieutenant by mistake at night in the square in an archway when he was drunk. Actually he hadn't even boxed his ears but only knocked his cap off. The artillery lieutenant happened to be standing at night under the archway and was apparently waiting for a prostitute. He had his back to him and the volunteer took him for a friend of his, another volunteer called Materna František.

'And he's a little tich, just like him,' he told Švejk, 'so I came up to him nicely from behind and knocked his cap off, saying: "Servus, Franci!" And the bastard was such a bloody fool that he at once started to whistle for the military police and they took me off.

'It may be,' the volunteer admitted, 'that in the course of that scuffle a few blows fell, but I don't think that affects the matter, since it was an obvious case of mistaken identity. He admits himself that I said: "Servus, Franci", and his Christian name is Anton. That's quite clear. The only thing which can get me into trouble is that I ran away from hospital, and if it gets out about that hospital book ...

'When I joined up,' he went on, 'I first of all rented a room in the town and tried to contract rheumatism. Three times in succession I got myself thoroughly pickled, went and lay down in a ditch outside the town when it was raining, and took my boots off. But that didn't help. And then in the winter I bathed by night in the Malše for a whole week, but I achieved just the opposite results. Old man, I got so hardened that for a whole night I could lie in the snow in the court-yard of the house where I lived, and when the people of the house woke me up in the morning my feet were as warm as if I had been wearing fur slippers. If I had only caught tonsillitis at least, but absolutely nothing came of it. And I couldn't even catch that bloody V.D. Every day I went to The Port Arthur. Some of my colleagues had already got inflammation of the testicles and had their balls cut off, but I still remained immune. It was hellishly bad luck, old man. And then one day at The Rose I met a disabled soldier from Hluboká. He told me to come and see him one Sunday and promised that the next day I'd have legs like cans. At home he had a needle and syringe and really I could hardly get home from Hluboká afterwards. That precious soul hadn't deceived me. And so in the end I got my muscular rheumatism. I was at once taken to the hospital and everything was hunky-dory. And then fortune smiled at me again. My brother-in-law, Dr Masák from Žižkov, was transferred to Budějovice and it's him I have to thank for my being able to stay in hospital so long. He could have spun it out so long as to get me discharged as unfit for service, if I hadn't ruined it with that damned hospital book. The idea was a good one, first class. I got hold of a big book, gummed a label on to it and wrote on it: "Hospital book of the 91st regiment". The headings and so on were all in order. I wrote in false names, temperature readings, diseases, and every afternoon after the doctor's visit I coolly went into the town with this book under my arm. At the gates the Landwehr men were keeping guard and so from that side I was completely secure too. I showed them the book and they even saluted me. Then I went to a chap I knew, an official in the tax office, changed into mufti and went to a pub, where in company I knew we carried on various treasonable conversations. After that I got so cool that I didn't even bother to change into mufti and went in uniform to pubs and about the town. I didn't get back to my bed in the hospital before the early hours and when the patrol stopped me at night I showed them my "Hospital book of the 91st regiment" and after that no one asked me any more. At the gates of the hospital I again silently showed the book and somehow I always managed to get back to my bed. My cheek increased so much that I thought no one could do anything to me. Then came that fatal mistake at night on the square beneath the archway, a mistake that clearly showed that no trees grow all the way up to heaven, old man. Pride goes before a fall. All flesh is as grass and all the glory of man as the flower of grass. Icarus burnt his wings. Man would like to be a giant – and he's nothing but a shit, old man. Don't trust to chance but pinch yourself morning and night to remind yourself that discretion is the better part of valour and that nothing's more harmful than excess. After debauches and orgies there always follows the moral hangover. That's the law of nature, old man. When I think that I ruined my chance of being exempted for life from active service, that I could have been rejected as C3. . . . What a tremendous break! I could have loafed about somewhere in an office in the Reserve Command but my carelessness tripped me up.'

The volunteer solemnly concluded his confession as follows:

'Carthage fell. Niniveh was reduced to ruins, old man, but thumbs up! Don't let anyone imagine that when they send me to the front I'll fire a single shot. Regimental report! Expulsion from the school! Long live Imperial and Royal cretinism! Why should I squat in their school and take their exams? Cadet, ensign, second lieutenant, lieutenant! I'll shit on them! Officers' school! Dealing with those pupils that have to repeat the whole year's course over again! Military paralysis! Should a rifle be carried on the left or right shoulder? How many stars does a corporal have? Checking up on lists of reservists! Himmelherrgott! There's nothing to smoke, old man! Would you like me to teach you to spit on the ceiling? Look, this is how it's done. Wish something while you're doing it and it will be granted. If you like drinking beer I can recommend you the excellent water there in the jug. If you're hungry and you want to enjoy your food I can recommend you the City Club. I advise you to write poetry as a cure against boredom. I've already written an epic:

> 'Is the warder at home? He sleeps the night through.
> We carry the brunt, till we hear from H.Q.
> That the battle is lost.
> And here against the enemy's raid
> From bunks he builds a barricade.
> When he's finished with his wall
> From his lips you hear the story:
> "Austria's might will never fall,
> God preserve its power and glory."

'You see, old man,' the fat volunteer went on, 'to hell with anyone who says that respect for our dear monarchy is disappearing among our people. Here's a man in prison, who has nothing to smoke and is waiting to go on regimental report, and he is giving the finest example of affection for the throne! He pays homage in his songs to his greater fatherland, at a moment when it is threatened with a walloping on all sides. He is deprived of his liberty, but all the same there flow from his lips verses of unswerving devotion. *Morituri te salutant, Caesar!* The dead salute you, Caesar, but the warder's a bastard. You've got bloody good menials in your service. The day before yesterday I gave him five crowns to buy me cigarettes and the bloody swine told me this morning that smoking was forbidden, that he would get into trouble if he did what I asked and that he'd return those five crowns to me when he got his pay. Yes, old man, I don't believe anything nowadays. The best slogans are turned upside down. Robbing prisoners! And into the bargain the bastard sings the whole day: "Where people sing you can sleep without wrongs. Folk who are wrong-uns have no songs!" Hound, gutter-snipe, scoundrel, traitor!'

The volunteer now asked Švejk what was his offence.

'You were trying to find your regiment?' he said. 'That must have been some hunt. Tábor, Milevsko, Květov, Vráž, Malčín, Čížová, Sedlec, Horažd'ovice, Radomyšl, Putim, Štěkno, Strakonice, Volyň, Dub, Vodňany, Protivín, Putim, Písek, Budějovice. A thorny path! And tomorrow you're on regimental report too? Brother, we'll meet together on the execution ground. Then our Colonel Schröder will have something to chuckle about. You've got no idea how worked up he gets by regimental affairs. He flies round the yard like a mad bloodhound and sticks his tongue out like a dying old pack-horse.

'And then his speeches, his exhortations, while all the time he spits about him like a slavering camel. His speeches never come to an end, and you could expect the whole of the Mariánské barracks to collapse at once. I know him well because I was on his regimental report once before. I joined up in top boots and wore a top hat because my tailor hadn't delivered my uniform in time. And so I came to the parade ground for the one-year volunteers' school dressed in top boots and a top hat and fell into line and marched with the others on the left flank. Colonel Schröder rode straight at me and nearly knocked me down. "Donnerwetter," he roared in German so that you could hear it far away in the Šumava, "what are you doing here, you bloody civilian?" I answered him politely that I was a one-year volunteer and that I was taking part in drill. And you should have seen him! He orated for half an hour and then for the first time he saw that I was saluting in my top hat. All he did was to shout out that the next day I must go on regimental report, after which he spurred his horse God knows where like a mad rider. Then he galloped up again, roared and rampaged once more, beat his breast and ordered me at once to clear out of the drill-grounds and to go to the guard-house. At regimental report he gave me fourteen days confined to barracks, made me put on impossible rags from the store and threatened to tear off my stripes.

' "A one-year volunteer," that bloody fool of a colonel went on drivelling aloud, "is something noble. They are the embryos of glory, military quality, heroism. The one-year volunteer Wohltat was promoted to the rank of corporal after passing the usual examination. He then volunteered for the front and took fifteen enemy prisoners. While he was handing them over he was torn to pieces by a shell. Five minutes later the order came that Wohltat was promoted cadet. And you too could expect the same glorious future, advancement,

decorations. Your name could be inscribed in the golden book of the regiment."'

The volunteer spat: 'You see, old man, what kinds of bastards are born under the sun. I don't care a damn about one-year volunteers' stripes and all the other privileges they give you: "Sir, you are an oaf." How fine that sounds: "Sir, you are . . ." and not just vulgarly, "Bloody oaf!" And after your death you will get the *Signum Laudis* or Great Silver Medal: the Imperial and Royal purveyors of corpses with or without stars. Why, any ox is better off. They kill it in the slaughterhouse and don't drag it beforehand to the drill-ground and to rifle practice.'

The fat volunteer rolled on to the other straw mattress and went on: 'It's obvious that one day it will all collapse. It can't last for ever. Try to pump glory into a pig and it will burst in the end. If I went to the front I should write on the carriage:

'Upon the fields your bones they'll put.
Eight horses or four dozen foot.'

The door opened and the warder appeared, bringing a quarter portion of army bread for both and some fresh water.

Without getting up from the mattress the volunteer apostrophized the warder in the following speech: 'How noble and beautiful it is to visit prisoners, St Agnes of the 91st regiment! Welcome, angel of charity, whose heart is full of compassion. Thou art bowed down under the hampers of food and drinks brought to alleviate our sufferings. We shall never forget the charity thou hast shown us. Thou art a radiant vision in our dark prison.'

'On regimental report you'll soon forget your sense of humour,' the warder grumbled.

'Keep your hair on, you miserable old screw,' the volunteer replied from his plank-bed. 'You'd better tell us what you'd do if you had to lock up ten one-year volunteers? Don't look so bloody silly, you turn-key of the Mariánské barracks. You'd lock up twenty and let out ten, you hamster. Christ, if I were the minister I'd see you had a wonderful war! You know the law that the angle of incidence equals the angle of reflection? I only ask you one thing: Show me and give me a firm point in this universe and I'll lift up the whole world with you in it, you conceited oaf!'

The warder's eyes bulged, he shook himself and banged the door.

'A mutual aid society for removing warders,' said the volunteer, dividing the portion of bread fairly in two parts. 'According to paragraph sixteen of prison regulations prisoners in the barracks have to be served full army rations until sentence is passed on them, but here it's the law of the jungle which rules: lucky the chap who's the first to wolf up the prisoners' rations.'

Švejk and he were sitting on the plank-bed and chewing the army bread.

'You can see best by the warder how war brutalizes a man,' the volunteer went on reflecting. 'No doubt before our warder was called up he was a young man with ideals, a fair-haired cherub, gentle and humane, defending the unfortunate, whom he always stood up for when at revels in his village there was a rough-house because of a girl. No doubt everybody respected him then, but today. . . . My God, how I itch to give him one across the jaw, bang his head on the plank-bed, throw him head-first into the rears. And that too, old man, is a proof of how in the military business your mentality gets completely brutalized.'

He started singing:

> 'Not even the Devil could scare her,
> Till she met an artillery man . . .

'Old man,' he went on, 'if we consider all this from the angle of our dear monarchy, we reach the inescapable conclusion that the situation is just the same as it was with Pushkin's uncle, of whom Pushkin wrote that, as he was a dying duck, there was nothing to do but:

> 'Sigh and keep on wondering,
> When the devil will carry you off!'

The rattle of a key in the door could be heard again and the warder lit the oil lamp in the corridor.

'A ray of light in the darkness!' shouted the volunteer. 'Enlightenment penetrates the army! Goodnight, Mr Warder, give my love to all the higher ranks and I wish you pleasant dreams – perhaps you'll dream that you've returned me those five crowns which I gave you to buy cigarettes with and which you've spent on drinking my health. Sweet dreams, you old monster.'

The warder could be heard muttering something about regimental report the next day.

'Alone once more,' said the volunteer. 'Now I shall devote the time

before sleep to an exposition and lecture on how the zoological knowledge of the N.C.O.s and officers increases every day. In order to dig
out new live war material and militarily conscious morsels for the
cannon's maw, profound studies of natural history are needed or of the
book *The Sources of Economic Prosperity*, published by Koči, where on
every page crop up the words: cattle, pig, swine. But recently we have
noted however that our progressive military circles have been introducing new nomenclature for recruits. In the 11th company Corporal
Althof uses the word "Engadine goat"; Lance-Corporal Müller, a
German schoolmaster from Kašperské Hory,[1] calls recruits "stinking
Czech swine"; Sergeant-Major Sondernummer "ox-headed toads" or
"Yorkshire porkers", promising in addition that he'll flay and stuff
every recruit. He does it with expert knowledge, as though he came
from a family of taxidermists. All our superior officers try in this way
to instil in us a love for our fatherland by means of special teaching aids
such as bellowing at recruits and dancing round them, a war-cry
reminiscent of the natives in Africa when they are about to skin an
innocent antelope or roast the haunches of a missionary who is being
dressed for the table. Such expressions never apply to Germans of
course. If Sergeant-Major Sondernummer uses the expression "pack
of swine" he always quickly adds the word "Czech", in case the
Germans should be offended and think it was meant for them. Then
all the N.C.O.s of the 11th company roll their eyes like a miserable dog
that has been greedy enough to swallow a sponge dipped in oil and
can't get it out of its throat. Once I heard a conversation between
Lance-Corporal Müller and Corporal Althof about the next steps in
the training of the men of the home defence. In this conversation the
following words stood out: "a couple across the jaw". I thought at
first they were having a row, that the German military monolith was
coming unstuck, but I made a great mistake. They were actually only
referring to the rank and file.

' "When a Czech pig like that" (these were the discreet instructions given by Corporal Althof) "does not learn after thirty 'flat
downs' to stand as straight as a candle it's not enough to give him a
few across the jaw. Deal him a sharp blow in the belly with the fist
of one hand and with the other knock his cap across his ears, saying: 'About turn!' As he turns round give him a kick up his backside

---

1. Bergreichenstein, a town in the Bohemian forest, where the Germans were in
an overwhelming majority.

and you'll see how he'll straighten up and how Ensign Dauerling will laugh."

'And now, old man, I must tell you something about Dauerling,' continued the volunteer. 'The recruits in the 11th company talk about him rather like a lonely old woman on a farm near the Mexican frontiers would romance about some famous Mexican bandit. Dauerling has the reputation of being a man-eater – an anthropophagus from the Australian tribes who devour the members of other tribes when they fall into their hands. His life story is marvellous. Not long after his birth his nurse fell down when she was carrying him, and little Konrad Dauerling knocked his head so hard that even today you can see a flattening on it as though a comet had struck the North Pole. Everybody doubted whether he would ever be fit to do anything, even if he survived the concussion of the brain. Only his father, a colonel, didn't lose hope and said that it wouldn't matter at all because, as a matter of course, when young Dauerling grew up he would go in for a military career. Young Dauerling managed to get into the cadet school at Hainburg after a frightful struggle with four classes of the lower technical school, for which he was coached by private crammers. The first of them grew prematurely grey and went mad, and the second grew so desperate that he wanted to jump off the St Stephen's Tower in Vienna. In the cadet school they never worried about previous education because it was generally unsuitable for Austrian regular officers. Their one military ideal was the Prussian drill-sergeant. Education ennobles the soul and this is useless in the army. The coarser the officers the better.

'In the cadet school Dauerling was no good even in those subjects of which every pupil had at least a smattering. Even there traces could be observed of his having given his head a knock in childhood.

'His answers at examinations spoke eloquently of his unfortunate accident. They were remarkable for their stupidity and were considered classic examples of crass idiocy and mental confusion, so that the professors at the cadet school never called him anything but "our dumb friend". His stupidity was so dazzling that it justified the hope that perhaps after a few decades he might make the Theresian Military Academy or the Ministry of War.

'When the war broke out and all the young cadets were made ensigns, Konrad Dauerling got himself on to the list of Hainburg cadets who were promoted and thus he found his way to the 91st regiment.'

The volunteer paused, and went on: 'The Ministry of War published a book, *Drill or Education*, in which Dauerling read that terror
was essential for soldiers. Training had success in proportion to the
degree of terror applied. And in this Dauerling always had success.
To avoid having to listen to his bellowing whole companies of soldiers
reported sick – a practice, however, which didn't exactly come off.
Anyone who reported sick received three days "severe". By the way do
you know what "severe" means? They chase you on the drill-ground
all day and then after that they lock you up at night. So it happened
that no one in Dauerling's company reported sick any more. Those
who did simply sat in clink. Dauerling always preserves on the drill-
ground that casual barracks tone, beginning with the word "swine"
and ending with that mysterious zoological enigma "swinehound".
But at the same time he's very liberal. He leaves to the soldiers their
freedom of decision. He says: "What do you want, you elephant, a
few bashes on the nose or three days 'severe'?" If anyone chooses
"severe" he gets two bashes on the nose as well, to which Dauerling
adds this explanation: "You bloody coward, I suppose you're afraid
of your snout? What are you going to do later on when the heavy
artillery strikes up?"

'Once, when he knocked out a recruit's eye he declared in German:
"Ugh! What a lot of fuss about a bastard that'll peg out anyhow."
Field Marshal Konrad von Hötzendorf used to say the same: "All
soldiers have to peg out sooner or later."

'A favourite and effective method of Dauerling's is to summon the
Czech rank and file and lecture them on Austria's military tasks, where
he explains the general principles of army education from handcuffing
to hanging and shooting. At the beginning of the winter before I went
to hospital we drilled on the drill-ground next to the 11th company,
and when there was a rest-pause Dauerling made a speech to his Czech
recruits:

' "I know," he began, "that you're scum and that I'll have to knock
out of your heads all your Czech bullshit. With Czech you won't even
get to the gallows. Our supreme commander is a German too. Are
you listening? Hell's bells! Flat down!"

'Everyone fell down flat, and when they were all lying on the ground
Dauerling walked in front of them and orated:

' " 'Flat down's' got to be 'flat down', even if you cut yourself to
pieces in the mud, you brigands. 'Flat down' existed even in ancient

Rome; in those days everyone had to join up and serve from seventeen to sixty. They had to serve thirty years in the field and weren't allowed to wallow about in the barracks like pigs. And at that time too there was one army language and command. If the men had tried to talk Etruscan to them, those Roman officers would have given them hell, and I too require all of you to reply in German and not in that double-Dutch of yours. You see how nice it is for you to lie in the mud, but just imagine what would happen if one of you didn't want to go on lying there and tried to get up. What would I do? I'd break his jaw up to his ears, because it would be an act of insubordination, mutiny, opposition, dereliction of duty for a good soldier, a breach of order and discipline and contempt for official instructions in general. From this it follows that a bastard like that is destined for the gallows and 'forfeiture of any claim to respect and civil rights'." '

The volunteer lapsed into silence and continued again after having obviously in the interval worked out his theme of the description of conditions in the barracks:

'It was under Captain Adamička. He was completely apathetic. When he sat in the office he usually stared blankly into space like a harmless lunatic and had an expression as though he was going to say: "I couldn't care less." At battalion report God knows what he was thinking about. Once a soldier of the 11th company presented himself on battalion report with the complaint that one evening in the street Ensign Dauerling had called him a Czech pig. He was a book-binder in civil life and a nationally conscious Czech worker.

' "And so that's how it is," said Captain Adamička quietly, because he always spoke very quietly. "He said that to you yesterday in the street. Now we shall have to see whether you had permission to go out of the barracks. Dismiss!"

'Some time later Captain Adamička summoned the man who had lodged the complaint.

' "It has been ascertained," he said again just as quietly, "that you had permission that day to absent yourself from the barracks until ten o'clock in the evening. And so you will not be punished. Dismiss!"

'After that, old man, it used to be said of Captain Adamička that he had a sense of justice, and so they sent him to the front and in his place came Major Wenzl. But he was a devil when people tried to stir up trouble between the nationalities. And it was he who hauled Ensign Dauerling over the coals. Major Wenzl has a Czech wife and is very much afraid of nationality disputes. Years ago when he served as a captain in Kutná Hora and was drunk he swore at a waiter in a hotel and called him "Czech scum". Let me mention that in society Major Wenzl never spoke anything but Czech, just as he did at home, and that his sons study in Czech. But nonetheless he uttered these words, and it got into the local paper. Then a deputy made an interpellation in the Vienna parliament about Captain Wenzl's behaviour in the hotel. Wenzl had a lot of unpleasantness because of it as it was just at the time of the debate on the army estimates, and right into the middle of it all came a sozzled Captain Wenzl from Kutná Hora.

'Later Captain Wenzl learned that all this was a put-up job by Zítko, one of the probationary cadets from the one-year volunteers, who sent it to the newspaper because there had been a feud between him and Captain Wenzl from the time when Zítko at a party in Wenzl's presence started reflecting that one only had to look at Mother Nature to observe how clouds cover the horizon, mountains rise high on the sky-line, waterfalls thunder in the forests and birds sing.

' "You only have to reflect," said probationary cadet Zítko, "what any captain is compared with sublime nature? Just as much of a zero as any probationary cadet."

'Because all the officer gentlemen were at that moment completely pickled, Captain Wenzl wanted to flog the unfortunate philosopher Zítko like a mule, and so the feud increased and the captain bullied Zítko whenever he could and all the more because Zítko's utterance became proverbial.

' "What is Captain Wenzl compared with sublime nature?" It was famous over the whole of Kutná Hora.

' "The bastard! I'll make him hang himself," Captain Wenzl used to say, but Zítko went into civil life and went on studying philosophy. But from then on Major Wenzl conceived a mad loathing for all junior officers. Not even a lieutenant was proof against his raging and raving, not to speak of cadets and ensigns.

' "I'll crush them like bugs!" says Major Wenzl, and woe betide that ensign who would drive anyone on to battalion report for any trifling offence. In Major Wenzl's eyes only an enormous and frightful offence has any significance – like for instance a soldier falling asleep on guard at the powder magazine or when he does something even more frightful like falling asleep when crawling at night over the wall of the Mariánské barracks and letting himself be caught by a patrol of the Landwehr or the artillery – in short, horrible things which would be a blot on the good name of the regiment.

'"For Christ's sake!" I heard him once roar in the corridor, "it's the third time he's been caught by the Landwehr patrol. Throw the reptile into the dungeon at once! The bastard must be sent away from the regiment to the train to cart dung somewhere. And he didn't even fight with them! They're not soldiers, these bastards, they're crossing-sweepers! Don't let him have anything to eat until the day after tomorrow. Take away his straw mattress and shove him into solitary confinement. Don't let him have a blanket, the rat!"

'Now just imagine, my friend, immediately after the major had come here, that idiotic Ensign Dauerling hounded on to battalion report a man who, allegedly, had intentionally failed to salute him when he was driving across the square in a fiacre one Sunday afternoon with a young lady! According to the N.C.O.s' accounts, battalion report on that occasion was like the day of the last judgement. The sergeant-major from the battalion office ran out into the passage with the registers and Major Wenzl roared at Dauerling:

'"I won't have this bloody nonsense, Himmeldonnerwetter! I utterly forbid it! Do you know, ensign, what battalion report is? Battalion report's not a Sunday-school treat! How the hell could he see you when you were driving across the square? Don't you know that you yourself were taught that officers are to be saluted only when met, and that doesn't mean that a soldier has got to gyrate like a top just to keep track of some ensign driving across a square. Be good enough to hold your tongue! Battalion report is a very serious institution. If the soldier has already stated to you that he didn't see you because at that moment he was saluting me on the corso and had turned his eyes in my direction – do you understand, Major Wenzl's, and if he said that he couldn't look behind at the fiacre you were driving in, then I think you've got to believe him. Next time, have the goodness not to bother me with such trifles."

'From that time on Dauerling changed.'

The volunteer yawned: 'We must have a good sleep before regimental report. I only wanted to tell you something of what it's like in the regiment. Colonel Schröder doesn't like Major Wenzl. He's altogether a funny bird. Captain Ságner, who looks after the volunteers' school, sees in Schröder the true type of soldier, although nothing in the world frightens Colonel Schröder more than the idea that he might have to go to the front. Ságner is a very smart customer indeed and hates reserve officers just like Schröder. He calls them "civilian stink". He regards volunteers as wild beasts out of which you have to make military robots, sew stars on their tunics and send them to the front to be liquidated instead of noble active officers who have to be preserved for stud purposes.

'All along the line,' said the volunteer, pulling the blanket over him, 'everything in the army stinks of rottenness. Up till now the wide-eyed masses haven't woken up to it. With goggling eyes they let themselves be made into mincemeat and then when they're struck by a bullet they just whisper, "Mummy!" Heroes don't exist, only cattle for the slaughter and the butchers in the general staffs. But in the end everybody will mutiny and there will be a fine shambles. Long live the army! Goodnight!'

The volunteer was quiet. Then he started to toss and turn under the blanket and asked:

'Are you asleep, old man?'

'No,' answered Švejk from the other bunk. 'I'm thinking.'

'What about, old man?'

'About the Great Silver Medal for valour which at the beginning of the war was conferred on a cabinet-maker from Vávrova Street at Vinohrady, Mlíčko by name, because he was the first in his regiment to have his leg torn off by a shell. He got an artificial leg and began to boast about his medal everywhere and to say he was the first and very first war cripple in the regiment. Once he came to the Apollo at Vinohrady and had a row with butchers from the slaughterhouse. In the end they tore off his artificial leg and clouted him over the head with it. The man who tore it off him didn't know it was an artificial one and fainted with fright. At the police station they put Mlíčko's leg back again, but from then on he was furious with his Great Silver Medal for valour and went and pawned it in the pawnshop, where they seized him and the medal too. He had some unpleasantness as a result. There was a kind of special court of honour for disabled soldiers and it sentenced him to be deprived of his Silver Medal and later of his leg as well...'

'How do you mean?'

'Awfully simple. One day a commission came to him and informed him that he was not worthy of having an artificial leg. Then they unscrewed it, took it off and carried it away.

'Or,' Švejk went on, 'it's awful fun too when the survivors of someone who has fallen in the war suddenly receive a medal like that with
an inscription saying that they are lent it so that they can hang it somewhere in an important place. In Božetěchova Street at Vyšehrad an
infuriated father, who thought that the authorities were making fun of
him, hung the medal up in the rears and a policeman who shared those
rears on the gallery with him denounced him for treasonable activities,
and so the poor fellow got hell.'

'From this we may conclude,' said the volunteer, 'that all flesh is as
grass and all the glory of man as the flower of grass. Now they have
published in Vienna *The diary of a one-year volunteer*, and in it there's
a fascinating poem in Czech translation:

> 'There was once a valiant volunteer
> Who gave his life for his country dear
> Thus showing how, without fear or fright,
> A man should for his country fight.
> They carry his corpse on to the gun.
> Prayers rise to heaven, one by one,
> As they pin an order on to the breast
> Of the man who fell at his monarch's behest.

'And so I think,' said the volunteer after a short silence, 'that our
military morale is declining. I therefore propose, old man, that in the
darkness of the night, in the silence of our prison, we sing a song about
the gunner Jabůrek. That will raise military morale. But we must bawl
it out as loud as we can so it can be heard all over the Mariánské
barracks. I accordingly recommend that we should station ourselves
close by the door.'

And from the prison there soon resounded such a powerful roar that
the windows in the corridor began to shake:

> 'And he stood by his gun
> And loaded on, on, on,
> And he stood by his gun
> And loaded on.
> In the midst of war's alarms
> A shell blew off his arms.
> But he stayed where he was
> And loaded on, on, on,
> And he stood by his gun
> And loaded on.'

In the courtyard could be heard steps and voices.

'That's the warder,' said the volunteer. 'With him is Lieutenant Pelikán who is on duty today. He's a reserve officer, a friend of mine from the Czech Club. In civilian life he's a mathematician in an insurance firm. We'll get cigarettes out of him. Let's go on bawling.'

And again could be heard: 'And he stood by his gun . . .'

When the door opened the warder, obviously upset by the presence of the officer on duty, let fly at them sharply:

'This isn't a menagerie!'

'Excuse me,' answered the volunteer, 'this is the local branch of the Rudolfinum. It's a concert in aid of prisoners. We've just finished the first number in the programme: War Symphony.'

'Stop that,' said Lieutenant Pelikán, pretending to be severe. 'I think you know that you have to be in bed at nine o'clock and not make a noise. Your concert number could be heard as far away as the square even.'

'Humbly report, sir,' said the volunteer, 'we didn't rehearse it properly, and if there's any lack of harmony . . .'

'He does that every evening,' said the warder, trying to put the officer up against his enemy. 'Altogether he behaves frightfully unintelligently.'

'Please, sir,' said the volunteer, 'I'd like to speak to you alone. Let the warder wait outside the door.'

When this was done the volunteer said familiarly:

'All right, then, cough up the cigarettes, Franta . . .

'Only Sportky? You're a lieutenant and you haven't got anything better? All right, then, for the time being, thanks very much. And matches too.'

'Sportky!' said the volunteer contemptuously, when the lieutenant had gone. 'Even in the direst straits a man must keep his spirits up. Have a smoke, old man, for the last time. Tomorrow the last judgement awaits us.'

The volunteer did not forget to sing before he fell asleep 'Mountains, valleys and lofty cliffs are my friends. But they cannot bring back to us what we once loved, my beloved sweetheart . . .'

If the volunteer characterized Colonel Schröder as a brute, he was wrong because Colonel Schröder had a partial sense of justice, which manifested itself clearly after those nights when he had been happy with the company in which he spent his evenings in the hotel. And when he had not been happy?

While the volunteer was delivering his crushing criticism of the conditions in the barracks, Colonel Schröder was sitting in the hotel in the company of officers and listening to Lieutenant Kretschmann, who had returned from Serbia with a wounded leg (a cow had gored him), relating how he saw the attack on the Serbian positions from the staff to which he was assigned.

'Yes, now they fly out of the trenches. Along the whole length of two kilometres they now climb over the barbed wire and hurl themselves on the enemy, hand grenades at their belts, gas-masks, rifles over their shoulders, ready to fire, ready for the attack. The bullets whistle. One soldier who jumped out of the trenches falls; another falls on the rampart which had been blown up; a third falls after a few steps, but his comrades sweep on with shouts of "hurrah!" through smoke and powder! And the enemy shoots from all sides, from the trenches and shell craters, and train their machine-guns on us. Again soldiers fall. A group try to reach an enemy machine-gun. They fall too. But their comrades are already in front. Hurrah! An officer falls. The rattle of rifle-fire can no longer be heard. Something frightful is in store. Again a whole group falls and the enemy machine-guns can be heard: ratatata . . . and there falls. . . . Pardon me, I can't go on, I'm drunk . . .'

And the officer with the wounded leg was silent and sat dully on his chair. Colonel Schröder smiled graciously and listened as Captain Spíra opposite him struck the table with his fist as though wanting to start up a quarrel and repeated something which had no meaning and from which it was impossible to deduce what it was intended to mean or what he wanted to say:

'Consider it carefully, please. We have fully mobilized the Austrian Landwehr Uhlans, the Austrian Landwehr, the Bosnian Rifles, the Austrian Rifles, the Austrian Infantry, the Hungarian Infantry, the Tyrolean Imperial Sharpshooters, the Bosnian Infantry, the Hungarian Honvéd Infantry, the Hungarian Hussars, the Landwehr Hussars, the Mounted Rifles, the Dragoons, the Uhlans, the artillery, the train, the sappers, the medical corps, the marines. Do you understand? And Belgium? The first and second levy form the operational army, the third looks after service at the base . . .'

Captain Spíra struck the table with his fist. 'The Landwehr carries out its duties at the base in time of peace.'

A young officer next to him was earnestly trying to convince the colonel that he was a hardened soldier and asserted very loudly to his neighbour: 'Consumptives should be sent to the front. It does them good and after all it's better for the sick to be killed than the fit.'

The colonel smiled, but suddenly he frowned and, turning to Major Wenzl, said: 'I'm surprised Lieutenant Lukáš avoids our company. Since he came here he has not been with us once.'

'He writes verses,' Captain Ságner remarked scornfully. 'Hardly had he come here when he fell in love with the wife of engineer Schreiter, whom he met in the theatre.'

The colonel frowned and stared into space: 'I've heard he can sing couplets.'

'Yes, in the cadet school he used to entertain us a lot with his couplets,' answered Captain Ságner, 'and he knows a lot of good stories. They're marvellous. I don't know why he doesn't join us.'

The colonel shook his head sadly: 'Today there's no longer the right spirit of comradeship among us. In the old days, as I remember, every one of us officers tried to make some contribution to our entertainment in the officers' club. One of them, as I remember, a Lieutenant Dankl, stripped himself naked, lay on the floor, stuck the tail of a herring in his backside and gave us a performance of a mermaid. Another, Lieutenant Schleisner, could wiggle his ears and whinny like a stallion, imitate the mewing of cats and the humming of bumble-bees. I also remember Captain Skoday. He always brought his girls into the mess whenever we wanted them. They were three sisters and he'd trained them like dogs. He put them on the table and they began to strip for us in time. He had a little conductor's baton with him and, all honour to him, he was a splendid bandmaster. And what didn't he do with them on the sofa! Once he had a tub of hot water brought into the middle of the room and each one of us, one after the other, had to go and take a bath with those girls. And he photographed us.'

Recalling this Colonel Schröder smiled ecstatically.

'And what bets we made in the tub,' he went on, smacking his lips lecherously and squirming in his chair. 'But today? Is there any fun at all? And even that coupletist doesn't appear. And the younger officers today don't even know how to hold their drink. It's not yet twelve o'clock and around this table as you see there are five people drunk already. There were times when we sat for two days and the more we drank the more sober we were. We went on pouring beer, wine and liqueurs into ourselves without stop. Today there's no longer the real military spirit. God knows why. No jokes, only everlasting talk without end. Just listen now how at the table down there they're talking about America.'

From the other end of the table someone's solemn voice could be heard saying: 'America can't come into the war. The Americans and British are at daggers drawn. America's not ready for it.'

Colonel Schröder sighed: 'That's the drivelling of reserve officers. It's enough to make you sick. Only yesterday a man like that was writing in a bank somewhere, making paper bags and selling spice, cinnamon and boot polish, or telling children in the school that hunger drives the wolves from the forests. Today he thinks he can be on the same footing as a regular officer, know everything and poke his nose into everything. And when we have a regular officer like Lieutenant Lukáš, he doesn't come and join us.'

Colonel Schröder went off home in an angry mood, and when he woke up the next morning he was in an even worse temper, because in the newspapers which he read in bed he found several times in the reports from the front the sentence that our troops had withdrawn to positions already prepared in advance. These were glorious days for the Austrian army, as like the days of Šabac[1] as two peas in a pod.

And it was under these impressions that at ten o'clock in the morning Colonel Schröder approached the act which, probably quite rightly, the volunteer had characterized as the last judgement.

Švejk and the volunteer stood in the courtyard and waited for the colonel. Already present were the N.C.O.s, the officer on duty, the regimental adjutant and the sergeant-major from the regimental office with the documents about the delinquents on whom the axe of justice – the regimental report – was about to fall.

At last the colonel appeared, frowning and accompanied by Captain Ságner from the volunteers' school. He was nervously striking the tops of his boots with his riding whip.

After having received the report he walked several times in death-like silence past Švejk and the volunteer, who did 'eyes right' or 'eyes left' according to the side from which the colonel appeared. They did this with unusual thoroughness and could easily have twisted their necks, because it lasted so long.

At last the colonel stopped in front of the volunteer who reported: 'One-year volunteer ...'

'I know,' said the colonel tersely. 'A one-year volunteer scum and reject. What do you do in civilian life? Do you study classical philosophy? So I suppose you're a boozed intellectual ...

'Captain,' he called to Ságner, 'bring the whole volunteers' school here.

'Of course,' he went on to the volunteer, 'a Lord High Student of classical philosophy, whom people like us have got to be contaminated with. About turn! Just what I expected! The folds on his greatcoat are not in order. It looks as if he had just left a woman or had been wallowing in a brothel. I'll teach you, you young upstart.'

The volunteers' school marched into the courtyard.

'Form a square!' ordered the colonel. They formed a narrow square round the accused and the colonel.

'Look at that man,' shouted the colonel, pointing to the volunteer with his riding whip. 'He has boozed away the honour of you volun-

1. A town in Serbia which was fought over by the Austrian and Serbian armies in 1914 and 1915.

teers, out of whom we have to train up a cadre of respectable officers who can lead the men to glory on the battlefield. But where would this fellow lead his men to, this drunken sot? From pub to pub. He'd soak up the men's whole rum ration. Have you anything to say in your defence? You haven't. Look at him. He can't even say anything in his own defence and in civilian life he studies classical philosophy. Truly a classic example.'

The colonel pronounced the last words slowly and emphatically and spat: 'A classical philosopher, who in a state of intoxication knocks officers' caps off their heads at night. My God! How lucky that it was only an artillery officer!'

Into that last remark was concentrated all the 91st regiment's loathing for the artillery in Budějovice. Woe betide the artilleryman who fell at night into the hands of the regimental patrols and vice versa. The hatred was frightful and irreconcilable; a vendetta, a blood feud which had been handed down from one year to another, accompanied on both sides with traditional stories, such as how the infantrymen threw the artillerymen into the Vltava or the reverse; how they fought in The Port Arthur, at The Rose and in other numerous places of entertainment in the Southern Bohemian metropolis.

'None the less,' continued the colonel, 'a crime like that must be punished in an exemplary way. The bastard must be expelled from the volunteers' school and morally annihilated. We've quite enough intellectuals of his kind in the army already. Regimental office!'

The sergeant-major from the regimental office advanced gravely with documents and pencil.

There was silence as in a court-room where a murderer is being tried and the judge says: 'I shall now pronounce the sentence.'

And in this very same tone of voice the colonel announced: 'One-year volunteer Marek is sentenced to twenty-one days' "severe". After serving his sentence he is to be sent to the kitchen to peel potatoes.'

Turning to the volunteers' school, the colonel gave the orders to dismiss. They could be heard quickly forming fours and marching off, while the colonel said to Captain Ságner that it was not properly done and in the afternoon he should repeat the march drill with them in the courtyard.

'It must thunder, captain. And one other thing more. I nearly forgot.

Tell them that the whole school has five days confined to barracks, so that they shall never forget their former colleague, the scoundrel Marek.'

But the scoundrel Marek stood by the side of Švejk and looked quite happy. It could not have turned out better for him. It was definitely better to peel potatoes in the kitchen, shape dumplings and take meat

off the bone than stand up to the hurricane fire of the enemy and roar out: 'Form two deep! Fix bayonets!' when one's trousers were full.

Returning from Captain Ságner, Colonel Schröder stopped in front of Švejk and observed him carefully. Švejk's figure at this moment was characterized by his full smiling face, bordered with great ears. They stuck out under his military cap, which was rammed down over his head. The whole created an expression of complete assurance and total ignorance of any offence. His eyes asked: 'Have I done something wrong, please?' His eyes spoke: 'Don't you see that I'm as innocent as a lamb?'

And the colonel concentrated his observations on the question he put to the sergeant-major from the regimental office: 'Idiot?'

And then the colonel saw the mouth of that good-natured face open before him.

'Humbly report, sir, yes, idiot,' Švejk answered for the sergeant-major.

Colonel Schröder nodded to the adjutant and drew him aside. They then called the sergeant-major and looked at the material on Švejk.

'Aha,' said Colonel Schröder. 'So this then is Lieutenant Lukáš's batman who, according to the lieutenant's report, got lost in Tábor. I think that officers must educate their batmen themselves. If Lieutenant Lukáš chose such a patent idiot for his batman he must suffer the consequences. He has plenty of time for it since he doesn't go anywhere. You haven't seen him in our company either, have you? Very well, then. He has quite enough time to train his batman.'

Colonel Schröder walked up to Švejk and looking into his good-natured face said: 'You mentally deficient animal, I give you three days' "severe", and when you have served that, go and report to Lieutenant Lukáš.'

And so Švejk met up again with the volunteer in the regimental prison and Lieutenant Lukáš was able to enjoy the opportunity of being told by Colonel Schröder, who had sent for him: 'Lieutenant, after your arrival in the regiment about a week ago you made an application for a batman, because your servant had got lost on the station in Tábor. Since he has returned ...'

'Sir ...' Lieutenant Lukáš answered pleadingly.

'I have decided,' the colonel went on with emphasis, 'to put him in gaol for three days and then send him back to you ...'

Lieutenant Lukáš staggered out of the colonel's office, completely shattered.

During the three days which Švejk spent in the company of the volunteer Marek he amused himself hugely. Every evening on their plank-beds they made patriotic demonstrations.

In the evening from the prison there could always be heard the strains of 'God save our Emperor' and 'Prince Eugène, the noble

Knight'. They sang also a whole series of military songs and when the warder came in they greeted him with:

> 'Our old warder
> Mayn't give up the ghost,
> Till the devil comes from hell
> And puts him on the roast.
> Comes up with his cart
> And knocks him on the ground.
> Oh, what splendid firewood
> Those devils in hell have found!'

And over the plank-bed the volunteer made a drawing of the warder and wrote underneath it the text of an old song:

> When I went to Prague a sausage for to buy
> Who should I meet but a funny old guy.
> That funny old guy our warder chanced to be,
> And if I hadn't run away he'd have bitten me.

And meanwhile, while they both were teasing the warder, just as in Seville they tease an Andalusian bull with a red cloth, Lieutenant Lukáš was waiting in agony for the moment when Švejk would turn up to report for duty again.

3

Švejk's Adventures in Királyhida

THE 91st regiment moved to Királyhida or Bruck an der Leitha.

Just three hours before Švejk was to be released after three days' confinement he was taken away with the one-year volunteer to the main guard-room and marched to the station under military escort.

'It was known a long time ago,' the volunteer said to him on the way, 'that we'd be transferred to Hungary. There they'll form march battalions, the soldiers'll be trained in field shooting, they'll brawl with the Hungarians and we shall go gaily to the Carpathians. The Hungarians'll come here to Budějovice to do garrison duty and the races'll get mixed. There's a theory that raping girls of another nationality is the best recipe against degeneration. The Swedes and Spaniards did it during the Thirty Years' War, the French under Napoleon and now in the Budějovice region the Hungarians'll do it too, and it won't be rape with gross violence. Everything will be all right in time. Fair exchange is no robbery. A Czech soldier will sleep with a Hungarian girl, an unfortunate Czech girl will take a Hungarian Honvéd into her bed, and centuries later there will be an interesting surprise for the anthropologists: why did people with protruding cheekbones appear on the banks of the Malše?'

'This cross-breeding,' observed Švejk, 'is a very interesting matter altogether. In Prague there is a negro waiter called Kristián, whose father was an Abyssinian king and who had himself exhibited in a circus at Štvanice in Prague. A schoolmistress who used to write verses in *Lada* about shepherds and a forest brook went with him to a hotel and fornicated with him, as it says in the Holy Scripture, and she was awfully surprised when she gave birth to a little boy who was completely white. All right, but after a fortnight the little boy began to get brown. He got browner and browner and then after a month he began to get black. Within half a year he was as black as his grandfather, the Abyssinian king. She went with him to the clinic for skin diseases in the hope that they'd be able to bleach him somehow, but there they told her that it was a real black nigger skin and there was nothing to be done. This drove her off her head; she began to write to the magazines for advice on what to do against niggers, and they took her away to Kateřinky[1] and put the little nigger boy in an orphanage, where they had an awful lot of fun with him. Then he learned to be a waiter and went dancing in night clubs. Today there are Czech mulattoes who have been successfully bred from him and are not as coloured as he was. A medico who used to go to The Chalice once told us that it's not quite as simple as all that. A half-breed like that brings half-breeds into the world again and they can't be distinguished from white people. But suddenly in a later generation a negro turns up. Imagine the catastrophe! You might get married to a young lady. The filly is quite white and suddenly she gives birth to a negro baby. And if before her ninth month she went without you to the Variety Theatre to watch wrestling where a negro was performing, I think the whole thing would give you something to think about.'

'The case of your negro, Kristián,' said the volunteer, 'has to be looked at from a war point of view too. Let's suppose they called that

---

1. Lunatic asylum at Prague.

negro up. He's from Prague and so he comes under the 28th regiment. But you've heard how the 28th regiment went over to the Russians. How surprised the Russians would be if they found they had taken the negro Kristián prisoner. The Russian newspapers would certainly write that Austria was driving into the war the colonial troops she hasn't got and was already drawing on her nigger reserves.'

'People used to say,' put in Švejk, 'that Austria did have some colonies somewhere in the north. Emperor Franz-Josephs-Land or something . . .'

'Lay off, boys,' said one of the escort soldiers. 'You'd better be careful not to speak about any Emperor Franz-Josephs-Land today. Don't mention any names and it'll be better for you . . .'

'Well, then, look at the map,' the volunteer put in. 'There really does exist a land of our most gracious monarch, the Emperor Franz Joseph. According to the statistics the only thing on it is ice which is exported from it on ice-breakers belonging to the Prague ice works. This ice industry is highly prized by foreigners, because it is a profitable, if dangerous, enterprise. The greatest danger occurs during the transport of the ice from Emperor Franz-Josephs-Land across the polar circle. Can you imagine it?'

The soldier from the escort muttered something unintelligible and the corporal, who accompanied the escort, came nearer and listened to the further remarks of the volunteer, who went on solemnly: 'This one and only Austrian colony can supply the whole of Europe with ice and is an outstanding national economic asset. Colonization is proceeding slowly of course, because colonists partly don't volunteer and partly get frozen to death. None the less, with the help of an adjustment of the climatic conditions, in which the Ministries of Trade and Foreign Affairs have a great interest, there is hope that the great areas of the icebergs will be appropriately exploited. By building several hotels heaps of tourists will be attracted. It will of course be necessary to lay out tourist paths and roads between the ice floes and to paint tourist signs on the icebergs. The only difficulty are the Eskimoes, who make the work of our local authorities impossible . . .

'The bastards won't learn German,' continued the volunteer, while the corporal listened with interest. He was an active man – a farm-hand in civil life. He was stupid and coarse, swallowed everything which he knew nothing about and his ideal was to grow old in Austrian service.

'The Ministry of Education, corporal, built a school for them at great expense and sacrifice. Five of the builders froze to death . . .'

'The bricklayers survived,' Švejk interrupted him, 'because they kept themselves warm with the pipes they lit.'

'Not all of them,' said the volunteer. 'Two of them unfortunately forgot to puff and their pipes went out. And so they had to be buried in the ice. But in the end the school was built out of ice bricks and re-inforced concrete, which holds together very well, but the Eskimoes lit a fire all round it out of the wood from merchant ships which were ice-bound, and achieved what they wanted. The ice on which the school was built melted away and the whole school with the headmaster and the government representative, who was to have been at the solemn consecration of the school the next day, fell into the sea. When he was up to his neck in water you could hear the government representative shout out: "*Gott strafe England!*" Now they'll probably send an army there to restore order among the Eskimoes. Of course it'll be a hard war with them. What will cause our troops the most damage will be the tame polar bears.'

'That would be the last straw,' the corporal observed wisely. 'As though there were not enough war inventions already. Take for instance gas masks for gas poisoning. You put one on your head and you're poisoned, as they told us in the N.C.O.s' school.'

'They're only trying to frighten you,' said Švejk. 'No soldier ought to be afraid of anything. Even if he falls into the rears while fighting he should only lick himself and go back into battle. And everyone's used to poison gas in the barracks, when they serve a ration of new bread and peas with groats. But now they say the Russians have got a new invention against N.C.O.s . . . .'

'Those are probably special electrical currents,' the volunteer added. 'When they are connected to the stars on the N.C.O.s' collars the stars explode because they're made out of celluloid. That'll be a new disaster.'

And although the corporal in civilian life was a cowman and a prize fat-head as well, he perhaps understood in the end that they were pulling his leg, left them, and went away to the head of the patrol.

Moreover they were drawing near to the station where the inhabitants of Budějovice were taking leave of their regiment. It had no official character, but the square in front of the station was filled with people who were waiting for the army.

Švejk's interest was concentrated on the crowds lining the streets. As was usually the case the good soldiers marched in the rear and those under arrest at the head. The good soldiers would later be squashed into cattle trucks and Švejk with the volunteer would be put into a special prisoners' van, which was always attached to the military trains just behind the staff carriage. In a prisoners' van of this kind there was always heaps of room.

Švejk could not help crying out '*Nazdar!*'[1] to the line of people and waving his cap. It worked so suggestively that the crowd repeated it loudly and '*Nazdar*' spread far and wide and thundered in front of the station. Far away people began to say: 'They're coming.'

The corporal from the escort was quite upset and shouted at Švejk to shut his mug. But the shouts spread like an avalanche. The gendarmes pushed the crowds back and made a path for the escort, but people went on shouting '*Nazdar!*' and waved their caps and hats.

It was a regular manifestation. From the windows of the hotel opposite the station some ladies waved their handkerchieves and cried: '*Heil!*' In the crowd too, '*Nazdar*' mingled with German '*Heil*' and one enthusiast who used the opportunity to shout out in German 'Down with the Serbs' was tripped up and slightly trampled on in the artificial log-jam.

And like an electric spark it flashed along: 'They're coming!'

And they came, Švejk under armed escort waving affably to the crowd and the volunteer solemnly saluting.

It was in this way they went into the station and to the military train appointed for them, where the band of the Sharpshooters, whose conductor was seriously confused by the unexpected manifestation, nearly started to play 'God save our Emperor'. Fortunately in the nick of time the senior chaplain, Father Lacina, from the 7th cavalry division, appeared in a black bowler and began to restore order.

His story was a simple one. He had come to Budějovice the day before and as though by chance attended a small banquet of the officers of the departing regiment. A voracious glutton, the scourge of all the officers' messes, he ate and drank for ten people and went in a more or less intoxicated condition to the officers' mess to try to wheedle some scraps out of the cook. He gulped down dishes of sauces and dumplings, tore the meat from the bones like a wild cat and finally got to the rum in the kitchen. When he had soaked up so much of it that he belched he

1. The greeting used by Czech patriots.

returned to the farewell party and distinguished himself there by a
fresh bout of boozing. He had rich experience of this sort of thing and
in the 7th cavalry division he always cost the officers a lot of money. In
the morning he got the idea that he must clean things up when the first
regimental carriages went off and so he sauntered along the whole length
of the crowd, and produced such an effect in the station that the officers
in charge of the regiment's transport shut themselves up in the station
master's office to get away from him.

And so he appeared again in front of the station just in time to tear
away the baton from the bandmaster of the Sharpshooters at the
moment when he was about to conduct 'God save our Emperor'.

'Stop!' he said. 'Not yet! Wait till I give you the word. Stand at
ease until I come back.' He went off into the station and set off after
the escort, which he stopped with his shout of 'Halt!'.

'Where are you off to?' he said severely to the corporal, who had
no idea what to do in the new situation.

The good-natured Švejk answered for him: 'They are taking us to
Bruck. If you'd like to come with us too, sir, you can.'

'Very well, then, I will,' said Father Lacina, and turning to the escort
added: 'Who says I can't? Forward march!'

When the senior chaplain found himself in the prisoners' van, he lay
down on the bench, and the good-natured Švejk divested himself of
his own greatcoat and put it under his head, while the volunteer
observed softly to the horrified corporal: 'Nursing service for senior
chaplains.'

Father Lacina, now comfortably stretched out on the bench, began
to expound: 'Ragout with mushrooms, gentlemen, is better the more
mushrooms there are, but the mushrooms must first be fried with
onions and only afterwards should bay leaves and onions be added ...'

'You've put the onions in already, sir,' said the volunteer. The
corporal looked at him in desperation, seeing in Father Lacina a drunk
indeed but at the same time his superior officer none the less.

The corporal's situation was really desperate.

'Yes,' put in Švejk, 'the senior chaplain is perfectly right. The more
onions the better. In Pakoměřice there lived a brewer who used to put
onions in the beer, because he said onions provoke thirst. The onion is
a frightfully useful thing altogether. Fried onions are used against
boils too ...'

Father Lacina was meanwhile talking in a half-whisper on the bench

as though in a dream: 'Everything depends on the spices, what spices it's seasoned with and the quantity. There shouldn't be too much pepper or too much paprika . . .'

As he went on he talked slower and more softly: 'Not too many cloves, not too much lemon, not too much allspice, not too much muscat . . .'

He never finished and fell asleep whistling through his nose when he stopped snoring from time to time.

The corporal looked at him with a glassy eye, while the men from the escort sat on their benches and laughed quietly.

'He's not going to wake up so quick,' said Švejk after a time. 'He's completely sozzled.

'It doesn't matter,' Švejk went on, when the corporal gave him an anguished sign to keep quiet. 'You can't do anything about it. He's as tight as a lord. He's got the rank of a captain. All these chaplains, never mind whether they're senior or junior, have the special gift from God of getting themselves stinking drunk at every opportunity. I served under Chaplain Katz and he could have drunk his own nose away. What this man's doing here is absolutely nothing compared with what the other used to do. Together we pawned the monstrance to get drink, and we'd have even pawned the Lord God himself, if anyone had advanced us money on him.'

Švejk approached Father Lacina, turned him over towards the wall and said with the confidence of an expert: 'He'll go on snoring until we get to Bruck.' Then he returned to his place, followed by the despairing look of the unfortunate corporal, who observed: 'Perhaps I should go and report it.'

'Don't think of doing so,' said the volunteer. 'You are in command of the escort. You mustn't leave us. And according to regulations you mustn't let any of the escorting guard go away to make a report until you have a replacement. As you see, this is a knotty problem. Nor can you fire a shot as a signal for someone to come, because that's not possible either. Nothing is happening here. On the other hand there's a regulation that apart from the prisoners and the escorts accompanying them no one else is allowed in the prisoners' van. Entrance is strictly forbidden to unauthorized persons. Moreover, if you wanted to cover up the traces of your delinquency and unobtrusively throw the senior chaplain out of the train while it's going you couldn't do that either, because here there are witnesses, who have seen that you let him come into the van where he doesn't belong. You'll certainly get demoted, corporal.'

The corporal replied in confusion that he had not allowed the senior chaplain to come into the van; he had come in of his own accord and he was after all a superior officer.

'You are the only superior here,' the volunteer asserted emphatically. And Švejk completed the utterance: 'Even if His Imperial Majesty wanted to come in you shouldn't let him. It's just like being on guard when an inspecting officer comes to a recruit and asks him to go and fetch cigarettes for him and the recruit asks him what sort he should bring him. For that you'll be put into the fortress.'

The corporal feebly objected that it had after all been Švejk who had been the first to tell the senior chaplain that he could join them.

'I can afford to do that, corporal,' answered Švejk, 'because I'm soft-headed, but no one would expect it from you.'

'Have you been a regular for long?' the volunteer asked the corporal in course of conversation.

'Three years. And now I expect to be promoted platoon sergeant.'

'You can put paid to that,' said the volunteer cynically. 'I tell you, it looks like demotion.'

'It's all the same,' said Švejk, 'whether you fall as an N.C.O. or as an ordinary soldier – but it's true that they push the demoted into the first ranks of the firing line.'

The senior chaplain stirred.

'He's snoozing,' said Švejk, when he had ascertained that everything was in the best order. 'Now he's certainly dreaming about some blow-out. I'm only afraid that he may do something here. When my chaplain Katz got sozzled, he didn't know what he was doing in his sleep. Once he . . .'

And Švejk began to relate his experiences with Chaplain Otto Katz in such detail and in such an interesting way that they did not notice that the train had started.

It was only the roar from the vans behind which interrupted Švejk's narrative. The 12th company, which consisted exclusively of Germans from Krumlov and Kašperské Hory, were bawling out:

> 'When I come, when I come,
> When I come, come again.'

And from another van a desperate fellow howled out towards disappearing Budějovice:

> 'And you, my dear,
>   Stay here.
>   Holaryo, holaryo, holo!'

It was such a frightful yodelling and screeching that his comrades had to drag him away from the open door of the cattle truck.

'I'm surprised we haven't had any inspection yet,' the volunteer said to the corporal. 'According to regulations, as soon as we got to the station you should have reported us to the commandant of the train and not have wasted your time on a drunken senior chaplain.'

The wretched corporal preserved an obstinate silence and went on staring stubbornly at the disappearing telegraph posts.

'When I think that we've not been reported to anybody,' continued the volunteer maliciously, 'and that at the next station the train commander will certainly come and see us, then all my soldier's blood rises up in protest. Why we're being treated like . . .'

'Like gipsies,' Švejk put in, 'or tramps. It's as though we were afraid of God's light and dared not report anywhere in case they lock us up.'

'Apart from that,' said the volunteer, 'pursuant to the decree of 21 November 1879 the following regulations have to be observed when arrested soldiers are being taken by train: first, the prisoners' van must be furnished with bars. This is as clear as daylight and has been carried out here according to regulations. We are behind perfect bars. And so that's in order. Secondly, supplementary to the Imperial and Royal decree of 21 November 1879 there must be a W.C. in every prison van. If there is not, the van must be fitted with a chamber pot with a lid for the discharge of the great and small bodily needs of the prisoners and the escort. In our case we can't really talk about a prison van where there might be a W.C. We're simply in a reserved compartment, isolated from the whole world. And there's no chamber pot here . . .'

'You can do it through the window,' the corporal said in despairing tones.

'You forget,' said Švejk, 'that no prisoner may approach the window.'

'Then thirdly,' continued the volunteer, 'a vessel with drinking water has to be provided. You haven't bothered about that either. By the way, do you know at what station they'll give us our mess portions? You don't? I knew you hadn't taken the trouble to find out . . .'

'And so you see, corporal,' observed Švejk, 'that conveying prisoners isn't just a Sunday-school treat. We have to be looked after. We're no ordinary soldiers who can look after ourselves. Everything has to be brought to our very noses, because there are decrees and clauses about it which everyone must observe, otherwise there would be no order. "A man under arrest is like a baby in swaddling clothes," a notorious ragamuffin said to me once. "He has to be looked after in case he catches cold or gets excited, so that he's content with his lot and no one insults him, poor little chap."'

'By the way,' said Švejk after a moment, looking in a friendly way at the corporal, 'would you be kind enough to tell me when it's eleven o'clock?'

The corporal looked at Švejk inquiringly.

'You obviously wanted to ask me, corporal, why you should tell me when it's eleven o'clock. From eleven o'clock onwards I belong to the cattle truck, corporal,' said Švejk with emphasis and went on in a solemn voice: 'On regimental report I was sentenced to three days. At eleven o'clock I started serving my sentence and today at eleven o'clock I must be released. After eleven o'clock I have no business here. No soldier may be detained longer than he has to be, because in the army discipline and order must be observed, corporal.'

The desperate corporal took a long time to recover from this blow, but finally voiced the objection that he had received no papers.

'My dear corporal,' said the volunteer, 'papers don't go to the escort commander of their own accord. If the mountain won't go to Mahommed the escort commander must go and fetch the papers himself. You're now faced with a new situation. Definitely you have no right to detain anyone who should be set free. On the other hand, according to current regulations no one may leave a prison van. Honestly, I don't know how you're going to get out of this awful situation. The further you go the worse it seems. Now it's half past ten.'

The volunteer pushed his watch back into his pocket: 'I'm very curious to know, corporal, what you are going to do in half an hour's time.'

'In half an hour's time I belong to the cattle truck,' Švejk repeated dreamily, whereupon the corporal, who was by now in a state of complete confusion and demoralization, turned to him and said:

'If it isn't inconvenient to you, I think it's much more comfortable here than in the cattle truck. I believe . . .'

He was interrupted by a shout from the senior chaplain who screamed in his sleep: 'More gravy!'

'Hushaby, hushaby,' said Švejk affably, putting under the senior chaplain's head the corner of his own greatcoat, which was falling from the bench. 'Go on dreaming something nice about guzzling.'

And the volunteer began to sing:

> 'Hushaby baby on the tree-top,
> When the wind blows the cradle will rock.
> When the bough bends the cradle will fall,
> Down comes baby, cradle and all.'

The desperate corporal no longer reacted to anything.

He stared blankly at the countryside and gave full rein to the utter disorganization in the prisoners' van.

By the partition the escort were playing 'flesh', and nimble and hefty swipes were falling on their buttocks. When he looked in their direction his eyes caught the provocative hindquarters of an infantryman. He sighed and turned back to the window again.

The volunteer thought for a moment about something and then addressed the crushed corporal: 'Do you know the magazine *The Animal World*?'

'That magazine,' the corporal answered with an obvious expression of pleasure that the conversation was taking another turn, 'used to be taken by the pub-keeper in our village, because he was frightfully keen on angora goats and they all pegged out. So he asked advice from it.'

'My dear fellow,' said the volunteer, 'the story I am now going to tell will prove to you as clearly as daylight that no one is free from faults! I'm convinced, gentlemen, that you in the back there will stop playing "flesh", because what I'm going to tell you now will be very interesting if for nothing else for the mere fact that you won't be able to understand many technical expressions in it. I'm going to tell you a story about *The Animal World* so that we can forget our war troubles of today.

'How I actually once became editor of *The Animal World*, a very interesting magazine, was for some time a pretty insoluble puzzle for me, until I had reached the conclusion that I could only have accepted the job in the completely demented state of mind into which I had been driven by my friendly affection for my old comrade Hájek. Up to that time he had edited the magazine quite decently, but while doing so he fell in love with the daughter of its owner, Mr Fuchs, who gave him an hour's notice on condition that he found a decent editor for him.

'As you can see there were strange labour relations at that time.

'When I was introduced to the owner of the magazine by my friend Hájek, he received me very courteously and asked me whether I had any idea at all about animals. He was very satisfied with my answer that I had always had a very high respect for animals and saw in them the transition stage to man. Particularly from the point of view of animal protection I had always respected their desires and wishes. No animal has any other wish than to be liquidated as painlessly as possible before it is eaten.

'From the day of its birth the carp is dominated by the idea that it is not nice of the cook to slit its belly while it's still alive. The custom of decapitating a cock is a step towards the principles of the Society for the

Prevention of Cruelty to Animals, that poultry should not have their throats slit bv unprofessional hands.

'The twisted forms of fried roaches prove that in the act of dying they protest against being fried alive in margarine in Podolí. To chase a turkey . . .

'At that moment he interrupted me and asked me whether I knew anything about poultry-keeping, dogs, rabbits, bee-keeping, miscellanea from the animal world; whether I could cut out of foreign magazines pictures for reproduction, translate expert articles in foreign journals about animals, consult the pages of Brehm and cooperate with him in writing leading articles about the life of animals in connection with Catholic saints' days, the varying seasons, horse-racing, hunting and shooting, the training of police dogs, national and church holidays – in short have a journalist's bird's-eye view of the situation and make use of it in a short meaty leader.

'I declared that I had already thought a great deal about how a magazine like *The Animal World* ought properly to be run, and that I could fully cope with all those columns and points, having perfectly mastered all the subjects he'd mentioned. My endeavour would be to raise the magazine to an unusually high standard. I would re-organize its contents and system.

'I would introduce new columns such as for instance: "Gay Animals' Corner", "Animals about Animals", always carefully taking the political situation into account.

'I would offer the readers surprise after surprise, so that they would not be able to recover breath from one animal to the next. A column, "A Day in the Life of the Animals", ought to alternate with "A New Programme for Solving the Question of Farm Animals" and "The Cattle Movement".

'Again he interrupted me and said that this would do perfectly and if I succeeded in carrying out only half of it he would give me a pair of bantam Wyandottes from the last Berlin poultry exhibition. They had won the first prize and their owner had been awarded a gold medal for excellent selective breeding.

'I can say that I did my best and kept to my action programme for running the magazine as far as lay within my powers. But I soon discovered that my articles went beyond my capabilities.

'Wishing to offer the public something completely new I invented animals.

'I proceeded from the basic assumption that animals like, for instance, the elephant, the tiger, the lion, the monkey, the mole, the horse, the pig etc. were already quite familiar creatures to the readers of *The Animal World* and that it was therefore necessary to stimulate the readers with something fresh, with new discoveries. And so I made an experiment with the Sulphur-Bellied Whale. This new kind of whale of mine was the size of a cod and was equipped with a bladder full of formic acid as well as a special cloaca through which it could make an explosive discharge of narcotic poisonous acid on small fishes which it wanted to devour. An English scientist, I've forgotten now what name I gave him, later gave this acid the name of whale acid. Whale blubber was already known to everybody, but the new acid aroused the attention of several readers, who asked for the name of the firm manufacturing it.

'I can assure you that the readers of *The Animal World* are in general very inquisitive.

'Shortly after the Sulphur-Bellied Whale I discovered a whole series of other animals. Among them I would mention the Artful Prosperian, a mammal of the kangaroo family; the Edible Ox, the ancient prototype of the cow; the Sepia Infusorian, which I characterized as a sort of sewer rat.

'My new animals multiplied daily. I was extremely surprised myself by my successes in these spheres. I never had any idea that it would be necessary to make such copious additions to the animal kingdom and that Brehm had left out so many animals from his book *The Life of Animals*. Did Brehm and all those who followed him know of my bat from Iceland, the Faraway Bat, or of my domestic cat from the peak of Mount Kilimanjaro called the Irritable Bazouky Stag-Puss?

'Did zoologists before have any idea of Engineer Khun's Flea, which I found in amber and which was completely blind, because it lived on an underground prehistoric mole, which was also blind because its great-great-grandmother had mated, as I wrote, with a blind underground olm from the Postumia caves, which at that time stretched as far as the Baltic Sea of today?

'From this trifling event there developed an extensive controversy between *Čas* and *Čech*,[1] because the latter in its feuilleton on miscellanea

1. *Čas* ('Time') was the newspaper which voiced the ideas of T. G. Masaryk and his 'Realist Party' from 1887 to 1923. *Čech* ('The Czech') was the organ of the conservative wing of the People's (Clerical) Party.

quoted the article about the flea I had discovered and stated: "What God does he does well." *Čas*, naturally in a purely realistic way, tore my flea to shreds together with the august *Čech*, and from that time it seemed that my lucky star as inventor and discoverer of new creations was deserting me. The subscribers to *The Animal World* began to get worried.

'This was due to my various small news-stories about bee-keeping and poultry-keeping, where I developed my new theories. They caused genuine panic, because after reading my simple pieces of advice the well-known bee-keeper, Mr Pazourek, had a stroke and bee-keeping in the Šumava and Podkrkonoší died out completely. The poultry was attacked by a pest and, in a word, everything began to peg out. The subscribers wrote threatening letters and refused to take the journal.

'I then threw myself into wild birds and I can still today remember my affair with the editor of *Peasant Horizon*, the clerical deputy and director, Josef M. Kadlčák.

'I cut out of the English magazine *Country Life* a picture of a little bird sitting on a walnut tree. I gave it the name of nutcracker, just as I wouldn't have hesitated logically to write that a bird sitting on a juniper tree was a junip or a gincracker.

'And what didn't happen after that? I was attacked by Mr Kadlčák, who wrote to me on an ordinary postcard and said that the bird was a jay and certainly no nutcracker, which was a mistranslation of the German *Eichelhäher*.

'I sent him a letter in which I expounded my whole theory about the nutcracker, interpolating frequent words of abuse and imaginary quotations from Brehm.

'Deputy Kadlčák replied with a leader in *Peasant Horizon*.

'My chief, Mr Fuchs, was sitting as usual in the café and reading the provincial press, because he had recently been spending an awful lot of time looking for references to my thrilling articles in *The Animal World*. When I came in he pointed to a copy of *Peasant Horizon* which was lying on the table and spoke quietly, looking at me with that sad expression which had latterly never left his eyes.

'I read aloud in the presence of all the public in the café:

'Honoured Sir,
I have drawn your attention to the fact that your journal is introducing an unusual and unjustifiable terminology, that it shows scant regard for the purity of the Czech language and that it is inventing animals of various kinds.

I cited as evidence that instead of the generally adopted old-established name of "jay" your editor has introduced the name "acorncracker" which has its origin in a mistranslation of the German name "*Eichelhäher*" – jay.

' "Jay," the owner of the newspaper repeated desperately after me.
'I went on reading calmly:

'Then I received from your editor of *The Animal World* a letter which was insufferably vulgar, personal and impertinent, in which I was criminally referred to as a bloody ignorant mule, which merits the sharpest of rebukes. This is not the way respectable people reply to objective scholarly criticisms. I should like to know which of us two is the bigger mule. It is true, perhaps, that I should not have made my reproaches on a postcard, but rather have consigned them to a letter, but through great pressure of work I overlooked this trifling matter. Now after the vulgar onslaught of your editor of *The Animal World* I am determined to pillory him in public.

'Your editor is making a frightful mistake if he imagines that I am an uneducated mule who has no conception of the nomenclature of this or that bird. I have occupied myself with ornithology for years and not from books but from observation in nature. In my cages I have kept far more birds than your editor has ever seen in all his life, he being a man who spends his life immured in Prague gin-palaces and pubs.

'But these are questions of secondary consideration, although it certainly would have done no harm if before starting to make these sallies with his pen your editor of *The Animal World* had taken the trouble to find out whom he was accusing of being a mule, in case it should be destined for Frýdland near Místek in Moravia, where before the appearance of this article your journal had subscribers too.

'It is not a question of personal polemics with some insane lout but of facts, and so I repeat once more that it is quite impermissible to invent names by translation, when we have in our own language the universally known name of "jay".

' "Yes, jay," said my chief in an even more despondent voice.
'I went on reading calmly without letting myself be interrupted.

'It is plain villainy when this is done by ignoramuses and vandals. Who ever called a jay a "nutcracker"? In the book *Our Birds* on page 148 there is the Latin name: ganulus glandarius[1] B.A. That is my bird – the jay.

'The editor of your journal will certainly acknowledge that I know my own bird better than any layman can know it. According to D. Bayer the nutcracker is called mucifraga carycatectes B.[2] and that "B" does not mean,

---

1. '*Garrulus* glandarius'.
2. *Nucifraga*.

as your editor wrote to me in his letter, the first letter of a certain word. Czech ornithologists know only the common jay and certainly not your "acorncracker", which is the brain-child of that very gentleman, to whom, in accordance with his theory, the initial letter "B" belongs. It is a piece of crude personal invective which does not alter the facts.

'Jay remains jay, even if the editor of *The Animal World* p—s with rage over it, and it only goes to prove how frivolously and unobjectively people can sometimes write, even if he has cited Brehm in an ostentatiously rude way. The lout has the impudence to write that, according to Brehm, the jay belongs to the family of the crocodiloids, page 452, where the reference is to the lesser grey shrike or common butcher-bird (lanius minor L.). Then this ignoramissimus, if I may use this euphemism, again cites Brehm as the authority for his statement that the jay belongs to the fifteenth family, whereas in fact Brehm assigns the crows to the seventeenth family which includes rooks and the jackdaw family. He is so vulgar as to call me a jackdaw (colaeus) and the genus of magpies, blue crows, the sub-family of moron ineptus, although on the same page the reference is to wood-jays and spotted magpies . . .

' "Wood-jays!" sighed my magazine-owner, putting his hands to his head. "Give it back so that I can finish reading it."

'I was afraid that he had lost his voice when he went on reading: "The ring ouzel or Turkish blackbird will always be in Czech translation ring ouzel, just as fieldfare will always be fieldfare."

' "The fieldfare ought to be called the junip or gincracker, sir," I interposed, "because it feeds on juniper from which you make gin."

'Mr Fuchs threw the newspapers on to the table and crawled under the billiard table, gasping out the last words he had read:

' "Turdus, ring ouzel."

' "No jay," he howled from underneath the billiard table. "Nut-cracker. I bite, gentlemen!"

'He was finally dragged out and two days later he expired from cerebral influenza in the bosom of his family.

'His last words in his last lucid moment were: "It is not a question of my personal interests but of the common weal. From that point of view be so good as to accept my judgement, which is as objective as . . ." – and he hiccupped.'

The volunteer paused and said maliciously to the corporal:

'I only meant by that that at some time or other everybody finds himself in a dicey situation and makes a blunder!'

All in all the only thing the corporal understood from all this was that he was the one who was making a blunder and so he turned back to the window and stared gloomily at the retreating landscape.

Švejk showed more interest in the story. The escort looked stupidly at each other.

Švejk began: 'Nothing remains hidden in the world. Everything comes to light in the end, as you've heard, and it even turns out that an idiotic jay like that is not a nutcracker. It's really very interesting that anyone could be taken in by a trick like that. It's true that inventing animals is a difficult thing to do, but presenting animals which have been invented is really much harder. Once some years ago in Prague there was a chap called Mestek who discovered a mermaid and exhibited her behind a screen in Havlíček Street in Vinohrady. In the screen there was an opening, and everybody could see in the half-light a common or garden sofa with a woman from Žižkov sprawling on it. Her legs were wrapped up in green gauze, which was supposed to represent a tail. Her hair was painted green and she had gloves on her hands with cardboard fins fitted on them, which were also green. And on her spine she had a kind of rudder fixed with a cord. Young people under sixteen were not allowed in, but all those who were over sixteen and had paid for their tickets were absolutely delighted to find that that mermaid had enormous buttocks on which was the inscription: "Au revoir!" As for her breasts they were nothing to shout about. They flopped down to her stomach like a worn-out trollop's. At seven o'clock in the evening Mestek shut the panorama and said: "Mermaid, you can go home." She changed and already at ten o'clock at night you could see her walking up and down Táborská Street and saying quite unobtrusively to every gentleman she met: "Darling, what about coming and playing philopena with me?" Because she didn't have a registration book Drašner locked her up with other tarts like her he had caught in a raid, and Mestek lost his business.'

At that moment the senior chaplain fell off the bench but went on sleeping on the floor. The corporal stared at him stupidly and then during the general silence lifted him on to the bench again without any help from the others. He had obviously lost all authority and when he said in a weak, hopeless voice: 'You might give me a hand,' all the escort looked woodenly and none of them stirred a finger.

'You should have left him snoozing where he was,' said Švejk. 'I never did anything else with my chaplain. Once I let him sleep in the W.C. Once he slept on top of the cupboard, another time in the washing trough in someone else's house and God knows where else he didn't lie and snooze.'

The corporal was suddenly seized by a fit of determination: he wanted to show that he was master here and so he said rudely: 'Shut your mug and don't drivel! Every batman blathers too much. You're worse than vermin.'

'Yes, of course, and you're God, corporal,' answered Švejk with the composure of a philosopher who wants to bring about universal peace throughout the world and launches into frightful arguments. 'You are the Madonna of the Seven Griefs.'

'Oh, God, our heavenly father,' the volunteer cried, wringing his hands, 'fill our hearts with love for all N.C.O.s, that we may not look upon them with loathing. Bless our congregation in this prison hole on wheels.'

The corporal flushed and jumped up: 'I forbid all remarks, you one-yearer.'

'You can't help it,' continued the volunteer in a soothing tone. 'Nature has denied many breeds and families of animals any intelligence whatsoever. Have you ever heard talk of human stupidity? Wouldn't it have been much better if you'd been born some other kind of mammal and not got the idiotic name of human being and corporal? It's a great mistake for you to think that you're the most perfect and most developed creature. If they take your stars away from you you're a mere cipher to be shot dead in any trench and on any front without anybody caring. If they give you another pip and make you into an animal that's called an "old sweat" it still won't be all right with you. Your mental horizon'll get still narrower and when somewhere on the front you lay down your culturally underdeveloped bones there won't be anyone in Europe to shed a tear for you.'

'I'll have you clapped in gaol,' shouted the corporal despairingly.

The volunteer smiled: 'Of course you'd like to clap me in gaol because I've called you names. But you'd be lying, because your mental faculties are quite incapable of grasping any insults and, apart from that, I'm willing to bet you what you like that you don't remember a single word of our conversation. If I said to you that you were an embryo, you'd forget it not just before we come to the next station but before the next telegraph post flashes past us. You're a piece of defunct grey matter. I can't imagine that you could ever report coherently what you've heard me say. Apart from that, you can ask anybody you like whether my words contain the slightest reference to your mental horizon and whether I have insulted you in any way.'

'Why, of course not,' confirmed Švejk. 'No one here said a single word to you on which you could possibly put a wrong construction. It's always bad when someone feels himself insulted. Once I was sitting in the night café The Tunnel and we talked about orang-outangs. There was a sailor sitting with us and he told us that you often can't tell an orang-outang from an ordinary citizen with a beard. An orang-outang has his chin covered with tufts like . . ."like," he went on, "shall we say, that gentleman sitting there at the next table." We all looked round and that man with the beard went up to the sailor and slapped his face. The sailor then broke his head with a beer bottle and the bearded gentleman fell down and lay unconscious. We said goodbye to that sailor, because he went away at once when he saw he had very nearly slain the man. Then we revived the gentleman, which we certainly shouldn't have done, because as soon as he was revived he called the police against all of us, although we had had absolutely nothing to do with it, and the police took us off to the police station. There he went on saying that we had taken him for an orang-outang and that we had been talking about nothing else but him. And so he went on. But we objected and said he wasn't an orang-outang. And he said, yes, he was one, he'd heard it. I asked the police commissioner if he would explain it to him. And he explained it to him quite good-naturedly, but even then that fellow wouldn't hear of it and told the commissioner that he didn't understand anything about it and was in league with us. And so the commissioner had him locked up to sober him, and we wanted to go back to The Tunnel, but we couldn't because we were put into clink too. So you see, corporal, what can come out of a small and unimportant misunderstanding, which is not worth mentioning. In Okrouhlice, too, there was a citizen who got offended when they told him in Německý Brod that he was an Indian python. There are a lot of other words like that which are not criminal at all. For instance, if we told you that you were a musk-rat, would you really have any reason to be angry with us?'

The corporal squealed. You could not say that he roared. Rage, fury, despair, all this merged in a series of powerful sounds and the concert number was completed by the whistling act which the snoring senior chaplain performed through his nose.

After this squealing total depression set in. The corporal sat down on

the bench and his watery expressionless eyes fixed themselves on the forests and mountains in the distance.

'Corporal,' said the volunteer, 'when you stare at the soughing hills and fragrant forests you remind me of the figure of Dante. The same noble face of the poet, a man of gentle heart and soul, susceptible to noble emotion. Please go on sitting there. It suits you very well. With what inspiration, without any affectation or pompousness, you stare out on the countryside. Certainly you are thinking how beautiful it will be in the spring when in the place of these barren spots a carpet of gaily coloured meadow flowers will unfold . . .'

'And that carpet will be hugged by a little brooklet,' observed Švejk, 'and the corporal will be licking his pencil, sitting on a tree-stump and writing a little poem to *The Young Reader*.'

The corporal became completely apathetic while the volunteer maintained that he had definitely seen the corporal's head modelled at a sculptural exhibition:

'Excuse me, corporal, isn't it true that you once sat for the great sculptor Štursa?'

The corporal looked at him and said sadly:

'No, I didn't.'

The volunteer was silent and stretched himself out on the bench.

The men from the escort were playing cards with Švejk. Out of despair the corporal kibitzed from time to time and even permitted himself the remark that Švejk had led the ace of spades and that it was a mistake. He ought not to have trumped, but kept the seven for the last trick.

'In pubs,' said Švejk, 'there used to be very good notices against kibitzers. I remember one of them: "Kibitzer, go and hold your jaw, or I'll knock you on the floor."'

The army train went into the station, where the vans were to be inspected. The train stopped.

'Well, of course,' said the volunteer mercilessly, giving a knowing glance at the corporal, 'we've got the inspection already . . .'

Inspectors entered the van.

Reserve officer Dr Mráz had been appointed by the staff to be commandant of the military train.

They always pushed reserve officers into stupid jobs like this. Dr Mráz had been driven off his rocker by it. He still could not account for one of the vans, though in civil life he was a teacher of mathematics at a secondary modern school. Besides, the number of men reported in the various vans at the last station did not tally with the number given after they had taken their places in the train at Budějovice. When he looked into his papers it appeared that suddenly out of the blue he had two field-kitchens too many. His discovery that in some mysterious way the horses had multiplied sent unpleasant shivers up his spine. In the list of officers he could not trace two missing cadets. In the first van where there was the regimental office they were all the time looking for a typewriter. All this chaos gave him a headache. He had already taken three aspirins and now he was inspecting the train with a painful expression on his face.

When he entered the prison van with his companion he looked at the papers and, receiving the report of the distraught corporal that he was escorting two prisoners and had such and such a number of men with him, he verified once more from the documents the correctness of the information and looked around him.

'Who on earth are you taking with you?' he asked severely, pointing to the senior chaplain who was sleeping on his belly and whose hind-quarters looked up provocatively at the inspectors.

'Humbly report, sir,' stuttered the corporal, 'it's thingum-a-bob . . .'

'What do you mean by "thingum-a-bob"?' growled Dr Mráz. 'Express yourself clearly.'

'Humbly report, sir,' Švejk replied for the corporal, 'this gentleman who is sleeping on his belly is a senior chaplain who is the worse for liquor. He hooked himself on to us and got into the van here and because he is our superior officer we couldn't throw him out in case there should be a breach of *super*ordination. He obviously confused the staff carriage with the prison van.'

Dr Mráz sighed and looked into his papers. There was no mention there of any senior chaplain who had to go by train to Bruck. His eye twitched nervously. At the last station there had suddenly been too many horses, and now senior chaplains sprang up out of the blue in the prisoners' van.

He could not brace himself to do anything more than order the corporal to turn the man over because from his present position where he was sleeping on his belly it was not possible to identify him.

After long efforts the corporal turned the senior chaplain over on his back, during which he woke up, and seeing the officer in front of him said in German: 'Hey, servus, Freddie, what's the news? Is dinner ready?' Then he closed his eyes again and turned to the wall.

Dr Mráz at once saw that it was the glutton from the officers' mess of the previous night, the notorious shark who wolfed up all the officers' mess portions, and he sighed quickly.

'For this you'll go on report,' he said to the corporal. He was just going away when Švejk stopped him:

'Humbly report, sir, I don't belong here. I'm supposed to be incarcerated only till eleven, because it's just today that my term expires. I've been locked up for three days and now I ought to go and sit with the others in the cattle truck. As it's already long past eleven I would ask you, sir, if I could be put out on to the track or sent forward either to the cattle truck where I belong or to Lieutenant Lukáš.'

'What's your name?' asked Dr Mráz, looking again at his papers.

'Švejk, Josef, humbly report, sir.'

'H'm, so you're that famous Švejk,' said Dr Mráz. 'It's true you should have been out by eleven. But Lieutenant Lukáš asked me not to let you out until Bruck. He said it'd be safer, because at least you wouldn't be up to any mischief on the way.'

After the inspectors' departure the corporal could not refrain from making the acid remark:

'So you see, Švejk, that it helped you a shit to apply to higher authority. If I'd have wanted to I could have made it very hot for both of you.'

'Corporal,' said the volunteer, 'throwing shit is a more or less credible form of argument, but an intelligent man shouldn't use such words if he is angry, or if he wants to attack anybody. And then that ridiculous threat of yours that you could make it hot for both of us. Why the hell didn't you do so, when you had the opportunity? This just shows your great intellectual maturity and your rare tact.'

'I've had enough of this!' the corporal said, jumping up. 'I can take you both off to prison!'

'And what for, ducks?' asked the volunteer innocently.

'That's my affair!' said the corporal, summoning courage.

'Your affair,' said the volunteer with a smile. 'Yours and ours. Just like that card game, "My aunt – your aunt!". I should rather say that the mention of your having to go on report has upset you, and that's why you are beginning to shout at us, of course in a way quite contrary to official regulations.'

'You're vulgar swine!' said the corporal screwing up his last courage to make himself appear frightening.

'I'll tell you something, corporal,' observed Švejk: 'I'm an old soldier. I served before the war and I tell you you never get anywhere with bad language. I can remember that when I served years ago there was an old sweat in our company called Schreiter. He served for the soup, as the saying goes. He could have gone home long ago as a corporal, but he was slightly cracked. That chap went for us men. He stuck to us like shit on a shirt. This thing wasn't right and then that was against all regulations. He bullied us like hell and used to say to us: "You're not soldiers but a pack of lousy watchmen." One day I lost my temper and went on company report. "What do you want?" asked the captain. "Humbly report, sir, it's a complaint against our Sergeant-Major Schreiter: after all, we're soldiers of the Emperor and not a pack of lousy watchmen. We serve His Imperial Majesty and we're not guarding fruit trees."

' "Listen, you vermin," the captain replied, "get out of my sight!" And so I asked him obediently if he would put me on battalion report.

'On battalion report, when I had explained to the lieutenant-colonel that we were not just watchmen but soldiers of the Emperor, he had me locked up for two days, but then I asked to be put on regimental report. When I explained things on regimental report the colonel roared at me that I was a bloody idiot and I could go to hell. And so I again countered: "Humbly report, sir, may I be put on brigade report?" He was afraid of that and at once had our Sergeant-Major Schreiter summoned to the office, who had to apologize to me in the presence of all the officers for the words "lousy watchmen". Afterwards he caught up with me in the yard and told me that from that day on he wouldn't swear at me but hound me to the garrison gaol. From then on I was on the look-out as you can imagine but I didn't watch carefully enough. I stood at sentry post by the stores and every sentry always wrote something on the wall. Either they drew female genitals or wrote a little rhyme. I couldn't think of anything and so out of sheer boredom I put my signature under the inscription: "Old sweat Schreiter is an oaf." And that swine of a sergeant-major at once denounced me, because he was tracking me like a bloodhound. By an unfortunate mischance on top of that inscription there was another one: "We're not going to war. We shit on it", and that was in 1912, when we were about to march to Serbia because of that consul

Prochaska.[1] And so they sent me at once to Terezín to the regional court. About fifteen times the gentlemen from the military court photographed that wall by the stores and its inscriptions with my signature on it, and ten times they made me write down: "We're not going to war. We shit on it" so that they could examine my handwriting. Fifteen times I had to write in front of them: "Old sweat Schreiter is an oaf", and in the end an expert in handwriting came and made me write: "It was 29 July 1897 when Dvůr Králové on the Elbe experienced the terrors of the Elbe in wild flood." "That's not enough," the judge advocate said. "What interests us is the shit. Dictate to him something where there are a lot of s's and h's." And so he dictated to me: "Sherry, sheik, shark, pasha, sheriff, shemozzle, shyster, riffraff." That handwriting expert from the court was driven quite crazy by it. He always looked round at the soldier standing behind him with a bayonet and finally said it would have to go to Vienna and I must write three times in succession: "And the sun begins to scorch too. It is beautifully warm." They sent all the material to Vienna and in the end the result was that as far as those inscriptions were concerned it was not my handwriting, but that the signature was mine because I had confessed to it. So I was sentenced to six weeks because I had signed it while on sentry duty and they said I couldn't be properly on guard at the time that I was doing it.'

'And so it's clear,' said the corporal with satisfaction, 'that all the same you didn't get off without being punished and that you are a proper criminal. If it had been me and not that court I'd have booked you not just for six weeks but for six years.'

'Don't be so awful,' the volunteer interposed, 'and think instead of how you'll end up yourself. Not long ago the inspector told you that you'd have to go on report. For a matter like that you ought to prepare yourself very seriously and ponder on the last moments of a corporal. What are you really in comparison with the universe, when you consider that the nearest fixed star is 275,000 times farther away from this army train than the sun and its parallax can make one second of arc? If you were a fixed star in the universe you'd certainly be too minute for even the best astronomical instruments to identify. Your insignificance in the universe defies definition. For half a year you'd make in the sky a

---

[1]. In 1912 the Austrian government unleashed a press campaign against Serbia on the unsubstantiated charge that their consul in Prizren, named Prochaska, had been mishandled. In fact nothing had happened to him.

tiny arc, in a year a very tiny ellipse which would be too small to be expressed in figures. Your parallax would defy measurement.'

'If that's the case,' observed Švejk, 'the corporal should be proud of the fact that no one could measure him, and however it may turn out on report he should be calm and not get excited, because all excitement is dangerous for the health, and now in wartime we must all take care of our health, because these war exertions require of every individual that he shouldn't be a lame duck.

'If they put you in gaol, corporal,' continued Švejk with a sweet smile, 'if you suffer any injustice, then don't lose heart, and if they have their own opinions, you stick to yours. I once knew a coalman who was locked up with me at police headquarters in Prague for high treason at the beginning of the war, František Škvor, and who later might have been executed because of a Pragmatic Sanction or something. When this man was asked at interrogation whether he had anything to object to in the statements, he said:

> ' "However it used to be, it used to be somehow.
> It never happened yet that it was no-how."

'After that they put him into a dark cell and gave him nothing to eat or drink for two days and again brought him back for interrogation. But he continued to insist that however it used to be, it used to be somehow. It never happened yet that it was no-how. Perhaps, after they had court-martialled him, he went with it to the gallows.'

'They say that they hang and shoot people a lot nowadays,' said one of the escort. 'Not long ago on the drill-ground they read us out an order that at Motol they had shot the reservist, Kudrna, because the captain slashed with his sabre his little boy, who was in his wife's arms when she came to say goodbye to him at Benešov and he lost his temper. And "politicals" are locked up as a matter of course. They also shot an editor in Moravia. And our captain said that the same fate's in store for others.'

'Everything has its limits,' said the volunteer ambiguously.

'You're right,' said the corporal. 'It serves editors like that right. They only stir the people up. Last year when I was still only a lance-corporal I had an editor under me and he called me nothing else but a disaster for the army, but when I taught him unarmed drill and he sweated, he always used to say: "Please respect the human being in me." But I gave him hell for his human being when the order was "flat down" and there were a lot of puddles in the barracks courtyard. I took him in front of a puddle like that and the bastard had to fall down into it until the water splashed like in a swimming pool. And in the afternoon he had to have everything on him glittering, his uniform had to be as clean as a new pin, and he rubbed and moaned and muttered. The next day he was again like a pig wallowing in the mud and I stood over him and said to him: "So you see, Mr Editor, what's more important, that disaster for the army or that human being of yours?" He was a regular highbrow, he was!'

The corporal looked triumphantly at the volunteer and continued: 'All because of his being a highbrow he lost his one-year stripes, for he wrote to the newspapers about the maltreatment of soldiers. But how could you help maltreating him when a learned chap like him couldn't even dismantle the breech of his rifle, not even when he was shown how to do it ten times. And when he was told: "Eyes left", he screwed his silly nut to the right as though on purpose and stared all the time like an old crow. And at rifle practice he never knew what to grasp first, the sling or his cartridge-pouch. And when you showed him how his arm had to go down on the sling he goggled at you like a calf at a new gate. He didn't even know which shoulder you carry your rifle on and he saluted like a monkey, and when he had to make turns, God help us, the movements he made when there was a march past and he was learning how to step! When he had to do about-turn it was all the same to him which of his shanks he did it with. Thud, thud, thud! He might take six paces forward and only then turn round like a cock on a swivel. And when he marched his step was like a chap's with gout or he danced about like an old whore at a parish fair.'

The corporal spat: 'He was purposely allocated a very rusty rifle from the store to learn how to clean it and he rubbed it like a dog does a bitch, but even if he had bought two kilos of tow more he wouldn't have been able to clean it properly. The more he rubbed it the worse and rustier it became and on report his rifle was passed from hand to hand and everyone was amazed how it was possible that it could be nothing but rust. Our captain used to tell him that he would never be a soldier, that it would be better if he went and hanged himself and that he was uselessly wasting the army bread. But he just blinked under his glasses. It was a red-letter day for him when he didn't get "severe" or confined to barracks. Then he usually wrote his articles to the newspapers about the manhandling of the troops until one day they searched his baggage. And, my God, all the books he had! Only about disarmament and international peace. Because of that he had to pop off quick to the garrison gaol and from then on he gave us peace until he suddenly reappeared in the office, where his job was to fill in ration forms so that the men shouldn't have any contact with him. That was the sad end of that highbrow. He might have become a very different gentleman altogether if he had not lost his volunteer privileges because of his stupidity. He could have become a lieutenant.'

The corporal sighed: 'He couldn't even get the folds right on his greatcoat. From Prague he ordered various liquids and polish for cleaning buttons and all the same his buttons looked as rusty and red as Esau. But couldn't he half jaw! And when he was in the office he did nothing else but philosophize. He had a liking for that before. As I said, he was always on about his "human being" and nothing else. Once when he was reflecting over a puddle in which he had to plop down when he did his "flat down" I said to him: "When you're always talking about a human being even when you're in the mud remember that man was created out of the dust of the ground and it must have been O.K. for him."'

Having said what he wanted, the corporal was pleased with himself and waited for what the volunteer would say. But it was Švejk who spoke:

'For the same sort of things, for manhandling like that, years ago a certain Koníček stabbed himself and his corporal in the 35th regiment. I read it in the *Courier*. The corporal had about thirty wounds in his body, of which over a dozen were mortal. Afterwards that soldier sat on the body of the dead corporal and stabbed himself on top of it. There was another case years ago in Dalmatia where they cut a corporal's throat and no one knows to this day who did it. It remained shrouded in secrecy and all that was known was that the corporal was called Fiala and came from Drábovna near Turnov. And then I know of another corporal in the 75th regiment called Rejmánek . . .'

This pleasant narration was interrupted by loud groans from the seat where the senior chaplain, Lacina, was sleeping.

The venerable father awoke in all his beauty and dignity. His awakening was accompanied by the same phenomena as the morning awakening of the young giant Gargantua as described by gay old Rabelais.

The senior chaplain farted, belched on the bench and gave an enormous yawn. At last he sat up and asked in surprise:

'Kruzilaudon, where am I?'

The corporal, seeing that the military gentleman had woken up, answered very servilely:

'Humbly report, sir, Your Reverence is pleased to be in the prison van.'

A gleam of astonishment passed over the venerable father's face. He sat for a moment in silence and tried hard to collect his thoughts. It was in vain. There was an ocean of obscurity between what had happened to him in the small hours and his awakening in a van the windows of which were covered with bars.

In the end he asked the corporal who was still standing servilely in front of him: 'And on whose orders am I here – I . . .'

'Humbly report, sir, on nobody's orders.'

The venerable father stood up and began to walk up and down between the benches muttering to himself that he could not understand.

He sat down again and said: 'Where are we actually going?'

'Humbly report, sir, to Bruck.'

'And why are we going to Bruck?'

'Humbly report, sir, the whole of our 91st regiment is transferred there.'

The venerable father tried hard again to ransack his memory of what had actually happened to him, how he got into the van and why on earth he was going to Bruck and of all things with the 91st regiment under an escort.

He had recovered sufficiently from his hangover to be able to distinguish the volunteer and so turned to him to ask:

'You are an intelligent person. Can you explain to me without further nonsense and without suppressing anything how I managed to get into your company?'

'With pleasure,' said the volunteer in an amiable tone. 'When we were getting into the train you joined up with us at the station in the morning because you had taken a drop too much.'

The corporal looked at him severely.

'You got into our van,' continued the volunteer, 'and the thing was done. You lay down on the bench, and Švejk here put his greatcoat under your head. When the train was inspected at the last station you were entered on the lists of officers travelling in it. You were, so to speak, officially discovered and our corporal will have to go on report because of it.'

'I see, I see,' sighed the venerable father. 'See that I am transferred to the staff carriage at the next station. You don't know by any chance whether lunch has already been served?'

'Lunch won't be served until Vienna, sir,' the corporal put in.

'And so it was you who put your coat under my head?' the venerable father said to Švejk. 'Thank you very much indeed.'

'I don't deserve any gratitude,' replied Švejk, 'I only acted as every soldier has to act when he sees that his superior officer has nothing under his head and that he's – what-d'ye-call-it. Every soldier has got to respect his superior, even if he's half-seas over. I have great experience with chaplains because I was the batman to the chaplain, Otto Katz. Chaplains are a merry and good-natured lot.'

The senior chaplain, who had got a fit of democracy as a result of his hangover from the day before, took out a cigarette and offered it to Švejk: 'Have a puff, my boy!'

'And you are going on report because of me, are you?' he said to the corporal. 'Don't worry. I'll get you off that. Nothing will happen to you.'

'And as for you,' he said to Švejk, 'I'll take you with me. You'll live with me like in a feather bed.'

Now he got a new fit of magnanimity and insisted that he would do something for each one of them. He would buy chocolate for the volunteer and rum for the escort. He would have the corporal transferred to the photographic section of the staff of the 7th cavalry division. He would free all of them and never forget them.

He began to distribute cigarettes from his case not only to Švejk but to all of them, and declared that he permitted all the prisoners to smoke, that he would do his best to see that their punishment was reduced and have them returned to normal military life.

'I don't want you to think badly of me. I have many connections and I won't let you down. You all of you impress me as being decent people whom the Lord loves. If you have sinned you are atoning for your acts and I see that you gladly and readily endure what God has visited you with.'

He turned to Švejk: 'On what grounds have you been punished?'

'The Lord visited me with a punishment,' answered Švejk piously, 'on regimental report, sir, as a result of my being late in reaching my regiment through no fault of mine.'

'God is boundlessly merciful and just,' said the senior chaplain solemnly. 'He knows whom he should punish and shows in this his wisdom and omnipotence. And why are you in gaol, volunteer?'

'Because,' answered the volunteer, 'merciful God was gracious enough to visit me with rheumatism and I waxed too proud. After serving my sentence I shall be sent to the kitchen.'

'What God ordains he ordains well,' said the venerable father enthusiastically when he heard about the kitchen. 'Even there a decent chap can make a career. The kitchen is just the place where they should put intelligent people because of all the possible combinations. What is important is not how one cooks but the love with which the food is put together and prepared and so on. Take sauces, for example. When an intelligent person makes onion sauce he takes all kinds of vegetables and fries them in butter. Then he adds spices, pepper, new spices, a little nutmeg and ginger. But an ordinary second-rate cook has the onion boiled and throws into it brown roux made with suet. Best of all I'd like to see you somewhere in an officers' mess. A man can live without intelligence in an ordinary occupation and in life, but in the kitchen he's shown up. Yesterday evening in Budějovice in the officers' mess they gave us among other things kidneys *à la madeira*. May God forgive all the sins of the man who cooked them. That was a really intelligent man and it is true that in the kitchen of that officers' mess there is a teacher from Skuteč. I had eaten the same kidneys *à la madeira* in the officers' mess of the 64th Landwehr regiment. They put caraway seed in them, like they do in an ordinary country pub when they make kidneys with pepper. And who did them? What was that cook in civil life? He was a cattle-fattener on a big estate.'

The senior chaplain stopped and then changed the conversation to culinary problems in the Old and New Testament, where particularly in those times they took a great deal of trouble with the preparation of tasty dishes after divine service and other church ceremonies. He then invited them all to sing something, whereupon Švejk, unfortunately as usual, started up:

'Naughty Caroline
Gave a little sign.
After her the vicar
Followed with the wine.'

But the senior chaplain did not get angry.

'If there was only a drop of rum here, we wouldn't need any wine,' he said, smiling in a completely friendly mood, 'and we could dispense with that Caroline too. She leads people to sin anyway.'

The corporal cautiously groped in his coat and drew out a flat bottle with rum in it.

'Humbly report, sir,' he said quietly, so that it could be felt what a sacrifice he was making. 'If you wouldn't take it amiss?'

'I'll certainly not take it amiss, my boy,' answered the reverend father joyfully, his voice assuming a cheery tone. 'I'll drink to our happy journey.'

'Jesus Mary,' gasped the corporal, observing that after a thorough swig half the bottle had disappeared.

'Oh, you rogue, you!' said the chaplain, smiling and winking knowingly at the volunteer, 'you're even taking the name of the Lord in vain into the bargain. The Lord must punish you for this.'

The venerable father again took a swig from the flat bottle and giving it to Švejk gave the imperious order: 'Bottoms up!'

'War is war,' Švejk said good-humouredly to the corporal as he returned him the empty bottle, the emptiness being confirmed by a strange glint in the corporal's eyes such as can only appear in a mental patient.

'And now I shall take forty winks until we get to Vienna,' said the senior chaplain, 'and I should be grateful if you would wake me as soon as we get there.

'You,' he turned to Švejk, 'will go to the kitchen of our mess, collect some knives and forks and fetch me my lunch. Say that it is for the senior chaplain, Lacina. Make sure that you get a double portion. If there are dumplings, don't take them from the ends. You only lose out on that. After that bring me a bottle of wine from the kitchen and take your mess-tin with you, so that they can pour rum into it.'

Father Lacina fumbled in his pockets.

'Listen,' he said to the corporal, 'I haven't any change. Lend me a guilder. Hey, here you are! What's your name? Švejk?

'Here you are, Švejk, here's a tip for you! Corporal, lend me another guilder. Look, Švejk, you'll get that second guilder when you've done your commission properly. And don't forget too to see that they give you cigarettes and cigars for me. If they are also serving out chocolate, bag a double portion and if there are any tins see that they give you smoked tongue or goose liver. If they're giving out Emmental cheese, see that they don't give you a piece from the edge, and when it comes to Hungarian salami don't take an end but a cut from the middle, where it's juicy.'

The senior chaplain stretched himself out on the bench and was asleep in a moment.

'I think that you must be quite pleased with our foundling,' said the volunteer to the corporal to the accompaniment of the reverend father's snores. 'He's alive and kicking.'

'He's already weaned, as the saying goes,' said Švejk. 'He's already taking the bottle.'

The corporal struggled with himself for a moment and suddenly, losing all humility, said harshly: 'Pretty fair sauce!'

'Not having any change he reminds me of a chap called Mlíčko, a mason from Dejvice,' said Švejk. 'He never had any change either, until he was up to his ears in debt and was gaoled for fraud. He ate up big money and never had any small change.'

'In the 75th regiment before the war,' said a man from the escort, 'the captain bust all the regimental funds on drink and was cashiered. Now he's a captain again. And a sergeant-major who robbed the army of cloth for facings – there were more than twenty packages of it – is now a staff sergeant-major. And not long ago they shot an infantryman in Serbia because he ate up his whole tin at one go when it was supposed to last him three days.'

'That's got nothing to do with it,' said the corporal, 'but it's true that to borrow from a poor corporal two guilders for a tip is . . .'

'Here you are. Here's the guilder,' said Švejk. 'I don't want to enrich myself at your expense. And if he gives me a second guilder I'll return that too, so that you shouldn't blub. You ought to be glad when one of your military superiors borrows money from you for his expenses. You are frightfully selfish. It's only a question of two miserable guilders. I'd like to see what you'd do if you had to sacrifice your life for your military superior, if he were lying wounded somewhere in the enemy lines and you had to save him and carry him away in your arms, when they were shooting at you with shrapnel and everything possible.'

'You'd shit with fright,' the corporal defended himself, 'you chicken-livered little batman.'

'There's a lot of shitting in every battle,' the man from the escort chimed in again. 'Not long ago one of the chaps who was wounded told us in Budějovice that when they were advancing he shitted three times in succession: first when they were climbing up from cover to the space before the barbed-wire entanglement; a second time when they started cutting the wire, and a third time when the Russians rushed at them with their bayonets and shouted "Hurrah." Then they began to run back to the trenches and in their unit there wasn't a single man who hadn't shitted. And a dead man, who lay on top of the cover with his legs hanging down and half of whose head had been torn off by shrapnel, just as though he'd been cut in half, he too in the last moment shitted so much that it ran from his trousers over his boots into the trenches mixed with blood. And half his skull together with his brains lay right underneath. A chap doesn't even notice how it happens to him.'

'Sometimes,' said Švejk, 'a chap gets ill in a fight. It nauseates him. A sick re-convalescent from Przemyśl told us in a pub called Outlook at Pohořelec in Prague that there was a bayonet assault somewhere under the fortifications and a Russian suddenly appeared facing him, a mountain of a man who went for him with his bayonet and had a huge drip on his nose. When he looked at that Russian's nose drip, at his snot, he suddenly began to feel sick and had to go to the first-aid post where they diagnosed him as suffering from cholera and sent him to the cholera barracks in Budapest, where he actually caught cholera.'

'Was that a common soldier or a corporal?' asked the volunteer.

'It was a corporal,' Švejk answered calmly.

'That could happen to any volunteer too,' said the corporal stupidly, but as he spoke he looked triumphantly at the volunteer, as if to say: 'One up to me. What d'you say to that?'

But the volunteer made no reply and lay down on the bench.

They drew near to Vienna. Those who were not sleeping observed from the window the barbed-wire entanglements and fortifications around Vienna, which obviously evoked feelings of depression throughout the train.

One could still hear from the vans the incessant roaring of the Boche from Kašperské Hory: '*Wann ich kum*', *wann ich kum*', *wann ich wieda*', *wieda*' *kum*',[1] but now it was hushed under the unpleasant impression of the barbed wire, with which Vienna was lined.

'Everything's in order,' said Švejk, looking at the trenches. 'Everything is in perfect order, except that these Viennese may get their trousers torn when they go out on trips on Sunday. A chap's got to be very careful here.

'Vienna is quite an important city,' he continued. 'Only think of the wild animals they have in their Schönbrunn menagerie! When I was in Vienna years ago I liked best of all to go and look at the monkeys, but when any personality drives out of the Imperial Palace they don't allow anybody through the cordon. I had with me a tailor from the tenth district and they put him in gaol because he was determined to see those monkeys at any price.'

'And have you been to the palace too?' asked the corporal.

'It's very beautiful there,' answered Švejk. 'I haven't been there, but someone who had been there told me all about it. The finest of all is the palace guard. Everyone must be two metres high and afterwards he gets a kiosk to run. As for princesses there are swarms of them.'

They passed through a station. Behind them could be heard the sounds of the Austrian hymn played by a band which had come here probably by mistake, because it took them a long time to get with the

---

1. When I come, when I come,
   When I come back again . . .

train into the station. They stopped, got their mess portions and a ceremonial welcome.

But it was not the same as it had been at the beginning of the war when soldiers on their journey to the front stuffed themselves at every station and when they were welcomed by maidens in stupid white dresses with still more stupid faces, by desperately stupid bunches of flowers and even stupider speeches from some lady, whose husband today pretends to be a great patriot and republican.

The reception party in Vienna consisted of three lady members of the society of the Austrian Red Cross, two members of a war society of Viennese ladies and girls, an official delegate from the Vienna magistracy and a military representative.

Fatigue could be seen on all these faces. Troop trains passed through day and night, ambulance coaches packed full of wounded every hour. At the stations they continually shunted trains of prisoners from one track to another, and members of all these various corporations and clubs had to be everywhere present. This went on from day to day and the initial enthusiasm degenerated into yawning. People attended in shifts and all who appeared on a Vienna station had exactly the same tired expression as those who were waiting that day for the train with the Budějovice regiment.

Soldiers peered out of cattle trucks with an expression of hopelessness like people going to the gallows.

Ladies came to them and doled them out gingerbread cakes with German inscriptions in sugar: 'Victory and Vengeance', '*Gott strafe England*', 'The Austrian has a Fatherland. He loves it and has good cause to fight for it.'

The men from Kašperské Hory could be seen stuffing themselves with gingerbread cakes, without losing their expression of hopelessness.

Then came the order to go by companies for mess portions to the field-kitchens, which stood behind the station.

There was also an officers' kitchen there, where Švejk went to carry out the orders of the senior chaplain, while the volunteer waited until he was fed, because two of the escort went to fetch the mess portions for the whole prison van.

Švejk carried out his orders correctly, and crossing the track saw Lieutenant Lukáš, who was walking between the lines and waiting to see whether there would be anything left for him in the officers' mess.

His situation was very unpleasant because for the time being he shared Lieutenant Kirschner's batman. The scoundrel only bothered about his own master and carried out complete sabotage when it was a question of anything for Lieutenant Lukáš.

'Who are you carrying that to, Švejk?' the unhappy lieutenant asked when Švejk put on the ground the pile of things which he had succeeded in wheedling out of the officers' mess and which he had wrapped up in his greatcoat.

Švejk was taken aback for the moment but immediately pulled himself together. His face was full of joy and peace when he replied:

'To you, humbly report, sir. Only I don't know where you have your carriage and I also don't know whether the commandant of the train won't make a fuss if I go with you. He must be a fair swine.'

Lieutenant Lukáš looked inquiringly at Švejk, who, however, went on affably and confidentially: 'He really is a swine, sir. When he came to inspect the train I informed him at once that it was already eleven o'clock and that I had by now served the whole of my sentence and should be either in the cattle truck or with you, and he snubbed me quite rudely and said that I must stay where I was, so that I shouldn't disgrace you again on the journey, sir.'

Švejk assumed a martyred expression: 'As though I had ever disgraced you, sir.'

Lieutenant Lukáš sighed.

'I've certainly never disgraced you,' continued Švejk. 'If anything ever happened, it was pure coincidence, nothing but a dispensation of God, as old Vaníček from Pelhřimov used to say when he had served his thirty-sixth sentence. I never meant any harm, sir. I always only wanted to do something helpful, something good, and it's not my fault if neither of us had any good out of it, but only misery and torment.'

'Don't cry so much, Švejk,' said Lieutenant Lukáš in a gentle voice, as they approached the staff carriage. 'I'll do everything to see that you're with me again.'

'Humbly report, sir, I'm not crying. It only dawned on me how sad it was that we are both the most unfortunate people of all in this war and under the sun and we can neither of us help it. It's a terrible fate, when I think that I've tried so hard for the best all my life.'

'Calm yourself, Švejk!'

'Humbly report, sir, if it were not insubordinate of me, I'd like to say I can't calm myself, but as things are I must say that following your instructions I'm already quite calm again.'

'Then go and get into the van, Švejk.'

'Humbly report, I'm getting in, sir.'

Night peace reigned over the military camp in Bruck. In the men's huts the soldiers shivered with cold and in the officers' quarters they were opening the windows because of the overheating.

From the various objects which were under guard there could be heard from time to time the steps of the patrol, who were marching to drive away sleep.

Down in Bruck an der Leitha shone the lights of the Imperial and Royal factory for tinned meat. Here they worked day and night and processed various kinds of offal. Because the wind blew from that quarter towards the alley in the military camp, it brought with it the stink of rotten sinews, hooves, trotters and bones which all went into the tinned soup.

From an abandoned little pavilion, where in peacetime a photographer used to photograph soldiers who were spending their youth here at the military shooting range, one could see down in the valley of the Leitha the red electric light of a brothel, The Maize Cob, which Archduke Stephen honoured with a visit during the great manoeuvres at Sopron in 1908, and where the officers foregathered every day.

It was the finest bawdy-house and ordinary soldiers or one-year volunteers were not permitted to patronize it.

They had to go to The House of Roses, the green light of which was also visible from the deserted photographer's studio.

There was the same class segregation as later at the front, when the monarchy could do nothing else to help its troops than provide them with transportable brothels assigned to the brigade staffs, the so-called 'puffs'.

Consequently there were 'Imperial and Royal Officers' Puffs', 'Imperial and Royal N.C.O.s' Puffs', and 'Imperial and Royal Men's Puffs'.

Bruck an der Leitha was bright with lights and on the other side beyond the bridge there glittered Királyhida, Cisleithania and Transleithania.[1] In both towns, Hungarian and Austrian, gipsy bands were playing, the windows of the cafés and restaurants gleamed with light, there was singing and drinking. The local burghers and officials brought their wives and grown-up daughters to the cafés and restaurants, and Bruck an der Leitha and Királyhida were nothing but one giant brothel.

In one of the officers' huts in the camp at night Švejk was waiting for his Lieutenant Lukáš, who had gone that evening to the theatre in the town and had not yet returned. Švejk had prepared the lieutenant's bed and was sitting on it while Major Wenzl's batman was sitting on the table opposite.

The major had returned to his regiment again, after his utter incompetence had been demonstrated on the Drina in Serbia. It was said that he had given orders for the dismantling and destruction of a pontoon bridge when half his battalion were still on the other side of it. Now he had been assigned to the military rifle range in Királyhida as commandant and also dealt with the camp's catering. The officers said that Major Wenzl would now make a packet. The rooms of Lukáš and Wenzl were in the same passage.

1. Austria was called Cisleithania, i.e. the lands on the nearer side of the Leitha. Hungary was Transleithania, i.e. the lands beyond it.

Major Wenzl's batman, Mikulášek, a pockmarked little fellow, was swinging his legs and swearing: 'I can't think why my old bastard hasn't come yet. I'd like to know where the old dodderer is gadding about all night. If he'd only given me the key of his room I could have gone to bed and had a few drops. He's got oceans of wine.'

'They say he flogs a lot,' Švejk observed, comfortably smoking one of his lieutenant's cigarettes because the latter had forbidden him to puff his pipe in the room. 'But surely you must know where he gets all that wine from?'

'I go where he sends me to,' said Mikulášek in a feeble voice. 'I get a warrant from him and then I go and draw supplies for the hospital and bring them to his home.'

'And if he were to order you to rob the regimental till,' Švejk asked, 'would you do it? You swear at him behind his back, but you tremble in front of him like an aspen leaf.'

Mikulášek blinked with his little eyes: 'I'd think twice about that.'

'There's nothing to think twice about, you silly coot!' Švejk shouted at him, but he suddenly stopped because the door opened and Lieutenant Lukáš came in. As could at once be observed he was in a high humour, because he had his cap on back to front.

Mikulášek was so scared that he forgot to jump down from the table and saluted in a sitting position, forgetting as well that he hadn't a cap on his head.

'Humbly report, sir, everything is in order,' announced Švejk, assuming a firm military appearance according to all regulations. Only the cigarette remained in his mouth.

Lieutenant Lukáš did not notice this however and went straight to Mikulášek who observed every one of his movements with goggling eyes and continued to salute while sitting on the table.

'Lieutenant Lukáš,' said the lieutenant, approaching Mikulášek with a not too firm gait. 'And what's your name?'

Mikulášek was silent. Lukáš brought a chair up for himself in front of Mikulášek, sat down and looking up at him said: 'Švejk, bring me my service revolver from my suitcase.'

The whole time that Švejk was looking for the revolver in the suitcase Mikulášek was staring in silent horror at the lieutenant. If he understood at this moment that he was sitting on the table it made him only the more desperate because his legs now were touching the knees of the seated lieutenant.

'Hi, what's your name, man?' the lieutenant shouted up to Miku-lášek.

But the batman wouldn't answer. As he afterwards explained he had a kind of fit of paralysis at the unexpected arrival of the lieutenant. He wanted to jump down and couldn't, he wanted to reply and couldn't, he wanted to stop saluting but couldn't manage it.

'Humbly report, sir,' Švejk put in, 'the revolver isn't loaded.'

'Then load it, Švejk.'

'Humbly report, sir, we haven't got any cartridges and it'll be difficult to shoot him down from the table. May I be permitted to add, sir, that he is Mikulášek, Major Wenzl's batman. He always loses the power of speech when he sees one of the officer gentlemen. He's too shy to speak. I tell you, the thing's a complete milksop and it's still wet behind the ears. Major Wenzl always leaves it standing in the corridor, when he goes anywhere in the town, and it always moons about miserably from batman to batman in the barracks. You could understand it if it had some reason to be startled, but really, you know, it hasn't done any mischief at all.'

Švejk spat, and from the tone of his voice and the fact that he spoke about Mikulášek in the neuter one could deduce his complete contempt for the cowardice of Major Wenzl's batman and his unmilitary bearing.

'If you permit, sir,' continued Švejk, 'I'll sniff him.'

Švejk dragged down Mikulášek, who went on looking idiotically at the lieutenant from the table, and, having placed him on the ground, sniffed his trousers.

'Not yet,' he asserted, 'but it's already starting. Should I throw him out?'

'Throw him out, Švejk.'

Švejk took the quaking Mikulášek out into the corridor, shut the door after him and said to him: 'There you are, you stupid bastard. I've saved your life. When Major Wenzl returns you'll bring me a bottle of wine and keep your mouth shut, do you understand? I'm not joking. I've saved your life, honestly I have. When my lieutenant's sozzled it's a bad thing. I'm the only chap who can deal with him then and no one else.'

'I'm...'

'You're a fart,' Švejk exclaimed contemptuously. 'Sit on the doorstep and wait until your Major Wenzl comes.'

'You've been away enough,' was Lukáš's greeting to Švejk. 'Now I want to talk to you. You don't have to go on standing at attention like a stuck pig. Sit down, Švejk, and cut out that "according to orders". Shut your mug and listen carefully. Do you know where Sopron Street is in Királyhida? For God's sake cut out your: "Humbly report, sir,

I don't." If you don't know then say: "I don't know", and that's enough. Write it down on a piece of paper: 16 Sopron Street. In that house there's an ironmonger's shop. Do you know what an ironmonger's shop is? Herrgott, don't say "Humbly report". Say "I do" or "I don't." And so you know what an ironmonger's shop is? You do? All right, then. That shop belongs to a Hungarian called Kákonyi. Do you know what a Hungarian is? Now, Himmelherrgott, do you or don't you? All right. Above the shop there is a first floor and that's where he lives. Do you know that? You don't know. Hell's bells! I'm telling you he lives there. Isn't that good enough for you? It is. Good. If it wouldn't have been good enough for you, I'd have had you clapped in gaol. Have you got it noted down that that bastard's called Kákonyi? Good. Very well, then, tomorrow morning at about ten o'clock you'll go down to the town, you'll find that house, you'll go upstairs to the first floor and you'll hand this letter to Mrs Kákonyi.'

Lieutenant Lukáš opened his pocket book and, yawning, put into Švejk's hand a white envelope without an address.

'It's a frightfully important matter, Švejk,' he went on. 'Caution is never out of place, and consequently, as you can see for yourself, there's no address there. I rely completely on your handing this letter over properly. Make a further note that the lady is called Etelka. And so now write "Mrs Etelka Kákonyi". Let me add that you're to hand this letter over discreetly without fail and to wait for an answer. It's already written in the letter that you're to wait for an answer. Anything more?'

'But what am I to do, sir, if they don't give me an answer?'

'Then you'll tell them that you've got to get an answer at all costs,' replied the lieutenant with a terrible yawn. 'Now I'm going to bed. I'm really fagged today. My God, what we haven't drunk! I think anyone'd be as tired as I am after an evening and night like that.'

Lieutenant Lukáš had not originally intended to stay long in the town. Towards the evening he had left the camp and gone to the Hungarian theatre in Királyhida, where they were giving a Hungarian operetta. The leading roles were performed by buxom Jewish actresses, whose fabulous distinction was that when they danced they threw their legs up in the air and didn't wear either tights or drawers, and for the greater gratification of the officers they shaved themselves underneath like Tartar women. If the gallery got no gratification out of this, all the more fell to the share of the officers of the artillery, who were sitting down in the stalls and had taken with them to the theatre their artillery field glasses for this beautiful spectacle.

But this kind of interesting smuttiness had not much of an appeal for Lieutenant Lukáš, because the opera glasses he had hired were not achromatic and instead of thighs he only saw one or two violet patches in motion.

In the interval after the first act he was more attracted by a lady who was dragging to the cloakroom the middle-aged gentleman who escorted her and insisting to him that they should go home at once, because she refused to look at such things. She expressed it rather loudly in German, whereupon her escort replied in Hungarian: 'Yes, my angel, let's go, I agree. It really is a very tasteless spectacle.'

'It's disgusting,' answered the lady in incensed tones, when the gentleman wrapped her theatre cloak around her. Her eyes blazed with indignation over this obscenity – those big black eyes, which went so well with her beautiful figure. As she said this she looked at Lieutenant Lukáš and repeated once more with some passion: 'Disgusting, really disgusting!' This was decisive for a short romance.

He learned from the cloakroom attendant that they were Mr and Mrs Kákonyi, and that the husband kept an ironmonger's shop at 16 Sopron Street.

'And he lives with Mrs Etelka on the first floor,' said the cloakroom attendant with the detailed knowledge of an old bawdy-house keeper. 'She's a German from Sopron and he's a Hungarian. Here everything's mixed.'

Lieutenant Lukáš took his coat from the cloakroom too and went into the town, where he met some officers of the 91st regiment in the large wine restaurant and café, The Archduke Albrecht.

He did not talk much but drank all the more instead, planning what he should write to that severe, moral and pretty lady who definitely attracted him more than all those monkeys on the stage, as the other officers described them.

In a very good mood he went away to a small café, At the Cross of St Stephen, where he went into a small *chambre séparée* and threw out of it a Rumanian woman, who offered to strip naked before him, after which he could do with her what he liked. Then he ordered some ink, a pen, some writing paper and a bottle of cognac. Finally after careful consideration he wrote the following letter which seemed to him to be the loveliest he had ever composed:

Dear Madam,

Yesterday in the Town Theatre I was present at the play which upset you so much. I watched you during the whole of the first act, you and your husband too. As I could observe . . .

'I won't pull my punches,' said Lieutenant Lukáš. 'What right has that bastard to have such a sweet wife. Why, he looks like a shaven baboon.'

He went on writing:

. . . your husband watched all the lewdness which was shown on the stage with complete understanding. But you, dear madam, were revolted by it because it was not art but disgusting exploitation of the most intimate human feelings.

'What breasts the woman has,' Lieutenant Lukáš thought. 'Why beat about the bush?'

Excuse me, dear lady, for writing so frankly to you, when you do not know me. I have seen many women in my life, but none of them have made such an impression upon me as you have, for your judgement and view of life are completely identical with mine. I am convinced that your husband is a rank egoist and drags you around with him . . .

'No, that won't do,' said Lieutenant Lukáš to himself. He crossed out: 'drags you around' and wrote instead:

. . . and in his own personal interests, dear lady, takes you with him to theatre performances which are on his own level of taste only. It is my custom to be frank. I do not wish to obtrude upon your private life and my only desire is to talk with you privately about pure art . . .

'It'll be no good in the hotels here. I'll have to carry her off to Vienna,' the lieutenant thought again. 'I'll fix up an official journey.'

And so I take the liberty, dear lady, of asking you if we could not meet and get to know each other better in all honour. You will surely not deny this to one who will soon be facing the sufferings of marching to the front and who, if you should accord him your gracious consent, will retain in the turmoil of battle the most beautiful memories of a soul who understood him just as he understood her. Your decision will be my command, your reply the decisive moment of my life.

He signed the letter, drank up his cognac, and ordered another bottle. Then, drinking glass after glass and reading over his last lines, he actually wept over every sentence.

It was nine o'clock in the morning, when Švejk woke Lieutenant Lukáš: 'Humbly report, sir, you've overslept your duty, and I must go with your letter to Királyhida. I called you once at seven, again at half past seven and then again at eight, as they went past for drill practice, but you just turned over on your other side. Sir . . . I say, sir . . . .'

Lieutenant Lukáš murmured something and wanted to turn over on his side again, but he did not succeed, because Švejk quite ruthlessly shook him and bellowed: 'Sir, I'm going with that letter to Királyhida.'

The lieutenant yawned: 'With that letter? Ah, yes, with my letter. This is a very discreet matter, you understand? A secret between us. Dismiss . . .'

The lieutenant wrapped himself up again in his blanket, from which Švejk had dragged him, and went on sleeping while Švejk went on his pilgrimage to Királyhida.

It would not have been difficult to find 16 Sopron Street if he had not by chance met on the way the old sapper, Vodička, who had been drafted to the 'Styrians' whose barracks were down in the camp. Years ago Vodička had lived in Prague at Na Bojišti, and so on the occasion of a meeting like this they both had to go to The Black Lamb in Bruck where the waitress Růženka was a friend of his. She was a Czech and was owed money by all the Czech volunteers in the camp.

Recently Sapper Vodička, who was an old slyboots, had been paying court to her and had a list of all the march battalions which were leaving the camp. He went to see the Czech volunteers at the appropriate time and reminded them that they must not disappear in the tumult of the battle without paying their debts.

'Where exactly are you bound for?' asked Vodička, after they had tasted their first draught of good wine.

'That's a secret,' answered Švejk, 'but I'll tell you, because you're my old friend.'

He explained everything to him in detail, and Vodička declared that he was an old sapper, that he could not desert him and that they would go together to hand the letter over.

They had a wonderful time discussing past times and everything seemed natural and easy to them when at about lunch-time they left The Black Lamb.

Apart from that they had inside them a firm conviction that they were not afraid of anyone. On the way to 16 Sopron Street Vodička expressed tremendous hatred of the Hungarians and told over and over again how he fought with them everywhere, where and when he had had rows with them and what at any time and at any place had happened to prevent him fighting with them.

'Once we had one of those Hungarian bastards by the throat in Pausdorf, where we sappers went for a drink. I wanted to sock him across the coconut with a belt in the dark – you see we had smashed the hanging lamp with a bottle as soon as it started – but all of a sudden he began to shout:

' "Tonda! Why, it's only me, Purkrábek, from the sixteenth Landwehr!" '

'A mistake was avoided by a hair's breadth. But instead we gave it fair and proper to those Hungarian clowns at Neusiedler See which we went to look at three weeks ago. In a village near by there was

stationed a machine-gun detachment of a Honvéd regiment, and we all happened to go to a pub where they were dancing their Csardas like mad and shooting their mouths off as they shouted: "*Uram, uram, biró, uram*", or "*Láňok, láňok, láňok a faluba*".[1] We sat opposite them; only we put our belts in front of us on the table and said to ourselves: "You bastards, we'll give it to you hot for your *láňok*", and a chap named Mejstřík who had a paw as big as the White Mountain immediately volunteered to dance and take away a girl from one of these

1. Hungarian songs: 'Mr, Mr, Mr Justice' and 'Girls, girls, girls from the village'.

lousy bastards in the middle of the dance. The girls were bloody neat pieces, you know, with plump calves and fleshy arses, and marvellous thighs and eyes. From the way those Hungarian bastards squeezed them you could see that those girls had breasts as full and firm as rubber balls, that they got a great kick out of it and knew their onions. And then our Mejstřík jumped into the dance and was just going to take the neatest piece away from one of the Honvéds. The Honvéd started to jabber something, but Mejstřík immediately socked him one across the jaw and the bastard fell down. We all of us at once seized our belts, twisted them round our hands so that the bayonets didn't slip out and leaped into the crowd. I shouted out: "Innocent or guilty, finish them off one by one!" From then on it went like a house on fire. They began to jump out of the windows, but we seized them by their legs and dragged them back into the hall again. Anyone who wasn't one of ours didn't half get it. Their mayor and a gendarme tried to intervene, but they got it across the backside. The landlord got a thrashing, because he started to swear in German and accused us of ruining the dance. Afterwards we went through the village and rounded up any who were trying to hide from us, like one of their platoon sergeants who we found buried in the hay in the loft of a farm right down in the village. He was betrayed to us by his girl because he'd gone and danced with another one. She had fallen for our Mejstřík and went with him afterwards on the way up to Királyhida below the forest where the haystacks stand. She dragged him into one of those haystacks and afterwards wanted five crowns from him. But he socked her one across the jaw instead. Afterwards he caught up with us at the top just before the camp and told us that he had always thought that Hungarian women had fire in them, but this cow had been as dead as a log of wood and only jabbered something all the time.

'To put it in a nutshell, the Hungarians are a pack of lousy bastards,' old Sapper Vodička concluded, whereupon Švejk observed: 'Many a Hungarian can't help being Hungarian.'

'Why can't he help it?' Vodička said angrily. 'Of course he can. That's stupid. I'd just like to see you getting into their clutches as I did when I came for courses here the first day. The very same afternoon they drove us into the school like a herd of cattle and some bloody fool started to make drawings and to explain what blindages are, how you lay foundations, how you take measurements and he said that if any-one didn't have it drawn the next morning exactly as he'd explained it, he would be gaoled and trussed. "Bloody hell," I thought. "Did I volunteer at the front for these courses just to get out of serving at the front or did I do it to make bloody silly drawings every evening in a bloody silly exercise book with a bloody silly pencil like a bloody silly schoolboy?" I got so furious, I lost my patience, I couldn't even look at the bloody idiot who was explaining it to us. I wanted to smash everything around me, I was so mad. I didn't even wait for coffee but went straight from the hut to Királyhida and in my fury I had only one thought and that was to find a quiet little pub in the town, drink myself sozzled there, kick up a row, sock someone across the jaw and then go home relaxed and satisfied. Man proposes, God disposes. By the river there among some gardens I found a place exactly like that, quiet as a chapel, just made for a row. There were only two guests sitting there and talking Hungarian which made me madder still, and into the bargain I was already more sozzled than I realized. And so it happened that I didn't notice – sozzled as I was – that next door there was another place where eight hussars came in while I was doing my best. When I socked those two guests across the jaw the hussars set on me. The bastards gave me such a beating up and chased me all over the gardens so I couldn't find my way home until the early morning and had to go at once to the medical depot, where I gave as an excuse that I'd fallen into a brick pit. Then for a whole week they wrapped me up in a wet sheet so that my back didn't get inflamed. O Lord, don't you ever get yourself mixed up with bastards like that! They are not human beings. They're animals.'

'All they that take the sword shall perish with the sword,' said Švejk. 'And so you shouldn't be surprised that they got worked up when they had to leave all their wine on the table and go and chase you all over the gardens in the dark. They should have beaten you up at once on the spot in the pub and then thrown you out. It would have been better for them and for you too if they'd finished with you at the table once and for all. I knew a chap called Paroubek who kept a pub in Libeň. Once a tinker got himself drunk in his bar on jalovcová¹ and began to swear and say that the jalovcová was weak, that Paroubek had put water in it and that if he had been going around as a tinker for a hundred years and for all his earnings had only bought jalovcová and had drunk it all up at one go, he would still be capable of walking on a tight-rope and of carrying Paroubek in his arms over it. After that he told Paroubek that he was a

1. Schnaps made out of juniper berries.

huncut[1] and the monster of Šaščín.[2] Then dear old Paroubek caught hold of him, knocked him across the skull with his mouse-traps and wires, kicked him out of the pub, beat him all the way to the Invalidovna with the pole for pulling down the shop shutters, chased him like a madman across the Invalidovna to Karlín up to Žižkov and from there across the Židovské pece[3] to Malešice, where he finally broke the stick on him and could return to Libeň. But in his blind fury he forgot of course that all the public were still in his pub and that all those thugs would be helping themselves. And when he finally got back he saw for himself that this had really been the case. The shutters were half-closed and two cops were standing there, who got pretty tight as well when they tried to put things in order inside. Half of all the stock was drunk up, in the street was an empty rum barrel, and under the counter Paroubek found two bastards who were completely sozzled. They had escaped the attention of the cops and when he dragged them out they wanted to pay him two kreutzers saying that they had not consumed more schnaps than this. That's the reward for hot-headedness. It's just like in war. First we defeat our enemy, then we pursue him on and on and in the end we can't run fast enough to get away from him.'

'I haven't forgotten those bastards,' said Vodička. 'If a single one of those hussars crossed my path I'd pay him out. We sappers are ugly customers when we get sore. We're not like the Iron Flies.[4] When we were at the front at Przemyśl we had with us a Captain Jetzbacher, a swine, the like of which you won't find again under the sun. He succeeded in bullying us so much that a chap called Bitterlich from our company, a German but a very good fellow, shot himself just because of him. And so we said to ourselves that when it began to whistle from the Russian side it would be all up with our Captain Jetzbacher. And as soon as the Russians started to fire at us we peppered him with five shots in the cross-fire. The monster was still alive after that like a cat with nine lives and we had to finish him with two further shots, so that there wouldn't be any trouble. He just growled but in a comic sort of way so that it was rather funny.'

1. A Hungarian word for a scoundrel.

2. Švejk seems to have got mixed up here but probably is alluding to Elisabeth Báthory of Čachtice who murdered young girls and bathed in their blood in order to make herself beautiful.

3. Literally 'Jewish furnaces' – a suburb of Prague.

4. 'Iron Flies' was a name for the Landwehr.

Vodička laughed: 'That happens every day at the front. One of my friends told me – he's with our company now – that when he was an infantryman at Belgrade his company shot their lieutenant in the middle of a battle. He was a cur of the same sort too who had shot two soldiers on the march, because they hadn't the strength to go on. And when he was about to expire he suddenly started to blow his whistle and give the signal for retreat. All the people around had a good laugh.'

During this absorbing and illuminating conversation Švejk and Vodička finally found the ironmonger's shop of Mr Kákonyi at 16 Sopron Street.

'I think you'd better wait here,' said Švejk to Vodička at the carriage entrance. 'I'll run up to the first floor and hand over the letter. I'll wait for an answer and be down in a moment.'

'Do you really imagine I'd desert you?' said Vodička in astonishment. 'You don't know the Hungarians, I keep on telling you. Here we've got to be very much on our guard with them. I'll sock him one.'

'Listen, Vodička,' said Švejk gravely. 'In this case it isn't to do with a Hungarian but with his wife. I told you everything when we sat together with that Czech waitress, didn't I? I'm carrying a letter from my lieutenant and it's absolutely essential to keep it secret. My lieutenant enjoined me strictly that no living soul must know about it and, after all, your waitress herself said that this was quite right and that it was a very delicate matter. Nobody must know that my lieutenant is corresponding with a married woman. And you approved and nodded your head in agreement. I've explained to you as is right and fitting that I'm faithfully carrying out my lieutenant's order and you suddenly insist at all costs on going upstairs with me.'

'You don't yet know me, Švejk,' answered old Sapper Vodička in very grave tones too. 'When I've once said that I won't leave you, you must remember that my word is my bond. Two are safer than one.'

'I'll talk you out of that, Vodička. Do you know where Neklanova Street is at Vyšehrad? The locksmith, Voborník, had his workshop there. He was a good and just man and when he returned home one day from a spree he brought with him another reveller. And then he lay in bed for a long time and every day when his wife dressed the wound on his head she said to him: "You see, Toníček, if there hadn't been two of you I'd have only given you a wigging and wouldn't have thrown the weighing machine at your head." And later when he was able to speak he said: "You're right, mum, next time when I go anywhere I won't bring anybody back with me." '

'Well, if that Hungarian bastard tried to throw something at our heads it would be the end, really,' said Vodička, starting to get worked up: 'I'll take him by the neck and throw him from the first floor down the steps, so that he'll fly like a piece of shrapnel. You mustn't take any chances with those Hungarian bastards. Kid-gloves are no use.'

'Vodička, you haven't drunk so much after all. I had two quarters of a litre more than you. Please consider carefully that we mustn't make any scandal. I'm responsible for this. Besides, it's a question of a lady.'

'I'll sock the lady one as well, Švejk. It makes no difference to me. You still don't know old Vodička. Once in Zábĕhlice in The Island of Roses some bitch didn't want to dance with me because I had a swollen jaw, she said. It's true that I did have a swollen jaw, because I'd just come there from a dance-party in Hostivař, but just imagine getting an insult of that kind from that whore. "Well, here's one for you too, noble lady," I said, "so that you shan't complain."

'When I socked her one she pulled down the whole table in the garden with all the glasses where she was sitting with her papa and mamma and two brothers. But I wasn't afraid of the whole Island of Roses; I had friends there from Vršovice and they helped me. We beat up about five families, children as well. It must have been heard all the long way to Michle and after that it was in the newspapers too about that garden party, which was held by a charity association of the citizens of some town or other. And so, as I say, as other people have helped me, so I always help any friend of mine if anything should happen to him. I won't desert you, God help me, I won't. You don't know these Hungarian bastards. . . . You can't surely push me off when we're seeing each other again after so many years and in circumstances like this into the bargain.'

'Very well, then, come with me,' Švejk decided, 'but please act carefully so that we don't have any unpleasantness.'

'Don't worry, old man,' said Vodička quietly, when they approached the steps. 'I'll sock him . . .'

And he added in an even quieter tone: 'You'll see, this Hungarian bastard won't give us any trouble.'

And if there had been anybody in the carriage entrance who understood Czech he would have heard from the stairway Vodička's slogan being loudly proclaimed: 'You don't know these Hungarian bastards

...', a slogan which came to Vodička in the quiet pub above the river Leitha, among the gardens of the famous Királyhida surrounded by mountains. Soldiers will always remember these mountains with curses, recalling all those 'exercises' before the world war and during the world war in which they received theoretical training for practical massacre and slaughter!

Švejk and Vodička stood before the door of Mr Kákonyi's flat. Before pressing the bellpush, Švejk observed: 'Vodička, have you ever heard that discretion is the better part of valour?'

'I'm not bothered,' answered Vodička. 'He mustn't be allowed time even to open his mug ...'

'I have no business with anybody here, Vodička.'

Švejk rang the bell, and Vodička said loudly, '*Ein, zwei* and he'll be down the stairs.'

The door opened, a maid appeared and asked in Hungarian what they wanted.

'*Nem tudom*,'[1] said Vodička scornfully. 'Learn to speak Czech, my good girl.'

'Do you understand German?' Švejk asked in broken German.

'A leettle,' the girl replied equally brokenly.

'Then tell lady I want speak lady. Tell her there is letter from gentleman outside in passage.'

'I'm amazed,' said Vodička, following Švejk into the hall, 'that you can waste your time talking to a little squit like that.'

They stood in the hall, shut the door to the passage and Švejk confined himself to observing:

'They're quite nicely set up here, even two umbrellas on the coat stand. And that picture of Jesus Christ isn't too bad either.'

From one of the rooms, from which could be heard the clatter of spoons and the clinking of plates, the maid emerged again and said to Švejk:

'Madam say she have no time. If there is anything you give it me and tell me.'

'Very well,' said Švejk solemnly, 'letter for madam, but mum's the word!'

He took out Lieutenant Lukáš's letter.

'I,' he said, pointing to himself, 'wait for answer in hall here.'

1. 'I don't speak [Hungarian].'

'Why don't you sit down?' asked Vodička, who was already sitting on a chair by the wall. 'There's a seat for you. You don't have to stand here like a beggar. Don't demean yourself before that Hungarian. You'll see, we're going to have trouble with him, but I'll sock him.

'Listen,' he said a minute later, 'where did you learn German?'

'I taught myself,' answered Švejk. There was a moment's silence again. Then from the room into which the maid had carried the letter there could be heard a tremendous shouting and uproar. Someone threw something heavy on the ground, then glasses could be clearly heard flying and plates splintering mixed with a bellowing of '*Baszom az anyát, baszom az istenet, baszom a Kristus Máriát, baszom az astyádot, baszom a világot!*'[1]

The door flew open and there flew into the hall a man in his best years with a napkin round his neck waving in his hands the letter which had been delivered a moment before.

Nearest to the door sat old Sapper Vodička, and consequently it was to him that the infuriated gentleman addressed himself first.

'What does this mean? Where is the bloody swine who brought this letter?'

'Gently now,' said Vodička, getting up. 'Don't shout so loud here, unless you want to be chucked out and if you wish to know who brought that letter ask my friend there. But talk to him politely or one, two, three, go, and you'll be out of the door.'

Now it was for Švejk to experience the rich eloquence of the gentleman with the napkin round his neck, who got fearfully tied up and said that they were just having lunch.

'We've heard that you're having lunch,' Švejk agreed in broken German, adding in Czech: 'It could also have occurred to us that we might perhaps be dragging you quite unnecessarily away from your meal.'

'Don't demean yourself!' said Vodička.

The infuriated gentleman, whose napkin as a result of his lively gesticulation hung around him only by one corner, went on to say that he had at first thought the letter contained something about army billeting in this house, which belonged to his wife.

'Quite a lot of soldiers could get in here,' said Švejk, 'but that was not what the letter was about, as you probably now see for yourself.'

1. A string of obscene Hungarian oaths. Literally, 'Fuck your mother, God, Christ, the Virgin Mary, father and the world.'

The gentleman put his hands to his head and uttered a whole series of reproaches, saying that he was also a reserve lieutenant, and that he would like to be serving now but that he had kidney disease. In his day the officers were not so profligate as to disturb the tranquillity of the family. He would send the letter to the regimental commander, to the Ministry of War, he would publish it in the newspapers.

'Sir,' said Švejk with dignity. 'It was me who wrote that letter. I wrote. Not lieutenant. The signature and name are false. I like your wife very much. *Ich liebe Ihre Frau.* I'm up to the ears in love with your wife, as Vrchlický [1] used to say. She's a capital woman.'

The infuriated gentleman wanted to hurl himself at Švejk, who stood calmly and happily in front of him, but old Sapper Vodička following his every movement tripped him up, tore from his hand the letter which he was continually waving and stuck it in his pocket. Then when Mr Kákonyi got up again Vodička seized him, carried him to the door and

1. Famous Czech poet.

opened it with one hand. Then something could be heard rolling down the steps.

It all happened as quickly as in fairy tales, when the devil comes to take someone off.

The only trace which remained of the infuriated gentleman was his napkin. Švejk picked it up, knocked respectfully on the door of the room from which five minutes ago Mr Kákonyi had emerged and where a woman's sobs could be heard.

'I'm bringing you the napkin,' Švejk said gently to the lady, who was weeping on the sofa. 'Someone might trample on it. My compliments, madam.'

He clicked his heels, saluted and went out into the passage. On the stairs no further traces of the struggle could be seen and just as Vodička had forecast the scene passed off quite smoothly. Only afterwards by the gate in the carriage entrance Švejk found a torn-off collar. Evidently the last act of this tragedy was performed here when Mr Kákonyi desperately held on to the house gate so as not to be dragged out into the street.

It was lively in the street however. Mr Kákonyi was dragged off to the carriage entrance of the house opposite, where they poured water on him, and in the middle of the street old Sapper Vodička fought like a lion against some Honvéds and Honvéd hussars who had rallied to their fellow-countryman. He defended himself in a masterly fashion with his bayonet hanging on his belt like a flail. And he was not alone. At his side there fought several Czech soldiers from various regiments who were just passing by in the street.

Švejk, as he later maintained, did not know himself how he came to get mixed up in this, nor how, not having a bayonet, he got hold of the stick of a panic-stricken passer-by.

It lasted quite a long time, but all good things have to come to an end. The military police came along and arrested them all.

Švejk carried with him the stick, which was pronounced by the commandant of the military police to be a *corpus delicti*, and marched side by side with Vodička.

He walked happily, carrying the stick on his shoulder like a rifle.

Old Sapper Vodička was stubbornly silent during the whole journey. It was only when they came to the guard-house that he said in a gloomy tone to Švejk: 'Didn't I tell you that you didn't know those Hungarian bastards?'

4

New Sufferings

COLONEL SCHRÖDER observed with satisfaction the pale countenance of Lieutenant Lukáš who had big rings under his eyes and in his embarrassment avoided the colonel's gaze. Instead, surreptitiously, as though he were studying something he eyed the plan of the disposition of the men in the camp, which was also the only ornament in the whole of the office.

On the table in front of Colonel Schröder lay some newspapers containing articles marked in blue pencil. The colonel scanned them once more and said, looking at Lieutenant Lukáš:

'And so you know already that your batman Švejk is under arrest and will probably be brought before divisional court-martial?'

'I do, sir.'

'But that does not of course close the matter,' the colonel said with emphasis, feasting his eyes on the pale face of Lieutenant Lukáš. 'The local community have certainly been shocked by the whole affair of your batman Švejk, and your name is quoted in that context as well, lieutenant. Divisional headquarters have already sent us certain material. We have here some journals which deal with this case. You may read them aloud to me.'

He handed to Lieutenant Lukáš the newspapers with the marked articles and the lieutenant began to recite them in a monotonous voice, as though he were reading from a child's reading primer the sentence: 'Honey is much more nourishing and more easily digestible than sugar.'

'WHERE IS THE GUARANTEE OF OUR FUTURE?'

'Is that in the *Pester Lloyd*?' asked the colonel.

'Yes, sir,' answered Lieutenant Lukáš and went on reading:

'The conduct of the war demands the cooperation of all classes of the population of the Austro-Hungarian Monarchy. If we are resolved to guarantee the security of the state, all the nationalities must render each other mutual support, and it is just in the spontaneous respect which one nationality feels for another that the guarantee of our future lies. The greatest sacrifices of our doughty warriors at the fronts, where they advance forward without respite, would not be possible if the base, which is the ancillary and political pulse of our glorious armies, were not united – if behind the backs of our troops

there were elements trying to break up the state monolith and by their male-volent propaganda undermine its authority as an integral unit and sow discord in the community of the nationalities of our Empire. In this historic hour we cannot pass over in silence a handful of people who out of local chauvinistic motives would like to try to destroy the unified efforts and struggle of all the nationalities of this Empire for the just punishment of those criminals who have attacked our Empire without just cause or reason with the object of robbing it of the whole heritage of its culture and civiliza-tion. We cannot ignore those disgusting manifestations of the outbursts of a pathological mentality which has no other aim but to disrupt the unanimity reigning in the hearts of our peoples. Already several times we have taken the opportunity to draw attention in our journal to the need for the military authorities to intervene with the utmost severity against those individuals in the Czech regiments, who in disregard of glorious regimental traditions and by their senseless and outrageous conduct stir up hatred in our Hungarian towns against the entire Czech nation, which as a whole is entirely innocent and which has always stood firmly for the interests of this Empire. This is proved by a whole series of outstanding Czech military personalities, among whom we recall the glorious figures of Marshal Radetzky and other defenders of the Austro-Hungarian Monarchy. In contrast to these shining lights there are a few scoundrels drawn from the depraved Czech rabble who in obedience to their lowest instincts have taken advantage of the world war to volunteer for service in the army and to spread chaos in the solidarity of the nationalities of the Monarchy. We have already once drawn attention to the outrageous behaviour of regiment no. . . . in Debrecen, whose disgraceful excesses were the subject of discussion and condemnation by the Budapest Diet and whose regimental standard was later – *confiscated* – at the front. Who is it that has this heinous sin on his conscience? – *confiscated*. Who drove the Czech soldiers to – *confiscated*. The brazen behaviour of this alien vermin in our Hungarian fatherland is best shown by the case in Királyhida, the Hungarian outpost on the Leitha. What was the nationality of those soldiers from the near-by military camp in Bruck an der Leitha who assaulted and tortured the local merchant, Mr Gyula Kákonyi? It is clearly the duty of the authorities to investigate this crime and to demand information from the military command, who must certainly be concerning themselves with this matter. We require to know the exact role played by Lieutenant Lukasch in this unprecedented agitation against citizens of the Kingdom of Hungary. This officer's name is being mentioned in the town in connection with the events of recent days, as we have been informed by our local correspondent, who has already collected voluminous material about the whole affair, which is a crying scandal in today's serious times. The readers of *Pester Lloyd* will certainly follow with interest the developments of the investigation and we wish to assure them that we shall inform them in detail about this affair which is of outstanding importance. Nevertheless we are still expecting official news of the crime at Királyhida, which was committed against the Hungarian population. It is obvious that the Budapest Diet will take the matter up, so that it can be established once and for all that Czech soldiers passing through the Kingdom of Hungary on their way to the front are not permitted to think that they hold the lands of the crown of St Stephen in fee. If however any representatives of that nationality who in Királyhida have so splendidly represented the partnership of all the nationalities of this Monarchy are still unable to understand the situation they had better keep extremely quiet, for in war people of this kind will be taught by the bullet, the gallows, gaol and the bayonet to obey and to subordinate their acts to the highest interests of our common fatherland.'

'Who has signed this article, lieutenant?'

'Béla Barabás, editor and parliamentary deputy, sir.'

'He's a notorious swine, lieutenant; but before the article found its way to the *Pester Lloyd*, it had already been published in the *Pesti Hirlap*. Now please read me the official translation from Hungarian of the article in the Sopron journal *Sopronyi Napló*.'

Lieutenant Lukáš read aloud the article, in which the editor took great pains to ensure that the following hotch-potch of expressions should figure prominently:

'The requirements of state wisdom', 'law and order', 'human degeneration', 'human dignity and feelings trampled underfoot', 'cannibalistic debauches', 'massacre of human society', 'pack of Mamelukes', 'behind the scenes you will recognize them'. And so it went on, as though the Hungarians were the most persecuted element on their own soil – as though the Czech soldiers had come and struck down the editor, trampling on his belly with their boots, while he was howling with pain, and someone had taken it all down in shorthand.

'There is a dangerous silence enshrouding some very important matters, and nothing is written about them,' was the wail of *Sopronyi Napló*, the daily paper of Sopron.

We all know what a Czech soldier is in Hungary and at the front. We all know what things the Czechs do, what is going on here, what the situation is with the Czechs and who is behind it all. The vigilance of the authorities is of course directed towards other important things, which however must not be isolated from the general control of events, so that what has happened these days in Királyhida may never happen again. Our article of yesterday was confiscated in fifteen places. That is why we have no alternative but to state that even today we still do not have on technical grounds many reasons for dealing in detail with the events in Királyhida. The reporter whom we sent out established on the spot that the authorities are showing genuine zeal in the whole affair and that the investigations are proceeding at full steam. The only strange thing is that some participators in the whole massacre are still at liberty. This is particularly the case with one gentleman who according to hearsay still remains unpunished in the military camp and still wears the insignia of his parrot-regiment,[1] and whose name was also published the day before yesterday in the *Pester Lloyd* and the *Pesti Napló*. We refer to the well-known Czech chauvinist, Lükáš, whose outrageous behaviour will form the subject of the interpellation by our deputy Géza Savanyú, who represents the district of Királyhida.

1. The 91st regiment wore parrot-green facings on their uniforms.

'The weekly in Királyhida and the Pressburg papers write just as amiably about you, lieutenant,' Colonel Schröder observed. 'But that won't interest you very much because it's all much of a muchness. There are political reasons for this, because after all we Austrians, whether we're Germans or Czechs, are, if you compare us with the Hungarians, still pretty ... You understand me, lieutenant, don't you? There's a certain tendency in all this. You might perhaps be more interested in an article in the *Komárno Evening News*, where they assert that you tried to rape Mrs Kákonyi right in her very dining-room during lunch in the presence of her husband, whom you had threatened with your sabre and forced to gag his wife's mouth with a towel to prevent her screaming. That's the latest news of you, lieutenant.'

The colonel gave a smile and went on: 'The authorities have not done their duty. Preventive censorship of the newspapers here is in the hands of the Hungarians too. They do what they like with us. Our officers enjoy no protection from the insults of a swine of a civilian Hungarian editor like this and it was only as a result of our sharp intervention, in other words on the basis of a telegram from divisional court-martial, that the Public Prosecutor's office in Budapest took the necessary steps to see that arrests were carried out among the editorial staffs of all the papers mentioned. The man who's going to catch it hottest is the editor of the *Komárno Evening News*. He will remember his *Evening News* to his dying day. Divisional court-martial has authorized me as your superior officer to hear your side of the case and at the same time has sent me all the documents concerning the investigation. Everything would have turned out all right if it had not been for your unfortunate Švejk. There was with him a certain sapper, Vodička. When they took that man to the guard-house after the brawl they found on him the letter you had sent to Mrs Kákonyi. Your Švejk alleged under cross-examination that it was not your letter, but that he had written it himself. However, when it was shown to him and he was asked to copy it to compare the handwriting in it with his own he ate it up. From regimental office your reports were later sent to divisional court-martial so that they could compare them with Švejk's handwriting and this is the result.'

The colonel turned over the pages of the documents and drew the lieutenant's attention to the following passage:

The accused, Švejk, refused to write the sentences dictated to him, claiming that during the night he had forgotten how to write.

'I really attribute no importance whatsoever to what your Švejk or
the sapper said at divisional court-martial, lieutenant. They alleged
that it was only a question of a little joke which had been misunder-
stood, and that they were themselves attacked by civilians and defended themselves to protect their military honour. In the course of the
investigation it was ascertained that that Švejk of yours is a fine rascal
altogether. Thus for example, when asked why he didn't confess, he
answered according to the report: "I'm in just the same position as the
servant of the academy painter Mr Panuška once was about some
pictures of the Virgin Mary. When it was a question of some pictures
he had allegedly embezzled he too couldn't answer anything except:
'Do you want me to spit blood?' " Of course on behalf of regimental
command I have seen to it that in the name of divisional court-martial
all newspapers must publish corrections of all these rubbishy articles
in the local papers here. Today these corrections will be sent out and I
hope I have done everything to repair what took place as a result of the
rascally conduct of those Hungarian civilian journalist bastards.

'I think I've formulated it well:

' "Divisional court-martial no. N and regimental command no. N
state that the article published in the local journals about alleged excesses on the part of the men of regiment N has no basis in fact and
is invented from A to Z, and that the proceedings brought against
those journals will result in the severe punishment of the guilty."'

'Divisional court-martial in its report to our regimental command,'
continued the colonel, 'has come to the conclusion that behind all
this there is nothing less than a systematic agitation against military
units coming from Cisleithania to Transleithania. Just compare how
many soldiers have gone to the front from our part of the country
and how many from theirs. I tell you that a Czech soldier is much more
to my taste than any pack of Hungarian bastards. It's enough for me
to remember how at Belgrade the Hungarians shot at our second march
battalion, who didn't know that it was the Hungarians who were
shooting at them and began to fire at the Deutschmeisters on the right
wing. Then the Deutschmeisters got muddled as well and opened fire
on the Bosnian regiment which stood alongside them. That was a nice
situation! At that very moment I was having my lunch at the brigade
staff. The day before we had had to be satisfied with ham and tinned
soup but that day we had a proper chicken soup, fillet with rice, and
little doughnuts with egg-flip. The evening before we'd hanged a

Serbian wine-merchant in the town and our cooks had found in his cellar wine which was thirty years old. You can imagine how we all looked forward to the lunch. We'd eaten the soup and were just digging into the chicken when suddenly there was a skirmish and a salvo of shots and our artillery, who hadn't the foggiest idea that it was our units who were shooting at each other, began to shoot into our lines and one shell fell quite close to our brigade staff. The Serbs probably thought that a mutiny had broken out on our side and so they began to fire at us from all sides and to cross the river towards us. The brigade general was called to the telephone, and the divisional commander kicked up a tremendous row about the shambles in the brigade sector. He said that he'd just got orders from army staff to begin the attack on the Serbian positions at 2.35 a.m. on the left flank. We were the reserve and we must at once cease fire. But in such a situation how can you hope to have "cease fire". Brigade telephone exchange reported that it couldn't get any connection anywhere but that the staff of the 75th regiment was reporting that it had received from the next division the order "stand firm", that it was not possible to communicate with our division, that the Serbs had occupied points 212, 226 and 327, that a battalion was required to act as liaison and provide telephone communication with our division. We transferred the call to the division but the connection was already broken, because in the meantime the Serbs had got behind us on both flanks and cut up our centre into a triangle. Inside that everything stayed, regiments, artillery and baggage train with the whole column of cars, the stores and the field-hospital. I was two days in the saddle and the divisional commander was captured together with our brigade commander. And that was all the fault of the Hungarians because they shot at our second march battalion. Of course, as you can imagine, they tried to blame it all on our regiment.'

The colonel spat:

'You've been able to see for yourself, lieutenant, what splendid use they have made of your little adventure in Királyhida.'

Lieutenant Lukáš coughed in embarrassment.

'Lieutenant,' the colonel said to him in a familiar tone. 'Hand on your heart, how many times did you sleep with Mrs Kákonyi?'

Colonel Schröder was in a very good mood today.

'Don't say, lieutenant, that you've only just begun to correspond with her. When I was your age, I spent three weeks in Erlau on a geometry course and you should have seen how during all those three weeks I did nothing else but sleep with Hungarian women. Every day with another one. Young ones, single ones, elderly ones, married ones, just as they came. I ironed them out so thoroughly that when I returned to my regiment I could hardly move my legs. It was the wife of a lawyer who took most out of me. She showed me what Hungarian women can do. She bit me on the nose in the process and didn't let me close my eyes the whole night.

'You just began to correspond . . .' the colonel said, patting him familiarly on the shoulder, 'we know that. You don't need to say anything. I have my opinion of the whole matter. You got involved with her, her husband came along, and that stupid Švejk of yours . . .

'But you know, lieutenant, that Švejk of yours must have character after all, when he pulled off such a trick with your letter. One really feels sympathy for such a man. I say it's a matter of upbringing. That's what I like about that bastard. Definitely the proceedings have to be stopped in this respect. Lieutenant, you have been vilified in the newspapers. Your presence here is quite unnecessary. In a week's time a march battalion will be sent to the Russian front. You're the most senior officer in the 11th company and you'll go with it as commander. Everything has been arranged at brigade headquarters. Tell the quartermaster sergeant-major that he should find you another batman instead of that Švejk.'

Lieutenant Lukáš looked gratefully at the colonel, who continued: 'I assign Švejk to you as company orderly.'

The lieutenant turned pale and the colonel got up and offered him his hand saying:

'Well, everything is settled now. I wish you good luck so that you can distinguish yourself on the Eastern front. And if by any chance we should meet again, come and join us. Don't avoid our company as you did in Budějovice . . .'

Lieutenant Lukáš repeated to himself all the way home: 'Company commander, company orderly.'

And vividly before his eyes there loomed the figure of Švejk.

Quartermaster Sergeant-Major Vaněk said, when Lieutenant Lukáš ordered him to find him a new batman instead of Švejk: 'I thought, sir, you were satisfied with Švejk.'

When he learnt that the colonel had nominated Švejk orderly to the 11th company, he cried out: 'God help us all!'

*

At the divisional court in a hut which was fitted with bars they got up according to regulations at 7 a.m. and put in order their straw mattresses which were lying about in the dust on the ground. There were no bunks. In a compartment in the long hall they were folding the blankets and placing them neatly on the straw mattresses according to regulations. The men who had finished their jobs were sitting on benches along the wall and either looking for lice (those who'd come from the front) or amusing themselves by relating various adventures.

Švejk with old Sapper Vodička sat on a bench near the door with a group of soldiers from various regiments and military units.

'Look at that Hungarian fellow there by the window, chaps,' said Vodička. 'See how the bastard prays to God that everything will go well with him. Wouldn't you like to break his mug open from ear to ear?'

'But he's a decent chap,' said Švejk. 'He's only here because he didn't want to join up. He's against the war, belongs to some kind of sect and he's been gaoled because he didn't want to kill people. He keeps God's commandment, but they're going to make God's commandment hot for him. Before the war there was a fellow called Nemrava living in Moravia who didn't even want to take a rifle on his shoulder, and when he was called up he said that it was against his principles to carry a rifle. Because of that he was gaoled until he was blue in the face and then brought up again to take the oath. But he said he wouldn't do it as it was against his principles and he held out so long that he got away with it.'

'He must have been a stupid chump,' said old Sapper Vodička. 'He could have taken the oath and then shitted on everything and the oath too.'

'I've already taken the oath three times,' an infantryman chimed in, 'and this is the third time I'm here for desertion, and if I hadn't got a medical certificate showing that fifteen years ago I beat my aunt to death in a fit of insanity maybe they'd have shot me three times at the front. But my late lamented aunt always helps me out of trouble and in the end I'll probably get out of this war safe and sound.'

'And why did you kill your auntie, old man?' asked Švejk.

'Why do people kill each other?' the pleasant man answered. 'You can guess for yourself. It was for money, of course. She had five savings-bank books, that old frump had, and they had just sent her the interest when I came to visit her and I was completely at the end of my tether. Except for her I didn't have a soul in the whole of God's world. And so I went to ask her if she'd take me into her care and the old bitch said that I was a young, strong, healthy man and ought to go out and work. Well, one word led to another and I only hit her over the head a few times with a poker, but I got her face into such a mess that I didn't know whether she was my aunt or not. And so I sat beside her on the ground and kept on saying to myself: "Is that Auntie or isn't it Auntie?" And that's how the neighbours found me next day, sitting beside her. Then I was put into the madhouse at Na Slupi and, when later, before the war, they sent us before a commission in Bohnice, I was pronounced cured and had at once to go and make up those years' service in the army which I had missed.'

A lean emaciated soldier with a care-worn appearance passed by carrying a broom.

'That's a teacher from the last march company,' said a rifleman who was sitting next to Švejk. 'Now he goes around sweeping up the floor under him. He's an awfully decent chap. He's here because of some stupid rhyme he wrote.

'Hallo, teacher, come here!' he called to the man with the broom, who approached the bench with a solemn expression. 'Tell us the rhyme of yours about the lice.'

The soldier with the broom cleared his throat and began:

> 'The army's all loused up, they're scratching at the front,
> And on our backs a monster louse is creeping.
> The general himself has had to join the hunt.
> The lice have made him toss and spoilt his sleeping.
> The lice are doing finely in the soldiers' huts.
> They're even getting used to the tough N.C.O.s.
> And the bastard Austrian he-louse,[1] if he's still got the guts,
> Can mate with the Prussian she-louse, I suppose.'

The care-worn soldier and teacher sat down on the bench and sighed: 'That's all it was. And because of that I've been examined four times already by the judge advocate.'

'That's really not worth talking about,' said Švejk nonchalantly. 'The question is only this: who will the people in the court think is the bastard Austrian he-louse? It's good that you put in that bit about mating. That'll confuse them completely and knock them off their

1. In Czech *všivák*, which also means (a) someone who has lice on him; (b) a bastard. The reference is of course a veiled one to the Emperor Franz Joseph.

rockers. You've just got to explain to them that the bastard he-louse is the male of the species and that the she-louse can only be mounted by a bastard he-louse. Otherwise you won't get away with it. You obviously didn't write that rhyme to insult anyone. That's quite clear. Just tell the judge advocate that you wrote it for your own personal amusement and that as the male of a pig is called a boar, so the male of a louse is called a bastard.'

The teacher sighed: 'But the trouble is that the judge advocate's Czech isn't very good. I've already tried hard to explain it to him in this way, but he just let fly at me and shouted that a male louse is called "*fešak*" in Czech. "You bloody idiot of a scholar, the feminine is '*ten feš*' and so the masculine is '*ta fešak*'.[1] Go and teach your grandmother to suck eggs!" '

'To put it in a nutshell,' said Švejk, 'you're in a jam, but you mustn't lose hope. It can still change for the better as the gipsy Janeček said in Pilsen when in 1879 they put the cord round his neck for double robbery with murder. He was right in his guess, because at the very last moment they took him away from the gallows, as they couldn't hang him, owing to its being the birthday of His Imperial Majesty which fell on the very same day when he ought to be hanged. And so they hanged him the following day after the birthday had passed. But just imagine the luck that bastard had, because on the third day he got a pardon and his case had to be taken up again, as everything pointed to the fact that it was another Janeček who had committed the crime. So they had to dig him out of the convicts' cemetery and rehabilitate him in the Catholic cemetery at Pilsen. But afterwards it turned out that he had been an evangelical and so they transferred him to the evangelical cemetery. And after that . . .'

'And after that you'll get a sock on the jaw,' said old Sapper Vodička. 'The things that bastard thinks up! A chap has trouble with divisional court-martial and when they took us away for interrogation yesterday the bloody fool starts explaining to me what the Rose of Jericho is.'

'But it wasn't me who explained it. The story comes from Matěj, the painter Panuška's servant, who told an old woman who asked him what the Rose of Jericho looked like:

'Take some dry cow shit, put it on a plate, pour water on it and it

1. The judge advocate, who is a German, gets the meaning and genders wrong, confusing *všivák* (he-louse or bastard) with *fešák* (dandy). The Czechs normally use for both he- and she-louse the word *veš*, which is feminine.

will become green and beautiful: that's the Rose of Jericho,' Švejk said, defending himself. 'It wasn't me who thought up that nonsense, and after all, we had to talk about something when we went to the interrogation. I only wanted to cheer you up, Vodička . . .'

'Wanted to cheer me up!' Vodička spat contemptuously. 'A chap has his head full of worries about how to get out of this jam, how to manage to get free so as to be able to pay out those damned Hungarian bastards and this bloody fool here wants to cheer him up with some cow shit!

'How can I pay those Hungarian bastards out if I'm sitting locked up here, and if into the bargain I've got to pretend to the judge advocate that I don't feel any hatred for the Hungarians? It's a dog's life, my God, really it is, but when I manage to get my paws on one of those Hungarian bastards I'll strangle him like a puppy. I'll teach them their "*Isten, ala meg a magyar*".[1] I'll be even with them. I won't allow them to forget old Vodička, I tell you!'

'Don't let's any of us have any worries,' said Švejk. 'Everything will sort itself out. The main thing is always to say in court what isn't true. Any chap who allows himself to be hoodwinked into confessing is always done for. Nothing good will ever come of that. Once when I worked in Moravská Ostrava there was the following case there: a miner beat up an engineer when he was alone with him so that there were no witnesses. And the lawyer who defended him insisted that if he denied it, nothing could happen to him. But the president of the senate kept on appealing to him that confession would be an extenuating circumstance. But the miner went on asserting that he couldn't confess and so he was acquitted, because he had established his alibi. On the very same day in Brno . . .'

'Jesus Mary,' cried Vodička in a fury. 'I can't stand it any longer. Why he tells all this bloody nonsense I can't understand. Yesterday at the investigation we had just the same sort of a fellow. When the judge advocate asked him what he was in civil life he said: "I blow at crosses." It took more than half an hour before he could explain to the judge advocate that he blew the bellows at a smith's called Cross, and when they asked him afterwards: "So in civil life you're an untrained worker?", he answered them: "Of course I don't work in the train. That's Franta Hybš." '

1. Hungarian for 'God bless the Hungarians' – the first words of the Hungarian national hymn.

From the passage could be heard steps and the shouting of the guard: 'New lot.' 'There'll be more of us again,' said Švejk happily. 'Perhaps these will have managed to keep some cigar stumps.'

The door opened and the volunteer who had sat with Švejk under

arrest in Budějovice, and was now destined for the kitchen of a march company, was pushed in.

'Praised be the Lord Jesus Christ,' he said on entering, upon which Švejk answered in the name of all: 'For ever and ever, amen.'

The volunteer looked happily at Švejk, put the blanket which he had brought with him on the ground and sat down on the bench next to the Czech colony. Then he unwound his puttees, took out the cigarettes which were artfully rolled in the folds and distributed them. Then he took out of his boots the striking part of a box of matches and one or two matches cunningly split down the centre from the top.

He struck a match, carefully lit a cigarette, gave a light to all of them and said nonchalantly: 'I'm accused of mutiny.'

'That's nothing,' said Švejk consolingly. 'That's just fun.'

'Of course it is,' the volunteer agreed. 'But I really don't know if it's the way to win the war with all these courts-martial. If they insist on trying me at any price, let them try me. Generally speaking one trial can't change the situation at all.'

'And how did you mutiny?' asked Sapper Vodička, looking at the volunteer with sympathy.

'I refused to clean the rears in the guard-house,' he answered. 'And so they took me all the way up to the colonel. And he was a pretty fair swine. He started to shout at me that I was locked up on the basis of a regimental report and that I was a common convict, that he was quite amazed that the earth still carried me and didn't stop turning round because of the shame that in the army there was a man with the rights of a volunteer who had claims to officer's rank, but who by his behaviour could only arouse revulsion and contempt in all his superiors. I replied that the rotation of the globe could not be interrupted by the appearance on it of a volunteer like myself, that the laws of nature were more powerful than the shoulder-straps of volunteers and that I would like to know who could compel me to clean a rear, if I had not shitted in it myself, although I might be entitled to do so after the filthy catering there was in the regiment and after all that rotten cabbage and soaked salted mutton they gave us. And then in addition I said to the colonel that his view as to why the earth still carried me was rather odd, since there would surely not be an earthquake because of me. The colonel didn't do anything during the whole of my speech except grind his teeth like a mare when it feels the chill of frozen turnips on its tongue, and then he roared at me:

' "Very well, then, are you going to clean the rear or aren't you?"

' "Humbly report, I'm not going to clean any rear."

' "You are going to clean it, you volunteer!"

' "Humbly report, I'm not."

' "Bloody hell, you're going to clean not only one rear but a hundred rears!"

' "Humbly report, I'm not going to clean either a hundred rears or one rear."

'And so it went on and on: "Are you going to clean it?" "I'm not going to clean it." Rears flew about all over the place as though it was a nursery rhyme by the writer Pavla Moudrá. The colonel ran up and down the office like a madman and finally sat down and said: "Think it over carefully. I'm going to send you to divisional court for mutiny. Don't imagine that you'll be the first volunteer to be shot in this war. In Serbia we hanged two volunteers of the 10th company and shot one of the 9th in cold blood. And why? All because of their pig-headedness. Those two who were hanged had hesitated to stab the wife and kid of a comitadji[1] near Šabac, and the volunteer from the 9th company was shot because he wouldn't advance and made the excuse that he had swollen legs and was flat-footed. Very well, then, will you clean the rears or not?"

' "Humbly report, I won't." '

'The colonel looked at me and said: "Listen, do you happen to be a Slavophil?" '

' "Humbly report, I don't." '

'After that they took me away and declared that I was accused of mutiny.'

'The best thing you can do now,' said Švejk, 'is to pretend to be an idiot. When I sat in the garrison gaol, we had with us a very intelligent and well-educated fellow who was a teacher at a commercial school. He "dissented" from the front and an awfully fine show trial was fixed up for him, so that he could be condemned and hanged as a warning to others. But he managed to get out of the whole mess in an awfully simple way. He started by pretending that he had got some congenital disease and when the staff doctor examined him he said he had not "dissented" but that from his earliest years he had liked to travel and had always had a longing to vanish in some faraway part of the world. Once he had woken up in Hamburg and another time in London and he had not known how he got there. His father had been an alcoholic and had committed suicide before his birth. His mother had been a prostitute who took to drink and died of *delirium tremens*. His younger sister drowned herself; his elder one threw herself under a train; his brother jumped from the railway viaduct at Vyšehrad; his grandfather murdered his wife, poured paraffin on himself and set himself on fire; his other grandmother used to gad about with the gipsies and poisoned herself in prison with matches; one cousin was condemned several times for arson and cut his jugular vein with a glass splinter in the Carthusian monastery prison; a female cousin on the father's side threw herself out of the sixth storey of a building in Vienna. He himself had had a frightfully neglected upbringing and couldn't speak until he was

1. A Balkan guerrilla.

ten, because once when he was six months old and they were changing
his nappies and left him alone on the table, a cat pulled him off it and
he knocked his head in the fall. He also had violent headaches from
time to time and on those occasions he didn't know what he was doing.
It was in a state like this that he went from the front to Prague and it
was only when the military police arrested him at the pub U Fleků
that he came to. My goodness, you should have seen how glad they
were to release him from army service. About five servicemen who
sat with him in the same cell for all eventualities made the following
notes on a piece of paper:

> 'Father alcoholic. Mother prostitute.
> 1st sister (drowned).
> 2nd sister (train).
> Brother (from bridge).
> Grandfather,† wife, paraffin, set fire.
> 2nd grandmother (gipsies, matches)† etc.

'And when one of them started to recite the same story to the staff
doctor he got no further than to the cousin, when the staff doctor, who
had heard it twice before, said: "You bloody bastard, your cousin on
the father's side threw herself out of the sixth storey of a building in
Vienna. You had a frightfully neglected upbringing and so you'll be
put right by 'special' treatment." And so they took him away to the
"special" wing and trussed him and immediately his frightfully neglected upbringing, his alcoholic father and his prostitute mother and all
the rest disappeared and he readily volunteered for the front.'

'In the army nowadays nobody believes any longer in hereditary
taints,' said the volunteer, 'because if they did all the general staffs
would have to be shut up in lunatic asylums, every one of them.'

The key in the reinforced iron door rattled and the warder came in
saying:

'Infantryman Švejk and Sapper Vodička to go to the judge advocate!'

They got up and Vodička said to Švejk: 'You see what these bastards
are like. Every day they have an interrogation and there's never any
result. Himmelherrgott, if only they would sentence us and not keep
on dragging us about. As it is we lie here the whole bloody day and
millions of those Hungarian bastards keep on running around . . .'

Continuing on the way to the interrogation in the office of the
divisional court which was situated in another hut on the other side

of the camp, Sapper Vodička and Švejk wondered when they would actually be brought before a proper court.

'It's always nothing but interrogation,' said Vodička, whipping himself up into a fury. 'If only something would come out of it at last. They waste heaps of paper and a chap doesn't even see the court. He rots behind the bars. Tell me honestly, is the soup eatable? And that cabbage with frozen potatoes? Bloody hell, I've never had such a blasted silly war. I thought it would be quite different.'

'As for me, I'm quite happy,' said Švejk. 'When years ago I was serving as a regular our old sweat Solpera used to say that in the army everybody must be conscious of his duties and he gave you at the same time such a sock on the jaw that you never forgot it. Or the late Lieutenant Kvajser, when he came to inspect the rifles, always lectured us too on how every soldier must show the greatest moral ruthlessness because soldiers were only cattle whom the government fed. They gave them something to guzzle, let them swill coffee and stuff tobacco in their pipes, and for that they had to obey and pull like oxen.'

Sapper Vodička reflected for a moment and said after a time:

'When you come before the judge advocate, Švejk, keep your head screwed on and don't forget to repeat what you said at the last interrogation so that I don't get into a mess. The main thing is that you saw how those Hungarian bastards attacked me. After all, we were together in this.'

'Don't worry, Vodička,' said Švejk consolingly. 'Take it calmly. Don't get nervy. What does it matter being brought before divisional court like this? You should have seen how smartly a court-martial like that worked years ago. There was a teacher called Herál on service with me. Once, when we were lying on our bunks because all of us who shared the room had been confined to barracks, he told us that in the Prague Museum there's a book of records of a military court like that from the time of the Empress Maria Theresa. At that time every regiment used to have its executioner who executed the soldiers of the regiment for one Maria Theresa thaler per head. And according to those records that executioner earned some days as much as five thalers.

'Of course,' Švejk added thoughtfully, 'at that time there were strongly-manned regiments and they were regularly filled with recruits from the villages.'

'When I was in Serbia,' said Vodička, 'some men in our brigade volunteered to hang comitadji for cigarettes. A soldier who hanged a comitadji bastard got ten cigarettes and five for a woman or a child. But later Supplies H.Q started economizing and the shootings took place *en bloc*. There was a gipsy who served in our company and for a long time we didn't know what dirty job he was doing. We only noticed that at nights they always summoned him to go to the office. At that time we were encamped on the Drina. And once in the night when he was away a fellow took it into his head to root about in his things and the swine had in his rucksack three whole cartons each with a hundred cigarettes. Later he returned to our barn towards morning and we made short shrift with him. We knocked him on the ground and a chap called Běloun strangled him with his belt. The bastard had as many lives as a cat.'

Old Sapper Vodička spat: 'You just couldn't strangle him. He shitted, his eyes bulged and still he was as live as a half-decapitated cock. And so they wrenched him in two like a cat. Two chaps took his head and another two took his legs and they broke his neck. After that we put his rucksack on his shoulder with the cigarettes in it and threw him into the Drina. Who would want to smoke those cigarettes? In the morning there was a search for him.'

'You should have reported that he'd "dissented",' said Švejk nonchalantly, 'that he'd already made preparations for it and had been saying every day that he would run away.'

'But who would have thought of that?' answered Vodička. 'We had done our bit and we weren't worried about anything else. It was really quite easy there. Every day somebody was missing and they didn't even fish them out of the Drina. A bloated comitadji floated peacefully down the Drina to the Danube side by side with one of our Landwehr men who had been torn to pieces. People who were new to it became a little feverish when they saw it for the first time.'

'You should have given them quinine,' said Švejk.

They were just entering the hut of the offices of divisional court and the patrol led them at once to office no. 8, where behind a long table with a pile of documents sat Judge Advocate Ruller.

A volume of the legal code lay before him, and a half-consumed glass of tea stood on top of it. On the table on the right stood a crucifix made out of imitation ivory with a dusty Christ, who looked despairingly at the pedestal of his cross, on which there were ashes and cigarette stubs.

To the renewed regret of the crucified Jesus Judge Advocate Ruller
was at this very moment flicking the ash from another cigarette on to
the pedestal of the crucifix. With his other hand he was raising the
glass of tea, which had got stuck to the legal code.

When he had freed the glass from the embrace of the code he turned
over the pages of a book which he had borrowed from the officers'
club.

It was a book by Franz S. Krause with the promising title: *Research
into the History of the Development of Sexual Morals.*

He was staring at the reproduction of naïve drawings of male and
female sexual organs with appropriate rhymes which the scholar
Franz S. Krause discovered on the walls of the W.C.s of the West
Berlin railway station, and so he did not pay any attention to the men
who entered the room.

He only pulled himself away from examining the reproductions
when Vodička coughed.

'What's the matter?' he asked, turning the pages further and looking for the continuation of the naïve and stupid drawings, sketches and designs.

'Beg to report, sir,' answered Švejk, 'my friend Vodička has caught cold and is now coughing.'

Judge Advocate Ruller only now looked at Švejk and at Vodička. He tried to assume an air of severity.

'And so you've at last come along, you bastards,' he said, ferreting about in the pile of papers on his desk. 'I had you summoned for nine o'clock and now it's almost eleven.

'What do you mean by standing like that, you bloody great ox?' he asked Vodička, who had taken the liberty of standing at ease. 'Only when I say "At Ease" can you do what you like with your shanks.'

'Humbly report, sir, he has rheumatism,' Švejk put in.

'You'd better shut your mug,' said Judge Advocate Ruller. 'You'll only speak when you're given permission. Three times you've come before me for cross-examination and it was like trying to get water from a stone. Well, am I going to find it or aren't I? You've given me a lot of work, you bloody bastards. But you'll pay for having troubled the courts without good reason!

'Now look, you bloody swine,' he said, when he had taken from a heap of documents a voluminous file with the inscription:

'*Schwejk & Woditschka.*'

'Don't think that because of a stupid brawl you'll be able to loll about in the divisional court and get out of front service for a time. All because of you I had to telephone all the way up to the army court, you bloody idiots!'

He sighed.

'Don't look so serious, Švejk. At the front you'll lose your taste for fighting with Honvéds,' he continued. 'The proceedings against you both are quashed. Each of you is going to his unit, where he will be punished at report and after that sent with a march company to the front. If ever you get into my clutches again, you vermin, I'll make such a mess of you that you won't be able to recognize yourselves. Here you have your release warrant and now behave yourselves respectably. Take them to no. 2.'

'Humbly report, sir,' said Švejk, 'we both take your words to heart and we thank you very much for your kindness. If this was in civil life

I would take the liberty of saying that you're a man of gold. And at the same time we must both beg your pardon for giving you so much bother. We really don't deserve your kindness.'

'Well, now get to hell out of it!' the judge advocate shouted at Švejk. 'If Colonel Schröder hadn't put in a word for you both I don't know what might have happened to you.'

Vodička only felt himself the old Vodička again when they were in the corridor and the patrol led them to office no. 2.

The soldier who escorted them was afraid he would be late to lunch and so he said:

'Come on, now, briskly there, you chaps, you crawl along like lice.'

Vodička told him not to open his trap as wide as that. He was lucky to be a Czech. If he had been a Hungarian he'd have torn him to pieces like a salted herring.

As the army writers in the office had already gone to mess, the soldier who had escorted them was obliged to bring them back temporarily to the divisional court gaol. This did not take place without oaths on his part which he addressed to the hated race of army writers.

'The others will have cleaned up all the fat from the soup,' he moaned in tragic tones, 'and instead of meat they'll leave me sinew. Yesterday too I escorted two people into the camp and while I was doing it someone ate up half the loaf which they had drawn for me.'

'It looks as if here in divisional court you only think about filling your bellies,' said Vodička, who was already his old self again.

When they told the volunteer what had happened to them he exclaimed: 'So it's the march company for you, my friends! This is just like in the journal for Czech tourists, "A Fair Wind!" The preliminary preparations for the journey are already completed. Everything has been managed and arranged by the glorious military administration. And you too have been specially picked to join the expedition to Galicia. Set out on your journey with easy minds and light and joyful hearts. Cherish special love for the regions where they will introduce you to the trenches. It's lovely and extremely interesting there. You will feel at home in those distant foreign lands as though you were in familiar parts, yes, almost as though you were in your dear fatherland. With exalted feelings you will begin your pilgrimage to those lands, of which even the good old Humboldt said: "In the whole world I've never seen anything more magnificent than that bloody silly Galicia." The numerous precious experiences which our glorious army acquired in the course of its retreat from Galicia during the first expedition will certainly be very helpful guide lines when we make our programme for the second expedition. Just follow your nose to Russia, and joyfully fire all your cartridges into the air.'

After lunch, before Švejk and Vodička left for the office they were approached by the unfortunate teacher who had written the rhyme about the lice. He took them both aside and said mysteriously: 'Don't forget when you're on the Russian side to say at once to the Russians: "Zdravstvuite, Russkie bratya, my bratya Chekhi, my nyet Avstritsy".'[1]

And when they came out of the hut Vodička, wanting to manifest his hatred towards the Hungarians and demonstrate that his confinement had not shaken his convictions, trod on the foot of the Hungarian who didn't want to serve at the front and roared out at him: 'Put on your boots, you bastard!'

'He ought to have said something to me,' Sapper Vodička grumbled afterwards to Švejk. 'He should have piped up and I'd have torn his Hungarian snout from one ear to another. But the idiotic bastard keeps mum and lets me trample on his boots. Herrgott, Švejk, I'm furious that I haven't been convicted. Why, it looks as though they were just laughing at us, as if what we did to the Hungarians was not worth a damn. And yet we fought like lions. It's your fault that they didn't convict us and gave us a clean chit as though we hadn't known how to fight properly. Who do they think we are? Why, it was quite a respectable roughhouse.'

'My dear old boy,' said Švejk affably, 'I can't understand why you're not glad that our divisional court officially recognized us as quite respectable people against whom they could have no charge. It's true that during the investigation I made all sorts of excuses, but that's what you have to do. Its your duty to lie, as the lawyer Bass tells his clients. When the judge advocate asked me why we broke into the apartment of that Mr Kákonyi I simply said to him: "I thought the best way for us to get acquainted with Mr Kákonyi was to go and see him." After that the judge advocate didn't ask me any further questions and had had enough of it.

'Remember,' Švejk continued reflectively, 'that at a court-martial no one must ever confess anything. When I was under arrest at garrison court there was a soldier in the next cell who confessed.

1. 'Hello, Russian brothers, we're your Czech brothers, we aren't Austrians.'

When the others learnt about it they gave him the blanket treatment and ordered him to withdraw his confession.'

'If I'd done something dishonest I wouldn't have confessed, of course,' said Sapper Vodička, 'but when that bastard of a judge advocate asked me straight out: "Did you fight?", I said: "Yes, I did." "Did you manhandle anybody?" "Certainly I did, sir." "Did you

wound anybody?" "Of course I did, sir." He should know who he's dealing with. And the real disgrace is that they acquitted us. It's as though he didn't want to believe that I broke my bayonet-belt over those Hungarian bastards, that I made pea soup, bumps and bruises out of them. You were there, weren't you, at the very moment when I had three of those Hungarian bastards on top of me and you could see after a short time how all of them fell on to the ground and I stamped on them. And after all that the swine of a judge advocate goes and quashes the proceedings. It's just as if he'd said to me: "You fight? Who d'you think you bloody well are?" When the war's over and I return to civilian life I'll find that swine somewhere and show him whether I know how to fight or not. And then I'll come here to Királyhida and make such a roughhouse here as the world has never seen. And people'll go and hide in their cellars when they learn that I have come to have a word with those bastards in Királyhida, those rats, those stinking swine.'

In the office all the formalities were completed very quickly. A sergeant-major with a mouth still greasy from lunch gave Švejk and Vodička their documents with a frightfully solemn expression on his face and did not let the opportunity slip of making a speech to both of them, in which he appealed to their military spirit. In doing so, as he was a *Wasserpolak*, he mixed up several expressions in his dialect, saying things like '*marekvium*', '*glupi rolmopsie*', '*krajcová sedmina*', '*sviňa porýpaná*' and '*dum vám baně na mjesjnuckov vaši gzichty*'.[1]

When Švejk said goodbye to Vodička and each of them was taken off to his unit he said: 'When the war's over come and see me. You'll find me every evening from six o'clock onwards in The Chalice at Na Bojišti.'

'Of course I will,' answered Vodička. 'Will there be any fun there?'

'Every day it goes with a bang there,' Švejk promised, 'and if it should turn out to be too quiet, we'll fix something.'

They parted, and when they were already several paces away from each other, old Sapper Vodička called after Švejk: 'Very well then, but see that you fix some fun when I come to see you!'

Upon which Švejk called back: 'But be sure you come as soon as the war's over!'

After that they went further away from each other and some time later Vodička's voice could be heard from round the corner of the other row of huts: 'Švejk, what kind of beer do they have at The Chalice?'

And Švejk's answer came like an echo: 'Velkopopovický.'[2]

'I thought they had Smíchovský!'[2] Sapper Vodička called from the distance.

'They've got girls there too!' shouted Švejk.

1. *Wasserpolak* (literally 'Water Pole') was a pejorative name for inhabitants of Southern and Western Silesia where a mixture of German and Polish was spoken.
2. Two famous brands of Czech beer.

'Very well, then, at six o'clock in the evening when the war's over!' shouted Vodička from below.

'Better if you come at half-past six, in case I should be held up somewhere,' answered Švejk.

And then Vodička's voice could be heard again this time from a great distance:

'Can't you come at six?'

'Very well then, I'll come at six,' Vodička heard his retreating friend reply.

It was in this way that the good soldier Švejk and the old Sapper Vodička parted. As the German saying goes, '*Wenn die Leute auseinandergehen, da sagen sie "Auf Wiedersehen".*'[1]

1. 'When people part, they say "Till we meet again".'

5

From Bruck an der Leitha to Sokal

LIEUTENANT LUKÁŠ strode angrily up and down the office of the
11th march company. It was a dark hole in the company's hut, par-
titioned from the corridor by boards. There were a table, two chairs,
a can of paraffin and a bunk.

Before him stood Quartermaster Sergeant-Major Vaněk, who here
drew up the records of the soldiers' pay, kept the accounts for the
men's kitchen, was finance minister for the whole company and spent
the whole blessed day in the office, sleeping there as well.

At the door stood a fat infantryman with bushy whiskers like
Krakonoš.[1] This was Baloun, the lieutenant's new batman, in civil life
a miller from the region of Český Krumlov.

'You've certainly picked me a wonderful batman,' said Lieutenant
Lukáš to the quartermaster sergeant-major. 'Thank you very much
for this kind surprise. The very first day I send him for my lunch from
the officers' mess he wolfs up half of it.'

'I spilled it, please, sir,' said the fat giant.

'Good, you spilled it. But you could only have spilled the soup or
the sauce, not the roast with the frankfurter stuffing. Why, you've
brought me a speck just small enough to fit in behind a finger-nail,
and what did you do with the Apfelstrudl?'

'Sir, I've...'

'Now, don't deny it. You've wolfed it up too.'

Lieutenant Lukáš pronounced the last words with such gravity and
in such a severe tone that Baloun involuntarily recoiled two steps.

'I asked in the kitchen what there was for lunch today. There was
soup with liver dumplings. What have you done with those dumplings?
You've filched them on the way, that's certain. And then there was beef
with gherkins. What have you done with that? You've bolted that up
too. And then there were two slices of roast with frankfurter stuffing.
And you've only produced half a slice, haven't you? Two pieces of

1. A giant in one of the Czech fairy tales.

Apfelstrudl! What have you done with them? You've stuffed yourself
up with them, you disgusting miserable swine! Speak out! What have
you done with the Apfelstrudl? What do you say? It fell in the mud,
did it? You verminous scab, you! Can you show me the spot where

it's lying in the mud? What do you say? A dog suddenly came up, did
it? By appointment, I suppose? And it seized it and carried it off?
Jesus Christ, I'll give you such a sock on the jaw that you'll have a
head like a wash-tub. And the swine still denies it! Do you know who
saw you? Quartermaster Sergeant-Major Vaněk here. He came to me
and told me: "Humbly report, sir, your swine, Baloun, is wolfing up
your lunch. I looked out of the window and there he was stuffing
himself as if he hadn't eaten for a whole week." Listen, you quartermaster sergeant-major, couldn't you really have picked out some other
animal for me than this prize bastard?'

    'Humbly report, sir, Baloun seemed the decentest chap in the whole
of our march company. He's such an idiot that he never can remember

any of the rifle positions. If you put a rifle in his hands there'd certainly be an accident. When we had the last exercise with blanks he nearly shot his neighbour's eye out. I thought that he'd at least be able to do this kind of duty.'

'And he'll wolf up his master's lunch every time,' said Lukáš. 'As if one portion wasn't enough for him. Perhaps you're still hungry?'

'Humbly report, sir, I'm hungry all the time. When anybody has bread to spare I buy it from him for cigarettes, and it still isn't enough. I'm like that by nature. I always think I'm full but it's wrong. In a jiffy, as though it were before a meal, my stomach begins to rumble and there it is again, the beast. Sometimes I think I've really had enough, I couldn't get anything more inside me, but it's no good. If I see somebody eating or if I only smell food my stomach feels at once as if it's been cleaned out. It starts to claim its rights and I could even eat nails. Humbly report, sir, I had already asked whether I could be allowed a double portion. Because of that I went to the regimental doctor at Budějovice and he gave me instead three days in the sick bay, prescribing for me only a little cup of clear soup for the whole day. "I'll teach you to be hungry, you vermin," he said. "Come here again and you'll see how you leave us again. You'll be as thin as a hop pole!" I don't have to look at any specially good things, sir, I've only got to see quite ordinary things and my mouth at once begins to water. Humbly report, sir, I respectfully beg to be allowed a double portion. If there isn't meat, could I at least have the garnishing, potatoes, dumplings, a little sauce. There's always plenty of that left . . .'

'Good. I've listened to these impudences of yours, Baloun,' answered Lieutenant Lukáš. 'Have you ever heard, quartermaster sergeant-major, of a soldier being on top of everything else as insolent as this bastard is? He's wolfed up my lunch and still has the cheek to demand I should give him a double portion. But I'll teach you, Baloun, what it means to be hungry.

'Quartermaster sergeant-major,' he turned to Vaněk, 'take him to Corporal Weidenhofer and tell him to tie him up firmly in the yard by the kitchen for two hours when they serve out goulash this evening. Let him tie him nice and high, so that he can only just stand on tip-toe and see how the goulash is cooking in the cauldron. And make sure that the bastard is kept tied up when the goulash is being doled out in the kitchen, so that his mouth can water like a starving cur's when it's sniffing at a delicatessen shop. Tell the cook to give away the bastard's own portion!'

'Very good, sir. Come along, Baloun!'

Just as they were leaving the lieutenant detained them in the doorway and, looking into the horrified face of Baloun, cried out triumphantly: 'You've done well for yourself, Baloun. I wish you a good appetite! And if you should ever try this on me again, I'll have you mercilessly court-martialled.'

When Vaněk returned and reported that Baloun was already tied up Lukáš said: 'You know me well, Vaněk, and you know I don't like doing things like this, but I can't help it. First you must admit that if you take a bone from a dog it growls. I don't want to have a low fellow about me, and next the fact that Baloun is tied up will have a great moral and psychological impact on all the rank and file. When those bastards are on march companies and know that the next day or the day after they'll go to the front they tend to do what they like.'

Lieutenant Lukáš appeared extremely care-worn and went on in a quiet voice: 'The day before yesterday, when we had night operations, we had as you know to manoeuvre against the volunteer school behind the sugar-refinery. The first group, the advance guard, marched quite noiselessly along the street, because I led them myself, but the second, which was supposed to go to the left and to send advance patrols below the sugar-refinery, behaved as if they were out on a picnic. They sang and stamped, so that they could probably be heard even as far away as the camp. After that on the right flank the third group went to reconnoitre the terrain below the wood. That was about ten good minutes away from us and even at that distance you could see how the bastards were smoking; they were fiery points in the dark. And the fourth group had to form the rear guard and God himself knows how it happened, but they suddenly appeared in front of our advance guard and were taken for the enemy, and I had to retreat from my own rear guard, which advanced against me. That's the 11th march company which I've inherited! What can I do with them? How are they going to show up in a real action?'

Lieutenant Lukáš clasped his hands and assumed a martyr's expression, while the point of his nose seemed to prolong itself.

'Don't worry too much about that, sir,' the quartermaster sergeant-major said, trying to console him. 'Don't let that give you a headache. I've already been on three march companies and every one of them was broken to pieces together with the whole battalion and so we had to go and form another again and again. And every march company was just the same as the other, not a single one of them was a hair better than yours, sir. The worst of all was the 9th. That carried off with it into captivity all the N.C.O.s and the company commander

as well. I was only saved because I had gone to the regimental train to draw rum and wine for the company, so they did their bit without me.

'And you don't know, sir, that during the last night operation, which you were talking about, sir, the volunteer school which was supposed to encircle our company got as far as the Neusiedler See? They went marching on until the next morning and their advance posts got as far as the marshes. It was Captain Ságner who led them. They'd probably have got to Sopron if daylight hadn't come,' continued the quartermaster sergeant-major in a mysterious voice. He took pleasure in such happenings and kept records of them.

'And do you know, sir,' he said, winking confidentially, 'that Captain Ságner is to become battalion commander of our march battalion? Some time ago they all thought, as Staff Sergeant-Major Hegner said, that you would be appointed, because you are the most senior officer we have, but later, they say, the order came from the division to the brigade that Captain Ságner had been appointed.'

Lieutenant Lukáš bit his lip and lit a cigarette. He knew all about that and was convinced that an injustice was being done to him. Captain Ságner had jumped over him twice in promotion; but he said nothing but: 'Well, of course, Captain Ságner . . .'

'I can't say I'm very pleased about it,' said the quartermaster sergeant-major confidentially: 'Staff Sergeant-Major Hegner said that Captain Ságner at the beginning of the war in Serbia wanted to distinguish himself somewhere in the mountains in Montenegro, and drove one company of his battalion after another on to the machine-guns of the Serbian positions, although it was quite unnecessary and the infantry there wasn't any damn use at all because only artillery could have dislodged the Serbs from those cliffs. Out of the whole battalion only eighty men survived; Captain Ságner himself was shot in the hand and later he got dysentery in hospital. And then again he appeared in Budějovice at the regiment and last night they say that he was telling in the officers' club how he was looking forward to the front, and that he'd show what he was worth and get the *Signum Laudis*, even if he had to leave the whole march battalion there. He'd got a ticking off because of Serbia, but now he'd either fall with the whole of the march battalion or be appointed lieutenant-colonel, but the whole march battalion would have to be ready to go west. I think, sir, that we face this risk too. Staff Sergeant-Major Hegner said not long ago that you don't get on very well with Captain Ságner and that he'll send our 11th company first into the attack and place it in the most dangerous positions.'

The quartermaster sergeant-major sighed: 'I believe that in a war like this, where there are so many armies and such a long front, you would gain more merely by proper manoeuvring than by desperate assaults. I saw that at Dukla when I was in the 10th march company. Then everything went off quite smoothly; an order came "Hold fire" and so no one shot and we all waited until the Russians came near to us. We could have taken them without firing a shot, but un-fortunately at that time we had next to us on the left flank the "Iron

Flies", and those stupid Landwehr men were so frightened that
the Russians were coming near us that they started to go down the
slopes of the hills in the snow like on a slide. We got the order that
the Russians had penetrated the left flank and we must try to reach the
brigade. I was then at the brigade itself, having the job of checking
the company catering accounts because I couldn't find our regimental
train. It was just then that the first men of the 10th march company
started coming to the brigade. By the evening 120 had come. The
others apparently lost their way in the retreat and slid down over the
snow like a toboggan somewhere into the Russian positions. It was
really frightful, sir. The Russians had positions in the Carpathians
above and below. And then, sir, Captain Ságner . . .'

'Oh, for God's sake stop talking about Captain Ságner,' said Lieutenant Lukáš. 'I know all that. And, by the way, don't think that next
time when there's an assault and fighting you'll again have the chance
of being somewhere in the regimental train drawing rum and wine.
I've already been told that you're a frightful soaker. Anyone looking
at your red nose can see at once the sort of chap he's dealing with.'

'That comes from the Carpathians, sir. We were forced to drink
there. We really were. By the time the mess portions reached us on top
there they were quite cold. Our trenches were under snow. We weren't
allowed to light fires. And so it was only the rum which kept us alive.
And if it hadn't been for me it would have been the same as in other
companies where they didn't even have rum and people got frozen.
That's why we all of us had red noses from the rum. But that also had
its disadvantage, because an order came from the battalion that only
men with red noses should go on patrols.'

'Now the winter's over,' the lieutenant observed significantly.

'I tell you, sir, rum is an indispensable thing at the front at any
season of the year and wine as well. It makes for good humour, so to
speak. For half a mess-tin of wine and a quarter-litre of rum people
will fight anybody. . . . Who's that mule knocking on the door
again? Can't you read what's written there: "Don't knock. Come in."'

Lieutenant Lukáš turned on his chair towards the door and observed
how it opened slowly and softly. And just as slowly and softly the good
soldier Švejk entered the office of the 10th march company. He was
saluting in the doorway and perhaps he was even doing so when he
knocked on the door and looked at the inscription 'Don't knock.'

His saluting was the full-blooded accompaniment to his everlastingly

contented and carefree face. He looked like the Greek god of theft in the sober uniform of an Austrian infantryman.

Lieutenant Lukáš shut his eyes for a moment at the sight of the good soldier Švejk who embraced and caressed him with his glances.

Probably with the same affection the lost and newly-found prodigal son looked at his father when he roasted a sheep on the spit in his honour.

'Humbly report, sir, I'm here again,' said Švejk with such sincere nonchalance that Lieutenant Lukáš suddenly came to again. From the time when Colonel Schröder had informed him he was going to send Švejk to him and that he would have him round his neck again, Lieutenant Lukáš had mentally tried every day to put off that meeting. Every morning he said to himself: 'He won't come today. He's probably been up to something again and they'll keep him there.'

But Švejk by his sweet and simple entry corrected all these calculations.

Švejk now looked at the quartermaster sergeant-major and turning to him with a pleasant smile handed him some documents which he drew from a pocket of his greatcoat: 'Sergeant-major, I have to give you these papers which they made out for me in the regimental office. They're to do with my pay and messing.'

Švejk moved as freely and sociably in the office of the 11th march company as if he had been Vaněk's best friend, to which the quartermaster sergeant-major reacted simply with the words: 'Put them on the table.'

'It will be best, quartermaster sergeant-major, if you leave me alone with Švejk now,' said Lieutenant Lukáš with a sigh.

Vaněk went away but remained standing outside the door to hear what the two would say to one another.

At first he heard nothing, because Švejk and the lieutenant were silent. Both observed each other closely for a long time. Lukáš stared at Švejk as though he was preparing to hypnotize him like a cock standing in front of a chicken and waiting to spring on it.

Švejk as usual looked at Lieutenant Lukáš with moist tender eyes as though wanting to say: 'United again, heart of mine! Now nothing will separate us, my pet.'

And when the lieutenant remained silent for a long time, Švejk's eyes spoke with sorrowful tenderness: 'Speak, my darling, say what you are thinking.'

Lieutenant Lukáš broke this embarrassing silence with the words into which he tried to inject a considerable dose of irony: 'Hearty welcome to you, Švejk. Thank you for the visit. Well, now, what a precious guest we have!'

He could not contain himself, however, and the anger of the past days exploded into a tremendous blow on the table with his fist, at which the inkstand jumped up and the ink was spilt all over the pay-list.

At the same time Lieutenant Lukáš jumped up, stood directly in front of Švejk and roared at him: 'You animal!' Then he began to march up and down in the restricted space of the office, spitting whenever he came anywhere near Švejk.

'Humbly report, sir,' said Švejk, when Lieutenant Lukáš went on walking up and down and furiously threw into the corner crumpled balls of paper, which he again and again came to the table to pick up, 'I handed the letter over as you instructed me. I was lucky enough to find Mrs Kákonyi and I can say that she's a very pretty woman although I only saw her when she was in tears . . .'

Lieutenant Lukáš sat down on the quartermaster sergeant-major's bunk and cried out in a hoarse voice: 'When is this going to end, Švejk?'

Švejk answered as though he had not heard: 'And then a little disagreeable thing happened to me, but I took the blame for it myself. They didn't believe I had corresponded with the lady and so at the investigation I thought it better to swallow the letter to put them off the scent. Then by pure chance – I can't explain it otherwise – I found myself involved in a small and very unimportant scuffle. But I got out of that too. They recognized my innocence, sent me on regimental report and quashed the whole proceedings in the divisional court. I had only been a few minutes in the regimental office when the colonel came. He swore at me a little, and then said I should at once report to you, sir, as orderly. He ordered me to tell you that he required you to come at once about the march comp. It's already more than half an hour ago, but the colonel didn't know that they would afterwards drag me off to the regimental office and that I would be sitting there another quarter of an hour still. You see the whole time I was under arrest I had my pay left there and I had to be paid by the regiment and not by the company, because I had been put under regimental arrest. Altogether they're in such a God Almighty mess there that it's enough to drive you barmy . . .'

When Lieutenant Lukáš heard that already half an hour ago he should have been with Colonel Schröder he dressed quickly and said: 'You've certainly done me a wonderful service again, Švejk.' He said it in such despairing tones, full of such hopelessness, that Švejk tried to soothe him with a friendly word, which he called out when Lieutenant Lukáš rushed out of the door: 'Don't worry. The colonel'll wait. He hasn't anything to do, anyway.'

A short time after the lieutenant's departure Quartermaster Sergeant-Major Vaněk entered the office.

Švejk was sitting on a chair and feeding the small iron stove, throwing bits of coal inside through its open door. The stove smoked and stank, and Švejk went on with this amusement, taking no notice of

Vaněk, who watched Švejk for a time. Then he kicked the door of the stove shut and told Švejk to remove himself.

'Sergeant-major,' Švejk said with dignity, 'allow me to inform you that even with the best will in the world I cannot carry out your order to remove myself from this room or altogether from the whole camp, as I am subject to higher orders. You see, I am orderly here,' he added

proudly. 'Colonel Schröder assigned me here to the 11th march company, to Lieutenant Lukáš, whose batman I used to be. Thanks to my natural intelligence I have been promoted company orderly. The lieutenant and me are old friends. What are you in civil life, sergeant-major?'

The quartermaster sergeant-major was so surprised by the familiar neighbourly tone of the good soldier Švejk that he forgot his dignity, which he was so fond of showing off to the soldiers of the company, and answered as though he had been Švejk's subordinate:

'I am Vaněk from Kralupy, the chemist.'

'And I was apprenticed to an apothecary too,' said Švejk, 'at a Mr Kokoška's at Na Perštýně in Prague. He was an awfully rum fellow and once when by mistake I set fire to a barrel of petrol in the cellar and the house burnt down he kicked me out. After that the guild wouldn't ever accept me anywhere and so because of that stupid barrel of petrol I couldn't finish my apprenticeship. Do you also manufacture herbs for cows?'

Vaněk shook his head.

'We used to manufacture herbs for cows together with holy images. Mr Kokoška, our chief, was a frightfully religious chap and once he read that St Pelegrinus helped when cattle got flatulent. So he had printed somewhere at Smíchov images of St Pelegrinus and had them consecrated at the Emmaus for two hundred guilders. And then we put them into the boxes of our herbs for cows. The herbs had to be diluted in warm water and given to the cows to drink from the tub, and at the same time a prayer to St Pelegrinus, which Mr Tauchen, our assistant, composed, was recited to the cow. Now, you see, when those images of St Pelegrinus were already printed some little prayer had to be printed on the reverse side. And so in the evening our boss, Kokoška, called Mr Tauchen and told him that by the next morning he must have a prayer written to put on the picture and to be served with the herbs. When he came to the shop at 10 a.m. it must be ready, so that it could be sent to the printers as the cows were already waiting for the prayer. For Mr Tauchen it was "either – or". If he did it well he would be given a guilder in hard cash; if not, he'd get a fortnight's notice. Mr Tauchen sweated the whole night and didn't sleep a wink. In the morning he came to open the shop and had nothing written. He even forgot what the saint for those cow-herbs was called. And so our porter Ferdinand helped him out of the mess. He could do anything. When we were drying camomile tea in the attic he always climbed up there, took off his boots and showed us how to stop our feet sweating. He caught pigeons in the attic, knew how to open the cash-drawer in the counter and taught us other small tricks with the goods. At that time I was only a boy and I had at home a chemist's set which I had brought home from the shop. Even the "Brother Hospitallers"[1] didn't have one like it. And Ferdinand helped Mr Tauchen. He just said: "Give it to me, Mr Tauchen, and let me look at it." Mr Tauchen immediately sent me to fetch a glass of beer for

1. A hospital in a monastery at Prague.

him. Before I had brought the beer Ferdinand had already finished half of it and was reciting:

> "I come from the kingdom above,
> And bring a message of love.
> Cow, calf and ox all need
> On Kokoška's herbs to feed.
> Kokoška's mixture once a day
> Keeps the veterinary away."

'And when he had drunk the beer and taken a pretty deep swig of tincture of amaranth he got on with it quickly and finished it very neatly in a trice:

> "To Pelegrinus offer vows
> And he will come and cure your cows.
> Praise St Pelegrinus who
> Has blessed this box for guilders two.
> Worship him in thought and word
> And beg his blessing on your herd."

'Then Mr Kokoška came and Mr Tauchen went with him to the office, and when he came out he showed us two guilders, not one as had been promised, and he wanted to share it fifty-fifty with Ferdinand. But when Ferdinand saw the two guilders he succumbed to the influence of Mammon. "No," he said, "either I get all or nothing." And so Mr Tauchen didn't give him anything and kept the two guilders for himself. Then he took me to the storehouse next door, gave me a box on the ears and said I would get a hundred more if I ever dared say that he didn't write it himself, and if Ferdinand should go and complain to the old man I should say that he was a liar. I had to swear an oath before some kind of jug of tarragon vinegar. And so that porter of ours started to revenge himself on those cow-herbs. We mixed it in big boxes in the attic and whenever Ferdinand was able to sweep up mouse droppings he brought them up there and mixed them into the herbs. And then he collected horse manure in the streets, dried it at home, pestled it in a mortar and threw all that too into our cow-herbs with the picture of St Pelegrinus. But that was not the end of it. He pissed into those boxes, shitted into them and stirred it all up together so that it was like a bran mash . . .'

The telephone rang. The quartermaster sergeant-major jumped to the receiver and threw it away in anger: 'I've got to go to the regimental office. All of a sudden like this! I don't like it at all.'

Švejk was alone again.

After a moment the telephone rang again.

Švejk began to speak into the receiver: 'Vaněk? He's just gone to the regimental office. Who's speaking? The orderly of the 11th march company. Who's calling? The orderly from the 12th march company? Servus, colleague. What's my name? Švejk. And yours? Braun. Are you any relation to the hatter, Braun, in Pobřežní Avenue in Karlín? You aren't? You don't know him ...? I don't know him either. I only went past the shop in the tram some time ago and the name of the firm struck me. What's the news? – I don't know anything. – What? When are we going? I haven't spoken with anybody yet about going. Where are we supposed to be going to?'

'With the march company to the front, you ninny.'

'I haven't heard anything about that.'

'Then you're a fine orderly. You don't know whether your lieutenant . . .'

'He's not a lieutenant, he's an *Oberleutnant*.'

'It's all the same. And so your *Oberleutnant* has gone to the colonel for a conference, has he?'

'The colonel called him over.'

'Well, there you are, you see! Ours was called over too and the lieutenant from the 13th march company as well. I've just spoken with the orderly on the telephone. I don't like this flap. And do you know whether the band is packing too?'

'I don't know anything.'

'Don't act like a bloody idiot. Your quartermaster sergeant-major already got the notice about the vans, didn't he? How many men have you got?'

'I don't know.'

'You bloody fool, d'you think I'm going to eat you up?' (The man at the telephone could be heard saying to someone else: 'Franta, take the other receiver, so that you can hear what a bloody mug of an orderly they have in the 11th march company.') – 'Hallo, are you asleep there or what? All right, then, answer when your colleague asks you a question! So you don't know anything yet? Now come clean. Didn't your quartermaster sergeant-major say anything to you about your going to draw tins? You didn't talk to him about any-

thing like that? You bloody oaf, you. It's no business of yours?'
(There was audible laughter.) 'You must have a screw loose. When
you hear anything, ring us in the 12th march company, my sonny
boy, my prize ass! Where do you come from?'

'From Prague.'

'Well, you ought to be brighter. . . . And one more thing: when was
your quartermaster sergeant-major called to regimental office?'

'Only a minute ago.'

'My God, and couldn't you have told me that before? Ours went
away a moment ago too. Something's in the wind. Haven't you
spoken with the train?'

'No.'

'Jesus Christ, and you say you're from Prague? You don't bother
about anything, do you? Where have you been hanging about all this
time?'

'I only came from divisional court an hour ago.'

'Ah, that's another story, old man, then I must come and see you today. Ring off twice.'

Švejk was just going to light his pipe when the telephone rang again.

'To hell with your ringing!' thought Švejk. 'Why should I waste my time on you?'

The telephone went on inexorably ringing until Švejk finally lost his patience. He took the receiver and shouted into the telephone:

'Hello, who's calling? This is Orderly Švejk of the 11th march company.' The answering voice Švejk recognized as belonging to Lieutenant Lukáš:

'What are you doing there? Where's Vaněk? Call him at once to the telephone!'

'Humbly report, sir, a minute ago the telephone was ringing . . .'

'Listen, Švejk, I've no time to waste with you. Telephone conversations in wartime aren't just a gossip like when we invite someone to come and have lunch. They must be clear and concise. There's no time for "Humbly report, sir" on the telephone in wartime. Well, Švejk, I am asking you, is Vaněk there with you? Let him come to the telephone at once!'

'Humbly report, sir, I haven't got him with me. A short time ago he was called away to the regimental office. It might have been less than a quarter of an hour ago.'

'When I'm back I'll deal with you, Švejk. Can't you express yourself concisely? Now, listen very carefully to what I say. Can you understand clearly so that you don't excuse yourself afterwards by saying that there was crackling in the telephone? As soon as you hang up the receiver . . .'

There was a pause and then renewed ringing. Švejk took the receiver and was drowned in a heap of abuse: 'You animal, you gutter-snipe, you blackguard, you. What the hell are you doing? Why do you break the connection?'

'Please, sir, you said I was to hang up the receiver.'

'I shall be back in an hour, Švejk, and then you'll see. . . . Now get cracking at once. Go to the hut and find a platoon sergeant, let's say Fuchs, and tell him at once to take ten men and go with them to the stores to draw tinned food. Now repeat what he's to go and do.'

'He's to go with ten men to the stores to draw tinned food for the company.'

'Now at last you're not talking drivel for once. Meanwhile I'll ring up Vaněk in the regimental office and tell him to go to the stores and take them over. If he should come to our hut in the meanwhile tell him to drop everything and rush at the double to the stores. Now you can hang up the receiver.'

For a long time Švejk vainly searched not only for Platoon Sergeant Fuchs, but for the other N.C.O.s too. They were in the kitchen, gnawing the meat from the bones and enjoying the sight of the tethered Baloun, who stood with his feet firmly on the ground, because they had taken pity on him, but who none the less presented a remarkable spectacle. One of the cooks brought him meat from a rib and pushed it into his mouth and the tethered bearded giant Baloun, who had no possibility of moving his arms, carefully pushed the bone around in his mouth, balancing it with the help of his teeth and his gums, in the course of which he gnawed the meat with the expression of a wild man of the woods.

'Who of you here is Platoon Sergeant Fuchs?' Švejk asked, when he finally got to them.

Sergeant Fuchs considered it beneath his dignity to reply, when he saw that he was being asked for by a common or garden infantryman.

'Hey,' said Švejk, 'how long am I going to stand here asking? Where the hell is Platoon Sergeant Fuchs?'

Sergeant Fuchs stepped forward and in all dignity began to deliver a volley of all kinds of oaths, saying that he wasn't just 'platoon sergeant', he should be addressed as 'sir', and that it was not for Švejk to say 'Where the hell is the platoon sergeant?' but 'Humbly report, sir, where is the platoon sergeant, sir?' In his platoon, if anyone didn't say: 'Humbly report, sir' he immediately got a sock on the jaw.

'Don't try that one on me,' said Švejk deliberately. 'Get cracking immediately. Go to the hut, take ten men and go with them at the double to the storehouse. You are to draw tinned food there.'

Platoon Sergeant Fuchs was so surprised that he could only manage to get out: 'What?'

'I don't permit any "Whats",' answered Švejk. 'I am the orderly of the 11th march company and just a minute ago I was speaking on the telephone with Lieutenant Lukáš and he said: "At the double with ten men to the stores." If you don't go, platoon sergeant, then I shall at once go back to the telephone. Lieutenant Lukáš explicitly wishes that you should go. It is unnecessary to talk about it. "A telephone conversation," says Lieutenant Lukáš, "must be concise and clear. If Platoon Sergeant Fuchs is told to go then he'll go. An order of this kind is not just a gossip on the telephone like when we invite somebody to come and have lunch. In the army, and especially in wartime, being late is a crime. If that Platoon Sergeant Fuchs doesn't go at once when you tell him, then ring me up immediately and I'll deal with him myself. There'll be nothing left of Platoon Sergeant Fuchs." My God, you don't know Lieutenant Lukáš.'

Švejk looked triumphantly at the N.C.O.s, who were really surprised and depressed by his performance.

Platoon Sergeant Fuchs mumbled something unintelligible and went away at a quick pace. Švejk called after him: 'Can I now ring the lieutenant that everything is in order?'

'I'll be at the store with ten men at once,' Platoon Sergeant Fuchs replied from the hut and Švejk without uttering another word left the group of N.C.O.s who were just as surprised as was Platoon Sergeant Fuchs.

'It's already starting,' said little Corporal Blažek. 'We shall be packing.'

When Švejk returned to the office of the 11th march company he again had no time to light his pipe because the telephone rang once more. Again it was Lieutenant Lukáš speaking:

'Where have you been running to, Švejk? It's the third time I've rung and no one's answered.'

'I've fixed it, sir.'

'Have they gone off?'

'You bet they've gone off, but I don't know yet whether they've got there. Shall I run and see once more?'

'Did you find Platoon Sergeant Fuchs?'

'I did, sir. First of all he said: "What?" and only when I had explained to him that telephone conversations must be concise and clear. . . .'

'Don't waste my time, Švejk. . . . Hasn't Vaněk returned yet?'

'He hasn't yet, sir.'

'Don't roar in the telephone. Don't you know where that damned Vaněk could have got to?'

'No, sir, I don't know where that damned Vaněk could have got to.'

'He was in the regimental office and has gone off somewhere else. I think he'll probably be in the canteen. Then go and find him, Švejk, and tell him that he must go at once to the stores. One thing more – find at once Corporal Blažek and tell him to untie Baloun immediately and send him to me. You can hang up the receiver now.'

Švejk really started to make things hum. When he found Corporal Blažek and conveyed to him the lieutenant's order regarding the untying of Baloun, Corporal Blažek growled: 'When it starts to get hot for them they get the jitters.'

Švejk went to see to the release of Baloun and accompanied him on the way, because it led to the canteen, where he was to try and find Vaněk.

Baloun looked on Švejk as his saviour and promised to share with him every packet which he got from home.

'They're going to do some slaughtering at home,' said Baloun in a melancholy voice. 'Do you like Speckwurst with blood or without?

Just say. I'll write home tonight. My pig ought to weigh about 150 kilos. It's got a head like a bulldog and pigs like that are the best. You don't find any duds among pigs like that. They are a very good race and hardy too. It'll have about eight fingers of fat. When I was at home

I used to make the jitrnice[1] myself and I always stuffed myself so full that I could have burst. Last year's pig weighed 160 kilos.

'Oh, that was a pig,' he said with enthusiasm, squeezing Švejk's hand in a powerful grip when they parted. 'I raised it on nothing but potatoes and was amazed myself how well it put on weight. I soaked the hams in brine and, I tell you, a nicely roasted piece of pork, taken out of the brine and served with cabbage and potato dumplings and sprinkled with cracklings, is the finest treat you can have. And then a

1. Jitrnice is a popular variety of Czech sausage, for which there is no translation. It is made of pork liver and various parts of the pig, is highly spiced and fastened at its ends with small wooden sticks.

lot of beer afterwards. A chap's so satisfied. And the war's taken all that away from us.'

The bearded Baloun sighed deeply and went off to the regimental office, while Švejk directed his steps towards the canteen through an old alley of tall lime trees.

Meanwhile Vaněk was sitting happily in the canteen and telling a staff sergeant-major friend of his how much one could make on enamel paints and cement washes before the war.

The staff sergeant-major was already half-seas over. In the morning a rich landowner from Pardubice who had a son in the camp had arrived and given him a respectable bribe, and the whole morning he had been hospitable to him down in the town.

Now he was sitting there in despair, because he had no more appetite; he did not even know what they were talking about and did not react at all to the conversation about the enamel paints.

He was occupied with his own ideas and babbled something about how a local railway line ought to go from Třeboň to Pelhřimov and back again.

When Švejk came in, Vaněk was once more trying to explain to the sergeant-major in figures how much profit could be made out of one kilogram of cement wash for buildings, whereupon the staff sergeant-major answered completely on the other track:

'And on the way back he died, leaving only letters behind him.'

Observing Švejk, he obviously mixed him up with someone whom he did not like and began to swear at him, saying that he was a ventriloquist.

Švejk came up to Vaněk, who was also pretty high but was at the same time very amiable and nice.

'Quartermaster sergeant-major,' Švejk reported, 'you are to go at once to the stores. Platoon Sergeant Fuchs is already waiting there with ten men. Tinned food will be drawn. You are to go at the double. The lieutenant has already telephoned twice.'

Vaněk burst out laughing: 'I'd be a bloody fool if I did, my dear boy. I'd have to swear at myself, my angel. There's plenty of time for everything, sonny boy. There's nothing on fire, my dear boy, is there? When Lieutenant Lukáš has got ready as many march companies as I have he can begin to talk. He won't bother a chap utterly pointlessly with his "at the double". In the regimental office I've already got the order that we are off tomorrow and that we must pack and quickly go and draw provisions for the journey. What have I done? I came here for a quarter-litre of wine and I am sitting here comfortably and letting things slide. Tins'll be tins, and supplies supplies. I know the stores better than the lieutenant does and I know what they talk about at those conferences between the officers and the colonel. It's only the colonel's imagination that there are any tins in the stores. Our regimental stores never had any but only got them from time to time from the brigade or borrowed them from other regiments which they got in touch with. We owe the Benešov regiment alone over three hundred tins. He he! Let them say what they like at their conference, only no flap, please! Why, the storekeeper himself will tell our people when they come there that they've gone mad. Not a single march company has ever got any tins for the journey.

'That's so, isn't it, you old potato,' he said, turning to the staff sergeant-major. But the latter was either falling asleep or getting a little delirious because he answered:

'While she was walking she held an open umbrella over herself.'

'The best thing you can do,' continued Vaněk, 'is to let everything just go its own sweet way. If today they said in the regimental office that we're to go tomorrow, then not even a baby should believe them. Can we go without trucks? While I was there they telephoned to the station. They haven't got a single spare truck there. It was just the same with the last march company. Then we stayed at the station for two whole days and waited till someone would take pity on us and send a train for us. And then we didn't know where we were going. Not even the colonel knew. After that we travelled all over the whole of Hungary and still no one knew whether we were going to Serbia or Russia. At every station we spoke direct to the staff of the division. We were just paper to cover up cracks. Finally we were sent near Dukla. There they cut us to pieces and we marched back to be re-formed. Only no flap, please! Everything will settle itself in time and there's no need for hurry. Yes, that's how it is. Here we are again!'

'Today they've got exceptionally good wine here,' Vaněk went on, not paying any attention to the staff sergeant-major, who was burbling to himself in German: 'Believe me, up to now I've had little from life. I am surprised at this question.'

'Why should I bother myself unnecessarily about the departure of the march battalion? Why, in the first march company I went with, everything was in complete readiness in two hours. In the other companies of our march battalion they took two days to get ready. But we had as company commander a Lieutenant Přenosil, a great dandy, and he said to us: "Don't hurry, boys," and everything went like a house on fire. We only started packing two hours before the departure of the train. Why don't you sit down as well? . . .'

'I can't,' said the good soldier Švejk with frightful self-sacrifice. 'I must go to the office. What if someone telephones?'

'Then go along, sonny boy, but remember for the whole of your life that it's not nice of you. A proper orderly should never be where he's needed. You mustn't be too zealous in your duties. There's really nothing more ugly, love, than a wild orderly who would like to eat up the whole war.'

But Švejk was already out of the door and rushing to the office of his march company.

Vaněk was left in solitude, because no one could possibly claim that the staff sergeant-major provided any company for him.

The latter was living in his own world and babbling the most ridiculous things in Czech and German without any connection and stroking his quarter-litre of wine:

'I walked through this village many times and didn't have an idea that it existed. In a half year's time I'll have passed my state examination and have done my doctorate. I've become an old cripple, thank you, Lucy. They are appearing in finely got-up volumes – perhaps there's someone among you who can remember it.'

Out of boredom the quartermaster sergeant-major drummed a march, but he did not have to be bored for long because the door opened and Jurajda, the cook from the officers' mess, came in and sank into a chair.

'Today we got the order to draw brandy for the journey,' he babbled. 'Because we hadn't a wicker rum bottle empty we had to empty one. That knocked us out! The men in the kitchen just passed out. I was a few portions short in my calculations, the colonel came late and there wasn't anything left for him. Now they're making him an omelette. I can tell you that that was fun and games.'

'It's a marvellous adventure,' observed Vaněk, who always liked beautiful words when he was drinking wine.

The cook Jurajda started to philosophize, which in fact matched his former occupation. Before the war he used to edit an occultist journal and a series of books called *The Mysteries of Life and Death*. When war broke out he shirked his way into the officers' kitchen of the regiment and very often burnt a joint while he was absorbed in reading a translation of the old Indian sutras *Pragnâ – Paramitâ* ('Wisdom Revealed').

Colonel Schröder liked him as a rarity in the regiment; for what officers' kitchen could boast an occultist as its cook? While probing into the mysteries of life and death, he so astounded everyone with his excellent sirloin of beef or ragout that Lieutenant Dufek when mortally wounded near Komarovo continually called for Jurajda.

'Yes,' said Jurajda out of the blue. He could hardly sit on his chair and he stank of rum a mile off. 'When there wasn't anything left for the colonel today and he saw only steamed potatoes he fell into the state of *gaki*. Do you know what *gaki* is? It is the state of starved spirits. And I said to him: "Sir, have you enough strength to overrule the predestination of fate that there's no roast veal left for you? It is written in *karma*, sir, that today you will be served for dinner a wonderful omelette with chopped and stewed calves' liver."

'Dear boy,' he said softly to the quartermaster sergeant-major after a while, involuntarily making a movement with his hand and knocking over all the glasses which stood in front of him on the table.

'There exists the non-being of all phenomena, forms and things,' the occultist cook said gloomily after this act. 'Form is non-being and non-being is form. Non-being is not different from form and form is not different from non-being. Everything that is non-being is also form and everything that is form is also non-being.'

The occultist cook wrapped himself in a shroud of silence, held his head in his hands and looked at the wet, stained table.

The staff sergeant-major continued to babble something which had neither rhyme nor reason: 'The corn has disappeared from the field, disappeared – in this mood he received an invitation and went to her – the Whitsun holidays are in the spring.'

Quartermaster Sergeant-Major Vaněk went on drumming on the table, drank, and occasionally remembered that ten men with a sergeant were waiting for him at the stores.

When this memory came to him he always smiled to himself and dismissed it with a wave of his hand.

When he returned late to the office of the 11th march company he found Švejk by the telephone.

'Form is non-being and non-being is form,' he managed to utter as he climbed fully dressed into his bunk and immediately fell sound asleep.

And Švejk continued to sit by the telephone, because two hours earlier Lieutenant Lukáš had said to him that he was still at the conference with the colonel and he had forgotten to tell him he could leave the telephone.

After that Sergeant Fuchs spoke to him on the telephone. He and his ten men had not only been waiting all that time in vain for the quartermaster sergeant-major but had also found that the stores were shut.

After that he went away and the ten men returned one by one to their hut.

Occasionally Švejk amused himself by taking off the receiver and listening. It was a telephone of a new system which had just been introduced into the army and had the advantage that you could hear quite clearly and intelligibly other people's telephone calls all over the line.

The train was exchanging abuse with the artillery barracks, the sappers were threatening the army post, the military rifle range was growling at the machine-gun section.

And Švejk went on sitting at the telephone . . .

The conference in the colonel's office went on longer and longer . . .

Colonel Schröder was developing his latest theories on field service and was emphasizing particularly the role of trench mortars.

He spoke without rhyme or reason about how the front stood two months ago in the south and east, about the importance of exact communications between individual units, about poison gas, shooting at enemy aeroplanes and catering for the men in the field. Then he passed to conditions among the troops.

He spoke of the relationship of the officers to the men, of the men to the N.C.O.s, of deserting to the enemy at the front, of political events and of the fact that fifty per cent of the Czech soldiers were 'politically suspect'.

'Yes, gentlemen, Kramář, Scheiner and Klofáč.'[1] Most of the officers were wondering all the time when the old dodderer would stop drivelling, but Colonel Schröder burbled on about the new tasks of the new march battalions, of the officers of his regiment who had fallen, of Zeppelins, of 'Spanish riders' and the soldier's oath.

When he reached that point Lieutenant Lukáš remembered that

1. Three Czech political leaders who were imprisoned for treason during the war.

when the whole battalion took the oath, the good soldier Švejk did not take part, because at that time he was under arrest at the divisional court.

And suddenly he couldn't help laughing. It was a kind of hysterical laughter which affected some officers among whom he sat and which caught the attention of the colonel, who just at that moment had gone over to the experiences acquired during the retreat of the German troops in the Ardennes. He got completely muddled and ended: 'Gentlemen, it's no laughing matter.'

Then they all went away to the officers' club because Colonel Schröder had been called to the telephone by brigade staff.

Švejk was still slumbering by the telephone when he was woken up by its ringing.

'Hallo,' he heard, 'regimental office speaking.'

'Hallo,' he answered, 'office of the 11th march company speaking.'

'Don't waste my time,' he heard a voice say. 'Take a pencil and write. Here is a telegram.

'The 11th march company . . .'

Now there followed in succession various sentences in a strange chaos, because they were mixed up with the conversations of the 12th and 13th march companies, which went on at the same time, and the telegram got completely lost in the panic of sounds. Švejk could not understand a single word. Finally everything quietened down and Švejk understood: 'Hallo, hallo, now read it through and don't waste my time!'

'What have I got to read through?'

'What have you got to read through, you bloody fool? The telegram!'

'What telegram?'

'Bloody hell, are you deaf? The telegram which I've just dictated to you, you crazy oaf!'

'I couldn't hear anything. Someone was talking here all the time.'

'You idiotic baboon. Do you think I'm just passing the time of day with you? Well, are you going to take the telegram or not? Have you got a pencil and paper? You haven't, you bastard, and so I've got to wait until you find it? That's a soldier for you, if you like. Well, are you going to take the message or not? Are you ready? At last you've woken up, you bloody bastard. You've been dolling yourself up, I suppose. Now listen. The 11th march company. Repeat that!'

'The 11th march company . . .'

'Company commandant . . . Have you got that? Repeat that.'

'Company commandant . . .'

'For conference tomorrow . . . Are you ready? Repeat that.'

'For conference tomorrow . . .'

'At 9 a.m. "*Unterschrift*." Do you know what "*Unterschrift*" is, baboon? It's "signature". Repeat that!'

'At 9 a.m. *Unterschrift*. Do you know what "*Unterschrift*" is, baboon? It's "signature".'

'Stupid mutt. Well, here you are, here's the signature: Colonel Schröder, bastard. Have you got that? Repeat that!'

'Colonel Schröder, bastard.'

'Good, you bloody mule. Who took the telegram?'

'Me.'

'Himmelherrgott, who's me?'

'Švejk. Anything further?'

'Thank the Lord, nothing. But your name ought to be Cow. What news is there?'

'Nothing. Just the same as before.'

'And you're glad, then, aren't you? One of your men was tied up today, they say?'

'It was only the lieutenant's batman. He guzzled up his lieutenant's mess portion. Do you know when we're going?'

'My dear boy, what a question! Why, even the old man himself doesn't know. Goodnight. Have you got fleas there?'

Švejk hung up the receiver and began to wake Quartermaster Sergeant-Major Vaněk, who furiously resisted. When Švejk began to shake him, he hit him in the nose. Then he lay on his stomach and kicked about in his bunk.

None the less Švejk succeeded in waking Vaněk so far that he rubbed his eyes, turned over on his back and asked in an alarmed voice what had happened.

'Nothing so far,' replied Švejk. 'I'd only like to consult you. We've just got a telegram that tomorrow at 9 a.m. Lieutenant Lukáš is to go to a conference with the colonel again. I don't know now where I stand. Am I to go and deliver the message at once or can I wait till the morning? I hesitated a long time whether I should wake you up when you were snoring so beautifully, but then I thought, never mind, better get his advice . . .'

'For God's sake, please let me sleep,' Vaněk groaned, and gave an enormous yawn. 'Go to him in the morning and don't wake me up.' He rolled over on his side and immediately fell asleep again.

Švejk went back to the telephone, sat down and began to nod at the table. He was woken by the bell.

'Hello, 11th march company?'

'Yes, 11th march company speaking. Who's there?'

'Thirteenth march company speaking. Hallo. What's the time? I can't get hold of the exchange. I've been waiting hours for them to relieve me.'

'Our clock's stopped.'

'Then you're in the same boat as we are. Do you know when we're going? Did you speak to regimental office?'

'There they don't know a shit more than we do.'

'Don't be vulgar, miss. Have you drawn your tins yet? They went there from our company and didn't bring anything back. The stores were shut.'

'Ours came back with nothing too.'

'All this flap is quite pointless. Where do you think we're going?'

'To Russia.'

'I think it's more likely to be Serbia. We'll see when we get to Budapest. If they take us to the right, then it looks like Serbia. If it's to the left it'll be Russia. Have you already got your bread sacks? They say that pay will be increased. Can you play Frische Viere?[1] You can? Then come here tomorrow. We play every evening. How many of you are there at the telephone? Only you? Then damn the telephone and go to bed. You certainly have funny arrangements where you are. What did you say? You got the job by pure fluke? And now at last they've come to relieve me. Have a sweet snore.'

And Švejk indeed fell into a sweet sleep by the telephone, forgetting to hang up the receiver, so that nobody disturbed him in his slumbers on the desk and the telephone operator in the regimental office swore when he could not get any answer from the 11th march company. He had a new telegram requiring that by twelve o'clock the next day the regimental office was to be informed of the number of those who had not been inoculated against typhus.

Meanwhile Lieutenant Lukáš was still sitting in the officers' club with the army doctor, Šancler, who, seated astride a chair, hit the floor

1. A German card game.

at regular intervals with a billiard cue and pronounced the following sentences in succession as he did so.

'The Saracen Sultan, Salah-Edin, recognized for the first time the neutrality of the medical corps.

'The wounded of both sides are to be cared for.

'Drugs and medical care for them are to be paid for against compensation from the other side.

'It should be permitted to send them doctors and their assistants with generals' passports.

'The wounded prisoners are to be sent back under the protection and guarantee of generals or exchanged. But they can afterwards go on serving.

'The wounded on both sides are not to be captured or liquidated but sent to safe shelter in hospitals and it should be permitted to leave them guards who, like the wounded, are to return with generals' passports. This applies also to chaplains, doctors, surgeons, chemists, nurses, assistants and other persons appointed to look after the sick. They may not be taken prisoner but must be sent back in the same way.'

Doctor Šancler had already broken two billiard cues and was still not finished with his peculiar treatise on the care of the wounded in war, continually mixing into it something about some generals' passports.

Lieutenant Lukáš drank up his black coffee and went home, where he found the bearded giant Baloun occupied with frying some salami in a pan on Lieutenant Lukáš's spirit stove.

'I've taken the liberty,' Baloun stammered, 'excuse me, humbly report. . . .'

Lukáš looked at him. And at that moment Baloun appeared to him like a big baby, a naïve creature, and suddenly he was sorry that he had had him tied up because of his enormous hunger.

'Just go on cooking, Baloun,' he said, taking off his sabre. 'Tomorrow I'll authorize you to draw an additional portion of bread.'

Lieutenant Lukáš sat down at the table and was in such a mood that he began to write a sentimental letter to his auntie:

Dear Auntie,

I've just got orders to be prepared to leave for the front with my march company. Perhaps this letter is the last you will get from me because there is fierce fighting everywhere and our losses are great. Therefore it is hard for me to end this letter with the words: 'Until we meet again!' It would be more appropriate to send you a last farewell!

'I'll finish it in the morning,' Lieutenant Lukáš thought and went to bed.

When Baloun saw that the lieutenant was fast asleep he began again to sneak and snoop about the apartment like black-beetles in the night. He opened the lieutenant's suitcase and took a bite of a bar of chocolate. Then when the lieutenant started in his sleep he got scared. He hastily put back into the case the half-bitten chocolate and was quiet.

Then he went noiselessly to see what the lieutenant had written.

He read it and was moved, especially by the 'last farewell!'.

He lay down on his straw mattress by the door and remembered his home and the slaughterings. He could not free himself of the vivid impression that he was making a hole in the Speckwurst to get the air out of it, so that it didn't burst when it was being cooked.

And with the memory of how once at his neighbour's house a whole

Speckwurst had burst and disintegrated he fell asleep in an uneasy slumber.

He dreamed that he had called in a clumsy butcher and that when he was filling the jitrnice with stuffing their guts began to burst. And then again he dreamed that the butcher had forgotten to make blood sausages, and that the fresh boiled pork disappeared and there were not enough little sticks to fasten the jitrnice. After that he dreamed of a drumhead court-martial, because they had caught him when he was taking a piece of meat from the field-kitchen. Finally he saw himself hanging on a lime tree in the alley of the military camp in Bruck an der Leitha.

When Švejk awoke with the breaking dawn, which came to him accompanied by the smell of cooked tinned coffee from all the company kitchens, he hung up the receiver mechanically as if he had only just finished a telephone conversation, and took a little early morning walk round the office, singing while he did so.

He started right in the middle of the text of the song: a soldier dresses up as a girl and goes to find his sweetheart in a mill, where the miller puts him to bed with his daughter, but before that he calls out to his wife:

> Mamma, go and cook some meat
> So the little girl may eat.

The miller's wife gives that mean rascal some food. And then follows the family tragedy:

> The miller and his wife were up by eight
> And found these words upon their gate.
> 'Your daughter, Anne, a maid before,
> Is now, alas, a maid no more.'

Švejk put into the end of the song so much voice that the office came to life: Quartermaster Sergeant-Major Vaněk woke up and asked what the time was.

'Just a moment ago they sounded the reveille.'

'Then I'll get up after I've had coffee,' decided Vaněk, who always had enough time for everything. 'Anyhow, they'll be bound to bully us, get us into a flap and push us around unnecessarily as they did yesterday about those tins...' Vaněk yawned and asked whether when he came home he hadn't talked too long.

'Only just a little off the beam,' said Švejk. 'You kept on saying something about some forms, that form wasn't form and what wasn't form was form and that form again wasn't form. But you got over it quite quickly and soon began to snore like a sawmill.'

Švejk was silent, walked to the door and back to the quartermaster sergeant-major's bunk, stopped before him and said:

'As far as I'm personally concerned, sergeant-major, when I heard that you were talking about those forms I remembered a certain Zátka, a gas worker; he had a job at the gas company at Letná and had to light the lamps and put them out again. He was an enlightened man and went to all sorts of pubs at Letná because between the lighting of the lamps and putting them out he had to kick his heels. In the morning when he got back to the gas company he used to talk in the same way as you did yesterday except that he said, "The cube is angularity and that's why the cube is angular." I heard it with my own eyes when a sozzled cop took me to the gas company instead of to the police station for committing a nuisance in the street.

'And after that,' said Švejk quietly, 'that Zátka came to a sad end. He joined the Congregation of the Virgin Mary and went with those sanctimonious nanny-goats to hear the sermons of Father Jemelka[1] at St Ignatius on Charles Square. Once when the missionaries were at St Ignatius he forgot to put out the gas lamps in his district so that the light blazed on the streets uninterruptedly for three days and three nights.

'It's bad,' continued Švejk, 'when a chap suddenly starts to get caught up in philosophizing. That always stinks of *delirium tremens*. Years ago they transferred to us a certain Major Blüher from the 75th. Once a month he always made us fall in and form a square. Then he discussed with us what military superiors were. He never drank anything else but slivovice. "Every officer," he used to tell us in the yard of the barracks, "is, as such, the most perfect being, my men, and has a hundred times more brain than all of you together. You cannot conceive anything more perfect than an officer, my men, even if you were to think about it all your lives. Every officer is a necessary being, whereas you, my men, are only incidental beings. You may exist but you may not. And if, my men, it came to a war and you were to give up your lives for His Imperial Majesty, good, then nothing would change very much. But if before that your officer were to fall, then

1. A notorious Jesuit preacher in Prague at the time.

you'd first see how dependent you are on him and what a loss it would be to you. The officer must exist and, in fact, you derive your existence exclusively from the officers; you spring from them. You cannot get on without them. You can't even fart without your military superiors. For you, my men, an officer is your moral law whether you understand it or not, and because every law must have its legislator, my men, it is only the officer to whom you feel and must feel entirely bound and whose every order you must obey unconditionally even if you shouldn't like it."

'Once when he had finished he went round the square and asked the men one by one:

' "How do you feel when you've taken a drop too much?"

'They gave him confused answers such as either they had never taken a drop too much or after drinking they always felt sick. One said he felt as though he was going to be confined to barracks etc. Major Blüher ordered all these to leave the ranks saying that in the afternoon they were going to do unarmed drill in the yard as a punishment for not being able to express what they felt. Before my turn came I remembered what he had discussed with us last time and when he came to me I said quite calmly:

' "Humbly report, sir, when I take a drop too much I always feel inside me a sort of nervousness, a fear and pricking of conscience. But if I'm given extended leave and then return properly to the barracks in time, a feeling of bliss comes creeping over me. I have complete spiritual peace."

'Everyone around me laughed and Major Blüher shouted at me:

' "It's more likely that you've got bugs creeping on you, you bastard, when you snore on your bunk. You miserable swine, you've got the bloody cheek to try to be funny."

'And for that I was put in irons and it wasn't half fun!'

'In the army it's got to be like that,' said the quartermaster sergeant-major, stretching himself lazily on his bed. 'It's an accepted thing that however you answer or whatever you do a dark cloud will always be hanging over you and the thunder will begin to peal. Without that you can't have discipline.'

'Very well said,' said Švejk. 'I shall never forget when they locked up a recruit called Pech. The lieutenant of the company was a chap called Moc and he collected the recruits and asked each of them where he came from.

' "You greenhorns of recruits, you godforsaken bastards," he told them. "You must learn to answer clearly and exactly, like at the crack of a whip. Now let's start. Where do you come from, Pech?" Pech was an intelligent man and answered: "Dolní Bousov, Unter Bautzen, 267 houses, 1936 Czech inhabitants, region Jičín, district Sobotka, former estate of Kost, parish church of St Katherine from the fourteenth century restored by Count Václav Vratislav Netolický, school, post, telegraph, station of the Czech Commercial Railway, sugar refinery, sawmill, an isolated farm called Valcha, and six annual fairs." And at the same moment Lieutenant Moc leaped at him and began to give him one sock after the other across the jaw and to shout: "That'll teach you for one of your annual fairs, here's for the second, here's for the third, the fourth, the fifth, the sixth." And Pech, although he was a recruit, applied to be sent on battalion report. In the office at that time there happened to be a gang of bastards with a sense of humour. They gave as reason for his going on battalion report the annual fairs in Dolní Bousov. The battalion commander was Major Rohell. "Well, what's up?" he asked Pech, who started off: "Humbly report, sir, in Dolní Bousov there are six annual fairs." And then Major Rohell thundered at him, stamped his feet and had him sent at once to the mental section of the military hospital. From that time on Pech became the worst soldier and went from one punishment to another.'

'Soldiers are difficult to educate,' said Quartermaster Sergeant-Major Vaněk, yawning. 'A soldier who has not been punished in the army is no soldier. It was perhaps true in peacetime that a soldier who had completed his service without any punishment could afterwards have an advantage in state service, but today it's different: the worst soldiers, those who in peacetime were never out of prison, become in wartime the best. I remember an infantryman called Sylvanus in the 8th march company. Before the war he always used to get punishment after punishment. And what punishments! He was not above stealing his comrades' last kreutzer. And when he got into action, he was the first to cut through the barbed-wire entanglements, took three chaps prisoner and shot one of them on the way, because he said he couldn't trust him. He was awarded the Great Silver Medal. They sewed on him two stars and if they hadn't later hanged him near Dukla he would have long ago become platoon sergeant. But there you are, they had to hang him because after one action he volunteered for reconnaissance and a patrol of another regiment caught him robbing corpses. They found on him about eight watches and many rings. And so they hanged him at brigade staff.'

'Which only goes to show,' Švejk observed wisely, 'that every soldier must do his utmost to win his place on the ladder.'

The telephone bell rang. The quartermaster sergeant-major went to the telephone and Lieutenant Lukáš's voice could be heard asking what had happened with the tins. After that there could be heard some reproaches.

'But really, there aren't any, sir!' Vaněk shouted into the telephone. 'Of course there aren't, sir. It's only just a flight of imagination from above on the part of Supply H.Q. It was utterly pointless to send those men there. I wanted to ring you up, sir. What, I was in the canteen? Who said that? That occultist cook from the officers' mess? Yes, I took the liberty of going there. You know, sir, what that occultist called that flap about the tins? "The horror of the unborn". Oh no, sir, not at all, I'm completely sober. What is Švejk doing? He's here. Shall I call him?'

'Švejk, come to the telephone!' said the quartermaster sergeant-major, and added in a whisper: 'And if he should ask you what state I was in when I came back say that I was O.K.'

Švejk at the telephone: 'This is Švejk, humbly report, sir.'

'Listen, Švejk, what happened about those tins? Is it all right?'

'No, sir, there isn't any sign of them.'

'Švejk, I want you to report to me every morning, as long as we're in the camp. Otherwise you are to be with me all the time during the journey. What did you do during the night?'

'I was at the telephone the whole night.'

'Was there any news?'

'There was, sir.'

'Švejk, for God's sake, don't start to be an idiot again. Was there anything important reported from anywhere?'

'Yes, sir, there was, but only for nine o'clock.'

'Why didn't you inform me at once?'

'I didn't want to disturb you, sir. It was the last thing I wanted to do.'

'Then for God's sake tell me what was there so important for nine o'clock?'

'A telegram, sir.'

'I don't understand you, Švejk.'

'I've written it down, sir: "Take down the telegram. Who's that at the telephone? Have you got it? Read it or something like that."'

'For God's sake, Švejk, you're the cross I have to bear. Tell me what was in it or I'll leap at you and give you such a sock! Well, what was it?'

'Another conference with the colonel, sir. This morning at nine o'clock. I wanted to wake you in the night, but then I thought better of it.'

'Well, it's your luck that you didn't have the insolence to try to disturb me for any kind of bloody nonsense when there was time enough in the morning. Another conference. To hell with it! Hang up the receiver and call Vaněk to the telephone!'

The quartermaster sergeant-major at the telephone: 'Quartermaster Sergeant-Major Vaněk speaking, sir.'

'Vaněk, find me at once another batman. That rogue Baloun wolfed up all my chocolate in the night. Should you tie him up? No! Let's send him to the medical corps. The bastard's a mountain of a man. He can easily drag the wounded out of the firing line. I'll send him to you at once. Arrange it with the regimental office and come back to the company at once. D'you think we're going to leave soon?'

'There's no hurry, sir. When we had to march off with the 9th march company they fooled around with us for four whole days. It was just the same with the 8th. It was only with the 10th that it was better. Then we were in full state of preparedness for the front. At noon we got the order and by the evening we'd gone. But afterwards they drove us over the whole of Hungary and didn't know which hole on what battlefield they wanted us to bung up.'

Ever since Lieutenant Lukáš had become commander of the 11th march company he had found himself in a state of mind called syncretism; which meant in philosophical terms that he tried to settle conceptual contradictions by means of compromises which were carried to a point when all views merged and lost their identity.

And so he replied: 'Yes, maybe it's like that. You don't think then that we'll be going today, do you? At nine o'clock we have a conference with the colonel. By the way, do you know that you are the sergeant-major on duty? I'm only telling you. Now find out for me. . . . Wait a moment, what should you find out for me? . . . Get a list of the N.C.O.s with information on their length of service. . . . Then the company's stocks. Nationality? Yes, yes, that as well. . . . But first of all send up this new batman. . . . What has Ensign Pleschner to do with the men today? Preparation for departure. Accounts? I'll come and sign them after mess. Don't allow anybody to go into the town. To the canteen in the camp? After mess for an hour. . . . Now call Švejk here! . . .

'Švejk, stay for the moment at the telephone.'

'Humbly report, sir, I've not yet had my coffee.'

'Then bring your coffee and stay in the office at the telephone until I call you. Do you know what an orderly is?'

'Something that runs about, sir.'

'Well, see that you're in your place whenever I call you. Tell Vaněk once more that he must find a batman for me. Švejk, hallo, where are you?'

'Here, sir. They've just brought the coffee.'

'Švejk, hallo!'

'I hear you, sir. The coffee's completely cold.'

'You know very well what a batman is, Švejk. Give him the once-over and then tell me afterwards what sort of fellow he is. Hang up the receiver.'

Vaněk, sipping the black coffee to which he added rum from a bottle with an inscription 'ink' (to take every precaution), looked at Švejk and said: 'Our lieutenant shouts rather into the telephone. I understood every word. You must know the lieutenant very well, Švejk.'

'We're hand in glove,' Švejk replied. 'One palm greases the other. We've gone through a lot together. How often they wanted to tear us apart, but we've always come together again. He always relies on me in everything, so that I'm often really quite surprised myself. And you certainly heard that I've got to remind you once more that you are to find him a new batman and that I must give him the once-over and report on him. The lieutenant won't be satisfied with any kind of batman.'

When Colonel Schröder called all the officers of the march battalion to a conference he did so again with great joy, because it offered him the chance of giving a lecture. Apart from that he had to take some decisions in the case of the volunteer Marek who had refused to clean the latrines and had been sent by him to the divisional court on the charge of mutiny.

Marek had arrived the night before from the divisional court at the main guard-house where he was held under guard. With him the regimental office received the report of the divisional court, which was colossally muddled and in which it was pointed out that in this case it was not a question of mutiny, because volunteers ought not

to clean latrines. None the less it was a case of 'breach of discipline', a delinquency which could be condoned on grounds of good conduct in the field. For this reason the accused volunteer Marek was being sent back to his regiment and the investigation into the case of breach of discipline was quashed until the end of the war. It would be taken up again the next time the volunteer Marek committed an offence.

And then there was another case. Together with the volunteer Marek the spurious Sergeant Teveles was taken to the main guard-house from the divisional court. He had appeared recently at the regiment where he had been sent from a hospital in Zagreb. He had the

Great Silver Medal, the stripes of a volunteer and three stars. He told of the heroic acts of the 6th march company in Serbia and said he was the only survivor from it. In the course of investigation it was established that at the beginning of the war a certain Teveles did actually go with the 6th march company, but that he did not have the rights of a volunteer. Information was then sought from the brigade under whose command the 6th march company came when the retreat took place from Belgrade on 2 December 1914, and it was ascertained that in the list of names of those recommended for the award of the Silver Medal or of those awarded it there was no Teveles. It could not, however, be confirmed whether the infantryman Teveles was promoted in the Belgrade war campaign to the rank of sergeant, because the whole of the 6th march company with all its officers disappeared near the church of St Sava in Belgrade. Before the divisional court Teveles defended himself by saying that the Great Silver Medal had really been promised to him and he had therefore bought one in hospital from a Bosnian. As for the volunteer's stripes, he sewed them on when he was drunk and went on wearing them because he was incessantly drunk, his constitution having been weakened by dysentery.

When the conference began Colonel Schröder, before discussing these two cases, announced that they would have to have more frequent contacts before their departure, which would not now be long delayed. He had received information from the brigade that orders were expected from the division. The men must be in a state of alert and company commanders must punctiliously ensure that no one was missing. Then he repeated once more everything that he had said the day before. He again made a survey of the military operations and said that nothing should be allowed to suppress fighting spirit and warlike initiative in the army.

On the table in front of him was fastened a map of the battlefield with flags on pins, but all the flags were overturned and the front lines shifted. Pins with flags were lying about under the table.

The whole battlefield had been frightfully messed up in the night by a tom cat which the writers kept in the regimental office and which, when it performed its own operations on the Austro-Hungarian battlefield, wanting to scratch and cover them over, tore out the flags and smeared the mess over all the positions. It stained the fronts and the bridgeheads and defiled all the army corps.

Colonel Schröder was very short-sighted.

Officers of the march battalion watched with interest as Colonel Schröder's fingers came nearer to these little mounds.

'From here, gentlemen, from Sokal to the Bug,' said Colonel Schröder prophetically and moved his finger from memory towards the Carpathians. In doing this he plunged his finger into one of those

little mounds with which the tom cat had tried to make the map of the battlefield a relief one.

'What's this, gentlemen?' he asked in astonishment when something had stuck to his finger.

'Probably cat droppings, sir,' Captain Ságner answered very politely for all of them.

Colonel Schröder rushed into the office next door, from where there could be heard tremendous thunderings and fulminations with frightful threats that he would make them lick up everything the cat had done.

The cross-examination was brief. It was ascertained that a fortnight ago the cat was brought to the office by the youngest writer, Zwiebel-fisch. When this had been ascertained Zwiebelfisch packed himself up lock, stock and barrel and the senior writer took him to the guard-house where he would sit until further orders from the colonel.

With that the whole conference was in fact finished. When Colonel Schröder returned to the officers, crimson in the face, he forgot that he had to discuss the fate of the volunteer Marek and the spurious Sergeant Teveles.

He said quite shortly: 'I request you, gentlemen, to be in a state of alert and to await my further orders and instructions.'

And so the volunteer and Teveles remained under guard at the guard-house and when Zwiebelfisch joined them later they were able to play mariáš together and after mariáš to bother their guards with the request to catch for them the fleas on the straw mattresses.

Then later Corporal Peroutka of the 13th march company was pushed in with them. When the news got around in the camp that they were going to the front, he had got lost and been found in the morning by the patrol at The White Rose at Bruck. He gave as an excuse that before they left for the front he wanted to see the famous greenhouses of Count Harrach at Bruck and on the way back he had lost his way. It was only in the early morning that he got to The White Rose in a state of complete exhaustion. (As a matter of fact he spent the night in bed with Růženka from The White Rose.)

The situation remained unclear. Were they going or weren't they? Švejk at the telephone in the office of the 11th march company heard various pessimistic and optimistic opinions. The 12th march company telephoned claiming that someone in the office had heard that they were waiting to do some shooting practice at moveable targets and that they would only leave after gunnery practice under front conditions. This optimistic view was not shared by the 13th march company which telephoned that Corporal Havlík had just returned from the town and had heard there from a railwayman that the trucks were already at the station.

Vaněk tore the receiver from Švejk's hand and shouted angrily that the railwaymen knew damn all about it and that he had just come back from the regimental office.

Švejk stayed at the telephone with true devotion and his answer to all questions about the news was that nothing definite was yet known.

He answered the lieutenant's question in the same way too when the latter asked:

'What news is there?'

'Nothing definite yet, sir,' Švejk answered in a stereotyped manner.

'You bloody mule. Hang up the receiver.'

Then came a series of telegrams which Švejk took after a lengthy period of misunderstanding. First of all there was the telegram which could not be dictated the night he failed to hang up the receiver and was sleeping. It concerned those who were inoculated and those who were not.

Then there was the delayed telegram about the tins which had been cleared up already the night before.

Finally there was a telegram to all battalions, companies and units of the regiment as follows:

Copy of brigade telegram no. 75692. Brigade order no. 172. In statistical reports about the running of the field-kitchens the following order must be observed in naming articles of consumption: 1 meat, 2 tins, 3 fresh vegetables, 4 dried vegetables, 5 rice, 6 macaroni, 7 groats and semolina, 8 potatoes, instead of previous: 4 dried vegetables, 5 fresh vegetables.

When Švejk read this to Quartermaster Sergeant-Major Vaněk the latter declared solemnly that as a rule telegrams like this are thrown down the rears:

'Some bloody fool on the army staff has thought that one up. Now it's going round all the divisions, brigades and regiments.'

Then Švejk received one more telegram which was so quickly dictated that he managed to get down on the notebook only what sounded like a cipher:

'As a result of more detailed it has been permitted or the same can on the other hand none the less be supplemented.'

'This is all pointless,' said Vaněk, when Švejk was frightfully puzzled by what he had written and read it out aloud three times in succession: 'Sheer stupidity, although God knows it could be in cipher, but in the company we're not equipped to receive cipher. You may throw it away as well.'

'I think so too,' said Švejk. 'If I were to report to the lieutenant that he has as a result of more detailed it has been permitted or the same can on the other hand none the less be supplemented, I think he'd perhaps feel offended.

'You wouldn't believe how frightfully fussy some people are,' continued Švejk, delving deep into his reminiscences again. 'Once I went by tram from Vysočany to Prague and in Libeň a certain Mr Novotný got in. As soon as I recognized him I went to him on the platform and started to get into conversation with him as we both came from Dražov. But he just shouted at me not to molest him and claimed that he didn't know me. I began to explain that he ought to remember, since when I was a kid I used to go and see him with my mother who was called Antonie and that my father was called Prokop and was a bailiff. But even then he didn't want to own that we knew each other. So finally I gave him closer details and said that in Dražov there were two Novotnýs, Tonda and Josef. He was Josef. They had written to me about him from Dražov and said he had shot his wife when she rebuked him for drinking. And then he raised his arm to hit me but I dodged and he broke the windscreen on the front platform – the big one in front of the driver. And so they pushed us both out and took us away. At the police station it turned out that why he had been so touchy was because he was not called Josef Novotný at all but Eduard Doubrava, and had come from Montgomery in America to visit his relatives from whom his family were descended.'

The telephone interrupted his narration and a hoarse voice from the machine-gun section again asked whether they would be going. There was a rumour that there was to be another conference with the colonel the next morning.

In the door there appeared the pale face of Cadet Biegler, who was the biggest ass in the company, because in the volunteers' school he always tried to show off his knowledge. He beckoned to Vaněk to come out in the passage, where he had a long conversation with him.

When Vaněk returned he smiled contemptuously.

'There's a bloody idiot for you,' he said to Švejk. 'We've certainly got some specimens in this march company of ours! He was at the conference too and when it broke up the lieutenant ordered all platoon commanders to make a rifle inspection and to make it a strict one. Now he's come to ask me whether he should tie up Žlábek because he cleaned his rifle with paraffin.'

Vaněk flared up.

'And he asks a bloody stupid thing like that when he knows we're going to the front. Well, the lieutenant thought twice about his having tied up his batman yesterday and I said to this young greenhorn that he should think twice about treating the men like cattle.'

'And while you're speaking about that batman,' said Švejk, 'do you happen to know whether you've found one for the lieutenant?'

'Keep your hair on,' answered Vaněk. 'There's plenty of time for everything. Besides, I believe the lieutenant will get used to Baloun. Now and again he'll guzzle up something of his and then he'll stop. He's bound to when we get to the front. There often neither of them will have anything to eat at all. When I say that Baloun is to stay, then there's nothing to be done about it. This is my business and the lieutenant has no say in it. Take it easy.'

Vaněk lay down on his bed again and said: 'Švejk, tell me a funny story about the army.'

'I might,' answered Švejk, 'but I am afraid someone might ring up again.'

'Then disconnect it, Švejk. Screw off the contacts. Take off the receiver.'

'Good,' said Švejk, taking off the receiver. 'I'll tell you something that's suitable for this situation, except that at that time instead of real war we only had manoeuvres. There was just the same sort of flap as there is today, because no one knew when we would move out of the barracks. Serving with me was a man called Šic from Poříčí, a good chap but religious and funky. He imagined that manoeuvres were something horrible, that people died of thirst on the march and the medical corps would pick them up like rotten fruit. And so he stoked himself up well with drink and when we went out on the manoeuvres from the barracks and came to Mníšek he said: "I can't take it, boys. Only the Lord God can protect me." Then we came to Hořovice and there we had two days' rest because there had been a mistake and we had advanced too quickly, so that we and the other regiments who marched with us on the flank could have taken the whole enemy general staff prisoner. This would have been a disgrace because our army corps was meant to get shat on and the enemy to win, because on the enemy side there was a worn-out old archdukelet. Now this is what that Šic did. When we were encamped there he set out to do some shopping in a village beyond Hořovice, returning to the camp at noon. It was hot and he was quite tight, and on the way he saw a pillar and on the pillar was a box and in it under the glass a small statue of St John of Nepomuk. He prayed in front of St John and said to him: "It must be hot for you here; you ought to drink a little. You're in the sun here. You must certainly be sweating all the time." And so he shook the field-flask, took a sip out of it and said: "I've left you a nip too, St John of Nepomuk." But then he got scared and drank it all up and there was nothing left for St John. "Jesus Mary," he said, "St John of Nepomuk, you must forgive me for this. I'll make it up to you. I'll take you with me to the camp and give you so gloriously much to drink that you won't be able to stand on your feet." And dear Šic, out of pity for St John of Nepomuk, broke the glass, pulled out the statue of the saint, put it under his tunic and carried it off to the camp. After that John of Nepomuk slept with him in the straw, he carried him in his sack on his marches, and he always had tremendous luck at cards. Wherever we were in camp he always won, until we came to the district of Prácheň and lay in Drahenice, and there he lost everything, lock, stock and barrel. When we moved off in the morning St

John of Nepomuk was strung up on a pear-tree by the road. Well, that's your funny story, and now I'll put back the receiver again.'

And the telephone again communicated the quiver of a new nervous activity, after the old harmony of peace in the camp had been disturbed.

During this time Lieutenant Lukáš was in his room studying the ciphers which he had just received from the regimental staff together with the instructions on how they were to be read, as well as secret ciphered instructions about the direction which the march battalion would take on its way to the Galician frontier (first stage):

7217 – 1238 – 475 – 2121 – 35 = Mošon
8922 – 375 – 7282 = Raab
4432 – 1238 – 7217 – 35 – 8922 – 35 = Komárno
7282 – 9299 – 310 – 375 – 7881 – 298 – 475 – 7979 = Budapest.

Deciphering this code Lieutenant Lukáš sighed: 'Bugger the whole bloody thing.'

Part III

THE GLORIOUS LICKING

I

Across Hungary

At last the moment came when they were stuffed into vans in the ratio of 42 men to 8 horses. The horses travelled more comfortably than the men of course because they could sleep standing, but what did it matter? A military train was again carrying off to Galicia another herd of men driven to the slaughter-house.

But it brought these creatures some relief none the less; when the train moved off it was at last something definite, whereas before there had only been uncomfortable uncertainty and panic as to whether the train would go that day, the next, or the following one. Some felt as though a death sentence had been passed on them and waited in fear and trembling for the moment when the executioner would come. And then calm resignation followed: soon everything would be over.

This was why one soldier shouted from the van like a madman: 'We're off, we're off!'

Quartermaster Sergeant-Major Vaněk was perfectly right when he told Švejk there was no hurry.

Before the moment came for them to get into the vans several days elapsed and all this time there were persistent rumours about tinned goulash. The experienced Vaněk declared that it was only imagination. How could there be any tinned goulash? There might perhaps be a drumhead mass, because there had been one for the previous march company. When there's tinned goulash the drumhead mass is dropped. Conversely, when there's no tinned goulash the drumhead mass is a substitute for it.

And so instead of tinned goulash Senior Chaplain Ibl appeared and killed three birds with one stone. He celebrated a drumhead mass for three march battalions at one go. Two of them he blessed for their march to Serbia and a third for their march to Russia.

On this occasion he delivered a highly inspired address and it was noticeable that he had taken the material from the army almanacs. It was such a moving speech that later, when they went off in the direction of Mošon, Švejk, who travelled with Vaněk in an improvised office in one of the vans, remembered the oration and said to him: 'Won't it be marvellous when, like the chaplain said, the day draws to its close, the sun with its golden beams sets behind the mountains, and on the battle-fields are heard, as he told us, the last breath of the dying, the death-rattle of the fallen horses, the groans of the wounded and the wailing of the population, as their cottages burn over their heads. I love it when people drivel utter bunkum.'

Vaněk nodded his head in agreement. 'It was a damned moving story.'

'It was very beautiful and edifying,' said Švejk. 'I've memorized it perfectly and when I return from the war I'll tell it at The Chalice. When the chaplain was declaiming there he had his shanks so wide apart that I was afraid one of them would slip and he would fall on to the field altar and crack his coconut on the monstrance. He gave us such a wonderful example from the history of our army at the time when Radetzky was still serving in it, the barns on the battlefield were burning and the blaze merged with the glow of sunset. It was just as if he had seen it with his own eyes.'

And the same day the senior chaplain was already back in Vienna telling another march battalion the moving story which Švejk referred to and which he loved so much that he called it 'utter bunkum'.

'My dear men,' the senior chaplain declaimed, 'imagine that it is the year 1848 and the Battle of Custozza[1] has ended in victory, where after a fierce battle lasting ten hours the Italian King Albert has had to aban-don the bloody battlefield to our warrior father, Marshal Radetzky, who in his eighty-fourth year has won such a glorious victory.

'And lo, my dear men, the veteran marshal has stopped on the hill before conquered Custozza! Around him are his faithful generals. The whole circle are held spellbound by the solemnity of the moment, for at no distance at all from the marshal, my dear men, a warrior can be seen wrestling with death. With his limbs shattered on the field of glory the wounded standard-bearer, Hrt, senses that the marshal's eyes are upon him. In a convulsive fit of enthusiasm the valiant wounded standard-bearer still clutches his Gold Medal firmly in his stiffening right hand. At the sight of the noble marshal the pulse of his heart quickens again, the last vestige of his strength suffuses his paralysed

1. In 1848 the Austrians under Marshal Radetzky defeated the army of King Charles Albert of Sardinia who was forced to evacuate Lombardy.

body and in his dying moments he strives with a superhuman effort to crawl towards his marshal.

' "Spare yourself these pains, my brave warrior!" the marshal calls to him, dismounting from his horse and about to shake his hand.

' "It's no good, sir," says the dying warrior. "Both my arms are shot away. But one thing I beg of you. Please tell me the full truth: is it total victory?"

' "Total, dear boy," says the marshal kindly. "It's a pity that your joy is marred by your wounds."

' "Of course, noble sir, my end has come," says the warrior in sombre tones as he smiles sweetly. "Are you thirsty?" asks Radetzky. "The day has been sultry, sir. We have had more than 30 degrees of heat." Radetzky then takes his adjutant's field-flask and hands it to the dying man, who drinks a powerful draught from it. "May God reward you a thousand times, sir!" he cries, striving to kiss the hand of his commander. "How long have you been serving?" the latter asks. "More than forty years, sir! At Aspern[1] I was awarded the Gold Medal. I was at Leipzig[2] too. I have the Artillery Cross also. I was mortally wounded five times but now it's all over with me. Oh, but what a joy and blessing it is that I've lived to see this day. What do I care about death now that we have won this glorious victory and the Emperor's territory is restored!"

'At that moment, my dear men, the mighty and noble strains of our anthem, "God save our Emperor", resound from the camp and are wafted over the battlefield. The fallen warrior, bidding farewell to life, tries once more to rally his strength.

' "*Vivat Austria!*" he shouts enthusiastically. "*Vivat Austria!* May it live on in this jewel of a song! Glory to our Marshal! Long life to our army!"

'The dying man bends once more towards the marshal's right hand and kisses it. Then he sinks down and a quiet last sigh escapes from his noble soul. The marshal stands there with bared head before the body of one of his most valiant warriors.

' "This beautiful passing is indeed to be envied," the marshal says with emotion, lowering his head to his clasped hands.

1. Napoleon was repulsed by the Austrian army in 1809 at the Battle of Aspern when he tried to cross the Danube and march on Vienna.

2. Napoleon was defeated at the Battle of Leipzig in 1813.

'My dear men, let me too wish all of you a beautiful passing like that.'

Remembering this speech by the senior chaplain, Švejk could justifiably, without the least offence to him, call him a driveller of utter bunkum.

After that Švejk began to talk of the famous orders which had been read out to them before they got into the train. One was the army order, signed by Franz Joseph, and another came from Archduke Joseph Ferdinand, the Supreme Commander of the Eastern Army and Group. Both concerned the events on the Dukla Pass on 3 April 1915, when two battalions of the 28th regiment including their officers went over to the Russians to the strains of their regimental band.

Both orders had been read to them in a tremulous voice and ran as follows in Czech translation:

ARMY ORDER OF 17 APRIL 1915

With a heart overflowing with grief it is my command that the Imperial and Royal Infantry Regiment no. 28 be struck off the roll of my army for cowardice and treason. The regimental standard is to be withdrawn from the dishonoured regiment and handed over to the War Museum. This day marks the end of the existence of a regiment which was morally poisoned by the atmosphere at home and went into the field to commit treason.

Franz Joseph I

ORDER OF THE ARCHDUKE JOSEPH FERDINAND

During the campaign in the field the Czech troops failed, especially in the last battles. They failed notably when defending positions where they had lain entrenched for a considerable time. The enemy took advantage of this to make contact and establish links with worthless elements among these troops.

Assisted by these traitors the enemy made a point of directing their attacks against those detachments at the front which were composed of troops of this kind.

The enemy was often successful in surprising our units and was thus able almost without resistance to penetrate our positions and take prisoner a remarkably large number of defence troops.

A thousandfold disgrace, shame and contempt upon these dishonourable wretches, who committed treason against their Emperor and Fatherland, and besmirched the honour, not only of the glorious standards of our noble and valiant army, but also of the nation to which they claim to belong.

Sooner or later they will perish by the bullet or the hangman's rope.

It is the duty of every single Czech soldier who possesses a shred of honour to denounce to his commander every such villain, agitator and traitor.

Anyone who fails to do so is himself a traitor and villain of the same kind. Let this order be read out to all the men of the Czech regiments.

By order of our Monarch the Imperial and Royal Regiment no. 28 has been struck off the roll of the army, and all the deserters from the regiment when they are captured will pay with their blood for their heavy guilt.

Archduke Joseph Ferdinand

'They read it to us a little too late,' said Švejk to Vaněk. 'I'm very surprised they only read it to us now, seeing that His Imperial Majesty issued the order as long ago as on 17 April. It might look as if for some reason or another they didn't allow it to be read to us immediately. If I were His Imperial Majesty I wouldn't let myself be brushed off like this. If I gave an order dated 17 April then on 17 April that order would have to be read out in all regiments, even if the sky fell down.'

Opposite Vaněk on the other side of the van the occultist cook from the officers' mess was sitting and writing. Behind him sat Lieutenant Lukáš's batman, the bearded giant Baloun, and Chodounský, who was assigned to the 11th march company as telephonist. Baloun was chewing a piece of army bread and explaining to Chodounský in fear and trembling that it was not his fault if in the bustle to get into the train he had not been able to reach the staff carriage where his lieutenant was.

Chodounský frightened him by saying that now the fun was over and that Baloun would get a bullet for it.

'If only there could be an end to this misery,' moaned Baloun. 'I was once nearly done for at the manoeuvres near Votice. There we were marching, hungry and thirsty, and when the battalion adjutant came up to us I shouted out: "Give us some water and bread!" He turned his horse on to me and said that if that had happened in wartime I should have had to fall out and he would have had me shot, but as it was he would put me in the garrison gaol. But I had wonderful luck because when he went to report it to the staff, his horse took fright on the way and he fell and broke his neck, thank the Lord.'

Baloun gave a heavy sigh and choked over a bit of bread. When he got over it he looked greedily at Lieutenant Lukáš's two bags, which he was looking after.

'The officer gentlemen have drawn their rations of liver pâté and Hungarian salami,' he said in a gloomy voice. 'How I'd love to have a bit!'

Meanwhile he was looking at his lieutenant's two bags as longingly as a dog which has been abandoned by everyone and sits hungry as a wolf at the door of a delicatessen shop, inhaling the vapour of the delicatessen as it is being cooked.

'It wouldn't do any harm,' said Chodounský, 'if they met us somewhere with a good lunch. When we went to Serbia at the beginning of the war we stuffed ourselves at every station because they stood us something everywhere. We took the goose's thighs they gave us, cut little cubes of the very best meat and played draughts with them on bars of chocolate. At Osek in Croatia two gentlemen from the Veterans' Association brought a big cauldron of roast hare into our van and then we couldn't control ourselves and poured all of it over their heads. Wherever we went we did nothing else but spew out of the train. Corporal Matějka in our van stuffed himself so full that we had to put a board across his belly and jump on it, just like when you tread on sauerkraut. That was the only thing that relieved him and it came out of him from on top and underneath. When we went through Hungary they threw roast chickens into our vans at every station. We only ate the brains. In Kaposfalva the Hungarians threw in whole chunks of roast pork and one chap got such a blow on his skull with a whole roast boar's head that he chased the donor across three tracks with his belt strap. In Bosnia on the other hand they didn't even give us water. But on the way there, although it was forbidden, we got various brands of spirit, to our hearts' content, and oceans of wine. I can remember that at one station some young madams and misses treated us to some beer and we went and pissed into their beer jugs. You should have seen how they flew away from the van!

'We were all of us quite muzzy the whole journey. I couldn't even recognize an ace of clubs. We hadn't even finished our game when suddenly before we knew where we were an order came to get out of the vans at once. A corporal, I can't remember what his name was, shouted at his men to sing in German: "And the Serbs must see that we Austrians are victorious, victorious!" But someone gave him a kick from behind and he fell over on to the rails. After that there was a shout that the rifles had got to be stacked in a pyramid, and the train immediately reversed and went back empty. But you know what happens in a flap! It carried off with it all our provisions for two days. And shrapnel began bursting about as close to us as those trees over there. The battalion commander rode up from the other end and called all his officers to a consultation. Then our Lieutenant Macek came up – he was as Czech as they make them, but he only spoke German. He was white as chalk and told us that we couldn't go any farther, because the rails had been blown up. The Serbs had got across the river in the night and were now on our left flank. But that was still far away from us. We should get reinforcements, he said, and then we would cut them

to pieces. If anything should happen no one must surrender; the Serbs, he said, cut off their prisoners' ears and noses and gouged out their eyes. Shrapnel was bursting near us, but we were not to worry about that. It was only our artillery ranging their guns, he said. Suddenly from somewhere behind the mountain there resounded a ta-ta-ta-ta-ta-ta-ta. That was our machine-guns ranging, he said. After that you could hear a cannonade from the left. It was the first time in our lives we'd heard it and we lay down flat on our stomachs at once. Several shells flew over us and set the station on fire. And then from our right side bullets began to whistle over us and in the distance you could hear salvos and the rattle of rifle fire. Lieutenant Macek ordered the pyramids to be unstacked and the rifles to be loaded. The officer on duty came up to

him and said that it couldn't be done as we had no munitions with us and he knew very well that we were only scheduled to draw our munitions at the very last staging point before taking up our positions. The munitions train had gone ahead of us and was obviously now in the hands of the Serbs. Lieutenant Macek stood for a moment, as though rooted to the spot, and then gave the order "Fix bayonets!" without knowing why and only out of desperation for something to do. Then we stood again on the alert for a long time, and after that lay down again on the sleepers because an aeroplane had appeared and the officers roared "Cover, cover, everything under cover!" Then it turned out that it was one of our own and had been shot down by our artillery in error. And after that we got up again, but there was no order, only "At ease!" From one side a cavalryman came galloping towards us. When he was still far away he shouted out: "Where is Battalion Command?" The battalion commander rode out to meet him. The cavalry-man handed him a document and then rode away to the right. The battalion commander read it on the way and suddenly, as if he'd gone off his head, drew his sabre and came flying in our direction.

' "General retreat! General retreat!" he roared at the officers. "To the hollow! Single file!" And then it started. They began to fire at us from all sides, as if they had only been waiting for that moment. On the left side was a maize field and that was a hell. Leaving our ruck-sacks on those blasted sleepers we crawled on all fours to the valley. Before you could say Jack Robinson Lieutenant Macek had stopped one in the head from the side. By the time we got away to the valley there were masses of dead and wounded. We left them there and went on running until the evening, and there wasn't a single one of our men left in the region. All of them had cleared out long before we came. The only thing we saw was a plundered baggage train. In the end we reached the station, where we got new orders to get into the train and go back to the staff, which we couldn't do because the whole staff had been taken prisoner the day before. We only learnt about that the next morning. After that we were like orphans. No one wanted anything to do with us and they assigned us to the 73rd regiment so that we could retreat with them. Of course we were jolly glad to do it, but first we had to march forward for about a day before we could get to the 73rd regiment. After that we . . .'

No one was listening to him any longer, because Švejk and Vaněk were playing two-handed mariáš. The occultist cook from the officers' mess went on writing a voluminous letter to his wife, who in his absence had begun to publish a new theosophical journal. Baloun slumbered on the bench, and so the telephonist could do nothing but repeat: 'Yes, I'll never forget it . . .'

He got up and started to kibitz those who were playing mariáš.

'You might at least light my pipe for me,' said Švejk in a friendly tone to Chodounský, 'since you're coming to kibitz. Two-handed mariáš is more important than the whole war and that blasted adventure of yours on the Serbian frontier. . . . Oh, my God, what a bloody fool I am! I could kick myself. Why didn't I wait a bit longer with that king? Now the knave has come. I really am a bloody idiot.'

Meanwhile the occultist cook had finished his letter and was reading it to himself, obviously satisfied that he had done a good job with it in face of the military censorship.

My darling wife,

When you get these lines I shall have already been several days in the train, because we are off to the front. I'm not too pleased about it because in the train I have to hang about and I can't be much use. You see, no cooking is done in our officer's mess and we get food at the various staging points. I should have liked to cook a Szeged goulash for our officers on the journey through Hungary, but there was nothing doing. Perhaps when we come to Galicia I shall have a chance of making a real Galician scholet, goose stewed in barley or in rice. Believe me, darling Helenka, I am really doing my utmost to make life more pleasant for our officers and help them overcome their troubles and strain. I have been transferred from the regiment to the march battalion, which was my most ardent desire, because I wanted with the modest resources at my disposal to put the officers' field-kitchen at the front in the best order. You remember, dear Helenka, that when I was called up to the regiment you wished me good superiors. Your wish has been granted. Not only have I nothing whatsoever to complain about, but on the contrary, all the officers are our real friends and to me especially they are like a father. As soon as possible I will let you know the number of our field post . . .

This letter had to be written because of the following circumstances: the occultist cook had got into Colonel Schröder's bad books for good and all. The colonel had protected him for a long time but by a most unfortunate mischance he had again failed to get his portion of rolled roast sirloin of veal at the farewell party with the officers of the march battalion. And so he had sent him with a march company to the front, entrusting the regimental officers' kitchen to an unfortunate teacher from the Institute for the Blind at Klárov.

The occultist cook read over once more what he had written and thought it sufficiently diplomatically phrased to keep him a bit further away from the battlefield, because, you may say what you like, even at the front there are opportunities for an easier life.

This was of course not affected by the fact that while he was still in civil life and working as editor and owner of an occultist journal devoted to knowledge of what was beyond the grave, he had written a long essay on how no one ought to fear death, and another one on the transmigration of souls.

Now he too started to kibitz. At that moment there was no difference in rank between the two players, Švejk and Vaněk. They no longer played two-handed mariáš but three-handed with Chodounský.

Orderly Švejk swore like a trooper at Quartermaster Sergeant-Major Vaněk: 'How can you be such a bloody fool? You do realize, don't you, that he's playing *betl*?[1] I haven't got a bloody diamond and, instead of

1. *Betl* (like *misère* in whist) means that the player must lose every trick in a no-trump game.

playing your eight of diamonds, like a bloody twat you throw away your knave of clubs and give that bastard the game.'

'What a lot of bloody fuss about one lost *betl*,' was the quartermaster sergeant-major's polite answer. 'Why, you're playing like a bloody half-wit yourself. D'you expect me to pull an eight of diamonds out of my hat when I haven't got a single diamond in my hand? I've only got court cards in spades and clubs, you fornicating fool.'

'Then you should have played *durch*, ' you bloody genius,' said Švejk with a smile. 'It's just like what happened once down at the restaurant, U Valšů. There was a prize oaf there who had a *durch* hand but didn't play it. Instead he always threw away all his lowest cards and made everyone play *betl*. And what hands he had! In every suit he always had the highest cards. And, just as I wouldn't have got anything out of it now, if you had played *durch*, so at that time I couldn't have got anything out of it, nor could anyone of us either. As the game went on we would have paid him all the time. At last I said to him: "Mr Herold, please do play *durch* and don't be a bloody fool." But he flew at me and said he'd play what he liked and I should keep my trap shut since he had had a university education. But he paid dearly for it. The landlord was our friend and the waitress could hardly have been on more familiar terms with us, so we were able to explain to the police patrol that everything was all right. We said first of all that it was a dirty trick of his to disturb the night peace by calling a patrol just because somewhere in front of the pub he had slipped on the ice, fallen on his nose and broken it. We hadn't done anything to him when he cheated at mariáš, but when he had been found out he had rushed out so quickly that he fell full length on the ground. The landlord and the waitress confirmed to us that we'd really been too gentlemanly to him. He had deserved all he got. He had sat from 7 p.m. to midnight, only ordered one glass of beer and one of soda water, and made out that he was a hell of a gentleman because he was a university professor. But he understood as much about mariáš as a goat about parsley. Well, whose turn is it to deal now?'

'Let's play Kaufzwick,'[2] the occultist cook proposed. 'Twenty hellers and two.'

'Much better if you tell us something about the transmigration of

---

1. *Durch* (like grand slam) means that the player must win every trick.
2. Kaufzwick was a gambling card game forbidden by the Austrian authorities.

souls,' said Vaněk, 'like you told the young lady in the canteen when you got yourself a bloody nose.'

'I've heard something about that transmigration of souls too,' Švejk put in. 'I made up my mind years ago to educate myself, if you'll permit the expression, because I didn't want to be left behind. And so I went to the reading room of the Industrial Union in Prague. But because I was ragged and the light shone through the holes in the seat of my trousers I couldn't educate myself. You see, they wouldn't let me in and showed me the door, because they thought that I had come to steal the overcoats. And so I put on my best suit, went one day to the Museum library, and together with a friend of mine borrowed a book about the transmigration of souls. There I read how an Indian emperor turned after death into a pig, and when they slaughtered that pig he turned into a monkey, and from a monkey he became a dachshund, and from a dachshund a minister. Afterwards when I was in the army I saw that there must be something in it, because everyone who had a star used to call the men swine or some other animal name. From that you might conclude that a thousand years ago these common soldiers had been famous generals. But when there's a war on, a transmigration of souls like that is an awfully silly business. God knows how many changes a man goes through before he becomes, let's say, a telephonist, a cook or an infantryman. Then suddenly he's torn to pieces by a shell and his soul goes into a horse in the artillery, and when the whole battery goes to a point somewhere a new shell bursts into it, and this again kills the horse which the late lamented had become incarnate in. And then his soul immediately moves into a cow in the baggage train, which they make goulash out of for the troops, and from the cow perhaps into a telephonist and from a telephonist . . .'

'I'd really like to know,' said Chodounský, who obviously felt offended, 'why I of all people have to be the butt of your idiotic jokes.'

'Tell me, are you by any chance related to the Chodounský who has a private detective agency with that eye like the Holy Trinity?' asked Švejk innocently. 'I like private detectives very much. I once served years ago in the army with a private detective, a fellow called Stendler. He had such a cockeyed head that our sergeant-major always said that he'd seen many soldiers with cockeyed heads during his twelve years, but a cockeyed head like his he could never have imagined in his wildest dreams. "Listen, Stendler," he always said, "if there didn't happen to be manoeuvres this year, your cockeyed nut wouldn't do for military service, but as it is, the artillery can at least range their guns by it when they come to a locality where there's no better orientation point." He had to put up with a lot of chaff like this from that sergeant-major. Sometimes during the march he sent Stendler five hundred paces in front and then gave the order: "Direction, cockeyed nut."

'But even Mr Stendler had awfully bad luck as a private detective. He often told us in the canteen that he'd had a lot of bother. He got commissions like this one for example: to find out whether the wife of one of his firm's clients, who came to see him in a state of fury, was having an affair with another man and, if she was, who it was she was having the affair with, and where and how. Or again the opposite: a very jealous woman wanted to find out who her husband was having an affair with, so as to make it hotter for him at home. Mr Stendler was an educated man, spoke exquisitely about breach of matrimonial fidelity and was nearly always on the brink of tears when he told us that all his clients wanted him to catch her or him *in flagrante*. Another chap might perhaps get a kick out of it if he came upon a couple *in flag-rante* and his eyes would pop out of his head, but this Mr Stendler, as he told us himself, was quite unhappy because of it. He said very intelligently that he could no longer look at these lewd debauches. When he told us all the various positions in which he'd found those couples our mouths often watered, like a dog slobbers when they carry boiled ham past it. When we were given "confined to barracks" he always used to draw them for us. "This is how," he said, "I saw Mrs So-and-So with this and that gentleman . . ." And he even told us their addresses. And he used to be so miserable about it. "The slaps on the face I got from both parties!" he always said. "But that didn't upset me half as much as the fact that I stooped to taking bribes. One bribe I shall never forget to my dying day. He was naked; she was naked. It was in a hotel and they hadn't bolted the door, the idiots! They couldn't fit on to the sofa because they were both too fat, and so they made love on the carpet like two kittens. And the carpet was all trampled on and full of dust, and there were cigarette stubs lying about on it. And when I came in both of them jumped up. He stood opposite me and held his hand in front of him like a fig-leaf. And she turned her back to me and you could see the whole network pattern of the carpet printed on her skin and a cigarette stub stuck to her backbone. 'Excuse me,' I said, 'Mr Zemek, I am private detective Stendler, from Chodounský's agency, and it is my official duty to catch you *in flagrante* on the basis of a tip-off from madam, your wife. This lady, with whom you are here maintaining an illicit relationship, is Mrs Grotová.' I've never in my life seen such a calm citizen. 'Excuse me,' he said, as though it were a matter of course, 'I am going to put on my clothes. It is my wife who has the sole responsibility for this. She drives me to this illicit relationship by her groundless jealousy. Goaded on by nothing more than mere suspicion she insults her husband with reproaches and mean distrust. There's no doubt now that this scandal can no longer be hushed up. . . . Where are my pants?' he asked calmly. 'On the bed there.' While he was putting on his pants he went on explaining to me: 'If a scandal cannot be hushed up, people say "divorce", but even in that case the slur of the disgrace cannot be hushed up. A divorce is always a risky thing any-way,' he went on as he dressed. 'The best thing for the wife is to arm herself with patience and do nothing to provoke a public scandal. But do as you like. I'll leave you here alone with the lady.' Meanwhile Mrs

Grotová had climbed into bed. Mr Zemek shook hands with me and left."

'I can't remember any longer how Mr Stendler explained everything and what he talked about after that, because he conversed with the lady in the bed in a very intelligent way. He said that marriage was not instituted to make everyone find happiness immediately and that it was our duty in marriage to suppress lust and to exorcize and sublimate the physical side. "And while I was saying that," Mr Stendler continued, "I gradually began to undress, and just when I was undressed, and was completely bemused and wild as a rutting stag, a Mr Stach whom I knew well came into the room. He was also a private detective from the agency of our rival, Mr Stern, and Mr Grot had turned to him for help over his wife who, he claimed, must have a lover. Stach said nothing more than, 'Ah, Mr Stendler *in flagrante* with Mrs Grotová. My congratulations!' He closed the door again quietly and went away.

' " 'You needn't dress so hastily,' Mrs Grotová said. 'It makes no difference now. There's a place here for you beside me.' 'My good lady, it's just my place that I'm worrying about,' I said and I hadn't any idea any more what I was talking about. I can only remember that I said something about that if there were quarrels between husband and wife, the babes' upbringing suffered through them." And afterwards he told us how he quickly dressed and took to his heels and decided at once to tell everything to his chief, Mr Chodounský, but went first to have a pick-me-up. But before he got back the fat was already in the fire. Stach had been there on orders from his chief, Mr Stern, to give Mr Chodounský a shock by telling him the kind of employee he had in his private detective agency. Mr Chodounský could think of nothing better than at once to send for Mrs Stendler, so that she could deal with her husband herself for having been sent somewhere on official duties and been caught *in flagrante* by a rival agency. "From that time," Mr Stendler always used to say when the subject came up, "my nut is even more cockeyed."

'Now, let's go on playing Five-ten.' And so they did.

The train stopped at the station of Mošon. It was already evening and no one was allowed out of the vans.

When they moved off a powerful voice could be heard from one of the vans. It was as though someone was trying to drown the rattle of

the train. In the pious mood of the evening a German soldier from
Kašperské Hory in a frightful caterwaul extolled the silent night as it
descended on the Hungarian plains:

> 'Good night! Good night!
> To the weary respite.
> As the hushed day closes
> The busy hand reposes
> Till the dawning light.
> Good night! Good night!'

'Shut your trap, you miserable bastard,' someone interrupted the
sentimental singer, who then lapsed into silence.

They dragged him away from the window.

But the busy hands did not repose until morning. Just as everywhere
else in the train they played cards by candlelight, so here Švejk and
the others continued to play Kaufzwick by the light of a small paraffin
lamp hanging on the wall. Whenever anyone burst when buying a card
Švejk said that Kaufzwick was the fairest of all games, because anyone
could swap as many cards as he liked.

'At Kaufzwick,' asserted Švejk, 'it's only the ace and the seven which
you have to buy, and after that you can throw your hand in. You don't
have to buy the other cards. You do that at your own risk.'

'Let's play "Blessing",'[1] Vaněk suggested amid general agreement.

'Seven of hearts,' said Švejk, cutting the cards. 'Everyone stakes
five hellers and gets four cards. Don't waste time so that we can have
a good game!'

And their faces looked so happy, as though there were no war on and
they were not sitting in a train which was taking them off to positions
in the great and bloody battles and massacres but at the card tables
in a Prague café.

'I never imagined,' said Švejk after one game, 'when I had nothing
in my hand and swapped all four of my cards, that I should pick up
an ace. What the hell did you think you would do to me with your
king? I smash your king before you know where you are.'

And while here they were smashing the king with the ace, far away
at the front kings were smashing each other with their serfs.

In the staff carriage, where the officers of the march battalion were
sitting, a strange stillness reigned from the start of the journey. Most of

---

1. A variety of Kaufzwick, where the stakes are higher.

the officers were engrossed in a small book in cloth binding entitled *The Sins of the Fathers*, a novelette by Ludwig Ganghofer, and all were simultaneously busy reading page 161. Captain Ságner, the battalion commander, was standing at the window and holding in his hand this same book, which he also had open at page 161.

He was looking at the landscape and thinking how actually he could explain to everyone in the clearest possible way what they had to do with that book. It was in fact strictly confidential.

Meanwhile the officers were reflecting that Colonel Schröder must have gone off his rocker for good and all. He had been pretty crazy for a long time, but there had surely been no reason to expect that it would take him suddenly like this. Before the departure of the train he called them to a last 'conference' and informed them that each of them would get a copy of the book *The Sins of the Fathers* by Ludwig Ganghofer, which he had had sent to battalion office.

'Gentlemen,' he said with a terribly mysterious expression, 'never forget page 161!' Engrossed as they all were in this page they could not make anything out of it. There a woman called Martha came to a writing-desk, took out a script and reflected aloud that the public must feel sympathy with the hero of the play. And then on the same page there appeared as well a certain Albert, who tried to make jokes all the time, which, divorced from the unknown action which preceded them, seemed such tripe that Lieutenant Lukáš bit his cigarette-holder in fury.

'The old man has really gone barmy,' all of them thought. 'It's all up with him. Now they'll transfer him to the Ministry of War.'

Captain Ságner got up from the window, after he had composed everything in his head to his satisfaction. He did not have much pedagogical talent, and so it took him a long time before he had in his head the whole plan of a lecture on the importance of page 161.

Before he began to explain he addressed them as 'Gentlemen', just as the old dodderer of a colonel used to do, although before they got into the train he called them 'My dear fellows.'

'Very well, then, gentlemen . . .' And he began to expound how, the evening before, he had received from the colonel instructions about page 161 in *The Sins of the Fathers* by Ludwig Ganghofer.

'Very well, then, gentlemen,' he continued solemnly. 'Strictly confidential information about the new system of ciphering telegrams in the field.' Cadet Biegler took out a notebook and a pencil and said in an exceptionally zealous tone: 'I am ready, sir.'

Everybody looked at that idiot, whose zeal in the volunteers' school bordered on imbecility. He volunteered for the army and when the commander of the volunteers' school was looking into the private circumstances of the students he took the first opportunity of letting him know that his ancestors were originally called Bügler von Leuthold and bore in their armorial bearings a stork's wing with a fish tail.

From that time onwards they christened him by the name of his armorial bearings and 'Stork's wing with fish tail' was mercilessly persecuted and became unpopular at once, because it did not in the least fit in with his father's respectable business in hare and rabbit skins. But the romantic enthusiast strove with great earnestness to devour the whole of military science, and not only did he excel in diligence and knowledge of everything which was taught him, but he also crammed his head more and more with the study of writings on military science and the history of warfare, which he always tried to talk about, until he was rapped down and crushed. In officers' circles he considered himself the equal of the senior ranks.

'You cadet there, keep quiet,' said Captain Ságner, 'until I give you permission to speak. No one asked for your opinion. But you're a damned bright soldier all the same. I'm giving you strictly confidential information and you're writing it down in your notebook. If you lose your notes you can expect to be brought before a drumhead court-martial.'

On top of everything else Cadet Biegler had the bad habit of always trying to convince everyone that his intentions were the best.

'Humbly report, sir,' he replied, 'even if I lost the notebook no one could decipher what I've written, because I use shorthand and no one can read my symbols. I use the English system.'

Everyone froze him with a look of contempt. Captain Ságner dismissed his remark with a wave of his hand and continued his lecture.

'I've already referred to the new system of ciphering telegrams in the field, and if it was perhaps not clear to you why you were recommended to read of all things page 161 of Ludwig Ganghofer's novel, *The Sins of the Fathers*, I can tell you, gentlemen, that it is the key to the new ciphering system, operative on the basis of a new directive from the staff of the army corps to which we are assigned. As you will be aware, there are many systems of ciphering important messages in the field. The latest one, which we are using, is the supplementary figure method. This supersedes the ciphers and the deciphering directives given you last week by the regimental staff.'

'Archduke Albrecht's system,' the sedulous Cadet Biegler mumbled to himself, '8922 = R, taken from Gronfeld's method.'

'The new system is exceedingly simple,' the captain's voice rang out through the carriage. 'I have personally obtained from the colonel Book II and the information.

'If, for example, we are to get the order: "On point 228 direct machine-gun fire to the left", we shall receive, gentlemen, the following telegram: "Thing – with – us – that – we – look – in – the – promised – the – Martha – you – that – anxious – then – we – Martha – we – him – we – thanks – well – steering committee – end – we – promised – we – improved – promised – really – think – idea – quite – rules – voice – last." You see, it's frightfully simple, without any unnecessary combinations. From the staff by telephone to the battalion, from the battalion by telephone to the companies. Having obtained this ciphered telegram the commander deciphers it in the following way. He takes *The Sins of the Fathers*, opens it at page 161 and starts from the top to look for the word "thing" on the opposite page, i.e. 160. Very well, then, gentlemen. The first time the word "thing" occurs on page 160 is at the 52nd word, and so he looks for the 52nd letter from the top on the opposite page, no. 161. Please note that it is "O". The next word in the telegram is "with" – that is – now follow me carefully, gentlemen, the 88th word on page 160, corresponding to the 88th letter on the opposite page 161 which is "n". And now we have deciphered "On". And we proceed in this way until we learn the order: "On point 228 direct machine-gun fire to the left." Very ingenious, gentlemen, simple, and impossible to decipher without the key: page 161 of Ludwig Ganghofer: *The Sins of the Fathers*.'

Everyone stared in silence at the unfortunate pages and pondered deeply over them. There was quiet for a moment, until all of a sudden Cadet Biegler called out in a worried voice: 'Sir, humbly report, Jesus Mary! It doesn't fit!'

And it was indeed exceedingly mysterious.

Try as they could, no one except Captain Ságner could find the words on page 160 and the corresponding letters on page 161 with which the key started.

'Gentlemen,' Captain Ságner stammered, when he had realized that

Cadet Biegler's despairing exclamation corresponded to the truth, 'what has happened? In my *Sins of the Fathers* by Ganghofer it's there and in yours it isn't?'

'Permit me, sir,' Cadet Biegler began again. 'May I take the liberty to draw your attention to the fact that the novel of Ludwig Ganghofer is in two parts. You can, if you wish, verify this by looking at the first

title page: "Novel in two parts". We have Part I and you have Part II,' continued the thorough-going Cadet Biegler. 'And so it's as clear as daylight that our pages 160 and 161 do not correspond with yours. We have something completely different. According to you the first word of the deciphered telegram ought to be "On" but ours has come out "Hi".'

Now it was quite clear to everyone that Biegler was not perhaps such an idiot after all.

'I have Part II from brigade staff,' said Captain Ságner, 'and clearly it's a question of a mistake. The colonel ordered Part I for you. Obviously,' he continued, as though it was clear as daylight and he had known it long before he gave the lecture on the very simple system of ciphering, 'there has been a muddle in brigade staff. They didn't inform the regiment that it concerned Part II and that is how it happened.'

In the meantime Cadet Biegler was looking triumphantly at everybody and Lieutenant Dub whispered to Lieutenant Lukáš that 'Stork's wing with fish tail' had put it across Ságner and no mistake – and serve him right!

'What a curious case, gentlemen,' Captain Ságner said again, as though he wanted to start a conversation, because the silence was very embarrassing. 'In brigade office they aren't very bright.'

'Permit me to add,' said the indefatigable Cadet Biegler once more, wanting to show off his knowledge again, 'that matters of this kind which are of a confidential nature, indeed a strictly confidential nature, should not go from division through brigade office. A matter which concerns the most confidential business of the army corps may be communicated by a strictly confidential circular to no one except commanders of divisions, brigades and regiments. I know the cipher systems used in the Sardinian and Savoy wars, in the Anglo-French campaign at Sebastopol, during the Boxer rising in China and in the last Russo-Japanese war. These systems were conveyed . . .'

'We don't care a tuppenny hoot about that, Cadet Biegler,' said Captain Ságner with an expression of contempt and displeasure. 'There's no doubt that the system in question which I have explained to you is not only one of the best but also, we can say, quite unrivalled. All the counter-espionage departments of our enemy staffs can now pack up. Even if they bust themselves, they won't be able to read our cipher. It's something quite new. These ciphers have no precedents.'

The assiduous Cadet Biegler coughed knowingly.

'May I be allowed to take the liberty, sir,' he said, 'to draw your attention to Kerickhoff's book on military ciphering. Anyone can obtain this book from the publishers of the *Encyclopedia of Military Science*. There you will find, sir, described in detail the method which you have just explained to us. Its inventor was Colonel Kircher, who served in the Saxon army in the time of Napoleon. Kircher's word cipher, sir. Every word of the telegram is explained on the opposite page by means of a key. The method was perfected by Lieutenant

Fleissner in his book, *The Handbook of Military Cryptography*, which anyone can buy at the publishers of the Military Academy in Wiener Neustadt. Excuse me, sir.' Cadet Biegler put his hand in his bag, drew out the book to which he was referring and continued: 'Fleissner gives the very same example. You may all wish to confirm it for yourselves. It is exactly the same example as we have just heard.

'Telegram: On point 228 direct machine-gun fire to the left.
Key: Ludwig Ganghofer, *The Sins of the Fathers*, Part II.

'And look further please: "Cipher: Thing – with – us – that – we – look – in – the – promised – the – Martha ..." and so on. Just as we heard a moment ago.'

There was no answer to this. The greenhorn 'Stork's wing with fish tail' was right.

One of the generals in the army staff had hit upon a labour-saving device. He had discovered Fleissner's book about military ciphers and the job was done.

All this time Lieutenant Lukáš appeared to be trying to overcome a strange inner tension. He bit his lip, seemed to want to say something but in the end started to speak about something different from what he had originally intended.

'We need not take this so tragically,' he said in strange embarrassment. 'While we were in camp at Bruck an der Leitha the systems of ciphering telegrams were changed several times. Before we reach the front new systems will again be introduced. But I think that anyhow there's no time for deciphering cryptograms like this in the field. Before any of us had time to decipher a telegram like the example given us the company battalion and brigade would long ago have ceased to exist. It has no practical significance!'

Captain Ságner nodded his head very reluctantly. 'In practice,' he said, 'at least as far as my experiences from the Serbian battlefield go, no one had time to decipher telegrams. I don't mean that ciphers wouldn't have their importance in the course of a prolonged stay in the trenches, when we dig ourselves in and wait. It's also true that ciphers are changed.'

Captain Ságner was retreating all along the line: 'A great deal of the blame for our staffs making less and less use of ciphers when they communicate with the troops in position rests on the inaccuracy and unreliability of our field telephones, particularly during artillery fire when they do not reproduce the individual syllables clearly. You don't hear anything at all and it causes unnecessary chaos.' He paused.

'Chaos is the worst thing that can happen in the field, gentlemen,' he added prophetically and was silent.

'In a moment,' he said, looking out of the window, 'we shall be in Raab. Gentlemen, here the men will get fifteen dekas of Hungarian salami. And there will be half an hour's rest.'

He looked at the schedule: 'At 4.12 we leave. At 3.58 everything must be in the vans. We shall leave the train by companies. The 11th and so on. By platoons. Direction: store number 6. Control over distribution: Cadet Biegler.'

Everyone gave Cadet Biegler a look which meant 'You'll have a nice picnic now, you milksop.'

But the assiduous Cadet Biegler had already taken out of his bag a sheet of paper and a ruler, drawn lines on the paper, divided it according to march companies and asked the commanders of the various companies how many men they had. None of them knew this offhand and they could only give Biegler the required figures from vague jottings in their notebooks.

Meanwhile Captain Ságner in despair began to read the unfortunate book, *The Sins of the Fathers*, and when the train stopped at the station in Raab, he closed it and observed: 'This Ludwig Ganghofer doesn't write at all badly.'

Lieutenant Lukáš was the first to rush out of the staff carriage and go to the van to find Švejk.

Švejk and the others had long ago stopped playing cards and Lieutenant Lukáš's batman, Baloun, was already so hungry that he was beginning to rebel against the military authorities and to tell the others that he knew exactly how those officer gentlemen stuffed their gullets. It was worse now than during serfdom. It hadn't been like that in the army in the old days. As his grandfather who lived at home in retirement always said, the officers in the war of 1866 used to share their chicken and bread with the soldiers. There was no end to his lamentations, until finally Švejk considered it proper to stand up for army life in the present war.

'You must have quite a young grandfather,' he said affably, when they got to Raab, 'if he can only remember the war of 1866. I know a chap called Ronovský, and his grandfather was in Italy under serfdom, and he served his twelve years there and came home as a corporal. As that grandfather had no job, his father took him into his own house to work for him. And once they went to do their *corvée* for their landlord and cart away tree trunks. One trunk, as that grandfather who was working for his father told us, was just like a colossus and they couldn't make it budge. And so he said: "Let's leave the blighter here. Who's going to sweat with it." And a gamekeeper who heard this began to shout at him, raised his stick and told him that he'd got to load that tree trunk. Well, Mr Ronovský's grandfather said nothing but: "You clumsy oaf, you. I'm an old army veteran." But a week later he was served with a summons and called up for service in Italy again. He remained there for another ten years and wrote home that when he came back he'd slog that gamekeeper over the head with an axe. It was a bit of luck that that gamekeeper died.'

At that moment Lieutenant Lukáš appeared in the door of the van.

'Švejk, come here,' he said. 'Stop telling your stupid stories, and come and explain something to me.'

'At your service, humbly report, sir.'

Lieutenant Lukáš took Švejk away and the look he gave him, as he followed him with his eyes, was full of suspicion.

During the whole course of Captain Ságner's lecture, which had ended in such a fiasco, Lieutenant Lukáš had developed a certain aptitude for detective work for which no elaborate speculation was needed, because the day before their departure Švejk had reported to him: 'Sir, there are some books in the battalion for the gentlemen lieutenants. I've fetched them from the regimental office.'

And so when they crossed the second track and got behind an abandoned locomotive, which had been already waiting a week for a munitions' train, Lieutenant Lukáš asked straight out: 'Švejk, tell me, what happened to those books you told me about?'

'Humbly report, sir, it's a very long story and you always are pleased to get angry when I go into a lot of detail. Like the time you wanted to hit me over the jaw when you had torn up the document about the war loan and I told you that I'd read once in a book that in the old days when there was a war on people had to pay for their windows, twenty hellers for every window, and the same amount for their geese . . .'

'Like this we'll never be finished, Švejk,' said Lieutenant Lukáš continuing his cross-examination, during which he resolved that what was strictly confidential must of course be kept completely concealed to prevent that bastard Švejk making some kind of use of it again. 'Do you know Ganghofer?'

'What should he be?' asked Švejk with interest.

'He's a German writer, you stupid bastard,' answered Lieutenant Lukáš.

'Upon my honour, sir,' said Švejk with the expression of a martyr, 'I don't know any German writer personally. I only once knew a Czech writer personally, a certain Ladislav Hájek from Domažlice. He was the editor of *The Animal World*, and I once sold him a mongrel as a thoroughbred pom. He was a very cheery and nice man. He used to go to a pub and always read his stories there, which were so sad that everybody roared with laughter at them. Afterwards he wept and paid for everybody in the pub and we had to sing for him: "The Domažlice gate's in a beautiful state. It's thanks to the art of the amorous heart of a painter I knew who the girls did pursue, and who can't now be found, as he's under the ground . . ." '

'You're not on the stage, do you realize that? You're bellowing like an opera singer, Švejk,' shouted Lieutenant Lukáš in horror when Švejk began to sing the last sentence: 'And who can't now be found, as he's under the ground.' 'That's not what I asked you about. I only wanted to know whether you had noticed that those books which you yourself mentioned to me were by Ganghofer. What happened to those books, then?' he burst out angrily.

'Do you mean those I fetched from regimental office and carried to the battalion?' asked Švejk. 'Yes, they were written by that man you asked me whether I knew, sir. I got a telegram phoned straight from regimental office. They wanted to send those books to battalion office, but no one was there. They were all away, even the N.C.O. on duty, because they had to go to the canteen, when they were leaving for the front, as no one knew if they would ever be sitting in the canteen again. And so they were there, sir, they were there and they were drinking. You couldn't get anyone by phone, not even anyone from any of the other march companies, but because you had ordered me to be orderly at the telephone for the time being until they assigned us a telephone operator, Chodounský, I sat there and waited until my turn came. From regimental office they swore and complained that they couldn't get hold of anybody anywhere and that they had a telegram which said that the march battalion office should fetch from regimental office some books for the officers of the whole march battalion. Because I know, sir, that in wartime you have to act quickly, I telephoned to regimental office that I would go and pick up those books myself and take them to battalion office. There I was given such a colossal sack that I could hardly drag it to our company office, where I had a look at those books. But I had ideas of my own about them. The regimental quartermaster sergeant-major at regimental office told me that according to the telegram to the regiment they certainly knew in the battalion which of these books had to be taken and *which part*. You see these books were in *two parts*. The first part separate and the second part separate. I've never laughed so much in my life, because I've read many books in my time, but I've never started a book from the second part. And he said to me once again: "Here you have the first part and there you have the second. The officers know already *which part* they have to read." And so I thought that they must all be tight, because when you have to read a novel from the beginning like the one I've brought about *The Sins of the Fathers* (because I understand German too), you have to begin with the *first* part. After all, we're not Jews and don't read backwards. And that's why I asked you, sir, on the telephone, when you returned from the officers' club and I reported to you about these books, whether perhaps now in wartime it isn't all upside down and whether books aren't read back to front, first the *second* part and only after that the *first* part. And you told me that I was a sozzled ox if I didn't know that in the Lord's Prayer "Our Father" came first and "Amen" afterwards.

'Are you feeling bad, sir?' asked Švejk with concern, when Lieutenant Lukáš, who had turned pale, steadied himself by holding on to the footplate of the boiler of the abandoned locomotive.

There was no sign of anger in his pale face. There was just hopelessness and desperation.

'Go on, go on, Švejk. It doesn't matter. It's quite all right . . .'

'I was, as I've said, sir, of the same opinion myself,' Švejk's soft voice could be heard saying on the abandoned track. 'Once I bought a blood-and-thunder novel about Róža Šavaň from the Bakony Forest and the first part was missing, so I had to guess the beginning, and even in a gangster story like that you really need the first part. And it was quite clear to me that it would have been useless for the officers to start reading the second part first and the first part afterwards, and that it would look very stupid if I had said in the battalion what they told me in regimental office, that the officers would know *which part* they had to read. Altogether with these books I found it frightfully suspicious and mysterious. I knew that the officer gentlemen read very little anyhow and in the tumult of the battle . . .'

'Cut out the drivel, Švejk,' Lieutenant Lukáš groaned.

'And you know, sir, that I asked you by telephone at once, whether you wanted immediately both parts at once and you said to me, just like

now, that I should cut out the drivel and not bother you about carting any books with us. And so I thought that if that was your opinion then the other officers must see it in the same light too. And I also asked our Vaněk, who after all has experience from the front, and he said that at the beginning all the officers thought that the whole war would be just a picnic and took with them to the front whole libraries of books as though they were going on their summer holidays. Archduchesses presented them with complete collections of various poets for the front, so that the wretched batmen doubled up under their weight and cursed the day when they were born. Vaněk said that these books were never of any use for rolling cigarettes, because they were printed on very swell thick paper, and in the W.C. people might, if you excuse the expression, sir, scrape off the whole of their backsides with such poems. But there wasn't a moment for reading, because they had to flee all the time, and so the books were thrown away, and after that it became the usual custom for the batmen to throw away all the light reading at once as soon as they heard the first cannonade. After hearing this I wanted to learn your opinion once again, sir, and when I asked you on the telephone what I was to do with these books you said that when I got something into my bloody stupid noddle I never let go of it until I got one across the jaw. And so, sir, I took only *the first part* of the novel to battalion office, and the second part I left for the time being in our company office. With the best intentions in the world I thought that when the officer gentlemen had read the first part they would be issued with the second part just like at a library, but suddenly there came the news that we had to go and there was a telegram to the whole battalion that everything superfluous must be put into the regimental stores. And so I asked Mr Vaněk again if he regarded the second part of that novel as superfluous and he said to me that after the unhappy experiences in Serbia, Galicia and Hungary no books of light reading were taken to the front, and those boxes which were put in towns for the collection of newspapers for the soldiers were the only things which were any use, because in the newspapers you could roll tobacco or hay, which is what the soldiers smoke when they are in the trenches. They had already distributed to the battalion the first part of that novel and so we carried the second part to the store.'

Švejk paused and at once added: 'There were all sorts of things in that store, sir, even the Budějovice choirmaster's top hat, the one he wore when he was called up to the regiment . . .'

'I'll tell you something, Švejk,' said Lieutenant Lukáš with a heavy sigh. 'You obviously haven't an inkling of the consequences of your action. I'm quite sick of calling you a bloody half-wit, but there are really no words to describe your idiocy. When I call you a half-wit I'm really paying you a compliment. You've done something so frightful that the most ghastly crimes you've committed while I've known you are like angels' harp-playing in comparison. If you only knew, Švejk, what you've done. . . . But you will never learn that. . . . And should there ever be any mention of these books, then don't you dare let out in your chatter that I said something to you about sending the second part. . . . If the subject should ever come up about what happened to the first and second part, just ignore it. You haven't any idea about anything, you don't know anything, you don't remember anything. Don't you dare involve me in anything, you, you . . .'

Lieutenant Lukáš spoke in such tones as though he had a bout of fever and Švejk used the moment when he stopped speaking to ask innocently: 'Humbly report, sir, please forgive me, but why shall I never learn what I've done that's so frightful? I only venture to ask, sir, so that next time I can avoid such a thing, since it's generally said that a man learns from his errors, like that iron-founder Adamec from Daňkovka, when by mistake he drank hydrochloric acid . . .'

He never finished because Lieutenant Lukáš interrupted his example from life with the words: 'You miserable bastard, you! I shan't explain anything to you. Get back into the van again and tell Baloun that when we come to Budapest he is to bring me in the staff carriage a roll and that liver pâté I have in tin foil in the bottom of my bag. Then tell Vaněk that he's a bloody mule. Three times I've asked him to give me the company's exact complement. And when I needed it today I only had the old schedule from last week.'

'At your orders, sir,' Švejk barked in German and slowly withdrew in the direction of his van.

Lieutenant Lukáš walked along the track thinking: 'I ought to have given him a few on the jaw, but instead I've been gossiping with him as though he were a friend.'

Švejk got solemnly into his van. He felt respect for himself. It did not happen every day that he committed something so frightful that he must never be allowed to learn what it was.

'Quartermaster sergeant-major,' said Švejk, when he was sitting in his place again, 'Lieutenant Lukáš seems to me to be in a very good mood today. He asked me to tell you that you are a bloody mule, because he asked you three times to give him the company's correct complement.'

'Herrgott,' said Vaněk in fury. 'I'll give those platoon sergeants hell. How can I bloody well help it if every lazy bastard of a platoon sergeant does what he likes and doesn't send me the correct complement of his platoon? Have I got to pull the complement out of my hat? That's how it is in our company! That can only happen in the 11th march company. But I suspected it, I knew it. I didn't doubt for a moment that things weren't in order with us. One day four portions are missing in the kitchen. The next there are three too many. If only these bloody swine would at least tell me if someone isn't in hospital. Last week I still had on my list a chap called Nikodem and it was only when it came to the issuing of pay that I learnt that that Nikodem had died of galloping consumption in the hospital at Budějovice. All that

time they had gone on drawing rations for him. We drew a uniform for him but God knows what happened to it. And after all that the lieutenant tells me I'm a bloody mule, when he can't himself put right the mess in his own company.'

Vaněk walked up and down the van in fury: 'If I were company commander! Then everything would have to go like clockwork. I'd keep a check on every man jack of them. The N.C.O.s would have to give me the company's complement twice a day. But what can you do when the N.C.O.s are utterly incompetent. The worst of all in our company is that platoon sergeant Zyka. All he does is to make jokes

and tell stories, and when he's told that Kolařík has been assigned away
from his platoon to the baggage train, he reports to me next day the
same complement, as though Kolařík had gone on loafing about in the
company and in his platoon. And when that happens every day and on
top of that I'm told that I'm a bloody mule.... The lieutenant isn't
going to make himself popular this way. The quartermaster sergeant-
major in a company isn't just a lance-corporal whom anyone can use
to wipe his ...'

Baloun, who was listening with his mouth wide open, now spoke for
Vaněk that lovely word which Vaněk did not get round to saying,
wishing with this to contribute to the conversation.

'You shut your mug,' said the infuriated quartermaster sergeant-
major.

'Listen, Baloun,' said Švejk, 'I've got a message for you too. When
we get to Budapest you're to bring to the lieutenant in his carriage a
roll and that liver pâté which he keeps in tin foil at the bottom of his
bag.'

The giant Baloun desperately swung his long chimpanzee-like arms,
bent his back and remained in this position for some time.

'I haven't got it,' he said in a quiet despairing tone, staring at the
dirty floor of the van.

'I haven't got it,' he repeated jerkily. 'I thought ... I undid it
before we left ... I smelt it ... in case it was spoiled ...

'I tasted it,' he cried out in such genuine despair that it was quite
clear to everybody what had happened.

'You wolfed it all up, tin foil and all,' said Vaněk, stopping in front
of Baloun. He was grateful that he no longer had to defend his view
that he wasn't a bloody mule, as the lieutenant had conveyed to him,
but that the cause of the unknown factor x (the complement of the
men) had deeper roots in other bloody mules. He felt relieved too that
the subject of the conversation had been changed and been shunted to
the guzzler Baloun and to a new tragic event. Vaněk was seized by a
strong desire to say something unpleasant and moralizing to Baloun.
But he was anticipated in this by the occultist cook, Jurajda, who put
down his beloved book, a translation of the old Indian sutras *Pragñâ –
Paramitâ*, and turned to the crushed Baloun, who was bending all the
more under the weight of fate: 'Baloun, you've got to look after yourself and see you don't lose confidence in yourself and your destiny.
You ought not to attribute to yourself what is the merit of others.

Whenever you find yourself faced with a similar problem which you have eaten up, always ask yourself: "In what relation does the liver pâté stand to me?"'

Švejk considered it fitting to round off these reflections with a practical example: 'You yourself, Baloun, recently said that they were going to slaughter and smoke meat at your home, and that as soon as you know the place of your destination and the number of the field post, they are going to send you a piece of ham. Now imagine they sent that ham from the field post to us in the company and we all of us, including the quartermaster sergeant-major, cut off a slice. Let's say we enjoyed it so much that we cut another slice, so that that ham would have incurred the same fate as a postman I knew called Kozel. He had bone decay, so they first cut off his leg under the ankle and then under the knee, and then his thigh, and if he hadn't died in time they'd have cut the whole of him like a broken pencil. And so just imagine, Baloun, that we had wolfed your ham like you did the lieutenant's pâté.'

The giant Baloun looked sadly at all of them.

'It's only thanks to my efforts and my merits,' said the quartermaster sergeant-major to Baloun, 'that you have remained the lieutenant's batman. You were to have been transferred to the medical corps to carry the wounded from the battles. At Dukla our medical corps went out three times for a wounded ensign who got shot in the belly in front of the barbed-wire entanglements, and all of them remained there with their heads shot. Only the fourth pair managed to bring him in, but before they had got him to the first-aid post he'd given up the ghost.'

Baloun could no longer control himself and sobbed loudly.

'Aren't you ashamed?' said Švejk with contempt, 'you, a soldier . . .'

'But I wasn't made for the army,' Baloun lamented. 'It's true I'm a glutton and always unsatisfied, but it's only because I've been torn away from respectable life. We have this in the family. My late papa once wagered in a pub at Protivín that at one go he would eat fifty smoked sausages and two loaves of bread, and he won. Once in a wager I ate four geese and two basins full of dumplings and cabbage. It happened to me at home that after lunch I suddenly felt I'd like to have just a tiny bit more. So I used to go into the larder, cut off a piece of pork, send for a jug of beer and in a minute I'd devoured two kilos of smoked pork. I had at home an old servant, Vomel, and he always warned me not to get so grand, not to stuff myself so full. He remembered how his grandfather told him a long time ago about a gluttonous peasant like that. And how later when there was a war, there was no crop for eight long years, and they used to make bread out of straw and of some odds and ends which were left from the flax seeds; and it was a red-letter day for them when they could crumble a little curd into their milk, when there was no bread. And immediately the famine started that peasant died within a week, because his stomach was not used to such frightful misery . . .'

Baloun raised his anguished face: 'But I believe that even if God punishes people, he doesn't abandon them.'

'God the Father brought gluttons into the world and God the Father will look after them,' observed Švejk. 'You've already been tied up once and now you deserve to be sent to the very front line. When I was the lieutenant's batman he could rely upon me in everything and it never occurred to him that I would have wolfed up anything of his. When something special was issued he always said to me: "You can have it, Švejk," or: "Well, I'm not so keen on it. Give me a bit and do what you like with the rest." And when we were in Prague and he sometimes sent me to a restaurant to get lunch for him, in case he should perhaps think the portion I was bringing him was small because I'd wolfed up half of it on the way, whenever the portion seemed to me to be small I bought an extra one out of my last heller so that he could have enough and not think badly of me. But one day he got to know about it. I always had to bring him the menu from the restaurant and he chose what he wanted from it. And that day he chose stuffed pigeon. And I thought when they gave me only a half that perhaps the lieutenant might think I'd guzzled the other half myself, so I bought an extra portion with my own money and brought such an enormous helping that Lieutenant Šeba, who was trying to find some lunch that day and came to see my lieutenant just before noon, had a good meal out of it as well. And when he'd finished his lunch he said: "Don't tell me that's a single portion. Nowhere in the world would you get on a menu a whole stuffed pigeon. If I manage to get some money today I'll send to that restaurant of yours for some lunch. But tell me honestly, it's a double portion, isn't it?" The lieutenant asked me in his presence to confirm that he had given me money only for one portion, because he had no idea that Lieutenant Šeba was coming. I answered that he had given me money for an ordinary lunch. "So you can see for yourself," said the lieutenant, "this is nothing special. Last time Švejk brought me two whole legs of goose for lunch. Just imagine:

noodle soup, beef with anchovy sauce, two legs of goose, dumplings and cabbage piled up to the ceiling and palatschinken!"'

'Oh, yum-yum-yum-yum!' said Baloun, smacking his lips.

Švejk continued: 'That was the big snag. Of course next day Lieutenant Šeba really did send his batman to that restaurant of ours to get lunch, and he brought him as the main dish only a tiny dab of

chicken pilaf, about as much as a six-week-old baby does in his swaddling clothes, in other words about two spoonfuls. And Lieutenant Šeba accused him of wolfiing up half of it himself. But he said he was innocent. And Lieutenant Šeba socked him across the jaw and held me up as an example. He said that the portions I brought Lieutenant Lukáš were decent ones. And so then the next day that innocent soldier, who'd been socked across the jaw, went to the restaurant where he'd gone to get the lunch and asked a lot of questions. And he told it all to his master who told it in his turn to my lieutenant. One evening I was sitting with my newspaper and reading the news from the battlefield

reported by the enemy's staffs, when my lieutenant came in deadly pale
and went for me at once, telling me to say how many of these double
portions I had paid for in the restaurant, that he knew all about it, that it
was no use my denying it and that he had long known I was a bloody
half-wit but it had never occurred to him that I was a complete lunatic.
I had disgraced him so much, he said, that his one desire was to shoot

first me and then himself. "Sir," I said to him, "when you accepted
me that very first day you said that every batman was a thief and a low
bastard. And when in this restaurant they really gave such small portions of the main dish, you might have thought that I was really one of
those low bastards too and that I'd wolfed it all up . . ."'

'My God in heaven,' whispered Baloun. He bent over Lieutenant
Lukáš's suitcase and took it with him to the back of the van.

'Then Lieutenant Lukáš began to forage about in all his pockets,'
Švejk continued, 'and when that produced nothing he searched in his
waistcoat and gave me his silver watch. He was so moved. "When I

get my pay, Švejk," he said, "write down how much I owe you. Take this watch as well. And next time don't be so silly." And once after that we were both of us in such straits that I had to take the watch to the pawnbroker's . . .'

'What are you doing there in the back, Baloun?' asked Vaněk.

Instead of answering, the unhappy Baloun began to choke. He had in fact opened the suitcase and was stuffing himself with Lieutenant Lukáš's last roll . . .

Another military train went through the station without stopping. It was crammed from top to bottom with the men of the Deutschmeister regiment, who were being sent to the Serbian front. They had not yet recovered from their enthusiasm at parting with Vienna and had been bawling all the way since without pausing for breath:

> 'Prince Eugène, the noble knight,
> Sought to win for his Emperor's might
> The town and fortress of Belgrade.
> And so he ordered a bridge to be built,
> Over which to ride full tilt
> Into the town with his cavalcade.'

A corporal with an aggressively twisted moustache, leaning out and supporting himself with his elbows on the men who swung their legs out of the van, was beating time and bawling lustily:

> 'And when the mighty bridge was done,
> And man and horse and cart and gun
> Could freely pass o'er the Danube stream,
> They pitched their camps by Semlin's gate
> And sealed the Serbian garrison's fate.'

But then he suddenly lost his balance, flew out of the wagon and with the full force of his flight hit his stomach on the points-lever, on which he remained transfixed and hanging, while the train went on and while in the rear vans they were singing another song:

> 'Count Radetsky, noble sword,
> Swore to sweep the savage horde
> Out of treacherous Lombardy.
> But in Verona he tarried long
> Till reinforcements came along.
> Then no braver Count than he . . .'

Spiked on the stupid points-lever, the bellicose corporal was already dead and a young soldier from the station command was soon standing guard over him with fixed bayonet. He took his responsibility very seriously, stood erect at the points and assumed a triumphant expression, as though the spiking of the corporal on the lever had been his own work.

He was a Hungarian and when the men from the train of the march battalion of the 91st regiment came to have a look he bawled in his mother tongue over the whole track: '*Nem szabat!* Not allowed! Military commission, not allowed!'

'He's had his war,' said the good soldier Švejk, who was also among the curious sightseers, 'and he has the advantage that having a bit of iron in his belly, everybody at least knows where he's buried. It's just on the railway line and you don't have to hunt for his grave all over the battlefields.

'He spiked himself very neatly,' said Švejk, walking round the corporal from the other side and observing him with a professional eye. 'His guts are in his trousers.'

'*Nem szabat, nem szabat!*' shouted the young Hungarian soldier. 'The Military Commission of the station. Not allowed!'

Behind Švejk a severe voice could be heard: 'What are you doing here?'

In front of him stood Cadet Biegler. Švejk saluted.

'Humbly report, we're looking at the late lamented, sir.'

'And what kind of agitation are you up to? What's your business here?'

'Humbly report, sir,' Švejk replied with dignified calm, 'I'm not up to a "gitation" of any kind.'

Behind the cadet several soldiers burst out laughing and Vaněk stepped forward and stood in front of him.

'Sir,' he said, 'the lieutenant sent the orderly Švejk here to tell him what had happened. I was just now in the staff carriage and the battalion orderly Matušič is looking for you with orders from the battalion commander. You are to go at once to Captain Ságner.'

Shortly afterwards the signal to embark was sounded and everybody went off to their vans.

As he went off with Švejk, Vaněk said: 'When there are crowds of people about, do for heaven's sake give up your brainwaves, Švejk. It could get you into real hot water. As that corporal belonged to the

Deutschmeisters they might have made out that you were glad about it. That Biegler's a frightful Czech-eater.'

'But I haven't said anything at all,' answered Švejk in a tone which banished all doubt, 'except that the corporal had spiked himself very neatly and his guts were in his trousers. . . . He could have . . .'

'Well, don't let's talk about it any more, Švejk.' And Vaněk spat.

'As a matter of fact it makes no difference,' Švejk observed once more, 'where exactly his guts come out of his belly for His Imperial Majesty. He did his duty all the same. . . . He could have . . .'

'Listen, Švejk,' Vaněk interrupted him, 'look how Battalion Orderly Matušič is rushing towards the staff carriage. I'm surprised he hasn't fallen over on to the track.'

Shortly before that there had been a very sharp exchange between Captain Ságner and the zealous Cadet Biegler.

'I'm surprised, Cadet Biegler,' said Captain Ságner, 'that you didn't come and inform me at once that those fifteen dekas of Hungarian salami were not being issued. I had to go out myself and find out why the men were returning from the stores. And the officers too, as though an order wasn't an order. Surely you heard me say: "To the stores by platoons, company by company." That meant that if we couldn't get anything at the stores then the men were to return to the vans by platoons, company by company. I ordered you, Cadet Biegler, to make sure that discipline was maintained, but you let everything slide. You were only too glad not to have to bother about counting up portions of salami and as I saw from the window you calmly went to have a look at the Deutschmeisters' corporal who'd spiked himself. And when I had you summoned afterwards you had nothing better to do than to drivel with your cadetish ideas about how you went to find out whether by any chance anyone was up to any agitation near that spiked corporal . . .'

'Humbly report, sir, the orderly of the 11th company, Švejk . . .'

'Shut up about Švejk,' shouted Captain Ságner. 'Don't imagine, Cadet Biegler, that you're going to be allowed to intrigue against Lieutenant Lukáš. We sent Švejk there. . . . You're looking at me as if you thought I had my knife into you. . . . Well, yes, I do have my knife into you, Cadet Biegler. . . . If you don't know how to respect your superior officer, if you try to make a fool of him, then I'll make the war so hot for you that you'll never forget Raab station as long as you live, Cadet Biegler. Swanking about your knowledge of theory! . . . Wait till we get to the front ... and I order you on officers' patrol through the barbed-wire entanglements. ... And what about your report? You didn't even submit a report when you came. ... Not even in theory, Cadet Biegler ...'

'Humbly report, sir,[1] instead of fifteen dekas of Hungarian salami the men received two picture postcards each. Here you are, sir ...'

Cadet Biegler handed the battalion commander two of the picture postcards which had been issued by the Office of War Archives in Vienna, where the infantry general, Wojnowich, was in command. On one side there was a caricature of a Russian soldier, a Russian muzhik with a full beard, who was being embraced by a skeleton. Under the caricature was the German text:

'The day when perfidious Russia expires will be a day of salvation for the whole of our Monarchy.'

The other picture postcard came from the German Reich. It was a present from the Germans to the Austro-Hungarian warriors.

On the top there was an inscription: '*Viribus unitis*', and below a picture showing Sir Edward Grey hanging on a gallows. Beneath him were an Austrian and a German soldier saluting gaily.

The poem underneath came from a book by Greinz, *The Iron Fist*, containing jokes against our enemies. The Reich papers wrote that Greinz's verses were like blows with a lash and were full of true unbridled humour and unsurpassable wit.

The text under the gallows in translation was as follows:

GREY

On these gallows, you might say,
Ought to swing Sir Edward Grey.
It's high time that he did so.
At the same time you should know
That no oak would lend its wood
For the hanging of this Jude.
Aspens tremble on the tree.
They're from France as you can see.

Captain Ságner had not yet finished reading these verses of 'unbridled humour and unsurpassable wit' when the battalion orderly Matušič charged into the staff carriage.

He had been sent by Captain Ságner to the telegraph exchange at

1. All conversations between the officers, of course, take place in German. (Author's note.)

the station military command in case by any chance there were any other instructions, and he brought with him a telegram from the brigade. It was unnecessary to have recourse to any key for the ciphers. The telegram read quite simply, unciphered: 'Quickly finish cooking and march to Sokal.' Captain Ságner shook his head thoughtfully.

'Humbly report, sir,' said Matušič, 'the station commander asks if he could speak to you. There's another telegram there.'

There then followed a conversation of a very confidential nature between the station commander and Captain Ságner.

The first telegram had to be delivered when the battalion was at the station in Raab, although its contents were very surprising: 'Quickly finish cooking and march to Sokal.' It was addressed unciphered to the march battalion of the 91st regiment with a copy for the march battalion of the 75th regiment, which was still behind. The signature was correct: 'Brigade Commander, Ritter von Herbert.'

'Strictly confidential, sir,' said the station commander mysteriously. 'Here's a secret telegram from your division. Your brigade commander has gone mad. He's been carried off to Vienna after having dispatched from the brigade several dozen telegrams like that in all directions. In Budapest you'll certainly find another telegram. All his telegrams should of course be cancelled, but we haven't received any instructions to this effect yet. I have, as I say, only the order from the division that unciphered telegrams should be disregarded. I have to deliver them because on that point I have not received any answer from *my* authorities. Through *my* authorities I have made inquiries of Army Corps Command and as a result proceedings are being taken against me . . .

'I'm a regular officer of the old Engineers,' he added. 'I took part in the construction of our strategic railway in Galicia. . . .

'Sir,' he said after a moment, 'for us old rankers it's only the front! Today in the Ministry of War civil engineers from the railways with one-year volunteer examinations are as plentiful as dogs. . . . Well, after all, in a quarter of an hour you've got to go on. . . . I only remember that once in the cadet school in Prague as a cadet of a senior year I helped you on to the horizontal bar. Then we were neither of us allowed out. You fought then with the Germans in the class.[1] Lukáš was there with you too. You used both of you to be the best of friends. When we got the telegram with the list of the officers of the

1. In the German conversation which these two carried on: 'At that time you fought with the German fellow cadets too.' (Author's note.)

march battalion who were passing through the station I remembered perfectly. . . . It's quite a number of years ago. . . . I liked Cadet Lukáš very much then . . .'

The whole conversation made a very painful impression on Captain Ságner. He recognized perfectly well the man who was talking to him and who had led the opposition against 'Austrianism' in the cadet school. Later their preoccupation with their careers knocked all this out of their heads. The most unpleasant thing for him was the mention of Lieutenant Lukáš, who for some reason or other had been always passed over as compared with him.

'Lieutenant Lukáš,' he said emphatically, 'is a very good officer. When is the train leaving?'

The station commander looked at his watch. 'In six minutes' time.'

'I'm going,' said Ságner.

'I thought you'd say something to me, Ságner.'

'All right, then, *nazdar!*'[1] answered Ságner and went out in front of the building of the station command.

When, before the departure of the train, Captain Ságner returned to the staff carriage he found all the officers in their places. They were playing Frische Viere in groups. Only Cadet Biegler was not playing.

He was looking through a heap of unfinished manuscripts about war scenes, because he wanted to make a name for himself not only on the battlefield but also as a literary phenomenom describing the war events. The man with the funny wings and the 'fish tail' wanted to be an outstanding writer on war topics. His literary attempts began with very promising titles, which reflected the militarism of those times, but which were not yet properly worked out, so that on the sheets of paper could only be found the names of the works which were going to emerge:

'The Characters of the Warriors of the Great War. – Who Began the War? – The Policy of Austria-Hungary and the Origin of the World War. – War Notes. – Austria-Hungary and the World War. – Lessons from the War. – Popular Lecture on the Outbreak of the War. – Military Political Reflections. – The Glorious Day of Austria-Hungary. – Slav Imperialism and the World War. – Documents from the War. – Documents for the History of the World War. – A Diary of the World War. – A Daily Survey of the World War. – The First World War. – Our Dynasty in the World War. – Peoples of the Austro-Hungarian

1. Greeting used by Czech patriots.

Monarchy under Arms. – The World Struggle for Power. – My
Experiences in the World War. – The Chronicle of My War Campaign.
– How the Enemies of Austria-Hungary Fight. – Who Will Be the
Victors? – Our Officers and Our Men. – Memorable Acts of My
Soldiers. – From the Times of the Great War. – On the Turmoil of
Battle. – The Book of Austro-Hungarian Heroes. – The Iron Brigade.
– A Collection of My Writings from the Front. – The Heroes of Our
March Battalion. – Handbook for Soldiers in the Field.– Days of
Battles and Days of Victory.– What I Have Seen and Experienced in
the Field. – In the Trenches. – An Officer Relates . . . – Forward with
the Sons of Austria-Hungary! – Enemy Aeroplanes and Our Infantry.
– After the Battle. – Our Artillery. – Faithful Sons of the Fatherland.
– Come All the Devils in the World against Us . . . – Defensive and
Offensive War. – Blood and Iron. – Victory or Death. – Our Heroes
in Captivity.'

When Captain Ságner came up to Cadet Biegler and scrutinized
everything, he asked why he had done this and what was he trying to do.

Cadet Biegler answered with genuine enthusiasm that every title
meant a book which he would write – as many books as there were titles.

'If I should fall in battle I should like a memorial to remain after me,
sir. My model is the German professor, Udo Kraft. He was born in the
year 1870, volunteered for service now in the world war and fell on
22 August 1914 at Anloy. Before his death he published a book: *Self-
Education in Dying for the Emperor*.'[1]

Captain Ságner took Cadet Biegler to the window.

'Show me what else you have, Cadet Biegler. Your activities are of
great interest to me,' Captain Ságner said with irony. 'What's that
notebook you've put under your tunic?'

'That's nothing, sir,' Cadet Biegler replied with a childish blush.
'Please see for yourself.'

The notebook had the following title:

Diagrams of the most outstanding and glorious battles
Of the troops of the Austro-Hungarian army
Compiled according to historical research
By the Imperial and Royal Officer Adolf Biegler.
Furnished with comments and explanations
By the Imperial and Royal Officer Adolf Biegler.

1. Udo Kraft: *Selbsterziehung zum Tod für Kaiser*, C. F. Amelang Publishing
House, Leipzig. (Author's note.)

The diagrams were frightfully simple.

From the Battle of Nördlingen, 6 September 1634, to the Battle of Senta, 11 September 1697, the Battle of Caldiero, 31 October 1805, the Battle of Aspern, 22 May 1809, the Battle of the Nations at Leipzig in 1813, the Battle of St Lucia in May 1848 and the Battle of Trutnov, 27 June 1866, up to the taking of Sarajevo, 19 August 1878.

The diagrams and blueprints of the plans of these battles were all the same. Everywhere Cadet Biegler had drawn rectangles, blank on one side and shaded on the other representing the enemy. On both sides were a left flank, a centre and a right flank. Then behind came the reserves with arrows here and there. The Battle of Nördlingen like the Battle of Sarajevo looked like the positioning of players on the field at a football match at the beginning of the game. The arrows seemed to be indicating in which direction each side was to kick the ball.

This at once struck Captain Ságner who asked: 'Cadet Biegler, do you play football?'

Biegler blushed still more and nervously blinked so that he gave the impression that he was going to cry.

Captain Ságner smilingly turned the pages of the notebook further and stopped at a note on the diagram of the Battle of Trutnov during the Austro-Prussian war.

Cadet Biegler had written: 'The Battle of Trutnov should never have been fought, because the mountainous terrain made the deployment of General Mazzucheli's division impossible. It was threatened by powerful Prussian columns which were stationed on the high ground surrounding the left flank of our division.'

'And so in your view,' said Captain Ságner with a smile, returning the notebook to Cadet Biegler, 'the Battle of Trutnov should only have been fought if Trutnov had been on level ground, you Benedek[1] from Budějovice.

'Cadet Biegler, it's very nice of you during the short time of your stay in the ranks of the army to have tried to probe into strategy, except that in your case it's like little boys playing soldiers and giving each other the titles of generals. You have certainly promoted yourself marvellously quickly. It's charming! Imperial and Royal Officer Adolf Biegler! Before we get to Budapest you'll be a field marshal. The day before yesterday you were still somewhere at home with your papa weighing cow-hides. Imperial and Royal Lieutenant Adolf Biegler! . . . Why, man, you aren't even an officer yet. You're only a cadet. You hang in the air between ensign and N.C.O. You're as far from being able to call yourself an officer as a lance-corporal is when in a pub somewhere he lets himself be called staff sergeant-major.

'Listen, Lukáš,' he said, turning to the lieutenant, 'you have Cadet Biegler in your company. Well, make it hot for the lad. He signs himself "officer". Let him win his spurs in battle. When there's a cannonade and we attack, let the brave lad and his platoon cut the barbed-wire entanglements. By the way, Zykán asked to be remembered to you. He's station commander in Raab.'

Cadet Biegler, perceiving that the conversation with him was over, saluted and, purple in the face, marched through the carriage, until he found himself at the very end in the cross corridor.

Like a sleep-walker he opened the door of the W.C. and looking on

1. General Benedek led the Austrian army during its defeat by the Prussians in 1866.

the German and Hungarian inscriptions: 'The W.C. is only to be used while the train is in motion', began to whimper, sob and finally weep silently. Then he took down his trousers. . . . He strained hard, wiping away his tears. After that he used up his notebook with the title: 'Diagrams of the most outstanding and glorious battles of the troops of the Austro-Hungarian army, compiled by the Imperial and Royal Officer Adolf Biegler'. It disappeared dishonoured into the hole. Falling on the track it fluttered between the rails under the disappearing military train.

Cadet Biegler washed his red eyes in the basin of the lavatory and went out into the corridor. He told himself that he must be strong, bloody strong. His head and stomach had been aching since the morning.

He went past the last compartment where the battalion orderly, Matušič, was playing the Viennese game of 'Schnapsen' (sixty-six) with the batman of the battalion commander Batzer.

He looked into the open door of the compartment and gave a cough. They turned round and went on playing.

'Don't you know what is required of you?' Cadet Biegler asked.

'I couldn't help it,' answered Captain Ságner's batman, Batzer, in his frightful German from Kašperské Hory. 'I ran out of trumps.

'It was required of me to play clubs, high clubs and then at once afterwards my King of Spades. . . . That's what I should have done.'

Cadet Biegler did not say a word more and crawled into his corner. When later Ensign Pleschner came to offer him a drink from his bottle of cognac which he had won at cards, he was surprised to see that he was busily reading Professor Udo Kraft's book: *Self-Education in Dying for the Emperor*.

Before they reached Budapest, Cadet Biegler was so drunk that he leaned out of the window of the carriage and kept shouting out to the deserted countryside: 'On, on, ye brave! In God's name, on!'

After that on the orders of Captain Ságner Matušič dragged him off into the compartment, where he and Batzer laid him down on the bench, and Cadet Biegler had the following dream:

CADET BIEGLER'S DREAM ON THE WAY TO BUDAPEST

He had been awarded the *Signum Laudis* and the Iron Cross, was now a major and was going to inspect a detachment of a brigade which had been assigned to him. He could not understand why he was still

only a major when he had a whole brigade under him. He suspected
that he was to be promoted major-general and that the word 'general'
had got lost somewhere in the rush in the field post.

He had to laugh to himself when he thought how in the train on the
way to the front Captain Ságner had threatened him with having to go
and cut through barbed-wire entanglements. Anyway on his proposal
at the division both Captain Ságner and Lieutenant Lukáš had been
long ago transferred to another regiment, another division and another
army corps.

Someone had also told him how both of them had perished miserably
in a bog somewhere while running away.

When he went by car to the front line to inspect the detachment of
his brigade everything was clear to him. He had in fact been specially
sent from the General Staff of the army.

Soldiers marched past and sang a song which he had read in a collection of Austrian soldiers' songs: 'Our duty'.

> 'Brothers, all your valour show!
> Hold together, crush the foe!
> Let the Emperor's banners fly . . .'

The landscape had the same character as on the pictures in *The
Vienna Illustrated*.

On the right side near a barn, artillery could be seen firing at the
enemy's trenches beside the road along which the car was travelling.
On the left stood a house from which shots were being fired, while the
enemy were trying to break open the door with rifle butts. By the side
of the road an enemy plane was on fire. On the horizon could be seen
cavalry and a burning village, and then the trenches of a march battalion with a small hill, where machine-guns were shooting at the enemy.
Farther on the enemy trenches stretched beside the road. The chauffeur
drove on with him along the road in the direction of the enemy.

He shouted through his speaking-tube to the chauffeur: 'Don't you
know where we're going? That's where the enemy is.'

But the chauffeur answered calmly:

'General, this is the only decent route. The road is in good condition. The tyres would never hold out on those side lanes.'

The nearer they came to the enemy positions the more violent became the fire. Shells blew up the avenue of plum trees over the trenches
on both sides of the road.

But the chauffeur calmly answered through the speaking-tube:
'This is an excellent road, general. We're doing swimmingly. If we turned off through the fields our tyres would burst.

'Look, general,' the chauffeur shouted into the speaking-tube, 'this road is so well built that not even a $30\frac{1}{2}$-centimetre mortar could do anything to us. It's like a threshing-floor, but on those stony roads in the fields our tyres would burst. In any case we can't go back now, general!'

'Bzzz – zumm!' Biegler heard, and the car made a tremendous bound.

'Didn't I tell you, general,' the chauffeur roared into the speaking-tube, 'that it's a devilishly well built road? A thirty-eighter has just exploded in front of us, but there's still no hole. The road's like a threshing-floor. But going over the fields would mean the end of the tyres. Now they're firing at us from a distance of four kilometres.'

'But where are we going?'

'That remains to be seen,' answered the chauffeur. 'As long as the road remains as it is, I take responsibility for everything.'

A bound, an enormous bound and the car stopped.

'General,' cried the chauffeur, 'haven't you got a staff map?'

General Biegler lit his electric torch. He saw that he had a staff map on his knees. But it was a naval map of the Heligoland coast from 1864 in the Austro-Prussian war against Denmark over Schleswig-Holstein.

'There's a cross-road here,' said the chauffeur. 'Both the roads lead to the enemy positions. What I am concerned about is a decent road, so that my tyres don't get ruined, general . . . I'm responsible for the staff car . . .'

Then came an explosion, a deafening explosion and there were stars as big as wheels. The Milky Way was as thick as cream.

Biegler was floating through the universe on the seat beside the chauffeur. The car had been cut in two right in front of the back seat as though by scissors. Only the bellicose, aggressive front part of it remained.

'What good luck that you showed me the map from behind,' said the chauffeur. 'You flew towards me and the other part exploded. It was a forty-twoer. . . . I knew at once that as soon as there was a cross-road the road wouldn't be worth a damn. After the thirty-eighter it could only have been a forty-twoer. Nothing bigger has yet been produced, general.'

'Where are you driving to?'

'We're flying to heaven, general, and must avoid the comets. They're worse than the forty-twoers.'

'Now we've got Mars underneath us,' said the chauffeur after a long silence.

Biegler felt at ease again.

'Do you know the history of the Battle of the Nations at Leipzig?' he asked, 'when Field Marshal Prince Schwarzenberg marched on Liebertkovice on 14 October 1813 and when on 16 October there was the Battle of Lindenau? Do you know the battles of General Merweldt, when the Austrian army was in Wachau and when Leipzig fell on 19 October?'

At that moment the chauffeur said gravely: 'General, we've just reached the gates of heaven. You must get out, sir. We can't drive in through the gates of heaven. There's a great crowd here. They're all soldiers.'

'Just run over some of them,' he shouted at the chauffeur. 'They're sure to get out of our way.'

And leaning out of the car, he shouted out in German: 'Look out, you pack of swine! What idiotic brutes they are! They see a general and won't do "eyes right".'

The chauffeur calmed him down: 'It's difficult, general. Most of them have their heads blown off.'

It was only then that General Biegler noticed that those who were pressing to get in through the gates of heaven were various disabled soldiers who had lost some parts of their bodies in the war and carried them with them in their rucksacks – heads, arms and legs. A righteous artilleryman, who was pressing at the gates of heaven in a torn greatcoat, had his whole belly and lower extremities folded up in his pack. From another pack, which belonged to a righteous Landwehr man, half of his hind quarters which he had lost at Lwów stared out at General Biegler.

'That's for the sake of order,' said the chauffeur again, driving through the dense crowds. 'It's certainly because of the divine super-inspection.'

At the gates of heaven people were allowed in only after giving the countersign, which came to General Biegler at once: 'For God and the Emperor.' The car drove into paradise.

'General,' said an officer-angel with wings, when they went past the barracks of angel-recruits, 'you must report to supreme command.'

They drove on past a parade ground, where it swarmed with angel-recruits learning to shout: 'Alleluia.'

They drove past a group, where a red-haired angel-corporal was just pitching into a clumsy angel-recruit, thumping him in the belly with his fist and roaring at him: 'Open your mug a bit wider, you swine of Bethlehem. Is that how you shout "Alleluia"? Just as though you had a dumpling in your trap! I'd like to know what bloody ox that was that let cattle like you into paradise. Try it once more. . . . Hlahlehuhya? What, you bastard, so you think we're going to let you whine through your nose here in paradise. . . . Try it once again, you bloody cedar of Lebanon, you.'

They drove on and behind them for a long time they heard the frightened caterwauling of the snuffling angel-recruit: 'Hla – hle – hlu – hja', and the bellowing of the corporal angel: 'A – lle – lu – ja, a – lle – lu – ja, you bloody Jordan cow!'

And then there was an enormous glow over a building as big as the
Mariánské barracks in České Budějovice and there were two planes
above, one on the left and the other on the right, and in the middle

between them was drawn an enormous banner with the colossal inscription:

IMPERIAL AND ROYAL HEADQUARTERS
OF THE LORD

General Biegler was taken from the car by two angels in the uniform
of the field gendarmerie. They took him by the collar and led him up
to the first storey of the building.

'Behave yourself in the presence of the Lord,' they said to him, when
he was upstairs in front of a door, and pushed him inside.

In the middle of the room, on the walls of which there hung por-
traits of Franz Joseph and Wilhelm, the heir to the Austrian throne,
Karl Franz Joseph, General Viktor Dankel, the Archduke Friedrich and

the Chief of the General Staff, Konrad von Hötzendorf, stood the Lord.

'Cadet Biegler,' said the Lord with emphasis, 'don't you recognize me? I am your former Captain Ságner from the 11th march company.'

Biegler was struck dumb.

'Cadet Biegler,' said the Lord again, 'who gave you the right to appropriate for yourself the title of major-general? Who gave you the right, Cadet Biegler, to drive in a staff car on the road through the enemy positions?'

'Humbly report . . .'

'Shut your mug, Cadet Biegler, when the Lord speaks to you.'

'Humbly report,' Biegler blurted out once more.

'And so you're not going to keep your mug shut?' the Lord bawled at him. Then he opened the door and shouted: 'Two angels, come here!'

Two angels entered with rifles hung over their left wings. Biegler recognized in them Matušič and Batzer.

And the lips of the Lord pronounced the words: 'Throw him into the rears!'

Cadet Biegler was falling down somewhere. There was a ghastly stench.

Opposite the sleeping Cadet Biegler, Matušič was sitting with Batzer, Captain Ságner's orderly. They were still playing 'sixty-six'.

'The bastard stinks like a codfish,' remarked Batzer, who observed with interest how the sleeping Cadet Biegler was wriggling gingerly. 'He must have done something. . . .'

'That can happen to anybody,' said Matušič philosophically. 'Leave him alone. You're not going to change his clothes anyhow. Go on and deal instead.'

The glow of the lights above Budapest came into view. A searchlight was moving about above the Danube.

Cadet Biegler was already having another dream, because he said in German in his sleep: 'Tell my brave army that they have built in my heart an imperishable monument of love and gratitude.'

Because, as he said this, he began to fidget again, Batzer caught a strong whiff in his nose. Spitting, he observed: 'He stinks like a lat cleaner, like a shitted-up lat cleaner.'

But Cadet Biegler began to wriggle all the more restlessly and his

new dream was exceedingly fantastic. He was defending Linz in the War of the Austrian Succession.

He saw redoubts, entrenchments and palisades around the town. His G.H.Q. had been turned into an enormous hospital. All around there were wounded lying about and holding their bellies. Below the palisades of the town of Linz the French dragoons of Napoleon I were riding by.

And he, the commander of the town, was standing over this havoc and holding himself by the belly too, shouting at a Frenchman who had come to parley: 'Tell your Emperor that I refuse to yield . . .'

And then it was as though his bellyache had suddenly stopped and he was rushing with his battalion over the palisades out of the town on the road to glory and victory. He saw Lieutenant Lukáš being dealt a blow on the chest by a French dragoon's sword. The blow was really meant for him, Biegler, the defender of beleaguered Linz.

Lieutenant Lukáš was dying at his feet and crying out in German:

'A man like you, colonel, is much more use than a completely useless lieutenant!'

Overcome with emotion the defender of Linz turned away from the dying man. At that moment a piece of shrapnel flew at him and hit him in the muscles of his buttocks.

Biegler mechanically reached with his hands to the seat of his trousers and felt something damp. There was something sticky on his fingers. He shrieked: 'Ambulance! Ambulance!' and fell off his horse . . .

Batzer and Matušič lifted Cadet Biegler up from the floor, where he had fallen from the bench, and put him back in his place again.

Then Matušič went to Captain Ságner and told him that queer things were happening to Cadet Biegler.

'It's probably not after the cognac,' he said. 'It's more likely to be cholera. Cadet Biegler drank water at every station. At Mošon I saw that he . . .'

'Cholera doesn't work as quickly as that, Matušič. Tell the doctor in the next compartment to go and have a look at him.'

The battalion had had assigned to it a 'war doctor', the old medico and former German student, Welfer. He knew how to drink and brawl and at the same time had medicine at his fingertips. He had gone through the medical faculties of various university towns in Austria-Hungary and had practised in the most diverse hospitals, but he never took his doctorate for the simple reason that in the will which his uncle left to his heirs it was stipulated that the medical student, Friedrich Welfer, was to be paid a yearly grant until he obtained his doctor's qualifications.

This grant was about four times as much as the salary of a junior doctor in a hospital and Welfer did his honourable best to postpone taking a doctorate till the Greek calends.

The heirs were furious. They declared him an imbecile, and tried to foist wealthy brides on him so as to get rid of him. But to annoy them all the more, Welfer, who was a member of about twelve German student clubs, published in Vienna, Leipzig and Berlin one or two collections of quite decent poems. He contributed to *Simplicissimus* and went on studying as if nothing had happened.

But then came the war, which was a shameful stab in the back for him.

The student of medicine, Friedrich Welfer, the poet and author of the collections, *Laughing Songs*, *Tankard and Learning* and *Fairy Tales and Parables*, was taken off to the war without further ado and one of the inheritors in the Ministry of War saw to it that the valiant medico was awarded a 'war doctorate'. It was done by correspondence. He had to fill out a questionnaire and everywhere wrote down the stereotyped answer in German: 'Kiss my arse!' After three days he was informed by the colonel that he had been awarded the Diploma of Doctor of General Medicine, that he had long ago been ripe for a doctorate, that the chief staff doctor would assign him to the reserve hospital and that rapid advancement would depend upon his conduct. The colonel added that it was true that he had had duels with officers in various university towns and that this was well known, but that now there was a war on and it was all forgotten.

The author of the collection of poems, *Tankard and Learning*, bit his lip and went off to the army.

Certain cases came to light where the doctor had behaved unusually indulgently to soldier patients, prolonging their sojourn in the hospital as long as possible at a time when the mottos were: 'Rather peg out in the trenches than hang about in hospital' and 'Rather peg out in the front line than in hospital.' As a result Welfer was sent with the 11th march battalion to the front.

The regular officers in the battalion looked upon him as an inferior creature. The reserve officers took no notice of him either and did not make friends with him, for fear that the gulf between them and the regular officers should grow wider.

Captain Ságner naturally felt himself frightfully superior to this former student of medicine who, during the long time of his studies, had slashed a number of officers with his sabre. When the 'war doctor' went past him he did not even honour him with a glance but went on talking to Lieutenant Lukáš about something quite unimportant, such as for instance that vegetable marrows were grown around Budapest. Lieutenant Lukáš answered that when he was in his third year as a cadet he went with some friends in mufti to Slovakia and visited an evangelical vicar, a Slovak. He served marrow with the roast pork and afterwards poured them out wine, saying:

> 'Marrow's a swine
> And likes plenty of wine.'

As a result of this Lieutenant Lukáš felt frightfully insulted.[1]

'We shan't see much of Budapest,' said Captain Ságner. 'They're taking us round it. According to the schedule we should stay here two hours.'

'I think they're shunting the vans,' answered Lieutenant Lukáš. 'We're coming on to the transit siding. Military transport station.'

At that moment the 'war doctor' went by.

'It's nothing,' he said with a smile. 'Those gentlemen who aspire in the course of time to become army officers and who already in the officers' club in Bruck boasted their knowledge of history and strategy ought to be warned that it is dangerous to eat at one go a whole consignment of sweets which their mummy has sent them at the front. Cadet Biegler, who, as he has confessed to me, has eaten thirty cream rolls since we left Bruck and has only drunk boiled water everywhere on the stations, captain, reminds me of a verse of Schiller's: ". . . Who speaks of . . ."'

'Listen, doctor,' Captain Ságner interrupted him. 'It's nothing to do with Schiller. What is in fact the matter with Cadet Biegler?'

The 'war doctor' smiled. 'The candidate for officer's rank, *your* Cadet Biegler, has shitted his trousers. . . . It's not cholera, it's not dysentery, it's just a common or garden shitting. He has drunk a little too much cognac, has *your candidate for officer's rank*, and he has

---

1. Captain Ságner's conversation with Lieutenant Lukáš was carried on in Czech. (Author's note.)

shitted his trousers. . . . He would certainly have shitted his trousers even without your cognac. He gorged all the cream rolls which were sent him from home. . . . He's a baby. . . . In the club, as I know for a fact, he always drank one quarter of a litre of wine. A teetotaller.'

Doctor Welfer spat. 'He used to buy Linzertorte.'

'And so it's nothing serious?' asked Captain Ságner, 'but at the same time a case like this. . . . What if it were to spread?'

Lieutenant Lukáš stood up and said to Ságner: 'Thank you for a platoon commander like this . . .'

'I helped him a little bit on to his legs,' said Welfer, whose smile did not leave his lips. 'You, sir, as battalion commander, will decide further action. . . . I mean, I shall send Cadet Biegler to a hospital here. . . . I shall write out a certificate that it's dysentery. A severe case of dysentery. Isolation. . . . Cadet Biegler will go to the disinfection hut . . .

'It's definitely better,' continued Welfer with the same detestable smile. 'You can have either a cadet who has shitted his trousers or a cadet who has contracted dysentery . . .'

Captain Ságner turned to Lukáš and said in a completely official tone: 'Lieutenant, Cadet Biegler of your company has gone down with dysentery and will stay in Budapest for treatment . . .'

Captain Ságner thought that Welfer was laughing frightfully provocatively but when he looked at the 'war doctor' he saw that he had assumed a completely disinterested expression.

'Then everything's in order, sir,' answered Welfer calmly. 'The candidate for officer's . . .'

He made a dismissing gesture with his hand: 'With dysentery everybody shits in his trousers.'

And so it happened that the valiant Cadet Biegler was carried off to the military isolation hospital at Új Buda.

His shitted trousers got lost in the vortex of the world war.

His dreams of great victories were confined in a hospital ward in the isolation huts.

When he learned that he had dysentery he was genuinely delighted.

It was immaterial whether in the course of carrying out his duties for His Imperial Majesty he was wounded or sick.

Then he had a piece of ill luck. As all the places for dysentery cases were full they transferred him to the cholera hut.

They gave him a bath and when they put a thermometer under his arm a Hungarian staff doctor shook his head: '37°!' With cholera the worst symptom is a serious fall in temperature. The patient becomes apathetic.

Cadet Biegler, it was true, betrayed no excitement. He was unusually calm, telling himself over and over again that in any case he was suffering for His Imperial Majesty.

The staff doctor gave instructions to put the thermometer into Cadet Biegler's rectum.

'It's the last stage of cholera,' thought the staff doctor to himself. 'Symptoms of the final collapse, extreme weakness when the patient is losing consciousness of his surroundings and his mind is clouded. He smiles in dying convulsions.'

During these manipulations Cadet Biegler was indeed smiling like a martyr, acting like a hero, when they thrust a thermometer up his rectum. But he did not move.

'Symptoms which in cholera lead gradually to death,' thought the staff doctor to himself. 'A passive state . . .'

He asked the Hungarian medical N.C.O. whether Cadet Biegler had vomited and had diarrhoea in the bath.

Receiving a negative answer he stared at Biegler. With cholera, when diarrhoea and vomiting cease, it is again like the previous symptoms, a replica of the course cholera takes in the last hours before death.

Cadet Biegler felt frozen when he was being carried stark naked from the hot bath to his bed. His teeth started to chatter and he had goose flesh all over his body.

'You see,' said the staff doctor in Hungarian, 'violent ague fit. His extremities are cold. This is the end.'

Leaning over Cadet Biegler he asked him in German: 'Well, how do you feel?'

'Ve-v-v-ery we-e-e-ll-ll,' Biegler said with chattering teeth, '. . . a-a-a b-b-blank-k-ket.'

'Reason partly clouded, partly preserved,' said the Hungarian staff doctor. 'Body much emaciated, lips and nails should be black. . . . This is the third case I've had of people dying of cholera without black nails and lips. . . .'

He leaned over Cadet Biegler again and continued in Hungarian: 'The second response above the heart has ceased . . .'

'A-a-a-a b-b-blan-k-k-ket,' said Cadet Biegler with chattering teeth.

'What he's saying now are his last words,' said the staff doctor in

Hungarian to the medical N.C.O. 'Tomorrow we'll bury him with Major Koch. Now he'll fall into a coma. Have you got his documents in the office?'

'They'll be there,' answered the N.C.O. calmly.

'A-a-a b-b-blank-k-ket,' Cadet Biegler moaned after them with chattering teeth as they were going away.

In the whole ward there were five people in sixteen beds. One of them was a corpse. He had died two hours before, was covered with a sheet and had the same name as the discoverer of the cholera bacillus. He was that Major Koch who according to the staff doctor would be buried tomorrow with Cadet Biegler.

Cadet Biegler got up on his bed and saw for the first time how people died of cholera for His Imperial Majesty, for of the four remaining two were dying. They struggled for breath and turned blue, trying to get something out, but it was not possible to identify what they said or the language they were trying to say it in. It was like the rattle of a gagged voice.

The other two with their conspicuously stormy reactions to their convalescence were reminiscent of people suffering from typhoid delirium. They shrieked unintelligibly and threw their emaciated legs out from underneath the blankets. Over them stood a bearded medical orderly, who spoke Styrian dialect (as Cadet Biegler recognized) and tried to calm them: 'I've had cholera like that, my fine gentlemen, but I didn't kick at my blankets. Now you're all right. You'll get leave when . . .

'Don't fling yourself about so,' he roared at one who kicked at his blanket so that it went over his head. 'It's not allowed here. Be glad you've got a temperature. It means that at least they won't carry you off to the sound of music. You're both high and dry now.'

He looked around.

'Over there another two have died. That's what we expected,' he said good-humouredly. 'Be glad that you're quit of it all. I must go for some sheets.'

Returning after a short time he covered with sheets those who had just died and who had completely black lips, took out their black-nailed hands which in their last agony of suffocation they had held on their erect penises, and tried to put their tongues into their mouths. Then he kneeled by the beds and started praying: 'Holy Mary, Mother of God . . .' And while doing so the old orderly from Styria looked at his recovering patients, whose delirium meant a reaction to new life.

'Holy Mary, Mother of God,' he was repeating, when a naked man suddenly tapped him on the shoulder.

It was Cadet Biegler.

'Listen,' he said, 'I . . . had a bath . . . that's to say, they gave me a bath. . . . I need a blanket . . . I'm cold.'

'This is a special case,' said the staff doctor half an hour later to Cadet Biegler who was resting underneath a blanket: 'You are a reconvalescent, cadet. Tomorrow we shall send you to the reserve hospital at Tarnov. You are a carrier of cholera germs. . . . We have made so much progress that we know all about it. You belong to the 91st regiment . . .

'The 13th march battalion,' answered the medical N.C.O. for Cadet Biegler, '11th company.'

'Write down the following,' said the staff doctor: 'Cadet Biegler, of the 13th march battalion, 11th march company, 91st regiment, to the cholera barracks in Tarnov for observation. A carrier of cholera germs . . .'

And thus it was that from an enthusiastic warrior Cadet Biegler became a carrier of cholera germs.

In Budapest

AT the military station in Budapest Matušič brought Captain Ságner a telegram from headquarters sent by the unfortunate brigadier who had now been transported to a sanatorium. It was unciphered and contained a similar message to the one at the last station: 'Quickly finish cooking and march towards Sokal.' And then followed: 'Incorporate baggage train in Eastern group. Intelligence service abolished. 13th march battalion to build bridge across river Bug. Further details in newspapers.'

Captain Ságner went off at once to the station command. He was received by a small fat officer with a friendly smile.

'He hasn't half been carrying on, that brigadier of yours,' he said, roaring with laughter, 'but we had to send you all that lunacy, because we've got no orders yet from the division to stop delivering his telegrams to the addressees. Yesterday the 14th march battalion of the 75th regiment passed through and the battalion commander got a telegram here that each man should be given six crowns as a special reward for Przemyśl. At the same time he got the order that out of these six crowns every man should deposit in the office here two crowns for the war loan. . . . According to reliable information your brigadier has got paralysis.'

'Sir,' said Captain Ságner, turning to the station commander, 'according to regimental orders and our schedule we're going to Gödöllö. The men have to get fifteen dekas of Emmentaler cheese here. At the last station they should have got fifteen dekas of Hungarian salami, but they didn't get anything.'

'I'm afraid they'll get nothing here either,' the major replied, continuing to smile pleasantly. 'I know nothing about any order of the kind *for the regiments from Bohemia.* Anyhow, that's not my affair. Apply to supply command.'

'When are we leaving, sir?'

'There's a train in front of you with heavy artillery bound for Galicia. We shall send it off in an hour, captain. On the third track there's a hospital train. It's leaving twenty-five minutes after the artillery. On the twelfth track we've a munitions train. That's leaving ten minutes after the hospital train. Twenty minutes after that your train will be going.

'That's to say, if there are no changes,' he added, continuing to smile so that Captain Ságner found him utterly revolting.

'Excuse me, sir,' asked Ságner, 'will you be so good as to explain to me how it comes about that you know nothing of any order of the kind for the issue of fifteen dekas of Emmentaler cheese *for the regiments from Bohemia*?'

'That's secret,' the station commander at Budapest replied, continuing to smile.

'I've made an ass of myself,' thought Captain Ságner to himself, as he left the building of the station command. 'Why the devil did I go and tell Lieutenant Lukáš to collect all the commanders with all the men and go with them to the supply detachment to draw fifteen dekas of Emmentaler cheese per head?'

But before Lieutenant Lukáš could implement Captain Ságner's order and instruct the men of the battalion to proceed to the stores to draw fifteen dekas of Emmentaler cheese per head, Švejk appeared before him together with the luckless Baloun.

Baloun was trembling all over.

'Humbly report, sir,' Švejk said with his usual ease, 'the matter I've come about is extremely important. I would be most grateful, sir, if we could settle *the whole affair somewhere on the side*, as my pal Špatina of Zhoř once said, when he was a witness at a wedding and suddenly in church had to . . .'

'Well, what's the matter, Švejk?' Lieutenant Lukáš broke in. He was already missing Švejk as much as Švejk was missing him. 'Let's go a little further away then.'

Baloun walked behind them and continued to tremble. This giant had completely lost his equilibrium and was swinging his arms in frightful and hopeless despair.

'Well, what is it, Švejk?' asked Lieutenant Lukáš, when they had gone on to the side.

'Humbly report, sir,' said Švejk, 'it's always better to confess to something before it gets out. You gave a certain order, sir, that when we came to Budapest Baloun should bring you your liver pâté and some rolls.'

'Did you get that order or not?' said Švejk, turning to Baloun.

Baloun began to swing his arms about even more violently, as though he wanted to ward off the blows of an attacking enemy.

'This order,' said Švejk, 'could not unfortunately be carried out, sir, because I've eaten up that liver pâté of yours myself ...

'I ate it up,' said Švejk, nudging the horrified Baloun, 'because I thought the liver pâté might go bad. I've read several times in the newspapers how a whole family has been poisoned by liver pâté. Once at Zderaz, once at Beroun, once at Tábor, once at Mladá Boleslav, once at Příbram. All of them succumbed to the poison. Liver pâté is the worst muck ...'

Baloun, trembling all over, stood at the side, put his finger down his throat and vomited at short intervals.

'What's the matter with you, Baloun?'

'I'm sp–sp–ewing, sir ... pewing, sir,' the unfortunate Baloun called out during the intervals. 'I – I ge–ge–guzzled it, ge–ge–guzzled it my–s–s–s–elf.'

Bits of tin foil and pâté came out of the luckless Baloun's mouth.

'As you see, sir,' said Švejk, losing nothing of his composure, 'every bit of the guzzled pâté comes up like oil on the surface of the water. I wanted to take the blame myself, but the bloody fool has gone and given the show away. He's quite a decent chap really, but he guzzles everything that's given to him. I once knew a man like him, who was a bank messenger. They could trust him with thousands of crowns. Once he drew money in another bank and by mistake they gave him a thousand crowns too much and he returned it on the spot. But if they sent him to buy some smoked ham for fifteen kreutzers he guzzled half of it on the way. When it came to food he was so greedy that when the officials sent him to get sausages, he cut them on the way with his pocket knife and stuck the holes together with sticking plaster. The plaster for five sausages cost him more than a whole sausage itself.'

Lieutenant Lukáš sighed and went away.

'Would you like to give me any orders, sir?' Švejk called after him, while the luckless Baloun continued to stick his finger down his throat.

Lieutenant Lukáš dismissed him with a wave of his hand and went off to the supply stores, in the course of which the strange idea came to him that if soldiers ate their officers' liver pâté Austria could not win the war.

Meanwhile Švejk took Baloun away to the other side of the military track and consoled him by saying that they could both go together, have a look at the town and bring back some Debrecen sausages for the lieutenant, since in Švejk's mind the concept of the capital of the Hungarian kingdom was naturally bound up with the concept of a special kind of sausage.

'But the train might go without us,' bleated Baloun, in whom insatiable hunger was combined with extreme stinginess.

'When you go to the front,' said Švejk, 'you're never left behind, because every train which leaves for the front thinks twice before bringing only half a trainful to its destination. But I understand you very well, Baloun. You're an old skinflint.'

But they didn't go anywhere because the signal for getting into the train suddenly sounded. The men of the various companies returned from the supply stores to their vans with empty hands once more. Instead of fifteen dekas of Emmentaler cheese, which should have been issued here, each one of them got a box of matches and a postcard, published by the War Graves Commission in Austria (Vienna XIX/4,

Canisiusgasse). Instead of fifteen dekas of Emmentaler cheese each one found himself with the West Galician warriors' cemetery at Sedlisk, with the memorial to the unfortunate Landwehr men, built by the scrimshanking sculptor, the one-year volunteer Sergeant-Major Scholz.

Outside the staff carriage too there was unusual excitement. The officers of the march battalion were collected around Captain Ságner who was excitedly explaining something to them. He had just returned from the station headquarters and had in his hand a very confidential, genuine telegram from brigade staff, containing a long-winded message of instructions and directives on how to carry on in the new situation in which Austria found itself on 23 May 1915.

Brigade had telegraphed that Italy had declared war on Austria-Hungary.

Already in the officers' club in Bruck an der Leitha there had been a lot of loose talk at lunches and dinners about the queer dealings and goings-on of the Italians but, when all was said and done, nobody expected that the prophetic words of that bloody fool Cadet Biegler would be fulfilled, when once at dinner he pushed away his plate of macaroni and said: 'The time to eat this will be when we are at the gates of Verona.'

After having studied the instructions which he had just obtained from the brigade, Captain Ságner gave the order for the alert to be sounded.

When all the men of the march battalion were assembled, they were drawn up in a square and Captain Ságner in an unusually exalted voice read them the order which he had received by telegram.

'With unexampled treachery and greed the King of Italy has forgotten the fraternal obligations which were binding on him as an ally of our Monarchy. From the outbreak of the war, when he should have stood at the side of our brave armies, the treacherous king played the role of a masked trickster, acting with duplicity and all along maintaining secret contacts with our enemies. This treachery culminated on the night of 22/3 May in his declaration of war on our Monarchy. Our supreme commander is convinced that our ever valiant and glorious armies will answer this contemptible treachery of a faithless enemy with such a blow that the traitor will come to recognize that by starting war against us in this shameless and treacherous fashion he has encompassed his own destruction. We believe firmly that with the help of God the day will soon dawn when the plains of Italy will see once more the victors of Santa Lucia, Vicenza, Novarra and Custozza. We want to win, we must win and win we certainly shall!'

After that came the usual 'Three cheers!', and the army got into the train once more, but in low spirits. Instead of fifteen dekas of Emmentaler cheese they had the war with Italy round their necks.

In the van where Švejk was sitting with Vaněk, Chodounský, Baloun and Jurajda, an interesting conversation began about Italy's entry into the war.

'There was a case like that in Táborská Street in Prague,' began Švejk. 'A shopkeeper called Hořejší lived there. A little way away on the other side of the street a shopkeeper called Pošmourný had his shop and between them both was a greengrocer called Havlasa. Well, the shopkeeper, Hořejší, once had the idea of joining up with the greengrocer, Havlasa, against the other shopkeeper, Pošmourný, and began to negotiate with him for the merger of the two shops under a single sign: "Hořejší and Havlasa". But Havlasa went to Pošmourný and told him that Hořejší was ready to give him twelve hundred crowns for his greengrocer's shop and wanted him to go into partnership with him. But if Pošmourný gave him eighteen hundred, he would rather go into partnership with him against Hořejší. And so they made a bargain and Havlasa was for some time round Hořejší's neck and acting as though he were his best friend, when in fact he was false to him all the time. When it came to the question of when they should go into partnership he always said: "Yes, we'll do that soon. I'm only waiting until the customers' families come back from their summer holidays." And when they came back, everything was really arranged for them to join forces as he had always promised Hořejší. But when Hořejší went down one morning to open his shop he saw over his rival's shop a big inscription, a giant sign: "Pošmourný and Havlasa".'

'We had a case like that with us too,' said the idiotic Baloun. 'I wanted to buy a heifer in the neighbouring village. I had the agreement all tied up but then a butcher from Votice came and snatched it away from me under my very nose.'

'Now that we have a new war again,' Švejk continued, 'now that we have one enemy more, now that we have a new front again, we'll have to be economical with our munitions. "The more children there are in the family, the more the rods are used," as grandpa Chovanec at Motol used to say, when for an all-in sum from the parents he gave all the children in the neighbourhood a good licking.'

'I'm only afraid,' said Baloun, trembling all over, 'that because of Italy the portions will be reduced.'

Vaněk pondered for a moment and said gravely: 'That might very well be the case, because our victory will now take rather longer.'

'Now we need another Radetzky,' said Švejk. 'He knew a thing or two about the Italian countryside: he understood very well where was the weak spot in the Italian defence, what had to be taken by storm and from which side. You see, it's not so hard to get in somewhere. Anyone can do that, but getting out again needs real military skill. When a chap gets in somewhere, he has to know about everything that's going on around him, so as not to find himself in a jam suddenly – what's called a catastrophe. Once at home in the house where I used to live before, they caught a thief in the attic. When he got in the bastard noticed that the builders were just repairing the air-shaft, and so he tore himself away from his pursuers, knocked down the house-portress, and dropped down the ladder into the air-shaft, from which he couldn't get out at all. But there wasn't a single path papa Radetzky didn't know. No one could catch him anywhere. There's a book where it's all written about that general, how he ran away from Santa Lucia, how the Italians ran away too and how he only realized that he had actually won on the second day when he couldn't find any Italians and couldn't see them through his telescope. And so he came back and occupied abandoned Santa Lucia. After that he was promoted marshal.'

'Well, Italy's a fine country, it certainly is!' said Jurajda. 'I was once in Venice and I know the Italian calls everybody a pig. When he gets angry everyone is a *porco maledetto*. For him even the Pope is a *porco*, even *Madonna mia è porco* and *Papa è porco*.'

Vaněk on the other hand spoke very favourably about Italy. At his chemist's shop in Kralupy he also manufactured lemon juice, which he made out of rotten lemons, and he always used to buy the cheapest and rottenest lemons from Italy. Now it would mean the end of the transport of lemons from Italy to Kralupy. There was no doubt that the war with Italy would bring various surprises, because Austria would want to take her revenge.

'It's easy to say "take her revenge",' Švejk said with a smile. 'A chap thinks he's going to take his revenge, but in the end it's the fellow he's chosen as the instrument of his vengeance who pays for it. When I lived years ago at Vinohrady, a house-porter lived on the ground floor and provided board for a petty official in a bank. This official went to a pub in Kramerius Street and had a quarrel there once with a gentleman who had an institute for the analysis of urine at Vinohrady. That gentleman never thought of or spoke of anything else except that institute and all the time carried about with him little test-tubes for urine. These he thrust under people's noses, urging them to make water and have their urine analysed, because the happiness of the man and his family depended on it and it was so cheap that it only cost six crowns. All the guests who came to the pub, as well as the landlord and his wife, had their urine analysed. Only that petty official still resisted, although the gentleman continually followed him to the urinal and when he came out said to him anxiously: "I don't know, Mr Skorkovský, but somehow I'm not very happy about your urine. You'd better make water into the test-tube, before it's too late!" Finally he persuaded him to do so. It cost that petty official six crowns and the gentleman made him suffer for it, as he did all the people in the pub, not excluding the landlord whose business he ruined, because with

every analysis he produced he always enclosed a report which stated
that it was a very serious case, that no one in that state should drink
anything but water; they shouldn't smoke, they shouldn't get married
and they should only eat vegetables. And so that petty official, like all
the rest, got furious with him and chose the house-porter as the instrument of his vengeance, because he knew he was a really nasty customer.
And so one day he told the gentleman who carried out the urine
analyses that the house-porter had not been feeling well for some time
and asked him to go and see him next day at seven o'clock and test his
urine. And so he went there. The house-porter was still sleeping when
the gentleman woke him up and said to him in a friendly way: "My
respects, Mr Málek. I wish you a good morning. Here's a test-tube for
you, please. Be so kind and make water into it and my charge is six
crowns." And what a shindy there was! The house-porter jumped out
of bed in his pants, seized the gentleman by the throat and threw him
at the cupboard so that he inlaid him in it! And when he pulled him
out of the cupboard again he seized a knout, went out as he was in his
pants and chased him down Čelakovská Street with the gentleman
yelling just like when you tread on the tail of a dog. In Havlíček
Avenue the gentleman jumped on to a tram and the house-porter was
caught by a policeman, fought with him and because he was only in his
pants and everything was peeping out, they threw him into the cart for
drunks and carried him off to the police station. When he was in the
cart he went on roaring like a bull: "You bastards, I'll teach you to
analyse my urine." He was in jug for six months for public violence
and for insulting the police. Afterwards when the sentence was pronounced he committed the further offence of insulting the Ruling
House, and it's very likely that he's still in jug today. And this is why I
say that if ever a chap wants to take his revenge on anybody it's always
the innocent party who pays for it.'

Meanwhile Baloun was furiously thinking about something till he
finally asked Vaněk in a panic: 'Excuse me, sergeant-major, please
could you be kind and tell me, do you *really* think that because of this
war with Italy we shall get smaller rations?'

'Yes, it's as clear as daylight,' answered Vaněk.

'Jesus Mary,' shrieked Baloun. He plunged his head into his hands
and sat quietly in the corner.

And this was how the discussion about Italy in the van came to a
final end.

In the staff carriage the discussion about the new war situation created by Italy's entry into the war would certainly have been very dull in the absence of the famous military theorist, Cadet Biegler, if he had not had a substitute in the person of Lieutenant Dub of the 3rd company.

Lieutenant Dub was in civil life a schoolmaster and teacher of Czech, and already at that time manifested an unusual alacrity for expressing his loyalty to the crown on all possible occasions.

For essays he set his pupils themes from the history of the house of Hapsburg. In the lower forms his pupils were frightened by the Emperor Maximilian, who climbed on to a cliff and could not get down, or Joseph II as the ploughman or Ferdinand the Benign. In the higher classes the themes were of course more sophisticated, as for example the exercise for the seventh form: 'Emperor Franz Joseph I, patron of the arts and sciences', which caused a member of the seventh form to be expelled from all secondary schools in the Austro-Hungarian empire for writing that this ruler's most glorious act was the building of the Emperor Franz Joseph I Bridge in Prague.

He always took good care to see that all his pupils sang the Austrian national anthem with great enthusiasm on all royal birthdays and at other similar Imperial ceremonies. In society he was unpopular, because people knew that he was a nark as well, and informed on his colleagues. In the town where he taught he was one of the members of a triumvirate of the biggest idiots and mules, consisting of the district hejtman, the headmaster of the grammar school and himself. In this narrow circle he learnt how to talk politics within the framework of the Austro-Hungarian Empire. Now too he began to reason with the voice and accents of a fossilized schoolmaster:

'All things considered I was not at all surprised at Italy's entry into the war. I expected it already three months ago. It had become obvious that Italy had been growing extremely arrogant latterly as a result of her victorious war with Turkey over Tripoli. In addition she relies too much on her navy and on the mood of the population in our maritime provinces and in the South Tyrol. Why, even before the war I discussed this with our district hejtman and urged that our government shouldn't underestimate the irridentist movement in the south. He said I was quite right, because any sensible man who had the preservation of our empire at heart should have realized long ago where our excessive lenience towards such elements was leading us. I remember well how about two years ago I said in a conversation with the district hejtman that Italy – it was at the time of the Balkan War during the affair of our consul Prochaska – was only waiting for the first opportunity to give us a treacherous stab in the back.

'And now it's come!' he shouted in such tones as though everyone had quarrelled with him, although while he was talking all the regular officers present were only thinking that as far as they were concerned this blithering idiot of a civilian could go to hell.

'It's true,' he continued in milder tones, 'that in most cases in our school essays they forgot our former relations with Italy, and those great days of our glorious victorious armies in 1848 and 1866, which are still mentioned in brigade orders to this day. But I at least always did my duty, and even before the end of the school year, that is to say at the very beginning of the war, I set my pupils the following essay: "Our heroes in Italy from Vicenza to Custozza, or . . .".'

And the idiotic Lieutenant Dub added solemnly in German: '. . . Blood and life for the Hapsburgs! For an Austria inviolate, united and great. . . .'

He paused and obviously expected that the others in the staff carriage would talk about the new situation, and he could show them once more how he had known five years ago that Italy would one day treat her ally like this. But he was completely disappointed, because Captain Ságner, to whom Matušič had brought the evening edition of *Pester Lloyd* from the station, looked into the paper and said: 'Look here, that Weiner girl who we saw in Bruck in a guest performance appeared here yesterday in the Little Theatre.'

And this was how the discussion about Italy ended in the staff carriage . . .

As well as those who sat in the back of the train Matušič and Batzer judged the war with Italy from the purely practical point of view, as once years ago while they were still in regular service they had both taken part in manoeuvres in South Tyrol.

'It'll be an awful sweat having to climb up those mountains,' said Batzer. 'Captain Ságner has a whacking great pile of cases. It's true I come from the mountains, but it's another story when you take a gun under your coat and go and see if you can't pot a hare on Prince Schwarzenberg's estate.'

'That's of course if they cart us down to Italy. I can't say it appeals to me either to go flying over mountains and glaciers carrying orders. And the grub down there! Why, it's only polenta and oil,' said Matušič gloomily.

'And why should they shove us of all people up on to those mountains?' said Batzer, getting angry. 'Our regiment's already been in Serbia and the Carpathians. I've already traipsed about the mountains with the captain's cases. Twice I've lost them; once in Serbia, another time in the Carpathians in some skirmish or other, and maybe now it's coming to me a third time on the Italian frontier. And as for the grub down there . . .' He spat. Moving nearer to Matušič he said to him in a familiar manner: 'You know, at home in Kašperské Hory we make sort of small dumplings out of raw potatoes. We boil them, dip them in egg and roll them well in breadcrumbs. After that we fry them with bacon.' He pronounced the last word in a mysteriously solemn tone.

'But they're best with sauerkraut,' he added in a melancholy voice. 'They can chuck their macaroni down the rears.'

And that was how the conversation about Italy ended here . . .

As the train had already been standing at the station for over two hours, there was only one opinion in the other vans and that was that it was probably going to be re-routed and sent to Italy.

This appeared to be confirmed too by the fact that strange things had been happening with the train in the meantime. Once more all the men were driven out of the vans, sanitary inspectors arrived with the disinfection corps and sprayed all the vans with lysol. This was very badly received, especially in those vans where the army bread was being carried.

However, orders are orders, the sanitary commission had given the order that all the vans of train number 728 had to be disinfected and so the piles of army bread and sacks of rice were quite happily sprayed with lysol. This indicated that something special was afoot.

After that the men were driven into the vans again and driven out again half an hour later because an aged general came to inspect the train. He was so old that Švejk quite naturally thought of a name for him. Standing in the rear line he remarked to Vaněk: 'That old boy's a death-watch.'

Escorted by Captain Ságner the old general proceeded along the line and stopped in front of a young soldier. In order somehow to inspire some enthusiasm in the men he asked him where he came from, how old he was and whether he had a watch. The soldier had in fact got one, but because he thought he might possibly get another from the old gentleman, he said he hadn't, whereupon the old death-watch, giving the same kind of super-idiotic smile which Emperor Franz Joseph used to give when he spoke to a mayor in some town or other, said: 'That's good, that's good,' whereupon he condescended to ask the corporal who was standing next to him whether his lady wife was well.

'Humbly report, sir,' bawled the corporal, 'I'm not married,' whereupon the general with his patronizing smile repeated: 'That's good, that's good.'

Then the general in his senility asked Captain Ságner to show him how the men numbered in twos, and a little later there could be heard: 'One – two, one – two, one – two.'

The old death-watch was delighted with this. He even had at home two lads whom he made line up in front of him and number by themselves: 'One – two, one – two' ...

Austria had masses of generals like that.

When the inspection was successfully over the general did not spare his praise when speaking to Captain Ságner, and the men were allowed to dismiss and move freely about the station area, because the news had come that they would not be leaving for another three hours. And so they wandered up and down and stared about them, because on the station there were quite a lot of people and here and there some of the soldiers cadged a cigarette.

It was evident that the first flush of enthusiasm, which had shown itself in the festive welcome for the trains at the stations, had faded considerably and declined to the point of beggary.

A deputation from the Society for the Reception of Heroes presented itself before Captain Ságner. It consisted of two frightfully jaded ladies, who handed over a gift for the train, in fact twenty boxes of sweet-smelling mouthwash pastilles, which were an advertisement for a Budapest sweet factory. The boxes were beautifully finished in metal. On the lid was painted a Hungarian Honvéd clasping the hand of an Austrian Landstürmer, while over them blazed the crown of St Stephen. Around them was the inscription in German and Hungarian: 'For Emperor, God and Fatherland.'

The sweet factory was so loyal that it gave precedence to the Emperor over the Almighty.

Every box contained eighty pastilles, so that about five pastilles fell to three men. Apart from that the care-worn and jaded ladies brought a huge bundle of printed copies of two prayers written by the Archbishop of Budapest, Géza of Szatmár-Budafal. They were in German and Hungarian and contained the most frightful imprecations on all enemies. They were written with such passion that the only thing missing in them was the trenchant Hungarian expression: '*Baszom a Kristus Máriát!*'[1]

According to the venerable archbishop the merciful Lord ought to cut the Russians, British, Serbs, French and Japanese into mincemeat, and make a paprika goulash out of them. The merciful Lord ought to bathe in the blood of the enemies and murder them all, as the ruthless Herod had done with the Innocents.

His Eminence, the Archbishop of Budapest, used in his prayers such beautiful sentences as for instance: 'God bless your bayonets that they may pierce deeply into your enemies' bellies. May the most just Lord direct the artillery fire on to the heads of the enemy staffs. May merciful God grant that all your enemies choke in their own blood from the wounds which you will deal them!'

That is why it should be repeated once more that the only thing missing in these little prayers was: '*Baszom a Kristus Máriát!*'

When both ladies had presented all this they expressed a desperate wish to be allowed to be present when the gifts were distributed. One of them even had the nerve to mention that she would like on this occasion to address the warriors, whom she referred to as 'our brave men in field grey'.

Both appeared frightfully offended when Captain Ságner turned down their request. For the time being their charitable alms found their

1. 'Fuck Christ and the Virgin Mary!'

way to the vans where the stores were kept. The venerable ladies passed down the line of soldiers and one of them could not resist patting a bearded soldier on the cheek. He was a man called Šimek from Budějovice, and having no idea of the ladies' exalted mission he let fall the following remark to his comrades after their departure: 'The

whores here are pretty fresh, I must say. It might be different if a monkey like that was anything to write home about but she's as scraggy as a stork. She's got nothing to show but her hocks, and looks like God's martyrdom. And an old hag like that has the cheek to try to start something with soldiers like us.'

There was a lot of bustle on the station. The Italian affair had caused some panic, because two trains with artillery had been kept back and sent to Styria. There was also a transport of Bosnians here, who for some unknown reason had already been waiting two days at the station and had been completely forgotten and lost. For two days these Bosnians had not drawn any rations and were going about cadging bread all over Új-Pest. And so you could hear nothing but the agitated voices of the forgotten Bosnians who were gesticulating violently and all the time cursing: '*Jebem ti boga, jebem ti dušu, jebem ti majku.*'[1]

Then the 91st march battalion were made to fall in again and go back to their vans. After a short time however Matušič returned from the station command with the news that they would be leaving in three hours' time. Because of this the men were again let out of the vans. Just before the departure of the train Lieutenant Dub came into the staff carriage in a great state of excitement and asked Captain Ságner to have Švejk clapped in gaol instantly. Lieutenant Dub, well known at his school as an old-established informer, loved getting into conversation with soldiers. In doing so he endeavoured to probe their opinions, seeking at the same time for an opportunity to teach them and explain to them why they were fighting and what they were fighting for.

In the course of his round he caught sight of Švejk behind the station building. He was standing by a lamp and looking with interest at a placard issued by a charity war lottery. The placard showed an Austrian soldier pinning to the wall a wide-eyed bearded Cossack.

Lieutenant Dub tapped Švejk on the shoulder and asked him how he liked the placard.

'Humbly report, sir,' answered Švejk, 'It's bloody silly. I've seen lots of asinine placards but never such tripe as this.'

'What don't you like about it?' asked Lieutenant Dub.

'What I don't like about this placard, sir, is the way that soldier there handles the arms entrusted to him. You know, he could easily break the bayonet on the wall and anyhow the whole thing is quite unnecessary. He would be court-martialled for it, because that Russian has his hands up and is surrendering. He's been taken prisoner and prisoners have to be treated decently, because after all they're human beings too.'

And so after that Lieutenant Dub decided to go on probing Švejk's views and asked him: 'So I suppose you're sorry for that Russian, aren't you?'

'I'm sorry for both of them, sir, for the Russian because he's spiked and for the soldier because he'll be gaoled for it. You know, sir, he certainly must have broken his bayonet in doing it. It's no good. You see it looks like a stone wall where he's thrusting his bayonet, and steel is brittle. Once, sir, before the war when I was in regular service we

---

1. Serbian oaths meaning literally: 'Fuck God, your soul and your mother.'

had a lieutenant in our company. Not even an old sweat of a sergeant-major could use such language as that lieutenant did. On the parade ground he used to say to us: "When it's 'attention', you bloody swine, you've got to roll your eyes like a cat shitting in the straw." But otherwise he was a very decent fellow. Once at Christmas he went mad and bought a whole wagon of coconuts for the company, and it's from that time that I know how brittle bayonets are. Half the company broke their bayonets on those coconuts and our lieutenant-colonel had the whole company clapped into gaol. For three months we weren't allowed out of the barracks and the lieutenant himself got house arrest . . .'

Lieutenant Dub stared in rage at the serene face of the good soldier Švejk and asked him angrily: 'Do you know me?'

'Yes, I know you, sir.'

Lieutenant Dub rolled his eyes and stamped: 'I tell you, you don't know me yet.'

Švejk answered once more with the serene calm of someone making a report: 'I know you, sir, humbly report. You are from our march battalion.'

'You don't know me yet,' Lieutenant Dub shouted again. 'You may perhaps know me from the good side, but wait till you know me from the bad side. I'm nasty. Don't imagine I'm not. I make everyone cry. Very well, then, do you know me or don't you know me?'

'I know you, sir.'

'I tell you for the last time that you don't know me, you mule, you. Have you any brothers?'

'Humbly report, sir, I have one.'

Infuriated at the sight of Švejk's calm unruffled expression, and unable to control himself any longer, Lieutenant Dub shouted out: 'And your brother must certainly be as big a bloody mule as you are. What was he?'

'A schoolmaster, sir. He was in the army too and passed the officers' exam.'

Lieutenant Dub looked at Švejk as though he wanted to run him through with his sabre. Švejk bore his furious look with dignified composure, so that for the moment their whole conversation ended with the word: 'Dismiss!'

Each of them then went his own way and had his own thoughts.

Lieutenant Dub thought he would ask the captain to have Švejk clapped into gaol, and Švejk for his part thought that he had seen many idiotic officers in his time but such a bloody ass as Lieutenant Dub must surely be unique in the regiment.

Lieutenant Dub, who had on this very day resolved that he must educate the men, found a new victim behind the station. There were two soldiers there from the regiment, but from another company, who

were haggling in the dark in broken German with two prostitutes, dozens of whom were roaming about the station.

As Švejk went away he heard clearly from the distance the shrill voice of Lieutenant Dub: 'Do you know me? . . . But I tell you, you don't know me! . . . But wait till you get to know me! . . . You know me perhaps only from the good side! . . . I tell you, wait till you get to know me from the bad side! . . . I'll make you cry, you bloody mules! . . . Have you any brothers? . . . Then they must be as big bloody mules as you! . . . What were they? . . . From the baggage train? . . . Very well then. . . . Remember that you're soldiers. . . . Are you

Czechs? . . . Do you know that Palacký said that if Austria had not existed we would have had to create it. . . . Dismiss! . . .'

Lieutenant Dub's round of inspection did not have an altogether positive result, however. He stopped some three more groups of soldiers and his educational attempts to 'make the men cry' proved a complete fiasco. The quality of the material being taken off to the front was such that Lieutenant Dub could read from the expression of every one of them that they all certainly had a very unpleasant opinion of him. He was stung in his pride and the result was that in the staff carriage before the departure of the train he requested Captain Ságner to have Švejk clapped into gaol. He tried to justify the need to isolate the good soldier Švejk by his extraordinarily arrogant behaviour, characterizing Švejk's honest answer to his last question as 'malicious remarks'. If this sort of thing were allowed to go on the officers' corps would lose all respect in the eyes of the men. Certainly none of the officers could have any doubts about that. Long before the war he had himself talked with the district hejtman about how every officer must endeavour to preserve a certain authority over his subordinates.

The district hejtman had been of the same opinion. Especially now in wartime the nearer one came to the enemy the more the soldiers should be kept in a state of terror. For this reason he asked that Švejk should be given disciplinary punishment.

Captain Ságner as a regular officer hated all these reserve officers from various branches of civilian life and therefore warned Lieutenant Dub that complaints of this nature could only be made in the form of a report and not in the odd fashion of a costermonger haggling about the price of potatoes. As for Švejk himself the first échelon of authority under whose jurisdiction he fell was Lieutenant Lukáš. A matter like this could only be done by report. From company it would go to battalion and the lieutenant was no doubt well aware of this. If Švejk had done something wrong, then he should go on company report, and if he appealed, on battalion report. But if Lieutenant Lukáš had no objections and would accept Lieutenant Dub's statement as an official notification for punishment, he would have nothing against Švejk being summoned and questioned.

Lieutenant Lukáš had no objection to this, but only observed that he knew very well from what Švejk used to tell him that Švejk's brother was in fact a schoolmaster and a reserve officer.

Lieutenant Dub wavered and said that he was asking for punishment only in the broader sense, and it was possible that the man in question, Švejk, could not express himself and that it was only his replies which left an impression of arrogance, malice and lack of respect for his superiors. Moreover, it was clear from the man's whole appearance that his intellect was clouded.

And so the whole storm passed over Švejk's head without his being struck by lightning.

In the van, which combined the functions of both office and battalion stores, the quartermaster sergeant-major of the march battalion, Bautanzel, very condescendingly handed out to two writers from the battalion a handful of mouthwash pastilles from the boxes which were supposed to be distributed to the men. It was common practice that everything destined for the men had to go through battalion office and be subject to similar manipulations.

This was something so normal everywhere in wartime that when after an inspection somewhere the finding was that there was no stealing going on, every one of the quartermaster sergeant-majors in all the offices was none the less under suspicion of having exceeded his budget and of being guilty of other fiddles to put the books straight.

And so here too, when they were all stuffing themselves with these pastilles so as at least not to waste the filth when there was nothing else to filch from the men, Bautanzel spoke about the unhappy conditions during this journey: 'I've already done two march battalions but I've never known such a rotten trip as this. My God, on those earlier journeys, even before we got to Prešov we had masses of everything you could think of. I had salted away ten thousand cigarettes, two whole Emmentaler cheeses and three hundred tins. Later when we marched to the trenches at Bardějov, the Russians who occupied Mušina cut off our communications with Prešov and you should have seen the trade we did! For the sake of appearances I gave up about a tenth of it to the march battalion and said it was the result of economies I had made. The rest I flogged in the baggage train. We had a Major Sojka over us and he was a swine if there ever was one. He was no hero and liked best of all to swan about with us in the baggage train, because up above bullets were whistling and shrapnel bursting. And so he kept on coming to see us on the excuse that he must make sure that the cooking for the men was in order. Usually he came down to see us whenever there was a report that the Russians were preparing something again. He trembled all over and had to drink rum in the kitchen before he could make an inspection of all the field-kitchens. They were grouped around the baggage train, because it wasn't possible to carry the cauldrons up to the trenches and the mess portions were carried up there by night. At that time we were living in such conditions that you couldn't really speak of any officers' mess. The only

road to the base which was still free was occupied by the Germans from the Reich. They'd seized all the best things which were sent to us from the base and guzzled them themselves, so we never got anything. All of us in the baggage train were left without officers' mess portions. During all that time I only succeeded in salting away one pig for ourselves in the office, which we had smoked, and to prevent Major Sojka finding out about it we had it hidden an hour's journey away with the artillery, where I had a friend who was sergeant-major.

'Whenever the major came to see us he always started to taste the soup in the kitchen. It's true there was not much meat to cook, only such pigs or skinny cows as we could scrounge in the neighbourhood. The Prussians made strong competition for us and when requisitioning cattle always paid twice as much as we did. So during the whole time we laid siege to Bardějov, I couldn't salt away on the sale of cattle more than a little over twelve hundred crowns. And into the bargain at that time we didn't give money but mostly vouchers with the battalion stamp on them, particularly later, towards the end, when we knew that the Russians were not far to the east of us in Radvaň and not far to the west in Podolín. It's really an awful job dealing with people like that living in that region who can't read or write and can only sign with three crosses. Of course, Supply Headquarters were in the know, so when we asked them for money I couldn't enclose forged receipts to prove I'd paid them. You can only do that where the people are better educated and know how to sign their names. And on top of all that, as I've already said, the Prussians always outbid us and paid in cash, but when we arrived at a village people looked at us as though we were brigands.

'And then Supply Headquarters issued instructions that receipts signed with crosses would have to be submitted to Field Accountant Control, and there were masses of those accountant bastards loafing around. Usually a bastard like that would come to us, wolf up our food and drink and go and inform against us the next day. That Major Sojka was always walking around our field-kitchens and, God's truth, believe me, he once took out of the cauldron the meat for the whole fourth company, he did. He started with a pig's head, which he said was underdone, and had it cooked for a bit longer. It's true that at that time we weren't cooking very much meat. There were about twelve decent portions of meat of the old size for the whole company, and he ate them all up. Then he tasted the soup and made a row saying that it was just like water and what sort of a state of affairs was this when meat soup hadn't any meat in it? He had the soup thickened and chucked into it my last macaroni, which I'd been saving up for ages. But what annoyed me much more was that in that browned flour there got swallowed up two kilos of finest quality butter which I'd been saving ever since the time when there had still been officers' mess portions. I had it on a shelf over my bunk, and he swore at me asking who it had belonged to. I told him that according to the last order of the division out of the budget for the men's victualling every man was entitled to a bonus of fifteen grammes of butter or twenty-one grammes of lard. And because the stocks of butter were not sufficient they had to be stored until the bonus of butter could be given in its full weight. Major Sojka got into a great rage, started to shout that I was obviously waiting till the Russians came, took away our last two kilos of butter and said it must be put into the soup at once, as there was no meat in it. And so I lost the whole stock and, believe me, that major always brought me bad luck whenever he appeared. He gradually developed such a nose that he knew at once about all my stores.

'Once I had managed to save from the men's rations an ox liver and we were going to stew it when he suddenly went and pulled it out from underneath my bunk. When he started shouting at me I told him that the liver was meant for burying, that in the morning it had been diagnosed and condemned by a blacksmith in the artillery who had gone through a veterinary course. The major took with him one of the men from the baggage train and they cooked the liver in the cauldrons up in the mountains underneath the cliffs. But that was his funeral, because when the Russian artillery saw the fire they shot at the major and his cauldron with an eighteener. Afterwards we went and had a look round, and no one could tell whether it was the ox's liver or the major's that was lying about on those cliffs.'

Later the news came that they would be leaving in about four hours' time. The track leading up to Hatvan had been blocked by trains carrying the wounded. Moreover, the rumour spread round the station that near Eger a hospital train carrying sick and wounded had collided with another train carrying artillery. Relief trains from Budapest were on their way.

Soon the imagination of the whole battalion began to work. People talked of two hundred dead and wounded and said the collision was pre-arranged so that the fiddle with the patients' provisioning shouldn't be discovered.

This provoked sharp criticism of the inadequate catering for the battalion and of thefts in the office and in the stores.

Most people were of the opinion that Quartermaster Sergeant-Major Bautanzel shared fifty-fifty with the officers.

In the staff carriage Captain Ságner announced that according to schedule they should now actually be already at the Galician frontier. At Eger they were due to draw a three days' ration of bread and tins for the men, but Eger was still ten hours away. It was in fact so full of trains with wounded after the offensive at Lwów that according to a telegram there was not a single loaf of army bread or tin left there. He had received orders to pay out 6 crowns 72 hellers per man instead of bread and tins. This was to be issued with their pay in nine days' time, that is to say if they got the money from brigade by that time. There was only a little more than twelve thousand crowns in the till.

'It's a bloody rotten trick of the regiment to send us out into the world in such a wretched state,' said Lieutenant Lukáš.

A whispered colloquy began between Ensign Wolf and Lieutenant Kolář to the effect that Colonel Schröder in the last three weeks had paid sixteen thousand crowns into his account in the Wiener Bank.

Then Lieutenant Kolář explained how economies are made. You filch six thousand crowns from the regiment and put them in your pocket. With inescapable logic you then order all kitchens to deduct three grammes of peas from every man's ration in every kitchen.

In a month that makes ninety grammes per man so that in the kitchen and in every company a store of at least sixteen kilos of peas should have been saved and the cook has to show this.

Lieutenant Kolář talked with Wolf only in general terms about certain cases which he had noticed.

But it was certainly true that the whole military administration was bursting at the seams with cases like this. It started with the quartermaster sergeant-major in some unfortunate company and ended with the hamster in general's epaulettes who was salting something away for himself for a rainy day when the war was over.

War demanded valour even in pilfering.

The controllers of supplies looked at each other affectionately, as if to say: 'We are one body and soul, we steal, old chap, we cheat, brother, but what can you do? It's hard to swim against the tide. If you don't salt it away someone else will, and people will say that the only reason why you've not salted anything away is that you've already salted enough.'

A gentleman with red and gold stripes on his trousers came into the carriage. It was again one of those generals travelling on inspection over all railway routes.

'Sit down, gentlemen,' he nodded affably, pleased that he had again surprised a train which he had not expected to find there.

When Captain Ságner wanted to make a report to him, he only waved his hand. 'Your transport is not in proper order. Your transport is not sleeping. Your transport should already be asleep. When transports stand at a station the men in them have to be asleep at 9 p.m. as in barracks.'

He spoke curtly: 'Before nine o'clock the men have to be taken out to the latrines behind the station. After that they have to go to bed. If not they commit a nuisance on the track during the night. Do you

understand me, captain? Repeat that to me. Or rather, don't repeat it to me. Just do what I ask. Sound the alarm, drive the men to the latrines, sound the retreat and lights out, control who is not sleeping and punish them! Yes. Is that all? Issue supper at six o'clock.'

He was speaking now of something which belonged to the past, something which no longer happened, which was, as it were, round some other corner. He stood there like a phantom from the world of the fourth dimension.

'Issue supper at six o'clock,' he continued, looking at his watch which showed ten minutes past eleven at night. 'At half past eight alarm, latrine shitting, then bed. For supper at six o'clock – goulash with potatoes instead of fifteen dekas of Emmentaler cheese.'

Then he gave the order 'stand to'. Again Captain Ságner had the alarm sounded and the inspecting general, watching the battalion falling in, strolled with the officers and talked to them all the time as though they were idiots and couldn't immediately understand. As he did so he pointed at the hands of his watch: 'Very well, now, look! At half past eight shitting and half an hour later bed. That's quite sufficient. In this time of transition the men have a thin stool anyhow. But I put the main stress on sleep. It fortifies them for further marches. As long as the men are in the train they must rest. If there's not enough space in the vans they must sleep *in shifts*. A third of the men can lie comfortably in the vans and sleep from nine to midnight and the others can stand and look at them. Then the first shift who have slept can give up their places to the next shift who will sleep from midnight to three o'clock in the morning. The third shift sleeps from three to six and then there's reveille and the men wash. No jumping out of the vans when – they're – in – motion! Station patrols along the train so that no one jumps out when – it's – in – motion! If the enemy breaks a soldier's leg . . . ' The general tapped himself on the leg: '. . . that's something praiseworthy, but crippling yourself by uselessly jumping out of a van when the train is in full motion is a penal offence.

'So this is your battalion?' he asked Captain Ságner, looking at the sleepy figures of the men, many of whom could not control themselves and having been whipped out of sleep were yawning in the fresh night air. 'It's a yawning battalion, captain. The men must go to bed at nine.'

The general took up a position in front of the 11th company, where Švejk stood on the left flank and yawned terribly, but while he was doing it he was good-mannered enough to hold his hand before his mouth. But from underneath his hand there resounded such a roar that Lieutenant Lukáš trembled all over in case the general should pay closer attention to it. It struck him that Švejk was yawning on purpose.

And the general, as though he knew it, turned round to Švejk and went up to him: 'Czech or German?'

'Czech, humbly report, sir,' Švejk replied in German.

'Goot,' said the general, who was a Pole and knew a little Czech, although he pronounced it as though it were Polish and used Polish expressions. 'You roars like a cow doess for hiss hay. Shot op! Shot your mog! Dawn't moo! Haf you already been to ze latrines?'

'Humbly report, I haven't, sir.'

'Vy didn't you go and sheet wiz ze ozer mens?'

'Humbly report, sir, Colonel Wachtl always used to tell us on manoeuvres at Písek, when during the rest period the men crept in among the corn, that a soldier mustn't think all the time only about shitting. A soldier must think about fighting. Besides, humbly report, what would we do in those latrines? There would be nothing to squeeze out of us. According to our march schedule we ought to have got supper at several stations, but instead we got nothing at all. It's no good going to the latrines on an empty stomach!'

Švejk, explaining the situation to the general in simple words, looked at him somehow so trustingly that the general sensed a wish on their part that he should help them. If the order was given that they should go to the latrines in march formation, then that order should have some internal build-up.

'Send them all back to the vans,' said the general to Captain Ságner. 'How did it come that they didn't get any supper? All the transports going through this station must get supper. This is a provisioning station. It's not possible otherwise. There is a definite plan.'

The general said this with an assurance which meant that although it was already approaching eleven o'clock at night, supper should have been served at six o'clock, as he had already previously observed, so that there was nothing to be done but to keep the train another night and day until six o'clock in the evening, so that the men could have goulash and potatoes.

'When you are transporting an army in wartime,' he said with enormous gravity, 'there's nothing worse than to forget about its provisioning. It's my duty to find out the truth and to see how it looks in the station commander's office, for you know, gentlemen, sometimes it is the transport commanders themselves who fail in their duties. When I inspected the station of Subotište on the Bosnian southern railway I discovered that six transports had not got supper because the transport commanders had forgotten to ask for it. Six times they cooked goulash and potatoes at the station and no one asked for it. And so they poured it away in masses. Gentlemen, there was a pit full of potatoes and goulash there, and three stations further on the soldiers from the transports which had just gone by those masses and mountains of goulash in Subotište were begging on the station for a piece of bread. In this case, as you see, it was not the fault of the military administration.'

He made an impetuous gesture with his hand: 'The transport commanders were not up to their duties. Let's go into the office.'

They followed him, wondering why it was that all generals went off their heads.

At the station command it turned out that really nothing was known about the goulash. It was true that today meals should have been cooked for all transports passing through, but then the order had come to subtract from the army catering accounts 72 hellers for every soldier, so that every detachment which passed through would have a credit of 72 hellers per man, which they would get paid out by the supply office on the next pay-day. As far as bread was concerned the men would get half a loaf at Watian.

The commander of the provisioning point was not afraid. He told the general straight out that orders changed every hour. It often happened that he had messing prepared for the transports and then an ambulance train would arrive, refer to higher orders and that was the end of it. The transport was then confronted with the problem of empty cauldrons.

The general nodded his head in agreement and observed that conditions were definitely improving and that at the beginning of the war it had been much worse. One could not expect everything to go right all at once. Experience and practice were of course required. In fact theory stood in the way of practice. The longer the war lasted the more things would be put into order.

'I can give you a practical example,' he said with obvious delight that he had hit upon something outstanding. 'Two days ago transports passing through the station of Hatvan got no bread at all, whereas you will be able to draw your rations of it there tomorrow. Let's go now to the station restaurant.'

In the station restaurant the general began to speak again about the latrines and to say how ugly it looked when there were cactuses everywhere on the track. Meanwhile he ate beef steak and all of them imagined that he had a cactus in his mouth.

He laid so much stress on latrines that you would think that the victory of the Monarchy depended on them.

As for the new situation with Italy he asserted that it was in our army's latrines that our undeniable superiority in the Italian campaign lay.

Austria's victory crawled out of her latrines.

To the general everything was so simple. The road to military glory ran according to the recipe: at 6 p.m. the soldiers get goulash and potatoes, at half past eight the troops defecate it in the latrines and at nine they go to bed. In the face of such an army the enemy flees in panic.

The general grew meditative, lit a cigar and looked for a very long time at the ceiling. He was trying to think what else he could say now he was here and how he could further educate the officers of the transport.

'The core of your battalion is sound,' he said suddenly, when everyone was expecting that he would continue to look at the ceiling and say nothing. 'Your complement's in perfect order. That man I was talking to, with his frankness and military bearing, offers the best hope that the whole battalion will fight to the last drop of blood.'

He paused and looked once more at the ceiling, leaning against the back of his chair and continuing in this position, while only Lieutenant Dub, obedient to the slavish instincts of his soul, looked at the ceiling too. 'But your battalion requires that its good deeds should not be buried in oblivion. Your brigade's battalions already have their history and yours must continue with it. But what you need is a man to keep exact records and write up the history of the battalion. All the strands of what every company in the battalion has done must go to him. He must be an intelligent fellow, not a mule or a cow. Captain, you must appoint a battalion historian in your battalion.'

Then he looked at the clock on the wall, the hands of which reminded the whole sleepy company that it was time to go.

The general had his inspection train on the track and asked the gentlemen to accompany him to his sleeping-car.

The station commander sighed. The general had forgotten to pay for his beef steak and bottle of wine, and the commander had to pay for it himself again. Every day there were several visits like this. They had already cost him two wagons of hay which he had had to shunt on to a side line and sell to the firm of Löwenstein, the army corn suppliers, as standing corn is sold. The army had bought these two wagons back again and he had left them standing there for all eventualities. Perhaps he would sometime have to sell them back to the firm of Löwenstein again.

But all the army inspectors who passed through this main station of Budapest used to tell each other that the station commander there always had good food and drink.

In the morning the transport was still standing at the station, the reveille was sounded and the soldiers washed out of their mess-tins at the pump. The general and his train had not yet left and he went personally to inspect the latrines, where according to Captain Ságner's order of the day to the battalion the men went 'by sections under the command of the section commanders' to give the major-general pleasure. To give Lieutenant Dub some pleasure too, Captain Ságner informed him that he would be the inspecting officer that day.

And so Lieutenant Dub supervised the latrines.

The extensive long latrines with their two rows accommodated two sections of one company. So now the soldiers sat neatly on their haunches, one beside the other over the dug-up pits, like swallows on telephone wires when they prepare for their autumn flight to Africa.

Every one of them had his trousers down and his knees showing, every one had his belt round his neck as though he was going to hang himself any moment and was just waiting for the order.

The whole procedure was manifestly characterized by iron military discipline and efficient organization.

On the left flank sat Švejk, who had got there by mistake and was reading with interest a scrap of paper torn from some novel or other by Růžena Jesenská:

> . . . ensive finishing school, young ladies unfortunately . . .
> . . . ontent not quite certain, but perhaps more rea . . .
> who were mostly reticent, and uncommunicative, lo . . .
> . . . rved lunch in their apartments, or perhaps would ha . . .
> devoted themselves to those doubtful delights. And if . . .
> . . . ed a man and only grief and sorrow for her hon . . .
> . . . ently she was getting better, but she did not want . . .
> as they themselves would have wished. Successfully
> . . . othing was more welcome to young Křička than . . .

When he managed to tear his eyes away from the scrap of paper he looked involuntarily at the exit from the latrines and was astounded. There stood the major-general of the night before in his full glory. He was accompanied by his adjutant and beside them stood Lieutenant Dub who was eagerly explaining something to them.

Švejk looked around him. All the men went on sitting calmly over the latrines and only the N.C.O.s were somehow rigid and motionless.

Švejk sensed the gravity of the situation.

He jumped up just as he was, with his trousers down and belt round his neck, and, having used the scrap of paper in the very last moment, he roared out: 'Halt! Up! Attention! Eyes right!' and saluted. Two sections with their trousers down and their belts round their necks rose over the latrines.

The major-general smiled affably and said: 'At ease! Carry on!' Lance-Corporal Málek was the first to give an example to his section and resume his original posture. Only Švejk continued to stand and salute, because from one side he was being approached menacingly by Lieutenant Dub and from the other by the major-general with his smile.

'I seess you last night,' the major-general said on observing Švejk's strange posture; whereupon the infuriated Lieutenant Dub turned to the major-general and said in German: 'Humbly report, sir, the fellow is feeble-minded and a well-known idiot. He is an unparalleled imbecile.'

'What are you saying, lieutenant?' the major-general roared suddenly at Lieutenant Dub and let fly at him, saying that the very opposite was true. It was a case of a man who knew his duties when he saw his superior officer, and of an officer who did not see him and ignored him. It was just like in the field. The ordinary soldier assumes command in time of danger. And it was Lieutenant Dub himself who should have given the order that soldier gave: 'Halt! Up! Attention! Eyes right!'

'Haf you viped your arsch?' the major-general asked Švejk.

'Humbly report, sir, everything is in order.'

'Von't you sheet no more?'

'Humbly report, sir, I've finished.'

'Vell, now pull your hoses op and shtand at attention again!' Because the major-general pronounced the word 'attention' rather louder, the men who were nearest started getting up over the latrine.

The major-general waved to them affably and said in a gentle, fatherly voice: 'No, no! At eess! At eess! Jost go on!'

Švejk in his full splendour was already standing in front of the major-general, who delivered a short address to him in German: 'Respect for superiors, knowledge of service regulations and presence of mind mean everything in wartime. And if added to that we have courage, there is no enemy we need fear.' Turning to Lieutenant Dub, he prodded Švejk's belly with his finger and said: 'Make a note of this: when you get to the front this man must be promoted at once and at the next opportunity his name should be put forward for the

Bronze Medal for meticulous execution of duties and perfect know-ledge of. . . . But you know what I mean. . . . Dismiss!'

The major-general went away from the latrines, while Lieutenant Dub gave orders in a loud voice so that the major-general could hear: 'First section up! Form fours! . . . Second section . . .'

Meanwhile Švejk went away and when he passed Lieutenant Dub he saluted as was right and proper, but Lieutenant Dub said all the same, 'As you were!' and Švejk had to salute again and hear once more: 'Do you know me? You don't know me! You know me from my good side, but wait till you get to know me from my bad side! I'll make you cry!'

At last Švejk went off to his van thinking: 'Once when we were still in the barracks in Karlín there was a lieutenant called Chudavý and he used to say something quite different when he got angry: "Lads, when you see me, always remember that I am a swine to you and I'll go on being a swine to you as long as you stay in the company." '

When Švejk passed the staff carriage, Lieutenant Lukáš called to

him to tell Baloun to hurry up with the coffee and close the tin of milk properly again so that it wouldn't go bad. Baloun was making coffee for Lieutenant Lukáš on a small spirit stove in Vaněk's van. When Švejk walked up to pass the message on he realized that while he had been away the whole van had been drinking coffee.

Lieutenant Lukáš's tins of coffee and milk were already half empty and Baloun who was sipping coffee from his cup dug about with his spoon in the tinned milk to make the coffee better.

Jurajda and Vaněk both promised that when the next supply of tinned coffee and milk came they would make it up to Lieutenant Lukáš.

Švejk was also offered coffee but declined it saying to Baloun: 'An order has just come from army staff that every batman who embezzles his officer's tinned milk and coffee will be hanged without delay within the next twenty-four hours. I have to convey this to you from the lieutenant who wants to see you immediately with the coffee.'

The panic-stricken Baloun tore out of the hands of Chodounský the portion of coffee which he had just poured for him a moment ago, put it on the stove to be heated up a little more, added some tinned milk and rushed off with it to the staff carriage.

With goggling eyes he served the coffee to Lieutenant Lukáš. As he did so the thought went through his head that Lieutenant Lukáš must be able to read in his eyes how he had treated his tins.

'I was held up,' he stammered, 'because I couldn't open them.'

'I suppose you've gone and spilt the tinned milk, haven't you,' asked Lieutenant Lukáš, drinking his coffee, 'or you've gorged it on a spoon like soup? Do you know what you're in for?'

Baloun sighed and moaned: 'Humbly report, I have three children, sir.'

'You'd better look out, Baloun. I must warn you once again about your voracity. Hasn't Švejk said anything to you?'

'He said I could be hanged in the next twenty-four hours,' Baloun answered in mournful tones, trembling in every limb.

'Don't quake in front of me here, you idiot,' Lieutenant Lukáš said with a smile, 'but try to reform. Put your greediness out of your head and tell Švejk to look around in the station or in the neighbourhood for something good to eat. Give him these ten guilders here. I shan't send you. You'll only go when you're crammed full to bursting point. Didn't you eat up my tin of sardines? You say you didn't? Then bring it here and show it to me!'

Baloun told Švejk that the lieutenant had sent him twenty crowns to find something good to eat on the station. Then with a sigh he took out of the lieutenant's case the tin of sardines and in low spirits carried it to the lieutenant for inspection.

The poor fool had been happily hoping that Lieutenant Lukáš might have already forgotten about the sardines, but now that dream was over. The lieutenant would probably keep them in his carriage and deprive him of them. He felt as if he had been robbed.

'Humbly report, sir, here are your sardines,' he said bitterly as he gave them to their owner. 'Should I open them?'

'All right, Baloun, don't open anything but take them back to where they belong. I only wanted to be sure that you hadn't looked at them. You see, I thought that when you brought me my coffee you had a greasy mouth. Has Švejk already gone?'

'Humbly report, sir, he has,' said Baloun, cheering up. 'He said that you would be satisfied, sir, and that everybody would be envious of you, sir. He went somewhere outside the station and said that he knew the whole countryside here as far as Rákospalota. If by any chance the train should go off without him he would get himself on to a motor column and catch us up by car at the next station. We shouldn't worry about him, he knew what was his duty, even if it meant taking a fiacre at his own expense and driving after the train to Galicia. The money could be deducted from his pay afterwards. You definitely don't need to have any worry about him, sir.'

'Go away,' said Lieutenant Lukáš sadly.

They brought the news from the office of the command that they would be leaving by 2 p.m. via Gödöllö–Aszód and that at the various stations they would draw two litres of red wine and a bottle of cognac for the officers. They said it was a stray consignment intended for the Red Cross. Whatever it may have been it was a gift from heaven and there was joy in the staff carriage. The cognac had three stars and the wine was Gumpoldskirchen.

Only Lieutenant Lukáš was rather uneasy all the time. An hour had already passed and Švejk had still not come. Half an hour later a strange procession emerged from the office of the station command and approached the staff carriage.

At the head walked Švejk, grave and sublime, like one of the early Christian martyrs being dragged into the arena.

On each side of him marched a Hungarian Honvéd with fixed bayonet. On the left flank was a sergeant from the station command and behind them a woman in a red skirt with accordion pleats and a man in boots with a round hat and a black eye. He carried a live hen which was squawking in a terrified way.

They were all getting into the staff carriage, but the sergeant bawled in Hungarian at the man with the hen and the woman to stay where they were.

Seeing Lieutenant Lukáš, Švejk started winking at him very significantly.

The sergeant wanted to speak with the commander of the 11th

march company. Lieutenant Lukáš took from him a document from the station commander. He read it and turned pale:

To the commander of the 11th march company of the Nth march battalion of the 91st infantry regiment for further action.

This is to present infantryman Švejk, Josef, according to his own statement the orderly of the same march company of the Nth march battalion of the

91st infantry regiment, accused of the crime of larceny, committed against the married couple István in Isatarcsa in the region of the station command.

Grounds: Infantryman Švejk, Josef, having taken possession of a hen which was running behind the house of the married couple István in Isatarcsa in the region of the station command and belonging to the married couple István [in the original was a gloriously formed new German word: 'Istvángatten'], and having been stopped by the owner, who tried to take the hen away from him, obstructed the owner of the hen, István, in this and hit him across the right eye. He was detained by the patrol, which had been called, and was marched off to his detachment, the hen being at the same time returned to the owner.

Signature of the duty officer.

When Lieutenant Lukáš signed the receipt for Švejk his knees shook under him.

Švejk stood so close that he could see that Lieutenant Lukáš had forgotten to write in the date.

'Humbly report, sir,' Švejk put in, 'today is the twenty-fourth. Yesterday was 23 May, the day Italy declared war on us. While I've been in the country, people have been talking about nothing else.'

The Honvéds went away with the sergeant and there remained below only the István couple who still wanted to get into the carriage.

'If you happened to have another five guilders on you, we could buy that hen. The rogue wants fifteen guilders for it, but he's adding another ten for his black eye,' said Švejk in his narrative style. 'But I think, sir, that ten guilders for an idiotic eye like that is pretty steep. At The Old Lady they broke turner Matěj's whole jaw and six teeth with a brick for twenty guilders, and at that time money had much greater value than it has today. Why, even the public executioner, Wohlschläger, charges only four guilders for hanging people.

'Come here,' Švejk motioned the man with the black eye and the hen, 'and you, you old hag, keep where you are!'

The man got into the carriage. 'He knows a little German,' observed Švejk, 'understands all the swear words and can himself swear pretty well in German.

'Very well then, ten guilders,' he said to the man in a mixture of German and Hungarian, 'five guilders hen, five eye. Five florins, you see, cockadoodledoo, five florins peep peep, yes? This is the staff carriage, you thief. Give me the hen!'

He thrust ten guilders into the surprised man's hand, took the hen from him, wrung its neck, and then pushed him out of the carriage, giving him a friendly and very forceful handshake: 'Cheerio, you old bastard, bye bye! Now get back to your old frump before I knock you down.

'And so, sir, you see that everything can be settled peacefully,' said Švejk to Lieutenant Lukáš. 'It's always best if everything passes off without a scene and a lot of fuss. Now Baloun and I are going to cook you such a wonderful chicken soup that you'll smell it all the way to Transylvania.'

Lieutenant Lukáš could no longer control himself and knocked the wretched hen out of Švejk's hand. Then he shouted: 'Do you know,

Švejk, what a soldier deserves who in wartime robs the peaceful population?'

'Honourable death by powder and lead, sir,' Švejk answered solemnly.

'It's the rope you deserve, of course, Švejk, because it was you who

first started to plunder. You scoundrel, you're a ... I really don't know what to call you. You've forgotten your oath. You give me a sick headache.'

Švejk looked at Lieutenant Lukáš with an inquiring glance and quickly replied: 'Humbly report, I've not forgotten the oath which our warrior people have to take. Humbly report, sir, I swore solemnly to my most illustrious prince and lord, Franz Joseph I, that I would faithfully and obediently serve him and also His Imperial Majesty's generals and indeed all my superior officers. I swore to honour them and protect them and to carry out all their orders and instructions in all services against any enemy whoever it might be and wherever the will of His

Imperial and Royal Majesty should demand it, on the sea, under the sea, on land, in the air, by night and day, in battles, in assaults, in fights and in all other enterprises and in all places whatsoever.'

Švejk picked the hen up off the ground and went on, standing at attention and looking straight into the eyes of Lieutenant Lukáš. 'I swore to fight valiantly and manfully every hour and on every occasion, never to abandon my army, my banners, my flags or my guns, never to enter into parley with the enemy, always to conduct myself as the army laws demand and as befits a good soldier, that I may live and die with honour, so help me God, Amen. And, humbly report, I didn't steal that hen, I didn't commit robbery. I behaved correctly in full knowledge of my oath.'

'Will you drop that hen, you mule,' Lieutenant Lukáš roared at him, taking the papers and hitting the hand in which Švejk held the late lamented hen. 'Look at these documents. Do you see it here in black and white? "This is to present infantryman Švejk, Josef, according to his own statement the orderly of the same march company . . . for the crime of larceny . . ." Now tell me, you brigand, you hyena – no, I'm going to murder you one day after all, *murder* you, do you understand? – tell me, you thieving blockhead, how could you have stooped so low as this.'

'Humbly report,' said Švejk affably, 'it definitely must be a question of a little mistake here. When I got your order to scrounge something good to eat somewhere and buy it for you, I began to wonder what could be the best for you. Behind the station there was absolutely nothing, only salami made of horsemeat and some dried donkey's meat. Humbly report, sir, I thought it all over very carefully. In the field something very nutritious is needed so that one can withstand the war strains better. So I wanted to give you a *grandiloquent* pleasure. I wanted to make chicken soup for you, sir.'

'Chicken soup,' the lieutenant repeated after him, grasping his head with his hands.

'Yes, humbly report, sir, chicken soup. I've bought some onions and five dekas of noodles. Here it all is, sir. In this pocket I've got the onions and in the other the noodles. We've got salt in the office and pepper as well. Nothing else was needed but to buy a hen. And so I went behind the station to Isatarcsa. It's actually a village, not like a town at all, in spite of it being written in the first street Isatarcsa *town*. I went through one street with gardens, then a second, a third, a fourth, a fifth, a sixth, a seventh, an eighth, a ninth, a tenth, an eleventh until finally in the thirteenth street at the very end, behind a house where the meadows begin, a flock of hens was walking about and feeding. I went and picked out the biggest and heaviest one. Please look at it, sir, it's pure fat. You don't need to feel it. You can see at one glance that they must have stuffed it with grain. And so I took it quite openly in the presence of the population, who shouted something at me in Hungarian. I held the hen by the legs and asked one or two people in Czech and German who the hen belonged to, so that I could buy it from them, when suddenly a man and a woman rushed out of that house at the end and the man began swearing at me first in Hungarian and then in German, saying I had robbed him of a hen in broad daylight. I told him not to shout at me, as I'd been sent to buy it for you, and I explained to him what the situation was. And while I was holding that hen by the legs, it suddenly began to flap its wings and wanted to fly away, and as I was only holding it quite lightly it knocked my hand up and tried to sit on its master's nose. And he at once began shouting that I'd given him one across the jaw with the hen. And then that woman started shrieking something and continued to screech at the hen: "Puta, puta, puta, puta." And at that very moment some silly fools who didn't understand what was happening called the patrol on me, the Honvéds, and I asked them to go with me to the station command so that my innocence would come to the surface like oil on the water. But it was quite impossible to talk to that lieutenant who was on duty there, even when I'd asked him to make inquiries of you whether it was true or not that you'd sent me to buy something good. He started shouting at me that I should shut my mug, and that as it was he could see in my eyes a strong branch with a stout cord hanging from it. He was obviously in a very bad temper, when he told me that a soldier who was as well fed as I was must obviously steal and rob. He said that there had been lots of complaints at the station. The day before yesterday, he said, someone had lost a turkey somewhere round about, and when I said to him that at that time we were still in Raab he said that an excuse like that wouldn't hold water with him. And so they sent me to you and on top of that a corporal I hadn't noticed bawled at me and asked me whether I'd realized who I was talking to. I told him that he was a corporal and that if he'd been in the Rifles he'd have been patrol commander and if he'd been in the artillery he'd have been a senior gunner.'

'Švejk,' said Lieutenant Lukáš after a moment, 'you've already had so many peculiar incidents and accidents, so many little "mistakes" and "errors" as you call them, that the only release for you from all your misadventures would be a stout piece of rope round your neck and full military honours in square formation. Do you understand?'

'Yes, humbly report, sir, a square out of a so-called closed battalion consists of four, exceptionally three or five, companies. Is it your order, sir, that I should put more noodles into the soup from this chicken and make it thicker?'

'Švejk, my orders are that you and your hen are to clear out or I'll knock you on the head with it, you bloody idiot . . .'

'As you order, sir, but humbly report I couldn't find any celery or carrots either! I'll put pota . . .'

Švejk did not have time to say 'toes' but flew out of the staff carriage together with his hen. Lieutenant Lukáš drank a wineglass of cognac in one gulp.

Švejk saluted outside the windows of the carriage and departed.

After a happily concluded struggle with his conscience Baloun was just about to open the tin of sardines belonging to his lieutenant when Švejk appeared with the hen. This naturally caused a flutter among all those present in the wagon, and all looked at it as though they wanted to ask the obvious question: 'Where did you pinch it?'

'Bought it for the lieutenant,' answered Švejk, taking the onions and noodles out of his pockets. 'I wanted to make him a soup out of it, but he doesn't want it and has given it to me instead.'

'Didn't it peg out of natural causes?' asked the quartermaster sergeant-major suspiciously.

'No, I wrung its neck myself,' answered Švejk, taking a knife from his pocket.

Baloun looked at Švejk with an expression of gratitude mingled with respect and began silently to prepare the lieutenant's spirit stove. Then he took some cups and went off to get some water.

Chodounský came up to Švejk and offered to help him pluck the hen, whispering in his ear confidentially: 'Is it far away from here? Do you have to climb over into a yard or is it out in the open?'

'But I bought it.'

'Oh, shut up, be a good sport. We saw how they took you away under escort.'

He helped enthusiastically with the plucking of the hen none the less. In the great and glorious preparations he was joined by Jurajda, who sliced the potatoes and onions for the soup.

The feathers thrown out of the van attracted the attention of Lieutenant Dub, who was on his round of inspection of the vans.

He shouted inside that whoever was plucking a hen should present himself and in the door appeared the happy face of Švejk.

'What's this?' Lieutenant Dub shouted, picking up from the ground the head of the decapitated hen.

'Humbly report,' answered Švejk, 'it's the head of a hen of the breed called Black Leghorns. They lay very well, sir, as much as 260 eggs a year. Would you please kindly look what a rich ovary it has.' Švejk held the hen's bowels and other intestines under Lieutenant Dub's nose.

Dub spat, went away and returned after a while.

'Who is that hen for?'

'Humbly report, it's for us, sir. Just look how much fat it has.'

Lieutenant Dub went away murmuring to himself: 'I will see thee at Philippi.'

'What did he say to you?' Jurajda asked Švejk.

'We've only arranged a meeting somewhere at "Philips". These smart gentlemen are generally queers.'

The occultist cook asserted that only aesthetes were homosexuals. It derived from the very nature of aestheticism.

Vaněk then told how pedagogues in Spanish monasteries violate children.

While the water in the cauldron on the stove began to boil Švejk mentioned how they had once entrusted a whole colony of orphaned Viennese children to a tutor and how he had violated every one of them.

'It can't be helped. It's a passion, you see. But it's worst of all when women get it. Some years ago in Prague II there were two abandoned women, divorced because they were whores. They were called Mourková and Šousková and one evening when the cherries were blooming in the alley at Roztoky they got hold of a hundred-year-old impotent organ-grinder, dragged him to a wood at Roztoky and violated him there. And there's nothing they didn't do to him! In Žižkov there is a Professor Axamit and he used to dig there, searching for the barrows of people in crouch burial, and he really dug out a few. And those ladies dragged that old organ-grinder to one of those barrows, violated him there and really wore him out. And Professor Axamit came the next day and when he saw something lying in the barrow he jumped for joy, but it was only the organ-grinder who had been tortured and martyred by those divorced ladies. Around him there was nothing else but pieces of wood. And five days afterwards the organ-grinder died and those Jezabels had the cheek to go to his funeral. That's perversion if you like.

'Have you put any salt in it?' Švejk asked, turning to Baloun, who had taken advantage of the general interest in Švejk's story to filch something and put it into his rucksack. 'Show me what you're doing there.

'Baloun,' said Švejk solemnly, 'what do you want with that chicken leg? Now look at him, the bastard. He's pinched that chicken leg from us so as to cook it himself secretly afterwards. Do you know, Baloun, what you've done? Do you know what the punishment is in war when someone robs his fellow comrades in the field? He's bound to the barrel of a gun and shot into the air with a shell. Now it's too late to sigh. When we meet the artillery somewhere at the front you'll report to the nearest chief gunner. Meanwhile you'll do some punishment drill. Get out of the van!'

The unhappy Baloun got out and Švejk sat at the door of the van and commanded: 'Attention! Easy! Attention! Eyes right! Attention! Eyes front again! Easy!

'Now you will stand and do unarmed drill. Right turn! Man! You're a cow! Your horns should be where your right shoulder was before. As you were! Right turn! Left turn! Right incline! Not like that, you ox! As you were! Right incline! Now, you see, you mule, that you can do it. Left incline! Left turn! To the left! To the front! Front, you bloody fool! Don't you know what's your front? Forward march! About turn! Kneel! Down! Sit! Up! Sit! Down! Up! Down! Up! Sit! Up! Easy!

'Now you see, Baloun, it's good for your health, as well as for your digestion.'

Crowds began to collect around them and broke into cheers.

'Be good enough to make way,' shouted Švejk. 'He's going to march. Now, Baloun, pay attention, so I don't have to say "As you were!" I hate bothering soldiers unnecessarily. Now:

'Direction – railway station! Look where I'm pointing. Forward march! Section, halt! Halt, for the love of Christ or I'll have you put in jug! Section, halt! At last you've stopped, you bloody fool. Shorten step! Don't you know what "shorten step" means? I'll teach you till you're blue in the face! Full step! Change step! Mark time! You elephant, you! When I say "Mark time!", then you must move your shanks up and down on the spot.'

Now there were already at least two companies gathered there.

Baloun sweated and had no idea what was happening to him, but Švejk went on giving orders:

'In step! Section, to the rear, march! Section, halt! Double! Section, quick march! Slow march! Section, halt! Easy! Attention! Direction – railway station, double march! Halt! About turn! Direction van! Double march! Shorten step! Section, halt! Easy! Now you can rest for a moment! And then we'll start again. Where there's a will there's a way.'

'What's happening here?' It was the voice of Lieutenant Dub who had come running up in alarm.

'Humbly report, sir,' said Švejk, 'we are practising a little so that we shouldn't forget our drill and waste precious time.'

'Get down from the van,' Lieutenant Dub ordered. 'I've really had enough of this. I'm sending you to the battalion commander.'

When Švejk appeared in the staff carriage, Lieutenant Lukáš left it by another door and went out on to the platform.

When Lieutenant Dub told Captain Ságner about the good soldier Švejk's strange tomfoolery, as he called it, the latter was in a very good mood because the Gumpoldskirchen had indeed been first-class.

'I see, so you don't want to waste precious time,' he said with a knowing smile. 'Matušič, come here!'

The battalion orderly received instructions to summon the sergeant-major of the 12th company, Nasáklo, known to be the greatest tyrant, and to equip Švejk at once with a rifle.

'This man here,' Captain Ságner said to Sergeant-Major Nasáklo, 'doesn't want to waste precious time. Take him behind the van and give him an hour's rifle drill. But no pity and no respite, mind you! The main thing is – one order smartly after the other: order arms, shoulder arms, order arms!'

'You'll see, Švejk, that you won't be bored,' he said to him as he went away. And a moment later from behind the van a harsh order resounded ceremoniously between the tracks. Sergeant-Major Nasáklo, who had just been playing vingt-et-un and had held the bank, bawled out into the wide spaces of the heavens: 'Order arms! Shoulder arms! Order arms! Shoulder arms!'

Then there was silence for a short time and the happy and meditative voice of Švejk could be heard saying: 'I learnt all that years ago on regular service. When it's "order arms", then the rifle rests on the right hip. The point of the butt is in a straight line with the point of the toe. The right arm is naturally stretched and holds the rifle so that the thumb hugs the barrel. The other fingers must hold the butt by its front part. And when it's "shoulder arms" the rifle hangs freely on its sling over the right shoulder, the mouth of the barrel upwards and the barrel at the back ...'

'Now you bloody well put a sock in it!' Sergeant-Major Nasáklo went on with his commands. 'Attention! Eyes right! Herrgott, what a mess you're making of it ...'

'I'm at "shoulder arms", and at "eyes right" my right hand slips down the sling and clasps the neck of the butt. I throw my head to the

right. When it's "Attention!" I take the sling again with my right hand
and my head looks straight at you.'

And again there resounded the voice of the sergeant-major: 'Trail
arms! Order arms! Trail arms! Shoulder – arms! Fix bayonets!
Unfix bayonets! Sheath bayonets! Prepare for prayer! Finish prayer!
Kneel down for prayer! Load! Shoot! Shoot half-right! Target staff
carriage! Distance 200 paces! Ready! Aim! Fire! Easy! Aim! Fire!
Aim! Fire! Easy! Sights normal! Cartridges in pouch! Easy!' The
sergeant-major rolled a cigarette.

Meanwhile Švejk looked at the number on the rifle and said: '4268!
It's the same number a railway engine in Pečky had on track no. 16.
They should have taken it away for repairs to the depot in Lysá nad
Labem but it didn't go so easily, because, you see, sergeant-major,
that engine-driver, who should have taken it away, had a very bad
memory for figures. And so the track supervisor called him to his
office and said to him: "On track no. 16 there's an engine no. 4268. I
know you have a bad memory for figures and if I write any figure down
on paper you lose the paper. Now listen carefully and as you're not
good at figures I'll show you that it's very easy to remember any number you like. Look: the engine that you are to take off to the depot in
Lysá nad Labem is no. 4268. Now pay careful attention. The first figure
is four, the second is two, which means that you have to remember 42.
That's twice two. That means that in the order of the figures 4 comes
first. 4 divided by 2 makes 2 and so again you've got next to each
other 4 and 2. Now, don't be afraid! What's twice 4? 8, isn't it? Well,
then, get it into your head that 8 is the last in the series of figures in
4268. And now, when you've already got in your head that the first
figure is 4, the second 2 and the fourth 8, all that's to be done is to be
clever and remember the 6 which comes before the 8. And that's frightfully simple. The first figure is 4, the second is 2, and 4 and 2 are 6. So
now you've got it: the second from the end is 6 and now we shall never
forget the order of figures. You now have indelibly fixed in your mind
the number 4268. But of course you can also reach the same result by
an even simpler method . . ." '

The sergeant-major stopped smoking, goggled his eyes and could
only stutter: 'Cap off!'

Švejk went on solemnly: 'So he then began to explain to him the
simpler method of how to remember the number of the engine 4268.
8 minus 2 is 6. And so now he already knew 68. 6 minus 2 is 4. So

now he knew 4 and 68, and only the two had to be inserted, which made 4 – 2 – 6 – 8. And it isn't too difficult either to do it still another way by means of multiplication and division. In this way the same result is reached too. "Remember," the track supervisor said, "that twice 42 is 84. The year has 12 months. Very well, then, subtract 12 from 84 and you have 72 left. Take away from that the 12 months and

you have 60. We're sure about the 6 and cross out the nought. Now we know 42, 68, 4. When we've crossed out the nought we also cross out the last four, and we again get quite easily 4268, the number of the engine which is due for the depot in Lysá nad Labem. And, as I told you, it's quite easy by division. We calculate the co-efficient by the customs tariff!" Aren't you feeling well, sergeant-major? If you like I can easily start with perhaps "Prepare to fire salvo! Load! Aim! Fire!" Oh, hell! The captain shouldn't have sent us to do this in the sun! I must go and fetch a stretcher.'

When the doctor came he found that it was a case of sunstroke or acute inflammation of the lining of the brain.

When the sergeant-major recovered consciousness Švejk stood by him and said: 'Let me finish my story. Do you really imagine, sergeant-major, that that engine-driver managed to remember the figures? He muddled them all up and multiplied them all by three, because he remembered the Holy Trinity. And so he never found that engine. It's still standing there on track no. 16.'

The sergeant-major shut his eyes again.

And when Švejk returned to his van and was asked why he had been away so long he answered: 'Who teaches another the "double" must himself do a hundred "shoulder arms".' In the back of the van Baloun was trembling. During Švejk's absence, when part of the hen was cooked and ready, he had eaten up half Švejk's portion.

Before the train's departure it was caught up by a mixed military transport with various detachments in it. They were either latecomers, soldiers from hospitals trying to catch up with their detachments, or other suspicious individuals returning from special duties or arrest.

Among those getting out of this train was the one-year volunteer, Marek, who had been accused of mutiny because he had refused to clean the latrines, but the divisional court had acquitted him, the proceedings had been quashed and so he now turned up in the staff carriage to report to the battalion commander. The volunteer had up till now belonged nowhere, because he had been continually taken from one arrest to another.

When Captain Ságner saw him and took from him the documents which concerned his arrival and had a very secret minute on them: 'Politically suspect! Caution!', he was not exactly delighted, but fortunately he remembered the latrine general, who had made the interesting recommendation that a 'battalion historian' should be added to the battalion's strength.

'You're very negligent, you one-year volunteer,' he said to him. 'In the volunteer school you were a thorough devil and instead of trying to do well and get promoted, as your intelligence deserved, you just drifted about from arrest to arrest. The regiment must really be ashamed of you, volunteer. However, you can rectify your faults if you carry out your duties in the proper way and so take your place again in the ranks of good warriors. Devote your efforts to the battalion and do so with love. I shall see what I can do with you. You're an intelligent young man and certainly have the talent to write in a good style. Let me tell you something. Every battalion at the front needs a man who can make a chronological survey of all the events of the war which distinguish a battalion's performance on the fields of battle. All the battalion's victorious campaigns, all the significant and glorious moments which it experiences and in which it plays a leading and eminent role, should be recorded so that they will gradually form a contribution to the history of the army. Do you understand me?'

'Humbly report, I do, sir. It's a question of episodes from the life of all units. The battalion has its history. On the basis of the history of its battalions the regiment compiles its history. The regiments make the history of the brigade, the brigades make the history of the division and so on and so on. I'll do my very best, sir.'

Marek placed his hand on his heart.

'I shall set down with true love the finest hours of our battalion, especially at this time, when the offensive is in full swing and when it's going to be tough and our battalion will strew the battlefield with the corpses of its heroic sons. I shall conscientiously record the course of all the events which will have to happen, so that the pages of the history of our battalion may be full of laurels.'

'You will be attached to the staff of the battalion, volunteer. You will note carefully who has been recommended for decorations, you will record – of course according to our own directives – the marches which will particularly illustrate outstanding examples of the warlike spirit and iron discipline of our battalion. This is by no means an easy task, volunteer, but I hope that you have enough talent for observation, so that when you have received from me certain directives you will be able to exalt our own battalion above other formations. I am sending a telegram to the regiment that I have nominated you "battalion historian". Report to Quartermaster Sergeant-Major Vaněk of the 11th company so that he can find room for you in the van. There's still plenty of room there. Tell him to come and report to me. Of course you will be included in the lists of the battalion staff. This will be done by a battalion order.'

The occultist cook was sleeping. Baloun was still trembling, because he had already opened the lieutenant's sardines. Vaněk had gone to see

Captain Ságner, and Chodounský, who had secretly laid hands on a bottle of borovička somewhere on the station, had drunk it up and was now singing in a sentimental mood:

'While I still erred in my sweet dreams,
Then all the world seemed true,
And faith alone breathed in my breast.
With love my eye flamed too.

But when the whole world seemed to me
As false as Judas' lie,
My love and faith did fade away
And I first learned to cry.'

Then he got up, went to Vaněk's table, and wrote on a piece of paper in large letters:

I herewith humbly request that I should be appointed and promoted battalion horn-player.
Chodounský, telegraphist.

Captain Ságner's conversation with Vaněk did not last too long. He did no more than inform him that provisionally the battalion historian, volunteer Marek, would be accommodated in the van with Švejk.

'I can only say this much to you, that that fellow Marek is, if I can put it in this way, suspect. Politically suspect. My goodness! There's nothing very remarkable in that today. Who is there who doesn't have that reputation? There are various suspicions like this. However, you do understand what I mean, don't you? I'm just telling you so that if by chance he should say something which, well, you understand what I mean, you will immediately sit on him so that I shan't have any trouble about it. Just tell him that he's to stop all talk of that kind and that will settle it. I don't mean that you should come running to me at once. Settle it with him in a friendly fashion. A friendly talk like that is always better than a stupid denunciation. In short I don't want to hear anything, because ... well, you understand. ... A thing like that always reflects on the whole battalion.'

And so when Vaněk returned he took Marek aside and said to him: 'Old man, you're under suspicion, but that doesn't matter. Only be careful what you say in front of that telegraphist, Chodounský.'

Hardly had he finished saying this when Chodounský came staggering in and fell into the arms of the quartermaster sergeant-major. He

was sobbing out in drunken tones what perhaps was meant to be a
song:

> 'When all the world abandoned me,
> Upon thy breast I sank my head.
> Upon thy heart, so warm and pure,
> Bitter, despairing tears I shed.
> A little flame burst in thine eye
> Like tiny stars which gleam and shine.
> I heard the whisper of coral lips:
> "I'll never leave thee. Thou art mine."'

'We'll never leave each other,' howled Chodounský. 'Whatever I
hear on the telephone I'll tell you at once. I shit on my oath.'

In the corner Baloun crossed himself in horror and began to pray
aloud:

'Mother of God, be not deaf to my anguished prayers, but hearken
mercifully unto me. Console me with Thy love, help me, miserable
sinner, who calls to Thee with living faith, firm hope and ardent love in
this vale of tears. Oh, heavenly Queen, by Thy intercession help me to
continue to walk in the grace of God and under Thy protection till the
last days of my life.'

The merciful Virgin did in fact take him under her protection, for a
little later the volunteer drew out of his poor haversack several tins of
sardines and distributed one to each of them.

Baloun resolutely opened Lieutenant Lukáš's case and put back
into it the sardines which had fallen from heaven.

But when the others had opened their tins and were enjoying their
sardines Baloun succumbed to temptation, opened both the case and
the sardines and gobbled them up voraciously.

And then the most merciful and sweet Virgin turned her face from
him, because at the very moment when he was drinking up the oil from
the tin Matušič appeared in front of the van and called up: 'Baloun,
you've got to bring the sardines to your lieutenant.'

'Now you're going to get your face knocked in,' said Vaněk.

'You'd better not go to him empty-handed,' Švejk advised. 'At least
take these five empty tins with you.'

'What have you done that God should punish you so?' said the
volunteer. 'There must have been some enormous sin in your past
life, surely? Didn't you perhaps commit sacrilege and eat up your
vicar's ham when it was hanging in his chimney? Or maybe you drank

the sacramental wine in his cellar? Or did you steal the pears in his orchard when you were a boy?'

Baloun tottered away with a desperate expression on his face, full of hopelessness. His agitated expression was heartbreakingly eloquent: 'When will all this suffering take an end?'

'This is all because you've lost touch with the Lord, my friend,' said the volunteer when he heard the luckless Baloun's words. 'You don't know how to pray properly for the Lord to take you away from this world as soon as possible.'

To this Švejk added: 'Baloun still can't decide to entrust his soldier's life, his military mentality, his words, his deeds, his soldierly death to the mercy of the maternal heart of the Almighty, as my Chaplain Katz used to say, when he started to get tipsy and by mistake jostled a soldier on the street.'

Baloun moaned that he had already lost faith in the Lord, because he had prayed so often for God to give him strength and somehow contract his stomach.

'It didn't start with this war,' he groaned. 'It's already an old disease, this voracious appetite of mine. Because of it my wife and children used to go on pilgrimages to Klokoty.'

'I know that place,' observed Švejk. 'That's near Tábor and they have a very rich Madonna with false diamonds there, and once a sexton from somewhere in Slovakia wanted to rob her. He was a very pious man. Well, he came there and thought that he'd perhaps get on better if he were first purified of all his old sins. And so he went to confession and confessed among other things that he was going to rob the Madonna the following day. He could hardly say Jack Robinson and finish praying those three hundred paternosters, which the priest gave him so that he shouldn't run away in the meantime, when the sextons came and took him straight off to the gendarmerie station.'

The occultist cook began to dispute with Chodounský whether it was a violation of the seal of confession which cried out to high heaven or whether it was something hardly worth talking about, when it was a question of diamonds which were false. In the end, however, he proved to Chodounský that it was all *karma*; in other words predestined by fate as long ago as the distant unknown past, when this unfortunate sexton from Slovakia had still been a mollusc on some other planet. And it had also been predetermined long ago, when that priest from Klokoty was perhaps still an echidna or some kind of marsupial, now extinct, that he must violate the seal of confession, although from the legal point of view absolution can be given according to canonic law even where monastery property is concerned.

To this Švejk added this simple observation: 'Why, of course, no one knows what he'll be up to in a few million years, and he shouldn't tempt providence. When we were still serving in Karlín in the Reserve Command, Lieutenant Kvasnička always said, when he taught us: "Don't imagine, you dung-eaters, you idle cattle and swine, that military service will end for you in this world. We shall meet each other again after death, and I'll make such a purgatory for you that you'll be completely cuckoo, you bastard scum, you." '

Meanwhile Baloun, who went on thinking in his hopeless despair that they were now talking only about him and that everything had to do with him, went on with his public confession: 'Not even Klokoty cured my inordinate greed. After my wife and children came back from the pilgrimage they immediately set about counting the hens. One or two of them were missing. But I couldn't help it, really. I knew that we needed them in the household for their eggs, but I went out, looked at them and suddenly felt an awful void in my stomach. After an hour I was all right again, but one of the hens was gnawed to the bone. Once when they were at Klokoty to pray that papa shouldn't guzzle up anything while they were away and cause fresh damage, I walked about the courtyard and suddenly my eye fell on a turkey. That time it might easily have cost me my life. Its thighbone stuck in my throat and if it hadn't been for the fact that my apprentice, quite a young chap, managed to get the bone out, I wouldn't be sitting here with you today, or have lived to see the world war. Yes, yes. That apprentice of mine was a smart nipper. He was small, chubby, dumpy, well-fed – . . .'

Švejk came up to Baloun: 'Show me your tongue!'

Baloun put out his tongue at Švejk, whereupon the latter turned to everyone who was in the van. 'I knew it. He even guzzled up his own apprentice. Confess, when was it that you did it? Once when your wife and children were at Klokoty again, wasn't it?'

Baloun wrung his hands and cried: 'Let me be, my friends! And to think that on top of everything else I should get this from my comrades.'

'We don't condemn you for it,' said the volunteer. 'On the contrary, you'll obviously make a jolly good soldier. When the French besieged Madrid in the Napoleonic wars the Spanish commander of the fortress at Madrid ate his own adjutant unsalted rather than be starved into surrendering the fortress.

'That was certainly a sacrifice, because an adjutant who was salted would have been definitely more digestible. Tell me, quartermaster sergeant-major, what's the name of our battalion adjutant? Ziegler? He's such a scraggy fellow that you wouldn't get enough portions out of him for a single march company.'

'Look!' said Vaněk, 'Baloun has a rosary in his hands.'

And, indeed, Baloun in his infinite grief sought salvation in the small beads of the rosary manufactured by the firm of Moritz Löwenstein of Vienna.

'It's from Klokoty too,' said Baloun sadly. 'Before they brought it to me, two goslings had gone, but that's no meat. It's only mush.'

A little later the order came through the whole train that they would be leaving in a quarter of an hour. Because nobody believed it, it happened that in spite of all precautions some men went wandering off. When the train moved off eighteen men were missing, including Sergeant-Major Nasáklo of the 12th march company. Long after the train had disappeared beyond Isatarcsa, he was still haggling with a prostitute in a shallow hollow in a small acacia grove behind the station. She wanted five crowns from him, whereas he was proposing as payment for the service already performed either a crown or a few smacks in the face. In the end, however, a settlement was reached in favour of the latter and with such vehemence that hearing the lady's screams people began to run up there from the station.

3

From Hatvan towards the Galician Frontier

THROUGHOUT the rail journey of the battalion which was to reap military glory when it marched from Laborce through Eastern Galicia to the front, strange, more or less treasonable conversations took place in the van in which the volunteer and Švejk were travelling. The same thing was happening in the other vans as well, although perhaps to a lesser extent. Even in the staff carriage dissatisfaction reigned because in Füzesabony an army order had come from the regiment reducing the ration of wine for each officer by an eighth of a litre. Of course the men were not forgotten either. Their ration of sago was reduced by one deka per head, which was all the more curious in that no one had ever seen any sago in the army at all.

None the less, Quartermaster Sergeant-Major Bautanzel had to be told of it and felt himself frightfully insulted and cheated, which he expressed by saying that sago was a rare commodity today and he could have got at least eight crowns for one kilo of it.

It was at Füzesabony that it came out that one company had lost its field-kitchen, because at this station the goulash and potatoes on which the 'latrine general' had placed such stress were at last to be cooked. Investigations revealed that the wretched field-kitchen had not left Bruck with them and probably to this very day it still stands somewhere behind shed 186, abandoned and cold.

A day before the departure the kitchen staff belonging to that same field-kitchen had been imprisoned in the guard-house for overexuberant behaviour in the town and had managed to arrange to remain incarcerated there until their march company was safe on its way through Hungary.

The kitchenless company was therefore assigned to another field-kitchen, which of course did not occur without a row. A violent disagreement arose among the men who were drafted from both companies to peel potatoes, one party having stated firmly to the other that they were not such bloody fools as to go and sweat their guts out for the others. Finally it turned out that the cooking of goulash and potatoes was in fact nothing more than a manoeuvre so that the men could gradually get used to the eventuality that when goulash was being cooked in the field in the face of the enemy the order 'general retreat!' might suddenly come, the goulash be poured away and no one get even a lick of it.

And so this was a kind of rehearsal, not tragic in its consequences, but none the less quite instructive, for at the very moment when the goulash was about to be distributed, the order came, 'into the vans', and the train went off to Miskolc. But even there no goulash was distributed, because a train with Russian vans stood on the track there. And so the men were not let out of the vans and their imagination soon got to work: the goulash would be distributed only when they got out of the train in Galicia, where it would be pronounced sour and unfit for consumption and poured away.

And so they took the goulash farther on to Tiszalök and Sambor, and when no one any longer expected that any goulash would be distributed the train stopped at Sátoraljaújhely, where fires were again lit under the cauldrons and the goulash was again heated and at last distributed.

The station was crowded. Two munitions trains had to be sent off first and after them two artillery transports and a train with pontoon detachments. It was certainly true to say that at this station trains were collected with troops from every possible unit of the army.

Behind the station Honvéd hussars were giving hell to two Polish Jews whose hamper of spirits they had plundered. They were in high humour and instead of paying for it were hitting them across the jaw. This was apparently permitted because quite close by their captain was standing and smiling affably at the whole scene, while behind the storehouse a few other Honvéd hussars were putting their hands under the skirts of the dark-eyed daughters of the same Jews who had been beaten.

There was also a train here with a detachment of aircraft. On other lines there stood trucks with the same objects, such as aircraft and guns but badly smashed. They were shot-down aircraft and howitzers with their barrels smashed. And so while everything fresh and new went up to the front, these remnants of glory travelled back to the base for repair and reconstruction.

To all the soldiers who crowded round the smashed guns and aeroplanes Lieutenant Dub of course explained that they were war booty. It did not escape his notice either that Švejk was again standing in a group near by and relating something. And so he went up there and could hear the discreet voice of Švejk saying: 'Whatever way you look at it, it's war booty after all. At first sight it looks a bit tricky

when you read here on the gun carriage "Imperial and Royal Artillery Division", but probably it was like this: the gun fell into the hands of the Russians and we had to win it back. Booty like that is much more valuable because . . .

'Because,' he said solemnly, when he observed Lieutenant Dub, 'nothing must ever be left in the hands of the enemy. That's like what happened in Przemyśl or with that soldier who had his field-flask torn off by the enemy in an engagement as long ago as in the Napoleonic wars. The soldier went by night into the enemy's camp and brought the field-flask back again. It was worth it, because during the night the enemy had drawn rations of spirit.'

Lieutenant Dub said nothing more than: 'See you make yourself scarce, Švejk, and I don't find you here again.'

'Just as you order, sir.' And Švejk went away to another group of vans, and if Lieutenant Dub had heard what he said afterwards he would certainly have jumped out of his uniform, although it was a completely innocent biblical saying: 'A little while, and ye shall not see me, and again a little while, and ye shall see me.'

After Švejk had gone Lieutenant Dub was, on top of all this, so stupid that he drew the soldiers' attention to a shot-down Austrian plane which had 'Wiener Neustadt' clearly marked on its metal ring.

'This one we shot down from the Russians at Lwów,' said Lieutenant Dub. His words were overheard by Lieutenant Lukáš, who came up and added aloud: 'And during the operation both Russian airmen were burnt to death.'

Then he walked on without a word, thinking to himself that Lieutenant Dub was a prize ox.

Behind the other van he ran into Švejk and tried to avoid him, because from Švejk's expression on seeing him it was clear that the man had a great deal on his chest which he wanted to unload on to him.

Švejk came straight up to him: 'Humbly report, sir, Company Orderly Švejk asks for further orders. Humbly report, sir, I've already been looking for you in the staff carriage.'

'Listen, Švejk,' said Lieutenant Lukáš, in a snubbing and unfriendly tone, 'do you know your name? Have you already forgotten what I called you?'

'Humbly report, sir, I've not forgotten a thing like that, because I'm not a volunteer Železný. Long before the war, when we were in the Karlín barracks, there was a colonel by the name of Fliedler von Bumerang or something erang.'

In spite of himself, Lieutenant Lukáš could not help smiling at the 'something erang' and Švejk went on: 'Humbly report, sir, that colonel of ours was half your height. He wore a long beard like Prince Lobkovic so that he looked like a monkey, and when he got angry he jumped twice as high as he was tall, so that we called him the india-rubber fossil. It happened to be the first of May and we were on alert. The evening before in the courtyard he delivered a great speech to us saying that the next day we must all remain in the barracks and not move a step outside, so that in case of need on highest orders we could shoot all the Socialist scum. And so if any soldier had extended leave of absence and instead of returning to the barracks stretched it out until the next day he would be committing high treason, because a drunken bastard like that wouldn't be able to hit a man when salvos were shot, but would shoot up into the air. So that volunteer Železný returned to his room and said that the india-rubber fossil had had a good idea after all. And it was quite true, you see: the next day they wouldn't let anybody into the barracks and so it was best not to come at all and, humbly report, sir, that is exactly what the smart fellow did with great gusto. But that Colonel Fliedler was such a lousy swine, God help us, that the next day he went all over Prague and looked for anybody from our regiment who might have dared to leave the barracks. Somewhere near the Powder Tower he had the luck to run into Železný and immediately let fly at him: "I'll give you hell! I'll teach you! I'll make it bloody hot for you!" He said a great deal more like this and dragged him off to the barracks. And the whole way he said to him all sorts of ugly threatening things and kept on asking him his name. "Železný, Železný. You'll shit for this. I'm delighted I've caught you. I'll teach you the first of May! Železný, Železný, now I've got you, I'll clap you into gaol – yes, into a lovely gaol." But it was all the same to Železný. And so as they went along Poříč, past U Rozvařilů, Železný jumped off into the carriage entrance of a house, ran away through a passage and cheated the india-rubber fossil of the enormous pleasure of clapping him in gaol. The colonel was so furious over his escape that in his rage he forgot the delinquent's name, got it mixed up, and when he came back to the barracks began to jump up to the ceiling. The ceiling was low and the duty officer was very surprised that the old fossil was suddenly speaking broken Czech and shouting: "Clap Měděný into gaol! Don't clap Měděný into gaol! Clap Olověný into gaol! Clap Cínový into gaol!"[1] And it was in this way the old fossil bullied his staff, keeping on asking them whether they had caught Měděný, Olověný and Cínový, and he even called up the whole regiment, but Železný, whom everybody knew about, had been drafted into the medical section because he was a dentist. And then one day a man from our regiment succeeded in stabbing in the pub U Bucků a dragoon who had been running after his girl. So they formed us into a square and everyone had to come on parade, even

1. 'Železný' means in Czech 'iron', 'měděný' 'copper', 'olověný' 'lead', and 'cínový' 'tin'. The colonel could not get the name right.

the sick, and if anyone was very ill, he was held by two others. And so there was no help for it: Železný had to fall in in the yard and they read us the regimental order that dragoons were soldiers too and it was forbidden to stab them, because they were our "comrades-in-arms". A one-year volunteer translated this and our colonel glowered at us like a tiger. First he went to the front line, then to the rear, then round the whole square, when suddenly he discovered Železný, that mountain of a man who was so colossal, sir, that it was really frightfully funny when he brought him into the middle of the square. The volunteer stopped translating and our colonel started jumping in front of Železný like a dog jumping at a horse and all the time he roared: "You can't get away from me now. You can't escape anywhere. Now I say again that you're Železný. I've kept on saying you were Měděný, Cínový, Olověný. He's Železný, the bloody bastard Železný. I'll give you Olověný, Cínový, Měděný, you bastard, you swine, you Železný!" And then he gave him four weeks' clink, but a fortnight later his teeth began to ache and he remembered that Železný was a dentist. And so he had him brought out of arrest to the medical department and wanted to make him pull his tooth out. Železný took about half an hour pulling it out so that they had to wash the old fossil about three times, but somehow or other he got tamed and let Železný off that second fortnight. And so that's what happens, sir, when a superior officer forgets the name of his subordinate. But a subordinate must never forget the name of his superior, just as that colonel used to tell us. He said we'd never forget for the whole of our lives that we had once had a Colonel Fliedler. – Wasn't that story perhaps a little too long, sir?'

'You know, Švejk,' Lieutenant Lukáš answered, 'the more I listen to you the more convinced I am that you don't respect your superior officers at all. A soldier ought only to speak well of his superiors, even years and years afterwards.'

Lieutenant Lukáš was obviously beginning to enjoy the conversation.

'Humbly report, sir,' said Švejk in an apologetic tone, 'Colonel Fliedler has been dead for a long time, but if you wish it, sir, I'll of course only sing his praises. He was a perfect angel to the soldiers, sir. He was as good as St Martin, who used to give geese to the needy and hungry at Martinmas. He shared his dinner from the officers' mess with the first soldier he met in the yard, and when we were tired of dumplings he ordered for us in the mess "grenadier march"[1] with pork. But it was at the manoeuvres that he really showed his generosity. When we came to Dolní Královice he gave orders that the whole brewery there should be consumed at his expense, and when

he had a birthday he treated the whole regiment to roast hare in cream sauce with bread dumplings. He was so good to the men, that once, sir . . .'

Lieutenant Lukáš tapped Švejk gently on the ear and said in a friendly voice: 'Well, get along now, you bastard. Drop all that about him.'

'Very good, sir!' And Švejk went away to his van. Meanwhile in front of the battalion train where all the telephone instruments and wires were locked up in a van the following scene was taking place: a sentry stood there because by orders of Captain Ságner everything had

---

1. Steamed potatoes, buttered noodles and browned onions.

to be kept on field alert. Consequently sentries were posted on both sides of the train according to the value of the transport and received their passwords from the battalion office.

On that particular day the first part of the password was 'copy' and the second 'Hatvan'. The sentry at the van with the telephones, who had to remember this, was a Pole from Kolomyje, who by some strange mischance had got to the 91st regiment.

Of course he could not know what 'copy' was, but because he had some faint idea of mnemonics he managed to remember all the same that the word began with a 'c', and when Lieutenant Dub, who was duty officer, came up to him and asked him the password of the day, he proudly answered 'coffee'. Of course this was only natural, because a Pole from Kolomyje could not forget the morning and evening coffee in the camp at Bruck.

And when he shouted out 'coffee' once again, and Lieutenant Dub came nearer and nearer to him, he remembered his oath and that he was on sentry duty, and called out menacingly 'Halt!' When Lieutenant Dub took two more steps towards him and still wanted him to say the password, the sentry aimed his rifle at him and not having perfect command of the German language shouted out in a strange mixture of Polish and German: 'I'm going to shit. I'm going to shit.'

Lieutenant Dub understood and began to edge away, calling out: "Commander of the guard! Commander of the guard!"

Then Sergeant Jelínek appeared, who had escorted the Pole to his post, and asked him what the password was. Lieutenant Dub did the same and the desperate Pole from Kolomyje replied to those questions with a roar which resounded all over the station: 'Coffee, coffee.' There were lots of transports there and men began to jump out of all of them with mess-tins and there was a frightful panic which ended in the worthy sentry being disarmed and led off to the arrest van.

But Lieutenant Dub harboured certain suspicions against Švejk, when he saw that he was the first to climb out of the van with his mess-tin. He was ready to bet his life that he had heard Švejk shout: 'All outside with mess-tins, all outside with mess-tins.'

After midnight the train moved off to Ladovce and Trebišov, where it was met at the station in the morning by a society of Hungarian veterans who had confused this march battalion with the march battalion of the 14th Hungarian Honvéd regiment, which had only just passed through the station during the night. Obviously the veterans were tight and woke up the whole train with their cater-wauling: '*Isten áldmeg a király.*'[1] A few more nationally conscious individuals leaned out of the vans and replied to them: 'Come and kiss our arses. *Eljén!*'[2]

Thereupon the veterans roared until the windows shook: '*Eljén! Eljén a tizenégyedek regiment!*'[3]

Five minutes later the train went on to Humenné. Here were already clearly visible traces of the fighting when the Russians had advanced to the valley of the Tissa. Primitive trenches stretched along the slopes, here and there a burnt-out farm could be seen, and a rapidly built shed nearby indicated that the owners had come back again.

When later at about lunchtime they reached Humenné, where the station showed the same traces of fighting, preparations were made for lunch and the men in the transport could in the meantime catch a glimpse of a public secret, and observe how after the departure of the Russians the authorities treated the local population, who were related to the Russian armies in speech and confession.

On the platform surrounded by Hungarian gendarmes stood a group of arrested Ruthenians from Hungary. It included priests, teachers and peasants from far and wide in the region. All of them had their hands tied behind their backs with cord and were fastened to each other in pairs. Most of them had broken noses and bumps on their heads, since immediately after their arrest they had been beaten up by the gendarmes.

A little further away a Hungarian gendarme was amusing himself with a priest. He had tied his left foot with a cord, held the cord in his hand and forced him with his rifle butt to dance a czardas. Then he tugged at the cord so that the priest fell on his nose, and as the priest had his arms tied behind his back he could not get up but made desperate attempts to turn on his back, perhaps to be able to raise himself from the ground. The gendarme laughed so heartily at this that tears ran from his eyes, and when the priest tried to get up he gave another tug at the cord and the priest was on his nose again.

At last a gendarmerie officer put an end to this and ordered the prisoners to be taken away to an empty barn behind the station until

1. 'God save the King.'
2. 'Hail!'
3. 'Hail to the 14th regiment!'

the train had passed. There they were to be beaten and pounded without anyone being able to see it.

This episode was a topic of conversation in the staff carriage and generally speaking most of the officers condemned it.

Ensign Kraus thought that if they were traitors they should at once be hanged on the spot without further maltreatment. On the other hand Lieutenant Dub was in full agreement with the whole scene and turned the conversation at once to the Sarajevo assassination, explaining that the Hungarian gendarmes at the station of Humenné were avenging the death of the Archduke Franz Ferdinand and his wife. To add weight to his words he said that he used to subscribe to a journal (Šimáček's *Four-Leaved Clover*) and that already before the war the July number, writing about this assassination, had said that the unparalleled crime of Sarajevo left a wound in people's hearts which would long remain unhealed. The wound was the more grievous because the crime caused the death not only of the representative of the executive power of the state but of his faithful and beloved consort too. Thus by the destruction of these two lives a happy, exemplary family life had been broken up and children, who were universally loved, were made orphans.

Lieutenant Lukáš only muttered to himself that no doubt here in Humenné the gendarmes had subscribed to Šimáček's *Four-Leaved Clover* with its touching article. Suddenly all this began to nauseate him and he felt nothing but an urge to get drunk so as to get rid of his *Weltschmerz*. He got out of the carriage and went to look for Švejk.

'Listen, Švejk,' he said to him, 'do you know where there is a bottle of cognac to be had? I'm not feeling very well.'

'Humbly report, sir, it's the change of weather. Maybe when we get to the battlefield you'll be feeling even worse. The farther one gets away from one's original military base the fainter one feels. A gardener in Strašnice, Josef Kalenda by name, once left his home in the same way. He went from Strašnice to Vinohrady[1] and called at the pub, At the Stop, but at that time he still felt all right. But as soon as he came to the water tower in Korunní Avenue, he called at every pub along the avenue as far as the Church of St Ludmila, and then he began to feel some lassitude. However, he was not put off by that, because the evening before in Strašnice at The Terminus he had bet a tram-driver that he could walk round the world in three weeks. And so he began to

1. Both districts of Prague.

go farther and farther away from his home until he came to The Black Brewery on Charles Square and from there he went to the Malá Strana to St Thomas's Brewery and then to the restaurant, U Montágů, and even higher to the pub, The King of Brabant, and then to The Beautiful View and from there to the brewery at the Strahov Monastery. But at that point the change of climate stopped doing him any good. He got as far as Loretta Square and there got such a fit of homesickness that he fell on the ground and began to roll about on the pavement crying: "Oh, no, no. I'll not go any further. As for that trip round the world," (if you'll excuse me, sir) "I don't care a bloody – spit." But if you like, sir, I'll rustle up some cognac for you, only I'm afraid that the train might start before I come back.'

Lieutenant Lukáš assured him that they would not be leaving for two hours and that cognac was being secretly sold in bottles just behind the station. Captain Ságner had already sent Matušič there and he had brought him a bottle of quite respectable cognac for fifteen crowns. Here were fifteen crowns and he should go, but not tell anybody that it was for Lieutenant Lukáš or that it was he who sent him, because strictly speaking it was forbidden.

'You can be assured, sir,' said Švejk, 'that everything will be all right, because if there's anything I love it is forbidden things. You see, I've always been mixed up in something forbidden without my even having known about it. Once in the Karlín barracks they forbade us...'

'About turn – quick march!' Lieutenant Lukáš interrupted him.

And so Švejk went behind the station repeating to himself on the way all the elements of his expedition: the cognac must be good and so he must taste it beforehand; it was forbidden and so he must be cautious.

Just as he was turning behind the station he met Lieutenant Dub once again. 'What are you fooling around here for?' he asked Švejk. 'Do you know me?'

'Humbly report,' answered Švejk, saluting. 'I don't want to get to know you from your bad side.'

Lieutenant Dub turned stiff with shock but Švejk stood unmoved, keeping his hands all the time at the peak of his cap. Then he continued: 'Humbly report, sir, I want to know you only from your good side so that you shouldn't make me cry as you said to me last time.'

Lieutenant Dub's head went dizzy at such audacity and he could only utter an indignant yell. 'Get away, you bastard! I'll have something to say to you later.'

Švejk went away behind the platform and Lieutenant Dub, having pulled himself together again, set out after him. Behind the station immediately by the road stood a row of rush baskets placed upside down, on which there were straw-plaited dishes, and on these dishes there were various delicacies which looked entirely innocent, as though all these good things had been intended for school children on an outing. Lying there were sweets of spun sugar, wafer cornets, little piles of acid drops and here and there on one or two trays slices of black bread with pieces of salami quite definitely of equine origin. Underneath, however, the baskets harboured various kinds of alcohol, bottles of cognac, rum, jeřabinka and other liqueurs and spirits.

Immediately behind the ditch bordering the road was a hut where all this business with illicit drinks was actually transacted.

The soldiers first of all started the dealings at the baskets, and a Jew with long curls drew out of the bottom of the basket an innocent-looking bottle of spirit and took it under his kaftan to the wooden shed, where the soldier hid it unostentatiously in his trousers or under his tunic somewhere.

It was here that Švejk went, while all the time Lieutenant Dub with his detective talent watched him closely from the station.

Švejk began straight away at the first basket. First he picked out some sweets, which he paid for and put in his pocket, while the gentleman with the long curls whispered to him: 'I've got some schnaps too, your honour.'

The negotiation was rapidly completed. Švejk went into the shed but did not hand over the money until the gentleman with the long curls had opened the bottle and let Švejk taste the contents. Švejk was satisfied with the cognac and returned to the station, having shoved the bottle under his tunic.

'Where have you been, you bastard?' said Lieutenant Dub, blocking his way to the platform.

'Humbly report, sir, I've been to buy some sweets.' Švejk fumbled in his pocket and brought out a handful of dirty, dusty sweets: 'May I offer you some, if they don't disgust you, sir. I've already tasted them and they're not bad. They've got a pleasant, special taste like plum jam, sir.'

Under his tunic were outlined the round contours of a bottle.

Lieutenant Dub slapped Švejk on the tunic: 'What are you carrying there, you bastard? Take it out!'

Švejk drew out the bottle with its yellow contents and its clear and explicit label, 'Cognac'.

'Humbly report, sir,' answered Švejk unintimidated, 'that I pumped a little drinking water into an empty cognac bottle. I still have a frightful thirst after that goulash we had yesterday. Only the water in that pump is rather yellow as you can see, sir. There must be some iron in it. Water with iron in it is very healthy and good for you.'

'If you really have such a thirst, Švejk,' said Lieutenant Dub, smiling devilishly and desiring only to prolong as long as possible a scene in which Švejk must finally be the loser for ever, 'go on and drink but drink properly. Drink the whole of it at one draught!'

Lieutenant Dub had already planned in advance how Švejk would take a few gulps and then be unable to go on, and how then he, Lieutenant Dub, would have a glorious victory over him and would say: 'Give me that bottle too, so I can drink a little. I am thirsty also.' He could imagine the expression on that bastard Švejk's face at that frightful moment for him, and then he would make a report and so on.

Švejk uncorked the bottle, put it to his lips, and gulp by gulp it disappeared down his throat. Lieutenant Dub stiffened. Švejk drank the whole bottle before his eyes without batting an eyelid and threw away the empty bottle across the road into the pond. Then he spat and said, as though he had drunk a glass of mineral water: 'Humbly report, sir, that water really had a taste of iron. In Kamýk nad Vltavou there was a pub-keeper who made water with iron in it for his summer guests by throwing old horseshoes into the well.'

'I'll give you old horseshoes! Come and show me that well where you got the water from!'

'It's only a little way from here, sir, just there behind that wooden shed.'

'March in front, you scum, so I can see whether you can walk straight!'

'This is really very strange,' thought Lieutenant Dub. 'You can't see anything on that miserable bastard.'

And so Švejk marched ahead, putting his fate into the hands of the Lord, but all the time something told him that there must be a well there, and so he was not a bit surprised when he actually found one.

There was even a pump there and when they got to it and Švejk began to pump, yellow water spurted out from it, so he could announce ceremoniously: 'Here is that iron water, sir.'

A panic-stricken man with long curls appeared and Švejk asked him in German to bring a glass as the lieutenant wanted to drink.

Lieutenant Dub lost his head so completely that he drank up the whole glass, after which there spread over his mouth the flavour of horse urine and manure. Then, driven completely silly by what he had experienced, he gave the long-curled Jew five crowns for that glass of water and turning to Švejk said: 'What are you standing here gaping for? Clear off home.'

Five minutes later Švejk appeared before Lieutenant Lukáš in the staff carriage and with a mysterious gesture beckoned him to come out of it. Outside he said to him: 'Humbly report, sir, in five, at the latest in ten, minutes I shall be completely gone, but I'll be lying down in my van. I would only beg you, sir, if you would be so kind as not to call me for the next three hours at least and not give me any orders, sir, until I've slept it off. Everything's in order, but Lieutenant Dub caught me. I told him that it was water and so I had to drink the whole bottle of cognac before him to show him that it really was water. Everything is all right, I haven't given anything away, just as you wished, sir, and I was also very cautious indeed. But now, humbly report, sir, I'm already beginning to feel it. My legs are starting to have pins and needles. Of course, beg to report, sir, I'm used to boozing because when I was with Chaplain Katz . . .'

'Get out of my sight, you brute!' Lieutenant Lukáš shouted, but without any anger. Lieutenant Dub, however, became fifty-per-cent more repugnant to him than before.

Švejk got cautiously into his van and lying down on his greatcoat and pack said to the quartermaster sergeant-major and the others: 'Once upon a time a man got sozzled and asked not to be disturbed . . .'

After these words he rolled over on his side and began to snore.

The gases which he emitted by belching soon filled the whole compartment, so that Jurajda, inhaling the atmosphere through his nostrils, declared: 'God! It certainly reeks of cognac here.'

Marek, who after all his tribulations had finally attained the rank of battalion historian, was sitting at a folding table.

He was engaged in writing up in advance the heroic deeds of the battalion, and it was obvious that he derived great pleasure from his look into the future.

Vaněk watched with interest how the volunteer was busily writing and laughing heartily in the process. Then he got up and leant over his shoulder. Marek started to explain to him: 'You know, it's enormous fun writing a history of the battalion in advance. The main thing is to proceed systematically. In everything there must be system.'

'A systematic system,' observed Vaněk with a more or less contemptuous smile.

'Oh, yes,' the volunteer said nonchalantly, 'a systemized systematic system of writing the battalion's history. We can't march off straight away with a magnificent victory. Everything must go gradually according to a definite plan. Our battalion cannot win this world war all at once. *Nihil nisi bene.* The main thing for a conscientious historian like me is first to draw up a plan of our victories. For example, here I describe how our battalion – this will perhaps be in two months' time – nearly crosses the Russian frontier, which is very strongly defended by, let's say, the Don regiments of the enemy, while a number of enemy divisions surround our positions. At first sight it looks as if it's all up with our battalion and that the enemy will make sausage-meat of us. But at this very moment Captain Ságner gives the following order to our battalion: "It is not the Lord's will that we should perish here. Let's flee." And so our battalion starts to flee, but when the enemy division, which has encircled us, sees that we are actually running after them, they begin to retreat in panic and fall into the hands of our army's reserve without firing a shot. It is at this point really where the whole history of our battalion begins. From unimportant events, to speak like a prophet, Mr Vaněk, far-reaching things develop. Our battalion goes from victory to victory. It will be interesting to read how it attacks the enemy when he is asleep. For this we obviously need the style of the *Illustrated War News*, which was published by Vilímek during the Russo-Japanese war. Well, as I said, our battalion attacks the camp of the enemy while he is asleep. Each man of us seeks out an enemy and with all his force thrusts a bayonet into his chest. The finely sharpened bayonet goes through him like a knife through butter. Only here and there a rib cracks. The sleeping enemy jerk convulsively in their death spasms. For a moment they roll and goggle their eyes, but they are eyes which no longer see anything. Then they give the death rattle and their bodies stiffen. Bloody saliva appears on their lips, and with this it's all over and victory is on the side of our battalion. Or it will be even better in, say, three months' time, when our battalion captures the Tsar of Russia. But we'll talk about that later, Mr Vaněk. Meanwhile I must prepare in advance small episodes which testify to the battalion's unexampled heroism. I'll have to think out an entirely new war terminology for it. I've already invented one new term. I intend to write about the self-sacrificing resolution of our men, who are riddled through and through with splinters of shrapnel. As a result of an explosion of an enemy mine one of our sergeants, shall we say, of the 12th or 13th company, has his head blown off.

'By the way,' he said, hitting himself on the head, 'I nearly forgot, sergeant-major, or if we're to talk on civilian terms, Mr Vaněk, that you must get me a list of all the officers and N.C.O.s. Give me the name of a sergeant-major of the 12th company. – Houska? Good.

Houska now will have his head blown off by that mine. His head flies off, but his body still marches one or two steps forwards, takes aim and shoots down an enemy plane. It's quite obvious that in the future these victories and their repercussions will have to be celebrated within the family circle at Schönbrunn. Austria has very many battalions, but there is only one battalion like ours, which distinguishes itself so much that in its honour a small intimate family celebration is held in the Imperial Household. I visualize it in the following way, as you can see in my notes: the family of the Archduchess Marie Valerie moves from Wallsee to Schönbrunn for this celebration: the function is a purely private one and takes place in the hall next to the Monarch's bedroom, which is lit with white candles, because, as is well known, they do not like electric bulbs at the court in case there should be a short circuit, to which the old monarch has strong objections. The ceremony in honour and praise of our battalion starts at six o'clock in the evening. At this moment His Majesty's grandchildren are brought into the hall, which is actually part of the suite of the late Empress. Now it's a question as to who will be present besides the Imperial Family. The Monarch's general adjutant, Count Paar, must and will be there, and because during such family and intimate receptions someone occasionally feels faint (by which of course I don't mean that Count Paar himself should vomit), the presence of the personal doctor, the Counsellor of the Court, Dr Kerzl, will be required. For the sake of decency, to ensure that the court footmen shouldn't permit themselves any liberties with the ladies-in-waiting present at the reception, the Marshal of the Court, Baron Lederer, the Chamberlain, Count Bellegarde, and the principal Lady-in-Waiting, Countess Bombelles, will appear. The latter fulfils the same role among the ladies-in-waiting as madame does in the Prague brothel, U Šuhů. As soon as these exalted gentry are assembled the Emperor is informed and appears accompanied by his grandchildren. He sits down at a table and proposes a toast in honour of our march battalion. After him the Archduchess Marie Valerie makes a speech in which she pays a special compliment to you, quartermaster sergeant-major. Of course, according to my notes our battalion will suffer heavy and severe losses, because a battalion without dead is no battalion at all. I shall still have to prepare a new article about our fallen. The history of a battalion should not consist merely of dry facts about victories, of which I have already recorded in advance some forty-two. You, for example, Mr

Vaněk, will fall by a small stream, and Baloun, who's staring at us here in such an extraordinary fashion, will die an entirely different death. It will not be by bullet, shrapnel or shell. He will be strangled by a lassoo, thrown down from an enemy plane at the very moment when he is wolfing his lieutenant's dinner.'

Baloun stepped back, waved his hands despairingly and remarked dejectedly: 'I'm sorry, you know, but I can't help my nature! Even when I was in regular service I used to turn up some three times for mess in the kitchen until they put me in gaol for it. Once I had boiled rib of beef for dinner three times and because of that I was in quod for a month. May God's will be done!'

'Don't be afraid, Baloun,' the volunteer consoled him. 'In the history of the battalion there'll be no mention of the fact that you perished when you were guzzling grub on the way from the officers' mess to the trenches. You'll be mentioned together with all the men of our battalion who fell for the glory of our Empire, as for instance Quartermaster Sergeant-Major Vaněk.'

'What kind of death are you preparing for me, Marek?'

'Don't rush me, please, sergeant-major. It doesn't go as quickly as all that.'

The volunteer thought for a moment: 'You're from Kralupy, aren't you? Then write home to Kralupy that you are going to be missing without a trace, but write cautiously. Or would you prefer to be seriously wounded and remain lying beyond the barbed-wire entanglements? You could lie beautifully like that with a broken leg the whole day. In the night the enemy lights up our positions with his searchlights and notices you; he thinks you're spying and begins to riddle you with shells and shrapnel. You have performed a tremendous service for the army, because the enemy has had to expend on you as large a quantity of munitions as would have been needed for a whole battalion. After all these explosions your bits float freely in the air over you and, penetrating it with their rotations, sing a paean of glorious victory. In short everybody will have his turn, everyone of our battalion will distinguish himself so that the glorious pages of our history will overflow with victories – although I really would much prefer them not to overflow, but I can't help it. Everything must be carried out thoroughly so that some memory of us will remain until, say, in the month of September there will be really nothing left whatsoever of our battalion, except these glorious pages of history which will carry a message to the hearts of all Austrians, making it plain to them that all those who will never see their homes again fought equally valiantly. And I've already written the end, you know, Mr Vaněk – the obituary notice. Honour to the memory of the fallen! Their love for the Monarchy is the most sacred love of all, for death was its climax. Let their names be pronounced with honour, as for instance the name of Vaněk. Those who felt deepest of all the loss of their breadwinners may proudly wipe away their tears. Those who fell were the heroes of our battalion.'

Chodounský and Jurajda were listening with great interest to the volunteer's exposition of the forthcoming history of the battalion.

'Come closer, gentlemen,' said the volunteer, turning the pages of his notes. 'Here is page 15. "The telephonist, Chodounský, fell 3 September together with the battalion cook, Jurajda." Now listen further to my notes: "Exemplary heroism. The former, at the sacrifice of his life, protects the telephone wires in his cover when left at his telephone for three days without relief. The latter, observing the danger threatening from an enemy encirclement of our flank, throws himself at the foe with a cauldron of boiling soup, scattering terror and scaldings in his ranks." That's a splendid death for both of them, isn't it? One torn to pieces by a mine, the other asphyxiated by poison gas which they put under his nose, when he had nothing to defend himself with. Both perish with the cry: "Long live our battalion commander!" The High Command can do nothing else but daily express its gratitude in the form of the order that all other units of our army should know of the courage of our battalion and follow our example. I can read you an extract from the army order which will be read out in all units of the army and which is very like the order of the Archduke Karl, when he stood with his army in 1805 before Padua and got a frightful drubbing the day after. Listen to what people will read about our battalion as a heroic unit, which is a glowing example for all armies. ". . . I hope that the whole army will follow the example of the above-named battalion, and in particular adopt its spirit of self-confidence and self-reliance, its unshakeable invincibility in danger and its qualities of heroism, love and confidence in its superior officers. These virtues, in which the battalion excels, will lead it on to glorious deeds for the victory and blest happiness of our Empire. May all follow its example!" '

From the place where Švejk lay a yawn resounded and he could be heard talking in his sleep: 'Yes, you're right, Mrs Müller, people are all alike. In Kralupy there lived a Mr Jaroš who manufactured pumps and he was like the watchmaker Lejhanz from Pardubice, as like as two pins. And Lejhanz again was strikingly like Piskora of Jičín, and all four together resembled an unknown suicide whom they found hanged and completely decomposed in a lake near Jindřichův Hradec, just underneath the railway line, where he probably threw himself under the train.' There resounded another yawn and it was followed by: 'And then they sentenced all the others to a huge fine, and to-morrow, Mrs Müller, please make me some noodles with poppy-seed.' Švejk turned over on the other side and went on snoring, while be-tween Jurajda and the volunteer a debate started about what would happen in the future.

Jurajda thought that even if at first sight it might seem nonsensical that just for a joke a man should write about what was going to happen in the future, it was nonetheless certain that even a joke like this often had in it some prophetic elements, when under the influence of mysterious forces the inner eye broke through the veil of the unknown. From that moment on Jurajda's conversation became nothing but veils. In every other sentence there appeared his veil of the future, until finally he went over to regeneration or the renewal of the human body. He brought in the capacity of infusorians to renew their bodies and ended with the statement that if anyone broke off the tail of a lizard it would grow again.

To that Chodounský remarked that people would have the time of their lives if they could do what the lizards could with their tails. Take war, for instance, when anyone's head or other parts were torn off. How frightfully glad the military administration would be, because there would then be no disabled soldiers. An Austrian soldier whose legs, arms and head went on growing again and again would be cer-tainly more valuable than a whole brigade.

The volunteer stated that today, thanks to advanced war technique, it was possible successfully to divide the enemy into, say, three diagonal parts. There was a law about the renewal of the bodies of stentors of the family of the infusorians, according to which every dis-membered part grew again, acquired new organs and became an independent stentor. By this analogy, after every battle it took part in, the Austrian army would be trebled or increased tenfold, and from every severed leg would grow a fresh infantryman.

'If Švejk heard you,' said Vaněk, 'he would certainly quote us some example of it.'

Švejk reacted to his name, mumbled 'Present!', and went on snoring after having uttered this expression of military discipline.

In the half-open door of the compartment appeared the head of Lieutenant Dub.

'Is Švejk here?' he asked.

'Humbly report, sir, he's sleeping,' replied the volunteer.

'When I ask for him, one-year volunteer, you must at once jump up and call him.'

'I can't, sir, he's asleep.'

'Then wake him up! I'm surprised, volunteer, that that did not occur to you at once. You must show more keenness towards your superior officer. You don't know me yet, do you? But wait till you get to know me!'

The volunteer began to wake Švejk.

'Fire, Švejk! Fire! Get up!'

'When the Odkolek mills were on fire that time,' Švejk muttered, turning again on to the other side, 'the fire brigade came all the way from Vysočany . . .'

'Please be good enough to see, sir,' the volunteer said affably to Lieutenant Dub. 'I'm trying to wake him but it's really not possible.'

Lieutenant Dub got angry. 'What's your name, volunteer? – Marek? – Ah ha, so you're that volunteer Marek who's all the time been sitting in gaol, are you?'

'Yes, sir, I've spent my one-year course – so to speak – in gaol and have been re-degraded. That means that since my release from the divisional court, where my innocence was proved, I have been appointed battalion historian while retaining the rank of one-year volunteer.'

'You won't be it long,' roared Lieutenant Dub, who was now quite red in the face. This change of colour gave the impression that his face was swelling after being slapped. 'I shall take care of that!'

'Please, sir, may I be sent on report?' said the volunteer gravely.

'Don't play with me!' said Lieutenant Dub. 'I'll teach you report! We'll see each other again and then I'll give you hell, because you'll get to know me, whereas now you don't yet know me!'

Lieutenant Dub went angrily away from the van, forgetting all about Švejk in his agitation, although a short time before he had had every intention of calling him and saying to him: 'Breathe on me!'

as a last means of establishing Švejk's illicit alcoholism. But now it was of course too late, because when he returned to the van half an hour later they had in the meantime distributed black coffee and rum to the men. Švejk was already up and at Lieutenant Dub's call jumped out of the wagon like a mountain goat.

'Breathe on me!' Lieutenant Dub roared at him.

Švejk breathed out on to him the whole storehouse of his lungs, like a hot wind carrying to the fields the fragrance of a distillery.

'And what do you smell of, you bastard?'

'Humbly report, sir, I smell of rum.'

'And so you see, you bloody scoundrel,' Lieutenant Dub called out triumphantly. 'I've got you at last!'

'Yes, sir,' said Švejk without any sign of disturbance. 'We've just drawn our rations of rum for the coffee and I had drunk the rum first. If, sir, there is a new order that coffee should be drunk first and rum afterwards, then please excuse me. It won't happen again.'

'And why were you snoring then when I was in the van half an hour ago? Why, they couldn't even wake you!'

'Humbly report, sir, I couldn't sleep the whole night because I was remembering that time when we were still doing manoeuvres in Veszprem. At that time the mock first and second army corps went through Styria and West Hungary and surrounded our fourth corps, which was in camp in Vienna and the surroundings, where we had fortifications everywhere. But they out-flanked us and got as far as the bridge which the sappers were making from the right bank of the Danube. We were supposed to launch an offensive and the armies from the north and later from Osijek in the south were supposed to come to our assistance. They read out in the order of the day that the third army corps would march to our aid, so that when we advanced against the second army corps they shouldn't smash us to pieces. But it was all no use; just as we were about to win they sounded the end of the manoeuvres and those who wore white armbands had won.'

Lieutenant Dub said nothing and went away shaking his head in embarrassment. But a moment later he came back again from the staff carriage and said to Švejk: 'You'd better all of you remember that a time will come when you will be whining before me!' He could not manage to say more and went away again to the staff carriage, where Captain Ságner was just interrogating an unfortunate man from the 12th company who had been brought to him by Sergeant-Major

Strnad. Starting already now to worry about his safety in the trenches this man had carried away from somewhere in the station the door of a pigsty which was reinforced with metal plating. Now he stood there panic-stricken with staring eyes and excused himself by saying that he had wanted to take it with him to his place of cover to shield himself against shrapnel.

Lieutenant Dub used the opportunity to deliver a lengthy sermon on how a soldier ought to conduct himself and what his duties were towards his fatherland and the Monarch, who was the supreme commander and highest military authority. Of course if there should be elements of this kind in the battalion they must be eradicated, punished and clapped into gaol. All this claptrap was so disgusting that the captain tapped the guilty man on the shoulder and said to him: 'Well, well, you obviously didn't mean anything bad, but don't do anything like it again. It was foolish of you. Put the door back again where you took it from and get to hell out of it!'

Lieutenant Dub bit his lip and thought to himself that the preservation of discipline in the battalion, which was on the point of collapse, depended only on himself. And so he went round the whole area of the station once more, and near a depot, where there was a large inscription in Hungarian and German that smoking was forbidden, he found a soldier sitting and reading a newspaper which covered him so completely that it was impossible to see his shoulder straps. Lieutenant Dub shouted at him 'Attention!', because it was a man from a Hungarian regiment which was stationed in Humenné in reserve.

Lieutenant Dub gave him a shaking. The Hungarian soldier stood up and did not even consider it proper to salute. He merely stuck the newspaper in his pocket and went off towards the road. Lieutenant Dub followed him as though in a trance, but the Hungarian soldier quickened his pace and then, turning round, put his hands up above his head in a mocking gesture so as not to leave Lieutenant Dub in any doubt that he had at once recognized him as belonging to one of the Czech regiments. After that the Hungarian trotted out of view among the huts close behind the road.

To show that this scene did not concern him Lieutenant Dub went majestically into a small shop by the road, pointed in some confusion to a large reel of black thread, put it into his pocket and paid for it. Then he returned to the staff carriage, where he made the battalion orderly call his batman Kunert, to whom he gave the thread and said: 'I have to see to everything. I know you've forgotten the thread.'

'Humbly report, sir, we've got a whole dozen.'

'Then show them to me immediately and be back here again with them at once. Do you imagine I believe you?'

When Kunert returned with a whole box of reels of thread, white and black, Lieutenant Dub said 'Now look here, you bastard. Carefully observe the threads which you brought and this big reel of mine. See how your threads are thin and how easily they break. Now look at mine. You've got to work very hard before you can break it. When we're in the field we don't want any rags. In the field everything must be solid. Very well, then, take away all those threads again and wait for my orders. And remember, next time don't you dare to do on your own anything which comes into your head, but come and ask me before you buy anything. And you'd better not wish to get to know me. You don't know my bad side yet.'

When Kunert went away Lieutenant Dub turned to Lieutenant

Lukáš: 'My batman is a very intelligent fellow. Occasionally he makes a mistake but otherwise he catches on to it quite well. The best thing about him is his absolute honesty. When we were in Bruck I got a parcel containing several roast goslings from my brother-in-law in the country, and, believe me, he didn't touch them at all. As I couldn't eat them so quickly he preferred to let them get rotten and stink. Of course it's a matter of discipline. An officer must give his soldiers proper training.'

Lieutenant Lukáš purposely turned to the window so as to make it plain that he was not listening to this idiot's claptrap. He said: 'Yes, it's Wednesday today.'

Lieutenant Dub, feeling the need to say at least something, turned to Captain Ságner, whom he asked in a quite familiar, comradely tone: 'Look, captain, what do you think . . .?'

'Excuse me for a moment,' said Captain Ságner, and went out of the carriage.

Meanwhile Švejk was talking to Kunert about the latter's master.

'Where have you been all the time when there wasn't a trace of you?' Švejk asked.

'But you know very well,' said Kunert. 'All the time I have bother with that old lunatic of mine. Every minute he calls you to him and asks you about things that aren't your business at all. He even asked me whether I was a friend of yours and I told him that we see very little of each other.'

'That was awfully sweet of him to ask about me. I like him very much, that lieutenant of yours. He's so kind, so good-natured, a real father to the soldiers,' said Švejk solemnly.

'Well, that's what you think,' objected Kunert. 'But I tell you, he's a bloody swine and a first-class idiot too. I'm fed up with him. He's always on at me.'

'Not really?' said Švejk in surprise. 'You know, I thought that he was really such a decent chap. It's funny the way you speak about your lieutenant, but perhaps it's natural. All batmen do the same. Take Major Wenzl's. He never says anything about his master except that he's a bloody idiotic fool. Or take Colonel Schröder's. Whenever he talked about his master he never called him anything else but a pissed bastard and a stinking shit. This is because every batman learns it from his master. If the master himself didn't swear, the batman wouldn't repeat it. When I was in regular service in Budějovice there was a Lieutenant Procházka there. He didn't swear very much: he only used to say to his batman: "You lovely cow, you." His batman, who was called Hibman, never heard any other word of abuse from him. And of course Hibman got so used to it than when he went back to civil life he used to say to his papa, mamma or sisters: "You lovely cow, you", and he said the same thing to his fiancée with the result that she broke with him and had him up for insulting her honour, because he had said it to her and her papa and mamma in public at a dance. And she never forgave him and before the court she stated that if he had called her a cow somewhere in private she might perhaps have been ready to consider a reconciliation, but as things were it meant a European scandal. Between ourselves, Kunert, I'd never have thought that of your lieutenant. He made such a nice impression on me the first time I spoke to him. He was like a smoked sausage, all fresh from the chimney, and when I spoke to him the second time he seemed very well read and a man of sensibility. Where do you actually come from? Direct from Budějovice? I'm always glad when someone comes direct from somewhere. Where do you live there? In the arcades? That's good. At least it's cool there in the summer. Have you got a family? A wife and three children? You're lucky, my friend. At least you'll have somebody to mourn you, as my dear Chaplain Katz always used to say in his sermons. And it's true of course, because I once heard a colonel talk like that when he was making a speech to the reserves at Bruck, who were going from there to Serbia: every soldier who leaves a family behind him and falls on the battlefield severs all his family ties – or rather his exact words were these: "If he iss a corpse, zen he iss a corpse of ze family. Ze family tice are gebroken, but he iss all ze more hero, because he hass zacrificed hiss life for ze greater family, for ze Vaterland." Do you live on the fourth floor? On the ground floor? Of course, I'd forgotten that in the square in Budějovice there isn't a single four-storied house. Are you going away already? Ah I see, your lieutenant is standing in front of the staff carriage and looking this way. Should he by chance ask you whether I've talked about him, of course tell him I have and don't forget to say how nicely I spoke of him, how I said that I'd rarely met an officer who behaved in such a friendly and fatherly way as he does. Don't forget to tell him that I consider him very well read and also say that I think he's very intelligent. Tell him too that I warned you to be good and to obey his slightest whim. Will you remember that?'

Švejk got into the van and Kunert went back again to his hole with the threads.

A quarter of an hour later they went on towards Nová Čabyna over the burned-out villages of Brestov and Veliký Radvaň. It was clear that they had had pretty tough fighting there. The Carpathian hillsides and slopes were furrowed with trenches running from valley to valley along the railway track with its new sleepers, on both sides of which were huge shell craters. The track followed the upper reaches of the Laborec and here and there across the streams flowing into it could be seen new bridges and the charred beams of those they had replaced.

On the way to Medzilaborce the whole valley was furrowed and the earth piled up as though armies of giant moles had been working there. The road behind the river was dug up and destroyed, and alongside it could be seen the vast trampled expanses left by the armies which had rolled over them.

Storm and rain had uncovered the torn shreds of Austrian uniforms lying on the edge of the shell craters.

Behind Nová Čabyna entangled in the branches of an old burnt-out pine there was hanging the boot of an Austrian infantryman with a piece of shin-bone.

Where the artillery fire had raged one could see forests without leaves or cones, trees without crowns and shot-up farmsteads.

The train went slowly over the freshly-built embankments so that the whole battalion could take in and thoroughly savour the delights of war. At the sight of the army cemeteries with their white crosses gleaming on the plains and on the slopes of the devastated hills all could prepare themselves slowly but surely for the field of glory which ended with a mud-bespattered Austrian cap fluttering on a white cross.

After Humenné the Germans from Kašperské Hory, who sat in the rear vans, grew powerfully silent. As recently as at the station of Milovice they had still been bawling as they came in, 'When I come, when I come, when I come back again . . .'

They understood that many of those whose caps were on the gravestones had sung like them of how nice it would be when they returned home and stayed there for ever with their sweethearts.

In Medzilaborce the stop was behind the smashed and burnt-out station. Twisted beams jutted out from its charred walls. The new long wooden shed, which had been quickly built to replace the burnt-out station, was pasted over with posters in all languages: 'Subscribe to the Austrian war loan.'

Another long shed housed the Red Cross depot. Two nurses and a fat military doctor stepped out of it. The nurses laughed uproariously at the fat military doctor, who was giving an imitation of various animal sounds for their amusement and was making an unsuccessful attempt to grunt.

At the bottom of the embankment in the valley of the river lay a smashed field-kitchen. Pointing to it Švejk said to Baloun: 'Look, Baloun, what we must expect in the near future. The men's mess portions were just on the point of being issued and at that very moment a shell flew in and made this kind of a mess.'

'It's frightful,' sighed Baloun. 'I never imagined that anything like this was in store for me. But it's all the fault of my cursed pride because, miserable brute that I am, I bought some kid gloves in Budějovice last winter. I thought I was too fine to put on my peasant paws the old gloves which my late papa used to wear and so I kept on hankering after those kid gloves from the town. Papa had to be satisfied with boiled peas but I couldn't stand peas at any price, I would touch nothing but poultry. I even turned up my nose at ordinary roast pork too; my old woman used to have to cook it for me with beer, God forgive me!'

Overcome with despair Baloun began to make a general confession: 'I blasphemed against the saints and martyrs. At Malše in a pub and in Dolní Zaháji I beat up the chaplain. I just managed to believe in God, I won't deny it, but I had doubts about St Joseph. At home I tolerated all the saints; only the picture of St Joseph had to be removed, and now God has punished me for all those sins of mine and for my immorality. All those immoral acts I committed in the grinding room! How often I swore at my papa and made his life a burden to him. How I bullied my wife.'

Švejk thought for a moment: 'You're a miller, aren't you? Then you ought to know that though the mills of God grind slowly they grind exceedingly small – if it was all because of you that the world war broke out.'

The volunteer joined the conversation: 'With all that blaspheming, Baloun, and your refusal to recognize all saints and martyrs you certainly did a bad service to yourself, because you must know that our Austrian army has been for years a purely Catholic army and finds its most glorious example in our supreme war leader. How can you be so brazen as to go into battle carrying in your heart the poison of hatred against some saints and martyrs, when the Ministry of War introduced Jesuit sermons for the officers at garrison commands and when we have witnessed the glory of the military resurrection? Are you sure you understand me, Baloun? Do you realize that you're committing a crime against the glorious spirit of our glorious army, as in the case of St Joseph, of whom you said his picture was not allowed to hang in your home? But surely, Baloun, you know that he's in fact the patron saint protecting all those who shirk military service. He was a carpenter and you know very well our expression: "Let's see where the carpenter has left a hole."[1] How many people let themselves be taken prisoner with this slogan. Surrounded on all sides, they saw the inevitability of it, and tried to preserve themselves, not out of any egoistic considerations, but just as members of the army, so that afterwards when they were released they could say to His Imperial Majesty: "We are here and we await your further orders." Now do you understand that, Baloun?'

'No, I don't,' sighed Baloun. 'I have a very thick head. For me you've got to repeat everything ten times.'

'Couldn't you manage with a little less?' asked Švejk. 'If so I'll try to explain it to you once again. Here you've been hearing that you have to act according to the spirit prevailing in the army, that you must believe in St Joseph and that when you are surrounded by the enemy you must look out for where the carpenter has left a hole, so that you can preserve yourself for His Imperial Majesty and for further wars. Now perhaps you understand and you would do best to confess to us in rather more detail what immoral acts you were actually up to in that grinding room. But don't you dare tell us anything like that story about the girl who went to the priest for confession and afterwards when she had confessed various sins blushed and said that every night she committed immoral acts. Now when the priest heard that, you can imagine how his mouth began to water at once, and he said: "No, feel no shame, my dear daughter. I am here in the place of God, and you can tell me the fullest details of your immoral acts." And then she burst into tears and said that she was ashamed, because it was such

1. Czech saying, meaning: 'Let's clear off!'

a frightfully immoral act, and he explained to her once more that he was her spiritual father. In the end after long reluctance she started to tell how she used to undress and creep into bed. And then again he could not get a word out of her and she only started to cry all the more. And he said once more that she shouldn't be ashamed, that man was by his very nature a sinful vessel but the grace of God was infinite. So she decided to speak and told him amid tears: "When I undressed and got into bed I began to pick the dirt out between my toes and smell it." And that was all her immorality. But I hope, Baloun, that in the grinding room you didn't do that and that you'll tell us something more substantial, a really immoral act.'

It turned out that Baloun according to his own description had committed immoral acts with peasant women in the grinding room, but his immorality consisted only in his adulterating their flour, which in his simpleness of mind he called immorality. The most disappointed man of all was Chodounský, who asked Baloun if he really hadn't been up to something with the peasant women on top of the flour sacks in the grinding room, whereupon Baloun swung his arms and replied: 'I was too stupid for that.'

The men were informed that lunch would be taken beyond Palota in the Lupkovský Pass, and the battalion quartermaster sergeant-major got out and went to the village of Medzilaborce accompanied by the cooks of all the companies and Lieutenant Cajthaml, who was responsible for the battalion's provisioning. Four men were assigned to them as patrol.

They returned in less than half an hour with three pigs tied by the back legs, a howling family of a Ruthenian, from whom the pigs had been requisitioned, and the fat military doctor from the Red Cross shed who was passionately explaining something to Lieutenant Cajthaml, while the latter was only shrugging his shoulders.

The whole dispute came to a climax outside the staff carriage, when the military doctor began to tell Captain Ságner straight out that those pigs were assigned to the Red Cross hospital. But the peasant would not admit this and demanded that the pigs should be returned to him. He insisted that they were his only property and that he certainly could not hand them over for the price which they had paid him.

Saying this he tried to thrust into Captain Ságner's hand the money which he had got for the pigs and which he was holding. The peasant woman held Captain Ságner's other hand and kissed it with that servility which has always distinguished this region.

Captain Ságner was quite scared by all this and it took a moment before he was able to push the old peasant woman away. But it was of no avail. In her place young forces came up and began to suck his hands again.

Lieutenant Cajthaml announced in a businesslike tone: 'That bastard has twelve more pigs and he was paid quite correctly according to the last division order, no. 12420, catering section. According to that order, paragraph 16, pigs are to be purchased in places outside the war zone at a price of not more than 2 crowns 16 hellers per kilo of live weight. In war-affected areas for every kilo of live weight there are to be added 36 hellers, which means 2 crowns 52 hellers per kilo. There is an additional note saying that, should there be cases documented where in war-affected areas farms have preserved intact their full complement of pigs and other stock and they can be delivered for purposes of catering units which are passing through, payment can be made for the requisitioned pork at the same rates as in places outside the war zone with a special extra payment of 12 hellers per kilo of live weight. If this situation is not completely clear a commission should at once be set up on the spot, consisting of the prospective purchaser, the commander of the military unit passing through and that officer or quartermaster sergeant-major (if it is a question of a smaller formation) who has charge of the catering.'

Lieutenant Cajthaml read all this from a copy of the divisional order which he always carried about on him. So he already knew almost by heart that in the front zone the price per kilo of carrots was increased by 15.30 hellers and the price of cauliflower for the officers' messing department by 1 crown 75 hellers.

Those who had drawn up these orders in Vienna imagined the front zone to be a land flowing with carrots and cauliflowers.

Lieutenant Cajthaml read this out of course in German to the enraged peasant and asked him if he understood it. When the latter shook his head he shouted at him: 'Do you want to have a commission then?'

The peasant understood the word commission and nodded his head affirmatively. And while his pigs had been dragged off only a moment ago to the field-kitchen for execution, he was now surrounded by bayoneted soldiers assigned on requisition duty. The commission set off for his farm to establish whether he should get 2 crowns 52 hellers per kilo or only 2 crowns 28 hellers.

Hardly had they reached the road leading to the village when there resounded from the field-kitchens the triple dying squeals of the pigs.

The peasant understood that it was all up and shouted out in desperation: 'Give me 2 Rhine guilders for each pig!'

The four soldiers ringed him in closer, and his whole family kneeled down in the dust of the road and obstructed the way for Captain Ságner and Lieutenant Cajthaml.

The mother and her two daughters embraced the knees of both, calling them benefactors, until the peasant shouted at them in the Ruthenian dialect of the sub-Carpathian Russians and told them to get up: let the soldiers gorge themselves on the pigs and come to a sticky end.

And so that was the end of the commission, but because the peasant suddenly began to be obstreperous and threaten them with his fist, he was beaten by one of the soldiers with a rifle-butt so that his sheep-skin coat resounded with the blow. Then the whole of his family made the sign of the cross and fled together with their father.

Ten minutes later the battalion quartermaster sergeant-major together with the battalion orderly, Matušič, were enjoying pig's brain in their van and while the former valiantly stuffed himself he said waspishly to the writers from time to time: 'You'd like a bite, wouldn't you? Well, my boys, this is only for the higher ranks. The cooks get the kidneys and liver, the quartermaster sergeant-majors the brain, head and neck, and the writers only double the ordinary men's portion of meat.'

Captain Ságner had already issued an order for the officers' mess: 'Roast pork with caraway seed. Select the top-quality meat so that it isn't too fat!'

And so it happened that when in the Lupkovský Pass the mess portions were given to the men, every soldier found in his portion of soup two tiny pieces of meat and whoever happened to be born under an unlucky star found only a piece of skin.

In the kitchen there prevailed the usual military nepotism which rewarded all those who were close to the ruling clique. The batmen appeared in the Lupkovský Pass with greasy lips. Every orderly had a stomach like a boulder. Things happened which screamed to high heaven.

Marek caused a scene in the kitchen, because he wanted to be fair, and when the cook put into his mess-tin of soup a fair-sized slice of roast joint with the remark 'This is for our historian', he declared that in the army all men were equal. This met with general support and provided a good excuse for swearing at the cooks.

The volunteer threw the slice of meat back, saying firmly that he didn't want any favouritism. This was not understood in the kitchen where they thought that the battalion historian was not satisfied, so the cook took him aside and told him that if he came afterwards when the mess portions had been distributed he would get a piece of leg.

The writers' muzzles were also shiny with grease, the medical orderlies snorted with affluence and all around this scene of cornucopia lay the traces of the most recent battles. Cartridge cases were lying about everywhere as well as empty tins, shreds of Russian, Austrian and German uniforms, parts of smashed carts, long bloody strips of gauze bandages and cotton wool.

Where the station had once stood there was now only a heap of rubble and an unexploded shell had lodged itself in an old pine tree. Everywhere could be seen splinters of shrapnel and somewhere in the immediate neighbourhood the corpses of soldiers must evidently have been buried, because it smelt frightfully of putrefaction.

And as the troops passed through and camped in the neighbourhood there could be seen everywhere little heaps of human excrement of international extraction belonging to all peoples of Austria, Germany and Russia. The excrement of soldiers of all nationalities and of confessions lay side by side or heaped on top of one another without quarrelling among themselves.

A half-smashed water reservoir, a wooden hut of a railway watchman and everything of any kind which had any walls were riddled with rifle bullets like a sieve.

To complete this impression of the delights of war, clouds of smoke were rising behind a hill not far away, as though a whole village was burning there and was the centre of large-scale military operations. In fact they were burning the cholera and dysentery huts to the great satisfaction of those gentlemen who were concerned with the setting up of that hospital under the patronage of the Archduchess Marie, and of those brigands who had salted away tidy sums by fiddling accounts for non-existent cholera and dysentery huts.

And now one group of huts was the victim for all the others, and in the stink of the burning straw mattresses there rose to high heaven all the thuggery of archducal patronage.

Behind the station the Germans from the Reich had lost no time in setting up on a rock a monument to the fallen Brandenburgers with the inscription 'The Heroes of the Lupkovský Pass' and a huge Reich German eagle cast out of bronze. On its plinth it was expressly stated that the emblem was made out of Russian guns captured during the liberation of the Carpathians by German regiments from the Reich.

In this strange atmosphere, to which they had not yet got accustomed, the battalion was resting in the vans after lunch and Captain Ságner and the battalion adjutant were exchanging cipher telegrams with the brigade base without being able to reach an understanding on the further advance of the battalion. The messages were so inaccurate that it looked as if the battalion should not have come to the Lupkovský Pass at all, but have travelled in a completely different direction from Sátoraljaújhely, because in the telegrams there was mention of the places: 'Csap – Ungvár, Kis-Berezna – Uzsok'.

Ten minutes later it turned out that the staff officer sitting at the brigade base was an utter nitwit, because a ciphered telegram came in asking whether they were the 8th march battalion of the 75th regiment (military cipher G.3). The nitwit at the brigade base seemed amazed at the answer that they were the 7th march battalion of the 91st regiment and asked who ordered them to go to Mukačevo along the military track road towards Stryj, when the march route was across the Lupkovský Pass towards Sanok in Galicia. The nitwit was awfully surprised that the telegram had come from the Lupkovský Pass and sent the ciphered message: 'March route unchanged, direction Lupkovský Pass – Sanok, where await further orders.'

After Captain Ságner's return there was talk in the staff carriage of some people having lost their heads and certain hints were dropped that if it had not been for the Reich Germans the East Army Group would have lost their heads completely.

Lieutenant Dub tried to defend the idiocy of the Austrian staff and burbled something to the effect that the terrain here was pretty devastated by recent battles and that it had not been possible to put the railway track into the required order yet.

All the officers looked at him pityingly as if to say: 'This gentleman can't help being a bloody fool.' Encountering no opposition Lieutenant Dub started to burble more about the magnificent impression which this devastated scenery left on him, since it proved the striking power of the mailed fist of our army. Again no one answered him, whereupon he repeated: 'Yes, to be sure, of course, the Russians fled here in complete panic.'

Captain Ságner resolved that at the next opportunity when the situation was really dangerous in the trenches he would send Lieutenant Dub as officer on patrol for reconnoitring the enemy's positions beyond the barbed-wire entanglements. He whispered to Lieutenant Lukáš, when they were both leaning out of the window of the carriage: 'These damned civilians are a bloody headache. The intellectuals among them are the biggest bastards of them all.'

It looked as if Lieutenant Dub would never stop talking. He went on to explain to all the officers what he had read in the newspapers about those Carpathian battles and the fight for the Carpathian passes during the Austro-German offensive on the San.

He spoke about it as though he had not only taken part in those battles but had even directed all the operations himself.

It was especially repulsive when he uttered sentences of this kind: 'Then we went towards Bukovsko to secure the line Bukovsko-Dynov, keeping contact with the Bardějov group at Velká Polanka where we smashed the Samara division of the enemy.'

Lieutenant Lukáš could not stand it any longer and remarked to Lieutenant Dub: 'And of course you talked about this already before the war with your district hejtman.'

Lieutenant Dub gave Lieutenant Lukáš an ugly look and left the carriage.

The military train stood on an embankment and down below some metres under the slope lay various objects thrown away by the retreating Russian soldiers, who must have retreated along this ditch. Here were rusty teapots, saucepans and cartridge pouches. Side by side with these various things lay rolls of barbed wire and more bloody strips of gauze and cotton wool. At one place a group of soldiers was standing over the ditch and Lieutenant Dub noticed at once that Švejk was there explaining something to them.

And so Lieutenant Dub went up to join them.

'What's happened here?' he said in a stern voice, standing directly in front of Švejk.

'Humbly report, sir,' answered Švejk for all of them, 'we're having a look.'

'And what are you having a look at?' shouted Lieutenant Dub.

'Humbly report, sir, we're having a look down into the ditch.'

'And who gave you permission to do that?'

'Humbly report, sir, it was the wish of our Colonel Schröder from Bruck. When we were about to leave for the battlefields he said good-bye to us and told us in his speech that when we walked over deserted battlefields we all of us ought to examine very carefully how the fighting took place and see what could be of use to us. And in this ditch we can see everything that every soldier has to throw away when he retreats. We can see here, humbly report, sir, how stupid it is when a soldier drags about with him all sorts of useless things. He's needlessly encumbered with them. It tires him unnecessarily and if he carts such a weight about with him he can't easily fight.'

The hope suddenly dawned in Lieutenant Dub's breast that he would at last manage to have Švejk brought before a wartime drum-head court-martial for treasonable anti-war propaganda, and so he asked quickly: 'And so you think that a soldier should throw away cartridges like these lying about here in the ditch or bayonets like those I see there?'

'Oh, of course not, oh no, humbly report, sir,' Švejk answered, smiling affably. 'But please look down here at that abandoned metal chamberpot.'

And under the embankment there was indeed lying provocatively a rusty chamberpot of beaten enamel among chips and fragments of other pots. All these articles, which were no longer suitable for domestic use, had been stacked up here by the station master as material for discussion for archaeologists in future ages who, when they discover this settlement, will be quite crazy about it and children in the schools will be taught about the age of enamel chamberpots.

Lieutenant Dub stared at this object but could not do otherwise than confirm that it really was one of those disabled war veterans which had spent their green youth under a bed.

This made a tremendous impression on everyone and when Lieutenant Dub said nothing Švejk piped up: 'Humbly report, sir, once there was a lot of fun with a chamberpot like that at Poděbrady spa. I heard about it in a pub at Vinohrady. At that time, you see, they'd started publishing in Poděbrady a provincial rag called *Independence*. A Poděbrady chemist was the main person behind it, and they made a certain Ladislav Hájek of Domažlice editor. And that chemist was such a queer fish that he used to collect old pots and other bits and pieces until he had a whole museum of them. And that Hájek of Domažlice once invited to Poděbrady spa a friend of his who was also a journalist, and they both got thoroughly pickled together, because they hadn't seen each other for a whole week. And the journalist promised his friend that in return for this binge he would write a feuilleton for *Independence*, that independent journal on which he was dependent. So he went and wrote a feuilleton about a collector who found in the sands on the bank of the Elbe an old metal chamberpot, thought it was the helmet of St Wenceslas, and made such a fuss about it that Bishop Brynych of Hradec came to look at it with a procession and banners. Then the chemist of Poděbrady thought that the feuilleton was about him and so both of them, he and Mr Hájek, had a row.'

Lieutenant Dub was dying to push Švejk down the embankment but he controlled himself and shouted at all of them: 'I tell you, you're not to waste your time standing and staring here! None of you know me yet, but wait till you get to know me . . .

'Švejk, you stay here!' he said in a frightful voice, when Švejk and the others were about to return to the vans.

They remained standing in front of each other and Lieutenant Dub was thinking hard what frightful thing he could say to him.

But Švejk cut in: 'Humbly report, sir, if only the weather would keep. It's not very hot in the daytime and the nights are really quite pleasant so that this is the most suitable time for warfare.'

Lieutenant Dub drew out his revolver and asked: 'Do you know what this is?'

'Humbly report, sir, I do. Lieutenant Lukáš has one like it, you know.'

'Then don't forget it, you bastard,' Lieutenant Dub said with gravity and dignity as he put his revolver back. 'You should know that something very unpleasant can happen to you if you continue with these propagandas of yours.'

Lieutenant Dub went away repeating to himself: 'Now I really put it well: "These propagandas of yours", yes, "these propagandas of yours".'

Before Švejk got into his van again he walked about for a short time muttering to himself: 'In what class should I put him?' And the more he thought about it the more clearly it came to him that his classification should be: 'A semi-fart.'

In the army vocabulary the word 'fart' had been in favourite use from time immemorial and in the main this honourable title was bestowed on colonels or senior captains and majors, and it indicated

a degree higher than the commonly used term: 'Bloody old man'. Without the adjective 'bloody' the appellation 'old man' indicated friendly appreciation of an old colonel or major who blew his top a lot but at the same time was fond of his men and protected them from other regiments, particularly when it came to other patrols rounding them up in pubs when they had not been given 'extended leave'. An 'old man' looked after the interests of his soldiers and insisted that their messing was in order, but he always had some kind of bee in his bonnet, was always on about something – and so he was 'the old man'.

But when the 'old man' gave the officers and men a lot of unnecessary hell, thought up night operations and other things like that, he became the 'bloody old man'.

From 'bloody old man', if he attained the highest degree of bloodiness, bullying and blockheadedness, he became a 'fart'. This word was full of meaning, and great was the difference between a 'fart' in civilian life and a 'fart' in the army.

The former, the civilian, was also a superior official and was given this name by messengers and subordinates in government offices. He was a bureaucrat and Philistine, who, for example, would complain that the draft was not properly dried with blotting paper and so on. He was a thoroughly oafish and bloody phenomenon in human society, because a mule like that at the same time pretended to be decent, wanted to understand everything, could explain everything and took offence at everything.

Anyone who has served in the army naturally understands the difference between this kind of phenomenon and the 'fart' in uniform. Here the word meant an 'old man' who was bloody, really bloody, and who made a thorough bastard of himself about everything, but all the same stopped before any obstacle. He did not like the men and wrangled with them without result. He could not gain any of the authority which the 'old man' and the 'bloody old man' enjoyed.

In some garrisons, as for example at Trento, instead of 'fart' the men used to say 'our old shit'. In all cases it was applied to an elderly person and when Švejk inwardly christened Lieutenant Dub 'a semifart' he quite logically diagnosed that in both age and rank, and in fact in everything whatsoever, Lieutenant Dub lacked fifty per cent of the quality of being a 'fart'.

Returning to his van with these thoughts in his head he met the batman, Kunert, who had a swollen face and muttered something unintelligible about how he had just run into his master, Lieutenant Dub, who had suddenly out of the blue socked him many times across the jaw, because allegedly he had proof that he was friendly with Švejk.

'If that's the case,' said Švejk calmly, 'we'll go on report. The Austrian soldier may permit himself to be hit in the face only in certain cases. But that master of yours has exceeded all bounds. As old Prince Eugène of Savoy used to say, "As far as so far." Now you must go yourself on report and if you don't I'll swipe you a few myself to teach you what discipline in the army means. In the barracks in Karlín there was once a lieutenant called Hausner and he had a batman too and swiped him across the jaw and kicked him. Once this batman had had so many across the jaw that he was knocked quite silly and he went on report and, getting mixed up, stated there that he'd been kicked. And so that master of his was able to prove that he was lying, since on that particular day he had not kicked him but only socked him on the jaw. As a result the good batman was jugged for three weeks for bringing a false charge.

'But that doesn't affect the case,' Švejk continued. 'It's just the very same thing as the medico Houbička always used to say, that when you cut someone up in the pathological institute it comes to the same thing whether he hanged or poisoned himself. But I'll go along with you. In the army a few socks on the jaw are no laughing matter.'

Kunert had been knocked stupid and let himself be led by Švejk to the staff carriage.

Leaning out of the window Lieutenant Dub roared out: 'What do you want here, you bastards?'

'Comport yourself with dignity,' Švejk urged Kunert, and pushed him forward to the carriage.

In the corridor Lieutenant Lukáš appeared with Captain Ságner behind him.

Lieutenant Lukáš, who had already had so much to do with Švejk, was frightfully surprised, for he no longer looked as good-naturedly solemn as usual; his face lacked its accustomed good-humoured expression and instead boded some new unpleasant developments.

'Humbly report, sir,' said Švejk, 'the matter's going on report.'

'For God's sake don't be a bloody fool again, Švejk. I'm fed up with that.'

'Would you mind permitting me, sir,' said Švejk. 'I am your company orderly. You are, sir, if you will kindly allow me to say so, the company commander of the 11th, if you please, sir. I can understand, sir, that this appears horribly strange, but I know too that Lieutenant Dub is under your command.'

'You've gone completely crazy, Švejk,' Lieutenant Lukáš interrupted. 'You're tight. You'd better go away! Do you understand, you bloody fool, you bastard, you.'

'Humbly report, sir,' said Švejk, pushing Kunert in front of him. 'It seems just like when in Prague they tried to use a protecting rail to stop people being run over by trams. The inventor himself fell a victim to the experiment and afterwards the City Council had to pay his widow compensation.'

Captain Ságner, not knowing what to say, nodded his head in agreement, while Lieutenant Lukáš looked desperate.

'Everything must go on report, sir,' continued Švejk inexorably. 'You told me already in Bruck, sir, that when I was company orderly I had other duties beyond just carrying out orders. You said I had to keep myself informed about everything that was happening in the company. On the basis of this instruction I would like to inform you, sir, that Lieutenant Dub has struck his batman across the jaw for no reason at all. Humbly report, sir, I might not have told you this. However, I saw that Lieutenant Dub is assigned to your command and I said to myself that it must go on report.'

'This is an odd business,' said Captain Ságner. 'Why are you pushing Kunert forward like this, Švejk?'

'Humbly report, sir, everything must go on report. He's been knocked silly. He had his jaw struck by Lieutenant Dub and he's not capable of going on report by himself. Humbly report, sir, you should look at him and see how his knees shake. He's got no life in him, because he has to go on report. And if it hadn't been for me he wouldn't probably have gone on report at all, like a chap called Kudela from Bytouchov. When he was in regular service he kept on going on report again and again until he was finally transferred to the navy, where he became a cornet and was later declared a deserter on an island in the Pacific. There he got married and talked also with the traveller Havlasa, who had no idea he was not a native. . . . It's of course extremely distressing when someone has to go on report just because of a few stupid swipes across the jaw. He didn't want to come here, because he said he wouldn't come here. Altogether he's been so bashed about and knocked so silly that he doesn't even know what swipes on the jaw he's complaining about. He wouldn't have come here at all. He didn't want to go on report. He would have let himself be swiped lots more times and lots more again. Humbly report, sir, look at him. He's all in a shit because of it. But on the other hand he really ought to have complained at once that he had got those swipes, but he was afraid to do so because he knew that it was better, as a poet once wrote, "to be a modest violet". He works for Lieutenant Dub, you see.'

Pushing Kunert in front of him Švejk said to him: 'Don't be all of a flutter like the aspen leaves of an oak!'

Captain Ságner asked Kunert to tell him how it had actually happened.

Kunert, however, shaking all over, asserted that they could ask Lieutenant Dub. He had never struck him across the face.

Continuing to tremble all over, the Judas, Kunert, even went so far in the end as to maintain that the whole thing was an invention of Švejk's.

Lieutenant Dub put an end to this embarrassing affair by appearing suddenly and roaring at Kunert: 'Do you want to get a few *more* across the jaw?'

The case was then completely clear and Captain Ságner told Lieutenant Dub quite simply: 'From today on Kunert is assigned to the battalion kitchen and as to the question of a new batman for yourself you'd better apply to Quartermaster Sergeant-Major Vaněk.'

Lieutenant Dub saluted and as he went out said to Švejk: 'I'm willing to bet that you'll be hanged one day.'

When he had gone Švejk turned to Lieutenant Lukáš and said in a gentle, friendly tone: 'Once in Mnichovo Hradiště there was a gentleman like that too and he spoke to another chap in the same way and got the answer: "We'll see each other on the execution ground."'

'Švejk,' said Lieutenant Lukáš, 'you really are a bloody fool, but don't you dare say as you usually do: "Humbly report, sir, I'm a bloody fool."'

'Remarkable,' said Captain Ságner as he leant out of the window. He would have liked to go away from the window, but had no time to do so because disaster appeared in the shape of Lieutenant Dub who stood under it.

Lieutenant Dub started by saying that he was very sorry that Captain Ságner had gone away and had not listened when he gave the reasons for the offensive on the Eastern front.

'If we are to understand this giant offensive,' Lieutenant Dub called up to the window, 'we have to realize how the offensive developed at the end of April. We had to break through the Russian front and found the line between the Carpathians and the Vistula the most convenient place for this break-through.'

'I'm not disputing it with you,' answered Captain Ságner drily, and left the window.

When half an hour later the journey towards Sanok continued Captain Ságner stretched himself out on the seat and pretended to sleep, so that in the meantime Lieutenant Dub might forget his hackneyed conclusions about the offensive.

In Švejk's van Baloun was missing. He had in fact begged and obtained permission to wipe the goulash cauldron clean with a piece of bread. He was now in the van with the field-kitchens in an unpleasant situation, because when the train started to move he flew headlong into the cauldron and his legs stuck out of it. However, he got used to this position and from inside the cauldron the licking of his lips could be heard. It was like a hedgehog chasing beetles. Later Baloun's pleading voice could be heard: 'For God's sake, chaps, be kind and throw me a piece of bread. There's an awful lot of sauce here still.' This idyll lasted until the next station where they arrived with the cauldron of the 11th company so spotlessly clean that the metal inside it gleamed like a mirror.

'God bless you, chaps,' said Baloun, thanking them heartily. 'It's the first time that fortune has smiled on me since I've been in the army.'

Nothing could have been truer. In the Lupkovský Pass Baloun managed to get two portions of goulash. Lieutenant Lukáš expressed his pleasure that Baloun had brought him an untouched portion from the officers' mess and left him a good half of it. Baloun was serenely happy, swung his legs which he stuck out of the train, and suddenly the whole war seemed to him something domestic and cosy.

The company cook began to tease him and say that when they came to Sanok another supper and one more lunch would be cooked to make up for the fact that throughout the journey they had had nothing. Baloun only nodded his head in assent and whispered: 'You'll see, chaps, that the Lord will not abandon us.'

Everybody laughed heartily at this and the cook sitting on the field-kitchen began to sing:

> 'Upida! Upidee!
> God won't abandon us, not he!
> If he chucks us in the dirt,
> He'll scrape us out, that's a cert.
> If he chucks us in the wood,
> He'll bite us out. I'm sure he could.
> Upida! Upidee!
> God won't abandon us, not he!'

Beyond the station of Szczawne new military cemeteries began to appear again in the valleys. Beneath Szczawne a stone cross with a headless Christ could be seen from the train. He had lost his head when the track was blown up.

The train increased its speed, hurrying down the valley to Sanok.

The horizons grew larger and at the same time the groups of destroyed villages on both sides of the landscape became more and more frequent.

Near Kulaszne a Red Cross train could be seen down in the stream. It had plunged down the railway embankment and been smashed to pieces.

Baloun goggled at this and was particularly astonished at the sight of the parts of the engine thrown around below him. The funnel was rammed into the railway embankment and stuck out of it like a twenty-eighter.

The phenomenon also aroused attention in the van where Švejk was. Jurajda got most excited by it: 'What, is it allowed to fire at Red Cross vans?'

'It's not allowed, but it can be done,' said Švejk. 'It was a perfect shot, and they will apologize afterwards, of course, and make the excuse that it was night time and the red cross couldn't be seen. There are lots of things in the world which are not allowed to be done but can be done. The main thing is that everybody should try to do what he's not allowed to do so that it can be done. During the Imperial manoeuvres at Písek an order came that soldiers on the march were not allowed to be trussed. But our captain had the idea that they could be, because an order like that was frightfully ridiculous. After all, any-one could see that a soldier who was trussed couldn't march. And so he didn't evade the order, but quite simply and sensibly had the trussed soldiers thrown into the trucks of the baggage train and in this way it was possible to go on marching with them. Or consider another case which happened in our street five or six years ago. A man called Mr Karlík was living on the first floor. One storey above there lived a good man called Mikeš who was a student at the conservatoire. He was very fond of women and among others began to run after the daughter of Mr Karlík, who had a carriers' business and a confec-tionery shop as well as a bookbinding firm under a completely different name somewhere in Moravia. When Mr Karlík learnt that the student was running after his daughter he went to see him in his flat and said to him: "You're not going to marry my daughter, you gutter-snipe. I shan't give her to you!" "All right," Mr Mikeš replied, "if I can't marry her what do you expect me to do? Do you expect me to break myself in half?" Two months later Mr Karlík called on him again and brought his wife with him. They both said to him with one accord: "You bastard, you've robbed our daughter of her honour." "Of course I have," he answered them. "I've taken the liberty of making a whore of her, madam." Then Mr Karlík started shouting at him quite gratuitously that he'd told him that he must not marry her and that he wouldn't give her to him, but Mr Mikeš answered quite correctly that he was not going to marry her and that at that time they had never discussed what he could do with her. There had been no bargaining about that. He would keep his word and they shouldn't worry as he wouldn't marry her. He was a man of character and not a straw in the wind. He would keep his word because when he said something it was sacred. And if he were persecuted for it it wouldn't matter to him because he had a clean conscience. His late mamma on her very death-bed had asked him to swear that he would never tell a lie in his life, and he had given her his hand of honour in promise and an oath like that was a valid one. In his family no one at all had told lies, and at school he had always had the best marks for moral conduct. And so you can see from that that lots of things aren't allowed but yet can be done, and that "though our ways may be different, let our endeavours be the same."'

'Dear friends,' said the volunteer, who was eagerly making notes, 'every cloud has a silver lining. This Red Cross train which was blown up and hurled half-burnt down the embankment enriches the glorious history of our battalion by adding a new heroic act for the future. I visualize that perhaps on 16 September, as I've already noted down, one or two ordinary soldiers from every company of our battalion led by a corporal will volunteer to blow up the enemy's armoured train which has been firing at us and preventing us crossing the river. Disguised as peasants they honourably discharge their mission.

'What do I see here?' the volunteer exclaimed, as he looked into his notes. 'How did our Mr Vaněk get here?

'Listen, sergeant-major,' he said, turning to Vaněk, 'what a fine little article there will be about you in the battalion history. I believe you've been already mentioned once, but this will be definitely finer and more substantial.' He read out in an exalted voice:

'HEROIC DEATH OF QUARTERMASTER SERGEANT-MAJOR VANĚK

'The plan to blow up the enemy's armoured train was a bold one and among others Quartermaster Sergeant-Major Vaněk volunteered to take part, disguised like the others in peasant costume. He was temporarily stunned by the explosion and when he recovered he found himself surrounded by the enemy. They immediately sent him off to their division staff, where face to face with death he refused to give any information about the position and numbers of our forces. Since he was in disguise he was condemned to be hanged as a spy, but in view of his high rank the sentence was commuted into one of death by shooting. The execution was carried out at once at the wall of the cemetery and brave Quartermaster Sergeant-Major Vaněk asked that his eyes should not be bandaged. When asked whether he had any wish he replied: "Convey my last greeting to my battalion through one of your truce negotiators. Say I die in the conviction that our battalion will continue to go forward on its path of glory. Also tell Captain Ságner that according to the last brigade order the portion of tins is increased daily to two and a half tins per man." So died our Quartermaster Sergeant-Major Vaněk. With his last dying sentence he instilled panic into the enemy who had thought that in stopping us from crossing the river they would cut us off from our supply points, quickly starve us out and sow demoralization in our ranks. The fact that before his execution he played Kaufzwick with the enemy staff officers is a testimony to the composure with which he faced death. "Give the sum I've won to the Russian Red Cross," he said, as he stood and looked down the muzzles of the firing squad. This noble magnanimity brought tears to the eyes of the military representatives present.

'Excuse me, Mr Vaněk,' the volunteer continued, 'for having taken the liberty of disposing of the money you won. I had been considering whether it shouldn't perhaps be given to the Austrian Red Cross, but in the end I assumed that from the humanitarian point of view it was all the same, provided it was given to some humane institution.'

'Our late sergeant-major could have given it to the Soup Institute of the City of Prague,' said Švejk, 'but it's better as it is, because probably with that sum the lord mayor might have bought a sausage for his elevenses.'

'Well, of course, they steal everywhere,' said Chodounský.

'And most of all in the Red Cross,' said Jurajda furiously. 'In Bruck I once knew a chef who cooked for the nurses in their hut and he told me that the matron and all the head nurses sent home whole trunks of Malaga and chocolate. This is what opportunity brings with it. It's the self-determination of man. Every man in the course of his eternal life undergoes countless changes and has to appear once in this world as a thief in certain periods of his activity. I've gone through this period myself.'

He took a bottle of cognac out of his pack.

'Here you can see the indisputable proof of my assertion,' he said, opening the bottle. 'Before our departure I took this bottle from the officers' mess. It is a cognac of the very best brand and was supposed to be used for icing on Linzertorte. But it was predestined that I should steal it, just as I was predestined to become a thief.'

'And it really wouldn't be a bad thing at all,' Švejk interposed, 'if we were predestined to be your accomplices. In any case I have a presentiment that we are.'

And the predestination proved to be a fact. The bottle was passed

round in spite of the protests of Quartermaster Sergeant-Major
Vaněk, who maintained that the cognac should be drunk out of the
mess-tins and be fairly shared between them, because there were five
men to one bottle, which, being an odd number, meant that it could
easily happen that one person might drink one swig more than the
others; whereupon Švejk put in: 'That's true, but if Mr Vaněk prefers
there to be an even number he might like to withdraw from the circle
– to avoid any unpleasantness or dispute.'

Vaněk then took back his proposal and made another suggestion
which was a generous one, that the donor, Jurajda, should put himself in the position where he could drink twice, but this caused a
storm of opposition, because Vaněk had had one swig already when he
tasted the cognac on opening the bottle.

In the end the volunteer's proposal that they should drink in alpha-
betical order was accepted. He justified it by saying that what a person
was called was really a question of predetermination too.

The bottle was finished by Chodounský who came first in alpha-
betical order. As he did so he cast a menacing glance at Vaněk, who
reckoned that as he was the last he would have one swig more. But
this was a bad mathematical error on his part, because there were
twenty-one swigs.

After that they played ordinary three-card Zwick. It turned out that
whenever the volunteer bought a card he accompanied the action with
pious quotations from the Scripture. When he bought a knave he called
out: 'Oh Lord, let me have this knave this summer too that I may
plough and dung him, that he bear me fruit.'

When they criticized him for having the audacity to buy an
eight, he called out in a great voice: 'Either what woman having ten
pieces of silver if she lose one piece doth not light a candle and sweep
the house and seek diligently till she find it? And when she hath found
it she calleth her friends and her neighbours together, saying, "Rejoice with me; for I have bought an eight and received as well the
king and ace of trumps!" So please give me the cards. You've all of you
burst.'

Marek had indeed great good fortune at cards. While the others were
trying to out-trump each other, he always out-trumped their out-
trumpings, so that they burst one after the other and he grabbed
stake after stake. He called out to those who had lost: 'And in the
places there will be great earthquakes, and tribulations of famine and

pestilence, and there will be great miracles from heaven.' In the end they had enough of it and stopped playing when Chodounský lost his pay for half a year in advance. He was crushed by this, and the volunteer demanded an I.O.U. from him so that Quartermaster Sergeant-Major Vaněk would pay Chodounský's pay packet to him.

'Don't be afraid, Chodounský,' Švejk comforted him. 'If you have any luck you'll fall in the first action and Marek won't get any pay packet from you. Just sign for him.'

The mention of his falling in battle upset Chodounský very much and he said firmly: 'I can't fall, because I'm a telephonist and telephonists are always in covered positions. Telephone wires are only put up or tested for faults after the action.'

The volunteer gave it as his opinion that telephonists were, on the contrary, exposed to great dangers, as it was mainly on them that the enemy concentrated their artillery fire. No telephonist was safe in his cover. If he were ten metres under the ground the enemy artillery would find him none the less. That telephonists died like flies was proved by the fact that when he left Bruck they were just opening the twenty-eighth course for telephonists.

Chodounský stared in front of him in dismay, which moved Švejk to make the friendly and good-natured remark: "You can't help it. It's all a dirty business anyway.' Chodounský answered affably: 'Shut up, auntie.'

'I shall look for the letters "ch" in my notes for the history of the battalion . . .' Marek observed. 'Chodounský, Chodounský, h'm, aha, here we are: "Telephonist Chodounský buried by a mine explosion. Telephones to the staff from his tomb: 'I'm dying and I congratulate my battalion on its victory!'"'

'Surely that's good enough,' said Švejk, 'or do you want more still? Do you remember that telephonist on the *Titanic*? After the ship had already sunk he went on telephoning down to the flooded kitchen to ask when lunch would be served.'

'It doesn't matter to me,' said the volunteer. 'If you like, Chodounský's dying words can be completed by his final call on the telephone: "Give my last greetings to our Iron Brigade!"'

4

Forward March!

WHEN they came to Sanok it turned out that in the van with the field-kitchen of the 11th company, where the bloated Baloun was farting with bliss, they had been quite right in thinking that supper would be served and that as well as supper there would even be an issue of army bread for all those days when the battalion had got nothing. When they got out of the vans they also found out that it was in Sanok that the staff of the 'Iron Brigade' was located, to which, according to its baptismal certificate, the battalion of the 91st regiment belonged. Although the railway connection to Lwów and northwards to Mościska was undisturbed it puzzled people why the staff of the Eastern sector had made dispositions for the 'Iron Brigade' with its staff to concentrate its march battalions 150 kilometres behind the lines, when the front then ran from Brody to the Bug and along the river northwards to Sokal.

This very interesting strategical question was cleared up in a frightfully simple way when Captain Ságner went to report the arrival of the march battalion to the brigade staff in Sanok.

The officer on duty was the brigade adjutant, Captain Tayrle.

'I'm extremely surprised, Captain Ságner,' said Captain Tayrle, 'that you did not get any definite information. The march route is fixed. Of course you should have reported to us beforehand the line of your advance. According to the dispositions of the High Command you've come *two days too early*.'

Captain Ságner blushed slightly, but it did not occur to him to repeat all those ciphered telegrams which he had been receiving throughout the journey.

'I must say, I'm really surprised, captain, that you . . .' said Adjutant Tayrle.

'I would expect,' Captain Ságner answered, 'that as a fellow-officer you would address me less formally.'

'Just as you like, old man,' said Captain Tayrle, 'but tell me, are you

a regular or a civilian? Regular? Well, that's another story then. . . .
You never can tell, you know. We've had so many bloody fools passing
through – reserve lieutenants. When we retreated from Limanowa and
Kraśnik all those "extra-lieutenants" lost their heads as soon as they
saw a Cossack patrol. At the staff we don't think much of parasites like
them. Some stupid bastard who's passed the army I.Q. test in the end
goes and gets himself on to the regular list or passes an officers' examination when he's a civilian. Of course he goes on being a bloody fool
of a civilian all the time. When war comes he shows he's no lieutenant
at all – just a cowardly shit!'

Captain Tayrle spat and patted Captain Ságner on the back in a
familiar way: 'You'll stay here for about two days. I'll show you all the
sights. We'll have some dancing. We've got some lovely little whores
here – "angel whores". And we've also got a general's daughter who
used to be a Lesbian. So we all dress up in women's clothes and
you'll see what she can do! But she's such a skinny sow that you'd
never imagine it of her. But she knows a thing or two, old man! She's
a bloody bitch – but of course you'll find that out for yourself!

'Excuse me,' he suddenly broke off, 'I must go and spew again. It's
the third time today already.'

To prove how gay it was here, he told Captain Ságner when he came
back that this was the result of a party last night, in which the sappers'
unit had taken part.

Captain Ságner very quickly got acquainted with the commander of
this unit, who also had the rank of captain. An enormously tall man in
uniform suddenly crashed into the office. He was in a daze, did not
notice the presence of Captain Ságner and said to Tayrle quite familiarly: 'What are you doing, you old swine? You certainly sewed up our
countess marvellously yesterday.' He sat down on a chair and said,
laughing uproariously and striking himself over the calves with a thin
cane: 'When I remember how you spewed into her lap . . .'

'Yes,' said Tayrle. 'We had a very jolly evening yesterday.' It was
only then that he introduced Captain Ságner to the officer with the
cane and they all of them left the office of the administrative section
of the brigade and went into a café which had very recently grown out
of a former beer-cellar.

When they went through the office Captain Tayrle took the cane
from the commander of the sappers' unit and brought it banging down
on to a long table, round which twelve military writers fell into line by

order. These were the chaps who had an eye for easy safe jobs behind the lines. They had large satisfied bellies and 'extra' uniforms.

Trying to show off in front of Ságner and the other captain, Captain Tayrle said to these twelve fat apostles of scrimshanking: 'Don't think that I keep you here just to fatten you. You bloody hogs, you'd better jolly well guzzle and booze less and run around more.

'Now I'll show you another training trick,' Tayrle told his companions.

He struck the table again with the cane and asked the twelve: 'When are you going to burst, you hogs?'

All the twelve answered in unison: 'At your orders, sir!'

Laughing at his own crass idiocy and stupidity Captain Tayrle went out of the office.

When they all three sat in the café Tayrle ordered a bottle of jeřabinka and called some young ladies who happened to be free. It turned out that the café was really nothing but a brothel and because none of the young ladies were free Captain Tayrle got exceedingly angry, swore at madame in the coarsest terms and shouted out: 'Who's with Miss Ella?' When the answer came that a lieutenant was with her, his vituperations increased.

It was in fact Lieutenant Dub who was with Miss Ella. When the march battalion was already in its sleeping quarters in a secondary school, he had summoned all the men of his unit and warned them in a long speech that the Russians, when they retreated, had set up brothels everywhere and staffed them with personnel infected with V.D. so as to cause the Austrian army heavy losses through this trick. He accordingly warned his men against visiting such places. Because they were in the front zone he would himself verify by personal inspection of these houses whether his order had been obeyed or not. Anyone who was caught would be brought before a drumhead court-martial.

And so Lieutenant Dub went to verify by personal inspection whether his orders had been obeyed, and for this reason he obviously chose as the point of departure for his journey of inspection the sofa in Ella's cubicle on the first floor of the so-called 'Town Café'. He was having a very good time on this sofa.

Meanwhile Captain Ságner went back to his battalion. Tayrle's company had dispersed. There was a search for Captain Tayrle at the brigade staff where the brigadier had been looking for his adjutant for over an hour.

New orders had come from the division and they had to determine finally the march route for the 91st regiment which had just arrived. According to the new dispositions, the march battalion of the 102nd regiment was to go by the route originally chosen for the 91st.

Everything was in a great muddle. The Russians were retreating very hastily in the north-east tip of Galicia so that some Austrian detatchments got mixed up with each other and in some places units of the German army drove wedges into them. The chaos was completed by the arrival of new march battalions and other military detachments. And in sectors of the front, which were farther in the rear, the same thing occurred as for example here in Sanok, where there unexpectedly arrived the reserves of the German Hanoverian division under the command of a colonel with such an ugly look that the brigadier was thrown into a state of complete confusion. The colonel of reserves of the Hanoverian division showed the dispositions of his staff, according to which his men had to be quartered in the secondary school, where at this very moment the battalion of the 91st had just been billeted. For the accommodation of his staff he requested the evacuation of the building of the Cracow Bank where the staff of the brigade were quartered.

The brigadier got into direct contact with the division and described the exact situation. After that the evil-eyed Hanoverian spoke to the division, as a result of which the brigade received the following order: 'The brigade is to evacuate the town at 6 p.m. in the direction of Tyrawa Wołoska – Liskowiec – Stara Sól – Sambor, where they are to await further orders. They will be accompanied by the march battalion of the 91st regiment which will afford them protection. The dispositions have been worked out in the brigade according to the following plan: the vanguard will leave at half past five in the direction of Tyrawa, preserving a distance of $3\frac{1}{2}$ kilometres between the southern and northern flank cover. The covering rear guard will leave at a quarter past six.'

And so there was a great flap in the secondary school and the only person missing at the conference of the officers of the battalion was Lieutenant Dub. Švejk was given the task of trying to find him.

'I hope you'll find him without any difficulties,' said Lieutenant Lukáš to Švejk, 'because there's always something going on between the two of you.'

'Humbly report, sir, may I ask for a written order from the company? This is just because there always *is* something going on between the two of us.'

While Lieutenant Lukáš copied out on a loose leaf of his notebook an order saying that Lieutenant Dub was to come at once to the school for an officers' conference, Švejk went on to say: 'Certainly, sir. As usual you don't need to have any worries. I shall find him, because soldiers are forbidden to go into brothels and he will certainly have gone into one to verify by personal inspection that none of his platoon wants to be brought before a drumhead court-martial, which is his usual threat. He himself declared to the men of his platoon that he would go through all the brothels and then woe betide them, because they would get to know him from his bad side. By the way, I know where he is. He is in that café just opposite, because all the men watched to see where he would go first.'

'The Combined Halls of Entertainment and Town Café', the establishment mentioned by Švejk, was divided into two parts. Anyone who did not want to go through the café went round the back, where an old lady was sunning herself. She spoke German, Polish and Hungarian and the gist of her remarks was as follows: 'Come along, soldier boy, we've got lovely young ladies here.'

When the soldier boy came in, she led him along the corridor to a reception hall and called to one of the young ladies, who came running up in her slip. She asked for the money in advance, which madame cashed on the spot, while the soldier boy took off his bayonet.

The officers went through the café. The route for these gentlemen was more complicated because it led through the *chambres séparées* at the back of the café where there was a choice of another category intended for the officers and where the slips were of lace, and wine or liqueurs were drunk. Madame would not allow anything to be done here. It all had to take place in the cubicles upstairs. In one of them Lieutenant Dub, in his pants, was rolling about on a sofa enjoying this particular form of paradise which was full of bugs, while Miss Ella related to him the tragedy of her life, which was entirely imaginary, of course, as always happens in these cases. She told him that her father was a manufacturer and she herself had been a schoolmistress at a girls' grammar school in Budapest, and had done this out of blighted love.

On a small table behind Lieutenant Dub within the reach of his hand was a bottle of jeřabinka and glasses. The facts that the bottle was half-empty, and that Ella and Lieutenant Dub were no longer in control of their speech, were incriminating proof that Lieutenant Dub could not carry his liquor. Judging by his speech it was evident that he was already mixing everything up and thought Ella was his batman, Kunert. He called her by Kunert's name and threatened his imagined batman in his usual way: 'Kunert, Kunert, you animal, wait till you get to know me from my bad side ...'

Švejk was expected to undergo the same procedure as all the other soldier boys who went round the back. However, he amiably tore himself away from a girl in a slip, whose screams brought the Polish madame running up. She denied brazenly to Švejk that she had any lieutenant as a guest.

'Don't shout at me like that, madame,' said Švejk affably, smiling sweetly at her, 'or else I'll sock you one on the jaw. In Prague where I lived they once beat up a madame in Platnéřská Street so much that she didn't know where she was. At that time it was a son who was looking for his father, who was called Vondráček and had a tyre business. That madame was called Křovánová. When they brought her round and asked her at the first-aid station what her name was, she said that it was something that began with "Ch". And may I ask your honourable name, please?'

The honourable matron set up a frightful wail, when Švejk, after saying this, pushed her aside and advanced gravely up the wooden staircase to the first floor.

Downstairs appeared the owner of the brothel himself, an impoverished Polish nobleman, who ran up the stairs after Švejk and tried to drag him back by the tunic, shouting at him in German that the rank and file were not allowed to go upstairs, that it was reserved for the officer gentlemen and that the men's place was on the ground floor.

Švejk let him know that he had come here in the interests of the whole army, that he was looking for a certain lieutenant, without whom the army could not proceed to the field, and, when the Pole became more and more aggressive, Švejk knocked him down the staircase and continued upstairs to inspect the locality. He verified that all the cubicles were empty except the one at the very end of the passage. Here he gave a knock, pressed the latch and half opened the door. The squealing voice of Ella could be heard: 'Engaged', and immediately afterwards the deep voice of Lieutenant Dub, who perhaps thought that he was still in his room in camp: 'Come in!'

Švejk entered, advanced to the sofa and handed Lieutenant Dub the loose leaf from the notebook. Looking askance at the various articles of uniform thrown on the corner of the bed, he announced: 'Humbly report, sir, you are to dress and, according to the instructions which I'm handing you, report immediately at our barracks in the secondary school. We have a big military conference there!'

Lieutenant Dub goggled the tiny pupils of his eyes at him but told himself that he was not so tipsy as to fail to recognize Švejk. He immediately imagined that they were sending Švejk to him on report and so he said: 'I'll deal with you immediately, Švejk. You'll see – what – will – happen – to – you . . .

'Kunert,' he shouted at Ella, 'pour – me – another – one!'

He took a drink and tearing up the written instructions laughed: 'That's an – apology? With us – no apologies – are of any use. We – are in the army – and not – at – school. And so – they – have caught you – in a brothel? Come – here – to me – Švejk – come – nearer – I – am going to give you – a few – swipes – across – the jaw. In – what – year – did Philip – of Macedon – defeat – the Romans? You don't – know that – do you – you stallion!'

'Humbly report, sir,' Švejk continued inexorably, 'this is the highest order from the brigade. The gentlemen officers are to put their clothes on and go to a battalion conference. We're leaving, you know, sir, and only now will they decide which companies will be advance guard, flank guard and rear guard. Now they're going to take a decision on this and I think, sir, that you too will have something to say about it.'

This diplomatic speech went some way towards reviving Lieutenant Dub and he began now to feel sure that he was not in the barracks after all. But out of caution he still asked: 'Where am I?'

'You have the honour to be in a brothel, sir. God moves in a mysterious way.'

Lieutenant Dub gave a heavy sigh, got down from the sofa and began to look for his uniform, which Švejk helped him to do. When he had finally dressed they both went out, but a little later Švejk returned for a moment. Taking no notice of Ella, who attributed an entirely different significance to his return and out of unrequited love immediately climbed back into bed, he quickly drank the jeřabinka remaining in the bottle and went out again after the lieutenant.

In the street Lieutenant Dub's head again became befuddled, because it was very hot. He talked to Švejk a lot of nonsense without any connection. He said that he had at home a postage stamp from Heligoland, and that immediately after passing his school-leaving examination they had gone to play billiards and had not taken their caps off to their

class master. To every one of his sentences he added: 'I think you follow me.'

'I certainly do,' Švejk answered. 'You talk rather like a tinsmith called Pokorný in Budějovice. Whenever people asked him: "Have you bathed this year in the Malše?" he answered: "I haven't, but there'll be a lot of plums this year." Or they asked him: "Have you eaten any mushrooms this year?" and he answered: "I haven't, but the new Sultan of Morocco is said to be a very good man."'

Lieutenant Dub stopped and managed to get out of himself: 'Sultan of Morocco? He's a back number now.' He wiped the sweat from his forehead and looking at Švejk with misty eyes murmured:

'I've never sweated like this even in winter. Do you agree? Do you follow me?'

'Yes, I do, sir. When we were at The Chalice an old man used to come there who was a retired official of the district council, and he asserted exactly the same thing. He always said he was surprised at the difference between the temperature in summer and winter. He thought it very strange that people hadn't yet realized it.'

At the school gate Švejk left Lieutenant Dub who reeled on the stairs up to the assembly hall, where the military conference was taking place. He immediately reported to Captain Ságner that he was completely drunk. Throughout the conference he sat with his head in his hands and during the discussion occasionally stood up to cry out: 'Your opinion is correct, gentlemen, but I am completely drunk.'

When all the dispositions had been worked out and Lieutenant Lukáš's company had to go as vanguard cover, Lieutenant Dub gave a sudden jerk, stood up and said: 'I recall, gentlemen, our form master in the first year of the grammar school. Hip hip hurrah, hip hip hurrah, hip hip hurrah!'

It occurred to Lieutenant Lukáš that for the time being the best thing to do would be to make Kunert lay Lieutenant Dub on the couch in the physics cabinet next door, where there was a guard posted to see that no one stole the already half-plundered collection of minerals. The units marching through were continually warned about this by the brigade.

This measure dated from the time when a Honvéd battalion, which had been billeted in the school, began to rifle the cabinet. The Honvéds had taken a particular fancy to the collection of minerals, the gaily-coloured crystals and pyrites, and had stuck them into their packs.

On one of the white crosses in the military cemetery there is the inscription: 'László Gargany'. A Honvéd who plundered the school collections and drank up all the methylated spirit from a jar in which the various reptiles were being preserved now sleeps his last sleep there.

In wiping out the human race the world war did not hesitate to use methylated spirit intended for preserving reptiles.

When all the others had gone away Lieutenant Lukáš had Lieutenant Dub's batman, Kunert, brought to him. He took away his lieutenant and stretched him out on the sofa.

Lieutenant Dub was suddenly like a small child; he took Kunert by the hand and began to look at his palm, saying that he could divine from it the name of his future wife.

'What's your name? Take out of the breast pocket of my tunic my notebook and pencil. You're called Kunert, aren't you? Well, then, come here in a quarter of an hour's time and I'll leave you here a piece of paper with the name of your lady wife.'

No sooner had he said this than he started to snore, but again he seemed to wake up and began to scribble in his notebook. He tore out what he had scribbled and threw it on the ground. Putting his finger mysteriously to his lips he babbled: 'Not now, but in a quarter of an hour's time. You'd better look for the paper blindfold.'

Kunert was such a well-meaning ox that a quarter of an hour later he actually appeared, and when he had unfolded the paper he read from Lieutenant Dub's hieroglyphics: 'The name of your future wife will be: Mrs Kunert.'

Švejk, when he showed this to him a moment later, told him to keep this piece of paper carefully. Documents of this kind from military gentlemen ought to be respected by everyone. In army life it had never been the case before that an officer corresponded with his batman and called him 'Mr'.

When all the preparations had been made for the departure according to the given dispositions, the brigadier, who had been so smartly dislodged by the Hanoverian colonel, made the whole battalion fall in in the usual square formation and made a speech to them. He loved making speeches and, when he did so, muddled everything up, and when he had nothing more to say he remembered the field post:

'My men,' he thundered out to the square, 'now we are nearing the enemy's front, from which we are only separated by a few days' march. Up till now on the march you have not had the opportunity, my men, of informing the dear ones whom you have left behind of your addresses, so that those far away from you may know where they are to write, and you may have pleasure from the letters of your dear bereaved ones.'

He got himself so tied up that he couldn't find a way out and repeated countless times: 'The dear ones whom you have left behind – your dear relatives – your dear bereaved ones' etc., until he finally broke out of the vicious circle by calling out vociferously: 'And that is why we have the field post at the front!'

The rest of his speech gave the impression that all these people in their grey uniforms should let themselves be killed with the greatest joy just because field posts were installed at the front, and if anyone had both his legs torn off by a shell it would be a beautiful thing for

him to die with the thought that his field post number was 72, and that perhaps a letter was lying there from home, from his dear ones far away, with a package containing a piece of smoked pork, bacon and home-made biscuits.

Then, after his speech, when the brigade music struck up the national anthem, three cheers were given for the Emperor, and these various groups of human cattle, which were destined for slaughter somewhere beyond the Bug, set out successively on the march, unit by unit, according to the dispositions made.

The 11th company left at half past five for Tyrawa Wołoska. Švejk trudged behind with the company staff and the ambulance, while Lieutenant Lukáš rode round the whole column, going to the rear every now and then to check on the ambulance, where on a cart under canvas they carried Lieutenant Dub to new heroic deeds of an unknown future. Lieutenant Lukáš also whiled away the journey by talking to Švejk, who patiently carried his pack and rifle and was telling Vaněk how fine it was when they marched on manoeuvres near Velké Meziříčí some years ago.

'It was just the same sort of country as here, only we didn't march with full field-equipment, because at that time we didn't even know what "reserve tins" meant. When we drew any tins, all of us in our platoon ate them at the very next night billet and we put a brick in our sacks instead. In one village inspectors came and threw out all the bricks from our packs. There were so many of them that one chap built a house out of them for his family.'

A little later Švejk marched energetically by the side of Lieutenant Lukáš's horse and talked to him about the field posts: 'That was a beautiful speech, and of course it's very nice for anyone at the front if he gets a kind letter from home. But when I was serving years ago in Budějovice I got only one letter in the barracks and I've still kept it.'

Švejk took out a greasy letter from his stained pocket book and read it aloud, at the same time keeping pace with Lieutenant Lukáš's horse, which had broken into a gentle trot:

'You bloody bastard, you dirty murderer and blackguard! Corporal Kříž came to Prague on leave. I danced with him at U Kocanů and he told me that they say you went dancing at Budějovice at The Green Frog with a stupid tart, and that you've completely thrown me over. For your information I'm writing this letter in the rears on the board next to the hole. It's all over between us. Your former Božena. What did I want to add? Yes, that corporal knows how to do it and he's going to give you hell, because I've asked him to. And what else did I want to say? Yes, when you come home on leave you won't find me among the living.'

'Of course,' Švejk continued at a gentle trot, 'when I came on leave she was still among the living and very living they were! I found her at U Kocanů too. Two soldiers of a foreign regiment were helping her to dress, and one of them was so very "living" that he was quite publicly putting his hand under her bodice just as though, humbly report, sir, he wanted to pluck the bloom of her innocence, as Věnceslava Lužická says,[1] or as a young girl of about sixteen once said with loud sobs to a schoolboy when he pinched her in the shoulder at

1. An authoress of novels for young ladies.

dancing class: "Sir, you have rubbed off the bloom of my virginity."
Of course everybody laughed and her mamma who was looking after
her took her out into the passage in the Union and gave the stupid
ninny a good kicking. However, I must say, sir, that I came to the
conclusion that the country wenches are all the same more sincere than
those worn-out young misses in the towns who go to dancing classes.
When years ago we were in camp at Mníšek I used to go dancing at
Starý Knín and went around with a girl called Karla Veklová, but she
didn't like me very much, I'm afraid. One Sunday evening when I took
her to the lake, we sat on the dam and when the sun was setting I asked
her whether she loved me. Humbly report, sir, the air was so balmy,
all the birds were singing and she replied with a horrible laugh: "I
love you about as much as a piece of straw in my arse, because you're
such an idiot." And I really was an idiot, such a frightful idiot that I
used to stroll with her, humbly report, sir, in the fields amid the
standing corn where there wasn't a living soul and we never sat down
once. I kept on showing her all that cornucopia and, stupid ass that I
was, all I did was to tell that peasant wench that this was rye, this was
wheat and that over there was oats.'

And as though confirming the remark about the oats there resounded
somewhere in front the voices of the company singing in unison. They
continued the song which Czech regiments sang when they marched
and bled for Austria at Solferino:

> 'And when the night was black,
> The oats jumped out of the sack.
> Hey, diddly dee,
> Every wench is free!'

And the others immediately joined in:

> 'Is free, is free, is free,
> And so why shouldn't she
> Plant a burning kiss
> On that cheek or on this?
>
> Hey, diddly dee,
> Every wench is free,
> Is free, is free, is free,
> And so why shouldn't she . . .'

After that the Germans started singing the same song in German.
This is an old, old soldiers' marching song which the *soldateska* used

to sing in all languages perhaps as long ago as in the Napoleonic wars.
Now it resounded hilariously on the dusty road on the way to Tyrawa
Wołoska in the Galician plain, where on both sides of the road as far as
the green hills in the south, the fields were trampled on and destroyed
under the hooves of horses and the soles of thousands and thousands of
soldiers' heavy boots.

'Once we made the same mess at the manoeuvres near Písek,' said
Švejk, looking about him. 'We had with us an Imperial Archduke. He
was such a fair gentleman that when for strategic reasons he rode
with his staff through the corn, the adjutant behind him at once calculated all the damage he'd caused. A peasant called Pícha was not at all
pleased at this visit and refused to accept from the government eighteen
crowns compensation for the hectare of land which had been trampled
down. You won't believe it, sir, but he wanted to go to law, sir, and he
got eighteen months for it.

'But I think, sir, that in fact he ought to have been grateful that
someone from the Imperial House came to see him on his land. Another peasant, a more conscientious one, would have dressed all his
girls in white dresses like bridesmaids, put bunches of flowers in their
hands and stationed them on his estate. And each of them would have
had to welcome the exalted gentleman, like I've read they did in India,
when the subjects of a ruler allowed themselves to be trampled on by
that elephant.'

'What on earth are you talking about, Švejk?' Lieutenant Lukáš
called down to him from his horse.

'Humbly report, sir, I mean that elephant which carried on his back
that ruler which I read about.'

'You've certainly got an explanation for everything, Švejk,' said
Lieutenant Lukáš and rode on ahead. There the column was already
getting broken up. After the rest in the train the unaccustomed march
in full and complete equipment resulted in them all getting sore
shoulders, and everyone tried to make himself as comfortable as he
could. They shifted their rifles from one side to the other. Most of them
no longer carried them by their slings but had them thrown over their
shoulders like a rake or fork. Some thought they would get on better by
marching in the ditch or on the meadows where the ground under their
feet felt softer than on the dusty road.

Most of them went with bowed heads and all suffered from enormous
thirst, because in spite of the sun having already set it was just as sultry

and stifling as if it had been mid-day and no one had a drop of water left in his field-flask. It was the first day of the march and this unaccustomed situation, which was a kind of prelude to greater and greater hardships, made all of them weaker and fainter the farther they went. They stopped singing and started to guess among themselves how far it could be to Tyrawa Wołoska, where they thought they would be spending the night. Some sat down for a time in the ditch and so as not to make a wrong impression undid their boots and acted at first glance like somebody who has put his puttees on wrong and tries to rewind them so that they will not pinch him on the march further on. Others shortened or lengthened their rifle slings or opened their packs and went through the objects contained in them, trying to persuade themselves that they were doing it to distribute the load better and to prevent the pack straps pulling on one or other of their shoulders. When Lieutenant Lukáš approached them they got up one after the other and reported that something was hurting them, if indeed the cadets or sergeants had not caught a glimpse of Lieutenant Lukáš's mare in the distance and already hounded them on.

Lieutenant Lukáš, as he rode by, asked them in a friendly tone to get up, telling them that it was another three kilometres to Tyrawa Wołoska and they would be able to rest there.

In the meantime Lieutenant Dub recovered consciousness through the constant shaking of the two-wheeled ambulance cart. He had not come round completely but he could already raise himself and lean out of the cart to call to the staff of the company. They were walking freely around, because all of them, beginning with Baloun and ending with Chodounský, had put their packs into the cart. Only Švejk went bravely ahead carrying his pack, holding his rifle by the sling across his chest in dragoon fashion, smoking his pipe and singing as he marched:

> 'When we marched to Jaroměř,
>   Believe it, folks, or not,
>   We reached the town at supper-time
>   And got it on the dot.'

More than five hundred paces in front of Lieutenant Dub clouds of dust rose on the road out of which there loomed the figures of soldiers. Lieutenant Dub, whose enthusiasm had returned to him, leaned his head out of the cart and began to shout at the dust on the road: 'My men, your noble task is a heavy one. Difficult marches are ahead. You will all of you experience deprivations and hardships of every kind. However, I am convinced that I can confidently rely on your pluck and grit.'

'You shit,' Švejk put in poetically.

Lieutenant Dub went on: 'For you, my men, there is no obstacle so powerful that you cannot overcome it. Once more, my men, I repeat to you that I am not leading you to easy victory. It will be a hard nut for you to crack, but crack it you will! You are the heroes of whom historians wrote.'

'Stick your finger down your throat,' Švejk put in poetically again.

And as though Lieutenant Dub had heard this he suddenly began to vomit into the dust of the road with his head bent down and when he had spewed it all out he shouted once more: 'On, soldiers, on! Hurrah!' Then he fell on to Chodounský's pack again and slept till Tyrawa Wołoska, where by order of Lieutenant Lukáš, who had a very long and difficult talk with him, they finally put him on his feet and took him out of the cart. He then recovered so much that he was able at last to declare: 'From a logical point of view I've committed an act of folly, which I shall redeem when we are face to face with the foe.'

He was not of course yet completely himself, because when he went back to his platoon he told Lieutenant Lukáš: 'You don't know me yet, but wait till you get to know me . . .!'

'If you want to know what you've done, you can get the information from Švejk,' Lukáš replied.

So before returning to his platoon Lieutenant Dub went to see Švejk and found him in the company of Baloun and Vaněk.

Baloun was just telling them that in his mill at home he always used to keep a bottle of beer in the well. The beer was so cold that it set his teeth on edge. In other mills in the evening they drank beer to wash down cottage cheese, but he, in his gluttony, for which the good Lord had punished him, always guzzled a sizeable piece of meat after it. Now God in his justice had punished him with tepid stinking water from the wells at Tyrawa Wołoska. As a protection against cholera they had to pour into it citric acid, which they had had distributed to them only a moment ago when the well water was issued to them by companies. Baloun expressed the view that the citric acid was no doubt intended to starve them. It was true indeed that he had managed to get a little to eat at Sanok and that Lieutenant Lukáš had even left him again half a portion of veal which he had brought him from the brigade, but it was dreadful because he had thought that when they came here and there was rest and night quarters they would cook something as well. He had been quite convinced of this when the cooks fetched water for the cauldrons, and had at once gone to the kitchens to ask about it. The answer he got was that they had only received an order to draw water for the time being and any minute another one might come ordering them to pour it away.

At this very moment Lieutenant Dub came up and, being very uncertain of himself, asked: 'Are you having a chat?'

'Yes, we are, sir,' Švejk answered for all of them. 'And our chat is in full swing. It's always best to have plenty of chat. Just now we're chatting about citric acid. No soldier can do without a chat. That's how he forgets all his tribulations.'

Lieutenant Dub told him to come a little of the way with him, because he had a few questions to ask him. When they were on one side he asked him in a frightfully uncertain voice: 'Isn't it me you're chatting about?'

'Oh no, sir, not at all, never, sir, only about citric acid and smoked pork.'

'Lieutenant Lukáš told me that I am supposed to have done something wrong and that you know all about it, Švejk.'

Švejk said very gravely and with great emphasis: 'You haven't done anything at all, sir. You were only visiting a house of ill fame. But it was most likely a mistake. It was just the same as what once happened to a tinsmith called Pimpr from Kozí Square in the Old Town of Prague. Whenever he went to buy metal sheets in the town they always used to search for him and always found him in the same kind of establishment, either at U Šuhů or at U Dvořáků, just as I found you. On the ground floor there was a café and upstairs there were tarts as in our case here. You were probably where you were by mistake, sir, because it was so hot and when someone's not used to drinking in hot weather like that he gets drunk on ordinary rum, to say nothing of jeřabinka, sir. And I got an order to deliver you a summons to come to the conference before we left and I found you with that tart upstairs. Because of the heat and the jeřabinka you didn't even recognize me and lay on the sofa without any clothes on. You didn't kick up a shindy there and you didn't even say: "You don't know me yet." A thing like this can happen to anybody when it's hot. Some people love doing it as a regular thing, while others just get into it by pure accident. If you had known old Vejvoda, sir, a builder's foreman from Vršovice – he once took it into his head that he wouldn't drink any drink which would make him drunk. And so he had his last wee dram for the road at home and set out on a journey to find some non-alcoholic drinks. He called first of all at a pub called At the Stop, had a quarter-litre of vermouth there and started his unobtrusive inquiries of the landlord about what sort of stuff those total abstainers actually drank. He was quite right in thinking that pure water was rather cruel fare even for total abstainers. The landlord then explained to him that total abstainers drink soda water, mineral water, milk and then various kinds of alcohol-free wines, cold clear soup and other beverages without spirit. Of this wide range of drinks it was the alcohol-free wine which most appealed to Vejvoda's taste. He asked one more question: whether there also existed spirits without alcohol. Then he had another quarter-litre of vermouth, talked with the landlord about how it was a real sin to get tight very often, whereupon the latter told him that he could endure everything in the world except a chap who goes and gets himself sozzled in another pub and only comes to him to get sober with a bottle of soda water and perhaps makes a terrible row as well. "Get sozzled in my pub," said the landlord, "and you are my man, but otherwise I won't have anything to do with you." Old Vejvoda finished his vermouth and went out to continue his journey until he came – just imagine it, sir – to a wine shop at Charles Square which he also used to visit from time to time. He asked there whether they didn't have wines without spirit. "Sorry, Mr Vejvoda," they told him, "we don't have any wines without spirit, just vermouth or sherry." Somehow or other old Vejvoda felt ashamed and so he had a quarter-litre of vermouth and a quarter-litre of sherry, and as he sat there he met one of those total abstainers. They got talking and drank another quarter-litre of sherry, and in the end it turned out that the gentleman knew a place where they served wines without spirit. "It's in Bolzanova Street," he said. "You get there down the steps and they have a gramophone there." In reward for this cheering information old Vejvoda ordered a whole bottle of vermouth and then they both walked to the place in Bolzanova Street, which was down the steps and where they had a gramophone. And it was quite true that they only served fruit wines there, not only free of spirit but without alcohol either. First of all each ordered a half-litre of gooseberry wine and then a half-litre of redcurrant wine, and when they had drunk another half-litre of spirit-free gooseberry wine they began to feel pins and needles in their legs after all the vermouth and sherry they had had before. And they began to shout that they must be given official confirmation that what they were drinking there was spirit-free wine. They were total abstainers and if they didn't get this at once they would break everything up including the gramophone. Finally the cops had to drag both of them up the steps again to Bolzanova Street. And they had to put them in the drunks' cart and chuck them into the isolation cell. Both had to be sentenced for being drunk and disorderly when they were total abstainers.'

'Why are you telling me this?' shouted Lieutenant Dub, who had been completely sobered up by this speech.

'Humbly report, sir, it's not really to the point, but I thought that while we were having this nice chat . . .'

At that moment it suddenly occurred to Lieutenant Dub, who had now nearly completely recovered, that Švejk had insulted him once again, so he shouted at him: 'One day you'll get to know me! What about the way you are standing?'

'Humbly report, I'm standing wrong. Humbly report, I've forgotten to put my heels together. I'll do it at once.' And Švejk was already standing at the best possible 'attention'.

Lieutenant Dub tried hard to think what he should say next but in the end confined himself to the remark: 'You'd better look out and see that I don't have to speak to you again,' and then he added a modified version of his old saying: 'You don't know me yet, but I know you.'

When Lieutenant Dub left Švejk he thought to himself in his state of hangover: 'Perhaps it would have had a greater effect on him if I'd said to him: "I've known you for a long time, you bastard, and from your bad side."'

Lieutenant Dub then had his batman Kunert called and ordered him to look for a jug of water.

To Kunert's credit let it be said that he spent a long time in scouring all Tyrawa Wołoska for both the jug and the water. In the end he managed to steal a jug from the vicar and filled it with water from a well which was completely nailed over with planks. To do this he had of course to tear off one or two of them. The well was in fact boarded up because the water in it was suspected of being typhus-infected.

Lieutenant Dub, however, drank up the whole jug without any further effects, which only confirms the saying: 'A good pig can swallow anything.'

It was a mistake to think that they might perhaps spend the night at Tyrawa Wołoska.

Lieutenant Lukáš called Chodounský, Vaněk, Švejk and Baloun. His orders were quite simple. They should leave their equipment by the ambulance cart, set out straight away to Mały Polanec by a path over the fields and then go along the stream down in a south-easterly direction towards Liskowiec.

Švejk, Vaněk and Chodounský were to be a billeting party. They were to find night billets for the company which would follow them in about an hour, or at the most an hour and a half. As for Baloun he was ordered to roast a goose at the house where Lieutenant Lukáš would spend the night. The other three had to keep an eye on him and see he did not wolf up half of it. Apart from this Vaněk and Švejk had to buy a pig within the limits of the quantity of meat allotted to the company. At night they were to make goulash. The night billets for the men must be up to the required standard: they should avoid lousy hovels so that the men could have a really proper rest, because the company would set out from Liskowiec as early as half past six in the morning over Krościenko in the direction of Stara Sól.

The battalion was no longer short of cash. The brigade supply office at Sanok had paid out to it advances in respect of the slaughter that was to come. In the company till there was more than a hundred thousand crowns and Vaněk had already received the order that when they were finally somewhere at their destination, by which they meant the trenches, he should settle accounts and pay the men the sums which were indisputably owing to them for the bread rations and the mess portions which they had not been issued with.

And while these four set out on their journey the local vicar appeared at company headquarters and distributed to the men leaflets with 'The Song of Lourdes' in all languages according to their nationality. He had a bundle of these songs, which had been left here by a high military clerical dignitary, who passed through ravaged Galicia in a car with some tarts. The local vicar was to distribute them to the military units which passed through.

> Where the river flows deep down in the dell
> The angels' message rings out on the bell.
> Ave, ave, ave Maria! – Ave, ave, ave Maria!
>
> The maiden Bernarda was led by the Lord
> Down to the bank through the fresh green sward. – Ave!
>
> There she sees on the rocks in a glow of grace
> A sublime being with a holy face. – Ave!
>
> Lovely she looks in her raiment of white
> With a cloud-coloured girdle, simple and bright. – Ave!
>
> She holds a rosary in hands serene,
> Our merciful and most gracious Queen. – Ave!
>
> A change comes over Bernarda's face.
> It is lit by the glow of Our Lady's grace. – Ave!
>
> She kneels and prays, and the Virgin sees,
> And addresses to her these words of peace. – Ave!

'My child, I conceived, spotless and true,
And shall now be the guardian for all of you. – Ave!

My pious people pass in procession.
They worship me and find salvation. – Ave!

In this dell I shall build a marble dome
In token that here I shall make my home. – Ave!

This bubbling spring calls thee down from above.
It shall be the gage and pledge of my love. – Ave!'

O glory to thee, most merciful dell,
In thee the Mother of God shall dwell. – Ave!

There in the rock is the cave of Thine.
Thou hast given us paradise, merciful Queen. – Ave!

Since this glorious and radiant day
Men and women come here to pray. – Ave!

Worshippers Thou shalt have in throngs.
Look down upon us and right our wrongs! – Ave!

O star of salvation, show us the way
To the throne of God, that we may pray! – Ave!

Most holy Mother, hold us dear
And shed Thy mercy on Thy children here!

In Tyrawa Wołoska there were many latrines and scattered all over them could be found the leaflets with 'The Song of Lourdes'.

Corporal Nachtigal, who came from somewhere near Kašperské Hory, had bought a bottle of spirit from a frightened Jew. Now he gathered together some of his comrades and they all started to sing 'The Song of Lourdes' after the German text without the refrain 'Ave!' and to the tune of 'Prince Eugène'.

It was a bloody awful journey when it got dark and those four, whose duty it was to find night accommodation for the 11th company, got to a spinney above a brook which was supposed to lead to Liskowiec.

Baloun, who found himself for the first time in a situation where he was going somewhere into the blue, and to whom everything, the darkness, the fact that they were going ahead to look for night billets, seemed suddenly extraordinarily mysterious, was seized by a frightful suspicion that things were not as they should be.

'Chaps,' he said quietly, as he stumbled along the path above the brook, 'they've sacrificed us.'

'What do you mean?' Švejk roared at him almost inaudibly.

'Oh chaps, don't let's make such a shindy,' Baloun begged in a whisper. 'I feel it in my bones. The enemy'll hear us and at once start shooting at us. Oh, I know it. They've sent us forward to see whether the enemy's there, and when they hear the firing they'll know at once that it's not possible to advance any further. Chaps, we're the *avant-garde* as Corporal Terna once taught me.'

'Well, go on *avant* then,' said Švejk. 'We'll follow you nicely and you can protect us with your body as you're such a giant. When you're shot, let us know, so that we have time to lie flat on the ground. You're not much of a soldier! He's afraid someone's going to shoot at him! But every real soldier ought to enjoy that frightfully. He must know that the more the enemy shoots the more ammunition he uses up. Every shot which the enemy fires at you reduces his fighting capacity. And he's glad too that he can shoot at you, because he doesn't have to drag his cartridges about with him and can run much easier.'

Baloun gave a heavy sigh: 'But I've got a farm at home.'

'Oh, damn that farm,' Švejk advised him. 'It's much better for you to give your life for His Imperial Majesty. Didn't they teach you that in the army?'

'They only mentioned it,' said the idiotic Baloun. 'They only took me to the drill-ground and after that I didn't hear anything any more about it, because I became a batman. . . . If only His Imperial Majesty would feed us better . . .'

'You're a bloody gluttonous pig. A soldier shouldn't be given any food at all before an engagement. We were told that years ago in the school by Captain Untergriez. He always used to say to us: "You bloody bastards, if there should be a war and you should get into a battle, you mustn't gorge yourselves before it. A chap who's overgorged and stops a bullet in his belly is done for at once, because all the soup and army bread fly out of his guts after a shot like that, and a soldier who stops one gets an inflammation and is finished at once. But if he's got nothing in his stomach then a shot there doesn't mean anything to him. It's just like when a wasp stings you, a pure pleasure." '

'I digest very quickly,' said Baloun. 'Nothing ever stays very long in my stomach. Just imagine, chaps, I might eat a whole dish of dumplings with pork and cabbage and half an hour later I don't shit out of me more than two or three soupspoons. The rest gets lost inside me. Some people say for instance that when they eat chanterelles they come out of them whole just as they went in. You can wash them and cook them again in sour sauce, but with me it's the opposite. I stuff myself so full with chanterelles that anyone else would burst, and when I go to the rears afterwards I just fart out a little yellow gruel like a baby. The rest gets lost inside me.

'You won't perhaps believe me,' Baloun told Švejk confidentially, 'but fishbones and even plum stones get dissolved in me. Once I purposely counted them. I ate seventy plum dumplings with their stones and when my time came I went behind the huts, poked about in it with a stick, separated the stones and counted them. Of those seventy stones more than half got dissolved inside me.'

A quiet long-drawn sigh escaped Baloun's lips. 'My old woman used to make plum dumplings out of potato-dough, to which she added a little curds to make it richer. She always preferred to sprinkle them with poppy seeds rather than with cheese, but I liked the opposite so that once I smacked her face because of it. . . . Oh, dear, I wasn't capable of appreciating my domestic bliss.'

Baloun stopped, licked his lips, rolled his tongue over his palate and said sadly and softly: 'You know, old man, now I don't have them I believe my wife was right and that they are better with poppy seed. Then I always imagined the poppy seeds stuck in your teeth but now I think if only they did. . . . Yes, my wife suffered lots of trouble with me. How often she wept when I insisted that she put more marjoram in the jitrnice and I always used to biff her one. Once I beat her up so much, poor thing, that she lay in bed for two days and it was all because she wouldn't slaughter a turkey for me for dinner and said that a cockerel would be good enough.

'Yes, old chap,' Baloun began to cry, 'if only I had jitrnice even without marjoram and cockerels now! Do you like dill sauce? You see, we always had rows about it and today I'd drink it like coffee.'

Baloun slowly forgot his fears of an imaginary danger and in the dead of the night, while they were still going down towards Liskowiec, he continued to tell Švejk with emotion what he had not appreciated before and would now like to eat, until his eyes were full of tears.

Behind him walked Chodounský with Vaněk.

Chodounský was saying to Vaněk that in his opinion the world war was bloody nonsense. The worst thing about it was that if a telephone wire was cut anywhere he had to get up in the night and put it right and what was even worse was that when there had been a war before searchlights had not been invented. But nowadays, just when you were mending those bloody wires, the enemy picked you out at once with searchlights and set their whole artillery on you.

Down in the village, where they had to find night billets for the company, it was dark and all the dogs started barking. This forced the expedition to stop and consider what they should do to cope with the brutes.

'What about going back?' whispered Baloun.

'Oh, Baloun, Baloun, if we reported what you've just said you'd be shot for cowardice,' said Švejk.

The dogs barked more and more the farther they went, and they started to bark even to the south beyond the river Ropa as well as in Krościenko and several other villages, for Švejk shouted out into the night quiet:

'Down – down – down,' as he used to shout at his dogs when he had a dog business.

The dogs only barked all the more, so that Vaněk said to Švejk:

'Don't shout at them, Švejk, you'll set the whole of Galicia a-bark.'

'Something similar happened to us on manoeuvres in the region of Tábor,' Švejk answered. 'We marched in the night to a certain village and the dogs started making an enormous racket. The region all round is fairly heavily populated so that the barking spread from village to village, always farther and farther on, and when the dogs in the village where we camped, who had already stopped barking, heard this barking from far away, perhaps even as far away as Pelhřimov, they started to bark again, and after a while there was nothing but barking over the whole area of Tábor, Pelhřimov, Budějovice, Humpolec, Třeboň and Jihlava. Our captain was a very nervous old man and couldn't stand the barking of dogs. He couldn't sleep the whole night but walked up and down asking the patrols: "Who's that barking? What's that barking?" The soldiers humbly reported that it was dogs who were barking, and this infuriated him so much that those of us who were then on patrol got confined to barracks when we returned from manoeuvres. After that he always chose out a "dog command" and sent them ahead. It had the task of informing the inhabitants in the village where we were going to stay overnight that no dog must be allowed to bark in the night otherwise it would be liquidated. I was also on one of those commands and when we came to a village in the region of Milevsko I got mixed up and told the mayor that every dog-owner whose dog barked in the night would be liquidated for strategic reasons. The mayor got frightened, immediately harnessed his horses and rode to headquarters to beg mercy for the whole village. They didn't let him in, the sentries nearly shot him and so he returned home,

but before we got to the village everybody on his advice had tied rags round the dogs' muzzles with the result that three of them went mad.'

They went down to the village after general acceptance had been accorded to Švejk's doctrine that dogs in the night fear the lighted points of cigarettes. Unfortunately none of them were smoking cigarettes, so that Švejk's advice had no positive effect. It turned out, however, that the dogs were barking out of joy, because they remembered with affection the troops who passed through and always left something behind for them to eat.

From a long way off the dogs sensed the approach of creatures who always left behind them bones and horse carcasses. Suddenly, as though they had come from nowhere, four huge dogs appeared and sprang on Švejk in a friendly fashion with their tails erect.

Švejk stroked them, patted them, and spoke to them in the dark as though they were children:

'So at last we're here. We've come to you to go bye-byes, to have our yum-yum. We'll give you delicious bonies and crusties, and the next morning we'll go on towards the enemy.'

In the cottages in the village, lights began to go on, and when they started to knock on the door of the first cottage to find out where the mayor lived, they heard from inside the squealing and shrill voice of a woman, who said in what was neither Polish nor Ukrainian that she had a husband in the army, her children had smallpox, the Russkies had taken everything away from her and that her husband before he went to the front ordered her not to open the door to anyone in the night. Only when they lent weight to their assault on the door by assuring her that they were 'billeteers' was the door opened by an unknown hand. When they got inside it turned out that it was actually here that the mayor lived. He vainly tried to persuade Švejk that it was not he who had imitated the squeaky woman's voice. He excused himself by saying that he slept in the hay and that when someone suddenly awoke his wife from sleep she didn't know what she was saying. As for night billets for the whole company the village was so teeny tiny, he said, that there was no space even for one soldier. There was no place to sleep at all. There was nothing to buy either. The Russkies had requisitioned everything.

Perhaps their gracious lordships would condescend to come with him to Krościenko. There were big farms there and it was only three-quarters of an hour away. There was plenty of room there. Every soldier could cover himself with a sheep skin and get a mess-tin of milk, as they had lots of cows there. The water was good there too. The officer gentlemen could sleep in the castle, but here in Liskowiec there was nothing but penury, the itch and lice. He himself had once had five cows, but the Russkies had requisitioned them all, so that even when he wanted milk for his sick children he had to go to Krościenko.

As though in confirmation of this the cows mooed next door in his cow-shed and a shrill woman's voice could be heard shouting at those unfortunate cows and wishing that the cholera would seize them.

However, the mayor did not let himself be disturbed by this and went on putting on his high boots:

'The only cow here is the one belonging to my next-door neighbour Vojciek. It's the one you have just heard mooing, my gracious lords. It's a sick and miserable cow. The Russkies took away her calf. Since then she doesn't give any milk, but the landlord doesn't like to slaughter her. He hopes that the Mother of God from Częstochowa will put everything right again.'

While he said this he put on his sheepskin coat:

'Let's go to Krościenko, my gracious lords. It isn't even three-quarters of an hour. What am I saying, sinner that I am? It won't even be half an hour. I know a way over the brook and then through the birch grove past the oak. . . . The village is a big one, and they've got very powerful vodka there in their pubs. Let's go, my gracious lords! Why delay? The soldier gentlemen of your glorious regiment must be able to go to bed in order and comfort. The Royal and Imperial soldier who fights with the Russkies undoubtedly deserves a clean bed and comfortable sleeping quarters . . . and here? Lice, the itch, smallpox and cholera. Yesterday in our cursed village here three peasants turned black from cholera . . . the most merciful Lord has placed a curse on Liskowiec . . .'

At this moment Švejk waved his hand majestically.

'Listen, my gracious lords,' he said, imitating the voice of the mayor. 'I once read in a book how in the Swedish wars, when orders had been given to billet the men in some village or other, the mayor began to make excuses and wouldn't give them help and so they hanged him on the nearest tree. And today in Sanok a Polish corporal told me that when the billeting party come the mayor has to summon all the members of the council, and they go with them into each cottage and say quite simply: "Three men can go here, four there, the officers will be billeted at the vicarage and everything must be ready in half an hour."

'My gracious lord,' said Švejk, turning solemnly to the mayor, 'tell me where is your nearest tree?'

The mayor did not understand the word 'tree' and so Švejk explained to him that a 'tree' was a birch, an oak, a pear-tree, an apple-tree, in short anything that had strong branches. The mayor again failed to understand, but when he heard the names of fruit trees he got startled because the cherries were already getting ripe and so he said he had no idea about anything like trees but there was an oak in front of his house.

'All right,' said Švejk, making with his hand the international sign

for hanging. 'We're now going to hang you in front of your house, because you must be aware that there's a war on and that we have orders to sleep here and not in any Krościenko. You won't change our strategic plans, you bastard. You're going to swing just as it happened in that book about the Swedish wars. . . . There was a case like that, gentlemen, once on the manoeuvres at Velké Meziříčí . . .'

At that moment Vaněk interrupted Švejk:

'You can tell us about that afterwards, Švejk,' he said, and turning to the mayor added: 'Very well, then, pull up your socks and produce the billets!'

The mayor began to tremble and stammered something about how he meant it for the best for their gracious lordships, but if there was no other way he could perhaps find something in the village so that all the gentlemen would be satisfied. He would immediately fetch his lantern.

When he went out of the room, which was very sparsely lit by a small paraffin lamp under the image of a saint, who was twisted on the picture like the most wretched cripple, Chodounský suddenly exclaimed:

'Where's Baloun got to?'

However, before they could look about them, the door behind the stove, which led somewhere outside, quietly opened and Baloun slipped in through it. He looked round him to see whether the mayor was there and said, sniffing as though he had a heavy cold:

'I've beed in the larder. I found somethig. I've god my moud idto id and now id's all stuck to my deed. Id isn'd sald or sweed. Id's bread dough.'

Vaněk shone the electric torch on him and all were able to convince themselves that they had never yet seen in their lives an Austrian soldier in such a filthy mess as he was. After that they got frightened because they saw that Baloun's tunic was blown up as though he were in the last stage of pregnancy.

'What's happened to you, Baloun?' Švejk asked him pityingly, prodding his bloated belly.

'It's the gherkins,' Baloun rattled, struggling for breath through the dough, which he couldn't get either up or down. 'Careful, they are salt gherkins. I ate three of them in a rush and I've brought you the others.'

Baloun began to take out from under his tunic gherkin after gherkin and handed them round.

The mayor stood in the doorway with his light. Seeing the scene he crossed himself and whined:

'The Russkies have robbed us and now our people do the same.'

They all went out to the village accompanied by a pack of dogs which clung obstinately to Baloun and jumped up at his trouser pocket, where he had a piece of bacon also obtained from the larder but kept secret from his comrades-in-arms due to his greediness.

'Why are the dogs running after you?' Švejk asked Baloun, who answered only after long reflection:

'They sense in me that I'm a good man.'

What he did not say was that he had his hand on the bacon in his pocket and that one of the dogs was continually snapping at it . . .

When they went round to look for billets they discovered that Liskowiec was a big settlement which had indeed been drained of everything by the war havoc. It had not suffered any fires, it is true, as miraculously enough neither warring parties had included it in their sphere of operations, but on the other hand the population of nearby villages which had been destroyed, such as Chyrów, Grabów and Hołubla, had been settled in it.

In some of the huts there lived as many as eight families in the greatest penury after all those losses which they had suffered through the predatory war, when a whole epoch of it hurled itself over them like the devastating waves of a flood.

The company had to be billeted in a small devastated distillery at the other end of the village, where half a company could be put into the fermenting room. The rest were billeted by tens in various farms where the rich nobility had refused to shelter the miserable riff-raff who had lost their homes and land and been reduced to beggary.

The company staff with all the officers, Vaněk, the batmen, the telephonist, the ambulance, the cooks and Švejk were billeted at the vicarage with the vicar, who had not taken in a single one of the destitute families from the neighbourhood either, although he had plenty of room.

He was a tall thin old gentleman in a faded and greasy cassock who out of stinginess hardly ate at all. He had been brought up by his father to detest Russians, but at once lost his hatred for them when they retreated and the Austrian army came and devoured all his geese and chickens. The Russians had not touched these, when several shaggy Cossacks from beyond Lake Baikal had been billeted on him.

His hatred for the Austro-Hungarian army increased still more when the Hungarians came to his village and took away from him all the honey from his beehives. Now he looked with loathing at his unexpected guests and it gave him pleasure to be able to walk past them, shrug his shoulders and say again and again: 'I've got absolutely nothing. I'm a complete beggar. You won't find even a crust of bread here, gentlemen.'

The man who was the saddest of all at this was Baloun, who nearly burst into tears at such penury. In his head he always had a vague idea of a roast sucking-pig with flesh which crackled and smelt like honey. All this time he was slumbering in the vicar's kitchen, where from time to time a lanky youth peeped in who worked for the vicar as servant and cook and had strict orders to keep an eye on the whole house and see that nothing got stolen.

Baloun could find nothing in the kitchen either except a little bit of paper with a pinch of caraway seed which was lying in a salt-cellar. He stuffed it into his mouth and its aroma awoke in him savoury hallucinations of sucking-pig.

In the courtyard of the small distillery behind the vicarage the flames blazed under the cauldrons of the field-kitchen. The water was already boiling but there was nothing to boil in it.

The quartermaster sergeant-major and the cook went up and down the whole village vainly scouring it for a pig. Everywhere they got the same answer that the Russkies had eaten everything up or taken it away.

They also woke up a Jew in a pub who began to tear his long curls and express desperate regret that he could not help the soldier gentlemen. In the end he made them buy from him an old centenarian of a cow, a scraggy living carcass, which was only skin and bones. He asked a horrific price for it, tore his beard and swore they would not be able to find a cow like it in the whole of Galicia, in the whole of Austria and Germany, in the whole of Europe, in the whole world. And all the time he howled, wept and swore solemnly that it was the fattest cow which had ever come to the world at Jehovah's bidding. He swore by all his ancestors that people came riding all the way from Wołoczyska to look at that cow, they talked about it in the whole region as a marvel, it wasn't really a cow at all but the most succulent of buffalos. Finally he knelt down before them and hugging their knees one after the other cried out:

'Kill the poor old Jew if you like, but don't go away without his cow.'

He confused all of them so much by his screaming that in the end they carried off that sorry beast to the field-kitchen, although any knacker would have refused it. But long afterwards, when he had already got the money in his pocket, he went on weeping before them and complaining that they had completely ruined him and destroyed

him and that he had been utterly beggared by selling such a magnificent cow so cheaply. He begged them to hang him for committing in his old age an act of such utter folly that his forefathers would turn in their graves.

After he had been grovelling in the dust before them he suddenly shook off all his self-pity, went home and said to his wife in the privacy of his room:

'My Elsa, my Elsakins, those soldiers are fools and your Nathan is a clever one.'

They had a lot of trouble with that cow. At times it looked as if it would not be possible to skin it. In flaying it they broke the skin several times and underneath appeared muscles as twisted as a dried-up hawser.

Meanwhile they dragged in a sack of potatoes from somewhere and began hopelessly to cook those sinews and bones, while nearby in a smaller kitchen the cook in utter despair tried to make officers' mess portions out of a piece of that skeleton.

This wretched cow, if that phenomenon of nature deserved the name of cow at all, remained indelibly impressed upon the memory of all who were there, and it is almost certain that if afterwards before the battle of Sokal the commanding officers had reminded the men of the cow from Liskowiec, the 11th company would have hurled itself with fixed bayonets at the enemy to the accompaniment of frightful bellows of rage.

The cow was such a disgrace that it was not even possible to make beef soup out of it. The longer the meat was cooked the more firmly it clung to the bones and grew into them. It grew as ossified as a bureaucrat who spends half a century pasturing on official red tape and devours nothing but official documents.

Švejk, who as courier maintained unbroken communication between the staff and the kitchen so as to ascertain when the meal would be cooked at last, announced to Lieutenant Lukáš:

'Sir, it's come out like porcelain. The cow is so tough that you could cut glass with it. When the cook, Pavlíček, tasted the meat with Baloun, he broke off his front tooth and Baloun lost his back molar.'

Baloun solemnly advanced before Lieutenant Lukáš and, stammering, handed him the broken tooth, which was wrapped up in 'The Song of Lourdes':

'Humbly report, sir, I've done what I could. I broke the tooth when we tried the officers' mess portions to see if it was possible to make a beefsteak out of the meat.'

At these words a melancholy figure rose from an armchair by the window. It was Lieutenant Dub, who had been brought in on an ambulance cart in a state of complete ruin.

'Please be quiet,' he said in despairing tones. 'I'm ill!'

He sat down again in the old chair in every crack of which there were thousands of bugs' eggs.

'I'm tired,' he said in a tragic voice. 'I'm sick and suffering. Please don't speak of broken teeth in my presence. My address is: Smíchov,

Královská 18. If I don't live to see tomorrow's day please see that my family are informed of it and that their feelings are spared. Don't forget to note on my gravestone that before the war I was a schoolmaster in an Imperial and Royal grammar school.'

He started to snore gently and could no longer hear the verse which Švejk quoted from an elegy for the dead:

'O Thou who saved the Virgin's soul
And led the robber to his goal,
Guide me to heaven and save my soul.'

After this Vaněk ascertained that the wonderful cow would have to be cooked two hours longer in the officers' kitchen. There was no question of there being any beefsteak from it and instead they would make goulash.

It was decided that before they sounded the signal for mess the men should be allowed to have a nap, because in any case supper would not be ready before morning.

Vaněk fetched a bundle of hay from somewhere, placed it beneath him in the vicar's dining-room, nervously twisted his moustache and said quietly to Lieutenant Lukáš who was resting above him on an old sofa:

'Believe me, sir, that in the course of the whole war I've never seen a cow like that . . .'

In the kitchen Chodounský was sitting by the lighted stump of a church candle preparing in advance a stock of letters for home so that he wouldn't have to bother about writing any when the number of their field post had been finally decided. He wrote:

Dear darling wife, fondest Boženka,

It is night time and I think incessantly of you, my treasure. I picture you thinking of me as you look at the empty bed beside you. You must forgive me if all sorts of thoughts spring into my mind. You know very well that I have been on military service in the field since the very beginning of the war and that I've already heard all sorts of things from my comrades who have been wounded and gone on leave. When they came back home they would rather have been in their graves than find that some rascally scamp had been at their wives. It's very painful for me to have to write this to you, darling Boženka. I wouldn't perhaps be writing like this but you know very well yourself that you confided to me that I was not the first man who knew you really well and that Mr Kraus from Mikulášská Avenue had you before me. When I think this very night how in my absence that lousy wretch might make some demands on you, I'm ready, darling Boženka, to strangle him on the spot. For a long time I've kept this to myself, but when I think that he might once more run after you, my heart turns to stone and I must warn you of one thing and that is that I will not have living with me a bitch who has gone a-whoring after all and sundry and brought a slur on my name. Pardon me, darling Boženka, for these sharp words, but take care I don't find out any-thing bad about you. If I do I shall be forced to hack the guts out of both of you because I'll stick at nothing even if it costs me my life. I kiss you a thousand times. Give my love to papa and mamma,

Your Tonouš

N.B. Don't forget that *I gave you my name!*

He went on writing further letters for the stock.

My dearest Boženka,

When you get these lines you will know that we already have behind us the great battle in which the fortunes of war turned in our favour. Among other things we've shot down about ten enemy planes and one general with a big wart on his nose. In the thick of the fighting when shrapnel burst over our heads I was thinking about you, dear darling Boženka, what you might be doing, how you were and what was the news at home. I often remember how we went together to St Thomas's beer hall, how you led me home and how next day your arm ached from all that effort. Now we are advancing again and so I have no more time to continue my letter. I hope you have been faithful to me, because you know very well that in this respect I'm a devil. But it's already time for the march. I kiss you a thousand times, dear Boženka, and you must hope that everything will turn out well.

Your loving Tonouš

Chodounský began to nod and fell asleep at the table.

The vicar, who could not sleep and all the time walked up and down in the vicarage, opened the door to the kitchen and for economy's sake blew out the burning stump of the candle beside Chodounský.

In the dining-room no one was sleeping except Lieutenant Dub. Vaněk, who had received in the brigade office at Sanok a new budget for the catering of the troops, was studying it carefully and found that the nearer the army got to the front the more the portions were reduced. He even had to laugh over one paragraph of the order in which it was forbidden to use saffron and ginger in making soup for the men. There was also a note appended to the instructions that in the field-kitchens the bones had to be collected and dispatched to the division stores at the base. It was rather vague because no one could know which bones were meant – the bones of human beings or of other slaughtered livestock.

'Listen, Švejk,' said Lieutenant Lukáš, yawning with boredom, 'before we start eating, you could perhaps tell me a story.'

'Oh dear,' Švejk answered, 'before we get any food I'd have time to tell you the whole history of the Czech nation, sir. But instead I know only a very short story about a postmaster's wife from the district of Sedlčany, who after the death of her husband took over the post office. I straightaway thought of her when I heard that speech about these field posts, although it has absolutely nothing to do with field posts.'

'Švejk,' said Lieutenant Lukáš from the sofa, 'you're starting to talk frightful tripe again.'

'I certainly am, humbly report, sir. The story really is frightful tripe. In fact I don't know how anything so tripish could come into my head or how I could talk of such a thing. Either it's my natural idiocy or else it's memories of my youth. There are, as you know, sir, people with various natures on our globe. And that cook Jurajda was after all right that time in Bruck when he was drunk and fell into the ditch, and when he couldn't get out and shouted from it: "Man is destined and chosen to know truth, that he may with his spirit rule the whole universe in harmony, that he may continually develop and educate himself and gradually rise to higher and higher spheres and more intelligent and affectionate worlds." When we wanted to drag him out he scratched and bit. He thought he was at home and it was only when we threw him back again into it that he began begging us to drag him out of it.'

'But what happened to that postmistress?' Lieutenant Lukáš cried in desperation.

'She was a very good woman, the only thing was that she was a bit of a bitch, sir. She carried out all her duties at the post office but she only had one fault, and that was that she thought everybody was persecuting her and had a down on her. And so after her day's work she denounced them to the authorities according to how the circumstances came about. Once she had gone in the early morning to the wood to pick mushrooms and had observed carefully how when she went past the school the schoolmaster was already up. He had greeted her and asked her where she was going so early in the morning. When she had told him that she was going to pick mushrooms, he had said that he would follow after. From that the silly old woman concluded that he had some indecent intentions towards her and afterwards when she saw him actually coming out of the bushes she took fright, ran away and at once wrote to the local school council denouncing him for having tried to rape her. The schoolmaster was summoned before a disciplinary board, but to prevent a public scandal the school inspector himself came to look into the case. He spoke to the sergeant of the gendarmerie and asked him to give his view whether that schoolmaster was likely to have done such a thing. The sergeant of the gendarmerie looked into the documents and said that he was incapable of it, because once already he had been accused by the priest of running after his niece, whom the priest used to sleep with, and the schoolmaster had obtained from the district doctor a certificate confirming that he'd been impotent since he was six, when he fell with wide-open legs from the loft down on to the shaft of a haycart. And so that bitch went and denounced the sergeant of gendarmerie, the district doctor and the school inspector for having all of them been bribed by the schoolmaster. They all of them took her to the courts where she was found guilty, but she appealed on the grounds that she was mental. She was examined by the medical experts and they issued an official certificate that although she was feeble-minded she could hold any office in the State service.'

Lieutenant Lukáš exclaimed:

'Jesus Mary!' and added afterwards: 'I'd like to say something to you, Švejk, but I don't want to spoil my supper', after which Švejk said:

'I warned you, sir, that what I was going to tell you was frightful tripe.'

Lieutenant Lukáš only waved his hand and said: 'You've dropped so many pearls of wisdom, Švejk.'

'Not every man can have wisdom, sir,' said Švejk convincingly. 'Stupid people have to exist too, because if everyone were wise then there would be so much good sense in the world that every other person would be driven crazy by it. If for instance, humbly report, sir, everyone knew the laws of nature and could calculate the distance of the heavenly bodies, then he would only be a trouble to those around him like a man called Mr Čapek who used to come to The Chalice, and whenever he went out of the pub on to the street at night he looked at the stars in the sky and when he came back went up to everyone and said to each of them: "Today Jupiter is shining beautifully. You've got no idea, you bastard, of what you've got over your head. Talk about distances! If they were to shoot you out of a gun with the speed of a shell, you lousy brute, you'd still have to fly for millions and millions of years to get there." When he said this he was so coarse and rude that afterwards he himself usually flew out of the pub with the usual speed of a tram, perhaps, sir, at about ten kilometres an hour. Or take for instance, sir, the ants...'

Lieutenant Lukáš raised himself on his sofa and put his hands together in prayer:

'I'm really surprised at myself for always talking to you, Švejk. After all, I've known you for so long, Švejk...'

Švejk nodded affirmatively:

'It's a question of habit, sir. It's due to the very fact that we have known each other for so long and that we've gone through a lot together. We've suffered a lot together and if we got into trouble it was always by a pure fluke. Humbly report, sir, I think it's fate. What His Imperial Majesty ordains, he ordains well. He brought us together and I wish nothing better for myself than to be able to be a really great help to you sometimes. Aren't you hungry, sir?'

Lieutenant Lukáš, who had meanwhile stretched himself out on the old sofa again, said that Švejk's last question was the best ending to this lamentable conversation, and that he should go and ask what had happened to the mess. It would certainly be better if Švejk could go out for a little and leave him, because the tripe which he kept on hearing from him exhausted him more than the whole march from Sanok. He would like to go to sleep for a bit, but he couldn't.

'It's all because of the bugs, sir. There's an old saying that vicars breed bugs. You'll not find anywhere so many bugs as you do at vicarages. In the vicarage in Horní Stodůlky the vicar, who was called Zamastil, even wrote a whole book about bugs. They were crawling on him even when he was preaching.'

'Well, what did I say, Švejk? Are you going to the kitchen or not?'

Švejk went out and behind him Baloun came out on tiptoe from a corner like his shadow...

When in the morning they left Liskowiec for Stara Sól and Sambor they carted in the field-kitchen with them the wretched cow which was still not cooked enough. It was resolved that they should cook it on the way and that they would eat it at the rest pause halfway between Liskowiec and Stara Sól.

For the journey they made the men black coffee.

Lieutenant Dub was again carried on the ambulance cart because he felt still worse after yesterday. The man who suffered most from him was his batman, who had continually to run beside the cart, while Lieutenant Dub shouted at him without cease that he had not looked after him at all yesterday and that when they reached their destination he would settle with him. Every moment he asked for water and when he drank it he vomited it up again.

'Who – what are you laughing at?' he shouted from the cart. 'I'll teach you. Don't play with me. You'll get to know me!'

Lieutenant Lukáš rode on horseback accompanied by Švejk, who marched sprightly forward, as though he could hardly wait for the moment when they were to fight the enemy. All the time he talked:

'Have you noticed, sir, that some of our people are really like flies? They have hardly thirty kilos on their backs and yet they can't stick it. They ought to be given lectures like the late Lieutenant Buchánek gave to us. He was the man who shot himself because of the advance which he got out of his future father-in-law for his marriage and which he spent on other tarts. And then he got another advance from another future father-in-law and was a bit more economical with it. He slowly lost it at cards and left the tarts alone. But he couldn't hold out for long and had to find a third future father-in-law for an advance. With this third advance he bought a horse, an Arab stallion, not a thorough-bred . . .'

Lieutenant Lukáš jumped down from his horse.

'Švejk,' he said in a menacing tone, 'if you start talking about a fourth advance I'll chuck you into the ditch.'

He jumped back on to his horse and Švejk went on solemnly:

'Humbly report, sir, there was no question of a fourth advance, because he shot himself after the third one.'

'At last,' said Lieutenant Lukáš.

'Not to forget what we've been talking about,' Švejk went on, 'the sort of lectures which Lieutenant Buchánek always used to give us whenever soldiers collapsed during the march ought, in my modest opinion, to be given to all the troops. He gave the order for "rest", made us all line up like chickens round a hen and began to explain to us: "You bastards, you're quite incapable of appreciating the fact that you're marching on this globe, because you're such uneducated scum that it's enough to make a chap vomit when he looks at you. You should be made to march on the sun! A man who weighs sixty kilos on our miserable planet weighs over seventeen hundred there. That'd do you all in. You'd have to march carrying in your packs over 280 kilos or about three quintals, and your rifle alone would be one and a half quintals in weight. You'd be groaning with your tongues hanging out like exhausted hounds." We had with us an unfortunate schoolmaster and he was so bold as to break in: "If you'll excuse me, sir, on the moon a man of sixty kilos weighs only thirteen kilos. On the moon we'd be able to march better because our packs would only weigh four kilos. On the moon we should not be marching at all, we should be floating in the air."

' "Tut! tut! That's really awful," the late Lieutenant Buchánek said. "You seem to be asking for a sock on the jaw, you lousy bastard. You can be glad I'm going to give you just an ordinary earth sock, because if I were to give you a moon sock with your light weight you'd fly as far as somewhere in the Alps and be smashed up there. If I were to give you a heavy sun sock your uniform would be changed into pea soup and your head would fly somewhere to Africa." And so he gave the Jimmy Knowall an ordinary earth sock, and he started blubbing and we went on marching. But during the whole march he blubbed and talked, sir, about human dignity or something like that, complaining that they were treating him as if he were a dumb creature. After that the lieutenant sent him on report and they gaoled him for fourteen days. He had six more weeks to serve but he didn't serve them because he got a rupture. Somehow or other they made him twist on the horizontal bars in the barracks and he couldn't take it and died as a malingerer in the hospital.'

'It's really very peculiar, Švejk,' said Lieutenant Lukáš, 'that as I've already told you so many times, you have a habit of speaking in a specially disparaging way about the officers' ranks.'

'Oh, no, I don't,' Švejk answered sincerely. 'I only wanted to tell you, sir, how in the old days in the army people drove themselves to ruin. That man whom I was talking about thought that he was more educated than the lieutenant. With his talk about the moon he wanted to lower him in the eyes of the troops, so because of that he got that earth sock on the jaw. And everybody sighed with relief. No one minded. On the contrary all were only glad that the lieutenant had made such a good joke about his earth sock: that's what you call "saving the situation". A chap has to have a sudden bright idea and then it's all right. Opposite the Carmelite Convent in Prague, sir, there used years ago to be a shop with rabbits and other birds kept by a Mr Jenom. He started walking out with the daughter of a bookbinder called Bílek. Mr Bílek didn't approve of the acquaintance and announced publicly in the pub that if Mr Jenom asked for the hand of his daughter he'd knock him down the stairs in a way the world had never seen. Mr Jenom then had a good drink to get his courage up and went to see Mr Bílek all the same. The latter welcomed him in the hall with a large knife which they used for trimming books and which looked like a chopper. He thundered at him and asked him what he wanted, and at that moment the good Mr Jenom farted so loudly that the pendulum on the grandfather clock stopped. Mr Bílek burst out laughing, shook his hand at once and from then on it was just: "Welcome, dear Mr Jenom – please come in, do take a seat – if you haven't cacked your trousers? You see I'm not such a bad chap after all. It's true I wanted to chuck you out but now I see that you're quite an agreeable gentleman. You're a rarity indeed! I'm a bookbinder and I've read many novels and stories, but I've never read in any book yet of a future bridegroom introducing himself in this way." Mr Bílek laughed so much that he nearly burst his sides and kept on saying with considerable relish that he felt as though they'd known each other since the day of their birth and were born brothers. He immediately offered him a cigar, sent for beer and sausages for him, called his wife and introduced him to her, giving her all the details of the fart. But she only spat and walked out of the room. After that he called his daughter and told her: "This gentleman has come to ask for your hand in such and such circumstances." The daughter immediately burst into tears and said she didn't want to know him, and had no wish even to see him, so there was nothing else for them both to do but drink up the beer, eat up the sausages, and part. Afterwards it brought shame upon Mr Jenom in that pub where Mr Bílek used to go, and in the end all over that quarter of the city people had no other name for him but "Shitter Jenom", and everywhere they talked about how he had tried to "save the situation".

'Human existence, beg to report, sir, is so complicated that the life of a single individual is nothing more than a bit of rubbish in comparison. Before the war a police sergeant called Mr Hubička used to come to The Chalice at Na Bojišti. Another regular guest there was an editor who collected stories of broken legs and people who were run over or committed suicide and reported them in his newspaper. He was a merry gentleman and happened to be more often at the police station than in his editorial office. One day he got the police sergeant, Hubička, completely drunk and they exchanged clothes in the kitchen, so that the police sergeant was in mufti and the editor became the police sergeant. All he did was to cover up the number on his revolver and set out on patrol in the streets of Prague. In Resslova Street behind the former Wenceslas prison he ran into an elderly gentleman in top hat and fur coat, who was walking in the middle of the night arm in arm with an elderly lady in a fur wrap. Both were hurrying home and not exchanging a word. He rushed up to them and shouted into the gentleman's ear: "Don't make such a shindy or I'll have you up!" Imagine, sir, what a shock they had! In vain they explained to him that there must be some mistake, because they were both returning from a dinner at the governor's. They had gone in their carriage as far as the National Theatre and now they wanted to take some fresh air. They lived not far away at Na Moráni: he was a senior counsellor in the governor's office and the lady was his wife. "You won't fool me," the disguised editor shouted at him. "All the greater shame on you if you are, as you say, a senior counsellor in the governor's office and behave like a young hooligan. I've been watching for a long time how you've been banging with your stick at the roller blinds of all the shops on your way and how your, as you call her, 'wife' has been helping you in it." "But I don't have any stick, as you can see. It must have been somebody else before us." "I should say you haven't," said the disguised editor, "when as I saw with my own eyes you broke it there round the corner on the head of an old woman who goes round the pubs with roast potatoes and chestnuts!" The lady was not even able to cry and the senior counsellor got so angry that he began to speak of "insolent rudeness", whereupon he was arrested and handed over to the next patrol in the district of the police station in Salmova Street. The disguised editor told the patrol that the couple should be taken off to the police station. He himself was from the police station at Svatý Jindřich and was on an official errand to Vinohrady. He had caught them both when they were disturbing the night peace and were involved in a night brawl. In addidition they had committed the offence of abusing the police. He would finish his business at the police station at Svatý Jindřich and

come in an hour's time to the police station in Salmova Street. And so they were both of them taken away by the patrol and locked up until the next day while they waited for that police sergeant who had in the meantime returned by roundabout ways to The Chalice at Na Bojišti. There he woke up the police sergeant, Hubička, and told him very delicately everything that had happened, that an investigation would be made and if he didn't keep his mug shut . . .'

Lieutenant Lukáš seemed to be already tired by the conversation and before he urged his horse into a trot to get in front of the vanguard he said to Švejk:

'If you were to go on talking until evening, the longer you went on the more rot you'd talk.'

'Sir,' Švejk called out after the departing lieutenant. 'Don't you want to know how the story ended?'

Lieutenant Lukáš got into a gallop.

Lieutenant Dub's condition improved so much that he got out of the ambulance cart, gathered round him the whole staff of the company and began to instruct them as though in a haze. He delivered an enormously long speech which weighed on them all more heavily than their ammunition and rifles.

It was a hash-up of various parables.

He began: 'The soldiers' love for their officers makes unbelievable sacrifices possible. But that's not the point. On the contrary, if this love does not come natural to the soldier it must be forced on him. In civil life compulsory love like, shall we say, a school janitor's love for the teaching staff, lasts only as long as the external power which imposes it. In the army, however, we observe precisely the contrary, because an officer must not allow a soldier the slightest relaxation of the love which binds him to his superior officer. This love is no ordinary love: it is in fact respect, fear and discipline.'

All this time Švejk walked beside him on the left and as Lieutenant Dub spoke he had his face constantly turned towards him in 'eyes right' position.

At first Lieutenant Dub did not notice this and went on with his speech:

'This discipline and obligation to obey, the compulsory love of the soldier for the officer, is succinctness itself, because the relationship between soldier and officer is a perfectly straightforward one – the one obeys, the other commands. Long ago we read in books on military science that military laconism, military straightforwardness are those very virtues which every soldier must acquire. For, whether he likes it or not, he must love his superior officer, who in his eyes must be the greatest, the most perfect and completely crystallized embodiment of a firm and flawless will.'

It was only now that he noticed Švejk's 'eyes right' fixed on him. It was extremely disagreeable to him, because he suddenly felt that he was getting muddled in his speech and could not get out of the rut of the soldier's love for his superior officer. And so he shouted at Švejk:

'What are you gawking at me for?'

'By your own orders, humbly report, sir. Once you yourself were good enough to warn me that when you speak I must follow your lips with my eyes. As every soldier must carry out the instructions of his superior officer and remember them for all future occasions I have to do this too.'

'Look the other way,' Lieutenant Dub shouted. 'Only for God's sake not at me, you stupid bastard. You know I don't like it and I can't bear to see you. I'll give you such hell . . .'

Švejk turned his head to the left and went on walking so stiffly beside Lieutenant Dub that the latter shouted out:

'Where are your eyes when I'm talking to you?'

'Humbly report, sir, by your own orders, I'm now doing "eyes left".'

'Oh, my God,' sighed Lieutenant Dub, 'what a cross you are to bear! Look straight in front of you and think this about yourself: "I'm such an idiot that if anything happens to me no one will be the worse." Will you remember that?'

Švejk looked in front of him and said:

'Humbly report, sir, am I expected to reply?'

'Don't you dare behave like this!' Lieutenant Dub roared at him. 'Don't you dare speak to me like that! What do you mean by it?'

'Humbly report, sir, I'm thinking only of your orders at a station once when you rebuked me and told me that I shouldn't answer when you had finished speaking.'

'And so you're frightened of me?' said Lieutenant Dub in delight. 'But you haven't yet learned to know me. You're not the only one to have trembled in front of me, remember that! I've succeeded in taming other bastards and so you'd better shut your mug, stay quietly behind, and keep out of my sight!'

And so Švejk stayed at the back by the ambulance and rode comfortably on its two-wheeled cart to the next rest halt, where at last everyone got what they'd been waiting for – the soup and meat from the miserable cow.

'This cow ought to have been soaked in vinegar for at least a fortnight, or if not the cow, the man who bought it,' said Švejk.

From the brigade a courier came riding up on horseback with a new order for the 11th company that the march route would be changed to the direction of Felsztyn. Wojałycze and Sambor should be left out, as it was not possible to billet the company there, because they had two regiments from Poznań there already.

Lieutenant Lukáš immediately made new dispositions. Vaněk and Švejk were ordered to look for night billets for the company in Felsztyn.

'Now don't you get up to any mischief on the way, Švejk,' Lieutenant Lukáš warned him. 'Above all, mind you behave decently to the civilian population.'

'Humbly report, sir, I'll try my best, though I had a frightful dream, when I was dozing a bit towards morning. I dreamt about a washing trough which was dripping water the whole night in the corridor of the house where I lived, until the water ran over and soaked the landlord's ceiling. And he at once gave me notice that very morning. There actually was, sir, a case like that in real life: in Karlín behind the viaduct...'

'Oh, cut out your stupid stories, Švejk, and look with Vaněk at the map to see where you've got to go. Now here you see these villages. From this village here you must go to the right towards the stream and then follow its course until you come to the nearest village. From there, at the spot where the first brook flows into it, which will be on your right hand, you must go along a path through the fields up the hill due north. Then you can't lose your way until you get to Felsztyn. Can you remember that?'

Švejk set off with Vaněk and followed the march route.

It was just after midday. The land was breathing heavily in the heat and a rotting stink came out of the badly heaped pits containing buried soldiers. The two men came to the region where the fighting had taken place during the advance on Przemyśl and where whole battalions had been mowed down by machine-guns. The havoc made by the artillery could be seen in the small spinneys along the stream. On the wide spaces and slopes there were some maimed stumps sticking out of the ground instead of trees and this wilderness was furrowed with trenches.

'It seems to be a bit different here from around Prague,' said Švejk, to break the silence.

'At home the harvest's already over,' said Vaněk. 'We begin first in the Kralupy region.'

'There'll be a very good harvest here after the war,' said Švejk after a while. 'They won't have to buy bone flour. It's a great advantage for the farmers when their fields are covered with the dust of a whole regiment; in other words it's a very good means of livelihood. The only thing which worries me is that the farmers shouldn't let themselves be cheated and sell these soldiers' bones unnecessarily for bone charcoal in the sugar refineries. In the barracks at Karlín there was a lieutenant called Holub. He was so learned that everybody in the company thought he was an idiot. You see, because of his learning he never learnt to swear at the soldiers and considered everything only from the academic point of view. Once the soldiers reported to him that the army bread which they had drawn was not eatable. Another officer would have flown in a passion at such insolence, but not he. He remained quite calm, didn't call anybody a pig or a swine, and didn't sock anybody on the jaw. He only called all his men together and told them in his pleasant voice: "First of all, my men, you must realize that the barracks aren't a delicatessen shop where you can choose pickled eels, sardines and sandwiches. Every soldier must be intelligent enough to swallow any ration he draws without complaining about its quality. And he must have enough self-discipline not to make a fuss about the quality of what's put before him. Just imagine, my men, if there were a war. The soil in which you'd be buried after the battle wouldn't care a hoot what kind of bread you were gorged with before you died. Mother Earth would decompose you and eat you up boots and all. In this world nothing is allowed to vanish completely. Out of you, my men, there'll grow new corn for bread rations for new soldiers who again like you perhaps won't be satisfied, will start complaining, and then come up against someone who'll clap them in gaol until kingdom come, because he's got the right to do that. Now, my men, I've explained everything to you nicely and I believe I need not remind you again that whoever comes and complains a second time will thank his lucky stars later when he's allowed out again into God's light." "If he'd only swear at us," the soldiers said to each other, and they didn't at all like all those refinements in the lieutenant's speeches. And so once they chose me from the company and asked me to go and tell him that they all liked him but it's not the army if people don't swear at you. And so I went to his house and asked him to cut out all this refinement; that the army must be as tough as nails and soldiers are used to being reminded every day that they're bastards and swine. If they aren't they lose respect for their superior officers. At first he defended himself, spoke about intelligence and said that the times had gone by when the birch rod ruled, but in the end he accepted it, gave me a sock on the jaw and threw me out of the door so as to bolster his prestige. When I told the others the result of the negotiations they were all very pleased, but the very next day he went and spoiled it all. He came to me and said in the hearing of all of them: "Švejk, I lost my temper yesterday. Here's a guilder for you. Go and drink my health. One's got to know how to treat the men."'

Švejk looked at the countryside.

'I think we're going wrong,' he said. 'The lieutenant explained it to us quite well. We've got to go uphill, then down, first to the left and then to the right, and then again to the right. After that to the left – but we're going straight ahead all the time. Or have we gone through all that while we were talking? I can certainly see here before me two roads to Felsztyn. I suggest we take the one to the left.'

Vaněk, as is always the case when two people find themselves at a crossroads, started insisting that they must go to the right.

'My path,' said Švejk, 'is more comfortable than yours. I shall walk along the little brook where forget-me-nots grow and you'll be fooling around in the waste land. I stick to what the lieutenant said, that we can't lose our way and if we can't lose our way then why should I climb up any hills? I shall stroll comfortably over the meadows, put a nice little flower on my cap and pick a whole bunch for the lieutenant. Anyhow, we shall see which of us is right and I hope we part here good friends. This is the kind of country where all paths must lead to Felsztyn.'

'Don't be crazy, Švejk,' said Vaněk, 'According to the map we've got to go to the right here, as I say.'

'A map can be wrong,' answered Švejk, going down to the valley of the brook. 'Once a pork butcher named Křenek from Vinohrady walked home at night from U Montágů on the Malá Strana and tried to find his way with a street plan of Prague and in the morning he got to Rozdělov near Kladno. There they found him quite stiff in the rye where he had fallen down in exhaustion. If you insist on your opinion and won't accept any advice, sergeant-major, we must part and we shall only see each other again at our destination in Felsztyn. Just look at your watch so that we know which of us gets there first. And if any

kind of danger should threaten you just fire into the air so that I know where you are.'

In the afternoon Švejk came to a small lake where he ran into an escaped Russian prisoner who was bathing there. At the sight of Švejk he immediately ran away as naked as he was when he came out of the water.

His Russian uniform was lying underneath the willows and Švejk was curious to know how it would suit him, so he took off his own and put on the uniform worn by the unfortunate naked prisoner, who had escaped from a transport which had been billeted in a village behind the wood. Švejk wanted to see his reflection in the water and so he walked such a long way along the dam of the lake that he was caught by a patrol of field gendarmerie, who were looking for the escaped Russian prisoner. They were Hungarians and in spite of his protests they dragged him off to the staff command at Chyrów where they put him among a transport of Russian prisoners, who were being sent off to work on the reconstruction of the railway line in the direction of Przemyśl.

Everything happened so quickly that it was only the next day that Švejk realized the situation and wrote with a piece of charcoal on the white wall of the schoolroom where the detachment of prisoners was billeted: '*Here slept Josef Švejk of Prague, company orderly of the 11th march company of the 91st regiment, who as a member of a billeting party was taken prisoner in error by the Austrians near Felsztyn.*'

Part IV

THE GLORIOUS LICKING
CONTINUED

I

Švejk in a Transport of Russian Prisoners

AND so when Švejk, clad in his Russian greatcoat and cap, had been taken for a Russian prisoner escaping from a village near Felsztyn, and was writing his despairing screams in charcoal on the wall, no one took any notice, and when at the transit point in Chyrów, as crusts of hard maize bread were being distributed, he tried to explain everything in detail to a passing officer, one of the Hungarian soldiers guarding the transport of prisoners prodded his shoulder with his rifle butt and said: '*Baszom az élet!* Get into line, you Russian pig!'

All this was in line with the way the Hungarians treated their Russian prisoners, whose language they did not understand.

And so Švejk went back to the ranks and turning to the nearest prisoner said:

'That chap there's carrying out his duties, but he's exposing his life to great risk. What if the rifle happened to be loaded and the safety-catch released? Then when he was beating somebody over the shoulder with it and had the barrel pointing at himself, it might quite easily go off, all the ammunition in it would fly into his mouth and he'd die in the act of carrying out his duties. In a quarry in the Šumava workers stole sticks of dynamite to have a supply to break up tree-stumps with in the winter. The guard in the quarry got the order to search every labourer when he came away from work and he did it with such gusto that he at once seized the first quarry-worker he saw and beat him over his pockets so violently that the sticks of dynamite inside went off and both of them were blown up sky-high. It looked as though in their very last moment they had their arms round each other's necks.'

The Russian prisoner looked at Švejk in full understanding of the fact that he could not understand a single word of what he said.

'No understand. I Crimean Tartar. *Allah achper*,' the Tartar said. Then he sat down, crossed his legs on the ground, folded his arms on his chest and began to pray, half in Russian and half in Tartar: '*Allah achper, Allah achper – bezemila – arachman – arachim – malinkin mustafir.*'[1]

'Well now, so you're a Tartar, are you?' said Švejk with compassion. 'Well, you're a fine customer then! How could you with your double-Dutch be expected to understand me then and I you, if you're a Tartar? Hm – do you know Jaroslav of Šternberk?[2] You don't, do you, you Tartar bastard? Well, he thrashed your arses below Hostýn. And then you Tartar bastards turned tail and fled head over heels out of Moravia. Obviously in your textbooks they don't teach you the same things as they used to teach us. Do you know Our Lady of Hostýn? Of course you don't! Well, she was there too. You'd better look out, you bastard of a Tartar. They'll baptize all of you now you're prisoners here.'

Švejk turned to another prisoner:

'Are you a Tartar too?'

The person addressed understood the word Tartar, shook his head and said half in Russian: 'No Tartar, Circassian, Circassian born and bred. I chop off heads!'

It was Švejk's luck that he found himself in the company of these various representatives of the Eastern peoples. The transport comprised Tartars, Georgians, Osetins, Circassians, Mordvins and Kalmyks.

But it was his ill luck that he could not make himself understood by any of them and was dragged off with the others to Dobromil, from where the railway line running through Przemyśl in the direction of Niżankowice was to be repaired.

In the office at the transit point of Dobromil the prisoners were registered one by one. This was a difficult process because of all the 300 prisoners who were driven to Dobromil not a single one understood the Russian of the sergeant-major who sat there at a table. This man had once reported that he knew Russian and was now acting as an interpreter in Eastern Galicia. Some three weeks ago he had ordered a German-Russian dictionary and conversation book, but they had not come yet, and so instead of Russian he spoke only broken Slovak. He had picked up only a smattering of this language when he represented

1. 'Great Allah, Great Allah – merciful – have pity – have mercy – simple soldier.'
2. According to legend the Virgin appeared in a vision to Jaroslav of Šternberk just before the battle with the Tartars beneath the hill of Hostýn in Moravia in 1240. The Tartars were routed.

a Vienna firm in Slovakia and sold images of St Stephen, fonts for holy water and rosaries.

He was quite aghast at these outlandish figures with whom he could not make himself understood. And so he went out and roared in German at a group of prisoners: 'Who knows German?'

Švejk stepped forward from the group and with a happy face rushed towards the sergeant-major, who told him to follow him at once into the office.

The sergeant-major sat down at his registers, which were a heap of forms about the prisoners' names, origin and nationality, and an amusing conversation in German began:

'You're a Jew, aren't you?' he started.

Švejk shook his head.

'You don't need to deny it,' the sergeant-major interpreter continued assertively. 'Every single one of you prisoners who has known German has been a Jew and that's that. What's your name? Schweich? Now look, why do you deny it, when you've got such a Jewish name? In Austria you don't need to be afraid of admitting it. In Austria there are no pogroms. Where do you come from? Oh, I see, Praga. I know. I know. It's near Warsaw. Only a week ago I had two Jews here from Praga near Warsaw. And what's the number of your regiment? 91?'

The sergeant-major took the classification list and looked through its pages: 'The 91st regiment comes from Erevan in the Caucasus. Its base is in Tiflis. Your eyes pop out, don't they, when you see that we know everything here.'

Švejk's eyes really did pop out in surprise at the whole thing and the sergeant-major continued with great gravity, giving Švejk his half-smoked cigarette: 'This is rather different from that *machorka* shag of yours, isn't it? – I'm the big chief here, Jew boy. When I say a word, everybody's got to tremble and crawl on their hands and knees. In our army we have a very different kind of discipline from yours. Your Tsar's a bastard but ours is a clever chap. Now I'll show you something, so that you can see what our discipline's like here.'

He opened the door to the next room and called out: 'Hans Löfler!'

The answer came: 'Present!' And a goitrous soldier stepped into the room. He was a Styrian and had the expression of a blubbering idiot. He was the maid-of-all-work at the transit point.

'Hans Löfler!' the sergeant-major ordered. 'Take my pipe there, put it in your mug like a dog fetching a stick and run round the table on all fours until I say "Halt!" And while you do it you must bark, but you mustn't let the pipe fall out of your mug. If you do I'll have you trussed.'

The goitrous Styrian went down on all fours and started to bark.

The sergeant-major looked triumphantly at Švejk: 'Didn't I tell you, Jew boy, that we had discipline?'

And the sergeant-major looked delightedly at the expressionless face of the soldier from an Alpine hut somewhere. 'Halt!' he said finally. 'Now sit up and beg and bring me my pipe! – Good, and now yodel!'

The office resounded with the roar: 'Holariyo, holariyo . . .'

When the performance was over the sergeant-major took four cigarettes out of the drawer and gave them magnanimously to Hans, after which Švejk began to explain to him in his broken German that in one regiment an officer had an obedient batman like that who did everything his master wished, but when he was asked once whether, if his master ordered him to do so, he would eat his excrement out of a spoon, he said: 'If my lieutenant ordered me to do that I'd eat it according to his orders, always provided I didn't find a hair in it. If I did, it would disgust me frightfully and I should be sick at once.'

The sergeant-major laughed: 'You Jews have quite good stories, but I'm ready to bet that the discipline in your army isn't as good as ours. But to come to the point – I appoint you in charge of the transport. By the evening you'll write down for me the names of all the other prisoners. You'll draw the mess portions for them. You'll divide them up by tens and personally go bail that none of them escapes. If anybody escapes, Jew boy, we'll shoot you.'

'I'd like to speak to you, sergeant-major,' said Švejk.

'Now don't haggle,' the sergeant-major answered. 'I don't like that and if you do I'll send you off to a camp. You seem to have acclimatized yourself jolly quickly here in Austria. You want to speak with me privately? . . . The nicer one is to you prisoners the worse it is. . . . Now, clear off quick! Here's some paper and a pencil. Make the list . . . ! What else do you want?'

'Humbly report, sergeant-major . . .'

'Get to hell out of it! Can't you see I'm busy?' The sergeant-major's face assumed the expression of a man who was utterly overworked.

Švejk saluted and went back to the prisoners, thinking to himself that all his patience in aid of His Imperial Majesty would one day no doubt bear fruit.

But it was, of course, a hard job to compile the list, as it took a long time for the prisoners to understand that they had got to give him their names. Švejk had experienced much in his life, but all the same

these Tartar, Georgian and Mordvin names simply would not stick in his head.

'No one will ever believe,' thought Švejk, 'that anyone could ever have names like these Tartars here: Muhlahaley Abdrachmanov – Beymurat Allahali – Djeredje Cherdedze – Davlatbaley Nurdagaljev and so on. After all we've got much better names at home. Think of that vicar at Živohošt who was called Vobejda.'[1] And again he went on walking along the ranks of the prisoners who shouted out one by one their surnames and first names: 'Djindraley Hanemaley – Babamuley Mirzahali,' etc.

1. 'Loafer' in Czech.

'Make sure you don't bite your tongue,' Švejk said to each of them with a friendly smile. 'Isn't it much better to be called like our people are – Bohuslav Stěpánek, Jaroslav Matoušek or Růžena Svobodová?'[1]

When after frightful suffering Švejk had finally listed all these Babula Halleis, Hudji Mudjis etc. he decided he would make one more try and explain to the interpreter sergeant-major that he had been the victim of an error. However, as had happened many times already on the journey, when they drove him in among the prisoners his appeals for justice were in vain.

Already before this the interpreter sergeant-major had had a drop too much and by now he had completely lost his capacity for judgement.

He had spread out before him the advertisement pages of a German newspaper and was singing the words of the advertisements to the music of the Radetzky March: 'A gramophone in exchange for a perambulator. – I buy broken pieces of white and green sheet glass. – If anyone wants to learn book-keeping he should do the written course in accountancy' etc.

Some of the advertisements were not suitable for a march tune, but the sergeant-major exerted himself to the utmost in an endeavour to overcome this and beat out the time with his fist on the table and stamped his feet. The tips of his moustache, which were sticky with kontušovka, stuck out on both of his cheeks as though someone had stuck a dry brush of gum into them. His puffy eyes noticed Švejk, it was true, but there was no reaction to this discovery except that he ceased beating with his fist and stamping his feet. To the tune of 'Ich weiss nicht, was soll es bedeuten...'[2] he drummed out another advertisement with his fingers on the chair: 'Karolina Dreger, midwife, respectfully offers her services to honourable ladies for all eventualities.'

Then he began to sing more and more softly until finally he stopped altogether and stared motionless at the whole space of advertisements in the newspaper. This gave Švejk the opportunity to talk about his own misfortunes, for which his sentences of broken German were barely adequate.

He started by saying that he had after all been quite right when he said they should have walked along the stream to Felsztyn, and it was not his fault if an unknown Russian prisoner escaped from captivity

1. Names of Czech writers of the time.
2. The beginning of the famous Lorelei song.

and went to have a swim in the lake. He, Švejk, had had to walk along the lake. It had been his duty to do so, when he was a member of a billeting party and had to take the shortest route to Felsztyn. The Russian ran away as soon as he saw him and left all his uniform in the bushes. Švejk had heard that the uniform of fallen enemies could be used at the

front for purposes of espionage, and so as an experiment he put on that cast-off uniform just to see how it would feel to be in a foreign uniform.

Having tried to explain his little mistake, Švejk realized that his efforts had been utterly in vain, since before he even reached the part about the lake the sergeant-major had long since fallen asleep. Švejk approached him and touched him familiarly on the shoulder, which was enough to cause him to fall on to the floor, where he went on sleeping peacefully.

'Excuse me, sergeant-major,' Švejk said, saluted and left the office.

Early in the morning the army building command changed its dispositions and decided that the group of prisoners to which Švejk belonged should be sent direct to Przemyśl to renew the track from Przemyśl to Lubaczów.

And so everything was just as it was before and Švejk continued his odyssey among the Russian prisoners. The Hungarian guards drove all of them on at a brisk tempo.

On a village green where they had a rest they met a detachment from a baggage train. An officer was standing in front of a group of carts and looking at the prisoners. Švejk jumped out of the ranks, posted himself in front of the officer and called out to him in German: 'Sir, humbly report . . .' He said no more, because two Hungarian soldiers immediately struck him in the back with their fists and thrust him among the prisoners again.

The officer threw him a cigarette stump, which another prisoner quickly picked up and finished smoking. Then the officer explained to a corporal who was standing next to him that in Russia there were colonies of Germans and they had to fight as well.

Later, throughout the journey to Przemyśl Švejk had no opportunity to complain to anyone that he was in fact the orderly of the 11th march company of the 91st regiment. He could only do this in Przemyśl, where in the evening they were driven to a fortress in the inner zone which was completely destroyed except for the artillery horses' stables.

Inside the stables the heaps of straw were so lice-ridden that the lice moved over the short stalks as though they were not lice at all but ants carrying material to build their nest.

The prisoners were each given a little black dishwash made out of nothing but chicory and a piece of stale maize bread.

Then Major Wolf, who was at that time in charge of all the prisoners working on the reconstruction of the fortress at Przemyśl and its surroundings, took charge of them. He was a man who did things thoroughly. He had with him a whole staff of interpreters who selected building specialists from the prisoners according to their abilities and previous training.

Major Wolf had the fixed idea that the Russian prisoners tried to conceal their literacy, because it used to happen that when he asked them through an interpreter 'Can you build a railway?' all of them gave the stereotyped answer: 'I don't know anything about anything.

I've never heard of anything like that. I've always lived honestly and decently.'

When, however, they all stood lined up before him and all his staff, he first of all asked them in German if any of them understood that language.

Švejk stepped forward resolutely, stationed himself in front of the major, saluted and reported that he did.

Major Wolf, visibly pleased, at once asked Švejk if he happened to be an engineer.

'Humbly report, sir,' answered Švejk, 'I'm not an engineer but the orderly of the 11th march company of the 91st regiment. I've been taken prisoner by us. It happened like this, sir . . .'

'What did I hear you say?' Major Wolf roared.

'Humbly report, sir, what happened was . . .'

'You're a Czech,' Major Wolf went on shouting. 'You've put on a Russian uniform.'

'Humbly report, sir, yes. It's perfectly correct. I'm really very glad indeed, sir, that you've at once appreciated my position. Perhaps our men are already fighting somewhere and I shouldn't like to be kicking my heels about here for the duration of the war. Let me please explain it properly to you, sir, once more.'

'That's enough,' said Major Wolf, and, calling two soldiers, he gave them the order to take the man off at once to the guard-house. And he himself followed slowly after Švejk, gesticulating violently while he talked with the officer accompanying him. In every one of his sentences there was something about 'Czech dogs', but at the same time from his words the other officer had the feeling that the major was delighted that it was his keen eye that had discovered one of those shady customers, about whose treasonable activities abroad the commanders of military detachments had received confidential reports for some months already. It had been ascertained that some deserters from Czech regiments, forgetting their oath, were joining the ranks of the Russian army and were now working for the enemy, affording him above all useful espionage services.

The Austrian Ministry of the Interior was still in the dark about whether a military organization of Czech deserters on the Russian front existed or not. Nothing definite was yet known about revolutionary organizations abroad and it was only in August that the battalion commanders on the line Sokal–Milijatin–Bubnów received the confidential report that the former Austrian professor Masaryk had fled abroad, where he was carrying out propaganda against Austria. A stupid ass from the division appended to it the following order: 'If captured he should at once be brought to division staff!'

I hereby bring this to the attention of President Masaryk, so that he may know what pitfalls and traps were laid for him between Sokal, Milijatin and Bubnów.[1]

At that time Major Wolf had no idea at all of what was being hatched against Austria by the deserters, who when they later met in Kiev or elsewhere and were asked 'What are you doing here?' answered cheerfully: 'I have betrayed His Imperial Majesty.'

It was only from secret reports like the above that he knew of the existence of these deserters and spies, one of whom they were taking off to the guard-house after he had fallen so easily into his trap. Major Wolf was a rather vain man and he pictured in his mind the praise he would get from his superiors and the decoration he would receive for his vigilance, foresight and intelligence.

By the time they reached the guard-house he was convinced that when he asked the question 'Who of you knows German?' he had done it on purpose, because when he inspected the prisoners it was this very one who at once appeared suspect.

The officer who was accompanying him nodded his head in agreement and said that they would have to report the arrest to garrison command for further action and bringing the accused before a higher court-martial, because it would definitely not be right to do as the major suggested, examine him in the guard-house and then hang him immediately behind it. He would be hanged of course, but by the due process of law, as laid down by court-martial procedure, so that before he was hanged the link with other criminals could be established with the help of a detailed cross-examination. Who could tell what else might come out of it all?

Major Wolf was overcome by a sudden fit of obstinacy. A latent brutality filled him and he announced that after the cross-examination he would have this deserter spy hanged at once on his own responsibility. This is something he could well afford to do, because he had friends in high places and nothing mattered very much to him. They should deal with the man here as they would have done at the front.

1. This 'personal message' from Hašek to President Masaryk has been omitted from recent editions of *The Good Soldier Švejk*.

If they had caught him immediately behind the battlefield, they would have interrogated him and hanged him on the spot without any fuss. Moreover, the captain must surely know that in a war zone the commanding officer, *any* commanding officer from captain upwards, had the right to hang any suspicious individual.

Major Wolf of course had got things slightly wrong when he spoke of the competence of officers to hang people.

In East Galicia the nearer they came to the front the more this competence was delegated to lower and lower ranks, until in the end there were cases where even a corporal in command of a sentry patrol ordered a twelve-year-old boy to be hanged because he had aroused his suspicions by cooking potato peelings in a tumble-down hut in a deserted and ransacked village.

The dispute between the captain and the major rose in intensity.

'You have no right to do that,' the captain shouted excitedly. 'He will be hanged on the basis of a legal verdict of a court-martial.'

'He's going to be hanged without any verdict at all,' Major Wolf hissed.

Švejk, who was being led in front of them and heard the whole of this conversation, said nothing to his escort except: 'Six of one and half a dozen of the other. We had the same sort of discussion at the pub Na Zavadilce in Libeň, when we couldn't decide whether, as soon as there appeared in the doorway a certain hatter named Vašák, who always made a nuisance of himself during the music and dancing, we should throw him out at once, or do it when he had had a glass of beer, paid for it and drunk it up, or whether we should give him the boot after he had danced the first dance. The landlord suggested we shouldn't chuck him out until the middle of the show, to give him time to run up a bill. Then he would have to pay up and leave at once. And do you know what that bastard did? He never turned up at all. What do you think of that?'

Both soldiers, who were from somewhere in the Tyrol, answered simultaneously: 'Nix Czech.'

'Do you understand German?' Švejk asked calmly in that language.

'Jawohl,' they both answered, upon which Švejk observed: 'That's good. You're lucky! At least you won't get lost among your own folk.'

In the course of these friendly conversations they all reached the guard-house, where Major Wolf continued his dispute with the captain about Švejk's fate, while Švejk sat modestly on a bench in the back.

Finally after all Major Wolf came over to the captain's view that the man should swing only after the longer procedure which is so sweetly called 'the process of law'.

If they had asked Švejk what he thought about it, he would have said: 'I'm very sorry, sir, because you have a higher rank than the captain, but he is the one who is right. Every hasty action only does harm. Once at a Prague district court one of the judges went mad. For a long time no one noticed it in him until it suddenly erupted during a libel action. A chap called Znamenáček met on the street a chaplain called Hortík, who had boxed his son's ears during religious instruction, and he said to him: "You bloody bastard, you dirty scum, you religious maniac, you filthy hog, you presbytery goat, you debaucher of Christ's teachings, you hypocrite and charlatan in a cassock!" And so the chaplain sued him. That mad judge was a very religious man. He had three sisters and they were all vicarage cooks and he had been a godfather to all their children. And so he got so infuriated that he suddenly lost his reason and roared at the accused: "In the name of His Majesty the Emperor and King you are condemned to death by hanging. There is no appeal." Then he called to the warder: "Mr Horáček, take this gentleman out and go and hang him there, you know, where they beat the carpets, and after that come back here and you'll get a tip!" Of course Mr Znamenáček and the warder stood rooted to the spot, but the judge stamped his foot and shouted at them: "Are you going to obey or not!" The warder was so frightened that he had already begun to drag Mr Znamenáček down, and if it hadn't been for the defending counsel who intervened and called an ambulance I don't know how it would have fared with Mr Znamenáček. And even when they were putting the judge into the ambulance he was still shouting: "If you can't find a rope, hang him with a bed-sheet. We'll credit it to you in the half-yearly returns . . ." '

And so Švejk had to sign a report drawn up by Major Wolf to the effect that as a serving member of the Austrian army he had in full knowledge of the consequences and without constraint changed into Russian uniform and been detained behind the front line by the field gendarmerie when the Russians retreated. And after that he was sent under escort to the garrison command.

All of this was holy truth, and Švejk, as an honest man, could not object to it. When the report was being drawn up he tried several times to supplement it by adding a statement which might perhaps

have explained the situation more precisely, but the major was at once ready with the order: 'Shut your mug. We're not asking your opinion about that. The case is quite clear.'

After that Švejk simply saluted and said: 'Humbly report, I'm shutting my mug and the case is quite clear.'

After they had brought him to garrison command, they took him away to some hole which had formerly been a rice store as well as a boarding-house for mice. Grains of rice were still scattered everywhere on the floor, and the mice were not at all afraid of Švejk and gaily ran about picking them up. Švejk had to go and fetch a straw mattress and when he looked around in the darkness he found that a whole family of mice had instantly moved into it. There was no doubt at all that they were trying to make a new nest here in the ruins of the glory of the rotten Austrian straw mattress. Švejk began to hammer on the locked door. A corporal came, who was a Pole, and Švejk asked to be transferred to other quarters, because otherwise he might lie on the mice in his straw mattress and cause damage to crown property, because everything in the military stores was crown property.

The Pole understood something of what he said and threatened Švejk with his fist in front of the closed door. Mentioning something about 'a shit-hole' he went away muttering angrily about cholera, as though Švejk had insulted him in some way.

Švejk passed a quiet night, because the mice made no great demands on him and obviously had their own programme for the night, which they celebrated in the store room next door. Military greatcoats and caps were stored there and the mice bit through them with great confidence and in great security, because it was only a year later that the quartermaster's office remembered to introduce into the military stores crown-property cats without pension rights, which were entered in the administration records under the heading: 'Imperial and Royal military store cats.' The rank of cat was in fact only a revival of an old institution which had been abolished after the war of 1866.

Earlier, in the reign of Maria Theresa, cats had been introduced into the military stores in wartime, when it was on the wretched mice that the gentlemen from the administration were blaming all their fiddles with uniforms.

But in many cases the Imperial and Royal cats failed to do their duties, and so it happened that once in the reign of Emperor Leopold six cats which had been assigned to the military stores at Pohořelec were hanged by the verdict of a court-martial. I can imagine that on that occasion all those who had had anything to do with the military stores laughed smugly in their sleeves . . .

With Švejk's early-morning coffee they pushed into his hole a man in a Russian cap and greatcoat.

The man spoke Czech with a Polish accent. He was one of those scoundrels who served in the counter-espionage of the army corps which had its headquarters in Przemyśl. He was a member of the military secret police and did not trouble much about any refined preliminaries before proceeding to grill Švejk. He began quite simply: 'I've got into a fine mess as a result of my carelessness. I served in the 28th regiment and immediately deserted to the Russians. Then I was stupid enough to get caught. I volunteered to go on advance patrol for the Russians . . . I served in the 6th Kievan division. Which Russian regiment did you serve in, old man? I have a feeling we must have met somewhere in Russia. I knew many Czechs in Kiev, who went to the front with us, when we went over to the Russians. I can't remember their names now or where they came from. Perhaps you can remember someone you were in contact with then? I'd very much like to know who there was from our 28th regiment.'

Instead of replying Švejk laid his hand anxiously on his visitor's forehead, felt his pulse, finally led him away to a little window and asked him to put out his tongue. The scoundrel made no resistance to this procedure, imagining that it was a case of certain conspiratorial signs. Then Švejk started to hammer on the door, and when the guard came to ask why he was making such a row, he asked him in Czech and German if they would call a doctor at once, because the man they had put into the cell with him was suffering from hallucinations.

It was no good. No one came to fetch the man. He remained there quite calmly and continued to babble something about Kiev and how he'd certainly seen Švejk there marching with the Russian soldiers.

'You must certainly have been drinking water from the marshes,' said Švejk, 'like a young man, Týnecký, whom I used to know a long time ago. He was quite a sensible chap otherwise, but suddenly out of the blue he set out on a journey and got as far as Italy. He didn't talk about anything else but Italy and said there was a lot of marshy water there, but otherwise nothing else worth seeing. And he too got fever from that marshy water. It attacked him four times a year – on

All Saints, St Joseph's, Peter and Paul and the Assumption of the Virgin. When he had these attacks, he thought he knew people who were completely strange and unknown to him, just like you. In a tram he might address someone, saying he knew him and that they had met on the station in Vienna. All the people he met on the street he'd seen either on the station in Milan or had sat with them in the Rathaus cellar in Steyr over a glass of wine. If, when this marsh fever came over him, he happened to be sitting in a pub, he knew all the guests. He'd seen all of them on a steamer when he sailed to Venice. There was only one remedy against it, and that was the one which a new male nurse used in the Kateřinky. He also had to look after a mental patient who did nothing else the whole day but sit in a corner and count: "One, two, three, four, five, six," and then again from the beginning: "One, two, three, four, five, six." He was a professor. That nurse nearly jumped out of his skin with fury when he found that that madman couldn't get beyond six. He started first by being nice to him and tried to get him to say: "Seven, eight, nine, ten." But what a hope! The professor didn't take any damned notice of him. He went on crouching in the corner and counting: "One, two, three, four, five, six," and then again: "One, two, three, four, five, six!" Then the nurse suddenly flew off the handle, jumped at his patient and when he got to the word "six" socked him one on the jaw. "Now you've got seven," he said, "and here's eight, nine, ten." And he got as many socks as there were numbers. The professor suddenly put his hands to his head and asked where he was. When they told him he was in the madhouse he immediately remembered everything and how he had got to the asylum all because of a comet, which he had reckoned would appear in a year's time on 18 July at 6 a.m., but they had proved to him that it had burnt itself out several million years ago. I knew that nurse. When the professor recovered completely and was released, he took him on as his servant. The only work he had to do was to mete out to the learned professor four socks on the jaw each morning. And he always discharged this duty conscientiously and precisely.'

'I know all your friends from Kiev,' the mercenary of the counter-espionage continued indefatigably. 'Didn't you have with you a very fat man and also a very thin one? I can't remember what their names were or from what regiment they came . . .'

'Don't worry about that,' Švejk consoled him. 'It can happen to anyone that he doesn't remember all the fat and thin people there are

and what their names are. Thin people are of course harder to remember, because there are more of them in the world. And so they
form a majority as the saying goes.'

'Old man,' the Imperial and Royal scoundrel said in a plaintive tone,
'you don't trust me. But after all we must both expect the same fate.'

'That's why we're soldiers,' said Švejk nonchalantly. 'It was for that
our mothers bore us – so that we could be made mincemeat of when we
were put into uniform. And we do it gladly, because we know that
our bones won't rot in vain. We shall fall for His Imperial Majesty
and His Royal Family, for whom we won Herzegovina. Out of our
bones they'll make bone charcoal for sugar refineries. Lieutenant
Zimmer told us about that years ago. "You pack of swine," he said,
"you barbarous hogs, you useless indolent monkeys! You twist your
shanks about as if they weren't worth anything. If you fall in the war,
they'll make half a kilo of bone charcoal out of each of them. Out of
every man jack of you there'll be more than two kilos, shanks and
paws together, and in the sugar refineries they'll filter sugar through
you, you bloody oafs. You haven't an inkling how useful you're going
to be to your descendants after your death. Your boys will drink
coffee with sugar which was filtered through your shanks, you godforsaken half-wits, you." It made me think a bit and he asked me what
I was thinking about. "Humbly report," I said, "I've been thinking
that the bone charcoal which is made out of you officer gentlemen must
be much more expensive than what's made out of us ordinary soldiers."
For that I got three days' solitary confinement.'

Švejk's companion beat on the door and had some discussions with
the guard, who called to the office.

After a while a staff sergeant-major came to fetch him away and Švejk
was left alone.

As he went out the reptile pointed to Švejk and said loudly to the
staff sergeant-major: 'It's my old mate from Kiev.'

For a whole period of twenty-four hours Švejk remained in solitude
except for those moments when they brought him something to eat.

During the night he came to the conviction that the Russian military greatcoat was warmer and more copious than the Austrian one
and that it isn't too unpleasant if in the night a mouse sniffs at the ear
of a sleeping man. To Švejk it appeared like a tender whisper, from
which he was woken in the grey light of morn when they came to fetch
him.

To this day Švejk cannot make out what kind of court it was before which he was dragged that depressing morning. That it was a court-martial there was no doubt. Even a general was sitting there, not to speak of a colonel, a major, a first and second lieutenant, a sergeant-major and an infantryman, who did nothing else but light the other persons' cigarettes.

Švejk was not asked many questions.

It was the major who showed rather more interest and spoke Czech.

'You are guilty of treason against His Imperial Majesty,' he barked at Švejk.

'Treason? Jesus Mary, when?' Švejk cried out. 'The idea that I should have committed treason against His Imperial Majesty, our most serene monarch, for whom I have already suffered so much!'

'Cut out that tomfoolery,' said the major.

'Humbly report, sir, treason against His Imperial Majesty is no tomfoolery. We men of the army have sworn an oath of loyalty to His Imperial Majesty and, as they sang in the theatre, "In loyalty my vow I have fulfilled".'[1]

'It's all here,' said the major. 'Here are the proofs of your guilt and of the truth.' He pointed to a voluminous bundle of papers.

The man whom they had put into Švejk's cell had produced the main material.

'And so you still refuse to confess?' the major asked. 'After all, you've confirmed yourself that you voluntarily changed into Russian uniform, although you were a serving member of the Austrian armed forces. I ask you for the last time: did you do this act under compulsion?'

'I did it without any compulsion.'

'Voluntarily?'

'Voluntarily.'

'Without any pressure?'

'Without any pressure.'

'You know that you're lost?'

'I know. They're certainly already searching for me in the 91st regiment. But will you permit, sir, a small observation on how people voluntarily put on other people's clothes. Sometime in July in 1908 a bookbinder Božetěch from Příčná Street in Prague was bathing at Zbraslav in the old channel of the Berounka. He left his clothes in some

1. Quotation from *Dalibor*, the opera by Bedřich Smetana.

willow bushes and was enjoying himself immensely in the water when later a gentleman came and joined him there. They got talking, frolicked together, squirted water at each other and ducked each other until evening. Then the stranger gentleman went out of the water saying that he had to go to dinner. Mr Božetěch remained sitting in

the water a little longer and then went to the willow bushes for his clothes. In their place he found some tramp's rags and a piece of paper. It contained the following message:

'I thought about it a long time: ought I to do it – or oughtn't I, when we were having such fun together in the water? So I tore off the petals of a marguerite. The last petal I tore off was "I ought!" and so I swopped togs with you. You needn't be afraid of putting them on. They were deloused a week ago in the district gendarmerie station at Dobříš. Next time be more careful about who you go bathing with. In the water every naked man looks like a member of parliament and may well be a murderer. You did not know who you were bathing with either. But the bathe was worth it. Now towards the evening the water is at its best. Run in once more so that you can come to your senses again.

'Mr Božetěch could do nothing else but wait until it got dark. Then he put on those tramp's rags and set out in the direction of Prague. He avoided the district road and went by paths across the fields, where he fell in with the gendarmerie patrol from Chuchle. They arrested him as a tramp and took him the next morning to the district court in Zbraslav, because anyone could say that he was Josef Božetěch, bookbinder from 16 Příčná Street, Prague.'

The clerk, who did not understand much Czech, took it that the accused was giving the address of his accomplice and asked once more in German: 'Is that correct? Prague no. 16, Herr Josef Bosetech?'

'I don't know if he still lives there,' Švejk answered, 'but he lived there at that time in 1908. He bound books jolly well, but it took him a long time, because he had to read them first and then bind them according to their contents. If he gave a book black edges, that meant that no one need read it. Then you knew at once that the novel would end very badly. Would you perhaps like to have still more details? Oh, by the way – he used to sit every day at U Fleků and tell people the contents of all the books which they had just sent to him for binding.'

The major went over to the clerk and had a whispered exchange with him. The latter then crossed out in his records the address of the new alleged conspirator, Herr Bosetech.

After that the strange court proceedings continued, following the fashion of the summary courts-martial held by the presiding general, Fink von Finkenstein.

Just as some people have a hobby of collecting matchboxes, so this gentleman's particular hobby-horse was to hold summary courts-martial, although in the majority of cases they were contrary to military regulations.

This general used to say that he did not need any judge advocates, that he would call the court together and in three hours every bastard must be swinging. As long as he was at the front there was never any lack of summary courts-martial.

Just as some people must regularly play a game of chess, billiards, or mariáš every day, so this excellent general had to hold summary courts-martial daily. He presided over them and with great solemnity and joy checkmated the accused.

If anyone wanted to be sentimental he could write that this man had many dozens of people on his conscience, especially in the East, where, to quote his own words, he fought with the Great Russian propaganda among the Ruthenians of Galicia. From his own point of view, however, we cannot say that he had anybody's life on his conscience.

A conscience simply did not exist for him. If on the verdict of his summary court-martial he sent a schoolmaster, a schoolmistress, an Orthodox priest or a whole family to the gallows, he returned peacefully to his quarters just like a keen mariáš player returns contentedly home from the pub and recalls how they called 'flek' and how he answered 're', how they called 'supre' and he 'tutti', how they called 'boty' and how he won everything and had a hundred and seven.[1] He regarded hanging as something simple and natural, a sort of daily bread, and in passing the sentences he often forgot His Imperial Majesty and even omitted to say: 'In the name of His Majesty you are condemned to death by hanging,' but declared: 'I condemn you.'

Sometimes he even saw the comic side in hanging and once wrote about it to his wife in Vienna:

... or for example, my darling, you cannot imagine what a good laugh I had recently when a few days ago I sentenced a teacher for espionage. I have a trained man who does the hanging. He's already had considerable practice. He's a sergeant-major and does it as a sport. I was in my tent when this sergeant-major came to see me after the verdict and asked me where he should hang the teacher. I told him to do it on the nearest tree. Now conceive the humour of the situation. We were in the middle of the steppe, where we could see nothing else far and wide except grass, and there wasn't a tree for miles. Orders are orders, and the sergeant-major took the teacher with him under escort and went to look for a tree.

He did not get back until the evening and had the teacher with him still. He came to see me and asked me again: 'What am I to hang this bastard on?' I swore at him and told him that he knew my orders: on the nearest tree. He said that he would try it next morning, and next morning he came to me white in the face and said that the teacher had disappeared in the early hours. I found it so funny that I forgave all those who had been guarding him and I even made the joke that the teacher must obviously have gone to look for a tree himself. So you see, my darling, we're not bored here in any way and you can tell little Willi that papa sends him a kiss and that he'll soon send him

1. There are various possible declarations which can be made in mariáš. One is 'a hundred and seven' which means that the player must win 100 points and take the last trick with the seven of trumps. When the declaration has been made the other players can double or multiply. If a player says 'flek' he means he will double. If another says 're', he means he will quadruple. 'Supre' multiplies 8 times, 'tutti' 16 times and 'boty' 32 times.

a live Russian which he can ride on like a pony. And that reminds me, my darling, of another comic incident. We recently hanged a Jew for espionage. The rascal happened to cross our path during our journey, although he had no business there, and gave the excuse that he was selling cigarettes. And so he swung, but only for a few seconds, because the cord broke and he fell down. But at once he recovered consciousness and shouted at me: 'Excellency, I'm going home. Now you've hanged me and according to the law I can't be hanged twice for one offence.' I burst out laughing and we let the Jew go. We have a lot of fun here, my darling . . .

When General Fink became commander of the garrison fort of Přemyśl he did not have the same opportunities of arranging circus shows like these and that was why he was very glad to seize on Švejk's case.

And so Švejk stood in front of this tiger, who sat at the head of the long table and smoked cigarette after cigarette. He ordered Švejk's confession to be translated to him and nodded his head in approval, as he listened to it.

The major proposed that, since the accused affirmed by his statements that he belonged to the 11th march company of the 91st regiment, they should telegraph to the brigade for information where that regiment now was.

The general opposed this and said that it would hold up the summary character of the proceedings and defeat the object of the whole institution. They had after all a complete confession on the part of the accused that he had put on Russian uniform, and they had in addition an important piece of evidence where the accused had admitted that he had been in Kiev. He proposed therefore that they should retire for discussion, so that the sentence could be pronounced and carried out immediately.

But the major insisted that it was necessary to establish the identity of the accused, since the whole matter was of unusual political importance. By doing this they might come on to the track of further contacts between the accused and his former comrades from his unit.

The major was a romantic dreamer. He went on to say that it was not enough merely to condemn the man but it was necessary to look for the threads. The sentencing itself was only the result of a definite investigation which involved threads and those threads. . . . He got rather tied up in those threads, but everyone understood him and nodded their heads in agreement, including even the general, who was so enamoured by the threads that he imagined that he could hang new summary courts-martial on them. And so he no longer protested against the idea of verifying at brigade headquarters whether Švejk actually belonged to the 91st regiment and in the course of what operation of the 11th march company he went over to the Russian side.

During the whole period of this debate Švejk was in the corridor under the guard of two men with bayonets. Afterwards he was again brought before the court and once more asked to which regiment he in fact belonged. Then they transferred him to the garrison gaol.

When General Fink returned home after the unsuccessful summary court-martial he lay down on the sofa and considered how he could expedite the whole case.

He was fully convinced that the answer would come soon, but none the less the proceedings would lack that speed which had otherwise distinguished his courts-martial, because afterwards they would have to offer the condemned man spiritual consolation and that would un-necessarily hold up the execution for two hours.

'It doesn't matter,' General Fink thought to himself. 'We can offer him spiritual consolation in advance before the verdict and before we get the information from the brigade. He'll swing anyway.'

General Fink summoned Chaplain Martinec before him.

This was an unfortunate catechist and chaplain from a village in Moravia who had had such a brute of a vicar over him that he preferred to join the army. He was a sincerely religious man who with pain in his heart remembered his vicar who was slowly but surely going down the drain. He remembered how the vicar used to swill slivovice like a fish and how once in the night he had insisted on putting into the chaplain's bed a vagabond gipsy girl whom he had picked up near the village when he was lurching out of a wine-cellar.

Martinec imagined that by having the duty of offering spiritual consolation to the wounded and dying on the battlefield he would redeem even the sins of his depraved vicar, who returning home at night had countless times woken him up and told him:

'Jan, Jan, my dear boy! A buxom wench is the joy of my life.'

His hopes were not fulfilled. They threw him about from one garrison to another, where he had nothing more to do than preach to the soldiers once a fortnight before mass in the garrison church and resist the temptation of the officers' club, where the conversations were such that in comparison his Moravian vicar's buxom wenches seemed like an innocent little prayer to a guardian angel.

Now he was usually summoned to General Fink during major operations on the battlefield when some victory of the Austrian army was to be celebrated, for General Fink was just as delighted to arrange festive drumhead masses as summary courts-martial.

That blackguard Fink was such a devout Austrian patriot that he refused to pray for the victory of the Reich German or Turkish arms. When the Reich Germans won a victory over the French or British anywhere he saw to it that it was ignored at the altar.

But every unimportant victorious skirmish between an Austrian reconnoitring patrol and a Russian advance patrol, which the staff blew up into a terrific soap-bubble defeat of a whole Russian army corps, provided General Fink with the occasion for festive services, so that the unfortunate Martinec had the impression that the general was not only commander of the fortress but also supreme head of the Catholic Church in Przemyśl.

General Fink also decided the order of service at such masses and would always have preferred something like a Corpus Christi with the octave.

When at mass the exaltation of the host was over, it was also his habit to gallop up to the altar on the parade ground and call out three times: 'Hurrah – hurrah – hurrah!'

Martinec, who was a pious and honest soul, and one of those few who still believed in the Lord, did not like going to see General Fink.

After the garrison commander had given him all his instructions he always had something strong poured out for him and afterwards told him the latest stories from the most stupid booklets which were published for the troops by the German comic paper *Lustige Blätter*.

He had a complete collection of such booklets with idiotic titles like: *Humour in the Haversack for Eyes and Ears, Hindenburg Stories, Hindenburg Mirrored in Humour, The Second Haversack Full of Humour, Loaded by Felix Schlemper, From our Goulash Gun, Succulent Shrapnel from the Trenches*, or the following rubbish: *Under the Double Eagle* and *Wiener Schnitzel from the Imperial and Royal Field-Kitchen, Warmed up by Artur Lokesch*. Sometimes he even sang to him out of his collection of gay army songs 'Victory must be ours!', while all the time continuing to pour out something strong and forcing Martinec to drink and caterwaul with him. Then he went over to telling smutty stories and with heavy heart Martinec remembered his vicar who was in no way inferior to General Fink where coarse words were concerned.

Martinec saw to his horror that the more he went to see General Fink the more morally debased he grew.

The unfortunate man began to take pleasure in the liqueurs which he drank with the general, and slowly but surely the general's conversation began to appeal to him. He began to entertain lecherous thoughts and, because of the kontušovka, jeřabinka and the cobwebs on the bottles of the old wine which General Fink served to him, he gradually began to forget the Lord, and the women from the general's stories began to dance before his eyes in between the lines of the breviary. His dislike of his visits to the general slowly began to wear off.

The general took a fancy to Martinec, who had at first appeared to him to be like a St Ignatius of Loyola, but who later gradually adapted himself to the general's environment.

One day the general invited two nurses from the field-hospital, who in fact did not work there but were only entered on the books for their wages and who increased their incomes by high-class prostitution, as was the custom in those difficult times. He summoned Martinec, who had already fallen so deep into the claws of the devil that after half an hour's fun he enjoyed both ladies one after the other, and got into such a state of rut that he slobbered all over the cushion on the sofa. Afterwards he reproached himself for a long time for having acted so dissolutely, although he was not able to make amends for it even when on his return that night he kneeled by mistake in the park in front of the statue of the builder and mayor of the town, the Maecenas Mr Grabowsky, to whom the city of Przemyśl owed a great debt in the eighties.

Only the stamping of the military patrol broke in on his ardent words: 'Do not judge Thy servant, for no man will be justified before Thee, if Thou dost not forgive him all his sins. I beg Thee that Thy verdict be not severe. I beg Thy help and entrust my soul into Thy hands, O Lord.'

From that time on, whenever he was called to General Fink he made various attempts to renounce all earthly pleasures and gave the excuse that he had a stomach upset. He considered this lie necessary so that his soul might be spared hellish sufferings, for he knew only too well that army discipline demanded that when a general said to a chaplain: 'Have a good booze, old man,' he must booze out of pure respect for his superior officer.

Sometimes of course he did not succeed, especially when the general after the glorious field services organized even more glorious gargantuan feasts at the expense of the garrison budget. Afterwards in the accounts department they somehow managed to sew it all together so that they could get a rake-off too. After these happenings the chaplain always imagined that he was morally buried before the face of the Lord and reduced to a quaking jelly.

Then he went about as though in a daze and without losing faith in God in this chaos began seriously to wonder whether he should not regularly flog himself every day.

It was in just such a mood that he now appeared in answer to the general's invitation.

General Fink went to meet him beaming all over with joy.

'Have you heard of my summary court-martial?' he called to him delightedly. 'We're going to hang one of your people.'

At the words 'your people' Martinec looked in anguish at the general. He had already many times rejected the assumption that he was a Czech and explained time without number that their parish in Moravia had two communities, a Czech and a German one, and that he often had to preach one week for the Czechs and another for the Germans. And because in the Czech district there was no Czech school but only a German one, he had to teach in German in both districts and therefore was no Czech. This piece of logic had once provoked a major at the table into observing that that chaplain from Moravia was really a shop with mixed groceries.

'Sorry,' said the general, 'I forgot. He's not one of your people. He's a Czech, a deserter, a traitor who has worked for the Russians and is going to hang. Meanwhile, purely as a matter of form, we are establishing his identity. But it doesn't matter. He'll hang at once as soon as we get the answer by telegram.'

Seating the chaplain beside him on the sofa the general continued gaily: 'When I hold a summary court-martial everything must be done to match its summary nature. That's my principle. When at the beginning of the war I was near Lwów I managed to have a bastard hanged only three minutes after the verdict. He was a Jew of course, but we once hanged a Ruthenian only five minutes after discussing his case.'

The general smiled good-humouredly: 'Neither of them happened to need spiritual consolation. The Jew was a Rabbi and the Ruthenian an Orthodox priest. The case we have now is of course quite a different one. Here it's a Catholic we're going to hang. I hit on the capital idea of offering him spiritual consolation beforehand, so as not to hold matters up afterwards, as I say, so as not to hold matters up.'

The general rang the bell and gave the following order to his servant: 'Bring two from yesterday's battery.'

And a moment later he filled the chaplain's glass with wine and said affably: 'Console yourself a little before you offer spiritual consolation . . .'

At this frightful time from the barred window behind which he sat on a straw mattress Švejk's song rang out:

> 'We're the boys who make the noise,
> Win the hearts of all the tarts,
> Draw our pay and then make hay!
> Hey, diddle de dee. One, two, three!'

2

Spiritual Consolation

IN the literal sense of the word Chaplain Martinec did not walk in to
see Švejk but floated into his cell like a ballerina on the stage. Heavenly
yearnings and a bottle of old Gumpoldskirchen made him as light as
a feather at this moving moment. He imagined that in this grave and
holy moment he was drawing nearer to God, when in fact he was drawing nearer to Švejk.

They shut the door behind him and left the two alone. The chaplain
said enthusiastically to Švejk, who was sitting on the bunk: 'My dear
son, I am Chaplain Martinec.'

On his way to Švejk this form of address had seemed to him to be
very suitable and somehow paternally touching.

Švejk got up from his bunk, shook hands energetically with the chaplain, and said: 'I'm very glad to meet you. I am Švejk, the orderly of the 11th march company of the 91st regiment. Recently they transferred the nucleus of our regiment to Bruck an der Leitha, so please make yourself comfortable beside me, Your Reverence, and tell me why you've been put into gaol. You have after all the rank of an officer and so you are entitled to officers' arrest in the garrison. You certainly should not be put here, because that bunk is full of lice. It sometimes happens of course that people don't know where prisoners properly belong either because there's been a muddle in the office or by pure chance. Once, sir, I was sitting in the regimental gaol in Budějovice when they brought a probationary cadet into my cell. A probationer like that was something like a chaplain, neither fish nor fowl nor good red herring. He roared at the men like an officer, but when anything happened they locked him up with the common rank and file. These probationers were such mongrels, sir, that they were not accepted in the N.C.O.s' mess. They had no right to go to the men's mess, they were too senior for that, and the officers' mess again wasn't suitable for them. We had five of them and to begin with they only lived on cheese in the canteen because they never got portions from the mess. But then Lieutenant Wurm got to know about them and forbade them to go there, because he said it was not compatible with a probationary cadet's honour to patronize the men's canteen. And so what could they do? They were not allowed into the officers' canteen. And so they just hung in the air and for a few days endured such a calvary that one of them jumped into the river Malše, and another ran away from the regiment and two months later wrote to the barracks that he was Minister of War in Morocco. After that there were four of them, you see, because the one who had jumped into the Malše was fished out again alive. In his excitement when he jumped into it he had forgotten that he knew how to swim and had passed a swimming test with honours. They put him into a hospital and didn't know what to do with him there, whether to cover him up with an officers' blanket or a men's one. But they found a way round and gave him no blanket at all. Instead they wrapped him up in a wet sheet, so that after half an hour he begged to be sent back to the barracks. And that was the man they put in with me when he was still completely wet! He sat there about four days and was very happy indeed because he at last got messing there. It's true it was prisoners' messing, but he could at least be sure of getting it. On the fifth day they came for him and half an hour later he returned for his cap and wept with joy. He said to me: "At last they have taken a decision about us. From today probationary cadets will be locked up in the guard-house with the officers and we shall pay extra to the officers' mess for our messing. We shall be admitted when the officers have finished their food. We shall sleep with the men, get our coffee from the men's mess and draw our tobacco rations with the men too." '

It was only now that Martinec had recovered sufficiently to be able to break in upon Švejk with a sentence, the contents of which had no relevance whatsoever to the preceding conversation: 'Yes, yes, dear son, there are things between heaven and earth of which it behoves us to think with glowing heart and confidence in the infinite mercy of God. I come, dear son, to offer you spiritual consolation.'

He paused, because all that seemed somehow inappropriate. On the way he had composed a complete draft of a speech, in which he had intended to bring the unfortunate man to the contemplation of his life and to the realization that he would be forgiven in heaven above if he would only repent and show real sorrow.

Now he was wondering how to go on, but Švejk anticipated him by asking whether he had a cigarette.

Martinec had not yet learned to smoke; it was the only thing he had retained of his former way of life. Once or twice when he was with General Fink and had had a drop too much he tried to smoke a cigar, but at once everything came out of him and he had the impression that his guardian angel was warningly tickling him in the throat.

'I don't smoke, dear son,' he answered Švejk with unusual dignity.

'I'm surprised,' said Švejk. 'I've known many chaplains and they smoked like the distillery in Zlíchov. I can't really imagine a chaplain who doesn't smoke or drink. I've only known one who didn't puff and he preferred to chew tobacco rather than smoke it, and when he was preaching he spat it out all over the pulpit. Where do you come from, Your Reverence?'

'From Nový Jičín,' answered the Imperial and Royal Reverend Martinec in a dejected tone.

'Then perhaps, sir, you once knew a Růžena Gaudrsová. Two years ago she was employed in a wine restaurant in Platnéřská Street in Prague and suddenly brought paternity actions against eighteen persons because she'd given birth to twins. One of those twins had one blue and one brown eye and the other had one grey and one black. And so she assumed that four gentlemen with eyes like that, who had visited the wine restaurant and had business with her, had been involved. And then one of the twins had a lame leg, like a city councillor who also used to go there, and the other had six toes on one foot, like a parliamentary deputy who was a daily guest there. And just imagine, sir, eighteen guests used to go to that wine restaurant and those twins had a small birthmark after each one of all those eighteen whom she kept company with either at home or in a hotel. In the end the court decided that in such a queue of people the father was anonymous and then finally she laid the blame on the proprietor of the wine restaurant where she worked and sued him. But he proved that he had been impotent for twenty years as a result of an operation for an inflammation of his lower extremities. After that they sent her under escort, sir, to you at Nový Jičín, and from that you can see very well that whoever strives for power usually gets a lemon. She should have stuck to one man only and not said in court that one of the twins was by the deputy and the other by the city councillor or by this person or that. You can always reckon up the birth of a baby. On such and such a date I was with him in the hotel and on such and such a date the child was born. That's of course if it's a normal birth, sir. In "transit hotels" like that you'll always get a witness for ten crowns, either a waiter or a chambermaid, who'll swear that he'd actually been with her that night and that when they went down the stairs together she said to him: "And what if something happens?", and he answered her: "Don't be afraid, my silly pet, I'll look after the baby." '

The chaplain thought for a moment and the whole of his spiritual consolation seemed to him now rather difficult, although he had had all worked out beforehand what he would say to his dear son and how he would say it. He had planned to speak of the supreme mercy on the day of the last judgement, when all army criminals would rise from their graves with ropes around their necks and because they had repented would be received with mercy like the robber in the New Testament.

He had prepared what was perhaps one of the most beautiful spiritual consolations and it was going to be in three parts. First of all he would explain that death by hanging is easy if a man is completely reconciled with God. Army law punishes the delinquent for his treason against His Imperial Majesty who is the father of his warriors. One must therefore regard the smallest offence of any warrior as an act of parricide and sacrilege to the father. After that he intended to go on and develop his theory that His Imperial Majesty was Emperor by the grace of God and was appointed by him to direct secular affairs, just as the Pope was appointed by him to direct spiritual affairs. Treason against the Emperor was treason against the Lord himself. And the army criminal must expect not only the rope but eternal punishment and eternal perdition as well. If, however, because of the requirements of military discipline secular justice could not quash the sentence and had to hang the criminal, everything was not yet lost as far as the other punishment in eternity was concerned. A man could improve his position by means of an excellent move – by repentance.

The chaplain pictured this very moving scene as something which might help him in heaven by obliterating all the traces of his activities and actions in General Fink's apartment in Przemyśl.

To start with he would shout at the condemned man: 'Repent, my son! Let us kneel together! Repeat after me, my son!'

And then this stinking lousy cell would resound with the prayer: 'O God, whose quality it is always to give grace and to forgive, I earnestly beg Thee for the soul of this warrior, whom Thou hast commanded to leave this world by the sentence of a summary court-martial in Przemyśl. Grant that this infantryman by his piteous and total repentance be spared from suffering the torments of hell and that he may partake of the everlasting joys.'

'If you allow me to say so, Your Reverence, you've been sitting like a stuck pig for five minutes as though you'd lost your capacity for speech. Anyone can see on you that this is the first time you've been in gaol.'

'I have come for spiritual consolation,' said the chaplain gravely.

'It beats me why you keep harping on this spiritual consolation, sir. I'm awfully sorry, sir, but I don't feel strong enough to be able to offer you any consolation at all. You're not the first or the last chaplain to get himself behind bars. And moreover, to tell the truth, sir, I don't have the eloquence to offer consolation to anyone in such a difficult situation. I once tried, but it didn't turn out very well. Now, come and sit down nicely here next to me and I'll tell you all about it. When I used to live in Opatovická Street, I had a friend called Faustýn, who was a porter in a hotel. He was a very decent fellow, very fair and hard-working. He knew every girl on the streets, and you could come to see him, sir, in the hotel at any time during his night duty and just tell him: "Mr Faustýn, I'd like a girl", and he would at once ask you very conscientiously whether you wanted a blonde, a brunette, a short one, a tall one, a thin one, a fat one, a German, a Czech, a Jewess, a married one, a divorced one, a widow, an intelligent one or an unintelligent one.'

Švejk nestled up to the chaplain in a familiar way and putting his arm round his waist continued: 'Let's say now, sir, that you had said: "I'd like a blonde with long legs, a widow without intelligence." Well, in ten minutes you'd have had her in bed with you with her birth certificate as well.'

The chaplain began to feel hot all over and Švejk went on talking, clasping the chaplain to him like a mother: 'And you wouldn't have guessed, sir, what a feeling for morality and decency Mr Faustýn had. He didn't take a single kreutzer tip from those women whom he bargained with and delivered to the rooms. And if ever one of those women forgot and wanted to slip him something, you should have seen how furious he got and how he started to shout at her: "You filthy bitch, you, when you sell your body and commit mortal sin don't imagine that ten kreutzers of yours are going to make any difference. I'm no bawd, you impudent whore, you. I only do this out of compassion for you, so that when you've sunk so low you won't have to display your shame to passers-by in public, be caught in the night somewhere by a patrol and spend three days scrubbing the floors of the police headquarters. Here at least you're warm and no one sees how low you've fallen." But he compensated himself at the expense of the guests when he refused to accept money like a bawd. He had his tariff: blue eyes cost ten kreutzers, black eyes fifteen. And he always made out a detailed bill on a piece of paper which he presented to the guest. Those were very reasonable agent's prices. For a woman without intelligence there was a surcharge of ten kreutzers because he took the view that a vulgar piece like that provided more fun than an educated lady. Well, once towards evening Mr Faustýn came to see me in Opatovická Street. He was in a very excited state and not at all himself, as though they had only a moment ago dragged him out from underneath the protecting rail on a tram and stolen his watch in the process. At first he didn't say a word, and then he drew out of his pocket a bottle of rum, took a swig at it, offered it to me and said: "Drink." And then we didn't say anything until we'd drunk up the whole bottle, when he suddenly said: "Old man, please do something for me. Open the window on to the street. I'll sit on the ledge here. You take me by the legs and throw me down from the third floor. I need nothing more in life. I've now got this last consolation that there's a true friend who can see me off out of this world. I can't go on living in it. Honest as I am, I have been accused of procuring like a bawd from the Jewish quarter. After all, our hotel's a first-class one. All the three chambermaids and my wife have police books and don't owe the doctor a single kreutzer for his visits. If you have any affection for me at all throw me down from the third floor and give me this last consolation." I told him to climb out on to the window-ledge and I threw him down on to the street. . . . Don't be afraid, Your Reverence.'

Švejk stood on the bunk and pulled the chaplain up with him: 'Look, Your Reverence, I seized him like this and – whizz bang, down he went!'

Švejk lifted up the chaplain and dropped him on the ground again, and while the horrified chaplain picked himself up from the floor Švejk went on saying: 'So you see, sir, that nothing happened to you, and nothing happened to him, to Mr Faustýn either, although it was three times as high. Mr Faustýn was completely tight and forgot that I was living on the ground floor in Opatovická Street and not on the third floor as I used to a year before, when I lived in Křemencova Street and he used to come and see me there.'

From the floor the chaplain looked up in alarm at Švejk, who stood over him on the bunk and waved his arms.

It flashed on the chaplain that he was dealing with a madman and so he stammered: 'Yes, my dear son, it wasn't even three times as high.' Then he shuffled slowly backwards to the door, began suddenly to bang on it and uttered such frightful shrieks that they at once opened it for him.

Švejk saw through the barred window how the chaplain hurriedly rushed across the courtyard escorted by a guard and gesticulating in a lively manner.

'And now they're probably taking him to the mental ward,' thought Švejk, as he jumped down from the bunk and marched around singing:

> 'I'll never wear that ring you gave me.
> Lor lummy, why ever not?
> When I get back to my reg-i-ment
> I'll load it in my gun . . .'

A few minutes later they reported to General Fink that the chaplain had come.

The general was again entertaining many guests among whom an eminent role was played by two pleasant ladies, not to speak of wine and liqueurs.

Here were met together all the officers who had formed the board of the summary court-martial, except the ordinary infantryman who had lit their cigarettes in the morning.

The chaplain floated into the gathering like a phantom in a fairy story. He was pale, tense and dignified like a man who is conscious that he has had his face slapped for no fault of his own.

General Fink, who had latterly behaved very familiarly to the chaplain, drew him beside him on the sofa and asked him in a drunken voice: 'What's the matter with you, old spiritual consolation?'

At the same time one of the gay ladies threw a cigarette at the chaplain. 'Have a drink, old spiritual consolation,' General Fink said again, pouring him out some wine in a large green goblet. As he did not start drinking at once, the general began to pour the wine down him, and if the chaplain had not imbibed very valiantly he would have made a nice mess over him.

It was only then that the inquiries began about how the condemned man had conducted himself while the spiritual consolation was being offered. The chaplain stood up and said in tragic tones: 'He's gone mad.'

'That must have been a brilliant spiritual consolation!' the general said with a loud guffaw, upon which all the others had fits of frightful laughter and both ladies began once more to throw cigarettes at the chaplain.

At the end of the table the major nodded in his chair. He had already taken a drop too much and now he woke up out of his apathy, quickly poured a liqueur into two wine glasses, made his way through the chairs to the chaplain and forced the confused servant of God to drink 'to brotherhood'[1] with him. After that he rolled back to his place and went on with his forty winks.

With this toast to 'brotherhood' the chaplain fell completely into the clutches of the devil, who stretched his arms out to him from all the bottles on the table and from the looks and smiles of the gay ladies who

1. Drinking 'to brotherhood' was a formal preliminary to the use of the second person singular in addressing someone or calling someone by his Christian name.

put their legs on the table opposite him, so that Beelzebub was even peering at him out of lace frillies.

Up to the very last moment the chaplain had not lost the conviction that his soul was at stake and that he was a martyr.

This he expressed in his meditations which ne addressed to the general's two batmen who carried him into the next room and laid him on the sofa: 'A sad but exalted spectacle is opening up before your eyes, when with an unprejudiced and pure mind you recall so many famous sufferers who became victims for their faith and who are known by the name of martyrs. In my case you can observe how a man can feel exalted over all his sufferings, when justice and virtue dwell in his heart, and armed with these he wins a glorious victory over his most frightful sufferings.'

Then they turned his face to the wall and he immediately fell asleep.

He had very disturbed slumbers.

He dreamt that in the daytime he was carrying out the duties of a chaplain and in the evening he was porter in the hotel in the place of Faustýn, whom Švejk had thrown out of the window from the third floor.

Complaints against him came to the general from all sides on the grounds that he had brought a guest a brunette instead of a blonde, and that instead of a divorced lady with intelligence he had supplied a widow without intelligence.

He woke up in the morning sweating like a pig and with a queasy stomach. It occurred to him that his vicar in Moravia was an angel compared with him.

3

Švejk back in his March Company

THE major who acted as judge advocate at the court proceedings with Švejk the previous morning was the same figure who at the general's evening party drank 'to brotherhood' with the chaplain and snoozed.

One thing was certain: no one knew at what hour and in what state the major left the general that night. They were all of them in such a condition that no one noticed his absence. The general was even confused about who of the company was speaking. The major had already been more than two hours away when the general, twirling his moustaches and smiling in an idiotic way, called out: 'Very well said, major.'

In the morning the major could not be found anywhere. His greatcoat hung in the hall, his sabre was on the hook and the only thing missing was his officer's cap. They thought he had perhaps gone to sleep in the W.C. in the house somewhere, and so they looked through all the W.C.s but failed to find him anywhere. Instead they discovered on the second floor a lieutenant who had been one of the general's guests and who was fast asleep in a kneeling position with his mouth in the hole, sleep having overtaken him just as he was vomiting.

The major seemed to have vanished from the face of the earth.

But if anyone had happened to look through the barred window into where Švejk was locked up they would have seen that under Švejk's Russian military greatcoat two persons were sleeping on one bunk and two pairs of boots were peeping out.

The boots with spurs belonged to the major, those without to Švejk.

Both men lay cosily together like two kittens. Švejk had his paw under the major's head and the major was embracing Švejk's waist, snuggling up to him like a puppy to a bitch.

There was nothing mysterious about this. The major was duty-conscious and that was all.

You must certainly have had the experience of sitting and drinking with someone the whole night until late the next morning, when suddenly your drinking companion puts his hands to his head, jumps up and shouts: 'Jesus Mary, I ought to have been in the office at eight o'clock.' This is the so-called fit of duty-consciousness which comes on as a by-product of a guilty conscience. A person who is seized by such a noble fit is not easily deflected from his sacred conviction that he must at once go to the office and make up for what he missed there. These are the hatless apparitions whom the porters in the offices catch in the corridor and tuck up on the sofa in their hole so that they can sleep it out.

And this was the sort of fit that had seized the major.

When he woke up in his chair it suddenly occurred to him that he must at once interrogate Švejk. This fit of official duty-consciousness bobbed up so quickly and suddenly and was implemented so promptly and decisively that no one noticed the major's disappearance.

But all the more conspicuously was the major's presence felt in the guard-house of the army gaol. He erupted there like a bomb.

The sergeant-major on duty was sleeping at the table and around him the rest of the men slumbered in various positions.

The major with his cap on one side let off such a volley of oaths that all stopped in the midst of their yawns and their faces acquired a grimacing expression. It was not a pack of soldiers who stared at him so hopelessly and so grotesquely but a pack of grinning apes.

The major struck the table with his fist and shouted at the sergeant-major: 'You indolent bastard, I told you a thousand times that your men are a pack of swinish shits.' Turning to the goggling men he shouted: 'Men! There's imbecility staring out of your eyes even when you're asleep, and when you're awake, you bastards, you look as if each one of you had wolfed up a truck of dynamite.'

After that there followed a long and copious sermon about the duties of all the men on guard and finally the order that they should at once open up for him the cell where Švejk was held, as he wanted to subject the delinquent to a new interrogation.

And so this was how the major got to Švejk's cell in the night.

He arrived there at the stage when everything was, so to speak, ripening within him. His final outburst was his order that the keys of the prison should be handed over to him.

In a last despairing recollection of his duties the sergeant-major refused to comply. This at once made a grandiose impression on the major.

'You swinish pack of shits!' he shouted into the courtyard. 'If you'd given me the keys I'd have shown you!'

'Humbly report, sir,' the sergeant-major answered, 'I am obliged to lock you up and to put a guard over the prisoner for the sake of your own safety. When you want to leave, sir, please just knock on the door.'

'You bloody half-wit,' said the major, 'you baboon, you camel, do you really imagine that I'm afraid of any prisoner and you have to station a guard to protect me when I'm going to interrogate him? Bloody hell! Lock me in and clear out quick!'

In the opening over the door in the barred lantern a petrol lamp with a short wick emitted a faint light which barely sufficed to enable the major to find Švejk who, awake and standing in military position by his bunk, patiently awaited what would actually come out of this visit.

Švejk remembered that the best thing to do would be to give the major a report and so he called out energetically: 'Humbly report, sir, one gaoled man and otherwise nothing to report.'

The major suddenly could not remember why he had come there and so he said: 'At ease! Where have you got that gaoled man?'

'Humbly report, it's me, sir,' said Švejk proudly.

The major however ignored this reply, for the general's wine and liqueurs were producing in his brain the final alcoholic reaction. He yawned so frightfully that any civilian would have sprained his jaw. In the case of the major, however, this yawning shunted his thoughts into those recesses of the brain where human beings preserve the art of song. Without any ceremony he fell on to Švejk's mattress on the bunk and screamed out in the tones of a slaughtered pig just before its final end:

> 'O Tannenbaum, o Tannenbaum,
> Wie schön sind deine Blätter!'[1]

He repeated this several times, punctuating the song with incomprehensible shrieks.

Then he rolled over on to his back like a small bear, made himself into a ball and began to snore at once.

'Sir,' Švejk said, waking him, 'humbly report, you'll get lice.'

It was no good. The major was dead to the world.

Švejk looked at him tenderly and said: 'Well, then, to bye-byes, old

1. This famous German folk song hardly needs translation: 'O fir tree, O fir tree, how lovely are thy leaves.'

toper,' and covered him with his greatcoat. Later he crept in beside him and it was in this position they found them next morning snuggled together.

At about nine o'clock, when the hunt for the major reached its climax, Švejk got up and thought it appropriate to wake him. He

shook him several times very thoroughly, pulled the Russian great-coat off him, until finally he sat up on the bunk and looking dully at Švejk tried to find out from him the solution to the enigma of what had actually happened to him.

'Humbly report, sir,' said Švejk, 'they've come here several times from the guard-room to make sure you're still alive. And so I've taken the liberty of waking you up now, because I don't know how long you generally sleep and I wouldn't like you to oversleep. There was once a cooper in a brewery at Uhříněves who always slept until six o'clock in the morning and should he happen to oversleep only a quarter of an hour more to a quarter past six, he went on sleeping until noon and did this for so long that they kicked him out of his job. After that he got angry and abused the church and a member of our Ruling House.'

'You dotty, no?' said the major in broken Czech, not without a touch of hopelessness, because he had a terrible hangover from the previous night and still could not find an answer to the question why he was actually sitting there, why people kept on coming here from the guard-room and why this fellow who was standing in front of him was drivelling such nonsense which was completely Greek to him. It all seemed frightfully queer. He remembered vaguely that he had already been there once in the night, but what on earth was the reason?

'I already be here night?' he asked in a tone of some uncertainty.

'According to instructions, sir,' Švejk answered, 'as I understood from your words, sir, humbly report, you came to interrogate me.'

And then it all suddenly dawned on the major and he looked at himself and behind him as though he were searching for something.

'Please don't worry about anything, sir,' said Švejk. 'You've woken up exactly as you were when you came in here. You arrived here without a greatcoat and without a sabre but with a cap. Your cap is over there. You see, I had to take it from your hand because you wanted to put it under your head. An officer's parade cap, sir, is like a top hat. There's only one man who could go to sleep on a top hat and that was a Mr Karderaz at Loděnice. He stretched himself out on a bench in a pub and put his top hat under his head. He used to sing at funerals, you see, and went to every funeral in a top hat. He put his top hat nicely under his head and impressed it on his mind that he musn't squash it. Then throughout the night in some way or other he kept the full weight of his body off it so that it wasn't damaged at all but rather benefited from it, because when he turned from one side to the other he slowly brushed it with his hair till he had completely ironed it.'

The major, who was now already grasping the whys and wherefores, continued to look dully at Švejk and could only repeat: 'You dotty, no? I now here. I go away.' He got up, went to the door and hammered on it.

Before they came to open it he had time to say to Švejk: 'If telegram no come that you're you then you hang!'

'Thank you very much indeed,' said Švejk. 'I know, sir, that you're taking very good care of me and if by any chance, sir, you should have caught one on this bunk you can be assured that if it's a small one and has little red buttocks it's a male. And if there's only one and you don't find a long grey one with reddish stripes on its belly then it's all right, because otherwise there would have been a pair and these bastards breed frightfully, even worse than rabbits.'

'Drop that,' the major said dejectedly in German to Švejk, when they opened the door for him.

In the guard-room the major made no further scenes. He just stiffly ordered them to get him a droshky, and during its vibrations on the wretched cobbles of Przemyśl he had only one thought in his head and that was that even if the delinquent was an imbecile of the first water he was probably only an innocent bastard after all. As far as he personally was concerned there was nothing else for him to do except either shoot himself as soon as he came home or send for his greatcoat and sabre from the general's apartment, take a bath in the town baths, stop at Vollgruber's wine-cellar afterwards, put his appetite in order again and book by telephone a ticket for the performance in the town theatre that evening.

Before he reached his apartment he decided on the latter.

But in his apartment a small surprise awaited him. He arrived just at the right moment . . .

In the corridor stood General Fink, who was holding the major's batman by the collar, manhandling him frightfully and roaring at him: 'Where have you put your major, you swine? Speak, you animal!'

But the animal did not speak, because he was blue in the face through the general suffocating him.

As he came in upon this scene the major saw that the unfortunate batman was firmly holding under his arm his greatcoat and sabre, which he had obviously brought from the general's vestibule.

The scene began to give the major a great deal of entertainment and so he stood in the open doorway and went on looking at the suffering of his faithful servant, who had the precious quality of having drawn on to himself the major's dislike on account of his various pilferings.

The general let go of the blue-faced batman only for a moment in order to take a telegram out of his pocket. He then began to pound the batman across the mouth and lips with it and to shout at him: 'Where have you put your major, you swine, where have you put your

major *judge advocate*, you bastard, so that you can hand him a telegram on an official matter?'

'Here I am,' Major Derwota called from the door. The association
of the words 'major', 'judge advocate' and 'telegram' reminded him
again of his duties.

'Ah,' shouted General Fink, 'so you're coming back, are you?'
There was so much malice in his tone that the major did not reply but
stood there irresolutely.

The general told him to follow him into the sitting-room and when
they sat down at the desk he threw on to the table the telegram with
which he had pounded the batman's face and said to him in a tragic
voice: 'Read it! This is your work.'

While the major read the telegram the general got up from his chair,
ran up and down the room, knocked over the chairs and stools and
shouted: 'But I'll hang him none the less!'

The telegram read as follows:

Infantryman Josef Švejk, orderly of the 11th march company, got lost on
the 16th of this month on the route Chyrów–Felsztyn while on an official
journey to look for billets. Send Infantryman Švejk to brigade headquarters
at Wojałycze without delay.

The major opened the drawer of his desk, drew out a map and reflected that Felsztyn was forty kilometres south-east of Przemyśl and
so it was a frightful mystery how Infantryman Švejk could have come
across a Russian uniform in an area more than 150 kilometres away
from the front, since the forward positions stretched along the line
Sokal–Turze–Kozlów.

When the major informed the general of this and showed him on
the map the place where according to the telegram Švejk had got lost
a few days ago, the general bellowed like a bull, because he felt that all
his hopes of having a summary court-martial had dissolved in smoke.
He went to the telephone, called up the guard-room and gave orders
that they should at once bring the prisoner Švejk to him in the major's
apartment.

Before the order was carried out the general amid a volley of frightful oaths gave full rein to his annoyance countless times: he should
have had him hanged on his own responsibility without any further
investigations.

The major opposed this view and said something to the effect that

law and justice must go hand in hand. He spoke eloquently in resounding periods about justice and the law courts, judicial murders
and everything he could possibly think of, because after the night
before he had a ghastly hangover which he felt an urge to relieve by
talking.

When they at last produced Švejk, the major demanded an explanation from him of what had happened near Felsztyn and the facts about
the Russian uniform.

Švejk duly explained this and corroborated it with a few examples
from his chronicle of human suffering. When afterwards the major
asked him why he had not stated this under cross-examination before
the court, Švejk answered that no one had in fact asked him how he
got into Russian uniform and that all the questions had been: 'Do you
admit that you voluntarily and without any pressure put on enemy
uniform?' Since that was true he could not say anything else but:
'Of course – yes – certainly – it was like that – undoubtedly.' This

was why he had rejected with indignation the accusations made in the court that he had betrayed His Imperial Majesty.

'The fellow is a complete imbecile,' said the general to the major. 'Only a bloody idiot would put on a Russian uniform left on the dam

of a lake by goodness knows whom and then get himself drafted into a party of Russian prisoners.'

'Humbly report, sir,' Švejk said, 'you are right. I do sometimes notice myself that I'm feeble-minded, especially towards evening when . . .'

'Shut up, you ox,' the major said to Švejk and turned to the general to ask what they should do with him.

'Let his brigade hang him,' the general decided.

An hour later the escort took Švejk to the station to conduct him to the staff of the brigade in Wojałycze.

In the gaol Švejk left behind him a small memorial of himself, having scratched on the wall with a piece of wood a list in three columns of all the soups, sauces and main dishes which he had eaten in civil life. It was a kind of protest against the fact that for twenty-four hours they had given him nothing whatsoever to eat.

The following document accompanied Švejk to the brigade:

In accordance with instructions contained in telegram number 469 the infantryman Josef Švejk, a deserter from the 11th march company, is forwarded to the brigade staff for further action.

The escort itself, which consisted of four men, was a medley of nationalities. It was made up of a Pole, a Hungarian, a German and a Czech. The last-named, who had the rank of a corporal and led the escort, tried to show his importance towards the prisoner who was his fellow-countryman by letting him feel his frightful superiority. When for instance Švejk expressed the wish at the station that he might be permitted to urinate, the corporal told him quite rudely that he could urinate when he came to the brigade.

'Very well,' said Švejk. 'You'll have to give me that in writing, so that when my bladder bursts it is established who is responsible for it. There is a law about that, corporal.'

The corporal, who was a simple cowman, was frightened by the word bladder and so the whole escort ceremoniously led Švejk to the W.C. on the station. Throughout the journey the corporal gave the impression of being a brutal fellow and he looked so stuck-up that you might have thought he was going to get at the very least the rank of commander of an army corps the very next day.

When they were sitting in the train on the line Przemyśl–Chyrów, Švejk remarked to him:

'Corporal, when I look at you, I'm always reminded of a certain Corporal Bozba, who used to serve in Trento. The first day they promoted him corporal he began suddenly to increase in girth. First his cheeks started to swell and then his belly blew up so that the next day his crown-property trousers weren't big enough for him. But what was worst of all was that his ears began to grow long. So they sent him to the sickroom and the regimental doctor explained that it was what usually happened to corporals. At first they blow up and with some corporals this passes over quickly, but this case of his was a very serious one and he might burst, because it was spreading from his star down to his navel. To save him they had to cut off his star and then he went down again.'

From that moment Švejk vainly tried to keep up a conversation with the corporal and to explain to him in a friendly way why it was a common saying that a corporal was a disaster for a company.

The corporal did not answer except to make dark threats about which of them would be the one to laugh when they came to the brigade. In short Švejk's fellow-countryman did not prove to be much good, and when Švejk asked him where he came from he answered that it was no business of his.

Švejk tried all kinds of methods on him. He told him that this was not the first time he had been led under escort and that he had always had a grand time with all those who had escorted him.

The corporal remained silent and Švejk went on: 'Well, now, I think, corporal, that some disaster in the world must have struck you if you've lost your power of speech. I've known many gloomy corporals but such a godforsaken disaster as you are, corporal – please excuse me and don't be angry that I'm saying it – I've never yet seen. Tell me frankly what's worrying you and perhaps I can advise you, because a soldier who is being led under escort always has more experience than those who are guarding him. Or do you know what, corporal? What about your telling us a story so that the journey can pass more pleasantly? Perhaps you could tell us something about what it looks like in the part of the country you come from, whether there are lakes there or whether there are the ruins of an old castle there and, if there are, you could tell us the legend about them.'

'I've had enough of this,' shouted the corporal.

'Then you're a happy man,' said Švejk. 'Many people never have enough.'

The corporal enveloped himself in complete silence after he had spoken his last word: 'In the brigade they'll explain it all to you and I shan't bother myself about you any more.'

There was very little fun in the escort altogether. The Hungarian talked with the German in a peculiar way, because the only words he knew in German were *Jawohl* and *Was?* When the German explained something to him, the Hungarian nodded his head and said: '*Jawohl*', and when the German stopped talking the Hungarian said: '*Was?*' and the German started again. The Pole in the escort behaved like an aristocrat. He took no notice of anyone and amused himself on his own by blowing his nose on the ground, very cleverly using for this purpose the fingers of his right hand. After that he gloomily smeared it with the butt of his rifle and in a well-bred manner wiped the sticky butt of the rifle on his trousers, muttering all the time: 'Holy Mother of God.'

'You aren't very clever at it,' said Švejk to him. 'At Na Bojišti there lived in a cellar apartment a crossing-sweeper called Macháček. He used to blow his nose on the window and smear it round so cleverly that he made out of it a picture of Libuše prophesying Prague's glory.[1] For every picture like that his wife gave him such an honorarium that he had a mug like a barn door. But he wouldn't give it up and went on perfecting himself in it. It was the only pleasure he had, you see.'

The Pole did not answer and finally the whole escort was plunged in deep silence, as though they were going to a funeral and were thinking pious thoughts about the late lamented.

It was in this state that they approached the brigade staff at Woja-łycze.

Meanwhile at the brigade staff there had been very considerable changes.

The command of the brigade staff had been entrusted to Colonel Gerbich. This was a gentleman of great military talents, which had gone to his legs in the form of gout. But he had some very influential friends in the ministry who saw to it that he did not retire but could knock about in the various staffs of the larger military units, draw increased pay together with various kinds of war bonuses and remain in each place until in a fit of gout he committed some act of complete asininity. Then he was again moved somewhere else and usually it was a kick upstairs. At lunch he never talked to the officers about anything except his swollen toe, which sometimes attained such frightful dimensions that he had to wear a special big boot.

At meals it was his favourite occupation to tell everybody how his toe oozed and continually sweated, so that he had to have it in cotton wool, and that these exudations smelt like sour oxtail soup.

This was why whenever he was transferred to another job the whole officers' corps always said a heartfelt goodbye to him. Otherwise he was a very jovial gentleman and behaved quite affably to the junior

1. Libuše, the legendary prophetess, was the first ruler of the Czechs and is the subject of Smetana's opera of that name.

officers, to whom he recounted the good things he used to drink and eat before he was attacked by gout.

When they brought Švejk to the brigade and, at the orders of the officer on duty, escorted him together with the necessary documents before Colonel Gerbich, Lieutenant Dub was sitting in the office.

During those few days since the march from Sanok to Sambor Lieutenant Dub had experienced one more adventure. Beyond Felsztyn the 11th march company met a transport of horses which were being led to the Dragoon Regiment in Sądowa Wisznia.

Lieutenant Dub himself hardly knew how it had happened that he had wanted to demonstrate his equestrian skill to Lieutenant Lukáš and how he had jumped on to a horse which disappeared with him down the valley of a stream, where they afterwards found him so firmly planted in a small bog that even the cleverest gardener would not have been capable of doing it. When with the help of ropes they dragged him out Lieutenant Dub had no complaints. He only groaned in a low voice, as though his last hour had come. As they marched by the staff of the brigade, they took him there and settled him in a small military hospital.

A few days later he recovered so that the doctor could say that they should rub his back and belly two or three times more with tincture of iodine after which he could go back to his unit.

Now he was sitting in Colonel Gerbich's office and was chatting with him about various illnesses.

When he saw Švejk he shouted out in a loud voice, because he knew all about his mysterious disappearance on the way to Felsztyn: 'So we've got you back again! Many go away as brutes and return as even bigger monsters. You're one of those, I suppose.'

For the sake of completeness it would be appropriate to add that Lieutenant Dub, as a result of his adventures on horseback, had suffered a slight concussion of the brain and therefore we must not be surprised if coming close to Švejk he called upon the Lord to struggle with Švejk and shouted out in verse: 'Father, look, I urge Thee. The cannons smoke and boom. The bullets whistle past me with a terrifying zoom. Lord of battles, Father, help me against this rogue! . . . Where have you been such a long time, you bastard? What's that uniform you've got on?'

It must also be recorded that the gout-stricken colonel had everything arranged very democratically in his office when he had no attacks. Officers and N.C.O.s of all ranks came to visit him to listen to his opinions about his swollen toe with its flavour of sour oxtail soup.

During the periods when Colonel Gerbich did not suffer attacks his office was always full of the most diverse ranks, because in such exceptional circumstances he was very gay and talkative and was glad

to have listeners around him to whom he could tell his dirty stories. This gave him a lot of pleasure and gave the others the satisfaction of being forced to laugh at his chestnuts, which were probably in circulation as long ago as the time of General Laudon.[1] It was very easy to serve under Colonel Gerbich at such times. Everybody did what they liked and wherever the colonel turned up in any staff everybody knew that people would flog and fiddle in every kind of way.

And so now, in addition to Švejk, who was brought before him, the

1. The renowned Austrian general in the eighteenth century who defeated Frederick the Great and was the subject of many army songs.

colonel's room was crowded with officers of the most varied ranks who waited to see what would happen, while the colonel studied the document addressed to the brigade staff and composed by the major from Przemyśl.

But Lieutenant Dub continued his conversation with Švejk in his usual charming way: 'You don't know me yet, but when you get to know me, you'll be dead stiff with horror.'

The colonel was completely flummoxed when he read the document from the major at Przemyśl, because the latter had dictated it when he was still under the influence of slight alcohol poisoning.

Colonel Gerbich was in a good mood none the less, because yesterday and today the unpleasant pains had eased and his toe was as quiet as a lamb.

'Well, what have you actually done?' he asked Švejk in such an affable tone that a dagger went through Lieutenant Dub's heart and impelled him to reply in the place of Švejk:

'This man, sir,' he said, presenting Švejk, 'pretends to be a half-wit for the sole purpose of concealing his rascality under the mask of imbecility. I am not acquainted with the contents of the document which has been sent with him, but none the less I presume that the blackguard has again committed some offence but this time on a larger scale. If you would allow me, sir, to familiarize myself with the contents of the document, I could surely give you, should you wish it, certain pointers to the way he should be handled.'

Turning to Švejk he said to him in Czech: 'You're sucking my blood, aren't you?'

'I am,' answered Švejk with dignity.

'So you can see what he's like, sir,' Lieutenant Dub continued in German. 'You can't ask him any questions. You can't talk to him at all. One day the scythe must strike against the stone and he will have to be punished in an exemplary fashion. Allow me, sir ...'

Lieutenant Dub buried himself in the document which had been drawn up by the major from Przemyśl and when he had finished reading it he called out triumphantly: 'Now it's amen for you, Švejk. What have you done with your crown-property uniform?'

'I left it on the dam of the lake when I was trying on these rags to see how a Russian soldier feels in them,' answered Švejk. 'It's really nothing more than a misunderstanding.'

Švejk began to tell Lieutenant Dub all the troubles he had had on account of this misunderstanding and when he had finished Lieutenant Dub roared at him:

'It is only now that you're really going to know me. Do you know what it means to lose crown property, you scoundrel, to lose your uniform in wartime?'

'Humbly report, sir,' answered Švejk, 'when a soldier loses his uniform he has to draw another one.'

'Jesus Mary,' shouted Lieutenant Dub. 'You hound, you reptile, how much longer are you going to play the fool with me? Do you want to serve another hundred years after the war?'

Colonel Gerbich, who up to this moment had remained sitting calmly and composedly at his table, suddenly grinned in a frightful way because his toe, which up to that time had been very quiet, was suddenly transformed by a fit of gout from a gentle and peaceful lamb into a roaring tiger, an electric current of six hundred volts, a limb which was being slowly crushed to rubble by a hammer. He just waved his hand and roared in the frightful voice of a man who is being slowly roasted on a spit: 'Get out everybody! Give me a revolver!'

Everyone already recognized the symptoms and so they all rushed out, including Švejk, whom the guard dragged out into the passage. Only Lieutenant Dub remained. The moment seemed to him a very favourable one to settle scores with Švejk and so he said to the grimacing colonel: 'Allow me to observe, sir, that this man . . .'

The colonel mewed and threw an inkpot at him, whereupon the horrified Lieutenant Dub saluted and said: 'Of course, sir,' and disappeared through the door.

After that roars and howls resounded from the colonel's office for a long time until finally the painful lamentations ceased. The colonel's toe was suddenly transformed back into a peaceful lamb. The fit of gout had passed. The colonel rang the bell and ordered Švejk to be brought back to him.

'Well, what's the matter with you?' he asked Švejk, as though a load had fallen from his shoulders. He was as free and happy as though he were rolling in the sand at the seaside.

Švejk smiled affably at the colonel and told him his whole odyssey; how he was the orderly of the 11th march company of the 91st regiment and how he had no idea how they could get on without him.

The colonel also smiled and then issued the following orders: 'Write out a railway warrant for Švejk via Lwów to Żółtańce, where his march company is due to arrive tomorrow, and give him a new uniform out of the store and 6 crowns 82 hellers for messing en route.'

When later, dressed in a new Austrian uniform, Švejk left the brigade staff to go to the station, Lieutenant Dub was hanging about the staff headquarters and was not a little surprised when Švejk reported to him in a strictly military fashion, showed him his documents and asked him solicitously whether he should take any message from him to Lieutenant Lukáš.

Lieutenant Dub could utter no word except: 'Dismiss!' When he looked after the disappearing figure of Švejk he muttered under his breath: 'You'll get to know me in time, Jesus Mary, you will . . .'

At the station of Żółtańce Captain Ságner's whole battalion was assembled except for the rearguard of the 14th company which had got lost somewhere when they marched round Lwów.

Arriving at the small country town Švejk found himself in a completely new environment because it was possible to observe from the general bustle that it was not very far from the front where people were massacring each other. All around the artillery and baggage trains had their encampments. Soldiers of various regiments came out of every house. Like an elite among them all Reich Germans were strolling about and aristocratically offering the Austrians cigarettes from their lavish supplies. In the Reich German field-kitchens in the square there were even whole barrels from which they tapped beer for the men, who fetched rations of it for their lunch and supper. The neglected Austrian soldiers with their bellies distended by filthy concoctions of sweet chicory hung around them like greedy cats.

Groups of Jews with hanging curls and in long kaftans pointed to the smoke clouds in the west and gesticulated with their hands. Everywhere they were shouting that on the river Bug the villages of Uciszków, Busk and Derewiany were on fire.

The thunder of guns could be clearly heard. They shouted that the Russians were bombarding Kamionka Strumiłowa from Grabów, that fighting was going on along the whole of the Bug and soldiers were stopping refugees who wanted to go back to their homes across the Bug.

Everywhere disorder and confusion reigned and no one knew for certain whether the Russians had not started a new offensive and halted their continuous retreat along the whole front.

Every moment field gendarmerie patrols brought to the main head-quarters of the town some frightened Jewish soul who was accused of having spread mendacious and false news. There they beat the wretched Jews until they were covered with blood and released them to go home with their hindquarters lacerated.

It was into this chaos that Švejk arrived and in this country town that he started his quest for his company. Already on the station he had nearly come into conflict with the transit command guard. When he came to the table where information was provided for soldiers looking for their units a corporal shouted at him from the table whether he didn't perhaps want him to go and look for his company for him. Švejk told him that he only wanted to know whereabouts in the town the 11th march company of the 91st regiment was billeted. 'It's very important for me to know where the 11th company is,' Švejk stressed, 'because I am its orderly.'

Very unfortunately a staff sergeant-major sat at the next table. He jumped up like a tiger and roared at Švejk: 'You blasted swine, you are an orderly and you don't know where your march company is!'

Before Švejk could answer, the staff sergeant-major had disappeared into the office and a moment later he brought out from it a fat lieu-tenant who looked as worthy as the owner of a large sausage factory.

The transit commands tended to be the collecting grounds for wild vagabond soldiers who might spend the whole war looking for their units and knocking about from one transit point to another. They would have liked most of all to wait in long queues by those tables at the transit commands, where there was the inscription: 'Payment for messing.'

When the fat lieutenant came in, the sergeant-major shouted out in German: 'Attention!' and the lieutenant asked Švejk: 'Where are your documents?'

When Švejk had shown them to him and the lieutenant was satis-fied as to the correctness of his march route from the staff of his brigade to his company in Żółtańce he returned them to Švejk and said patronizingly to the corporal at the table: 'Give him the informa-tion he requires,' and again shut himself in the office next door.

When the door closed after him the staff sergeant-major took Švejk by the shoulder and leading him to the door gave him the following information: 'See that you clear out of here quick, you stinking bastard!'

Švejk found himself once more in the chaos and started to look for someone whom he knew from the battalion. He walked for a long time on the streets until in the end he staked everything on one card.

He stopped a colonel and asked him in his broken German if by

any chance he knew where his battalion and company were quartered.

'You can speak Czech to me,' the colonel said. 'I'm Czech too. Your battalion is quartered nearby in the village of Klimontów behind the railway. It's not allowed in the town because people from one of your companies fought with the Bavarians in the town square the very day they arrived.'

And so Švejk set off to Klimontów.

The colonel called after him, put his hand in his pocket and gave him five crowns to buy cigarettes with. Then he said a friendly goodbye to him and went away from him, thinking to himself: 'What a nice lad.'

Švejk continued his journey to the village and thinking about the colonel drew the inference that twelve years ago in Trento there was a Colonel Habermaier who behaved just as nicely to the soldiers but turned out in the end to be a homosexual, because in the baths near the Adige he had tried to violate a cadet probationer, using 'service regulations' as blackmail.

Walking slowly, and absorbed in these gloomy thoughts, Švejk reached the nearby village and had little trouble in finding the staff of his battalion because, although the village was very extensive, there was only one decent building in it, a big elementary school, which the Galician local administration had built in this purely Ukrainian area as part of an intensive drive to make the community more Polish.

The school had gone through various phases during the war. Various Russian and Austrian staffs had been quartered there and the former gymnasium had been turned into an operating theatre at the time of the great battles which decided the fate of Lwów. They cut off legs and arms and carried out skull trepanning there.

Behind the school building in the garden was a huge funnel-shaped crater caused by the explosion of a shell of heavy calibre. In the corner of the garden stood a very large pear-tree and on one of the branches hung a piece of cut rope. Not long ago the local Greek Catholic vicar had been hanged on it as a result of a denunciation by the head-master of the local Polish school, who accused him of being a member of the group of Old Russians and of having during the Russian occupation celebrated a mass in the church for the victory of the arms of the Russian Orthodox Tsar. It was in fact not true, because the accused had not been there at the time but had been undergoing a cure for his gallstones at a small spa in Bochnia Zamurowana, which was untouched by the war.

Various elements played their part in the hanging of the Greek Catholic priest: nationalism, religious strife and a hen. Shortly before the war the unfortunate vicar had killed in his garden one of the head-master's hens which was pecking up the melon seeds he had just sown.

After his death the vicarage building stayed empty and it could be said that everyone took something away in memory of him.

One Polish peasant even took home the old piano, the top board of which he used for repairing the door of his pigsty. Some of the furniture was chopped up by the soldiers, as was the custom, and it was a stroke of luck that the stove in the kitchen was not ruined. It was big and had an excellent cooker, because the Greek Catholic vicar was no different from his Roman Catholic colleagues and enjoyed his yum-yum. So he liked to have many pots and pans on the cooker and in the oven.

Thus it became a tradition that all units of the army which passed through here used this kitchen for cooking for their officers. Upstairs in one big room was a sort of officers' club. The tables and chairs were collected from the inhabitants of the village.

That very day the officers of the battalion were having a banquet. They had clubbed together and bought a pig and Jurajda was making a pork feast for them. He was surrounded by various hangers-on from those ranks who served the officers, among whom the quartermaster sergeant-major played a prominent part. He advised Jurajda how to carve the pig's head so that a piece of its snout was left for him.

The eyes which goggled most were those of the insatiable Baloun.

He had the same lustful and longing look as cannibals must have when they see a missionary roast on a spit and the fat runs down and gives out a pleasant smell when it is being fried. Baloun felt like a dog leading a milk-cart when a boy from the delicatessen shop goes past with a basket of pieces of freshly smoked meat on his head. A string of smoked sausages hangs out of the basket over his back and the dog would jump and snap at it, were it not for the nasty straps in which it is harnessed and its horrible muzzle.

The initial phase of the jitrnice was the preparation of the sausage-meat, and here it lay on the baking board – an enormous embryo smelling of pepper, fat and liver.

And Jurajda with his rolled-up sleeves was so solemn that he could have served as a model for a painting of how God created the world from chaos.

Baloun could not contain himself and began to sob. Then his sobs grew into a heart-rending wailing.

'What are you bellowing like a bull for?' Jurajda asked him.

'It reminds me of home,' Baloun answered sobbing, 'how I was always at home at such times as this and never wanted to send a hamper even to my best neighbour. I always wanted to wolf it all myself, and so I did. Once I filled myself up so much with jitrnice,

blood sausage, pig's head and trotters that everyone thought I was
going to burst, and they drove me up and down and round the courtyard with a whip just like a cow that's blown up after eating clover.

'Mr Jurajda, please let me scoop up a little of this sausage-meat, and
after that I don't mind if they truss me. Otherwise I shan't be able to
stand the suffering.'

Baloun got up from the bench and swaying as if he were drunk
stepped towards the table. He stretched out his paw in the direction
of the heap.

Then there came a tough struggle. It was only with the greatest
difficulty that all those present could prevent him from hurling himself at the sausage-meat. None the less, when they were dragging him
out of the kitchen they were not able to hold him and in his desperation he managed to have a grab at the pot with guts which were being
prepared for filling with the sausage-meat.

Jurajda was so angry that he threw a whole bundle of sausage-
sticks at the fleeing Baloun and roared after him: 'Go and stuff yourself on sausage-sticks until you burst, you bastard.'

By that time the officers of the battalion were already assembled
upstairs and were waiting solemnly for that marvel which was being
born in the kitchen below. In the meantime, for want of other alcohol
they drank a crude corn spirit coloured yellow with onion peel juice,
which the Jewish merchant maintained was the most delicious and
most genuine French cognac which he had inherited from his father,
who in his turn had had it bequeathed to him by his grandfather.

'You bastard, you,' said Captain Ságner on this occasion, 'if you
go on saying that your great-grandfather bought it from the French
when they retreated from Moscow, I'll have you clapped in gaol
until the youngest in your family becomes the oldest.'

While after every sip they cursed the enterprising Jew, Švejk
was already sitting in the battalion office, where there was no one else
except Marek who, as the battalion historian, was using the sojourn
at Żółtańce to write up a stock of victorious battles which would
obviously break out in the future.

For the time being he was making certain preliminary notes and
when Švejk came in he had just written down: 'If in our mind's eye
we conjure up all these heroes who took part in the battles at the
village of N, where alongside our battalion there fought a battalion of
regiment N and another battalion of regiment N, we shall find that

our Nth battalion displayed the most brilliant strategic abilities and contributed undeniably to the victory of the Nth division, the object of which was the final consolidation of our position in sector N.'

'And so I'm back again, you see,' said Švejk to the volunteer.

'Allow me to smell you,' said Marek, pleasurably touched. 'Hum, you certainly stink of the dungeon-hole.'

'As usual,' said Švejk, 'it was only a matter of a small misunderstanding. And what are you doing?'

'As you see,' answered Marek, 'I'm making a rough cockshy about the heroic defenders of Austria, but somehow or other it doesn't hang together and the result's pure drivel. I am stressing the letter "N", which has attained extraordinary perfection in both the present and the future. In addition to my former talents Captain Ságner has discovered in me an unusual gift for mathematics. I have to control the battalion accounts and I've come to the conclusion so far that the battalion is completely in the red and is only waiting for the time when it can reach a settlement with its Russian creditors, because most stealing takes place after a defeat or a victory. However, it makes no difference whatsoever really. Even if we were wiped out to the last man the documents of our victory are still in existence here, because in my capacity of battalion historian I am honoured to be able to write: "Again fortune has turned against the enemy at the very moment when he was thinking that victory was in his grasp. A sortie by our soldiers and a bayonet attack are the matter of a moment. The enemy flee in despair and throw themselves into their own trenches. We bayonet them without mercy so that they abandon their trenches in disorder leaving wounded and unwounded prisoners in our hands. It is one of the most glorious moments." Whoever survives all this will write a letter home by field post: "They caught it square on their arses, dear wife! I am well. Have you weaned our little brat yet? Only, don't teach him to call strangers 'papa' because that would be difficult for me." Afterwards the censorship will black out the words "Caught it square on their arses", because no one knows who got it and it could be liable to various interpretations owing to its not being clearly expressed.'

'The really important thing is to speak unequivocally,' Švejk said. 'When the missionaries were at the church of St Ignatius in Prague in 1912 there was a preacher there who said from the pulpit that he would probably not meet anybody again in heaven. There was present

at that evening spiritual exercise a tinker named Kulíšek and after the
service he said at a pub that that missionary must have been up to
quite a lot in his time, if he could declare in the church like at a public
confession that he wouldn't meet anybody again in heaven. Why did
they allow such people up into the pulpit? People ought always to
speak clearly and distinctly and never in any kind of conundrums.
At U Brejšků there was a head cellarman years ago and when he was
sozzled and went home after his work he had the habit of stopping at
a night café and drinking toasts with strangers. And he always said
at each toast: "We'll . . . on you, and you'll . . . on us . . ." and because
of that he once got such a swipe across the jaw from a respectable
gentleman from Jihlava that when the café proprietor swept up the
teeth the next morning he called his daughter who went to the fifth
class of the elementary school and asked her how many teeth a grown-
up man had in his mouth. Because she couldn't tell him he knocked out
two of her teeth and on the third day got a letter from that head cellarman in which he apologized for all the unpleasantness he had caused
and said he had not wanted to say anything coarse but that the public
didn't understand him, because what he had in fact meant to say was
just this: "We'll have a down on you and you'll have a down on us."
Anyone who speaks ambiguously has got to think carefully before he
opens his mouth. A straightforward chap who calls a spade a spade
seldom gets a swipe across the jaw. But if he happens to get one
several times, then he's careful and prefers to keep quiet when he's in
company. It's true that people think that a fellow like that must be
up to some trick or other, and that he often gets beaten up too, but
that's what his deliberation and self-control bring him. After all, he
has to reckon that he's on his own and that he has against him a lot
of people who feel they've been insulted by him, and if he started to
fight with them he'd get twice as much in return. A chap like that has
got to be modest and patient. In Nusle there is a certain Mr Hauber
and once on a Sunday on the road at Kundratice they stabbed him
with a knife by mistake, when he was returning from a trip to Bar-
tůněk's Mill. He came home with the knife stuck in his back and when
his wife took off his coat she drew it cleanly out of his back. That same
afternoon she was using it to chop the meat for goulash, because it
was made out of Solingen steel and beautifully sharpened and their
knives at home were all saw-edged and blunt. After that she wanted to
have a whole set of such knives in her household and she kept on

sending him every Sunday on a trip to Kundratice, but he was so modest that he never went further than to U Banzetů at Nusle, where he knew that when he was sitting in the kitchen old Banzet would chuck him out before anyone could lay hands on him.'

'You haven't changed at all,' the volunteer said to him.

'I haven't,' answered Švejk. 'I haven't had the time to. They even wanted to shoot me, but that was not the worst. I've not had any pay since the twelfth.'

'And you won't get it here either, because we're going to Sokal, and the pay will only be issued after the battle. We've got to economize. If I reckon that the fighting will break out in a fortnight, they'll save 24 crowns 72 hellers on every fallen soldier, including the bonus.'

'And what's the news here otherwise?'

'First our rear-guard got lost, then the officers' corps is having a pork feast at the vicarage, and the men are dispersed all over the village and are committing all sorts of immoralities with the local female population. This morning they trussed a soldier from your company because he climbed up to the attic after a seventy-year-old woman. The fellow is innocent because in the order of the day it was never stated up to what age it's permitted.'

'Of course the chap's innocent,' said Švejk, 'because when an old woman like that climbs up on a ladder he can't see her face. We had just the same sort of case at the manoeuvres near Tábor. One of our platoons was quartered in a pub and a woman was scrubbing the floor in the hall when a fellow called Chramosta came up to her and spanked her on her – what should I say? – her petticoat. She had a very well developed petticoat and when he spanked her on it she didn't register at all. He spanked her a second time and then a third time and she still didn't register, as though it didn't concern her. And so he resolved to start operating, but she went on calmly scrubbing the floor around. Afterwards she turned round to him, looked him straight in the eyes and said: "Ever been had, soldier?" The woman was over seventy and she told this story all over the village.... And now I'd like to ask you whether during my absence you haven't been gaoled too?'

'There was no opportunity,' Marek apologized, 'but on the other hand as far as you're concerned I have to inform you that the battalion has issued an arrest warrant for you.'

'It doesn't matter,' Švejk put in. 'They're quite right to have done so. The battalion had to do it. It had to issue an arrest warrant for me.

It was their duty, because no one knew where I was for such a long time. That was no hasty act on the part of the battalion. . . . Well, did you say that all the officers are at the vicarage having a pork feast? Then I must go there and present myself to show that I'm back again. I am sure that Lieutenant Lukáš has anyhow been very worried about me.'

Švejk set off for the vicarage with a firm military step, singing:

> 'Now look at me, my treasure, look at me!
> My treasure, look at me!
> See how they've made a gentleman of me . . .
> A gentleman of me . . .'

After that Švejk entered the vicarage and went up the stairs to the room above, from where the voices of the officers could be heard.

They were talking about everything on earth and were just going on about the brigade and the muddle there was at the staff. Even the brigade adjutant added fuel to the attack by observing: 'We telegraphed yesterday because of that fellow Švejk. Švejk . . .'

'Present!' Švejk called out from the half-open door and repeated as he came in: 'Present! Humbly report, Infantryman Švejk, company orderly to the 11th march company.'

Seeing the bewildered faces of Captain Ságner and Lieutenant Lukáš, in which could be descried a certain mute despair, he did not wait for any questions and called out:

'Humbly report, they wanted to shoot me for having betrayed His Imperial Majesty.'

'For Jesus Christ's sake, what on earth are you talking about?' Lieutenant Lukáš shouted in despair. He was deathly pale.

'Humbly report, it was like this, sir . . .'

And Švejk began to describe in detail what had actually happened to him.

They looked at him with staring eyes and he told his story with all possible detail, not even forgetting to mention that forget-me-nots were blooming on the dam of the lake where his misfortune had happened. When afterwards he mentioned the names of the Tartars he had got to know on his pilgrimage, like Hallimulabalibay, to which he added a whole string of names he had himself invented, like Valivolavalivey, Malimulamalimey, Lieutenant Lukáš could not stop himself from saying: 'I'll kick your backside, you mule. Go on, but be brief and to the point!'

And Švejk went on with his customary consistency, and when he came to the summary court-martial, the general and the major, he mentioned that the general squinted in his left eye and that the major's eyes were blue.

'And they looked me through and through,' he added afterwards in rhyme.

Lieutenant Zimmerman, the commander of the 12th company, threw a mug at Švejk. He had drunk out of it strong spirit bought from the Jew.

Švejk went on quite unruffled and explained how afterwards there had been spiritual consolation, and how the major slept in his embrace till the morning. Then he made a fine defence of the brigade, where he had been sent when the battalion reported him missing and demanded his return. Handing over the documents to Captain Ságner to prove that he had been cleared of all suspicion by the highest authority of the brigade he added: 'Humbly report, I take the liberty to inform you that Lieutenant Dub is in the brigade with concussion of the brain and asks to be remembered to you. May I now have my pay and tobacco money, please?'

Captain Ságner and Lieutenant Lukáš exchanged questioning glances but at that moment the door opened and they brought the steaming hot pork soup in in a kind of tub.

That was the beginning of all those delights for which they had been waiting so long.

'You godforsaken bastard,' Captain Ságner said to Švejk. He was in a mellow mood before the forthcoming treat. 'It's only the pork feast which has saved you.'

'Švejk,' Lieutenant Lukáš added, 'if anything more happens, it'll be a bad day for you.'

'Humbly report, it will have to be a bad day for me,' Švejk said, saluting. 'When a man is in the army he has to be conscious and aware of . . .'

'Clear off!' Captain Ságner roared at him.

Švejk cleared off and went down to the kitchen. There the crushed Baloun had returned and was asking if he could wait on his Lieutenant Lukáš at the feast.

Švejk arrived at the very moment when Jurajda was arguing with Baloun.

In the course of the argument Jurajda used some pretty incomprehensible terms.

'You're a *hodulus vorax*,' he said to Baloun. 'You'd go on stuffing yourself until the sweat poured out of you, and if I were to let you take the jitrnice upstairs you'd be *beelzebubbing* with them on the stairs.'

The kitchen now had quite another appearance. The battalion and company quartermaster sergeant-majors were nibbling in accordance with their rank and Jurajda's carefully elaborated plan. Out of a rusty wash-basin the battalion writers, company telephonists and one or two N.C.O.s were greedily gulping the pork soup, which had been thinned with boiling water so that they all could get a mouthful or two.

'Hallo!' said Vaněk to Švejk as he gnawed a pig's claw. 'A moment ago Marek was here and said you'd come back and had a new uniform on. That means you've got me into a pretty mess. He's been frightening me by saying that we shan't be able to get our accounts straight with the brigade because of that uniform. Your old uniform was found on the dam of the lake and we've already reported that to the brigade through the battalion office. I had entered you as drowned while bathing. You had no business to come back and make trouble for us with two uniforms. You have no idea what you've done to the battalion. Every part of your uniform is entered in our books. It's registered as an extra in the list of uniforms which I have for the company. The company has one whole uniform in excess. I've reported this to the battalion. Now we shall get a notification from the brigade that you've got a new uniform there. And because in the meantime the battalion will show in its equipment records that there's one complete uniform in excess.... I can imagine what that can mean: we could get an inspection because of it. Over a trifle like this Supply Headquarters would come and inspect us. If two thousand pairs of boots are lost no one worries about it at all . . .

'But we've lost your uniform,' said Vaněk tragically, sucking the marrow from a bone which had fallen into his hand, and digging out the rest with a matchstick which he used instead of a toothpick. 'For a trifle like that there's sure to be an inspection. When I was in the Carpathians there was an inspection just because the order had not been carried out that frozen soldiers should have their boots pulled off without damage to the boots. They tried to pull them off, pulled and pulled – and on two of the men the boots burst while this was being done and one of them had had broken boots even before he died. And so the mischief was done. A colonel came from Supply Headquarters and if it hadn't happened that as soon as he arrived he stopped one in the head from the Russians and rolled down into a valley, I don't know what might have come out of it.'

'Did they take his boots off as well?' Švejk asked with interest.

'They did,' said Vaněk pensively, 'but no one knew who had done it, so we couldn't show the colonel's boots in our accounts either.'

Jurajda returned from upstairs again and his first glance fell on the prostrate Baloun who sat, a miserable wreck, on a bench by the stove and gazed at his emaciated belly in frightful despair.

'You should belong to the sect of the Hesychasts,' said the learned cook compassionately. 'They too spent whole days looking at their navel until they got to imagine that a halo shone round it. After that they supposed they had reached the third degree of perfection.'

Jurajda reached into the oven and took out a small piece of blood sausage.

'Now put that into your maw, Baloun,' he said affably. 'Have a good glut until you burst. Choke yourself, you greedy guts.'

Tears came to Baloun's eyes.

'At home when we slaughtered,' he said plaintively, as he gobbled up the small piece of blood sausage, 'I always ate first a good piece of boiled pig's head, its whole snout, its heart, its ear, a bit of its liver, its kidneys, its spleen, a slice of its ribs, its tongue and afterwards . . .'

And he added in a hushed voice as though he were telling a fairy tale: 'Afterwards it was the turn of the jitrnice, six, ten pieces, and then pot-bellied blood sausages stuffed with meat and pearl barley or breadcrumbs, so that you didn't know which to bite into first, those with breadcrumbs or those with barley. Everything melted on your tongue, everything smelled so good – and you went on stuffing and stuffing.

'So I think the bullets will spare me,' Baloun went on lamenting, 'and it will be hunger that'll get me and I'll never more in my life come across such a roaster of blood-sausage meat as I had at home. As for brawn I didn't like it too much, because it only shakes like jelly and you get nothing out of it. My wife on the other hand would die to get brawn and I wouldn't let her put even a piece of pig's ear into it because I wanted to wolf everything up myself in the way I liked it best. I didn't appreciate those delicacies, that good living, and once I even refused to let my old father-in-law have his pig. I slaughtered it and wolfed it all up myself and I was so greedy that I didn't even send him a tiny hamper – and afterwards he prophesied that when I kicked the bucket it would be of starvation.'

'And that's the situation,' said Švejk, from whose lips nothing but rhymes seemed to flow involuntarily that day.

Jurajda had already got over his sudden fit of sympathy for Baloun, because the latter nimbly slipped towards the stove, took out of his pocket a piece of bread and tried to dab the whole of it in the sauce, which was nestling up to all sides of the great lump of roast pork in the huge roaster.

Jurajda hit him over the hand, so that Baloun's slice of bread fell into the sauce just like a swimmer jumping from a diving board into a river.

Before Baloun had an opportunity of snatching the delicacy out of the roaster Jurajda seized him and threw him out of the door.

The crushed Baloun saw through the window how Jurajda took out on a fork the piece of bread which had become brown in the sauce, gave it to Švejk and put on it a piece of meat which he had cut off from the top of the roast, saying:

'Eat, my dear old modest friend!'

'Holy Mary, Mother of God,' Baloun lamented behind the window, 'my bread's gone down the drain.' Swinging his long arms he went to find a titbit in the village.

As he ate Jurajda's noble gift Švejk said with his mouth full: 'I'm truly glad that I'm back again among my own folk. I should really have hated it if I couldn't have gone on rendering the company my effective services.' Wiping from his chin the drops of sauce and fat which fell from the bread he continued:

'I really can't imagine what you'd have done without me if they had held me somewhere and the war had continued a few years longer.'

Vaněk asked with interest:

'How long do you think the war will go on, Švejk?'

'Fifteen years,' answered Švejk. 'That's obvious because once there was a thirty years' war and now we're twice as clever as they were before, so it follows that thirty divided by two is fifteen.'

'Our captain's batman told us that he'd heard that as soon as we occupy the frontiers of Galicia we shan't advance any further,' said Jurajda. 'Then the Russians will begin to sue for peace.'

'In that case it wouldn't be worth while having a war at all,' said Švejk emphatically. 'When there's a war on, let it be a war. I certainly won't hear of peace until we are in Moscow or Petrograd. After all, when there's a world war on it's not really worth it just to sit about on our arses near the frontiers. Let's take for example the Swedes during the Thirty Years' War. Look how far away they came from when they got to Německý Brod and Lipnice, where they made such a breach that to this very day they talk Swedish in the pubs after midnight there and don't understand each other. Or take the Prussians. They weren't exactly our next-door neighbours and yet in Lipnice they managed to leave behind them bags of Prussians. They even got as far as Jedouchov and America and back again.'

'Besides,' said Jurajda, who was today completely driven off balance by the pork feast and was in a mental muddle, 'all people are descended from carps. Take for instance Darwin's theory of evolution, chaps . . .'

His further meditations were interrupted by the sudden entry of Marek:

'The devil take the hindmost,' Marek called out. 'A moment ago

Lieutenant Dub arrived in a car at the battalion staff and brought with him Cadet Biegler in his shitted bags.

'It's terrible with him,' Marek went on. 'When they got out of the car he rushed into the office. You know very well how when I went away from here I told you I was going to take forty winks. Well, I stretched myself out on a bench in the office and began happily to doze, when suddenly he hurled himself on me. Cadet Biegler roared: "Attention!" and Dub made me get up and then let fly at me: "You're surprised, are you, that I've caught you in the office in dereliction of duty? Sleeping is permitted only after the last post." Thereupon Biegler added: "Section 16 paragraph 9 of barrack regulations." Then Dub hammered with his fist on the table and shouted: "Perhaps you wanted to try and get rid of me from the battalion. Don't imagine that it was concussion of the brain I had. My skull can take anything." In the meantime Cadet Biegler went through the papers on the table and read aloud to himself from one of the documents: "Order for division no. 280." Dub, thinking that Biegler was making fun of him, because of his last sentence, that is to say that his skull could take anything, started rebuking him for his unworthy and insolent behaviour towards senior officers and is now taking him to the captain to complain about him.'

A moment later they came to the kitchen, which they had to go through if they went upstairs to where the whole officers' corps was sitting and where after the roast pork the chubby Lieutenant Malý was singing an aria from the opera *Traviata* and belching as well after the cabbage and rich banquet.

When Lieutenant Dub entered the kitchen Švejk shouted: 'Attention! Up all of you!'

Dub came very close to Švejk so that he could shout at him right in his face: 'Now you'll catch it! Now it's amen for you! I'm going to have you stuffed as a memorial for the 91st regiment.'

'Just as you command, sir,' Švejk said saluting. 'Humbly report, I once read that there was a great battle in which a Swedish king fell together with his faithful horse. They sent both corpses back to Sweden and now they both stand stuffed in the Stockholm museum.'

'Where did you get that knowledge from, animal?' shouted Lieutenant Dub.

'Humbly report, sir, from my schoolmaster brother.'

Lieutenant Dub turned round, spat, and pushed Cadet Biegler in front of him up the stairs leading to the big hall. But he could not help turning round in the door and looking at Švejk. With the inexorable severity of a Roman emperor deciding the fate of a wounded gladiator in a circus he made a gesture with a finger of his right hand and shouted to Švejk: 'Thumbs down!'

'Humbly report,' Švejk called out after him, 'I'm already putting them down!'

Cadet Biegler was in a weak state. During all this time he had gone through the various cholera stations and got fully accustomed to all the manipulations they used on him as a cholera suspect. As a result he had begun to discharge continually and involuntarily into his trousers. When at one of these observation stations he finally came into the hands of a specialist who could not find any cholera bacilli in his excrement, the latter bound his intestines with tannin, as a shoemaker binds broken shoes with pitch thread, and sent him to the nearest transit command. Although Biegler was as weak as steam over a pot the specialist pronounced him fit for service. He was a kind-hearted man.

When Cadet Biegler told him that he felt very weak he said with a smile: 'You'll still be able to carry off the Gold Medal for valour. After all, you volunteered for front service, didn't you?'

And so Cadet Biegler set out to try to earn the Gold Medal.

His steeled intestines no longer ejected a thin fluid into his trousers, but he still suffered from frequent urgent calls, so that from the last transit station to the staff of the brigade, where he met Lieutenant Dub, it was in actual fact a whistle-stop journey to all possible W.C.s. Several times he missed his train because he was sitting in the station W.C. so long that it went off without him. Several times he failed to change trains, because he was sitting in the train W.C.

But in spite of all that and in defiance of all those W.C.s which were hampering his journey Cadet Biegler none the less came nearer and nearer to the brigade.

Lieutenant Dub should have remained a few days longer under treatment at the brigade, but the same day that Švejk went off to the battalion, the staff doctor had second thoughts about Lieutenant Dub, when he learned that in the afternoon an ambulance car would be going in the direction of the battalion of the 91st regiment.

He was very glad to get rid of Lieutenant Dub, who as usual supported his various assertions with the words: 'I talked with the district hejtman about this already before the war.'

'You can kiss my arse with your district hejtman,' the staff doctor thought, and he was very grateful for the fortunate chance that ambulance cars were going up to Kamionka Strumiłowa via Żółtańce.

Švejk never saw Cadet Biegler at the brigade, because for two hours the latter was again sitting in one of the brigade officers' W.C.s. One can be bold enough to claim that Cadet Biegler never wasted his time in those places because he always rehearsed to himself all the glorious battles of the heroic Austro-Hungarian armies from the Battle of Nördlingen on 6 September 1634 to Sarajevo on 19 August 1888.

When he had pulled the chain of the water closet innumerable times and the water gushed into the pan with a roar, he shut his eyes and imagined he heard the battles' din, the assaults of cavalry and the thunder of artillery.

Lieutenant Dub's meeting with Cadet Biegler was not too delightful and no doubt explained a certain sourness in their future relations both on and off duty.

It happened that when Lieutenant Dub was vainly trying to get to the W.C. for the fourth time he shouted out in exasperation: 'Who's there?'

'Cadet Biegler, 11th march company, battalion N, 91st regiment,' came the proud reply.

The competitor announced himself in front of the door. 'This is Lieutenant Dub of the same company.'

'I'll be ready in a moment, sir.'

'I'm waiting!'

Lieutenant Dub looked impatiently at his watch. No one would have believed how much energy and tenacity was required to hold out a further fifteen minutes in such a situation in front of the door, and after that another five, and then a further five more, and after knocking, beating and kicking on the door to receive always the same answer: 'I'll be ready in a moment, sir.'

Lieutenant Dub became feverish, notably when after a hopeful rustling of the paper a further seven minutes went by without the door opening.

Into the bargain Cadet Biegler was so tactful that he still did not pull the chain.

Lieutenant Dub in a slight fever started to reflect whether he shouldn't perhaps complain to the commander of the brigade, who might then order the door to be broken open and Cadet Biegler to be taken out. It also occurred to him that it might perhaps be an act of insubordination.

Only after a further five minutes did Lieutenant Dub in fact realize that he could no longer perform anything inside the door and that his urge had long since passed. He remained however in front of the W.C. out of some kind of principle and continued to kick on the door, from which there always came back the identical reply: 'I'll be ready in a moment, sir.'

At last Biegler could be heard pulling the chain and after a short time they met face to face.

'Cadet Biegler,' Lieutenant Dub thundered at him, 'don't imagine that I am here for the same purpose as you. I have come here because you failed to report to me when you arrived at brigade staff. Are you ignorant of the regulations? Do you know to whom you have to give priority?'

Cadet Biegler searched his memory for a time to try to recall whether he had really done something which was not compatible with discipline and with the regulations concerning relations between junior and senior officers.

In this respect there was a vast vacuum and gap in his memory.

In the school no one had ever lectured to them on how junior officers should behave towards senior officers in a case like this. In such circumstances should he stop shitting in the middle of the process and fly out of the door of the W.C., holding his trousers in one hand and saluting with the other?

'Will you please answer, Cadet Biegler!' Lieutenant Dub called out challengingly.

And then Biegler remembered a very simple answer which solved everything: 'Sir, I was not informed after my arrival at brigade staff that you were here and when I had completed my business in the office I went at once to the W.C. where I remained until your arrival.'

And then he added in a solemn voice: 'This is Cadet Biegler reporting to Lieutenant Dub.'

'You know it's not just a mere trifle,' Lieutenant Dub said acidly. 'In my view, Cadet Biegler, as soon as you got to brigade staff you should have asked in the office whether by chance there wasn't any officer of your battalion or company there. We shall decide about your conduct in the battalion. I am going there by car and you will come with me. "But"? I don't want to hear any "buts" from you, please!'

In fact Cadet Biegler objected that he had obtained from the office of the brigade staff a march route which indicated that he should go by rail and that this method of travelling seemed much more suitable in view of the uncertainty of his bowels. Every child knows perfectly well that cars are not equipped for such cases. Before you go 180 kilometres you've already done it in your trousers.

Heaven knows how it happened, but when they drove off the shaking of the car had initially no effect on Biegler.

Lieutenant Dub was in complete despair at not being able to carry out his plan of vengeance.

When they drove off he thought to himself. 'Just wait, Cadet Biegler! When you find it's coming on, don't imagine I'm going to have the car stopped for you.'

It was in this sense that to the extent permitted by the speed of the car, which was eating up the kilometres, Dub started a pleasant conversation with Biegler: army cars with a fixed scheduled route must not waste petrol and cannot make any stops anywhere.

Cadet Biegler quite correctly objected that when a car stops anywhere for anything it does not use up petrol, because the chauffeur switches off the engine.

'But if it has to arrive at its destination at the scheduled time,' Lieutenant Dub continued inexorably, 'it mustn't stop anywhere on the way.'

There was no answer on the part of Cadet Biegler.

And so they raced through the air for more than a quarter of an hour, until suddenly Lieutenant Dub felt he had a very distended stomach and that it would be desirable to stop the car, get out, go into a ditch, take down his trousers and seek relief.

He controlled himself like a hero as far as the 126th kilometre, when he resolutely pulled the driver by the coat and shouted into his ear: 'Stop!'

'Cadet Biegler,' said Lieutenant Dub graciously as he jumped rapidly out of the car down into the ditch, 'now you have your opportunity too.'

'No, thank you,' Cadet Biegler answered. 'I would not like to hold the car up unnecessarily.'

Cadet Biegler, who was also at the end of his tether, said to himself under his breath that he would rather mess up his trousers than miss this marvellous opportunity of making a fool of Lieutenant Dub.

Before they got to Żółtańce Dub stopped the car twice and after the last stop he said doggedly to Biegler: 'For lunch I had bigos cooked in the Polish way.[1] From the battalion I shall make a complaint by telegram to the brigade. The sauerkraut was bad and the pork not fit for eating. The insolence of these cooks exceeds all bounds. Whoever doesn't yet know me, will soon get to know me.'

'Field Marshal Nostitz-Rhieneck, the elite of the reserve cavalry, published a paper called "What is bad for the stomach in war",' Biegler replied, 'and in it he recommended that during war troubles and strains pork should not be eaten at all. Every excess on the march is harmful.'

Lieutenant Dub did not say a word in reply. He only thought to himself: 'I'll soon deal with all your erudition, you bastard.' Then he

---

1. Szeged goulash made out of fat pork and sauerkraut.

had second thoughts and replied to Biegler with a very stupid question: 'And so you think, Cadet Biegler, that an officer to whom you must regard yourself as subordinate in rank eats immoderately? Didn't you want to say, Cadet Biegler, that I'd overgorged myself? I am grateful to you for this rudeness. Be assured that I shall settle accounts with you. You don't know me yet, but when you get to know me you won't forget Lieutenant Dub.'

As he said the last word he very nearly bit his tongue, because they suddenly flew over a hole in the road.

Cadet Biegler did not answer, which in its turn stirred up Lieutenant Dub, who asked rudely: 'Listen, Cadet Biegler, I think that you have learnt that you have to answer the questions of your superior officer.'

'Of course,' said Cadet Biegler, 'there is such a passage. But of course it's necessary first to analyse our mutual relations. As far as I am aware I have not yet been assigned anywhere and so there can be no question whatsoever of my being directly subordinated to you, sir. The most important thing of course is that in officers' circles questions asked by superiors need only be answered when they concern matters of duty. As we two are sitting here in the car we do not represent any battle component of any precise military unit. Therefore there is no official relationship between us. We are both going to our units, and it would certainly be no official utterance if I were to answer your question whether I perhaps meant that you have overgorged yourself, sir.'

'Have you finished, you, you . . . ?' Lieutenant Dub roared at him.

'Yes, I have,' Cadet Biegler stated with assurance. 'Don't forget, sir, that an officers' court of honour will no doubt pronounce on what has taken place between us.'

Lieutenant Dub was almost beside himself with rage and fury. When he got angry he had the special habit of talking even greater nonsense and idiocy than when he was calm.

And so he muttered: 'It will be a court-martial which will decide on your case.'

Cadet Biegler used this opportunity to give him the final knock-out by saying in the most familiar tone possible: 'You're joking, old man.'

Lieutenant Dub shouted at the chauffeur to stop.

'One of us must walk,' he gibbered.

'I shall go in the car,' Cadet Biegler answered calmly. 'As for you, old man, you can do what you like.'

'Drive on,' Lieutenant Dub bawled at the chauffeur as though in a delirium. Thereafter he enveloped himself in dignified silence like Julius Caesar, when the conspirators approached him with daggers to stab him.

And it was in this way they arrived at Żółtáńce, where they came on to the track of the battalion.

While Lieutenant Dub and Cadet Biegler were still disputing on the stairs whether a cadet who had not yet been assigned anywhere had a right to draw any portion of the amount of jitrnice which fell to the officers of individual companies, down in the kitchen they were already stuffed full. They had stretched themselves out on the spacious benches, were talking about everything possible and puffing at their pipes like billyo.

Jurajda declared: 'Well, today I've made a wonderful discovery. I think it's going to make a complete revolution in cooking. You know very well, Vaněk, that I couldn't find any marjoram for the jitrnice anywhere in this cursed village.'

'*Herba majoranae*,' said Vaněk, remembering that he was a chemist.

Jurajda continued: 'No one has ever made a proper study of how in an emergency the human mind seizes on the most various means, how new horizons appear before it, how it begins to discover all sorts of impossible things, which humanity has not dreamed of up to now. . . . Well, I tried to look for marjoram in all the houses here. I ran around, searched and explained to them what it was needed for and what it looked like . . .'

'You should have gone on to describe the smell,' Švejk chimed in from the bench. 'You should have said that marjoram smells like when you sniff at an ink-bottle in an alley of flowering acacias. On the hill of Bohdalec near Prague . . .'

'But please, Švejk,' Marek interrupted him imploringly, 'let Jurajda finish.'

Jurajda went on: 'At one farm I came across an old pensioned soldier from the time of the occupation of Bosnia and Herzegovina. He did his military service in the Uhlans at Pardubice and still remembered his Czech. He began to argue with me and say that in Bohemia they put camomile in jitrnice and not marjoram. Honestly, I had no idea what to do because among all the spices which are put into jitrnice really any sensible and unprejudiced person must consider marjoram as champion: I had at once to find some substitute, which would give that striking spicy taste. And then I found in a farm hanging under the picture of a saint a wedding-garland of myrtle. They had been newly married, and the sprigs of myrtle on the garland were still fairly fresh. And so I put the myrtle into the jitrnice. Of course I had to steam the whole wedding-garland three times in boiling water so that the leaves should get soft and lose their too acrid smell and taste. Naturally, when I took away from them that myrtle wedding-garland of theirs for the jitrnice it caused a lot of heartache. When we parted they were convinced that for such sacrilege I should be killed by the very next bullet, as the garland was consecrated. But you have eaten my pork soup and not one of you realized that it smelt of myrtle instead of marjoram.'

'In Jindřichův Hradec,' Švejk put in, 'years ago a pork butcher called Josef Linek had two boxes on his shelf. In one he had a mixture of all the spices he put into jitrnice and blood sausages. In the other box he had insect powder, because he had found out several times that his clients had eaten bugs or beetles in his sausages. He used to say that as far as bugs were concerned they had a taste of the bitter almonds they put in cakes, but beetles in smoked sausages smelt like mildewy old bibles. And that was why he was so keen on cleanliness in his workshop and strewed that insect powder everywhere. But once he was making blood sausages and had a cold. And so he took the box of insect powder and shook it into the sausage-meat for blood sausages and ever since then people in Jindřichův Hradec only went to Linek for their blood sausages. They absolutely stormed his shop. And he was so cunning that he twigged that it was the insect powder that did it, and from that time on he ordered whole cases of the powder cash on delivery, after having previously told the firm from which he ordered it to write on the cases: "Indian Spices". That was his secret and he went with it to the grave. And the most interesting thing was that all those families who bought his blood sausages were free of beetles and bugs. Since then Jindřichův Hradec has been one of the cleanest cities in the whole of Bohemia.'

'Have you finished?' asked Marek, who obviously wanted to join the conversation.

'Well, I'd be ready with this particular case,' answered Švejk, 'but

I know a similar case in the Beskydy Mountains, but I'll tell you about that when the fighting begins.'

Marek began to speak: 'Culinary art is best appreciated in wartime especially at the front. Allow me to make a small comparison. In

peacetime we've read and heard of so-called iced soups, i.e. soups to which they add ice and which are very popular in North Germany, Denmark and Sweden. And you see the war came and this winter in the Carpathians the men had so much iced soup that they wouldn't touch it, although it's such a delicacy.'

'You can eat frozen goulash,' Vaněk objected, 'but not for too long – I should think a week at the most. That was why our 9th company gave up their positions.'

'In peacetime,' said Švejk with unusual gravity, 'the whole army service centred on the kitchen and various dishes. We had in Budějovice a Lieutenant Zákrejs and he was always hanging around the officers' kitchen and whenever any soldier did anything wrong he made him stand at attention and started off at him: "You bastard, you do that once more and I'll make a nice piece of beaten steak out of your mug. I'll stamp you into a potato mash and then make you eat it. Giblets and rice will come out of you and you'll look like a larded hare in a roaster. And so you'd better improve if you don't want people to think that I've made meat hash with cabbage out of you."'

Further explanations and interesting discussion about the use of the menu before the war for educating warriors was interrupted by a huge scream upstairs where the glorious dinner was drawing to an end.

Out of the confused chorus of voices there rang the shrieks of Cadet Biegler: 'Already in peacetime a soldier must know what war will demand of him, and in wartime he must not forget what he learnt on the parade ground.'

Then could be heard the snorting of Lieutenant Dub: 'I insist that it be noted that this is the third time I have been insulted!'

Great events were happening upstairs.

Lieutenant Dub, who as we well know cherished treacherous intentions towards Cadet Biegler in relation to the battalion commander, was received immediately on his entry with a great roar by the officers. The spirit provided by the Jew was having a wonderful effect on everybody.

One on top of the other they shouted, referring to Lieutenant Dub's equestrian skill: 'It's no good without a groom!' – 'The skittish mustang!' – 'How long did you spend among the cowboys in the West, old man?' – '*Haute école!*'

Captain Ságner quickly poured into him a glass of the cursed spirit and the offended Lieutenant Dub sat down at the table. He moved up an old broken chair beside Lieutenant Lukáš who welcomed him with the friendly words: 'We've eaten everything up already, old chap.'

The figure of that melancholy knight, Cadet Biegler, was somehow overlooked in spite of the fact that strictly according to regulations he had officially reported himself to Captain Ságner and the other officers round the table. Although all of them saw and knew him he kept on repeating several times in succession: 'Cadet Biegler has arrived at the battalion staff.'

Biegler took a full glass, sat down quite modestly by the window and waited for a suitable moment to air some of his knowledge from the textbooks.

Lieutenant Dub, who felt that the awful concoction was going to his head, knocked with his finger on the table and addressing Captain Ságner said out of the blue:

'The district hejtman and I always used to say: "Patriotism, fidelity to duty, victory over oneself, these are the weapons that matter in warfare." I am reminded of that especially today when our troops will in foreseeable time be crossing the frontier.'

*

This was the point reached by Jaroslav Hašek in dictating The Good Soldier Švejk and his Fortunes in the World War. *He was already ill and death silenced him for ever on 3 January 1923. It prevented him from completing one of the most famous and widely-read novels published after the First World War.*